GAUNT'S GHOSTS

The Saint

THIS OMNIBUS EDITION collects the second sequence of Gaunt's Ghosts novels following the story of the Tanith First-and-Only regiment and their charismatic commissar, Ibram Gaunt. Nick-named the Ghosts, due to their skills in scouting, the regiment journey from warzone to warzone in the Chaos-infested Sabbat Worlds system, using their skills to aid the massed ranks of the Imperium stamp out Chaos. The Ghosts must risk all and carry out the most dangerous of missions in the war against Chaos, all in the name of the Emperor.

Men of Tanith, do you want to live forever?

More Dan Abnett from the Black Library

· GAUNT'S GHOSTS ·

Colonel-Commissar Gaunt and his regiment, the Tanith First-and-Only, struggle for survival on the battlefields of the far future.

The Founding

(Omnibus edition containing Books 1-3:
FIRST AND ONLY, GHOSTMAKER and NECROPOLIS)

The Saint

(Omnibus edition containing Books 4-7:
HONOUR GUARD, THE GUNS OF TANITH,
STRAIGHT SILVER and SABBAT MARTYR)

The Lost

Book 8 – TRAITOR GENERAL

Book 9 – HIS LAST COMMAND

Book 10 – THE ARMOUR OF CONTEMPT

· EISENHORN ·

In the nightmare world of the 41st millennium, Inquisitor Eisenhorn hunts down mankind's most dangerous enemies – the alien, the heretic and the daemon.

EISENHORN
(Omnibus edition containing *XENOS*,
MALLEUS and *HERETICUS*)

· RAVENOR ·

Inquisitor Gideon Ravenor and his warband fight a desperate battle to protect the Imperium from its most deadly enemies.

Book 1 – RAVENOR

Book 2 – RAVENOR RETURNED

Book 3 – RAVENOR ROGUE

A WARHAMMER 40,000 ANTHOLOGY

GAUNT'S GHOSTS

The Saint

Dan Abnett

A Black Library Publication

This omnibus edition published in Great Britain in 2007 by
BL Publishing,
Games Workshop Ltd.,
Willow Road,
Nottingham, NG7 2WS, UK.

10 9 8 7 6 5 4 3 2 1

Cover illustration by Clint Langley.

Honour Guard, Guns of Tanith and *Straight Silver* maps by Ralph Horsley.

Sabbat Martyr map by Nuala Kinrade.

A CIP record for this book is available from the British Library.

ISBN 13: 978 1 84416 479 0
ISBN 10: 1 84416 479 9

Distributed in the US by Simon & Schuster
1230 Avenue of the Americas, New York, NY 10020, US.

IT IS THE 41st millennium. For more than a hundred centuries the Emperor has sat immobile on the Golden Throne of Earth. He is the master of mankind by the will of the gods, and master of a million worlds by the might of his inexhaustible armies. He is a rotting carcass writhing invisibly with power from the Dark Age of Technology. He is the Carrion Lord of the Imperium for whom a thousand souls are sacrificed every day, so that he may never truly die.

YET EVEN IN his deathless state, the Emperor continues his eternal vigilance. Mighty battlefleets cross the daemon-infested miasma of the warp, the only route between distant stars, their way lit by the Astronomican, the psychic manifestation of the Emperor's will. Vast armies give battle in his name on uncounted worlds. Greatest amongst His soldiers are the Adeptus Astartes, the Space Marines, bio-engineered super-warriors. Their comrades in arms are legion: the Imperial Guard and countless planetary defence forces, the ever-vigilant Inquisition and the tech-priests of the Adeptus Mechanicus to name only a few. But for all their multitudes, they are barely enough to hold off the ever-present threat from aliens, heretics, mutants – and worse.

TO BE A man in such times is to be one amongst untold billions. It is to live in the cruellest and most bloody regime imaginable. These are the tales of those times. Forget the power of technology and science, for so much has been forgotten, never to be re-learned. Forget the promise of progress and understanding, for in the grim dark future there is only war. There is no peace amongst the stars, only an eternity of carnage and slaughter, and the laughter of thirsting gods.

CONTENTS

AUTHOR'S INTRODUCTION

WELCOME BACK.

This is the second trip by omnibus into the wartorn domains of the Sabbat Worlds Crusade. It's been over ten years since I first roamed out this way, as I mentioned in the introduction to the first compilation, and back then, let me tell you, this was all fields.

It wasn't until the eighth book in this series (*Traitor General*) that we formally adopted the idea of these novels working as discrete story arcs, and began to label them as such. A little retrospective planning divided the previous seven into two arcs for the purposes of collection: the first three books (*First and Only, Ghostmaker* and *Necropolis*) became 'The Founding', and the next four (*Honour Guard, The Guns of Tanith, Straight Silver* and *Sabbat Martyr*) became 'The Saint'. The third arc ('The Lost') comprises *Traitor General, His Last Command* and *The Armour of Contempt,* and concludes with *Only in Death,* to be published this autumn.

Why did we break the series into arcs? For ease of handling, essentially. An eleven (and counting) book series can be a little daunting, but seen as three self-contained chunks, it becomes more manageable.

Another reason is because that's where the story breaks naturally fell. Though many ongoing character threads and themes continue right through the series as a whole, there are distinct plot shapes inside each story arc. By the time I got to *Sabbat Martyr,* I knew it was going to conclusively punctuate plot lines that had begun in *Honour Guard*. Both *Sabbat Martyr* and *Only in Death* were specifically written to be the endstops of epic adventures.

Each of the four books in this omnibus has its own story to tell, overarching themes notwithstanding. When I wrote *Honour Guard,* I was beginning to experiment with what I could do in each Ghosts adventure: if each book had to be a battlefield story about Imperial Guardsmen (and it did), how could I keep them all fresh and different? Mainly, I started to play around with mission parameters, locations, and types of military undertaking, which is why *Honour Guard* is a road trip, *The Guns of Tanith* an airborne operation, *Straight Silver* a trench war campaign and *Sabbat Martyr* a city fight. Over all, they march the valiant Tanith First closer and closer to the very core of the Crusade.

These books are also where many of the central characters really start to develop. Verghastites such as Kolea, Soric, Criid and Curth emerge in the front rank of importance, and other characters appear for the first time, such as Viktor Hark and Lijah Cuu.

Ah, Cuu. At the risk of repeating myself (I've written about this before) Cuu is one of those characters that makes writing fun. It goes like this... I'd written most of *Honour Guard*, heading for my deadline, and my computer ate the manuscript, all of it. No, I hadn't backed up. Yes, I realise that was a bit stupid. To keep the schedules on track, I rewrote the book from scratch in a month, and a couple of odd things happened. One was that the second version turned out to be much, much better than the lost original, despite the rush. The other was that, although I stuck to the same plot outline, new things happened. Characters – especially Cuu – just appeared in the new version of the story, took on lives of their own, and refused to go away. Cuu came to determine a great deal of what went on in the next three books. You couldn't make it up and, in Cuu's case, I don't think I really did.

Each of these four books occupies a particular place in my creative memory. *Honour Guard* has the best, most symmetrical symbolic plan of any book I've ever written (*Riders of the Dead* comes close); *The Guns of Tanith* spawned its own spin-off (*Double Eagle*) AND features the most shocking thing I'd done to date (I still get letters); *Sabbat Martyr*, as befits the series climax, was the most intense and, well, climactic, book I was capable of producing.

Straight Silver, and I take it out of sequence deliberately, is the only Ghosts book I ever hear less than favourable comments about. I find this odd, as I think it's one of the very best written of the entire run. I think what gets people is not so much what I do in it as what I *don't* do. That, I assure you, was quite deliberate. It would have been too easy to play to the stalls. I wanted to twist the knife just a little longer. I hope that, reading it as part of this omnibus sequence, the gainsayers might re-evaluate it. It's got some of my all-time favourite Ghost moments in it, especially the siege in the little woodland house.

Also in this collection you'll meet the Blood Pact for the first time, and you'll start to learn to say goodbye.

These are the books where people begin to die. These are the books where we realise that all bets are off, and no one is safe.

And on that cheerful note, enjoy the trip.

Dan Abnett
Paris, April, 2007.

HONOUR GUARD

For Colin Fender, honorary Guardsman
and Marco, patience of a saint

'THE MONUMENTAL IMPERIAL *crusade to liberate the Sabbat Worlds cluster from the grip of Chaos had been raging for over a decade and a half when Warmaster Macaroth began his daring assaults on the strategically vital Cabal system. This phase of reconquest lasted almost two whole years, and featured a bravura, multi-point invasion scheme devised by Macaroth himself. Simultaneous Imperial assaults were launched against nineteen key planets, including three of the notorious fortress-worlds, shaking the dug-in resolve of the numerically superior but less well-orchestrated enemy.*

'From his war room logs, we know that Macaroth fully appreciated the scale of his gamble. If successful, this phase of assault would virtually guarantee an overall Imperial victory for the campaign. If it failed, his whole crusade force, an armed host over a billion strong, might well be entirely overrun. For two bloody, bitter years, the fate of the Sabbat Worlds Crusade hung in the balance.

'Serious analysis of this period inevitably focuses on the large-scale fortress-world theatres, most particularly on the eighteen month war to take the massive fortress-world Morlond. But several of the subsidiary crusade assaults conducted during this phase are deserving of close study, especially the liberation of the shrineworld Hagia and the remarkable events that afterwards unfolded there...'

— from *A History of the Later Imperial Crusades*

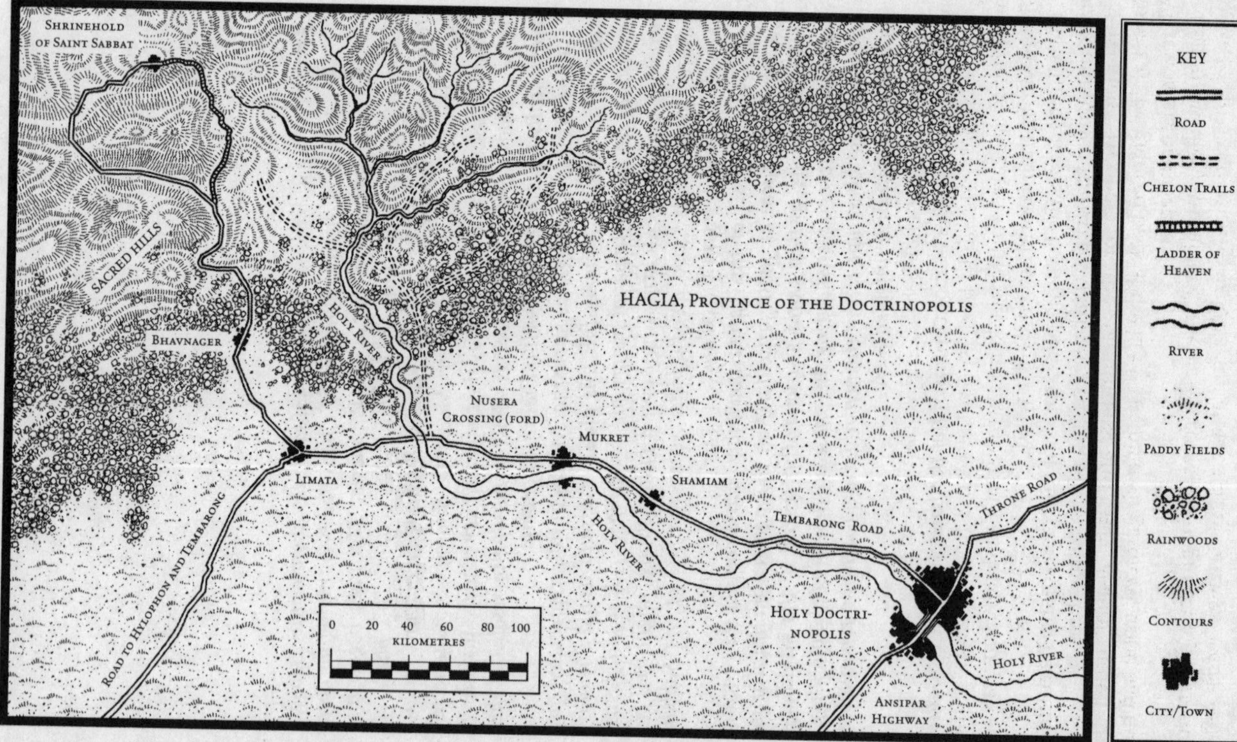
HAGIA, Province of the Doctrinopolis
Shrinehold of Saint Sabbat
Sacred Hills
Bhavnager
Holy River
Nusera Crossing (ford)
Mukret
Limata
Shamiam
Tembarong Road
Throne Road
Road to Hylophon and Tembarong
Holy River
Holy Doctri-nopolis
Holy River
Ansipar Highway
0 20 40 60 80 100
kilometres
KEY
Road
Chelon Trails
Ladder of Heaven
River
Paddy Fields
Rainwoods
Contours
City/Town

ONE
A DAY FOR HEROES

'Betwixt the wash of the river and the waft of the wind,
let my sins be transfigured to virtues.'

— Catechism of Hagia, bk I, chp 3, vrs xxxii

THEY'D STRUNG THE king up with razor wire in a city square north of the river.

It was called the Square of Sublime Tranquillity, an eight-hectare court of sun-baked, pink basalt surrounded by the elegant, mosaic walls of the Universitariate Doctrinus. Little in the way of sublime tranquillity had happened there in the last ten days. The Pater's Pilgrims had seen to that.

Ibram Gaunt made a sharp, bat-like shadow on the flagstones as he ran to new cover, his storm coat flying out behind him. The sun was at its highest and a stark glare scorched the hard ground. Gaunt knew the light must be burning his skin too, but he felt nothing except the cool, blustering wind that filled the wide square.

He dropped into shelter behind an overturned, burnt-out Chimera troop carrier, and dumped the empty clip from his bolt pistol with a flick-click of his gloved thumb. He could hear a popping sound from far away, and raw metal dents appeared in the blackened armour of the dead Chimera's hull. Distant shots, their sound stolen by the wind.

Far behind, across the cooking pink stones of the open square, he could see black-uniformed Imperial Guardsmen edging out to follow him.

His men. Troopers of the Tanith First-and-Only. Gaunt noted their dispersal and glanced back at the king. The high king indeed, as he had been. What was his name again?

Rotten, swollen, humiliated, the noble corpse swung from a gibbet made of tie-beams and rusting truck-axles and couldn't answer. Most of his immediate court and family were dangling next to him.

More popping. A hard, sharp dent appeared in the resilient metal next to Gaunt's head. Crumbs of paint flecked off with the impact.

Mkoll ducked into cover beside him, lasrifle braced.

'Took your time,' Gaunt teased.

'Hah! I trained you too fething well, colonel-commissar, that's all it is.'

They grinned at each other.

More troopers joined them, running the gauntlet across the open square. One jerked and fell, halfway across. His body would remain, sprawled and unmourned in the open, for at least another hour.

Larkin, Caffran, Lillo, Vamberfeld and Derin made it across. The five scurried in beside the Ghosts' leader and Mkoll, the regiment's scout commander.

Gaunt assayed a look out past the Chimera cover.

He ducked back as distant pops threw rounds at him.

'Four shooters. In the north-west corner.'

Mkoll smiled and shook his head, scolding like a parent. 'Nine at least. Haven't you listened to anything I've told you, Gaunt?'

Larkin, Derin and Caffran laughed. They were all Tanith, original Ghosts, veterans.

Lillo and Vamberfeld watched the apparently disrespectful exchange with alarm. They were Vervunhivers, newcomers to the Ghosts regiment. The Tanith called them 'fresh blood' if they were being charitable, 'scratchers' if they weren't really thinking, or 'cannon trash' if they were feeling cruel.

The new Vervunhive recruits wore the same matt-black fatigues and body armour as the Tanith, but their colouring and demeanour stood them apart. As did their newly stamped, metal-stocked lasguns and the special silver axe-rake studs they wore on their collars.

'Don't worry,' said Gaunt, noting their unease and smiling. 'Mkoll regularly gets too big for his boots. I'll reprimand him when this is done.'

More pops, more dents.

Larkin fidgeted round to get a good look, resting his fine, nalwood-finished sniper weapon in a jag of broken armour with experienced grace. He was the regiment's best marksman.

'Got a target?' Gaunt asked.

'Oh, you bet,' assured the grizzled Larkin, working his weapon into optimum position with a lover's softness.

'Blow their fething faces off then, if you please.'

'You got it.'

'How... How can he see?' gasped Lillo, craning up. Caffran tugged him into cover, saving him an abrupt death as las-shots hissed around them.

'Sharpest eyes of all the Ghosts,' smiled Caffran.

Lillo nodded back, but resented the Tanith's cocky attitude. He was Marco Lillo, career soldier, twenty-one years in the Vervun Primary, and here was a kid, no more than twenty years old all told, telling him what to do.

Lillo shuffled round, aiming his long lasgun.

'I want the king, high king whatever-his-name-is,' said Gaunt softly. Distractedly, he rubbed at a ridge of an old scar across his right palm. 'I want him down. It's not right for him to be rotting up there.'

'Okay,' said Mkoll.

Lillo thought he had a shot and fired a sustained burst at the far side of the square. Lattice windows along the side of the Universitariat exploded inwards, but the hard breeze muffled the noise of the impacts.

Gaunt grabbed Lillo's weapon and pulled him down.

'Don't waste ammo, Marco,' he said.

He knows my name! He knows my name! Lillo was almost beside himself with the fact. He stared at Gaunt, basking in every moment of the brief acknowledgement. Ibram Gaunt was like a god to him. He had led Vervunhive to victory out of the surest defeat ten months past. He carried the sword to prove it.

Lillo regarded the colonel-commissar now: the tall, powerful build, the close-cropped blond hair half hidden by the commissar's cap, the lean cut of his intense face that so matched his name. Gaunt was dressed in the black uniform of his breed, overtopped by a long, leather storm coat and the trademark Tanith camo-cape. Maybe not a god, because he's flesh and blood, Lillo thought... but a hero, none the less.

Larkin was firing. Hard, scratchy rasps issued from his gun.

The rate of fire spitting over their ducked heads reduced.

'What are we waiting for?' asked Vamberfeld.

Mkoll caught his sleeve and nodded back at the buildings behind them.

Vamberfeld saw a big man... a very big man... rise from cover and fire a missile launcher.

The snaking missile, trailing smoke, struck a coronet on the west of the square.

'Try again, Bragg!' Derin, Mkoll and Larkin chorused with a laugh.

Another missile soared over them, and blew the far corner of the square apart. Stone debris scattered across the open plaza.

Gaunt was up and running now, as were Mkoll, Caffran and Derin. Larkin continued to fire his expert shots from cover.

Vamberfeld and Lillo leapt up after the Tanith.

Lillo saw Derin buckle and fall as las-fire cut through him.

He paused and tried to help. The Tanith trooper's chest was a bloody mess and he was convulsing so hard it was impossible for Lillo to get a good grip on him. Mkoll appeared beside the struggling Lillo and together they dragged Derin into cover behind the makeshift gibbet as more las-fire peppered the flagstones.

Gaunt, Caffran and Vamberfeld made it to the far corner of the square.

Gaunt disappeared in through the jagged hole that Bragg's missile had made, his power sword raised and humming. It was the ceremonial weapon of Heironymo Sondar, once-lord of Vervunhive, and Gaunt now carried it as a mark of honour for his courageous defence of that hive. The keening, electric-blue blade flashed as it struck at shapes inside the hole.

Caffran ducked in after him, blasting from the hip. Few of the Ghosts were better than him in storm clearance. He was fast and ruthless.

He blocked Gaunt's back, gun flaring.

Niceg Vamberfeld had been a commercia cleric on Verghast before the Act of Consolation. He'd trained hard, and well, but this was all new to him. He followed the pair inside, plunging into a suddenly gloomy world of shadows, shadow-shapes and blazing energy weapons.

He shot something point blank as he came through the crumpled stone opening. Something else reared up at him, cackling, and he lanced it with his bayonet. He couldn't see the commissar-colonel or the young Tanith trooper any more. He couldn't see a gakking thing, in fact. He started to panic. Something else shot at him from close range and a las-round spat past his ear.

He fired again, blinded by the close shot, and heard a dead weight fall.

Something grabbed him from behind.

There was an impact, and a spray of dust and blood. Vamberfeld fell over clumsily, a corpse on top of him. Face down in the hot dirt, Vamberfeld found his vision returning. He was suffused in blue light.

Power sword smoking, Ibram Gaunt dragged him up by the hand.

'Good work, Vamberfeld. We've taken the breach,' he said.

Vamberfeld was dumbstruck. And also covered in blood.

'Stay sane,' Gaunt told him, 'It gets better...'

They were in a cloister, or a circumambulatory, as far as the dazed Verghastite could tell. Bright shafts of sunlight stippled down through the complex sandstone lattices, but the main window sections were screened with ornately mosaiced wood panels. The air was dry and dead, and rich with the afterscents of las-fire, fyceline and fresh blood.

Vamberfeld could see Gaunt and Caffran moving ahead, Caffran hugging the cloister walls and searching for targets as Gaunt perused the enemy dead.

The dead. The dreaded Infardi.

When they had seized Hagia, the Chaos forces had taken the name Infardi, which meant 'pilgrims' in the local language, and adopted a green silk uniform that mocked the shrineworld's religion. The name was meant to mock it too; by choosing a name in the local tongue, the enemy were defiling the very sanctity of the place. For six thousand years, this had been the shrineworld of Saint Sabbat, one of the most beloved of Imperial saints, after whom this entire star cluster – and this Imperial crusade – were named. By taking Hagia and proclaiming themselves pilgrims, the foe were committing the ultimate desecration. What unholy rites they had conducted here in Hagia's holy places did not bear thinking about.

Vamberfeld had learned all about Pater Sin and his Chaos filth from the regimental briefings on the troop ship. Seeing it was something else. He glanced at the corpse nearest him: a large, gnarled man swathed in green silk wraps. Where the wraps parted or were torn away, Vamberfeld could see a wealth of tattoos: images of Saint Sabbat in grotesque congress with lascivious daemons, images of hell, runes of Chaos overstamping and polluting blessed symbols.

He felt light-headed. Despite the months of training he had endured after joining the Ghosts, he was still out of shape: a desk-bound cleric playing at being soldier.

His panic deepened.

Caffran was suddenly firing again, splintering the dark with his muzzle-flashes. Vamberfeld couldn't see Gaunt any more. He threw himself flat on his belly and propped his gun as Colonel Corbec had taught him during Fundamental and Preparatory. His shots rattled up the colonnade past Caffran, supporting the young Tanith's salvoes.

Ahead, a flock of figures in shimmering green flickered down the cloister, firing lasguns and automatic hard-slug weapons at them. Vamberfeld could hear chanting too.

Chanting wasn't the right word, he realised. As they approached, the figures were murmuring, muttering long and complex phrases that overlapped and intertwined. He felt the sweat on his back go cold. He fired again. These troops were Infardi, the elite of Pater Sin. Emperor save him, he was in it up to his neck!

Gaunt dropped to his knee next to him, aiming and firing his bolt pistol in a two-handed brace. The trio of Imperial guns pummelled the Infardi advance in the narrow space.

There was a flash and a dull roar, and then light streamed in ahead of them, cutting into the side of the Infardi charge. Blowing another breach in the cloister, more Ghosts poured in, slaughtering the advancing foe.

Gaunt rose. The half-seen fighting ahead was sporadic now. He keyed his microbead intercom.

There was a click of static that Vamberfeld felt in his own earpiece, then: 'One, this is three. Clearing the space.' A pause, gunfire. 'Clearance confirmed.'

'One, three. Good work, Rawne. Fan inward and secure the precinct of the Universitariat.'

'Three, acknowledged.'

Gaunt looked down at Vamberfeld. 'You can get up now,' he said.

DIZZY, HIS HEART pounding, Vamberfeld almost fell back out into the sunlight and wind of the square. He thought he might pass out, or worse, vomit. He stood with his back to the hot cloister stonework and breathed deeply, aware of how cold his skin was.

He tried to find something to focus his attention on. Above the stupa and gilt domes of the Universitariat thousands of flags, pennants and banners fluttered in the eternal wind of Hagia. He had been told the faithful raised them in the belief that by inscribing their sins onto the banners they would have them blown away and absolved. There were so many... so many colours, shapes, designs...

Vamberfeld looked away.

The Square of Sublime Tranquillity was now full of advancing Ghosts, a hundred or more, spilling out across the pink flagstones, checking doors and cloister entranceways. A large group had formed around the gibbet where Mkoll was cutting the corpses down.

Vamberfeld slid down the wall until he was sitting on the stone flags of the square. He began to shake.

He was still shaking when the medics found him.

MKOLL, LILLO AND Larkin were lowering the king's pitiful corpse when Gaunt approached. The colonel-commissar looked dourly at the tortured remains. Kings were two a penny on Hagia: a feudal world, controlled by city-states in the name of the hallowed God-Emperor, and every town had a king. But the king of Doctrinopolis, Hagia's first city, was the most exalted, the closest Hagia had to a planetary lord, and to see the highest officer of the Imperium disfigured so gravely offended Gaunt's heart.

'Infareem Infardus,' Gaunt muttered, remembering at last the high king's name from his briefing slates. He took off his cap and bowed his head. 'May the beloved Emperor rest you.'

'What do we do with them, sir?' Mkoll asked, gesturing to the miserable bodies.

'Whatever local custom decrees,' Gaunt answered. He looked about. 'Trooper! Over here!'

Trooper Brin Milo, the youngest Ghost, came running over at his commander's cry. The only civilian saved from Tanith, saved by Gaunt personally, Milo had served as Gaunt's adjutant until he had been old enough to join the ranks. All the Ghosts respected his close association with the colonel-commissar. Though an ordinary trooper, Milo was held in special regard.

Personally, Milo hated the fact that he was seen as a lucky charm.

'Sir?'

'I want you to find some of the locals, priests especially, and learn from them how they wish these bodies to be treated. I want it done according to their custom, Brin.'

Milo nodded and saluted. 'I'll see to it, sir.'

Gaunt turned away. Beyond the majestic Universitariat and the clustering roofs of the Doctrinopolis rose the Citadel, a vast white marble palace capping a high rock plateau. Pater Sin, the unholy intelligence behind the heretic army that had taken the Doctrinopolis, the commanding presence behind the entire enemy forces on this world, was up there somewhere. The Citadel was the primary objective, but getting to it was proving to be a slow, bloody effort for the Imperial forces as they claimed their way through the Doctrinopolis street by street.

Gaunt called up his vox-officer, Raglon, and ordered him to patch links with the second and third fronts. Raglon had just reached Colonel Farris, commander of the Brevian Centennials at the sharp end of the third front pushing in through the north of the city, when they heard fresh firing from the Universitariat. Rawne's unit had engaged the enemy again.

FOUR KILOMETRES EAST, in the narrow streets of the quarter known as Old Town, the Tanith second front was locked in hard. Old Town was a warren of maze-like streets that wound between high, teetering dwellings linking small commercial yards and larger market places. A large number of Infardi, driven out of the defences on the holy river by the initial push of the Imperial armour, had gone to ground here.

It was bitter stuff, house to house, dwelling to dwelling, street to street. But the Tanith Ghosts, masters of stealth, excelled at street fighting.

Colonel Colm Corbec, the Ghost's second-in-command, was a massive, genial, shaggy brute beloved of his men. His good humour and rousing passion drove them forward; his fortitude and power inspired them. He held command by dint of sheer charisma, perhaps even more than Gaunt did, certainly more than Major Rawne, the regiment's cynical, ruthlessly efficient third officer.

Right now, Corbec couldn't use any of that charismatic leadership. Pinned by sustained las-fire behind a street corner drinking trough, he was cursing freely. The microbead intercom system worn by all Guardsmen was being blocked and distorted by the high buildings all around.

'Two! This is two! Respond, any troop units!' Corbec barked, fumbling with his rubber-sheathed earpiece. 'Come on! Come on!'

A drizzle of las-blasts rocked the old sandstone water-tub, scattering chips of stone. Corbec ducked again.

'Two! This is two! Come on!'

Corbec had his head buried against the base of the water-tub. He could smell damp stone. He saw, in sharp focus, tiny spiders clinging to filmy cones of web in the tub's bas-relief carvings, inches from his eyes.

He felt the warm stone shudder against his cheek as las-rounds hit the other side.

His microbead gurgled something, but the broken transmission was drowned by the noise of a tin ladle and two earthenware jugs falling off the edge of the trough.

'Say again! Say again!'

'–chief, we–'

'Again! This is two! Say again!'

'–to the west, we–'

Corbec growled a colourful oath and tore out his earpiece. He sneaked a look around the edge of the tub and threw himself back.

A single lasround whipped past, exploding against the wall behind him. It would have taken his head off if he hadn't moved.

Corbec rolled back onto his arse, his back against the tub, and checked his lasrifle. The curved magazine of the wooden-stocked weapon was two-thirds dry, so he pulled it out and snapped in a fresh one. The right-hand thigh pocket of his body armour was heavy with half-used clips. He always changed up to full-load when there was a chance. The half-spent were there at hand for dug-in resistance. He'd known more than one trooper who'd died when his cell had drained out in the middle of a firefight, when there was no time to reload.

There was a burst of firing ahead of him. Corbec spun, and noted the change in tone. The dull snap of the Infardi weapons was intermingled with the higher, piercing reports of Imperial guns.

He lifted his head above the edge of the tub. When he didn't get it shot off, he rolled up onto his feet and ran down the narrow alleyway.

There was fighting ahead. He leapt over the body of an Infardi sprawled in a doorway. The curving street was narrow and the dwellings on either side were tall. He hurried between hard shadow and patches of sunlight.

He came up behind three Ghosts, firing from cover across a market yard. One was a big man he recognised at once, even from the back.

'Kolea!'

Sergeant Gol Kolea was an ex-miner who'd fought through the Vervunhive war as a part of the 'scratch company' resistance. No one, not even the most war-weary and cynical Tanith, had anything but respect for the man and his selfless determination. The Verghastites practically worshipped him. He was a driven, quiet giant, almost the size of Corbec himself.

The colonel slid into cover beside him. 'What's new, sarge?' Corbec grinned over the roar of weaponsfire.

'Nothing,' replied Kolea. Corbec liked the man immensely, but he had to admit the ex-miner had no sense of humour. In the months since the new recruits had joined the Ghosts, Corbec hadn't managed to engage Kolea at all in small talk or personal chat, and he was pretty sure none of the others had managed it either. But then the battle for Vervunhive had taken his wife and children, so Corbec imagined Kolea didn't have much to laugh or chat about any more.

Kolea pointed out over the crates of rotting produce they were using as cover.

'We're tight in here. They hold the buildings over the market and west down that street.'

As if to prove this, a flurry of hard-round and laser fire spattered down across their position.

'Feth,' sighed Corbec. 'That place over there is crawling with them.'

'I think it's the merchant guild hall. They're up on the fourth floor in serious numbers.'

Corbec rubbed his whiskers. 'So we can't go over. What's to the sides?'

'I tried that, sir.' It was Corporal Meryn, one of the other Ghosts crouched in the cover. 'Sneaked off left to find a side alley.'

'Result?'

'Almost got my arse shot off.'

'Thanks for trying,' Corbec nodded.

Chuckling, Meryn turned back to his spot-shooting.

Corbec crawled along the cover, passing the third Ghost, Wheln, and ducked under a metal handcart used by the market's produce workers. He looked the market yard up and down. On his side of it, Kolea, Meryn and Wheln had the alley end covered, and three further squads of Ghosts had taken firing positions in the lower storeys of the commercial premises to either side. Through a blown-out window, he could see Sergeant Bray and several others.

Opposing them, a salient of Infardi troops was dug into the whole street-block. Corbec studied the area well, and took in other details besides. He had always held that brains won wars faster than bombs. Then again, he also believed that when it really came down to it, fighting your balls off never hurt.

You're a complex man, Sergeant Varl had once told him. He'd been taking the piss of course, and they'd both been off their heads on sacra. The memory made Colm Corbec smile.

Head down, Corbec sprinted to the neighbouring building, a potter's shop. Shattered porcelain and china fragments littered the ground inside and out. He paused near a shell hole in the side wall and called.

'Hey, inside! It's Corbec! I'm coming in so don't hose me with las!'

He swung inside.

In the old shop, troopers Rilke, Yael and Leyr were dug in, firing through the lowered window shutters. The shutters were holed in what seemed to Corbec to be a million places and just as many individual beams of light shafted in through them, catching the haze of smoke that lifted through the dark shop's air.

'Having fun, boys?' Corbec asked. They muttered various comments about the wanton proclivities of his mother and several other of his female relatives.

'Good to hear you're keeping your spirits up,' he replied. He began stamping on the pottery-covered floor.

'What the sacred feth are you doing, chief?' asked Yael. He was a youngster, no more than twenty-two, with a youngster's insubordinate cheek. Corbec liked that spirit a lot.

'Using my head, sonny,' smiled Corbec, pointing to his size eighteen field boot as he stomped it again.

Corbec raked away some china spoil and dragged up a floor-hatch by the metal yoke.

'Cellar,' he announced. The trio groaned.

He let the hatch slam down and crawled up to the window with them.

'Think about it, my brave Tanith studs. Take a look out there.'

They did, peering though the shredded shutter-slats.

'The market's raised... a raised podium. See there by that pile of drums? Gotta be a hatch. My money's on a warren of produce cellars under this whole market... and probably under that guild hall too.'

'My money's on you getting us all dead by lunchtime,' growled Leyr, a hard-edged, thirty-five year old veteran of the Tanith Magna militia.

'Have I got you dead yet?' asked Corbec.

'That's not the point–'

'Then shut up and listen. We'll be here til doomsday unless we break this deadlock. So let's fight smart. Use the fact this cess-pit of a city is a trazillion years old and full of basements, crypts and catacombs.'

He keyed his microbead intercom, adjusting the thin wire arm of the mike so it was close to his lips.

'This is two. You hearing me, six?'

'Six, two. Yes I am.'

'Bray, keep your men where they are and give the front of that hall a good seeing to in about... oh, ten minutes. Can you do that?'

'Six, got it. Firestorm in ten.'

'Good on you. Two, nine?'

'Nine, two.' Corbec heard Kolea's tight voice over the channel.

'Sarge, I'm in the pottery vendor's down from you. Leave Meryn and Wheln put and get over here.'

'Got you.'

Kolea scrambled in through the shell hole a few seconds later. He found Corbec shining his lamp-pack into the open cellar hatch.

'You know about tunnels, right?'

'Mines. I was a miner.'

'Same difference, it's all underground. Prep, we're going down.' He turned to Leyr, Rilke and Yael. 'Who's got a yen for adventure and a satchel full of tube-charges?'

Again, they groaned.

'You're safe, Rilke. I want you popping at those windows.' Rilke was a superb sniper, second only to the regimental marksmanship champion Larkin. He had a long-pattern needle-las. 'Give up any tubes you got to these plucky volunteers.'

Leyr and Yael moved back to the hatch. Each of them, like Corbec and Kolea, wore twenty kilos of matt-black composite body armour over their fatigues and under their camo-cloaks. Most of that weight came from the modular webbing pouches filled with ammo, lamp-packs, sheathed blades, waterproof microbead sets, coiled climbing rope, rolls of surgical tape, ferro-plastic binders, Founding-issue Imperial texts, door-spikes, flashbombs, and all the rest of the standard issue Imperial Guard kit.

'Gonna be tight,' mused Leyr sourly, looking down into the hole where Kolea's flashlight played.

Kolea nodded and pulled off his camo-cloak. 'Ditch anything that will get hung up.' Leyr and Yael did so, as did Corbec himself. The cloaks went onto the floor, as did other loose items. All four copies of the Imperial Infantryman's Uplifting Primer hit the cloaks at the same time.

The men looked at Corbec, almost ashamed.

'Ahh, it's all up here,' Corbec said, tapping his temple.

Sergeant Kolea tamped a spike into the tiled floor and ran the end of his climbing rope through the eye. He dropped the snake of cable down into the hole.

'Who's first?' he asked.

Corbec would have preferred to let Kolea lead, but this was his call and he wanted them to know he trusted it.

He grabbed the rope, slung his lasrifle over his shoulder, and clambered down into the hole.

Kolea followed, then Leyr. Yael brought up the rear.

The cellar shaft was eight metres deep. Almost immediately, Corbec was struggling and sweating. Even though he had ditched a lot of kit, the sheer bulk of his webbing and body armour was confining him and screwing with his centre of balance.

He landed on a floor in the darkness and switched on his lamp-pack. The air was thick and foetid. He was in a cellar space four metres wide, dripping with ancient fluid and rot. His boots sloshed through semi-solid waste and murk.

'Oh feth!' spat Leyr as he made the ground.

There was an arched conduit snaking off towards the underyard. It was less than a metre high and only half a metre wide. With kit and weapons, even stripped down, they had to hunch and edge in sideways, single file. The liquid ooze on the floor sucked up around their boot-tops.

Corbec attached his lamp-pack to the bayonet fitting under his lasgun's muzzle. He swung the weapon back and forth as best he could side on, bent over, and led them on into the soupy darkness.

'Probably wasn't the best idea in the galaxy to send either of us on this,' said Kolea behind him.

It was the closest Corbec had ever heard to a joke from the scratch sergeant. Apart from 'Try Again' Bragg, he and Kolea were the biggest men in the Tanith First. Neither Leyr and Yael topped out over two metres.

Corbec smiled. 'How did you manage? In the mines?'

Kolea slid round, passing Corbec in an awkward hunch. 'We crawled when the seams dipped. But there are other ways. Watch me.'

Corbec shone his light onto Kolea so that he and the two Tanith behind him could see. Kolea leaned back against the conduit wall until he was almost in a sitting position. Then he skirted along through the muck, bracing his back against the wall so that the top half of his body could remain upright. His feet ran against the foot of the far wall to prevent him slipping out.

'Very saucy,' said Corbec in admiration.

He followed suit, and so did Leyr and Yael. The quartet slid their way down the conduit. Overhead, through the thick stone, they heard heavy fire. The ten minutes were up. Bray had begun his promised firestorm.

They were behind, too slow.

The conduit fanned and then opened out into a wide box. The stinking ooze was knee deep. Their flashlights found bas-relief markers of old saints on the walls.

At least the roof was higher here.

Straightening up, they headed forward through the tarry fluid. They were directly under the centre of the market yard now, by Corbec's estimation.

Another conduit led away towards what he presumed was the guild hall. Now Corbec led the way, double-time, back-crawling down the low conduit as Kolea had taught them.

They came on a shaft leading up.

By flashlight, they could see the sides were smooth brick, but the shaft was narrow, no more than a metre square.

By force of thighs alone, it was possible to edge up the shaft with back braced against one wall and feet against the other. Corbec led again.

Grunting and sweating, he climbed the shaft until his face was a few centimetres from a wooden hatch.

He looked down at Kolea, Yael and Leyr spidered into the flue below him.

'Here goes,' he said.

He pushed the hatch up. It didn't budge initially, then it slumped open. Light shone down. Corbec waited for gunfire but none came. He shuffled up the last of the shaft, shoulderblade by shoulderblade, and pushed out into the open.

He was in the guild hall basement. It was boarded up and empty, and there were several corpses on the floor, drizzled with flies.

Corbec pulled himself out of the shaft into the room. The others followed.

Rising, their legs wet and stinking from the passage, they moved out, lasguns ready, lamp-packs extinguished.

The percussive throb of las-fire rolled from the floor above.

Yael checked the corpses. 'Infardi scum,' he told the colonel. 'Left to die.'

'Let's help their pals join them,' Corbec smiled.

The four took the brick stairs in the basement corner as a pack, guns ready. A battered wooden door stood between them and the first floor.

His foot braced against the door, Corbec looked back at the three Ghosts clustered behind him.

'What do you say? A day for heroes?'

All three nodded. He kicked in the door.

TWO
SERVANTS OF THE SLAIN

'Let the sky welcome you, for therein dwells the Emperor and his saints.'

— Saint Sabbat, proverbs

Brin Milo, his lasgun slung muzzle-down over his shoulder, made his way against the press of traffic approaching the square from the south. Detachments of Tanith and light mechanised support from the Eighth Pardus Armoured were pouring into the Universitariat district from the fighting zones to the south-west, moving in to support the commissar's push. Milo ducked into doorways as troop carriers and Hydra batteries grumbled past, and slid sideways to pass platoons marching four abreast.

Friends and comrades called greetings to him as they moved by, a few breaking step to quiz him on the front ahead. Most of them were caked in pink dust and sweating, but morale was generally high. Fighting had been intense during the last fortnight, but the Imperial forces had made great gains.

'Hey, Brinny-boy! What lies in store?' Sergeant Varl called, the squad of men with him slowing into a huddle that blocked the street.

'Light stuff, the commissar's opened it up. The Universitariat is thick with them though, I think. Rawne's gone in.'

Varl nodded, but questions from some of his men were drowned by an air horn.

'Come on, move aside!' yelled a Pardus officer, rising up in the open cab of his Salamander command vehicle. A line of flamer tanks and tubby siege gun platforms was bottling up behind him. More horns sounded and the coughing motors raised pink dust in the air of the narrow street.

'Come on!'

'All right, feth it!' Varl responded, waving his men back against the street wall. The Pardus machines rumbled past.

'I'll try and leave some glory for you, Varl!' the armour officer called out, standing in the rear of his bucking machine and throwing a mock salute as he went by.

'We'll be along to rescue you in a minute, Horkan!' Varl returned, raising a single digit in response to the salute that all the Tanith in his squad immediately mimicked.

Brin Milo smiled. The Pardus were a good lot, and such horseplay typified the good humour with which they and the Tanith co-operated in this advance.

Behind the light armour came Trojans and other tractor units hauling heavy munitions and stowed field artillery, then Tanith pushing handcarts liberated from the weavers' barns. The carts were laden with ammunition boxes and tanks of promethium for the flamers. Varl's men were called over to help lift a cart out of a drain gutter and Milo moved on.

Hurrying against the flow of men and munitions, the young trooper reached the arch of the great red-stone bridge over the river. Shell holes decorated its ancient surface, and sappers from the Pardus regiment were hanging over the sides on ropes, shoring up its structure and sweeping for explosives. In this part of the Doctrinopolis, the river surged through a deep, man-made channel, its sides formed by the basalt river walls and the sides of the buildings. The smooth water was a deep green, deeper than the shade of the Infardi robes. A sacred river, Milo had been told.

Milo took directions from the Tanith corporal directing traffic at the junction, and left the main thoroughfare by a flight of steps that brought him down onto a riverwall path leading under the bridge itself. The water lapped at the stone three metres below and reflected ripples of white off the dark underside of the bridge.

He made his way to an archway overlooking the water further along the wall. It was the river entrance to one of the lesser shrines and tired, hungry-looking locals loitered around the entrance.

The shrine had been turned into a makeshift hospital early in the assault by local physicians and priests, and now, on Gaunt's orders, Imperial medical personnel had moved in to take charge.

Troops and civilians were being treated side by side.

'Lesp? Where's the doc?' Milo asked, striding into the lamp-lit gloom and finding the lean Tanith orderly at work sewing up a Pardus trooper's scalp laceration.

'In the back there,' Lesp replied, blotting the sutured wound with a swab of alcohol-soaked cloth. Stretcher parties were arriving all the time, mostly with civilian injured, and the long, arched shrine was filling up. Lesp looked harried.

'Doctor? Doctor?' Milo called. He saw Hagian priests and volunteers in cream robes working alongside the Imperial medics, and attending to the particular customs and rites of their own people. Army chaplains from the Ecclesiarchy were ministering to the needs of the off-world Imperials.

'Who's calling for a doctor?' asked a figure nearby. She rose, straightening her faded red smock.

'Me,' said Milo. 'I was looking for Dorden.'

'He's in the field. Old Town,' said Surgeon Ana Curth. 'I'm in charge here.' Curth was a Verghastite who had joined the Tanith along with the Vervunhive soldiery at the Act of Consolation. She'd taken to combat trauma well during the hive-siege and Chief Medic Dorden had been amazed and grateful at her decision to join.

'Will I do?' she asked.

'The commissar sent me,' answered Milo with a nod. 'They've found...' he dropped his voice and steered her into a private corner. 'They've found the local lord. A king, I think. He's dead. Gaunt wants his body dealt with according to local custom. Dutiful respect, that sort of thing.'

'Not really my field,' Curth said.

'No, but I figured you or the doc might have got to know some of the locals. Priests, maybe.'

She brushed her fringe out of her eyes and led him through the infirmary crowds to where a Hagian girl in the coarse cream robes of a scholar was re-dressing a throat wound.

'Sanian?' The girl looked up. She had the long-boned, strong-featured look of the local population, with dark eyes and well-defined eyebrows. Her head was shaved except for a bound pony-tail of glossy black hair hanging from the back of her skull.

'Surgeon Curth?' Her voice was thin but musical.

She's no older than me, Milo thought, but with the severe shaved head it was difficult to guess an age.

'Trooper Milo here has been sent by our commanding officer to find someone with a good knowledge of Hagian lore.'

'I'll help if I can.'

'Tell her what you need, Milo,' said Curth.

MILO AND THE Hagian girl went out of the hospital into the hard sunlight of the river wall. She put her hands together and made brief nods of respect to the river and the sky before turning to him.

'You're a doctor?' Milo asked.

'No.'

'Part of the priesthood, then?'

'No. I am a student, from the Universitariat.' She gestured to her pony-tail. 'The braids mark our station in life. We are called esholi.'

'What subject do you study?'

'All subjects, of course. Medicine, music, astrography, the sacred texts... is that not the way on your world?'

Milo shook his head. 'I have no world now. But when I did, students at advanced levels specialised in their study.'

'How... strange.'

'And when you've finished your study, what will you become?'

She looked at him quizzically.

'Become? I have become what I will become. Esholi. Study lasts a lifetime.'

'Oh.' He paused. A line of Trojans rattled by over the bridge above them. 'Look, I have some bad news. Your king is dead.'

The Hagian put her hands to her mouth and bowed her head.

'I'm sorry,' Milo said, feeling awkward. 'My commander wants to know what should be properly done to... to care for his remains.'

'We must find the ayatani.'

'The who?'

'The priests.'

A WAILING NOISE made Rawne swing round, but it was only the wind.

He felt the movement of air against his face, gusting down the stone hallways and vaults of the Universitariat. Many windows had been blown out, and shell holes put through the walls, and now the windy air of Hagia was getting in.

He stood for a thoughtful moment, stealth cape swept back over one shoulder, lasgun slouched barrel-down across his belly staring into...

Well, he didn't rightly know what. A large room, scorched and burned out, the twisted, blackened limbs of fused sconces adhering to the sooty walls like stomped spiders. Millions of glass fragments littered the burnt floor. There were seared tufts of carpeting around the room edges.

What great purpose this room had once had was no longer important. It was empty. It was clear. That was all that mattered.

Rawne turned and went back out into the hallway. The wind, leaking through shell holes and exposed rafters, whined after him.

His clearance squad moved up. Feygor, Bragg, Mkillian, Waed, Caffran.. and the women.

Major Rawne still hadn't sorted his head out about the women. There were a fair number of them, Verghastites who had elected to join the Ghosts during the Act of Consolation. They could fight – feth! – he knew that much. They'd all been baptised in combat during the war for Vervunhive, common workers and habbers forced into fighting roles.

But still they were women. Rawne had tried to speak to Gaunt about it, but the colonel-commissar had droned on about various illustrious mixed or all female units in Guard history blah blah blah and Rawne had pretty much blanked him out.

He wasn't interested in history. He was interested in the future. And in being there to enjoy it.

Women in the regiment put a strain on them all. Cracks were already showing. There had been a few minor brawls on the troop ships: Verghastite men protecting the 'honour' of their women; men falling out over women; women fighting off men...

It was a powder keg and soon there'd be more than a few split lips and broken teeth to show for it.

Bottom line was, Rawne had never really trusted women much. And he'd certainly never trusted men who put too much trust in women.

Caffran, for example. One of the youngest Ghosts: compact, strong, a fine soldier. On Verghast, he'd gotten involved with a local girl and they'd been inseparable ever since. A couple, would you believe? And Rawne knew for a fact the girl had a pair of young children who were cared for amongst the other non-combatants and camp-followers in the regimental escort ships.

Her name was Tona Criid. She was eighteen, lean and hard, with spiky bleached hair and gang tattoos that spoke of a rough life even before the Vervunhive war. Rawne watched her as she walked with Caffran down the shattered Universitariat hallway, covering each other, checking doors and alcoves. She moved with easy grace. She knew what she was doing. The black Ghost uniform fitted her well. She was... good-looking.

Rawne turned away and scratched behind his ear. These women were going to be the death of someone.

The clearance squad prowled forward, picking their way down empty halls over the glass of broken windows and the kindling of shattered furniture. Rawne found himself moving level with the other female in his squad. Her name was Banda, an ex-loom worker from Vervunhive who'd fought in the famous guerilla company run by Gol Kolea. She was lively, playful, impetuous with close-cut curly brown hair and a figure that was a tad more rounded and feminine than that of the lithe ganger Criid.

Rawne signalled her on with a silent gesture and she did so, with a nod and a wink.

A wink!

You didn't wink at your commanding officer!

Rawne was about to call a halt and shout into her face when Waed signalled.

Everyone fell into shadows and cover, pressing against the hallway walls. They were reaching a turn. A wooden, red-painted door lay ahead, closed, and then further down the corridor, around the turn, there was an archway. The carpet in the halls had been rucked up and was stained and stiff with dried blood.

'Waed?'

'Movement. In the archway,' Waed whispered back.

'Feygor?'

Rawne's adjutant, the ruthless Feygor, nodded to confirm.

Rawne gestured some orders in quick succession. Feygor and Waed moved up, hunched low, hugging the right-hand wall. Bragg took the corner as cover and got his big autocannon braced. Banda and Mkillian went up the left side of the corridor until they reached the cover of a hardwood ottoman pushed against the wall.

Caffran and Criid slung their lasrifles over their shoulders, drew their blunt-nosed laspistols and went to the red door. If, as seemed likely, it opened into the same room as the archway, this could open their field of fire. And double checking it covered their arses.

Total silence. They were all Ghosts, moving with a Ghost's practiced stealth.

Caffran grasped the door handle, turned it, but didn't open it. He held it fast as Criid leaned down and put her ear to the red-painted wood. Rawne saw how she brushed her bleached hair out of the way to do it. He–

He was going to have to fething concentrate, he realised.

Criid looked round and made the open-handed sign for 'no sound'.

Rawne nodded, made sure all the squad could see him, raised three fingers and then dropped them one by one.

As the third finger dropped, Criid and Caffran went through the door low and fast. They found themselves in a large stone chamber that had once been a scriptorium before rockets had blown out the vast lancet windows opposite the door and shattered the wooden desks and writing tables. Caffran and Criid dropped for cover amid the twisted wooden wreckage. Las-shots spat their way from an archway at the far end of the room.

At the sound of gunfire from the room, Rawne's team opened up at the corridor arch. Fire was hastily returned.

'Caffran! What have you got?' Rawne snarled into his vox-link.

'The room doesn't go right along to your archway, but there's access through.'

Caffran and Criid crawled forward, popping the occasional shot off at the doorway over the broken lecterns and cracked stools. The floor was soaked with spilled ink and their palms were quickly stained black. Criid saw how the explosions had blown sprays of ink up the walls of the scriptorium: spattered patterns like reversed-out starmaps.

Caffran pulled open his hip-case and yanked out a tube-charge.

'Brace for det!' he yelled, ripping the foil strip off the chemical igniter and tossing the metal tube away through the doorway.

There was a bang that shook the floor and clouds of vapour and debris burst out of the hallway arch. Feygor tried to move forward to get a look in.

Criid and Caffran had risen and approached the inner doorway. Smoke wreathed the air and there was a pungent smell of fyceline. Just short of the doorway, Criid unslung her lasrifle and took something out of her pocket. It was the pin-mount of a brooch or a medal, the surface polished into a mirror. She hooked it over the muzzle of her weapon and pushed it into the room ahead of her. A turn of the wrist and the mirror slowly revealed the other side of the doorway.

'Clear,' she said.

They moved in. It was an annex to the scriptorium. Metal presses lined one wall. Three Infardi, killed by Caffran's charge, lay near the doorway. They were spattered and drenched by multi-coloured inks and tinctures from bottles exploded by the blast.

Rawne came in through the hallway arch.

'What's through there?' he asked, pointing to a small curtained door at the back of the annex.

'Haven't checked,' Caffran replied.

Rawne went to the door and pushed the curtain aside. A burst of las-fire pelted at him, punching through the cloth.

'Feth!' he cried, taking cover behind a mixing table. He fired through the doorway with his lasrifle and saw an Infardi crash sideways into a rack of vellum, spilling the whole lot over.

Rawne and Caffran went through the door. It was a parchment store, with no other exits. The Infardi, his green robes yanked up over his face, was dead.

But there was still shooting.

Rawne turned. It was outside in the corridor.

'We've picked up some–' MKillian's voice spat over the link.

'Feth!' That was Feygor.

Rawne, Criid and Caffran hurried to the corridor archway, but the force of crossfire outside prevented them from sticking their heads out. Las-shots smacked into the archway's jamb and ricocheted back into the annex room. One put a burn across Rawne's chin.

'Feth!' He snapped back in, smarting, and keyed his microbead. 'Feygor! How many!'

'Twenty, maybe twenty-five! Dug in down the hall. Gods, but they're putting up a wall of fire!'

'Get the cannon onto it!'

'Bragg's trying! The belt-feed's jammed! Oh crap–!'

'What? What? Say again?'

Nothing but ferocious las-fire for a second, then Feygor's voice crackled over the link again.

'Bragg's down. Took a hit. Feth, we're pinned!'

Rawne looked around, exasperated. Criid and Caffran were over by the blasted window arches in the main scriptorium. Criid was peering out.

'What about this?' Caffran called to the major.

Rawne hurried over. Criid was already up and out on the ledge, shuffling along the stone sill.

'You've got to be kidding...' Rawne began.

Caffran wasn't. He was up on the sill too, following Criid. He reached a hand down for Rawne.

The major put his rifle strap over his shoulder and took the hand. Caffran pulled him up onto the stone ledge.

Rawne swore silently. The air was cold. They were high up. The stone flanks of the Universitariat dropped away ninety metres below the scriptorium window, straight down into the green, opaque channel of the river. Above the scriptorium's sloping, tiled roof, domes and spires rose. Rawne swayed for a second.

Criid and Caffran were edging down the ledge, stepping gingerly over leaded rainwater spouts and gutter trays. Rawne followed them. Bas-relief wall carvings, some in the form of saints or gargoyles, all weathered by age, stuck out, in some places wider than the ledge. Rawne found they had to go sidelong with their backs to the drop so they could hunch and belly around such obstructions.

He felt his foot go into nothingness and put his arms round a saint's stone neck, his heart thundering, his eyes closed.

When he looked again, he could see Caffran about ten metres away, but there was no sign of the girl Criid. Feth! Had she fallen off? No. Her bleached-blonde head appeared out of a window further down, urging them on. She was back inside.

Caffran pulled Rawne in through the broken window. He ripped his kneecaps on the twisted leading and toothy stubs of glass in the frame and it took him a minute to get his breathing rate down again. He looked around.

A seriously big artillery shell had taken this chamber out. It had come through the windows, blown out the floor and the floor beneath. The room had a ring of broken floorboards jutting out around the walls and a void in the centre. They worked their way round on the remains of the floor to the hallway door. The firing was now a way behind them.

Caffran led the way out into the corridor. The shell blast had blown the room's wooden door, complete with frame, out across the hall and left it propped upright against the far wall. The three Ghosts scattered back down the hall at a run, coming in behind the enemy position that was keeping the rest of their team pinned.

The Infardi, twenty-two of them, were dug in behind a series of barricades made from broken furniture. They were blazing away, oblivious to anything behind them.

Rawne and Caffran drew their silver Tanith knives. Criid pulled out her chain-dagger, a gang-marked legacy of her low-life Vervunhive days. They went into the cultists from behind and eight were finished before the rest became aware of the counter-attack.

Then it came to hand to hand, a frantic defence. But Rawne and Criid had begun to open fire with their lasguns and Caffran had pulled out his pistol.

An Infardi with a bayonet charged Rawne, screaming, and Rawne blew his legs and belly out, but the momentum of the charge threw the body into the major and knocked him down.

He tried to scramble out from under the slippery, twitching body. Another Infardi appeared above him, swinging down with one of those wicked, twist-bladed local axes.

A headshot toppled him.

Rawne got up. The Infardi were dead and his squad was moving up.

'Feygor?'

'Nice move, boss,' Feygor replied.

Rawne said nothing. He could see no point in mentioning that the sneak attack had been Caffran's and Criid's idea.

'What's the story?' he asked.

'Waed's taken a scratch. He's okay. But Bragg's got a shoulder wound. We'll need to vox up a team to stretcher him out.'

Rawne nodded. 'Good headshot,' he added. 'That bastard had the drop on me there.'

'Wasn't me,' said Feygor, jerking a dirty thumb at Banda. The ex-loom girl grinned, patted her lasgun.

And winked.

'Well... Good shooting,' Rawne mumbled.

IN A PRAYER yard east of the Universitariat precinct, Captain Ban Daur was controlling traffic when he heard the colonel-commissar calling his name.

Colonel Corbec's second front push had woken up the Old Town, and civilians who had been hiding there in cellars and basements for the best part of three weeks were now fleeing the quarter en masse.

In the long narrow prayer yard, the tide of filthy, frightened bodies moved west in slow, choked patterns.

'Daur?'

Ban Daur turned and saluted Gaunt.

'There are thousands of them. It's jamming up the east-west routes. I've been trying to redirect them into the basilica at the end of that street. We've got medical teams and aid workers from the city authorities and the Administratum down there.'

'Good.'

'There's the problem.' Daur pointed to a row of stationary Hydra battery tractors from the Pardus unit drawn up against the far side of the yard. 'With all these people, they can't get through.'

Gaunt nodded. He sent Mkoll and a group of Tanith away into a nearby chapel and they returned with pews which they set up as saw-horses to channel the refugees away.

'Daur?'

'Sir!'

'Get down to this basilica. See if you can't open up some of the buildings around it.'

'I was taking a squad into the Old Town, sir. Colonel Corbec has asked for more infantry team support in the commercia.'

Gaunt smiled. Daur meant market district, but he used a term from Vervunhive. 'I'm sure he has, but the war will keep. You're good with people, Ban. Get this working for me and then you can go get shot at.'

Daur nodded. He respected Gaunt beyond measure, but he wasn't happy about this order. It seemed all too characteristic of the jobs he'd found himself doing since joining the Ghosts.

In truth, Daur felt empty and unfulfilled. The fight for Vervunhive had left him hollow and grim, and he'd joined the Tanith mainly because he couldn't bear to stay in the shell of the hive he had called home. As a captain, he was the senior ranking Vervun Primary officer to join the Tanith, and as a result he'd been given a place in the regimental chain of command on a par with Major Rawne, as officer in charge of the Verghast contingent, answering only to Corbec and Gaunt.

He didn't like it. Such a role should have gone to a war hero like Kolea or Agun Soric, to one of the men who had pulled himself up by his bootstraps to earn the respect of the men in the scratch companies. The majority of the Verghastite men and women who had joined the Ghosts were workers turned warriors, not ex-military. They just didn't have the sort of respect for a Vervun Primary captain they had for a hero like Gol Kolea.

But that wasn't the way it was done in the guard, apparently. So Daur was caught in the middle, with a command role he didn't like, giving orders to men who he knew should be his commanders, trying to keep the rivalry between Tanith and Verghastite under control, trying to win respect.

He wanted to fight. He wanted to badge himself with the sort of glory that would make the troops look up to him.

Instead, he found most of his days spent on squad details, deployment orders, refugee supervision. He could do that kind of thing well, and Gaunt knew it. So he was always the one Gaunt asked for when such tasks came up. It was as if Gaunt didn't think about Ban Daur as a soldier. Just as a facilitator. An administrator. A people person.

Daur snapped out of his reverie as shots rang out and the refugees around him scattered and screamed. Some of Mkoll's makeshift sawhorses pitched over in the press. Daur looked around for a sniper, a gunman in the crowd...

One of the gun crew officers on the stationary Pardus vehicles was taking pot-shots with his pistol at the clusters of votive kites and flags that fluttered over the prayer yard. The flags and banners were secured on long tether-lines to brass rings along the temple wall. The officer was pinking at them for the entertainment of his crew.

'What the gak are you doing?' Daur shouted as he approached the Hydra mount. The men in their baggy tan fatigues and slouch caps looked down at him in puzzlement.

'You!' Daur yelled at the officer with the pistol in his hand. 'You trying to cause a panic?'

The man shrugged. 'Just passing the time. Colonel Farris ordered us up to help assault the Citadel Hill, but we're not getting anywhere, are we?'

'Get down here,' Daur ordered.

With a glance to his men, the officer holstered his service pistol and climbed down from the tractor. He was taller than Daur, with pale, freckled skin and blond hair. Even his eyelashes were blond.

'Name?'

'Sergeant Denil Greer, Pardus Eighth Mobile Flak Company.'

'You got a brain, Greer, or do you get through life with only that sneer?'

'Sir.'

Gaunt approached and Greer lost some of his bluster. His sneer subsided.

'Everything in order, Captain Daur?'

'High spirits, commissar. Everything's fine.'

Gaunt looked at Greer. 'Listen to the captain and be respectful. Better he reprimands you than I do.'

'Sir.'

Gaunt moved away. Daur looked back at Greer. 'Get your crews down and help us get these people off the road in an orderly fashion. You'll move all the quicker that way.'

Greer saluted halfheartedly and called his men down off the parked vehicles. Mkoll and Daur quickly got them to work moving civilians off the thoroughfare.

Daur moved through the filthy crowd. No one made eye contact. He'd seen that shocked, war-wrecked, fatigued look before. He'd worn it himself at Vervunhive.

An old woman, stick-thin and frail, stumbled in the crowd and went over, spilling open a shawl full of possessions. No one stopped to help. The refugees plodded on around her, stepping over her reaching hands as she tried to recover her possessions.

Daur helped her up. She was as light as a bag of twigs. Her hair was shockingly white and pinned back against her skull.

'There,' he said. He stooped and picked up her few belongings: prayer candles, a small icon, some beads, an old picture of a young man.

He found she was looking at him with eyes filmed by age. None of them had found his eyes out like that.

'Thank you,' she said, her voice richly flavoured with antique Low Gothic. 'But I don't matter. We don't matter. Only the saint.'

'What?'

'You'll protect her, won't you? I think you will.'

'Come on now, mother, let's move you along.'

She pressed something into his hand. Daur looked down. It was a small figurine, made of silver, worn almost featureless.

'I can't take this, it's–'

'Protect her. The Emperor would will it of you.'

She wouldn't take the trinket back, damn her! He almost dropped it. When he looked round again, she had disappeared into the river of moving bodies.

Daur looked about, confused, searching the moving crowd. He thrust the trinket in his pocket. Nearby, waving refugees past him, Daur saw Mkoll. He started to ask the scout leader if he'd seen the old woman.

A woman fell against him. A man just ahead dropped to his knees suddenly. Nearby in the crowd, someone burst in a puff of cooked blood.

Daur heard the shooting.

Not even twenty metres away, through the panicking crowd, he saw an Infardi gunman, shooting indiscriminately with a lasrifle. The killer had dragged back the dirty rags that had been concealing his green silk robes. He'd snuck in amid the refugee streams like a wolf coming through in the thick of a herd.

Daur drew his laspistol, but he was surrounded by jostling, screaming people. He heard the rifle firing again.

Daur fell over a body on the flagstones. He stumbled, looking through the running legs around him, catching sight of green silk.

The cultist's gunfire brought down more of the shrieking people. It made a gap.

Clutching his laspistol two-handed, Daur fired and put three shots through the gunman's torso; at almost exactly the same moment, Mkoll put a las-round through his skull from another angle.

The killer twisted and fell down onto the pink stones. Gleaming blood leaked out of him and threaded between the edges of the flags. There were bodies all around him.

'Sacred soul!' said Mkoll, moving through. Other Tanith troopers ran past, pushing through the crowd and heading for the north-east end of the yard. The vox-link buzzed and crackled.

More shooting, fierce exchanges, from the direction of the Old Town Road.

Daur and Mkoll pushed against the almost stampeding flow of refugees. At the north-east end of the prayer yard, a large sandstone pylon led through onto a long colonnade walk between temple rows. Ghosts were grouped in cover around the pylon, or were daring short runs down into the colonnade to shelter around the bases of black quartzite stelae spaced at regular intervals.

Gunfire, like a blizzard of tiny comets, churned up and down the colonnade. The long sacred walkway was littered with the bodies of native Hagians, sprawled out in twisted, undignified heaps.

More Ghosts ran up behind them, and some of the Pardus artillery men too, pistols drawn. Daur glimpsed Sergeant Greer.

'Go! Go left!' Mkoll yelled across at Daur, and immediately darted along from the arch towards the plinth of the nearest right-hand stelae. Four of his men gave him covering fire and a couple ran after him. Las-shots stitched across the walkway's flags and smacked chippings off the ancient obelisk.

Daur moved left, feeling the heat of a close round across his neck. He almost fell into the shadows of the nearest obelisk plinth. Other Ghosts tumbled in with him: Lillo, Mkvan and another Tanith whose name he didn't know. A Pardus crewman attempted to follow, but he was clipped in the knee and collapsed back into cover yelping.

Daur dared a look out, and glimpsed green movement further down the colonnade. The heaviest fire seemed to be coming from a large building on the left side of the colonnade which Daur believed was a municipal census hall.

'Left, two hundred metres,' Daur barked into his link.

'I see it!' Mkoll replied from the other side of the colonnade. Daur watched as the scout leader and his fireteam tried to advance. Withering fire drove them back into cover.

Daur ran again, reaching the next obelisk plinth on the left side. Shots were suddenly coming across him from the right and he turned to see two Infardi straddling the sloping tiles of a building, raking shots down into the shadows of the street.

Daur fired back, hastily, dragging his lasrifle off his shoulder. Lillo and Nessa reached his position around the same time and joined his fire. They didn't hit either of the Infardi but they drove them back off the roof out of sight. Broken tiles from the section of roof they had bombarded slithered off and crashed down onto the flagstones.

Mkvan reached their position too. The crossfire was intense, but they were a good twenty metres closer to the census hall than Mkoll's fireteam.

'This way,' Daur said, making sure he signed the words as he did so. Nessa was an ex-hab worker turned guerilla and like a fair number of the Verghastite volunteers, she was profoundly deaf from enemy shelling at Vervunhive. Signed orders were a scratch company basic. She nodded she understood, her fine, elfin features set in a determined frown as she slid a fresh ammunition cell into the port of her sniper-pattern lasgun.

Running stooped and low, the quartet left the main colonnade and ventured through the airy cool and shadows of a hypostyle hall. This temple, and the next which they crossed into via a small columned passage, was empty: what decoration and ornament the faithful hadn't taken and hidden prior to the invasion had been plundered by the Infardi during their occupation. Lamp braziers were overturned, and puddles of loose ash dotted the ceramic tiles of the floor. Splintered wood from broken furniture and prayer mats was scattered around. Along one east-facing wall, in a pool of sunlight cast by the hypostyle's high windows, a row of buckets and piles of rags showed where local people had attempted to scrub the Infardi's heathen blasphemies off the temple walls.

The four of them moved in pairs, providing bounding cover, two stationary and aiming while the other two swept forward to the next contact point.

The back of the second temple led into a subsidiary precinct that connected to the census hall. Here, the walls were faced in black grandiorite, but some Infardi hand had taken a sledgehammer to the ancient wall-carvings.

The Infardi had posted lookouts at the back of the census hall. Mkvan spotted them, and brought the Ghosts into cover as laser and solid shots cut into the arched doorway of the precinct and blew dusty holes in the ashlar.

Nessa settled and aimed. She had a good angle and two single shots brought down a couple of the enemy gunmen. Daur smiled. The vaunted Tanith snipers like 'Mad' Larkin and Rilke would have to guard their reputations against some of the Verghastite girls.

Daur and Mkvan ran forward through the archway, back into the bright sunlight, and tossed tube-charges in through the rear doors of the census hall. A row of small glass windows overlooking the alley blew out simultaneously and smoke and dust rolled back out of the doors.

The four Ghosts went in, knives fixed as bayonets, firing short bursts into the smoke. They came into the Infardi position from behind. The intense firefight began to split the airy interior of the census hall.

DAUR'S STRIKE IMMEDIATELY diluted the Infardi barrage from the front of the building, allowing the pinned forces in the colonnade ample chance to push in. Three fireteams of Ghosts, including Mkoll's, circled in down the colonnade.

By then, Gaunt had moved up to the front line amongst the stelae. 'Mkoll?'

'The front's barricaded firmly, sir,' the scout leader reported over the link. 'We've got their attention turned away from us... I think that's Daur's doing.'

Gaunt crouched behind a stelae and waved a signal down the line of crouching Ghosts ranged along the side of the colonnade. Trooper Brostin ran forward, the tanks of his flamer unit clanking.

'What kept you?' Gaunt asked.

'Probably all the shooting,' Brostin replied flippantly. The colonel-commissar indicated the census hall facade.

'Wash it out, please.'

Brostin, a big man with ursine shoulders and a ragged, bushy moustache, who always reeked of promethium, hefted the flamer around and thumbed the firing toggle. The tanks made a coughing gurgle and then retched a spear of liquid fire out at the census hall. The jet of flame arced downwards with yellow tongues and noxious black smoke curling off it like a mane.

Fire drizzled and trickled across the boarded front of the hall. Painted panels suddenly scorched black and caught fire. Paint peeled and beaded in the heat. The tie-beams over the door burst into flames.

Brostin took a few steps forward and squirted flame directly in through some of the tight firing slits in the hall's defences. Gaunt liked watching Brostin work. The burly trooper had an affinity with fire, an understanding of the way it ran and danced and leapt. He could make it work for him; he knew what would combust quickly and what slowly, what would burst in fierce incandescent flames and what would smoulder; he knew how to use wind and breeze to fan flames up into target dugouts. Brostin wasn't just hosing an enemy emplacement with flames here, he was artfully building an inferno.

According to Sergeant Varl, Brostin's skill with fire came from his background as a firewatcher in Tanith Magna. Gaunt could believe this. It wasn't what Trooper Larkin said, though. Larkin said Brostin was an ex-convict with a ten-year sentence for arson.

The fire, almost white, coiled up the hall front and caught the roof. A significant section of the front wall blew out into the street as fire touched off something volatile, perhaps an Infardi's satchel of grenades. Another section guttered and fell in. Three green-clad men came out of the hall door mouth, firing las-weapons down the colonnade. The robes of one of the trio were burning. Ghost weapons opened up all around and the three toppled.

A couple of grenades flew from the burning hall and exploded in the middle of the street. Then two more Infardi tried to break out. Mkoll killed both within seconds of them appearing at the doorway.

Now, under Gaunt's orders, the Ghosts were firing into the burning facade. A Pardus Hydra platform clanked down the centre of the colonnade, trailing a bunch of prayer-kite tails that had snagged on its barrels and aerial mount, and rolled in beside Gaunt's position.

Gaunt climbed up onto the plate behind the gunner and supervised as the NCO swung the four long snouts of the anti-aircraft autocannons down to horizontal.

'Target practice,' Gaunt told him.

The gunner tipped a salute and then tore the front of the census hall into burning scraps with his unforgiving firepower.

INSIDE, AT THE rear of the hall, Daur and his comrades were moving back the way they had come in. Thick black smoke boiled out from the main body of the hall. Daur, choking, could smell promethium and knew a flamer had been put to good work. Now there was a hell of a noise out front. Heavy fire, and not something man-portable.

'Come on!' he rasped, waving Nessa, Lillo and Mkvan back. The four staggered through the smoke wash, coughing and spitting, half blind. Daur prayed they hadn't lost their sense of direction.

They were remarkably unscathed. Mkvan had a scratch across the back of his hand and Lillo was cut along the forehead, but they'd hit the Infardi hard and lived to tell of it.

More heavy firing from the colonnade side. A couple of murderously powerful shots, glowing tracers, tore through a wall behind them and passed over their heads. The shots had passed right through the bulk of the census hall.

'Gak!' cried Lillo. 'Was that a tank?'

Daur was about to reply when Nessa gave out a gasping cry and doubled over. He swung around, eyes stinging with the smoke and saw five Infardi rushing them from the main hall area. Two were firing lasrifles. Another's robes had all been burnt off his seared body.

Daur fired, and felt the kiss of a las-round past his shoulder. Daur's gunfire blew two of the Infardi over onto their backs. Another charged Mkvan and was impaled on the Tanith's out-thrust bayonet. Thrashing, fixed, the Infardi shot Mkvan through the face point-blank with his pistol. Both bodies toppled over in the smoke.

Lillo was borne down by the other two who, weaponless, clawed at him and ripped into his clothes and skin with dirty, hooked fingernails. One got his hands on Lillo's lasrifle and was trying to pull it free, though the sling was hooked. Daur threw himself at the rebel and they went over, crashing back through the doorway and into the fire-swamped main hall.

The heat took Daur's breath away. The Infardi was hitting and biting and clawing. They rolled through fire. The enemy had his hands around Daur's throat now. Daur thought about his knife, but remembered it was still attached to the bayonet lug of his lasrifle, and that was lying out in the next room next to Mkvan's corpse.

Daur rolled, allowing the frantic Infardi to get on top of him, and then bucked and reeled, kicking up with his legs, throwing the cultist headfirst over the top of him. The cultist bounced off a burning table as he landed, throwing up a cloud of sparks. He got up, muttering some obscene oath, a smouldering chair leg in his hands, ready to wield as a club.

The roof came in. A five tonne beam, rippling from end to end with a thick plumage of yellow and orange flame, crushed the Infardi into the ground.

Daur scrambled up. His tunic was on fire. Little blue flames licked down the sleeve and the cuff, and around the seams of the pockets. He beat at himself, stumbling towards the door. He hadn't taken a breath in what seemed like two or three minutes. His lungs were full of searing heat.

In the annex at the back of the census hall, Lillo was trying to drag Nessa out through the back portico. Tarry black smoke was gusting out of the rafters and the air was almost unbearably toxic.

Daur stumbled towards them, over the burning bodies of the Infardi. He helped Lillo manhandle Nessa's dead weight. She'd been shot in the stomach. It looked bad, but Daur was no medic. He had no idea how bad.

A dull rumble echoed through the blazing hall as another roof section collapsed, and a gust of smoke, sparks and superheated air bellowed out around them. As they staggered through the portico into the rear yard, Daur heard something fall from his tunic and clink on the ground behind him.

The trinket. The old woman's trinket.

They dragged Nessa clear across the yard and Lillo collapsed by her side, coughing from the bottom of his lungs and trying to vox for a med-team.

Daur crossed back to the flaming portico, tearing off his smouldering tunic. The heat and flames had scorched the fabric and burst the seams. One of the pockets was hanging off by singed threads and it was from there that the silver trinket had fallen.

Daur saw it on the flagstones, lying just inside the portico. He hunkered down under the seething mass of black smoke that filled the upper half of the archway and roiled up into the windy blue sky. He reached for it and closed his fingers around the trinket. It was painfully hot from the blaze.

Something bumped into him and knocked him to his knees. He turned to face an Infardi cultist, his flesh baked raw and bloody, who had come blindly out of the inferno.

He reached out his blistered hands, clawing at Daur, and Daur snapped his laspistol from its holster and put two rounds through his heart.

Then Daur fell over.

Lillo ran across to him, but Daur couldn't hear what the trooper was shouting.

He looked down. The engraved hilt of the ritual dagger was sticking out of his ribcage and blood as dark and rich as berry juice was pumping out around it. The Infardi hadn't just bumped into him at all.

Daur started to laugh inanely, but blood filled his throat. He stared at the Infardi weapon until his vision became like a tunnel and then faded out altogether.

THREE
PATER SIN

'Fortune deliver you by the nine holy wounds.'

— ayatani blessing

HIS FATHER TURNED from the workbench, put down a greasy spanner and smiled at him as he wiped his oily hands on a rag. The machine shop smelled of cog-oil, promethium and cold metal.

He held out the piping hot cup of caffeine, a cup so big his small hands clutched it like a chalice, and his father took it gratefully. It was dawn, and the autumn sun was gliding up over the stands of massive nalwood trees beyond the lane that led down from the river road to his father's machine shop.

The men had arrived at dusk the previous night, eight raw-palmed men from the timber reserve fifteen leagues down river. They had a big order to meet for a cabinet maker in Tanith Magna and their main woodsaw had thrown its bearings. A real emergency... could the best mechanic in Pryze County help them out?

The men from the reserve had brought the saw up on a flatbed wagon, and they helped his father roll it back into the workshop. His father had sent him to light all the lamps. It was going to be a late hour before work would be finished.

He waited in the doorway of the shop as his father made a last few adjustments to the woodsaw's big motor and then screwed the grille cover back in place. Collected sawdust had spilled out of the recesses of the cover and the room was suddenly perfumed with the pungent fragrance of nalwood.

As he waited for his father to test the saw, he felt his heart beating fast. It had been the same as long as he could remember, the excitement of watching his father perform magic, of watching his father take dead lumps of metal and put them together and make them live. It was a magic he hoped he'd inherit one day, so that he could take over when his father had done with working. So that he'd be the machinesmith.

His heart was beating so fast now, it hurt. His chest hurt. He clutched the doorframe to steady himself.

His father threw the switch on the sawblock and the machine shrilled into life. Its rasping shriek rattled around the shop.

The pain in his chest was quite real now. He gasped. It was all down one side, down the left, across his ribs. He tried to call out to his father, but his voice was too weak and the noise of the running saw too loud.

He was going to die, he realised. He was going to die there in the doorway of his father's machine shop in Pryze County with the smell of nalwood in his nose and the sound of a woodsaw in his ears and a great big spike of impossible pain driving into his heart–

COLM CORBEC OPENED his eyes and added a good thirty-five years to his life. He wasn't a boy any more. He was an old soldier with a bad wound in a grim, grim situation.

He'd been stripped to the waist, with the filthy remnants of his undershirt still looped about his shoulders. He'd lost a boot. Where the feth his equipment and vox-link had gone was anybody's guess.

Blood, scratches and bruises covered his flesh. He tried to move and pain felled him back. The left side of his ribcage was a mass of purple tissue swelling around a long laser burn.

'D-don't move, chief,' a voice said.

Corbec looked around and saw Yael beside him. The young Tanith trooper was ash-white and sat with his back against a crumbling brick wall. He too had been stripped down to his breeches and dried blood caked his shoulders.

Corbec looked around. They were sprawled together in the old, dead fireplace of a grand room that the war had brutally visited. The walls were shattered skins of plaster that showed traces of old decorations and painting, and the once-elegant windows were boarded. Light stabbed in through slits between the planks. The last thing Corbec remembered was storming into the guild hall. This, as far as he could tell, wasn't the guild hall at all.

'Where are we? What h–'

Yael shook his head gently and gripped Corbec's arm tightly.

Corbec shut up fast as he followed Yael's look and saw the Infardi. There were dozens of them, scurrying into the room through a doorway out of sight to his left. Some took up positions at the windows, weapons ready.

Others moved in, carrying ammo crates and bundles of equipment. Four were manhandling a long and obviously heavy bench into the room. The feet of the bench scraped on the stone floor. The Infardi spoke to each other in dull, low voices.

Now he began to remember. He remembered the four of them taking the main chamber of the guild hall. God Emperor, but they'd punished those cultist scum! Kolea had fought like a daemon, Leyr and Yael at his side. Corbec remembered pressing ahead with Yael, calling to Kolea to cover them. And then–

And then pain. A las-shot from almost point-blank range from an Infardi playing dead in the rubble.

Corbec pulled himself up beside Yael, wincing at the pain.

'Let me look,' he whispered, and tried to see to the young man's injury. Yael was shaking slightly, and Corbec noticed that one of the boy's pupils was more dilated than the other.

He saw the back of Yael's head and froze. How was the boy still alive?

'Kolea? Leyr?'

'I think they got out. I didn't see...' Yael whispered back. He was about to say something else, but he fell suddenly dumb as a sigh wafted through the room.

Corbec felt it rather than heard it. The Infardi gunmen had gone quiet and were backing to the edges of the chamber beyond the fireplace, heads bowed.

Something came into the room, something the shape, perhaps, of a large man, if a man can be clothed in a whisper. It was something like a large, upright patch of heat haze, fogging and distorting the air, humming like the low throb of a drowsy hornet's nest.

Corbec stared at the shape. He could smell the way it blistered reality around itself, smell that cold hard scent of the warp. The shape was simultaneously translucent and solid: vapour-frail but as hard as Imperator armour. The more Corbec looked, the more he saw in the haze. Tiny shapes, twinkling, seething, moving and humming like a billion insects.

With another sigh, the refractor shield disengaged and dissolved, revealing a large figure wrapped in green silk robes. The compact generator pack for the body-shield swung from a belt harness.

It turned to face the two guard prisoners in the empty fireplace.

Well over two metres, built of corded muscle, with skin, where it showed past the rich emerald silk, decorated with the filthy tattoos of the Infardi cult.

Pater Sin smiled down at Colm Corbec.

'You know who I am?'

'I can guess.'

Sin nodded and his grin broadened. An image of the Emperor tortured and agonised was tattooed across his left cheek and forehead, with Sin's bloodshot left eye forming the screaming mouth. Sin's teeth were sharpened steel implants. He smelled of sweat and cinnamon and decay. He hunched down in front of Corbec. Corbec could feel Yael quaking with fear beside him.

'We are alike, you and I.'

'I don't think so...' said Corbec.

'Oh yes. You are a son of the Emperor, sworn to his service. I am Infardi... a pilgrim devoted to the cults of his saints. Saint Sabbat, bless her bones. I come here to do homage to her.'

'You come here to desecrate, you vile bastard.'

The steel grin remained even as Sin lashed out and kicked Corbec in the ribs.

He blacked out. When his mind swam back, he was crumpled in the centre of the room with Infardi all around him. They were chanting and beating time on their legs or the stocks of their rifles. He couldn't see Yael. The pain in his ribs was overwhelming.

Pater Sin reappeared. Behind him was the bench his minions had dragged in. It was a workbench, Corbec now saw. A stonecutter's bench with a big rock drill clamped to it. The drill whined. The noise had been in Corbec's dream. He had thought it was a woodsaw.

'Nine holy wounds the saint suffered,' Sin was saying. 'Let us celebrate them again, one by one.'

His men threw Yael on the bench. The drill sang.

There was nothing Corbec could do.

To the north of its area, the Old Town rose steeply, clinging to the lower scarps of the Citadel plateau. A main thoroughfare called, confusingly enough, Infardi Mile, curved up from the Place of Wells and the livestock markets and climbed through a more salubrious commercial neighbourhood, the Stonecutters Quarter.

One glimpse of the temples, the stelae, the colonnades – any of the Doctrinopolis's triumphant architecture – told a visitor how exalted the work of the stonecutters and the masonic guilds was. The most massive work, the great sarsens and grandiorite blocks, were brought in by river or canal from the vast upland quarries, but in their workshop houses on the skirts of the Citadel mount, the stonecutters carved their intricate statuary, gargoyles, ceiling bosses, cross-facings and lintels.

At the bottom end of Infardi Mile, the Tanith chief medic Tolin Dorden had set up a field aid-post in a ceramic-tiled public washhouse. Some of the men had carried in buckets or helmets full of water from the fountain pools in the square to sluice the washrooms out. Dorden had personally taken a disinfectant rub to the worktops where the clothes had been scrubbed. There was a damp, stale scent to the place, undercut by the warm, linty aroma that drifted from the drying cupboards over the heating vents.

He was just finishing sewing up a gash on Trooper Gutes's thumb when a Verghastite Ghost wandered in from the harsh sunlight in the square. The rattling thump of Pardus mortars shelling the Citadel rolled in the distance. Out in the square, Dorden could see huddles of Tanith resting by the fountains.

He sent Gutes on his way.

'What's the trouble?' he asked the newcomer, a broad-faced, heavy jawed man in his thirties.

'It's me arm, doc,' he replied, his voice full of the Verghastite vowel-sounds.

'Let me take a look. What's your name?'

'Trooper Tyne,' the man replied, dragging up his sleeve. The upper part of his left arm was a bloody, weeping mess, with infection setting in.

Dorden reached for a swab to start cleaning.

'This is infected. You should have brought it to me before now. What is it, a shrapnel wound?'

Tyne shook his head, wincing at the touches of the alcohol-soaked swab. 'Not really.'

Dorden cleaned a little more blood away and saw the dark green lines and the knife marks. Realising what it was, he cleaned a little more.

'Didn't the commissar issue a standing order about tattoos?'

'He said we could mark 'em if we knew how to do it.'

'Which you clearly don't. There's a man in eleven platoon, one of yours, what's his name... Trooper Cuu? They say he does a good job.'

'Cuu's a gak-head. I couldn't afford him.'

'So you did it yourself?'

'Mm.'

Dorden washed the wound as best he could and gave the trooper a shot. The Tanith were, to a man, tattooed. Mostly these were ritual or family marks. It was part of the culture. Dorden had one himself. But the only Verghastite volunteers with tattoos were gangers and slum-habbers wearing their allegiances and clan-marks. Now almost all of them wanted a mark – an axe-rake, a Tanith symbol, an Imperial aquila.

If you didn't have a mark, the sentiment went, you weren't no Ghost.

This was the seventeenth infected home-made mark Dorden had treated. He'd have to speak to Gaunt.

Someone was shouting out in the square. Trooper Gutes ran back in. 'Doc! Doc!'

Outside, everyone was on their feet. A group of Tanith Ghosts had appeared from the direction of the fighting down in the merchant market, carrying Trooper Leyr on a makeshift stretcher. Gol Kolea was running beside the prostrate man.

There was shouting and confusion. Calmly, Dorden pushed his way through the mob and got the stretcher down on the ground so he could look.

'What happened?' he asked Kolea, as he started to dress the las-wound in Leyr's thigh. The man was hurt, battered, covered in minor wounds and semi-conscious, but he wouldn't die.

'We lost the colonel,' Kolea said simply.

Dorden stopped his work abruptly and looked up at the big Verghastite. The men all around went quiet.

'You what?'

'Corbec took me and Yael and Leyr in under the guild hall. We were doing pretty well but there were too many. I got out with Leyr here, but Colonel Corbec and the lad... They got them. Alive. As we shot our way out of the hall, Leyr saw the bastards dragging both of them away.'

There was murmuring all around.

'I had to get Leyr to an aid-station. That's done. I'm going back for Corbec now. Corbec and Yael. I want volunteers.'

'You'll never find them!' said Trooper Domor, stunned and miserable.

'The bastards were taking them north. Into the high part of the Old Town, towards the Capital. They're holding positions up there. My guess is they're going to interrogate them. Means they'll be alive for a while yet.'

Dorden shook his head. He didn't agree with the brave Verghastite's assessment. But then he'd seen a great deal more of the way Chaos worked.

'Volunteers! Come on!' Kolea snapped. Hands went up all around. Kolea selected eight men and turned.

'Wait!' said Dorden. He moved forward and checked the minor wounds on Kolea's face and chest. 'You'll live. Let's go.'

'You're coming?'

Corbec was pretty much beloved by all, but he and the old doctor had a special bond. Dorden nodded. He turned to Trooper Rafflan, the vox-operator. 'Signal the commissar. Tell him what we're doing and where we're going. Tell him to get a medic down here to man the aid-post and an officer to supervise.'

Dorden gathered up a makeshift kit and hurried after the troopers moving out of the square.

'You're behind schedule, Gaunt,' said the clipped voice from the vox speaker. The lips of Lord General Lugo's three-dimensional holographic image moved out of sync with his utterance. Lugo was speaking via vox-pictor from Imperial Base Command at Ansipar City, six hundred and forty kilometres south-west of the Doctrinopolis, and atmospherics were causing a communications lag.

'Noted, sir. But with respect, we're inside the Holy City four days ahead of your pre-assault strategy prediction.'

Gaunt and the other officers present in the gloomy command tractor waited while the lag coped with the reply. Seated in harness restraints to the rear, astropaths mumbled and muttered. The hologram flickered and jumped, and then Lugo spoke again.

'Quite so. I have already applauded the work done by Colonel Furst's Pardus units in breaking you in.'

'The Pardus have done excellent work,' Gaunt agreed smoothly. 'But the colonel himself will tell you the Infardi put up little outer resistance. They didn't want to meet our armour head on. They fell back into the Doctrinopolis where the density of the buildings would work to their advantage. It's going street by street with the infantry now, and by necessity, it's slow.'

'Two days!' the vox crackled. 'That was the estimate. Once you'd entered the walls of the Holy City, you said you'd need two days to retake and consolidate. Yet you're not even near the Citadel!'

Gaunt sighed. He glanced around at his fellow officers: Major Kleopas, the squat, plump, ageing second-in-command of the Pardus armour; Captain Herodas, the Pardus's infantry liaison officer; Major Szabo of the Brevian Centennials. None of them looked comfortable.

'We're shelling the Citadel with mortars,' Szabo began, his hands in the patch-pockets of his mustard drab jacket.

Herodas cut in. 'That's true. We're getting medium firepower close to the Citadel. The heavies will pull in once the infantry have cleared the streets. Commissar Gaunt's representation of the theatre is accurate. Getting into the city proved to be four days easier than you estimated. Getting through it is proving harder.'

Gaunt shot the young Pardus captain an appreciative nod. A calm, united front was the only way to deal with tactically obsessed top brass-hole like Lugo.

The holographic figure jerked and fizzled again. A phantom of green light and mist, Lord General Lugo stared out at them. 'Let me tell you now that we are all but done here at Ansipar. The city is burning and the shrines are ours. My troops are rounding up the enemy stragglers for execution as we speak. Furthermore, Colonel Cerno reports his forces are within a day of taking Hylophan. Colonel Paquin raised the aquila above the royal palace at Hetshapsulis yesterday. Only the Doctrinopolis remains in enemy hands. I gave you the job of taking it because of your reputation, Gaunt. Was I wrong?'

'It will be taken, lord general. Your faith was not misplaced.'

A lag-pause. 'When?'

'I hope to begin full assault on the Capital by sundown. I will advise you of our progress.'

'I see. Very well. The Emperor protects.'

The four officers repeated the abjuration in a mumbled chorus as the hologram fizzled out.

'Damn him,' Gaunt murmured.

'He's there to be damned,' Major Kleopas agreed. He pulled down one of the metal frame slouch-seats from the wall of the tractor hull, sat his rotund bulk down and scratched at the scar tissue around the augmetic implant that served as his left eye. Herodas went to fetch them all caffeine from the stove rack by the rear hatch.

Gaunt took off his peaked and braided cap, set it on the edge of the chart display and tossed his leather gloves into it. He knew well what Kleopas meant. Lugo was new blood, one of the 'New Minted' generals Warmaster Macaroth had brought with him when he superseded Slaydo and took command of the Sabbat Worlds Crusade almost six sidereal years before. Some, like the great Urienz, had proved themselves just as able as the Slaydo favourites they replaced. Others had proved only that they were book-learned tacticians with years of campaign in the war-libraries of Terra and none at the front line. Lord General Lugo was desperate to prove himself, Gaunt knew. He'd botched command of his first theatre, Oscillia IX, turning a sure-thing into a twenty-month debacle, and there were rumours that an enquiry was pending following his lightning raids on the hives of Karkariad. He needed a win, and a victor's medal on his chest, and he needed them quickly before Macaroth decided he was dead weight.

The liberation of Hagia was to have been given to Lord Militant General Bulledin, which was why Gaunt had gladly approved his Ghosts for the action. But at the last minute, presumably after much petitioning behind the scenes by Lugo's faithful, Macaroth had replaced Bulledin and put Lugo in charge. Hagia was meant to be an easy win and Lugo wanted it.

'What do we do?' asked Szabo as he took a cup from Herodas.

'We do as we're told,' Gaunt replied. 'We take the Citadel. I'll pull my men back out of Old Town and the Pardus can shell it to pieces. Clear us a path. Then we'll storm the Citadel.'

'That's not how you want it to go, is it?' asked Kleopas. 'There are still civilians in that district.'

'There may be,' Gaunt conceded, 'but you heard the lord general. He wants the Doctrinopolis taken in the next few days and he'll make us scapegoats for any delay. War is war, gentlemen.'

'I'll make arrangements,' said Kleopas grimly. 'Pardus armour will be rolling through Old Town before the afternoon is old.'

There was a metallic rap at the outer hatch. A Tanith trooper on duty opened it and spoke to the figure outside as cool daylight streamed into the dim tactical chamber.

'Sir?' the trooper called to Gaunt.

Gaunt walked to the hatch and climbed down out of the massive armoured mobile command centre. The tractor, a barn-sized hull of armoured metal on four massive track sections, had been parked in a narrow street beside the basilica where the city's refugees were now being housed. Gaunt could see rivers of them still issuing from the Old Town district, pouring into the massive building under the supervision of Ghost troopers.

Milo was waiting for him, accompanied by a local girl in cream robes and a quartet of old, distinguished men in long gowns of austere blue silk.

'You asked for me?' Gaunt said to Milo.

The young Tanith nodded. 'This is ayatani Kilosh, ayatani Gugai, ayatani Hilias and ayatani Winid,' he said, indicating the men.

'Ayatani?' Gaunt asked.

'Local priests, sir. Devotees of the saint. You asked me to find out about–'

'I remember now. Thank you, Milo. Gentlemen. My trooper here has undoubtedly explained the sad news I bear. For the loss of Infareem Infardus, you have my commiserations.'

'They are accepted with thanks, warrior,' ayatani Kilosh replied. He was a tall man, bald save for a silver goatee. His eyes were immeasurably weary.

'I am Colonel-Commissar Ibram Gaunt, commander of the Tanith First and over-all commander of the action here at the Doctrinopolis. It is my wish that your high king, so miserably murdered by the arch-enemy, should receive every honour that is due to him.'

'The boy has explained as much,' said Kilosh. Gaunt saw how Milo winced at the word 'boy'. 'We appreciate your efforts and your respect for our customs.'

'Hagia is a holy world, father. The honour of Saint Sabbat is one of the primary reasons for our crusade. To retake her homeworld is my chief concern. By honouring your customs, I do no more than honour the God-Emperor of Mankind himself.'

'The Emperor protects,' the four priests echoed in concert.

'So what must be done?'

'Our king must be laid to rest in sanctified soil,' said Gugai.

'And what counts as sanctified?'

'There are a number of places. The Shrinehold of the Saint is the most holy, but here in the Doctrinopolis, the Citadel is the high hallowed ground.'

Gaunt listened to Kilosh's words and turned to look out past the jagged roofs of the Old Town towards the towering plateau of the inner Citadel. It was swathed in smoke, the white after-fog of heavy mortar shelling wisping away into the windy blue air.

'We have just drawn plans to retake the Citadel, fathers. It is our imperative. As soon as the way is clear, I will allow you through to perform your rites and lay your gracious ruler to rest.'

The ayatani nodded as one.

There, thought Gaunt. It's decided for me. Hell take Lugo's wishes, we have a need to recapture the Citadel now. Kloepas, Herodas and Szabo had emerged from the command tractor now and Gaunt waved them over. He signalled to his waiting vox-officer too.

'We're go for the Citadel,' Gaunt told the officers. 'Get the armour ready. I want shelling to begin in an hour from now. Beltayn?'

The Tanith vox-officer stepped up. 'Signal the Tanith units in the Old Town area to withdraw. The word is given. Armour assault begins in an hour.'

Trooper Beltayn nodded and hitched his vox-set around to his hip, coding in the orders for transmission.

'THAT ONE'S YOUR leader?' Sanian asked Milo as they waited in the shadow of the command tractor.

'That's him.'

She studied Gaunt thoughtfully. 'It is his way,' she said.

'What?'

'His way. It is his way and it suits him. Do you not have a way, Trooper Milo?'

'I... I don't know what you mean...'

'By "way", the esholi means destined path, boy,' said ayatani Gugai, looming at Milo's left side. Sanian bowed her head in respect. Milo turned to the old priest.

Gugai was by far the most ancient of the four priests Sanian had found for him. His skin was wizened and deeply scored with innumerable lines. His eyes were clouding and dim, and his body, beneath the blue silk robes, was twisted and hunched from a lifetime that had been both long and hard.

'I'm sorry, father... with respect, I still don't understand.'

Gugai looked cross at Milo's reply. He glanced at the bowed Sanian. 'Explain it to the off-worlder, esholi.'

Sanian looked up at Milo and the old priest. Milo was struck by the peerless clarity of her eyes.

'We of Hagia believe that every man and woman born in the influence of the Emperor–' she began.

'Fate preserve him, may the nine wounds mark his fortune,' intoned Gugai.

Sanian bowed again. 'We believe that everyone has a way. A destiny preordained for them. A path to follow. Some are born to be leaders, some to be kings, some to be cattlemen, some to be paupers.'

'I... see...' Milo said.

'You don't at all!' Gugai said with contempt. 'It is our belief, given to us by the saint herself, that everyone has a destiny. Sooner or later, God-Emperor willing, that destiny will realise itself and our way become set. My way was to become a member of the ayatani. Commander Gaunt's way, and it is clear, is to be a warrior and a leader of warriors.'

'That is why we esholi study all disciplines and schools of learning,' Sanian said. 'So that when our way becomes apparent to us, we are ready, no matter what it brings.'

Milo began to understand. 'So you have yet to find your... way?' he asked Sanian.

'Yes. I am esholi yet.'

Gugai sat his old bones down on an empty ammo box and sighed. 'Saint Sabbat was a low-born, daughter of a chelon herdsman in the high pastures of what we now call the Sacred Hills. But she rose, you see, she rose despite her background, and led the citizens of the Imperium to conquest and redemption.'

The best part of six years in the Sabbat Worlds Crusade had told Milo that much. Saint Sabbat had, six thousand years before, come from poverty on this colony world to command Imperial forces and achieve victory throughout the cluster, driving the forces of evil out.

He had seen images of her, bare-headed and tonsured, dressed in Imperator armour, decapitating the daemons of filth with her luminous sword.

Milo realised the girl and the old priest were staring at him.

'I have no idea of my way,' he said quickly. 'I'm a survivor, a musician... and a warrior, or that's what I hope to be.'

Gugai stared some more and then shook his head. It was the strangest thing. 'No, not a warrior. Not simply a warrior. Something else.'

'What do you mean?' asked Milo, disarmed.

'Your way is many years hence...' Gugai began, then stopped abruptly. 'You'll find it. When the time comes.' The old priest rose stiffly and wandered away to rejoin his three brethren, talking together quietly in the stepped portico of the basilica.

'What the feth was that about?' Milo barked, turning to the girl.

'Ayatani Gugai is one of the Doctrinopolis elders, a holy man!' she exclaimed defensively.

'He's an old madman! What did he mean I wasn't a warrior? Was that some kind of prophecy?'

Sanian looked at Milo as if he'd just asked the dumbest question in the entire Imperium.

'Of course it was,' she said.

Milo was about to reply when his earpiece squawked and combat traffic crackled into his link. He listened for a moment and then his face went dark.

'Stay here,' he told the girl student. He hurried towards Gaunt, who stood with the other Imperial officers at the rear steps of the command tractor. Sunlight barred down between the high roofs of the temple district and made pools on the otherwise dark street. Rat-birds, their plumage grey and dirty, fluttered between the eaves or roosted and gurgled in the gutters.

As Milo strode towards Gaunt he could see that the Tanith commander was listening to his own headset.

'You heard that, sir?'

Gaunt nodded.

'They've got Colonel Corbec. Kolea's leading a rescue party.'

'I heard.'

'So call off the withdrawal. Call off the armour.'

'As you were, trooper.'

'What?'

'I said – As you were!'

'But–' Milo began and then shut up. He could see the dark, terrible look in Gaunt's face.

'Milo... if there was a chance of saving Corbec, I'd hold up the entire fething crusade. But if he's been taken by the Infardi, he's already dead. The lord general wants this place taken quickly. I can't suspend an attack in the slim hope of seeing Colm again. Kolea and his team must pull out with the others. We'll take the Citadel by nightfall.'

There were many things Brin Milo wanted to say. Most of them were about Colm Corbec. But the look of Colonel-Commissar Gaunt's face denied them all.

'Corbec's dead. That's the way of war. Let's win this in his name.'

'SIGNAL HIM "NO",' Kolea drawled.

'Sir?' vox-officer Rafflan queried.

'Signal him a "no", gak take you! We're not withdrawing!'

Rafflan sat down in a corner of the ruined Old Town dwelling they had secured. Trooper Domor and four others moved past to the cracked and bare windows and aimed their lasguns. The old doctor, Dorden, weighed down with his medicae kit and loose-fitting black smock, was last into the building.

'I can't, sir, with respect,' said Rafflan. 'The colonel's signalled a priority order, code Falchion, verified. We are to withdraw from the Old Town now. Shelling is to commence in forty-six minutes.'

'No!' Kolea snapped. The men looked round from their positions.

Dorden settled in beside Kolea on the slope of plaster and rubble under the window.

'Gol... I don't like this any more than you, but Gaunt's made an order.'

'You never break one?'

'An order from Gaunt? You're kidding!'

'Not even on Nacedon, when he ordered you to abandon that field hospital?'

'Feth! Who's been talking?'

Kolea paused for a moment. 'Corbec told me,' he said.

Dorden looked down and ran a hand through his thinning grey hair. 'Corbec, huh? Damn it...'

'If they start shelling, we'll be hit by our own guns,' Trooper Wheln said.

'It's Corbec,' Dorden said simply.

'Don't signal,' said Kolea, reaching forward and unplugging Rafflan's headset. 'Just don't signal, if it makes you feel better. We've got to do this. You just never got the order.'

Mkvenner and Sergeant Haller called back that the street was clean. They were on the edge of the Stonecutters' district.

'Well?' Dorden looked at Kolea.

'Come on!' he replied.

TWO HOURS AFTER the midday chimes had peeled from the dozen or more clock towers in the Universitariat district, to be echoed by the clocks of the Old Town and beyond, the Pardus armour was unleashed.

Led by Colonel Furst aboard the legendary Shadow Sword super-heavy tank *Castigatus*, a storm-shoal of fifty Leman Russ Conquerors, thirty-eight Thunderer siege tanks and ten Stygies-pattern Vanquishers slammed into the southern lip of the Old Town.

Long-range bombardment from Basilisk units and Earthshaker platforms out in the marshes south of the city perimeter fell for twenty minutes until the tank squadrons were poised at the limits of the Old Town district. By then, firestorms were boiling through the street blocks from the livestock market north to Haemod Palisade and all the way across to Infardi Mile.

The tank groups plunged forward, their main weapons blasting as they went. Vanquishers and Conquerors followed the street routes, churning up the Mile like determined beetles under a rising pall of smoke and firedust that quickly shrouded the entire city. The hefty siege tanks ploughed straight through terraced habitation blocks and ancient dwelling towers with their dozer blades, bricks and building stone and tiles cascading off them. The thump and roar of the tank guns quickly became a drum beat heard by all of the citizens and soldiery in the Doctrinopolis. The Ghosts had fallen back into the suburbs south of the Old Town, and the Brevians had withdrawn clear of the firefield to the Northern Quarter above the Universitariat. Vox-officers reported to the tactical teams that Sergeant Kolea's team had not been recorded.

The fire splash of the tank wave rippled through the Old Town all the way up to the base of the Citadel. Twenty thousand homes and businesses burned or were flattened by shelling. The Chapel of Kiodrus Militant was blown apart. The public kitchens and the studios of the iconographers were blasted through and trampled under churning tracks. The Ayatani Scholam and the subsidiaries of the esholi were destroyed, and their brick litter toppled into the holy river. The ancient stones of the Indehar Sholaan Sabbat Bridge were hurled a hundred and fifty metres into the air.

The Pardus armour ploughed on, directed by Colonel Furst and Major Kleopas. They were one of the best armour units in this segmentum.

Old Town, and everything and everyone in it, didn't stand a chance.

FOUR
THE COLONEL AT BAY

'Lay a fire within your soul and another between your hands,
and let both be your weapons.
For one is faith and the other is victory and neither
may ever be put out.'

— Saint Sabbat, lessons

THE ROOM SHOOK. The walls and floor jarred slightly. Dust dribbled from the rafters. Onion-flasks full of water clinked against each other.

No one seemed to notice at first, except Corbec himself. He was sprawled on the floor, and he could feel the flagstones stirring under his palms and fingertips.

He looked up, but none of the Infardi had felt it. They were too busy with Yael. The boy was dead now; for that much Corbec was thankful, though it meant it would soon be his own turn on the bench. But the Infardi were still finishing their ritual butchery, adorning the corpse with shunned symbols while they muttered verses from polluted texts.

The room shook again. The bottles clinked. More dust trickled down.

Despite the gravity of his situation, perhaps even because of it, Colm Corbec smiled.

A shadow fell across him.

'Why do you smile?' Pater Sin asked.

'Death's coming,' Corbec replied, spitting a wad of bloody saliva into the floor dust.

'Do you welcome it?' Sin's voice was low, almost breathless. Corbec saw that Sin's metal teeth were so sharp they cut the inside of the bastard's own lips.

'I welcome death all right,' Corbec said. He sat up slightly. 'Takes me away from you for one thing. But I'm smiling 'cause it's not coming for me.'

The room shook again. Pater Sin felt it and looked around. His men stopped what they were doing. With curt words and gestures, Sin sent three of them hurrying from the room to investigate.

Corbec didn't need anyone to tell him what it was. He'd been close to enough mechanised assaults in his time to know the signs. The hard shocks of shells falling, the background vibration of heavy armour...

The room shook yet again, and this time there was a triple-peal of noise loud enough to be clearly identified as explosions. The Infardi were gathering up their weapons. Sin stalked over to one man who had a light vox unit and exchanged calls with other Infardi units.

By then, the shaking and the sound of the explosions was a constant background noise.

Sin looked over at Corbec.

'I expected this, sooner or later. You presume it's taken me by surprise, but in fact it's precisely what I...'

He paused, as if unwilling to give away secrets even to a half-dead old footslogger.

Sin made several guttural noises – Corbec decided they must be command words in the Infardi's private combat-code – and the gunmen made ready to leave en masse. Four of them grabbed Corbec and dragged him up with them. Pain flared through his torso, but he bit his lip.

His captors pulled and shoved him along dirty hallways and across an open courtyard behind the main body of the Infardi gunmen. In the yard, the sunlight was harsh and painful to Corbec, and the open air brought the sounds of the Imperial assault to him with greater clarity: the overlapping, meaty thump of explosions, the swooping air-rush of shells, the clanking grind of tracks, the slithering collapses of masonry.

Corbec found himself almost hopping along, trying to favour the foot with the boot on it. The Infardi punched and jabbed him, cursing him. They wanted to move faster than he could go. Besides, keeping one hand on him meant they each had only one hand free to manage ammo satchels, lasrifles and their other accoutrements.

They pressed on through the interior of a stonecutter's workshop where everything was coated thumb-deep in white stone dust, before emerging through a set of wooden shutters into a steep, cobbled street.

Above, not more than two kilometres away, rose the Citadel. It was the closest Corbec had been to the building. Its bleached cliff edges, fringed in mauve mosses and feathery lichens, thrust up above the skirt of roofs and towers formed by Old Town and the eastern hill quarters of the Doctrinopolis, supporting the ashlar-dressed pillars and temples of the holy city's royal precincts. The monumental buildings were flesh-pink against the blue of the sky. Sin's men must have taken him and Yael a good way north through the Old Town.

Looking the other way, the street swept down through the jumbled old dwellings and massy stoneshops towards the river plain where the Old Town started. The sky that way was a whirling haze of black and grey smoke. Fire licked through the town's flanks. Corbec could see series after series of shell-strikes fan in ripples through the streets. Geysers of flame, smoke, earth and masonry blew up into the air.

His guards pulled at him again and forced him up the slope of the street. Most of the other Infardi had already disappeared into the surrounding buildings.

The gunmen jostled him off the street, through a cast-iron gate into a level yard where stones and tiles were stacked ready for use. To one side, under an awning, sat three flat-pan work barrows and some cutter's tools; to the other, a pair of heavy old-pattern servitors that had been deactivated.

The men pushed Corbec down on the barrows. Pater Sin reappeared with eight other men, moving from an inner door across the yard, and words were exchanged.

Corbec waited. The barrows were covered in dusty sacking. The masons' tools were nearby: four big adzes, a worn mallet, some chisels, a diamond-bladed trowel. Even the smaller items were not small enough for him to conceal.

A whistling scream shook the yard as a shell passed directly overhead. It detonated in the neighbouring building and blew brick chips and smoke back over them with a boneshaking roar. Corbec pressed his head down into the sacking.

He felt something under the sacking, reached for it.

A heavy weight, small, about the size of a child's fist or a ripe ploin, with a cord attached. A stonecutter's plumb-line; a hard lead weight on the end of four metres of plaited silk string. Trying not to let them see, he tugged it out of the sacking on the barrow and wound it into his hand.

Pater Sin barked some more orders to his men, and then engaged his body-shield, effectively vanishing from view. Corbec saw his hazy shape, crackling in the dustclouds kicked up from the near-hit, leave the yard by the far side, accompanied by all but three of the men.

They turned back to him, approaching.

A salvo of tank shells fell on the street around with numbing force and noise. Luck alone had caused them to bracket the yard or, Corbec realised, he and his captors would have been pulped. As it was, all three Infardi were knocked over on their faces. Corbec, who had a more experienced ear for shelling times and distances than the cultists, had braced himself at the first whistle of the incoming shells.

He leapt up. One of the Infardi was already rising groggily, lasrifle swinging up to cover the prisoner.

Corbec spun the looped plumb-line in his hand quickly, letting the lead soar free on the third turn. It smashed into the gunman's left cheek with a satisfying crack and sent him tumbling back to the floor.

Corbec now spun the line over his head at the full length of its cord. He had built up enough force by the time the second gunman jumped up that it wrapped four times around his throat and cinched tight.

Choking, the cultist fell, trying to get the tough, tight cord off his throat.

Corbec grabbed his lasrifle, and managed to roll with it and fire off a pair of shots as the first Infardi got up again. He was firing as he rose, the dent of the plumb-weight bruising his face. Corbec's shots went through his chest and tossed him over on to his back.

Clutching his captured weapon, Corbec stood up. More shells fell close by. He put a shot through the head of the Infardi who was still trying to get the line off his neck.

The third was face down, dead. The close blast had buried a piece of tile in his skull.

The rolling thunder of the barrage was coming closer. There was no time to search the bodies for ammo or liberate a replacement boot. Corbec figured if he headed up the Old Town hill he could get around the side of the Citadel plateau and perhaps stay alive. It was undoubtedly what the Infardi were doing.

He went through the doors on the far side of the yard, in the direction Sin had taken. He kept hopping as shards of debris dug into the sole of his unprotected foot. He passed down a tiled hallway where the force of the blasts had brought the windows and blinds in, then on into a bay area where iron scaffolding was stored near to a loading ramp.

Between the beat of explosions, close and distant, he heard voices. Corbec crouched and peered through the loading area. The outer doors, tall and old and wooden, had been levered open, and a pair of eight-wheel cargo trucks had been backed in. Infardi, about a dozen of them, were loading sheet-wrapped objects and wooden crates into the rear of the vehicles.

There was no sign of Pater Sin.

Corbec checked the power-load of his appropriated weapon. Over three-quarters yield.

Enough to make them sit up and take notice at least.

THE BURNING STREETS were alive. Humans, locals, fleeing from their devastated homes and hiding places with bundles of possessions, driving thin, scared livestock before them.

And vermin... tides of vermin... pouring out of the inferno, sweeping down the hill streets of Old Town towards the river.

Kolea's team moved against the tide.

Chasing uphill at a run, with rebreather masks buckled over their faces to shut out the searing smoke, they tried to head away from the blast front of the encroaching armour brigade while steering a path towards the masons' district.

Now and then, shells fell so close they were all thrown off their feet by the shockwaves. Torched dwellings collapsed across streets to block their route. In places, they waded through living streams of rodents, guard-issue boots crunching on squirming bodies.

The eight Ghosts sprinted across another street junction, wafer-shreds of ash billowing around them, and took shelter in a leather worker's shop. It had been gutted by shells, just an empty ruin.

Dorden pulled off his rebreather and started coughing. By his side, Trooper Mkvenner rolled onto his side and tried to pull a shard of hot glass shrapnel out of his thigh.

'Let me see to it,' Dorden coughed. He used his medicae kit tweezers to tug the sliver out and washed the deep cut with antiseptic from a spray bottle.

Dorden sat back, mopping his brow.

'Thanks, doc,' whispered Mkvenner. 'You okay?'

Dorden nodded the question away. He felt half-cooked, wilted, choked. He couldn't draw breath properly. The heat from the burning buildings all around was like an oven.

By an exploded doorway in the far wall, Kolea and Sergeant Haller looked out.

'It's clear that way,' Kolea muttered, pointing.

'For now,' Haller conceded. He waved up troopers Garond and Cuu and sent them dashing over to secure the premises next door.

Dorden noted that Haller, a Verghastite recruit himself, and a veteran of the Vervun Primary regiment, favoured the troops he knew from his homeworld: Garond and Cuu, both Verghastites.

Haller was a cautious soul. Dorden felt the sergeant sometimes had too much respect for the heroic Tanith to give them orders.

The old medic eyed the other members of the squad: Mkvenner, Wheln, Domor and Rafflan, the other Tanith men. Harjeon was the only other Vervunhiver. A small, blond man with a wispy moustache, Harjeon cowered in the shelled out corner of the premises.

Dorden noted he could see a pecking order now. Kolea's in charge, and he's a war hero, so no one argues. Haller's ex-hive military, and so's Garond. Cuu... well, he's a law unto himself, an ex-ganger from the lowest hive levels, but no one doubts his mettle or his fighting smarts.

Harjeon... An ex-civilian. Dorden wasn't sure what Harjeon's calling had been in pre-guard life. A tailor? A teacher? Whatever, he rated lowest of all.

If they ever got out of this alive, Dorden knew he'd have to talk to Gaunt about evening up the prejudices that the new influx brought with them.

Volcanically, shells splashed down across the end of the street. They were showered with debris.

'Let's move!' Haller cried and took off after Cuu and Garond. Kolea waited, waving Harjeon and the Tanith past.

Dorden reached the doorway, and looked at Kolea as he adjusted his rebreather mask.

'We really should go back...' he began.

'Into that, doctor?' Kolea asked, gesturing back at the firestorm that boiled up through Old Town after them.

'We're out of options, I'm afraid,' Kolea said. 'Just to stay alive, we've got to keep ahead of the shells. So we might as well keep on and see if we can find Corbec.'

They ran through a wall of heat into the next ruin. Dorden saw the bare skin on his wrists and forearms was blistering in the crisping air.

They darted into the next building. It was remarkably intact and the air within mercifully cool. From the window, Dorden watched as shells slammed down close by. The building across the street seemed to shunt sideways, whole and complete, before disintegrating.

'Close, huh, Tanith?'

Dorden glanced round and met the eyes of Trooper Cuu.

Trooper Cuu. Lijah Cuu. Something of a legend already in the regiment. Just under two metres, slim, corded with muscle. Lean with a face like a bad lie. That's how Corbec had described him.

Cuu had been a ganger in Vervunhive before the war. Some said he'd killed more men in gang fights than he had in battle. He was tattooed extensively, and sold his ability with ink and needle to appreciative Verghastites. A long scar split his face top to bottom.

Trooper Cuu called everyone 'Tanith', like it was a scornful insult.

'Close enough for me,' Dorden said.

Cuu flexed around and checked over his lasrifle. His movements were feline and quick, Dorden thought. A cat, that's just what he is. A scarred and ragged tomcat. Even down to his chilly green eyes. Dorden had spent the last odd years in the company of exceptionally dangerous men. Rawne, that ruthless snake... Feygor, a soulless killer... but Cuu...

A casebook sociopath, if ever he'd seen one. The man had made a life of gang-fights and blade-wars long before the crusade had come along to legitimise his talents. Just being close to Cuu with his vivid tattoo gang marks and cold, lifeless eyes made Dorden uneasy.

'What's the matter, doc? Got no stomach for it?' Cuu chuckled, sensing Dorden's unease. 'Better you stayed at your nice safe aid station, huh?'

'Absolutely,' Dorden said and moved across to a place between Rafflan and Domor.

Trooper Domor had lost his eyes on Menazoid Epsilon, and augmetic surgeons had rebuilt his face around a pair of military gauge optic sensors. The Tanith men called him 'Shoggy', after the bug-eyed amphibian they decided he now resembled.

Dorden knew Domor well, and counted him a friend. He knew that Domor's implants could read heat and movement through stone walls and brick facades.

'You see much?'

'It's all empty ahead,' Domor replied, the milled focus rings of his implants whirring as they moved around on automatic. 'Kolea should put me up front. Me and Mkvenner.'

Dorden nodded. Mkvenner was one of the Tanith's elite scout troopers, trained by the infamous Mkoll himself. Between his senses and Domor's augmetic sight, they could be moving ahead with a great deal more confidence.

Dorden decided to speak to Kolea and Haller about it. He moved forward towards the bulky shape of the big miner and the lean figure of Haller, who still wore his spiked Vervun Primary helmet as part of his battledress.

A shockwave threw him off his feet into the far wall. Plaster smashed and slid away as he hit it.

For a fleeting, peaceful second, he saw his wife, and his daughter, long gone with Tanith itself and his son Mikal, dead these last few months on Verghast far away...

Mikal smiled, and detached himself from the embrace of his sister and his mother. He stepped towards his father.

'Sabbat Martyr,' he said.

'What?' Dorden replied. His mouth and nose were full of blood and he couldn't talk clearly. The joy and pain of seeing his son was making him cry. 'What did you say?'

'Sabbat Martyr. Don't die, dad. It's not your time.'

'Mikal, I...'

'Doc! Doc!'

Dorden opened his eyes. Pain shuddered through his waking body. He couldn't see.

'Oh feth,' he gurgled, blood filling his mouth.

Rough hands yanked his mask off and he heard liquid pattering on the rubble. He blinked.

Wheln and Haller were bent over him, anxious looks on their faces. 'W-what?' Dorden mumbled.

'Thought you were fething dead!' Wheln cried.

They helped him sit up. Dorden wiped his face and saw his hand came away bloody. He checked his face and realised his nose was streaming blood. The nosebleed had filled his mask and blinded his eye-slits.

'Feth!' he snarled, getting up. His head swam and he sat back.

'Who did we lose?' he asked.

'No one,' Haller said.

Dorden looked around. The shell had taken out the west wall of the building, but all his comrades were intact: Kolea, Cuu, Garond, Rafflan, Mkvenner, Harjeon.

'Charmed lives,' said Cuu with a chuckle.

With the help of Wheln and Haller, Dorden got to his feet. He felt like the spirit had been blasted out of him.

'You all right?' Kolea asked.

Dorden spat clotted blood and wiped his face. 'Just dandy,' he said. 'If we're going, let's just go, right?'

Kolea nodded, and signalled the party to their feet.

Firestorms were ripping down both sides of the street by them, and further shells were adding to the inferno. Behind the dwelling, they found that the shell had blown open a watercourse gurgling below street level in a brick defile.

Kolea and Mkvenner leapt down into it. The brackish water, perhaps an ancient tributary of the holy river, surged around their boots.

Dorden followed them down. It was cooler here, and the moving water seemed to wash away the thick smoke.

'Let's move along it,' Kolea suggested. No one argued.

In a tight line, the seven Ghosts tracked up the watercourse through the fires.

They'd gone no more than a hundred metres when Trooper Cuu suddenly held up his hand. The crude tatts of a skull and crossbones marked his knuckles.

'Hear that?' he asked. 'Las-fire!'

Corbec's shots tore through the loading bay. Two Infardi were slammed back off the side of one of the trucks. Another toppled, dropping the crate he had been carrying.

They started firing back almost immediately, pulling handguns from their sashes or grabbing the lasrifles leaning up against the wall. Glittering laser fire and whining hard rounds hammered into the stacked scaffolding around Corbec.

He didn't flinch. Kicking over a stack of scaffolding, he ran down the length of the bay's side wall, firing from the hip. Another Infardi clutched his throat, fell on his back and slithered off the bed of one of the trucks.

A bullet creased his tricep. A las-round tore through the thigh pocket of his combat pants.

He threw himself into cover behind an archway pillar.

It went unpleasantly quiet. Gunsmoke and the coppery stink of las discharge filled the air.

Corbec lay still, trying to slow his breathing. He could hear them moving around.

An Infardi came around the pillar and Corbec shot him through the face. A torrent of shots poured in his direction and the Tanith colonel started to crawl on his hands and knees down the stone passage. The wood-panelled walls above began to splinter and shred into the air as solid and energy rounds rained into them.

There was a doorway to his left. He rolled across into it, and got up. His hands were shaking. His chest hurt so much he could barely think any longer.

The room was an office of some sort. There were book cases and a large clerical desk lined with pigeon holes. Sheets of paper coated the floor, some fluttering in the breeze from the small, broken window high in the end wall.

There was no way out. The window was about large enough for him to stick his arm out of and that was it.

'Feth me..' Corbec murmured to himself, wiping a hand through his matted beard. He hunched down behind the heavy desk and laid the barrel of his weapon over the desktop, pointing at the doorway.

The gun's power cell was all but a quarter spent now. It was an old, battered Imperial issue job, with an L-shaped piece of metal brace welded on in place of the original stock. The makeshift brace jutted into his collarbone, but he aimed up as best he could, remembering all the things Larkin had taught him about spot shooting.

A figure in green silk darted across the door mouth, too fast for Corbec to hit. His wasted shot smacked into the far wall. Another swung round into the doorway, firing on auto with a small calibre machine pistol. The spray of bullets went high over Corbec's head and destroyed a bookshelf. Corbec put a single round into the Infardi's chest and threw him back out of sight.

'You messed with the wrong man, you bastards!' he yelled. 'You should have finished me when you had the chance! I'm gonna take the head off anyone who comes through that door!'

I just hope they don't have grenades, he thought.

Another Infardi ducked in, fired twice with his lasgun and jumped back out. Not fast enough. Corbec's shot didn't kill him but it went through his arm. He could hear whimpering outside.

Now a lasgun came around the doorframe, held out blind and firing. Two shots hit the desk hard enough to jerk it back against him. He shot back and the gun disappeared.

Now he could smell something. An intense chemical stink.

Liquid promethium.

They had a flamer out there.

GOL KOLEA SNAPPED his fingers and made three quick gestures.

Mkvenner, Harjeon and Haller sprinted forward to the left, down the side of the stonemason's shop. Domor, Rafflan and Garond ran right, around to the gaping entrance of the loading bay that opened onto the narrow back street. Cuu headed forward, jumped up onto a rainwater tank and from there swung up onto the sloping roof.

With Dorden at his heels, Kolea moved after them. The chatter of las and solid firing from inside the buildings was audible over the roar of the advancing tank assault down the hill behind them.

Domor, Rafflan and Garond rushed the bay doors, firing tight bursts. They came in on half a dozen Infardi who turned in abject surprise to meet their deaths.

Mkvenner, Harjeon and Haller kicked in big leaded windows and fired into the bay, cutting down a trio of Infardi who were running back through, alerted by the sudden firing.

Cuu shot in a skylight and began picking off targets below.

Kolea went in through a side door, firing twice to drop an Infardi trying to flee that way.

Dorden watched the Ghosts at work with awe. It was a stunning display of precision tactics, exactly the sort of work that the Tanith First-and-Only was famous for.

Caught from several angles at once, the enemy panicked and started to die.

One of the trucks spluttered into life and spun its heavy wheels as it started to speed out of the bay. Domor and Rafflan were in its way, and stood their ground, firing their lasguns from the shoulder, peppering the cab. Garond, to the side, raked the vehicle as it ran past.

Sharp-edged punctures stung the cab's metalwork. The windows shattered. It veered drunkenly, smashing a crate waiting to be stacked and rolling over the sprawled corpses of two Infardi with nauseating crunches.

At the last moment, Rafflan and Domor dived aside. The truck sped right across the back alley and battered nose-first into the opposite wall, which caved in around it.

Rafflan and Domor advanced into the bay, joining up with Garond and then with Kolea and Dorden. The soldiers formed a straggled knot, firing safety shots into corners where the collecting weapon-smoke blocked vision.

Dorden felt his pulse racing. He felt exposed, and more, he felt elated. To be part of this. Killing was misery and war was a bestial waste, but glory and valour... they were something else. Pleasures so intense and so fundamentally contiguous with the horrors he abominated, they made him feel guilty to cherish them. At times like this, he understood why mankind made war, and why it celebrated its warriors above all others. At times like this he could understand Gaunt himself. To see well-trained men like Kolea's squad take down a significantly larger force with discipline, skill and daring....

'Check the other vehicle,' Kolea snapped, and Rafflan turned aside to do so. Domor went ahead and covered the corner into a short passageway.

'Flamer!' he cried, leaping back, and a moment later fire gouted out of the passageway mouth.

Kolea pushed Dorden into cover and keyed his microbead.

'Haller?'

'Inside, sir! We're coming at you from the east. A little light opposition.' From the bay they could all hear the las exchanges.

'Go slow: we've got a flamer.'

'Understood.'

'I can get him, sure as sure,' Cuu's voice crackled.

'Do it,' Kolea instructed.

Trooper Cuu moved across the shop roof and swung his lithe body down through a gap between broken shutters. He could see the Infardi with the flamer now, cowering in a passageway outside some kind of office with two other gunmen.

Cuu could smell the sweet promethium reek.

From thirty metres, he put a las-round through the flamer operator's skull, then picked off the other two as they stumbled up in alarm.

'Clear!' he reported, gleefully. He crept forward.

'Who's out there?' a hoarse voice called from the office.

'That you, colonel?'

'Who's that? Lillo?'

'Nah, it's Cuu.'

'Is it clear?'

'Clear as clear.'

Corbec limped cautiously out of the doorway, gun raised, glancing around.

'Gak, ain't you a mess, Tanith,' smiled Cuu. He flicked open his bead.

'I found Colonel Corbec. Do I win a prize?'

'THAT'LL DO UNTIL we reach a proper aid post,' Dorden said, taping the last dressing tightly across Corbec's chest. 'You can forget about the war, colonel. This'll see you bed-ridden for a good two weeks.'

Weary and broken by pain, Corbec simply nodded. They were seated on crates in the bay while the other Ghosts regrouped. Cuu and Wheln were checking bodies.

'You find Sin?' Corbec asked.

Kolea shook his head. 'We count twenty-two dead. No sign of Sin, leastways not anybody who matches your description.'

Outside, the tremulous rumble of the armour wave was closer.

'What's Gaunt doing sending the infantry ahead of the tanks?' Corbec asked.

Kolea didn't reply. Rafflan looked away, embarrassed.

'Sergeant?'

'This is unofficial,' Dorden replied for Kolea. 'We came hunting for you.'

Corbec shook his head. 'Against orders?'

'The Pardus armour is putting Old Town to the torch. The assault on the Citadel has begun. The commissar ordered all infantry groups out.'

'But you came looking for me? Feth, was this your idea, Kolea?'

'We all kind of went along,' said Dorden.

'I thought you had more sense, doc,' Corbec growled. 'Help me up.'

Dorden supported Corbec as he shuffled over to the bay doors.

The colonel took a long look down the hill at the nightmare of fire and destruction moving up towards them.

'We're dead if we stay here,' Corbec said glumly.

'Right enough,' Mkvenner said. 'I reckon we should use that truck. Drive on over the hill, away from the assault.'

'That's Infardi territory!' Garond exclaimed.

'True, but I rate our chances that way higher. Besides, I'd guess they were falling back by now.'

'What's the matter, colonel?' Dorden asked, seeing a look on Corbec's face.

'Pater Sin,' he said. 'I can't figure it. We thought he was up in the Capital. I don't understand why he was down here in Old Town.'

'Driving his men? Hands-on, like Gaunt?'

Corbec shook his head. 'There was something else. He almost told me.'

Haller got up into the cab of the truck and turned the engine over. On the flatbed, Harjeon had opened one of the crates.

'What's this?' he called.

The crate was full of icons and holy statuettes, prayer texts, reliquaries. The men opened the other crates and found them all to be full of similar artefacts.

'Where is this all from?' asked Rafflan.

Kolea shrugged.

'The shrines of the Citadel. They must have plundered them all.' Corbec gazed down into one of the open crates.

'But why? Why take all this stuff? Why not just smash it? It's not sacred to them, is it?'

'Let's work it out later.'

The Ghosts climbed up into the rear of the truck. Haller took the wheel with Wheln riding shotgun beside him.

They rolled out of the battle-torn bay onto the backstreet, edged around the wreck of the other truck, and sped away up the hill.

Just after six o'clock, local time, a brigade-strength force of Brevian Centennials led by Major Szabo scaled the Holy Causeway and entered the Citadel. They met no resistance. The storm assault of the Pardus tanks had broken the back of the Infardi grip on the Doctrinopolis. Sixteen square kilometres of the city, the areas of Old Town flanking the noble plateau, were on fire and dead. Scout recons estimated what little numbers the Infardi could still muster had fled north, out of the city and into the rainwoods of the hinterland.

A victory, Gaunt realised, as Szabo's initial reports were relayed to him by the vox-operator. They had taken the Doctrinopolis and driven the foe out. Pockets of resistance remained – there was a hell of a street fight raging in the western suburbs – and it would take months to hunt out the Infardi who had gone to ground outside the city. But it was a victory. Lord General Lugo would be pleased. Or at least satisfied. In short order, Szabo's men would raise the Imperial standard above the Citadel, and under the fluttering aquila, the place would be theirs again. Hagia was theirs. A world liberated.

Gaunt climbed down from the command tractor and wandered alone down the street. He felt oddly out of sorts. There had been precious little glory in this theatre. His men had acquitted themselves well, of course, and he was happy to see the Tanith working confidently and efficiently alongside the Verghastite newcomers.

But it hadn't gone the way he would have liked. It might have cost him more in time and casualties, but he resented the fact that Lugo hadn't allowed him to clear Old Town and make a clean job of it. The Pardus were exemplary soldiers, and they'd cracked this nut. But the city had suffered unnecessarily.

He stood alone for a while in a prayer yard, watching the votive flags and kites dancing in the wind. The yard was littered with chips of stained glass thrown out when tank shells had gutted a nearby shrine.

This was the sacred beati's world, Saint Sabbat's world. He would have taken it whole, out of respect for her, not ruined it to crush the foe.

The darkening evening sky was thick with sooty smoke. Thanks to Lugo and his hunger for victory, they had razed a third of one of the most holy sites in the Imperium. He would resent this all his life, he realised. If Lugo had left him alone, he could have liberated the Doctrinopolis and left it standing.

Macaroth would hear of this.

Gaunt stepped into the cold silence of the ruined shrine and removed his brocaded cap before advancing down the temple aisle. Glass shards cracked under his jack boots with every pace. He reached the altar and knelt down.

Sabbat Martyr!

Gaunt started and looked round. The whisper had come from right behind him, in his ear.

There was no one in sight.

His imagination...

He settled back onto one knee. He wanted to make his peace with the saint in this holy place, to see if he could make amends for the excessive way they had driven out the infidel. And there was Corbec too, a loss that he would really feel.

But his mouth was dry. The words of the Imperial catechism would not form. He tried to relax, and his mind sought out the words of the

Throne Grace he'd been taught as a child at the Scholam Progenium on Ignatius Cardinal.

Even that simple, elementary prayer would not come.

Gaunt cleared his throat. The wind moaned through the broken window lights.

He bowed his head and–

Sabbat Martyr!

The hiss again, right beside him. He leapt up, drawing his boltgun and holding it out at arm's length.

'Who's there? Come out! Show yourself!'

Nothing stirred. Gaunt snapped his aim around, left, right, left again.

Slowly, he slid the heavy hand gun back into his leather button-down holster. He turned back to the altar and knelt again.

He let out a long breath and tried to pray again.

'Sir! Commissar, sir!'

Vox-trooper Beltayn was running frantically in through the temple doors, his vox-set falling off his shoulder and swinging round on its strap to bump against the end of the pews.

'Sir!'

'What is it, Beltayn?'

'You've got to hear this, sir! Something's awry!'

Awry. Beltayn's favourite word, always used as a masterpiece of understatement. 'The invading orks have killed everyone, sir! Something's awry!'... 'Everything's been awry since the genestealers turned up, sir...!'

'What?'

Beltayn thrust out the headset to his commander.

'Listen!'

MAJOR SZABO'S BREVIANS moved into the Citadel, fanning out, weapons ready. The towering shrines were silent and empty, pinkish stone gleaming in the light of the setting sun.

As they moved out of the sunlight into the slanted shadows of the temple pylons, Szabo felt a chill, as cold as anything he'd suffered in the winter-wars on Aex Eleven.

The men had been chatting freely and confidently as they advanced up the Citadel hill. Now their voices were gone, as if stolen by the silence of these ancient tombs and empty temples.

There was nothing, Szabo realised. No priests, no Infardi, no bodies, not even a speck of litter or a sign of damage.

He fanned the Brevians out with a few brisk hand signals. In their mustard-drab fatigues and body armour, the fire-teams clattered forward down parallel avenues of stelae.

Szabo selected a vox-channel.

'Brevia one. Zero resistance in the Citadel. It's damn quiet.'

He looked around, and sent Sergeant Vulle ahead into the lofty Chapel of the Avenging Heart with twenty men. Szabo himself advanced into a smaller chapter house where the Ecclesiarchy choir had lived.

Inside the portico, he saw the row of empty alcoves where the household shrine should have been.

Vulle voxed in from Avenging Heart. Every holy item, every icon, every text, every worship statuette, had been removed from the famous chapel. Other fire-teams voxing in from around the temple precinct reported the same. Altars were empty, votive alcoves were bare, relic houses were empty.

Szabo didn't like it. His men were edgy. They'd expected some fighting, at least. This was meant to be Pater Sin's bolt hole, the place where he'd make his last stand.

The Brevians spread out through the vast colonnades and temple walks. Nothing stirred except the wind across this high plateau.

With a lag-team of eight men, Szabo entered the main shrine, the Tempelum Infarfarid Sabbat, a towering confection of pink ashlar and cyclopean pillars, rising three hundred metres above the heart of the Citadel precinct. Here too the altar was bare. The size of a troop carrier, the colossal, gilt-swathed altar bore no branches of candelabras, no censers, no triptych screen, no aquila.

There was an odd scent in the air, a tangy smell like thick oil being fried, or pickled fish.

Szabo's lips were suddenly moist. He licked them and tasted copper.

'Sir, your nose...' his scout said, pointing.

Szabo wiped his nose and realised blood was weeping out of it. He looked around and saw that every man in his squad was leaking blood from their nose or their eyes. Someone started whimpering. Trooper Emith suddenly pitched over onto his face, stone dead.

'Great God-Emperor!' Szabo cried. Another of his men fell in a faint as blood poured out his tear ducts.

'Vox-officer!' shouted Szabo. He reached out. The smell was getting stronger, a thousand times more intense. Time seemed to be slowing down. He watched his own hand as he reached it out in front of him. How slow! Time and the very air around them seemed to have become treacle-thick and heavy. He saw his men, slowed down in time like insects in sap. Some half-fallen, limbs outstretched, some convulsing, some on their knees. Perfect, glinting droplets of blood hung in the air.

Someone had done this. Someone had been ready. They'd stripped the shrines of their holy, warding charms. And left something else in their place.

Something lethal.

'A trap! A trap!' Szabo yelled into the vox. His mouth was full of blood. 'We've set something off by coming in here! We–'

The choking overwhelmed him. Szabo let go of the vox handset and retched blood onto the polished floor of the Tempelum Infarfarid Sabbat.

'Oh Holy Emperor...' Szabo mumbled. There were maggots in the blood.

Time stopped dead. Over the Doctrinopolis, night fell prematurely.

In a flare of blue light, like the petals of a translucent orchid a kilometre across, the Citadel exploded.

FIVE
THE BECKONING

'From this high rock, from this peak, let the light of worship shine so that the Emperor himself might see it from his Golden Throne.'

— dedication on the high altar of the Tempelum Infarfarid Sabbat

THE CITADEL BURNED for many days. It burned without flames, or at least without any flames known to mankind. Mist-blue and frost-green tongues of incandescent energy leapt kilometres into the air like some flailing part of an aurora display anchored to the plateau. They fluttered helplessly in the wind. Their glare cast long shadows in daylight, and illuminated the night. At their base, the blues and greens became white hot, a blistering inferno that utterly consumed the temples and buildings of the Citadel, and the heat could be felt half a kilometre away down the hillslopes.

No one could approach closer than that. The few scout squads that ventured nearer were driven back by nausea, spontaneous bleeding or paroxysms of insane fear. Observations made from a safe distance by scopes or magnoculars revealed that the stone cliffs of the plateau were melting and twisting. Rock bubbled and deformed. One observer went mad, raving that he'd seen screaming faces form and loom out of the oozing stone.

At the end of the first day, a delegation of local ayatani and ecclesiarchs from the Imperial Guard retinues set up temporary shrines around the slopes of the Citadel and began a vigil of supplication, appeasement and banishment.

A dismal mood of defeat settled on the Doctrinopolis. This was an unparalleled disaster, worse even than the Infardi's annexation of the holy city. This was desecration. This was the darkest possible omen.

Gaunt was withdrawn. His mood was black and few dared to disturb him, even his most trusted Ghosts. He lurked in private chambers in the Universitariat, brooding and reviewing reports. He slept wretchedly.

Even the news that Corbec had been recovered, injured but alive, failed to lift his spirits much. Many believed that Gaunt's mood was so dark he would now mete severe punishment on Kolea's unit for disobeying the withdrawal orders, despite the fact they had saved the colonel.

The ayatani conducted a service of thanksgiving for the holy icons and relics Kolea's unit had brought back in the captured truck. It was a small, redemptive consolation in the face of the Citadel's destruction. The items were solemnly rededicated and placed in the Basilica of Macharius Hagio at the edge of the Old Town.

The surviving Brevians, two brigades who had not deployed into the Citadel with Szabo, entered into a ritual of remorseful fasting and mourning. A mass funeral oration was made on the second day, during which the roll of the fallen was read out, name by name. Gaunt attended, in full dress uniform, but spoke to no one. The guns of the Pardus Armour thundered the salute.

On the morning of the fourth day, Brin Milo crossed the Square of Sublime Tranquillity and hurried up the steps of the Universitariat's south gate with a feeling of dread inside him. Tanith sentries at the gatehouse let him past, and he walked through echoing halls and drafty chambers where teams of esholi worked in silence to salvage what they could of the books, papers and manuscripts the Infardi had left torn and scattered in the ransacked rooms.

He saw Sanian, industriously picking paper scraps from a litter of glass chips under a shattered window, but she didn't acknowledge him. Afterwards, he wondered if it had actually been her. With their white robes and shaved heads, the female esholi affected an alarming uniformity.

He turned at a cloister corner, trotted up a set of stone stairs under the watchful, oil-painted stares of several ex-Universitariat principals, and crossed a landing to a pair of wooden doors.

Milo took a deep breath, tossed the folds of his camo-cape over his shoulder and knocked.

The door opened. Trooper Caffran let him through.

'Hey, Caff.'

'Brin.'

'How is he?'

'Fethed if I know.'

Milo looked around. Caffran had let him into a small anteroom. A pair of shabby couches had been pulled up under the window to serve as makeshift daybeds for the door guards. On a side table were a few dirty mess trays, some ration packs, and some bottles of water and local wine. Sergeant Soric, Caffran's partner on watch duty, sat nearby, playing Devils and Dames Solo with a pack of buckled cards. He was using an upturned ammo box as a table.

He looked up and grinned his one eyed, lop-sided grin at Milo.

'He hasn't stirred,' he said simply.

Milo didn't have the measure of Soric yet. A squat, slabby barrel of a man, Agun Soric had been an ore smeltery boss on Verghast, then a guerrilla leader. Though overweight, he had massive physical power, the legacy, like his hunched posture, of hard years at the ore face as a youth. And he was old, older than Corbec, older even than Doc Dorden, who was the oldest of the Tanith. He had the same avuncular manner as Corbec, but was wilder somehow, more unpredictable, more given to anger. He'd lost an eye at Vervunhive, and had refused both augmetic implant or patch. He wore the puckered wink of scar tissue proudly. Milo knew the Verghastite Ghosts adored him, maybe even more than they did the noble, taciturn Gol Kolea, but he sensed Soric was still a Verghast man in his heart. He'd do anything for his own men, but was less forthcoming with the Tanith. To Milo, he typified the few amongst both Tanith and Verghastite who perpetuated the divide rather than seeking to close it.

'I have to see him,' Milo said. He wanted to say that Major fething Rawne had told him to come and see Gaunt because Major fething Rawne didn't fancy doing it himself, but there was no point getting into it.

'Be my guest,' Soric grinned disparagingly, gesturing to the inner doors.

Milo looked at Caffran, who shrugged. 'He won't let us in except to bring him meals, and he doesn't eat half of those. Gets through a feth of a lot of these, though.' Caffran pointed to the empty wine bottles.

Milo's unease grew. He'd been worried about disturbing Gaunt when his mood was bad. No one wanted to confront an ill-disposed Imperial commissar. But now he was worried about Gaunt himself. He'd never been a drinker. He'd always had such great composure and confidence. Like all commissars, he had been created to inspire and uplift.

Milo knew things here on Hagia had turned bad, but now he was afraid they might have taken Gaunt with them.

'Do you knock, or should I just–' Milo began, pointing at the inner doors. Caffran backed off with a shrug and Soric pointedly refused to look up from his dog-eared cards.

'Thanks a lot,' Milo said, and walked to the doors with a sigh.

THE INNER CHAMBERS were dark and quiet. The drapes were drawn and there was an unpleasantly musty smell. Milo edged inside.

'Colonel-commissar?'

There was no answer. He walked further in, blind in the gloom as his night vision tried to adjust.

Groping his way, he slammed into a book stand and sent it crashing over.

'Who's there? Who the feth is there?'

The anger in the voice made Milo start. Gaunt loomed in front of him, unshaven and half-dressed, his eyes fierce and bloodshot.

He was pointing his bolt pistol at Milo.

'Feth! It's me, sir! Milo!'

Gaunt stared at Milo for a moment, as if he didn't recognise him, and then turned away, tossing his gun onto a couch. He was wearing only his jackboots and uniform breeches, and his braces dangled slackly around his hips. Milo glimpsed the massive scar across Gaunt's trim belly, the old wound he had taken at Dercius's hands on Khed 1173.

'You woke me,' Gaunt growled.

'I'm sorry.'

Gaunt lit an oil lamp with clumsy fingers and sat down on a tub chair. He began leafing urgently through an old, hide-bound tome. Gazing at the book, he reached out without looking to snatch up a glass tumbler from a side table. He took a deep swig of wine and set it down again.

Milo moved closer. He saw the stacks of unread military communiqués piled by the chair. The top few had been torn into long shreds, and many of these paper tassels now marked places in the book Gaunt was studying.

'Sir–'

'What?'

'Major Rawne sent me, sir. The lord general is on his way. You should make ready.'

'I am ready.' Gaunt took another swig, his eyes never leaving the book.

'No you're not. You need a wash. You really need a wash. And you look like shit.'

There was a very long silence. Gaunt's hands stopped flipping the pages. Milo tensed, regretting his boldness, waiting for the other shoe to drop.

'This doesn't answer anything, you know.'

'What, sir?' Milo asked, and realised Gaunt was referring to the old book.

'This. The Gospel of Saint Sabbat. I felt sure there would be an answer in here. I've been through it line by line. But nothing.'

'An answer to what, sir?'

'To this,' Gaunt said, gesturing about himself. 'To this... monstrous disaster.' He reached for his glass again without looking and succeeded in knocking it onto the floor.

'Feth. Get me another.'

'Another?'

'Over there, over there!' Gaunt snapped impatiently, pointing to a sideboard where numerous bottles and old glasses stood.

'I don't think you need another drink. The lord general's coming.'

'That's precisely why I need another drink. I don't intend to spend a moment of my time in the company of that turd-brained insect if I'm sober.'

'I still don't–'

'Feth you, you Tanith peasant!' Gaunt snapped venomously and got up, tossing the book to Milo as he strode over to the sideboard.

Milo caught the book neatly.

'See if you can do better,' Gaunt hissed as he went through the bottles one by one until he found one that wasn't empty.

Milo looked at the book, thumbing through, seeing the passages Gaunt had feverishly underlined and scribbled over.

'Defeat is but a step towards victory. Take the step with confidence or you will not ascend.'

Gaunt swung round sharply, sloshing the overfilled glass he had just poured.

'Where does it say that?'

'It doesn't. I'm paraphrasing one of your speeches to the men.'

Gaunt hurled the glass at Milo. The boy ducked.

'Feth you! You always were a clever little bastard!'

Milo dropped the book onto the seat of the tub chair. 'The lord general's coming. He'll be here at noon. Major Rawne wanted you to know. If that's all, I request permission to leave.'

'Permission granted. Get the feth out.'

'WHAT DID HE say? How was he?' Caffran asked as Milo stepped out of the inner rooms and closed the doors behind him.

Milo just shook his head and walked on, out through the ruined hallways of the Universitariat, into the windy sunlight.

TEN MINUTES BEFORE noon, the sound of distant rotors thumped across the Doctrinopolis. Five dots appeared in the sky to the south-west, but in the glare of the Citadel fire it was hard to resolve them.

'He's here,' Feygor called.

Major Rawne nodded and smoothed the front of his clean battledress, made sure the campaign medals were spotless, and carefully put on his cap. He took one last look at himself in the full-length mirror. Despite the crazed cracks in it, he could tell he still looked every fething centimetre the acting first officer of the Tanith First Regiment.

He turned, and strode out of the derelict dressmaker's shop that had served as his ready room.

Feygor, Rawne's adjutant, whistled and fell in step beside him. 'Look out ladies, here comes the major.'

'Shut up.'

Feygor smiled. 'You're looking very sharp, I must say.'

'Shut up.'

They marched down a debris-strewn side street and out onto the massive concourse of the high king's royal summer palace on the holy river. The area had been cleared to allow the lord general's aircraft to land. Round the edges of the concourse, four platoons of Ghosts, two platoons of Brevians and three platoons of Pardus stood as an honour guard, along with delegations of local officials and citizens. There was a military band too, their brass instruments winking as they caught the sunlight.

The uniforms of the honour guard were clean and spotless. Colonel Furst, Major Kleopas and Captain Herodas had all put on dress kit. Medals were on show.

Rawne and Feygor approached them across the concourse.

'When you put on your cap, it was just the way Gaunt does it. Brim first.'

'Shut up.'

Feygor smiled and shrugged.

'And fall in,' added Rawne. Feygor, his own matt-black Ghost battle dress immaculate, double-timed and took his place at the end of the Ghost file. Rawne joined the officers. Furst nodded to him and Herodas stepped back to make room.

The band started to play. The old hymn 'Splendid Men of the Imperium, Stand Up and Fight'. Rawne winced every time they missed the repeated harmonic minor in the refrain.

'I didn't know you were a music lover, Major Rawne,' Captain Herodas said quietly.

'I know what I like,' Rawne said through gritted teeth, 'and what I'd like right now is for someone to jam that bass horn up the arse of the bastard who's molesting it.'

All four officers coughed as they stifled their laughter.

The lord general's transport approached.

The four ornithopter gunships flying escort thundered overhead, tearing the air with the beating chop of their massive rotors. They were painted ash-grey with a leopard pattern of khaki blotches. Rawne admired their power, and the bulbous gun turrets on their chins and the ends of their elongated tails.

Lord General Lugo's aircraft was a massive delta wing with a spherical glass cockpit at the prow. It was matt silver with beige jag-stripes and yellow chevrons on the wingtips alongside the Imperial aquila.

Its shadow fell across the honour guard as it paused in mid-air and the giant jet turbines slowly cranked around in their gimbal mounts from a horizontal position. With jets now flaring downwards, the huge transport descended, whirling up dust and extending delicate landing struts from cavities in the underwing.

It bounced slightly once, settled, and the screaming jets slowly powered down. A ramp set flush into the sky-blue painted belly gently unfolded and seven figures emerged.

Lord General Lugo strolled down the ramp, a tall, bony man in a white dress uniform, his chest burdened by the weight of medals on it. At his heels, two battle-armoured troopers in red and black from the Imperial Crusade staff marched in escort, hellguns raised. Behind them came a towering, stick-thin woman of advancing years dressed in the black leather and red braid of the Imperial tacticians, two colonels from the Ardelean Colonials with glittering breastplates and bright sashes of orange satin, and a thickset man in the uniform of an Imperial commissar.

The group advanced across the concourse and saluted the visitors.

Lugo eyed them all suspiciously, particularly Rawne.

'Where's Gaunt?'

'He... Sir... He...'

'I'm here.'

Dressed in full ceremonial uniform, Ibram Gaunt strode out across the concourse flagstones. From the attentive ranks of the honour guard, Milo sighed. He was relieved to see that Gaunt was clean and shaved. Gaunt's silver-trimmed black leather uniform was immaculate. Perhaps the unpleasant incident in the Universitariat had been just an aberration...

Gaunt saluted the lord general and introduced his fellow officers. The band played on.

'This is Imperial Tactician Blamire,' said Lugo, indicating the tall, elderly woman. She nodded. Her face was lean and pinched and her greying hair was cropped.

'I am here because of that...' Lugo said flatly, turning to look across the concourse and the holy city beyond to the flaring aurora flames flickering over the Citadel.

'That, lord, is an abomination we all regret,' Gaunt said.

'You will bring me up to speed, Gaunt. I want a full report.'

'And you'll have it,' said Gaunt, guiding the lord general across the concourse to the waiting land cars and their Chimera escort.

Lugo sniffed suddenly.

'Have you been drinking, Gaunt?'

'Yes, sir. A cup of altar wine during the morning obeisance conducted by the ayatani. It was symbolic and expected of me.'

'I see. No matter then. Now show me and tell me what I need to know.'

'Starting where, sir?'

'Starting with how this simple liberation turned into a pile of crap,' said Lugo.

* * *

'YOU REALISE IT's a signal,' said Tactician Blamire, lowering her magnoculars.

'A signal?' echoed Colonel Furst.

'Oh yes. The adepts of the Astropathicus have confirmed it as such... it's generating a significant psychic pulse with an interstellar range.'

'For what purpose?' asked Major Kleopas.

Blamire fixed him with a craggy gaze, a patient smile on her lips. 'Our imminent destruction, of course.'

The party of officers stood on the flat roof of the treasury, escorted by over fifty guardsmen. Prayer kites and votive flags cracked and shimmied in the air above them.

'I don't follow,' said Kleopas, 'I thought that it was just a spiteful parting gift from the enemy. A booby trap to sour our victory.'

Blamire shook her head. 'Well, it's not, I'm afraid. That phenomenon–' she gestured to the flickering blaze on top of the Citadel plateau. 'That phenomenon is an operating instrument of the warp. An astropathic beacon. Don't think of it as fire. What happened up there four days ago wasn't an explosion in any conventional sense. Its purpose wasn't to destroy the Citadel, or to kill those unfortunate Brevian troops. Its purpose is to beckon.'

'Beckon who?' asked Furst.

'Don't be dense,' said Gaunt quietly. He fixed Blamire with a direct gaze. 'The site was significant, of course. Sacred ground.'

'Of course. The warp-magic of their ritual required the desecration of one of our shrines.'

'That was why they removed all the relics and icons?'

'Yes. And then withdrew to wait for the Brevian Centennials to move in and act as the blood sacrifice to set it off. This Pater Sin clearly planned this contingency well in advance when it looked like his forces would be ousted.'

'And is it working?' Gaunt asked.

'I'm sorry to say it is.'

There was a long silence broken only by the whip and buffet of the flags and kites above them.

'We have detected an enemy fleet massing and moving through the immaterium towards us,' said Lord General Lugo.

'Already?' queried Gaunt.

'This summons is clearly something they don't intend to ignore or be slow about responding to.'

'The fleet... How big?' There was an anxious tone on Kleopas's voice. 'What is the scale of the enemy response?'

Blamire shrugged, rubbing her gloved hands together uncomfortably. 'If it is even a quarter the size we estimate, the combined liberation force here will be obliterated. Without question.'

'Then we need to reinforce at once! Warmaster Macaroth must retask crusade regiments to assist. We–' Lugo cut Gaunt off.

'That is not an option. I have communicated the situation to the Warmaster, and he has confirmed my fears. The reconquest of the Cabal system is now fully underway. The Warmaster has committed all the crusade legions to the assault. Many are already en route to the fortress-worlds. There are categorically no reinforcements available.'

'I refuse to accept that!' Gaunt cried. 'Macaroth is fully aware of this world's sacred significance! The saint's home world! It's a vital part of Imperial belief and faith! He wouldn't just let it burn!'

'The point is moot, colonel-commissar,' said Lugo. 'Even if the Warmaster was able to assist us here – and I assure you, he is not – the nearest Imperial contingents of any useful size are six weeks distant. The arch-enemy's fleet is twenty-one days away.'

Gaunt felt helpless rage boil up inside him. It reminded him in the worst way of Tanith and the decisions he had been forced to make there. For the greater good of the Sabbat Worlds Crusade, another whole damned planet was going to be sacrificed.

'I have received orders from the Warmaster,' said Lugo. 'They are unequivocal. We are to commence immediate withdrawal from this planet. All Imperial servants, as well as the planetary nobility and priesthood, are to be evacuated with us, and we are to remove the sacred treasures of this world: relics, antiquities, holy objects, works of learning. In time, the crusade will return and liberate Hagia once more and, at such a time, the shrines will be restored and rededicated. Until then, the priests must safeguard Hagia's holy heritage in exile.'

'They won't do it,' said Captain Herodas. 'I've spoken to the local people. Their relics are precious, but only in conjunction with the location. As the birthplace of Saint Sabbat, it is the world that really matters.'

'They will be given no choice,' snapped Lugo. 'This is no time for flimsy sentiment. An intensive program of evacuation begins tonight. The last ship leaves here no later than eighteen days from now. You and your officers will all be given duties overseeing the smooth and efficient running of said program. Failure will result in the swiftest censure. Any obstruction of our work will be punishable by death. Am I safe to assume you all understand what is required?'

Quietly, the assembled officers made it clear they did.

'I'm hungry,' Lugo announced suddenly. 'I wish to dine now. Come with me, Gaunt. I wish to explain your particular duties to you.'

'LET'S BE FRANK about this, Gaunt,' said Lugo, deftly shucking the shell of a steamed bivalve harvested from celebrated beds a few kilometres down river. 'Your career is effectively over.'

'And how do you figure that, sir?' Gaunt replied stiffly, taking a sip of wine. His own dish of gleaming black shellfish lay largely untouched before him.

Lugo looked up from his meal at Gaunt and finished chewing the nugget of succulent white meat in his mouth before replying. He dabbed his lips with the corner of his napkin. 'I assume you're joking?'

'Funny,' said Gaunt, 'I assumed you were, sir.' He reached for his glass, but realised it was empty, so instead picked up the bottle for a refill.

Lugo chased a morsel of food out of his cheek with his tongue and swallowed. 'This,' he said, with an idle gesture that was intended to take in the entire city rather than just the drafty, empty dining chamber where they sat, 'this is entirely your fault. You never were in particular favour with the Warmaster, despite your few colourful successes in the last couple of years. But there's certainly no coming back from a disgrace like this.' He took up another bivalve and expertly popped the hinged shell open.

Gaunt sat back and looked around, knowing if he spoke now it would be the beginning of a swingeing rant that would quite certainly end with him at the wrong end of a firing squad. Lugo was a worm, but he was also a lord general. Shouting at him would achieve nothing productive. Gaunt waited for his anger to subside a little.

The dining chamber was a high-ceilinged room in the summer palace where the high king had once held state banquets. The furniture had been cleared except for their single table with its white linen cloth. Six Ardelean Colonial infantrymen stood watch at the doors, letting through the serving staff when they knocked.

With Lugo and Gaunt at the table was the heavily-built commissar who had arrived with the lord general's party. His name was Viktor Hark, and he had said nothing since the start of the meal. Nothing, in fact, since he had stepped off the aircraft. Hark was a few years younger than Gaunt, with a short, squat stature that suggested a brute muscular strength generously upholstered in the bulk of good living. His hair was thick and black and his heavy cheeks and chin were cleanly shaven. His silence and refusal to make any kind of eye contact was annoying Gaunt. Hark had already finished his shellfish and was mopping up the cooking juices from the dish with chunks of soda bread torn from a loaf in the basket on the table.

'You're blaming me for the loss of the Citadel?' Gaunt asked gently.

Lugo widened his eyes in mock query and replied through his mouthful. 'You were the commanding officer in this theatre, weren't you?'

'Yes, sir.'

'Then who else would I blame? You were charged with the liberation of the Doctrinopolis, and the recapture, intact, of the holy Citadel. You failed. The Citadel is lost, and furthermore, your failure has led directly to the impending loss of the entire shrineworld. You'll lose your command, naturally. I think you'll be lucky to remain in the Emperor's service.'

'The Citadel was lost because of the speed with which it was retaken,' Gaunt said, choosing every word carefully. 'My strategy here was slow and methodical. I intended to take the holy city in such a way as to leave it as intact as possible. I didn't want to send the tanks into the Old Town.'

'Are you,' Lugo paused, washing his oily fingers in a bowl of petal-scented water and drying them carefully on his napkin, 'are you possibly trying to suggest that I am in some way to blame for this?'

'You made demands, lord general. Though I had achieved my objectives ahead of the planned schedule, you insisted I was running behind. You also insisted I ditch my prepared strategy and accelerate the assault. I would have had the Citadel scouted and checked in advance, and such care may have resulted in the safe discovery and avoidance of the enemy trap. We'll never know now. You made demands of me, sir. And now we are where we are.'

'I should have you shot for that suggestion, Gaunt,' said Lugo briskly. 'What do you think, Hark? Should I have him shot?'

Hark shrugged wordlessly.

'This is your failure, Gaunt,' said Lugo. 'History will see it as such, I will make sure of that. The Warmaster is already demanding severe reprimand for the officer or officers responsible for this disaster. And, as I pointed out just now, you're hardly a favourite of Macaroth's. Too much of old Slaydo about you.'

Gaunt said nothing.

'You should have been stripped of your rank already, but I'm a fair man. And Hark here suggested you might perform with renewed dedication if given a task that offered something in the way of redemption.'

'How kind of him.'

'I thought so. You're a capable enough soldier. Your time as a commanding officer is over, but I'm offering you a chance to temper your disgrace with a mission that would add a decent footnote to your career. It would send a good message to the troops, too, I think. To show that even in the light of calamitous error, a true soldier of the Imperium can make a worthy contribution to the crusade.'

'What do you want me to do?'

'I want you to lead an honour guard. As I have explained, the evacuation is taking with it all of the priesthood, the what do you call them...?'

'Ayatani,' said Hark, his first spoken word.

'Quite so. All of the ayatani, and all the precious relics of this world. Most precious of all are the remains of the saint herself, interred at the Shrinehold in the mountains. You will form a detail, travel to the Shrinehold, and return here with the saint's bones, conducted with all honour and respect, in time for the evacuation transports.'

Gaunt nodded slowly. He realised he had no choice anyway. 'The Shrinehold is remote. The hinterlands and rainwoods outside the city are riddled with Infardi soldiers who've fled this place.'

'Then you may have trouble on the way. In which case, you'll be moving in force. Your Tanith regiment, in full strength. I've arranged for a Pardus tank company to travel with you as escort. And Hark here will accompany you, of course.'

Gaunt turned to look at the hefty commissar. 'Why?'

Hark looked back, meeting Gaunt's eyes for the first time. 'For the purposes of discipline, naturally. You're broken, Gaunt. Your command judgment is suspect. This mission must not be allowed to fail and the lord general needs assurance that the Tanith First is kept in line.'

'I am capable of discharging those duties.'

'Good. I'll be there to see you do.'

'This is not–'

Hark raised his glass. 'Your command status has always been thought of as strange, Gaunt. A colonel is a colonel and a commissar is a commissar. Many have wondered how you could perform both those duties effectively when the primary rationale of a commissar is to keep a check on the unit's commander. For a while, Crusade command has been considering appointing a commissar to the Tanith First to operate in conjunction with you. Events here have made it a necessity.'

Gaunt pushed back his chair with a loud scrape and rose.

'Won't you stay, Gaunt?' Lugo asked with a wry smile. 'The main course is about to be served. Braised chelon haunch in amasec and ghee.'

Gaunt nodded a curt salute, knowing that there was no point saying he had no appetite for the damned meal or the company. 'My apologies, lord general. I have an honour guard to arrange.'

SIX
ADVANCE GUARD

'What raised me will rest me. What brought me forth will take me back. In the high country of Hagia, I will come home to sleep.'

— Saint Sabbat, epistles

THE HONOUR GUARD left the Doctrinopolis the next morning at daybreak, crossing the holy river and travelling west out of the Pilgrim Gate onto the wide track of the Tembarong Road.

The convoy was almost three kilometres long from nose to tail: the entire Ghost regiment, carried in a line of fifty-eight long-body trucks: twenty Pardus mainline battle tanks, fifteen munition Chimeras and four Hydra tractors, two Trojans, eight scout Salamanders and three Salamander command variants. Their dust plume could be seen for miles and the throaty rumble of their collective turbines rolled around the shallow hills of the rainwoods. A handful of motorcycle outriders buzzed around their skirts, and in their midst travelled eight supply trucks laden with provisions and spares and two heavy fuel tankers. The tankers would get them to Bhavnager, two or three days away, where local fuel supplies would replenish them.

Gaunt rode in one of the command Salamanders near the head of the column. He had specifically chosen a vehicle away from Hark, who travelled with the Pardus commander, Kleopas, in his command vehicle, one of the Pardus regiment's Conqueror-pattern battle tanks.

Gaunt stood up in the light tank's open body and steadied himself on the armour cowling against the lurching it made. The air was warm and sweet, though tinged with exhaust fumes. He had twenty-five hundred infantry in his retinue, and the force of a mid-strength armour brigade. If this was his last chance to experience command, it was at least a good one.

His head ached. The previous night he'd retired alone to his chambers in the Universitariat and drunk himself to sleep over a stack of route maps.

Gaunt looked up into the blue as invisible shapes shrieked over, leaving contrails behind them that slowly dissipated. For the first hour or two, they'd have air cover from the navy's Lightnings.

He looked back, down the length of the massive vehicle column. Through the dust wake, he could see the Doctrinopolis falling away behind them, a dimple of buildings rising up beyond the woodlands, hazed by the distance. The flickering light storm of the Citadel was still visible.

He'd left many valuable men back there. The Ghosts wounded in the city fight, Corbec among them. The wounded were due to be evacuated out in the next few days as part of the abandonment program. He was going to miss Corbec. He was sadly struck by the notion that his last mission with the Ghosts would be conducted without the aid of the bearded giant.

And he wondered what would happen to the Ghosts after his removal. He couldn't imagine them operating under a commander brought in from outside, and there was no way Corbec or Rawne would be promoted. The likelihood was the Tanith First would simply cease to be once he had gone. There was no prospect for renewal. The troopers would be transferred away into other regiments, perhaps as recon specialists, and that would be that.

His looming demise meant the demise of his beloved Tanith regiment too.

In one of the troop trucks, Tona Criid craned her head back to look at the distant city.

'They'll be fine,' said Caffran softly. Tona sat back next to him in the bucking truckbed.

'You think?'

'I know. The servants of the Munitorium have cared for them so far, haven't they?'

Tona Criid said nothing. At Vervunhive, thanks to circumstance, she had become the de facto mother of two orphaned children. They now accompanied the Tanith First war machine as part of the sizeable and extended throng of camp followers. Many of that group, the cooks and mechanics and munition crew, were travelling with them, but many had been left behind for the evacuation. Children, wives, whores, musicians, entertainers, tailors, peddlers, panders. There was no place for them on this stripped-down mission. They would leave Hagia on the transports and, God-Emperor willing, would be reunited with their friends, and comrades and clients in the First later.

Tona took out the double-faced pendant she wore around her neck and looked wistfully at the faces of her children, preserved in holoportraits and set in plastic. Yoncy and Dalin. The babe in arms and the fretful young boy.

'We'll be with them again soon,' Caffran said. He thought of them as his too now. By extension, by the nature of the relationship he had with Tona, Dalin called him Papa Caff. They were as close to an actual family unit as it was possible to get in the Imperial Guard.

'Will we, though?' Tona asked.

'Old Gaunt would never lead us into harm, not if he thought he could get out of it,' Caffran said.

'The word is he's finished,' said Larkin from nearby, overhearing. 'Word is, we're finished too. He's a broken man. Dead on the wire, so to speak. He's going to be stripped of command and we're going to be kicked around the Imperial Guard in search of a home.'

'Are we now?' said Sergeant Kolea, moving down the truck bay, catching Larkin's words.

'S'what I heard,' said Larkin defensively.

'Then shut up until you know. We're the fighting Tanith First, and we'll be together until the end of time, right?'

Kolea's words got a muted chorus of cheers from the troops in the truck.

'Oh, you can do better than that! Remember Tanith! Remember Vervunhive!'

That got a far more resounding cheer.

'What's that you've got, Criid?' Kolea asked as he shambled back down the truck.

She showed him the pendant. 'My kids, sir.'

Kolea looked into the pendant's portraits for a curiously long time.

'Your kids?'

'Adopted them on Verghast, sir. Their parents were killed.'

'Good... good work, Criid. What are their names?'

'Yoncy and Dalin, sir.'

Kolea nodded and let go of the pendant. He walked to the end of the lurching truck and looked out into the rainwoods and irrigated field systems as they passed.

'Something the matter, sarge?' asked Trooper Fenix, seeing the look on Kolea's face.

'Nothing, nothing...' Kolea murmured.

They were his. The children in the pendant portrait were his children. Children he thought long gone and dead on Verghast.

Some god-mocking irony had let them survive and be here. Here, with the Ghosts.

He felt sick and overjoyed all at the same time.

What could he say? What could he begin to say to Criid or Caffran or the kids?

Tears welled in his eyes. He looked out at the rainwoods sliding by and said nothing because there was nothing he could say.

THE TEMBARONG ROAD ran flat, wide and straight through the arable lowlands and rainwoods west of the Doctrinopolis. The lowlands were formed by the broad basin of the holy river, which irrigated the fields and ditch systems of the local farmers every year with its seasonal floods. There was a fresh, damp smell in the air and for a lot of the way, the road followed the curving river bank.

Sergeant Mkoll ran ahead of the main convoy in one of the scout Salamanders with troopers Mkvenner and Bonin and the driver. Mkoll had used Salamanders a couple of times before, but he was always impressed with the little open-topped track-machines' turn of speed. This one wore Pardus Armour insignia on its coat of blue-green mottle, carried additional tarp-wrapped equipment slouched like papooses to the side sponsons, and had its pair of huge UHF vox-antennas bent back over its body and tied off on the rear bars. The driver was a tall, adenoidal youth from the Pardus Armour Aux who wore mirrored glare-goggles and drove like he wanted to impress the Tanith.

They dashed down the tree-lined road at close to sixty kph, waking out a fan tail of pink dust behind them off the dry earth surface.

Mkvenner and Bonin clung on, grinning like fools and enjoying the ride. Mkoll checked his map book and made notes against the edges of the glass-paper charts with a wax pencil.

Gaunt wanted to make the most of the Tembarong Road. He wanted a quick motorised dash for the first few days as far as the sound highway lasted. Their speed was bound to drop once the trail entered the rainwoods, and after that, as they wound their way up into the highlands things might get very slow altogether. There was no way of telling what state the hill roads were in after the winter rains, and they were hoping to pass a great many tonnes of steel along them.

As scout commander, Mkoll had special responsibilities for route-tasking and performance. He'd spent a while talking to Captain Herodas the night before, assessing the mean road and off-road speeds the Pardus could manage. He'd also spoken to Intendant Elthan, who ran the Munitorium's freight motorpool. He and his drivers were crewing the troop trucks and tankers. Mkoll had taken their conservative estimates of speed and mileage and revised them down. Both Herodas and Elthan were imagining a trip of five or six days to travel the three hundred or so kilometres to the Shrinehold, roads permitting. Mkoll was looking at seven at least, maybe eight. And if it was eight, they'd have barely a day to collect up what they'd come for and turn around for the home run, or they'd miss Lord General Lugo's eighteen-day evacuation deadline.

For now, the going was clear. The sky was still violet blue, and a combination of low altitude and the trees kept the breezes down. It was hot.

At first they passed few people on the road except the occasional farmer, or a family group, and once or twice a drover with a small train of livestock. The farmfolk had tried to maintain cultivation during the Infardi occupation, but they had suffered, and Mkoll saw that great areas of the field-stocks and water beds were neglected and overgrown. The few locals they saw turned to watch them pass and raised a hand of greeting or gratitude.

There was no sign of Infardi, many of whom had apparently fled out this way. The road and its environs showed some sign of shelling and air damage, but it was old. The war had passed over this area briefly months ago, but most of the conflict on Hagia had been focused on the cities.

Every once in a while, their passing engines scared flocks of gaudy-feathered fliers up out of trees and roosts. The trees were lush green and roped with epiphytes, their trunks tall, curved and ridged. To Mkoll, raised in the towering, temperate nalwood forests of Tanith, they seemed slight and decorative, like ornamental shrubs, despite the fact that some of them were in excess of twenty metres tall.

At regular intervals through the trees, they caught racing glimpses of the sunlight on the river. Along one half kilometre stretch where the highway ran right beside the water's edge, they motored past a line of fishermen wading out into the river stream, casting hand nets. The fishers all wore sunhats woven from the local vineleaves.

The river dictated the way of life in the floodplains. The few roadside dwellings and small settlements they went through were built up on wood-post stilts against the seasonal water rise. They also passed ornately carved and brightly painted boxes raised three metres high on intricately carved single posts. These were occasional things, appearing singly by the roadside or in small groups in glades set from the highway.

In the hour before noon, they ran through an abandoned village of overgrown, unkept stilt houses and came around one of the road's sharper bends, almost head-first into a herd of chelons and their drovers.

The Pardus driver gave out a little gasp, and hauled on the steering yoke, pulling the Salamander half up onto the bushy verge, into the foliage and to an undignified halt. Unconcerned, the chelons, more than forty of them, lowed and grunted as they shambled past. They were the biggest Mkoll had yet seen on Hagia, the great bell-domed shells of the largest and most mature towering above their vehicle. The smallest and youngest had blue-black skins that gleamed like oil and a fibrous dark patina to their shells, while the elders' hides were paler and less lustrous, lined with cracks and wrinkles, their massive shells limed almost white. A haze of dry, earthy animal smells wafted from them: dung, fodder, saliva in huge quantities.

The three drovers ran over to the Salamander the moment it came to rest, waving their jiddi-sticks and exclaiming in alarm. All three were tired, hungry men in the earth-tone robes of the agricultural caste.

Mkoll jumped down from the back step and raised his arms to calm their jabberings while Mkvenner directed the Pardus driver as he reversed the light tank back out of the thorn breaks.

'It's fine, no harm done,' Mkoll said. The drovers continued to look unhappy, and were busy making numerous salutes to the Imperials.

'Please... If you feel like helping, tell us what's ahead. On the road.' Mkoll pulled out his mapbook and showed the route to the men, who passed it between themselves, contradicting each other's remarks.

'It's very good,' said one. 'The road is very clear. We come down now this month from the high pastures. They say the war is over. We come down in the hope that the markets will be open again.'

'Let's hope so,' said Mkoll.

'People have been hiding in the woods, whole families, you know,' another said. His ancient weather-beaten skin was as lined and gnarled as that of the chelons he drove. 'They were afraid of the war. The war in the cities. But we have heard the war is over and many people will come out of the woods now it is safe.'

Mkoll made a mental note. He had already suspected that a good proportion of the rural population might have fled into the wilderness at the start of the occupation. As the honour guard pressed on, they might encounter many of these people emerging back into the lowlands. With the threat of Infardi guerrillas all around, that made their job harder. Hostiles and ambushes would be harder to pick out.

'What about the Infardi?' Mkoll asked.

'Oh, certainly,' said the first drover, cutting across the gabble of his companions. 'Many, many Infardi now, on the road and in the forest paths.'

'You've seen them?' Mkoll asked with sharp curiosity.

'Very often, or heard them, or seen the signs of their camps.'

'Many, you say?'

'Hundreds!'

'No, no... Thousands! More every day!'

Feth! Mkoll thought. A couple of pitched fights will slow us right down. The chelon-men might be exaggerating for effect, but Mkoll doubted it. 'My thanks to you all,' he said. 'You might want to get your animals off the road for a while. There's a lot more of this stuff coming along,' he pointed to the Salamander, 'and it's a fair size bigger.'

The men all nodded and said they would. Mkoll was a little reassured. He wasn't sure who would win a head-on collision between a Conqueror and a mature bull chelon, but he was sure neither party would walk away smiling. He thanked the drovers, assured them once more they had done him and his men no harm, and got back aboard the Salamander.

'Sorry,' the driver grinned.

'Maybe a tad slower,' Mkoll replied. He pulled out the handset for the tank's powerful vox set and sent a pulse hail to the main convoy. Mkvenner was still standing in the road, gently and politely trying to refuse the honking chelon calf that one of the drovers was offering him to make amends.

'Alpha-AR to main advance, over.'

The speaker crackled. 'Go ahead Alpha-AR.' Mkoll immediately recognised Gaunt's voice.

'Picking up reports of Infardi activity up the road. Nothing solid yet, but you should be advised.'

'Understood, Alpha-AR. Where are you?'

'Just outside a village called Shamiam. I'm going ahead as far as Mukret. Best you send at least a couple more advance recon units forward to me.'

'Copy that. I'll send Beta-AR and Gamma-AR ahead. What's your ETA at Mukret?'

'Another two to three hours, over.' Mukret was a medium-sized settlement on the river where they had planned to make their first overnight stop.

'God-Emperor willing, we'll see you there. Keep in contact.'

'Will do, sir. You should be aware that there are non-coms on the road. Families heading back out of hiding. Caution advised.'

'Understood,'

'And about an hour ahead of you, there's a big herd of livestock moving contra your flow. Lots of livestock and three harmless herdsmen. They may be off road by the time you reach them, but be warned.'

'Understood.'

'Alpha-AR out.' Mkoll hung up the vox-mic and nodded at the waiting Pardus driver. 'Okay,' he said.

The driver throttled the Salamander's turbine and pointed her nose up the brown mud-cake of the highway.

A GOOD FIFTEEN kilometres back down the Tembarong Road, the honour guard convoy slowed and came to a halt. The big khaki troop trucks bunched up, nose to nose, and shuddered their exhaust stacks impatiently as they revved. A few sounded their horns. The sun was high overhead and gleamed blindingly off the metalwork. To the left of the convoy, the blue waters of the holy river crept by on the other side of a low levee.

Rawne got up in the back of his transport and climbed up on the guardrail so he could look out along the length of the motorcade over the truck's cab. All he could see was stationary armour and laden trucks right down to the bend in the road three hundred metres away.

He keyed his microbead as he glanced back down at Feygor.

'Get them up,' Rawne told his adjutant.

Feygor nodded and relayed the glib order to the fifty or so men in the transport cargo area. The Ghosts, many of them sweating and without headgear, roused and readied their weapons, scanning the tree-line and field ditches to the right of the road.

'One, three,' said Rawne into his link. There was a lot of vox traffic. Questioning calls were running up and down the convoy.

'Three, one,' replied Gaunt from up ahead.

'One, what's the story?'

'One of the munition Chimeras has thrown a track section. I'm going to wait fifteen minutes and see how the techs do. Longer than that, I'll leave them behind.'

Rawne had seen the battered age of the worn Chimeras they'd been issued by the Munitorium motorpool. It would take more than fething fifteen minutes to get one running in his opinion.

'Permission to recreationally disperse my men along the river edge.'

'Granted, but watch the tree-line.'

Setting two men on point to cover the right-hand side of the road, Rawne ordered the rest of his troops off the truck. Joking, pulling off jackets and boots, they jogged down to the river edge and started bathing their feet and throwing handscoops of water on their faces. Other troop trucks pulled off the hardpan onto the levee shoulder and disembarked their men. A Trojan tank tractor grumbled past, edging up along the length of the stationary column from the rear echelon to assist with the spot repairs.

Rawne wandered down the line of vehicles to where Sergeants Varl, Soric, Baffels and Haller stood on the levee. Soric was handing out stubby cigars from a waxed card box and Rawne took one. They all smoked for a while in silence, watching the Ghosts, both Verghastite and Tanith, engage in impromptu water fights and games of kickball.

'Is it always like this, major?' Soric asked, jerking a thumb at the unmoving convoy. Rawne didn't warm to people much, but he liked the old man. He was a capable fighter and a good leader, but he wasn't afraid to ask questions that revealed his inexperience, which in Rawne's book made him a good student and a promising officer.

'Always the same with motorised transportation. Breakdowns, bottlenecks, bad terrain. I always prefer to shift the men by foot.'

'The Pardus equipment looks alright,' said Haller. 'Well maintained and all.'

Rawne nodded. 'It's just the junk transports the Munitorium found for us. These trucks are as old as feth, and the Chimeras...'

'I'm surprised they've made it this far,' said Varl. The sergeant gently windmilled his arm, nursing the cybernetic shoulder joint the augmeticists had given him on Fortis Binary several years before. It still hurt him in humid conditions. 'And we'll be fethed without them. Without the munitions they're carrying, anyway.'

'We're fethed anyway,' said Rawne. 'We're the Imperial fething Guard and it's our lot in life to be fethed.'

Haller, Soric and Varl laughed darkly, but Baffels was silent. A stocky, bearded man with a blue claw tattoo under one eye, Baffels had been promoted to sergeant after old Fols was killed at the battle for Veyveyr Gate. He still wasn't comfortable with command, and took his duties too seriously in Rawne's opinion. Some common troopers – Varl was a good example – were sergeants waiting to happen. Baffels was an honest footslogger who'd had responsibility dumped on him because of his age, his dependability and his good favour with the men. Rawne knew he was finding it hard. Gaunt had had a choice when it came to Fols's replacement: Baffels or Milo, and he'd opted for Baffels because to give the lead job to the youngest and greenest Ghost would have smacked of favouritism. Gaunt had been wrong there, Rawne thought. He had no love for Milo, but he knew how capable he'd proved to be and how dearly the men regarded him as a lucky totem. Gaunt should have gone with his gut – ability over experience.

'Good smoke,' Varl told Soric, glancing appreciatively at the smouldering brown tube between his fingers. 'Corbec would have enjoyed them.'

'Finest Verghast leaf,' smiled Soric. 'I have a private stock.'

'He should be here,' Baffels said, meaning the colonel. Then he glanced quickly at Rawne. 'No offence, major!'

'None taken,' Rawne replied. Privately, Rawne was enjoying his newfound seniority. With both Corbec and that upstart Captain Daur out of the picture, he was now the acting second of the regiment, with only the Pardus Major Kleopas and the outsider Commissar Hark near to him in the taskforce pecking order. Mkoll was the Ghosts' number three officer for the duration, and Kolea had been given Daur's Verghastite liaison tasks.

It still irked Rawne that he was forced to maintain the callsign 'three' to Gaunt's 'one'. Gaunt had explained it was to preserve continuity of vox recognition, but Rawne felt he should be using Corbec's 'two' now.

What irked him more was the notion that Baffels was right. Corbec *should* be here. It went against Rawne's impulse, because he'd never liked Corbec that much either, but it was true. He felt it in his blood. What everyone knew and none wanted to talk about was that this seemed likely to be the last mission of the Tanith First. The lord general had broken Gaunt, and Rawne would lead the applause when they came to march Gaunt away in disgrace, but still...

This was the Ghosts' final show.

And, feth him, Corbec should be here.

* * *

MAD LARKIN SAT, hot and edgy, in the rear of a vacated truck, his long-pattern las resting on the bodywork. Kolea had left him and Cuu on point while the others ran to the river to cool down and blow off steam.

Larkin searched the far side of the road with his usual obsessive methods, sectioning the tree-line and the expanse of water-field by eye and then scanning each section in turn sequentially. Thorough, careful, faultless.

Each movement made him tense, but each movement turned out to be flapping forkbills or scampering spider-rats or even just the breeze-sway of the fronded leaves.

He passed the time with target practice, searching out a target and then following it through his scope's crosshairs. The red-crested forkbills were fine enough, but they were an easy target because of their white plumage and size. The spider-rats were better: creepy eight-limbed mammals the size of Larkin's hand that jinked up and down the tree trunks in skittering stop-start trajectories so fast they made a sport out of it.

'What you up to?'

Larkin looked round and up into Trooper Cuu's arrogant eyes.

'Just... spotting,' Larkin said. He didn't like Cuu at all. Cuu made him nervous. People called Larkin mad, but he wasn't mad like Cuu. Cuu was a cold killer. A psycho. He was covered in gang tatts and had a long scar that bisected his narrow face.

Cuu folded his lean limbs down next to Larkin. Larkin thought of himself as thin and small amongst the Ghosts but Cuu was smaller. There was, however, a suggestion of the most formidable energy in his wiry frame.

'You could hit them?' he asked.

'What?'

'The white birds with the stupid beaks?'

'Yeah, easy. I was hunting the rats.'

'What rats?'

Larkin pointed. 'Those things. Creepy fething bugs.'

'Oh yeah. Didn't see them before. Sharp eyes you got. Sharp as sharp.'

'Goes with the territory,' Larkin said, patting his sniper weapon.

'Sure it does. Sure as sure.' Cuu reached into his pocket and produced a couple of hand-rolled white smokes which he offered in a vee to Larkin.

'No thanks.'

Cuu put one away and lit the other, drawing deep. Larkin could smell the scent of obscura. He'd used it occasionally back on Tanith, but it was one of Gaunt's banned substances. Feth, but it smelled strong.

'Colonel-commissar'll have you for that stuff,' he said.

Cuu grinned and exhaled ostentatiously. 'Gaunt don't frighten me,' he said. 'You sure you won't...?'

'No thanks.'

'Those gakking white birds,' Cuu said after a long interval. 'You reckon you could hit them easy?'

'Yeah.'

'I'm betting they could be good in the pot. Bulk up standard rations, a few of them.'

It was a decent enough idea. Larkin keyed his link. 'Three, this is Larks. Cuu and I are going off the track to nab a few waterbirds for eating. Okay with you?'

'Good idea. I'll advise the convoy you're going to be shooting. Bag one for me.'

Larkin and Cuu dropped off the side of the truck and wandered across the road. They slithered down the field embankment into an irrigation ditch where the watery mud sloshed up around their calves. Forkbills warbled and clacked in the cycad grove ahead. Larkin could already see the telltale dots of white amongst the dark green foliage.

Skeeter flies buzzed around them, and sap-wasps droned over their heads. Larkin slid his sound suppressor out of his uniform's thigh pouch and carefully screwed it onto the muzzle of his long-las.

They came up around a clump of fallen palms and Larkin nestled down in the exposed root system to take aim. He scope-chased a spider-rat up and down a tree bole for a moment to get his eye in and then settled on a plump forkbill.

The trick wasn't to hit it. The trick was to knock its head off. A las-round would explode a forkbill into feathers and mush if it hit the body, like taking a man out by jamming a tube-charge down his waistband. Shoot the inedible head off and you'd have a ready-to-pluck carcass.

Larkin squared up, shook his head and shoulders out, and fired. There was a slight flash and virtually no noise. The forkbill, now with nothing but a scorched ring of flesh and feathers where its head should have joined on, dropped off into the shallow water.

In short order, Larkin pinked off five more. He and Cuu sloshed out to gather them up, hooking them by the webbed feet into their belts.

'You're gakking good,' Cuu said.

'Thanks.'

'That's a hell of a gun.'

'Sniper variant long-las. My very best friend.'

Cuu nodded. 'I believe that. You mind if I take a try?'

Cuu held his hand out and Larkin reluctantly handed the long-las to him, taking Cuu's standard lasrifle in return. Cuu grinned at the new toy, and eased the nalwood stock against his shoulder.

'Nice,' he sighed. 'Nice as nice.'

He fired suddenly and a forkbill exploded in a mass of white feathers and blood.

'Not bad, but–'

Cuu ignored Larkin and fired again. And again. And again. Three more forkbills detonated off their perches.

'We can't cook them if you hit them square,' Larkin said.

'I know. We've got enough for eating now. This is just fun.'

Larkin wanted to complain, but Cuu swung the long-las round quick fire and destroyed two more birds. The water under the trees was thick with blood stains and floating white feathers.

'That's enough,' said Larkin.

Cuu shook his head, and aimed again. He'd switched the long-las to rapid fire and when he pulled the trigger, pulse after pulse whined into the canopy.

Larkin was alarmed. Alarmed at the misuse of his beloved weapon, alarmed at Cuu's psychopathic glee...

...and most of all, alarmed at the way Cuu's wildfire blasted and crisped a half dozen spider-rats off the surrounding tree trunks. Not a shot was wasted or went wide. Skittering targets even he'd have to think twice about hitting were reduced to seared, blood-leaking impacts on the trees.

Cuu handed the weapon back to Larkin.

'Nice gun,' said Cuu, and turned back to rejoin the road.

Larkin hurried after him. He shivered despite the sun's heat that baked down over the highway. Cold killer. Larkin knew he'd be watching his back from now on.

AT THE FRONT end of the immobile convoy, Gaunt, Kleopas and Herodas stood watching the tech-priests and engineers of the Pardus regiment as they struggled to retrack the defective Chimera. A workteam of Pardus and Tanith personnel had already unloaded the armoured transport by hand to reduce its payload weight. The Trojan throbbed and idled nearby like a watchful parent.

Gaunt glanced at his chronometer. 'Another ten minutes and we'll move on regardless.'

'I might object, sir,' Kleopas ventured. 'This unit was carrying shells for the Conquerors.' He gestured to the massive stack of munitions the work-team had removed from the Chimera to get it upright. 'We can't just leave this stuff.'

'We can if we have to,' said Gaunt.

'If this was a payload of lasgun powercells, you'd say different.'

'You're right,' Gaunt nodded to Kleopas. 'But we're on the tightest of clocks, major. I'll give them twenty minutes. But only twenty.'

Captain Herodas moved away to shout encouraging orders at the engineer teams.

Gaunt pulled out a silver hip flask. It was engraved with the name 'Delane Oktar'. He offered it to Kleopas.

'Thank you, colonel-commissar, no. A little early in the day for me.'

Gaunt shrugged and took a swig. He was screwing up the cap when a voice from behind them said, 'I hear shooting.'

Gaunt and Kleopas looked around at Commissar Hark as he approached them.

'Just a little authorised foraging,' Gaunt told him.

'Do the squad leaders know? It might trigger a panic.'

'They know. I told them. Regulation 11-0-119 gamma.'

Hark made an open-handed shrug. 'You don't need to cite it to me, colonel. I believe you.'

'Good. Major Kleopas... perhaps you'd explain to the commissar here what is happening. In intricate detail.'

Kleopas glared at Gaunt and then turned to smile at Hark. 'We're retracking the Chimera, sir, and that involves a heavy lifter as you can see...'

Gaunt slipped away, removing himself from the commissar's presence. He walked back down the line of vehicles, taking another swig from the flask.

Hark watched him go. 'What are your thoughts on the legendary colonel-commissar?' he asked Kleopas, interrupting a lecture on mechanised track repair.

'He's as sound a commander as ever I knew. Lives for his men. Don't ask me again, sir. I won't have my words added to any official report of censure.'

'Don't worry, Kleopas,' said Hark. 'Gaunt's damned any way you look at it. Lord General Lugo has him in his sights. I was just making conversation.'

Gaunt walked back a hundred metres and found Medic Curth and her orderlies sitting in the shade cast by their transport.

Curth got up. 'Sir?'

'Everything fine here?' Gaunt asked. He was unhappy with the fact that Dorden had stayed behind in the Doctrinopolis to see to the wounded. Curth was a fine medic, but he wasn't used to her being in charge of the taskforce's surgical team. Dorden had always been his chief medic, since the foundation of the Ghosts. Curth would take a little getting used to.

'Everything's fine,' she said, her smile as appealing as her heart-shaped face.

'Good,' said Gaunt. 'Good.' He took another swig.

'Any of that going spare?' Curth asked.

Surprised, he turned and handed her the flask. She took a hefty slug.

'I didn't think you'd approve.'

'This waiting makes me nervous,' she said, wiping her mouth and handing the hip flask back to Gaunt.

'Me too,' Gaunt said.

'Anyway,' said Curth. 'Trust me. It's medicinal.'

* * *

ALPHA-AR PULLED INTO Mukret in the late afternoon. The Salamander rolled down to a crawl and Mkoll, Mkvenner and Bonin leapt out, lasguns raised, trailing the light tank down the main highway as it passed through the jumble of stilt houses and raised halls. A slight breeze had picked up with the approach of evening, and it lifted dust and leaf-litter across the bright sunlit road and the dark spaces of shadow between and under the dwellings.

The sun itself, big and yellowing, shone sideways through a stiff break of palms and cypresses towards the river.

The township was deserted. Doors flapped open and epiphytic creepers roiled around window frames and stack posts. There was broken crockery on the house-walks, and litters of ragged clothing in the gutters. At the far end of the town sat long, brick and tile smokehouses. Mukret's main industry was the smoke-drying of fish and meats. The Tanith could still pick out the tangy background scent of woodsmoke in the air.

Behind the rolling tank, the three scouts prowled forward, lasguns held in loose, fluid grips. Bonin swung and aimed abruptly as forkbills mobbed out of a tree.

The Salamander rumbled.

Mkoll moved ahead and switched Bonin left down a jetty walk to the river itself with a coded gesture.

Ahead, something stirred. It was a chelon, an immature calf, wandering out into the main road, dragging its reins in the dust. A short-form clutch saddle was lashed to its back.

It wandered past Mkoll and Mkvenner, trailing its bridle. Mkoll could hear sporadic knocking now. Mkoll signalled for Mkvenner to hold back as cover and walked forward towards the noise.

An old man, skinny and gnarled, was hammering panels into place on an old and ransacked stilt-chapel. It looked like he was trying to board up broken windows using only a length of tree-limb as a hammer.

He was dressed in blue silk robes. Ayatani, Mkoll realised. The local priesthood.

'Father!'

The old man turned and lowered his tree-limb. He was bald, but had a triumphantly long, tapering white beard. It was so long, in fact, that he'd tucked it over his shoulder to keep it out of the way.

'Not now,' he said in a crotchety tone, 'I'm busy. This holy shrine won't just repair itself.'

'Maybe I can help you?'

The old man clambered back down to the roadway and faced Mkoll. 'I don't know. You're a man with a gun... and a tank, it appears. You may be intending to kill me and steal my chelon which, personally speaking, I would not find helpful. Are you a murderer?'

'I'm a member of the Imperial liberation force,' Mkoll replied, looking the old man up and down.

'Really? Well now...' the old man mused, using the tip of his long beard to mop his face.

'What's your name?'

'Ayatani Zweil,' said the old man. 'And yours?'

'Scout Sergeant Mkoll.'

'Scout Sergeant Mkoll, eh? Very impressive. Well, Scout Sergeant Mkoll, the Ershul have fouled this shrine, this sacred house of our thrice-beloved saint, and I intend to rebuild it stick by stick. If you assist me, I will be grateful. And I'm sure the saint will be too. In her way.'

'Father, we're heading west. I need to know if you've seen any Infardi on the road.'

'Of course I have. Hundreds of them.'

Mkoll reached for his vox link but the old man stopped him.

'Infardi I've seen plenty of. Pilgrims. Flocking back to the Doctrinopolis. Yes, yes... plenty of Infardi. But no Ershul.'

'I'm confused.'

The ayatani gestured up and down the sunlit road through Mukret. 'Do you know what you're standing on?'

'The Tembarong Road,' said Mkoll.

'Also known in the old texts of Irimrita as the Ayolta Amad Infardiri, which literally means the "approved route of Infardi procession" or more colloquially the Pilgrim's Way. The road may go to Tembarong. That way. Eventually. Who wants to go there? A dull little city where the women have fat legs. But that way–' He pointed the direction Mkoll had appeared from.

'In that direction, pilgrims travel. To the shrines of the Doctrinopolis Citadel. To the Tempelum Infarfarid Sabbat. To a hundred places of devotion. They have done for many hundreds of years. It is a pilgrim's way. And our name for pilgrims is "Infardi". That is its proper sense and I use it as such.'

Mkoll coughed politely. 'So when you say Infardi you mean real pilgrims?'

'Yes.'

'Coming this way?'

'Positively flocking, Scout Sergeant Mkoll. The Doctrinopolis is open again, so they come to give thanks. And they come to prostrate themselves before the desecrated Citadel.'

'You're not referring to soldiers of the enemy then?'

'They stole the name Infardi. I won't let them have it! I won't! If they want a name, let them be Ershul!'

'Ershul?'

'It is a word from the Ylath, the herdsman dialect. It refers to a chelon that consumes its own dung or the dung of others.'

'And have you seen... uhm... Ershul? On your travels?'

'No.'

'I see.'

'But I've heard them.' Zweil suddenly took Mkoll by the arm and pointed him west, over the roofscape of Mukret, towards the distant edges of the rainwoods, which were becoming hazed and misty in the late afternoon. A dark stain of stormclouds was gathering over the neighbouring hills.

'Up there, Scout Sergeant Mkoll. Beyond Bhavnager, in the Sacred Hills. They lurk, they prowl, they wait.'

Mkoll involuntarily wanted to pull away from the old man's tight grip but it was strangely reassuring. It reminded him of the way Archdeacon Mkere used to steer him to the lectern to read the lesson at church school back on Tanith, years ago.

'Are you a devout man, Scout Sergeant Mkoll?'

'I hope I am, father. I believe the Emperor is god in flesh, and I live to serve him in peace and war.'

'That's good, that's good. Contact your fellows. Tell them to expect trouble on their pilgrimage.'

TWENTY KILOMETRES EAST, the main convoy was moving again. The munitions Chimera had been repaired well enough for the time being, though Intendant Elthan had warned Gaunt it would need a proper overhaul during the night rest.

They were making good time again. Gaunt sat in the open cab of his command Salamander, reviewing the charts and hoping they'd make it to Mukret before nightfall. Mkoll had just checked in. Alpha-AR had reached Mukret and found it deserted, though the dour scout had repeated his warning about Infardi sightings.

Gaunt put the maps aside and turned to his battered, annotated copy of Saint Sabbat's gospel, as he had done many times that day. Trying to read the text in the jolting Salamander made his head hurt, but he persisted. He flicked through to the most recent of the paper place-markers he'd left. The mid-section, the Psalms of Sabbat. Virtually impenetrable, their language both antique and mysteriously coded with symbols. He could read everything and nothing into them as meaning, but nothing was all he took away.

Except that it was the most beautiful religious verse he'd ever read. Warmaster Slaydo had thought so too. It was from him that Gaunt had got his love of the Sabbat psalms. His hands lowered the book to his knees as he looked up and remembered Slaydo for a moment.

He felt a lurch as the tank slowed suddenly, and stood up to look. His mount was third from the front of the convoy, and the two scout Salamanders ahead had dropped speed sharply. Red brake lights came on behind their metal grilles, stark and bright in the twilight.

A large herd of massive chelons was coming towards them, driven by several beige-robed peasants. It was half blocking the road. The convoy leaders were being forced to pull into tight single file against the riverwards edge of the highway.

Mkoll had warned him about this. Lots of livestock and three harmless herdsmen, he'd said, though he'd seemed certain they'd be off the road before the convoy met them.

'One to convoy elements,' Gaunt said into his vox on the all-channel band. 'Drop your speed and pull over to the extreme left. We've got livestock on the road. Show courtesy and pass well clear of them.'

The drivers and crews snapped back responses over the link. The convoy slowed to a crawl and began to creep along past the straggled line of lowing, shambling beasts. Gaunt cursed this fresh delay. It would be a good ten minutes until they were clear of the obstruction.

He looked out at the big shell-backs as they went by close enough to lean out and touch. Their animal odour was strong and earthy, and Gaunt could hear the creak of their leathery armour skin and the gurgle of their multi-chambered stomachs. They broke noxious wind, or groaned and snuffled. Blunt muzzles chewed regurgitated cuds. He saw the drovers too. Large labourers in the coarse off-white robes of the agrarian caste, urging the beasts on with taps of their jiddi-sticks, their hoods and face-veils pulled up against the dust. A few nodded apologetically to him as they passed. Most didn't spare the Imperials a look. Religious war and sacred desecration ravages their world and for them, it's business as usual, thought Gaunt. Some lives in this lethal galaxy were enviably simple...

Lots of livestock and three harmless herdsmen. He remembered Mkoll's report with abrupt clarity. Three harmless herdsmen.

Now he was level with them, he counted at least nine.

'One! This is one! Be advised, this could be–'

His words were cut off by the bang-shriek of a shoulder-launched missile. Two vehicles back, a command Salamander slewed wildly and vomited a fierce cone of flame and debris out of its crew-space. Metal fragments rained down out of the air, tinking off his own vehicle's bodywork.

The vox-link went mad. Gaunt could hear sustained bursts of las-fire and auto weapons. Herdsmen, suddenly several dozen in number, were surging out from the cover of their agitated animals. They had weapons. As their robes fell away, he saw body art and green silk.

He grabbed his bolt pistol.

The Infardi were all over them.

SEVEN
DEATH ON THE ROAD

'Let me rest, now the battle's done.'

— Imperial Guard song

HIS DROVER'S DISGUISE flapping about him, an Infardi gunman clambered up the mudguard of the command Salamander and raised his autopistol, a yowl of rabid triumph issuing from his scabby lips. He stank of fermented fruit liquor and his eyes were wild-white with intoxicated frenzy.

Gaunt's bolt round hit him point-blank in the right cheek and disintegrated his head in a puff of liquidised tissue.

'One to honour guard units! Infardi ambush to the right! Turn and repel!'

Gaunt could hear further missile impacts and lots of small arms fire. The chelons, viced in by the road edge on one side and the Imperial armour on the other, were whinnying with agitation and banging the edges of their shells up against vehicle hulls. 'Turn us! Turn us around!' Gaunt yelled at his driver.

'No room, sir!' the Pardus replied desperately. A brace of hard-slug shots sparked and danced off the Salamander's cowling.

'Damn it!' Gaunt bellowed. He rose in the back of the tank and fired into the charging enemy, killing one Infardi and crippling a mature chelon. The beast shrieked and slumped over, crushing two more of the ambushers before rolling hard into the Chimera behind. It began to writhe, baying, shoving the tank into the verge.

Gaunt swore and grabbed the firing grips of the pintle-mounted storm bolter. Infardi were appearing in the road ahead and he raked the hardpan, dropping several. Some had swarmed over the leading scout tank ahead and were murdering the crew. The vehicle slewed to a drunken, sidelong halt.

A tank round roared off close behind him. He heard the hot detonation of superheating gas, the grinding clank of the recoiling weapon, the whoosh of the shell. It fell in the ditchfield to the right of the road and kicked up a huge spout of liquid muck. More tanks now fired their main guns, and turret-mounted bolters chattered and sprayed. Another big chelon, hit dead centre by a tank shell, exploded wholesale and a big, stinking cloud of blood mist and intestinal gas billowed down the convoy.

Gaunt knew they had the upper hand in terms of strength, but the ambushers had been canny. They'd slowed the convoy down with the livestock and pinned it against the road wall so it couldn't manoeuvre.

He fired the weapon mount again, chopping through an Infardi running up to position a missile launcher. Dead fingers convulsed anyway and the missile fired and immediately dropped, blowing a deep crater in the road.

Something grabbed Gaunt from behind and pulled him off the storm bolter. He fell back into the tank's crewbay, kicking and fighting for his life.

THE FIRST THIRD of the honour guard convoy was under hard assault, jammed and slowed to such an extent by the herd that the trailing portion of the convoy, straggled back to a more than four kilometre spread now, couldn't move up to successfully support.

Larkin found himself next to Cuu, firing down from their troop truck body into the weeds as Infardi swarmed up out of the waterline, shooting as they came. Cuu was giggling gleefully as he killed. An anti-tank rocket wailed over their heads, and las-fire exploded around them, killing a trooper nearby and blowing out the windows of the truck cab.

'Disperse! Engage!' Sergeant Kolea yelled, and the Tanith leapt from the trucks en masse, charging the attackers with fixed bayonets and blazing las-fire.

Criid and Caffran charged together, hitting the first of the Infardi hand to hand, clubbing and gutting them. Caffran dropped for a wide shot that sent another ambusher tumbling back down the ditch into the field. Criid fell, got up, and laced las-blasts into the shins of the Infardi stampeding towards them. A Pardus tank roared nearby, blindly shelling the herd.

Rawne's truck, further down the line, was mobbed by Infardi. The cargo bed rocked as bodies piled onto it. Rawne fired his lasgun into the thick press, and saw Feygor rip an enemy's throat out with his silver Tanith knife. The darkening evening air was crisscrossed by painfully bright las-fire. A second later, gusting flames surged down the roadside gulley. From Varl's truck, Trooper Brostin was washing the roadline with bursts from his flamer.

Major Kleopas tried to turn his Conqueror, but a massive chelon, bucking and hooting, slammed into his bull-bars and shunted the entire tank around. For a full five seconds, the tank's racing tracks dragged at thin air as the weight of the bull chelon drove its nose into the road.

Then the tracks grabbed purchase again. Kleopas's tank lurched forward.

'Ram it!' Kleopas ordered.

'Sir?'

'Screw you! Full power! Ram it!' Kleopas barked down at his driver.

The Conqueror battle tank, named *Heart of Destruction* according to the hand-painted hull logo, scrambled sideways in a vast spray of dust and then drove its bulldozer blade into the legs of the big bull chelon. Kleopas's tank maimed the animal and rammed it off the highway, though the Conqueror dented its hull plating against the chelon's shell in the process.

Squealing, the chelon fell down into the waterfield ditch and rolled over on its back, squashing eight Infardi troopers in the irrigation gulley.

The *Heart of Destruction* dipped off the roadside and down into the waterbed, tracks churning. As his main gunner and gun layer pumped shells into the breaks of trees beyond the road, Kleopas manned the bolter hardpoint and blasted tracer shots across the irrigation ditches.

His manoeuvre began to break the deadlock. Three tanks followed him through the gap he'd cut and rattled round into the tree-line off the road, wasting the dug-in Infardi with turret bolters and flamers.

In the closed truck carrying the medical supplies, Ana Curth flinched as stray shots punched through the hardskin and her racks of bottled pharmaceuticals. Glass debris spat in all directions. Lesp stumbled to his knees, a dark line of blood welling across his cheek from a sliver of flying glass.

Two Infardi clambered up the rear gate of the truck. Curth kicked one away with a boot in the face, and then dragged out a laspistol Soric had given her and fired twice. The second Infardi attacker fell off the truck.

Curth turned to see if Lesp was all right. She saw the alarm in his face, half-heard the warning shout coming from his mouth, and then felt herself grabbed and pulled bodily out of the truck.

Her world spun. Terror viced her. She was jerked upside down, held carelessly by the legs, her face in the dirt. The Infardi were all over her, clawing and tearing. She could smell their wretched sweat-stink. All she could see was a jumble of green silk and tattooed flesh.

There was a sudden glare of hard blue light and a sizzling sound. Hot liquid sprayed over her, and she realised, with professional detachment, that it was blood. She swung as the grip on her half-released.

The blur of blue light carved the air again and something yelped. She collapsed onto the road, flat on her belly, and rolled up in time to see Ibram

Gaunt raking his glowing power sword around in an expert figure-six swing that felled an Infardi like a tree. Gaunt had lost his cap and his clothes were torn. There was an unnerving look of unquenchable fury in his eyes. He wielded the sacred blade of her home-hive two-handed now, like a champion of antique myth. Dismembered bodies piled around him and the gritty sand of the road was soaked with gore for metres in every direction.

A hero, she thought abruptly, realising it truly in her mind for the first time. Damn Lugo and his disdain! This man is an Imperial hero!

Lesp, his face running with blood, appeared suddenly behind the commissar in the back gatehatch of the medical truck and began laying down support fire with his lasgun. Gaunt staked his power sword tip-down in the road and knelt next to it, scooping up a fallen Infardi lasrifle. His short, clipped bursts of fire joined Lesp's, stinging across the road and into the mob of Infardi. Green-clad bodies tumbled onto the road or slithered back down the trench into the field.

Curth scrambled over to Gaunt on her hands and knees. Once she was safely beside him, she too knelt and began firing with a purloined Infardi weapon. She had none of the Commissar's trained skill with an assault las, nor as much as Trooper Lesp, but she made a good account of herself with the unfamiliar weapon nevertheless. Gaunt, grim and driven, handled his firing pattern with an assured expertise that would have shamed even a well-drilled infantryman.

'You didn't scream,' Gaunt said to her suddenly, firing steadily.

'What?'

'You didn't scream when they grabbed you.'

'And that's good – why?'

'Waste of energy, of dignity. If they'd killed you, they'd have taken no satisfaction in it.'

'Oh,' she said, nonplussed, not sure if she should be flattered.

'Never give the enemy anything, Ana. They take what they take and that's more than enough as it is.'

'Live by that, do you?' she asked sourly, twitching off another burst of unsteady but enthusiastic shots.

'Yes,' he replied, as if he was surprised she should ask. Sensing that, she felt surprised too. At herself, for her own stupidity. It was obvious and she'd known it all along if she'd but recognised it. That was Gaunt's way. Gaunt the Imperial hero. Give nothing. Never. Ever. Never let your guard down, never allow the enemy the slightest edge. Stay firm and die hard. Nothing else would do.

It wasn't just the commissar in him. It was the warrior, Curth realised. It was Gaunt's fundamental philosophy. It had brought him here and would carry him on to whatever death, kind or cruel, the fates had in store for him. It made him what he was: the relentless soldier, the celebrated leader, the terrifying slayer.

She felt unbearably sad for him and in awe of him all in the same moment.

Ana Curth had heard about the disgrace awaiting Gaunt at the end of this mission. That made her saddest of all. She realised he was going to be absolutely true to his duty and his calling right to the end, no matter the shadow of dishonour hanging over him. He would not falter.

Gaunt would be Gaunt until death claimed him.

FIFTY METRES AWAY, Captain Herodas fell out of a burning Salamander a few moments before a second anti-tank rocket whooshed out of the roadside trees and blew it apart.

Almost immediately, a hard-slug tore through his left knee and threw him into the dust. He blacked out in pain for a second and then fought back, trying to crawl. The Pardus trooper next to him was face down in a pool of blood.

'Lezink! Lezink!'

Herodas tried to turn the man over, but the limbs were loose and the body was hollow and empty. Herodas looked down and saw the horror of blown-out meat and bone shards that was all that remained of his own leg joint. Las-shots zinged over his head. He reached for his pistol but his holster was flapping open.

There were tears in his eyes. The dull pain was rising to overwhelm him. From all around came the sounds of screaming, shooting, killing.

The ground shook. Herodas looked up in disbelief at the cow chelon that was stampeding towards him from the trapped, terrified herd. It was a third the size of the big bulls, but still weighed in at over two tonnes.

He closed his eyes tight and braced for the bone-splintering impact that was about to come.

A thin beam of hot red energy stabbed across the road and hit the hurtling brute with such force it was blown sideways off its feet. The shot disintegrated a huge hole in the chelon and left it a smouldering husk, dripping fatty mush.

Plasma fire! thought Herodas. Thrice-damned gods! That was plasma fire!

He saw the stocky shape of Commissar Hark striding down the roadway, dark in the rising dust and evening light, his long coat rippling around him. Hark was calling out commands and pointing as he directed the units of sprinting Tanith infantry down the road and into the enemy flank. He held an ancient plasma pistol in his right hand.

Hark halted and sent three more troop units on past him as they ran up, forking them wide to disperse them into the roadside gutter. He turned and waved two Pardus Conquerors forward off the road with quick, confident gestures.

Then he spun round abruptly, brought up his weapon, and cremated an Infardi who had risen from the roadside weeds with a rifle.

Hark crossed to Herodas.

'Stay still, help's on the way.'

'Get me up, and I'll fight!' Herodas complained.

Hark smiled. 'Your courage does you credit, captain, but believe me, you're not going anywhere but to a medic cot. Your leg's a mess. Stay still.'

He turned and fired his plasma gun into the trees again at a target Herodas couldn't even see.

'They're all over us,' Herodas said.

'No, they're breaking. We've got them running,' Hark told him, holstering his plasma gun and kneeling down to apply a tourniquet to Herodas's thigh.

'The fight's out of them,' he reassured the captain, but Herodas had blacked out again.

THE FIGHT WAS indeed out of them. Overmatched and repulsed, leaving two-thirds of their number dead, the Infardi ambushers fled away into the off-road woodland, hunted by the Pardus shelling and the staccato thrash of the Hydra batteries.

The front section of the convoy was a mess: two scout Salamanders and a command Salamander ruined and burning, a supply Chimera overturned and blown out, two trucks ablaze. Twenty-two Pardus dead, fifteen Ghosts, six Munitorium crewmen. Six Ghosts and three Pardus severely injured and over eighty light wounds sustained by various personnel.

Listening to the roll call of deaths and injuries on his microbead, Gaunt strode back to his vehicle, retrieving his cap, and exchanging his torn storm coat for a short leather bomber jacket.

He sat on the rear fender of his Salamander as sweating troopers carried out the bodies of his driver and navigator.

Smoke and blood-fumes lingered over the scene. Infardi bodies were strewn everywhere, as well as the stricken chelon, some dead, some mortally hurt. The rest of the herd had broken into the waterfield and were disappearing as they moved away in the diminishing light. Gaunt could hear the snap of las-fire and the grumble of tanks as they cleared the low lying woods.

During the course of the fight, the sun had gone down, and the sky was now a smooth, luminous violet. Night breezes came up from the river and shivered the trees. They were badly behind schedule, a long way short of the planned night stop. It would be well after full dark before they reached Mukret now.

Gaunt heard someone approach and looked up. It was Intendant Elthan, wearing the stiff grey robes of the Munitorium, and a look of disdain.

'This is unacceptable, colonel-commissar,' he said briefly.

'What is?'

'The losses, the attack.'

'I'm afraid I don't follow you, intendant. War isn't "unacceptable". It's dirty and tragic and terrifying and often senseless, but it's also a fact of life.'

'This attack!' Elthan hissed, his lips tight around his yellowed teeth. 'You were warned! Your scout detail warned you of the enemy presence. I heard it myself on the vox-link. This should never have happened!'

'What are you suggesting, intendant? That I'm somehow culpable for these deaths?'

'That is exactly what I'm suggesting! You ignored your recon advice. You pressed on–'

'That's enough,' said Gaunt, getting to his feet. 'I'm prepared to put your comments down to shock and inexperience. We should just forget this exchange happened.'

'I will not!' Elthan relied. 'We all know the mess you made of the Doctrinopolis liberation. That shoddy leadership has cost you your career! And now you–'

'Menazoid Epsilon. Fortis Binary. Vervunhive. Monthax. Sapiencia. Nacedon.'

They both looked around. Hark stood watching them.

'Other examples of shoddy leadership, in your opinion, intendant?'

Elthan went a little red around the edges and then blustered on. 'I expect your support on this, commissar! Are you not here for the express purpose of disciplining and supervising this... this broken man?'

'I am here to discharge the duties of an Imperial commissar,' said Hark simply.

'You heard the recon reports!'

'I did,' said Hark. 'We were warned of enemy activity. We moved judiciously and took precautions. Despite that, they surprised us. It's called an ambush. It happens in war. It's part of the risk you take in a military action.'

'Are you siding with him?' asked Elthan.

'I'm remaining neutral and objective. I'm pointing out that even the best commander must expect attacks and losses. I'm suggesting you return to your vehicle and supervise the resumption of this convoy.'

'I don't–'

'No, you don't understand. Because you are not a soldier, intendant. We have a saying on my home world: sometimes you get the carniv and sometimes the carniv gets you.'

Elthan turned disdainfully and stalked away. Down the road, a trio of Pardus tanks had lowered their dozer blades and were ploughing the chelon carcasses off the thoroughfare. Headlamps gleamed like little full moons in the dusk.

'What's the matter?' Hark asked Gaunt. 'You look... I don't know... startled, I suppose.'

Gaunt shook his head and didn't reply. In truth, he was startled at the way Hark had come to his defence. Elthan had been talking a lot of crap, but he'd been spot on about Hark's purpose here. It was common knowledge. Hark himself had been brutally matter-of-fact about it from the outset. He was Lugo's punisher, here to oversee the end of Gaunt's command. Gaunt knew little of Hark's background or past career, but the same was clearly not true in reverse. Hark had casually reeled off the most notable actions of the Ghosts under Gaunt from memory. And he'd spoken with what seemed genuine admiration.

'Have you made a particular study of my career, Hark?'

'Of course. I have been appointed to serve the Tanith First as commissar. I'd be failing in that duty if I did not thoroughly acquaint myself with its history and operations. Wouldn't I?'

'And what did you learn from that study?'

'That, despite a history of clashes with the upper echelons of command, you have a notable service record. Hagia is your first true failure, but it is a failure of such magnitude that it threatens to eclipse all you have done before.'

'Really? Do you really believe I deserve sole blame for the disaster in the Doctrinopolis?'

'Lord General Lugo is a lord general, Gaunt. That is the most complete answer I can give you.'

Gaunt nodded with an unfriendly smile. 'There is justice beyond rank, Hark. Slaydo believed that.'

'Rest his good soul, the Emperor protects. But Macaroth is Warmaster now.'

The candid honesty of the response struck Gaunt. For the first time, he felt something other than venom towards Commissar Viktor Hark. To be part of the Imperial Guard was to be part of a complex system of obedience, loyalty and service. More often than not, that system forced men into obligations and decisions they'd otherwise not choose to make. Gaunt had butted up against the system all his career. Was he now seeing that mirrored in another? Or was Hark just dangerously persuasive?

The latter notion seemed likely. Charisma was one of the chief tools of a good commissar, and Hark seemed to have it in spades. To say the right thing at the right time for the right effect. Was he just playing with Gaunt?

'I've detailed some platoons to bury the dead here,' Hark said. 'We can't afford to carry them with us. A small service should do it, consecrated by the Pardus chaplain. The wounded are a bigger problem. We have nine serious, including Captain Herodas. Medic Curth tells me at least two of them won't live if they don't reach a hospital by tomorrow. The others will perish if we keep them with us.'

'Your suggestion?'

'We're less than a day out from the Doctrinopolis. I suggest we sacrifice a truck, and send them back to the city with a driver and maybe a few guards.'

'That would be my choice too. Arrange it, please, Hark. Select a Munitorium driver and one Ghost trooper, one single good man, as armed escort.'

Hark nodded. There was a long pause and Gaunt thought Hark was about to speak again.

Instead he walked away into the gathering gloom.

It was approaching midnight when the last elements of the honour guard convoy rolled in to the deserted village of Mukret. Both moons were up, one small and full, the other a large, perfect geometric semi-circle, and dazzling ribbons of stars decorated the dark blue sky.

Gaunt looked up at them as he jumped down from his command vehicle. The Sabbat Worlds. The battleground he had come to with Slaydo all those years before. The starscape of the crusade. For a moment he felt as if it all depended on this little world, on this little night, on this little continent. On him.

They were the Sabbat Worlds because this was Sabbat's world. The saint's place. If ever a soldier had to face his final mission, none could be more worthy. Slaydo would have approved, Gaunt considered. Slaydo would have wanted to be here. They weren't storming some fortress-world or decimating the legions of the arch-enemy. Such worthy glories and battle honours seemed slight and meaningless compared to this.

They were here for the saint.

Alpha-AR had secured the empty town. The tanks and carriers rolled in, choking the cold night air with their thunderous exhausts and dazzling lamps.

The main town road was full of vehicles and disembarking troops. Braziers were lit, and pickets arranged.

Mkoll saluted Gaunt as he approached. 'You had some trouble, sir.'

'Sometimes the carniv gets you, sergeant,' Gaunt replied.

'Sir?'

'From tomorrow, we run a spearhead under your command. Hard armour, fast moving.'

'Not my way, sir, but if you insist.'

'I do. We were caught napping. And paid for it. My mistake.'

'No one's mistake, sir.'

'Perhaps. But it can only get worse from here. Spearhead, from Mukret, at dawn. Can you manage that?'

Mkoll nodded.

'Do you want to choose the formation or do you trust me to do it?'

The scout sergeant smiled. 'You call the shots, sir. I've always preferred it that way.'

'I'll consult Kleopas and let you know.'

They walked through the bustle of dismounting personnel.

'I've met a man here,' Mkoll said. 'A sort of vagrant priest. You should talk to him.'

'To confess my sins?'

'No sir. He's... Well, I don't know what he is, but I think you'll like him.'

'Right,' said Gaunt. He and Mkoll sidestepped as Tanith troopers backed across their path carrying ammo boxes and folded mortars for the perimeter defence.

'Sorry, sir,' said Larkin, struggling with a heavy shell crate.

'As you were, Larks,' Gaunt smiled.

'Tough luck about Milo,' said Larkin.

Gaunt felt his blood chill. For one dreadful moment, he wondered if he'd missed Brin's name on the casualty roll.

'Tough luck?'

'Him going back to the city like that. He'll miss the show.'

Gaunt nodded warily, and called over Sergeant Baffels, Milo's platoon commander. 'Where's Trooper Milo?'

'Heading back to the Doctrinopolis with the wounded. I thought you knew, sir.' Baffels, chunky and bearded, looked awkwardly up at the colonel-commissar.

'Hark selected him?'

Baffels nodded. 'He said you wanted a good man to ride shotgun for the wounded.'

'Carry on, sergeant.'

Gaunt walked through the busy activity of the convoy, away, down to the river's edge, where the rippling water reflected back the moons and the chirrup of night insects filled every angle of the darkness.

Milo. Gaunt had always joked about the way the men saw Brin Milo as his lucky charm. He'd teased them for their superstitious foolishness. But in his heart, silently, he'd always felt that it was actually true. Milo had a charmed life. He had the pure flavour of lost Tanith about him. He was their last and only link to the Ghosts' past.

Gaunt had always kept him close for that reason, though he'd never, ever admitted it.

Hark had chosen Milo to be the one to return to the holy city. Accident? Coincidence? Design?

Hark had already stated he had studied the Tanith records. He had to know how psychologically important Brin was to the Ghosts. To Gaunt.

Gaunt had a nasty feeling he'd been deliberately undermined.

Worse still, he had a feeling of doom. For the first time, they were going out without Milo. He already knew this mission was going to be his last.

Now, with a sense of terrifying premonition, he felt it was going to turn bad. Very bad indeed.

FAR AWAY NOW, chasing back down the Tembarong Road towards the Doctrinopolis, the lone troop truck thundered through the night.

Milo had ridden in the cab for the first part of the overnight journey, but the obese Munitorium driver had proved to be surly and taciturn, and then had begun to exhibit a chronic flatulence problem that would have been offensive even in an open-topped car.

Milo had climbed back to spend the rest of the trip with the wounded men.

Commissar Hark had singled him out for this duty. Milo wondered why. There were any number of troopers who could have done the job.

Milo wondered if Hark had chosen him because he hadn't been a proper trooper long. Despite his uniform, some of the Ghosts still regarded him as the token civilian. He resented that. He was a fething Imperial Guardsman and he'd take physical issue with anyone who doubted that. Even more, he resented missing out on what he knew would be the last action of the Tanith Ghosts under Ibram Gaunt. He doubted there would be much glory in the mission, but still he yearned to be there.

He felt cheated.

Then, as he watched the moons' light flickering on the river dashing by, he wondered if Gaunt had told Hark to select him. His encounter with Gaunt in the Universitariat still stung. Had Gaunt really wished him away?

Most of the wounded were unconscious or asleep. Milo sat beside Captain Herodas in the back of the rocking truck. The captain was pale from blood loss and trauma and his face was pinched. Milo was afraid Herodas wasn't going to make it back to the Doctrinopolis, despite Medic Curth's ministrations. He'd lost so much blood.

'Don't you go dying on me, sir,' he growled at the supine officer.

'I won't, I swear it,' Herodas murmured.

'Just a bad wound. They'll fix you up. Feth, you'll get an augmetic knee, soon as look at you!'

Herodas laughed but no sound came out of him.

'Sergeant Varl in my mob, he's got an augmetic shoulder. The latest fething bionics!'

'Yeah?' whispered Herodas. Milo wanted to keep him talking. About anything, any old nonsense. He was worried what might happen if Herodas fell asleep.

'Oh yes, sir. The latest thing! Claims he can crack nalnuts in his armpit now, he does.'

Herodas chuckled. 'You're gonna miss all the fun coming back with us,' he said.

Milo grimaced. 'Not so much fun. The colonel-commissar's swansong. No great glory in being there for that.'

'He's a good man,' mumbled Herodas, moving his body as much as the pain allowed to resettle more comfortably. 'A fine commander. I didn't know him well, but from what I saw, I'd have been proud to be numbered as one of his.'

'He does his job,' said Milo.

'And more. Vervunhive! I read the dispatches about that. What an action! What a command! Were you there for that?'

'Hab by fething hab, sir.'

Herodas coughed and smiled. 'Something of note. Something to be proud of.'

'It was just the usual,' Milo lied, his eyes now hot with angry tears.

'Glory like that, you take it with you to the end of your days, trooper.' Herodas fell silent and seemed to be sleeping.

'Captain? Captain?'

'What?' asked Herodas, blinking up.

'I– nothing. I see the lights. I see the Doctrinopolis. We're almost there.'

'That's good, trooper.'

'Milo. It's Milo, sir.'

'That's good, Milo. Tell me what you see.'

Milo rose up in the flatbed of the bouncing truck and looked out through the windy dark at the lambent flames burning distantly on the Citadel. They made a beacon in the night.

'I see the holy city, sir.'

'Do you?'

'Yes, I see it. I see the lights.'

'How I want to be there,' Herodas whispered.

'Sir? What did you say? Sir?' Milo looked down out of the wind, holding on tight to the truck's stanchions.

'My name is Lucan Herodas. I don't feel like being a "sir" any more. Call me by my name.'

'I will, Lucan.'

Herodas nodded slowly. 'Tell me what you see now, Milo.'

'I see the city gates. I see the roofs and towers. I see the temples glowing like starflies in the dark.'

Lucan Herodas didn't reply. The truck rolled in under the Pilgrim Gate. Dawn was just a suggestion at the horizon.

Ten minutes later, the truck drew up in the yard of the western city infirmary.

By then, Herodas was dead.

EIGHT
THE WOUNDED

'As I have been called to the holy work,
so I will call others to me.'

— Saint Sabbat, epistles

'A FINE, FAIR, bright morning, Colm, you old dog,' Dorden announced as he walked into the little side room that had been reserved for the Tanith second-in-command. Early daylight poured in like milk through the west facing casement. The air was cool with the promise of a hot day ahead. A smell of antiseptic wafted in from the hospital halls.

There came no immediate reply, but then Corbec was a notoriously heavy sleeper.

'Did you sleep well?' Dorden asked conversationally, moving towards the cabinet beside the gauze-veiled bed.

He hoped the sound of his voice would slowly, gently rouse the colonel so he could check him over. More than one orderly had received a slap in the mouth for waking Corbec too abruptly.

Dorden picked up a small pottery flask of painkillers. 'Colm? How did you sleep? With all the noise, I mean?'

The sounds of the relentless evacuation had gone on all night, and even now, he could hear the thump of equipment and bustle of bodies in the street outside. Every half hour, the ascending wail of transporter jets roared over the Doctrinopolis as bulk transports lifted away into the sky.

The considerable, gothic manse of the Scholam Medicae Hagias lay on the west bank of the holy river facing the Universitariat, and thus occupied the heart of one of the most populated and active city quarters. A municipal infirmary and teaching hospital attached to the Universitariat, the Scholam Medicae was one of the many city institutions sequestered by the Imperial liberation force to treat wounded men.

'Funny, I don't seem to be sleeping at all well myself,' Dorden said absently, weighing the pill-bottle in his hand. 'Too many dreams. I'm dreaming about my son a lot these days. Mikal, you know. He comes to me in my dreams all the time. I haven't worked out what he's trying to tell me, but he's trying to tell me something.'

Below the little room's window, an argument broke out. Heated voices rose in the still, clear air.

He went to the window, unlatched the casement and leaned out. 'Keep it down!' he yelled into the street below. 'This is meant to be a hospital! Have you no compassion?'

The voices dropped away and he turned back to face the veiled bed.

'This feels light to me,' he said softly, gesturing with the flask. 'Have you been taking too many? It's no joke, Corbec. These are powerful drugs. If you're abusing the dose...'

His voice trailed off. He stepped towards the bed and pulled back the gauzy drapes.

The bed was empty. Rucked, slept in, but empty.

'What the feth–?' Dorden murmured.

THE BASILICA OF Macharius Hagia was a towering edifice on the east side of the Holyditch chelon markets. It had four steeples clad in grey-green ashlar, a stone imported from off-world and which contrasted starkly with the pinks and russets and creams of the local masonry. A massive statue of the Lord Solar in full armour, raising his lightning claws to the sky in a gesture of defiance or vengeance, stood upon a great brick plinth in the entrance arch.

Inside, out of the day's rising heat, it was cold and expansive. Doves and rat-birds fluttered in the open roof spaces and flickered across the staggeringly broad beams of sunlight that stabbed down into the nave.

The place was busy, even at this early hour. Blue-robed ayatani bustled about, preparing for one of the morning rites. Esholi fetched and carried for them, or attended the needs of the many hundreds of worshippers gathering in the grand nave. From the east side, the breeze carried the smells of cooking fish and bread, the smells of the public kitchens adjoining the temple, whose charitable work was to produce alms and free sustenance twice a day for the visiting pilgrims.

The smells made Ban Daur hungry. As he limped in down the main colonnade amidst the other faithful, his stomach gurgled painfully. He stopped for a moment and leaned hard on his walking stick until the dizzying discomfort passed. He hadn't eaten much since taking his wound, hadn't done much of anything, in fact. The medics had banned him from even getting out of bed, but he knew best how he felt. Strong, surprisingly strong. And lucky. The ritual blade had missed his heart by the most remarkably slim margin. The doctors worried the wound might have left a glancing score across the heart muscle, a weakness that might rupture if he exerted himself too soon.

But he could not just lie in bed. This world, Hagia... It was coming to an end. The streets were full of military personnel and civilians trying to pack up and ship out the contents of their lives. There was fear in the air, and a strange sense of unreality.

He started to walk again, but had to stop quickly. He was still light-headed, and sometimes the wound ache in his chest came in bitter waves.

'Are you all right, sir?' asked a passing esholi, a teenage boy in cream silk robes. There was concern in the eyes of the shaven-headed youth.

'Can I help you to a seat?'

'Mmmh... Perhaps, yes. I may have overdone things.'

The student took his arm and guided him across to a nearby bench. Daur lowered himself gratefully onto it.

'You're very pale, sir. Should you even be on your feet?'

'Probably not. Thank you. I'll be fine now I'm sitting.'

The student nodded and moved on, though Daur saw him again some minutes later, talking to several ayatani and pointing anxiously Daur's way.

Daur ignored them and sat back to gaze up at the high altar. The shortness of breath was the worst thing. Exertion got him out of breath so quickly and then he couldn't catch it back because taking deep breaths was agony on his wound.

No, that wasn't the worst thing. A knife in the chest wasn't the worst thing. Being injured in battle and missing the last mission of his regiment.... even that wasn't the worst thing.

The worst thing was the thing in his head, and that wouldn't leave him alone.

He heard voices exchanging hard words nearby and looked round. So did all the worshippers in earshot. Two ayatani were arguing with a group of officers from the Ardelean Colonials. One of the Colonials was repeatedly gesturing to the reliquary. Daur heard one of the priests say '...but this is our heritage! You will not ransack this holy place!'

Daur had heard the same sentiments expressed several times in the last day or so. Despite the abominable evil that moved towards them with the clear intent to engulf the entire world, few native Hagians wanted the evacuation. Many of the ayatani, in fact, saw the removal of icons and relics for safekeeping tantamount to desecration. But Lord General Lugo's decrees had been strict and inflexible. Daur wondered how long it would be before a Hagian was arrested for obstruction or shot for disobedience.

He felt an immeasurable sympathy for the faithful. It was almost as if his wounding had been an epiphany. He'd always been a dutiful man, dutiful to the Imperial creed, a servant of the God-Emperor. But he'd never thought of himself as especially... devout.

Until now. Until here on Hagia. Until, it seemed to Ban Daur, the very moment an Infardi dagger had punched between his ribs. It was like it had changed him, as if he'd been transformed by sharp steel and his own spilt blood. He heard about men undergoing religious transformations. It scared him. It was in his head and it wouldn't leave him alone.

He felt he needed to do something about it, desperately. Limping his way from the infirmary to the nearest temple was a start, but it didn't seem to achieve much. Daur didn't know what he expected to happen. A sign, perhaps. A message.

Such a thing didn't seem very likely.

He sighed, and sat back with his eyes closed for a moment. He was scheduled to join a troop ship with the other walking wounded at six that evening. He wasn't looking forward to it. It felt like running away.

When he opened his eyes, he saw a familiar figure amongst the faithful at the foot of the main altar. It was such a surprise, Daur blinked in confusion.

But he was not mistaken. There was Colm Corbec, his left arm webbed in a sling tight against his bandaged chest, the sleeve of his black fatigue jacket hanging empty, kneeling in prayer.

Daur waited. After a few minutes, Corbec stood up, turned, and saw Daur sitting in the pews. A look of puzzlement crossed the grizzled giant's face. He came over at once.

'Didn't expect to see you here, Daur.'

'I didn't expect to see you either, colonel.'

Corbec sat down next to him.

'Shouldn't you be resting in bed?' Corbec asked. 'What? What's so funny?'

'I was about to ask you that.'

'Yeah, well...' Corbec murmured. 'You know me. Can't abide to be lying around idle.'

'Has there been any word from the honour guard?'

Corbec shook his head. 'Not a thing. Feth, but I...'

'You what?'

'Nothing.'

'Come on, you started to say something.'

'Something I don't think you'd understand, Daur.'

'Okay.'

They sat in silence for a while.

'What?' Daur looked round sharply at Corbec.

'What what?' growled Corbec.

'You spoke.'

'I didn't.'

'Just then, colonel. You said–'

'I didn't say anything, Daur.'

'You said "Sabbat Martyr". I heard you.'

'Wasn't me. I didn't speak.'

Daur scratched his cheek. 'Never mind.'

'What... what were those words?'

'Sabbat Martyr. Or something like that.'

'Oh.'

The silence between them returned. The basilica choir began to sing, the massed voices shimmering the air.

'You hungry, Ban?'

'Starving, sir.'

'Let's go to the public kitchens and get some breakfast together.'

'I thought the temple kitchens were meant to serve the faithful.'

'They are,' said Corbec, getting to his feet, an enigmatic half-smile on his lips. 'Come on.'

THEY GOT BOWLS of fish broth and hunks of crusty, huskseed bread from the long-canopied counters of the kitchens, and went to sit amongst the breakfasting faithful at the communal trestle tables under a wide, flapping awning of pink canvas.

Daur watched as Corbec pulled what looked like a couple of pills from his coat pocket and gulped them down with the first sip of broth. He didn't comment.

'There's something not right in my head, Ban,' Corbec began suddenly through a mouthful of bread. 'In my head... or my gut or my soul or wherever... somewhere. It's been there, off and on, since I was a held captive by Pater Sin, rot his bones.'

'What sort of thing?'

'The sort of thing a man like me... a man like you too, would be my guess... has no idea what to do with. It's lurked in my dreams mostly. I've been dreaming about my father, back home on lost Tanith.'

'We all have dreams of our old worlds,' said Daur cautiously. 'It's the guard curse.'

'Sure enough, Ban. I know that. I've been guard long enough. But not dreams like this. It's like... there's a meaning to be had. Like... Oh, I dunno...' Corbec frowned as he struggled to find adequate words.

'Like someone's trying to tell you something?' Daur whispered softly. 'Something important? Something that has to be done?'

'Sacred feth!' growled Corbec in amazement. 'That's it exactly! How did you know?'

Daur shrugged, and put his bowl down. 'I can't explain. I feel it too. I didn't realise... Well, I didn't until you started describing it there. It's not dreams I'm having. Gak, I don't think I'm dreaming much at all. But a feeling... like I should be doing something.'

'Feth,' murmured Corbec again.

'Are we mad, do you think? Maybe what we both need is a priest who's a good listener. A confessor. Maybe a head-doctor.'

Corbec dabbed his bread into the broth distractedly. 'I don't think so. I've nothing to confess. Nothing I haven't told you.'

'So what do we do?'

'I don't know. But I know there's no way in feth I'm getting on that troop ship tonight.'

HE'D STOLEN A few hours' sleep in a corner of the western city infirmary's entrance hall. But as the sun rose and the noise of people coming and going became too much to sleep through, Brin Milo shouldered his pack and rifle and began the long walk up the Amad Road into the centre of the Doctrinopolis.

Hark had told him to report to Guard command once he'd escorted the wounded party to safety. He was to present himself and arrange his place on an evacuation ship.

The city seemed like a place of madness around him. With the fighting over, the streets had filled up with hurrying crowds, honking motor vehicles, cargo trains hauled by servitors, processions of worshippers, pilgrims, protesters, refugees. The city was seething again, like a nalmite nest preparing to swarm.

Milo remembered the last, final hours in Tanith Magna, the same atmosphere of panic and activity. The memories were not pleasant. He decided he wanted to be out of here now, on a troop ship and away.

There was nothing here now he wanted to stay for, or needed to stay for.

A flustered Brevian Centennial on crowd control duties told him that Evacuation command had been established in the royal treasury, but the roads approaching that edifice were jammed with foot traffic and vehicles. The commotion was unbearable.

Transport shuttles shivered the sky as they lifted up over the holy city. A pair of navy fighters screamed overhead, low and fast.

Milo turned and headed for the Scholam Medicae where the Tanith wounded were being cared for. He'd find his own men, maybe Colonel Corbec, he decided. He'd leave with them.

'BRINNY BOY!' A delighted voice boomed behind him, and Milo was snatched up off his feet in a one-armed bear hug of crushing force.

'Bragg!' he smiled, turning as he was released.

'What are you doing here, Brin?' beamed Trooper Bragg.

'Long story,' said Milo. 'How's the arm there?'

Bragg glanced contemptuously at his heavily bandaged right shoulder.

'Fixing up. Fething medics refused to let me join the honour guard. Said it was a safe ticket out for me, feth 'em! It's not bad. I could've still fought.'

Milo gestured to the busy hallway of the Scholam Medicae Hagias they stood in. 'Anyone else around?'

'A few. Most of 'em in a bad way. Colonel's here somewhere, but I haven't seen him. I was in a bed next to Derin. He's on the mend and cussing his luck too.'

'I'm going to try and find the colonel. What ward are you in?'

'South six.'

'I'll come and find you in a bit.'

'You better!'

Milo pushed on through the hectic hallway, through the smells of blood and disinfectant, the hurrying figures, the rattling carts. He passed several doors that opened onto long, red-painted wards lined with critically injured guardsmen in rows of cots. Some were Ghosts, men he recognised. All were too far gone from pain and damage to register him. After asking questions of several orderlies and servitors, he found his way to Dorden's suite of offices on the third floor. As he approached, he could hear the shouting coming from inside down the length of the corridor.

'...don't just get up and walk off when you feel like it! For the Emperor's sake! You're hurt! That won't heal if you put a strain on it!'

An answering mumble.

'I will not calm down! The health of the regimental wounded is my business! Mine! You wouldn't disobey Gaunt's orders, why the feth do you think you can disobey mine?'

Milo walked into the office. Corbec was sitting on an examination couch facing the door, and his eyes opened wide when he saw Milo. Dorden, shaking with rage, stood facing Corbec and turned sharply when he read Corbec's expression.

'Milo?'

Corbec leapt up. 'What's happened? The honour guard? What the feth's happened?'

'There was an ambush on the road last night. We took a few injured, some bad enough Surgeon Curth wanted them brought back here. Commissar Hark volunteered me to ride shotgun. We got back here at dawn.'

'Are you meant to return?'

Milo shook his head. 'I'd never catch up with them now, colonel. My orders are to join the evacuation now I'm here.'

'How were they doing? Apart from the ambush, I mean?'

'Not so bad. They should've made it to the overnight stop at Mukret.'

'Did we lose many in the attack?' Dorden asked softly. His anger seemed to have dulled.

'Forty-three dead, fifteen of them Ghosts. Six Ghosts amongst the injured I brought back.'

'Sounds bad, Milo.'

'It was quick and nasty.'

'You can show me on the map where it happened,' Corbec told him.

'Why?' snapped Dorden. 'I've told you already, you're not going anywhere. Except to the landing fields this evening. Forget the rest, Colm. I mean it. I have seniority in this, and Lugo would have my fething head. Forget it.'

There was a loaded pause.

'Forget... what?' Milo dared to ask.

'Don't get him started!' Dorden roared.

'The boy's just asking, doc...' Corbec countered.

'You want to know, Milo? Do you?' Dorden was livid. 'Our beloved colonel here has this idea... No, let me start at the beginning. Our beloved colonel here decides he knows doctoring better than me, and so gets himself out of bed against my orders this morning! Goes wandering around the fething city! We didn't even know where he was! Then he shows up again without so much as a by your leave, and tells me he's thinking of heading up into the mountains!'

'Into the mountains?'

'That's right! He's got it into his thick head that there's something important he's got to do! Something Gaunt, an armour unit and nigh on three thousand troopers can't manage without his help!'

'Be fair, I didn't quite say that, Doc...'

Dorden was too busy ranting at the rather stunned Milo. 'He wants to break orders. My orders. The lord general's orders. In a way, Gaunt's own orders. He's going to ignore the instructions to evacuate tonight. And go chasing up into the Sacred Hills after Gaunt. On his own! Because he has a hunch!'

'Not on my own,' Corbec growled in a whisper.

'Oh, don't tell me! You've persuaded some other fools to go along with you? Who? Who, colonel? I'll have them chained to their fething beds.'

'Then I won't tell you who, will I?' Corbec yelled.

'A... hunch...?' Milo asked quietly.

'Yeah,' said Corbec. 'Like one of me hunches...'

'Spare us! One of Colonel Corbec's famous battle-itches–'

Corbec wheeled round at Dorden and for a moment, Milo was afraid he was going to throw a punch. And even more afraid that the medic was going to throw one back. 'Since when have my tactical itches proved wrong, eh? Fething when?'

Dorden looked away.

'But, no... It's not like that. Not an itch. Not really. Or it's like the grandaddy of all battle-itches. It's more like a feeling–'

'That's all right then! A feth-damned feeling!' said Dorden sarcastically.

'More like a calling, then!' bellowed Corbec. 'Like the biggest, strongest calling I've ever had in me life! Pulling at me, demanding of me! Like... like if I've got the wit to respond, the balls to respond, I'll be doing the most important thing I could ever do.'

Dorden snorted. There was a long, painfully heavy pause.

'Colm... it's my job to look after the men. More than that, it's my pleasure to look after them. I don't need orders.' Dorden sat down behind his desk and fiddled with a sheaf of scripts, not making eye contact with either of the others. 'I came into Old Town with Kolea – broke orders to do it – because I thought we might get you out alive.'

'And you did, doc, and feth knows, I owe you and the boys that one.'

Dorden nodded. 'But I can't sanction this. You – and anyone else you may have talked to – you all need to be at the muster point for evacuation at six tonight. No exceptions. It's an order from the office of the lord general himself. Any dissenters. Any absentees... will be considered as having deserted. And will suffer the full consequences.'

He looked up at Corbec. 'Don't do this to me, Colm.'

'I won't. They ask you, you don't know a thing. I'd have liked you to join me, doc, really I would, but I won't ask that of you. I understand the impossible position that'd put you in. But what I feel isn't wrong...'

'Corbec, please–'

'The last few nights, me dad's been in my dreams. Not just a memory, I mean. Really him. Bringing me a message.'

'What sort of message?' asked Milo.

'All he says is the same thing, over and over. He's in his machine shop, back in Pryze County, working the lathe there. I come in and he looks up and he says "sabbat martyr". Just that.'

'I know what's going on,' said Dorden. 'I feel it myself, it's perfectly natural. We both know this is Gaunt's last show. That Lugo's got his balls in a vice. And that means, let's face it, the end for the Ghosts. We all want to be there with Gaunt this last time. The honour guard, the last duty. It doesn't feel right to be missing it. We'd do anything... we'd think of any excuse... to get out there after him. Even subconsciously, our minds are trying to magic up ways to make it happen.'

'It's not that, doc.'

'I think it is.'

'Well then, maybe it is. Maybe it is me subconscious trying to jinx up an excuse. And maybe that's good enough for me. Gaunt's last show, doc. You said it yourself. They can court martial me, but I won't miss that. Not for anything.'

Corbec glanced at the silent Milo, patted him on the arm, and limped out of the office.

'Can you talk some sense into him, do you think?' Dorden asked Milo.

'From what I've just heard, I doubt it. In all candour, sir, I doubt I want to.'

Dorden nodded. 'Try, for my sake. If Corbec's not at the muster point tonight, I won't sell him out. But I can't protect him.'

CORBEC WAS IN his little room, sorting his pack on the unmade bed. Milo knocked at the half-open door.

'You coming with me? I shouldn't ask. I won't be offended if you say no.'

'What's your plan?'

Corbec half-shrugged. 'Fethed if I know. Daur's with me. He feels the same. Really, he feels the same, you know?'

Milo said nothing. He didn't know.

'Daur's seeing if he can find any others crazy enough to come. We'll need able men. It won't be an easy ride.'

'It'll be hell. A small unit, moving west. The Infardi are everywhere. They didn't think twice about hitting a target the size of the taskforce.'

'We could so do with a scout. Local knowledge, maybe. I don't know.'

'Assuming we make it through, all the way to the Shrinehold. What then?'

'Feth me! I hope by then me dad will have told me more! Or maybe Daur will have figured it out. Or it'll be obvious...'

'It sure isn't obvious now, sir. Whatever it is, if Gaunt and the taskforce can't do it, how could we hope to?'

'Maybe they don't know. Maybe... they need to do something else.'

Corbec turned and smiled at Milo. 'You realise you've been saying "we", don't you?'

'I guess I have.'

'Good lad. It wouldn't be the same without you.'

'WELL, FETH BLESS my good soul!' said Colm Corbec. He was so touched by the sight before him, he felt he might cry. 'Did you all... I mean, are you all...?'

Bragg got up from the base of the pillar he was sitting against and stuck out his hand. 'We're all as crazy as you, chief,' he smiled.

Corbec gripped his meaty paw hard.

'Daur and Milo asked around. We're the only takers. I hope we'll do.'

'You'll do me fine.'

They stood in the shadows of the Munitorium warehouse on Pavane Street, off the main thoroughfare, out of sight. The contents of the warehouse had been evacuated that morning. It had been arranged as the rendezvous point. It was now close to six o'clock.

Somewhere, a troop ship was waiting for them. Somewhere, their names were being flagged on the commissariat discipline lists.

Corbec moved down the line as the assembled troopers got up to greet him. 'Derin! How's the chest?'

'Don't expect me to run anywhere,' smiled Trooper Derin. There was no sign of injury about him, but his arms moved stiffly. Corbec knew a whole lot of suturing and bandages lay under his black Tanith field jacket.

'Nessa... my girl.'

She threw him a salute, her long-las resting against her hip. *Ready to move out, colonel sir*, she signed.

'Trooper Vamberfeld, sir,' said the next in line. Corbec grinned at the pale, slightly out of condition Verghastite.

'I know who you are, Vamberfeld. Good to see you.'

'You said you needed local knowledge,' Milo said as Corbec reached him. 'This is Sanian. She's esholi, one of the student body.'

'Miss,' Corbec saluted her.

Sanian looked up at Corbec and appraised him frankly. 'Trooper Milo described your mission as almost spiritual, colonel. I will probably lose my privileges and status for absconding with you.'

'We're absconding now, are we?' The troopers around them laughed.

'The saint herself is in your mind, colonel. I can see that much. I have made my choice. If I can help by coming with you, I am happy to do it.'

'It won't be easy, Miss Sanian. I hope Milo's told you that much.'

'Sanian. I am just Sanian. Or esholi Sanian if you prefer to be formal. And yes, Milo has explained the danger. I feel it will be an education.'

'Safer ways of getting an education...' Derin began.

'Life itself is the education for the esholi,' said Milo smartly.

Sanian smiled. 'I think Milo has been paying too much attention to me.'

'Well, I can see why,' said Corbec, putting on the charm. 'You're welcome here with us. Do you know much about the land west of here?'

'I was raised in Bhavnager. And the western territories of the Sacred Hills and the Pilgrim's Way are fundamental knowledge for any esholi.'

'Well, didn't we just win the top prize?' grinned Corbec. 'So,' he said, turning to face the six of them. 'I guess we wait for Daur. He's in charge of transport.'

The group broke up into idle chatter for a minute or two. Suddenly, they all heard the clatter of tracks in the street outside. All of them froze, snatching up weapons, expecting the worst.

'What do you see?' Vamberfeld hissed to Bragg.

'It's the commissariat, isn't it?' said Derin. 'They're fething on to us!'

An ancient, battered Chimera rumbled into the warehouse. Its turbines coughed and rasped as they shut down. It was the oldest and worst kept piece of Munitorium armour Milo had ever seen, and that included the junk piles that had been given to the honour guard convoy.

The back hatch opened, and Daur edged out as gracefully as his aching wound allowed.

'Best I could do,' he said. 'It was one from the motorpool they're going to abandon in the evacuation.'

'Feth!' said Corbec, walking around the dirty green hulk. 'But it goes, right?'

'It goes for now,' replied Daur. 'What do you want, Corbec, miracles?'

A second man climbed out of the Chimera. He was a tall, blond, freckled individual in Pardus uniform. His head was bandaged.

'This is Sergeant Greer, Pardus Eighth Mobile Flak Company. I knew none of us could handle this beast, so I coopted a driver. Greer here... kind of owes me.'

'That's what he says,' Greer said sulkily. 'I'm just along for the ride.'

'Where'd you get the hurt?' Corbec asked him.

Greer touched his bandage. 'Glancing shot. During the action to take the census hall a few days back.'

Corbec nodded. The same action Daur had been hurt in. He shook Greer's hand.

'Welcome to the Wounded,' he said.

AT AROUND HALF past six, the names of troopers Derin, Vamberfeld, Nessa and Bragg, and of Captain Daur and Colonel Corbec, were noted in the log of the evacuation office as overdue. The lift shuttle left without them.

At a muster point further east across the Doctrinopolis, the Pardus chief surgeon noted the absence of Driver-Sergeant Greer.

Both reports were sent to Evacuation command and entered into the night log. The officer of the watch wasn't unduly taxed by this. He had over three hundred names on his list of absentees by then, and it was growing with each passing shuttle call. There were many reasons for missed muster: badly relayed orders; confusion as to the correct muster point; delays because of traffic in the holy city; un-logged deaths from the guard infirmaries. Indeed, some names on the evacuation lists were of troopers who had died in the liberation fight and as yet lay undiscovered and unidentified in the rubble.

Some, a very few, were deserters. Such names were passed to the discipline offices and the lord general's staff.

The officer of the watch passed these latest names on. It was unusual for senior officers like a colonel to fail to report.

By eight o'clock, the list had dropped onto the desk of Commissar Hychas, who was away at dinner. His aide passed it to the punishment detail, who by nine thirty had sent a four-man team led by a commissar-cadet down to the Scholam Medicae Hagias to investigate. A report was copied to Lord General Lugo's staff, where it was read by a senior adjutant shortly before midnight. He immediately voxed the punishment detail, and was told by the commissar-cadet that no trace of the missing personnel could be found at the Scholam Medicae.

At one in the morning, a warrant was issued for the arrest of Colonel Colm Corbec of the Tanith First-and-Only, along with six of his men. No one thought or knew to tally this with the warrant out for Sergeant-Driver Denic Greer of the Pardus Eighth. Or the theft report of a class gamma transport Chimera from the Munitorium motorpool.

By then, Corbec's Chimera was long gone, heading west down the Tembarong Road, five hours out from the city perimeter, thundering into the night.

It had made one stop, in the half-empty, wartorn suburb streets just short of the Pilgrim Gate. That had been around seven at night, with deep, starless dusk falling.

At the helm, Greer had seen a figure in the road ahead, waving at them. Corbec had popped the turret hatch and looked out, almost immediately calling down at Greer to pull over.

Corbec had dropped down from the waiting Chimera, his boots kissing the road dust, and had walked to meet the figure face to face.

'Sabbat martyr,' Dorden had said, tears in his eyes. 'My boy told me to. Don't think for a minute you're going without me.'

NINE
APPROACHING BHAVNAGER

'If the road is easy, the destination is worthless.'

— Saint Sabbat, proverbs

FROM MUKRET, THE highway ran due west to the Nusera Crossing where the holy river twisted across it. North of the crossing, the river's course snaked up to the headwaters in the hills, one hundred and fifty kilometres away.

The second day of the mission dawned soft and bright, with the lowland plains of the river valley dressed in thick white fogs. The scout spearhead under Mkoll left Mukret through the early fogs, travelling at a moderate rate because of the reduced visibility.

Gaunt and Kleopas had assembled three scout Salamanders carrying a dozen Ghost troopers between them, two Conqueror tanks and one of the two Destroyer tank hunters in the Pardus complement. The main taskforce set out from Mukret an hour behind them.

Gaunt's intention was to reach the farming community of Bhavnager by the second night. This meant a run of nearly ninety-five kilometres, on decent roads. But already the mists were slowing their progress. At Bhavnager, so intelligence reported, they could refuel for the later stages of the journey. Bhavnager was the last settlement of appreciable size on the north-west spur of the highway. It marked the end of the arable lowlands and the start of the rainwood districts that dressed the climbing edges of the Sacred Hills. From Bhavnager, the going would become a lot tougher.

Ayatani Zweil had agreed to accompany the main taskforce, and rode with Gaunt in his command Salamander at the colonel-commissar's personal invitation. He seemed intrigued by the Imperial mission: no one had told him of the intended destination, but he clearly had ideas of his own, and once they took the north-west fork at Limata, there would be no disguising where they were heading.

'How long do these fogs last, father?' Gaunt asked him as the convoy ran through the pale, smoke-like mists. It was bright, and the fogs glowed with the sunlight beyond, but they could see only a few dozen metres ahead of themselves. The sounds of the convoy engines, amplified, were thrown back on them by the heavy vapour.

Zweil toyed with his long, white beard.

'In this part of the season, sometimes until noon. These, I think, are lighter. They will lift. And when they lift, they go suddenly.'

'You're not much like the other ayatani I've met here, if you'll forgive me saying so. They all seemed tied to a particular shrine and places of worship.'

Zweil chuckled. 'They are tempelum ayatani, devoted to their shrine places. I am imhava ayatani, which means "roving priest". Our order celebrates the saint by worshipping the routes of her journeys.'

'Her journeys here?'

'Yes, and beyond. Some of my kind are up there.' He pointed a gnarled finger at the sky, and Gaunt realised he meant space itself, space beyond Hagia.

'They travel the stars?'

'Indeed. They pace out the route of her Great Crusade, her war pilgrimage to Harkalon, her wide circuit of return. It can take a lifetime, longer than a lifetime. Few make the entire circuit and return to Hagia.'

'Especially in these times, I imagine.'

Zweil nodded thoughtfully. 'The return of the arch-enemy to the Sabbat Worlds has made such roving a more lethal undertaking.'

'But you are content to make your holy journeys here?'

Zweil smiled his broad, gap-toothed smile. 'These days, yes. But in my youth, I walked her path in the stars. To Frenghold, before Hagia called me back.'

Gaunt was a little surprised. 'You've travelled off this world?'

'We're not all parochial little peasants, Colonel-Commissar Gaunt. I've seen my share of the stars and other worlds. A few wonders on the way. Nothing I'd care to stay for. Space is overrated.'

'I tend to find that too,' Gaunt grinned.

'The main purpose of the imhava ayatani is to retread the routes of the saint and offer assistance to the believers and pilgrims we find making their way. Guardians of the route. It is, I think, small-minded for a priest to stay at a shrine or temple to offer aid to the pilgrims who arrive. The journey is the hardest part. It is on the journey that most would have need of a priest.'

'That's why you agreed to come with us, isn't it?'

'I came because you asked. Politely, I might add. But you're right. You are pilgrims after all.'

'I wouldn't call us pilgrims quite–'

'I would. With devotion and resolve, you are following one of the saint's paths. You are going to the Shrinehold, after all.'

'I never said–'

'No, you didn't. But pilgrims usually travel east.' He gestured behind them in the vague direction of the Doctrinopolis. 'There's only one reason for heading this way.'

The vox squawked and Gaunt slid down into the driving well to answer it. Mkoll was checking in. The spearhead had just forded the holy river at Nusera and was making good speed to Limata. The fogs, Mkoll reported, were beginning to lift.

When Gaunt resumed his seat, he found Zweil looking through his ragged copy of Sabbat's gospel.

'A well-thumbed book,' said Zweil, making no attempt to set it aside. 'Always a good sign. I never trust a pilgrim with a clean and pristine copy. The texts you've marked are interesting. You can tell much of a man's character by what he chooses to read.'

'What can you tell about me?'

'You are burdened... hence the numerous annotations in the Devotional Creeds... and burdened by responsibility and the demands of office in particular... these three selections in the Epistles of Duty show that you seek answers, or perhaps ways of fighting internal daemons... that is plain from the number of paper strips you've used to mark the pages of the Doctrines and Revelations. You appreciate battle and courage... the Annals of War, here... and you are sentimental when it comes to fine devotional poetry...'

He held the book out open to show the Psalms of Sabbat.

'Very good,' said Gaunt.

'You smile, Colonel-Commissar Gaunt.'

'I am an Imperial commander leading a taskforce of war on a mission. You could have surmised all that about me without even looking at the bookmarks.'

'I did,' laughed Zweil. He carefully closed the gospel and handed it back to Gaunt.

'If I might say, colonel-commissar... the gospel of our saint does contain answers. But the answers are often not literal ones. Simply reading the book from cover to cover will not reveal them. One has to... feel. To look around the bare meanings of the words.'

'I studied textual interpretation at Scholam Progenium...'

'Oh, but I'm sure you did. And from that I'm sure you can tell me that when the saint talks of the "flower incarnadine" she means battle, and when she refers to "the fast-flowing river of pure water" she means true human faith. What I mean to say is the lessons of Saint Sabbat are oblique mysteries, to be unlocked by experience and innate belief. I'm not sure you have those. The answers you seek would have come to you by now if you had.'

'I see.'

'I meant no disrespect. There are high ayatani in the holy city who do no more than read and reread this work and fancy themselves enlightened.'

Gaunt didn't reply. He looked out of the rocking tank and saw how the fog was beginning to burn off with remarkable haste. Already the tree-lines at the river were becoming visible.

'Then how do I begin?' Gaunt asked darkly. 'For, truth be told, father, I have need of answers. Now more than ever before.'

'I can't help you there. Except to say, start with yourself. It is a journey you must make, standing still. I told you you were a pilgrim.'

Half an hour later, they reached the crossing at Nusera. The highway came down to a wide, shallow pan of shingle that broke the fast flowing water in a broad fording place. Groves of ghylum trees clustered at either bank, and hundreds of forkbills broke upwards into the sky in an explosive fan at the sound of the motors, their wings beating the air with the sound of ornithopter gunships.

A lone peasant with an ancient cow chelon on a pull-rein waved them past. One by one, the vehicles of the honour guard ploughed over the ford, spraying up water so hard and high that rainbows marked their wake.

LIMATA WAS ANOTHER dead town. Mkoll's spearhead reached it just before eleven thirty. The fogs had vanished. The sun was climbing and the air was still. This day was going to be even hotter than the last.

The baking roofs of Limata lay ahead, dusty and forlorn, their tiles bright pink in the sunlight. No breeze, no sounds, no telltale fingers of cookfire smoke rising above the village. Here, the Tembarong Road divided, one spur heading southwest towards Hylophon and Tembarong itself. The other broke north-west into the highlands and the steaming tracts of the rainwoods. Forty-plus kilometres in that direction lay Bhavnager.

'Slow to steady,' Mkoll snapped into his vox. 'Troopers arm. Load main weapons. Let's crawl in.'

Captain Sirus, commanding the Pardus elements, voxed in immediately from his Conqueror. 'Allow us, Tanith. We'll drive 'em down.'

'Negative. Full stop.'

The vehicles came to a halt six hundred metres short of the town perimeter. The Ghosts dismounted from the Salamanders. Idling engines rumbled in the hot, dry air.

'What's the delay?' Sirus snapped over the vox.

'Stand by,' replied Mkoll. He glanced around at Trooper Domor, one of the disembarked troopers. 'You sure?'

'Sure as they call me Shoggy,' Domor nodded, carefully using a felt cloth to wipe dust grit from the lenses of his augmetic eyes. 'You can see the way the road surface there is broken and repacked.'

Most eyes couldn't but Mkoll's were sharper than any in the regiment. And Domor's field specialisation was in landmines.

'Want me to sweep?'

'Might be an idea. Unship your kit, but don't advance until I say.'

Domor went over to his Salamander with troopers Caober and Uril to unpack the sweeper sets.

Mkoll fanned fire-teams out into the acestus groves on either side of the roadway, Mkvenner to the left and Bonin to the right, each with three men.

Within seconds of entering the dappled shadows of the fruit trees, the men were invisible, their stealth cloaks absorbing the patterns around them.

'What's the delay?' asked Captain Sirus from behind. Mkoll turned. Sirus had dismounted from his waiting Conqueror, the *Wrath of Pardua*, and had come forward to see for himself. He was a robust man in his early fifties, with the characteristic olive skin and beak nose of the Pardus. He seemed a little gung-ho to Mkoll, and the scout sergeant had been disappointed when Kleopas had appointed him to Mkoll's spearhead company.

'We've got road mines in a tight field there. And maybe beyond.' Mkoll gestured. 'And the place is too quiet for my liking.'

'Tactics?' Sirus asked briefly.

'Send my sweepers forward to clear the road for you and infiltrate the village from the sides with my troops.'

Sirus nodded sagely. 'I can tell you're infantry, sergeant. Bloody good at it too, so I hear, but you haven't the armour experience. You want that place taken, my *Wrath* can take it.'

Mkoll's heart sank. 'How?'

'That's what the Adeptus Mechanicus made dozer blades for. Give the word and I'll show you how the Pardus work.'

Mkoll turned away and walked back to his Salamander. This wasn't his approach to recon patrols. He certainly didn't want the Pardus heavies lighting up the hill for all to see with their heavy guns. He could take Limata his way, by stealth, he was sure. But Gaunt had urged him to co-operate with the armour allies.

He reached into the Salamander and pulled out the long-gain vox mic.

'Recon Spear to one.'

'One, go ahead.'

'We've got possible obstruction here at Limata. Certainly a minefield. Request permission for Captain Sirus to go in armoured and loud.'

'Is it necessary?'

'You said to play nice.'

'So I did. Permission granted.'

Mkoll hung up the mic and called to Domor's group. 'Pack it away. It's the Pardus's turn.'

Griping, they began to disassemble the sweeper brooms.

'Captain?' Mkoll looked over to Sirus. 'It's all yours.'

Sirus looked immensely pleased. He ran back to his revving tank.

At his urging, riding high in the open hatch of his turret, the two Conquerors clanked past the waiting Salamanders and headed down the highway. The grim Destroyer waited behind them, turbines barely murmuring.

The two battle tanks lowered their hefty dozer blades as they came up on the mined area and dug in, driving forward.

Captain Sirus's mine clearance methods were as brutal as they were deafening. The massive dozer blades ploughed the hardpan of the road and kicked up the buried munitions which triggered and detonated before them. Clouds of flame and debris swirled up around the advancing tanks. If the mines had been triggered under a passing vehicle, they would have crippled or destroyed it, but churned out like the seeds of a waterapple or flints turned up by a farrier's plough, they exploded harmlessly, barely scorching the thrusting dozer blades.

It was an impressive display, Mkoll had to admit.

Smoke and dust drifted back down the road over Mkoll and the waiting Salamanders. Mkoll shielded his eyes and purposely kept his off-road fireteams in position.

In less than six minutes, the *Wrath of Pardua* and its sister tank *Lion of Pardua* were rolling into Limata, the road buckled and burning behind them.

Mkoll got up on the fender of his Salamander and ordered all three light tanks to move forward after them.

He looked round. The Destroyer had disappeared.

'What the feth?' How did something that big and heavy and ugly disappear?

'Recon Spear command to Destroyer! Where the feth are you?'

'Destroyer to command. Sorry to startle you. Standard regimental deployment. I pulled off-road to lie low. Frontal assaults are the Conquerors' job, and Sirus knows what he's doing.'

'Read that, Destroyer.' Mkoll, who was generally inexperienced when it came to tank warfare, had already noted the clear differences between the Conqueror battle tanks and the low-bodied Destroyers. Where the Conquerors were high and proud, stately almost, with their massive gun turrets, the Destroyers were long-hulled and sleek, their one primary weapon not turret-mounted but fixed out forward from their humped backs. The Destroyers were predators, tank hunters, armed with a single, colossal laser cannon. They were, it seemed to Mkoll, the tank equivalent of an infantry sniper. Accurate, cunning, hard-hitting, stealthy.

The Destroyer appointed to the Recon Spear was called the *Grey Venger*. Its commander was a Captain LeGuin. Mkoll had never seen LeGuin face to face. He just knew him by his tank.

Through the rising pall of smoke, Mkoll saw the Conquerors were in the village now. They were kicking up dust. Abrupt small arms fire rained against their armoured bodies from the left.

The *Wrath of Pardua* traversed its turret and blew a house apart with a single shell. Its partner began shelling the right flank of the town's main drag. Stilt houses disintegrated or combusted. The sponson-mounted flamers on both Conquerors rippled through the close-packed buildings and turned them into torched ruins.

Captain Sirus's whoops of triumph came over the vox. Mkoll could see him in his turret, supporting his main weapon's blasts with rakes from the pintle mount.

'That's just showing off,' Domor said beside him.

'Tank boys,' murmured Caober. 'Always wanting to show who's boss.'

Advancing, they found the bloody, burnt remnants of maybe three dozen Infardi in the ruins Sirus had flattened. Limata was taken. Mkoll signalled the news to Gaunt and advanced the spearhead, bringing his fire-teams in and reforming the force with the Salamanders at the front. The Destroyer trundled out of hiding and joined the back of the column.

'Next stop Bhavnager!' Sirus warbled enthusiastically from his Conqueror.

'Move out,' ordered Mkoll.

WELL OVER A day behind them, Corbec's thrown-together team rolled past the site of the ambush, skirting around the wrecks of the Salamanders and the Chimera that the taskforce's Trojans had pushed to the roadside verges.

Corbec called a halt. The Chimera's turbine was overheating anyway, and the troopers dismounted for a rest.

Corbec, Derin and Bragg wandered over to the roadside where a plot of dark earth and rows of fresh-cut stakes marked the graves of the fallen.

'One we missed,' said Derin.

Corbec nodded. This site marked the first Ghosts action that he hadn't been a part of. Not properly. All the way from Tanith he'd come, to be with his men. Here, they'd fought and died while he had been lying in his bed miles away.

His chest hurt. He swallowed a couple more pain-pills with a swig of tepid water from his flask.

Greer had dismounted from the Chimera on the road and had yanked back its side cowlings to vent greasy black smoke. He reached in with a wrench, trying to soothe its ailing systems.

Milo thought he'd talk to Sanian, but the esholi had wandered down to the water's edge with Nessa. It looked like the Verghastite girl was teaching the student the rudiments of sign language.

'She likes to learn, doesn't she?'

Milo looked round and met Captain Daur's smile. 'Yes, sir.'

'I'm glad you found her, Brin. I don't think we'd last long without a decent guide.'

Milo sat himself down on a roadside stump and Daur sat next to him, cautiously nursing his wounded body down.

'What do you know, sir?' Milo asked.

'About what?'

'About this mission. Corbec said you knew as much as him. That you – uh – felt the same way.'

'I can't offer you an explanation, if that's what you're asking for. I just have this urge in my head...'

'I see.'

'No, you don't. And I know you don't. And I love you like a brother for daring to come this far in such ignorance.'

'I trust the colonel.'

'So do I. Have you not had dreams? Visions?'

'No, sir. All I have is my loyalty to Corbec. To you. To Gaunt. To the God-Emperor of mankind...'

'The Emperor protects,' Daur put in dutifully.

'That's all. Loyalty. To the Ghosts. That's all I know. For now, that's all I need.'

'But you delivered to us our guide,' a calm, frail voice said suddenly.

'I did what?'

Daur paused and blinked.

'What?' he asked Milo, who was looking at him mistrustfully.

'You said "but you delivered to us our guide"... just then. Your voice was strange.'

'Did I? Was it?'

'Yes, sir.'

'I meant Sanian...'

'I know you did, but that was a pretty odd way of saying it.'

'I don't remember... Gak, I don't remember saying that at all.'

Milo looked at Daur dubiously. 'With all respect, captain, you're weirding me out here.'

'Milo, I think I'm weirding myself out,' he said.

* * *

'Doc.'

'Corbec.'

They stood in the groves overlooking the burial place. It was the first chance they'd got to talk alone since leaving the Doctrinopolis.

'Your son, you say? Mikal?'

'My son.'

'In your dreams?'

'For days now. I think it started when I was looking for you in Old Town, you old bastard.'

'You haven't dreamt of Mikal before?'

Mikal Dorden had died on Verghast. He had been the only Ghost to escape the destruction of Tanith with a blood relative alive. Trooper Mikal Dorden. Chief Medic Tolin Dorden. Ghosts together, father and son, until... Vervunhive and Veyveyr Gate.

'Of course. Every night. But not like that. This was like Mikal wanted me to know something, to be somewhere. All he said was "sabbat martyr". When you said the words too, I realised.'

'It's going to be hard,' said Corbec softly, 'getting up there.' He pointed up towards the Sacred Hills, which lingered distantly, partly obscured by the smudge of a rainstorm over the woods.

'I'm ready, Colm,' Dorden smiled. 'I think the others are too. But keep your eye on Trooper Vamberfeld. His first taste of combat hasn't gone down well. Shock trauma. He may get past it naturally, but some don't. I don't think he should be here.'

'In truth, none of us should. I took what I could get. But point taken. I'll be watching him.'

'I RESPECT YOU.'

'I'm sure you do, buddy,' said Greer, nursing the old Chimera's engines back to health.

'But I do, I respect you,' repeated Trooper Vamberfeld.

'And why's that?' asked Greer off-hand as he unclamped a fuel pipe.

'To join this pilgrimage. It's so holy. So, so holy.'

'Oh, it's so holy sure enough,' growled Greer.

'Did the spirit of the saint speak to you?' Vamberfeld asked.

Greer looked round at him with a cynical eyebrow cocked. 'Did she speak to you?'

'Of course she did! She was triumphant and sublime!'

'That's great. Right now, I've got an engine to fix.'

'The saint will guide your work...'

'Will she crap! The moment Saint Sabbat manifests here and helps me flush out the intercooler, then I'll believe.'

Vamberfeld looked a little crestfallen. 'Then why do you come?'

'The gold, naturally,' Greer said, over-stressing each word as one would to a child.

'What gold?'

'The gold. In the mountains. Daur must've told you about it?'

'N-no...'

'Only reason I'm here! The gold ingots. My kind of come-on.'

'But there is no treasure. Nothing physical. Just faith and love.'

'Whatever you reckon.'

'The captain wouldn't lie.'

'Of course he wouldn't.'

'He loves us all.'

'Of course he does. Now if you'll excuse me...'

Vamberfeld nodded and walked away obediently. Greer shook his head to himself and returned to work. He didn't get these Tanith, too intense for his liking. And ever since he'd arrived on Hagia he'd heard men rambling on and on about faith and miracles. So, it was a shrineworld. So what? Greer didn't hold with that sort of stuff much. You lived, you died, end of story. Sometimes you got lucky and lived well. Sometimes you got unlucky and died badly. God and saints and fricking angels and stuff was the sort of nonsense men filled their with heads with when bad luck came calling.

He wiped his hands on a rag, and cinched the hose clamp tighter. This mob of losers was a crazy lot. The colonel and the doctor and that complete sad-case Vamberfeld were mooning on about visions and saints, clearly all out of their heads. The deaf girl he didn't get. The big guy was an idiot. The boy Milo was way too up himself, and only here because he had the hots for that local girl, who was incidentally a nutjob in Greer's humble opinion. Derin was the only one who seemed remotely okay. Greer was sure that was because Derin was along for the gold too. Daur must have persuaded the rest of the lunatics to sign on by buying into their saint fixations.

Daur was a hard case. He looked all clean-cut and stalwart, the very model of a young, well-bred officer. But under the surface ticked the heart of a conniving bastard. Greer knew his type. Greer hadn't liked Daur since the moment they'd met in the prayer yard. Dressing him down in front of his men like that. Greer had only ended up wounded because he'd been going balls-out in the fight to prove his mettle and win back his rep. But Daur had needed a driver, and he'd cut Greer in on the loot. Temple gold, stacks of ingots, taken secretly from the Doctrinopolis treasury to a place of hiding when the Infardi invaded. That's what Daur had told him. He'd got the inside track from a dying ayatani. Worth deserting for in Greer's book.

He wouldn't be surprised if Daur intended to waste the others once they were home and dry. Greer would be watching his back when the time came. He'd get in first if he had to. For now though, he knew he was safe. Daur needed him more than any of the others.

Vamberfeld was the one he worried about most. Daur had recruited everyone except Sanian and Milo from the hospital, from amongst the injured, and they all had bandaged wounds to prove it. Except Vamberfeld. He was a psych case, Greer knew. The timid behaviour, the thousand-metre stare. He'd seen that before in men who were on the way to snapping. War fever.

Greer didn't want to be around when the snap came.

He closed the engine cowling. 'She's running! Let's go if we're going!'

The company moved back to rejoin the Chimera. For the umpteenth time that day, Corbec wondered what he had got himself into. Sometimes it felt so decisively right, but the rest of the time the doubts plagued him. He'd broken orders, and persuaded eight other guardsmen to do the same. And now he was heading into enemy country. He wondered what would happen if they got into a situation. Milo was sound and able bodied, but the doc and Sanian were non-combatants. Nessa was strapped up with a healing las-wound in her belly, Bragg's shoulder was useless, Daur and Derin had chest wounds that slowed them down badly, Greer had a head-wound, and Vamberfeld was teetering on the edge of nervous collapse. Not to mention his own, aching wounds.

Hardly the most able and fit fire-team in the history of guard actions. Nor the best equipped. Each trooper had a lasrifle – in Nessa's case a long-las sniper model – and Bragg had his big autocannon. They had a box of tube-charges but were otherwise short on ammo. As far as he knew they had only half a dozen drums for the cannon. The Chimera had a storm bolter on its pintle, but given its performance so far, Corbec wasn't sure how much longer it would be before they were all walking.

He wondered what Gaunt would do in this situation. He was pretty sure he knew.

Have them all shot.

Through the trees, thick roadside glades of acestus and slim-trunked vipirium, they began to see the outlines of Bhavnager.

It was late afternoon, the sun was infernally bright and hot, and the heat haze was distorting every distance. The Recon Spear had made excellent time, and word on the vox was that the main convoy was only seventy minutes behind them.

Mkoll pulled them to a halt and headed out into the groves with Mkvenner to do a little scouting. They crouched in the slanting shadows of the wild fruit trees and panned their magnoculars around. The air was still and breathless, as dry and hot as baked sand. Insects ticked like chronometers in the gorse thickets.

Mkoll compared what he saw with the town plan on his map. Bhavnager was a large place, dominated by a large white-washed temple with a golden stupa to the east and a massive row of brick-built produce barns to the south-west. Prayer kites and flags dangled limply from the golden dome in the breeze-less air. The road they were following entered in the south-eastern corner, ran in south of the temple to what looked like a triangular market place which roughly denoted the town centre, and then appeared again north of large buildings on the far outskirts that Mkoll took to be machine shops. A streetplan of smaller roads radiated out from the market, lined with shops and dwellings.

'Looks quiet,' said Mkvenner.

'But alive this time. Figures there, in the market.'

'I see them.'

'And two up there, on the lower balcony of the temple.'

'Lookouts.'

'Yeah.'

The pair moved forward and down a little, parallel to the highway. Once the road came out of the fruit groves it was open and unprotected for over fifteen hundred metres right down to the edge of the town. Trees had been felled and brush cleared.

'They don't want anyone sneaking up on them, do they?'

Mkoll held up his hand, the signal for quiet. They both now detected movement in the trees twenty metres to their right, right on the road itself.

With Mkvenner a few paces behind him in cover, las raised, Mkoll slid forward silently through the dry undergrowth. He slipped his silver blade from its sheath.

The man was watching the road from a small culvert under the trees, His back was to Mkoll. The vehicles of the Recon Spear were out of sight beyond the road turn, but he must have heard their engines. Had he sent a signal already or was he waiting to see what came around the bend?

Mkoll took him out with a fast, sudden lunge. The man didn't have time to realise he was dead.

He was dressed in green silk, his filthy skin livid with tattoos.

Infardi.

Mkoll checked the corpse and found an old autorifle but no vox set. Tucked into a hand-dug hole in the side of the culvert was a round mirror. Simple but effective signalling, perhaps to another invisible spotter down the road. How many others? Had they already rolled in past some?

He looked back at the town in time to see sunlight glint and flash off something on the temple balcony. A minute or so later, it repeated.

An answer? A question? A routine check? Mkoll wondered whether to use the mirror or not. He'd tip them off if he got the signal wrong, but would a lack of response be as bad?

The flash from the temple came again.

'Chief?' Mkvenner hissed over the headset vox.

'Go.'

'I see flash-signals.'

'On the temple?'

'No. Far side of the road from you, about thirty metres, right where the tree-line ends.'

Mkvenner had a better angle. Mkoll moved back out of the culvert softly and edged down a little way, his stealth cloak pulled around him. He could see the man now, on the far side of the road under a swathe of camo-netting. The man was looking up the highway and seemed not to have made out Mkoll yet.

Mkoll sheathed his blade and took up his lasrifle. The sound suppressor was screwed in place. He seldom took it off in country.

He waited for the man to shift around and raise his mirror again and then put a single shot through his ear. The Infardi spotter tumbled back out of sight.

The scouts headed back to the Recon Spear. Sirus was waiting, with the commander of the other Conqueror.

'No idea of numbers but the place is held by the enemy,' explained Mkoll. 'We picked off a couple of lookouts on the road. They're watching the approach carefully and they've made the south edge of the town clear. I'd prefer to take the time to disperse my troops into the woods here to clear for other spotters and maybe make a crawl approach after dark, but I think the clock's against us. They'll notice their spotters are quiet before long, if they haven't already.'

'We'll have the whole bloody convoy bunching up behind us in less than an hour,' said Sirus.

'Maybe that's how to play it,' said the other commander, a short man called Farant or Faranter, Mkoll hadn't quite caught it. 'Wait until the main elements arrive and then just go in, full strength.'

It made sense to Mkoll. They could waste a lot of time here trying to be clever. Maybe this was an occasion where sheer brute force and might were the best course. Simple, direct, emphatic. No messing about.

'I'll get on the vox and run it past the boss,' he said, and walked over to his Salamander.

There was a faint, distant bang, muffled by the dead air of the hot afternoon. A second later, a whooping shriek came down out of the sky.

'Incoming!' Sirus yelled. All the men broke for cover.

With a roar, the shell hit the roadline twenty-five metres short of them and blew a screen of trees out onto the track. After a moment, two more exploded in the trees to their left, hurling earth and flames into the cloudless blue.

Soil drizzled down over them. Both Conquerors came around the Salamanders, the *Wrath of Pardua* leading the way. More shells now, detonating all around them. The enemy had either done an excellent job of range-finding or had just got very lucky.

'Hold! Sirus, hold back!' Mkoll yelled into the vox as his Salamander lurched forward. He had to duck as debris from a perilously close shell rattled across the hull.

This was shelling from more than one gun. Multiple points, field guns maybe, large calibre ordnance by the size of the shell strikes. Where the hell were they hiding a battery of artillery?

Farant's Conqueror suddenly came apart in a huge fireball. The explosion was so fierce the shockwave punched Mkoll off his feet. Splintered armour shards rained down. Caober cried out as one ripped his forehead.

The blazing remains of the Pardus tank filled the centre of the road, turret disintegrated, bodywork fused and twisted, tread segments disengaged and scattered. The *Wrath* was beyond it, moving down the roadway.

'Enemy armour! Enemy armour!' Sirus bawled over the vox-link.

Mkoll saw them. Two main battle tanks, painted bright lime green, main guns roaring as they tore their way out through the fruit tree stands and onto the road ahead.

That was why he'd seen no artillery positions. It wasn't artillery.

The Infardi had armoured vehicles. Lots of them.

TEN
THE BATTLE OF BHAVNAGER

'Do not shirk! Do not falter!
Give them death in the name of Sabbat!'

— Saint Sabbat, at the gates of Harkalon

HEEDLESS OF THE 105mm shells tearing into the highway and trees around him, Sirus confronted the Infardi armour head-on. The *Wrath of Pardua* sped forward with a clank of treads and fired its main gun. The hypervelocity round hit the nearest of the two enemy vehicles, exploding into the rear mantlet of its turret with such force the entire turret mount spun round through two hundred and ten degrees. The tank clearly retained motive power, because it continued to churn along the road, but its traverse system was crippled and the turret and weapon swung around slackly with the motion. The *Wrath* fired again, mere seconds before a shell from the second tank glanced lengthways along its starboard flank. The hit buckled and tore its track guards and then fragmented off into the trees.

The *Wrath's* second shot had missed. The disarmed Infardi machine was closing to less than forty metres now, and its hull-mounted lascannon began to spit bolts of blue light at Sirus's Conqueror. The other enemy tank was trying to pull around its wounded colleague for a clearer shot, knocking down a row of saplings and small acestus trees as it hauled half its bulk off the highway and through the verge underbrush. Heavy shelling from as yet unseen Infardi units continued to lacerate the position.

With furious las-fire from the injured tank now splashing off the *Wrath of Pardua's* front casing, Sirus ordered his layer to address the other tank coming around the first. Re-laying the gun took a vital second. In that time, the second tank fired again and hit the *Wrath* squarely. The impact was enough to lurch all sixty-two tonnes of armoured machine several metres sideways. But it didn't penetrate the twenty-centimetre-thick armour skin. Inside, the crew was dazed, and they'd lost most of the forward scopes. Sirus bellowed to retask, but the tank was now right on them and looming for the kill.

A devastating lance of laser fire raked past the *Wrath* and cut through the assaulting vehicle below the turret. Internally stored munitions went off and the tank exploded with such force that the main body and track assemblies cartwheeled over in a blistering fireball. The blast wake and shrapnel cleared a semicircle of woodland twenty metres in radius.

The Destroyer *Grey Venger* had struck.

From the open cab of his rapidly reversing Salamander, Mkoll saw the long, low Destroyer prowl past, palls of heat discharge spuming from the vent louvres around its massive fixed laser cannon. It nudged aside the burning wreck of Farant's dead Conqueror and came up alongside the *Wrath*.

But the crew of the *Wrath of Pardua* had recovered their wits and swiftly nailed the remaining aggressor hard at short range, blowing out its port track sections and shunting it away lame with the shell impact. It began to burn.

By then, the trio of scout Salamanders had reversed far enough to be able to turn.

'Break off and retreat!' Mkoll shouted into the vox. 'Fall back to waymark 00.58!'

LeGuin immediately acknowledged, but Mkoll got nothing from Sirus.

Fething idiot wants to stay in the fight, Mkoll thought. From his machine's tactical auspex, he counted at least ten good-size targets moving up towards their position from Bhavnager.

But Sirus suddenly appeared out of the *Wrath's* top hatch, looking back through the gusting smoke to Mkoll. The last hit had taken out his vox system and intercom. Mkoll made damn sure Sirus understood his hand signals.

The *Grey Venger* stood its ground and walloped two more incandescent blasts down the road at targets Mkoll couldn't see. Probably just discouragement tactics, he thought. Who wants to ride an MBT into woodland cover when you know an Imperial Destroyer is waiting for you?

The *Wrath of Pardua* reversed hard and swung around to follow the Salamanders, traversing its turret to the rear to cover their backs. Then, as it too began bravura discouragement shelling, the *Venger* came about and trundled after them all so fast its hull rocked and rose nose up on its well-sprung torsion bar traction.

Deafened and a little bloodied, the Recon Spear made off down the highway away from the bombardment, which continued for some fifteen minutes after they had withdrawn. There was no sign of pursuit.

Mkoll voxed the bad news to Gaunt.

KEEPING A WEATHER eye on the northern approaches for signs of the enemy, the Recon Spear waited to rendezvous with the main honour guard strength at waymark 00.58, a west-facing escarpment of grass pasture fifteen kilometres south of Bhavnager.

The sun was beginning to sink and the intense heat of the day was dissipating. A southerly was blowing cooler air down from the misty shapes of the Sacred Hills, which now could be seen rising above the wide green blanket of the rainwoods on the northern horizon.

Mkoll got out of his Salamander, passing Bonin who was field stitching the gash in Caober's face, and walked towards the *Wrath of Pardua*. He took the time to gaze at the Sacred Hills: dark uplands seventy kilometres away, then behind them, higher peaks fading to an insubstantial grey in the distance. Behind them still, about a hundred kilometres beyond, the majestic jagged summits of the Sacred Hills proper: transparent, icy titans with their heads lost in ribbons of cloud, nine thousand metres above sea level.

It was quite a prospect.

The fact that getting there involved struggling past at least one enemy tank unit dug into their only guaranteed fuel depot, then rainwood jungle, then increasingly high mountains, made it all the more chilling.

Thunder, the reveille call of a too hot day in summer, crackled around the neighbouring hills. The taste of rain was a promise on the rising breeze. Swells of grey cloud, as mottled as Imperial air-camo schemes, rolled in from the north, staining a sky that had otherwise been cloudless and blue since the fogs lifted that morning.

Small chelons and goat-like herbivores grazed and ruminated in the lush meadows beyond the raised pasture of the waymark point. Their throat bells clanged dully as they moved.

Sirus and his men were running emergency repairs to the great, wounded *Wrath of Pardua*. They were joking and laughing with their captain, revelling in the details of the recent combat and the fact they had come away alive. No one spoke of the dead crew. There would be due time for recognition later. Mkoll felt sure that once the obstacle of Bhavnager was done with, there would be more than one Conqueror to mourn.

A figure approached him across the wind-shivered grass. Mkoll knew at once it was the so far unseen LeGuin. He was a short, well-made man in his thirties, dressed in tan Pardus fatigues and a fleece-lined leather coat. He unbuttoned his leather skull-guard as he approached, unplugging the wire of his headset. His skin was darker than most of the Pardus men, his eyes glittering blue.

'Cool head, sergeant,' he said, offering Mkoll his hand.

'Looked mighty tight there for a minute,' Mkoll replied.

'It was, but so are the best fights.'

'I thought Sirus might blow it,' Mkoll ventured.

LeGuin smiled. 'Anselm Sirus is a bravo and a glory hound. He's also the best Conqueror boss in the Pardus. Except maybe for Woll. They have a rivalry. Both multi-aces. But permit Sirus his heroics. He's the very best.'

Mkoll nodded. 'I know similar infantrymen. I thought they'd got him there, though. But for you.'

'My greatest pleasure in life is using my girl's main mount to effect. I was just doing my job.'

The *Grey Venger* lay nearby, hull down in a grassy lea, its massive muzzle pointing north up the road. Mkoll reflected that if he'd ever been schooled into armour, a Destroyer would have been his machine of choice. As far as fifty-plus tonnes of rattling armoured power could be said to be stealthy, it was a silent predator. A hunter. Mkoll had a kinship with hunters. He'd been one all his adult life before the guard and, in truth, he'd been one ever since too.

Some of the grazers in the meadow below suddenly looked up and began to move away west.

A minute later, they heard the gathering thunder from the south.

'Here they come,' said LeGuin.

THE HONOUR GUARD assembled at the waymark, spreading its strength out in a firm defensive line facing the north. As the tanks took up station, the Hydra batteries behind them, the infantry dismounted and dug in.

'Now we'll see fun, sure as sure,' Trooper Cuu informed Larkin as they took position in the grasses.

'Not too much fun, I hope,' Larkin mumbled back, test-sighting up his long-las.

As the force secured the position, Gaunt called his operational and section chiefs for a briefing. They assembled around the back of his Salamander: Kleopas, Rawne, Kolea, Hark, Surgeon Curth, tank commanders, squad leaders, platoon sergeants. Some brought dataslates, some charts. Most clutched tin cups of fresh brewed caffeine or smokes.

'Opinions?' he asked, drawing the briefing to order.

'We've got no more than four hours of light left. Half of that will go getting into position,' Kleopas said. 'I take it we're looking at dawn instead.'

'That means we're looking at noon at least to refuel and turn around, provided we can break Bhavnager,' replied Rawne. 'That's half a day chopped off our timetable just like that.'

'So what?' Kleopas asked cynically. 'Are you saying we rush ahead and hit them up tonight, major?'

Some of the Pardus laughed.

'Yes,' Rawne answered coldly, as if it was so obvious Kleopas must be a fool to miss it. 'Why lose the daylight we have left? Is there another way?'

'Airstrike,' said Commissar Hark. To a man, the tank soldiers moaned.

'Oh, please! This is a prime opportunity to engage with armour,' said Sirus. 'Leave this to us.'

'I'll tell you what it is, captain,' said Gaunt darkly. 'This is a prime opportunity to discharge a mission for the God-Emperor as expediently and efficiently as we can. What it's not is an opportunity to let you heap up glory by forcing a tank fight.'

'I don't think that's what Sirus meant, sir,' said Kleopas as Sirus scowled.

'I think it's exactly what he meant,' said Hark lightly.

'Whatever he meant, I've been talking to navy strike command at Ansipar. The air wing is tied up with the evacuation. They wouldn't tell me more than that. We might get an airstrike if we wait two days. As Major Rawne pointed out, time is not for wasting. We're going to take Bhavnager ourselves, the hard way.'

Sirus smiled. There was murmuring.

Gaunt consulted the assessment reports on-slate. 'We know they have at least ten armour units. Non-Imperial MBTs.'

'At least ten,' repeated Sirus. 'I doubt they would have fielded their entire complement to chase off a raid.'

'Type and capability?' Gaunt asked, looking up.

'Urdeshi-made tanks, type AT70s,' said LeGuin. 'Indifferent performance and slow on the fire rate. 105-mil guns as standard. They're common here in this subsector and favoured by the arch-enemy.'

'They've been cranking them out of the manufactories on Urdesh ever since the foe took that world,' said LeTaw, another tank officer.

'The Reaver model by the look of the ones I saw,' LeGuin went on. 'Promethium guzzlers with cheap armour, and loose in the rear on a turn. Our Conquerors outclass them. Unless they have the numbers, of course.'

'From the hammering we got on the road, I'd say they had a minimum of five self-propelled guns too,' said Sirus.

'At the very least,' said LeGuin. 'But there's another thing. They continued to shell the roadway for quite a time after we pulled back. I bet that's because they didn't know we'd gone. They had an efficient string of spotters and lookouts, but my guess is their onboard scanners are very much lower spec than ours. No auspex. No landscape readers. Until they or their spotters actually see us, they're blind. We, on the other hand...'

'Noted,' said Gaunt. 'Okay, here's how we're going to play it. Head-on assault following the roadline. Tonight. If we think it's dicey leaving it so close to nightfall, you can bet they won't expect it. Armour comes out of the woods and spreads. Infantry behind, supporting with anti-tank weapons. I want two full strength troop assaults pushing ahead into the south of the town here. Kolea? Baffels? That's you. Around the warehouse barns.'

He pointed to his chart.

'Here's the winner. A side thrust. Maybe four or five tanks, in from the east, with infantry support and the Salamanders. Objective is the temple and then pushing through to the fuel stores. Hydra batteries will slug down from the roadline here.'

'What about civilians?' asked Hark.

'I haven't brought any, have you?'

The men laughed.

'Bhavnager is a clear and open target. I'll say it now so there's no mistake about it. We prosecute this town with maximum prejudice. Even if there are civilians, there are no civilians. Understood?'

The officers assented quickly. Gaunt ignored Curth's dark look.

'Kleopas, you have command of the main charge. I'll bring the Ghosts in behind you. Rawne? Sirus? You have the side thrust. Varl? I want you to play watchdog with a platoon on the road. Stay behind the Hydras and cover the transport and supply train. Bring them in only when we signal the town as secure. Go word is "Slaydo". Support advance is "Oktar". Retreat command is "Dercius". Vox channel is beta-kappa-alpha. Secondary is kappa-beta-beta. Any questions?'

THERE WERE NONE. With under two hours of daylight left, sunset burning off the mountains and rain on the wind, the honour guard fell upon Bhavnager.

LeGuin's *Grey Venger*, and the company's other Destroyer, the name *Death Jester* painted in crimson on its plating skirts, went in first along the highway, cleaning off the outer perimeter. Between them, they made eight kills, all Infardi MBTs covering the fruit groves on the road.

Mkoll led a scout platoon in with them. They rode on the Destroyers' hulls until they reached the treecover and then scattered into the spinneys. The Ghosts rolled forward in a wave alongside the hunting tank killers, locating and cutting the observation posts of the enemy signal line by stealth.

Venger and *Jester* bellied down at the edge of the trees overlooking Bhavnager as the main assault force swooped in past them, the *Heart of Destruction* leading the way. The ground shook, and mechanical thunder rolled through the still air. Troops dismounted in full strength from the trucks behind them, and then the transporters retreated to waymark 00.60, where Varl and his unit guarded the Chimeras, Trojans and tankers.

The word was given and the word was 'Slaydo'. Under Kleopas, twelve battle machines charged towards Bhavnager from the south, eleven Conquerors and the company's single Executioner, an ancient plasma tank nicknamed *Strife*.

By then, the enemy had seen the smoke and flash of the Destroyer kills in the woods and had launched out in force. Thirty-two AT70 Reavers, all painted gloss lime, plus seven model N20 halftracks mounting 70-mil anti-tank cannons. Major Kleopas considered ruefully that this was considerably more than Captain Sirus's estimate of 'at least' ten Reavers and five self-propelled guns. This was going to be a major engagement. A chance to snatch glory from the din of battle. A chance to find death. The sort of choice the Pardus were bred to make.

Despite the appalling odds, Kleopas grinned to himself.

The Imperial Hydras, dug-in and locked out, sprayed their drizzle of rapid fire over the town from the tree-line. Two thousand Ghosts fanned out over the open approach in the wake of Kleopas's charging armoured cavalry. Already, small arms fire was cracking at them from the town edge.

The tank fight began in earnest. Kleopas's squadron was formed in a trailing V with the *Heart of Destruction* at the tip. They had the slight advantage of incline in the cleared ground between the fruit groves and the town edge and were making better than thirty kph. The enemy mass, in no ordered formation, churned up the slope to meet them, kicking rock chips and dry soil out behind them as their tracks dug in. They played out in a long, uneven line.

In the command seat of the *Heart*, Kleopas checked the readings of his auspex, glowing pale yellow in the half-light of the locked down turret, against the eyeball view through his prismatic up-scope. He used his good right eye for this, not his augmetic implant, an affectation his crew often joked about. Kleopas then adjusted his padded leather headset and flicked down the wire stalk of the voice mic.

'Lay on and fire at will.'

The Conqueror phalanx began to fire. A dozen main weapons blasting and then blasting again. Bright balls of gas-flame flashed from their muzzles and discharge smoke streamed back from their muzzle brakes, fuming in long white trails of slipstream over their hulls. Three AT70s sustained direct hits and vanished in flurries of metal and fire. Two more were crippled and foundered, beginning to burn. A halftrack lurched lengthways as a round from the Conqueror *Man of Steel* punched through its crew bay and shredded it like a mess tin hit by a las-shot.

The elderly Pardus Executioner tank *Strife*, commanded by Lieutenant Pauk, was slower on its treads than the dashing Conquerors, and trailed at the end of the left-hand file. Its stubby, outsized plasma cannon razed a gleaming red spear of destruction down the slope and explosively sheared the turret off an AT70 in a splash of shrapnel and spraying oil.

The enemy mass began firing back uphill with resolved fury. The main weapons of the AT70s were longer and slimmer than the hefty muzzles of the Imperial Conquerors. Their blasts made higher, shrieking roars and sparked star-shaped gas-burns from the flash-retarders at the ends of their barrels. Shells rained down across the Imperial charge.

LeGuin had been right. Examples of old, sub-Imperial standard technology, the Reavers lacked any auspex guidance or laser rangefinding. It was also clear they had no gyro stabilisers. Once the Conqueror guns were aimed, they damn well stayed aim-locked thanks to inertial dampers, no matter how much bouncing and lurching the tank was experiencing. That meant the Conquerors could shoot and move simultaneously without any appreciable loss of target lock. The AT70s fired by eye and any movement or jarring required immediate aim revision.

In the *Heart of Destruction*, Kleopas smiled contentedly. The enemy was chucking hundreds of kilos of munitions up the slope at them, but most of it was going wide or overshooting. They were not designed for efficient mobile shooting. If their supremo had only had the good sense to stop his armour dead and fire on the Imperial charge from stationary locks, he would have been ahead on points by now.

Even so, more by luck than judgement, the enemy scored hits. The Conqueror known as *Mighty Smiter* was hit simultaneously by two rounds from different adversaries, exploded and slewed to an ugly halt, greasy black smoke pouring out of the hatches. *Drum Roll*, another Conqueror, under the command of Captain Hancot, was hit in the starboard tread section and lost its tracks in a shower of sparks and steel fragments. It lurched and came to a stop, but continued to fire.

Captain Endre Woll made his second kill of the day and his crew let out a cheer. Woll was a tank ace, adored by the Pardus regiment, and Sirus's chief rival. Under the stencil reading *Old Strontium* on the side of his steed was a line of sixty-one kill marks. Sirus and the *Wrath of Pardua* claimed sixty-nine. Electric servos swung *Old Strontium's* turret basket around and Woll executed a perfect kill on a veering AT70. The noise in the Conqueror turret was immense, despite the sound-lagging and the crew's ear-protectors. When it fired, the breech of the main gun hurtled back into the turret space with one hundred and ninety tonnes of recoil force. The novice loaders and gun layers at Pardus boot camp quickly trained themselves to be alert and nimble. As the breech slammed back, a battered metal slide funnelled the red-hot spent shell case into the cartridge hopper and the loader swung round with a fresh shell from the water-jacketted magazine, thumping it into place with the ball of his palm. The layer consulted the rangefinder and the crosswind sensor, and obeyed Woll's auspex-guided instructions. Woll always kept one eye on the target reticule displayed on his up-scope. Like all good soldiers, he only trusted tech data so far.

'Target at 11:34!' Woll instructed.

'11:34 aye!' the layer repeated, jerking the recoil brake. The gun roared.

Another Reaver was reduced to a rapidly expanding ball of fire and scrap.

The Pardus armour men were trained for mobile cut and thrust. The Conquerors' time-honoured torsion-bar suspension systems and high power to weight ratio meant they were more nimble than most of the adversaries they encountered, whether super-heavy monsters or lacklustre mediums like the ones the Infardi were fielding. That meant the Conquerors were perfect cavalry tanks, built to fight on the move, to charge, to out-manoeuvre and overwhelm the foe.

But there came a crucial moment in any armour-cav charge where the decision had to be made to halt, break or break through. Kleopas knew that moment was at hand. The dream intention of any armour charge was to utterly crush the target formation. But the Infardi outnumbered them three to one, and more tanks were massing at the edge of the town. Kleopas cursed... the Infardi had mustered in division strength at Bhavnager. The major had to keep revising Sirus's original estimate up and up. Forget about major engagement, this was becoming historic.

The Conquerors were about to meet the enemy head-on. Kleopas had three choices: stop dead and fight it out standing, break through the enemy line and turn to finish the job, or separate and pincer.

A stand-up fight was a worst case option. It would allow the Reavers to play to their strengths. Breakthrough was psychologically strong, but it meant reversing the playing field, and the Pardus would then be fighting back up hill, risking their own infantry coming in behind.

'Pincer three-four! Pincer now!' Kleopas instructed his squadron. The left-hand edge of the V formation carried on with Kleopas at the head, crashing past and between the Infardi machines. The right edge, under Woll, spread wide in a lateral line and slowed right down.

Gearboxes and differentials grinding, the tanks of Kleopas's wing rotated almost on a point, spraying up loose earth, and presented at the hindquarters of the enemy line. All Leman Russ pattern tanks, like the Conquerors, delivered deliciously low ground pressure through their track arrangement, and possessed fine regenerative steering. These almost balletic turns were a trademark move. Six more AT70s blew out as they were struck from the rear, and two more and a halftrack fell to Woll's straggler line.

The sloping field south of Bhavnager became a tank graveyard. Flames and debris covered the ground, and burning wrecks littered the incline. Huddles of Infardi crew, ejected from escape hatches, ran blindly for cover. Some of the Reavers, lurching on their old-style volute spring suspension, tried to come about to engage Kleopas's line, and were blown apart from both sides. The front formation of the Infardi armour was overrun and slaughtered.

But the day was nothing like won yet.

The *Man of Steel* shuddered and lost its front end in a spurting fireball. From the edge of the town, an N20 halftrack, sensibly bedded down and unmoving, had hit it squarely with its anti-tank cannon.

Kleopas blanched as he heard Captain Ridas screaming over the vox-net as fire swamped his turret basket. Moments later, the conqueror

Pride of Memfis was destroyed by a traversing AT70. Plasma spitting out with searing brilliance, Lieutenant Pauk's *Strife* evened the score.

As Kleopas's tanks hauled around on their regenerative steering again, Woll's line came through the kill-field, crunching and rolling over enemy wrecks. Eighteen more AT70s were spread around the town's southern limits and were bombarding steadily from standing. The shell deluge was apocalyptic. Woll counted nine Usurper-pattern self-propelled guns firing from positions behind the AT70 front. The boxy Usurpers carried howitzers, crude but efficient copies of Imperial Earthshakers, slanting forward out of their gun pulpits. Behind them came twelve more N20s, moving in a file down the marketplace road.

It was going to get worse before it got better.

'LINE UP, LINE up!' Gaunt cried, and his call was repeated down the infantry file from platoon leader to platoon leader. The Ghosts had formed in position at the edge of the tree-line, behind the four rattling Hydra batteries, and had been watching in awe and admiration for the last ten minutes as the tank fight boiled across the approach field below.

'Men of Tanith, warriors of Verghast, now we do the Emperor's duty! Advance! By file! Advance!'

Starting to jog, and then to run, the massed force of Ghosts came down the field, through the blasted landscape, bayonets fixed.

A few shells dropped amongst them. Glaring tracers spat overhead. The air was filthy with smoke. Kolea led the left-hand point of the advance, Sergeant Baffels the right, with Gaunt somewhere between them.

Gaunt allowed his designated assault leaders to move ahead, confident in their abilities, while he took time to pause and turn to yell encouragement and inspiration to the hundreds of troopers streaming down the slope. He brandished his power sword high so they could see it.

Right then, he missed Brin Milo. Milo should be here, he thought, piping the Ghosts into battle. He yelled again, his voice almost hoarse.

Commissar Hark was advancing with Baffels's mob. His shouts and urgings lacked the rousing fire of Gaunt's. He was new to them, he hadn't shared what Gaunt had shared with them. Still he urged them on.

'Destroyers signal their advance in our support,' Vox-officer Beltayn reported to Gaunt as they ran forward. Gaunt looked back to see the *Grey Venger* and the *Death Jester* rise up on their torsion springs and begin to prowl in at the heels of the infantry. It made a change to advance under armour, Gaunt thought. This was the Imperial Guard at its most efficient. This was inter-speciality co-operation. This was victorious assault.

ANA CURTH AND the medical party pushed down in the wake of the charging Ghosts. The ground they were covering was ruined by the furious tank fight and stank of fuel and fyceline. Shells had torn it up, so that the chalky bed rock was ploughed up over the black topsoil in white curds and lumps. It looked to Curth as if the very entrails of the earth had been blown out and exposed. This was a dead landscape, and they would undoubtedly extend and enlarge it before they were finished with Bhavnager.

Lesp darted to the left as a Ghost went down. Another two fell to an overshot tank round immediately ahead and Chayker and Foskin ran forward.

'Medic! Medic!' the scream rose from the massed confusion of manpower before her.

'I have it!' Mtane called to her, scrambling over the broken ground to a Ghost who was hunched over a squealing, disembowelled friend.

This is hell, Curth thought. It was her first taste of open war, of full-scale battle. She'd been through the urban horrors of Vervunhive, but had only ever read about the experience of pitched war in exposed territory. Battlefields. Now she understood what the term meant. It took a lot to shock Ana Curth, and death and injury wasn't enough.

What shocked her here was the raging, callous fury of the battle. The scale, the size, the gak-awful noise, the mass charge.

The mass wounding. The randomness of pain and hurt.

'Medic!'

She pulled open her field kit, running forward between the plumes of fire kicked up by falling shells and heavy las-fire.

Every time she thought she knew the horrors of war, it gleefully exposed new ones. She wondered how men like Gaunt could be even remotely sane after a life of this.

'Medic!'

'I'm here! Stay down, I'm here!'

FROM WAYMARK 07.07, the side thrust began their assault. They congregated a kilometre to the east of Bhavnager at an outlying farm. Even from this distance, the thunder of the main assault four kilometres away was shaking the ground.

Rawne spat in the dust and picked up the lasrifle he had lent against the farmyard's drybrick perimeter wall.

'Time to go,' he said.

Captain Sirus nodded and ran back towards his waiting tank, one of six Conquerors idling behind the abandoned farmstead.

Feygor, Rawne's adjutant, armed his lasgun and roused up the troops, close on three hundred Ghosts.

The wind was up, and the sun setting. Gold light radiated from the bulbous stupa of the temple a kilometre away.

Rawne adjusted his vox. 'Three to Sirus. You see what I see?'

'I see the eastern flank of Bhavnager. I see the temple.'

'Good. If you're ready... go!'

The six Conquerors roared out of their holding position and charged across the open fields and meadows towards the eastern edge of the town. Behind them came the convoy's eight remaining Salamanders. Rawne hopped up onto the running boards of one of the command Salamanders and rode it in, turning back to supervise the infantry group advancing behind him.

The five Conquerors chasing Sirus's *Wrath of Pardua* were named *Say Your Prayers, Fancy Klara, Steel Storm, Lucky Bastard* and *Lion of Pardua*, the latter the *Wrath's* sister tank. Rocking over terrain humps and irrigation gullies, the Pardus machines began firing, their shots hammering at the looming temple and its precincts. Puffs of white smoke plumed from the distant hits silently.

Almost immediately, four AT70 tanks appeared around the northern side of the temple. Two spurred forward into the edges of the wet, arable land, the others stopped dead and commenced shelling.

The *Fancy Klara*, commanded by Lieutenant LeTaw, crippled one of the moving tanks with a beautiful long range shot that would have made Woll himself proud. But then, as it bounced up over a tilled field, a tungsten-cored tank round hit the *Klara* squarely, penetrating the turret mantle and puncturing down through the basket. LeTaw lost his right arm and his gunlayer was instantly liquidised. The incandescent shell pierced the water jackets of the *Klara's* magazine and didn't explode.

The Conqueror swerved to a halt. LeTaw was numb with shock. He could barely pull aside his seat harness to look round. The interior of the turret was painted with a slick film of gore, the only remaining physical trace of his layer.

The loader had fallen from his metal stool, and was curled foetally on the floor of the basket, drenched in blood.

'Holy Emperor,' LeTaw murmured, looking down through the crisp-edged hole in the side of the magazine. Filthy water from the jackets dribbled out, diluting the blood on the floor. He could see sizzling fire inside the hole, the heat-shock residue of the impact.

'Get out!' he cried.

The loader looked blank, shocked out of his mind.

'Get out!' LeTaw repeated, reaching for the escape hatch pull with an arm that was no longer there.

Laughing at the macabre oddness of it, he swung around and reached up with his remaining hand. He heard the driver scrambling out through the forward hatch.

With a pop, heat-exchanger conduits in the side of the turret, weakened by the shell impact, burst. Scalding water spurted out, hitting LeTaw in the face before cascading down to broil his loader.

LeTaw tried to scream. The loader's shrieks echoed around the tank interior.

The shell had severed electrical cables in the footwell of the turret. The swirling water met the fizzling ends. LeTaw and his loader were electrocuted even as they writhed and screamed and blistered.

Targeting a stationary AT70, the *Steel Storm* exchanged shot after shot with it. Lieutenant Hellier, commanding the *Steel Storm*, realised his inertial dampers were damaged and that his auspex must consequently be out.

He shut the electronic systems down and began to aim through the reticule of the up-scope. He called out lay numbers to his aimer and was about to make a confident kill when the tank exploded, flipped over and broke apart.

The *Steel Storm* had hit the edge of the so-far undetected mine-field east of Bhavnager. The *Wrath of Pardua* crossed into the field immediately behind it, losing track pins and part of its side plating to an exploding mine.

Gunning its drive into full reverse, it was able to limp backwards a few metres while Sirus called an urgent dead stop.

The three remaining Conquerors slewed up behind him.

Bouncing up to their rear, the Salamander formations drew out in a line abreast, the infantry herding in around them. Shells from the three AT70s on the far side of the mine-field splashed all around them, chewing up the muddy irrigation system of the farmland which had already been scored with deep furrows by the hurtling armour.

'Sweepers! Sweepers forward!' Rawne ordered into his vox. Two specialist squads of three, one led by 'Shoggy' Domor, the other by a Verghastite trooper named Burone, immediately went ahead under fire.

'Infantry units! Support!' Rawne yelled.

The Ghosts began firing at the edge of the town with lasrifles, and with the heavier infantry support weapons they had brought up: four heavy stubbers and three missile launchers, plus the heavy bolters and the autocannons hull-mounted on the Salamanders.

The sweeper squads were miserably exposed, working their delicate magic as tank rounds and small arms fire whooshed around them. They had the expertise to clear a corridor through the field... if they lived long enough.

The second front advance was now dangerously delayed.

More AT70s appeared in support of the existing trio, as well as a quartet of heavy Usurper self-propelleds. Sirus wondered just how much bloody armour the enemy had to draw on at Bhavnager.

Deadlocked by the mines, the four Conquerors began free-firing at the enemy position with main guns and coaxial mounts. In the space of a few seconds, the *Lion of Pardua* comprehensively destroyed a self-propelled gun thoroughly enough to ignite its munition pile, and the *Lucky Bastard* knocked out an AT70. The detonation of the self-propelled gun was severe enough to spray shrapnel out over the minefield and trigger a few of the buried munitions off.

The *Say Your Prayers* and Sirus's *Wrath of Pardua* slung over some tank rounds that blew out the north retaining wall of the temple. The *Wrath's* driver and a Pardus tech-priest from the Salamanders took the opportunity to rig running repairs on the Conqueror's damaged track section.

IN A SHELL-DUG foxhole near to Rawne's Salamander, Criid, Caffran and Mkillian prepped one of the foot support missile launchers, known as 'tread-fethers' in the regimental slang. It was a shoulder tube of khaki-painted metal with a fore-scope, a trigger brace and fluted venturi at the back end to vent the recoil exhaust.

Heavy support weapons like this weren't commonly deployed by the stealth-specialist Ghosts; in fact Bragg was often the only trooper carrying one. But they were in the middle of a tank fight now. Caffran shouldered the tube and aimed via the crude wire crosshairs at the AT70 that had duelled with the late, lamented *Steel Storm*. Like many Ghosts, Caffran had become familiar with tread-fethers during the street-to-street war at Vervunhive, where he'd used one to knock out five Zoican siege tanks.

In fact he'd been fielding one in the burning habs when Criid had turned up to save his life from Zoican storm troops. They'd been together ever since.

Over the roar of the fighting, he heard her say 'For Verghast' as she kissed the armed rocket-grenade Mkillian handed to her. She slammed it into the launcher pipe.

'Loaded!' she yelled.

Caffran had his target. 'Ease!' he ordered.

Everyone nearby echoed the word, so that their mouths would be open when the tube fired. Anyone with closed mouths risked burst eardrums from the sudden firing pressure.

With a hollow, whistling cough, the tread-fether shot the rocket grenade at the enemy, leaving a slowly dissolving con-trail of smoke behind it. The hit was clean, but the rocket exploded impotently off the heavy front armour of the Reaver. As if goaded, the AT70 came around.

'Load me!'

'Loaded!' Criid yelled.

'Ease!'

Now that was better. The AT70 shuddered and began to burn. Its cannon muzzle drooped, as if the tank itself was feigning death.

'Load me! Just to be sure!'

'Loaded!'

'Ease!'

The burning AT70 now shivered and exploded in a blizzard of machine parts, armour plating, track segments and fire.

A cheer rippled down the infantry lines.

Then, above the ceaseless warring, the sound of another, louder cheer.

Rawne leapt out of his Salamander to investigate, running hunched as tracer fire crackled over his position.

Larkin had scored magnificently with his first shot of the engagement.

'I saw it for definite,' Trooper Cuu told Rawne excitedly, tapping his lasgun's scope. 'Larks got the officer, dead as dead.'

At a distance of over three hundred metres, Larkin had put a hot-shot las round through the sighting grille of the pulpit armour on one of the Usurpers and killed the artillery officer in charge. It was one hell of a shot.

'You go, Larks!' Trooper Neskon yelled. One of the unit's flamer troopers, Neskon was reduced to firing his laspistol, his flame-gun pretty much redundant in these mid- to long-range conditions.

'Could you do better closer?' Rawne asked Larkin.

'I'd feel better further away, major... like on another planet, maybe,' Larkin said sourly.

'I'm sure, but...'

'Yes, of course, sir!' Larkin said.

'Follow Domor's team out into the field. Feygor? Form up a five-man intruder team around Larkin. Get another sniper in there if you can. Move out down the swept corridor and give the sweeper boys cover. Use the reduced range to do some real damage. I want officers and commanders picked out and killed.'

'Don't we all, major,' replied Feygor as he leapt up to obey. The voice of Rawne's adjutant had always been deep and gravelly, but ever since the final fight for Veyveyr Gate, he'd spoken through a voicebox deformed and twisted with las-burn scar tissue. He was permanently monotone and deadpan.

Feygor scrambled around and selected Cuu, Banda and the Verghast sniper Twenish to accompany himself and Larkin.

Under the storm of fire, the quintet moved out into the killing field. Domor's party, working alongside Burone's, had cleared a ten metre wide channel that ran thirty metres into the field, its edges carefully denoted by staked tapes laid by Trooper Memmo. One of Burone's squad was already dead and Mkor in Domor's had taken shrapnel in his left thigh and shoulder.

Domor's team was slightly ahead of Burone's, and this competition was a matter of pride between Tanith and Verghastite minesweepers. Domor, of course, had the advantage of his heat-reading augmetic eyes to back up the sweeper brooms.

Feygor's intruder team joined them, Larkin and Twenish immediately digging in and sighting up as Cuu and Banda gave them cover fire. The vulnerable sweepers were glad of the additional support.

'Couldn't have brought a fat stub or a tread-fether with you, I suppose?' Domor asked.

'Just keep sweeping, Shoggy,' Feygor growled.

Twenish was a damn good shot, Larkin noted. He was one of the very few Verghastite newcomers to have specialised in sniper school before the Act of Consolation. A long-limbed, humourless fellow, Twenish was ex-Vervun Primary, a career soldier. His long-las was newer than Larkin's nalwood-furnished beauty; a supremely functional weapon with grotesquely enlarged night-scope array, a bipod stand and a ceramite stock individually tailored to fit its user.

The two snipers, products of entirely diverging regimental schools and training, began firing at the enemy armour. From three shots, Larkin dropped a Usurper gunlayer, an infantry leader, and the commander of an AT70 who had made the mistake of spotting from his turret hatch.

Twenish fired in quick double-shots. If the first didn't kill, it at least found range and drew his aim to his target for the second. From three of these paired shots, he made two excellent kills, including an Infardi priest rousing his men to combat. But to Larkin, it seemed like wasted effort. He knew about the double-shot method, and also was aware that many guard regiments taught the approach as standard. In his opinion, it gave the enemy too much warning, no matter how quickly you adjusted for the second squeeze.

As he lined up again, Larkin began to find the crack-pause-crack of Twenish's routine off-putting. Twenish was obsessive in his care, laying out a sheet of vizzy-cloth beside his firing position that he used to polish clean the scope lenses between each double-shot. Like a fething machine... crack-pause-crack.... polish-polish... crack-pause-crack. Enough with the precious rituals! Larkin felt like yelling, though he had more than enough of his own.

Larkin snuggled in again and with one shot killed the driver of a halftrack that was moving into the opposition line.

Banda, Cuu and Feygor knelt in the folds of soil, blazing suppressing fire freely at the enemy.

Banda was an excellent shot, and like many of her kind – female Verghastite conscripts, that was – she had wanted to specialise in marksmanship on joining the Ghosts. As it was, there was a strict limit on numbers for that specialisation and she'd been denied, although, to Banda's delight, her friend Nessa had made it. Most of the marksman places went to Vervun Primary snipers like Twenish who were carrying their specialisation over into the Ghosts with them. But Banda could shoot damn well, even with a standard, bulk-stamped las-rifle... a fact she'd proved to the gak-ass Major Rawne in the Universitariat clearance.

A swathe of autogun fire rippled across the position of the sweepers and the intruder team and every one threw themselves down. The remaining member of Burone's team was shredded, and Burone himself was hit in the hip. As they all got up again, Banda was first to realise that Twenish was dead; hammered into the soil in his prone position by the stitching fire that had raked over them.

Without hesitating, she leapt forward and prised the Verghastite long-las from Twenish's stiff grip.

'Do you know what you're doing?' Larkin called to her.

'Yes, gak you very much, Mr Tanith sniper.'

She took aim. The stock, molded for Twenish's longer reach, was awkward for her, but she persisted. This was a long-las, gak it!

No double-shots for her. An Infardi artillery officer running from one Usurper to the other crossed her sighting reticule and she blew his head off.

'Nice,' approved Larkin.

Banda smiled. And took an Infardi gunman off the balustrade of the temple at four hundred metres.

'Beat 'cha at yer own game, Larks,' Cuu simpered at Larkin. 'Sure as sure.'

'Feth off,' said Larkin. He knew how brilliantly – if psychotically – Cuu could shoot. If Cuu wanted a piece of it, let him get his belly dirty and use the damn long-las. At least Banda was eager. And damn good. He'd always suspected that about her. Since the day he'd first met her at street junction 281/kl in the suburbs of Vervunhive. The cheeky fething bitch.

As Domor's squad continued forward with their unenviably deadly task, and a fresh sweeper team ran forward to replace Burone's unit, the two Ghost snipers plied their precise and murderous trade across the enemy positions.

'THREE, ONE. WE'RE deadlocked!' Rawne told Gaunt via his Salamander's powerful voxcaster set.

'How long, three?'

'At this rate, an hour before we're even at the temple, one!'

'Continue as you are and await orders.'

SOUTH OF BHAVNAGER, the infantry forces were swarming into the town itself on the smoking heels of the Pardus main armour. Tanks were engaging the enemy at short range now, in the limiting spaces of the narrow market area streets. Woll's *Old Strontium* knocked out three N20 anti-tankers during this phase of close armour, and hit a Usurper before it could train its huge tank-killing weapon down to fire.

Kloepas's *Heart of Destruction* was caught in a firefight with two Reavers, and the Conquerors *Xenophobe* and *Tread Softly* smashed down low corral walls and single-storey brick-built houses as they moved to support it.

The Executioner tank *Strife*, flanked by the Conquerors *Beat the Retreat* and P48J, crushed a squadron of halftracks and broke into the compound of the south-western produce barns. Kolea's troop spearhead swiftly moved up to support them, enduring a series of fierce, close range fights through the echoing interiors of the barns. Mkoll's scout force pushed through towards the town centre marketplace after an ambiguous but deadly confrontation in the yards of the warehouses, where bales of dried vines were stacked. A platoon under Corporal Meryn fought their way in after them, meeting a counter-assault massed by fifty Infardi gunmen.

The flame-troopers, typified by Brostin and Dremmond and the Verghastite Lubba, excelled themselves during this part of the fight, sweeping clean the hard-locked barns of any Infardi resistance.

Accompanied by Vox-officer Beltayn, Gaunt advanced through the promethium smoke and the fyceline discharge. He took the handset from Beltayn as it was offered.

'One to seven!'

'Seven, one!' Sergeant Baffel's replied, his voice eerily distorted by electromagnetics.

'Three's counter-punch is deadlocked. We need to secure the fuel depot stat. I want you to push ahead and cut us a way through. How do you feel about that?'

'Do our best, one.'

'One, seven. Acknowledged.'

SERGEANT BAFFELS TURNED to his prong of the advance, as heavy shelling whipped over them.

'Orders just got interesting, people,' he said.

They groaned.

'What the gak are we expected to do now, Baffels?' asked Soric.

'Simple,' said Baffels. 'Live or die. The fuel depot. Let's look like we mean business.'

AT WAYMARK 00.60, standing amid the parked tankers, Chimeras, Trojans and troop trucks, they could hear the rumble of battle from away through the trees at Bhavnager.

Varl's defence section stood about aimlessly, talking with the waiting Munitorium drivers, smoking, cleaning kit.

Varl paced up and down. He so fething wanted to get down there and into it. This was a good duty and all, but still...

'Sir?' Varl looked round. Trooper Unkin was approaching.

'Trooper?'

'He says he wants to advance.'

'Who does?'

'Him, sir.' Unkin pointed at the ragged old ayatani, Zweil.

'I'll deal,' Varl told his point man.

He wandered down to the old priest. 'You have to stay here, father,' he said.

'I have to do no such thing,' Zweil replied. 'In fact, it's my duty to get down there, on the path of the Ayolta Amad Infardiri.'

'The what, father?'

'The Pilgrim's Way. There are pilgrims in need of my ministry.'

'There's no such–'

A distant, powerful explosion shook the air.

'I'm going, Sergeant Varl. Right now. To do less would be desecration.'

Varl groaned as the elderly priest strode away from him and began heading down the highway through the fruit groves towards Bhavnager. Gaunt would have Varl's stripes if anything happened to the ayatani.

'Take over,' Varl told Unkin and began running after the retreating figure of the priest.

'Father! Father Zweil! Wait up!'

CAUSTIC SMOKE WAS rolling down the length of the side street, obscuring Kolea's view. Somewhere down there, somewhere close to the point where the street met the main through road just off the market square, an enemy halftrack was sitting and chopping fire from its pintle-mount at anything that moved. Every now and then, it fired its anti-tank gun too.

The wretched smoke was pouring out of a threshing mill close by. Lasfire whimpered down the thoroughfare. The tightly packed buildings in the side street degraded vox-quality. It reminded Kolea rather too much of the fighting in the outhabs of Vervunhive.

Corporal Meryn's platoon, fresh from their firefight in the barns, moved up behind Kolea's bunch. Kolea signalled Meryn by hand to force a way through the buildings to the left and out onto the street running parallel to the one that currently stymied the advance. Meryn acknowledged.

Bonin, one of the scouts, had peeled to the right and found a walk-through breezeway that opened onto a small area of open wasteland behind the street buildings. Hearing this over the vox, Kolea immediately sent Venar, Wheln, Fenix and Jajjo through to link up with Bonin. Fenix carried a 'tread-fether' in addition to his lasrifle.

From cover, Kolea continued to scrutinize the billowing smoke for signs of the gakking N20. After a while, he began to fire off rounds into the section of smoke his instinct said concealed it. He was sure he could hear his shots impacting off hull metal. A heavy burst of stub fire raked back in response, chewing into the rubble and debris on the street. Almost immediately, it was followed by a whistling bang as the anti-tank weapon fired. The shell, travelling, it seemed to Kolea, at head height, impacted explosively in a burnt-out hut behind Kolea's position. As it sped through the smoke, the projectile left behind a bizarre corkscrew wake pattern.

'Come forward, come forward, you bastard...' Kolea urged the 'track, under his breath.

'Confirmed foot targets!' the vox hiss came in his ear. Marksman Rilke, dug into cover close by Kolea, had seen movement down by the burning mill. He'd challenged by vox, using the day's code word, in case it was some of their own out of position and crossing the line of battle. No identifiers came back. Rilke lined up his long-las and began firing.

Others in Kolea's formation joined in: Ezlan and Mkoyn over a broken wall near Rilke; Livara, Vivvo and Loglas from the windows of a livery; the loom-girls Seena and Arilla from a fox hole to Kolea's right. Las and auto fire began to ripple down the street at them. Platoon-strength opposition at least.

Seena and Arilla formed, respectively, the gunner and loader of a heavy stubber team. They'd learned the skills in the Vervun war, as part of one of the many 'scratch' companies of the resistance. Seena was a plump, twenty-five year old girl who wore a black slouch cap to keep her luxuriant bangs out of her eyes; Arilla was skinny, barely eighteen.

Somehow it looked wrong for the frailer, shorter girl to always be the one lugging the hollow plasteel yoke laden with ammo hoppers. But they were an excellent team. Their matt-black stubber was packed into the lip of the foxhole tightly to prevent the tripod skating out during sustained fire. Those old-pattern stubbers could buck like a riled auroch. Seena was squirting out tight bursts, interspersing them with longer salvoes that she sluiced from side to side on the gunstand's oiled gimbal.

Ezlan and Mkoyn tossed out a few tube-charges that detonated with satisfying thumps and collapsed the street facade of a farrier's shop.

Kolea got a few shots off himself, moving along the defence line. Another anti-tank round screamed low overhead. Kolea hoped the infantry clash would bring the halftrack up in support of its troops. He got Loglas and Vivvo to prep their missile tube.

'Nine, seventeen?'

'Seventeen,' Meryn answered over the link.

'What have you got?'

'Access to the next street. Looks quiet. Advancing.'

'Steady does it. Keep in vox-touch.'

A particularly heavy spray of las-fire stippled the wall behind him, and Kolea ducked flat. He heard the stubber barking out in response.

'Nine, thirty-two?'

'Reading you, nine.'

'Any luck with that halftrack yet, Bonin?'

'We're crossing the wasteground. Can't find a route back onto the street to come in behind them. We... Hold on.'

Kolea tensed as he heard fierce shooting distorted by the vox.

'Thirty-two? Thirty-two?'

'...vy fire! Heavy fire in this area! Feth! We've got m–' Bonin's response came back, chopped by the vox-bounce off the buildings.

'Nine, thirty-two. Say again! Nine, thirty-two!'

The channel just bled white noise. Kolea could hear staccato crossfire from behind the structures to his right. Bonin's fire-team needed help. More particularly, if they were overrun, Kolea needed to make sure the gap to his flank was plugged.

'Nine, I require fire support here! Map-mark 51.33!'

Within two minutes, a platoon had moved up from the warehouses along the route his team had already cleared. Kolea's old friend Sergeant Haller was at the head of it. Kolea quickly outlined the situation and the suspected position of the N20 to Haller and then grouped up a fire-team of Livara, Ezlan, Mkoyn and, from Haller's detail, Trooper Surch and the flamer-man Lubba.

'Take over here,' Kolea told Haller, and immediately led his ready-team right, down through the breezeway and onto the open ground beyond.

As if it had been waiting for the Verghastite hero to go, the halftrack suddenly clanked forward through the pungent brown smoke and fired its main mount at the Ghost line. Two of Haller's new arrivals were killed and Loglas was wounded by flying debris. Haller ran head-down through the rain of burning ash, and scooped up the missile tube as Vivvo got the dazed Loglas into cover.

'Loaded?' Haller yelled at Vivvo.

'Hell, yes sir!' Vivvo confirmed.

Haller sighted up. He put the crosshairs on the box-armoured view-slits of the N20's cab.

'Ease!'

The rocket tore open the halftrack's cab armour like a can-opener, and exploded out with enough force to spin the entire anti-tank mount around. Seena and Arilla hosed the stricken machine with stub-fire.

There was a ragged ripple of cheers from the Ghosts.

'Load me up again,' Haller told Vivvo. 'I want to make certain and kill it twice.'

BONIN'S ADVANCE TEAM had run into ferocious and extraordinary opposition centring on a shell-damaged building at the edge of the wasteground. More than twenty Infardi weapons had fired on them and then, incredibly, dozens of green-clad warriors had charged out, brandishing cleavers, pikes and rifle bayonets.

The five Ghosts reacted with extreme levels of improvisation. Fenix had been winged in the initial fire, but he was still fit to fight, and dropped to his knees, presenting a smaller target as he fired at the mob rushing them. Wheln and Venar had already fixed bayonets and countered directly, uttering blood-chilling yells as they drove forward, slashing and impaling.

Bonin sprayed his lasgun on full auto, draining out the powercell swiftly but harvesting the opposition. Jajjo was carrying the loaded tread-fether and decided not to waste the stopping power. Yelling 'Ease!' he shouldered the tube and fired the anti-tank round into the face of the building the Infardi had charged out of. The back-blast took out several of the skirmishers and collapsed a section of the wall. Then Jajjo tossed his tube aside and leapt into the close fighting, his silver blade in his hand.

His powercell depleted, Bonin joined in the hand to hand too, clubbing with his gunstock. The Imperials, trained by the likes of Feygor and Mkoll at this sort of fighting, outclassed the cultists, despite the latter's superior numbers and bigger, slashing blades. But the Infardi had frenzy in them, and that made them lethal opponents.

Bonin broke a jaw with a swing of his lasgun, and then smacked the muzzle of his weapon into the solar plexus of another attacker. What the feth had made them charge out like this, he wondered? It was bizarre, even by the unpredictable standards of the Chaos-polluted foe. They had cover and they clearly had guns. They could have taken Bonin's intruder unit in the open.

The brutal melee lasted for four minutes and only ended when the last of the Infardi were dead orunconscious. Bonin's team were all splashed with the enemy's gore and the wasteground was soaked. Corpses sprawled all around. The Ghosts had all sustainedcuts and contusions: Bonin had a particularly deep laceration across his left upper arm and Jajjo had a broken wrist.

'What the hell was that about?' Venar groaned, stooping over, out of breath.

Bonin could feel the adrenalin surging through his body, the rushing beat of his own heart. He knew his team must be feeling the same way too, and wanted to use it before they ebbed out of that intense combat edge. He slammed a fresh powercell into his weapon.

'Don't know but I want to know,' he told Venar. 'Let's get in there and secure the damn place fast. Jajjo, use your pistol. Wheln, carry the tread-fether.'

Fenix suddenly switched round at movement behind them, but it was Kolea's support section.

'Gak me!' said Kolea, looking at the bloody evidence of the fight. 'They charge you?'

'Like fething maniacs, sir,' Bonin said, pausing to put a lasround through the head of a stirring Infardi.

'From there?'

Bonin nodded.

'Protecting something?' Ezlan suggested.

'Let's find out,' said Kolea.

'Fenix, get yourself and Jajjo back to the rear and find medics. Bonin, Lubba, you've got point.'

The nine men advanced into the ruin through the hole Jajjo's rocket had made.

Lubba's flamer stuttered and then surged cones of fire into the dark spaces.

They found the Infardi troop leader sprawled unconscious amid the blast damage. His personal force shield had been overwhelmed by the rocket blast, and the portable generator pack lay shattered nearby.

He'd sent his men out in a suicidal charge to cover his own escape.

Kolea looked down at the unconscious man. Tall, wiry, with a shaved head and a pot belly, his unhealthy skin was covered with unholy symbols. Bonin was about to finish him with his silver blade but Kolea stopped him.

'Vox the chief. Ask him if he wants a prisoner.'

IN THE NEXT street over, Meryn's unit had caught up with Mkoll's scout section and they moved forward together. The sounds of close fighting rolled in from the neighbouring street, but Haller had informed Meryn that the N20 had been killed and advised him to press on.

Night was now falling fast, and the darkening sky was lit all around by firelight, the flashes of explosions and the glimmer of tracers. By Mkoll's guess, the fight was not yet even half done. The Tanith were still a long way from taking Bhavnager or securing their primary objective, the fuel depot.

Strangely, the street they advanced down, a narrow lane lined with empty dwellings and plundered trading posts, was untouched by the fighting, intact, almost peaceful.

Mkoll wished urgently for full darkness. This phase of the day when light turned into night was murder on the eyes. Night vision refused to settle in. The bright moons were up, shrouded by palls of rising smoke that turned them blood red.

Meryn suddenly made a movement and fired. Swiftly, all the Ghosts opened up, moving into secure cover. Odd bursts of gunfire came back at them, chipping the bricks and stucco walls of the commonplace buildings.

Then something made a whooping bang and a building to Meryn's left dissolved in a fireball that took two Ghosts with it.

'Armour! Armour!'

Squat and ominous like a brooding toad, the AT70 crumpled a fence as it rolled out onto the road, traversing its turret to fire down on them again. The blast destroyed another house.

'Missile tube to order!' Meryn yelled as brick chips drizzled down over him.

'Firing jam! Firing jam!'

'Feth!' Meryn growled. The one tool they had that might make a dent in the tank was down. They were caught cold.

Infardi troops streamed in behind the Reaver, blasting away. A serious small arms firefight developed, lighting up the dim street with its strobing brilliance.

The tank rolled on, crushing heedlessly over the dead or wounded forms of its own foot troops. Meryn shuddered. It would soon be doing the same to his boys.

From his position, he could hear Mkoll urgently talking over the vox. He waited until Mkoll broke off before patching in. 'Seventeen, four. Do we fall back?'

'Four, seventeen. See if we can hold out a few minutes more. We can't let these infantry numbers in at our flank.'

'Understood. What about the tank?'

'Let me worry about that.'

Easy for Mkoll to say, Meryn thought. The tank was barely seventy metres away now, its 105-mil barrel lowered to maximum declension. It fired again, putting a crater in the road, and its coaxial weapon began chattering. Meryn heard two Ghosts cry out as they were hit by the spray of bolter rounds. The Infardi troops were moving up all around. This was turning into a full-on counter thrust.

Meryn wondered what the feth Mkoll intended to do about the tank. He hoped it wasn't some insane, suicidal run with a satchel of tube-charges. Even Mkoll wouldn't be that crazy, would he? Then again, he hoped Mkoll had something up his guard-issue sleeve. The AT70 was going to be all over them in a moment.

His vox crackled. 'Infantry units, brace and cover for support.'

What the feth...?

A horizontal column of light, as thick as Meryn's own thigh, raked down the narrow street from the rear. It was so bright its afterimage seared Meryn's retinas for minutes afterwards. There was a stink of ozone.

The AT70 blew up.

Its turret and main gun, spinning like a child's discarded rattle, separated from the hull in the fireball and demolished the upper storey of a house. The hull itself split open like a roasting nalnut shell in a campfire and showered flames and metal fragments everywhere.

'Feth me!' Meryn stammered.

'Moving up, stand aside,' the vox said.

LeGuin's *Grey Venger* rolled up the street, a dark predatory shape, unlit.

'Drinks are on me,' Meryn heard Mkoll vox to the tank.

'Hold you to that. Form up and follow me in. Let's get this finished.'

The Ghosts moved out of cover and ran up behind the advancing tank destroyer, firing suppression bursts into the surrounding houses. The *Venger* crunched over the remains of the Reaver. The Infardi were in flight.

Meryn smiled. In a second, the flow of battle had completely reversed. Now they were the ones advancing with a tank.

HALF A KILOMETRE away, the *Heart of Destruction* and the P48J finally broke through into the market place. Their steady advance had been delayed for a while by a trio of N20s, and the *Heart's* hull carried the blackened scars of that clash.

Kleopas looked away from the prismatic up-scope for the first time in what seemed like hours.

'Load?' he asked.

'Down to the last twenty,' his gun layer said after checking the shells left in the water-jacketted magazine.

Small arms fire began to rattle off the mantlet. Kleopas scoped around and identified at least three fire-teams of Infardi troops on the northern side of the market place. The two Conquerors smashed forward through the empty wooden market stalls, shattering them and tearing off the canvas awnings. P48J dragged one like a pennant.

The *Heart's* gun-team loaded and layed at one of the enemy fire-teams.

'Don't waste a shell on soft targets, we're low on ammo,' Kleopas growled. He pulled open a fire-control lever and aimed up the coaxial bolter. The heavy cannon destroyed one Infardi position in a blizzard of dust. The P48J followed suit – she must be running low on shells too, Kleopas decided darkly – and between them, the armoured pair pulverised the outclassed foot troops.

Kleopas's auspex suddenly showed two fast-moving blips. A pair of Urdeshi-made light tanks, SteG 4s, each bouncing along on three pairs of massive tyres, sped into the square, headlamps blazing. Their tiny turrets mounted only stick-like 40-mil cannons, but if they had tungsten-cored ammo, or discarding sabots, they might still hurt the hefty Imperial machines.

'Lay up on that one,' said Kleopas, indicating his backlit target screen as he checked the up-scope. 'Now we use our muscle.'

SERGEANT BAFFELS FELT he was under intense pressure to perform. He was sweating profusely and he felt sick. The ferocious combat was bad enough, but he'd seen plenty of that before. It was the command responsibility that troubled him.

His eastern prong of the infantry assault had pushed up through Bhavnager far enough to cross the main highway. Now, with the temple on their right, they fought through the streets north of the market towards the fuel depot. Gaunt himself had charged Baffels with clearing the route to the depot. He would not fail, Baffels told himself.

The colonel-commissar had given him squad command on Verghast. He didn't want it much, but he appreciated the honour of it every waking moment. Now Gaunt had tasked him with the battle's crucial phase. It was an almost impossibly heavy burden to carry.

Almost a thousand Ghosts were pouring into the town behind him, platoon supporting platoon. The original plan had been that they, and a similar number under Kolea, would drive open, parallel wounds into

Bhavnager's defences and crack the place wide, while Rawne took the northern depot. Now with both Kolea and Rawne basically bogged down, it was down to him.

Baffels thought about Kolea a lot, usually with envy tingeing his mood. Kolea, the great war hero, took to command so effortlessly. The troops loved him. They would do anything for him. To be fair, Baffels had never seen a trooper disobey one of his own orders, but he felt unworthy. Until Vervunhive, he'd been a common dog-soldier too. Why the feth should they do as he told them?

He thought about Milo too. Milo, his friend, his squad buddy. Milo should have had this command, he often thought.

Baffels's brigade had struggled up through the streets east of the market, winning every metre hard. Baffels had Commissar Hark with him, but he wasn't sure Hark helped much. The men were afraid of him, and suspected him of all sorts of dreadful motives. It was good to have a healthy fear of commissars, Baffels knew that much. That's what commissars were there for. And the regiment's new commissar, give him his due, was doing his job and doing it well. As he had proved the day before during the ambush, Hark was almost unflappable and he had a confident and agile grasp of field tactics. Not only was he urging the rear portions of Baffel's group on, he was directing and focussing their efforts in a way that entirely complemented the sergeant's lead.

But Baffels could tell that the men despised Hark. Despised what he stood for. Baffels knew this because it was how he felt himself. Hark was Lugo's agent. He was here to orchestrate Gaunt's demise.

The leading edge of Baffels's assault had run into especially fierce fighting at an intersection between the abandoned halls of an esholi school and the market's livestock pens. Despite monumental efforts by Soric's platoon, they had lodged tight, coming under heavy fire from N20 halftracks and several curious, six-wheeled light tanks.

Hark, picking out a squad of Nehn, Mkendrick, Raess, Vulli, Muril, Tokar, Cown and Garond, had attempted to leap-frog Soric's unit and break the deadlock. They found themselves pinned down almost immediately.

Then, more by luck than plan, Pardus armour tore up through the eastern roadway to support them – the Executioner *Strife*, the Conquerors *Tread Softly* and *Old Strontium*, the Destroyer *Death Jester.* Between them, they made a terrific mess of the north-eastern streets and left burning tank and light tank carcasses in their wake. Baffels moved his forces in behind them as they made the last push to the depot, just a few streets away. It had been bloody and slow, but Baffels had done what Gaunt had asked of him.

The delay had given Gaunt himself the opportunity to move up with the front. Baffels was almost overjoyed to see him and Hark immediately deferred to the colonel-commissar.

Gaunt approached Baffels's position as enemy las-fire crisscrossed the night air.

'You've done a fine job,' Gaunt told the sergeant.

'It's taken fething ages I'm afraid, sir,' Baffels countered.

'It was going to. The Ershul aren't giving up without a fight.'

'Ershul, sir?'

'A word ayatani Zweil taught me this afternoon. Smell that?'

'I do, sir,' said Baffels, scenting the stink of promethium fuel on the wind.

'Let's go finish it,' Gaunt said.

Supported by the blistering firepower of the Pardus, the Ghosts moved forward towards the depot. Leading one line, Gaunt found himself suddenly face to face with Infardi who had laid low and dug in, now springing out in ambush to the file. His power sword sang and his bolter spat. Around him, Uril, Harjeon, Soric and Lillo, some of the best of the Verghastite new blood, proved themselves worthy Ghosts. It was the first of seventeen separate hand-to-hand engagements the prong would encounter on the way up.

At the fifth, a messy firefight to clear a cul de sac, chance brought Gaunt and Hark up side by side in the mayhem. Hark's plasma pistol seared into the shadows.

'I'll say this, Gaunt... you fight a good fight.'

'Whatever. The Emperor protects,' Gaunt murmured, decapitating a charging Infardi with the power sword of House Sondar.

'You still don't trust me, do you?' Hark said, destroying an enemy stubnest with a single, volatile beam.

'Are you really very surprised?' Gaunt replied tartly and, without waiting for a response, rallied his Ghosts for the next assault.

Sergeant Bray was the first platoon leader in Baffels's group to break his men through to the fuel depot proper. He found a row of massive sheds and chubby fuel tanks, guarded by over a hundred dug-in Infardi, supported by three AT70s and a pair of Usurpers.

Bray's rocket teams got busy. This was the heaviest resistance they'd yet encountered, and the attack had hardly been a picnic up until then. Bray called up for armour support.

Gaunt, Baffels, Soric and Hark clawed in, each driving a solid formation of Ghosts up to the rear of Bray's position. Gaunt could taste victory, and defeat too, intertwined. Experience told him that this was the moment, the make or break. If they endured and pushed on, they would win the town and destroy the foe. If not...

Shell, las and hard-round fire whipped into his formation. He saw the Pardus go forward, smashing through chain-link fences and across ditches as they breached the depot compound. *Strife* killed a Usurper, and *Death Jester* crippled a Reaver. The night sky was underlit by a storm of explosions and tracers.

'Regroup! Regroup!' Baffels was yelling as the shells scourged the air. Soric's section made gains, charging in through the southern fence, before being driven back by heavy fire from Infardi troops. Hark's section was backed into a corner.

Gaunt saw the Baneblade before anyone else.

His blood ran cold.

Three hundred tonnes of super-heavy tank, a captured, corrupted Imperial machine. It trundled casually out from behind the depot, its massive turret weapon rising.

A monster. A steel-shod monster from the mouth of hell.

'Baneblade! Enemy Baneblade at 61.78!' Gaunt yelled into his vox. Captain Woll, commanding the *Old Strontium*, couldn't believe his ears.

His auspex picked up the behemoth a second before it fired and obliterated the Conqueror *Tread Softly*.

Woll layed in and fired, but his tank round barely made a dent on the massive machine's hull.

The Baneblade's secondary and sponson turrets began to fire on the Imperial positions. The immediate death toll was hideous. Staunch, loyal Ghosts broke in terror and ran as the Baneblade rolled forward.

'Stand true! Stand true, you worthless dogs!' Hark yelled at the fleeing Tanith around him. 'This is the Emperor's work! Stand true or face his wrath at my hand!'

Hark was suddenly jerked backwards as Gaunt seized his wrist tightly and spoiled the threatened aim of his plasma pistol.

'*I* punish the Ghosts. Me. Not you. Besides, it's a fething Baneblade, you moron. I'd be running too. Now, help me.'

Soric's and Bray's sections hurled anti-tank missiles at the looming giant, to no great avail. *Death Jester* hit it with two blinding shots and still it rolled on. The Infardi armour and infantry advanced behind it.

Gaunt realised he had been right. This had been the moment. The make or break.

And they had broken.

Weapons thumping and spitting, the Infardi Baneblade drove the Tanith First into abject retreat.

Baffels would not let go. He was still determined to prove Gaunt right in selecting him for command. He was going to win this, he was going to take the target. He was–

As men fled around him, he grabbed a fallen tread-fether, loaded up a rocket and took aim on the monster tank. It was less than twenty metres away now, a giant, fire-spitting dragon that blotted out the stars.

Baffels locked the crosshairs on a slit window near what he assumed was the driver's position. He held the tube steady and fired.

There was a bright blast of flame and for one jubilant moment, Baffels thought he'd been successful. That he'd become a hero like fething Gol Kolea.

But the Baneblade was barely bruised. One of its secondary coaxial cannons killed Baffels with a brief spurt of shots.

RAWNE'S COUNTER PUNCH finally reached the Bhavnager temple at nine thirty-five. It was dark by then, and the town was alive with firestorms and shooting.

Their slow progression through the minefield had sped up when Larkin and Domor had hit upon an improvised plan. Domor's augmetic eyes could pick out many mines just under the soil surface. He talked Larkin onto them and Larkin and Banda then set them off with pinpoint shots.

The sweepers had advanced another thirty metres and by that time, with the sun gone, Sirus's tank mob had dealt with the opposition armour. Then the tanks rolled in down the channel Domor had cleared, and lowered their combat dozer blades to clear the last few metres now they were no longer under fire.

The temple was a mess. Golden fish-scale tiles trickled off the burst dome of the once glorious stupa. Incendiary shells burned in the main nave. Prayer flags smouldered and twitched in the breeze.

The counter punch drove in at last towards the fuel depot from the east.

Captain Sirus, his tracks now repaired, thundered forward in the *Wrath of Pardua*. He had heard the strangled, unbelievable transmission from the southern front that they'd met a Baneblade.

If it was true, he wanted a piece of that. Something Woll could never beat.

The *Wrath of Pardua* came at the enemy Baneblade in the open space of the depot field. Sensing the *Wrath* by auspex, the Baneblade had begun to turn.

Sirus loaded augur shells, armour busters, into his breech, and punched two penetrating holes in the massive enemy tank's mantlet. Few Pardus tank commanders carried augur shells as a matter of course, because few ever expected to meet something genuinely tougher than themselves. Sirus was a philosophically tactical man. He was happy to sacrifice a few valuable places in his magazine for augur shells, just in case.

Now the trick was to target the holes made by the augurs and blow the enemy out from the inside with a hi-ex tank round.

The wounded Baneblade traversed its turret, locked on to the *Wrath of Pardua*, and destroyed it with a single shot from its main weapon.

Sirus was laughing in victory as he was incinerated. An instant. An instant of success all tank masters dream of. He had wounded the beast. He could die now.

The *Wrath of Pardua* exploded, skipping armour chips out around itself in the blast wake.

Old Strontium purred out from behind the shattered buildings south of the depot. Woll had never carried augur rounds as standard, like Sirus. But he was damn well going to use the advantage. Ignoring his auspex and sighting only by eye, referring to his rangefinder and crosswind indicator, Woll punched a hi-ex shell through one of the profound holes Sirus had made in the Baneblade's armour.

There was a brief pause.

Then the super-heavy tank blew itself to pieces in a titanic eruption of heat and noise and light.

GAUNT AND SORIC, with the help of Hark and the squad leaders, managed to slow the Ghosts' panic and bring them around towards the fuel depot. Soric himself led the charge back down the yard towards the depot, past the flaming remains of the Baneblade.

By then, Rawne's counter punch had chased in after the valiant *Wrath of Pardua*, and was cleaning out the last Infardi in the depot. It was a running gun-battle, and Rawne knew he had time to make up.

He vox-signalled seizure of the depot just before eleven.

Surviving Infardi elements fled north into the rainwoods beyond Bhavnager. The town was now in Imperial hands.

AS THE MEDICS moved around him in the smoke-stained night, Gaunt found ayatani Zweil kneeling over the ruptured corpse of Sergeant Baffels. Sergeant Varl stood attentively nearby, watching.

'Sorry, chief. He insisted. He wanted to be here,' Varl told Gaunt.

Gaunt nodded. 'Thanks for looking after him, Varl.'

Gaunt walked over to Zweil.

'This man is a special loss,' Zweil said, turning to rise and face Gaunt. 'His efforts were crucial here.'

'Did someone tell you that or do you just feel that, father?'

'The latter... Am I wrong?'

'No, not at all. Baffels led the way to the depot. He did his duty, beyond his duty. I could not have asked for more.'

Zweil closed Baffels's clouded eyes.

'I felt as much. Well, it's over now,' he said. 'Sleep well, pilgrim. Your journey's done.'

ELEVEN
THE RAINWOODS

'Though my tears be as many as the spots of rain
Falling in the Hagian woods,
One for every fallen soul, loyal to the Throne
There would not be enough.'

— Gospel of Saint Sabbat, Psalms II vii.

UNDER COVER OF darkness, the sky lit up, over a hundred and fifty kilometres away. Flashes, sudden flares, spits of light, accompanied by the very distant judder of thunder.

Once it had been going on for an hour, they all agreed it wasn't a storm.

'Full-scale action,' Corbec murmured.

'That's one feth of a fight,' Bragg agreed.

They stood in the dark, at the edge of the holy river, insects chorusing around them, as Greer and Daur worked on the engine.

'What I wouldn't give...' Derin began, and then shut up.

'I know what you mean, son,' said Corbec.

'Bhavnager,' said Milo, joining them with a flashlight and an open chart-slate.

'Where, boy?'

'Bhavnager. Farming town, in the approach to the foothills.' Milo showed Corbec the area on the chart.

'It was meant to be our second night stop,' he said. 'There's a fuel depot there.'

An especially big flash underlit the clouds.

'Feth!' said Bragg.

'Bad news for some poor bastard,' said Derin.

'Let's hope it was one of theirs,' said Corbec.

DORDEN HAD WALKED away down to the river, and stood casting stones aimlessly into the inky water.

He started as someone came up beside him in the close dark. It was the esholi, Sanian.

'You are no fighter, I know that,' she said.

'What?'

'I worked with the lady Curth. I saw you. A medic.'

'That's me, girl,' Dorden smiled.

'You are old.'

'Oh, thanks a bunch!'

'No, you are old. On Hagia, that is a mark of respect.'

'It is?'

'It shows you have wisdom. That, if you haven't wasted your life, you have used it to collect up learning.'

'I'm pretty sure I haven't wasted my life, Sanian.'

'I feel like I have.'

He looked round at her. She was a shadow, a silhouette staring down into the river.

'What?'

'What am I? A learner? A student? All my life I have studied books and gospels... and now my world ends in ruin and war. The saint doesn't watch over us. I see men like Corbec, Daur, even a young man like Brin. They scold themselves because all they have learned is the art of war. But war is what matters. Here. On Hagia, now. But for the art of war-making, there is nothing.'

'There's more to life than–'

'There is not, doctor. The Imperium is great, its wonders are manifold, but what of it would remain but for war? Its people? Its learning? Its culture? Its language? Nothing. War encompasses all. In this time, there is only war.'

Dorden sighed. She was right. After a fashion.

'War has found Bhavnager,' she remarked, looking briefly at the flashes underlighting the distant clouds.

'You know the place?'

'I was born there and raised there. I left there to become esholi and find my way. Now, even if my way in life is revealed to me, there will be nothing for me to return home to, when this is done. Because it will never be done. War is eternal. It is only mankind that is finite.'

* * *

'NOTHING ON THE VOX,' Vamberfeld said.

Corbec nodded. 'You've tried all channels?'

'Yes sir. It's dead. I don't know if it's dead because we're out of range or because the Chimera's vox-caster is a pile of junk.'

'We'll never know,' said Derin.

Vamberfeld sat down on a tree stump at the edge of the road. Rain was in the air, and a true storm was gathering in defiance of the man-made one to the west. The wind stirred their hair and the first few spats of rain dropped around them.

Under the raised cowling of the Chimera, Daur and Greer worked at the engines.

Vamberfeld could hear Corbec talking to Milo just a few steps away from where he sat. It would be, he supposed, the easiest thing in the world just to stand up, get the colonel's attention, and talk to him, man to man.

The easiest thing...

He couldn't do it.

Even now, he could feel the terror crawling back into him, in through his pores, in through his veins, squirming and slithering down along his gut and up into the recesses of his mind. He began to shake.

It was so unfair. On Verghast, in the towering hive, he'd enjoyed a quiet life, working as Guilder Naslquey's personal clerk in the commercia, signing dockets, arranging manifests, chasing promissory notes. He'd been good at that. He'd lived in a decent little hab on Spine Low-231, with a promise of status promotion. He'd been very much in love with his fiancée, an apprentice seamstress with Bocider's.

Then the Zoican War had taken it all away. His job, his little hab, to an artillery shell; his fiancée to...

Well, he didn't know what. He'd never been able to find out what had happened to his dear, sweet little seamstress.

And that was all terrible. He'd lived through days and nights of fear, of hiding in ruins, of running scared, of starving. But he'd lived through them, and come out sane.

Because of that, he'd decided he was man enough to turn his back on the ruins of his life and join the Imperial Guard when the Act of Consolation made that possible. It had felt like the right thing to do.

He'd known fear during the war, and renewed the acquaintance again. The fear of leaving Verghast, never to return. The anxiety of warp travel in a stinking, confined troop ship. The trepidation of failing during the bone-wearying first week of Fundamental and Preparatory.

The true terror, the unexpected terror had come later. The first time, wriggling and chuckling at the back of his scalp, during the Hagia mass landings. He'd shaken it off. He'd been through hell on Verghast, he told himself. This was just the same kind of hell.

Then it had come again, in the first phase of the assault on the Doctrinopolis. In real fighting, for the first time, as a real soldier. Men died alongside him or, worse still as it seemed to Vamberfeld, were dismembered or hideously mutilated by war. Those first few days had left him shaking inside. The terror would not now leave him alone. It simply subsided a little between engagements.

Vamberfeld had decided that he needed to kill. To make a kill, as a soldier, to exorcise his terror. The chance had finally come when he'd been with Gaunt as they breached the Universitariat from across the Square of Sublime Tranquillity. To be baptised in war, to be badged in blood. He had been willing, and eager. He had wanted combat. He had wanted relief from the terror-daemon that was by then riding his back all the time.

But it had only made things worse.

He'd come out of that encounter shaking like an idiot, unable to focus or talk. He'd come out a total slave to that daemon.

It was so bloody unfair.

Bragg and Derin had recruited him from the hospital wards for this mission. He could hardly have refused them... he was able-bodied and that made him useful. No one seemed to see the cackling, oil-black terror clinging to him. Bragg and Derin had said Corbec had an important mission, and that was alright. Vamberfeld liked the colonel. It seemed vital. The colonel had talked about holy missions and visions. That was fine too. It had been easy for Vamberfeld to play along with that. Easy to pass off his nervousness and pretend the saint had spoken to him as well, and ear-marked him for the task.

It was all a sham. He was just saying what he thought they wanted to hear. The only thing that really spoke to him was the cackling daemon.

The words of the driver, Greer, had alarmed him. His talk of gold, of complicity with Captain Daur. Vamberfeld wondered if they were all mocking him. He was now pretty sure they were all bastard-mercenaries, breaking orders not because of some lofty, holy ideal but because of a base lust for wealth. And so he felt a fool for acting the part of the dutiful visionary.

His hands shook. He tucked them into his pockets in the hope that no one would see. His body shook. His mind shook. The terror consumed him. He cursed the daemon for fooling him into throwing in with a band of deserters and thieves. He cursed the daemon for making him shake. He cursed the daemon for being there at all.

He wanted to get up and tell Corbec about his terror, but he was shaking so much he couldn't.

And even if he could, he knew they'd most likely laugh in his face and shoot him in the bushes.

'Drink?'

'What?' Vamberfeld snapped around.

'Fancy a drink?' Bragg ask, offering him an open flask of the Tanith's powerful sacra.

'No.'

'You look like you could use some, Vambs,' Bragg said genially.

'No.'

'Okay,' said Bragg, taking a sip himself and smacking his lips in relish.

Vamberfeld realised the rain was falling hard now, bouncing off his face and shoulders.

'You should get in,' Bragg observed. 'It's coming down in buckets.'

'I will. In a minute. I'm okay.'

'Okay,' said the big Tanith, moving away.

Warm rainwater began to leak down Vamberfeld's neckline and over his wrists. He turned his face up to look into the downpour, wishing that it would wash the terror away.

'SOMETHING'S UP WITH the hive-boy, chief,' Bragg said to Corbec, passing him the flask.

Corbec took a deep swig of the biting liquor and used it to swallow a handful more painkillers. He was sucking in way too many of them, he knew. He hurt so, he needed them. Corbec followed Bragg's gesture and looked across the rain-pelted road at the figure seated with its back to them. 'I know, Bragg,' he said. 'Do me a favour. Keep an eye on him for me, would you?'

'SO... HOW MUCH?' whispered Greer, tightening a piston nut.

'How much what?' replied Daur. He was soaked by the rain now.

'Don't make me say it, Verghast... The gold!'

'Oh, that. Keep your voice down. We don't want the others hearing.'

'But it's a lot, right? You promised a lot.'

'You can't imagine the amount.'

Greer smiled, and wiped the rain off his face with a cuff that stained the streaks of water running down his brow with machine oil.

'You haven't told the rest, then?'

'Ah... Just enough to get them interested.'

'You gonna cut them out when the time comes?'

'Well, I'm considering it.'

'You can count on me, Verghast, time comes... If I can count on you, that is.'

'Oh, yeah. Of course. But look for my signal before you do anything.'

'Got it.'

'Greer, you will wait for my signal, won't you?'

Greer grinned. 'Absolutely, cap. This is your monkey-show. You call the play.'

* * *

'SLOW DOWN, GIRL, slow down!' Corbec smiled, sheltering from the rain under the open hatch of the Chimera. Her hand signs were too quick for him as usual.

Is the saint really calling to you? Nessa signed, more slowly this time.

'Feth, I don't know! Something is...' Corbec had still not truly mastered the sign codes used by the Verghastites, though he'd tried hard. He knew his clumsy gestures only conveyed the pigeon-essence of his words.

Captain Daur says he has heard her, she signed expressively. *He says you and the doctor have too.*

'Maybe, Nessa.'

Are we wrong?

'I'm sorry, what? Are we wrong?'

Yes. She looked up at him, her face running with rainwater, her eyes bright.

'Wrong in what way?'

To be here. To be doing this.

'No, we're not. Believe that much at least.'

ONLY HIS HAND shook now. His left hand. By force of will, Vamberfeld had focused all the terror and the shakes down into that one extremity. He could breathe again. He was controlling it.

Down the track, through the heavy rain, he saw something stir in the darkness. He knew he should reach for his weapon or cry out, but he didn't dare in case it let the shaking spill out through him again.

The movement resolved and became visible for a second. Two yearling chelon calves, no higher than a man's knee, waddling down the muddy track towards them.

And then a girl, aged twelve or thirteen, dressed in the dingy robes of the peasant caste, rounding the calves in with her crook.

She pulled them back before they came too close to the parked Imperial transport. Just a smudge in the rainy night. A peasant girl, bringing in her herd, trying not to risk contact with the soldiers driving through her pastures.

Vamberfeld stared at her in fascination. Her eyes came up and found his.

So young. So very grimy and spattered with mud. Her eyes piercing and...

The Chimera roared into life, engines turning and racing and spitting exhaust. Vapour streamed up into the rainfall in thick geysers of steam. The main lamps and headlights burst into life.

'Mount up! Mount up!' Corbec yelled, calling them all back to the repaired transport.

Vamberfeld woke up suddenly, finding himself lying on his side in the rain-pounded mud. He'd passed out and fallen from the tree stump. He got to his feet, weak and shivering, fumbled for his gun and ran back towards the brightly lit transport.

He cast a final look back into the dark trees. The girl and her chelons had vanished.

But the daemon was still there.

Pulling his shaking hand into his jacket to hide it, he climbed into the Chimera.

DAYBREAK, STREAMING RAIN in lament over the smoking battleground, came up on Bhavnager.

Waking early in his tent, Gaunt leapt up suddenly and then remembered the battle was done. He sat back on the tan canvas seat of his folding stool and sighed. A half-empty bottle of amasec sat on the map table nearby. He began to reach for it and then decided not to.

Beyond his tent, he heard the grumble of tank engines being overhauled by the tech-priests. He heard the clank of the fuel bowsers as they replenished the transports. He heard the whine of hoists as tank magazines were reloaded from the Chimeras. He heard the moan of the wounded in Curth's makeshift infirmary.

Vox-officer Beltayn stuck his head in through the tent flap cautiously. 'Oh five hundred, sir,' he said.

Gaunt nodded distractedly. He got up, pulling off his blood-, soot- and oil-streaked vest, replacing it with a fresh one from his kit. The braces of his uniform pants dangling loose around his hips, he washed his face with handfuls of water from the jug and then slipped the braces up, putting on a shirt and his black dolman jacket with its rows of gold buttons and frogging.

Bhavnager. What a victory. What a loss.

He was still shaking from the combat, from the ebbing adrenalin and the weariness.

He had slept for about three hours, and that fitfully. Mad dreams, confused dreams, dreams spawned by extreme fatigue and the memories of what he had been through.

He had seen himself on a narrow shelf of ice, with the world far below, clinging on, about to fall, hurricanes of fire falling around him.

Sergeant Baffels had appeared, alive and whole. He'd been on the lip of ice, and had reached over to grab Gaunt's hands. He'd pulled Gaunt up, onto solid ground.

'Baffels...' he'd managed to gasp out, frozen to the marrow.

Baffels had smiled, just before he'd vanished.

'Sabbat Martyr,' he'd said.

Gaunt grabbed the bottle and poured a deep measure into his dirty shot glass.

He swigged it down.

'Now the ghosts of Ghosts are haunting me,' he murmured to himself.

* * *

UNDER KOLEA'S INSTRUCTION, the honour guard buried their dead – almost two hundred of them – in a mass grave beside the temple at Bhavnager. The Trojans could have dug the pit, but the Pardus Conquerors *Old Strontium, Beat the Retreat,* P48J and *Heart of Destruction* did the honours with their dozer blades, even though their crews were half dead with fatigue. Ayatani Zweil was prevailed upon to make the service of the dead. The Ghosts dutifully staked small crosses cut from ghylum wood in rows across the turned earth, one for each of the dead who slept beneath.

THE DAY CAME up, warm, muggy and blighted with heavy rain. Gaunt knew it would take weeks for a unit to recover from the shock of an action as fundamentally brutal as Bhavnager, but he didn't have weeks.

He barely had days.

At nine in the morning, he called the honour guard to order for an hour's prep and sent the Recon Spear out in advance into the rainwoods above the town. Though tired, the men in his command seemed generally to be in good spirits. A solid victory, and against such odds, would do that, despite the losses. The Pardus were more sombre than the Ghosts: they seemed more to be mourning the beloved machines they'd lost rather than the men.

Gaunt crossed the town square and stopped by a small timber store where Troopers Cocoer, Waed and Garond were guarding the Infardi officer Bonin's squad had taken the night before. No other Infardi troops had been taken alive. Gaunt presumed that was because the Infardi took their wounded with them or killed them.

The vile, tattooed thing was chained up like a canid at the back of the shed. 'Anything from him?'

'No sir,' said Waed.

Rawne and Feygor had made a preliminary attempt at interrogation the previous night, after the fight, but the prisoner hadn't responded.

'Get him ready for shipping. We'll take him with us.'

Gaunt walked up towards the depot. Major Kleopas, Captain Woll and Lieutenant Pauk stood on the sooty apron of the machine sheds as the unit's Trojans towed in the *Drum Roll* and the *Fancy Klara*. Both tanks could be repaired, Gaunt had been told. The *Drum Roll's* damaged starboard track section was a buckled, dragging mess, and the crew, led by Captain Hancot, rode on the turret of their wounded steed. Though immobilised early in the fight, they had continued to fire and make kills effectively.

But for an oddly neat hole punched into the plating of its turret, the *Klara* seemed intact. Only her driver had survived. Shutting off the electrics, tech-priests and sappers had disarmed the unexploded enemy shell that had, both directly and indirectly, killed LeTaw and his gun crew. Once it had been extracted safely from the ruptured magazine, and the magazine picked over for damaged munitions, the *Klara* was towed into Bhavnager for turret repairs. A replacement crew was assembled from survivors of slain tanks.

Gaunt crossed to the watching tank officers and properly congratulated the Pardus commander for his part in the victory. Kleopas looked tired and pale, but he gladly shook Gaunt's hand.

'One for the casebooks in the Armour Academy on Pardua,' Gaunt said.

'I imagine so.'

'I have a... a question, I suppose, colonel-commissar,' said Kleopas.

'Voice it, sir,' said Gaunt.

'You and I... all of us were briefed that while Infardi forces were still at large in the hinterlands, their numbers wereminimal. The opposition they raised here at Bhavnager was huge in scale, well organised and well supplied. Not the sort of show you'd expect from a broken, running enemy.'

'I agree completely.'

'Damn it, Gaunt, we moved in on this target expecting a hard fight, but not an all-out battle. My machines faced numerical odds greater than they've ever known. Don't get me wrong, there was great glory here and I live to serve, the Emperor protects.'

'The Emperor protects,' echoed Gaunt, Woll and Pauk.

'But this isn't what they told us was out here. Can you... comment at least?'

Gaunt looked at his boots thoughtfully for a moment. 'When I was with Slaydo, just before the start of the crusade, we fell upon Khulen in winter time. I served with the Hyrkans then. Brave soldiers all. The enemy had vast numbers dug into the three main cities. It was snow-season and hellish cold. Two months it took, and we drove them out. Victory was ours. Slaydo told us to maintain vigil, and none of the command echelon knew why. Slaydo was a wily old goat, of course. He'd seen enough in his long career to have insight. His instincts proved correct. Within a month, three times as many enemy units fell upon our positions. Three times as many as we had driven out in the first place. They'd given up, you see? They'd abandoned the cities and fallen back before we'd had time to rob them of their full strength, regrouped in the wilderness, and come back in vast numbers.'

'What happened?' asked Pauk, fascinated.

'Slaydo happened, lieutenant,' smiled Gaunt and they all laughed.

'We took Khulen. A liberation effort turned into an all-out war. It lasted six months. We destroyed them. Now, consider this, a year later at the start of this crusade, liberating Ashek II. Formidable enemy strengths in the hives and the trade-towns of the archipelago. Three months' hard fighting and we were masters of the world, but the Imperial tacticians warned that the lava hills might provide excellent natural defences in which the enemy could regroup. We battened down, ready for the counter sweep. It never came. After a lot of recon we discovered that the enemy hadn't fallen back at all. They'd fought to the last man in the hives and we'd vanquished them entirely on the first phase. They hadn't even thought to use the landscape that so favoured them.'

'I'm beginning to feel like a child in tactica class,' smiled Woll.

'I'm sorry,' said Gaunt. 'I was simply illustrating a number of points.'

'That any enemy twisted by Chaos is always unpredictable?' suggested Kleopas.

'That, for one thing.'

'That because the enemy is so unpredictable, we might as well hang all the Imperial tacticians now?' chuckled Woll.

'Exactly, Woll, for two.'

'That this is what's occurring here?' asked Kleopas.

Gaunt nodded. 'You all know I have no love of Lugo. I have personal reason to object to the man.'

'Make no apologies for him,' Kleopas said. 'He's a new minted upstart with no experience.'

'Well, you said it, not me,' grinned Gaunt. 'The point is... whatever our lord general's failings... the spawn of Chaos is never predictable, never logical. You can't out-think them. To try would be madness. You can only prepare for any event. My clumsy examples were meant to illustrate that. If I failed at all at the Doctrinopolis, it was that I didn't cover every possibility.'

'I was with you, Gaunt. You were given orders that prevented you from using your experience.'

'Gracious. Thank you. That's what I feel we have here. A misguided expectation on the part of Lugo that the enemy will behave like an Imperial army. He thinks it will hold the cities until it is beaten. It will not. He thinks that only defeated remnants will flee after the battle. Not true again. I believe that the Infardi gave up the cities when they realised we had the upper hand, and purposefully backed up their main strengths into the outlying territories. Hence the weight of numbers at Bhavnager.'

'Lugo be damned,' said Woll.

'Lugo ought to listen to his officers, that's all,' said Gaunt. 'That's what made Slaydo Slaydo... or Solon Solon... the ability to listen. I fear that's lacking from the crusade's senior ranks now, even lacking in Macaroth.'

The Pardus officers shuffled uneasily.

'I'll blaspheme no more, gentlemen,' Gaunt said and drew smiles from them all. 'My advice is simply this. Prepare. Expect the unexpected. The arch-enemy is not a logical or predictable foe, but he has his own agenda. We can't imagine it, but we can suffer all too well when it takes effect.'

He stepped back as Rawne, Kolea, Varl, Hark and Surgeon Curth approached across the rockcrete apron to join them, and an impromptu operations meeting came to order. Curth handed a personnel review to the colonel-commissar.

They had two hundred and twenty-four wounded, of whom seventy-three were serious. Curth told Gaunt frankly that although they could move all the wounded with them, at least eighteen would not survive the transit more than a day. Nine would not survive the transit, period.

'Your recommendations, surgeon?'

'Simple, sir. None of them travel.'

Rawne shook his head with a dry laugh. 'What do we do? Leave them here?'

Kolea suggested they establish a stronghold at Bhavnager, where the injured might be tended in a field hospital. Though it meant leaving a reduced force at the town, vulnerable to the roaming Infardi, it might be the only hope of survival for the casualties. Besides, the honour guard would need Bhavnager's fuel resources for the return trip.

Gaunt conceded the merit of this idea. He would leave one hundred Ghosts and a supporting armoured force at Bhavnager to guard the fuel dump and the wounded while he pushed on into the Sacred Hills. Curth immediately insisted on staying, and Gaunt allowed that, selecting Lesp as the ongoing mission's chief medic. Captain Woll volunteered to command the armour guard of the Bhavnager fastness. Gaunt and Kleopas arranged to leave the *Death Jester*, *Xenophobe* and the mid-repairs *Drum Roll* and *Fancy Klara* under his command. Gaunt chose Kolea to command the position, with Sergeant Varl as his second.

Kolea accepted the task obediently, and went off to gather up the platoons under his immediate command. Varl was rather more against the choice, and as the meeting broke up, took Gaunt quietly to one side and begged to be allowed to join him on this final mission.

'It's not my final mission, sergeant,' Gaunt said.

'But sir–'

'Have you ever disobeyed an order, Varl?'

'No, sir.'

'Don't do it now. This is important. I trust you. Do this for me.'

'Yes sir.'

'For Tanith, like I know you remember her, Varl.'

'Yes, sir.'

'For Tanith.'

Then Gaunt roused up the main force and pushed on into the rain-woods, leaving the lowlands and Bhavnager behind in their dust.

Knots of Ghost and Pardus personnel watched the convoy depart. Varl stood watching for a long time after the last vehicle had vanished from sight and only dust clouds showed their progress.

'Sergeant?'

He swung around out of his reverie. Kolea and Woll had grouped squad leaders and tank chiefs around a chart table on the steps of the battered town hall.

'If you'd care to join us?' Kolea smiled. 'Let's figure out how best to get this place defended.'

FROM BHAVNAGER, THE wide road made a sharp incline for five or six kilometres as it ran north. Gaunt noticed that already the land to either side of the road was becoming less open. Field systems and cultivated areas began to disappear, except for a few well-watered paddocks and meadows, where lush stands of woodland began to flourish. Cycads and a larger variant of acestus predominated, often lush with sphagnum moss or skeins of a dark epiphyte known locally as priest's beard. Luminously coloured flowers dotted the thickets, some unusually large.

The air became increasingly humid. The woods to either side grew thicker and taller. Within the first hour after departure, sunlight began to flicker down on the travelling convoy, slanting through the ladder of the trees.

After three hours, the track levelled out and became damp sand and mud rather than dust. The air was heated and still, and clothing began to stick and cling with the airborne moisture. Every now and then, without warning or overture, heavy, warm rain began to fall, straight down, sometimes so hard visibility dropped to a few metres and headlamps went on. Then, just as abruptly, the rain would stop, as if it had never been there. Ground mist would well up almost immediately. Thunder rumbled in the heat-swollen air.

Past noon, they stopped, circulating rations and rotating driving teams. The rainwoods to either side of the trail were mysterious realms of green shadow, and a sweetly pungent vegetable smell permeated everything. Between the showers, the place was alive with wildlife: whirring beetles with wings like rubies, rivers of colonial mites, arachnids and grotesquely large shelled gastropods that left trails of glistening glue on the barks of the trees. There were many birds too: not the riverine forkbills, but shoals of tiny, coloured fliers that buzzed as they hovered and darted. Their tiny forms were small enough to be clenched in a man's fist, except their long, thin down-curved beaks which were almost thirty centimetres long.

Standing by his Salamander as he drank water and ate a ration bar, Gaunt saw eight-limbed lizards, their scaled flesh as golden as the stupa of Bhavnager's temple, flickering through the undergrowth. The whoops, whistles and cries of larger, unseen animals echoed intermittently from the woods.

'It surprises me you left Kolea at the town,' Hark said, appearing beside Gaunt. Hark had slipped off his heavy coat and jacket and stood, in shirt sleeves and a silver-frogged waistcoat, mopping sweat from his brow with a white kerchief. Gaunt hadn't heard him approach, and Hark's conversations tended to start like that, in the middle, without any hail or hello.

'Why is that, commissar?'

'He's one of the regiment's best officers. Ferociously loyal and obedient.'

'I know.' Gaunt took a swig of water. 'Who better to leave in charge of an independent operation?'

'I'd have kept him close by. Rawne is the one I'd leave behind.'

'Really?'

'He's a good enough soldier, but he fights from the head, not the heart. And there's no missing the fact he has issues with you.'

'Major Rawne and I have an understanding. He – and many other Ghosts – blame me for the death of their world. Time was, I think, Rawne would have killed me to avenge Tanith. But he's grown into command. Now, I think, he accepts that we just simply don't like each other and gets on with it.'

'I've studied his files and, over the last few days, I've studied the man. He's a cynic and a malcontent. I don't think his issues with you have subsided at all. His knife still itches for your back. The time will come. He's just become very good at waiting.'

'There was a saying Slaydo used to like: "Keep your friends close..."'

'"...and your enemies closer". I am familiar with that notion, Gaunt. Sometimes it does not work well at all.'

The cry went down the convoy to remount. 'Why don't you travel the next part in my carrier?' Gaunt asked Hark. He hoped none of the remark's irony would be lost.

FORTY MINUTES NORTH of the main convoy, the Recon Spearhead was slowing to a crawl. Rawne had chosen to accompany Mkoll's forward unit. For this, the third day, the spear comprised two scout Salamanders, a Hydra flak tractor, the Destroyer *Grey Venger* and the Conqueror *Say Your Prayers*.

The track was narrowing right down, so tight that the tree cover was beginning to meet overhead and the hulls of the big tanks brushed the foliage.

Mkoll kept checking the chart-slates to make sure they weren't off course.

'There was no other track or road,' said Rawne.

'I know, and the locator co-ordinates are right. I just didn't expect things to close down so tightly so fast. I keep feeling like we must have missed the main way and come off onto a herding trail.'

They both had to duck as a sheath of low-hanging rubbery green leaves brushed over the crewbay.

'Looks like fast-growing stuff,' said Rawne. 'You know what tropical flora can be like. This stuff may have come up in the last month's wet season.'

Mkoll looked over the side of the Salamander at the condition of the track itself. The rainwoods were packed into the spur gorges of the foothills, and that meant there was a slight gradient against them. The centre of the trackway was eroded into a channel down which a stream ran, and heavier flood-aways had brought down mud, rock and plant materials. The Salamanders were managing fine, and so was the Hydra, but the two big tanks were beginning to slip occasionally. Worse still, the track was beginning to disintegrate under their weight. Mkoll thought darkly about the weight of machines behind them, particularly the fifty-plus long-body troop trucks, which had nothing like the power or traction of the tracked vehicles.

Scintillating beetles sawed through the air between scout leader and major. Rawne kept one eye on the auspex. Both he and Mkoll knew considerable elements of Infardi had fled north into these woodlands after the battle, but no trace whatever had been found of them on the track. Somehow they'd got troops and fighting vehicles out of sight.

A cry came up from ahead and the spearhead stopped. Standing the scout troops and the armour to ready watch, Rawne and Mkoll went forward on foot. The lead Salamander had rounded a slow bend in the trail to find a massive cycad slumped across the track. The mass of rotting wood weighed many tonnes.

'Can you ram it aside?' Rawne asked the Salamander driver.

'Not enough purchase on this incline,' the driver replied. 'We'll need chains to pull it out.'

'Couldn't we cut it up or blast it?' asked Trooper Caober.

Mkoll had moved round to the uplifted rootball of the fallen trunk, which was sticky with peat-black soil and wormy loam. There were streaks of a dry, reddish oxide deposit on some of the root fingers. He sniffed it.

'Maybe we could get the Conqueror past. Lay in with its dozer blade,' Brostin was saying.

'Down! Down!' Mkoll yelled.

He'd barely uttered the words when las-fire stung out of the undergrowth alongside them. Rounds spanged off the vehicle hulls or tore overhanging leaves. The driver of the lead Salamander was hit in the neck and fell back into his machine's crewbay with a shriek.

Mkoll dived into cover behind the cycad trunk next to Rawne.

'How did you know?' Rawne asked.

'Fyceline traces on the tree roots. They used a charge to bring it over and block us.'

'Sitting fething target...' Rawne cursed.

The Ghosts were firing back now, but they could see nothing to aim at. Even Lillo, who happened to be in the crewbay of the lead Salamander and therefore had an auspex to refer to, could find no target. The auspex gave back nothing except a flat reading off the hot, dense mass of foliage.

'Cannons!' Rawne ordered, over his vox.

The coaxial and pintle mounts of the machines stuttered into life, raking the leaf canopy to shreds with heavy washes of fire. A moment later, Sergeant Horkan's Hydra drowned them all out as it commenced firing. The four, long barrelled autocannons of its anti-aircraft mount swivelled around and blasted simultaneous streams of illuminator rounds into the woodlands at head height, cropping trees, shredding bushes, pulverising ferns, liquidising foliage. A stinking mist of vaporised plant matter and aspirated sap filled the trackway, making the troops choke and retch.

After thirty seconds' auto-fire, the Hydra ceased. Apart from the drizzle of canopy moisture, the collapse of destroyed plants and the clicking of the Hydra's autoloader as it cycled, there was silence. The Hydra was designed to bring down combat aircraft at long range. Point-blank, against a soft target of vegetation, it had cut a clearing in the rainwood fifty metres deep and thirty across. A few denuded, broken trunks stood up amid the leaf-pulp.

Mkoll and Caober moved forward to check the area. The partially disintegrated remains of two Infardi lay amid the green destruction.

There was no sign of further attack.

Just a little ambush; just a little harrying, delaying tactic.

'Get chains round that tree!' Rawne ordered. At this rate, if the damn Infardi dropped a tree every few kilometres, it was going to take weeks to cross these rainwoods.

ABOUT A HUNDRED and twenty kilometres south of the rainwoods, a lone Chimera coughed its way down the dusty highway through an empty, abandoned village called Mukret. Since the dawn-stop that morning, it had borne the name 'the Wounded Wagon' on its flank, daubed in orange anti-rust lacquer by a hasty, imprecise hand.

The day was glaring hot, and Greer kept a close eye on the temp-gauges. The old heap's panting turbine was red-lining regularly, and twice now they'd had to stop, dump the boiling water-mix in the coolant system and replace it with water drawn from the river in jerry cans. Now they were out of coolant chemicals, and the mix in the flushed out system was so dilute it was essentially running on river water alone.

Greer pulled the vehicle to the roadside under the shade of a row of tree-ferns before the needles went past the point of no return.

'Fifteen minute break,' he called back into the cargo space. He needed to stretch his legs anyway, and maybe there would be time to show Daur a little more of the skills needed to drive the machine. An ability to swap drivers meant they would be able to keep going longer without rest stops.

Corbec's team dismounted into the sunlight and the dry air, seeking shelter at once under the ferns. The cabin fans and recirculators in the Chimera weren't working either, so it was like going on a long journey in an oven.

Corbec, Daur and Milo consulted the chart. 'We should get to Nusera Crossing by dark. That would be good. If they're in the rainwoods now, it means their rate of speed will have dropped, so we might just start catching them,' said Corbec. He turned aside, unpopped his water flask and knocked down a pill or two.

'The far side of the river bothers me,' Daur was saying. 'Seems likely that's where the mass of Infardi are concentrated. Things could get hotter for us too once we make the crossing.'

'Noted,' said Corbec. 'What are these here?'

Milo peered. The colonel was indicating a network of faint lines that followed the river north when it forked that way at Nusera. They radiated up into the Sacred Hills, echoing, though not precisely, the branches of the holy river's head waters. 'I don't know. It says "sooka" on the key. I'll ask Sanian.'

NEARBY, AT THE river's edge, Vamberfeld stood in the shallows skipping stones out over the flat water between the reed beds. A slight breeze stirred the feathery rushes on the far bank, which were starkly ash-white against the baked, blue sky.

He made one skip four times. Concentrating on simple actions like that helped him to control the shaking in his hand. The water was soothingly cool against his legs.

He skipped another. Just before it made its fifth bounce, a much larger stone flew out over his head and fell with a dull splash into the river. Vamberfeld looked round.

On the bank, Bragg grinned at him sheepishly.

'Never could do that.'

'So I see,' said Vamberfeld.

Bragg gingerly stepped out into the shallows, steering his clumsy bulk unsteadily over the loose stones of the bed.

'Maybe you could teach me?'

Vamberfeld thought for a moment. He took another couple of flat stones from his pants pocket and handed one to the big Tanith.

'Hold it like this.'

'Like this?' Bragg's meaty fingers dwarfed Vamberfeld's.

'No, like this. Flat to the water. Now, it's in the wrist. Make it spin as you release. Just so.'

Three neat splashes. Paff-paff-paff.

'Nice,' said Bragg, and tried. The stone hit the water and disappeared.

Vamberfeld fetched out two more stones. 'Try again, Bragg,' he said, and when the big man laughed he realised he had unwittingly made a joke.

Vamberfeld skipped a few more, and slowly, Bragg managed it too. One throw where Vamberfeld made four or five. The Verghastite suddenly, joyfully, realised that he was relaxed for the first time in recent memory. Just to be here, calm, in the sunlight, casually teaching a likeably gentle man to do something pointless like skip stones. It reminded him of his childhood, taking vacations up on the River Hass with his brothers. For a moment, the shaking almost stopped. Bragg's attention was fixed entirely on Vamberfeld's hands and demonstrations.

From the corner of his eye Vamberfeld saw the white rushes on the far side of the river sway in the breeze again. Except there was no breeze.

He didn't want to look.

'Hold it a little tighter, like that.'

'I think I'm getting it. Feth me! Two bounces!'

'You are getting it. Try another.'

Don't look. Don't look and it won't be there. Don't look. Don't look. Don't look.

'Yes! Three! Ha ha!'

Ignore the green shapes in amongst the rushes. Ignore them and they won't be there. And this moment won't end. And the terror won't come back. Ignore them. Don't look.

'Good shot! Five there! Can you do six?'

Don't look. Don't say anything. Ignore that urge to shout out: you know it will just start you shaking again. Bragg hasn't noticed. No one has to know. It'll go away. It'll go away because it isn't even there.

'Try again, Bragg.'

'Sure. Hey, Vambs... Why's your hand shaking?'

'What?'

It isn't. Don't look.

'Your hand's really starting to shake, pal. You okay? You look kinda sick. Vambs?'

'It's nothing. It's not shaking. Not. Try again. Try again.'

'Vambs?'

No. No. No no no no.

Shockingly loud, a lasrifle fired right behind them, the echo of the snap-roar rolling across the wide river. Bragg reeled round and saw Nessa crouched in a braced position on the bank, her long-las resting across a twist of roots. She fired again, out across the water.

'What the feth?' Bragg cried. His vox-link came alive.

'Who's shooting? Who's shooting?'

Bragg looked round. He saw the green shapes in the rushes over the river. There were silent flashes of light and suddenly las rounds were skipping like well-thrown stones in the water around him.

'Feth!' he cried again. Nessa fired a third, then a fourth shot. Derin appeared, scrambling down the bank behind her, lasgun in hand.

'Infardi! Infardi on the far shore!' Derin was yelling into his link.

Las-fire was punching up and churning the water right across the shallows. Bragg turned to Vamberfeld and saw to his horror the man was frozen, his eyes rolled back, his entire body spasming and vibrating. Blood and froth coated his chin. He'd bitten through his tongue.

'Vambs! Ah, feth it!'

Bragg grabbed the convulsing Verghastite and threw him over his shoulder. His wound screamed out in protest but he didn't care. He started struggling his way towards the shore. Derin was now firing on auto with his assault las in support of Nessa's hot-shots. Enemy rounds cut through the trunk and branches of the old trees above them with a peculiar, brittle sound.

Corbec, Daur and Milo appeared at the top of the bank, weapons raised. Dorden came bouncing and scrambling down the shady bank on his arse, and splashed out into the water, reaching for the lumbering Bragg.

'Pass him here! Pass him here, Bragg! Is he hit?'

'I don't think so, doc!'

A las-shot grazed Bragg's left buttock and he yowled. Another missed Dorden's head by a hand's breadth and a third hit the doctor's medikit and blew it open.

Dorden and Bragg manhandled Vamberfeld ashore and then dragged him up the bank into the cover of the roadwall. The five Ghosts behind them unleashed a steady salvo of fire at the far bank. Glancing back, Bragg saw at least one raft of green silk floating in the water.

Greer ran up from the Chimera, clutching Bragg's autocannon. Sanian followed him, a stricken look of fear on her face.

'What the hell's going on?' Greer asked, gazing in sick horror at the weirdly vibrating Vamberfeld. Vamberfeld's shaking hands were twisted into claw-shapes by the extreme muscular spasm. He'd wet himself too.

'Ah, feth. The nutter's lost it,' Greer said.

'Shut the feth up and help me!' Dorden snarled. 'Hold his head! Hold his head, Greer! Now! Make sure he doesn't smash it into anything!'

Bragg snatched the autocannon from Greer and ran back to the bank, locking in a drum-mag. The enemy fire was still heavy. Ten or twelve shooters, Bragg estimated. As he settled down to fire, he saw another Infardi tumble into the river, hit by Nessa. Clouds of downy white fibre were rising like wheat chaff from the rushes where the Imperial firepower was mashing it.

Bragg opened fire. His initial burst chopped into the river in a row of tall splashes. He adjusted his aim and began to reap through the rush stands, chopping them down, exposing and killing three or four green-clad figures.

'Cease fire! Cease fire!' Corbec yelled.

The gunfire from the opposite bank had stopped.

'Everyone okay?'

A muted chorus of answers.

'Back to the vehicle,' Corbec shouted. 'We have to get moving.'

THEY DROVE WEST out of Mukret for three kilometres and then pulled off the road, tucking the Chimera into the cover of a stand of acestus trees. Everyone was still breathing hard, faces shiny with sweat.

'Good pick up, girl,' Corbec said to Nessa. She nodded and smiled.

'Didn't you see them, Bragg?'

'I was talking to Vambs, chief. He started to go off weird on me and next thing they were shooting.'

'Doc?'

Dorden turned round from the supine Vamberfeld who was laid on a bed roll on the floor of the cargo bay.

'He's stopped fitting. He'll recover soon.'

'What was it, the trauma again?'

'I think so. An extreme physiological reaction. This poor man is very sick, sick in a way that's hard for us to understand.'

'He's a nut job,' said Greer.

Corbec turned his considerable bulk to face Greer. 'Any more talk like that and I'll break your face. He's one of us. He needs our help. We're going to give it to him. And we're not going to make him feel bad when he comes round either. Last thing he needs to feel is that we're somehow against him.'

'Spoken like a true medicae, Colm,' said Dorden.

'Right. Support. Can we all do that? Greer? Good.'

'What now?' asked Daur.

'We keep on for the crossing. Problem is, they likely know we're around now. We gotta play careful.'

IT TOOK THE rest of the afternoon to reach Nusera. They moved slowly and made frequent stops. Milo kept his ear to the old vox-caster, listening for the sound of enemy transmissions. There was nothing but white noise. He dearly wished they had an auspex.

They stopped about a kilometre short of the crossing, and Corbec, Milo and Nessa moved ahead on foot to scout. Sanian insisted on accompanying them. They crossed several irrigated fields, and a pasture gone to weed where the skeletal remains of two chelons lay, their vast shells calcifying in the sun. They passed through one wooded stretch where boxes of ornately carved wood were raised on stout, decorated posts. Corbec had seen many like them along the Tembarong Road.

'What are they?' he asked Sanian.

'Post tombs,' she replied. 'The last resting places of pilgrim-priests who die along the holy way. They are sacred things.'

The quartet edged through the glade, skirting the shadows of the silent post tombs. Sanian made a gesture of respect to each one.

Pilgrims who died along the way, Corbec thought. Miserably, he could identify with that all too well.

Passing through another dense stand of woods, Corbec thought he could smell the river. But his nose had been impaired by way too many years smoking cheap cheroots. Nessa had it spot on.

Promethium, she signed.

She was right. It was the stink of fuel. Another few hundred metres, and they began to hear the rumble of engines.

They crossed the mouth of an overgrown trail that joined the road from the north, and then bellied down in the final approach through the undergrowth to the crossing.

On the far side of the river, a column of lime green painted armour and transport elements was feeding onto the Tembarong Road from the arable land to the south. Corbec counted at least fifty vehicles, and those were only the ones in view. Infardi troopers milled about the slow moving procession, and over the growl of engines he could hear the chanting and the praise-singing. A refrain kept repeating, a refrain that featured the name Pater Sin over and over.

'Pater fething Sin,' Corbec murmured.

Milo watched the spectacle with a chill in his blood. After the Doctrinopolis, despite the catastrophe at the Citadel, the Infardi here were supposed to be broken, just fleeing remnants in the hinterlands. Here was a damn army, moving north with a purpose. And from the signs of battle the night before, Gaunt's force had encountered at least as many up in Bhavnager.

It seemed to Milo that the Infardi may have actually allowed the cities of Hagia to fall so that they might regroup ready for the approaching fleet-scale reinforcements. It was a wild idea, but one that smacked of truth. No one could ever predict the illogical tactics of Chaos. Faced with an imposing Imperial liberation force, had they simply given up the cities, left foul booby-traps like the Citadel behind them, and gone to ground ready for the next phase?

A phase they knew they would certainly win.

'No going through that way,' Corbec whispered, turning back to look at his companions. He sighed and looked down, apparently defeated.

'Feth... We might as well give up.'

'What if we follow the river north instead of the road?' Milo asked.

'There's no track, boy.'

'Yes, yes there is, chief. The... the whatcha call 'em. The sooka. Sanian, what are they?'

'We passed one just a while back. They are the herdsman trails, older even than the road of pilgrimage. The routes used by the drovers to take the chelon herds up into the high pastures, and bring them down again for market each year.'

'So they run up into the Sacred Hills?'

'Yes, but they are very old. Not made for machines.'

'We'll see,' said Corbec, his eyes bright again. He punched Milo on the arm playfully. 'Good head you got there, Brin. Smart thinking. We'll see.'

So IT WAS that the *Wounded Wagon* began to thread its way up north along the sooka after dark that night, running east of the holy river. The track was very narrow for the most part, and its course worn into a deep trough by millennia of plodding feet. The Chimera slithered and bounced, jarring violently. Once in a while, members of the team had to dismount and clear overgrowth by the light of the hull searchlight.

They were now over a hundred and fifty kilometres behind the honour guard advance, travelling slower, and diverging steadily away to the north.

Vamberfeld slept. He dreamed of the herd-girl, her calf chelons and her piercing eyes.

TWELVE
THE HOLY DEPTHS

'One aching vista, everlasting.'

— Saint Sabbat, Biographica Hagia

GHOSTS. ICE-CLAD GHOSTS. Giants looming, impossibly tall, out of the dry, distant haze.

It had taken two full days for the honour guard column to crawl and squirm its way up through the dense, dark, smelly rainwoods. There had been sixteen random, inconsequential ambushes along the way. Gaunt's forces had skirmished with unseen harriers who left only a few dead behind. The progress lost Gaunt eighteen more men, one scout Salamander and a Chimera. But now, at dawn on the sixth day out from the Doctrinopolis, the honour guard began the laborious climb out of the rainwoods' humid mist and into the feet of the Sacred Hills. Above and around them, the mountain range rose up like silent monsters. They were already passing three thousand metres above sea-level. Some of the surrounding mountains topped out at over ten thousand metres.

The air was cool and dry, and the highland path ran through flat raised valleys where the soil was desiccated and golden. Few plants grew, except a wind-twitching gorse, rock-crusting lichens and a ribbony kelp-like weed.

It was temperate, cool and clear. Visibility was up to fifty kilometres. The sky was blue, and the ridges of mountains stood clear of the lower rainwood fogs like jagged white teeth.

Six thousand years before, a child called Sabbat, daughter of a high pasture herdsman, had lived up in these inhospitable and awesomely beautiful highlands. The spirit of the Emperor had filled her, and caused her to abandon her herds and track her way down through the filthy swamps of the rainwoods on the start of a course that would lead her, in fire and steel and ceramite, to distant stars and fabulous victories.

One hundred and five years later, she had made the return journey, borne on a palanquin by eight Space Marines of the Adeptus Astartes White Scars chapter.

A saint, even from the moment of her martyrdom. An Imperial saint carried in full honour to her birthplace by the Emperor's finest warriors.

The local star group that now twinkled above her mountains in early evening was named after her. The planet was made sacred in her memory.

Saint Sabbat. The shepherd girl who came down from the mountains of Hagia to shepherd the Imperium into one of its most punishing and fast-moving crusades. One hundred inhabited systems along the edge of the Segmentum Pacificus. The Sabbat Worlds. A pan-planet civilisation.

Gaunt stood up in the crewbay of his lurching Salamander, gazing at the wide, high, clear scenery, the refreshing wind in his face. The sweat of two days in the rainwoods needed blowing away.

Gaunt remembered Slaydo reciting her history to him, back in the early days, as their crusade was being formed. It was shortly after Khulen. Everyone was talking excitedly about the new crusade. The High Lords of Terra were going to select Slaydo as Warmaster because of Khulen. The great honour would fall to him.

Gaunt remembered being called to the study office of the great lord militant commander. He had been just a commissar back then.

The study office, aboard the Citadel ship *Borealis*, was a circular wooden library of nine levels, lined with fifty-two million catalogued works. Gaunt was one of two thousand and forty officers attending the initial meeting.

Slaydo, a hunched but powerful man in his late one-forties, limped up to the lectern at the heart of the study office in his flame yellow plate armour.

'My sons,' he began, not needing a vox-boost in the perfect acoustics of the study office. 'It seems the High Lords of Terra approve of the work we've done together.'

A monumental cheer exploded out across the chamber.

Slaydo waited for it to die down.

'We have been given our crusade, my sons... the Sabbat Worlds!'

The answering shout deafened Gaunt. He remembered yelling until he was hoarse. No sound he'd ever experienced since, not the massed forces of Chaos, not the thunder of titans, matched the power of that cheer,

'My sons, my sons.' Slaydo held his augmetic hand up for peace. 'Let me tell you about the Sabbat Worlds. And first, let me tell you about the saint herself...'

Slaydo had spoken with passionate conviction about Saint Sabbat, the beati as he called her. It had seemed to Gaunt even then that Slaydo held her in a special regard. He was a dutiful man, who honoured all the Imperial worthies, but Sabbat was somehow dearest to him.

'The beati was a warrior,' Slaydo had explained to Gaunt months later, on the eve of the liberation of Formal Prime. 'She exemplifies the Imperial creed and the human spirit better than any figure in the annals. As a boy, she inspired me. I take this crusade as a personal matter, a duty greater than any I have yet undertaken for the Golden Throne. To repay her inspiration, to walk in her path and make free again the worlds she brought from darkness. I feel as if I am... a pilgrim, Ibram.'

The words had never left him.

THE WIDE, BARE plateau allowed them to make back time, but it lent them a sense of vulnerability too. In the lowlands, on the roads and tracks, the heavy column of armoured machines and carriers had seemed imposing and huge, dominating the environment. But out here, in the majestic uplands, they seemed lonely and small, exposed in the treeless plains, dwarfed by the location.

Already, Lesp had reported the first few cases of altitude sickness. There was no question of stopping or slowing to assist acclimatisation. Surgeon Curth, ever the pragmatic thinker, had included decent quantities of acetazolamide in the drugs carried on the medical supply truck. This mild diuretic stimulated oxygen intake, and Lesp began prescribing it for the men worst affected by the thinner air.

Landmarks on the plateau itself were few, and their appearance became almost hypnotically fascinating to the troops. They stared as shapes spied distantly slowly resolved as they came closer. Usually they were nothing more than large boulders, erratics left by long departed glaciers. Sometimes they were single post tombs. Many of the Ghosts watched for hours as these lonely objects slowly receded from view in the distance behind them.

By mid-afternoon on the fifth day of travel, the temperature again dropped sharply. The air was still clear blue and the sun was bright, so bright in fact that several Ghosts had burned without realising it. But there was a biting wind now, moaning over the flatness, and the great shapes of the mountains no longer glowed translucent white in the brilliance. They had become a shade or two darker and duller, greying and misting.

'Snow,' announced ayatani Zweil, travelling with Gaunt. He stood up in the back of the Salamander, swaying at the motion, and sniffed the air. 'Snow definitely.'

'The air looks clear,' said Gaunt.

'But the mountains don't. Their faces are dark. Snow will be with us before the day's done.'

It was certainly colder. Gaunt had put on his storm coat and and his gloves.

'How bad? Can you tell?'

'It may flurry for a few hours. It may white out and murder us all. The mountains are capricious, colonel-commissar.'

'She calls them the Holy Depths,' Gaunt said idly, meaning the saint.

'She certainly does. Several times in her gospel, in fact. She came from up here and went down into the world. It's typical of her to think about them from the point of looking down. In her mind, the Sacred Hills rise up over everything. Even space and other planets.'

'I always thought it was a metaphor too. The great elevation from which the Emperor looks down on us all, his lowly servants toiling in the depths.'

Zweil grinned and toyed with his beard. 'What a profoundly bleak and inhospitable cosmos you inhabit, colonel-commissar. No wonder you fight so much.'

'So – it's not a metaphor.'

'Oh, I'm sure it is! I'm sure that stark image is precisely its meaning. Remember, Saint Sabbat was an awful lot more like you than like me.'

'I take that as a compliment.'

Zweil gestured at the ring of peaks. 'Actually, being at the top of a great mountain means only one thing.'

'Which is?'

'It means there's a long way to fall.'

As the light began to fail, they made camp at the mouth of the next ascending pass. Mkoll estimated that the Shrinehold was still two days away. They raised tents and a strong perimeter. Heater units were put to work and chemical fires lit. No one had thought to bring kindling from the foothills and there was no wood to gather up here.

The snow began just before dark, billowing silently from the north. A few minutes before it began, a trooper on watch saw what he thought were contacts on the wide-band auspex. By the time he'd called up Gaunt and Kleopas, the snow had closed in and the sensor was blind.

But for the short time it lasted, it had looked like contacts. A mass of vehicles, moving north across the plateau behind them, twenty kilometres away.

'Back! Back now!' cried Milo, trying his best not to get caught in the sheets of liquid mud the Chimera's tracks were kicking up. Wheezing and puffing, the transport's turbines gunned again, and it slithered from side to side in the steep rut.

'Shut it down! Shut it down before it overheats!' shouted Dorden, exasperated. The engine whined and cut out. Quiet returned to the sooka trackway. Birds warbled in the gorse thickets and the gnarled vipiriums.

Greer jumped down from the back hatch and came around the side of the Wounded Wagon to survey the problem. A fast-moving stream, running directly alongside this stretch of sooka, had undercut the trail and the weight of the Chimera had collapsed it, leaving the machine raked over at a drunken angle.

They'd been on the sooka for over two days now, since Corbec's decision to avoid the Infardi at Nusera, and this was by no means the first time the transport had fallen foul of the track. But it was the first time they hadn't been able to right it again first time.

The chelon trails led up into the holy river headwaters and were for the most part steep. The narrow and sometimes winding trail had taken them up into wooded country where there was no other sign of human life. Using Sanian's knowledge, they had taken a route that avoided the worst of the lower spurs and gorges where the thick and unwholesome rainwoods flourished. Instead, they kept to more open ground where the shelving land was clad in breaks of trees, or small deciduous woods through which the trails rambled. The water was never far away: hectic rills and streams that sometimes shot out over lips in the crags and poured in little silver falls; or the mass of the main water itself, crashing down the sloping land and turning sudden drops into seething cataracts.

Each time they moved clear of tree cover, it was possible to look back and see the vast green and yellow plain of the river basin below them.

'Maybe we could find a tree trunk and lever it,' suggested Bragg.

Greer looked at the big Tanith, then at the Chimera, and then back at the Tanith. 'Not even you,' he said.

'Does that work?' Corbec asked, pointing to the power-assisted cable drum mounted under the Chimera's nose.

'Of course not,' said Greer.

'Let's try and pack stuff under the tread there,' Corbec said, 'then Greer can try it again.'

They gathered rocks and logs from the trail and pieces of slate from the stream bed and Derin and Daur wedged them in under the track assembly.

The team stood clear and Greer revved the engines again. The tracks bit. There was a loud crack as a log fractured, and then the machine lurched forward and onto the trail. There was a half-hearted cheer.

'Mount up!' Corbec called.

'Where's Vamberfeld?' Dorden asked. The Verghastite had said little since the episode at Mukret and had kept to himself.

'He was here a second ago,' said Daur.

'I'll go look for him,' Milo volunteered.

'No, Brinny,' said Bragg. 'Let me.'

As the rest made ready, Bragg pushed off the side of the trail and lumbered into the glades. Birds called and piped in the leafy canopy at the tops of the tall, bare trunks. The place was full of sunlight and striated shadows.

'Vambs? Where'd you go, Vambs?' Bragg had taken a propriatorial interest in Vamberfeld's welfare since the stone skipping. The colonel had asked him to keep an eye on Vamberfeld, but to Bragg it wasn't an order he was following any more. He was a generous-hearted man, and he hated seeing a fellow Ghost in such a bad way.

'Vambs? They're all waiting!'

THROUGH THE GLADE, the land opened out into a wide, banking pasture dotted with wildflowers and heaps of stone. In one corner, against the line of the trees, Bragg saw the ruin of an old lean-to, a herdsman's shelter. He made his way towards it, calling Vamberfeld's name.

THERE WERE MANY chelon in the pasture, Vamberfeld noted. Not enough to be worth the drive to market, but the basis of a good herd. The cows were nosing together piles of leaf mulch ready to receive the eggs they would lay before the next new moons.

The girl sat cross-legged outside her lean-to, and sprang up warily the moment she saw Vamberfeld approaching.

'Wait, wait please...' he called. The words sounded funny. His tongue was still swollen from the bite he'd put through it in his fit, and he was self-conscious about the way it made his voice sound.

She disappeared into her hut. Cautiously, he followed.

The hut was empty except for old leaf-litter and a few sticks. For a moment, he thought she might be hiding, but there was nowhere to hide, and no loose boards at the rear through which she might have slipped. A couple of old jiddi-sticks lay on the floor inside the door, and on a hook on the wall hung the head-curl of a broken crook. It was very old, and the jagged end where it had snapped was dirty and worn. He took it down and turned it over in his hands.

'Vambs? Vambs?'

It took him a minute to realise the voice outside was calling his name. He went back out into the sunlight.

'Hey, there you are,' said Bragg. 'What were you doing?'

'Just... just looking,' he said. 'There was a girl and she...' He stopped. He realised that the pasture was empty now. There were no lowing chelons, no leaf-nests. The field was growing wild with weeds.

'A girl?'

'No, nothing. Don't worry about it.'

'Come on, we're ready to go now.'

They walked back to the sooka and rejoined the Chimera. Vamberfeld felt strangely dislocated and confused. The girl, the livestock. He'd definitely seen them, but...

It was only when they were underway again that he realised he was still holding the broken crook. He suddenly felt painfully guilty, but by then it was too late to go back and return it.

DESPITE CURTH'S BEST efforts, another of the casualties had died. Kolea nodded when she came to tell him and made an entry in the mission log. Night was falling over Bhavnager, the fourth since the honour guard had gone ahead. No vox contact had been made with them since then, though Kolea was confident that they might be well up into the Sacred Hills by now.

He'd just come back from an inspection tour of the stronghold. They'd made a good job of securing the town. The two Hydras Gaunt had left him guarded the approach highway where the Ghosts themselves had come in. The armour waited in the market place, ready to deploy as needed, except the Destroyer *Death Jester*, which was lurking on watch in the ruins of the temple precinct. Both south and north edges of the town were well defended by lines of Ghosts in slit trenches and strongpoints. Available munitions had been divided up so there was no single, vulnerable armoury point, and the emptied Chimera carriers retasked as troop support. The Conquerors had used their dozer blades to push rubble and debris into roadblocks and protective levees, drastically reducing the possible points of entry into the town. Chances were, if an attack came, they would be outnumbered. But they had the fabric of the town itself working for them and had made the best use of their weapons.

'When did you last sleep?' Kolea asked the surgeon, offering her a chair in the little ground floor room of the town hall that he'd taken as his command post. A long-gain vox-caster set burbled meaninglessly to itself in the corner next to the sideboard where his charts were laid out. Grey evening light poked in through the sandbags piled at the glass-less window.

'I can't remember,' she sighed, sitting down and kicking off her boots. She massaged her foot through a threadbare sock and then realised what she was doing.

'I'm sorry,' she said. 'That was very undignified.'

He grinned. 'Don't mind me.'

She sat back and stretched out her legs, gazing down over her chest at her toes as she wiggled them. The socks were worn through at the toes and heels.

'Gak! Look at me! I was respectable once!'

Kolea poured two generous glasses of sacra from a bottle Varl had given him and handed one to Curth.

'That's where you have me beat. I was never respectable.'

'Oh, come on!' she smiled, taking the glass. 'Thanks. You were a star worker back home, respectable mine worker, family man...'

'Well...'

'Gak!' she said suddenly, through a sip of the liquor. Her heart-shaped face was suddenly serious. 'I'm sorry, Gol, I really am.'

'What for?'

'The family man thing... That was really very crass of me...'

'Please relax. It's alright. It's been a while. I just think it's interesting, the way war is such a leveller. But for war, you and I would never have met. Never have spoken. Never have even been to each other's sectors of the city. Certainly never sat down with a drink together and wiggled our dirty toes at each other.'

'Are you saying I was a snob?' she asked, still smiling at his last remark.

'I'm saying I was an out-habber, a miner, lowest of the workforce. You were a distinguished surgeon running an inner hab collective medical hall. Good education, decent social circles.'

'You make me sound like some pampered rich kid.'

'I don't mean to. I just mean, look at what we were and now look at where we are. War does some strange things.'

'Admittedly.' She paused and sipped again. 'But I wasn't a snob.'

He laughed. 'Did you know any out-habbers well enough to call them by their first name?'

She thought hard. 'I do now,' she said, 'which is the real point. The point I have a feeling you were making anyway.'

He raised his glass to her and she toasted him back.

'To Vervunhive,' he said.

'To Vervunhive and all her hivers,' she said. 'Gak, what is this stuff?'

'Sacra. The poison of choice for the men of Tanith.'

'Ah.'

They sat a moment more in silence, hearing the occasional shouted order or chatter outside.

'I should be getting back to the infirmary,' she began.

'You need rest, Ana. Mtane can manage for a few hours.'

'Is that an order, Sergeant Kolea?'

'It is. I'm getting quite the taste for them.'

'Do you... think about them still?' she asked suddenly.

'Who?'

'Your wife. Your children. I'm sorry, I don't mean to pry.'

'It's alright. Of course I do. More than ever, just these last few days in fact.'

'Why?'

He sighed and stood up. 'The strangest thing has happened. I haven't told anyone. I haven't been sure what to say, or do for that matter.'

'I'm intrigued,' she said, leaning forward and cupping her glass.

'My dear Livy, and my two children... they all died in Vervunhive. I mourned them. I fought to avenge them for a long time. Just that vengeance took me through the resistance fighting, I think. But it turns out... my children aren't dead.'

'They're not? How? How do you know?'

'Here's where it gets strangest of all. They're here.'

She looked around.

'No, not in the room. Not on the planet now, I hope. But they're with the Ghosts. They've been with the Ghosts ever since Vervunhive. I just didn't know it.'

'How?'

'Tona Criid. You know her?'

'I know Tona.'

'She has two children.'

'I know. They're with the regimental entourage. I gave them their jabs myself during the medical screening. Healthy pair, full of... of... oh, Gol.'

'They're not hers. Not by birth. Bless Criid's soul, she found them in the warzone and took them into her protection. Guarded them throughout the war and brought them with her when she joined up. They regard her as their mother, unquestioningly now. Young, you see. So very young. And Caffran, he's as good as a father to them.'

She was stunned. 'How do you know this?'

'I found out by chance. She has holos of them. Then I asked around, very circumspectly, and got the story. Tina Criid rescued my kids from certain death. They now travel with our regiment in the support convoy. The price I pay for that blessing is... they're lost to me.'

'You've got to talk to her, tell her!'

'And say what? They've been through so much, wouldn't this just ruin what chances for a stable life they have left?'

Shaking her head, she held out her glass for a top-up. 'You have to... They're yours.'

He poured the bottle. 'They're content, and they're safe. The fact that they're even alive is such a big deal for me. It's like a... a touchstone. An escape from pain. It messed me up when I first found out, but now it... it seems to have released me.'

She sat back thoughtfully.

'This goes no further, of course.'

'Oh, of course. Doctor-patient confidentiality. I've been doing that my whole career.'

'Please, don't even tell Dorden. He's a wonderful man, but he's the kind of medic who'd... do something.'

'My lips are sealed,' she began to say, but a vox signal interrupted. Kolea ran out into the square, leaving Curth to pull her boots back on.

Mkvenner, his unit's chief scout, hurried up to him.

'Outer perimeter south has spotted movement on their auspex. Major movement. An armoured column of over a hundred vehicles moving this way.'

'Gak! How far?'

'Twenty kilometres.'

'And... I have to ask... Not ours, by any chance.'

Mkvenner smiled one of his lightless, chilling smiles. 'Not a chance.'

'Make ready,' Kolea said, sending Mkvenner on his way. Kolea adjusted his vox-link microbead. "Nine to all unit chiefs. Respond.'

'Six, nine,' replied Varl.

'Eighteen, nine.' That was Haller.

'This is Woll, sergeant.'

'All stations to battle ready. Prime defences. Arm weapons. Deploy armour to a southern line, plan alpha four. The Infardi are coming. Repeat, the Infardi are coming.'

THIRTEEN
ERSHUL IN THE SNOW

'More snowflakes fall on the Holy Depths in a day than there are stars left for me to conquer.'

— Saint Sabbat, Biographica Hagia

THEY WERE HALFWAY up the pass when the enemy began firing on them from the rear of the column.

It was ten o'clock on the morning of the seventh day, and the honour guard had been slow getting started. Snow had blown in all night and lay at least forty centimetres deep, drifting to a metre in the open wind. Before dawn, with the Ghosts and Pardus shivering in their tents, the snow had stopped, the sky had cleared and the temperature had plummeted. Minus nine, the air caking the rocks and metal with first frost and then hard folds of ice.

The sun rose brightly, but took none of the edge off. It had taken over an hour to get some of the trucks and the old Chimeras started. The men were slow and hangdog, grumbling at every move. Reluctantly, they tossed their packs up into the troop transports and leapt up to take their places on ice-cold metal benches.

A heated oat and water mix had been distributed, and Feygor brewed up a churn of bitter caffeine for the officers. Gaunt tipped a measure of amasec into each cup as it was handed round, and no one, not even Hark, protested.

Thermal kit and mittens had been brought as standard. The Munitorium had not underestimated the chill or the altitude, but the biggest boon to all the Ghosts was their trademark camo-cape which now served each man as a cold weather poncho. Zipped up to their throats in their fleece-lined crew-jackets and tank-leathers, the Pardus looked at the Ghosts enviously.

They had broken camp at eight forty, and extended their column up through the snow-thick pass. Occasional flurries whipped across them. The landscape was featureless and white, and the snow reflected the sunlight so fiercely that glare-shades came out before the issue-order was even given.

No trace of the phantoms from the night before could be found on the auspex. The convoy moved ahead at less than ten kph, churning and sliding as it groped for a track that was no longer identifiable.

The first few shells kicked up glittering plumes of snow. Near the head of the column, Gaunt heard the distinctive crack-thump, and ordered his machine to come around.

There was still no visual contact with the chasing enemy, and nothing on the auspex, though Rawne and Kleopas agreed that extreme cold made the sensor systems slow to function. It was also possible that the snow cover was bouncing signals wildly, cheating and disguising the auspex returns.

Gaunt's Salamander, bucking and riding over the snowfield and kicking up a wake of ice crystals, approached the back end of the file in time to see a salvo of high explosive shells thump across the rank. One of the heavy Trojans was hit and exploded, showering the white field with shrapnel and flaming scraps.

'One, four!'

'Four, one, go ahead.'

'Mkoll, keep your speed and pull the column ahead as fast as you can.'

Mkoll was riding a Salamander at the head of the line.

'Four, one. Acknowledged.'

Gaunt exchanged voxes with the Pardus, and four tanks peeled back to support him: the *Heart of Destruction*, the *Lion of Pardua*, the *Say Your Prayers* and the Executioner *Strife*.

'Full stop!' Gaunt told his driver, the heat of his breath billowing in clouds through the freezing air. As the light tank slid to a halt, Gaunt turned to ayatani Zweil, who, with Commissar Hark and the Tanith scout Bonin, was riding with him.

'This is no place for you, father. Bonin, get him down and escort him to the rear trucks.'

'Don't fret, Colonel-Commissar Gaunt,' said the old man, smiling. 'I'd rather take my chances here.'

'I...'

'Honestly, I would.'

'Right. Fine.'

More shells whoomed into the snow cover. A munitions Chimera trundling slowly towards the rear of the van was hit a glancing blow but continued to struggle on.

'Auspex contact,' reported Hark from the lower level of the crewbay.

'Size? Numbers?'

'Nine marks, closing fast.'

'Roll!' Gaunt told the driver.

The command Salamander moved off, churning through the virgin snow. The three Conquerors and the old plasma tank were circling round from the convoy after them.

The enemy came into view through the mouth of the pass. Four fast-moving SteG 4s, the six-wheeled light tanks, fanning out ahead of three AT70s and a pair of Usurpers.

Their bright green paint jobs made them stand out starkly against the general white glare.

The SteGs, their big wheels wrapped in chains, were firing their light 40-mil weapons. Hypervelocity tank rounds whistled over the command Salamander.

Gaunt heard the deeper crump of the 105-mil Reavers and the even deeper, less frequent thunder of the big Usurpers.

Explosions dimpled the snow all around them.

'Tube!' Gaunt yelled to Bonin. Since Bhavnager, he'd kept a tread-fether in his machine. The scout brought it up loaded.

'Take us close,' Gaunt told the driver.

An AT70 made a hit on the *Say Your Prayers*, but the shot was stopped by the Conqueror's heavy armour.

The *Heart of Destruction* and the *Lion of Pardua* fired almost simultaneously. The *Heart* overshot but the *Lion* struck a SteG squarely and blew it over in the air.

With distance closing, Gaunt rose and aimed the tube at the nearest SteG. It was surging towards his bucking machine, turret weapon firing.

'Ease!'

Gaunt fired.

His rocket went wide.

'You're a worse fething shot than Bragg!' cursed Bonin.

Zweil started to laugh uproariously.

'Load me!' instructed Gaunt.

'Loaded!' Bonin yelled, slamming the armed rocket into the breach.

The sky, mountainside and ground suddenly exchanged places. Gaunt found himself tumbling over and over in the snow, winded.

A round from the SteG had hit the side of the Salamander, jerking it over hard. It had righted itself, but not before Gaunt had been thrown clear. The wounded Salamander chugged to a halt, a sitting duck.

The SteG galloped up, swivelling its little turret to target the listing Salamander.

Spitting out snow, Gaunt got to his feet dazed. He looked about. The rear end of the missile launcher was jutting out of the snow ten metres away from him. He ran over and pulled it out, feverishly tapping the packed snow out of the tube mouth and the venturi.

Then he shouldered it and took aim, hoping to hell the fall hadn't dented the tube or misaligned the rocket. If it had, the tread-fether would explode in his hands.

The speeding SteG closed on the Salamander for the kill. Gaunt could see Hark standing up in the crewbay, firing his plasma pistol desperately at the attacking vehicle.

Gaunt braced and put the crosshairs on the SteG.

It exploded, kicking up an enormous gust of snow and debris.

Gaunt hadn't fired.

The *Heart of Destruction* roared past him in a spray of snow, smoke fuming from its muzzle break.

'You okay, sir?' Kleopas voxed.

'I'm fine!' Gaunt snapped, running towards the Salamander. Hark pulled him aboard.

'Are we alive still?' Gaunt snarled at Hark.

'Your scout's down,' said Hark. Bonin lay in the footwell, concussed from the impact.

Zweil smiled through his beard and held up his wizened hands. 'Me, I'm just dandy!' he declared.

'Could you see to Bonin?' Gaunt asked, and the ayatani jumped down, nursing Bonin into a braced, safe position.

'Move on!' cried Gaunt.

'S-sir?' the driver looked back out of the cave of the cockpit, terrified. Hark swept round and pointed his plasma pistol at the Pardus crewman. 'In the name of the Emperor, drive!' he yelled.

The Salamander roared away across the snow. Gaunt looked out and took stock of the situation.

The *Heart of Destruction* and the *Lion of Pardua* had knocked out the last two SteGs, and *Strife* had blown up a Reaver. The *Say Your Prayers* had been hit twice by Usurper shells and had come to a standstill. It looked intact, but ominous black smoke was pouring out of its engine louvres.

As Gaunt's Salamander slewed around, *Strife* fired on the nearest Usurper and detonated its munitions. Shrapnel whickered down over several hundred metres.

Gaunt braced himself and fired at the nearest AT70. The rocket hit its track guard. The battle tank reared up in the drifts and swung its turret around at the speeding Salamander. A heavy round blew into the snow behind them.

'Load me!' Gaunt demanded.

'Loaded!' Hark answered, and Gaunt felt the jolt of the rocket slamming home.

He took aim at the Infardi battle tank and fired.

Trailing smoke, the missile sped over the snow and hit the tank at the base of its turret. Internal explosions blew the hatches out and then burst the barrel off the tank-head.

Zweil whooped.

'Load me!' said Gaunt.

'Loaded!' said Hark.

But the battle was all done. The *Lion of Pardua* and the *Heart of Destruction* targetted and killed the remaining Usurper pretty much simultaneously and the *Say Your Prayers*, suddenly coughing back into life, crippled and then killed the last of the Reaver AT70s. Mechanical wrecks, sobbing out plumes of black smoke, marred the sugar-white perfection of the pass.

Kleopas's Conqueror turned hard around in a swirl of snow and bounced back alongside Gaunt's Salamander.

Kleopas appeared in the top hatch, holding his field cap in his hands and tugging at it. He pulled something off and tossed it to Gaunt.

Gaunt caught it neatly. It was the cap-badge of the Pardus regiment, worked in silver.

'Wear the mark proudly, tank killer!' Kleopas laughed as his machine sped away.

Through his scope, Kolea saw the musters of the enemy as they came down through the fruit glade onto Bhavnager. So many machines, so many troops. Despite his defences and his careful preparation, they would be overwhelmed. There was a horde of them. A gakking horde, with armour to match.

'Nine to all units, wait for my command. Wait.'

The Infardi legion advanced and spread out. They were almost on top of them. Kolea held fast. They would at least make a good account of themselves.

'Steady, steady...'

Without breaking stride, the enemy passed by.

They bypassed Bhavnager and continued up into the rainwoods. In under a half-hour, they were gone.

'Why so sad?' asked Curth. 'They left us alone.'

'They're going after Gaunt,' Kolea said.

She knew he was right.

It was like fething Nusera Crossing all over again. The way ahead was blocked. Through his scope, Corbec could see a long line of green-painted armour and transport units crawling northwards up the wide, dry pass below him. A legion strength force.

He shuffled back from the lip of the cliff and rose. Dizziness swirled through him for a moment. This cold, thin air was going to take quite some getting used to.

Corbec crunched down the slope of scree and down onto the sooka where the Wounded Wagon was drawn up. His team, pinch-faced and huddled in coats and cloaks, waited expectantly.

'We can forget it,' Corbec said. 'There's a fething great mass of enemy machines and troops heading north up the pass.'

'So what now?' whined Greer.

They'd been making good time up the sooka trails through the high pastures of the foot hills. The old Chimera seemed to respond better in the cooler climate. About an hour earlier they'd passed the edge of the tree-line, and now vegetation of any kind was getting thin and rare. The landscape had become a chilly, rock-strewn desert of pink basalt and pale orange halite, rising in great jagged verticals and sheer gorges that forced the ancient herding path to loop back and forth upon itself. The wind groaned and buffeted. Beyond, the awesome peaks of the Sacred Hills were dark and smudged with what Sanian said were snowstorms at the higher altitude levels.

They huddled around the chart-slates, discussing options. Corbec could feel the welling frustration in his team, especially in Daur and Dorden who, it seemed to him, were the only ones who felt the true urgency of the mission in their hearts.

'These here,' said Daur, pointing to the glowing screen of the chart with numb fingers. 'What about these? They turn east about six kilometres above us.'

They studied the radiating pattern of sooka branches that stretched out like thread veins.

'Maybe,' said Milo.

Sanian shook her head. 'This chart is not current. Those sooka are old and have been blocked for years. The herdsmen favour the western pastures.'

'Could we clear a way through?'

'I don't think so. This section here is entirely fallen away into the gorge.'

'Feth it all!' Daur murmured.

'There is perhaps a way, but it is not for our machine.'

'You said that about the sookas.'

'I mean it this time. Here. The Ladder of Heaven.'

Five thousand metres higher up and sixty kilometres to the north-west, the honour guard column climbed the ragged high passes in the driving snow. It was past dark on the night of the seventh day, but still they pressed on at a desperate crawl, headlamps blazing into the dark. Blizzarding snow swirled through the beams of their lights.

According to the last reliable auspex reading, an enormous enemy force was half a day behind them.

The route they were following, known as Pilgrim's Pass, was becoming treacherous in the extreme. The track itself, climbing at an incline of one in six, was no more than twenty metres broad. To their left rose the sheer cliffs of the mountainside. To their right, invisible in the dark and the snow, it fell away in a scree-slope that tumbled almost vertically down to the floor of the gorge six hundred metres below.

It was hard enough to read the road in the day. Everyone was tense, expecting a wrong turn to send a vehicle tumbling off into the chasm. And there was also the chance of a rockslide, or a simple loss of grip in the snow. Every time the troop truck wheels slid, the Ghosts went rigid, expecting the worst... a long, inexorable slide to oblivion.

'We have to stop, colonel-commissar!' Kleopas urged over the link.

'Noted, but what happens if it continues like this all night? Come the dawn, we might be so buried in snow we can't move again.'

Another hour, perhaps two, Gaunt thought. They could risk that much. In terms of distance, the Shrinehold was close now. The duration of the journey was more determined by the conditions.

'Sabbat does love to test her pilgrims on the path,' chuckled Zweil, huddled up in a bed roll in the back of the Salamander's compartment.

'I'm sure,' said Gaunt. 'Feth take her Holy Depths.'

That made the old priest laugh so heartily he started coughing.

If anything, the snow seemed to be getting heavier.

Suddenly, there came a series of unintelligible bursts on the vox. Rear-lamps ahead of them in the pelting flakes flashed and swung.

'Full stop!' Gaunt ordered and clambered out. He trudged forward into the wind and the driving snow, his boots sinking thirty or forty centimetres into the drifts.

Revealed only at the last minute by the groping auspex and by the driver's struggling eyesight, the track swung hard around a spur, almost at forty-five degrees. Even this close, Gaunt could barely see it himself. One of the pair of scout Salamanders fronting the column was dangling over the edge of the chasm, most of one entire track section hanging in space. Gaunt hurried up through the headlamp beams of the machines behind, joined by other Ghosts and vehicle crews. The four occupants of the stricken light tank: the Pardus driver, Vox-officer Raglon and Scout Troopers Mklane and Baen, were standing in the crewbay of the teetering machine, frozen in place, not daring to move.

'Steady! Steady, sir!' Raglon hissed as Gaunt approached. They could all hear rock and ice crumbling under the body of the scout machine.

'Get a line attached! Come on!' Gaunt yelled. A Pardus driver hurried forward with a tow-hook, playing out the plasteel-mesh cable. Gaunt took the hook and gently reached out, sliding it in place over one of the Salamander's hardpoint lugs.

'Tension! Tension!' he cried, and the electric drum of the vehicle behind them started to rotate, taking up the slack on the cable until the line was taut. The Salamander tilted back a little onto the track.

'Out! Now!' Gaunt ordered, and Raglon's crew scrambled out onto the snowy trail, dropping to their knees and gasping with relief.

The crews around them now began the job of hauling the empty machine back onto the path.

Gaunt helped Mklane up.

'I thought we were dead, sir. The road just wasn't there any more.'

'Where's scout one?' asked Gaunt.

They all stopped dead and turned to look out into the darkness. They'd been so busy saving one machine, no one had realised the other had vanished entirely.

He'd forced the pace, Gaunt reflected, and the scout crew had paid the price.

'Gaunt to convoy. Full stop now. We go no further tonight.'

'Maybe we do,' said ayatani Zweil, suddenly appearing at Gaunt's side. He pointed up into the darkness and the blizzarding snow. There was a light. Strong, yellow, bright, shining in the night above them.

'The Shrinehold,' said Zweil.

FOURTEEN
SHRINEHOLD

'In war, one must prepare for defeat. Defeat is the most insidious of our foes. It never comes the way we expect.'

— Warmaster Slaydo,
from *A Treatise on the Nature of Warfare*

THE HONOUR GUARD approached the Temple of the Shrinehold of Saint Sabbat Hagio at first light. The snows had stopped, and the mountain scenery was perfect, sculptural white under a golden sky.

The Shrinehold was a towering structure rising out of the basalt of a promontory spur that ran down from the ice-capped peak above. The road ran along the crest to a hefty gatehouse in the lower of two concentric walls. Within those walls stood the close-packed buildings of the Shrinus Basilica, the monastery of the tempelum ayatani shrinus, and a great square-sided tower topped by a golden gambrel roof with up-swept eaves. Prayer flags and votive kites fluttered from the tower. The buildings and walls of the Shrinehold were pink basalt. Shutters and doors were painted a bright gloss red and their frames edged in white. Beyond the walls and the tower, at the very edge of the promontory, stood a massive stone pillar of black corundum on top of which the eternal light of the signal fire burned.

Gaunt halted the column on the causeway before the gate and approached on foot with Kleopas, Hark, Zweil, Rawne and an escort of six Ghosts. True to Sergeant Mkoll's estimate, it had taken eight days to make the journey. They needed to expedite the business here if they were going to make it back to the Doctrinopolis in the ten days remaining before complete evacuation. Gaunt didn't even want to start thinking about how hard that journey was going to be. The Infardi were closing on their heels in huge numbers and as far as he knew there was no other way down from the Sacred Hills.

The gigantic red doors under the grim carved aquila on the gatehouse swung open silently as they approached, and they strode in up the steps. Six blue robed ayatani brothers bowed to them but said nothing. They were taken up a wide flight of stone steps, which had been brushed clear of snow, to the gate in the inner wall, and then through into a lofty entrance hall.

The place was smoky brown and gloomy, with light entering through high windows, cold and pure. Gaunt could hear chanting, and the sporadic chiming of bells or gongs. The air was full of incense smoke.

He removed his cap and looked around. Colourful gleaming mosaics decorated the walls, showing the saint at various points in her hallowed life. Small holographic portraits set into lit alcoves along one wall depicted the great generals, commanders and Astartes who had served during her crusade. The great banner standard of Sabbat, an ancient and worn swathe of material, was suspended from the arched roof.

Ayatani of the tempelum ayatani shrinus entered the hall through the far doors, approached the Imperial retinue and bowed. There were twenty of them, all old, calm-faced men with tight, wrinkled skin worn by wind and cold and altitude.

Gaunt saluted. 'Colonel-Commissar Ibram Gaunt, commander of the Tanith First, Imperial Crusade Liberation Army. These are my chief officers, Major Rawne, Major Kleopas and Commissar Hark. I am here under orders from Lord Militant General Lugo.'

'You are welcome to the Shrinehold, sir,' said the leader of the brothers, his blue robes a deeper shade of violet. His face was as weatherbeaten as his colleagues', and his eyes had been replaced by an augmetic visor that made his stare milky and blank, like chronic cataracts. 'My name is Cortona. I am ayatani-ayt of this temple and monastery. We welcome you all to the shrine, and praise your diligence in making the arduous trek here at this time of year. Perhaps you will take refreshment with us? You are also free to make devotion at the shrine, of course.'

'Thank you, ayatani-ayt. Refreshment would be welcome, but I should make clear that the urgency of my mission means I have little time to spare, even for pious observances.'

The Imperials were taken through into an anteroom where soda farls, dried fruit and pots of a warm, sweet infusion were laid out on low, painted tables. They sat: Gaunt and his men on squat stools; the ayatani, including Zweil, on floor mats. Refreshment was passed round by junior esholi in white robes.

'I am touched that your lord general has seen fit to be concerned for our welfare,' Cortona continued, 'but I fear your mission here has been a waste of effort. We are fully aware of the enemy forces that seek to overrun this world, but we have no need of defence. If the enemy comes, the enemy comes and that will be the way of things. Our holy saint believed very much in natural fate. If it is decreed by destiny that this Shrinehold should fall to the enemy, and that our lives are to be forfeit, then it is decreed. No amount of tanks and soldiers can change that.'

'You'd let the Chaos breed just walk in?' Rawne asked, incredulously.

'Watch your mouth, major!' Hark hissed.

'It is an understandable question,' said Cortona. 'Our belief system may be hard to comprehend for minds versed and schooled in war.'

'Saint Sabbat was a warrior, ayatani-ayt,' Gaunt pointed out smoothly.

'She was. Perhaps the finest in the galaxy. But she is at rest now.'

'Your concerns are moot anyway, with respect, father,' Gaunt went on. 'You have misjudged our purpose here. We have not been sent to defend you. Lord General Lugo has ordered me to recover the relics of the saint and escort them with full honour to the Doctrinopolis, prior to the evacuation of Hagia.'

The calm smile never left Cortona's face. 'I fear, colonel-commissar, that I can never allow that to happen.'

'YOU QUITE TOOK my breath away,' murmured Zweil. 'I never imagined that was why you were coming to the Shrinehold! Beati's blood, colonel-commissar! What were you thinking?'

'I was obeying orders,' said Gaunt. They stood together on the terrace of the Shrinehold's inner wall, looking out across the bright snows towards the gorge.

'I thought you'd been sent to protect this place! I knew the templum ayatani would be none too pleased with a military intervention, but I left that to you.'

'And if I'd told you my full purpose, would you have advised me to turn back?'

'I would have told you what ayatani-ayt just told you. The saint's relics can never be taken from Hagia. It's one of the oldest doctrines, her deathbed prophecy. Even the likes of this General Lugo, or your esteemed Warmaster Macaroth, would be fools to break it!'

'I've read it. You know I've read the gospels closely. I just assumed it was... a whim. A minor detail.'

Zweil shook his head. 'I think that's where you keep going wrong, my boy. Half the time you read the scriptures hunting for absolute literal sense, the other half you try too hard to decipher hidden meanings! Textual interpretation indeed! You need balance. You need to understand the fundamental equilibrium of faith as it matters to us. If you expect the ayatani to devoutly and strictly keep the customs and relics and traditions of the beati alive, then you must equally expect us to treat the instruction of her scriptures with absolute conviction.'

'It is written,' Gaunt began thoughtfully, 'that if the remains of Saint Sabbat are ever taken from Hagia, if they are ever removed by accident or design, the entire Sabbat Worlds will fall to Chaos forever.'

'What's not clear about that?'

'It's an open prophecy! A colourful myth designed to intensify devotion and worship! It couldn't actually happen!'

'No?' Zweil gazed out across the Sacred Hills. 'Why not? You believe in the saint, in her works, in her incorruptible sanctity. Your belief in her and all she represents shines from you. It brought you here. So why wouldn't you believe in her deathbed prophecy?'

Gaunt shrugged. 'Because it's too... insane! Too big, too far-fetched! Too unlikely...'

'Maybe it is. Tell me, do you want to test it by taking her from this world?'

Gaunt didn't reply.

'Well, my boy? Do you know better than the sector's most venerated martyr? Does Lugo or the Warmaster? Will you risk losing everything, a thousand inhabited systems, forever, just to find out? Never mind your orders or their seniority, have they the right to take that risk either, or order you to do it?'

'I don't believe they do. I don't believe I do,' replied Gaunt quietly after a long pause.

'I don't believe you even have to consider the question,' said Hark, approaching them from behind. 'You have utterly unambiguous orders, sir. They leave no room for interpretation. Lugo made your duty plain.'

'Lugo made a mistake,' Gaunt said, fixing Hark with a clear, hard stare. 'It's not one I care to take any further.'

'Are you breaking orders, sir?' asked Hark.

'Yes, I am. It hardly matters. My career's over, my regiment's finished, and there's every chance we won't get out of here alive anyway. I'm breaking orders with a clear conscience, because it's about fething time I showed a bit of backbone and stopped blindly obeying men who are clearly and demonstrably wrong!'

Zweil's gaze darted back and forth between the two Imperial officers in total fascination, hanging on every word. Hark slowly put on his silver-braided cap, sighed heavily, and moved his hand to open the button-down cover of his holster.

'Oh, don't even bother, Hark,' Gaunt snarled contemptuously and walked away.

* * *

THEY WERE HIGH enough now for the snow that Sanian had warned them about to become a reality. It was light but persistent, and settled on their clothes and eyelashes. Further up the pass, snow clouds choked visibility so badly the great mountains themselves were temporarily invisible, masked out by the storm.

They had finally said goodbye to the Wounded Wagon two hours earlier, abandoning it at a point on the sooka where an old rockslide had long since carried the last of the negotiable track away. Loading up with everything they could carry, they had continued on foot.

The track was as thin and desolate as the air. To their right towered the sheer south faces of the innermost and highest Sacred Hills. To their left, a great slope of scree and bare rock arced downwards into the mysterious shadows of gorges and low passes far below. Every few steps, one of them caught a loose stone with their toe, and it would skitter and slither away down the decline.

The Ladder of Heaven had been cut by early pilgrims soon after the foundation of the Shrinehold six millennia before. They had engineered the work with zealous enthusiasm, seeing it as a sacred task and an act of devotion. A fifty kilometre staircase rising four thousand metres up into the peaks, right to the Shrinehold. Few used it now, Sanian had explained, because the climb was arduous, and even hardy pilgrims preferred the march up the passes. But that softer option wasn't open to them now.

Sanian led them to the foot of the Ladder as the first snows began.

It didn't look like much. A narrow, worn series of steps carved into the mountainside itself, eroded by weather and age. Lichens clung like rust to the surfaces. Each step was about sixteen centimetres high, a comfortable enough pace, and the steps were uniformly two metres deep from front to back, except where they sectioned and turned. The Ladder wove up through the rocks and disappeared above them.

'This looks easy enough,' said Greer, stepping lightly up the first few.

'It isn't, I assure you. Especially with the weather closing like this. Pilgrims used to choose this approach as an act of chastening,' said Sanian.

They started up, Greer eagerly hurrying ahead, followed by Daur, Corbec and Dorden, then Milo and Sanian, Nessa, Derin and finally Vamberfeld and Bragg.

'He'll kill himself if he doesn't pace his climb,' Sanian told Milo, pointing to Greer far ahead of them.

The main group fell into a rhythm. After about twenty minutes, Corbec began to feel oppressed by the sheer monotony of the task. He started to roam with his mind, trying to occupy his thoughts. He considered the distance and altitude, the depth and width of the steps. He did a little sum or two in his head.

'How many steps do they say there are?' he called back to Sanian.

'They say twenty-five thousand.'

Dorden groaned.

'That's just what I made it,' Corbec beamed, genuinely pleased with himself.

Fifty kilometres. Troops could cover that in a day, easy. But fifty kilometres of steps...

This could take days. Hard, painful, bone-numbing days.

'I maybe should have asked you this about five hundred metres ago, Sanian, but how long does this climb usually take?'

'It depends on the pilgrim. For the dedicated... and the fit... five or six days.'

'Oh sacred feth!' Dorden groaned aloud.

Corbec concentrated on the steps again. Snow was beginning to settle on them. In five or six days, when they reached the Shrinehold, Gaunt should be virtually all the way back to the Doctrinopolis if he was going to make the evac. They were wasting their time.

Then again, there was no way in creation Gaunt's honour guard was going to get down the mountain past that Infardi host. Chances were he'd use the Shrinehold as his base and fight it out from there.

They'd have to wait and see. There was no point in going back now. There was nothing to go back for.

ALONE, IBRAM GAUNT pulled back the great old bolt and pushed open the door of the Shrinehold's sepulchre. The voices of male esholi filtered out, singing a solemn, harmonius, eight-part chant. Cold wind moaned down the monastery's deep airshafts.

He didn't know what to expect. He realised he had never imagined coming here. Slaydo, the Emperor rest him, would have been envious.

The room was surprisingly small, and very dark. The walls were lined with black corundum that reflected none of the light from the many rows of burning candles. The air smelled of smoke, and musty dryness, the dust of centuries.

He stepped in, closing the door after him. The floor was made of strange, lustrous tiles that shimmered in the candlelight and made an odd, plastic sound as he walked on them. He realised they were cut and polished sections of chelon shell, pearlescent, with a brown stain of time.

To either side of where he stood were alcove bays in the corundum. In each glowed a life-size hologram of a White Scars Space Marine, power blades raised in salutes of mournful triumph.

Gaunt walked forward. Directly ahead of him was the reliquary altar. Plated with more polished chelon shell, it shone with ethereal luminescence. Inlaid on its raised front was a beautiful mosaic of coloured shell pieces depicting the Sabbat Worlds. Gaunt had no doubt it was cartographically precise. Behind the altar rose a huge, domed cover that overhung the altar block like a cowl. It was fashioned from a single chelon shell, a shell that had come from an incredibly massive animal, far larger than anything Gaunt had seen on Hagia. Beneath it, behind the altar, lay the reliquary itself, a candlelit cavern under the shell. At the front were two hardwood stands with open lids in which, behind glass, lay original manuscripts of the gospels.

Gaunt realised his heart was beating fast. The place was having an extraordinary effect on him.

He moved past the gospel stands. To his left stood a casket on which lay various relics half-wrapped in satin. There was a drinking bowl, a quill pen, a jiddi-stick worn black with age, and several other fragments he couldn't identify.

To his right, on top of another, matching casket, lay the saint's Imperator armour, painted blue and white. It showed the marks of ancient damage, blackened holes and grooves, jagged dents where the paint had been scraped off. The marks of the nine martyring wounds. There was something odd about it. Gaunt realised it was... small. It had been purpose-built for a body smaller than the average male Space Marine.

Ahead of him, at the very rear of the shell dome, lay the holy reliquary, a bier covered in a glass casket.

Saint Sabbat lay within.

She had wanted no stasis field or power suspension, but still she was intact after six thousand years. Her features had sunk, her flesh had desiccated, and her skin was dark and polished. Around her skull there were traces of fine hair. Gaunt could see the rings on her mummified fingers, the medallion of the Imperial eagle clasped in her hands across her bosom. The blue of her gown had almost entirely faded, and the dry husks of ancient flowers lay around her on the velvet padding of the bier.

Gaunt didn't know what to do. He lingered, unable to take his eyes off the taut, withered but incorruptible form of the beati.

'Sabbat. Martyr,' he breathed.

'She's under no obligation to answer you, you know.'

He looked around. Ayatani Zweil stood beyond the altar, watching him.

Gaunt made a dignified, short bow to the saint and walked back out past the altar to Zweil.

'I didn't come for answers,' he whispered.

'You did. You told me so, as we were coming from Mukret.'

'That was then. Now I've made my choice.'

'Choices and answers aren't the same thing. But yes, you have. A fine choice, may I add. A brave one. The right one.'

'I know. If I doubted that before, I don't now I've seen this. We have no business moving her. She stays here. She stays here as long as we can protect her.'

Zweil nodded and patted Gaunt on the arm. 'It's not going to be a popular choice. Poor Hark, I thought he was going to shit out a kidney when you told him.' Zweil paused, and looked back at the reliquary. 'Forgive my coarse language, beati. I am but a poor imhava ayatani who ought to know better in this holy place.'

They left the sepulchre together, and walked down the drafty hall outside.

'When will you make your decision known?'

'Soon, if Hark hasn't told everyone already.'

'He may remove you from command.'

'He may try. If he does, you'll see me breaking more than orders.'

NIGHT WAS FALLING, and another storm of snow was racing down from the north-west. Ayatani-ayt Cortona had allowed the Imperial forces to pitch their camp inside the outer wall of the Shrinehold, and the space was now full of tents and chemical braziers. The convoy vehicles had been drawn up in the lea of the wall outside, except for the fighting machines, which had ranged out and dug in, hull down, to guard the approach up the gorge to the promontory. Troop positions had also been dug in the snow banks outside, and the heavy weapons fortified. Anything coming up the pass was going to meet heavy resistance.

Making use of an anteroom in the monastery, Gaunt assembled the officers and section chiefs of the honour guard. The Shrinehold esholi brought food and sweet tea, and none of the priesthood complained about the amasec and sacra being portioned around. Ayatani-ayt Cortona and some of his senior priests had joined them. The lamps twitched and snowstorm winds banged at the shutters. Hark stood at the back of the room, alone, brooding.

Before he went in to join them, Gaunt took Rawne to one side, out in the chilly hall.

'I want you to know this first,' Gaunt told him. 'I intend to disobey Lugo's orders. We are not moving the saint.'

Rawne arched his eyebrows. 'Because of this fething stupid old prophecy?'

'Exactly because of this fething stupid old prophecy, major.'

'Not because it's all over for you?' asked Rawne.

'Explain.'

Rawne shrugged. 'We've known from the start that Lugo's got you cold. When you return to the Doctrinopolis, be it empty-handed or with this old girl's bones, that's the end. End of command, end of you, end of story. So as I see it, you really haven't got anything to lose, have you? Not to speak of. Telling Lugo to feth off and shove his orders up his own very special Eye of Terror isn't going to make things any worse for you. In fact, it might leave you feeling better when they come to drag you away.'

'You think I'm doing this because I don't care any more?' asked Gaunt.

'Well, do you? This last week, you've not been the man I started serving under. The drinking. The rages. The foul, foul fething moods. You failed. You failed badly. At the Doctrinopolis, you fethed up good and proper. You've been a wreck ever since. Oh...'

'What?' growled Gaunt.

'Permission to speak candidly, sir. With effect retroactive.'

'Don't you always, Rawne?'

'I fething hope so. Are you still drinking?'

'Well, I...'

'You want me to believe you're right, that you're doing this for real reasons and not just because you couldn't give a good feth about anything any more, then smarten up. Clean up. Work it out. I've never liked you, Gaunt.'

'I know.'

'But I've always respected you. Solid. Professional. A warrior who works to a code. Sure, because of that code Tanith burned, but you stuck by it no matter what anyone else thought. A man of honour.'

'That's the closest you've ever come to complimenting me, major,' said Gaunt.

'Sorry sir, it won't happen again. What I need to know is this... Is it that code now? Is it honour? This fething mission is an honour guard... Do you mean it to deserve that title?'

'Yes.'

'Show me then. Show us all. Show us this isn't just spite and bile and frustration coming out of you because you fethed up and they caught you for it. Show us you're not just a drunken wreck going down fast and bitterly trying to take everything and everyone with you. It's over for you, any way you cut it, but it isn't for us. If we go along with you, the lord general will have us all court-martialled and shot. We've got something left to lose.'

'I know,' said Gaunt. He paused for a moment, and watched the driving snowflakes build and pile up against the glass of the hall windows.

'Well?'

'Would you like to know why this matters to me, Rawne? Why I took the disaster at the Doctrinopolis so badly?'

'I'd be fascinated.'

'I've given the better part of the last two decades to this crusade. I've fought hard every step of the way. And here on Hagia, the blind stupidity of one man... our dear lord general... forced my hand and ruined all that work. But it's not just that. The crusade that I've devoted these years to is in honour of Saint Sabbat, intended to liberate the planets she first made Imperial worlds six thousand years ago. I hold her in special regard, therefore, and am dedicated to her honour, and that bastard Lugo made me fail on the very world sacred to her. I didn't just feth up during a crusade action, major. I fethed up during a crusade action on the saint's own holy shrineworld. But it's not just that either.'

He paused and cleared his throat. Rawne stared at him in the gloom.

'I was one of Slaydo's chosen, hand-picked to wage this war. He was the greatest commander I've ever known. He took on this crusade as a personal endeavour because he was absolutely and utterly devoted to the saint. She was his totem, his inspiration, the role model on which he had built his military career. He told me himself that he saw this crusade as a chance to pay back that debt of inspiration. I will not dishonour his memory by failing him here. Here, of all places.'

'Let me guess,' said Rawne. 'It's not just that either, is it?'

Gaunt shook his head. 'On Formal Prime, in the first few months of the crusade, I fought alongside Slaydo in a fierce action to take the hive towers. It was one of the first big successes of the crusade.

'At the victory feast, he brought his officers together. Forty-eight of us, the chosen men. We caroused and celebrated. We all got a little drunk, Slaydo included. Then he... he became solemn, that bitter sadness that afflicts some men when they are at their worse for drink. We asked him what was wrong, and he said he was afraid. We laughed! Great Warmaster Slaydo, afraid? He got to his feet, unsteady. He was one hundred and fifty years old by then, and those years had not been kind. He told us he was afraid of dying before finishing his work. Afraid of not living long enough to oversee the full and final liberation of the beati's worlds. It was his one, consuming ambition, and he was afraid he would not achieve it.

'We all protested... he'd outlive us all! He shook his head and insisted that the only way he could ensure the success of his sacred task, the only way he could achieve immortality and finish his duty to the saint, was through us. He called for an oath. A blood oath. We used bayonets and fething table knives to cut our palms and draw blood. One by one we clasped his bleeding hand and swore. On our lives, Rawne, on our very lives. We would finish his work. We would pursue this crusade to its end. And we would damn well protect the saint against any who would harm her!'

Gaunt held out his right hand, palm open. In the blue half-light, Rawne could still make out the old, pale scar.

'Slaydo fell at Balhaut, that battle of battles, just as he feared he would. But his oath lives on, and in it, Slaydo too.'

'Lugo's making you break your pact.'

'Lugo made me ride rough-shod through the saint's Doctrinopolis and set ablaze her ancient temples. Now Lugo wants me to defy the beati and disturb her final rest. I apologise if I seemed to take any of that badly, but now perhaps you can see why.'

Rawne nodded slowly.

'You had better tell the others,' he said.

* * *

GAUNT WALKED INTO the centre of the crowded anteroom, declined a drink offered to him by an esholi, and cleared his throat. All eyes were on him and silence fell.

'In the light of developments in the field and... other considerations, I hereby inform you I am making an executive alteration to our orders.'

There was a murmur.

'We will not be proceeding as per Lord General Lugo's instruction. We will not remove the Shrinehold relics. As of now, my orders are that the honour guard digs in here and remains in defence of the Shrinehold until such time as our situation is relieved.'

A general outburst filled the room. Hark was silent.

'But the lord general's orders, Gaunt–' Kleopas began, rising.

'Are no longer viable or appropriate. As field commander, judging things as they stand here on the ground, it is within my purview.'

Intendant Elthan rose, quivering with rage. 'But we'll be killed! We have to return to the Doctrinopolis landing fields by the timetable or we will not be evacuated! You know what's coming, colonel-commissar! How dare you suggest this!'

'Sit down, Elthan. If it helps, I'm sorry that non-combatants such as yourself and your driver crews have been caught in this. But you are servants of the Emperor. Sometimes your duty is as hard as ours. You will obey. The Emperor protects.'

A few officers and all the ayatani echoed the refrain.

'Sir, you can't just break orders.' Lieutenant Pauk's voice was full of alarm. Kleopas nodded urgently at his junior officer's words. 'We'll all face the strictest discipline. Lord General Lugo's orders were simple and precise. We can't just disobey them!'

'Have you seen what's coming up the pass behind us, Pauk?' Everyone turned. Captain LeGuin was standing at the back of the room, leaning against the wall. 'In terms of necessity alone, I'd say the colonel-commissar was making a sound decision. We can't get back to the Doctrinopolis now even if we wanted to.'

'Thank you, captain,' nodded Gaunt.

'Stuff your opinions, LeGuin!' cried Captain Marchese, commander of the Conqueror P48J. 'We can always try! That's what the lord general and the Warmaster would expect! If we stay here and fight it out, we might resist for the next week or so. But once that fleet arrives, we're dead anyway!'

Several officers, Ghosts among them, applauded Marchese's words.

'We follow orders! We take up the relics and we break out now! Let's take our chances in a stand-up fight against the Infardi! If we fail, we fail! Better to die like that, in glory, than to wait it out for certain death!'

Much more support now.

'Captain Marchese, you should have been a commissar. You turn a good, rousing phrase.' Gaunt smiled. 'But I am commissar. And I am commander here. We stay, as I have instructed. We stay and fight.'

'Please reconsider, Gaunt!' cried Kleopas.

'But we'll die, sir,' said Sergeant Meryn.

'And die badly, come to that,' growled Feygor.

'Don't we deserve a chance, sir?' asked Sergeant Soric, pulling his stout frame upright, his cap clasped in his hands.

'Every chance in the cosmos, Soric,' said Gaunt. 'I've considered all our options carefully. This is the right way.'

'You're insane!' squealed Elthan. He turned and gazed imploringly at Hark. 'Commissar! For the Emperor's sake, do something!'

Hark stepped forward. The room went quiet. 'Gaunt. I know you've considered me an enemy all along. I can see why, but God-Emperor knows I'm not. I've admired you for years. I've studied how you've made command choices that would have been beyond lesser men. You've never been afraid of questioning the demands of high command.'

Hark looked round at the silent room and then his gaze returned to Gaunt.

'I got you this mission, Gaunt. I've been with the lord general's staff for a year now, and I know what kind of man he is. He wants you to shoulder the blame for the Doctrinopolis to cover his own lack of command finesse.

'After the disaster at the Citadel, he would have had you drummed out on the spot. But I knew damn well you were worth more than that. I suggested a final mission, this honour guard. I thought it might give you a chance to redeem yourself, or at least finish your career on a note of respectability. I even thought it might give Lugo time to reconsider and change his mind. A successful salvation of the shrineworld relics from under the nose of an overwhelming enemy force could even be turned into a famous victory with the right spin. Lugo might come out a hero, and you, consequently, might come out with your command intact.'

Hark sighed and straightened the front of his waistcoat. 'You break orders now, there's no coming back. You'll put yourself right where Lugo wants you. You'll turn yourself into the scapegoat he needs. Furthermore, as an officer of his personal commissariate, I cannot allow it. I cannot allow you to continue in command. I'm sorry, Gaunt. All the way along, I've been on your side. You've just forced my hand. I hereby assume control of the honour guard, as per general order 145.f. The mission will continue to the letter of our orders. I wish it could have been different, Gaunt. Major Rawne, relieve Colonel-Commissar Gaunt of his weapons.'

Rawne rose slowly. He walked across the packed room to Gaunt and then stood at his side, facing Hark. 'I don't think that's going to happen, Hark,' he said.

'That's insubordination, major,' murmured Hark. 'Follow my instructions and relieve Gaunt of his weapons now or I'll have you up on charges.'

'I can't have been clear,' said Rawne. 'Go feth yourself.'

Hark closed his eyes, paused, opened them again and drew his plasma pistol.

He raised it slowly and aimed it at Rawne. 'Last chance, major.'

'Who for, Hark? Look around.'

Hark looked around. A dozen sidearms were pointing at him, aimed by Ghost officers and a few Pardus, including LeGuin and Kleopas.

Hark holstered his weapon. 'I see you give me no choice. If we survive, this incident will be brought to the attention of the Crusade commissariate, in full and frank detail.'

'If we survive, I'll look forward to that,' said Gaunt. 'Now let's make ready.'

OUT IN THE blizzarding night, at waymark 00.02 at the head of the pass, Scout-trooper Bonin and Troopers Larkin and Lillo were dug into an ice bunker. They had a chemical heater puffing away in the base of the dugout, but it was still bitterly cold. Bonin was watching the portable auspex unit while Larkin hunted the flurrying darkness with the night scope of his long-las. Lillo chaffed his hands, waiting by the tripod-mounted autocannon.

'Movement,' Larkin said quietly.

'Nothing on the screen,' replied Bonin, checking the glowing glass plate of the auspex.

'See for yourself,' said Larkin, moving aside so that Bonin could slide in to view through the scope of the positioned sniper weapon.

'Where?'

'Left a touch.'

'Oh feth,' murmured Bonin. Illuminated in ghostly green, he could see blurs of light on the pass below. Hundreds of lights were moving up the precipitous track towards them. Headlamps glaring in the falling snow.

'There's lots of them,' said Bonin, moving back.

'You haven't seen the half of it,' mumbled Lillo, staring at the auspex screen. Bright yellow sigils wobbled around the contour lines of the holomap. The tactical counter had identified at least three hundred contacts, but the number was rising as they watched.

'Get on the vox,' said Larkin. 'Tell Gaunt all fething hell is coming up the pass.'

FIFTEEN
THE WAITING

'Actual combat is a fleeting part of war.
The bulk of soldiering is waiting.'

— Warmaster Slaydo,
from *A Treatise on the Nature of Warfare*

WHEN THE SNOWING stopped just before dawn, the Infardi advance guard began their first assault up the top of the pass. A bombardment was launched by their reserve tanks and self-propelled guns, but most of it fell short of the Shrinehold walls. Six SteGs and eight Reavers churned through the snow towards the promontory, and a hurrying line of four hundred troops followed them.

They were met by the Pardus armour and the dug-in sections of the Tanith First-and-Only. Hull-down, *Grey Venger* picked off the first four armour units before they were even clear of the spur. Their burning carcasses dirtied the snowfield with blackened debris and fire.

Heavy weapon emplacements opened up to meet the infantry. In a quarter of an hour, the white slopes were scattered with green-robed dead.

A SteG and an AT70 pushed in past the outer defence, behind *Grey Venger's* field of fire. They were met and destroyed by Kleopas's *Heart of Destruction* and Marchese's P48J.

The Infardi fell back.

GAUNT STRODE INTO the tent where Ghost troopers were guarding the Infardi officer taken prisoner at Bhavnager. The wretch was shivering and broken.

Gaunt ordered him to be released and handed him a small data-slate.

'Take this back to your brethren,' he said firmly.

The Infardi rose, facing Gaunt, and spat in his face.

Gaunt's punch broke his nose and sent him tumbling onto the snowy ground.

'Take this back to your brethren,' he repeated, holding out the slate.

'What is it?'

'A demand for them to surrender.'

The Infardi laughed.

'Last chance... Go.'

The Infardi got up, blood from his nose spattering the snow, and took the slate. He went out through the gate and disappeared down the slope.

The next time the Imperials saw him, he was strung spread-eagled across the front of an AT70 that was ploughing up the approach to the outer line. The tank waited, stationary, as if daring the Imperials to shoot or at least daring them to notice.

Then it fired its main gun. The screaming Infardi officer had been tied with his torso over the muzzle of the tank cannon.

A conical spray of red gore covered the snow. The AT70 turned and trundled back to its lines.

'An answer of sorts, I suppose,' Gaunt said to Rawne.

ON THE LADDER, barely a quarter of the way up, Corbec's team woke in the chill of dawn to find themselves half buried in the overnight snow. Each of them had lain down on a step in their bedroll. Shaking and slow, they got up, cold to the marrow. Corbec looked up the winding stairs. This was going to be murder.

FOR FIVE STRAIGHT days, the Infardi made no attempt to attack again. Gaunt was beginning to believe they were stalling until the fleet's arrival. For the Imperials dug in behind the Shrinehold defences, the waiting was becoming intolerable.

Then, at noon on the fourteenth day of the mission, the enemy tried again.

Armour ploughed up out of the gorge, and shells wailed at the Shrinehold. Caught in the initial rush, the Conqueror *Say Your Prayers* and two Chimera were lost. Smoke from the wreck of the dead Conqueror trailed up into the blue.

The rest of the Pardus armour met the assault and slugged it out. Ghosts under Soric and Mkoll ran forward from their ice trenches and countered the enemy push on foot up the pass.

From their dug-outs, the Tanith snipers began to compete. Larkin could outscore Luhan easily enough, but Banda was something else. Seeing a competition, Cuu put money on it. His wager, Larkin was furious to discover, was on the Verghastite loom-girl.

It took two straight hours for the Imperials to repulse the attack. They were exhausted by the end of it.

ON THE SIXTEENTH day, the Infardi tried yet again, in major force. Shells hit the Shrinehold's walls and tower. A blizzard of las-fire streaked the air, raining on the Imperial lines. Once they could see they were hurting their enemy, the Infardi charged, five or maybe six thousand cultist-warriors, pouring in through the advancing files of their war machines. From the wall, Gaunt saw them coming.

It was going to be bloody.

HIGH UP ON the punishing Ladder of Heaven which seemed to go on forever, Corbec stopped to get his breath back. He'd never known exhaustion like this, or pain, or breathlessness. He knelt down on the snow-covered step.

'Don't... don't you dare go... go quitting on me now!' Dorden exclaimed, vapour gusting from his lips, as he tried to pull Corbec to his feet. The chief medic was thin and haggard, his skin drawn and pale, and he was struggling for breath.

'But doc... we should never... never have even tried...'

'Don't you dare, Corbec! Don't you dare!'

'Listen! Listen!' Daur called back to them. He and Derin were about forty steps above them, silhouetted against the bright white sky.

They heard a rolling roar that wasn't the constant wind. A buffeting, thunderous drone, mixed over what they slowly realised were the voices of thousands of howling, chanting men.

Corbec got up. He wanted to just lie down and die. He couldn't feel his feet any more. But he got up and leaned against Dorden.

'I think, my old friend, we might be there at last. And I think we've arrived at a particularly busy time.'

A few steps behind them, the others had caught up, all except Greer who was now lagging a long, long way behind. Bragg and Nessa sat down in the snow to catch their breaths. Vamberfeld stood panting with his eyes closed. Milo looked at Sanian, whose weary face was clouded by what he supposed to be grief.

It wasn't. It was anger.

'That's the sound of war,' she wheezed, fighting her desperate fatigue. 'I know it. Not enough that war comes to my world, that it tears through my home town. Now it comes here, to the most sacred place of all, where only peace should be!'

She looked up at Dorden. 'I was right, you see, doctor? War consumes everything and everyone. There is only war. Nothing else even matters.'

* * *

THEY CLAMBERED ON, up the last few hundred metres of curling staircase, soul-weary and delirious with cold and hunger. But to know the end was at hand lifted them up for that last effort.

The sounds of the combat grew louder, magnified by the echoes that came off the mountain faces and the gorge.

They readied their weapons with trembling, clumsy hands, and advanced. Corbec and Bragg covered the way ahead, taking one step at a time.

The steps ended in a wide snow-covered platform of rock, the cliff edge of which showed the ancient traces of a retaining wall. They were climbing up onto a great promontory of rock, a flat-topped buttress of mountain that stuck out from the mountainside above a vast gorge. A walled, keep-like structure that could only be the Shrinehold itself lay to their left, dominating the promontory. Between it and the place where the wide promontory extended out from the top of the pass, full-scale battle raged. They were bystanders, hidden from view half a kilometre from the edge of the fighting. Banks of sooty smoke and ash rolled through the freezing mountain air.

A tide of Infardi war machines and troops, inexorable as a glacier, was moving forward from the head of the pass and up the promontory past them. In the sloping snowfield in front of the Shrinehold, the Chaos forces were being met head-on by the Imperial defenders. Shell holes had been torn in the Shrinehold's outer wall, and vehicles were on fire. The fighting was so thick they could barely make sense of it.

'Come on,' said Corbec.

'We're going into that?' moaned Greer. 'We can barely walk any more, you crazy bastard!'

'That's Colonel Crazy Bastard to you, pal. No, we're not going into that. Not directly. We'll follow the edge of this promontory around. But that's where we're going, and we've got to get in there sooner or later. Dead on my damned feet I may be, but I've come a fething long way to be part of this.'

GAUNT WAS IN the thick of the fighting at the foot of the outer wall. He hadn't been in a stand-up fight this fierce since Balhaut. It was so concentrated, so direct. The noise was bewildering.

Nearby, Lieutenant Pauk's Executioner was firing beam after beam of superheated plasma into the charging ranks, leaving lines of mangled corpses in the half-melted snow. Both the *Heart of Destruction* and the *Lucky Bastard* had run out of main gun shells, and were reduced to bringing in their bulk and coaxial weapons in support of the Ghosts. Brostin, Neskon and the other flame troopers were out on the right flank, spitting gouts of yellow flame down the field that turned the hard-packed snow to slush and sent Infardi troops screaming back, their clothes and flesh on fire.

The Imperials were holding, but in this hellish confusion, there was a chance that command coherency could be lost as wave after wave of the Chaos-breed stormed forward.

Gaunt saw the first couple of enemy officers. Just energised blurs moving amongst their troops, each one protected in the shimmering orb of a refractor shield. Nothing short of a point-blank tank round could touch them. He counted five of them amid the thick echelons of advancing enemy. Any one of them might be the notorious Pater Sin, come all this way to snatch his final triumph.

'Support me!' Gaunt cried to the fireteam at his heels, and they pushed out in assault, tackling the Infardi, sometimes hand to hand. Gaunt's bolt pistol fired shot after shot, and the power sword of Heironymo Sondar whispered in his fist.

Two Ghosts beside him were cut down. Another stumbled and fell, his left arm gone at the elbow.

'For Tanith! For Verghast! For Sabbat!' Gaunt yelled, his breath steaming the air. 'First-and-Only! First-and-Only!'

There was good support to his immediate left. Caffran, Criid, Beltayn, Adare, Memmo and Mkillian. Flanking them, Sergeant Bray's section, and the remains of a fireteam led by Corporal Maroy.

Scything with his sword, Gaunt worried about the right flank. He was pretty sure Corporal Mkteeg was dead, and there was no sign of Obel's section, or of Soric who, with Mkoll, had operational command of that quarter.

One of the Infardi officers was close now, cackling aloud, invisible in his ball of shield energy against which the Imperial las-fire twinkled harmlessly. Using him as mobile cover, the Ershul foot troops were pounding at the Ghosts. Memmo tumbled, headshot, gone, and Mkillian dropped a second later, hit in the thigh and hip.

'Caffran! Tube him!' Gaunt yelled.

'It won't breach the shield, sir!'

'Put it at his feet, then! Knock the fether over!'

Caffran hurled a tube-charge, spinning it end over end. It bounced in the thick snowpack right at the Infardi officer's feet and went off brightly.

The blasts didn't hurt the Ershul officer, but it effectively blew the ground out from under him and he fell, his refractor shield hissing in the snow.

Gaunt was immediately on him, yelling out, stabbing down two-handed with his power blade. Criid, Beltayn and Adare were right at his heels, gunning down the Ershul-lord's bodyguard.

Power sword met refractor shield. The shield was a model manufactured by Chaos-polluted Mechanicus factories on the occupied forgeworld Ermune. It was powerful and effective. The power sword was so old, no one knew its original place of manufacture. It popped the shield like a needle lancing a blister.

The fizzling cloak of energy vanished and Gaunt's sword blade plunged on, impaling the screaming Infardi revealed inside.

Gaunt wrenched the sword out and got up. The Infardi nearby, those who hadn't yet been dropped by his Ghosts, backed off and ran in fear. By killing the officer in front of their eyes, he'd put a chink in their insane confidence.

BUT IT WAS a tiny detail of triumph in a much greater battle-storm. Major Rawne, commanding units nearer to the main gate, could see no respite in the onslaught. The Infardi were throwing themselves at his position as fast as his troops in the snow-trenches and on the wall parapet could fire on them. A row of self-propelled guns was working up behind the enemy infantry, and their munitions now came whistling down, throwing up great bursts of ice and fire. Two shells dropped inside the wall and one hit the wall itself, blowing out a ten-metre chunk.

Rawne saw the *Grey Venger* advancing over the snow, streaking titanic stripes of laser fire at the Usurper guns. One was hit and sent up a fiery mushroom cloud. Rocket grenades slapped and banged off the *Venger's* hull. The *Lion of Pardua* smashed directly through a faltering pack of Infardi troopers, dozer blade lowered, fighting to get a shot at the heavy gun units too. A tank round, coming from Emperor alone knew where, destroyed its starboard tracks and it lurched to a stop. The shrieking Infardi were all over it, mobbing the hull, their green figures swarming across the crippled tank. Rawne tried to direct some of his troop fire to assist the Conqueror, but the range was bad and they were too boxed in. Tank hatches were shot or blasted open, and the mob of Infardi dragged the *Lion's* crew out screaming.

'Feth, no!' Rawne gasped, his warm exhalation becoming vapour.

Without warning, another tank round hit the *Lion*, and blew it apart, exploding several dozen Infardi with it. Killing the Imperial armour seemed to be all the enemy cared about.

In a snow-trench ten metres left of the major, Larkin cursed and yelled out 'Cover me!' as he rolled back from his firing position. Troopers Cuu and Tokar moved up beside the prone Banda and resumed firing.

The barrel of Larkin's long-las had failed. He unscrewed the flash suppressor and then twisted and pulled out the long, ruined barrel. Larkin was so practiced at this task he could swap the XC 52/3 strengthened barrels in less than a minute. But his bag of spares was empty.

'Feth!' He crawled over to Banda, shots passing close over his head. 'Verghast! Where're your spare rods?'

Banda snapped off another shot, and then reached round and pulled the clasp of her pack open. 'In there! Down the side!'

Larkin reached in and pulled out a roll of vizzy-cloth. There were three XC 52/3s wrapped in it.

'This all you got?'

'It's all Twenish was carrying!'

Larkin locked one into place, checked the line, and rescrewed his suppressor. 'They're not going to last any fething time at this pace!' he grunted.

'Should be more in the munition supplies, Tanith,' said Cuu, clipping a new power cell into his weapon.

'Yeah, but who's going back into the Shrinehold to get them?'

'Point,' murmured Cuu.

Larkin blew on his mittened hands and began firing again.

'What's the tally?' he hissed at Banda.

'Twenty-three,' she said without looking round.

Only two less than him. Feth, she was good.

Then again, who wouldn't score when they had this many damned targets to fire at?

Rawne got a fireteam forward as far as the cover provided by one of their own burning Chimeras. Lillo, Gutes, Cocoer and Baen dropped into the filthy snow beside him, firing through the raging smoke that boiled out of the machine. A moment later, Luhan, Filain, Caill and Mazzedo moved up close and provided decent crossfire under Feygor's command.

Rawne waved a third team – Orul, Sangul, Dorro, Raess and Muril – round to the far side of the Chimera. They were reaching position when an Infardi counter-push hit. Two rounds from an AT70 erupted like small volcanoes in their midst. Filain and Mazzedo were obliterated instantly. Cocoer was gashed by flying metal and fell screaming. Steam rose from his hot blood in the chill air. Gutes and Baen ran forward to drag the bawling, bloody Tanith into cover, but Gutes was immediately hit in the leg by a las-round. Baen turned in surprise and took two hits in the lower back. His arms lurched up and he fell on his face.

Infardi troops rushed in from the left, weapons blazing. In the savage short-range firefight that followed, first Orul and then Sangul were killed by massive torso injuries. Dorro managed to get Baen and Cocoer into cover and then he was hit in the jaw with such destructive force his head was virtually twisted off.

Rawne found himself pinned with Luhan, Lillo, Feygor and Caill, firing in support of Raess and Muril who were closer to the trio of wounded Ghosts.

'Three! This is three! We're pinned!'

The blackened wreckage of a Munitorium troop truck fifty metres ahead splintered and rolled as something big pushed it aside. For a moment, Rawne felt relief, sure it was one of the Pardus Conquerors.

But it wasn't. It was a SteG 4, squirming through the heavy snowcover on tyres that were encrusted with slush, oil and blood.

'Feth! Back! Back!'

'Where the gak to, sir?' Lillo wailed.

The SteG fired and the whooping shell slammed through the dead Chimera.

There was a chilling wail from behind Rawne's position. Part animal shriek, part pneumatic hiss, a sound that swooped from high pitch to low. The output of a powerful beam weapon ripped into the front of the SteG and a rush of pressurised flame blew out the side panels. It bounced to a halt, streaming smoke.

'Fall back! Get clear!' Commissar Hark yelled to Rawne and his soldiers as he fired again into the midst of a charging Infardi platoon. They half carried and half dragged Gutes, Cocoer and Baen back the twenty metres to the nearest snow-work cover.

'I'm surprised to see you,' Rawne told Hark flatly.

'I'm sure you are, major. But I wasn't just going to sit in the Shrinehold and wait for the end.'

'You won't have to wait long, commissar,' said Rawne, changing clips. 'I'm sure you'll be pleased to note that this is it. The last stand of Gaunt and his Ghosts.'

'I...' Hark began and then fell silent. As a commissar, even an unpopular, unwelcome one, it was his foremost duty to rally, to inspire the men and to quell just that kind of talk. But he couldn't. Looking out at the forces that swept in to overrun and slaughter them, there was no denying it.

The cold-blooded major was right.

In the very heaviest part of the battle, Gaunt knew it too. Troopers fell all around him. He saw Caffran, wounded in the leg, being dragged to cover by Criid. He saw Adare hit twice, convulse and drop. He saw two Verghastite Ghosts thrown into the air by a shell burst. He almost fell over the stiffening corpse of Trooper Brehl, the blood spats from his wounds frozen like gemstones.

A las-round hit Gaunt in the left arm and spun him a little. Another passed through the skirt of his storm coat.

'First-and-Only!' he yelled, his breath smoking in the cold. 'First-and-Only!'

Something happened to the sky. It changed abruptly from frozen chalk-white to fulminous yellow, swirling with cloud patterns. A sudden, almost hot wind surged up the gorge.

'What the gak is that?' Banda murmured.

'Oh no,' mumbled Larkin. 'Chaos madness. Fething Chaos madness.'

Silent auroras of purple and scarlet rippled across the sky. Crimson blooms swirled out and stained the sky like ink spots in water.

Lightning strikes, searing violet-white, sizzled and cracked down, accompanied by thunderclaps so loud they shook the mountain.

The savage fighting foundered and ceased. Beneath the alien deluge, the Infardi fled back down to the pass, leaving their wounded and their crippled machines behind them. The mass exodus was so sudden, they had cleared the approach fields of the Shrinehold in less than ten minutes.

The Imperials cowered in terror beneath the twisting lightshow. Vehicle engines stalled. Vox signals went berserk in whoops of interference and swarms of static. Many troopers wrenched their microbead ear-plugs out, wincing. Vox-officer Raglon's ears were bleeding by the time he'd managed to pull off his headset. Wild static charge filled the air, crackling off weapons, making hair stand on end. Greenish corposant and ball lightning wriggled and flared around the eaves and roofs of the Shrinehold.

In the face of final defeat, something had saved Gaunt's honour guard, or at least allowed it a temporary reprieve.

Ironically, that something was Chaos.

'I HAVE CONSULTED the monastery's sensitives and psyker-adepts,' said ayatani-ayt Cortona. 'It is a warp storm, a flux of the empyrean. It is affecting all space near Hagia.'

Gaunt sat on a stool in the Shrinehold's main hallway, stripped to the waist as Medic Lesp sutured and bound up his arm. 'The cause?'

'The arch-enemy's fleet.' replied Cortona.

Gaunt raised an eyebrow. 'But that's not due to reach us for another five days.'

'I don't believe it has. But a fleet of that size, moving through the aether, would create a massive disturbance, like the bow wave of a great ship, pushing the eddies and swirls of the warp ahead of it.'

'And that bow wave has just broken over Hagia? I see.' Gaunt stood up and flexed his bandaged arm. 'Thanks, Lesp. Immaculate needlework as ever.'

'Sir. I don't suppose there's any point advising you to rest it?'

'None whatsoever. We get out of this, I'll rest it all you like.'

'Sir.'

'Now get to the triage station and do some proper work. There are many more needy than me.'

Lesp saluted, collected up his medicae kit and hurried out. Pulling on his shirt, Gaunt walked with Cortona to one of the open shutters and gazed out at the seething, malign fury of the sky above the Sacred Hills.

'No getting off planet now.'

'Colonel-commissar?'

Gaunt looked round at the elderly high priest. 'There's nothing good about that storm, ayatani-ayt, but there's some satisfaction to be derived from it at least. If I had followed my orders and returned to the Doctrinopolis, I wouldn't have reached it until tomorrow, even under the best conditions. So even if I'd got in before the evacuation deadline, I'd have been trapped.'

'Like Lugo and the last few hundred ships undoubtedly are,' said Hark, suddenly there and in the conversation. A typical Hark-esque no-warning appearance.

'You sound almost pleased, Hark.'

'Hagia is about to be wiped from space, sir. Pleased is not the right word. But, like you, I wager, there is some cruel delight to be drawn from the idea of Lord General Lugo suffering along with us.'

Gaunt began to button up the braid froggings of his tunic. 'Major Rawne, another bête noir of yours, told me you did us proud in the fight today. Saved him and a good many others.'

'It wasn't service to you. It was service to the Golden Throne of Terra. I am a soldier of the Imperium and will make a good account of myself until death, the Emperor protects.'

'The Emperor protects,' nodded Gaunt. 'Look, commissar... for whatever it's worth, I have no doubts as to your courage, loyalty or ability. You've fought well all the way along. You've tried to do your duty, even if I haven't liked it. It took, I have to admit, a feth of a lot of guts to stand up in that room and try and take command off me.'

'Guts had nothing to do with it.'

'Guts had *everything* to do with it. I want you to know that you'll receive no negative report from me... if and when I ever get to make one. No matter what kind of report you choose to make. I bear you no ill will. I've always taken my duty to the Emperor fething seriously. Completely fething seriously. How could I possibly resent another man doing the same?'

'I... thank you for your civility and frankness. I wish things could have been... and could yet be... different between us. It would have been a pleasure to serve with you and the First-and-Only without this cloud of resentment hanging over me.'

Gaunt held out his hand and Hark shook it.

'I think so too.'

The doors to the hall swung open and cold air billowed in, bringing with it Major Kleopas, Captain LeGuin, Captain Marchese and the Ghost officers Soric, Mkoll, Bray, Meryn, Theiss and Obel. They stomped their boots and brushed flakes from their sleeves.

'Join me,' Gaunt told Hark. They joined the officers.

'Gentlemen. Where's Rawne?'

'There was some perimeter alert, sir. He went to check it out,' said Meryn.

Gaunt nodded. 'Any word on Corporal Mkteeg?'

'He was found alive, but badly shot up. They slaughtered his squad but for two other men,' said Soric.

'What is this, sir?' asked Corporal Obel. 'What drove the Infardi back? I thought they had us there, I really did.'

'They did, corporal. They honestly did. But for the damndest luck.' Gaunt quickly explained the nature of the storm effects as best as he understood it. 'I think this sudden warp storm shocked the Ershul. I think they thought it was some apocalyptic sign from their Dark Gods and simply... lost it. It is an apocalyptic sign from their Dark Gods, of course. That's the down side. Once they've regrouped, they'll be back, and stronger too, would be my wager. They'll know almighty hell is coming to help them.'

'So they'll assault again?' asked Marchese.

'Before nightfall would be my guess, captain. We must restructure our force disposition in time to meet the Ershul's next attack.'

'Is that what we're calling them now, sir?' asked Soric.

'Call them whatever you like, Soric.'

'Bastards?' suggested Kleopas.

'Scum-sucking warp-whores?' said Theiss.

'Targets?' said Mkoll quietly.

The men laughed.

'Whatever works for you,' said Gaunt. Good, there was some damn morale left yet.

'Bray? Obel? Drag over that table there. Captain LeGuin, I see you've brought charts. Let's get to work.'

They'd just spread out the tank hunter's maps when Gaunt's vox beeped.

'One, go.'

It was Vox-officer Beltayn. 'Major Rawne says to get out front, sir. Something's awry.'

Awry! Always with that nervous, understated awry! 'What's actually awry this time, Beltayn?'

'Sir... it's the colonel, sir!'

Gaunt ran out down the steps, through the snow lying between the inner and outer walls, towards the gate.

Rawne and a section of men were just coming in, bringing with them ten haggard, stumbling figures, caked in dirt and rime, half-starved and weary.

Gaunt's eyes widened. He came to a halt.

Trooper Derin. Try Again Bragg. The Verghastite Ghosts Vamberfeld and Nessa. Captain Daur, supporting a half-dead Pardus officer Gaunt didn't know. Dorden... Great God-Emperor! Dorden! And Milo, Emperor protect him, carrying a Hagian girl in his arms.

And there, at the head of them, Colonel Colm Corbec.

'Colm? Colm, what the feth are you doing here?' Gaunt asked.

'Did... did we miss all the fun, sir?' Corbec whispered, and pitched over into the snow.

SIXTEEN
INFARDI

'It was always her greatest weapon. Surprise, you would call it, I suppose. The scope of her ability to produce the unexpected. To turn the course of an engagement on its head, even the worst of defeats. I saw it happen many times. Something from nothing. Triumph from disaster. Until the very end, when at the last, she could no longer work her miracles. And she fell.'

— Warmaster Kiodrus, from *The Path to the Nine Wounds: A History of Service with the Saint*

THE NIGHT OF the sixteenth day fell, but it was not proper night. The surging maelstrom of the warp storm lit the sky above the Shrinehold with pulses and cyclones of kaleidoscopic light and electromagnetic spectres. The snows had ceased, and under the silent, flickering glare, the embattled Imperials stood watch at battle-readiness, gazing at the reflections of the rapidly fluctuating colour patterns on the snowfield and the ice of the Sacred Hills.

It was the stillest time, almost tranquil. Vivid colour roiled and swelled, broke and ebbed, all across the heavens. Barely a breeze stirred. Perhaps as a result of the warp-eddies, the temperature had risen to just above zero.

In an anteroom in the monastery, ayatani carefully lit the oil lamps and then left without a word.

Gaunt put his cap and gloves on a side table. 'I... I'm very pleased you're here, but the commissar in me wants to know why. Feth, Colm! You were wounded and you had orders to evacuate!'

Corbec sat back on a daybed under the bolted, gloss-red shutters, his camo-cloak pulled around him like a shawl, and a cup of hot broth in his hands.

'Both facts true, sir. I'm afraid I can't really explain it.'

'You can't explain it?'

'No, sir. Not without sounding so mad you'll have me clapped in irons and locked in a padded cell immediately.'

'Let's risk that,' said Gaunt. He'd poured himself a glass of sacra, but realised he didn't really want it. He offered it to Rawne, who shook his head, and then to Dorden, who took it and sipped it. The Tanith chief medic sat near the central fire pit. Gaunt had never seen him look so old or so tired.

'Tell him, Colm,' Dorden said. 'Tell him, damn it. I didn't believe you at first either, remember?'

'No, you didn't.' Colm sipped his broth, put it down, and pulled a box of cigars from his hip pouch. He offered them around.

'If I may,' said ayatani Zweil, rising up from his floor mat to take one. With a surprised grin, Corbec lit it for him.

'Haven't had one for years,' smiled Zweil, enjoying the first few puffs. 'What's the worst it could do? Kill me?'

'Least of your worries now, father,' said Rawne.

'Too true.'

'I'm waiting, Colm,' said Gaunt.

'I... ah... let me see... how best to put it... I... well, the thing of it was... at first...'

'The saint spoke to him,' said Dorden abruptly.

Zweil exploded in a coughing fit. Corbec leaned forward to thump the old priest on the back.

'Corbec?' growled Gaunt.

'Well, she did, didn't she?' said Dorden. He turned to Gaunt and Rawne. 'Don't look at me like that, either of you. I know how mad it sounds. That's how I felt when Colm told it to me. But answer me this... What in the name of the good God-Emperor would make an old man like me come all this way too? Eh? It almost killed me. The fething Ladder of Heaven! It nearly killed all of us. But none of us are mad. None of us. Not even Colm.'

'Oh, thanks for that,' said Corbec.

'I need more,' began Gaunt.

'A whole fething lot more,' agreed Rawne, helping himself to a stiff drink after all.

'I had these dreams. About my old dad. Back on Tanith, Pryze County,' said Corbec.

'Aha. Here we go...' said Rawne.

'Get out if you don't want to listen!' spat Dorden. Rawne shrugged and sat. The mild old medic had never spoken to him like that before.

'He was trying to tell me something,' Corbec went on. 'This was right after I'd been through the clutches of that Pater Sin.'

'Trauma, then?' suggested Gaunt.

'Oh, very probably. If it makes it easier for you, we can pretend I slogged three hundred fething kilometres just because I wanted to be with you at the last stand of the Ghosts. And these people were fool enough to follow me.'

'That is easier to pretend,' said Rawne.

'Agreed, major,' said Gaunt. 'But humour us, Corbec, and tell us the rest.'

'Through my father, in my dreams, the saint called me. I can't prove it, but it's a fact. She called me. I didn't know what to do. I thought I was cracking up. Then I discovered Daur felt the same way. From the moment he was injured, he'd been taken by this niggle, this itch that wouldn't go away, no matter how hard he tried to scratch it.'

'Captain?' asked Gaunt. Daur sat over in the corner and so far he'd said nothing. The cold and fatigue of his hard journey had played hell with his wound-weakened state.

'It's as the colonel describes. I had a... a feeling.'

'Right,' said Gaunt. He turned back to Corbec. 'And then what? This feeling was so strong you and Daur broke orders, deserted, and took the others with you?'

'About that,' admitted Corbec.

'Breaking orders... Where have I heard that recently?' murmured Zweil, relighting his cigar.

'Shut up, father,' said Gaunt.

'Corbec told me what was going on,' said Dorden quietly. 'He told me what was in his head and what he planned to do. I knew he was trying to rope in able-bodied troopers to go with him. I tried to argue him out of it. But...'

'But?'

'But by then the saint had spoken to me too.'

'Feth me!' Rawne exclaimed.

'She'd spoken to you too, Tolin?' asked Gaunt steadily.

Dorden nodded. 'I know how it sounds. But I'd been having these dreams. About my son, Mikal.'

'That's understandable, doctor. That was a terrible loss for the Ghosts and for you.'

'Thank you, sir. But the more Corbec talked to me about his own dreams, the more I realised they were like mine. His dead father. My dead son. Coming to each of us with a message. Captain Daur was the same, but in a different way. Someone... something... was trying to communicate with us.'

'And so the three of you deserted?'

'Yes sir,' said Daur.

'I'm sorry about that, sir,' said Corbec.

Gaunt breathed deeply in contemplation. 'And the others? Were they spoken to?'

'Not as far as I know,' said Corbec. 'We just recruited them. Milo had come back with the wounded and desperately wanted to rejoin the company, so he was easy to convince. He brought in the girl, Sanian, her name is. She's esholi. We knew we needed local knowledge. But for her guidance we'd have been dead many times over by now. Shot, or frozen on the mountainside.'

'She found our way for us,' joked Dorden darkly. 'I pray to the Golden Throne she finds her own now.'

'Bragg, well, you know Try Again. He'd do any damn thing I tell him,' said Corbec. 'He was so eager to help. Derin, too. Vamberfeld, Nessa. When you've got a colonel, a captain and a chief medic asking you to break the rules and help them out, life or death, I think you go for it. None of them are to blame. None should be punished. They gave their all. For you, really.'

'For me?' asked Gaunt.

'That's why they were doing it. We'd convinced them it was a life or death mission above and beyond orders. That you'd have approved. That you'd have wanted it. That it was for the good of the Ghosts and for the Imperium.'

'You say you had to convince them, Corbec,' said Rawne. 'That implies you had to lie.'

'None of us lied, major,' said Dorden bluntly. 'We knew what we had to do and we told them about it. They followed, because they're loyal Ghosts.'

'What about the Pardus... Sergeant Greer is it?'

'We needed a driver, sir,' Daur said. 'I'd met Greer a little while before. He didn't need much convincing.'

'You told him about the saint and her messages?'

'Yes, sir. He didn't believe them, obviously.'

'Obviously,' echoed Rawne.

'So I...' Daur faltered, ashamed. 'I told him we were deserting to go and liberate a trove of ayatani gold from the Sacred Hills. Then he went along willingly, just like that.' Daur clicked his fingers.

'At last!' said Rawne, refilling his shot glass. 'A motivation I can believe.'

'Is there a trove of ayatani gold in the Sacred Hills?' Zweil asked, blowing casual but perfect smoke rings.'

'I don't believe so, father,' said Daur miserably.

'Oh good. I'd hate to be the last to know.'

Gaunt sat down on a stool by the door, ruminated, and stood up again almost at once. Corbec could tell he was nervous, edgy.

'I'm sorry, Ibram...' he began.

Gaunt held up a commanding hand. 'Save it, Colm. Tell me this... If I believe this miraculous story one millimetre... What happens now? What are you all here for?'

Corbec looked at Dorden, who shrugged. Daur put his head in his hands.

'That's where we all kind of run out of credibility, sir,' said Corbec.

'That's where it happens?' Rawne chuckled. 'Excuse me, Gaunt, but I thought that moment had passed long ago!'

'Perhaps, major. So.... none of you have any idea what you're supposed to do now you're here?'

'No, sir,' said Daur.

'Not a clue,' said Corbec.

'I'm sorry,' said Dorden.

'Very well,' said Gaunt. 'You should return to the billets arranged for you and get some sleep.'

The three members of the Wounded Wagon party nodded and began to get up.

'Oh no, no, no!' said Zweil suddenly. 'That's not an end to it! Not at all!'

'Father,' Gaunt began. 'It's late and we're all going to die in the morning. Let it go.'

'I won't,' said Zweil. He stubbed out his cigar butt in a saucer. 'A good smoke, colonel. Thank you. Now sit down and tell me more.'

'This isn't the time, father,' said Gaunt.

'It is the time. If this isn't the time, I don't bloody know what is! The saint spoke to these men, and sent them out after us on a holy cause!'

'Please,' said Rawne sourly.

'A holy cause! Like it or not, believe it or not, these men are Infardi!'

'They're what?' cried Rawne, reaching for his laspistol as he leapt up.

'Infardi! Infardi! What's your word for it...? Pilgrims! They're bloody pilgrims! They have come all this way in the name of the hallowed beati! Don't spurn them now!'

'Sit down, Rawne, and put the sidearm away. What do you suggest we do, Father Zweil?'

'Ask them the obvious question, colonel-commissar.'

'Which is?'

'What did the saint say to them?'

Gaunt ran his splayed hands back though his cropped blond hair. His left arm throbbed. 'Fine. For the record... What did the saint say to you?'

'Sabbat Martyr,' Dorden, Corbec and Daur replied in unison.

Gaunt sat down sharply.

'Oh sacred feth,' he murmured.

'Sir?' queried Rawne, getting up. 'What does that mean?'

'That means she's probably been speaking to me too.'

'SANIAN?' MILO CALLED her name as he edged down the dim corridors of the Shrinehold.

The wind outside wailed down the flues of the airshafts. Bizarre reflections of light from the warp storm outside spilled across the tiled floor from the casements. He saw a figure sitting on one of the hallway benches.

'Sanian?'

'Hello, Milo.'

'What are you doing?'

He could see what she was doing. Clumsily and inexpertly, she was field-stripping and loading an Imperial lasrifle.

She looked around at him as he approached, put down the chamber block and the dirty vizzy-cloth, and kissed him impetuously on the cheek. Her fingers left a smudge of oil on his chin.

'What was that for?'

'For helping me.'

'Helping you to do what?'

She didn't reply immediately. She was trying to screw in the rifle's barrel the wrong way.

'Let me,' said Milo, reaching around her to grip the weapon. 'So what have I helped you to do?'

She watched as his expert hands locked the rifle system together.

'Praise you to the saint, Brin. Praise you.'

'Why? What have I done?' he asked as she took the weapon from his hands.

'You,' she smiled. 'You and your Ghosts. From them, I have found my way. I am esholi no longer. I see the future. I see my way at last.'

'Your way? So... what is it?'

Outside, the warp storm blistered across the night sky.

'It's the only way there is,' she said.

'I'M SORRY, BUT this is crazy!' Rawne cried, hurrying to catch up with Gaunt, Dorden, Corbec, Zweil and Daur as they strode down the long cloisters of the Shrinehold heading for the holy sepulchre.

'What is this commotion?' asked an ayatani, coming out of a pair of inner doors.

'Go back to bed,' Zweil told him as they rushed past.

Gaunt stopped dead and they slammed into him from behind.

He turned around. 'Rawne's right! This is fething stupid! There's nothing in it!'

'You said yourself some voice has murmured "Sabbat Martyr" to you several times,' reminded Dorden.

'It did! I thought it did! Feth! This is madness!'

'How long have we been thinking that?' Dorden looked aside at Corbec.

'It doesn't matter how stupid it feels,' Zweil said. 'Get in there. Into the sepulchre! Test it!'

'I've already been there! You know that!' said Gaunt.

'On your own, maybe. Not with these other Infardi.'

'I wish you'd stop using that word,' said Rawne.

'And I wish you'd bugger off,' Zweil told him.

'Stop it! All of you!' cried Gaunt. 'Let's just go and see what happens...'

'VAMBS?' WHISPERED BRAGG, pushing open the heavy, red door of the sepulchre. He wasn't sure where he was, but it looked a feth of a lot like a place he shouldn't be.

The chamber was dark, the air was smoky and the floor was squeaky. Bragg edged across the shiny tiles carefully. They looked valuable. Too valuable for his big boots. 'Vambs? Mate?'

Scary holos of Space Marines loomed out of alcoves in the black walls.

'For feth's sake! Vambs?'

Behind the polished altar and under a big hood of what looked to Bragg like bone, he saw Vamberfeld, bending over a small hardwood casket in the shadows.

'Vambs?' Bragg approached the altar. 'What are you doing in here?'

'Look, Bragg!' Vamberfeld held up an object he had taken from the casket. 'It's her jiddi-stick! The cane used by Sabbat herself to drive her chelon to market.'

'Great. Uhm... I reckon you oughta put that back...' Bragg said.

'Should I? Maybe. Anyway, look at this, Bragg! Remember that broken crook I found? See? It matches exactly the broken haft they have here! Can you believe it? Exactly! I think I found a piece of the saint's actual crook!'

'I think I should get you to the doc, mate,' Bragg said carefully. 'We shouldn't be in here.'

'I think we should. I think I should.'

The sepulchre door creaked open behind them.

'Feth! Someone's coming in,' said Bragg, worried. 'Stay here. Don't touch anything else, okay? Not a thing.' He walked back into the main area of the sepulchre.

'What the feth are you doing here?' Vamberfeld heard Bragg ask a few seconds later.

He turned and stared out of the gloomy reliquary. His friend Bragg was talking to someone.

'Same as you, Tanith. I've come for the gold.'

'The gold? What fething gold?' Vamberfeld heard Bragg reply.

'Don't screw with me, big guy!' the other voice said.

'I have no intention of screwing with you. Put that auto down, Greer. It's not funny any more.'

Don't. Not in here, Vamberfeld thought. Please not in here. His hand was starting to shake.

He got up and came out of the reliquary. Greer was standing inside the big red door, which he'd closed behind him. He looked sick and desperate and twitchy. His skin was haggard and blotchy from the ordeal they'd all been through. He was pointing a guard-issue autopistol at Bragg.

The moment Vamberfeld appeared, Greer flicked the muzzle to cover him as well.

'Two of you, huh? I expected as much, that's why I came down here. Trying to cheat me out of my cut, huh? Did Daur put you up to this or are you stabbing him in the back too?'

'What the good feth are you talking about?' asked Bragg.

'The gold! The damn gold! Stop playing innocent!'

'There is no gold,' said Vamberfeld, trying to stop his hand shaking. 'I told you that.'

'Shut up! You're not right in the head, you psycho! You've got nothing I wanna hear!'

'Why don't you put the gun down, Greer?' asked Bragg, taking a step forward. The gun switched back to cover him.

'Don't move. Don't try that crap. Show me the gold! Now! You got here before me, you must've found it!'

'There is no gold,' Vamberfeld repeated.

'Shut the hell up!' spat Greer, swinging the gun back to cover the Verghastite.

'This is getting out of hand,' said Bragg. 'We gotta calm down...'

'Okay, okay,' Greer seemed to agree. 'Look, we'll split it three ways. Gold's heavy. I can't carry it all, and there's no way I'm staying here tonight. Chaos is going to be all over this shithole any time. Three way split. As much as we can take. You help me carry it back down the Ladder to the Chimera. What do you say?'

'I'd say... One, you know we'd never make it back all that way, especially laden down... Two, the whole planet's falling to Chaos, so there's nowhere to run to... And three, there is no fething gold.'

'Screw you, then! I'll take what I can myself! As much gold as I can carry!'

'There is no gold,' said Vamberfeld.

'Shut up, you head-job!' screamed Greer, aiming the gun at Vamberfeld. 'Make him shut up, Tanith! Make him stop saying that!'

'But it's true,' said Vamberfeld. His hand was shaking so much. So hard. Trying to make it stop, he pushed it into his pocket.

'What the hell? Are you going for a weapon?' Greer aimed the gun straight-armed at Vamberfeld, his finger squeezing.

'No!' Bragg lunged at Greer, grappling frantically at his weapon.

The pistol discharged. The round hit Vamberfeld in the chest and threw him over onto his back.

'Vambs!' Bragg raged in horror. 'God-Emperor feth you, you bastard!' His massive left fist crashed into Greer's face, hurling the Pardus back across the sepulchre with blood spurting from his broken nose and teeth. The gun fired again twice, sending one bullet through Bragg's right thigh and the other explosively through the front of the chelon-shell altar in a spray of lustrous shards.

Bragg lunged at Greer again, big hands clawing.

The Pardus sergeant's first shot didn't even slow Bragg down, even though it went right through his torso. Neither did the second. The third finally brought Bragg down, hard on his face, at Greer's feet.

'You stupid pair of bastards!' Greer snarled contemptuously at the fallen men, trying to staunch the blood pouring out of his smashed face.

The Verghastite lay on the floor beside Bragg, face up, staring at the roof shadows high above through sightless eyes. Bragg was face down. A wide and spreading lake of blood seeped out across the ancient, precious tiles from each of them. The Pardus sergeant strode in towards the sepulchre.

'WHAT THE FETH! Did you hear that?' Corbec cried.

'Shooting! From the sepulchre,' said Gaunt. He pulled his bolt pistol out and started to run. The others raced after him, Dorden lagging, his weary legs too leaden.

They burst into the sepulchre, Gaunt's boot slamming the massive door wide.

'Oh, feth me, no! Doc!' bellowed Corbec, gazing at the bodies and the blood.

'Who would do this?' Zweil gasped.

'There! Down there!' cried Rawne, his laspistol already drawn.

In the reliquary itself, Greer dived for cover behind the altar. He'd overturned the hardwood relic casket in his frantic search, spilling the ancient pieces across the floor. The glass covers over the gospel stands were smashed. The venerated Imperator armour was half-slumped off its palanquin.

'Where is it? Where's the gold, you bastards?' he screamed, ripping off several shots. Rawne cried out in pain as he was twisted round off his feet. Gaunt grabbed Zweil and threw himself down on top of the old priest as a shield. Corbec and Daur ducked hard. Dorden, just reaching the door, sought cover behind the frame.

'Greer! Greer! What the feth are you doing?' bawled Corbec.

'Back off! Back the hell off or I'll kill you all!' yelled Greer, firing three more shots that punched into the shrine's door or chipped the black corundum of the walls.

'Greer!' cried Daur. 'It's me! Daur! What are you doing?'

Several more shots whined over his head.

Daur had his laspistol out. He glanced at Corbec, hunched on the polished tiles next to him.

A meaningful look.

'Greer! You'll blow everything! You'll ruin it for us!'

'Where is it, Daur?' shouted Greer, slamming a new clip into his sidearm's grip. 'It isn't here!'

'It is! Gak it, Greer! You're screwing up all the plans!'

'Plans?' murmured Rawne through gritted teeth. Dorden was hastily dragging him back into the cover of the doorway. The bullet had punched through Rawne's forearm.

'You weren't going to do anything until I gave you the word!' Daur yelled, trying to edge forward. Greer fired again, crazing several six thousand year old shell-tiles.

'Plans change! You Ghosts were gonna ditch me!'

'No! We can still do this! You hear me? You want to? I can show you the gold! Go with me on this!'

'I dunno...'

'Come on!' cried Daur, and leapt upright, turning to point his laspistol at Corbec, Gaunt and the others.

'Drop the guns! Drop them!'

'What?' stammered Gaunt.

'I guess you got us, Daur,' said Corbec, tossing aside his laspistol and staring at Gaunt as hard as he could.

'I got them covered, Greer! Come on! We can run for it! Come on! I'll take you to the gold and we can leave these bastards to die! Greer!'

Greer rose from behind the altar, his gun in his hand. 'You know where the gold is?'

Daur turned, his aimed weapon swinging from the sheltering Ghosts to point at Greer.

'There is no gold, you stupid bastard,' he said, and shot Greer between the eyes.

Dorden ran into the room and knelt by the bodies of Bragg and Vamberfeld. 'They're a mess, but I've got pulses on both. Thank the Emperor the maniac wasn't packing a las. We need medic teams here right now.'

Standing in the doorway, clutching his bloody arm, Rawne spoke into his microbead. 'Three, in the sepulchre. I require medical teams here right now!'

Gaunt got back to his feet, and helped the winded Zweil up.

'Captain Daur, perhaps you'd give me a warning next time you plan to play a bluff that wild. I almost shot you.'

Daur turned to the colonel-commissar and held out his laspistol, butt-first. 'I doubt there'll be a next time. This is my fault. I led Greer on. I knew he was dangerous, I just didn't realise how gakking far he'd go.'

'What are you doing, Daur?' asked Gaunt, looking at the gun.

'It's a court-martial offence, sir,' said Daur.

'Oh, at least,' said Corbec, with a wide grin. 'Saving the lives of your commanding officers like that.'

'Nice,' Rawne nodded at Daur. 'I never realised you were such a devious bastard, captain.'

'We'll talk about this later, Daur,' said Gaunt, and walked past the altar and Greer's spread-eagled corpse. He stared in dismay at Greer's wanton desecration.

'Just so I'm absolutely sure,' Zweil whispered to Daur. 'There really isn't a trove of ayatani gold here, is there?'

Daur shook his head. 'Just, you know, checking.'

Gaunt righted the relic casket and began putting the scattered fragments back reverently.

'What's keeping Lesp?' growled Dorden. He was trying to keep compression on Bragg's most serious injury. 'I need a medicae kit. Both of them are bleeding out! Colm! Get some pressure there on Vamberfeld's chest. No, higher. Keep it tight!'

The sound of running footsteps came from outside. Milo and Sanian burst in through the doorway and stopped dead.

'I heard shooting,' said Milo, out of breath. 'Oh, great God-Emperor! What's happened? Bragg!'

'Everything's under control, lad,' said Corbec, his hands drenched in Vamberfeld's blood. He wasn't convinced. In the reliquary, Gaunt seemed almost beside himself with agony as he tried to set things right.

'What was that?' asked Rawne sharply, looking around.

'What was what?' said Corbec.

'That noise. That hum.'

'I didn't... Oh, yeah. That's kind of scary.'

'A vibration!' said Rawne. 'The whole place is shaking!'

'It must be the Infardi attacking!' said Milo.

'No,' said Zweil with remarkable calm. 'I think it must be the Infardi reaching the sepulchre.'

The candles flickered and went out all at once. Pale, undersea light washed through the ancient tomb, green and cold. The holograms of the Adeptus Astartes dissolved and vanished, and in their place columns of bright white hololithic light extended from floor to ceiling. The black stone walls sweated and a pattern of previously invisible geometric blue bars glowed into life out of the stone, all the way around the chamber. Everything shook with the deep, ultrasonic growl.

'What the feth is happening?' stammered Rawne.

'I can hear...' Daur began.

'So can I,' said Dorden, looking up in wonder. Silent, phantom lights like ball lightning shimmered and circled above their heads.

'I can hear singing,' said Corbec. 'I can hear my old dad singing.' There were tears in his eyes.

In the reliquary, Gaunt slowly rose to his feet and gazed at the bier on which Saint Sabbat lay.

He could smell the sweet, incorruptible fragrance of spices, acestus and islumbine. The body of the saint began to shine, brighter and brighter, until the white radiance was too bright to stare at.

'Beati...' Gaunt murmured.

The light streaming out from the bier was so fierce, all the humans within had to close their eyes. The last thing Corbec saw was the faint silhouette of Ibram Gaunt, kneeling before the saint's bier, framed by the white ferocity of a star's heart.

THE LIGHT DIED away, and the sepulchre returned to the way it had been before. Blinking, speechless, they gazed silently at each other.

For the time it had lasted, no more than a few seconds, a calm but inexorable psychic force of monumental power had penetrated their minds.

'A miracle,' murmured Zweil, sitting down on the floor. 'A proper miracle. A transcendant miracle. You all felt that, didn't you?'

'Yes,' sobbed Sanian, her face streaming with tears.

Dorden nodded.

'Of course we did,' said Corbec quietly.

'I don't know what that was, but I've never been so scared in my life,' said Rawne.

'I'm telling you, Major Rawne. It was a miracle,' said Zweil.

'No,' said Gaunt, emerging from the reliquary. 'It wasn't.'

SEVENTEEN
SABBAT'S MARTYR

'There are no miracles. There are only men.'

— Saint Sabbat, epistles

THE ERSHUL'S FINAL assault began at two o'clock on the morning of the seventeenth day. In the silence of a snow-less, clear night, under the spasming auroras of the warp storm, they committed their entire strength to the attack on the Shrinehold. Support columns of reinforcements had been pushing up the pass all day and into the night. The Ershul were legion-strength. Nine thousand devotee-warriors. Five hundred and seventy armoured machines.

Just under two thousand able-bodied Imperial troops defended the Shrinehold, supported by the last four Conquerors, one Executioner, one Destroyer, and a handful of Chimeras, Salamanders and Hydra batteries. All they had on their side was the strategic strength of their walled position and the comparative narrowness of the approach across the promontory.

The staggering power of the Ershul bombardment hammered down onto the Imperial lines. The honour guard did not fire back. They were so low on ammunition and shells they had to wait to pick their targets. The Ershul host advanced towards them.

Standing on the inner wall, Gaunt surveyed their approaching doom through his scope. Even by his best estimate, they would be able to hold out for no more than twenty or thirty minutes.

He turned and looked at Rawne and Hark. Rawne's arm was thickly bandaged.

'I don't really think it matters how we fight this now, but I want you both to head down and rally the men for as long as you can. Do anything you can to buy time.'

The men nodded.

'The Emperor protects,' Gaunt said, shaking them both by the hand.

'We're not done yet, sir,' said Hark.

'I know, commissar. But remember... sometimes the carniv gets you.'

The officers strode away down the wall steps together.

Walking towards their deaths, Gaunt thought, taking one last look at the major and the commissar. And I should be there with them.

He turned and hurried back to the sepulchre where the others were waiting.

'A MIRACLE!' AYATANI-AYT Cortona was declaring yet again, his principal clerics gathered around him.

'I keep telling you it's not,' growled Zweil, 'and I have it on good authority.'

'You are just imhava! What do you know?' snapped Cortona.

'A feth of a lot more than you, tempelum,' said Zweil.

'You've been hanging out with the wrong crowd, picking up filthy language like that,' Corbec said to Zweil.

'Story of my woebegotten life, colonel,' said Zweil.

Gaunt entered the sepulchre and everyone turned to him.

'There is so little time, I have to be brief. This was not a miracle.'

'But we all felt it! Throughout the Shrinehold! The blessed power, singing in our minds!' cried Cortona.

'It was a psychic test pattern. The activation signature of an ancient device that I believe is buried under the shrine.'

'A what?' asked one of the ayatani.

'The Adeptus Mechanicus constructed this place to house the saint. I believe they laced the entire rock underneath us with dormant psyker technology the power – and purpose – of which we can only guess at. Was I the only one who got that from the psychic wave? It seemed quite clear.'

'Technology to do what?' sneered Cortona.

'To protect the beati. In the event of a true catastrophe, like this influx of the warp. To safeguard her final prophecy.'

'Preposterous! Why did we not know of it then?' asked another Shrinehold priest. 'We are her chosen, her sons.'

'Six thousand years is a long time,' said Corbec. 'Time enough to forget. Time enough to turn facts into myths.'

'But why now? Why does it manifest now?' asked Cortona.

'Because we came. Her Infardi. Gathered together in her sepulchre, we triggered the mechanism.'

'How?'

'Because our minds responded to the call. Because we came. Because through us, the mechanism recognised the time for awakening had come.'

'That's nonsense! Blasphemy, even!' cried the ayatani-ayt. 'It presumes you soldiers are more holy than the sacred brotherhood! Why would it wake for you when it has never woken for us?'

'Because you're not enlightened. Not that way,' said Zweil, drawing a gasp from the priests. 'You tend, and keep vigil, and reread the texts. But you do so out of inherited duty, not belief. These men really believe.' He gestured to Corbec, Daur and Gaunt.

There was a lot of angry shouting.

'There's no time to debate this! You hear that? The forces of Chaos are at the gates! We have a chance to use the technology the saint has left for us. We have barely any time to figure out how.'

'Sanian and I have been studying the holograms, sir,' said Milo. He gestured to the glowing bars of light in the shrine's corundum walls, lights that had not yet faded.

'There are depictions of her holy crusade,' said Sanian, tracing certain runes. 'The triumphs of Frenghold, Aeskaria and Harkalon. A mention of her trusted commanders. Here, for instance, the name of Lord Militant Kiodrus...'

'You're going to have to cut to the chase,' Gaunt interjected. 'We've only got a few minutes left.'

Sanian nodded. 'The activation mechanism for the technology appears to be here.' She pointed to a small runic chart glowing on the wall. 'The pillar of the eternal flame, at the very tip of the promontory.'

'How are we to use it?'

'Something must be put in place,' said Sanian, frowning. 'Some trigger-icon. I'm not sure what this pictogram represents.'

'I am,' said Daur. He rose from his stool and took the silver trinket from his pocket. 'I think this is what we need.'

'You seem remarkably sure, Ban' said Gaunt.

'I've never been so sure about anything, sir.'

'Right. No more time for talk. Pass me that and I'll–'

'Sir,' said Daur. 'It was given to me. I think I'm supposed to do this.'

Gaunt nodded. 'Very well, Ban. But I'm coming with you.'

'RALLY! RALLY, MY brave boys and girls!' Soric yelled above the roar of explosions. Infardi shells had torn the gate and the front part of the inner wall away. 'This is what we were born for! Deny the arch-enemy of mankind! Deny him now!'

GAUNT, CORBEC, MILO, Sanian and Daur approached the back gate of the outer Shrinehold wall. The din of battle behind them was deafening.

They readied their weapons. Sanian hefted up her lasrifle.

'We're going to get killed out there,' Milo told her. 'Are you sure you want to do this?'

'My way, remember? War. War is the only true way and I have found it.'

'For Sabbat!' cried Gaunt and threw open the gate.

'POWER BATTERIES HAVE failed!' Pauk's gunner told him.

'Restart them! Restart them!' the lieutenant shouted.

'The couplings have burnt out! We've put too much stress on them!'

'Hell, there's got to be a way to–' Pauk began.

He never finished his sentence. Usurper shells atomised the old Executioner tank *Strife*.

'PULL THE LINE back! Feygor, pull the line back!' Rawne yelled. The Ershul or whatever their fething name was were all over their positions now.

THE PILLAR SEEMED a hundred kilometres away across the snow, gleaming at the very end of the jagged promontory. Gaunt and his party ran forward in the snow, las-fire from the circling enemy flank zapping over and between them.

'Come on!' Gaunt yelled, firing his bolt pistol at the green-clad Ershul storming forward to cut them off.

'No! No!' Corbec yelped as a las-round hit his leg and brought him down.

Sanian turned and fired her gun on full auto, ripping into the enemy. She wasn't used to the recoil and it threw her over into the snow.

'Sanian! Sanian!' Milo stopped to pull her up as Gaunt and Daur ran on. 'Come on! I'll get you back to the–'

The butt of her gun hit Milo in the side of the head and he fell over unconscious.

'Bless you, Milo, but you won't rob me of this,' she muttered. 'This is my way. I'm going to take it, in the name of the saint. Don't try to stop me. Forgive me.'

She ran after the others, leaving Milo curled in the snow.

Twenty metres ahead of her, Daur was hit. He fell sideways into the snow, screaming in anger.

Gaunt stopped and ran back to him. The wound was in his side. He was yelling. There was no way he was going to be able to carry on.

'Ban! Give me the trigger-icon! Ban!'

Daur held the silver trinket out, clasped in his bloody fingers.

'Whoever does this will die,' he said.

'I know.'

'The psychic burst told me that. It needs a sacrifice. A martyr.'

'I know.'

'Sabbat's martyr.'

'I know, Ban.'

'The Emperor protects, Ibram.'

'The Emperor protects.' Gaunt took the silver figurine and began to run towards the pillar. Ban Daur tried to rise. To see. The las-fire of the enemy was too bright.

THE THUNDER OF war, of armageddon, shook the walls. Hands bloody, Dorden fought to save Bragg's life in the Shrinehold antechamber Lesp had turned into a makeshift infirmary.

'Clamp! Here!'

Lesp obeyed.

It was futile, Dorden knew. Even if he saved Bragg's life, they were all dead.

'Foskin!' Dorden yelled over as he worked. 'How's Vamberfeld doing?'

'I thought you had him,' said Foskin, jumping up from his work on another of the injured.

'He isn't here,' said Chayker.'

'Where the feth has he gone?' Dorden cried.

THROUGH THE PRISMATIC scope of his sight, LeGuin saw Captain Marchese's P48J blow out in a swirl of sparks.

Barely a second later, the same AT70 that had killed Marchese and his crew put a shell through the side of the *Grey Venger*. LeGuin's layer and loader were both disintegrated. The Destroyer lurched and stopped dead, its turbines failing for the very last time. Fire swirled through the compartment, up under LeGuin's feet. His hair was singed.

He tried the hatch above him. It was jammed shut.

Resignedly, Captain LeGuin sat back in his command chair and waited for the end.

Freezing cold air gusted in around him as the hatch opened.

'Come on! Come on!' Scout Sergeant Mkoll yelled down at him, his arms outstretched. LeGuin looked around himself for a moment at the ruined interior of his beloved tank. 'Goodbye,' he said, and then reached up and allowed Mkoll to pull him out.

Mkoll and LeGuin had got twenty metres from the *Grey Venger* when it exploded and flattened them both.

'TOO MANY! Too many! cried Larkin, firing through his last remaining barrel.

Beside him, a las-shot struck Trooper Cuu in the shoulder and threw him back into the bloody snow.

'Oh, feth! Too many!' Larkin murmured.

'No, Tanith,' smiled Banda beside him as she fired again and again. 'Not nearly enough.'

'Think I win my wager,' croaked Cuu, staring up at the warp storm that blistered overhead. 'Sure as sure.'

* * *

GAUNT WAS JUST thirty metres from the pillar, running through the blitz of shots. Infardi were closing all around him.

He didn't feel the las-round hit his shin, but his leg went dead and he fell, tumbling over and over in the drifts.

'No,' he cried out. 'No, please...'

A figure bent over him. It was Sanian, her lasrifle trained on the advancing enemy. She sprayed off a burst and then turned to Gaunt.

'I'll take it. Let me.'

Gaunt knew he couldn't move unaided. 'Just help me up, girl. I can make it.'

'Give it to me! I can move faster alone! It's what she wants!'

Hesitating, Gaunt reached out his hand, the trigger-icon in it.

'Do it right, girl,' he said through pain-gritted teeth.

She took the silver icon.

'Don't worry, I–'

Fierce las-fire exploded in the snow around them.

Three Ershul troopers were just a few metres away.

Sanian turned to fire, the unfamiliar lasrifle awkward in her hands.

The closest Ershul aimed his weapon to kill her. She threw herself down in desperation.

Pin-point las-fire toppled her would-be killer and the two Ershul behind him.

Spraying las-shots into the face of the enemy, Milo ran to them both, blood streaming from his head.

'Good work, Milo,' said Gaunt, struggling for breath and rising on his elbow to fire his bolt pistol.

'The icon! Where is it?' Milo called, looking around. 'I can make it! It's not far! Where the feth is it?'

'It was here! I had it in my hand!' Sanian replied, groping about in the snow as blisteringly intense shots fell around them.

'Where is it? Oh, God-Emperor! Where the hell is it?'

MAJOR KLEOPAS WAS smiling. He didn't need his augmetic implant to see it. The view through the scope was clear. The last round fired from the *Heart of Destruction* had destroyed a Reaver in a bloom of fire.

But it was the last round. The last round ever.

His valiant crew was dead. Flames filled his turret basket, igniting his clothes. He couldn't move to escape. Shrapnel had destroyed his legs and severed his spine.

'Damn. You. All. To. Hell,' he gasped out, word by word, as the inferno surged up around him and consumed him.

THE GHOSTS AROUND him were falling back in panic in the face of the overwhelming host.

'There's nowhere to run to,' mumbled Commissar Hark, firing at the foe. Blood from a head wound was running down his cheek and he'd lost his cap.

An Ershul officer, another swirling ball of shield energy, loomed ahead of him. He'd killed three of its kind so far. Hark hoped this was Pater Sin.

'For the saint! For the Ghosts! For Gaunt!' he bellowed at the top of his voice.

He fired his plasma pistol and the shield exploded.

HALF-BURIED IN the snow under the enemy onslaught, Sanian cried out, 'Oh my lord! Look! Look!'

Returning fire, Gaunt and Milo both looked around.

'Good feth,' Gaunt stammered.

IT WAS COLD out there, on the edge of the promontory. From below the lip, howling gorge winds cut like knives. Overhead, the warp storm blistered the heavens.

The pillar stood just ahead, a massive finger of corundum, fire flaming from the top of it.

Close now.

It was hard going. He'd been hurt badly. Including the chest wound Greer had dealt him, he had seven wounds. Las-fire from the Ershul had stabbed at him ferociously these last ten metres.

Daur's silver trinket was clamped tightly in his hands. It had just been lying there, in the snow, as if it was waiting for him.

A las blast clipped his calf. *Eight*.

Almost there.

He could see her piercing eyes. The little girl, the herder. He could smell the wet stink of the chelons' nests and the cold wind of the high pastures.

He could smell the fragrances of acestus and wild islumbine.

Vamberfeld slumped against the cold, hard side of the watch flame pillar. He uncurled his fingers from the silver trinket and placed it in the recess, just like he had been shown during the miracle.

His hand wasn't shaking any more.

That was good.

An Ershul bolter round blew out the back of his head.

Vamberfeld fell back into the snow, a sad smile on his face.

Nine.

EIGHTEEN
HONOUR GUARD

'Taken at face value, we were clearly mad.
Actually, I believe we're clearly mad most of the rest of the time,
so go fething figure.'

— Colm Corbec, at Hagia

FROM DEEP INSIDE its planetary core, obeying ancient instructions, the mechanisms of the saint came alive. Vast psychic amplifiers woke and broadcast their signal.

For just an instant.

An instant enough to send abject fear into the souls of the Chaos spawn infesting the planet.

An instant enough to cremate the minds of Ershul hosts choking up across the promontory.

An instant enough to blow back the warp storm with such force that the advancing fleet was tumbled aside.

An instant enough to show Tolin Dorden his smiling son again, to show Colm Corbec one last glimpse of his father, to show Ban Daur a final vision of the old woman with the shockingly white hair in the refugee crowd.

To show Trooper Niceg Vamberfeld the hard, penetrating eyes of the chelon herdsgirl in the last moment of his life.

OUTSIDE THE SHRINEHOLD, under a cold, blue sky, Ibram Gaunt limped out, and down a churned-up mass of snow and stone that used to be steps. He was clad in full dress uniform.

The remnants of the convoy waited below.

Beyond them, littered across the snows of the promontory, lay the fused and charred skeletons of nine thousand Chaos-touched humans and the blackened wrecks of over five hundred war machines.

'Hark?'

Hark stepped up and saluted the colonel-commissar.

'Units present and numbers correct, sir.'

'Very good.' Gaunt paused and looked back along the promontory at the lonely post tomb the tempelum ayatani had erected in the snow and rock beside the corundum pillar of the eternal watch fire.

Gaunt climbed up into his waiting Salamander.

'Honour guard, mount up!'

'As the commander orders, mount up and make ready!' Hark relayed down the line. Cries came back.

'Column ready to move out, sir,' Hark reported.

Gaunt thought of Slaydo for a moment and the old blood pact. He touched the scar on his palm. Then he took one last look back at Vamberfeld's lonely post tomb.

'Honour guard, advance!' he cried, making a sweeping gesture with his hand.

The units began to rumble forward, under a spotless sky of frozen blue, down towards the head of the pass.

THE GUNS OF TANITH

FOR TANITH • FOR THE EMPEROR

For Ben Stampton, with thanks for Larkin and the Angel

'LATE IN THE *sixteenth year of the Sabbat Worlds Crusade, Warmaster Macaroth's incisive advance on the strategically vital Cabal system, which had been so strong and confident in its initial phase, juddered to a halt. Three-quarters of the target planets, including two of the infamous fortress-worlds, had been taken by Imperial Crusade forces and the occupying armies of the Chaos arch enemy routed or put to flight. But, as many Navy commanders had warned, the push had overreached itself, creating as it did a salient vulnerable on three sides.*

'Orlock Gaur, one of the arch enemy's most able warlords, making good use of the vicious loxatl mercenaries, drove an inspired counter-offensive along the advance's coreward flank, taking, in quick succession, Enothis, Khan V, Caius Innate and Belshiir Binary. Vital supply lanes, especially those providing fuel resources for the stretched Crusade fleet, were cut. Macaroth's valiant gamble, which he had hoped might win him the campaign outright, now seemed foolhardy. Unless fresh supply lines could be forged, and new fuel resources made available, the hard-won Cabal Salient would crumble. At best, the Imperial advance would be forced into retreat. At worst, it would collapse and be overrun.

'Warmaster Macaroth hastily redeployed significant elements of his spinward flank in a make or break effort to open up new lines of supply. All those involved knew the outcome of this improvised action would certainly decide the fate of the Cabal Salient, and perhaps the war itself.

The key target worlds were the promethium-rich planets of Gigar, Aondrift Nova, Anaximander and Mirridon, the forge world Urdesh, Tanzina IV and Ariadne with their solid fuel reserves, and the vapour mills of Rydol and Phantine...'

— from *A History of the Later Imperial Crusades*

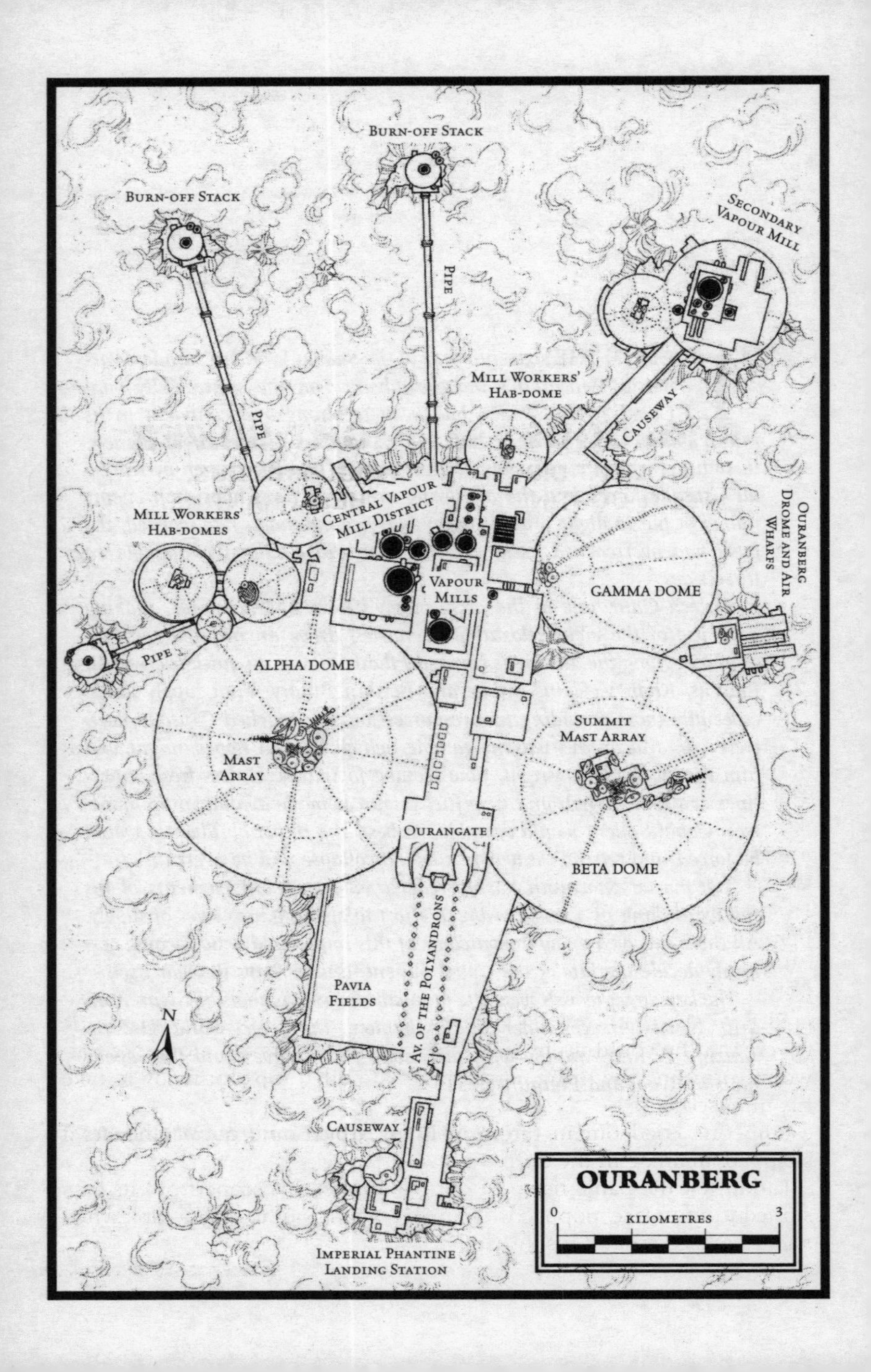

Burn-off Stack
Burn-off Stack
Secondary Vapour Mill
Pipe
Pipe
Mill Workers' Hab-dome
Causeway
Central Vapour Mill District
Mill Workers' Hab-domes
Ouranberg Drome and Air Wharfs
Vapour Mills
Gamma Dome
Pipe
Alpha Dome
Summit Mast Array
Mast Array
Ourangate
Beta Dome
Av. of the Polyandrons
Pavia Fields
N
Causeway
Imperial Phantine Landing Station
OURANBERG
0
Kilometres
3

PROLOGUE: STRAIGHT SILVER

COMBAT DISPERSAL DROGUE NIMBUS, WEST CONTINENTAL REACHES, PHANTINE, 211.771, M41

'I don't think any of us knew what we were getting into. Feth, I'm glad I didn't know what we were getting into.'

– Sgt. Varl, 1st Team leader, Tanith First

A CHOKE-HOLD was the last thing he expected.

Trooper Hlaine Larkin landed with a jarring thump in a place so dark he couldn't even see his hand in front of his face. He immediately got right down like the colonel had told him in practice. Belly down.

Somewhere in the dark, to his right, he heard Sergeant Obel scolding the men in the fireteam to hug cover. That was a joke for starters. Cover? How could they find cover when they couldn't even see the arse of the man in front?

Larkin lay down on his front and reached about until his fingers found an upright surface. A stanchion, maybe. A bulkhead. He slithered towards it, and then unshipped his long-las from its soft plastic cover. That he could do by touch alone. His fingers ran along the nalwood furniture, the firing mechanism, the oiled top-slot ready to take his nightscope.

Someone cried out in the darkness nearby. Some poor feth who'd snapped an ankle in the drop.

Larkin felt the panic rising in him. He pulled his scope from its bag, slotted it into place, popped the cap, and was about to take a look when an arm locked around his throat.

'You're dead, Tanith,' said a voice in his ear.

Larkin twisted, but the grip refused to break. His blood thudded in his temples as the choke-hold tightened and pinched his windpipe and carotid arteries. He tried to call 'Man out!' but his throat was shut.

There was a popping sound, and illumination flares banged off overhead. The drop area was suddenly, starkly lit. Pitch-black shadows, angular and hard, stabbed across him.

He saw the knife.

Tanith silver, straight, thirty centimetres long, hovering in front of his face.

'Feth!' Larkin gurgled.

A whistle blew, shrill and penetrating.

'GET UP, YOU idiot,' ordered Commissar Viktor Hark, striding down the field line of the bay with the whistle in his hand. 'You, trooper! Get up! You're facing the wrong damned way!'

The roof-lamps began to fizzle on, drenching the wide bay with stale yellow light. In amongst the litter of packing crates and corrugated iron, soldiers in black combat fatigues blinked and got to their feet.

'Sergeant Obel!'

'Commissar?'

'Get up here!'

Obel hurried forward to meet the commissar. Behind Hark, harmless low-pulse las-fire flashed in the gloom.

'Stop that!' Hark yelled, turning. 'They're all dead anyway! Cease fire and reset your position to starting place two!'

'Yes, sir!' a voice floated back from the enemy side.

'Report?' Hark said, looking back at the red-faced Obel.

'We dropped and dispersed, sir. Theta pattern. We had cover–'

'How wonderful for you. Do you suppose it matters that eighty per cent of your unit was facing the wrong way?'

'Sir. We were... confused.'

'Oh dear. Which way's north, sergeant?'

Obel pulled his compass from his fatigues. 'That way, sir.'

'At last. Those dials glow in the dark for a reason, sergeant.'

'Hark?'

Commissar Hark snapped to attention. A tall figure in a long storm coat walked across the bay to join him. He looked for all the world like Hark's shadow, drawn out and extended by the bad lights.

'How do you think you did?' asked Colonel-Commissar Ibram Gaunt.

'How do I think I did? I think you slaughtered us. And deservedly.'

Gaunt covered a smile. 'Be fair, Hark. Those men there are all behind cover. They'd have soon realised which way was up if that'd been real las-fire.'

'That's generous, sir. I figure it a good seventy-five point win to the passive team.'

Gaunt shook his head. 'No more than fifty-five, sixty points. You still had an opening you could have used.'

'I hate to correct you, sir,' said a tall, lean Tanith in a camo-cape who wandered casually out of Obel's lines. He was screwing the top back onto a paint stick.

'Mkvenner?' Gaunt greeted the grim scout, one of Sergeant Mkoll's elite. 'Go on then, disabuse me.'

Mkvenner had the sort of long, high cheek-boned face that made everything he said seem chilling and dark. He had a blue half-moon tattoo under his right eye.

Many reckoned he looked a lot like Gaunt himself, though Mkvenner's hair was Tanith black where Gaunt's was straw blond. And Gaunt was bigger too: taller, wider, more imposing.

'We heard them drop in during the blackout, and I got five men in amongst them.'

'Five?'

'Bonin, Caober, Doyl, Cuu and myself. Knives only,' he added, gesturing with the paint stick. 'We splashed a good eight of them before the lights came on.'

'How could you see?' asked Obel plaintively.

'We wore blindfolds until the lights went out. Our night vision was adjusted.'

'Good work, Mkvenner,' sighed Gaunt. He tried to avoid Hark's stern look.

'You had us cold,' said Hark.

'Evidently,' replied Gaunt.

'So... they're not ready. Not for this. Not for a night drop.'

'They'll have to be!' Gaunt growled. 'Obel! Get your sorry excuses for soldiers up into those towers again! We'll reset and do it over!'

'Yes, sir!' Obel replied smartly. 'Uhm... Trooper Loglas snapped his shin in the last exercise. He'll need a medic.'

'Feth!' said Gaunt. 'Right, go. Everyone else, reset!'

He waited for a moment as medics Lesp and Chayker carried the moaning Loglas out of the bay. The rest of Obel's detachment were clambering up the scaffolding of the sixteen metre tall drop towers and recoiling the rappelling cables, ready to resume drop positions.

'Lights down!' yelled Gaunt. 'Let's do this again until we get it right!'

'YOU HEARD HIM!' gasped Larkin. 'It's over! We're going again!'

'Lucky for you, Tanith.'

The choke-hold relaxed and Larkin fell sideways at last, panting for breath.

Trooper Lijah Cuu stepped over him and sheathed his silver blade.

'Still, I got you, Tanith. Sure as sure.'

Larkin gathered up his weapon, coughing. The whistle was shrilling again.

'Fething idiot! You nearly killed me!'

'Killing you was the point of the exercise, Tanith,' Cuu grinned, fixing the flustered master-sniper with his feline gaze.

'You're supposed to tag me with that!' Larkin snapped, nodding at the unopened paint stick hooked in Cuu's webbing.

'Oh, yeah,' marvelled Cuu, as if he'd never seen the stick before.

'Larkin! Trooper Larkin!' Sergeant Obel's voice sang across the bay. 'Do you intend to join us?'

'Sir!' Larkin snapped, stuffing his long-las back into its cover.

'Double-time, Larkin! Come on!'

Larkin looked back at Cuu, another surly curse forming in his mouth. But Cuu had disappeared.

OBEL WAS WAITING for him at the base of one of the towers. The last few men were clambering up the scaffold, encumbered by full assault kit. A couple had stopped at the foot of the tower to take sponges from a water can and smear away the tell-tale traces of red paint from their fatigues.

'Problem?' asked Obel.

'No, sir,' said Larkin, adjusting the sling of his gun-case. 'Except that Cuu's a fething menace.'

'Unlike the actual enemy, who is soft and cuddly. Get your scrawny butt up that tower, Larkin.'

Larkin heaved himself up the metalwork. Overhead, the lighting rigs were shutting off, one by one.

Sixteen metres up, there was a grilled shelf on which the men were forming up in three lines. Ahead of them was a scaffolding arch that was supposed to simulate the size and shape of a drop-ship's exit hatch, and which led out to a stepboard ramp that someone had dryly named 'the plank'. Gutes, Garond and Unkin, the three point men, were crouching there, drop-cables coiled on their laps. One end of each cable was secured to locking clamps on the gantry above the plank.

'In line, come on,' Obel muttered as he moved down the fireteams. Larkin hurried to take his place.

'Dead, Larks?' asked Bragg, making space for him.

'Feth, yes. You?'

Bragg patted a red stain on his tunic that he hadn't managed to sponge out.

'Never even saw 'em,' he said.

'Quiet in the line!' barked Obel. 'Tokar! Tighten that harness or you'll hang up. Fenix... where are your fething gloves?'

The last of the lights were going out. Down below somewhere, Hark was blowing his whistle. Three short bursts. The two minutes ready call.

'Stand by!' Unkin called back down the waiting rows.

Larkin couldn't see the men on the neighbouring towers. He couldn't even see the towers themselves. The gloom was worse than even the most moonless night back on Tanith.

'Make way,' whispered a voice behind them. A hooded flashlight cast a small green glow and showed another man joining them on the tower shelf.

It was Gaunt.

He moved in amongst them. 'Listen up,' he hissed, just loud enough for them all to hear. 'I know you're new to this drill, and that none of you like it, but we've got to get it down by the numbers. There'll be no landing at Cirenholm. I can guarantee that. The pilots are first class, and they'll get us in as close as possible, but even then it might be a lot further than sixteen metres.'

Several troopers groaned.

'The drop cable's thirty metres,' said Garond. 'What happens if it's further than that, sir?'

'Flap your arms,' said Gaunt. There was some chuckling.

'Hook up and slide fast. Keep your knees bent. And move. The drop-ships can't stay on station any longer than is absolutely necessary. You're going out three at a time, and there may be more than one man on a cable at any time. When you reach the deck, move clear. Is that a bayonet, trooper?'

'Yes sir.'

'Put it away. No fixed blades until you're down, not even in the real thing. Weapons on safety. If you've got folding stocks, fold them. Get all your harness and webbing straps tight and tuck them in. And remember, when the real thing comes, you'll all be in gas-hoods, which will add to the fun. I'm sure Sergeant Obel has told you all this.'

'It tends to sink in when you repeat it, sir,' said Obel.

'I'm sure it does.' Gaunt took off his storm coat and his cap and buckled on a hook-belt. 'Loglas is out, so you're a man short. I'll stand in.' He took his place in the number four slot of the right hand squad. Hark's whistle wailed out one long note. Gaunt snapped off his lamp. It was pitch dark.

'Let's go,' he hissed. 'Call the drill, sergeant.'

'Over the DZ!' Obel instructed, now speaking via the vox-headsets. 'Deploy! By the front! Cables out!'

'Cables away!' chorused the point men in the dark, spilling their lines down expertly from the plank. They were already hooked up.

'Go!'

Larkin could hear the abrasive buzz of the cables as they went taut and took the weight of the first men.

'Go!'

Drizzles of low-pulse fire twinkled in the darkness below. Larkin stepped up under the arch, holding the tunic tail of the man in front. Then the man was gone.

'Go!'

He groped for the line, found it, and snapped his arrestor hook around it.

'Come on!'

Larkin pulled his harness tight and went over into space. He swung wildly. The hook bucked and whined as its brake disk clamped at the cable. He could smell nylon burning with the friction.

The impact seemed even harder than the last time. The deck smacked the wind out of him. He struggled to release his hook, and rolled clear just before the man after him came hissing down.

He was on his belly again, like last time. His shoulder nudged a hard surface as he crawled forward and he moved his back against it. Where were the flares? Where were the fething flares?

His long-las was out of its cover, and the scope in place. Someone ran past him and his vox ear-piece was busy with man to man signals.

Larkin sighted. The night scope gave him vision, showed him the world as a green, phantom swirl. The enemy gun flashes were hot little spikes of light that left afterimages on the viewfinder.

He saw a figure in cover to his left, down behind some oil drums.

It was Mkvenner, with a paint stick in his hand.

'Pop!' said Larkin, and his gun fizzled a low-energy charge.

'Feth!' said Mkvenner, and sat back hard. 'Man out!'

Flares burst overhead. Crackling, blue-white light shimmered down over the DZ.

'Up and select!' Obel ordered curtly over the vox-link.

Larkin looked around. They were in place, facing the right fething way this time.

Men moved forward. Larkin stayed put. He was more use to them static and hunting.

He saw Bonin stalking two of his team and popped him out of the game too.

Flash charges went off down to Larkin's right. The bay rang. Some of Obel's squad, along with men from the neighbouring tower, had engaged full-on with the passive team. Larkin heard the call 'Man out!' five or six times.

Then he heard someone cry out in real pain.

Hark's whistle was blowing. 'Cease! Cease and stay put!'

The lights came on again, slowly and feebly.

Hark appeared. 'Better. Better, Obel.'

The men began getting up. Bonin moved past Larkin. 'Nice one,' he said.

Gaunt walked out into one of the pools of light. 'Mkvenner?' he called. 'Score it up.'

'Sir,' said Mkvenner. The scout looked unhappy.

'You get tagged?' Gaunt asked.

'Think it was Larkin, sir. We got about thirty points that time, all told.'

'That should make you a bit happier,' Gaunt said to Hark.

'Medic!'

Everyone turned. Bragg stumbled out from behind some empty munition boxes, clutching a deep red stain on his shoulder that wasn't paint.

'What happened?' asked Gaunt.

'Cuu stuck me,' growled Bragg.

'Trooper Cuu, front and centre!' Hark bellowed.

Cuu emerged from cover. His face, split by an old scar from top to bottom, was expressionless.

'You want to explain?' Hark asked him.

'It was dark. I tussled with the big f… with Bragg. I was sure I had my paint stick in my hand, sir. Sure as sure.'

'He jabbed me with his fething blade,' Bragg complained sourly.

'That's enough, Bragg. Go find a medic,' said Gaunt. 'Cuu. Report to me at sixteen hundred for discipline detail.'

'Sir.'

'Salute, damn you.'

Cuu made a quick salute.

'Get into line and don't let me see that blade again until we're in combat.'

Cuu wandered back to the passive unit. As he passed Larkin, he turned and glared at the sniper with his cold, green eyes.

'What are you looking at, Tanith?'

'Nothing,' said Larkin.

'LET ME EXPLAIN,' said Sergeant Ceglan Varl. He laid his guard-issue lasrifle on the counter of the Munitorium store and brushed the backs of his fingers down the length of it like a showman beginning a trick. 'This here is a standard pattern mark III lascarbine, stamped out by the armourers of Tanith Magna, God-Emperor rest their oily fingers. Notice the wooden stock and sleeve. That's nice, isn't it? Real Tanith nalwood, the genuine article. And the metalwork, all buffed down to reduce shine. See?'

The Munitorium clerk, a paunchy, dimpled man with greasy red hair and starchy robe, stood on the other side of the counter and stared back at Varl without any show of interest.

'Here's the thing,' said Varl, tapping the weapon's ammunition slot. 'That's a size three power port. Takes size three power cells. They can be short, long, sickle-pattern, box-form or drum, but they have to be size three or they won't fit. Size three. Thirty mil with a back-slant lock. With me so far?'

The clerk shrugged.

Varl took a power clip from his musette bag and slid it across the counter.

'You've issued my company with size fives. Size fives, you see? They're thirty-four mil and flat-fronted. You can tell they're not threes just by looking at the size of them, but if you're in any doubt, the fething great "5" stencilled on the side is a handy guide.'

The clerk picked up the clip and looked at it.

'We were instructed to issue ammunition. Eight hundred boxes. Standard pattern.'

'Standard size three,' said Varl patiently. 'That's standard size five.'

'Standard pattern, they said. I've got the docket.'

'I'm sure you have. And the Tanith First-and-Only have got boxes and boxes of ammo that they can't use.'

'It said standard pattern.'

Varl sighed. 'Everything's standard pattern! This is the Imperial fething Guard! Standard pattern boots, standard pattern mess-tins, standard pattern bodybags! I'm a standard pattern infantryman and you're a standard pattern no-neck, and any minute now my standard pattern fist is going to smack your nose bone back into your very sub-standard pattern brain!'

'There's no need to be abusive,' said the clerk.

'Oh, I think there might be,' said Sergeant Gol Kolea quietly, joining Varl at the counter. Kolea was a big man, an ex-miner from Verghast, and he towered over his Tanith comrade. But it wasn't his size that immediately alarmed the clerk. It was his soft tone and calm eyes. Varl had been spiky and aggressively direct, but the newcomer oozed potent wrath held in restraint below the surface.

'Tell him, Gol,' said Varl.

'I'll show him,' said Kolea and waved his hand. Guardsmen, all of them the so-called Ghosts, began to troop in, lugging ammo boxes. They started to stack them on the counter until there wasn't any more room. Then they started to pile them on the deck.

'No, no!' cried the clerk. 'We'll have to get counter-signed dockets before you can return these.'

'Tell you what,' said Kolea, 'let's not. Let's just swap these for boxes of size threes.'

'We... we don't have size threes,' said the clerk.

'You what?' Varl cried.

'We weren't told to carry any. On Phantine, size five is the–'

'Don't say standard pattern. Don't say it!' warned Varl.

'You're saying the blessed and hallowed Munitorium has no ammunition for the entire Tanith regiment?' asked Kolea.

'Feth!' Varl cursed. 'We're about to assault... what's it called?'

'Cirenholm,' said Kolea helpfully.

'That's the place. We're about to assault it and this is what you tell us? What are we supposed to use?' Varl pulled his Tanith knife from its sheath and showed the clerk the long, straight silver blade. 'Are we supposed to take the city using these?'

'If we have to.'

The Ghosts snapped to attention. Major Elim Rawne had wandered silently into the store. 'We've had to do worse. If Tanith straight silver is all I have, then it's all I need.'

The major looked at the clerk and the clerk shivered. Rawne's gaze tended to do that. There was a touch of snake about him, in his hooded eyes and cold manner. He was slim, dark and good-looking and, like many of the Tanith men, had a tattoo. Rawne's was a small blue star under his right eye.

'Varl, Kolea... get your men back to the billet. Round up the other squad leaders and run an inventory. I want to know just how much viable ammunition we've got left. Account for all of it. Don't let any of the men stash stuff in socks or musette bags. Pool it all and we'll distribute it evenly.'

The sergeants saluted.

'Feygor,' said Rawne, turning to his sinister adjutant. 'Go with them and bring the count back to me. Don't take all day.'

Feygor nodded and followed the troopers out.

'Now,' said Rawne, facing the clerk again. 'Let's see what we can sort out...'

TROOPER BRIN MILO, the youngest Ghost, sat down on his cot and looked across at the young man on the next bunk.

'That's very nice,' said Milo, 'and it will get you killed.'

The other man looked up, puzzled and wary. He was a Verghastite by the name of Noa Vadim, one of the many new Ghosts recruited after the siege of Vervunhive to replenish the ranks of the Tanith regiment. There was still a lot of rivalry between the two camps. The Tanith resented the new intake, and the Verghastites resented that resentment. In truth, they were slowly fusing now. The regiment had endured the fight for the shrineworld of Hagia a few months before and, as is ever the case with war, comradeship and a common goal had alloyed the Tanith and Verghast elements into one strong company.

But still, Verghastites and Tanith were breeds apart. There were so many little differences. Like accents – the gruff Vervunhive drawl beside the sing-song Tanith lilt. Like colouring – the Tanith were almost universally pale skinned and dark haired where the Verghastites were a rather more mixed lot, as was typical with a hive city of such size. The Verghastites' weapons had folding metal stocks and hand-plates where the guns of Tanith had sturdy nalwood furniture.

Vadim held the biggest difference in his hands: the regimental pin. The recruits from Vervunhive wore a silver axe-rake design denoting their home world. The Tanith wore a gold, wreath-surrounded skull backed by a single dagger that carried the motto 'For Tanith, for the Emperor'.

'What do you mean, "killed"?' asked Vadim. He'd been polishing his axe-rake pin with a hank of vizzy-cloth until it shone. 'There's a dress inspection at twenty hundred.'

'I know... and there's a night assault in the next day or two. Something that shiny will pick up any backscattered light.'

'But Commissar Gaunt expects–'

'Gaunt expects every man to be battle-prepped when we fall in. That's what the inspection's for. Ready for war, not ready for the parade ground.'

Milo tossed his own slouch cap across to the Vadim and the young Vervunhiver caught it. 'See?'

Vadim looked at the Tanith badge pinning back the brim-fold. It was clean, but non-reflective, dulled like granite.

'A little camo-paint and spit. Or boot-wax. Takes the shine right off.'

'Right.' Vadim peered more closely at Milo's pin. 'What are these rough edges here? On either side? Like something's been snapped off.'

'The skull was backed by three daggers originally. One for each of the original founded regiments. The Tanith First, the Tanith Second and the Tanith Third. Only the Tanith First made it off the home world.'

Vadim had heard the story secondhand a few times, but he had never plucked up the nerve to ask a Tanith about it directly. In honour of his service to Warmaster Macaroth's predecessor, Gaunt had been given personal command of the Tanith forces. That in itself was unusual, a commissar in command. Commissars were political officers. It explained why Gaunt's official rank was colonel-commissar.

On Tanith, about six years earlier, on the very day of the Founding, the legions of the arch-enemy had swept in. Tanith was lost, there was no question. For Gaunt, there had been a choice: stay and die with every man, or withdraw with what strengths he could save to fight another day. He had chosen the latter, and escaped with only the men of the Tanith First. The Tanith First-and-Only. Gaunt's Ghosts.

Many of the Ghosts had hated Gaunt for that, for cheating them out of the chance to fight for their world. Some, like Major Rawne, still did. But the last few years had shown the wisdom of Gaunt's decision.

Gaunt's Ghosts had chalked up a string of battlefield victories that had significantly helped the Crusade endeavour. He'd made them count, which made sense of saving them.

And at Vervunhive, perhaps Gaunt's most lauded victory so far, the Ghosts had benefited from new blood. The Verghastite recruits: scratch company guerillas, ex-hive soldiery, dispossessed civilians, all given the chance to join by Warmaster Macaroth as a mark of respect for the shared defence of the great hive.

'We snapped the side daggers off the crest,' said Milo. 'We only needed one piece of Tanith straight silver to remind us who we were.'

Vadim tossed the cap back to Milo. The billet room around them was a smoky haze of men lolling in bunks or finessing kit. Domor and Brostin were having a game of regicide. Nehn was playing a little box-pipe badly.

'How you finding the drills?' Milo asked Vadim.

'The drop stuff? It's okay. Easy enough.'

'You think? We've done rope deployments before a few times, but not in the dark. And they say the drop could be a long one. I hate heights.'

'I don't notice them,' said Vadim. He'd taken a tin of boot-wax out of his kitbag and was beginning to apply it to his pin as Milo had suggested.

'Why?'

Vadim grinned. He wasn't much older than Milo, perhaps early twenties. He had a strong nose and a generous mouth, and small, dark mischievous eyes. 'I was a roofer. I worked repairing the masts and plating on the Main Spine. High level stuff, mostly without a harness. I guess I'm used to heights.'

'Feth!' said Milo, slightly impressed. He'd seen Vervunhive Main Spine himself. There were smaller mountains. 'Any tips?'

'Yeah,' said Vadim. 'Don't look down.'

'Twenty-three hundred hours tomorrow night will be D-hour,' said Lord General Barthol Van Voytz. He folded the fingers of his white-gloved hands together, almost as if in prayer. 'May the Emperor protect us all. Field muster begins at twenty thirty, by which time, given advance meteorology, the drogues should be manoeuvring into the dispersal field. I want drop-ships and support air-ready by twenty-one thirty, when mount up commences. First wave launch is at twenty-two hundred, with second wave ten minutes after that and third wave at twenty-two thirty.'

He glanced around the wide, underlit chart table at his officers. 'Questions?'

There were none, not immediately anyway. Gaunt, two places to Van Voytz's left, leafed through his copy of the assault orders. Outside the force-dome surrounding the briefing session, the bridge crew of the mighty drogue manned their stations and paced the polished hardwood decks.

'Let's remind ourselves what's on offer,' said the lord general, nodding to his adjutant. Like the lord general, the aide was dressed in a crisp, emerald green Navy dress uniform with spotless white gloves. Each gold aquila button on his chest twinkled like a star in the soft, white illumination. The adjutant pressed a button on a control wand, and a three dimensional hololithic view of Cirenholm rose from the chart table's glass top.

Gaunt had been over the plans a hundred times, but he still took the opportunity to study this relief image. Cirenholm, like all the habitations still viable on Phantine, was built into the peaks of a mountain range that rose dramatically above the lethal atmospheric oceans of pollution covering the planet. It had three main domes, the two largest nestled together and the third, smaller, adjoining at an angle on a secondary peak. The domes were fat and shallow, like the lids of forest mushrooms. Their skirts projected out over the sides of the almost vertical mountains. The apex of each dome was spined with a cluster of masts and aerials, and a thicket of flues, smoke-stacks and heat exchangers bloomed from a bulge in the upper western slopes of the secondary dome. It had a population of two hundred and three thousand.

'Cirenholm is not a fortress,' said Van Voytz. 'None of the cities on Phantine are. It was not built to withstand a war. If it was simply a matter of crushing the enemy here, we'd be doing it from orbit, and not wasting the time of the Imperial Guard. But... and I think this is worthy of repetition... our mission here is to recapture the vapour mills. To drive out the enemy and reclaim the processors. The Crusade desperately needs the fuel-gases and liquid chemicals this world produces.'

Van Voytz cleared his throat. 'So we are forced into an infantry assault. And in infantry terms, Cirenholm is a fortress. Docking and hangar facilities are under the lips of the domes and well protected, so there is no viable landing zone. That means cable drops.'

He took out a hard-light pointer and indicated the narrow decks that ran around the rim of the domes. 'Here. Here. And here. These are the only viable drop zones. They look small, I know. In reality, they're about thirty metres broad. But that will look small to any man coming out of a drop ship on an arrestor hook. The last thing we need tomorrow night is inaccuracy.'

'Can I ask, sir, why tomorrow has been chosen as a go?' The question came from Captain Ban Daur, the Verghastite fourth officer of the Tanith regiment. Gaunt had brought him along as his aide. Corbec and Rawne were busy readying the men and Daur, Gaunt knew, had a cool head for strategy and soaked up tactics like a sponge.

Van Voytz deferred to the person on his immediate left, a short, fidgeting man dressed in the black leather and red braid of the Imperial Tacticians cadre. His name was Biota. 'Long range scans indicate that weather conditions will be optimal tomorrow night, captain,' said Biota. 'Low cloud, and no moonlight. There will be a crosswind from the east, but that should keep the cloud cover behind us and shouldn't pick up. We're unlikely to get better conditions for another week.'

Daur nodded. Gaunt knew what he was thinking. They could all do with a few more days' practice.

'Besides,' said the lord general, 'I don't want to keep the drogues out in open sky any longer than I have to. We're inviting attack from the enemy's cloud-fighters.'

Admiral Ornoff, the drogue commander, nodded. 'Every day we wait multiplies the chance of interception.'

'We have increased escort patrols, sir,' objected Commander Jagdea. A small woman with close-cropped black hair, Jagdea was the chief officer of the Phantine Fighter Corps. Her aviators had been providing protection since the drogues set out, and they would lead the raid in.

'Noted, commander,' said Van Voytz. 'And we are thankful for the efforts of your flight officers and ground crews. However, I don't want to push our luck.'

'What sort of numbers do the enemy have at Cirenholm?' Gaunt asked quietly.

'We estimate between four and seven thousand, colonel-commissar,' said Biota. 'Mostly light infantry from the Blood Pact, with close support.'

'What about loxatl?' Daur asked.

'We don't think so,' said the tactician.

Gaunt noted the number down. It was vague, and he didn't like that. The Blood Pact was the backbone of the Chaos forces in this subsector, the personal retinue of the infamous warlord Urlock Gaur.

They were good, so the reports said. The Ghosts had yet to face them. Most of the opposition the Tanith had met so far had been extreme fanatics. The Infardi, the Zoicans, the Shriven, the Kith. Chaos zealots, demented by their foul beliefs, who had taken up weapons. But the Blood Pact was composed of soldiers, a fraternal military cult, every one of them sworn to Gaur's service in a grisly ritual that involved cutting their palms against the jagged edges of his ancient Space Marine armour.

They were well-drilled, obedient, efficient by Chaos standards, blindly devoted to both their dark daemon-gods and their twisted warrior creed. The Blood Pact elements on Phantine were said to be commanded by Sagittar Slaith, one of Urlock Gaur's most trusted lieutenants.

The loxatl were something else. Xenos mercenaries, an alien breed co-opted by the arch-enemy as shock troops. Their murderous battle lust was fast becoming legendary. Or at least, the meat of barrack room horror stories.

'As you have read in your assault orders, the first wave will strike at the primary dome. That's you and your men, Colonel Zhyte.'

Zhyte, an ill-tempered brute on the other side of the table, nodded. He was the field commander of the Seventh Urdeshi Storm-troop, a regiment of nine thousand men. He wore the black and white puzzle-camo of his unit like he meant it. The Urdeshi were the main strength of the Imperial war on Phantine, if only numerically, and Gaunt knew it. Numbering little more than three thousand, his Ghosts were very much light support.

Urdesh, the famous forge world, had fallen to the arch-enemy several years before. Gaunt's men had already fought the products of the captured weapon shops and tank factories on Hagia. The Urdeshi regiments, eight of them, were famously good shock troops, and, like the Tanith, were dispossessed. The difference was that the Urdeshi still had a home world to win back.

Even now, the Urdeshi Sixth, Fourth Light and Tenth were engaged upon the liberation of their world. Zhyte's filthy demeanor was probably down to the fact he wished he and his men were all there, instead of here, fighting to free up some stinking vapour mills.

Still, Gaunt wished his men had been given the main assault. He felt in his bones they'd do it better.

'Second wave goes here. The secondary dome. That's your Tanith, Gaunt. The secondary dome houses Cirenholm's vapour mill, but, ironically, that's not your primary objective. It goes against what I said earlier, I know, but we need to secure Cirenholm as a staging position. It's vital. Our real trophy will be Ouranberg, and we don't have a hope of taking that unless we have a base in this hemisphere to operate out of. Cirenholm is the doorway to victory on Phantine, my friends. A stepping stone to triumph.'

Van Voytz pointed his stick towards the smallest dome. 'Third wave takes the tertiary dome. Major Fazalur's Phantine Skyborne will lead that one in, supported by Urdeshi storm-troops.'

Fazalur, next to Gaunt, smiled at last. He was a weathered man with shaven hair. He wore the quilted cream tunic of the local army. Gaunt was aware of the terrible loyalties being stretched in this force-screened room. Zhyte, longing to be in a war elsewhere, a war that actually mattered to him and his men. Daur – and Gaunt himself – wishing the Ghosts weren't going in so underprepared. Fazalur, yearning for his men to have the honour of leading the liberation of his own fething world. But the Phantine Skyborne numbered less than six hundred. No matter how brave or driven, they would have to allow others to win back their high cities for them.

'Any other comments?' asked the lord general.

There was an uneasy pause. Gaunt knew that at least three men around that table ached to unburden themselves and complain.

No one spoke.

'Right,' said the lord general. He waved to his aide. 'Let's collapse the force screen now and bring in some refreshments. I think we should all drink to D-hour.'

THE DRINKS AFTER the briefing had been intended to be convivial, to break the ice between commanders who knew little about one another. But it had been stiff and awkward.

Turning down the lord general's vintage amasec, Gaunt had withdrawn early, walking down the hardwood floor of the bridge deck and up a screwstair onto the drogue's forward observation deck.

He stood on a metal grille suspended by tension hawsers inside an inverted dome of armoured glass. Outside, the endless skies of Phantine boiled and frothed. He looked down. There was no land to see. Only millions of square kilometres of dimpled, stained cloud.

There were fast moving ribbons of pearly sculpture, dotting puffs of yellow fleece, iridescent bars of almost silver gas. Murky darkness seeped up through parts of the cloud, unwholesome twists of smog and venting corruption. Far below, occasional flares of ignited gas blossomed in the dense, repellent cloud.

Phantine had been an industrial world for fifteen centuries, and now it was largely inhospitable to human kind. Unchecked resource mining and rapacious petrochemical overproduction had ruined the surface and created a lethal blanket of air pollution five kilometres deep.

Only the highest places remained. Spire-like mountains, or the uppermost tips of long-dead hives. These spires and tips protruded from the corrosive gas seas and formed remote islands where mankind might just continue the habitation of the world its greed had killed. Places like Cirenholm and Ouranberg.

And the only reason for those precarious habitations was so that mankind could continue to plunder the chemical resources of Phantine.

Sliding under the handrail, Gaunt sat down on the edge of the walkway so that his boots were dangling. Craning out, he could just see back down the vast underbelly of the drogue. The pleated gas sacks. The armoured canvas panels. They glowed ochre in the unhealthy half-sun. He could see one of the huge engine nacelles, its chopping propeller blades taller than a warlord titan.

'They said I'd find you up here, Ibram.'

Gaunt glanced up. Colonel Colm Corbec hunkered down next to him.

'What's the word, Colm?' asked Gaunt, nodding to his second-in-command.

The big, thick-bearded man leaned against the handrail. His bared forearms were like hams and decorated, under the hair, with blue spirals and stars.

'So, what did Lord General Van Voytz have to say?' said Corbec. 'And what's he like?' he added, sitting down next to Gaunt and letting his legs swing off the grille.

'I was just wondering that. It's hard to know, sometimes, what a commander is like. Dravere and Sturm, well, they don't fething count. Bastards, the both of them. But Bulledin and Slaydo... they were both fine men. I always resented the fact Lugo replaced Bulledin on Hagia.'

'Lugo,' growled Corbec. 'Don't get me started on him.'

Gaunt smiled. 'He paid. Macaroth demoted him.'

'The Emperor protects,' grinned Corbec. He plucked a hip flask from his trouser pocket, took a swig, and offered it to Gaunt.

Gaunt shook his head. He'd abstained from alcohol with an almost puritanical conviction since the dark days on Hagia several months before. There, he and his Ghosts had almost paid the price for Lord General Lugo's mistakes. Cornered and frustrated, and tormented by an over-keen sense of responsibility invested in him by his mentors Slaydo and Oktar, Gaunt had come closer to personal failure than at any time in his career. He'd drunk hard, shamefully, and allowed his men to suffer. Only the grace of the Emperor, and perhaps of the beati Saint Sabbat, had saved him. He'd fought back, against the forces of Chaos and his own private daemons, and routed the arch-enemy, driving back their forces just hours before Hagia could be overrun.

Hagia had been spared, Lugo disgraced, and the Ghosts had survived, both as an active unit and as living beings. There was no part of that hard path Gaunt wanted to retrace.

Corbec sighed, took back the flask and sipped again. He missed the old Gaunt, the commander who would kick back and drink the night away with his men as hard as he'd fight for them the next day. Corbec understood Gaunt's caution, and had no wish to see his beloved commander turned back into a raging, drunken malcontent. But he missed the comradely Gaunt. There was a distance between them now.

'So... this Van Voytz?'

'Van Voytz is a good man, I think. I've heard nothing but good reports about him. I like his style of command–'

'I sense there's a "but", Ibram.'

Gaunt nodded. 'He's sending the Urdeshi in for first kill. I don't think their hearts are in it. He should trust me. And you. The Ghosts, I mean.'

'Maybe he's on our side for once.'

'Maybe.'

'Like you said, it's often hard to get the measure of your commander on first sight.'

Gaunt turned to look at Corbec. 'Meaning?'

'Look at us.'

'Look at us, what?'

Corbec shrugged. 'First time I saw you, I thought I'd been saddled with the worst bum-boil of a commander in the Imperium.'

They both snorted with laughter.

'Of course, my planet was dying at the time,' said Corbec as their amusement subsided. 'Then it turned out you were–'

'What?'

'Okay.'

Gaunt toasted Corbec with an imaginary glass. 'Thanks for that underwhelming vote of confidence.'

Corbec stared at Gaunt, all the laughter gone from his eyes. 'You're the best fething commander I've ever seen,' he said.

'Thanks, Colm,' said Gaunt.

'Hey...' said Corbec quietly. 'Look, sir.'

Outside, the sun had come out and the noxious clouds had wafted away from the ports. They looked out and saw the vast shape of the drogue escorting them, a kilometre long dirigible painted silver on the belly and white on the top. It had a ribbed, hardwood frame and extended out at the front in a fluked ram the size of a giant nalwood. They could see the eight motor nacelles along its belly beating the air with their huge props. Beyond it, in the suddenly gleaming light, they could see the next drogue in formation.

Floating islands, armed and armoured, each carrying upwards of four thousand men.

'Feth!' Corbec repeated. 'Pinch me. Are we aboard one of them?'

'We are.'

'I knew it, but it takes seeing it to know it, you know what I mean?'

'Yes.'

Gaunt looked up at Corbec.

'Are we ready, Colm?'

'Not really. I'm not even going to tell you about the ammunition situation. But... well, we're as ready as we can be.'

'Then that's good enough for me.'

DZ OR DEAD

CIRENHOLM, WEST CONTINENTAL REACHES, PHANTINE
212 to 213.771, M41

'There was a lot of shouting, a lot of jostling, a lot of activity at first. After that, everyone just went quiet. We knew what was coming. Then we went in. Down the rope. Gak! Holy gak! That was a ride.'

– Jessi Banda, sniper, Tanith First

One

NIGHT HAD FALLEN three hours before. Moonless, as Tactician Biota had promised. A light easterly. The immense gloom outside was a profound black, broken only, from far below, by the faint foam of polluted cloud bars and lustrous mist.

The lumbering drogues, running dark with blackout shutters closed, blinds drawn and rigging lights off, swung slowly around over a six hundred square kilometre cloud bank designated as the dispersal field. They faced north. They faced Cirenholm. It was twenty-one ten hours Imperial.

COMMANDER JAGDEA, DRESSED in a bulky green pressure suit, her crimson helmet on the deck at her feet, finished up her final briefing, and clasped hands with each of the Halo Flight personnel in turn. They had been grouped around her in a huddle at the edge of drogue *Nimbus's* secondary flight deck, and now they rose from perches on jerry cans and cannon-shell pallets to take her hand.

The secondary flight deck was brightly lit, and throbbed with noise and activity. Deck crews ran back and forth, releasing anchor lines, uncoupling feeder hoses, and pushing empty munition carriages out of the way. Pressure-powered drivers and ratchets wailed and stuttered as the last few plates and panels were screwed into place. Ordnance teams moved down the chevron of waiting warplanes, arming and blessing the wing-slung munitions. A group of deck servitors followed the tech-magi, collecting up the priming pins, each marked with a tag of yellow vellum, that the armourers left in their wake.

The six Marauder fighter-bombers of Halo Flight were set in a herringbone pattern down the length of the deck in greasy locking cradles. Three faced port, three faced starboard, all of them raked at a forty-five degree angle from the rear.

The flight crews, half a dozen for each forty tonne beast, ran down the centre line of the deck and climbed into their designated aircraft.

A buzzer sounded, followed by a quick whoop of klaxons. Cycling amber lights in a row down the centre ridge of the bay roof began flashing.

Jagdea scooped up her helmet and retreated to the far end of the deck, behind an angled blast-board.

The main lighting went off abruptly, as the buzzer had warned. Lines of low-power deck lights winked on, casting their feeble glow up through the grille of the floor. Deck crew with light poles moved down the line, flagging signals. Hatches and canopies began to close, techs leapt down and rolled away the lightweight access stairs. The massive thrust-tunnel turbines, four on each ship, began to turn over. A whine rose, shaking the deck.

Jagdea pulled on her vox-earpiece so she could listen in.

'Halo Two, at power.'

'Halo Four, check.'

'Halo Five, at power now.'

'Halo Three, power, aye.'

'Halo Six, at power.'

'Halo Leader, confirming I have power. Twenty seconds. Standby to mark.'

The roar was bone-shaking now. Jagdea could feel every organ in her torso vibrating. She loved that feeling.

'Control, Halo Leader. The word is Evangeline. Deck doors opening.'

'Halo Leader, control. I hear Evangeline. Praise be the Emperor. Flight confirm.'

'Halo Two, the word Evangeline.'

'Halo Five, I hear it.'

'Halo Six, aye, Evangeline.'

'Halo Three, Evangeline.'

'Halo Four, I hear Evangeline.'

'Halo Leader. Go with grace.'

The deck doors opened. Shutters peeled back along both sides of the deck, and hydraulic doors yawned underneath the cradles. The tumultuous inrush of high altitude wind and exterior prop noise drowned the engine roar.

'Control, Halo Leader. Execute.'

'Halo Leader. We have launch execute. Set to release cradles. Count off from three. Three, two–'

There was a lurch, and a series of concussive bangs. The huge warplanes tilted as their cradles tipped and disengaged, sliding them out of the deck space, dropping them like stones. Three dropped out to port, the other three to starboard. The huge drogue barely trembled as it released the weight.

They fell for a second into the blackness and then fired their engines, belching thrust, pulling hard G's as they took lift and climbed away from the airship.

The deck doors began to close. Jagdea took a last, wistful look at the retreating specks of afterburner glow that twinkled out there in the dark, like stars.

Another thirty minutes and it would be her turn.

Cirenholm was about fifty minutes' flying time from the dispersal field at a comfortable cruising speed, but Halo Flight were pushing their tolerances. In a long, vee formation they burned north, gaining altitude in the lightless air.

A little turbulence. The airframes rattled. On Halo Leader, Captain Viltry made a miniscule adjustment and scribed a mark on his thigh pad chart with a wax pencil. There were wind-whorls at this height. Counter-turning cones of cold, super-fast air.

There was frost on his canopy, stained yellow by air pollutants, and his limbs were stiff with altitude shock and air-burn.

He sucked hard on his mask.

To his side and just below, his navigator Gammil was hunched over his station, studying the hololithic charts by the light of a hooded spotlamp.

'Turn two two zero seven,' Gammil voxed.

'Halo Leader, Halo Flight. Turn two two zero seven. Make your height forty-four fifty.'

Viltry's sensors showed the first hard returns of the Cirenholm promontory. Nothing by eye.

'Halo Leader, Halo Flight. Make ready.'

Viltry noted with satisfaction the ten green lights that flashed live on his munition screen. Serrikin, his payload officer, had done his job perfectly.

'Two minutes,' Viltry announced.

Another patch of turbulence. Harder. The cabin shook. The glass on a dial cracked.

'Steady. One minute twenty.'

Viltry kept glancing at the locator. An enemy cloud-fighter now would be disastrous.

'Forty seconds.'

Something blurry crept across the sweeping display. An interceptor? Pray to the God-Emperor it was just a falling ice-cloud, echoing on their sensor patterns.

'Halo Two, Halo Leader. West quadrant. Nine by nine by six.'

'I see it, Halo Two. Just an ice-cloud. Twenty seconds.'

The Marauder bucked again, violently. The bulb in Gammil's spotlamp burst and the cabin below Viltry went dark.

He saw the snowy pleats of the filth clouds below, violet in the night. He made the sign of the aquila. He thumbed back the safety covers on the ten release switches.

'At ten seconds! Ten, nine, eight, seven…'

Halo Flight banked a tad, holding pattern.

'…three, two, one… drop! Drop! Drop!'

Viltry threw the release switches. His Marauder rose with a lurch as it loosed the weight. He nursed it back.

Halo Flight banked away west, turning and reforming for the run back to the drogue.

Behind them, colossal clouds of feathery nickel filaments bloomed out in the air, blinding the already half-blind sensors of Cirenholm.

THE MUSTER-DECK of the *Nimbus*, lit a cold, merciless white, was thronging with Ghosts. They were arranged by squad in rows marked by pew-like benches. It was twenty-one twenty-five hours.

Ibram Gaunt entered the muster hall and walked down the rows, chatting and exchanging pleasantries with the men. He was dressed for the drop in a hip-length, fur collared leather jacket, his cap still on. His bolt pistol was holstered under his left armpit in a buckled rig, and his power sword, the trophy weapon of House Sondar, was webbed across his back. He already wore his drop-harness, the heavy arrestor hook banging against his thigh.

The Tanith seemed ready. They looked fine. No one had the nervous look Gaunt always watched for.

Each Ghost was prepping up, and then turning to let his neighbour in the squad double-check his harness and couplings. They were all buttoned up and beginning to sweat. Lasguns were cinched tight across their chests. Gloves were going on. Each trooper had a balaclava and a rubberised gas-hood ready to pull on, his beret tucked away. Camo-cloaks were rolled like bedding into a tight tube across the backside.

Gaunt saw Obel checking Bragg down.

'How's the arm, Try?' asked Gaunt.

'Good enough to fight with, sir.'

'You can manage that?' Gaunt indicated the autocannon and tripod that Bragg was to carry down the rope. Support weapon troopers and vox-officers would have the hardest time tonight.

'No problem, sir.'

'Good.'

Caill was Bragg's ammo-humper. He had drum magazines strung over both shoulders.

'Keep him fed, Caill.'

'I will, sir.'

On the far side of the chamber, Gaunt saw Scout Sergeant Mkoll closing his final briefing with the Tanith scouts, the regiment's elite troopers. He made his way over, passing Doc Dorden and Surgeon Ana Curth, who were inoculating every trooper in turn with altitude sickness shots – acetazolamide, their systems more than used to it since the Holy Depths of Hagia – together with counter-toxin boosters and an anti airsickness drug.

Dorden was tossing spent drug vials into a plastic tray. 'You had a shot yet, colonel?' he asked Gaunt, fitting a fresh glass bulb into the metal frame of his pneumatic needle.

Deliberately, Gaunt hadn't. The venerable doctor had visited him in his cabin half an hour earlier to administer the shot, but Gaunt considered it more appropriate for him to be seen taking it in front of the men.

Dorden was just acting out his prearranged part.

Gaunt peeled off his glove and hauled back his sleeve.

Dorden fired the delivery spike into the meat of Gaunt's exposed forearm and then swabbed the blood-welling dot with a twist of gauze. Gaunt made sure he didn't flinch.

'Any shirkers?' he whispered to Dorden as he slid his sleeve back down.

'A few. They'll bayonet anything, but the sight of a needle–'

Gaunt laughed.

'Keep it going. Time's against us.'

Gaunt nodded to Curth as he moved on. Like Dorden, she wouldn't be making the drop. Instead, she'd have the unenviable task of waiting in the *Nimbus's* empty, silent infirmary for the wounded to roll in.

'The Emperor protect you, Colonel-Commissar,' she said.

'Thank you, Ana. Let him guide your work when the time comes.'

Gaunt liked Curth, and not because she was one of the most attractive things in the regiment. She was good. Damn good. Fething good, as Corbec might say.

And she'd left a rewarding life in Vervunhive to tend the Tanith First.

Delayed slightly by goodwill exchanges for troopers like Domor, Derin, Tarnash and the stalwart flame-trooper Brostin, Gaunt finally reached the gathering of scouts.

They stood around Sergeant Mkoll in an impassive circle. Bonin, Mkvenner, Doyl, Caober, Baen, Hwlan, Mkeller, Vahgnar, Leyr and the others. Not necessarily the best fighters in the regiment, but the reason for its reputation. Stealth. Special operations. And, so far, all Tanith-born. No Verghastite recruit had yet displayed enough raw ability to join Mkoll's elite scouts. Only a few, Cuu amongst them, had shown any real potential.

Gaunt stepped in amongst them and they all drew to salute. He waved them down with a smile.

'Stand easy. I'm sure I'm just repeating what Mkoll has told you, but I have a gut feeling this will be down to you. The lord general, and the other regimental commanders, are looking at this like a nut to crack by force. Wrong. I think it's going to take smarts. This is city fighting. Cirenholm may be stuck up on a fething mountain, but it's a city nevertheless. You've got to kill clever. Lead us in. Make the place ours. The lord general refused the idea of giving anyone under command rank the city plans, but I'm breaking that.'

Gaunt handed out tissue-thin copies of the schematics to the scouts.

'Feth knows why he doesn't want you to see this. Probably doesn't want troopers acting with initiative over and above command. Well, I do. Here's the thing. This won't be a fight where command can sit and shout orders. This isn't a battlefield. We're going into a complex structure full of hostiles. I want it closed down and secured in the name of the God-Emperor as fast as possible. That means on-the-hoof guidance. That means scouting and recon. That means decision making on the ground. When we've won the day, burn those maps. Eat them. Wipe your arses with them and flush them away. Tell the lord general, if he asks, you got lucky.'

Gaunt paused. He looked round, took them eye by eye. They returned his look.

'I don't believe in luck. Well... I do, as it goes. But I don't count on it. I believe in tight combat practice and intelligent war. I believe we make our own luck in this heathen galaxy. And I believe that means using you men to the limit. If any of you... I mean, *any* of you... voxes an order or instruction, I'll make sure it's followed. The squad leaders and commanders know that. Rawne, Daur and Corbec know that. What we take tonight, we take the Ghost way. The Tanith way. And you are the fething brains of that way.'

He paused again. 'Any questions?'

The scouts shook their heads.

'Give them hell,' said Gaunt.

The scouts saluted and strode off to join their squads. Gaunt and Mkoll shook hands.

'You're first in,' said Gaunt.

'Seems as if I am.'

'Do this for Tanith.'

'Oh, count on it,' Mkoll said.

ALERT LIGHTS WERE coming on. A buzzer sounded. The Ghosts, squad by squad, rose up and began to file out into the departure bay. A last few shouts and good lucks bounced between drop-teams.

Gaunt saw Trooper Caffran break ranks for a second to kiss the mouth of the Verghastite Tona Criid. She broke the kiss and slapped him away with a laugh. They were heading for separate drop-ships.

He saw Brostin helping Neskon to sit his flamer tanks just right over his back.

He saw Troopers Lillo and Indrimmo leading the Vervunhivers in one last hive war-chant.

He saw Rawne and Feygor marching their detail through the boarding gate.

He saw Kolea and Varl, each at the head of his own squad, exchanging boasts and dares as they filed to their designated ships.

He saw Seena and Arilla, the gun-girls from Verghast, carrying the light support stubber between them.

He saw the snipers: Larkin, Nessa, Banda, Rilke, Merrt... each one marked out amid the slowly moving files by the awkwardly bagged long-lasrifles they carried.

He saw Colm Corbec on the far side of the muster room, clapping his hands above his bearded head and raising up a battle anthem.

He saw Captain Daur, joining in with the singing as he rushed to pull on his balaclava. Daur left his cap on one of the vacant benches.

He saw them all: Lillo, Garond, Vulli, Mkfeyd, Cocoer, Sergeant Theiss, Mkteeg, Dremmond, Sergeant Haller, laughing and singing, Sergeant Bray, Sergeant Ewler, Unkin, Wheln, Guheen, Raess... all of them.

He saw Milo, far away through a sea of faces.

They nodded to each other. That was all that was needed.

He saw Sergeant Burone running back for the gloves he had forgotten.

He saw Trooper Cuu.

The cold, cat eyes.

Ibram Gaunt had always believed that it was a commander's duty to pray for all his men to return safely.

Not Cuu. If Cuu fell at Cirenholm, Gaunt thought, God-Emperor forgive me, I won't mourn.

Gaunt took off his cap and pushed it into his jacket. He turned to follow the retreating files out of the muster bay. Passing the entrance of the Blessing Chapel, he was almost knocked down by the shambling bulk of Agun Soric, the old, valiant Verghast gang boss.

'Sir!'

'As you were, sergeant. Get to your men.'

'I'm sorry, sir. Just taking a last blessing.'

Gaunt smiled down at the short, thick-set man. Soric wore an eye-patch and disdained augmetic work. He had been an ore-smeltery boss on Verghast, and then a scratch squad leader. Soric had courage enough for an entire company of men.

'Turn around,' said Gaunt, and Soric did so smartly.

Gaunt patted down Soric's harness, and made a slight adjustment to the buckles of his webbing.

'Get going,' he said.

'Yes sir,' said Soric, lurching away after the main teams.

'Hold on there,' said a dry, old voice from the Blessing Chapel.

Gaunt turned.

Ayatani Zweil, wizened and white-bearded, hopped out beside him, and put his hands either side of Gaunt's face.

'Not now, father–'

'Hush! Let me look in your eyes, tell you to kill or be killed, and make the sign of the aquila at least.'

Gaunt smiled. The regiment had acquired Ayatani Zweil on Hagia, and he had become their chaplain. He was imhava ayatani, a roving priest dedicated to Saint Sabbat, in whose name and memory this entire crusade was being fought. Gaunt didn't really understand what made the old, white-bearded priest tick, but he valued his company.

'The Emperor watch you, and the beati too,' said Zweil. 'Don't do anything I wouldn't do.'

'Apart from killing, slaughtering, engaging in firefights and generally being a warrior, you mean?'

'Apart from all that, naturally.' Zweil smiled. 'Go and do what you do. And I'll stay here and wait to do what I do. You realise my level of work-load depends upon your success or failure?'

'I've never thought of it that way, but thank you for putting it into such perspective.'

'Gaunt?' the old, ragged priest's voice suddenly dipped and became stifled.

'What?'

'Trust Bonin.'

'What?'

'Don't "what" me. The saint herself, the beati, told me... you must trust Bonin.'

'Alright. Thanks.'

The final siren was sounding. Gaunt patted the old priest's arm and hurried away to the departure bay.

* * *

THE DEPARTURE BAY was the *Nimbus's* primary flight deck. Down its immense, echoing length lay drop-ships. Sixty drop-ships: heavy, trans-atmospheric shuttles with a large door hatch in each flank. The deck crews were still milling around them. Engines were test-starting. The previous day, each one of the drop-ships had been wearing the colour pattern of the Phantine Skyborne. Now each one was drabbed down with an anti-reflective pitch.

The Ghosts were mounting up.

Fifty drop-troopers were appointed to each transport, two squads of twenty-five per ship. The squads mounted, in reverse order, via the hatch they would eventually exit through. Staging officers held up metal poles with stencilled number plates on the end so that the Ghosts could form up in the right detail, at the right ship, and on the correct side for mounting.

There were still a few minutes to wait for some squads. They sat down on the apron next to their appointed craft, daubing on camo-paint, making a last few equipment checks or just sitting still, their minds far away. The point men from each squad were checking, and in some cases, re-tying the jump-ropes secured above the hatch-doors. The ground crews had already done this perfectly well, but the point men took their responsibilities for the ropes very solemnly. If they and their comrades were going to depend on a knot for their survival, it had better be one they had tied themselves.

It was twenty-one forty hours. By now, on two of the *Nimbus's* sister drogues, the Urdeshi storm-troops would already be aboard their drops.

Gaunt checked his chronometer again as he walked down the deck to his drop-ship. Admiral Ornhoff had just voxed down that the operation was still running precisely to schedule, but there was a report that the cross wind had picked up a little in the last thirty minutes. That would make transit rough and roping out harder, and it would clear away more quickly the sensor-foxing chaff that Halo Flight had spread earlier on.

Gaunt called in Hark, Rawne and Corbec for a final word.

All of them looked ready, though Rawne was eager to get to his flight. Hark was still very unhappy about the disastrous ammunition situation. After rationing out all the size threes held by the regiment, and scouring the Munitorium stores of all the drogues, the Ghosts had a grand total of three clips per trooper. Due to a mis-relayed order, the taskforce Munitoria had stocked with size fives, the type used by both the Urdeshi and the Phantine. There had not been time to send back to Hessenville for extras, and no way of rearming the Tanith with alternative weapons.

'It could kill morale,' said Hark. 'I've heard a lot of grumbling.'

'It may actually focus them,' said Corbec. 'They know that more than ever, they have to make everything count.'

Commissar Hark didn't seem too convinced by the colonel's take, but he had not been with the regiment long enough to fully appreciate Colm

Corbec's instinctive wisdom. Hark had been attached to them on Hagia, essentially as the instrument of a command structure bent on bringing Gaunt down. But Hark had redeemed himself, fighting valiantly alongside the Ghosts at Bhavnager and the battle for the Shrinehold. Gaunt had kept him on after that. With Gaunt's leadership role split between command and discipline, it was useful to have a dedicated commissar at his side.

A buzzer began sounding. Some of the men whooped.

'Let's go, gentlemen,' said Gaunt.

IT WAS TWENTY-TWO hundred. The first wave of drop-ships, carrying the mass of the Urdeshi forces, spilled out of their drogues into the high altitude night.

Colonel Zhyte, aboard drop 1A, craned to look out of the thick-glassed port. He could see little except the inky volume of the sky and the occasional flare of thrusters from the drop-ships around him. The drogues were blacked out and invisible. There had been a tense last few moments between final boarding and launch as all lights on the landing deck shut down so that the launch doors could be opened without giving away position. An uneasy twilight, oppressive, ending only with the violent thump of gravity when the drop-ships plunged away.

Zhyte moved forward into the cockpit, past the rows of his troopers sitting in the craft's main body. In the low-level green illumination, their faces looked pale and ill.

In the cockpit, visibility was a little better. The lightless, limitless cold ahead was punctuated by sudden and swift-passing curls of smoky cloud or little darting wisps. Zhyte could see thirty or forty wavering, dull orange glows spread out ahead and below: the engine glares of the drop-ship formation.

The ship rattled and vibrated sporadically, and the pilot and his servitor co-pilot murmured to each other over the vox. That crosswind was picking up, and there was a hint of headwind now too.

'Over the DZ in forty-one minutes,' the pilot told Zhyte. The Urdeshi colonel knew that estimate would creep if the headwind got any stronger. The heavily laden drop-ships would be straining into it.

Zhyte studied the sensor plate, looking at the milky display of formation ships, scared of seeing something else. If an enemy cloud-fighter lucked onto them now, it would be a massacre.

TWENTY-TWO TEN Imperial. The exit doors of the drop-ships had been shut and locked three minutes before. Everything was vibrating with the noise of the massed transporter engines.

In drop-ship 2A, Gaunt took his seat, a fold-down metal bracket at one end of the row of men. Someone was muttering an Imperial prayer. Several of the men were turning over aquila symbols in their shaking hands.

A curt voice spoke over the vox-link. Gaunt couldn't make out what it said over the roar, but he knew what it meant.

There was a gut-flipping lurch as they seemed to fall, and then a slamming wall of gravity that threw them backwards.

They were in flight.

They were en route.

This was it.

COMMANDER JAGDEA PULLED a hard left turn and her two wingmen swooped with her. The three Lightnings of the Imperial Phantine Air Defence banked sharply and swept in alongside the dispersal drogue *Boreas*.

Jagdea had eight three-wing flights in the air now, escorts for the wallowing shoals of drop-ships lumbering and climbing away from the stationary drogues.

Visibility was so bad she'd been flying by instruments alone, but now she could see the twinkling burner flares of the troop transports, hundreds of them glowing like coals against the boiling darkness below.

'Control, Umbra Leader,' she said into her vox. 'I see a little spread in the troop formations. Urge them to correct for the crosswind.'

'Acknowledged, Umbra Leader.'

Some of the drop-ships had wandered on release, driven by the gathering turbulence. They were straggling out to the east.

Keep them tight or we'll lose you, she willed.

Every few seconds, she scanned the dome of sky above for contacts. As far as they knew, Cirenholm had no idea what was coming its way. But enemy aircraft might blow that advantage at any moment.

Not while she was airborne, Jagdea decided.

HALO FLIGHT HAD circled around to the west for the return loop to the drogue hangars, following a wide arc to avoid crossing the massed, inbound formations of drop-ships.

Captain Viltry adjusted the airspeed of his Marauder. They were running into toxic smog banks, and nuggets of dirt were rattling off his hull armour.

There was a brief vox blurt.

'Halo Leader, say again.'

Viltry waited. He felt himself tense up.

'Halo Leader to Halo Flight, say again.'

A few answers came back, all of them confused.

'Halo Leader. Halo Flight, double up your visual checking.'

'Halo Three, Halo Leader. Have you seen Halo Five?'

Viltry paused. He glanced down at Gammil, and his navigator checked the scanner carefully before shaking his head.

Shit. 'Halo Leader, Halo Five. Halo Five. Respond. Suken, where the hell are you?'

White noise filled Viltry's ears.

'Halo Leader, Halo Four. Can you see Suken from where you are?'

'Hold on, Halo Leader.' A long pause. 'No sign, Halo Leader. Nothing on the scope.'

Where the hell had–

'Contact! Contact! Eight eight one and closing!'

The shout came from Halo Two.

Viltry jerked around, searching the darkness, frantic.

There was a flash to his port. He looked round in time to see a little chain of tracer fire sinking away down into the clouds like a flock of birds.

There was another wordless fizzle of static and then an airburst ignited in the sky two hundred metres to Viltry's starboard wing.

Something very bright and fast passed right in front of him.

'Halo Three's gone! Halo Three's gone!' he heard one of his gunners yelling.

'Break, break, break!' he ordered. The world turned upside down and Viltry was pressed back into his grav-seat by the force of the spinning dive. He saw the dying fireball that had been Halo Three streaming away in the headwind in bands of blue flame.

His control console lit up and alarms blared. Viltry realised he was target locked. He cursed and flipped the Marauder over, hearing Gammil squeal in pain as he was thrown headlong out of the navigator seat.

They were tumbling. The altimeter was spinning like a speeded up chronometer. They were dropping fast, almost beyond the point of recovery.

Viltry hauled on the squad and fired the burners, slamming the Marauder back up and out of its evasive plummet. He tore off his breather mask and vomited as the extreme G forces pumped his guts empty.

His pounding ears suddenly became aware of a screaming on the vox-link. Halo Four.

'He's behind me! He's on me! Holy God-Emperor, I can't lose him! I can't–'

A wash of white fire blistered across the clouds behind them.

'Halo Leader to Control! Halo Leader to Control! Enemy raiders in the dispersal field! I say again, enemy raiders in the dispersal field!'

The target lock alarm sang out again.

Halo Leader slammed forward so hard Viltry bit through his own lips. He saw his blood spiralling away and spattering against the canopy as the stricken Marauder went into a lengthways spin.

He could smell burning cabling and a cold, hard stink of high altitude air.

He leaned into the controls and levelled the warcraft out.

One of his engines was on fire. Over the vox, he could hear his aft gunner wailing. He turned to look down at Gammil. The navigator was crawling back to his seat.

'Get up! Get up!' Viltry barked.

'I'm trying.'

Viltry's hands were slick with sweat inside his gloves. He looked up, searching the sky, and saw the lancing shadow right on them.

'For god's sake–' Gammil began, seeing it in the same instant.

White hot cannon shells sliced down through the cabin, mincing the navigator and his station in a welter of steel splinters, blood and smoke. The entire lower fuselage of Halo Leader sheared off, shredding into the freezing night. Viltry saw Serrikin tumbling away in a cloud of debris, dropping into the corrosive darkness far below.

The freezing air howled around him.

He reached for his ejector lever.

The canopy exploded.

Two

ANA CURTH WASHED her hands under the infirmary's chrome tap for the third time in fifteen minutes and then dusted them with sterilising talc. She was fidgety, restless.

The infirmary hall was a quiet vault, well-lit and ranged with rows of freshly laundered beds.

Curth checked a few drug bottles on the dispensary cart, then sighed and walked down the length of the bay. Her boots rang out cold, empty beats and her red surgical gown billowed out behind her like a lord palatine's cape.

'You'll drive yourself mad,' said Dorden.

The Tanith chief medic was lying serenely on his back on one of the beds, staring at the ceiling. Swathed in green scrubs, he lay on top of the well-made sheets so as not to disturb them.

'Mad?'

'Raving. The waiting quite addles the mind.'

Curth paused at the end of the bed Dorden occupied.

'And this is how you deal with it?'

He tilted up his head and looked down the length of his body at her.

'Yes. I meditate. I consider. I ruminate. I serve the God-Emperor, but I'm damned if I'll waste my life waiting to be of service.'

'You recommend this?'

'Absolutely.'

Curth hesitatingly laid herself out on the bed next to Dorden. She stared at the ceiling, her heels together, her arms by her side.

'This isn't making me much calmer,' she admitted.

'Patience, and you might learn something.'

'Like what?'

'Like... there are five hundred and twenty hexagonal divisions in the pattern of the ceiling.'

Curth sat up.

'What?'

'There are five hundred–'

'Okay, I got that. If counting roof tiles does it for you, I'm happy. Me, I have to pace.'

'Pace away, Ana.'

She walked away down the length of the bay. At the stern door, the regiment's medicae troopers Lesp, Chayker and Foskin were grouped outside the plastic door screen, smoking lho-sticks.

'Can I cadge one?' she asked, joining them.

Lesp raised his eyebrows and offered her one.

She lit up.

'They'll be almost there by now,' Chayker reflected. 'Right at the DZ.'

Lesp looked at his wristwatch. 'Yup. Right about now.'

'Emperor help them,' Curth murmured, drawing on her lho-stick. Now she'd have to wash her hands again.

TWENTY-THREE SIX Imperial. Not a bad delay. The pilot of drop 1A listened to his co-seat for a moment over the headset and then turned to give Zhyte a nod.

'Three minutes.'

The Urdeshi commander could still see nothing out of the front ports except vague cloud banks and the light-fizz of other drop-ships surging their engines. The headwind was climbing.

But Zhyte trusted his flight crew.

He moved back into the carrier hold and threw the switch that lit the amber light over the hatch. Make ready.

The men got to their feet in the blue gloom, nursing out the slack on their arrestor hook cords and pulling on their gas-hoods. Zhyte took his own gas-hood out of its pouch, shook it out, and fitted it over his head, adjusting it so the plastic eyeslits sat squarely and the cap didn't foul his vox-set. He squeezed shut the popper studs that anchored its skirts to his shoulders and zipped the seal.

Now he was more blind than ever, shrouded in a treated canvas cone that stifled him and amplified the sounds of his own breathing.

'Count off,' he announced into his vox.

The men replied quickly and efficiently by squad order, announcing their number and confirming that their hoods were in place. Zhyte waited until the last few had fastened up the seals.

'Hatches to release.'

'Release, aye!' the point men crackled back over the link.

There was a judder and a lurch as the side hatches were slid open and the craft's trim altered. Air temperature in the carrier bay dropped sharply, and the light took on an ochre tinge.

'Ready the ropes! Ninety seconds!'

The point men were silhouettes against the gloomy yellow squares of the open hatches, their battledress tugged by the slipstream.

Zhyte took out his bolt pistol, held it up clumsily in front of his face plate to check it, and put it back in his holster.

Almost there.

THE HARD SNAP of the inflator jerked Captain Viltry back into consciousness. His head swam, and his body felt curiously weightless. He had no idea where he was.

He tried to remember. He tried to work out what the hell he was doing. It was cold and everything was pitch dark. Drunkenly, his neck sore, he looked up and saw the faint shape of the inflator's spherical sac, from which he hung.

He'd ejected. Now he remembered. God-Emperor, something had taken his bird apart... and his wing men too. He looked around hoping to catch a glimpse of another aircraft. But there was just the high altitude void, the filmy cloud, the curling darkness.

He checked his altimeter, the one sewn into the cuff of his flight suit. He was a good two thousand metres below operational altitude, almost at the envelope of the toxic atmospheric layer. His inflator must have fired automatically, the pressure switch triggered by his fall.

The safety harness was biting into his armpits and chest. He tried to ease it, and realised he was injured. His shoulder was cut, and some of the harness straps were severed. He was lucky to still be wearing the rig.

Parachutes were pointless on Phantine. There was nowhere to drop to except corrosive death in the low altitude depths, the Scald, as it was known. Flyers wore bailing rigs that inflated globular blimps from gas bottles that would, unpunctured, keep them drifting above the lethal atmospheric levels of the Scald until rescue.

Viltry was an experienced flyer, but he didn't need that experience to tell him the coriolis winds, savage at this height, had already carried him far away from the flight paths. He tried to read the gauge on his air tanks, but he couldn't make the dial out.

Windwaste, he thought. That was him. Windwaste, the worst fate any combat pilot on Phantine could suffer. Drifting away, alive, beyond the possibility of recovery. Flyer lore said that men caught in that doom used their small arms to puncture their inflators so that they could have a quick death in the Scald's poison acid-gases below.

But there was still a chance he'd get picked up. All he had to do was activate his distress beacon.

A toggle pull would do it.

Viltry hesitated. That simple toggle pull might bring him rescue, but it would also be heard by the enemy at Cirenholm. They'd know that a flyer was in distress. And therefore that at least one Imperial aircraft was up tonight.

He didn't dare. Ornoff had told the pilot fold that surprise was the key to storming Cirenholm. Short range ship-to-ship vox chatter was safe, but powerful, ranged transmissions like the amplified vox-blink of his distress beacon might ruin that surprise. Alert the enemy. Kill thousands of Imperial Guardsmen.

Viltry drifted through the cold air desert, through the dark. Ice was forming on the inside of his goggles.

He had to stay silent. Even though that meant he would be windwaste.

'UMBRA LEADER TO flight, pickle off your tanks,' Jagdea said into her mask.

Umbra flight was threading the rear echelons of the troop ship formations. They were almost over the DZ now. The raised bulk of Cirenholm was a loud blur on her instruments.

The three Lightnings dumped their empty fuel tanks and rose above the drop-ship flocks. They were running on internal tanks now, which meant they had just another sixteen minutes of range left... less if they were called to burn hard into combat.

Jagdea was jumpy. Halo Flight should have made the return run by now, but there had been no sighting of the overdue Marauder flight.

Commander Bree Jagdea had fifteen thousand hours of combat flight experience. She was one of the best pilots ever to graduate from the Hessenville Combat School. She had instinctive combat smarts that no measure of training could ever teach. Those instincts took over now.

'Umbra Leader to Umbra Flight. Let's nose ahead for one last burn. Chase the Urdeshi formations. I've got a sick feeling there's opposition aloft tonight.'

'Understood, Umbra Leader.'

The trio of Imperial fighters swung west. Hundreds of lives were about to be lost. But, running on instinct, Jagdea had just saved thousands more.

'FINAL PREP,' SAID Sergeant Kolea, walking down the carrier hold of drop 2F at the trailing edge of the Tanith formation.

'Three minutes to the DZ. I want hoods in place and hooks ready in thirty. Door duty to active. Point men, stand by.'

The amber rune had not yet come on. Kolea strapped on his gas-hood, and went down the line checking his Ghosts, one by one.

* * *

THE SIDE HATCH of drop 2D was already open. Trooper Garond shivered in the slip-stream blast, and made ready with the rope as Sergeant Obel gave the signal. Outside, he could see cloud whipping past and several drop-ships lying abeam, men crouched in their open hatches, ready and prepped.

ABOARD DROP 2B, Colm Corbec fitted his gas-hood and ordered the hatches open. The squads took their positions, on their feet. Mkoll was at the head of the second squad, ready to lead the scout fireteam in.

Corbec nodded to him and uttered a final prayer.

IN DROP 2X, Sergeant Ewler looked over at Sergeant Adare. The two squad leaders shook hands.

'See you on the far side,' said Adare.

VILTRY WOKE AGAIN and found his face and shoulder were beginning to burn with the cold. He didn't want to die like this. Not alone, discarded, like a wind-blown seed. His numb fingers closed around the toggle.

He snatched his hand away and cursed his selfishness.

Unless...

If dispersal command-control heard his distress beacon, they'd know that something had happened to Halo Flight. They'd realise there were hunters loose.

He'd be warning them.

Filled with a sense of duty, Viltry pulled the toggle. It came away in his hand.

Shrapnel had ripped away the beacon's trigger switch.

SUDDENLY, THERE WAS a creamy glow below them. Available light was reflecting off the primary dome of Cirenholm in frosty midnight shine. The drop-ship's braking jets wailed so loud Zhyte could hear them through his hood. They were stationary, as stationary as the headwind allowed, right over the drop zone. Zhyte prayed they were low enough.

The green rune lit up.

'Deploy!' Zhyte growled.

There was a bright flash outside. Then another.

Shener, Zhyte's starboard point man, looked out and saw the drop-ship beside them splinter and fall apart, cascading luminous debris down into the darkness.

'Interceptors!' he screamed into his link.

Another Urdeshi drop-ship suddenly became visible in the night as it caught fire and burned down like a comet. A moment later, Cirenholm's defences woke up and lit the air with a ferocious cross-stitching of tracer fire.

Shells whacked into drop 1A's fuselage next to Shener. He had been coiling out the rope. A terrible, exposed cold filled his legs and lower torso and he looked down to see that there was an extraordinarily large, bloody hole in his gut.

Shener toppled out of the hatch wordlessly and fell away into the gloom below.

Zhyte reached the hatchway, battered by the wind. Shener was gone, and the two men first up the squad had been exploded across the bay. There were punctures in the hull.

Outside, a storm of enemy fire bloomed up at them.

Zhyte clipped his arrestor hook to the rope. He should have been last man out, but his point was gone and the troopers were milling, disorientated.

'Go!' yelled Zhyte. 'Go! Go! Go!'

He leapt into space.

DROP 1C ROCKED as its neighbour exploded. Whinnying scraps of outflung debris punched through the drop's hull. Sergeant Gwill and three other troopers were killed instantly. Corporal Gader, half-blinded in his hood, suddenly realised he was in charge.

The green rune was on.

He ordered the men out.

Two thirds of the squads had exited when cannon shells ripped drop 1C open. Gader was thrown out of the hatch.

He gestured tragically with his arrestor hook as he fell. But there was no rope.

Gader dropped like a stone, right down the face of Cirenholm's primary dome, bouncing once off an aerial strut.

DROP 1K MISJUDGED the headwind and came in too low, mashing against the side of the dome in a seething blister of fire.

Just behind it, drop 1N braked backwards in a flurry of jets and then trembled as a rain of cannon shells peeled off its belly, spilling men out into the darkness.

Drop 1M faltered, and tried to gain height. Its men were already deploying out of the hatches. Sliding down the ropes, they discovered that the drop was not only too high, it was also fifty metres short of the DZ. Each man in turn came off the end of the dangling rope and fell away into the void.

The pilot of drop 1D saw the enemy cloud-fighter with perfect clarity as it powered in, weapons flickering. He had no room to either pull up or bank. His troops were already on the ropes and heading down. Drop 1D exploded under the withering fire of the passing interceptor. Men were still hooked to the ropes as they snapped and fell away from the detonation.

* * *

'TARGETS! TARGETS! TARGETS!' Jagdea urged as she swept down across the Urdeshi troop ships. Drops were exploding all around, picked off by the Phantom interceptors or hit by Cirenholm's defence batteries.

The night had lit up. It was flickering hell here, beneath the vast dome of Cirenholm's primary hab.

Jagdea smoked in wide, avoiding a drop that blew apart in the air. She had target lock on a spinning cloud-fighter and the guns squealed as she let rip.

It was turning so hard it evaded her fire, though her marching tracers pummelled their way up the curve of the dome.

Jagdea inverted and, pulling two Gees, flipped round onto the cloud-fighter's tail. It was heading out to pick off more of the vulnerable troop ships in the van of the flock.

She jinked, lined it up, and hit the afterburner so that her streams of gunfire would rake its length as she swept past it.

The enemy fighter became a fireball with wings, that arced away down into the poisonous Scald below.

Jagdea banked around. Her wingmen were shouting in her headset.

Halo Two had just splashed an enemy interceptor, dogging it turn for turn and chewing off its tail with sustained cannon fire. The stricken fighter tried to end its death dive by ramming a drop, but it missed and trailed fire away into the clouds.

Jagdea hung on her wingtip, and dropped, hunting visually and instrumentally for targets. She powered down through the drop-ship fleet, her target finder pinging ever more rapidly as she bottomed out and swung in on the tail of a cloud-fighter that was flaring around to fire up at the bellies of the troop ships.

Jagdea killed it with a fierce burst of fire.

She yawed to port, out-running the tail of the troop ship dispersal before banking back to come in again beneath it. Her Lightning screwed over and her instruments wailed as cannon shots battered into her flank.

Red runes on all systems. She'd been killed.

She peddled out, pulled back, and gave the dead craft all the lift its wingspan would permit. She was now gliding towards the bulk of Cirenholm, about to stall out.

Jagdea squeezed the weapon toggles on her yoke and emptied her magazines into the dome, for what good it would do.

Her engines blew, and fire streamed along one wing.

She ejected.

HELL WAS REACHING up to them with thousands of fingers made of fire. The night was a strobing miasma of darkness and flashes. The wind was screaming, a dull roar through the gas-hoods. Every few seconds, there was a shell burst so bright the descending Urdeshi could see forever: the great domed face of Cirenholm; the swarming drop-ships; the dangling strings of men, hanging like fruit-heavy vines from the tightly packed ships.

Zhyte came off the rope end hard and slammed sideways into a balustrade. It ran around the lip of the dome's lowest outer promenade, and Zhyte realised that a few metres to the left and he would have missed the city structure entirely.

He'd cracked a rib on landing. He winced a few paces forward and troopers thumped and rolled around him. The vox-lines were frenetic with distorted chatter.

He tried to marshal his men and group them forward, but he'd never known confusion like it. Bitter, hard fire rained down from an elevated walkway twenty metres west, and dozens of his men were already sprawled and twisted on what had once been a regal, upper class outer walk with stratospheric views.

'Singis!' Zhyte yelled into his vox. 'Move them in! Move them in!'

Singis, his young, cadet-school trained subaltern, ran past, trying to get the men up. Zhyte saw a two-man stub-team attempting to erect their weapon, hampered by the men who were dropping all around them and sometimes on top of them. Indeed, there were so many men coming down now that the immediate DZ was filling up. Penned in by the city wall, the edge of the balustrade and the defending gunfire, they were rapidly filling up every precious metre of the drop area. Deployed troopers were being knocked down by the wave behind them. One man was pushed out over the balustrade, and was only just clawed back by his desperate comrades.

Zhyte could feel the powerful downwash of the drop-ships as they came in overhead, jostling for position.

The Urdeshi commander could see for about a kilometre along the length of the curving promenade. All the way along, drop-ships were clustering and roping out the strings of his puzzle-camoed troops. He saw a firefight around a hatchway fifty metres away as his fifth platoon tried to storm entry. He saw the flash of four grenades. He saw a drop-ship pummelled by tube-shot rockets, saw it burn as it tilted sideways, tearing through the drop-ropes of two other ships, cascading men to their deaths. As he watched, it exploded internally and fell, glancing off the promenade with enough force to shake the deck under his feet. A fireball now, it pitched sideways and fell off the city shelf into the abyss.

A trooper to Zhyte's left had lost his gas-hood in the descent. He was choking and frothing, yellow blisters breaking the skin around his lips and eyes.

Zhyte ran forward, ignoring the las-rounds exploding around him.

He got into cover behind a low wall with four of his squad's troopers.

'We have to silence that position!' he rasped, indicating the elevated walkway with a gloved hand. The man immediately right of him was suddenly hit twice and went tumbling back. A second defence position had opened up, raking 50-cal autocannon fire into the unprotected throng of the landing troops.

They were dying. Dying so fast, Zhyte couldn't believe what he was seeing. They were packed in like cattle, without cover, with nowhere to move to.

With a curse that came from somewhere deep in his guts, Zhyte ran into the open towards the walkway. Tracer fire stippled the ground at his feet. He hurled a grenade and the back blast knocked him down.

Two men grabbed him and dragged him into cover. The walkway was on fire and sagging. Urdeshi troops poured forward from the dense, corralled mob at the DZ.

'You're a bloody maniac,' a trooper told him. Zhyte never did find out who it was.

'We're inside!' Singis voxed.

'Move up, by squad pairs!' Zhyte ordered. 'Go!'

IBRAM GAUNT WAS the first man out, the first onto the ropes. The secondary dome of Cirenholm lay below. A huge fog of light and fire throbbed in the night sky behind the silhouetted curve of the more massive primary dome. The Urdeshi assault had been met with huge force.

Gaunt hit the DZ clean, and ran clear of the rope end as his men came down. Las-fire was beginning to spit down at them from gun positions higher up the dome slope. The Tanith were landing, as per instructions, on a wide balcony that ran entirely around the widest part of the dome's waist. Over the vox came a curt report announcing that both Corbec and Mkoll's squads were on the balcony too, about a hundred metres away.

Troopers Caober and Wersun were right behind Gaunt. He waved them wide to the right, to set up covering fire. He could see Sergeant Burone's drop-ship lining up ahead, hatches open as it came in over the balcony. Through the stiff, treated canvas of his hood, he could feel the air resonate with its whining thrusters.

'Hot contact!' the message buzzed over the vox. It was Sergeant Varl, somewhere behind him. A lattice of laser fire lit up the night maybe two hundred metres east, flickering along the balcony.

Gaunt saw figures ahead of him, armed men rushing out onto the balcony shelf. They were shadows, but he knew they weren't his own.

His bolt pistol barked.

'Move up!' he yelled. 'Engage!'

VARL'S SQUAD HAD come down into the middle of a firefight. Kolea's unit was dropping to their right, and Obel's somewhere behind.

Varl scurried forward, popping off random shots with his rifle. The enemy was secured around one of the major hatchways leading off the balcony walk into the dome. They were in behind flakboard and sandbags.

The Tanith edged forward, using ornamental planters and windscreens as cover, pumping fire at the entrance. Varl saw Ifvan and Jajjo scrambling up onto a walkway and running to get good shooting positions.

He ducked in behind a potted fern that had long since been eaten away by acid rain, and fired a sustained burst at a section of flakboard. Five other troopers, also in cover, joined him and the emphatic fire they laid up between them smashed the blast fence down. Bodies fell behind it.

'A flamer! I need a flamer!' Varl voxed. 'Where the feth is Brostin?'

HALF A KILOMETRE east of Gaunt, Rawne's assault units were dropping into the worst resistance offered by the secondary dome. A dozen men were shot off the ropes before they'd even reached the deck. Drop 2P had its belly shot out by ground fire and limped away, dragging streamers of men behind it.

There were enemy forces out on the balcony itself, firing up at the troop ships as they came over. And there were at least four multi-barrel autocannon nests firing out of windows further up the dome's surface.

Rawne paused in the hatchway of his ship.

'Sir?' Feygor asked, behind him.

'No fething way are we going down into that,' Rawne said sharply. Vertical las-fire hissed past the hatch.

'Charges! Give me charges!' Rawne said, turning back inside.

Feygor moved down the waiting squad with an open musette bag, getting every man to toss in one of his tube charges. When it was satisfyingly full, it was passed back up the line to Rawne at the door.

'Pilot to squad leader! Why aren't you going out? We can't hold this station for ever!'

'Feth you can! Do it!' Rawne growled back into the vox.

'I've got ships backing up behind him, and we're sitting ducks!' the voice on the vox complained.

'My heart bleeds,' replied Rawne, stripping the det-tape off one last charge, dropping it into the bag and tossing it out. 'Don't make me come up front and make your heart bleed too, you craven sack of crap.'

The satchel landed right in the midst of the ground troopers firing up from the balcony. Rawne could see it clearly. When it went off, it spewed out a doughnut shaped fireball that ripped fifty metres in every direction.

Rawne locked his arrestor hook to the rope.

'Now we go,' he said.

DROP 2K HAD come in too eagerly behind the troop ships halted by Rawne's delay. The pilot realised the flotilla ahead had cut to hover mode too late, and had to yaw hard, breaking out of line. In the back of the drop, the waiting lines of Ghosts were sent sprawling sideways. Trooper Nehn, crouching at the open hatch as point man, was thrown out, but managed to hold on to the rope. He was slammed back hard against the hull like a pendulum but maintained his frantic grip though the breath had been smashed out of him.

2 K's pilot tried to avoid fouling the other ships and turned wide. Angry and confused, the men in the drop bay had only just regained their feet when the ship threw them over again. They had dropped down into range of the dome defence, and taken two missiles in the flank.

The drop was ablaze. Domor, the commanding officer, yelled at the men to stay calm. Bonin and Milo were trying to drag Nehn back inside.

'We have to get down!' someone yelled.

'There's nowhere to put down!' Domor replied.

'We've fething well overshot!' bawled Haller, the commander of 2K's other squad.

Domor grabbed a leather roof strap and hung on, his heavy musette bag, cinched lasgun and arrestor hook banging and flapping against his body as the drop wallowed and pitched. Trooper Guthrie was on the deck, blood leaking down inside his hood from a scalp wound he'd received head-butting a seat restraint on the first wild jolt.

'Medic! Here!' Domor cried, and then clambered over the backs of several sprawled men to reach the port hatch. Milo and Bonin had just succeeded in dragging Nehn back inside.

Domor looked out. Their drop, spewing sheets of flame from somewhere near the ventral line, was limping slowly forward up over the patched, greasy roof plates of the secondary dome itself. They were already a good three hundred metres past the DZ. Looking back, Domor saw the waves of Tanith ships coming in, roping out into a spasming fuzz of light. Domor's vox-set was awash with radio traffic from the assaulting forces. He recognised voices, coded deployments, call-signs. But it all sounded like it was coming from men who were fading away into a distance, like a party he was leaving too soon. The curve of the dome was chopping the transmissions.

They had missed. They'd had their chance and they'd fethed it. There was no going back, no reversing back through the deploying lines. They were overshooting up and across the target city-dome itself.

Under such circumstances, standing orders applied and they were clear: abort and pull out along 1:03:04 magnetic, and return to the base drogue. That's it, boys. Nice try, but no thanks. Go home and better luck next time.

But abort wasn't an option. Domor craned out. They'd clearly damaged a fuel-line, and that was on fire. And from the sway of the old, heavy drop, the pilot had lost a good proportion of his attitude control.

They'd never make it back to the drogue. Not in a million years.

Even if there was a chance, and Domor was fething sure there wasn't, a pull-out at this height and crawl rate would glide them right over the dome's lip-guns as a nice, slow, fat, fire-marked target.

They were dead.

VARL DUCKED. CHUNKS of stone and scabs of plasteel spattered from the archway above his head. Down the hall, someone was the proud owner of a heavy autocannon.

They'd broken the rim defence and forced access into one of the main hatches leading off the secondary dome's balcony. His squad was the first one inside, though from the sound of the vox-traffic, Rawne was making headway further around the dome edge.

The hatch they'd fought their way in through gave onto a wide lobby dressed with polished ashlar and set with angular, cosmetic pillars. The floor was littered with brick chips and dust, and the bodies of the enemy dead.

Varl knew he was facing the troops of the notorious Blood Pact. He'd paid special attention in the briefings. The Blood Pact weren't enflamed zealots. They were professional military, soldiers sworn to the badges of Chaos. He could tell from the tight, well-orchestrated resistance alone that he was dealing with trained warriors.

They were holding the lobby with textbook authority: light support weapons blocking the main throughway, peppering the hatch opening with measured, tight bursts.

Varl ran to the next pillar, and watched in dismay as gunfire chewed away a good chunk of its stone facing.

Stone splinters sprayed from the damage. He pulled himself in.

'Brostin!' he voxed. The flamer had got them through the opening. If they could move Brostin further forward into the lobby's throat, they might take the next mark.

Las-fire and solid rounds spat past him. Varl could see Brostin in cover three pillars away.

Varl peered out, and took a hit to his shoulder that toppled him back. He writhed back into cover, patting out the smouldering hole in his uniform. His augmetic shoulder, heavy and metallic, had absorbed the shot.

'Nine, six!'

'Six, nine!' Kolea voxed back.

'Where are you, nine?' Damn these gas-hoods! Varl couldn't see a fething thing.

'Behind you, on the other side,' Kolea returned. Crouching around, Varl could see the big Verghastite, ducked down behind a pillar on the right, with two other men from his squad.

Cannonfire pounded down the hallway, filling the air with dust and flying chips. Despite his hood, Varl could hear the clinking rain of spent cases the enemy gun was spilling out onto the marble deck. Varl slid round onto his knees and started to prep a tube charge.

There was a sudden increase in resistance fire, and the flooring between the pillar rows was speckled with the ugly mini-craters of heavy fire. Varl looked up and saw, to his disbelief, that Kolea had successfully run forward into the maw of the enemy, and was now two pillars ahead of him on the other side. Kolea stood with his back to the chipped, punished pillar and lobbed a grenade out over his shoulder.

The blast welled flame down towards them. Varl sprang up and ran through the smoke, dropping down behind a pillar ahead of Kolea. Seeing him, Kolea swung out and drew level, then moved one ahead.

It was like some stupid fething competition, like the brainless games of devil-dare Varl had played as a teenager. There was no skill in this. No tactics, no battle-smarts. It was just sheer balls. Running into gunfire, damning the bullets, shaming the devil and taunting him. They were edging ahead simply by dint of bravado, simply through luck that neither of them had been hit.

Kolea looked back at Varl.

Devil-dare. Bullets whickered all around.

Varl ran out, sidestepped a tight burst and then pushed his already thread-thin luck further in order to dive behind the next pillar up. He could feel it vibrate against his back as cannonfire punched into the far side.

Devil-dare. Devil-fething-dare. But enough was enough. The Emperor, may he be ever vigilant, had smiled on them this far, but that was it. Another step would be suicide. Varl knew luck was a soldier's friend. It'd stick by you, but it was fickle, and it hated being asked for favours.

'Nine, six. Stay in cover. I think I–'

Autocannon shots barked out and chewed the wall. Kolea had just made a mad dash down the wall-side of the pillars on his half of the lobby and slid in safe behind a pillar ten metres further forward.

'Nine!'

'Six?'

'You're a mad fething fool!'

'It's working, isn't it?'

'But it shouldn't be working and it won't keep working if we do it again!'

'Cold feet, Tanith?'

'Feth you, Kolea!'

Of all the Ghosts, Varl and Kolea epitomised the best aspects of the Tanith/Verghastite rivalry. There were a good few from both backgrounds who manifested the uglier resentments, prejudices or simple racial enmities that made up the worst. Sergeant Varl and Sergeant Kolea had been friends from an early stage, but their friendship was catalysed in rivalry. Each was a notable soldier, popular with the men. Each enjoyed a good relationship with Gaunt. And each was in charge of a section that was considered by all to be fine, solid and second-string.

There was nothing formal about the distinction. It was just a given that a handful of platoons formed the regimental elite: Mkoll's scouts, Rawne's merciless band, Corbec's dedicated unit, Bray's tightly-drilled, tightly-disciplined squad and the determined, courageous mob schooled by Soric. They were the best, the 'front five' as they were often called. Kolea and Varl both yearned to elevate their own squads into that illustrious upper echelon. It was all fine and dandy to be regarded as part of the solid, dependable backbone. But it wasn't enough for either of them.

In combat, that competition came out. It didn't help that both had missed the epic battle for the Shrinehold on Hagia. They had formed the rearguard then, and done a fine job, but they had not been there to share the glory of the big fight. To prove their worth.

And so now it came down to devil-dare. Stupid, dumb-ass devil-dare games, urging fate and luck and all the other monsters of the cosmic firmament to make one a hero-winner and the other a loser-corpse.

Varl had come up from the ranks. He had fought for his stripes, and not just been given them due to his record as a scratch-company hero like Kolea.

But enough was enough.

'No more, nine! No more, you hear?'

'You're breaking up on me, six,' Kolea voxed back.

'We need to get a flamer up, Kolea–'

'Do what you like... I'm going ahead–'

'Nine!'

Varl looked out from cover, and saw a fountain spray of las-fire and tracers vomit down the hallway. He saw Kolea running forward, somehow, impossibly, alive in the midst of it. He saw thousands of individual impacts as soot and dust and mortar was smashed out of the bullet-holes in the floor, the roof and the walls.

Kolea ran on. He'd lost his wife at Vervunhive and, he had believed, his children too. Some cruel twitch of fate had allowed them to survive and to end up in the care of the female trooper Tona Criid and her devoted Tanith partner Caffran.

Cruel wasn't the word. It was too cruel. It was beyond cruel. He'd only discovered the fact on Hagia, and pain had sealed his mouth. Those kids – Dalin and Yoncy – had been through so much, believing their parents lost and gaining fine new ones in the form of Criid and Caffran, Kolea had decided never to disturb their world again.

He had avoided them. He had stayed away. No one had ever found out the truth, except for Surgeon Curth, in whom he had confided.

It was better that way. It freed him.

Freed him to fight and die and serve the Emperor.

Kolea ran on into a rain of fire. He was a big man who had served a long time in the mines of Verghast. Grim, largely humourless, powerful. He should have formed a huge target, but somehow the enemy fire missed him. Shots ripped the air around him, cast sparks from the pillars, blew stone chips from the floor.

He lived.

He thought about diving for cover, but he was so nearly there it didn't seem to matter.

Kolea came on the enemy position from the side, leapt over the horseshoe of sandbags and shot the two cannon gunners down.

A third lunged at him from the left and Kolea's bayonet tip punched through his forehead with a crack.

These brutes were Blood Pact. They wore old but well maintained suits of armour-plated canvas dyed a dark red, drapes of ammo-belts and munition pouches secured on black nylon webbing, and crimson steel bowl helmets with sneering, hook-nosed blast-visors. Chaos insignia glinted on their sleeves and chests.

More Blood Pact troops rushed out at Kolea, assuming they had been stormed by force. Their red-tunicked forms twisted away as Varl ran forward, firing his lasgun on auto, yelling the names of his sisters, his father, his mother and his homestead farm.

Raflon, Nour and Brostin were right behind him. Raflon made a stupendously good shot that burst the skull of a Blood Pact trooper who was turning out of cover from behind a doorpost.

Then Brostin washed the hallway beyond with a bright belch of promethium flame. Something exploded. Two Blood Pact troopers staggered into the main hall, their red uniforms ablaze, the armour plating falling out of the burning canvas of their sleeves.

Wordlessly, Varl and Kolea heaved the enemy autocannon around on its tripod and blitzed down into the corridor beyond: Varl firing, his hands clamped to the yoke, Kolea feeding the belts from the use-bruised panniers.

The big old cannon had huge power. Varl knew that. A minute before he'd been running into it.

Heavy support fire blasted from their left. Bragg was alongside them now, firing his autocannon from the hip, his feeder Caill fighting to keep up the supply of fresh drum mags.

'On! In!' Kolea barked. Nour and Bragg, Caill, Raflon, Hwlan, Brostin and Brehenden, Vril and Mkvan, a dozen more, ran past them into the inner hall, covering and firing.

Varl threw the emptied cannon aside and looked at Kolea.

'You're mad, Gol.'

'Mad? War's mad. We broke them, didn't we?'

'You broke them. You're mad. Crazy. Insane.'

'Whatever.'

They picked up their lasguns and moved on after the point men. 'When I tell Gaunt what you did–' Varl began.

'Don't. Please, don't.'

Kolea looked round, and Varl could see his eyes, dark and serious behind the misted plates of his gas-hood.

'Just don't.'

'WE ROPE OUT. Now.' said Domor. Drop 2K lurched again as cannon fire struck it.

'Rope out?' Sergeant Haller returned, horrified.

'Just shut up and do it or we're dead.'

'Onto the dome?'

'Yes, onto the dome!'

'But we've missed the DZ! We should–'

'Should what?' snapped Domor, turning to stare at Haller. 'Abort? Take your chances with that if you like, Verghast. I don't think so–'

'Air speed's dropping!' Milo cut in.

'Thrusters are failing. I can't get lift!' the pilot called back from the cockpit.

'Go!' said Domor. Haller was at one hatch, Bonin and Nehn at the other. The burning drop was wallowing over the dome, in darkness now, the curve of the dome eclipsing the flare of the main fight. They couldn't see a thing. They might as well be over the edge of the dome for all they could tell. The night was awash of black with no solid edges.

'We have to–' Domor said.

IT SEEMED TO Commander Bree Jagdea that the fight was happening a long way away, on another planet. Flares and flashes lit up the night sky to her right, but they were a long, long way away.

She lay on the curved metal surface of one of Cirenholm's habitat domes, the secondary one she guessed. It was cold and the crossing night wind bit deep. Her arm and several ribs were boken from the ejected landing. Her flight suit was torn.

Her blimp-chute had barely had time to deploy as she had fired up out of the seat of her dead fighter. Smack, the dome had come up to meet her hard.

And here, she presumed, she would stay until the midnight frosts made her a brittle part of the dome roof decoration.

When Jagdea saw the drop-ship, it was already on fire and coming in low over the dome towards her, spitting debris and flame, crawling crippled from the main fight.

She saw the hatches were open, saw figures in the hatches. Men about to rope out.

They were going long. They were going long, off the edge of the dome, into the Scald.

She didn't think. She pulled the toggle on the canister in her chute webbing and popped bright incandescent fire across the dome roof around her.

'Here!' she screamed, flailing her one good arm, like someone in need of rescue. 'Here!'

In truth, she was the one doing the rescuing.

'FETH! WE JUST got a DZ!' Bonin yelped.

'What?' Haller said, pulling at his hood to get a clear view.

'There, sergeant!' Bonin pointed.

'Steer us to port! To port!' Domor voxed the pilot.

Drop 2K yawed left, up and over the side of the secondary dome, a dark hemisphere below it. There was a splash of almost fluorescent light on the surface of the dome, a fizzle of flare just now beginning to sputter away.

The men roped out. Milo led the squad out of the port, his hook whizzing down the cable until he slammed into the curving roof and tumbled off. Domor was behind him, then Bonin, then Ezlan.

On the starboard side, Haller came out, followed by Vadim, Reggo and Nirriam.

The men thumped down onto the roof, scrabbling for handholds, desperate not to slide off into the night. Twenty men down, twenty-five. Thirty. Thirty-five.

The drop's engines failed. Clinging to the curve of the roofing panels on his belly, Domor heard the pilot scream. He looked back. The dropship simply fell out of the air and smashed into the roof, crushing a half-dozen of the roping men under it.

Then it began to slide.

Three

AN AWFUL CREAKING, screeching sound filled the air, metal on metal. There were still at least twenty men attached to the ropes, their arrestor hook locks biting the loose cables because of the sudden slackening. The men were tangled, and being dragged. Domor, Nehn and Milo struggled up and watched the blazing drop slowly sliding and shrieking away down the curve of the dome, hauling Guardsmen after it.

The pilot was still screaming.

'Cut the ropes! Cut the fething ropes!' Domor yelled.

Bonin cut the rope with his Tanith blade and fell free. He rolled, and managed to seize hold of an icy roof strut. Eight of Haller's men sawed their way clear of the snarling ropes too. Ezlan lost his knife, but managed to writhe himself out of his webbing.

The moment his blade severed it, the drop rope came whipping out of Dremmond's arrestor hook because it was under too much tension. The blow left him sprawled on the roof with a long, deep slash from the hawser across his collar.

Six more of Haller's men and nine more of Domor's managed to cut themselves free of the straining ropes and cling onto the roofing panels.

Then the drop went off over the side of the dome under its own massive weight, jerking threads of shrieking men after it.

Silence.

Milo got to his feet, unsteady. It was suddenly very dark and cold. The raked roof underfoot was slick with frost. The only light came from the burning tatters of debris outflung across the steeper pitches of the dome, and the sky glow of the battle they had become detached from. Despite the figures struggling up around him, he felt monstrously alone. They were, in effect, castaways on a mountaintop at night.

'Sound off!' Domor stammered over the vox. One by one, out of order, the survivors reeled off their call-signs. Fifteen of Domor's squad had survived. Haller had fourteen. The soldiers began to congregate on a flat decking area behind a vox-mast that protruded from the dome like a corroded thorn. Everyone was unsteady on their feet and there were some heart stopping slips.

Ezlan and Bonin joined the group, carrying an injured female aviator between them. Her name was Jagdea. Her Lightning had been brought down and she'd ejected onto the roof. She'd been the one who'd popped the flare and guided them in.

Her arm was broken and she was slipping into shock, so she barely heard the mumbled gratitude of the Guardsmen.

Milo glanced round sharply as he heard a thump. Dremmond, wounded and weighed down by his flamer, had risen only to lose his feet on the ice. He'd gone down hard and was starting to slide, slowly but definitely, down the dome's curve.

'Feth! Oh feth!' he burbled. His gloved hands scrabbled at the slippery metal and plasteel, frantic for purchase. 'Oh feth me!'

Milo moved. Dremmond had already slid right past two troopers either too stunned to move or too aware of their own tenuous footing. Dremmond's dangling arrestor hook and promethium tanks were squealing over the roof metal.

Milo slithered down towards him. He heard several voices yell at him. His feet went out and he landed on his backside, sliding down himself now. Unable to stop, he banged into Dremmond, who clutched at him, and they slid together. Faster. Faster.

The lip of the roof looked hideously close. Milo could see the burnt score marks where the weight of the drop-ship had gone over just moments before.

They jerked to a halt. Breathing hard, Milo realised his lasgun strap had fouled a rusty rivet standing proud of the plating. Dremmond clung to him. The canvas strap began to stretch and fray.

Something heavy bounced down the frosty roof beside them. It was a length of salvaged drop-rope, playing out from the darkness above.

'Grab it!' Milo heard a voice call from above. He got his hands around it. Looking up, he saw a trooper edging hand over hand down the rope towards them. It was the Verghastite, Vadim. A huddle of shadows further up the slope showed where Bonin, Haller, Domor and several of the others were anchoring the other end of the rope under the vox-mast.

Vadim reached them.

'Like this, like this,' he said, showing them how to coil the rope around their palms so that it wouldn't work loose. 'You all tight?'

'Yes,' said Milo.

'Hang on.'

To Milo's incredulity, Vadim continued on down the rope past them, making for the very edge of the roof lip. The air-exchanger on the back of his rebreather hood puffed clouds of steam and ice crystals out as he exerted himself.

Vadim reached the lip, wound the trailing end of the rope around his ankle like an aerialist, and then rolled onto his belly, so that he was hanging out over the abyss headfirst.

'What the feth is he doing?' Dremmond stuttered.

Milo shook his head – a futile response for a man in a gas-hood – but he was lost for words. They could only hold on and watch.

Vadim moved again, rolling upright and freeing his ankle only to lash the rope end around his waist, using his arrestor hook as a double lock. Then he reached into his webbing and dug out a roll of cable, a metal reinforced climbing line much narrower in gauge than the drop rope, a standard issue part of every Guardsman's kit. He fiddled with it a moment, securing it to the lifeline the men above were holding out, and then swung back over the side.

'Taking the weight, you hear me, sergeant?' Vadim suddenly voxed.

'Understood,' voxed Haller.

'Make sure you're gakking well anchored,' Vadim said.

'We're tied back to a goddamn mast here.'

'Good. Then smooth, hard pulls. Count off three between and do them together or we'll all end up down there somewhere.'

'Got it.'

'Go.'

The main rope jerked. Slowly, Milo realised they were sliding up the dome again, a few centimetres at a time. He clung on and felt Dremmond's hands tighten on him.

'Come on!' Vadim urged from below.

It seemed to take an age. Milo felt numb. Then hands were reaching for him and dragging him and Dremmond up amongst the cluster of bodies around the mast where the rope was tied off.

When he looked back down at Vadim, Milo was astonished to see he wasn't alone. He was dragging two more figures with him. Milo immediately added his own strength to the steady, regular heaves.

Vadim had found Seena and Arilla, the two Verghastite women from Haller's squad who crewed the autocannon. They'd been dragged off the dome by the drop-ship, but their section of rope had parted and snagged around a vent under the lip. They'd been left hanging in space. Vadim had heard their desperate calls on his way down to Milo and Dremmond.

The Ghosts pulled the trio to comparative safety. Vadim lay flat for a moment, exhausted. Fayner, the one surviving field medic, checked the girls over and then packed Dremmond's ugly wound, the exposed areas of which were beginning to blister.

The Ghosts began to light lamp packs and check over their weapons and equipment. Haller and Domor were consulting pocket compass and viewers, looking up the massive swell of the dome. Domor called Bonin over. He was one of the best scouts in the regiment, one of Mkoll's chosen.

'What are we going to do?' Nehn asked Milo.

'Find a way in?' Milo shrugged.

'How?' growled Lillo, one of the veteran Vervunhive troopers from Haller's squad.

Bonin heard him and looked round. He held up a flimsy fold of paper. 'The Emperor has blessed us. Or rather, Gaunt has. I have a map.'

THERE WAS NO one there.

Zhyte peered out of cover, but the corridor ahead, a wide access way, was empty. Singis voxed in a confirmation from the far side.

Zhyte edged forward. The Urdeshi main force had been on the ground in the primary dome for almost an hour now and they'd advanced barely three hundred metres from the DZ itself. True, they were inside the dome. But it had taken time and men. They'd lost so many to the enemy night-fighters on the run into the DZ, and then so many, many more in the brutal fight to storm the hatchways.

Now, it seemed as if the enemy had simply given up and vanished.

Zhyte crawled on his knees and elbows over to Singis, who was logging the situation on a data-slate as his vox-officer Gerrishon whispered information from the other units.

'Let me see,' Zhyte said, taking the slate anyway. His number two, Shenko, was still held fast in a hard fight along the promenade. Zhyte could hear the ragged fighting and weapon discharge from outside. Three forces, including his own, had penetrated the dome proper through main hatchways, meeting fierce resistance from squads of the Blood Pact scum, nightmarish in their red battledress and snarling, hook-nosed masks. There were status reports from Gaunt's mob at the secondary DZ and Fazalur's at the tertiary, and it seemed they had ground to a halt too, but Zhyte didn't much care. This was his baby. The primary dome was the main objective, and the Seventh Urdeshi had been given that honour. It was a matter of pride. They would take this blasted place.

But it had all gone so quiet. Ten minutes before, these access halls had been the scene of ferocious, almost hand-to hand-killing. The corpses and the battle damage all around testified to that.

And then, the Blood Pact had simply melted away.

'They may have fallen back. Perhaps to better defensive positions deeper in the dome,' Singis suggested.

Zhyte nodded but he didn't honestly give a little pebble crap for that idea. If the Blood Pact had wanted to hold them off, they'd been in a position to do it from the beginning. The Urdeshi had managed a few tricks, forced a few advantages, but it was nothing much. The enemy defence had been superb, and viable. It made no sense for them to have abandoned it for 'better positions'. Singis was talking out of his arse.

Zhyte tossed the slate back to his adjutant. Though it hurt his pride to think it, this had been a disaster all round. His entire force might by now be impact-splats down in the Scald levels if it hadn't been for the Phantine Lightnings that had driven the enemy nightfighters off. Not that he'd ever admit it to that sour bitch aviator Jagdea. Thanks to the air support, he'd got a good proportion of his men down. He'd lost hundreds rather than thousands.

And now this. Like his storm-troops were being toyed with.

He yanked the vox-mic from Gerrishon.

'Belthini? Rhintlemann? You hearing me?' The officers commanding the other two intruder forces voxed back affirmatives immediately.

'I don't know what the good crap is going on, but I'm not going to roll about here all night. Three minute count, on my mark from now. We're going to push ahead. Stir 'em up at least.'

They confirmed the order. Enough of this creeping around, Zhyte thought, exchanging his weapon's clip for a fresh one. He had a pack satisfyingly full of fresh ones.

'Go left,' he told Singis. 'Take groups three and four. Six and two advance with me. First port of call is that main hatch there. I want it secure and I want the support weapons up smart to set up along that colonnade.'

'Yes sir.'

'While we're at it... Kadakedenz?'

The recon-officer crouching to Singis's left looked up.

'Sir?'

'Hand pick six men and push in through that side hatch. They could be lying in wait, hoping to enfilade us.'

'Enfilade us, sir?'

'Shoot us sideways in the arse, Kadakedenz!'

'I don't think that's what enfilade means, sir. Not technically–'

'I don't know what "shut the crap up you sag-arsed tosser" means, Kadakedenz. Not technically. But I'm going to say that too. Can you whip up a side team and skidaddle it sideways to support my move, or are you too busy making inadvertent crap-streaks in your britches?'

'I can do it, sir, yes sir.'

Zhyte looked at his wrist-chrono. The beater hand was ticking towards the static marker needle he'd punched and set while giving Belthini and Rhintlemann the order mark.

'Let's move like we mean business.'

In a side hall off the main access to the secondary dome, gun smoke drifting in the cool air, Trooper Wersun was loading his last clip. 'Last chance box?' asked Gaunt, moving up next to him. Wersun reacted in surprise.

'Yes, sir. Last clip, sir.'

'Use it sparingly.' Gaunt huddled down next to him and slid a fresh sickle pattern magazine for his bolt pistol out of his ammo web. He'd sheathed his power sword for the moment.

As far as Gaunt knew, most of his men were now, like Wersun, down to their last. If he ever got out of this, he'd use the power blade of Heironymo Sondar to put on a novelty ventriloquist show for the Ghosts, using the Munitorium chief at Hessenville as the screaming puppet.

Gaunt's blood was up. This should have been easier. The Blood Pact were damn good. He'd been through a fight in the outer hatches that had been as hard and nasty as anything in his notable career.

'Caober?'

'Sir,' replied the Tanith scout, huddled up against a fallen pile of ceiling girders.

'Anything?'

'No, sir. Not a fething sign. Where did they go?'

Gaunt sat back against a block of bullet-chipped masonry. Where indeed? He was overheating in the hood now, and sweat was dribbling down his spine.

Beltayn, his vox-man, was nearby. Gaunt waved him over.

'Mic, sir?'

'No, plug me in.'

Beltayn wound a small cable from his heavy, high-gain vox-pack and pushed the jack into a socket on the side of Gaunt's hood. Gaunt's head-set micro-bead now had the added power of Beltayn's unit.

'One, two?'

'Two, one.'

'Colm? Tell me you see bad guys.'

'Not so much as a murmur, boss,' Corbec replied over the link. His force was advancing slowly down the access halls parallel to Gaunt's.

'Keep me advised. One, three?'

'Three,' responded Rawne.

'Any good news where you are?'

'Negative. We're at the mouth of an access tunnel. Five zero five if you've got your map handy. Where did they go?'

'I'm open to offers.'

'Four, one.'

'Go ahead, Mkoll.'

'We've got the promenade clear. Bray, Tarnash and Burone are holding the west end, Soric and Maroy the east. I think Kolea, Obel and Varl got their squads in through a hatch west of you.'

'I'll check. Any movement?'

'It all went quiet about ten minutes ago, sir.'

'Stay on top of them, Mkoll.'

'Understood.'

'Nine? Six? Twelve?'

Kolea, Varl and Obel responded almost simultaneously.

'We've still got contact here, sir!' Varl said urgently. 'We– feth!'

'Six? Six, this is one?'

'Six, one! Sorry. It's hot here. Got us a firefight in an antechamber, heavy fire, heavy cover.'

'One, six, report position. Six?'

'Twelve, one,' Obel cut in. 'Varl's under fire. Kolea's boys are moving in support. We're through to access 588.'

Gaunt waved a hand and Beltayn passed him the chart slate.

Five eight eight. Bless Varl, Obel and Kolea. They were hard in, deeper than any Ghost unit. And from the look of Beltayn's log, deeper than any Imperial force. They were almost into the main habs inside the secondary dome. Excluding casualties, Gaunt had perhaps seventy-five men almost a kilometre inside the city.

'Right,' said Gaunt. 'They've set the pace. Let's close it up.'

* * *

It was the small, dead hours of the night, and a hard crust of frost had formed over the outer surface of Cirenholm's secondary dome. The air was black-cold, and polluted snow crystals twinkled down.

The survivors of drop 2K moved slowly up the bowl of the vast superstructure, their progress hampered by the treacherous conditions and by the injured: Commander Jagdea, who had to be carried: Dremmond with his lacerated shoulder; Guthrie with his head wound; Arilla, who had dislocated an elbow when the drop went down.

Bonin moved ahead, at point. The whole, vast roof was creaking as the temperature contracted the metal. On occasions, their rubber soled boots stuck fast if they stood in one place too long.

The light wash in the sky from the main assault behind the curve of the dome seemed to have died down. Had they lost? Won? All Bonin could see were the bars of smoke drifting up from the domes and the fathomless night punctuated by stars.

His mother, God-Emperor rest and protect her, had always said he had been born under a lucky star. She said this, he was sure, because his life had not been easy from the start.

His had been a difficult birth, during a cold spring in County Cuhulic, marked by inauspicious signs and portents. Berries out late, haw-twist turning to white flowers without seeding, the larisel hibernating until Watchfrost. While still a babe in arms, he had been blighted by illness. Then, while he was still in the cradle, forest fires had taken their home in the summer of 745. The whole county had suffered then, and the Bonin family, fruiters by trade, had suffered with the best. It had taken two hard years of living in tents while his father and uncles rebuilt the homestead.

Until the age of eight, Bonin had been known as Mach by all the family. His mother had always had this thing about Lord Solar Macharius, especially since a copy of his *Life* had been the only thing she had been able to save from the family home during the fire. An often bewildered and contradictory devotee of the fates, his mother had considered this another of her signs.

At eight, as was the custom with most old Tanith families, Bonin had been baptised and given his true names. It was considered that a child grew into the names he or she would need, and formally naming a child at birth was premature. The custom wasn't observed much now.

Bonin stopped his reverie and gazed up at the cold night sky. The custom wasn't observed at all now, he corrected himself. All those billions of lights up there, and not one of them was Tanith.

He remembered the day of his baptism. Coming down to the river on a chilly spring afternoon, the sky over the nalwoods a sullen white. Shivering in his baptismal smock, his older sisters hugging him to keep him warm and stop his tears.

The village minister at the waterside.

His mother, in her best dress, so proud.

Dunked in freezing, rapid river water and coming up crying, he had been given the name Simen Urvin Macharius Bonin. Simen, after his father. Urvin after a charismatic uncle who had helped rebuild their home.

Bonin remembered his mother, soft, warm and excited, drying him off after the baptism in the private shrine of their house, under the painted nalwood panels.

'You've been through so much, you're lucky. Lucky. Born under a lucky star.'

Which one, Bonin wondered now, halting and looking up at the curve of the dome as the ice gleamed.

Not Tanith, that was certain.

But the luck had never left him. He was sure his mother had rubbed raw luck into him that day with the rough folds of the towel.

He had survived the fall of Tanith. On Menazoid Epsilon, he had walked away without a scratch when a concussion round vapourised the three men in the fox-hole with him. On Monthax, he had seen a las-bolt pass so close to his face he could taste its acrid wake. On Verghast, he had been part of Gaunt's and Kolea's team in the assault on the Heritor's Spike. During the boarding, he had lost his grip and fallen off. He should have died. Even Gaunt, who'd seen him fall, presumed him lost, and was stunned to find out he had survived.

There were sixteen vertebrae in his back made of composite steel, and an augmetic socket on his pelvis. But he was alive. Lucky. Fated. Just like his mother had always told him. A sign.

Born under a lucky star.

But, he often wondered, how long would it burn?

The deck under his boots was glossy wet, not caked in frost.

Bonin knelt down and felt the roof plating. Even through his glove, he could feel the warmth.

Ahead, a quarter of a kilometre away, rose the stacks and smoking flues of Cirenholm's vapour mill. The drizzle of wet heat was keeping this part of the roof thawed.

Bonin consulted the map Gaunt had given him. The mill superstructure was the only thing that penetrated the roof of the secondary dome. There were inspection hatches up here, ventilator pipes.

A way inside.

Whatever the star was, it was still watching over him.

THE ACCESS TUNNEL marked on the map as 505 gave out into what had once been an ordered little park. High overhead, in the girders of the dome roof, sunlamps and environment processors hung in bolted cages, but they had long since been deactivated and the trimmed fruit trees and arbors had died off. Leaf litter, grey and dry, covered the mosaic paths and the areas of dead grass. Brittle-branched grey-trunked trees filled the beds, grim as gravestones.

Rawne moved his squad out into the park, using the trees as cover. Feygor swung to the left at the head of a fireteam. ready to lay down protective fire on the main force. Leyr, the platoon's scout, edged forward. The air was cold and dry.

Tona Criid, on the right hand edge of the formation, suddenly started and turned, her weapon rising.

'Movement, four o'clock,' she whispered briefly into her micro-bead.

Rawne held his hand out, palm down, and everyone dropped low. Then he pointed to Criid, Caffran and Wheln, circled his hand and pointed ahead with a trident of three fingers.

Immediately, the three troopers rose and ran forward, fanning out, keeping their heads low. Criid dropped behind a rusty bench, and Caffran tucked down behind the plinth of a stone centaur whose rearing forelimbs had been shot off. Wheln got in behind a brake of dead trees.

Rawne glanced to his left and saw Neskon crawling forward with the hose of his flamer ready. Leclan was covering him. To Rawne's right, Banda had her long-las resting on the elbow of a low branch. Like Criid, Jessi Banda was one of the Verghastite females who had joined the Ghosts. They seemed to have a particular expertise for marksmanship, and sniper was the one regimental speciality where there were as many Verghastites as Tanith. And as many women as men.

Rawne's opposition to women in the regiment was so old now it was gathering dust and everyone was tired of hearing it. He'd never questioned their fighting ability. He just didn't like the added stress of sexual tension it put on the ranks.

Jessi Banda was a good example. Cheerful, sharp tongue, playful, she was a good-looking girl with short, curly brown hair and curves that the matt-black battledress couldn't hide. She'd been a loom-worker in Vervunhive, and then a member of Kolea's scratch company guerillas. Now she was a specialist sniper in the Imperial Guard, and a damn good one. The death of one of the Tanith snipers had forced her rotation into Rawne's platoon.

He found her distracting. He found Criid, the surly ex-gang girl, distracting. Both of them were very easy on the eye. He tried not to think about Nessa, the sniper in Kolea's unit. She was downright beautiful...

'Sir?' whispered Banda, cocking her head at Rawne. Through the lenses of her gas-hood, Rawne could see a smile in her eyes.

Feth! I'm doing it again! Rawne cursed himself. Maybe it wasn't them. Maybe it was him...

'Anything?' he asked.

She shook her head.

'Movement!' Wheln hissed over the vox.

Rawne saw them for a brief moment. Four, maybe five enemy troopers in muddy red, moving hurriedly down the walkway on the far right hand edge of the park.

Wheln's lasrifle cracked, and Caffran and Criid quickly opened up too.

One of the figures buckled and dropped and las-shots splintered against the wall of the park. Two of the others turned and started to fire into the park. Rawne saw their iron-masked faces, sneering above the flashing muzzles of their weapons.

There was a loud report from his right. Banda had fired, loosing one of the sniper-variant long-las's overpowered 'hot shot' rounds. One of the firing enemy was thrown back against the wall as if he'd been struck by a wrecking ball.

A flurry of fire whipped back and forth through the park edge now. There must have been more than five of them, Rawne decided. He couldn't see. He ran forward, dodging between tree trunks. A sapling just behind him ruptured at head height and swished back and forth from the recoil like a metronome arm.

'Seven one, three!'

'Seven one, sir!' Caffran responded. Rawne could hear the background fire echoed and distorted over the vox-link.

'Sit-rep!'

'I count eight. Five in the bushes at my ten, three back in the doorway. We've splashed another four.'

'I can't eyeball! Call it!' Rawne ordered.

From behind the statue's plinth, Caffran glanced around. Whatever faults you could lay at Major Rawne's door – and heartlessness, lack of humour, deceit and cruelty would be amongst them – he was a damn fine troop leader. Here, with no view of his own, he was devolving command to Caffran without hesitation, allowing the young private to order the deployment. Rawne trusted Caffran. He trusted them all. That was enough to make him a far greater leader than many of the so-called 'good guys' Caffran had seen in his Guard career.

'Wheln! Criid! Tight and right. Hit the door. Leclan! Osket! Melwid! Concentrate on those bushes! Neskon, up and forward!'

There was a crackle of barely verbal acknowledgements. The las-fire coming out of the park's tree-line into the path-edge bushes increased in intensity.

Caffran got off a few more shots, but something heavy like a stubber was bracketing his position, chipping shards of stone off the plinth and gouging divots out of the dead grass. He threw himself back as one rebounding shell scarred his boot and another pinged hard off his warknife's blade, leaving an ugly notch in the fine-honed edge.

'Banda! See the panels on the end wall?'

'Got 'em, Caff.'

'Fifth one in from the left, middle rivet. Aim on that, but drop the shot about five metres.'

'Uh huh...'

There was another sharp whine-crack and part of the straggled bushes blew apart as the hot-shot went through it. The stub fire ceased. If she hadn't actually killed him, Banda had certainly discouraged the bastard.

'Got one!' whooped Melwid meanwhile.

Criid fired from behind the bench until a trio of close shots splintered the seat-back. She got down onto her belly in time to see two of the enemy running from the doorway towards another clump of bushes near the end of the path. She flicked her toggle to full-auto and raked them from her prone position. One of them dropped a stick grenade he had been about to toss, and the blast threw fine grit and dry clumps of dirt into the park.

Rawne had moved in close now, into the stands of dead trees by the edge of the fighting. Leyr was nearby. With a coughing rush, flames spewed out across the line of bushes as Neskon finally got range. Rawne heard harsh, short screams and the firecracker blitz of ammunition cooking off.

'Breakers!' Leyr shouted.

Rawne turned, and caught a glimpse of two red-tunicked figures sprinting from the path into the trees, moving past them into the park. He jumped up and ran, leaping fallen boughs and kicking up stones and dead leaves.

'Left! Left!' he shouted to Leyr who was running too.

Rawne ran on. Breathing came hard when you exerted yourself in a rebreather. Running jarred the hood so that visibility was impaired.

He caught a glimpse of red, and fired once, but the shot simply skinned the bark of a tree. Leyr fired too, off to his left.

Rawne came round the side of a particularly large tree and slammed into the Blood Pact trooper who had been dodging the other way. They went sprawling.

Swearing, Rawne grappled with the man. The enemy trooper was hefty and strong. His arms and body seemed hard, as if packed with augmetic systems. His big, filthy hands were bare and showed the scar tissue of deep, old wounds across the palms, made during his ritual pledge of allegiance to the obscenity Urlock Gaur.

He fought back, kicking Rawne hard and spitting out a string of curses in a language Rawne didn't know and had no intention of looking up later.

They rolled in the dirt. Rawne's weapon, clamped between them, fired wildly. All Rawne could see was the front of the foe's tunic: old, frayed, stained a dull red the colour of dried blood. It occurred to Rawne that it probably *was* dried blood.

Rawne got an arm free and threw a short but brutal punch that lurched the growling brute off him. For a moment, he saw the man's face: the battered iron grotesque fashioned in the shape of a hook-nosed, leering fright mask, hinged in place under a worn bowl helmet covered in flaking crimson paint and finger-daubed runes of obscenity.

Then the Blood Pact trooper head-butted him.

Rawne heard a crack, and felt the stunning impact and a stab of white-hot pain in his left eye. He reeled away. The hooked nose of the iron grotesque had punched in through the left lens of Rawne's gas-hood like a blunt hatchet, breaking the plastic and digging deep. His head was swimming. He couldn't see out of his left eye and he could feel blood running down inside his hood.

Raging, Rawne threw a hooking punch that hit the enemy in the side of the neck. His assailant fell sideways, choking.

Rawne drew his silver Tanith knife, grabbed the man around the left elbow to yank his arm up against the side of his head, and stabbed the blade up to the hilt in the man's armpit.

The soldier of Chaos went into violent spasms. Rawne rolled back onto his knees.

Leyr came out of the bushes nearby. 'The other one's dead. Ran straight into Feygor. I–feth! Medic!'

Leclan was the platoon's corpsman, one of the troopers trained in the rudiments of field aid by Dorden and Curth. As soon as he saw Rawne, he checked the brass air-tester sewn into the side of his kit.

'Air's clean. Stale but clean. Get that hood off.'

Leyr pulled Rawne's gas-hood off and Leclan took a look at the face wound.

'Feth!' Leyr murmured.

'Shut up. Go and do something useful,' Rawne told him. 'How is it?'

'Looks a right mess, sir, but I think it's superficial.' Leclan took out some tweezers and started removing slivers of lens plastic from Rawne's face. 'You've got blood in your eye from the cuts, and your eyelid is torn. Hang on, this'll smart.'

Leclan sprayed counterseptic from a puffer bottle and then taped a gauze pad over Rawne's eye.

'I haven't lost the eye then.'

'No, sir. But Dorden needs to look at it.'

Rawne got up and tucked his gas-hood away in his belt. He'd had enough of it anyway. He went over to the corpse and pulled out his knife, twisting the grip to break the suction and free the blade.

Feygor was moving the platoon up. The fight on the path was over.

'We got them all,' Caffran reported.

'Any casualties?'

'Only you,' said Feygor.

'You can all lose the hoods if you want,' said Rawne. He walked down to the path. Criid, Wheln, Neskon and Melwid were examining the bodies.

'Made a mess of this,' said Neskon, indicating the charred bush and the three blackened corpses behind it. 'I think they were carrying something.' Rawne knelt down and took a look, ignoring the reek of promethium and the spicy stink of seared meat. It was some kind of equipment box, scorched with soot and burned out. Rawne could see melted cables and broken valves inside.

'Sir,' said Feygor quietly. The platoon had tensed at movement from the south door, but it was more Ghosts. Captain Daur's squad, supported by Corporal Meryn's which had brought Commissar Hark along with it.

'This park area's secure,' Rawne told them. Hark nodded.

'Does that hurt?' asked Daur.

'You ask some damn fool questions sometimes, Verghast,' Rawne snapped, though he knew full well that the young, handsome captain was exercising his trademark ironic wit.

'Your men are unhooded,' observed Hark, holstering his plasma pistol.

'A necessity with me. But the air's clean.'

Hark almost ripped his own hood off. 'Damn well glad to get rid of that,' he said, trying to hand-comb his thick, dark hair before putting his cap on. He smiled at Rawne. 'We've been so busy I hadn't even checked the gauge.'

'Me neither,' said Rawne. 'Come and take a look at this. I could use a–'

'Good eye?' Daur finished for him. Rawne heard Banda and Criid snigger.

'Get the men to unhood, captain, if you please,' Hark told Daur. Daur nodded and walked away, smiling.

'Insufferable feth,' Rawne growled as he walked the commissar over to the path.

'In the God-Emperor's illustrious brotherhood of warriors, we are all kindred, major,' returned Hark smoothly.

'A little boost from the holy primers?'

'No idea. I'm getting so good at this I can make lines like that up off the cuff.'

They both laughed. Rawne liked Hark, probably about as much as he disliked Daur. Daur, good-looking, popular, efficient, had entered the regiment's upper command like a virus, dumped there on an equal footing to Rawne himself, thanks to Gaunt's generous efforts to integrate the Verghastites. Hark, on the other hand, had come in against Gaunt's will, indeed his original task had been to turn Gaunt out of rank. Everyone had hated him at first. But he'd proved himself in combat and also proved himself remarkably loyal to the spirit of the Tanith First. Rawne had been pleased when Gaunt had invited Hark to stay on as regimental commissar in support of Gaunt's own split role.

Rawne welcomed Hark's presence in the Ghosts because he was a hard man, but a fair one. He respected him because they'd risked their lives for each other in the final battle for the Shrinehold on Hagia.

And he liked him because, if only technically, he was a thorn in Ibram Gaunt's side.

'You really don't like the Verghastites, do you, Rawne?' said Hark.

'Not my place to like or dislike, sir. But this is the Tanith First,' Rawne replied, stressing the word 'Tanith'. 'Besides, I've only seen a handful of them that can fight as hard or as well as the Tanith.'

Hark nodded slyly over at Banda and Criid. 'I see you keep the decorative ones in your platoon though.'

Now it was Hark's turn to joke at Rawne's expense, but somehow it didn't matter. Rawne would have floored Daur for a quip like that.

Hark crouched down and looked at the half-melted box.

'Why do we care what this is?' he asked.

'They were moving it through the park. That way,' Rawne added, indicating the direction the Imperials had been advancing. 'Must have been important because they were breaking cover to move it.'

Hark drew his blade. It was a standard issue, broad-bladed dress dagger, a pugio with a gold aquila crest. He was the only man in the regiment who didn't have a silver Tanith warknife. He picked at the edge of the box-seal with the pugio's top.

'Vox set?'

'Don't think so, sir,' said Rerval, the vox-officer in Rawne's squad.

'It's a generator cell for a void shield.'

They looked round. Daur had rejoined them.

'Are you sure, captain?' asked Hark dubiously.

Daur nodded. 'I was a garrison officer on the Hass West Fort, sir. Part of my daily duty was to test start the voids on the battery nests.'

Smug know-all bastard, Rawne thought.

'So what were they doing w–'

'Sir!' Caffran called down the pathway. He was with Feygor's fireteam at the end hatch.

They hurried down to join him. Meryn and Daur deployed their troops out across the park to cover all the access points.

The hatch was open and its arch was dim. Beyond it, Rawne could see a corridor with a grilled floor leading deeper into the dome structure.

'Cables, there, inside the jamb,' said Feygor, pointing out what they'd all missed. Feygor had notoriously sharp eyes. He had been able to spot a larisel at night at a hundred metres back home in the Great West Nals. And kill it with a dirty look. Feygor should have been in the scout section, but Rawne had worked determinedly not to lose his lean, murderous ally to Mkoll's bunch. And it was just as likely Mkoll didn't want Feygor anyway.

'Booby trap,' Caffran said, speaking what they were all thinking. A quick vox-check confirmed that all the accessways off the northside of the park showed similar signs of tampering.

Daur called Criid over. 'Permission to risk my health recklessly,' he asked Hark lightly.

'Don't wait on my account,' Rawne muttered.

'You have an idea, captain?' Hark asked.

'Get everyone to fall back from the doorways,' Daur said. He borrowed Criid's lasrifle and the small, polished brooch mount she kept in her pocket. It was her little trademark, and Daur requisitioned it now, sending her back into cover.

Daur fixed the mount to the bayonet lug of the rifle as he had seen Criid do and then gingerly extended the gun out at arm's length.

'Pray to the Golden Throne...' Hark whispered to Rawne, down in cover.

'Oh, I am,' said Rawne.

The brooch-mount had been polished to a mirror, and it was a canny tool for seeing round corners without risking a headshot. Rawne knew that several Ghosts had copied Criid's idea, realising how useful such a thing was for room to room clearance. Scout Caober used a shaving mirror.

Daur peered in via the little mirror for a few seconds and then ran back to the line.

'Thanks, Tona,' he said, handing the brooch and the weapon back to Criid.

'The door's rigged with a void shield,' Daur told them. 'It's not active yet, but it's charged.'

'You know because?'

'Smell of ozone.'

'So they're intending to block our advance in this section with shields. We better get in there and disable them,' Feygor said.

'Unless they're waiting for us to try,' said Daur.

'Might explain why they've fallen back so suddenly,' said Hark. 'Bringing us forward, luring us, so they can cut us off.'

'Or in two,' said Daur.

'What?' asked Rawne.

'You ever been standing in a void field when it was activated, major?'

'No.'

'It was a rhetorical question. The field edge would cut you in half.'

Rawne looked at Hark. 'I say we run it. Get as many through as we can.'

'So that those who get through can be cut down with nowhere to run because there's a void at their backs?' Daur asked sourly.

'You got a better idea, Verghast?'

Daur smiled at him without warmth and tapped the pips on his coat.

'Address me as "captain", major. It's a small courtesy, but I think even you should be capable of it.'

Hark held up his hand. 'Enough. Get me the vox-officer.'

FREE OF THE damn gas-hood at last, Gaunt set his cap on his head, brim first. He glanced at his watch, took a sip of water from his flask, and looked down the hallway.

Two storeys high, it was ornate with gilt and floral work, and the floor was a chequerboard of red and white pouskin tiles. Crystal chandeliers hung every ten metres, blazing out twinkly yellow light that shone from the huge wall mirrors.

Gaunt glanced back. His platoon was in cover down the length of the hall, using the architraves and pillars for shelter. Wersun and Arcuda were guarding a side door which led into a section of staterooms that had already been swept. There was a scent in the air. Fading perfume.

Cirenholm had been a rich place once, before Gaur's Blood Pact had overrun it. Here in the palatial halls of the secondary dome, the elegance lingered, melancholy and cold.

Caober reappeared, coming back down the hall, hugging the shadows. He dropped down next to Gaunt.

'Shield?'

Caober nodded. 'Looks like what Commissar Hark described. It's wired into the end doorway, and to the pair adjoining. There was a staircase, but I didn't fancy checking that without a fireteam.'

'Good work,' said Gaunt and took the mic Beltayn held out.

'One, four?'

'Four, one,' Mkoll replied. 'All exits north of 651 are wired for shields.'

'Understood. Stay where you are.' Gaunt looked at his chart, and ran a finger around a line that connected the sites his men had reported as covered by shields. They'd all found them: Corbec, Burone, Bray, Soric. Sergeant Theiss's squad had actually passed one, and then fallen back rapidly once Gaunt had alerted them. Only the spearhead formed by Obel, Kolea and Varl had gone beyond, too far beyond to call back now.

'What are they up to, d'you think, sir?' asked Beltayn. 'Something's awry.'

'Yes it is, Beltayn.' Gaunt smiled at the vox-officer's use of his favourite understatement. He looked at the chart again. His company – with the exception of the spearhead – had penetrated about two-thirds of a kilometre into the dome and had all come up against prepared shield emplacements, no matter what level they were on. Soric's mob were six levels lower thanks to a firefight and the chance discovery of a cargo lift. It was as if the enemy had given up the outer rim of the dome to lure them in against this trap.

But what kind of trap? Was it meant to stop them dead? Cut their force in half? Pull them on and trap them without hope of retreat?

Gaunt took the mic again. 'Boost it. I want Zhyte and Fazalur,' he told the vox-man.

'1A, 3A... this is 2A. Respond. Repeat, 1A, 3A, this is 2A.'

White noise. Then a burp of audio.

'...A... repeat this is 3A. Gaunt?'

'Confirmed, Fazalur. What's your situation?'

'Advancing through the tertiary dome. Low resistance.'

'We've found shields here, Fazalur. Void shields laid across our path. Any sign there?'

'Active shields?'

'Negative.'

'We've seen nothing.'

'Watch for them and stay in contact.'

'Agreed, 2A, I stand advised. Out.'

'1A this is 2A, respond. 1A respond this channel. 2A to 1A, respond...'

'I'VE GOT COMMISSAR Gaunt on the primary channel, sir,' Gerrishon called.

'Tell him I'm busy,' snorted Zhyte, waving the next squad forward. His unit was now a kilometre into Cirenholm's primary dome, exploring the marble vaults and suspiciously derelict chambers of the sky-city's commercial district. Ten minutes before, he had linked up with Belthini's group, and together they'd begun sectioning the outer dome. There was still no sign of the enemy. No sign of anyone, in fact, apart from his own puzzle-camoed troops. His skin was starting to crawl.

'He's quite insistent, sir. Says something about shields.'

'Tell him I'm busy,' Zhyte repeated. His men were executing bounding cover as they played out down the wide hallway, passing under vast holo-portraits of Phantine's great and good.

'Busy with what, sir?'

Zhyte stopped with a heavy sigh and turned to look at his suddenly pale vox-officer. 'Inform the stubborn little pool of canid-piss that I'm taking a masterful dump down the neck of Sagittar Slaith and I'll call him back when I've finished the paperwork.'

'I, sir–'

'Oh, give me that, you limpoid!' Zhyte spat and snatched the mic, cuffing Gerrishon for good measure.

'This had better be good, Gaunt,' he snarled.

'Zhyte?'

'Yes!'

'We've found shields, Zhyte, dug into doorways along marker 48:00 which would correlate to 32:00 on your map–'

'Do you have a point or are you calling for advice?'

'I'm calling to warn you, colonel. Secondary dome is wired for shields and tertiary may be too. Watch for them. Slaith, Emperor rot him, is no fool, and neither are the Blood Pact. They're planning something, and–'

'Do you know the name of my regiment, Gaunt?'

'Say again?'

'Do you know the name of my unit?'

'Of course. The Urdeshi Seventh Storm-troop. I don't see w–'

'The Urdeshi Seventh Storm-troop. Yes, sir. Our name is woven in silver thread on an honour pennant that hangs amongst the thousand flags beside the Golden Throne on Terra. We have been an active and victorious unit for a thousand and seventy-three glorious years. Is the Tanith First marked on an honour pennant, Gaunt?'

'I don't believe it is–'

'I know for a damn fact it isn't! You were only born yesterday and you're nothing! Nothing! There's only a bloody handful of you anyway! Don't you dare presume to tell me my business, you piece of shit! Warning me? Warning me? We are taking this bastard city piece by piece, hall by hall, with our blood and our sweat, and the last thing I want to hear is you whining about something that's making you soil your britches because you're too scared to do a soldier's job and get on with it!

'You hear me, Gaunt? Gaunt?'

GAUNT CALMLY HANDED the mic back to Beltayn.

'You get him, sir?'

'No. I got some fething idiot who's about to die,' said Gaunt.

ZHYTE CURSED AND threw the mic back at his vox-officer. The handset hit Gerrishon in the face and he fell down suddenly.

'Get up, you pile of crap! Gerrishon! On your feet!'

Zhyte paused abruptly. There was a widening pool of blood spreading out across the floor under Gerrishon's head. The vox-man's face was tranquil, as if he was sleeping. But there was a blackened hole in his forehead.

'God-Emperor!' Zhyte howled and turned. A las-round hit him in the shoulder and slammed him to the floor.

Everything, every last damn bloody thing, was exploding around him. He could hear screams and weapons fire. Laser shots spluttered along the walls, shattering ancient holo-plate portraits out of their frames.

Zhyte crawled round. He saw three of his advance guard topple as they ran. Mists of blood sprayed out of them. One was hit so hard his left leg burst and came spinning off.

His men were firing. Some were screaming. All were yelling. A grenade went off.

Zhyte got up and ran back down the hallway, firing his weapon behind him. He ducked behind a pillar and looked back to see Blood Pact troopers spilling into the hall from all sides. They were bayoneting the Urdeshi men in cover, and firing wild but effective bursts at those trying to retreat.

'Regroup! Regroup!' Zhyte yelled into his micro-bead. 'Hatch 342! Now!' Three four two. There was a gun nest there. Support fire.

He turned and fell over a corpse. It was Kadekadenz, his recon man. His carcass had been messily eviscerated by sidelong las-fire, and ropes of steaming entrails spilled out of it like the tentacles of some beached cephalopod.

'Singis! Belthini! Group the men!' Group them, for g–'

A blow to the shoulder slammed him over. Zhyte rolled, and saw the iron mask of a Blood Pact trooper gurning at him as he plunged his bayonet down.

The rusty blade stabbed through the flesh of Zhyte's thigh and made him shriek. He fired twice and blew the Chaos soldier off him, then tore the blade from his leg. Blood was squirting from a major artery.

Zhyte got up, and then fell over, his boots slipping in his own blood. He grasped the Blood Pact soldier's fallen rifle, the smeared bayonet still attached, and rolled over, firing.

He hit one, then another, then a third, swiping each one off his feet with the satisfying punch of a solid las-hit.

Singis grabbed him and began to half-drag, half-carry him back towards the hatch. There were corpses all around. Down the hall, Zhyte could see nothing but a mob of charging Blood Pact troopers, chanting and howling as they came on, firing, guns at belly height.

He saw his men, littering the marble floor of the hallway. Zofer, on his back, jaw-less. Vocane, doubled-up and hugging the belly wound that had killed him. Reyuri, his legs in tatters, groping at the air. Gofforallo, just upper body and thighs attached by a smouldering spine. Hedrien, stapled to the wall by a broken bayonet blade through the chest. Jeorjul, without a face or a left foot, his gun still firing in spasming hands. He saw a man he couldn't recognise because his head had been vapourised. Another that was just pieces of meat and bone wrapped in burning shreds of puzzle-camo.

Zhyte screamed and fired. He heard heavy weapon fire, and laughed like a maniac as tracers whinnied down the hall and tore through the front ranks of the advancing Blood Pact.

'Shut up! Shut up!' Singis yelled at him. 'Get on your feet and help me!'

Zhyte fell dumb, like a stunned drunk, shock setting in. His trousers were soaked red with his blood. Dyed red. Like the Blood Pact.

They were in the doorway. Three four two. Belthini was dragging him through. He couldn't see Singis, but he fell sidelong across the hatch opening, and saw Bothris and Manahide manning the .50 cal cannon, raking the enemy with tracer fire. Three four two. His support weapon pitch.

'Give the bastards hell!' he said. At least he thought he said it. He couldn't hear his own voice and they didn't seem to hear him.

There was blood welling up in his throat.

Everything went quiet. Zhyte could see the furious flashes of the .50's barrel. The lancing tracers. The las impacts all around. He could see men's mouths moving, yelling. Manahide. Bothris. Belthini, in the doorway, over him, a look on his face that seemed touchingly concerned.

Between Belthini's legs, Zhyte saw the Blood Pact. They had Rhintlemann. They were hacking him apart with their bayonets. He was vomiting gore and screaming.

Zhyte couldn't hear him.

He could hear nothing but his own pounding heart.

He sagged. Belthini stooped over him. Belthini said something.

Zhyte suddenly realised he could smell something. Something sharp, pungent.

Ozone.

It was ozone.

His head fell sideways. His skull bumped against the floor, and glanced off the sill of the hatch.

He saw the little box in the hatch frame, wired to the power sockets in the wall. There was a light flickering inside it.

Ozone.

He crawled. Crawled forward. He was sure he said something important, but Belthini was looking over at the gun team and didn't hear him.

There was a flash.

Just a bright flash, as if light had suddenly become solid, as if the air had suddenly become hard. He tasted smoke and heat.

Zhyte looked back in time to see the void shield engage across the doorway, chopping Manahide and Bothris in two, along with their .50, which exploded. It was quite amazing. A boiling fog of blood and atomised metal. Men falling apart, torsos and skulls cut vertically like scientific cross-sections. He saw smoothly severed white bone, sectioned brains, light coming in through Manahide's open mouth as the front of his face and body spilled forward on the other side of the shield.

Two sliced portions of human meat slumped back next to him, their edges curled and sizzling from the void field.

Zhyte looked up and saw Belthini trapped on the other side of the shield, his image distorted and blurred by the energy. He was shouting, desperate, hammering his fists. No sound came through.

Belthini was hit from behind by about six or seven las-rounds. Blood sprayed up the shield and he fell against it, sliding down like a man sliding down a pane of glass.

'Oh shit,' said Zhyte, hearing himself for the first time.

He realised the pain in his leg was gone.

And then he realised that was because his legs were still on the other side of the shield.

Four

He was the only one in the group who could see the stars.

They were hidden behind the black on black cloud cover that roiled across the heavens above the secondary dome, but he, and only he, could detect their light spill.

Sergeant Dohon Domor was known affectionately as Shoggy Domor by the men of the regiment. He'd been blinded in action back on Menazoid, years ago now as it seemed to him. He'd become quite used to the bulbous augmetic optics that crudely replaced his eyes.

Shoggy Domor. A shoggy was a little amphibian with bulging eyes found in the woodland pools on Tanith. He corrected himself: an *extinct* amphibian. The nickname had stuck.

Domor tried his micro-bead one last time, but there was nothing but static fizzle. They were out of range, and their main gain vox-sets, both of them, had gone down with the drop, still attached to vox-officers Liglis and Gohho.

He walked with careful steps up the dome's treacherous curve to rejoin the team. His augmetic eyes whirred and adjusted to reduce the light glare from the mill stacks ahead. The tips of the chimneys showed as flaring yellow, the stacks themselves as orange. The figures of the men were red shadows and beyond them the night cooled into shapes of blue, purple and black.

'Anything?' asked Sergeant Haller.

'No,' Domor replied. His limbs were beginning to ache from the cold and he could feel the throb of raw bruises.

All their uniforms and the canvas of their gas-hoods were begining to stiffen with hoarfrost.

With Bonin leading the way, flanked by Vadim, the survivors of drop 2K climbed cautiously into the scaffolding superstructure surrounding Cirenholm's vapour mill. Steamy gusts of hot, wet air exhaled over them, thawing their ice-stiff clothes and making them sweat suddenly. They could feel the thunder of massive turbines underfoot, shaking the roof housing. Meltwater and condensation drooled off every surface.

The beams of their lamp packs twitched nervously back and forth. It seemed more than a little likely that the enemy would have positioned sentries around the roof access here.

Commander Jagdea was back on her feet. Fayner, the corpsman, had given her a shot of dexahedrene and bound her broken right arm up across her chest in a tight brace. She carried her snub-snouted automatic pistol in her left hand.

They moved in under a dripping stanchion onto a massive grilled exhaust vent that steamed away in the cold of the night. Amber heat glowed far below down the shaft. Domor's energy sensitive vision adjusted again.

'Ah, feth!' Nehn shuddered.

The edges of the vent and all the girders around were thick with glistening, writhing molluscs, each one the size of an ork's finger. They turned towards the lights, fleshy mouthparts twitching and weeping viscous slime. They were everywhere, thousands of them. Arilla brushed one from her sleeve and it left a streak of ooze that hardened quickly like glue. The fat slug made a disgusting, meaty sound as it bounced off the roof.

'Thermovores,' said Jagdea, her breathing shallow and rapid. 'Vermin. They cluster around the heat exchangers feeding off the bacteria in the steam.'

'Charming,' said Milo, crushing one underfoot and really wishing he hadn't.

'They're harmless, trooper,' said the aviator. 'Just watch for skinwings.'

'Skinwings?'

'The next link of the food chain. Pollution mutants. They feed on the slugs.'

Milo thought about this. 'And what feeds on the skinwings?'

'Scald-sharks. But we should be all right. They don't usually come in close to the cities. They're deep sky hunters.'

Milo wasn't sure what a shark was. Indeed, he wasn't really sure what the Scald was either, but he was conscious of the stress Jagdea put on each word.

Bonin had stopped to consult the map, conferring with the sergeants and with Corporal Mkeller, the Tanith scout assigned to Haller's squad.

'That way,' Bonin said, and Mkeller concurred. The troop followed the scouts under a series of dripping derricks that rose up from the skin of the dome into the freezing night. Navigation lights winked on the mast tops, and on the fatter, higher columns of the chimneys. The slugs squirmed around them, following their lights, dribbling slime and forming glittering snot-bubbles around their snouts.

Bonin stopped by a raised vent and used his knife blade to scrape off the clusters of thermovores. Together with Mkeller, he managed to break the vent grille away and toss it aside.

Bonin peered in. 'It's tight, but we can make it. Break out ropes.'

'No,' said Vadim.

'What?'

'Let me look at that map,' Vadim said. He turned the thin paper sheet Bonin offered him in his gloved hands.

'That's a hot gas out-flue.'

'So?'

'So, we'll be dead if we go down there.'

'How do you reckon that?' asked Mkeller.

Vadim looked up so that Bonin and Mkeller could see his eyes behind the lenses of the hood. 'It's a fifty metre vertical climb. With our numbers and our impediments–' he glanced over at Jagdea, 'it'd take us upwards of two hours to get down there.'

'So?'

'I don't know how often this thing vents, but none of us want to be halfway down it when the hot gas comes up. It'd broil us. Clothes, armour, skin, flesh... all cooked off the bones.'

'How the feth do you know so much?' asked Mkeller.

'He was a roofer, back at Vervunhive,' Milo said quickly. 'He knows about this kind of thing.'

'I did some work on the heating systems. Vox-masts and sensor blooms mostly, but heating too. Look at the way the grille you pulled off is made. The louvres curl up... out. It's an out-flue.'

Bonin seemed genuinely impressed. 'You know this stuff, then? Good. You call it.'

Vadim looked at the map again, pausing to wipe condensing vapour from the eye plates of his hood. 'Here... here. The big intakes. Intake shafts for the cooler coils. It's a longer climb, and we'll have to be wary of duct fans and inrush–'

'What's inrush?' asked Domor.

'If they cycle up the fans for extra cooling, we could be caught in a wind tunnel effect. I'm not saying it's safe, but it's safer.'

There was a sudden bang and a howl of heat. The flue Bonin and Mkeller had been contemplating suddenly voided a thick cloud of superheated gas-flame and soot. It seemed, comically, to underscore the validity of Vadim's advice.

Bonin watched the donut of expelled gas-flame wobble up into the sky.

'I'm convinced,' he said. 'Let's go with Vadim's plan.'

ALL ACROSS THE secondary dome, the shields were lit, blocking them in and penning them in the outer limits of the dome. An anxious vox-signal from Fazalur in the tertiary dome confirmed that it was happening there too.

And then the signal cut off abruptly.

There was nothing from the Urdeshi at primary except a strangled mess of incoherent panic.

'Form up and move in!' Gaunt ordered, swinging his squad around. He voxed ahead to Corbec and Bray, instructing them to sweep laterally along the edge of the shield block and converge on him.

'Can't raise the spearhead,' Beltayn said.

Gaunt wasn't surprised. The shield effects distorted vox-links badly. The platoons led by Varl, Kolea and Obel were cut off from the main force, deep in the heart of the enemy-held dome.

As he moved his men around, down a wide stairwell and across a series of ransacked aerodrome hangars, Gaunt tried to work out the enemy tactics. Part of it seemed blindingly obvious: allow the Imperial forces a foothold in the perimeter of the dome, and then deprive them of advance. The question was... what next?

He didn't have to wait long to find out.

The Blood Pact had been waiting. They hadn't withdrawn at all. They'd concealed themselves in false floors and behind wall panels.

Now the Imperial invaders were penned in, they sprung their ambush, coming out in the midst of the confused guard units.

Guard units who no longer had any room to manoeuvre.

THE TROOPER NEXT to Colonel Colm Corbec turned to speak and then fell silent forever as a tracer round blew his head off. A brittle rain of las-fire peppered down onto Corbec's squad from balcony positions all along the mezzanine floor he was moving across.

'Down! Down and cover! Return fire!' Corbec yelled.

He saw three troopers drop, and watched in horror as the metal-tiled flooring all around ruptured and punctured in a thousand places under the cascade of enemy shots.

Corbec crawled behind an overturned baggage cart that shook and bucked as rounds struck it. He tugged out his las-pistol and blasted through the mesh at indistinct figures on the gallery above.

Trooper Orrin was beside him, firing selective rounds from his lasrifle.

'Orrin?'

'Last chance box, sir,' Orrin answered.

Corbec fired another few shots with his pistol and tugged his remaining clip from his ammo-web, handing it to Orrin.

'Use it well, lad,' he said.

Corbec was pretty sure none of his men had any more than a single clip of size three left after the initial assault. Loaded, they might do this. They might hold.

But running empty... it would be a matter of minutes until they were totally overwhelmed.

Already, he could see two or three of the best men in his squad – Cisky, Bewl, Roskil, Uculir – crouching in cover, heads down, their ability to resist gone.

They were out of ammo.

Corbec prayed with all his heart that someone, someone in authority... Ornoff, Van Voytz, maybe even Macaroth himself, would punish the simpletons in the Munitorium who, for want of a signed docket, had hung them all out to dry.

Corbec crawled forward to the end of the cart. Someone was crying out for a medic, and Corpsman Munne was darting through the rain of fire to reach him, aid bag in his hand.

Corbec fired his las-pistol up at the gallery. He had six clips – size twos – left for the handgun and that was his only arm now he'd given his last rifle pack to Orrin. There had been a plentiful supply of size two/pistol format in the drogue's stores. But few of the regular men carried pistols.

He saw Uclir firing a solid-ammo revolver at the enemy. A trophy gun, taken on some past battlefield. A lot of Ghosts cherished captured weapons. He hoped Uclir wasn't the only man in his squad to have kept his trophy with him and in working order.

There was a blast of serious firepower from his left. Surch and Loell had managed to get the light support .30 onto its brass stand and were firing. Their peals of tracers chased along the upper levels and several dismembered red figures tumbled down into the air shaft along with sections of stonework.

Told of the shortage of standard rifle packs before lift-off, Corbec had wisely assigned troopers Cown and Irvinn to hump extra boxes of .30 shells for the support weapon. At least his land-hammer had some life in it yet.

Lancing beams of terrible force, bright white and apocalyptic, shafted down from the massing enemy. A tripod-mounted plasma weapon was Corbec's best guess. He saw two of his men blown into flakes of ash by it.

Corbec fired his pistol twice more and then ran, braving the torrent of indiscriminate fire, back to a marble portico where Muril crouched with the platoon scout Mkvenner.

'Up there!' Corbec yelled as he skidded in beside them.

'Where?' Muril asked, swinging her long-las.

Muril, a female Vervunhiver with a heroic track record from the Zoican War, was Corbec's chosen sniper. Rawne had once asked Corbec why he'd personally selected Muril for the second platoon – Rawne seemed to have an unseemly interest in the female soldiers these days – and Corbec had laughed and told him it was because Muril had a deliciously dirty laugh and red hair that reminded him of a girl he'd been a fething fool to leave behind in County Pryze.

Both facts were true, but the real reason was that Corbec believed Muril to have a shooter's eye second only to Mad Larkin, and that given a well-maintained lasrifle and a generous crosswind, she could pick off anything, anywhere, clean and true.

'Get the fething heavy weapon!' Corbec urged her.

'I see it... gak!' She took the weapon off her shoulder.

'What?' asked Corbec.

'The gakking discharge from it... so bright... just about blinding me through the scope every time it fires. Screwing the scope's photoreceptors...'

Corbec watched in horror as Muril calmly uncoupled the bulky power-scope from her weapon and aimed it again, by naked eye, down the barrel to the foreplate.

'You'll never make it...' he whispered.

'As you Tanith would say, fething watch me–'

Muril fired.

Corbec saw a spray of dust and stone chips burst from the gallery overhead.

'Yeah, yeah, okay–' Muril growled. 'I was just getting my eye in.'

The plasma weapon fired again, blowing a hole out of the lower gallery and sending Trooper Litz into the hereafter, incinerated.

'I see you,' said Muril, and fired again.

The hot-shot round blew the head off one of the Blood Pact gunners and he dropped out of sight. Another iron-masked warrior ran over to recrew the gun as the loader yelled out, but Muril had already used her first hit as a yard-stick and she was firing again. Once, twice...

The third round hit the weapon's bulky power box and a whole section of the upper gallery exploded in a cone of energy. The floor level blew out, and thirty or more Blood Pact warriors tumbled to their deaths in an avalanche of blistered stone.

'I could kiss you,' Corbec murmured.

'Later,' Muril replied, adding a 'sir' that was lost in her dirty, triumphant laughter.

Leaving her to refit her scope, Corbec and Mkvenner ran towards the stairhead, where the team with the .30 autocannon was doing its level best to stem the tide of the Blood Pact stormers charging down at them. The stairs were littered with bodies, body parts and gore.

Loell was winged and knocked down by a stray round, but Cown leapt up to take over the ammo feed.

The .30 was chattering, its air-cooled barrel glowing red-hot.

Then it jammed.

'Oh feth–' stammered Corbec.

The Blood Pact were all over them.

'Straight silver! Straight silver!' Corbec ordered, and shot the nearest enemy soldier with his pistol as he drew his warknife. The troops in his squad pressed forward, those that had power left firing, those that didn't using their lasrifles like spears, their warknives locked to the bayonet lugs.

There was a brief, brutal struggle at the stairs. Corbec stabbed and fired, at one point ending up with a Blood Pact trooper's iron mask caught around his knife, the blade through the eye-slit.

He saw Cisky drop, trying to hold in his ripped guts. He saw Mkvenner halfway up the stairs, firing his last few rounds and killing an enemy with each one. He saw Uclir clubbing the brains out of a Chaos trooper with his solid-ammo revolver, his last few bullets used up.

A spear of flame ripped up the staircase, consuming the tide of enemy troops descending on them. Furrian, Corbec's flamer-man, advanced into the press, blitzing his drizzles of fire across the screaming foe, driving them back.

'Go, Furrian! Go, boy!' Corbec bellowed.

Furrian had grown up in the same wood-town as Brostin, and shared his unhealthy enthusiasm for naked flames. The tanks on his back coughed and spat liquid promethium that the burner head in his hands ignited into blossoms of incandescent fire.

Now we're turning this, thought Corbec, now we're fething turning this.

A las-round hit Furrian in the head. He twisted and fell, the flamer spurting weak dribbles of fire across the floor.

Then another las-round hit the tanks on Furrian's back.

The blast-wash of fire knocked Corbec down. Uclir screamed as his clothes caught fire and he pitched off the staircase, a blazing comet of struggling limbs. Orrin lost his face to the flames, but not his life. He rolled on the floor, shrieking and squealing through a lip-less mouth, choking on the melted fat of his own skin.

The Blood Pact poured in. They were met by Mkvenner, Cown and Surch, the only men still standing at the stairhead after the blast. Corbec struggled up, gasping, and saw something that would remain in his mind until his dying day: the most heroic display of last stand fighting he would ever witness.

Mkvenner was by then out of ammo, and Cown had nothing but his Tanith blade.

Surch was firing a laspistol, and had attached his warknife to a short pole.

Mkvenner swung his lasgun and decapitated the first enemy on him with the bayonet, las-rounds passing either side of him. He spun the weapon and smashed a Chaos soldier down with the butt-end before ramming the blade into the belly of another.

Cown opened the torso of a Blood Pact trooper with a downward slash, and then punched his knife through the eye-slit of the iron grotesque that followed. There were enemy troopers surging all round them.

Surch shot two, then pistol-whipped another when his handgun ran dry. He drove an iron mask back into the face behind it with the dumb end of his makeshift spear shaft and then sliced it round to cut the right hand off another of their visored foes.

The warknife flew out of Cown's hand as a Blood Pact trooper with a short sword all but tore his arm off. Cown fell down, cursing, and then grabbed a drum magazine from beside the .30. He used it to beat the swordsman to death before passing out across him.

Surch killed four more and wounded a fifth before a las-shot hit him in the knee, dropped him and exposed him to the butt of an enemy gun.

Mkvenner... Mkvenner was terrifying. He was using his lasrifle as a quarter staff, spinning it and doing equal damage with the stock end as with the blade. Urlock Gaur's chosen finest tumbled away from him on either side, cut, clubbed or smashed over by his heavy boots. Lanky and long, Mkvenner kicked like a mule and moved like a dancer. Mkoll had once told Corbec that Mkvenner had been trained in the martial tradition of cwlwhl, the allegedly lost fighting art of the Tanith wood-warriors. Corbec hadn't believed it. The wood-warriors were a myth, even by Tanith's misty standards.

But as he gazed at Mkvenner then, Corbec could believe it. Mkvenner was so fast, so steady, so direct. Every hit counted. Every swing, every strike, every counter-spin, every stab. The wood-warriors of ancient Tanith lore had fought in the old feudal days, using only spear-staves tipped with single edged silver blades. They had united Tanith and overthrown the Huhlhwch Dynasty, paving the way for the modern democratic Tanith city-states.

Mkvenner seemed to Corbec like a figure from the fireside tales of his childhood. The Nalsheen, the wood-warriors, the fighters of legend, masters of cwlwhl.

No wonder Mkoll had such a special admiration for Mkvenner.

But even he, even a Nalsheen, couldn't withstand the assault forever.

Corbec stumbled to join him, firing wildly with his laspistol.

He fell, halfway up the steps.

Then light and dazzling streams of las-fire sliced into the pouring foe from the top of the stairs.

Sergeant Bray's platoon had found them, moving along a higher level to fall on the Blood Pact from the rear. Twenty-five strong, Bray's squad quickly slaughtered the enemy and wiped the upper gallery clear.

Bray himself hurried down the steps, pausing only to finish off a couple of wheezing, twitching Blood Pact fallen, and joined Corbec.

'Just in time, I think,' Bray smiled.

'Yeah,' panted Corbec. The colonel clambered up the stairs and helped the exhausted, gasping Mkvenner to his feet.

'Brave lad,' Corbec told him. 'Brave, brave lad...'

Mkvenner was too breathless to reply.

Supporting Mkvenner, Corbec looked back at Bray.

'Get ready,' he said. He could hear snare drums now, and the ritual hollering of the enemy as they regrouped in the galleries and halls around them. 'Get your platoon into position. Scare up as many working weapons and viable ammo as you can from the enemy dead. This is just beginning.'

'D'you ever consider,' murmured Varl, taking a lho-stick out of a little wooden pocketcase and putting it between his lips, 'that we might have been too good?'

Kolea shrugged. 'What do you mean?'

Varl pursed his lips around the lho-stick, but he didn't light it. He wasn't that stupid. It was just a comfort thing, trying to block out just how much he really wanted a smoke right then. 'Well, we sure pushed ahead, didn't we? Right into the heart of them, leading the way. And look where it's got us.'

Kolea knew what the Tanith-born sergeant meant. They were, it seemed, cut off from the main force now. The last few transmissions received from Gaunt had spoken about shields or something. Now there was nothing but ominous vox-hiss. The three platoons under Varl, Kolea and Obel, numbering some seventy men, were deep in the secondary dome and utterly without support.

They had moved, cautiously, through block after block of deserted worker habitats, places that had presumably been looted and abandoned when the Blood Pact had first taken Cirenholm. Little, tragic pieces of evidence were all that showed this had once been an Imperial town: a votive aquila from a household shrine tossed out and smashed in the street; two empty ale bottles perched on a low wall; a child's toy lasgun, carved from monofibre; clothes hanging on a washing line between habs that had been left so long they were dirty again.

On the end wall of one hab-terrace was a large metal noticeboard that had once proudly displayed the workforce's monthly production figures, along with the names of the star workers. The words 'Cirenholm South Mill Second Shift' were painted in gold leaf along the top, and under that the Phantine flag and the motto, 'Our value to the beloved Emperor'. Someone had taken a lasgun to the sign, holing it repeatedly, before resorting to a flamer to burn off most of the paint.

Kolea looked at it sadly. Both it, and the hab area they were in, reminded him of the low-rent hab-home he had lived in with his family in Vervunhive. He'd worked Number Seventeen Deep Working for over a decade. Sometimes, at night, he'd dream of the smell of the ore-face, the rumble of the drills. Sometimes, he'd dream of the faces of his workmates, Trug Vereas, Lor Dinda. There'd been a proudly maintained production notice in their hab-block too. Kolea's name had appeared on it more than once.

The workers who had lived here had been employed by Cirenholm's vapour mill. Kolea wondered where they had gone, how many of them were still alive. Had the Blood Pact slaughtered the population of Cirenholm's domes, or were the poor devils penned up somewhere?

He looked back down the street block. It was broken and ruined, and made all the more dingy by the dirty yellow light shining down from the girdered roof. At least when his exhausting shifts down Number Seventeen Deep Working had been done, he'd risen to daylight and open air, to the sun rising or setting behind the artificial mountain of Vervunhive.

The Ghosts were prowling down the streets, checking the habs on either side. Varl had insisted on room-to-room checking, and it made sense. They hadn't seen an enemy since they'd first broken into the inner dome areas. The Blood Pact could be dug in anywhere. This hadn't turned into the straight fight they had been expecting. Not at gakking all.

Obel stood with a fireteam at the head of the street, looking out into a small market yard that had served the worker habs. Shops and businesses were boarded up or ransacked.

'Look at this,' Obel said, as Kolea approached. He led him into a broken down store that had once been the paymaster's office.

Munitorium crests were painted on the walls. Kolea scowled when he saw them. His opinion of the Imperial Munitorium was miserably low. He didn't know a man in their section of the company who had more than one las-cell remaining now.

Obel opened a drawer in the paymaster's brass desk, a raised mechanical lectern, with cable-sockets that showed it had once needed a cybernetic link to an authorised official in order to operate. The clamps had been broken and the drawer now rolled free and loose. Kolea was amazed to see the slots were still full of coins.

'They ransacked the city and they didn't loot the money?' Kolea wondered.

Obel picked a coin out of the tray and held it up. It was defaced. Someone with a makeshift tool, formidable strength and an obsessive amount of time on their hands, had crushed the coin and obliterated the Emperor's head. In its place was a crudely embossed rune. It made him queasy just to look at it.

Obel tossed the coin back. 'I guess that says something for the discipline of these bastards. They're more interested in leaving the mark of their maker everywhere than getting rich.'

Kolea shuddered. Every coin in the tray was the same. It was a strangely little thing, but somehow more horrifying than the sights of destruction and desecration he'd seen in his time. The arch-enemy wanted to take the Imperium and reshape every last little piece of it in his own image.

Outside, Kolea saw the hand-daubed words that the Blood Pact had painted on the walls. Words he didn't understand, made of letters he didn't know, mostly, but some were written in Low Gothic. Names. 'Gaur' and 'Slaith'.

Urlock Gaur, he knew, was the warlord controlling the main enemy strengths in this sector of the war, a fiend who commanded the loyalty of the Blood Pact. Gaunt had spoken of him with a mixture of revulsion and respect. From the recent turn of fortune the Crusade had experienced, it was clear this Urlock Gaur was a capable commander.

'Slaith' he wasn't too sure about. The commanding officers had mentioned several of Gaur's field commanders, and Kolea was pretty certain Slaith had been one of them. Perhaps he was the devil behind the war here on Phantine.

Varl wandered up and joined the both of them. 'What d'you think, eh?' he asked them. Obel shrugged.

'We've got to be closing on the vapour mill,' Kolea replied. 'I say we push on and take that.'

'Why?'

'Because we're on our own, and there doesn't seem a way back. If we're going to go down, I say we go down doing something that matters.'

'The mill?' asked Varl.

'Yes, the mill. Think how bad it could be. We could be the only ones left, and if we are, that means we'll not be getting out of here in one piece. Let's hurt them with what we have left. Let's take out their main power supply.'

On the far side of the marketplace, Larkin scooted in through the doorway of another smashed shop, taking care not to kick up the broken glass on the floor. He held his long-las ready. Baen and Hwlan, the scouts from Varl and Kolea's squads, had moved forward with fireteams to clear the west side of the market, and they'd taken the snipers with them.

Larkin looked round and saw Bragg behind him in the doorway, covering the line of open street with his heavy cannon. Caill was close by, shouldering the ammo hoppers for Bragg's support weapon.

'Anything, Larks?' Bragg hissed.

Larkin shook his head. He stepped back out onto the street. Fenix, Garond and Unkin hurried past, covering each other as they went into the next tumbled set of premises. Larkin could see Rilke and Nessa, his fellow snipers, positioned in good cover behind a stack of rotting crates, guarding the northern approach to the market hub.

Larkin moved on, slightly more comfortable with the idea of Bragg and his firepower flanking him. His sharp eyes suddenly caught something moving in a shop that Ifvan and Nour had supposedly already cleared.

'With me, Try,' Larkin hissed. As a rule, Mad Larkin didn't do brave. He preferred to lie back, pick his targets and leave the hero stuff to the likes of Varl and Kolea. But he was getting edgy. He wanted something to shoot at before he snapped, or before the tension dredged up another of his killer headaches from the dark sludge at the bottom of his brain.

He licked his lips, looked over at Bragg, who nodded reassuringly over the heavy barrel of his .50, and kicked in the old wooden door.

Larkin swept his long-las from side to side, peering into the gloom.

Dust swirled up in the sickly light that shafted in through the door and the holes in the shutters.

'Gak you, Tanith. You nearly gave me a cardiac.'

'Cuu?'

Trooper Cuu loomed out of the shadows at the back of the shop, his feline eyes appearing first.

'What the feth are you doing back there?'

'Minding my own business. Why aren't you minding yours, Tanith?'

Larkin lowered his weapon. 'This is my business,' he said, trying to sound tough, though there was something about Lijah fething Cuu that made him feel anything but.

Cuu laughed. The grimace put a nasty twist in the scar that ran down his face. 'Okay, there's enough to share.'

'Enough what?'

Cuu gestured to a small iron strong box that lay open on the shop counter. 'I can't believe these brain-donors left all this behind, can you?'

Larkin looked into the box. It was half full of coins. Cuu began pocketing some more and tossed a handful down the dirty counter to Larkin.

Larkin picked one up. It seemed like an Imperial coin, but the faces had been messed up. Cut, reworked, with a clumsy sign he didn't like.

'Take some,' said Cuu.

'I don't want any.'

Cuu looked round at him, a nasty sneer on his face. 'Don't you go trying to cut in on my action and then get high and mighty about it,' he hissed.

'I'm not–' Larkin began.

'Looting is contrary to regimental standing orders,' Bragg said softly. He was looking in through the doorway behind Larkin.

'Gak me, it's big dumbo too.'

'Shut up, Cuu,' Bragg said.

'What's the matter, big dumbo? You going all holy on me like Larkin?'

'Put the coins back,' Bragg said.

'Or what? You and Mad Larks don't got nothing that can threaten me, sure as sure.'

'Just put them back,' Bragg said.

Cuu didn't. He pushed past Larkin, and then stepped past Bragg into the street. As he did so, he paused, grinning up at the massive support gunner. 'Let's hope we don't meet up on some exercise again any time soon, eh, big dumbo?'

'What does that mean?' asked Bragg.

'Don't want to cut you with my paint stick again,' said Cuu.

Bragg and Larkin watched him walk away. 'What was that about?' asked Caill, striding up. Bragg shook his head.

'That guy's a–' Larkin paused. 'Someone needs to teach him a lesson,' he finished. 'That's all I'm saying.'

Five

An invisible plume of hard, cold air was tearing at him. Somewhere far below in the amber darkness, he could here a steady, dreadful 'whup! whup! whup!', the sound of beating fan blades.

Milo's fingers were going stiff. The climbing cable cut into his palms, even though he was sure he was holding it the way Vadim had shown him.

'Left!' hissed a voice. 'Milo! Left! Move your feet left!'

Milo floundered around, trying not to kick the hollow metal walls of the great vent, but still making what seemed to him was the sound of heavy sacks of root vegetables bouncing down a tin chute.

'Left! For gak's sake! There's a rim right there!'

Milo's left foot found the rim and he eased his right over on to it.

'Vadim?' he gasped.

'You're there. Now let go of the cable with your left hand.'

'But–'

'Gakking do it! Let go and reach out. There's a bulkhead right beside you.'

Milo was perspiring so hard now he felt like his whole skin might just slip off. He couldn't see anything except the darkness, couldn't feel anything except the cable biting into his hands and the sill under his toes, and couldn't hear anything except his own frantic breathing and the threatening 'whup! whup! whup!' from below.

That, and the persistent voice. 'Milo! Now!'

He reached out, and his fingers found reassuringly solid metal.

'Now slide round. Slide round to me... that's it.'

Milo tried, but his balance was shot. He lunged as he started to fall. 'Feth!'

Strong hands grabbed him and dragged him over the edge of a hard metal frame.

'Got you! I got you! You're down!'

Milo rolled on his back, panting, and saw Vadim looking down at him in the sub-light. The Verghastite was smiling.

'Good job, Milo.'

'Feth... really?'

Vadim helped him up. 'That's no easy climb. I wouldn't have wished it on many of the guys I used to roof with. Damn sight more sheer than I was expecting, and gakking few grab-holds. Not to mention that in-rush. You feel it?'

Milo nodded. He looked back through the inspection plate Vadim had hauled him in through. Below, far below, now he had a better angle, he could see the massive turning blades of the fan. Whup! Whup! Whup!

'Feth–' he breathed. He looked back. 'Where's Bonin?'

'Here,' said the scout, emerging from the shadows. Bonin and Vadim had gone down first. 'Wasn't easy, was it?' Bonin asked, as if it had been a walk in the fields.

Vadim nudged Milo aside and reached into the vent again, pulling out Lillo, whose face was pink and sweaty with fear and exertion.

'Never again...' Lillo murmured, crouching down to rest and wiping his brow.

'I don't think we should bring anyone else down,' Vadim said to Bonin. 'It's taking too long.'

Bonin nodded and activated his micro-bead.

'You hear me, Shoggy?'

'Go ahead. Are you down?'

'Yeah, all four of us. Rest of you stay put for now. It's no easy ride. We'll scope around and see if we can't find a proper roof access to let you in by.'

'Understood. Don't take too long.'

The four Ghosts checked their lasrifles and unwrapped their camo-cloaks. They were inside Cirenholm's vapour mill now, moving along the gantries and catwalks like shadows. The thunderous purring of the main turbines covered the slight sounds they made as they spread out.

Bonin gestured them into cover, then waved Vadim and Milo forward. They had reached a main deck area suspended over the primary drums of the turbines. The air was damp and smelled of oil and burned dust.

Lillo crossed the other way at Bonin's signal. When he was in place, Bonin started forward again.

He spotted a skeletal stairwell that looked promising. Roof access, perhaps.

Bonin got in cover behind a bulkhead and signalled the others forward. Lillo drew up to flank the scout, and Vadim and Milo hurried past, making for the end of the deck walkway.

Milo dropped again, but Vadim moved on. Milo cursed silently. The Verghastite had moved too far and broken rhythm of the smooth, bounding cover they were setting.

'Vadim!' he hissed over his link.

Vadim heard him and stopped, realising he had gone too far. He looked for good cover and hurried round into the mouth of an airlock.

The airlock hatch suddenly opened.

Light flooded out.

Vadim turned and found himself face to face with six Blood Pact warriors.

In the gloom, Milo saw the abruptly spreading patch of light shine out from the airlock where Vadim had gone to ground. A moment later, Vadim flew into view, diving frantically headlong, firing his lasrifle behind him with one hand.

A burst of answering las-fire exploded out after him. Milo saw the gleaming red bolts sizzling in the air, spanking off the grille deck and a hoist assembly, and snapping the handrail of the deck. He wasn't sure where Vadim had ended up, or if he'd been hit.

'Vadim? Vadim?'

Several figures moved out of the airlock onto the deck, fast and proficient, in a combat spread. Milo glimpsed red battledress, gleaming crimson helmets, the glint of black ammo-webbing, and dark faces that looked like they had been twisted into tortured expressions of pain. Two of them fired from the hatchway, down the length of the deck, providing protective fire for the others who ran out into the open.

Milo raised his weapon, but Bonin's terse voice came over the micro-link. 'Milo! Hold fire and stay low! Lillo… open up from where you are!'

Milo looked behind him. Lillo was further back down the deck than either himself or Bonin. The Verghastite started firing on semi-auto, squirting quick bursts of fire at the figures emerging from the airlock. The shots streamed down the deckway past Milo at hip height.

The enemy troops immediately focused their attention on Lillo, firing at him and moving down the deck towards him, hugging cover. Milo could see Bonin's simple but inspired tactic at once. Lillo was drawing the enemy out, stringing them between Milo and Bonin's firing positions.

'Wait… Wait…' Bonin murmured.

The enemy were closer now. Milo could see their faces were in fact metal masks, cruel and rapacious. He could smell the stink of their sweat and unwashed clothes. These have to be Blood Pact, he thought.

'Wait…'

Milo was crouched so low his legs were beginning to cramp. His skin crawled. He tightened his grip on his lasrifle. Laser bolts criss-crossed the air around him – blue-white from Lillo's Imperial weapon, flame-red from the Chaos guns.

'Now!'

Milo swept round and fired. His ripple of shots punched into a bulkhead, missing the Blood Pact trooper who hunched against it. The masked warrior whipped around at the now close source of opposition and Milo corrected his hasty aim, putting two rounds into the enemy's face.

Bonin had opened up too, deftly cutting down two of the Blood Pact as they were crossing for better cover and a better angle on Lillo.

A sudden silence. By Milo's reckoning, there were still three of them left. He could hear one creeping slowly towards the row of fuel drums concealing Bonin, but his own cover blocked his view. Milo got down and slowly pulled himself round on his belly. He could almost see his target. A shadow on the deck showed that the trooper was almost on top of Bonin.

Milo lunged out of cover, firing twice. He hit the Blood Pact trooper and sent him tumbling over, wildly firing the full-auto burst he had been saving for Bonin.

There was a fierce cry. Milo looked round to see another of the Blood Pact charging him, shooting. Las-rounds exploded off the plating behind him, nicking the stock of Milo's weapon and burning through his left sleeve.

Bonin appeared out of nowhere, leaping off the barrels full length. He smashed into the charging foe, the impact carrying them both over hard into the deck's handrail. The scout threw a savage uppercut, and his silver warknife was clenched in his punching fist. Screaming, the enemy clutched his neck and face and fell backwards off the deck.

A single las-shot rang out. The last Blood Pact trooper had been running back for the airlock. Lillo had cut him down with one, well-judged round.

Lillo hurried forward. 'Check the airlock,' Bonin told him, wiping his blade clean before sheathing it.

'Thanks,' said Milo. 'I thought he'd got me.'

'Forget it,' smiled Bonin. 'I'd never have got that one sneaking up on me.'

They joined Lillo at the airlock. 'Think we got them all. This one's an officer, I think.' He kicked the body of the one he had brought down in flight.

'Where's Vadim?' Milo asked.

They looked round. Desperate for cover, Vadim had thrown himself out of the airlock hatchway. It seemed to all three of them that in his panic, Vadim had gone clean off the edge of the deck into space.

'Hey!'

Milo got down and looked over the rail. Vadim was swinging by one hand from one of the deck's support members about five metres down.

'Feth!' said Milo. 'Get a rope!'

BONIN SEARCHED THE bodies of the dead Blood Pact, and found a ring of digital keys in the pocket of the officer's coat.

'Sorry,' Vadim said to everyone, now back on the deck. 'Got a bit ahead of myself.'

Bonin said nothing. He didn't have to. Vadim knew his mistake.

They approached the massive metal staircase and followed it up into the roof space. The captured keys let them through locked cage doors one by one. It would have taken them hours to cut or blow their way through.

At the top of the stairwell there was a greasy metal platform with a ladder up to a ceiling hatch. Bonin climbed up and tried the keys until he found one that disengaged the blast-proof lock on the hatch. 'Hoods,' he advised, and all four of them struggled back into their rebreathers before he opened the hatch. Orange hazard lights began spinning and flashing around the platform as the hatch opened to the night and freezing air billowed in.

'Someone's going to notice this,' Lillo said.

There was no helping it. Time was against them. The team they'd taken out would be missed soon anyway.

Bonin climbed out onto the roof and voxed to Domor and the main force. It took about fifteen minutes for them to struggle up through the mill's superstructure and get into the hatch. Bonin sent the first few troopers to arrive down the stairwell with Milo and Lillo to secure the base and the access to the deck. As soon as the last man was inside, Bonin closed and relocked the hatch. The hazard flashers shut down.

Down on the deck, those troopers – like Seena and Arilla – who had come through the drop crash minus weapons helped themselves to the battered, old-pattern lascarbines belonging to the Blood Pact. Avoiding the airlock, they continued on down the stairwell until they reached the main floor of the turbine chamber. It was dark and oily, with a low-level smog of exhaust smoke, but the darkness and the noise swallowed them up. Mkeller and Bonin, working from the map, snaked them through the sump levels of the mill, between the turbine frames, under walk-frames, over coils of pressurised pipes. Moisture dripped down, and unwholesome insect vermin scuttled in the corners.

Somewhere high above them, light shone out. The Ghosts froze. Light from an opened hatch or airlock spread out across one of the upper catwalks, and they saw a line of figures hurrying along the walk onto a raised deck level. A moment later, and more light appeared. Another group, more soldiers, lamps bobbing as they crossed an even higher walkway, moving to support the first.

Bonin and Milo had dumped the Blood Pact dead off the deck into the darkness of the sump, but there had been no disguising the las-damage to the deck area.

Once it seemed safe to move again, they filed along the narrow companionways of the sump, and reached an inner hatch that opened with a turn of the digital keys.

In fireteam formations now, Jagdea protected in one of the middle groups, they went through into a main service corridor, round in cross-section with heavy girder ribs. Dull blue lights glowed out of mesh boxes along the backbone of the roof.

The corridor wound away, passing junctions, crossways, stairwells and elevator hatches. Haller grew increasingly uncomfortable, and he could see it in the faces of the Verghastites too. It was a maze. They'd turned so many times, he wasn't even sure of basic compass orientation anymore. But the Tanith seemed confident. Corbec had once told Haller that the Tanith couldn't get lost. It wasn't in their genes, he reckoned. Something to do with the perpetually mystifying pathways of that homeworld forest they were forever banging on about.

Now he believed it. Bonin, who like all the Tanith scouts had a grim-set face that never seemed to find much to be cheerful about, didn't even consult the map any more. He paused occasionally to check stencilled wall signs, and once backed them up and rerouted them up a level via a stairwell. But his confidence never wavered.

They came at last to a small side hall that seemed particularly dingy and long out of use. They were, by Haller's estimation, in the very basement levels of the city dome, lower even than the mill sump levels. Racks of old, cobwebbed work coveralls and crates of surplus industrial equipment had been stacked there out of the way. Most of the rooflights had gone. There was a door at the far end. A metal hatch, painted blue with a flaking white serial stencil.

Bonin paused, and looked over at Mkeller. The other scout, an older man with greying hair shaved in close to the sides of his head, returned the look with a nod.

'What is this?' whispered Haller.

'Rear service access to the mill's main control chamber.'

'Are you sure?'

'I don't need to open the door to prove it's the rear service access to the mill's main control chamber, if that's what you mean, sir.'

'Okay, okay...' Haller glanced at Domor. 'What do you think?'

'I think it's the closest thing to a target that we're going to get. Unless you'd care to hide in these sub-basements until, oh, I don't know... the end of time?'

Haller smiled. 'Point taken. And as our beloved colonel-commissar is so fond of saying... do you want to live forever?'

THE BLAST RIPPED down the length of the stateroom, shredding the painted wood panelling, dashing up the polished floor tiles and tearing one of the crystal chandeliers off the roof. The chandelier crashed and rolled like a felled, crystal tree. Its twin wilted and swayed from the ceiling.

The wispy blue smoke began to clear.

Gaunt blinked away the tears that the smoke had welled up, and coughed to clear his throat. He looked around. Though some were brushing litter off themselves, the Ghosts in his squad seemed to have weathered the powerful explosion.

'Form and point, by threes. Let's go!' Gaunt growled over his microbead. 'Soric, watch our behinds.'

'Read you, sir,' crackled Soric's reply. His squad, along with those of Theiss, Ewler and Skerral, were dug in at their heels, holding off the mounting assaults of the Blood Pact.

Drawing his sword and powering it up, Gaunt ran forward with Derin and Beltayn, following the lead team of Caober, Wersun and Starck. Debris crunched underfoot. Gaunt's boot caught a crystal twig of chandelier and it went tinkling away across the dust.

Before he'd even reached the grand doorway at the end, he heard Caober's snarl of frustration and knew what it meant. The shield was still intact. They'd brought down the entire frontice of the doorway, frame and all, with the combined tube charges and det-sticks of the entire platoon and still the energy screen fizzled at them, untroubled.

'Sir?' asked Beltayn.

Gaunt thought fast. There had been a protocol for retiring – Tactician Biota had coded it 'Action Blue Magus' – but there was no point giving that signal. They were penned into the outer levels of the secondary dome by the shield wall to one side and the Blood Pact to the other. There was nowhere to retire to, and no hope of calling up an evac. Even if the drop fleet had returned to the drogue and refuelled, as they were supposed to do, the enemy held the DZ now, the only viable landing zone.

Biota had expected them to win, Gaunt thought. Dammit, he had expected them to win. Cirenholm should have been tough, but not this fething tough. They had seriously underestimated the resolve and strategic strength of the Blood Pact.

Gaunt took the mic from Beltayn.

'One to close units, by mark 6903. Shield is not breached. Repeat, not breached. Stand by.'

He consulted his data-slate chart, as Beltayn hurried to import updated troop positions from his vox-linked auspex. It was tight. Too tight. The Ghosts were entirely hemmed in by the enemy, and they were slowly being squeezed to death against the shield line.

With virtually no room to play with, Gaunt knew he had to make the best of what defensive positions he had.

'This is one,' Gaunt continued. 'Soric, Theiss, Skerral, hold your line. Ewler, angle west. The chart shows a service well two hundred metres to your right. I want it blocked and covered. Maroy, hold and provide protective fire for Ewler's move. Confirm.'

They did so in a rapid stutter of overlapped responses.

'One, further... Burone, you hear me?'

'Sir!'

'What's it like there?'

'Low intensity at present, sir. I think they're trying to flank us.'

'Understood. Try not to lose any more ground. Fall back no further than junction hall 462.'

'Four six two, confirmed.'

'Tarnash, Mkfin, Mkoll. Try to spread south to the vestibule at 717. There's a series of chambers there that look like they could be held.'

'Understood, sir,' replied Mkfin.

'Read you, one,' said Mkoll.

'Tarnash? This is one. Confirm.'

Crackling noise.

'Tarnash?'

Gaunt looked at Beltayn, who was adjusting the tuning dial. The harried vox-officer shook his head.

'One, twenty?'

'Go ahead, one.'

'Soric, Tarnash may be down, which means there may be a dangerous hole in your left flank.'

'We stand advised, sir.'

'Mkendrick, Adare... press your gain to the right. Soric needs the cover.'

'Understood, sir. It's fething hot this way,' Adare responded.

'Do your best. Wix, you still holding that loading dock?'

'Down to our last dregs of ammo, sir. We can give you ten minutes' resistance at best before it comes down to fists and blades.'

'Selective five, Wix. Use your damn tube charges, if you have to.'

A transmission cut across abruptly. 'Ten-fifty, one!'

'Go ahead, Indrimmo.'

The Verghastite's voice was frantic. Gaunt could hear rattling autofire over the link. 'We're out! My squad is out! Count zero on all las! Gak! They're on all sides now, we–'

'Indrimmo! Indrimmo! One, ten-fifty!'

'Channel's dead, sir,' murmured Beltayn.

Gaunt looked desperately back at the shield, the real enemy. It was denying him every possibility of constructing a workable defence. For a moment, he considered striking at the cursed shield with his power sword, but he knew that was no way to finish the life of Heironymo Sondar's noble weapon.

'Ideas?' he asked Caober.

The scout shook his head. 'All I figure is this shield system must be running off the city power supply. It must be sucking up a feth of a lot of juice to stay this coherent.'

Gaunt had worked that much out. If only he could reach the spearhead, Varl, Obel and Kolea... if they were still alive. Maybe they could hit in as far as the vapour mill and...

No. That was just wishful thinking. If the three squads of the spearhead were still alive, they'd be fighting for their lives now, alone in the heart of the enemy-held dome. Even if the shields hadn't been blocking their vox-broadcasts and he could talk to them, hoping they could storm the mill was futile.

Gaunt snapped round from his reverie, as what seemed like a grenade blast ruptured in across the stateroom from the left. Before the smoke had even cleared, he saw red-clad figures moving through the breach in the shattered wall.

The Imperial maps of Cirenholm were good, but the Blood Pact owned the turf, and knew every last vent chute and sub-basement. They'd got into the stateroom wall space somehow, behind the rearguard of Soric and the rest.

And they were storming out into the middle of his strung-out platoon.

He didn't have to issue instructions. His men reacted instinctively, even as some of them were cut down by the initial firing. Wersun ran forward, clipped twice by las-rounds, firing tight bursts that knocked at least three of the Blood Pact infantry off their feet. Caober and Derin went in head to head, stabbing with fixed blades and loosing random shots.

Vanette, Myska, Lyse and Neith leapt up and chattered their shots into the wall-breach. Myska was hit in the left forearm and fell over but was back on his feet again almost at once, using a soot-streaked jardiniere as a rest for his weapon now he was firing one-handed.

Starck fell, hit in the throat. Lossa was caught in the forehead by a las-round, stumbled blindly holding his head, and then had his legs shot out from under him by two Blood Pact at close range.

Those enemy soldiers both died quickly as successive rounds from Gaunt's bolt pistol burst their torsos.

Gaunt leapt over Wersun, who was now lying in a pool of blood, panting, and sliced his sword at the next black metal grotesque he saw.

The blue-glow of the blade glimmered in the air and was followed by a sharp stench of burnt blood. There was another to his left, raising a las-carbine that was quickly cut in half, along with the forearms clutching it.

Gaunt recoiled, the power-blade deflecting a las-round, and ran at the next group of enemies. Three of them, stumbling through the smoke-filled gap in the wall. One doubled over, hit by Derin's shots. Gaunt impaled another on his blade and slammed bodily into the third. That one tried to fire, but Gaunt dragged the sword and the heavy corpse draped on it absorbed the shots at point blank range. Gaunt punched the muzzle of his bolt pistol into the black visor and fired.

It was feral confusion now. Many of his Ghosts were dry. They fell into the mob of Blood Pact pressing through the breach with blades, fists or lasrifles swung like clubs.

A shot crisped through the sleeve of his jacket. Gaunt fired again, blowing a figure back into his comrades so they all fell like bowling pins. He fired again, but there was nothing now except a dull clack.

He was out. There was no time to change bolt clips.

He scythed with the power sword, severing bayonets, gun-muzzles and wrists. Two of the Chaos filth jumped on him, trying to bring him down. One got too near to his sword and tumbled off, eviscerated.

The other went limp suddenly, and Caober pulled him away, his straight silver in his hand.

Gaunt rose. Almost immediately, Beltayn cannoned into him and dragged him down again.

There was the chugging roar of a .30, and then the whoosh of a flamer. Bool and Mkan, manning the support weapon, and Nitorri, the squad's flame-trooper, had at last been able to move up from their positions at the end of the stateroom and address the assault. Gaunt crawled back to cover as the heavy cannon and the flames drove the enemy back into the wall.

Nitorri's left shoulder sprayed blood as a parting shot struck him. He slumped over. Lyse, one of the female Verghastites, a veteran of the Vervunhive Civil Defence Cadre, ran forward, knelt by Nitorri's shuddering body, and scooped up the flamer's hose. She swept it back and forth across the breach, igniting the panelwork and combusting the last two Blood Pact troopers who had dared to linger.

Gaunt wished he had a few more tube charges left.

'Cover that hole!' he yelled at the crew of the .30. 'You too, Trooper Lyse. Good work.'

'Sir! Commissar Gaunt sir!'

'Beltayn?'

The vox-officer held out his headset urgently.

'Sir,' he said. 'It's Scout Trooper Bonin.'

'SAY AGAIN, SIR! I can barely hear you!' Bonin kept the headset pressed to his ear and looked over with a desperate shrug to Nirriam, who was trying to adjust the big vox-unit.

There was another brief snatch of Gaunt's voice.

'Stand by, sir. We'll try and raise you on another channel.'

Bonin cut the link. 'Can you boost it?' he asked Nirriam. Nirriam raised his eyebrows, like a man who'd just been asked to inflate a drogue with lung-power.

'I dunno,' said the Verghastite. A basic infantryman, Nirriam had once done a secondary skills course in vox use, which meant he was the best qualified operator Haller and Domor's sections could rustle up. And that wasn't saying much.

Nirriam pulled up a metal-framed operator's chair and perched on it as he tried to familiarise himself with the vox unit. It was the mill control's main communication desk, so old it was almost obsolete. Time and use had worn all the switch and dial labels blank. It was like some fiendish, inscrutable puzzle.

Bonin waited impatiently, and glanced around the room. The chamber was a fan vault, two storeys high, and provided workstation positions for the mill's thirty tech-priests. Everything was finished in brass, with shiny cream enamel coating the extensive pipework running up and down the walls. The floor was paved in grubby green ceramic tiles. It had a faded air of elegance, a relic of a more sophisticated industrial age.

There were four exit points: a hatch on the upper gallery overlooking the main chamber and three on the ground floor, including the old service access they had come in through. Domor had spread the squads out to cover them all. Lillo, Ezlan and Milo were dragging the corpses into a corner.

There had been five adepts on duty, along with two Blood Pact sentries and an officer with a silver grotesque and shabby gold frogging down his tunic front. Bonin and Mkeller hadn't been in the mood for subtlety. Most of the shooting was done by the time the main body of the party got into the chamber.

Commander Jagdea was looking dubiously at the dead and the blood decorating the tiles. Milo had taken it to be disgust at first, but she was a warrior too, and had undoubtedly seen her fair share of death.

Her face pale with pain from her injury, she had looked at Bonin angrily. 'We could have questioned them.'

'We could.'

'But you killed them.'

'It was safer.' Bonin had left it at that and moved away.

Now the wisdom of her remarks was chafing at him. If they'd kept the adepts alive – adepts, indeed, who may have been loyal Imperial citizens working under duress – one of them might have been able to operate the control room's vox-unit.

No point regretting that now, Bonin thought. He silently prayed his lucky star was still with him.

'Nirriam?'

'Give me a chance, Bonin.'

'Come on–'

'Gakking do it yourself!' the Verghastite complained, now down under the desk unplugging the switch cables one by one to blow on them.

Domor came over, pausing to check on Dremmond, Guthrie and Arilla who sat on the floor leaning against the wall, resting. Fayner was checking their wounds.

'Anything?' Domor asked.

Bonin made an off-hand gesture in the direction of Nirriam. 'He's working on it,' he said.

'Try it now!' Nirriam snorted. Bonin was certain the sentence had actually finished with a silent 'gak-face'.

Bonin put the headset back on and keyed the mic.

'Thirty-two, one. Thirty-two, one, do you read?'

Nirriam leaned past him and gently turned a dial, as if it might actually do some good.

Bonin was surprised to find it did.

'-irty-two. One, thirty-two. You're faint but audible. Do you read?'

'Thirty-two, one. We hear you. Messy channel, but it's the best we can do.'

'There's serious void shield activity in the dome, and it's blocking the signals. Micro-beads are down. Are you getting through on your main vox?'

'Negative. We're using a captured system. Must have enough power to beat the interference.'

As if to prove it wasn't, there was a sudden yowl of trash noise before Gaunt's voice continued.

'...were dead. Report location.'

'Say again, one.'

'We thought you were dead. I was told your drop had gone down in the run. What's your situation and location?'

'Long story, one. Our drop did go in, but Haller and Domor got clear with about thirty bodies. Minimal casualties on the survivors. We're inside the–' Bonin paused. He had suddenly realised that the channel might not be anything like secure.

'One, thirty-two. Repeat last.'

Bonin took out his crumpled map. 'Thirty-two, one. We're... around about 6355.'

There was a long pause. The vox-speakers whined and hissed.

'One, thirty-two. Standby.'

GAUNT SPREAD HIS map out on the top of a damaged side table. His gloves were bloody, and left brown smears on the thin paper where he flattened it.

Six three five five. 6355. There was no fething 6355 on the chart. But Bonin had said 'around about'...

Gaunt reversed the sequence. 5536. Which meant...

The mill. The main control room of the vapour mill.

Feth!

Gaunt looked round at Beltayn and took the mic from him.

'One, thirty-two. We're blocked in by an enemy shield wall ignited along marker 48:00. It's sourcing power from the main city supply. We need that supply cut, and fast if we're going to survive much past the next quarter hour. Do you understand?'

'Thirty-two, one. Very clear, sir. I'll see what we can do. Standby.'

Gaunt could feel his pulse racing. Had the Ghosts just been cut the luckiest fething break in Imperial combat history? He realised he had become so resigned to defeat and death in the last few minutes that the idea they could still turn this around genuinely shook him.

He could suddenly taste victory. He could see its shadow, feel its heat.

He suddenly remembered the things that made the burden of command and the grind of service in the Emperor's devoted Guard worthwhile.

There was a chance. Could he trust it? Making best use of it would require him to trust it, but if that trust was misplaced, his men would be slaughtered even more swiftly and efficiently than before.

And then he remembered Zweil. The old ayatani, stopping him outside the drogue *Nimbus's* Blessing Chapel.

Let me look in your eyes, tell you to kill or be killed, and make the sign of the aquila at least.

Gaunt felt a sudden gnawing in his gut. He realised it was fear. Fear of the unknown and the unknowable. Fear of the supernature that lurked beyond the galaxy he was familiar with.

Zweil had said *trust Bonin.*

How could he have known? How could he have seen...

But the old priest's words echoed in his head, rising from holy depths to make themselves heard above the aftershock of the hours of combat that had flooded his conscious mind.

The saint herself, the beati, told me... you must trust Bonin.

He'd dismissed it at the time. He had barely remembered it as they approached the DZ, tense and busting fit to scream. It had gone from his head during the rush of the drop and the ever thicker combat that had followed.

But now it was there. Zweil. In his head. Advising him. Giving him the key to victory.

He had to trust it.

Gaunt grabbed the vox-mic from his waiting com-officer and began to order a series of retreats, across the board, to all the squads he could reach. Dismayed complaints came in from many units, especially from Corbec, Hark and Soric. Gaunt shouted them down, aware that Beltayn was staring at him as if he was mad.

He checked the chart, surveying the spaces and chambers currently inaccessible behind the shield wall. He ordered all his men to pull back against the shield, with nowhere to run, and gave them quick instructions of how to deploy once they were able to move again.

Something in his tone and his confidence shut them up. They listened.

Upwards of a hundred squad officers, suddenly seeing a chance to live and to win.

'Fall back, hold on, and pray. When I give the word, follow your deployment orders immediately.'

The sound of explosions rocked down the length of the stateroom. Sensing a change in the dispersal of the Ghosts, the Blood Pact had renewed their assaults, bringing up heavy support weapons and seeding grenades.

Gaunt shouted orders to his squad. All we have to do is hold them, he thought.

And all I have to do is trust Bonin.

Six

'IDEAS?' BONIN ASKED. He was answered by sighs and shaken heads.

'They might have known,' Jagdea said quietly, looking over at the heap of corpses in the corner.

Fething woman! Bonin thought he might strike her. He detested an 'I told you so'. He looked around the control room, trying to perceive the mysteries of the vast mechanism. He felt like a child. It was hopeless. Dial needles quivered mysteriously, gauges glowed inscrutibly, levers and switches seemed to be set 'just so'. He was a soldier, not a fething tech-priest. He had no idea how to shut down a vapour mill.

'If we had tube charges, we could blow it,' said Ezlan.

'If we had tube charges,' Lillo echoed.

'Then what?' Haller groaned. He strode over to the nearest workstation and pulled a brass lever. There was absolutely no perceptible change in anything. He shrugged.

'If–' Milo began.

'If what?' said about ten people at once.

'If the Blood Pact rigged their shields into the main supply, it would be non-standard. I mean, cut in, intrusive. You know, like when we hike a breaker cable in to wire a door release.'

Domor nodded.

'I hear Milo,' said Vadim. 'If they hooked it in, it would look jury-rigged. We might be able to recognise it.'

Bonin had been considering a desperate ploy of connecting all the power cells they had and forcing an overload. In the light of Milo's more subtle idea, he put the notion of an improvised bomb to the back of his mind.

'Let's try then, shall we?' he asked. Then he paused. Haller and Domor, sergeants both, were actually in charge here. He had overstepped the line. He glanced at them, embarrassed.

'Hey, I'm with Bonin,' Domor said.

'He's got my vote,' said Haller.

'Then... go!' Bonin exclaimed.

The Ghost survivors of drop 2K scurried off in every direction as if they'd all been simultaneously slapped on the behinds. Inspection panels were prised off, service hatches pulled out, lamp packs shone up under workstations.

The only ones not searching were the sentries: Seena at the upper door, Mkeller and Lwlyn at the lower main doors and Caes, with Dremmond's flamer, at the service hatch.

Bonin came out from under a work console and turned his attention to a wall plate. The wing nuts were stiff, and he had to use the pommel of his warknife like a mallet to move them.

Beside him, Vadim was investigating the guts of a relay position, up to his wrists in bunches of wires.

'Of course,' Vadim said cheerfully, 'we could just turn every dial and switch to zero.'

'I thought of that. I also thought we could simply shoot the living feth out of everything in sight.'

'Might work,' Vadim sighed.

'Can I just say–' said a voice behind them. Bonin glanced round. It was Jagdea, her slung arm looking more uncomfortable than ever.

'What, commander?'

'I'm an aviator so I don't know much about vapour mills, but I think I know a little more than you, having lived on Phantine all my life. The mill is a gas generator. It produces billions of litres of gas energy under extreme pressure. The priesthood that maintains the Phantine mills are privy to thousands of years of lore and knowledge as to their governance.'

'And your point... because I'm sure you have one somewhere,' said Bonin, finally forcing the wall plate off.

'It's an ancient system, working under millions... I don't know... billions of tonnes of pressure. Blow it up, shoot it up, shut it down... whatever... it's likely that the system will simply explode without expert control. And if this vapour mill explodes... well, I don't think there'll be a Cirenholm left for the taking.'

'Okay,' said Bonin, with false sweetness, 'Thanks for that.' He turned to resume his work. Damn woman was going to get his knife in her back if she didn't shut up. He knew she didn't like him. Damn woman.

Damn woman had a point. They were playing around, fiddling in ignorance, with a power system that kept an entire city alive. That was real power. Jagdea was right. If they got this wrong, there wouldn't be anything left of Cirenholm except a smouldering mountain peak.

'Feth!' Bonin cursed at the thought.

'What?' said Jagdea from behind him.

'Nothing. Nothing.'

'Of course,' Jagdea continued, 'if that boy was correct–'

'Milo.'

'What?'

'Trooper Brin Milo.'

'Okay. If Milo was correct, and the enemy has wired their shields into the mill systems, isn't it likely they did it at source in the main turbine halls rather than down here in the control room?'

Bonin dropped the wall plate wth a clang and rose, turning to face her. 'Yes. Yes it is. Very likely. But we're here and we're trying our damnedest. We can't go back now, because the foe is everywhere. So we work with what we have. Have you any other comments to make, because, if you haven't, quite frankly I'd love it if you shut up now and helped us look. You're really pissing me off.'

She looked startled.

'Oh. Well. All right. What would you like me to do?'

Bonin glanced about. 'Over there. Between Nirriam and Guthrie. Take a look at that desk, if you'd be so kind.'

'Of course,' she said, and hurried over to it.

'Way to go with the lady, Bonin,' laughed Vadim.

'Shut the feth up,' said Bonin.

'Sarge! Sarge!' They all heard Seena sing out.

'What?' replied Haller, looking up from a maintenance vent he had been buried to his shoulders in.

Seena was up on the gallery, watching the upper doorway.

'We've got company.' Her voice was sweetly sing-song.

What it meant was anything but.

'COME ON! COME on!' Corbec was yelling, standing up and waving his arms despite the enemy crossfire splashing all around. The Ghosts in his squad, along with Bray's troops, dashed back through the hatchway, a rain of fire dropping around them.

Irvinn stumbled, and Corbec dragged him through the hatch by the scruff of his neck.

'Is the shield down, chief?' he babbled.

'Not yet, son.'

'But Commissar Gaunt said it would be! He said it would be!'

'I know.'

'If the shield isn't down, we're backing ourselves into a trap, chief, we–'

Corbec cuffed the young trooper around the side of the head. 'Gaunt'll come through. That's what he does. He'll come through and we'll live! Now get in there and take your position!'

Irvinn scrambled on.

Corbec looked back in time to see two more Ghosts fall on their way to the hatch. One was Widden, whose body was struck so hard by .50 fire it was deformed completely. The other was Muril. She was hit and thrown in a cartwheel that ended with her lying on her face.

'No!' Corbec roared.

'Colm! Wait!' Sergeant Bray yelled.

'Get them back in, Bray, get them back in!' Corbec howled, running out from the hatchway towards Muril. Las-fire ripped up the deck around him, filling the air with a fog of atomised tiles.

Somehow, he reached Muril. He rolled her over. Her face was white with dust and dotted with blood that soaked into the dust like ink into clean blotting paper. Her eyelids flickered.

'Come on, girl! We're going!' he shouted.

'C-colonel–'

He looked her over, and saw the wound in her upper thigh. Bad, but survivable. He hoisted her onto his shoulders.

One of his legs gave way suddenly and they both fell over into the dust, kicking up a serene cloud of white mist.

Everything seemed to slow down. Everything seemed to go quiet.

Corbec saw the enemy las-rounds swirling through the dust in what seemed like slow motion; crackling barbs of red light, eddying wakes behind them in the dust; the oozingly slow on-off flashes of explosions; the strobe of tracers; the drops of bright red blood falling from Muril onto the floor, making soft craters in the dust.

He lifted her up again, and ran, but it was hard work. His leg didn't want to move.

There was a sudden pain in his back, and then another really biting lance of agony through his left shin.

He toppled in through the hatchway, into Bray's arms. Merrt and Bewl ran forward, mouths open, managing to catch Muril before she hit the ground.

'Medic! Medic!' Bray was yelling.

Corbec realised he couldn't move. Everything felt strangely warm and soft. He lay on his back, looking at the panelled roof.

It seemed to slide up and away from him.

The last thing he heard was Bray still screaming for a medic.

VIKTOR HARK FIRED his plasma pistol into the knots of foe around the doorway. The combined squads of Rawne, Daur and Meryn were spread out and dropping back through the dead park. There was nothing behind them except shield-blocked hatches.

They'd given up valuable ground on Gaunt's orders. There had been nothing in return.

Hark fired again. They were going to be killed. One by one, with the shield at their backs.

SERGEANT AGUN SORIC, hero of Vervunhive, sat back against the wall. The wound in his chest was sucking badly, and bloody foam was bubbling around the seared entry hole. Slowly, he raised his lasgun in one hand, but the weight of it was too much.

Men in red with metal grotesques were prowling forward towards him through the smoke.

Sergeant Theiss knelt beside him, coming out of nowhere. He fired at the enemy, forcing them into cover.

'Pull him up!' Soric heard Theiss yell.

Soric felt himself being lifted. Doyl and Mallor were under him, and Lanasa had his feet.

Theiss, with Kazel, Venar and Mtane, laid down backing fire.

'Are we through?' gurgled Soric. 'The shield...?'

'No,' said Doyl.

'Well...' said Soric, his eyes fading. 'It's been a good run, while it lasted...'

'Soric!' Doyl yelled. 'Soric!'

THE FIRST OF the Blood Pact hit the vapour mill control chamber along the upper passage.

Seena returned their fire until Ezlan and Nehn joined her. Her gunfire was punctuated with curses about the .30 she should have been firing.

It was a narrow hall, and the three Ghost guns could hold it... unless the enemy brought up something more punishing.

Three minutes after the upper hatch was assaulted, the lower main door guarded by Mkeller came under fire. He saw a grenade slung his way in time to slam the heavy iron hatch shut. The blast shook the door. Haller ran up and helped Mkeller throw the lock bolts on the corners of the hatch.

'That won't hold them long,' said Mkeller, and as if to prove it, the thump of beating fists and gun-stocks began against the door.

Lwlyn, stationed in the other main floor doorway, suddenly fell back on his backside with a curse. Blood soaked out across his battledress from his left shoulder.

'I'm hit,' he said, then fainted.

Ferocious las-fire ripped in through his hatchway. Two bolts struck Lwlyn's unconscious form sprawled in the open and made sure he would never wake up.

Guthrie reached the door and yanked it shut as las-fire hammered on the outside.

'If we're going to do something, we'd better do it now!' Guthrie yelled.

Bonin glanced at Domor. Domor shrugged. The chamber was a mess, with spools of wires draped out of every corner.

'For what it's worth, soldier,' said Jagdea, sitting down against the wall, 'I think you did your best.' She slid her short-bladed survival knife from her boot-top and slit open the cuff of her pressure suit. Bonin saw her tumble two white tablets out of the hollow cuff and tip them into her palm. She raised them to her mouth.

Bonin leapt forward and slapped them aside.

'What the feth are you doing?'

'Get off me!'

'What the feth are you doing?'

'Taking the honourable route out, soldier. We're dead. Worse than dead. Fighter Command give us those tablets in case we have to ditch behind enemy lines. The Blood Pact don't take prisoners, you know.'

'You were going to kill yourself?'

'Skinwing venom, concentrated. It's quite painless, so I'm told.'

Bonin slowly shook his head. Upon the gallery, Seena, Ezlan and Nehn were blasting away.

'Suicide, Commander Jagdea? Isn't that the coward's way out?'

'Screw you, soldier. How much clearer do you need it? We're dead. Dee-ee-ay-dee. I'd rather die without pain than greet the death they're bringing.'

Bonin dropped down in a crouch in front of her and scooped up the poison pills. He rolled them in his palm.

'Colonel-Commissar Gaunt taught me that death was something to be fought every last step of the way. Not welcomed. Not invited. Death comes when it comes and only a fool would bring it early.'

'Are you calling me a fool, Bonin?'

'I'm only saying that all is not yet lost.'

'Really?'

'Really. It may only be a soldier's ignorant philosophy, but in the Guard, we keep fighting to the end. If we die, we die. But suicide is never an option.'

Jagdea stared up at him.

'Give me the pills.'

'No.'

'I think I outrank you.'

'I hardly care.' Bonin dropped the tablets onto the floor and crushed them with his heel.

'Damn you, Bonin.'

'Yes, commander.'

'Do you really think something's going to change here? That we might be miraculously rescued?'

'Anything's possible, as long as you allow for it. My mother told me I was born under a lucky star. That luck's never left me. There have been times I should have died. At Vervunhive. I can show you the scars.'

'Spare me.' Her voice was thin and frail now.

'I believe in my luck, Jagdea. Tanith luck.'

'Screw you, we're all dead. Listen to that.'

Bonin heard the furious hammering at the doors, the frantic resistance of the trio on the gallery.

'Maybe. If we are, I promise you won't suffer.'

'You'll do me yourself? How gallant.'

Bonin ignored the sarcasm. 'Tanith First-and-Only, ma'am. We look after our own.'

ON THE GALLERY, Nehn flinched back, winged. Seena saw a Blood Pact trooper charging them… only to fall. In all the worlds, it looked to her like he had been hit in the back of the head by a hot-shot.

The assault lapsed.

Her micro-bead chirped. 'Who's down there?'

It was the Imperial Guard channel.

'Twenty-fourteen, come back?' she whispered.

'Nine, twenty fourteen. That you, Seena?'

'Sarge?'

'Large as life and twice as ugly, girl.'

'It's Kolea! It's Kolea!' Seena sang out to the chamber.

THE COMBINED SQUADS of Obel, Kolea and Varl moved in through the upper gallery and joined up with Haller and Domor's units. It was all very calm, matter of fact. There were a few handshakes and greetings. No whooping, no cheering, nothing to betray the elation they all felt. Nothing to acknowledge the dazzling fortune that had just turned their way.

By then, nearly psychotic levels of Blood Pact opposition were thrashing in at the main ground floor hatchways. Varl sent the flamers to subdue it.

'Of course,' Kolea was saying.

'Really?' asked Haller, who'd been his second in the Vervunhive scratch units.

'You don't work mines and power plants all your life and not know how the generator flow-systems work.'

Kolea walked over to what seemed like a side console and threw a nondescript lever.

The lights dimmed. The gauges dropped. The thundering pant of the turbines pitched away.

He turned from the console and saw the dumbstruck faces all around.

'What? What?'

THE SHIELDS WENT down.

THERE WAS AN electrical crackle and a sudden, violent rush of air as the shield at the end of the stateroom vanished and pressure equalised.

'Now,' yelled Ibram Gaunt. 'Now, now, now! Men of Tanith, Men of Verghast! The tables turn!'

'Show me what the Imperial Guard can do!'

A REAPPRAISAL OF COMBAT POLICY

CIRENHOLM CITY OCCUPATION, PHANTINE
214 to 222.771, M41

'Cirenholm was taken after seven hours of determined assault. A handsome victory for the Imperial Guard. That's what the textbooks will say. However, the crucial gains that enabled the victory were achieved not by mass assault, but by the stealthy application of highly trained, highly disciplined individuals who were sensibly trusted with an unusual degree of command autonomy, and who used their polished covert skills to disable the enemy defences more completely than ten thousand slogging infantry units could ever have managed. It's just a shame we didn't plan it that way.'

– Antonid Biota, Chief Imperial Tactician,
Phantine Theatre

One

SWOLLEN PLUMES OF brown fire-smoke drifted up from the south-facing edges of Cirenholm's trio of domes, and diluted into yellow smog in the hard morning sunlight.

From the upper observation deck of the primary dome, it was difficult to believe Phantine was a toxic world. The bright sun made the high altitude sky powder-blue and, down below the sculptural curves of the domes, great oceans of knotted white cloud spread out as far as the eye could see. Only occasionally was there a dark stain or a ruddy surge of flame visible beneath the clouds as the inferno of the Scald underlit them.

Like a pod of great sea mammals, the drogues were coming in. Eight of them, each a kilometre long from nose-ram to tail fins, coasting along on the morning wind, their taut silver and white skins gleaming. Pairs of tiny, fast moving Lightnings crossed between them, making repeated low passes over the city. Gunships, weapon-mounted variants of the drops that had brought them to Cirenholm, slunk along beside the vast drogues in escort.

It was cold up on the observation deck. The city's heating systems were still off-line. It was taking a long time to get the vapour mill running back to optimum after the sudden shutdown.

Gaunt pulled his long storm coat tight. Ice crystals were forming on the glass of the observation port, and he wiped them off with a gloved hand. There was something infinitely relaxing about watching the drogues approach. He could just hear the distant chop of their massive prop banks. Every now and then, the glass vibrated as a Lightning burned low overhead.

'Ibram?'

Gaunt turned. Hark had entered the observation gallery, cradling two beakers of steaming caffeine.

'Viktor, thank you,' Gaunt said, taking one.

'Quite a sight,' noted Hark, blowing the steam off his caffeine as he sipped it.

'Indeed.'

A pilot tug had just fluttered out to anchor the nose of the lead drogue and drag it into the hangar decks under the lip of the primary dome. Gaunt watched the letters painted on the drogue's nose – ZEPHYR – slowly disappear one by one as it passed into the deep shadow under the lip.

Gaunt drank his hot caffeine gingerly. 'What's the latest?' He'd remained on station with Beltayn for six hours, supervising the comm-traffic, before catching a few, restless hours of sleep in an unaired room off the grand states in secondary. Since he'd risen, he'd tried to stay away from the babbling voxes. He needed calm.

'Some fighting still in the northern sectors. Rawne's pretty much cleared the last of secondary. Tertiary is clean, and Fazalur's moving his forces up into primary to bolster the Urdeshi. Heaviest resistance is up in the north block of primary. Some bad stuff, but it's just a matter of time. We found the citizens, though. Kept in mass pens in the tertiary dome. Fazalur liberated them. We're beginning rehousing and repopulation.'

Gaunt nodded.

'What?' asked Hark.

'What what?'

Hark smiled. It was a rare expression for him. 'That look in your eyes. Sadness.'

'Oh, that. I was just pitying the Urdeshi. They had the worst of it, all told. What's the count now?'

'Twelve hundred dead, another nine hundred wounded.'

'And us?'

'Twenty-eight dead. Two hundred wounded.'

'How's Corbec?'

Hark sighed. 'It's not looking good. I'm sorry, Ibram.'

'Why? You didn't shoot him. What about Agun Soric?'

'They've crash resuscitated him twice already. He should have died on the spot, the wound he took.'

'Agun's a tough old feth. He'll go when he wants to.'

'Let's hope it's not yet, then. I don't know which we'd miss most.'

Gaunt frowned. 'What do you mean?'

Hark shrugged. 'Corbec's the heart of the Tanith First. Everyone loves him. We lose him, it'd be a body blow to all. But Soric is cut from the same cloth. He means a lot to the Verghastites. If he dies, I think it'll knock the stuffing out of the Verghast sections of the regiment. And we don't want that.'

'They have other leaders: Daur, Kolea.'

'And they're respected. But not like Soric. He's their father figure, like the Tanith have Corbec. Kolea could make more of himself, but I don't think he wants to be a totem. I honestly think Kolea would be happier as a basic trooper.'

'I think so too, sometimes.' Gaunt watched the next drogue, the *Boreas*, as it was tugged in under the hangar housing.

'Daur's a good man too,' Hark continued. 'I like him, but he's... I don't know. Perky. Eager. The Verghastites don't like that very much. He's not grounded like Soric. And the Tanith positively despise him.'

'Daur? They despise Daur?' Gaunt was shocked.

'Some of them,' said Hark, thinking of Rawne. 'Most of the Tanith genuinely appreciate the Verghast new blood, but none of them can really shake the notion of intrusion. Intrusion into their regiment. Daur landed authority equal to Major Rawne. To many, he exemplifies the invasion of the First-and-Only by the Vervunhivers.'

'To Rawne, you mean?'

Hark grinned. 'Yes, him especially. But not just him. It's an honour thing. Surely you've noticed it?'

Gaunt nodded without replying. He was well aware of the way Hark was testing him. Hark was a loyal man, and had begun to perform his duties as regimental commissar impeccably. But he was always testing boundaries. It pleased Hark to think he was more in tune with the First's spirit than Gaunt.

'I know we've got a good way to go before the Tanith and Verghastite elements of this regiment reach comfortable equilibrium,' said Gaunt after a long pause. 'The Tanith men feel proprietorial about the regiment. Even the most broadminded of them see the Verghastites as outsiders. It's their name on the standard and the cap badge, after all. And it's got nothing to do with ability. I don't think any Tanith would question the fighting spirit of the Vervunhivers. It's just a matter of... pride. This is and always was the Tanith regiment. The new blood we brought from Verghast is not Tanith blood.'

'And, in reverse, the same goes for the Verghastites,' agreed Hark. 'This isn't their regiment. They've got their own insignia, but they'll never get their name on the standard placard. They feel the resentment of the Tanith... they feel it because it's real. And they understand it, which makes things worse. They want to make a mark for themselves. I'm actually surprised the divide hasn't been more... difficult.'

Gaunt sipped the last of his drink. 'The Verghastites have made their mark. They've helped our sniper strength grow enormously.'

'Yes, but who's given them that edge? The women, for the most part. Don't mistake me, the girl snipers are a goddamned blessing to this combat force. But male Verghast pride is dented because the women are the best they can offer. They've made no scouts. And that's where the true honour lies. That's what the First is famous for. The Tanith scouts are the elite, and have the Verghasts produced even one trooper good enough to make that cut? No.'

'They've come close. Cuu.'

'That bastard.'

Gaunt chuckled. 'Oh, I agree. Lijah Cuu is a fething menace. But he's got all the qualities of a first-rate scout.'

Hark set his beaker down on the windowsill and wiped his lips. 'So... have you given any thought as to how we can improve the regimental divide?'

You're testing again, Gaunt thought. 'I'd welcome ideas,' he told Hark diplomatically.

'A few promotions. I'd make Harjeon up to squad rank. And LaSalle. Lillo too, maybe Cisky or Fonetta. We'll need a few fresh sergeants now Indrimmo and Tarnash are gone.'

'Cisky's dead. More's the pity. But I agree in principle. Not Harjeon. An ex-pen pusher. The men don't have any respect for him. Lillo's a good choice. So's Fonetta. LaSalle, maybe. My money would be on Arcuda. He's a good man. Or Criid.'

'Okay. Arcuda. Makes sense. I don't know about Criid. A female sergeant? That might cause more problems than it solves. But I think we should fast-track two or three into the scout corps.'

'Viktor, we can't do that if there isn't the talent. I'm not going to field point men who haven't got the chops for the job.'

'Of course. But Cuu, like you said. There are others. Muril.'

'Isn't she wounded?'

'Getting a brand new steel hip, but she'll make it. Also Jajjo, Livara and Moullu.'

Gaunt frowned. 'They're possibles. Some of them. Muril's got potential, and Livara. But I've never known a man as clumsy as Moullu, for all that he's light on his feet. And Jajjo? I'd have to think about that. Besides, the cut's not down to me. It's Mkoll's call. Always has been.'

'You could order him t–'

'Viktor, enough. Don't push it. The scout elite has always been Mkoll's area. I happily bow down to his expertise, I always have. If he thinks any of that list can make the grade, he'll take them. But if he doesn't, I'm not going to force them on him.'

'That's fine. Mkoll knows his stuff.'

'He does. Look, I'll keep my eyes open. I'll do everything I can to balance out the Verghastite/Tanith mix. Positive discrimination if necessary. But I won't risk damaging the combat core by advancing those who aren't ready or good enough.'

Hark seemed satisfied with this, but then he surprised Gaunt with a final comment. 'The Verghast need to know you value them as much as the Tanith, Ibram. Really, they do. What will destroy them is the idea they're latecomers who can't make the grade. They feel like second-class elements of this regiment. That's not good.'

Gaunt was about to reply, taken aback by the remark, but the deck's inner door slid open and a vox-officer dressed in the fur-trimmed uniform of the Phantine Skyborne entered and saluted.

'Lord General Barthol Van Voytz is coming aboard, Colonel-Commissar Gaunt. He requests your company.'

THE DROGUE NIMBUS was already edging in towards the vast hangar bay under the primary dome, a little tug-launch revving its over-powered thrusters as it heaved the vessel home. The drogue's immense aluminium propeller spars were making deep, whispering chops as they slowed to a halt.

Van Voytz had flown ahead. Escorted by two Lightnings that veered away sharply once it had reached the hangar mouth, his chequer-painted tri-motor purred in under the shadow. It was a stocky transport plane with a bulbous glass nose, and it made a heavy but clean landing on the deck way, its powerful double-screwed props chattering into reverse as soon as its tail hook caught the catch-line.

Gaunt stood waiting in the gloom of the hangar, a hangar which already accommodated the massive bulk of the drogue *Aeolus* without seeming full.

The tri-motor's engines were still roaring as the footwell slapped down from the hull and Van Voytz emerged.

'Guard, attention!' Gaunt barked and the honour detail of Ghosts – Milo, Guheen, Cocoer, Derin, Lillo and Garond, under the supervision of Sergeant Theiss – smacked their heels together and shouldered arms smartly. Theiss held the company standard.

The lord general bent low under the downwash of the props and hurried forward up the ramp, flanked by his aide, Tactician Biota and four splendid bodyguard troopers with blue-black tunics, hellguns and gold braid around the brims of their shakos.

'Gaunt!'

'Lord general.'

Van Voytz shook his hand. 'Damn fine job, soldier.'

'Thank you, sir. But it wasn't me. I have a list of commendations.'

'They'll all be approved, Gaunt. Mark my words. Damn fine job.' Van Voytz gazed up around him as if he'd never seen a hangar deck before. 'Cirenholm. Cirenholm, eh? One step forward.'

'One step back for the Urdeshi, with respect.'

'Ah, quite. I'll be having words with Zhyte once he's out of surgery. He screwed up, didn't he? Man's a blow-hard menace. But you, Gaunt... you and your Ghosts. You turned this fiasco on its head.'

'We did what we could, lord.'

'You did the Guard proud, colonel-commissar.'

'Thank you, sir.'

'You quite pulled a fast one, didn't you?'

'Sir?'

'You and your covert experts. He quite pulled a fast one, didn't he, Biota?'

'He seems to have done, lord general,' Biota replied mildly.

'Making us do a rethink, Gaunt. A radical rethink. Ouranberg awaits, Gaunt, and your work here has prompted us to make a hasty reappraisal of combat policy. Hasn't it, Biota?'

'It has, lord general.'

'It has indeed. What do you think of that, Gaunt?'

Ibram Gaunt didn't know quite what to think.

ONTI FLYTE REGARDED herself as a true Imperial citizen, and had raised her three children in that manner. When the arch-enemy had come to Cirenholm, and overrun it so fast, she'd felt like the sky had fallen in. Her husband, a worker in the mill, had been killed by the Pact in the initial invasion. Onti, her children and her neighbours, had been herded out of their habs by the masked brutess and shut up in a pen in the bowels of tertiary.

It had been hellish. Precious little food or water, no sanitation. The place had stunk like a drain by the end of the first day.

After that there had been disease and dirt, and the stench had become so high she could no longer smell it.

Now, as the Imperial Guard escorted them back to their habs, she could smell the stink. It was in her clothes and in her hair. She knew the street-block shower would have queues, and the laundry would be full to bursting, but she wanted her kids clean and dressed in fresh clothes. That meant getting the outhouse tub full, and hard work with the press.

A nice young Guardsman in black called Caffran had seen her and the kids back to their hab. Onti had kept apologising for the way they smelled. The boy, Caffran, had been so polite and kind.

It was only when she was back in her place, in the little parlour of her terraced hab, that she'd cried. She realised how much she missed her husband, and she was haunted by what the arch-enemy had undoubtedly done to him.

Her children were running around. She wanted them to quiet down. She was beside herself. The nice soldier – Caffran – looked in on her as the streets outside swarmed with people returning to their homes under escort.

'Do you need anything?' he asked.

'Just a handsome husband,' Onti had joked, painfully, but trying hard.

'Sorry,' the nice soldier said. 'I'm spoken for.'

Onti had put her head in her hands when he was gone and sobbed over the parlour table.

Her eldest, Beggi, had run in to tell her that the tub was almost full. He'd put the soap crystals in, the special ones, and all the kids said they wanted their mam to have the first bath.

She kissed them all in turn, and asked Erini to warm up a pot of beans for them all.

Onti went out into the yard and saw the steam wallowing from the outhouse where the tub sat. She could smell the peppermint vapours of the soap crystals.

On the other side of the yard fence, her neighbour, an old pensioner called Mr Absolom, was sweeping out his back step.

'The mess they made, Ma'am Flyte,' he cried.

'I know, Mr Absolom! Such a mess!'

Onti Flyte went into the outhouse and dragged off her filthy clothes.

Naked and wrapped in a threadbare towel, she was testing the water with her hand when she heard the creak.

She looked up and froze, realising someone was crouching in the back of the outhouse.

She felt vulnerable. She felt open. For a terrifying moment, she thought it was one of the arch-enemy, gone to ground. One of the foul, masked Blood Pact.

But it wasn't.

The figure stepped out of the shadows.

It was a fine young Guardsman. Just like the lovely young man who had escorted her and the kids back to her hab.

'Well, you shouldn't be in here, sir,' she said. 'You know what people say about a fine soldier boy...'

She sniggered.
The soldier didn't.
Onti Flyte suddenly realised that she was in trouble. Really bad trouble. She opened her mouth, but nothing came out.
The soldier stepped forward. He was very distinctive looking.
He had a knife. A long, straight silver knife that shone against the black fabric of his battledress.
She felt a scream building inside her. This wasn't right. This wasn't how it worked.
'Don't,' he said.
She screamed anyway. For a very short time.

Doc Dorden held the chipwood tongue depresser in the same confident way Neskon held his flamer. 'Say "Aaargh",' he said.
'Sgloot–' Milo managed.
'No, boy. "Aaargh"... "AAARGH"... like you've been stuck with an ork bayonet.'
'Aaargh!'
'Better,' smiled Dorden, taking the stick out of Milo's mouth and tossing it into a waste sack taped to the side of his medikit. He grabbed Milo by the head with both hands and examined his eyes, dragging the lids aside with firm fingertips.
'Any nausea?'
'Only now.'
'Ha ha... any cramps? Blood in your spittle or stools? Headaches?'
'No.'
Dorden released his head. 'You'll live.'
'Is that a promise?'
Dorden smiled. 'Not one in my power to give, I'm afraid. I wish–'
The old Tanith doctor added something else, but his words were lost in the background hubbub of the billet hall. Milo didn't ask him to repeat it. He was sure from the doc's sad eyes it had had something to do with his son, Mikal Dorden, Ghost, dead on Verghast.
It was the third day after the raid. The Tanith First had been assigned billets in a joined series of packing plants in the secondary dome. Hundreds of wood bales had been laid down in rows for cots and the Munitorium distribution crews had dropped a pair of thin blankets on each one. Most Ghosts had supplemented this meagre bedding with their camo-cloaks, bedrolls and musette bags stuffed with spare clothing.
The noise in the chamber was huge. In Milo's alone there were nine hundred men, and the wash of their voices and their activities filled the air and echoed off the high roof. The men were relaxing, cleaning kit, field stripping weapons, smoking, dicing, arm-wrestling, talking, comparing trophies, comparing wounds, comparing deeds...

Dorden, Curth and the other medics were moving through the billets, chamber by chamber, doing the routine post combat fitness checks.

'It's amazing how many troopers hide injuries,' Dorden was saying as he collected his kit together. 'I've seen five flesh wounds already that men didn't think were worth bothering me with.'

'Honour scars,' said Milo. 'Marks of valour. Lesp's such a good needleman, they're afraid they'll not have the marks to show and brag about.'

'More fool them, Brin,' said Dorden. 'Nour had a las-burn that was going septic.'

'Ah, there, you see?' replied Milo. 'Verghast. They want the scars most of all, to match our Tanith tattoos.'

Dorden made a sour face, the sort of sour face he always made when confronted by naive soldier ways. He handed Milo two pill capsules of different colours and a paper twist of powder.

'Take these. Basic vitamins and minerals, plus a hefty antibiotic boost. New air, new germ pool. And sealed and recirculated, which is worse. We don't want you all coming down with some native flu that your systems have no defence against. And we don't know what the scum brought here with them either.'

'The powder?'

'Dust your clothes and your boots. The Blood Pact had lice and now they're gone, the lice are looking for new lodgings. The poor Phantine found their billets in tertiary were infested.'

Milo swigged the pills down with a gulp from his canteen and then set about obediently sprinkling his kit with the powder. He'd been halfway through stripping his lasrifle when the doc reached his cot in the line, and he wanted to get back to it. Troops were being pulled out every few hours to assist in Major Rawne's final sweep of the primary dome. Milo was sure he would be called soon.

Dorden nodded to Milo and moved on to Ezlan at the next cot.

Milo looked across the busy activity of the cot rows. Two lines away, Surgeon Curth was checking a trooper's scalp wound. Milo sighed. He liked Doc Dorden a lot, but he wished Curth had reached his row first. He would have enjoyed being examined by her.

He pushed his half-stripped las to one side and lay back on his cot with his hands behind his head, staring at the roof and trying to blot out the noise. Try as he might, over these last few months, he had been unable to stop thinking about Esholi Sanian, the young scholar who had guided them to the Shrinehold on Hagia, their last battlefield. He'd liked her a lot. And he had been sure the feeling was mutual. The fact that he would never, ever see her again didn't seem to matter to Milo. She wouldn't leave his mind and she certainly wouldn't leave his dreams.

He'd never spoken about it to anyone. Most of the Tanith had lost wives or sweethearts on the home world, and most of the Verghastites had left their loves and lives behind. There were females in the regiment now, of course, and every last one of them was the object of at least one trooper's affection. There were some romances too. His friend Caffran's was the best. His first love Laria had perished with Tanith, and he'd been as forlorn as the rest for a long time. Then on Verghast, right in the thick of the hive-war, he'd met Tona Criid. Tona Criid… ganger, hab-girl, scratch fighter, mother of two young kids. Neither Caffran nor Criid, both of whom Milo now counted amongst his closest friends, had ever described it as love at first sight. But Milo had seen the way they looked at each other.

When the Act of Consolation had been announced, Criid had joined the Ghosts as standard infantry. Her kids came along, cared for during times of action by the Ghosts' straggling entourage of cooks, armourers, quartermasters, barbers, cobblers, musicians, traders, camp followers and other children. Every Guard regiment had its baggage train of non-combatants, and the Ghosts' now numbered over three hundred. Regiments accreted non-combatant hangers-on like an equine collected flies.

Now Caff and Criid were together. It was the Ghosts' one, sweet love story. The troops might smile at the couple, but they respected the union. No one had ever dared get in between them.

Milo sighed to himself sadly. He wished that Sanian had been able to come along with him that way.

He thought for a moment about going down to the hangar deck where the entourage was encamped. He could get a meal from the cook-stoves, and maybe visit one of the overly-painted women who followed the regiment and saw to the men's needs.

He rejected the idea. He'd never done that and it didn't really appeal except at the most basic level.

Anyway, they weren't Sanian. And it wasn't sex he was after. Sanian was inside his head, like it mattered she should be there. He didn't want to do anything that might eclipse her memory.

And he couldn't for the life of him explain why the memory of her refused to fade. Except… the prophecy. The one the old ayatani priests of Hagia had made. That Milo would find some way, some purpose, in years to come.

Milo hoped that had something to do with Sanian. He hoped that was why she remained bright in his mind. Maybe, somehow, she was his way.

Probably not. But it made him feel better to think of it like that.

'Now that looks like trouble,' he heard Doc Dorden say from the next cot along.

Milo sat up and looked. Far away, at the entrance to the billet hall, he could see Captain Daur talking seriously with a pair of Imperial commissars Milo had never seen before. The commissars were flanked by eight armed Phantine troopers.

'On whose authority?' Daur snapped.

'Imperial Taskforce Commissariate, captain, Commissar Del Mar. This is an internal security matter.'

'Does Colonel-Commissar Gaunt know about this?'

The two commissars looked at each other.

'He doesn't, does he?' smiled Daur. 'What about Commissar Hark?'

'You are delaying us, captain,' said the shorter of the two commissars. His name, he had told Daur, was Fultingo, and he was attached to Admiral Ornoff's staff. The other one, taller and gawkier, and wearing the pins of a cadet-commissar, had fresh Urdeshi insignia sewn onto his coat.

'Yes, I am. I want to know what this is about,' said Daur. 'You can't just march in here and start questioning my troops.'

'Actually, sir, we can,' said Fultingo.

'This is Gaunt's regiment, these are Gaunt's men...' Daur said quietly. 'Ibram Gaunt, the only commissar I know of to hold a command rank. Don't you think simple courtesy would have you approve it via him?'

'The God-Emperor's exalted Commissariate has little time for courtesy, captain.' Daur turned and saw Hark strolling up behind him. 'Unfortunately. However, as assigned Tanith First commissar, I intend to make sure that courtesy is extended.'

'They want to search the billet,' Daur said.

'Do they? Why?' Hark asked.

'A matter of internal security,' said Fultingo's cadet quickly.

Hark raised his eyebrows. 'Really... why?'

'Commissar Hark, are you refusing to cooperate?' asked Fultingo.

Hark turned. He took off his cap and tucked it under his arm. He fixed Fultingo with a poisonous stare.

'You know me?'

'We were briefed.'

'Yet I don't know you, or your... junior.' Hark waved his cap at the cadet.

'I am Commissar Fultingo, from the admiral's general staff. This is Cadet Goosen, who was serving under the Urdeshi Commissar Frant.'

'And Frant couldn't be bothered to attend?'

'Commissar Frant was killed in the assault,' said Goosen nervously, adjusting his collar.

'Oh, thrust into the limelight, eh, cadet?' smiled Hark.

'Not in any way I would have wished,' said Goosen. Daur thought that was a particularly brave response from the junior officer. Hark was in the process of bringing his full, withering persona to bear.

'So... Fultingo... what's this all about?' asked Hark softly.

'Something to do with that child, I should think,' said Curth. She'd joined them from the billet rows, her brow knotted. She pushed past the officers and the escort and knelt beside a small, grubby boy who was holding onto the last trooper's coat tails and trying not to cry.

'My name's Ana. What's your name?' she whispered.

'Beggi...' he said.

'Did you know that?' she asked Fultingo caustically.

Fultingo consulted his data-slate. 'Yes. Beggi Flyte. Eldest son of Onti Flyte, Cirenholm mill-wife.'

The boy was shuddering with tears now.

'He's deeply traumatised!' Curth spat, holding the child. 'Why did you see fit to drag him around these billets and–'

'He's deeply traumatised, ma'am,' said Fultingo, 'because his mother is dead. Murdered. By one of the Ghosts.

'Now... can we proceed?'

THE ENTOURAGE CAMP was a heady, smoky place half filling a cargo hangar. Cooks were roasting poultry and boiling up stews along a row of chemical stoves, and their assistants were dicing vegetables and herbs on chopping stands nearby. There was music playing, pipes, mandolins and hand-drums, and behind that there was the steady chink-chink of the armourers in their work-tents. Ghosts milled about, eating, drinking, getting their weapons sharpened, dancing and laughing, chatting conspiratorially to the painted women.

Kolea moved through the press. A fire-eater retched flame into the air and people clapped. The sounds reminded Gol of flamers in battle.

Someone offered him a smoked chicken portion for a credit but he waved them aside. Another, dressed in gaudy robes and sporting augmetic fingers, tried to interest him in a round of 'find the lady'.

'No thanks,' said Gol Kolea, pushing past.

A bladesmith was sharpening knives on a pedal-turned whetstone. Sparks flew up. Kolea saw Trooper Unkin waiting in line behind Trooper Cuu for his straight silver to be edged. Cuu's blade had already been rubbed in oil and was now set at the grinder, sparking.

He moved on. Black marketeers offered him size three clips.

'Where the gak were you?' he snarled, sending them away with a cuff.

Others had candy, porn-slates, exotic weapons, booze.

'Real sacra! Real, ghosty-man! Try it!'

'Can't stand the stuff,' growled Kolea, shouldering through.

A one-legged hawker showed off talismans of the Emperor, Tanith badges and aquila crests. Another, his face sewn together, produced chronometers, nightscopes and contraband micro-beads.

Yet another, limbless and moving thanks to a spider-armed augmetic chassis, displayed lho-sticks, cigars and several stronger narcotics.

A juggler tumbled past. A mime artist, her face yellow and stark, performed the death of Solan to an appreciative crowd. A small boy ran through the crowd, running a hoop with a stick. Two little girls, neither of them more than five years old, were playing hop-square.

'Going my way, handsome?'

Kolea stopped in his tracks. His Livy had always called him 'handsome'. He looked round. It wasn't Livy.

The camp-girl was actually pretty, though far too heavily made-up. Her dark-lashed eyes were bright and vivid. A beauty spot sat on her powdered cheek. She smiled at Kolea, her long skirt bunched up either side of her hips in her lace-gloved hands as she posed coquettishly. Her large, round breasts might as well have been bared given the flimsiness of the satin band that restrained them.

'Going my way?'

Her perfume was intoxicatingly strong.

'No,' said Kolea. 'Sorry.'

'Ball-less gak,' she hissed after him.

He tried to ignore her. He tried to ignore everything.

Aleksa was waiting for him in her silk tent.

'Gol,' she smiled. She was a big woman, fast approaching the end of her working days. No amount of powder, paint or perfume could really sweeten her rotund bulk. Her petticoats were old and threadbare, and her lace and holiathi gown was faded. She cradled a cut-crystal glass of amasec against her colossally exposed bosom with a wrinkled, ringed hand.

'Aleksa,' he said, closing the hems of her tent behind him.

She wriggled around on her pile of silk cushions. 'The usual?' she asked.

Gol Kolea nodded. He took the coins from his safe-belt, counted them again and offered them to her.

'On the nightstand, please. I don't like to get my gloves dirty.'

Kolea heaped the coins on the side table.

'Okay then... off you go,' she said.

He climbed on to the heap of cushions, and crawled across past Aleksa. She lay back, watching him.

Kolea reached the wall of the tent and parted the silk around the slit Aleksa had made for him.

'Where are they?'

'Right there, Gol.'

He angled his head. Outside, across the walkway, two children were playing a nameless game in a gutter puddle. A small boy and a toddler, laughing together.

'They've been okay?'

'They've been fine, Gol,' said Aleksa. 'You pay me to look after them so I do. Yoncy had a cough last week, but it's cleared up.'

'Dalin... he's getting so big.'

'He's a feisty one, no doubt. Takes a lot of watching.'

Kolea smiled. 'Which is all I do.'

He sat back on the cushions. She leaned forward and rubbed his shoulders with her hands.

'We've been through this, Gol. You should say something. You really should. It's not right.'

'Caff and Tona... they're doing right by them?'

'Yes, yes! Believe me, they're... I was going to say they were the best parents those kids could get... but you know what I mean.'

'Yeah.'

'Oh, Gol, come on.'

He looked round at her. 'They're mine, Aleksa.'

She grinned. 'Yes, they are. So go out there and claim them.'

'No. Not now. I won't gak up their lives any more. Their daddy's dead. It has to stay that way.'

'Gol... it's not my place to say this–'

'Say it.'

Aleksa grinned encouragingly. 'Just do it. Criid will understand. Caffran too.'

'No!'

'Criid's a good woman. I've got to know her, the time she spends here. She'd understand. She'd be... oh, I don't know. Grateful?'

Kolea took one last look through the slit. Dalin had made a paper boat for Yoncy and they were sailing it down the murky gutter.

'Too late,' breathed Kolea. 'For their sakes, and for mine, too late.'

THE PARTY REACHED the end of the last Ghost billet hall. Off-duty troopers watched them curiously as they passed by the cots. The boy had done little except stare and occasionally shake his head.

'Nothing?' asked Hark.

'No one he recognises,' said Fultingo.

'Satisfied, then?' snapped Curth.

'Not at all.' Fultingo dropped his voice. 'That boy's mother was killed in a frenzied knife attack. The wounds match exactly the pattern and dimensions of a Tanith warknife.'

'Knives can be stolen. Or lost in battle. Or taken from the dead. Some of the Ghosts may be missing their blades...' Hark said confidently. Daur knew it was for show. A warknife was a Ghost's most treasured possession. They didn't lose them. And they made sure their dead always went to the grave with their straight silver.

Fultingo wasn't put off anyway. 'Several witnesses saw a man in Tanith First battledress leaving the area of the habs. A man in a hurry.'

'Large? Small? Bearded? Clean-shaven? Tanith colouring or Verghast? Distinguishing marks? Rank pins?' Hark demanded.

'Lean, compact. Clean-shaven,' Goosen read from his notes. 'No one got a clear look. Except the boy. He's the best witness.'

Hark looked round at Daur and Curth. 'I deplore this crime, commissar,' he said to Fultingo. 'But this witch hunt's gone far enough. The boy's been through the halls and he hasn't recognised anyone. There's been a mistake. Your killer isn't a Ghost.'

Hark led them out into the corridor away from the men. It was cold, and condensation dribbled from the heating pipes that ran along the wall.

'I suggest you check with other regiments and explore other avenues of enquiry.'

Fultingo was about to reply, but they had to move aside as a platoon of weary Ghosts thumped down the corridor, dirty and smelling of smoke. A clearance squad returning from the fighting in the primary dome. Some were wounded or at least blood-stained.

'We haven't seen all of the men,' said Fultingo as they clomped past. 'There's still a number in the active zone and–'

'What is it? Beggi?' Curth said suddenly, crouching by the boy. He was pointing. 'What did you see?'

The boy didn't speak, but his finger's aim was an inexorable as a long-las.

'Detachment, halt!' Hark shouted, and the returning platoon came up sharp, turning in fatigued confusion.

'Is there a problem, commissar, sir?' asked Corporal Meryn, moving back from the head of the line.

'Is that him, Beggi?' asked Curth, warily.

'Is that the man?' echoed Hark. 'Son, is it?'

Beggi Flyte nodded slowly.

'Trooper! Come over here,' Hark growled.

'Me?' asked Caffran. 'Why?'

Two

The great bells of the Phantine Basilica pealed out into the morning across a municipal square at the heart of primary dome, and the sound of them raised cheering from the great gathering of Cirenholmers. The bells had been cast seventeen centuries before to serve the original Basilica some five kilometres below at a time when Phantine culture had occupied the surface of the planet. Since then, the cities had been serially abandoned and rebuilt on higher and ever higher ground to escape the rising blanket of pollution, and each time, the bells had been removed and transported up to the newly consecrated church.

Now they rang for joy. And they rang to signal the end of the service of deliverance that had been held to formally mark the liberation of Cirenholm. The night before, the last of the Blood Pact dug into the northern edges of the primary dome had been slaughtered or captured. Cirenholm was free.

Ecclesiarchs from Hessenville had conducted the service as all the Imperial priests in Cirenholm had been butchered during the invasion. The worthies of the city attended, some still sick and weak from their suffering during the occupation. So many citizens had come, the majority had been forced to congregate outside in the square and listen to the service via brass tannoys.

Hundreds of Imperial officers from the liberation force had also attended as a gesture of respect. Van Voytz, dignified in his dress uniform, had risen to say a few words. Diplomatically, his speech mentioned the efforts of the Tanith, Phantine and Urdeshi without differentiation. This was not a time for rebukes.

When the service was over and the bells were ringing, Gaunt rose from his pew and followed the crowds outside into the square. He paused briefly to speak to Major Fazalur, the stoic Phantine troop leader, and to a young officer called Shenko who was now, apparently, acting commander of the Urdeshi.

'How's Zhyte?' Gaunt asked.

'His fighting days are over, sir,' Shenko replied, with obvious awkwardness. 'He's to be shipped off-world to a veterans' hospice on Fortis Binary.'

'I hope his time there is happier than mine was,' said Gaunt with a reflective smile.

'Sir, I–' Shenko fumbled for the words.

'I don't bite, despite what you may have heard.'

Shenko grinned nervously. 'I just wanted to say... Zhyte was a good commander. A damn good commander. He saw us through hell several times. He always had a temper and his pride, well... I know he made a mistake here, sir. But I just wanted to say–'

'Enough, Shenko. I have no animosity towards the Urdeshi. I've actually admired their fortitude since Balhaut–'

'You saw action on Balhaut?' asked Shenko, his eyes wide.

'I did. I was with the Hyrkans then.' Gaunt smiled. Was he so old his past actions had a ring of history in the ears of younger men?

'Ask one of your veterans to tell you about Hill 67 sometime. The Hyrkans to the west of the ridge, the Urdeshi to the east. I don't bear a grudge, and I'm certainly not going to damn a whole regiment because of the attitude and actions of one man. Zhyte should have... ah, never mind. Your boys paid for his mistake here. Feth, Zhyte paid too, come to think of it. Just do me a favour.'

'Sir?'

'Be what he wasn't. We're going into the next theatre together soon. I'd like to think the Urdeshi will be allies, not rivals.'

'You have my hand on it, colonel-commissar.'

Gaunt walked away down the steps, through the throngs of people, stiff in his braided dress uniform.

Confetti streamed in the wind, and citizens pushed forward to hang paper garlands around the necks of their liberators and kiss their hands. Real flowers had vanished from Phantine eight centuries before, except for a few precious blooms raised in specialist hortivatae. But the paper mills still functioned.

With a garland of paper lilies around his neck, Gaunt made his way slowly through the crush on the square, shaking the hands thrust at him. He caught sight of a particularly striking officer dutifully shaking hands. It was Rawne. Gaunt smiled. He so seldom saw Rawne in full ceremonial regalia, it was a shock.

He moved over to him.

'Nice pansies,' he whispered mockingly in Rawne's ear as he shook the eager hands.

'Speak for yourself,' returned Rawne, glancing from his own garland to Gaunt's. The suturing around his blood-shot eye made his glare even angrier than usual.

'Let's get out of here,' said Gaunt, still smiling outwardly at the crowd.

'Good idea! Where to?' said Ayatani Zweil, appearing out of the press of reaching hands. Zweil had a half dozen garlands round his neck.

THEY PUSHED TO the edge of the crowd and, with hands aching, made off down a side street. Even then they were stopped several times to be kissed, hugged or thanked.

'If this is the upside of a soldier's life, no wonder you like it,' said Zweil. 'I haven't been worshipped this much since I was a missionary on Lurkan, walking the beati's path. Of course, at that time, I was much better looking, and it helped that the locals were expecting the return of a messiah named Zweil.'

Gaunt chuckled, but Rawne wasn't amused. He tore off his garland and tossed it into the gutter.

'The mawkish praise of sweaty hab-folk isn't why I signed up,' he sneered. 'That rabble probably thanked the Blood Pact just as effusively when they arrived. It always pays to be nice to the armed men controlling the place you live in.'

'You truly are the most cynical devil I've ever met, major,' Zweil remarked.

'Life sucks, holy father. Wake up and smell the flowers.'

Zweil toyed wistfully with the paper blooms around his neck. 'If only I could.'

'If you didn't sign up to enjoy the adulation of the Imperial common folk, Rawne,' Gaunt said, 'what did you do it for?'

Rawne thought for a moment.

'Feth you,' was all he could come up with.

Gaunt nodded. 'My thoughts exactly.' He stopped. 'This will do,' he told them.

It was a tavern. Built into the basement of a shabby records bureau, there was a steep set of steps running down from street level to the door. It had been closed since the Blood Pact occupation, and Gaunt had to pay the nervous owner well to get them in.

The place was dismal and littered with smashed glasses and broken furniture. The heathens had caroused their nights away, breaking everything they were finished with. Two girls, the owner's teenage daughters, were sweeping up debris. They'd already filled several sacks. The owner's brother was furiously scrubbing the walls with a bristle-brush dipped in caustic soda, trying to obliterate the obscenities that had been daubed on the plastered walls.

Gaunt, Rawne and Zweil took seats on a high bench beside the bar.

'I shouldn't be open,' the owner said. 'But for the saviours of Cirenholm, I'll gladly make an exception.'

'A double exception, I hope,' said Zweil.

'What will you have?'

'You have any sacra?' Gaunt asked.

'Uhh... no, sir. Not sure what that is.'

'No matter. Amasec?'

'I used to,' the owner said ruefully. 'Let me see if there's any left.'

'What are we doing here?' Rawne growled.

'Our duty,' Gaunt told him.

The bar owner returned with a pathetically dented tray on which sat three shot glasses of different sizes and a bottle of amasec.

He set the glasses down in front of the trio. 'My apologies. These are the only glasses I could find that haven't been broken.'

'In that case,' Gaunt assured him, 'they will be perfect.'

The owner nodded, and filled each glass up with the strong liquor.

'Leave the bottle,' Zweil advised him.

Rawne turned his glass slowly, eyeing the serious measure of alcohol. 'What are we drinking to?' he asked.

'The glorious liberation of Cirenholm in the name of the God-Emperor!' Zweil declared, smacking his lips and raising his shot.

Gaunt arrested his rising arm with a hand. 'No, we're not. Well, not really. At battle's end, Colm Corbec would have sniffed out the nearest bar and done just that. Today, he can't. So we're going to do it for him.'

Gaunt took up his glass and studied it dubiously, like it was venom. 'Colm Corbec. First-and-Only. Would that he was here now.'

He knocked back the shot in a single gulp.

'Colm Corbec,' Rawne and Zweil echoed and sank their shots.

'How is he?' Rawne asked. 'I've been at the front until now... not had a chance to... you know...'

'I went by the infirmary on my way here,' Gaunt said, playing with his empty glass. 'No change. He's probably going to die. The medics are amazed he's lasted this long.'

'Won't be the same without him...' Rawne muttered.

Gaunt looked round at him. 'Did I just hear that from Major fething Rawne?'

Rawne scowled. 'There's no shame in admitting we'll be poorer without Corbec. Now, if it was you that was at death's door, I'd be buying drinks for the whole fething regiment.'

Gaunt laughed.

'Speaking of which,' Zweil said, refilling their glasses.

Gaunt held his glass but didn't drink. 'I made a point of seeing Raglon earlier. Gave him brevet command of second platoon. He's got the chops for it, and as Corbec's adjutant, he's the obvious choice.'

Rawne nodded.

'And, on the record for a moment, I hereby give you second command, major. Until further notice.'

'Not Daur?' asked Zweil.

'Feth Daur!' Rawne spat, knocking back his drink.

'No, ayatani. Not Daur,' said Gaunt. 'Any reason it should be?'

Zweil sipped his drink and shrugged. 'The divide, I suppose.'

'The what?' asked Rawne, refreshing his own glass.

'The divide between the Tanith and the Verghastites,' Zweil explained. 'The Vervunhive mob feel like they're always in second place. In terms of morale, raising Daur to second would have pleased them.'

Rawne snorted. 'Fething Verghasts.'

Gaunt looked round at Zweil. The priest's remarks had reminded him forcefully of Hark's comments on the observation deck a few days before. Had Hark and Zweil been talking? 'Look, ayatani-father... I admire you and trust you, I use your advice and seek your council... spiritually. But when it comes to regiment protocol, I trust myself. Thank you for your opinion though.'

'Hey, I was just saying–' said Zweil.

'The Tanith First is the Tanith First,' said Gaunt. 'I want to make sure there's a balance, but when it comes to second officer, it has to be a Tanith in the role. Elevating Daur would give the wrong message to the men.'

'Well, you know what you're doing, Ibram. Be careful of that balance, though. Don't lose the Verghasts. They already feel they're second-class Ghosts.'

'They are,' said Rawne.

'Enough, Rawne. I expect you to use the Verghastites as well as you use the Tanith.'

'Whatever.'

'How's Soric?' Zweil asked.

Gaunt raised his drink. 'Dying, like Corbec. Faster, perhaps.'

'Here's to the soul of the Verghasts, then,' said Zweil. 'Agun Soric.'

They toasted and drained their shots.

Rawne made to top up their glasses from the bottle. 'And a toast to the next action, God-Emperor save us. Ouranberg. May it be half of Cirenholm.'

'It won't be,' said Gaunt. He covered his empty glass to stop Rawne filling it. One for Colm, one for Soric. That would do. 'It will be hell. The lord general's struck with some idea involving the Ghosts that he won't explain. I have a bad feeling about it. And it's been confirmed that Sagittar Slaith is in personal command of Ouranberg.'

'Slaith himself?' muttered Rawne. 'Feth.'

'There is some good news,' Gaunt said. 'A drogue arrived from Hessenville this morning with twenty thousand size three clips in its hold.'

'Praise be!' said Rawne humourlessly.

'Praise be indeed,' Gaunt said. 'The invasion drop is imminent and I'm just glad the Ghosts will be going in well supplied.'

'I just hope the business with Caffran is done by then,' said Rawne.

'What business?' Gaunt asked.

'Oh, the murder thing?' said Zweil. 'That was just ghastly.'

'What "business"? What "murder thing"?' Gaunt growled.

'Oh dear,' teased Rawne. 'Did I say too much? Has Hark been keeping it from you?'

'Keeping what?'

'The First-and-Only's dirty laundry,' said Rawne. 'I'm surprised at Caffran, actually. Didn't think he had it in him. Son of a bitch has plentiful grazing in that Criid woman without looking elsewhere. And murder? He has to be really fethed up to do that sort of shit. Heyyy!'

Gaunt had pushed Rawne off the end of the bench to get past him.

'Gaunt? Gaunt?' Zweil cried. But the colonel-commissar was running up the steps into the street and gone.

VIKTOR HARK BACKED across the room, bumped into a filing cabinet and realised there was nowhere left to retreat to.

'When were you intending to tell me, Viktor?' asked Gaunt.

Hark rose slowly. 'You were busy. With the lord general. And politically, I thought you could do with being distanced from it.'

'I brought you into this unit to serve as a political officer I could trust. Play all the spin you like, Viktor. But don't you ever dare keep me out of the loop again.'

Hark straightened his jacket and looked at Gaunt. 'You don't want this, Ibram,' he said softly.

'Feth that! I am the Ghosts! All the Ghosts! If it affects any one of them, it affects me.'

Hark shook his head. 'How did you ever get this far being so naive?'

'How did I ever think to trust you that you don't know that?' said Gaunt.

Hark shook his head sadly. He reached to the desk and handed Gaunt a data-slate. 'A hab-wife called Onti Flyte was butchered three nights ago. Stabbed with a Tanith knife. Witnesses saw a Ghost running from the premises. The victim's son positively identified Caffran. Case closed. I didn't bother you with it because it was just a minor incident. That's what I'm here for, sir. Taking care of the crap while you focus on the bigger picture.'

'Is that so? What will happen to Caffran?

'Commissar Del Mar has ordered his execution by las-squad at dawn tomorrow.'

'And it didn't occur to you that I'd question the loss of a trooper as valuable as Caffran?

'Given his crime, no sir.'

'And what does Caff say?'

'He denies it, of course.'

'Of course... he'll deny it particularly if he was innocent. I take it at least a routine investigation is being carried out? Witnesses can sometimes be mistaken.'

'Del Mar's staff is running the case. A Commissar Fultingo is lea–'

'You've just washed your hands of it?'

Hark fell silent.

'Local, civil law enforcement and the task force Commissariate have jurisdiction, of course. But this is also squarely a regimental matter. A matter for us. If there's a chance Caffran is innocent, I'm not going to let it go. Leave me the slate and get out of here,' Gaunt said.

Hark tossed the data-slate onto the table and walked out. 'Sir?' he asked, pausing in the doorway. 'I know Caffran's been with you from the start. I know he's well-liked and that he's a good soldier. But this is open and shut. The Tanith First are a remarkably well-behaved group of soldiers, you know. Sure, we get to deal with brawling and drinking, a few feuds and thefts, but nothing compared to some units I've served with. Summary execution for capital offences is almost routine in other regiments. Murder, manslaughter, rape. The Guard is full of killers and many of them can't help themselves. Dammit, you know that! Strict, rapid discipline is the only way to maintain control. I repeat, this is just a minor incident. It is nothing compared with the vital nature of the holy war we're undertaking. You shouldn't be wasting your time on this.'

'I'm wasting my time, Hark, precisely because it is so uncommon in this regiment. Now get the feth out of my sight for a while.'

VARL FOUND HIS way to the infirmary by following the scent of disinfectant. It was confusing at first, because almost every hallway and access in the secondary dome smelled of the stuff. There were Munitorium and civil work gangs all over the city hosing down floors and scrubbing away the reek and filth of the enemy.

But the infirmary had a stink of its own. Disinfectant. Blood.

The taskforce medicae had occupied an apprentices' college on one of the mid-level floors, close by the dome skin. The walls and roofs of some of the larger rooms demonstrated the gentle curve of the city's shape. Flakboard and shielding raised by the enemy had been stripped away from the windows to let in the cool light. Outside, through thick, discoloured armourglas, the pearly cloudscape spread away as far as the eye could see.

The place was busy. Varl edged his way in between weary nurses and arguing orderlies, bustling corpsmen resupplying their field kits from a dispensary, cleaning crews, walking wounded. Every chamber he passed was full of casualties, mainly Urdeshi, supported in crude but functional conditions. The worst cases were screened off in side wards.

The smell of pain was inescapable, and so was the low, background murmur of groans.

Varl slid his back to a wall to allow two medicae orderlies hurrying along with a resuscitrex cart to pass, and then entered the gloom of an intensive ward. The lighting was low-level, and trained around the individual beds. There was a steady, arrhythmic bleep of vitalators and the asthmatic wheeze and thump of the automatic respirator bellows.

Corbec lay on a rumpled cot, half-tangled in khaki sheets, like a shroud-wrapped pieta in an Imperial hero shrine. His limbs were sprawled, knotted in the fabric, as if he had turned restlessly in his dreams. Drips and monitor cables were variously anchored into his massive arms and chest, and his mouth and nose were plugged with larger, thicker tubes. It looked as if they were choking him. Corbec's eyes were sealed with surgical tape. Through his thick, black body hair it was possible to see the yellowing bruises and the hundreds of little, scabby cuts that marked his skin.

Varl stood looking at him for a long time and realised he couldn't think of anything to say or do. He wasn't even sure why he'd come.

He was halfway down the corridor on his way out when Dorden called out to him.

'Looking in on the chief, Varl?' the old doctor asked, coming over, his attention half on a data-slate he was reviewing.

Varl shrugged. 'Yeah, I–'

'You're not the first. Been Tanith in here all morning. In ones or twos. A few Verghastites too. Paying their respects.'

Varl breathed out deeply and stuck his hands in his pockets of his black combat pants. 'I don't know about respects,' he said. 'I don't mean that nasty, doc. I mean I… I think I just came to see.'

'To see Colm?'

'To see if it was true. Corbec's dying, they say. But I couldn't picture it. Couldn't see it in my head to believe it.'

'And now?' asked Dorden, handing the slate to a passing nurse.

'Still can't.' Varl grinned. 'He's not going to die, is he?'

'Well, we should all keep hoping and praying–'

'No, doc. I wasn't looking for no reassurance. If he's going to die, I hope you'd tell me. I just don't feel it. Standing there, I just don't. It doesn't feel like his time. Like he's not ready and he's fething well not going to let go.'

It was Dorden's turn to smile. 'You saw that too, huh? I haven't said that to anyone because I didn't want to get hopes up unfairly. But I feel it that way as well.'

'Doesn't seem hardly fair, does it?' said Varl. 'Corbec takes some punishment. He almost missed the show on Hagia and I know those injuries have only just healed. Now this.'

'Colm Corbec is a brave man and he takes risks. Too many risks, in my opinion. Mainly because, like all good officers, he leads by example. You know he got messed up this way saving Muril's life?'

'I heard.'

'Take risks, Varl, and sooner or later you get hurt. In Corbec's case sooner and later.'

Varl nodded, threw a half-salute, and turned to go. Then he hesitated.

'Doc?'

'Yes, sergeant?'

'About taking risks. I, uh… look, if I tell you something, it's just between us, right?'

'I can offer standard medicae confidentiality, Varl, providing it doesn't conflict with Guard security issues. And… I'm your friend.'

'Right, good.' Varl drew Dorden to one side, off the main corridor, into the entrance to one of the critical wards. He dropped his voice.

'Kolea.'

'Shoot.'

'He's a fine soldier. One of the best.'

'Agreed.'

'Good leader too.'

'No arguments.'

'We'd never have pushed the assault as far as we did if it hadn't been for him. He really… he did a real Corbec, if you know what I mean.'

'I do. You men pulled off a great victory. Getting in as far as the mill to support Domor and Haller's squads. Lucky break for us all. I hear Gaunt's going to commend a bunch of you. Don't tell him I told you.'

'It's just, well... Kolea was taking risks. Big risks. Crazy risks. Like he didn't care if he lived or died. I mean, he was insane. Running into enemy fire. It was a miracle he wasn't hit.'

'Some men deal with battle that way, Varl. I refer you to our previous conversation about Corbec.'

'I know, I know.' Varl struggled for the words. 'But this wasn't brave. This was... mad. Really fethed up. So mad, I said something to him, said I'd tell Gaunt what a crazy stunt he'd pulled. And he swore me not to. Begged me not to.'

'He's modest–'

'Doc, Gol lost his wife and his kids on Verghast. I think... I think he doesn't care any more. Doesn't care about his own life. I think he's looking for the reunion round.'

'Really?'

'I'm sure of it. And if I'm right, he's not only going to get himself dead, he's going to become a risk to the men.'

'It's good you told me this, Varl. Leave it with me for now. I'll be discreet. Let me know if you catch any more behaviour like it from him.'

Varl nodded and made his way out.

The canvas curtain behind Dorden slid back and Curth came through, peeling off bloody surgical gloves and tossing them into a waste canister.

'I didn't know you were there,' Dorden said.

'Assume I wasn't.'

'That was a confidential chat, Ana.'

'I know. It'll stay that way. I'm bound by the same oaths as you.'

'Good.'

'One thing,' she said, moving across to a trolley rack and sorting through data-slates. 'What's a reunion round?'

Dorden shook his head with a sigh. He scratched the grey stubble of his chin.

'Guard slang. It means... it means Kolea doesn't want to live without his lost loved ones. His dead wife, kids. He wants to be with them again. And so he's throwing himself into every fight that comes along without heed for his own safety, doing whatever he can do, until he finally catches that reunion round he's praying to find. The one that will kill him and reunite him with his family.'

'Ah,' said Curth. 'I had a nasty feeling that's what it was.'

'WHAT DID YOU do?'

Caffran slowly rose to his feet, mystified. The shackles linking his wrists clanked and drew tight where they ran down to his ankle-hobble. He'd been stripped down to his black vest and fatigue pants. His boot laces and belt had been removed.

'What do you mean?' he asked. His voice was dry and thin. The air in the dingy cell was damp and the light bad. A hunted look on Caffran's face showed that he was still dealing with the shock of the accusations.

'I mean what did you do? Tell me.'

'I didn't do anything. I swear.'

'You swear?'

'I swear! Nothing! Why... why have you come here, asking me that?'

Kolea stared at him. The shadows made it impossible for Caffran to read his expression.

Kolea was just a furious, threatening presence in the little cell.

'Because I want to know.'

'Why?'

Kolea took a menacing step forward. 'If I find out you're lying... if you hurt that woman–'

'Sergeant, please... I didn't do anything!'

'Sergeant Kolea!'

Kolea stopped a few paces from Caffran. He turned slowly. Silhouetted, Gaunt stood in the cell doorway.

'What are you doing here, Kolea?' Gaunt asked, stepping into the cell.

'I–' Kolea fell silent.

'I asked you a question, sergeant.'

'The men in my troop were... concerned... about what Caffran had done... I–'

Gaunt held up a hand. 'That's enough. You're out of line being here, Kolea. You should know that. Get out. Tell your men I'll talk to them.'

'Sir,' Kolea murmured and left.

Gaunt took off his cap and swung round to look at Caffran.

'Any idea what that was about, trooper?'

'No, sir.'

Gaunt nodded. 'Sit down, Caffran. You know why I'm here.'

'To ask the same questions Kolea did, probably.'

'And?'

Caffran slowly sat down on the cell's ceramic bench. He cleared his throat and then looked up, meeting Gaunt's gaze.

'I didn't do it, sir.'

There was a long silence. Gaunt nodded. 'All I needed to hear, Caff.'

He walked back to the door and put his cap back on.

'Keep your spirits up, Caff. If it's in my power to get you out of this, I will.'

'Thank you, sir.'

Gaunt stepped out into the brig hall. The Commissariate guards closed the heavy door, threw the bolts and ignited the shield. They saluted Gaunt, but he ignored them as he strode away.

* * *

In the rain, the mill-habs looked especially dismal. It wasn't real rain, naturally. Every two days, each section of the hab-district was sluiced with water from the dome's ceiling pipes. The idea was to maintain hygiene and keep the streets washed down.

It simply made everything glisten with wet and smell like a stale toilet stall.

The Flyte household had been boarded, and aquila seals stamped to the doors. The kids had been sent to stay with neighbours.

He jumped over the back fence into the rear yard and looked about, his cloak pulled up over his head against the downpour. If the outhouse was well roofed, then there might be some traces left to find. If it wasn't, the rain would have rinsed everything of value away.

He looked around, peering in through the cracked rear windows of the hab. All sorts of litter and broken debris was scattered in the weed-rife yard.

He went into the outhouse, breaking the aquila seal and ignoring the stencilled Commissariate warning notice. Inside, it smelled of rotting fibreboard and mineral waste. There was no light. It wasn't particularly watertight, but he could still see the dark stains on the wall, the floor, and the rim of the old, battered tub. One was a handprint. A perfect handprint. A woman's.

He looked around. The rafters were low, and there was a gash in one of them right above the bath. He took out a lamp pack and shone it up, probing the cut with the tip of his Tanith knife, and carefully teased out a tiny sliver of metal that he put in his hip pouch.

He sniffed the air. He sniffed the fibreboard wall. He got down on his hands and knees and shone the lamp-pack under the tub.

Something glinted.

He reached for it.

'Don't move! Not a bloody centimetre!'

Torchlight shone in at him.

'Out, slowly!'

He obeyed, keeping his hands in the open.

The young cadet commissar in the doorway looked very scared, an automatic pistol aimed at him. But credit where credit was due. He'd come up fething quietly.

'Who are you?' the cadet said.

'Sergeant Mkoll, Tanith First,' Mkoll replied quietly.

'Goosen? What's going on in there?' shouted a voice outside.

An older man, another commissar in a long, dripping storm coat, appeared behind the twitchy cadet. He almost took a step back in surprise when he saw Mkoll.

'Who the hell are you?'

'One of the neighbours reported an intruder, sir,' said Goosen. 'Said he thought it was the killer come back.'

'Cuff him,' said the older man bluntly. 'He's coming with us.'

'May I?' Mkoll said, gesturing to his battledress pocket.

Goosen covered him carefully as Mkoll reached into the pocket and drew out a folded document. He held it out to the older man.

'Signed authorisation from Colonel-Commissar Gaunt, my unit commander. His instructions for me to conduct an evidential search of the scene, pursuant to the case.'

The commissar looked it over. He didn't seem convinced. 'This is irregular.'

'But it's a fact. Can I lower my hands now?'

Goosen looked at the commissar. The older man shrugged.

'Let him be.'

The commissars looked round. Captain Ban Daur stood at the yard's back gate. He had no weapon drawn but, despite the rain, his coat was pulled back for easy access to his holstered laspistol.

Daur sauntered in, put his hand on Goosen's weapon and slowly pointed it down.

'Put it away,' he advised.

'Are you with him?' the commissar asked, indicating Mkoll.

'Yes, I am, Fultingo. Gaunt's rostered a team of us to carry out a regimental inspection of the case.'

'There's no time. The execution is–'

'Postponed. Gaunt obtained a delay order from Commissar Del Mar's office an hour ago. We have a grace period to assess all the evidence.'

Fultingo sneered at Mkoll. 'You sent a trooper into a crime scene?'

'Mkoll's unit chief of the Tanith scouts. Sharpest eyes in the Imperium. If there's something to find, he'll find it.'

'Who's in charge of your investigation?' asked Fultingo. He looked angry, thwarted. 'I'm going to lodge a formal complaint. You, captain? No... Hark, I'll bet.'

'Gaunt has taken personal charge of the case,' said Daur. Mkoll had lowered his hands and was inspecting the outside of the shed.

'Gaunt?' queried Fultingo. 'Gaunt himself? Why is he bothering with this?'

'Because it matters,' said Mkoll without looking round.

Fultingo stared at Daur, the dome-water dripping off his nose and capbrim. 'This is a criminal waste of resources. You haven't heard the last of it.'

'Tell someone who cares,' hissed Daur.

Fultingo turned on his jackbooted heel and marched out of the yard, Goosen scurrying after him, kicking up wet gravel.

'Thanks,' said Mkoll.

'You were handling it.'

Mkoll shrugged. 'Any progress?'

'Hark's done what Gaunt asked him to do. Everything's so tied up with red tape, Caff's safe for a few days. Dorden's examining the victim's body this evening. Hark's now circulating a questionnaire to the Ghosts just to see if anything flags up.'

Mkoll nodded. Daur shivered and looked about. The artificial rain was trickling to a stop, but the air was still filmy and damp. Steam rose from heating vents and badly insulated roofing. Water stood in great, black mirrors along the uneven street and in the ruts of the yard-back lane. Daur could smell stove fires and the faint, unwholesome aroma of ration meals cooking. Somewhere, children squealed and laughed as they played.

Although he couldn't see them, Daur could feel the eyes in all the back windows of the hab-street, eyes peering out from behind threadbare drapes and broken shutters, watching them.

'Gakking miserable place,' Daur remarked.

Mkoll nodded again and looked up. 'The worst kind. No sky.'

That made Daur smile. 'Mkoll,' he said. 'Since we're out here, off the record, as it were, you think Caffran did it?'

Mkoll turned his penetrating gaze round and directed it at the taller Verghastite officer. Daur had always admired and liked the chief scout. But for a moment, he was terrified.

'Caffran? Do you even have to ask?' said Mkoll.

'Yeah, right. Sorry.'

Mkoll wiped his wet face with a fold of his camo-cloak. 'I'm done here, sir.'

'Right. We can go back then. Did you turn up anything?'

'The prosecutors did a lousy job… unless someone's been in there since. They could have taken prints off the blood marks. Too late now, the damp's got in. But they missed… or ignored… a knife scar in the beams. I dug out a shard of metal.'

'From the knife?'

'I think so. The frames of all these buildings are made of surplus ceramite sheathed in paper pulp. The core's hard enough to nick a blade. Whoever did it was in a frenzy. And has a notch in his knife.'

'Well, gak! That's a start!'

'I know,' agreed Mkoll. 'More interestingly, I found this. Right under the tub.'

He held out his hand, palm up, and showed what he had found to Daur. A gold coin.

'An Imperial crown?'

Mkoll smiled. 'A defaced Imperial crown,' he said.

* * *

Three

LORD GENERAL VAN Voytz had chosen a generous High Gothic style manse in the upper levels of Cirenholm's primary dome for a command headquarters. Painted eggshell green, and supported by some of the integral pillars that rose up into the dome's roof structure, the manse was one of forty that overlooked a vast, landscaped reservoir complete with lawns and woodlands of aug-cultivated trees.

This lakeland habitat, complete with pleasure yachts rocking in coves at the timber jetties, had been the playground of Cirenholm's wealthiest and most influential citizens before the Blood Pact's arrival. Two planetary senators, a retired lord general, a worthy hierarch, six mill tycoons and the city governor had all owned homes around the shore.

All of them were dead now. There was no one left to object to Van Voytz's occupation. Not that any of them would have. The liberating lord general had power and, more crucially, influence, over them all.

An Imperial transport speeder still wearing its invasion camouflage skimmed Gaunt over the lake. Evening had fallen, and lights from the shoreline twinkled out over the dark water. Despite the gloom, Gaunt could see the burnt-out ruins of some of the properties, grim as skulls. He could also see the silhouettes of crosses dotted along the shore. No one had found the time yet to take down the murdered worthies of Cirenholm.

The speeder slowed and ran up the little beach in front of the manse in a wash of spray. Shielding their eyes from the drizzle, Urdeshi sentries waved the vehicle in. The speeder crossed a lawn and some low box hedges and settled on the arc of mica-shingled driveway outside the manse.

Gaunt stepped out into the night air, pulling on his storm coat. He could smell the water and the fading ozone reek of the cooling engines. Two staff limos were pulling away from the front steps, and speeder bikes and other Imperial transports sat parked under wet trees.

There were more sentries on the steps. Two of them, and Van Voytz's junior aide, hurried down to meet him.

'The lord general is waiting for you in the library, colonel-commissar. Go through. Have you eaten?'

'Yes, with the men.'

'A drink then?'

'I'm fine.'

Gaunt walked into the light of the hall. It was a stunning interior of polished rethuric panels, gold-laced shaniffes and displays of antique porcelain. He wondered how the hell any of this had survived unbroken.

The trompe l'oeil ceiling showed him vistas of the Empyrean, complete with dogged starships. The hall floor was piled with Guard-issue locker crates and roll-bags full of clothes.

'Through here,' the aide said.

Gaunt passed a side room which was bare apart from an enormous ormulu fireplace and a single escritoire lit by a floating glow-globe.

The tactician, Biota, sat working at the desk, veiled by holo displays and charts. He didn't look up.

Two Urdeshi storm-troops hurried past in full kit. They broke step only to salute.

The aide stopped outside a towering pair of gordian-wood doors. He knocked briefly and listened to his micro-bead.

'Colonel-Commissar Gaunt,' the aide said into his vox-mic. A pause. 'Yes, sir.'

The aide opened the doors and ushered Gaunt inside.

As libraries went, this one was contrary. The huge, arched roof, three storeys high, encased a wide room lined with shelves, with wrought iron stairwells and walkways allowing a browser access to the upper stacks.

But the shelves were empty.

The only books were piled on top of a heap of army crates in the centre of the parquet floor.

Gaunt took off his cap and wandered in. Lamps glowed from wall-brackets and autonomous glow-globes circled and hovered around him like fire-flies. At the end of the room, under the big windows, was a recently unpacked tactical desk. Its power cables snaked off and were plugged into floor sockets. A half-dozen library chairs were drawn up around it.

An open bottle of claret and several glasses, one half full, sat on a salver on a side table.

There was no sign of Van Voytz.

Gaunt looked around.

'A tragedy, isn't it?' said Van Voytz, invisible.

'Sir?'

'This house belonged to Air Marshal Fazalur, the father of our friend Major Fazalur. A splendid soldier, well decorated, one of the planet's heroes. An even more splendid bibliophile.'

Van Voytz suddenly appeared from under the wide tactical desk. Just his head and shoulders. He grinned at Gaunt and then disappeared again.

'Dead now, of course. Found his corpse on the beach. Most of his corpse, anyway.' Van Voytz's voice was partially muffled by the table.

'He had the most amazing collection of books, charts, data-slates and first editions. A wealth of knowledge and a real treasure. You can tell by all the empty shelves what size his collection was.'

'Extensive,' Gaunt said.

'They burned them all. The Blood Pact. Took all the slates, all the books, ferried them out into the woodland behind the manse, doused them with promethium, and burned them. There's a huge ring of ash out there still. Ash, melted plastic, twists of metal. It's still hot and smoking.'

'A crime, sir.'

Van Voytz appeared again.

'Damn right a crime, Gaunt!' He reached over, took a swig of wine from the glass, and then dropped out of sight once more.

Gaunt wandered over to the pile of books and lifted one. '*The Spheres of Longing*... Ravenor's greatest work. Feth, this is a first edition!'

'You've read Ravenor, Gaunt?'

'A personal favourite. They spared some things then? This volume alone is priceless.'

'It's mine. I couldn't bear the place looking so empty so I had some of my own library freighted up from Hessenville.'

Gaunt put the book down carefully, shaking his head. He couldn't imagine the sort of power that could order the Imperial Munitorium to fast ship a person's private book collection to him in a war zone. Come to that, he couldn't imagine the sort of power that would enable one to own a first edition of *The Spheres of Longing.*

He glanced at some of the other books. *The Life of Sabbat,* in its folio print. *The Considerations of Solon,* mint. Garbo Mojaro's *The Chime of Eons*. A perfect copy of *Liber Doctrina Historicas*. The complete sermons of Thor, cased. *Breaching the Darkness* by Sejanus. An early quarto of the *Tactica Imperium,* with foil stamps and plates complete. A limited issue of Slaydo's treatise on Balhaut, on the original data-slate.

'You like books, Gaunt?'

'I like these books, sir.'

Van Voytz emerged from under the desk and gave the display machine's cold flank a slap.

'Bloody thing!' He was clad in dress-uniform breeches and boots, but stripped down to an undershirt. Gaunt saw the lord general's tunic was hung over the back of one of the chairs.

'They shipped this thing in,' said Von Voytz, sweeping up his glass and sipping it as he flapped an arm at the tactical desk. 'They shipped it in and left it here. Did they plug it in and test start it? No. Can I get the holo-display to work? No. I tried. You saw me under there.'

'It's really a tech-magos's job, sir.'

Van Voytz grinned. 'I'm a lord general, Gaunt. I can do anything!'

They both laughed.

'Where are my manners?' said the general. He sloshed some of the contents of the bottle into one of the empty glasses. Gaunt took it. He realised he was still holding the copy of the *Tactica Imperium*.

'Cheers,' said Van Voytz.

'Your health, sir. The Emperor protects.'

'You like that one?' Van Voytz asked, pointing at the book Gaunt was holding.

'It's beautiful–'

'Keep it. It's yours.'

'I couldn't. It's priceless.'

'I insist. It's mine to give. Besides, you deserve it. A gift to recognise your efforts here on Phantine so far. I'm serious. Keep it.'

'I... thank you, sir.'

Van Voytz waved a hand. 'Enough of that. Damn desk.' He took a sip of claret and kicked the offending piece of furniture. 'I had holo graphics of Ouranberg to show you. The whole assault plan.'

'I could come back tomorrow, sir.'

'Don't be silly, Gaunt. You've got your hands full. I'll speak. You'll listen. You'll get the gist. It'll be like it was back in the days of Sejanus and Ponthi. You're Ponthi.'

'An honour, s–'

'I'm kidding, Ibram. Just kidding. I asked you here to talk about the Ouranberg assault. Biota's been totting things up, and he says I'm crazy. But I have an idea. And it involves your mob.'

'So you said, sir.'

'Don't look so... constipated, Ibram. You'll like this. I had the idea when I was reviewing your attack report. Damn fine men you've got there.'

'Thank you.'

'Good at stealth work. Smart. Capable. If we're going to take Slaith down, we'll need all of that.'

Gaunt put the book back on the pile and gulped his drink. 'It is Slaith then, sir?'

'Oh, you betcha. Probably with loxatl mercenaries. Ouranberg's going to be a real party.'

Van Voytz refilled his glass. 'Before we get into the planning, I hear there's a problem in your regiment.'

'A problem?'

'A fellow up on capital charges.'

'Yes sir. I'm dealing with it.'

'I know you are. And you shouldn't have to. It's a company level matter. Just let him hang.'

'I can't, sir. I won't.'

The lord general swigged his wine again and sat down on one of the chairs. 'You're a regimental officer now, Gaunt. Trust your staff to deal with it.'

'This matters to me, sir. One of my men has been falsely accused. I have to clear him.'

'I know all about it. I spoke with Commissar Del Mar this afternoon. I'm afraid you're wasting your time, Ibram.'

'Caffran's innocent, sir, I sw–'

'This man... Caffran is it? He's a dog soldier. A common trooper. The case against him is las-proof.

'You have more important things to be devoting your time to.'

'With respect, lord, I haven't. I stand where I stand today because of the common dog soldiers. I would not be me without their efforts. And so I make sure I look after every last one of them.'

Van Voytz frowned. 'Well, shame on me–'

'Sir, I didn't mean–'

Van Voytz waved his hand. 'I'm hardly offended, Gaunt. Actually, it's refreshing to hear an officer remember the basics of good command. The Imperial Guard is nothing without the Imperial Guardsmen. No one should get so high and mighty they forget that. Your personal code of honour is unusually robust. I just hope...'

'Sir?'

Van Voytz rose and started to put his jacket back on. 'I was going to say I hope it doesn't get you killed. But, you know, it assuredly will. Eventually, I mean. That's the curse of a code of honour as resolute as yours, colonel-commissar. Stick by it, and you'll end up dying for it.'

Gaunt shrugged. 'I always supposed that was the point, sir.'

'Well said,' Van Voytz replied, fiddling with the buttons of his frogging. 'Your dual role is a problem, though. Say the word and I'll transfer you out of the Commissariate. You'll be Brigadier Gaunt... no, let's not mess around, shall we? You'll be Lieutenant-General Gaunt, sectioned to me, Guard and Guard alone. A full Imperial Guard officer with commissars at your beck and call.'

Gaunt was mildly stunned.

'The uniform would suit you, Gaunt. Lieutenant-General, Tanith First-and-Only. No more fussing over discipline matters. No more wasting command time.'

Gaunt sat down. 'I'm flattered, sir. But no. I'm happy where I am.'

Van Voytz shrugged. He didn't seem put out. 'If you say so. But don't dwell on this man Caffran, please. I won't have it. Now... let me tell you my ideas about Ouranberg...'

FOR ALL DORDEN's efforts with the powder, the lice had taken hold. While fumigation crews filled the billets with noxious chemical clouds, the Ghosts reported en masse to a grand municipal bathhouse in primary. Kit was stripped off for steam-cleaning, and the troops, shivering in their shorts and vests, lined up in the cold stone atrium to have their heads shaved. The buzz of three dozen clippers filled the air above the chatter. Servitors shunted back and forth, sweeping up the hair for incineration.

Once shaved, the troops were sent through into the steaming shower blocks armed with cakes of tar-soap, their boots slung by the laces around their necks. On the far side of the shower blocks were halls lined with rush mats where stiffly-old but clean towels were stacked. Munitorium aides stood by at trestle tables piled with clean reserve kit that stank of yet more powder.

Gaunt and Daur walked into the drying halls and there was a general fuss and shuffling as naked or half-dressed troops tried to come to attention.

'As you were,' Gaunt called out, and they relaxed back to their ablutions. Gaunt nodded to Daur and the captain consulted a data-slate.

'Listen up,' Daur called out. 'If you hear your name, get dressed and assemble at the exit. I'll only call this once...'

Still toweling off their newly bald heads, the troops paid attention.

'Mkvenner! Doyl! Bonin! Larkin! Rilke! Nessa! Banda! Meryn! Milo! Varl! Cocoer! Kuren! Adare! Vadim! Nour! That's it! Fast as you like!'

Larkin was tugging a clean black vest over his bony torso and scowled at Bragg as he heard his name called. 'Oh, what now?' he grumbled. Larkin looked mean and cadaverous with his hair cropped.

'What have you done, Larks?' Bragg chuckled.

'Fething nothing!' snapped Larkin, struggling to pull on starch-stiff fatigue pants. Buckling his belt, he shuffled over to join the others in unlaced boots.

'That's everyone,' said Daur to Gaunt and the colonel-commissar nodded. Painfully aware of the shaven heads around him, Gaunt pointed to his own hair. 'Don't worry, it's my turn next,' he said. 'Lice have no respect for rank.' The Ghosts smiled. They all looked like raw recruits again, their scalps unhealthy white. Gaunt felt especially sorry for the women.

'Very well,' he said. 'Imperial Command has assigned an operation to us. Details later, for now it's enough for you to know the lord general conceived it himself and considers it a critical mission. Its successful execution has priority over all other Imperial operations at this point.'

A few eyes widened. Larkin made a soft, disheartened moan. Banda elbowed him.

'I've personally selected you all for this operation, for reasons that will become obvious to each of you. The operational name is Larisel. You will not speak about it in general or specific terms to anyone, even other Ghosts outside this group. I want you all assembled at sub-hangar 117 by 18.30 with full kit, gear and personal effects. I mean everything, prepped for transport. You won't be going back to the billet.'

'Is that because this is a... one-way mission?' asked Varl euphemistically.

'I won't lie, sergeant. Larisel will be ultra-high risk. But the reason you won't be going back to the regimental billet is that I'm moving you all to secondary billet for speciality training and mission-specific instruction. Okay?'

There were mumbles and nods.

'Any questions? No? Okay, good. I have supreme confidence in you all: your abilities and your characters. I'll say it again before you get underway, but good fortune to you all. The Emperor protects.'

Gaunt glanced round at Daur. 'Anything you want to add at this stage, captain?'

'Just one thing, sir.' Daur stepped to the front, reaching one hand into the patch pocket of his black tunic jacket. 'Regarding Trooper Caffran. As you know, we've been doing the rounds, asking questions, collecting data. I fully expect some valuable information to come out that way. Word of mouth, trooper to trooper. But from here in, you're going to be effectively separated from the regimental main force, so there's going to be much less opportunity to keep you in the loop as far as the ongoing investigation is concerned. Therefore, for now... I want to inspect everyone's warknife. I want to hear from any of you who has noticed notching or damage to the warknives of any other trooper. And has anyone seen one of these before?'

He took a small waxed envelope from his pocket, opened it and held up a gold coin.

'Imperial crown, local issue... purposely defaced on both head and reverse. Does anyone have one like it? Does anyone know anything about its origin? Does anyone know of another trooper who has one? If you're uncomfortable about speaking out now, see me, or the colonel-commissar, or Commissar Hark, in confidence. That's all.'

'Dismissed,' Gaunt said.

The group broke up, muttering to one another. Daur and Gaunt turned together and walked off down the outer hall.

'I've got hopes about the coin,' confided Daur. 'We already know from a dozen Ghosts, including Obel and Kolea, that there were more of the same in the business premises of the adjacent mill sector. But all of them swear they left the coins well alone because of the markings.'

'We'll see. If anyone did get greedy, he'll not want to admit it. They know how strict I am about looting. Did you check Caffran's blade?'

Daur sighed. 'It's notched. He said it happened during the firefight in the park at 505, but we've only got his word. Del Mar's staff will be all over that like a bad rash if it gets out.'

'Then don't let it out,' said Gaunt. 'They've got all the rope they need as it is. Don't give them any more.'

'WHAT DO WE do?' Larkin whispered anxiously to Bragg as he finished lacing up his boots. Bragg leaned beside him, pulling on his vest.

'We tell Gaunt,' Bragg answered simply.

'We can't!'

'Why not?' Bragg asked.

'Because we don't betray our own. I've never been a rat in my life, and I don't intend to start now.'

'I don't think that's the reason, Larks,' Bragg said. He smiled. 'We'd rat if it got Caffran off. No, I think you're scared of him.'

'I am not!'

'I think you are. I know I am.'

Larkin's eyes widened. 'You're scared of Cuu?'

'All right, not scared exactly. But wary. He's a mean piece of work.'

Larkin sighed. 'I'm scared of him. He's a maniac. If we report him, and he gets off later, he'll come for us. He'll fething come for us. It's not worth it.'

'It's worth it to Caff.'

'I'm not crossing Cuu. Not for anything. There's something about him. Something sick. He could go to the firing squad and then come back and haunt me.'

Bragg laughed.

'You think I'm joking.'

Bragg shook his head. 'Cuu's a fething maniac, Larks. If anyone in this mob is capable of that killing, it's him. If he's guilty, we don't have to worry about it. If he's innocent, well, then he gets off. And honestly, what would he do then? Kill us? Get off a murder charge and then commit a double murder?'

'I'm not doing it,' Larkin hissed firmly.

Bragg fingered the new, pink skin healing on the gash in his shoulder. 'Then I might,' he said. 'He's no friend of mine.'

THE BILLET HALL was fairly quiet except for the occasional cough or sneeze. The stink of the recent fumigation still clung to the air.

Milo expertly stowed the last of his kit in his backpack, lashed it shut and then secured the tightly rolled tubes of his bed-roll and camo-cloak to it.

Vadim, already packed and ready to go, wandered over to him. 'You ever been picked for special ops before, Milo?'

'Some. Not quite like this.' Milo pulled on his tunic, checking the contents of the pockets, and then strapped on his webbing. 'Sounds... high profile,' he added, hooking his gloves to his webbing before rolling his beret and tucking it through the epaulette of his tunic. He hoisted up his backpack, shook the weight onto his shoulders and then did up the harness.

'Sounds suicidal to me,' Vadim muttered darkly. He rubbed his sandpaper scalp. The lack of hair had altered the proportion of his head and made his strong nose seem almost beak-like. He looked like a dejected crow.

'We'll see, won't we?' Milo said, cinching the sling of his lasrifle before shouldering it. He inspected his makeshift cot one last time to make sure he hadn't left anything. 'I tend not to worry until I know I've got something to worry about.'

Fully prepped and weighed down with kit, Nour and Kuren moved across the billet to join them. They shook hands and exchanged banter with other Ghosts as they crossed the hall. None of them had explained where they were going and no one had asked, but it was clear they were shipping out for some special duty_and that prompted numerous farewells and wishes of luck.

Kuren had put on his drop-issue balaclava, rolled up into a tight woollen hat. 'Fething lice,' he grumbled, 'my fething head's cold.'

'Set?' Milo asked the three of them. They nodded. It was just after 18.00 and time to leave.

Milo looked across to Larkin's cot. The master sniper was finishing up his almost obsessive prep on his gun, packing up the cleaning kit and sliding the long foul-weather cover over the weapon. 'Larks? You ready?'

'Be right there, Milo.'

Bragg sat down on the cot next door. 'You... you have a good time now, Larks.'

'Oh, funny.'

'Just... come back again, okay?'

Larkin noticed the look in Bragg's eyes.

'Oh, I fething well intend to, believe me.'

Bragg grinned and held out a big paw. 'First and Only.'

Larkin nodded and slapped Bragg's palm. 'See you later.'

He walked over to the others. Trooper Cuu, who had been lying on his back gazing at the roof, sat up suddenly and grinned at Larkin as he went by.

'What?' asked Larkin, stopping sharply.

Still grinning, Cuu shook his head. 'Nothing, Tanith. Not a thing, sure as sure.'

'Come on, Larkin!' Nour called.

Larkin scowled at Cuu and pushed past him.

'Trooper Cuu!'

The sudden shout made the five troopers stop and turn. Hark had entered the billet with Sergeant Burone and two other Ghosts. All three troopers carried weapons. They marched down the aisle towards Cuu's bunk.

'What's this?' Vadim whispered. There was a general murmur of interest all around.

'Oh feth,' Larkin mumbled.

Cuu got up, staring at the approaching detail, confused.

'Kit inspection,' Hark told him.

'But I–'

'Stand aside, trooper. Burone, search his pack and bed-roll.'

'What is this?' Cuu blurted.

'Stand to attention, trooper!' Hark snarled and Cuu obeyed. His eyes flicked back and forth as he stood there rigidly. 'Pat him down,' Hark told one of the men with him.

'This is out of order,' Cuu stammered.

'Silence, Cuu. Give me his knife.' The trooper frisking Cuu unbuckled Cuu's warknife from his sheath and passed it to the commissar. Hark inspected the blade.

'Nothing, sir,' Burone reported. Cuu's entire kit was spread out across his cot, wherever possible taken apart. Burone was checking the lining of Cuu's backpack and musette bag.

'The blade's clean,' Hark said, as if disappointed.

'He had it ground and sharpened the other day.'

Hark glanced round. Kolea stood prominently in the group of Ghosts who had gathered to watch. 'I saw him, sir,' Kolea said. 'You can check with the knife grinder.'

Hark looked back at Cuu. 'True?'

'So fething what? It's a crime to keep your blade sharp these days?'

'That insolence is pissing me off, trooper–'

'Sir...' the trooper frisking Cuu called. He yanked up the top of Cuu's left pant leg. A tight cloth bag was taped to his shin above the top of the boot.

Hark bent down and pulled the tape off. Coins, heavy and gold, spilled out into his hand.

Turning the coins over, Hark rose again. He looked at Cuu.

'Anything to say?'

'They were just... no.'

'Take him in,' Hark told his detail.

Burone's men grabbed Cuu. He began to struggle.

'This is unfair! This is not right! Get off me!'

'Behave! Now! Or things will get even messier!' Hark warned him.

Cuu stopped thrashing and the men frog-marched him forward. Hark and Burone fell in behind. As they swept past Milo's group, Cuu's cat-eyes found Larkin. 'You? Was it you, you gak?' Larkin shuddered and looked away.

Then Cuu was being taken past Bragg. Bragg was smiling.

'You? You gak! You filthy gak! Big dumbo's set me up! He's set me up!'

'Shut up!' Hark roared and they swept him out of the hall.

Bragg looked across at Larkin and shrugged. Larkin shook his head unhappily.

'Well that was interesting,' Vadim said.

'Yeah,' said Milo. He checked his watch. 'Let's go.'

SUB-HANGAR 117 WAS low down on the west skirts of Cirenholm secondary, close to one of the dome's main recirculator plants. There was background throb in the air, and a constant vibration. Extractor vents moved warm, linty air down the access corridor and across the entrance apron.

By the time Varl arrived with Cocoer, it was almost 18.30 and most of the others were already there. Banda and Nessa stood talking to the Tanith sniper Rilke, and Corporal Meryn and Sergeant Adare sat on their kit-packs with their backs to the wall, smoking lho-sticks and chatting. Doyl, Mkvenner and Bonin, the three scouts, lounged over near the other wall in a huddle, conversing privately about something. Secret scout lore no doubt, Varl thought.

'Boys,' he nodded to them and they returned his greeting.

'Hey, Rilke, girls,' he said approaching the snipers. He threw a brief wave over at Adare and Meryn.

'We're a few short, aren't we?' said Cocoer, setting down his pack.

'Not for long,' Rilke said. Milo, Larkin and the others were approaching along the rust-streaked tunnel.

'Well, what do we think, eh?' asked Varl. 'Think Gaunt has arranged a nice day out and a picnic for us?'

Banda snorted. Nessa, who had been deafened on Verghast, had to lip-read and so smiled gently a heartbeat after Banda's derisive noise.

'Let's see… three scouts, four snipers, and eight dog standards like me and Cocoer,' Varl said, looking around. 'What does that sound like to you?'

'It sounds like an infiltrate and sanction detail,' said a voice from behind him. Mkoll strode purposefully up onto the apron, his field boots ringing on the metal plating. 'And it's four scouts, actually. I'm in this too.' Like all of them, Mkoll wore full matt-black fatigues and high-laced boots, and heavy-pouched webbing, with a full field kit and weapons on his back. The sleeves of his tunic were neatly rolled up past the elbows. He did a quick head count and then consulted his wristwatch. 'Everyone here and it's bang on 18.30. We got the first part right then.'

They followed him through the hatch into the hangar. It was cold and dim in the echoey interior, and they could see little except for the area just inside the hatch which was illuminated by a bank of overhead spots. Four men were waiting for them in the patch of light.

They were all big, powerful young men wearing cream-coloured quilted jackets and baggy, pale canvas pants bloused into the tops of high jump-boots. The sides of their heads were brutally shaved, leaving just a strip on their crowns. Not as a result of lice treatment, Varl thought. These men kept their hair that way. They were Phantine troopers. Skyborne special-ists.

Mkoll greeted them and the four Phantines snapped back smart salutes.

'Major Fazalur sends his compliments, sir,' said one with a silver bar on his sleeve under the Phantine regimental patch. 'He asked us to wait for you here.'

'Fine. Why don't you introduce yourselves?' Mkoll suggested.

'Lieutenant Goseph Kersherin, 81st Phantine Skyborne,' the large trooper replied. He indicated his men in turn. 'Corporal Innis Unterrio, Private first class Arye Babbist, Private first class Lex Cardinale.'

'Okay. I'm Mkoll. Tanith First. You boys'll get the hang of the others soon enough.' Mkoll swung round and faced the waiting Ghosts. 'Drop your packs for now and loosen off. Let's get you into groups. Four teams. Sergeant Varl, you're heading first team. Sergeant Adare, third team. Second team is yours, Corporal Meryn. Fourth team is mine. Now the rest of you... Doyl, Nessa, Milo, you're with Adare. Mkvenner, Larkin, Kuren... Meryn. Varl gets Banda, Vadim and Bonin. Which leaves Rilke, Cocoer and Nour for me. Let's group up so we get used to it. Come on. Good. Now, as you will have spotted, each team contains a leader, a trooper, a sniper and a scout. The bare minimum for light movement, stealth and insertion. None of us will enjoy the back-up of a support weapons section or a flamer on this. Sorry.'

There were a few groans, the loudest from Larkin.

'So,' said Mkoll with what seemed like relish. 'Let's get onto the fun bit. Lieutenant?'

Kersherin nodded and walked over to a dangling control box that hung down from the roof on a long, rubber-sleeved cable. He thumbed several switches. There were a series of loud bangs as the overhead light rigs came on one after another, quickly illuminating the entire, vast space of the hangar with cold, unfriendly light.

On the far side, rising some thirty-five metres above a floor layered with foam cushion mats, stood a large scaffolding tower strung with riser cables and pulleys.

'You see?' said Larkin to the Ghosts around him. 'Now I do not like the look of that.'

Four

THE EXECUTION YARD was an unprepossessing acre of broken cement, walled in on three sides by high curtains of pock-marked rockcrete, and by the Chamber of Justice on the fourth.

The Chamber of Justice, Cirenholm's central law court and arbites headquarters, had suffered badly during the Blood Pact occupation. The uppermost floors of the tall, Gothic revival building were burnt out, and the west end had been heavily shelled. Most of the office and file rooms were ransacked. An immense chrome aquila, which had once hung suspended on the facade over the heavy portico, had been shot away by determined stubber fire, and lay crumpled and flightless on the main steps. On one side of the entry court sat a chilling heap of dented arbites riot helmets, a trophy mound raised by the Blood Pact after their defeat of the lightly armed justice officers who had staunchly held out to the last to defend this sector of the city.

Despite all that, the prison block below ground was still functioning and it was the only true high security wing that Cirenholm could offer, and so the taskforce Commissariate had been forced to occupy the Chamber as best it could.

From a window at the rear of the first floor, Gaunt looked down onto the execution yard. The six-man firing squad, hooded and dressed in plain grey fatigues that lacked patches, insignia or pins, took absolution from the waiting Ecclesiarch official with routine gestures, and then lined up and took aim.

There was no fuss or ceremony. The hawkish commissar in charge, a black silk cloth draped over his balding pate, raised a sabre and gave the command in a tired voice.

The prisoner hadn't even been blindfolded or tied up. He just cowered against the back wall with nowhere to run.

Six las-shots, in a simultaneous flurry, spat across the yard and the prisoner toppled, rolling back to slide clumsily down the wall. The presiding commissar yelled out something else, and was already sheathing his sabre and taking off his black cloth as the squad filed off and servitors rolled a cart out to collect the body.

Gaunt let the scorched brocade curtain fall back against the broken window and turned away. Daur and Hark, who had been watching from the neighbouring window, exchanged a few words and went to look for something to sit on. Half-broken furniture was piled up along one wall of the battered stateroom.

The tall, ten-panelled door opened and Commissar Del Mar strode in. He was a lean man of advanced years, white-haired and reliant on augmetic limb reinforcements, but he was still striking and imposing. A good hand-span taller than Gaunt, he wore black dress uniform with a purple sash and a long cloak lined with red satin. His cap and gloves were arctic white.

'Gentlemen,' he said immediately, 'sorry to keep you waiting. Today is full of punishment details and each one requires my authority and seal. You're Gaunt.'

'Sir,' Gaunt saluted and then accepted Del Mar's handshake. He could feel the rigid armature of Del Mar's artificial hand through the glove.

'We've met, I believe?' said Del Mar.

'On Khulen, the best part of a decade ago. I was with the Hyrkans then. Had the pleasure of hearing you address the Council of Commissars.'

'Yes, yes,' Del Mar replied. 'And also on Canemara, after the liberation. Very briefly, at the state dinner with the incoming governors.'

'I'm impressed you remember that, sir. It was... fleeting.'

'Oktar, God-Emperor rest his soul, had nothing but praise for you, Gaunt. I've kept my eye out. And your achievements in this campaign have brought you recognition, let's face it.'

'You're very kind, sir. May I introduce my political officer, Viktor Hark, and Captain Ban Daur, acting third officer of my regiment.'

'Hark I know, welcome. Good to know you, captain. Now, shall we? We've a busy morning of what might be described as testimonial sifting to get through. Tactician Biota is here, along with a whole herd of staff officers, and Inquisitor Gabel is ready to present his working party's findings.'

'One extra matter I'd like to deal with before we get down to business,' said Gaunt. 'The case of Trooper Caffran.'

'Ah, that. Gaunt, I'm surprised that–' Del Mar stopped. He glanced round at Hark and Daur. 'Gentlemen, perhaps you'd give us a moment? Fultingo?'

Commissar Fultingo appeared in the doorway. 'Show the commissar and the captain here to the session hall, if you would.'

Commissar Del Mar waited until they were alone. 'Now then, this Trooper Caffran business. I'll be blunt, it's beneath you, Gaunt. I know I'm not the first person on the senior staff to caution you about this. Commissar or not, you're an acting field commander, and you should not be occupying your time or thoughts with this. It is a minor matter, and should be left to the summary judgement of your commissar.'

'I have Hark's support. I'm not going to back down. Caffran is a valuable soldier and he's innocent. I want him back in my regiment.'

'Do you know how many individuals I've had shot since we arrived, Gaunt?'

'A half-dozen. That would be the average for a taskforce this size.'

'Thirty-four. True, twenty of those were enemy prisoners who we were done with interrogating. But I've been forced to put to death seven deserters, four rapists and three murderers. Most of them Urdeshi, but a few Phantine too. I expect that kind of statistic. We command killers, Gaunt – violent, dangerous men who have been trained to kill. Some snap and desert, some attempt to slake their violent appetites on the civilian population, and some just snap. Let me tell you about the murderers. One, a Phantine private, wounded, went berserk and killed two orderlies and a nurse in the tertiary hospital. With a gurney. I can't begin to imagine how you kill someone with a gurney, but I guess it took a great deal of rage. The second, an Urdeshi flame-trooper, decided to ignite a public dining house in secondary and toasted four members of Cirenholm's citizenry who had every right to believe the danger was now past. The other, another Urdeshi, shot a fellow trooper during an argument over a bed-roll. My justice was swift and certain, as the honourable tradition of the Commissariate dictates and Imperial law demands. Summary execution. I'm not a callous man, Gaunt.'

'I didn't presume you were, commissar. Neither am I. As a sworn agent of the Commissariate, I do not hesitate to dispense justice as it is needed.'

Del Mar nodded. 'And you do a fine job, clearly. The Tanith First have a nearly spotless record. Now one of them steps out of line, one bad apple. It happens. You deal with it and move on. You forget about it and put it down as a lesson to the rest of the men. You don't tie up my office with demands for grace periods and the constant, deliberate interference of Commissar Hark.'

'Hark plagued you on my instruction, sir. And I'm glad he did. Caffran is innocent. We managed to buy enough time to identify the real killer.'

Del Mar sighed. 'Did you now?'

'He was arrested last night, sir. Trooper Cuu, another of my regiment. A Verghastite.'

'I see.'

'Those Tanith that are alive today, sir, are alive because I plucked them from their home world before it died. I consider them a precious resource. I will not give up any of them unless I know for sure it's right. This isn't right. Caffran's blameless. Cuu's the killer.'

'So... what are you asking me, Gaunt?'

'Release Caffran.'

'On your word?'

'On my recognisance. Try Cuu for the crime. The evidence against him is far more damning.'

Del Mar gazed out of the window. 'Well, now... it's not that simple any more, Gaunt,' he said. 'It's not that simple because you've made an issue of this. One crime, one suspect, that's routine. One crime, two suspects... that's an inquiry. A formal one. You've forced this, Gaunt. You must have realised.'

'I had hoped we might skip the formalities. Proceed to Cuu's court-martial and have done.'

'Well, we can't. We now have to depose this Caffran first and clear him and then try the other one. And given the impending attack on Ouranberg, I don't think you can afford the time.'

'I'll do whatever it takes,' Gaunt said, 'for victory at Ouranberg... and for my men.'

GAUNT ESCORTED COMMISSAR Del Mar to the session hall where Inquisitor Gabel's briefing was set to begin. Gabel had been interrogating the captured Blood Pact since the first day of occupation and was now ready to present his findings so that the Taskforce's senior officers and the strategic advisors could deliberate how the data might impact the plans for the assault on Ouranberg.

The session hall was a badly ventilated room packed with bodies, smoke and bad odours, but it was the only room in the Chamber of Justice large enough to contain the officers and support a large grade tactical holo-display.

Gesturing through the press of bodies, Gaunt brought Hark over to him. 'You're excused this. I'll stay and record the findings.'

'Why?' Hark asked.

'Because Del Mar's not going for it. He's insisting we clear Caff formally before they commit Cuu. I need you out there, working up the case on my behalf.'

'Ibram–'

'Dammit, Viktor, I can't not be here now. They keep telling me I should depend on my staff. Feth, you keep telling me. So go do it and do it well. I want to expend no more than a morning on Caffran's deposition. I can't afford any more. Van Voytz's been talking about going on Ouranberg in less than a week. Make a watertight case for Caff so we can get it done with quickly and I can turn my full attention to the invasion.'

'What about Cuu?'

'Cuu can go to hell, and I wash my hands. Caffran's my only concern. Now get along and do it.'

Hark paused. There was a strange expression on his face that Gaunt had never seen before. It was strangely sympathetic, yet baffled.

'What?'

'Nothing,' said Hark. 'They're starting. I'll go. Trust me, Ibram.'

'I do, Viktor.'

'No, I mean trust me to do this. Don't change your mind later.'

'Of course.'

'Okay. Okay, then.' Hark saluted and pushed his way out of the room.

Gaunt shouldered his way over to Daur.

'Everything okay, sir?'

'I believe so.'

A hush fell as Inquisitor Gabel, a cadaverous monster in matt-rose powered plate armour, stalked to the centre of the room and activated the tactical desk with his bionic digits. A hololithic display of Ouranberg city flickered into life.

'Soldiers of the Emperor,' Gabel rasped through his vox-enhancer, 'this is Ouranberg, the primary vapour mill city on this world, a vital target which we must recapture intact. It is held by a minimum of five thousand Blood Pact warriors under the personal command of the brute Slaith. We believe at least three packs of loxatl mercenaries support him. Now, here is what we have learned from the interrogated enemy prisoners...'

* * *

VARL WAS FALLING to his death.

He yowled out in terror, tried to address his fall and snagged so that he ended up dropping side on. Two metres from the ground, the counterweight pulley began to squeal as it rode the cable and bounced him to a halt, upside down, with his head mere centimetres from the mat.

Lieutenant Kersherin walked over to him and knelt down in front of him.

'Know what that was, sergeant?'

'Uh... exhilarating?'

'No. Hopeless,' Kersherin rose and gestured to the waiting Unterrio to clear Varl from the harness. Then he looked up at the figures perched on the top of the tower.

'Next one in sixty seconds!'

Thirty-five metres up, Milo stood on the tower's unnecessarily narrow and flimsy stage, holding on to the rail with one hand. He was next. Banda, Mkvenner and Kuren were waiting on the back of the stage behind him for their turns.

The Phantine trooper with him, Cardinale, beckoned Milo over as the pulleys were reset and the counterweight balanced.

He checked Milo's harness and tightened one of the straps.

'Don't look so worried. You've done this three times already. Why so unhappy?'

'Because it's not getting any better. And because I only own three pairs of undershorts and we're going for a fourth try.'

Cardinale laughed and hooked Milo up to the running line. 'Remember, face down, limbs out, even if that mat looks like it's coming up really fast. Then curl in and roll as you land. Come on, show that loudmouth Varl how it's done.'

Milo nodded and swallowed. Holding on to the riser wires, he set first one foot and then the other at the lip of the stage. What had they called it, back in drop instruction? The plank? That had been bad enough, and those practice towers had only been half the height. This tower was five metres higher than the longest possible rope drop they could have made. Also, this wasn't roping. This was jumping. Jumping out into space, hands empty. No one, not Mkoll, not Kersherin, had said anything to them yet about what Operation Larisel was specifically about, but they were clearly training for more than a long rope. The wires and cables and pulleys involved in this training were simply there to provide the simulation. Where they were going, it would be rope free.

And that, not the mats thirty-five metres underneath his toes, was the truly alarming prospect.

Babbist, a dot below them, flashed a green bat-board.

'Go!' Cardinale said.

Milo tensed.

'Go! The Emperor protects!'

'I–'

Cardinale helpfully shoved him off the plank.

'Better,' noted Kersherin, watching Milo's drop from a distance below. Beside him, Mkoll nodded.

'Milo's picking it up. Some of the others too. Nessa. Bonin. Vadim.'

'That Vadim's a natural,' Kersherin agreed.

'He has a head for heights. Apparently used to work the top spires of Vervunhive. That's why Gaunt picked him for this. Meryn and Cocoer aren't too shabby either. And to my complete surprise, Larkin's getting it too.'

'Self preservation, I think. Fear is a wonderful concentrator.'

'That much is certain.'

Milo was picking himself up and taking a jokey bow to the scattered applause of his comrades. Banda had taken her place up on the plank.

'The weakest?' Mkoll asked.

'Oh, Varl and Adare, by a long way. Doyl is too stiff. Banda tries way too hard and it throws her out. You could do with pulling your knees up.'

Mkoll grinned. 'Duly noted. Can we get them ready in time?'

'Tall, tall order. Skyborne training was six months. We've got barely as many days. We'll do what we can. No sense in cutting any out now in the hope of nosing out better candidates. We'd be starting over with them.'

'Here she goes,' Mkoll said, pointing.

They watched as Banda leapt off the tower and whizzed down on the tension of the pulleys. It was cleaner, though she bounced hard on landing.

'That's a lot better,' Kersherin remarked. 'She'll get there.'

A LITTLE LATER, once Mkvenner and Kuren had also made their fourth drops, Kersherin gathered them round and sat them down on the mats in a semi-circle. Water bottles and ration wraps were passed out. There was a lot of chatting and joking as adrenalin fizzed its way out of them.

'Listen up!' Kersherin said. 'Theory time. Private Babbist?'

Babbist came forward to the front of the semi circle, and Unterrio hurried in to deposit a field-kit sized crate in front of him before backing out.

Babbist opened the crate and lifted something out for them all to see. It was a compact but heavy metal backpack with a fearsome harness that included thigh loops, and a hinged arm with a moulded handgrip on the left side. The backpack sprouted two blunt, antler-like horns from the shoulders that ended in fist-sized metal balls. It was painted matt-green.

'What we have here, friends and neighbours,' said Babbist, patting the old, worn unit, 'is a classic type five infantry jump pack. Accept no imitations. Formal spec, for those that need it, is Type Five Icarus-pattern Personal Descent Unit with dual M12 gravity nullers and a variable-vent compressor fan for attitude control. Which, I gather, many of you need.'

There were some laughs, but the Ghosts' attention was fixed on the device.

'Manufactured on Lucius forge world,' Babbist continued, 'it's the standard Guard variant of the assault jump pack. Smaller and lighter, not to mention more compact, than the heavy jobs used by the Adeptus Astartes. The Marines, Emperor bless 'em, need heavier duty babies to hold them in the air. Besides which, we're not gods. We wouldn't be able to stand up with one of the Astartes packs yoked to us.'

Babbist leant the pack against his knees and opened his hands to his audience. 'Remember how in Fundamental and Preparatory they told you your las was your best friend? Look after it and it'd look after you? Right, forget that. This is your new best friend. Get to know him intimately or you'll end up a stain on the landscape. If your old friend the las complains, remind him that without your new friend here, he's not going to see any action.'

Larkin slowly raised a hand.

Babbist frowned, surprised, and glanced at Mkoll.

'Out with it, Larks,' Mkoll said.

'Uh... is this just an interesting little lecture to occupy our minds during snack break... or should we conclude that at some point in our approaching yet ever fething shortening future, we're going to be strapped to one of those things and thrown into the sky? Just asking. I mean, would we be right off the mark in connecting the... thrilling wire jumps we've been making off that lovely tower with a situation that combines one of those with a lot of screaming and looseness of bowel?'

There was a well-judged pause. 'No,' said Mkoll directly, and everyone, even Larkin, laughed despite the spears of anxiety that suddenly stabbed through them.

'I see Trooper Larkin has sussed out what Operation Larisel has in store for you all,' said Babbist. 'As a prize, he can come up here and help me demonstrate this baby.'

Urged on by the Ghosts around him, Larkin got to his feet. 'I'm not jumping out of anything,' he said as he walked over to Babbist.

'Legs in the yokes, one step, two step...' Babbist said, directing Larkin's hesitant motions. 'And up we go... good. Forestraps over your shoulders as you take the weight.'

'Feth!' baulked Larkin.

'Hold it while I do up the waist cinch... okay, now feed those forestraps over to me.' Babbist snapped the metal tongues of the shoulder strap buckles into the spring-loaded lock that now rested against Larkin's chest. 'Then the leg straps up like so...' These too clunked into the chest lock. 'Right. Just pull the yokes in a bit. That's it. How does it feel?'

'Like Bragg is sitting on me,' Larkin said, staggering with the weight.

More laughing.

'The type five weighs about sixty kilos,' Babbist said.

'I'm dying here,' Larkin moaned, shifting uncomfortably.

'That's sixty kilos dormant,' Babbist added. He reached over and pulled down the pack's hinged control arm. It now stuck out at waist height on Larkin's left side, the joystick handgrip extending vertically in exactly the right place for his left hand to grasp it comfortably. The handgrip was a finger-moulded black sleeve of rubber set on a collar of milled metal with a fat red button sticking from its top.

'Let's try it active,' said Babbist. He lifted a small plate marked with a purity seal on the right flank of the pack and threw two rocker switches. Immediately the pack began to whine and throb, as if turbine power was building up inside it. Babbist closed the plate again.

'Feth me!' Larkin said, alarmed.

'Relax,' said Babbist. 'That's just the fan rising to speed.' Babbist had a gentle grip on the handstick. He softly depressed the red button.

'How's that?'

'Holy–' Larkin stammered. 'The weight's gone. I can't feel it any more.'

'That's because the antigrav units–' Babbist indicated the two metal balls that projected out above Larkin's shoulders on their blunt antlers, 'are taking the weight. The red button determines grav lift, people. I'm just touching it and it's taking the weight of the pack. A tad more–'

'Feth!' Larkin gurgled to more laughter. He had risen twenty centimetres off the ground and hung there, feet dangling.

Babbist kept hold of the handgrip. 'It's touch sensitive. Depressing it just a little, like this, gives Larkin hover. If he was, say, dropping at terminal velocity, he'd probably need to depress it by two thirds for the same effect.'

'So he could jump from a drop, press that red button, and hover?' Milo asked.

'Yes. And pushing the button all the way gives lift,' said Babbist. He squeezed the button and Larkin rose again.

'It's a subtle thing. You'll get the hang of how much thumb pressure works… deceleration, hover, lift. There'll be time to practise. The other aspect of the pack is direction. There's a powerful compressor fan inside there.' Babbist swung the floating Larkin around so they could see the pack on his back. 'Here,' he said, 'and here, here, here, here, and here.' He indicated louvres on the top, bottom and four corners of the pack. 'Whether you're pressing the red button or not, angling the handgrip will direct the internal fan via these ducts. In other words, you point the handgrip, like a joystick, whichever way you want to go and the compressor fan will give you the appropriate thrust.'

Babbist yanked on the grip slightly and Larkin gusted sideways slightly. He yelped.

'The combination of controls means that you can jump from a ship, control your rate of descent and manoeuvre yourself onto the target. Questions so far?'

'How often do they fail?' Banda asked.

'Virtually never,' said Babbist.

'Call me Miss Virtually,' said Banda to a round of sniggering.

'What about crosswinds?' asked Mkvenner.

'With enough practice, you'll know how to compensate for windshear with a balance of lift and directional thrust.'

'When do we get to have a go?' asked Vadim gleefully.

VIKTOR HARK SET down his stylus and sat back in his chair. It was late, the dome lights had dimmed, and his office, a makeshift corner of a machine shop near the regiment billets, was getting cold.

Hark pushed aside the reams of notepaper and documents he had managed to accumulate, and picked up a data-slate. His thumb on the speed-scroll button, he surveyed the data. Caffran, Cuu, the evidence and witnesses for and against each of them. He sighed and tossed the slate aside. 'You haven't thought about Cuu, Gaunt,' he murmured to himself. 'You're so damn keen to get Caffran freed, you haven't thought about the consequences.'

Hark got to his feet, pulled on his leather storm coat and looked about for his cap. Unable to locate it, he decided he'd do without it. He walked to the door, went out, locked it carefully behind him, and made off in the direction of the stairs. No going back now.

'Gaunt?'

He halted in his tracks and looked down.

'No, father, he's not here.'

Zweil appeared below, moving up the staircase. 'Oh, Viktor. I'm sorry. I thought you were Ibram.'

'He's out still, with Daur and Rawne. The second day of tactical briefings.'

'A soldier's lot is never done,' Zweil sighed. He had drawn level with Hark and now sat down on the steps.

Hark paused. He hadn't got time for this.

He'd have to make time. He sat down on the gritty stairs next to Zweil.

'How're things?' Zweil asked.

'Bad. Next big show is coming up and we're still tied down to the stuff with Caffran and Cuu.'

'Caffran didn't do it, you know,' Zweil said.

'You have evidence?'

'Only the best kind,' Zweil tapped his forehead. 'He told me. I believe him.'

'That's what we're working on.' Hark said. 'What about Cuu? Is he clean?'

Zweil seemed to sulk.

'Father ayatani?'

'Cuu I don't know,' Zweil said. 'I've never met a man like him. I can't read him.'

'So he could be hiding something?'

'He could also be a difficult person to read. Everyone seems convinced that Cuu is the guilty one.'

'He is,' said Hark.

'Maybe, Viktor.'

Hark tried to control his anxious breathing. 'Father… how far would you go?'

'On a date? I'm a man of the cloth! Although, it has to be said that in my youth–'

'Forget your youth. Ayatani Zweil… you say you're with us to answer the spiritual needs of the men. In clerical confidence, I believe? Answer this–'

'Off you go.'

'A man is blameless, palpably so, but you've been instructed to prove that innocence. And there is no solid proof you can find. How far do you go?'

'Is this about Caffran?'

'Let's keep it hypothetical, father.'

'Well… if I knew an innocent man was going to be punished for something he didn't do, I'd fight it. Down to the wire.'

'With no proof?'

'Proof denies faith, Viktor, and without faith the God-Emperor is nothing.'

'So if you were convinced you were in the right, you'd fight to correct that injustice however you could?'

'Yes, I would.' Zweil was quiet for a while, studying the profile of Hark's face. 'Is this about Caffran?' he repeated.

'No, father.' Hark got up from the steps and walked away.

'Viktor? Where are you going?'

'Nowhere that needs to concern you.'

Five

THE COURT CHAMBER was nothing special. A square room hung with black drapes. A raised stage in the centre of the room, with seats and long desks on three sides for the opposing councils and the presiding officials. No banners, no standards, no decoration. It was depressingly banal and plain, depressingly rudimentary.

Gaunt took his seat on the defence side with his adjutant Beltayn and Captain Daur. There were four chairs, but no one had seen Hark since the previous night. The prosecution council – Fultingo and two aides – arranged themselves opposite Gaunt. A Commissariate clerk was laying out papers on the court table while another adjusted and set the vox/pict drone that hovered at the edge of the platform to document the proceedings.

'All rise and show respect!' one of the clerks announced, and chairs scraped back as Commissar Del Mar and two senior commissars strode in and took their places behind the centre table.

'Be seated,' said Del Mar curtly. He flicked through the papers laid out in front of him and handed a data-slate to one of the clerks.

'I have a time of 09.01 Imperial, 221.771 M41. Mark that. Court is now in session. Clerk of the court, please announce the first case on the docket. Let the accused be brought in.'

'Imperial Phantine Taskforce, courts martial hearing number 57, docket number 433.' The clerk read from the slate in a loud, nasal voice. 'Trooper Dermon Caffran, 3rd Section, Tanith First Light Infantry, to answer a charge of murder, first degree.'

As he was speaking, armed Urdeshi soldiers walked Caffran into the hall and stood him in the middle of the open side of the stage facing Del Mar. His wrists were manacled, but he had been allowed to shave and put on his number one uniform. He looked pale but determined. In fact, his face looked strangely expressionless. Lad's scared stiff, Gaunt thought. And no wonder. He nodded to Caffran and the young man made a very brief, nervous response, a little tilt of his chin.

There was something odd about Caffran, and it took a moment for Gaunt to realise it was the fact that the boy still had thick hair. Locked away, he'd missed the shearing and fumigation. Gaunt smiled to himself wryly, feeling the itch of his own fresh-shaved scalp.

'Where's Hark?' he whispered aside to Daur.

'Damned if I know, sir.'

Del Mar cleared his throat. 'A word to both councils before we get into this. I don't wish to appear as if I'm diminishing the gravity of the crime, but this case has become unnecessarily protracted. I want it finished. Speedily. That means no delaying antics, and a minimum of witnesses.' Del Mar made a light gesture in the direction of the papers in front of him, one of which was the call-list of witnesses Gaunt had submitted to the clerk. 'No character witnesses. Expert and eye witnesses only. Is that clear, colonel-commissar?'

'Yes, sir.' It was clear. Gaunt didn't like it but it was clear. Bang went the majority of names on his list.

'And you, Fultingo,' said Del Mar. 'I expect decent procedure from you too. Don't start in on anything that will provoke the defence council into... digressions.'

'Yes, sir.'

'Read the particulars, please.'

The clerk rose again. 'Be it known to the courts martial that on the night of 214 last, citizen Onti Flyte, resident of the Cirenholm South Mill second shift workforce housing, was assaulted and stabbed to death in her place of habitation.'

'Commissar Fultingo?'

Fultingo rose to his feet, and took a data-slate from his aide. 'Onti Flyte was a widow and a mother of three. Like all the residents of that district, she had just been rehoused by the liberation forces, following detention under the enemy occupation. The resident families were brought back to the South Mill habitat under escort during the course of that evening. Only a short while after returning to her home – we judge somewhere between 21.50 and 23.00 – she was attacked and murdered in her outhouse. The murder was committed using a long, straight knife, matching in all particulars the distinctive warknife carried by all Tanith infantry. An individual fitting the description of a Tanith trooper was seen leaving the vicinage at that time. The victim's eldest son, Beggi Flyte, later positively identified Trooper Caffran as the assailant. Deployment logs for the night show that Trooper Caffran was one of the escort detail assigned to South Mill.'

Fultingo looked up from the slate. 'In short, lord commissar, there seems to be little room for doubt. We have the right man. I urge you to rule so that punishment may be carried out.'

He sat down. Caffran hadn't moved. 'Gaunt?' Del Mar invited.

Gaunt got up. 'Lord, no one, not even Caffran himself, denies that he was present in the area that night. Futhermore, Caffran admits seeing and speaking with the victim and her family. He remembers escorting her to her home and making sure she was settled. The prosecution depends squarely on the identification made by the victim's son. The boy is very young. Given the terrible stress suffered by all Cirenholmers during the occupation, and adding to that the ghastly death of his mother, he is deeply, pitifully traumatised. He may easily have identified the wrong man. He had seen Caffran close up during the rehousing. When asked to pick out a Tanith trooper, he chose Caffran because he was the only one whose face he clearly recognised. I move we drop the charge and release Trooper Caffran. The real killer is yet to be prosecuted.'

Fultingo was back on his feet before Gaunt had even sat down. 'There we have the whole meat and drink of it, lord commissar. Gaunt expects us to believe this bright, intelligent boy would forget the face of his mother's killer, and simply recall the face of a soldier who helped them briefly earlier the same night. We really are wasting time. A mass of circumstantial evidence points to Trooper Caffran, and the positive ID clinches it. The defence can offer nothing, I repeat, nothing substantial in the way of evidence to contradict the prosecution's case. Just this whimsical theory of trauma-related mistaken identity. Please, sir, may we not simply end this now?'

Del Mar waved Fultingo back into his seat and looked at Gaunt. 'I am tempted to agree, Gaunt. Your point has some merit, but it's hardly an ironclad defence. The soldier admits that he was "helping out in the area until about midnight". Many saw him, but not so positively or for so long that he could not have found the time to carry out this heinous act. If you've nothing else to add, I will close the session.'

Gaunt stood up again. 'There is one piece of evidence,' he said. 'Caffran couldn't have done it. With respect to your comments about character, I have to insist on stating the fact that Caffran is a sound, moral individual with a spotless record. He is simply not capable of such a crime.'

'Objection,' growled Fultingo. 'You've already said character has no relevance, lord.'

'I am aware of what I said, commissar,' Del Mar replied. 'Seeing as Gaunt has chosen to ignore my instruction, may I remind him that for all his spotless character, Caffran is a soldier. He is a killer. Killing is not beyond him.'

'Caffran serves the Emperor as we all do. But he understands the difference between killing on a battlefield and predatory murder. He could not do it.'

'Gaunt!'

'Lord, would you send a basic infantryman to crew a mortar or a missile rack? No. He wouldn't have the ability. Why then would you maintain so staunchly that Caffran had done something he simply doesn't have the moral or emotional ability to undertake?'

'That's enough, Gaunt!'

The door at the back of the room opened suddenly and Hark hurried in. As quietly as possible, he took his seat next to Gaunt.

'My apologies,' he said to the court.

'You might as well have not bothered showing up at all, Hark. We're done here.'

Hark rose and handed a slip of paper to the clerk, who brought it round to Del Mar.

'Craving your patience, lord commissar, I submit the name of one last witness to be appended to the list.'

Gaunt looked surprised.

'Objection!' snapped Fultingo.

'Overruled, Fultingo,' said Del Mar reading the slip. 'It's late and it's annoying, but it's not against the rules. Very well, Hark, with Colonel-Commissar Gaunt's permission, let's see what you've got.'

IT WAS COLD out in the gloomy hall outside the courtroom. Tona Criid sat on a side bench under an oil painting of a particularly ugly Chief of Arbites and fidgeted. She'd come to give Caff her support, maybe even speak up for him if she was allowed, although Daur had advised her that character witnesses were unlikely to be heard.

But she hadn't even been permitted to observe.

Dorden was with her. He'd come to read his statement on the examination of the body if that proved relevant. And Kolea was there too. He was sitting right down at the end of the hall on his own. She wasn't sure why. Caff's section leader was Major Rawne. She supposed that with Rawne busy running the regiment up to speed, Kolea had been sent in his stead as a serving officer to bear witness to Caff's good character.

'It'll be fine,' said Dorden, sitting down next to her. 'Really,' he added.

'I know.'

'Who's that man, do you think, doc?' she added after a moment, whispering.

A hunched, elderly civilian sat on the benches opposite them.

He'd arrived a few minutes before with Commissar Hark, who'd set him on the seat and hurried into the court chamber.

'I don't know,' said Dorden.

The court door opened and Criid and Dorden looked up expectantly. A clerk looked out. 'Calling Cornelis Absolom. Cornelis Absolom. Is he present?'

The old man got up and followed the clerk into the court.

'State your name for the record.'

'Cornelis – ahm! – Cornelis Absolom, sir.'

'Occupation?'

'I am retired, sir. These last three years. Before that I worked for seventeen years as a night watchman at the vapour mill gas holders.'

'And how did you get that post, Mr Absolom?'

'They were looking for a man with military training. I served nine years in the Planetary Defence Force, Ninth Phantine Recon, but I was injured during the Ambross Uprising, and left the service.'

'So it's fair to say you are an observant man, Mr Absolom? As a night watchman and before that, in the recon corps?'

'My eyes are sound, sir.'

Commissar Hark nodded and walked a few paces down the stage thoughtfully.

'Could you describe to the lord commissar and the court your relationship with the deceased, Mr Absolom?'

'Ma'am Flyte was my next door neighbour.'

'When was the last time you saw the deceased?'

The old man, who had been given a chair to sit on because of his unsteady legs, cleared his throat.

'On the night of her murder, Commissar Hark.'

'Could you describe that?'

'We had just returned to the habs. The place was a mess, a terrible mess. I wanted to sleep, but I had to sweep out my parlour first. The smell... I was in my backyard and I saw her over the fence. She was going to the outhouse. We exchanged a few words.'

'About what, Mr Absolom?'

'The mess, sir.'

'And you didn't see her again?'

'No, sir. Not alive.'

'Can you tell the court what happened later that night, Mr Absolom?'

'It wasn't much afterwards. I'd filled a sack with rubbish, mostly food that had rotted in my pantry. I went out into the yard to dump it down by the back fence.

'I heard a sound from Ma'am Flyte's outhouse. A thump. Followed by another.

'I was worried, so I called out.'

'And then?'

'A man came out of the outhouse. He saw me at the fence, and ran off down the back lane.'

'Can you describe the man?'

'He was wearing what I know now to be the uniform of the Tanith First, sir. I had seen them earlier that night. They escorted us back to our homes.'

'Did you see the man's face?'

Absolom nodded.

'Please voice your answer for the vox-recorder, Mr Absolom,' Del Mar prompted softly.

'I'm sorry, lord. Yes, I did. I did see him. Not clearly, but well enough to know him.'

'Mr Absolom, was it the accused, Trooper Caffran?'

The old man shuffled round to take a look at Caffran.

'No sir. The man was a little taller, leaner. And older.'

Hark looked back at Commissar Del Mar. 'No further questions, lord.'

Fultingo got up at once. 'Mr Absolom. Why did you not come forward with this information earlier? You raised the alarm and alerted the authorities about the death. You were questioned, by me and my assistant, and claimed not to have seen any suspect.'

Absolom looked down the stage to the commissar. 'May I be honest, lord?'

'This court expects no less, sir,' said Del Mar.

'I was scared. We'd been through weeks of hell at the hands of those heathens. Ma'am Flyte didn't deserve what happened to her, no sir, but I didn't want to get involved. The tough questions of the commissars, the searches... and I didn't want to risk the man coming back.'

'To silence you?'

'Yes, lord. I was terribly afraid. Then I heard a man had been arrested and I thought, that's an end to it.'

Del Mar had been scribbling a few notes. He put the holo-quill back in its power-well. 'Your answers have a ring of truth to them, Mr Absolom. Except for one thing. Why did you come forward now?'

'Because Commissar Hark came to see me. He said he thought they might have the wrong man. When he showed me this lad's picture, I knew he was right. You hadn't caught the killer at all. I came forward today so that justice would not let this young man down. And because I was afraid again. Afraid that the real killer was still at large.'

'Thank you, Mr Absolom,' Del Mar said. 'Thank you for your time and effort. You are excused.'

'Lord, I–' Fultingo began.

Del Mar held up a hand. 'No, Fultingo. In the name of the God-Emperor of Terra, whose grace and majesty is everlasting, and by the power invested in me by the Imperial Commissariate, I hereby declare this case concluded and the accused cleared of all charges.'

FROM THE COURT doorway, Gaunt watched Criid hugging Caffran, and Dorden shaking the young man's hand. He turned to Daur and Beltayn.

'Thanks for your efforts, both of you. Beltayn, take Caffran back to the billet and see he has a good meal and a tot of sacra. Give him and Criid twelve-hour liberty passes too. He'll want to see his kids.'

'Yes, sir.'

'Ban, escort Mr Absolom back to his home and repeat my thanks.'

'I'd like that duty, Ibram,' Hark said. 'I promised the old man a bottle of beer and the chance to tell me his war stories.'

'Very well.' Gaunt faced Hark. 'You pulled it off.'

'I did what was asked of me, Ibram.'

'I won't forget this. Caffran owes his life to you.'

Hark saluted and made his way over to the old man.

'The clerk tells me Cuu's trial has been set for tomorrow morning, sir,' said Daur. 'They want that cleared away too. Shall I prepare the defence notes?'

'I won't be defending.'

Daur frowned. 'Sir?'

'Cuu's guilty. His crimes nearly cost us Caffran. The Commissariate can deal with him. I'll have Hark cover the formalities.'

'I see,' said Daur stiffly.

Gaunt caught his arm as he began to move away. 'You have a problem, captain?'

'No, sir. Cuu's probably guilty, as you say. I just thought–'

'Ban, I regard you as a friend, and I also expect all my officers to be open with me on all matters. What's on your mind?'

Daur shrugged. 'You just seem to be dismissing Cuu. Leaving him to his fate.'

'Cuu's a killer.'

'Most likely.'

'He'll get justice. The justice he deserves. Just like Caffran did.'

'Yeah,' said Daur. 'I guess he will.'

Down at the end of the hallway, Kolea watched the people spilling out of the court. He saw Caffran embracing Criid and the smiles on the faces of Daur and Gaunt.

He sighed deeply and went back to the billet.

GAUNT PUSHED OPEN the hatch to sub-hangar 117 and went inside. The cargo servitor escorting him followed, carrying the munition crate. The servitor wore the painted insignia of the Munitorium on its torso casing.

It was cold inside the hangar, and for a moment, Gaunt thought he had come to the wrong place. There were a few equipment packs and lasrifles heaped up along one wall, but no sign of anybody.

Then he looked up.

Twenty human figures were floating and bobbing up in the rafters of the hangar.

One saw him, turned and swooped down. As he approached, Gaunt heard the rising whine of a compressor fan. The man executed a decent turn and landed neatly on his feet, taking a few scurrying steps forward to slow himself. Gaunt recognised him as Lieutenant Kersherin.

Keeping his left hand on the jump-pack's control arm, the Skyborne specialist threw a neat salute.

'Colonel-commissar!'

'Stand easy, lieutenant. You seem to be making progress.'

'At a variable rate. But yes, I'd say so, sir.'

'I'd like to talk to them. If they're not too busy.'

Kersherin said a few words into his micro-bead and the floating figures began to descend. The three other Phantines made perfect, experienced landings. The Ghosts mostly made hesitant groundfalls, though Vadim, Nessa and Bonin reached the ground like experts. Varl and Adare thumped down hard and clumsily and made Gaunt wince.

They helped each other off with their jump packs, and the Skyborne trainers went round to double-check all the circuits had been shut down properly.

'Gather in,' said Gaunt. He slid a chart out of his pocket and began to unfold it. They grouped around in a half-moon.

'First of all, I thought you'd like to know that Caffran was cleared of all charges this morning.'

There were appreciative claps and cheers from the Ghosts.

'Next thing. More important to you. The time's come to tell you a little more about Operation Larisel. You've worked out by now that it's going to involve a grav-drop. And I'm sure you've guessed the target.'

Gaunt opened out the chart and laid it on the floor.

'Ouranberg, the primary target here on Phantine. A city five times larger than Cirenholm. Well defended. Strongly garrisoned. Not an easy target, but that's why they give us shiny medals.'

The Ghosts peered in to get a look at the chart of Ouranberg's sprawling, multi-domed plan.

'You'll get copies of this soon, and the chance to get decent familiarisation on a holo-simulation. For now, this is the target. Or rather, where the target can be found. Operation Larisel, as the name doubtless suggests to the Tanith amongst you, is a hunting mission. A grav drop, a stealth insertion and then a hunt.'

'What for?' asked Varl.

'In about a week, the taskforce will begin its assault on Ouranberg. The strength of resistance will depend on the morale and spirit of the Blood Pact and their allied units. At the moment, that's very high. Unbreakably high, perhaps. The rumours you may have heard are true. The enemy forces at Ouranberg are personally commanded by the Chaos General Sagittar Slaith, one of Warlord Urlock Gaur's most trusted lieutenants. His foul charismatic brand of leadership inspires almost invincible devotion and loyalty from his troops. If we move against a dug-in force under his command, the cost will be high, punishing. Even if the assault is successful, it will be a bloodbath. But if Slaith is removed from the equation, we face a much more vulnerable foe.' Gaunt paused. 'The purpose of Operation Larisel is to locate Slaith and eliminate him in advance of the invasion. To decapitate the enemy forces and break their spirit right at the start of the main military advance.'

No one said anything. Gaunt looked at their faces, but they were all taking this in and their expressions gave nothing away.

'Briefings on how to locate and identify Slaith will follow in the next day or so. We have a lot of data that we think will be invaluable to you. Operation Larisel will take the form of four teams – I believe you're already divided up – that will deploy to different insertion points in the city. Four mission teams, coming in from four different angles. Four times the chance of success.'

Gaunt turned to the crate that the waiting servitor was carrying and popped open the lid. 'One last thing for now, something to factor in to your training. It's been confirmed, I'm sorry to say, that loxatl mercenaries are active under Slaith's command at Ouranberg. Tac reports and battlefield intelligence have shown that these alien scum are particularly resistant to las-fire.'

Gaunt lifted a bulky weapon from the crate. It was an autorifle, almost a small cannon, with a heavy gauge barrel and a folding skeleton stock. He slapped a fat drum magazine into the slot behind the gnurled metal of the foregrip.

'This is a U90 assault cannon. Old, but powerful. Fires .45 calibre solid rounds at semi and full auto. Kicks like a bastard. The drum-pattern clip holds forty rounds. I've borrowed these four from the Urdeshi. They're manufactured on their home world. Not a terribly good weapon and prone to fouling, but with plenty of stopping power and the best trade-off of power against weight we could manage. Each team should assign one member to carry one in place of his or her standard las. The drums marked with a yellow cross carry standard shells.' He took another out of the crate and held it up. 'The ones with the red cross are drummed with explosive AP shells. We think these old solid-slug chuckers, firing armour piercing, will be your best chance against the loxatl. Designated troopers should get practice with them as soon as possible.'

Gaunt put the weapon and the spare drum back in the crate.

'I'll be back to continue briefing tomorrow. We'll deal with DZ specifics then, and begin a survey of the target landscape. Until then... keep up the good work.'

'Oh feth,' Larkin said, 'this keeps getting better and better.'

FOR THREE DAYS, supply barges from Hessenville had been arriving to dock in the hangars along Cirenholm's skirts. Those that arrived under escort on the morning of the 221st were accompanied by the drogue *Skyro*, carrying two Urdeshi and one Krassian regiment to bolster the invasion forces.

Many of the barges had been lugging aerial ordnance and parts to strengthen the taskforce's air wing, along with some eighteen Marauders and twenty-seven Lightnings. Since the afternoon of the 215th, the strike wings had been flying sorties north of Cirenholm to wrest air superiority from the Ouranberg squadrons, and now long-range night raids had begun on the city itself. Admiral Ornoff's intention was to soften the city's defences and neutralise as much of the enemy's air power as possible prior to the main assault, 'O-Day' as it was called.

The effect of the bombing raids was difficult to judge. In three nights of missions over three hundred thousand tonnes of explosives were dropped on Ouranberg at a cost of four Marauders.

The fighter sorties were somewhat easier to evaluate. Unless scrambled to meet a detected raid, which were few and far between, the Lightnings went up in four-ship patrols, hunting enemy traffic as directed by Sky Command Cirenholm's modar, astrotachographic and long range auspex arrays. Twenty-nine enemy planes of varying types were claimed as kills during the first five days, for a loss of two Lightnings. On the afternoon of the 220th, four wings of Phantine Lightnings were rushed up to intercept a mass raid by fifty enemy dive bombers and escort fighters. Eight more Lightnings and six Marauders were fast-tracked up to join them as the battle commenced. The northern perimeter guns of Cirenholm blistered the cloud cover with flak.

The engagement lasted forty-eight minutes and was punishingly hard-fought. The enemy was utterly routed before they could land a single item of munitions on Cirenholm. They lost a confirmed tally of thirty-three planes. The Phantine lost six, including the decorated ace Erwell Costary. Flight Lieutenant Larice Asch personally shot down four enemy aircraft, raising her career score to make her one of the few female Phantine aces, and Pilot Officer Febos Nicarde succeeded in notching up seven kills. Ornoff awarded him the Silver Aquila. It took hours for the twisted contrails and exhaust plumes created by the vast air battle to dissipate.

Inside the Cirenholm hangars, Munitorium workers, Imperial Guardsmen and volunteer citizens alike toiled in shifts to unload, process and store the vast influx of material. Some of the Hessenville barges also brought food and medicae supplies for the wounded population.

Mid-afternoon on the 221st, just about the time Caffran was being discharged, five platoons of Ghosts under the supervision of the Munitorium were off-loading crates from a barge's cargo hold and wheeling them on trolleys through to a sub-hangar.

Rawne had put his adjutant Feygor in charge, partly to ensure that the Ghosts got the pick of the inventory for their support weapons and rocket launchers. The air was a racket of clattering carts, raised voices, whirring hoists and rattling machine tools. The Ghosts were stripped to their vests, sweating hard to heft the laden trolleys up through the arch of the sub-hangar and then riding them back down the ramp empty with whoops and laughs. The sub-hangar was beginning to look like a mad warlord's pipe dream. Across the wide floor, rows of ammo crates and munition pods alternated with rows of carefully lined-up rockets. Along one wall, rack-carts with thick, meaty tyres carried fresh-painted bombs and missiles destined for underwing mounting. Some of the men had not been able to resist the temptation of chalking their names on the warheads, or writing such taunts as 'One from the Ghosts' or 'Goodbye fethhead' or 'If you can read this, scream'. Others had drawn on fanged mouths, turning the missiles into snarling predators. Others, touchingly, had dedicated the bombs as gifts to the enemy from fallen comrades.

'Running out of floor space,' Brostin told Feygor, mopping the perspiration from his brow.

Feygor nodded. 'Don't break your rhythm. I'll see to it.' He went in search of a Munitorium official, who agreed to open up the next sub-hangar along.

Feygor took Brostin with him to open up the sliding metal partition into the next sub-space. They passed Troopers Pollo and Derin wheeling a cart of grenade boxes out into the back corridor.

'Where the feth are you going with that?' Feygor asked.

'The hall,' Pollo replied as if it was a daft question. 'We're getting too full in here...'

Feygor looked out into the gloomy access hall behind the hangar. Already, work crews had lined up nine carts of munitions along one wall.

'Oh, feth... this isn't right,' Feygor growled. 'Take them back inside. All of them.'

The two men groaned.

'Rustle up some others to help you. We're going through into that sub-hangar there,' Feygor said, pointing. 'I have no idea why you thought this was a good place to dump stuff.'

'We were just following the others,' Derin said.

'What?'

'The guys ahead of us. There was a Munitorium fether with them, and they seemed to know what they were doing.'

'Go and get that guy over there,' snapped Feygor, indicating the Munitorium chief he'd spoken to. Derin hurried off.

Fifty metres down the back corridor from them, another hatch opened off the sub-hangar. As Feygor waited for the clerk to arrive, he saw three Ghosts wheeling another cart through, accompanied by a Munitorium aide.

'Ah, feth...' Feygor said. He was about to shout out when Pollo said 'They must be hot.'

There was something about Pollo's tone that made Feygor look again. The three Ghosts were wearing full kit, including tunics and wool hats.

'With me,' Feygor said to Brostin and Pollo, and moved forward at a jog. 'Hey, hey you there!'

The Ghosts seemed to ignore him. They were intent on getting their cart of missiles into a service elevator.

'Hey!'

Two of them turned. Feygor didn't recognise either of them. And Feygor prided himself on knowing every face in the regiment.

'What the feth...?' he began.

One of the 'Ghosts' suddenly pulled a laspistol and fired on them.

Feygor cried out and pulled Brostin into the wall as the shots blistered past them.

Pollo had been a nobleman's bodyguard back on Verghast, a trained warrior of House Anko. Expensive neural implants, paid for by his lord, gave him a reaction time significantly shorter than that of unaugmented humans. With a graceful sweep that combined instinct and immaculate training, he drew an autopistol from his thigh pocket and returned fire, placing his body without thinking between the assailants and his comrades.

He dropped the shooter with a headshot. The others fled.

'After the bastards!' Feygor bellowed. He was on his feet, his laspistol ripped from its holster. Brostin had wrenched a fire-axe from a wall bracket.

The interlopers pounded away down a side hall and into a stairwell. As he ran, Feygor keyed his headset. 'Alert! Security alert! Hangar 45! Intruders heading down-block to level thirty!' The sub-hangar behind them erupted in commotion.

They burst into the stairwell and heard feet clattering on the steps below. Feygor took the stairs three at a time, with Pollo close on his heels and Brostin lumbering after.

Feygor threw himself against the banister and fired down the airspace. Two hard-round shots ricocheted back up at him. They heard a door crash open.

The lower door led into a service area, a wide machine shop that seemed menacingly quiet and dark, and which glistened with oil. Feygor charged through the door and was almost killed by the gunman who had ducked back to lie in wait behind the hatch. Two bullets hissed past the back of his head and made him stumble. A moment later, Brostin came out of the door and pinned the gunman to the wall with one splintered whack of the fire-axe.

Shots rattled back across the machine shop. Feygor spotted one muzzle flash in the semi-gloom, dropped on one knee and fired his laspistol from a double-handed brace. The target lurched back against a workbench and fell on his face.

There was no sign of the third one. Pollo and Feygor prowled forward. Both swung around as they heard a door squeak. For a moment, a figure was framed against the light outside. Pollo's handgun roared and the figure flew out of sight as if yanked by a rope.

Brostin found the machine shop lights.

Pollo checked that the man he'd hit at the door was dead, and returned to find Feygor rolling his kill over on the oily floor. There was no mistaking the man's grizzled face, or his hands, thick with old scars. The Ghost uniform didn't even fit him particularly well. But it was a Ghost uniform. Right down to the straight silver warknife in his belt case.

'Feth!' said Feygor.

'Look at that,' said Pollo. He knelt down. Near to the bloody hole Feygor had put through the corpse, the black Tanith tunic had another rent, a scorched puncture that had been hastily sewn up with back thread.

'This isn't the first time this tunic's been worn by a dead man,' he said.

Six

HALF-DECENT FOOD was an understandable rarity on Cirenholm, but the late lunch placed in front of Gaunt and Zweil looked surprisingly inviting.

'You've excelled yourself, Beltayn,' Gaunt told his adjutant.

'It's not much, sir,' said Beltayn, though he was obviously pleased by the compliment. 'If an adj-officer can't rustle up some proper meat and a little fresh bread for his chief, what good is he?'

'Well, I hope you saved some for yourself too,' said Gaunt, tucking in. Beltayn blushed.

'If an adj-officer can't fill his own stomach, what good is he to his chief?' Gaunt reassured him.

'Yes sir.' Beltayn paused, and then produced a bottle of claret. 'Don't ask where I got this,' he said.

'My dear Beltayn,' said Zweil, pouring himself a glass. 'This act alone will get you into heaven.'

Beltayn smiled, saluted and left.

Zweil offered the bottle to Gaunt, who shook his head. They were sitting at a table in the stateroom of the merchant's house Gaunt had co-opted for his officers. It was a little cold and damp, but well appointed. Zweil smacked his lips and ate with gusto.

'You're pleased about Caffran?' he said.

'A weight off my mind, father. He says to thank you for the spiritual support you've offered.'

'Least I could do.'

'You'll be busy the next few days,' Gaunt said. 'The invasion hour approaches, and men will be looking for blessing and counsel.'

'They've already started coming. Every time I go to the chapel, there are Ghosts waiting for me.'

'What's the feeling?'

'Good, good... confident. The men are ready, if that's what you want to hear.'

'I want to hear the truth, father.'

'You know the mood. How's Operation Larisel shaping up?'

Gaunt put down his cutlery. 'You're not meant to know about that.'

'Oh, I know. No one is. But in the last two days Varl, Kuren, Meryn, Milo, Cocoer and Nour have all come to say penance and receive benediction. I couldn't really not know.'

'It'll be fine. I have every confidence.'

There was a knock at the door and Daur came in. He looked excited.

'Captain. Pull up a chair and pour yourself a drink. I can call Beltayn back, if you're hungry.'

'I've eaten,' said Daur, sitting with them.

'Then report.'

'A little disturbance on the hangar decks earlier. Feygor rumbled some interlopers trying to steal munitions.'

'Indeed?'

'They were Blood Pact, sir.'

Gaunt pushed away his plate and looked at the Verghast officer. 'Seriously?'

Daur nodded. 'Three of them dressed as Ghosts and another disguised as a Munitorium clerk. They're all dead. A bit of a firefight, I hear.'

'Feth! We should–'

Daur raised a hand. 'Already done, sir. We scoured the vicinity with fireteams and smoked out a cell of them hiding in the basement levels. They must have been there since the liberation, lying low. They didn't go without a fight. We found they had sneaked about three tonnes of explosive munitions down there. Probably intended to cause merry hell when they were up to strength.'

Gaunt sat back. 'Have you alerted the other commanders?'

Daur nodded. 'We're coordinating a fresh sweep of the entire city to check for any others that may have slipped the net the first time. No traces yet, so we may be clean. It may have been an isolated group. We have, however, already identified six locals who were assisting them.'

'By the throne!'

'I think the Blood Pact had threatened them, but they'd also paid them well for their troubles. In defaced gold coins.'

Gaunt pushed his unfinished meal aside. 'This has all been handed on to Del Mar?'

'I believe the interrogations and executions are already underway.'

'Extraordinary...' Zweil mused. 'We free them from these monsters, and still the taint persists.'

'Sir,' said Daur, choosing his words carefully, 'the Blood Pact were using disguises. Stolen clothes and equipment. They had obtained at least nine full sets of Tanith uniform.'

'Where from?'

'The morgue, sir. When we checked, nine bodybags had been opened and the corpses stripped.'

'The fething heathens...'

'Sir, they had everything. Ghost fatigues, webbing, even warknives.'

Gaunt realised where this was heading. The realisation stunned him. He looked at Daur.

'You're talking about Cuu, aren't you?'

Daur sighed. 'Yes sir, I am. A man dressed in Tanith uniform, wielding a warknife, carrying defaced coin. It's no longer so simple.'

'Oh feth,' Gaunt murmured and poured himself a glass of wine. 'It is. Cuu's a stone killer. We've got him.'

'With respect,' said Daur. 'Maybe we haven't. I don't like Cuu, but he maintains that all he is guilty of is looting the coins. What if he's innocent? There's now a reasonable doubt.'

'Yes, but–'

'Colonel-commissar, you went to the wire for Caffran on the basis of reasonable doubt. Doesn't Cuu deserve that kind of loyalty too? He's a Ghost, just like Caffran.'

'But–'

'But what? He's a Verghastite? Is that it?' Daur rose angrily.

'Sit down, Daur! That's not what I meant.'

'Really? Tell that to all the Verghastites in this regiment tomorrow when Cuu goes to the wall.'

He marched out and slammed the door.

'What?' Gaunt growled at Zweil.

The old father shrugged. 'Man's got a point. Cuu's a Ghost. He should expect the great and honourable Ibram Gaunt to fight his corner just as much as he did for Caffran.'

'Cuu's a killer,' Gaunt echoed.

'Maybe. If you're expecting me to confirm or deny that on the basis of confession, forget it. I am a sponge for secrets, for the good of men's souls, but I do not leak. Otherwise men would not trust me. Only the God-Emperor hears what I hear.'

'The Emperor protects,' said Gaunt.

'Are you biased?' Zweil asked impertinently.

'What?'

'Biased? Towards the Tanith? It's often thought you are. You favour the Tanith over the Verghastites.'

'I do not!'

Zweil shrugged. 'It's just the way it seems sometimes. To the Vervunhivers especially. You value them, appreciate them, even like some of them, men like Daur. But you always look to the Tanith first.'

'They've been with me longer.'

'No excuse. Are the Verghastite second-class members of this regiment?'

'No!' Gaunt slammed down his glass and got up. 'No, they're not.'

'Then stop making it seem as if they are. Quickly, before the Tanith First comes apart at the seams and splits down the middle.'

Gaunt was silent. He gazed out of the window.

'How many times in the last week have you mentioned Corbec in your addresses to the men? Keeping them updated on his progress? And how many times have you mentioned Soric? Two chief officers, both beloved of the men, both ostensibly valued by you... both dying. But Corbec is in every rousing speech you make. Soric? Forgive me, Ibram, but I can't remember the last time you even mentioned him.'

Gaunt turned round slowly. 'I refuse to accept that I'm as biased as you say. I have done everything to induct the Verghastites properly and fairly. I damn well know there is rivalry... I–'

'What, Ibram?'

'If you can even think this is true... and if Daur thinks it too, as he most obviously does, I will do what I have to. I will show the regiment that there is no division. I will demonstrate it so there is no doubt. I will not have anyone believing that I somehow favour the Tanith. The Ghosts are the Ghosts. Always and forever, first and only. It doesn't matter where they come from.'

Zweil toasted Gaunt and drained his glass. 'I take it you know how to do that?'

'Yes, though it goes against my ethical judgment and sticks in my throat, I do. I have to fight for Cuu's life.'

* * *

THEY NOTCHED UP twenty kilometres doing circuits of the secondary dome's promenade and then picked up the pace and took the thirty flight central dome stairwell at a sprint.

By the time Kolea's section arrived back in the withered park ground set aside for exercise, they were panting and drenched with sweat.

'Fall out,' Kolea said, his own breaths coming in gasps. He leaned over against his knees so that his dog-tags swung from his neck, and spat on the ground.

The men flopped down in the dust or shambled off to find water. Across the grey, dead grass, Skerral and Ewler's sections were doing callisthenics, directed by Sergeant Skerral's booming voice.

Hwlan tossed Kolea a water bottle and the sergeant nodded his thanks before taking a big gulp.

The section felt light, and he didn't like it. There had been a few casualties during the assault, but Rawne had promised to rotate some men up from lower platoons to make up the balance.

What Kolea particularly noticed was the gaping hole left by the three who had disappeared since their arrival on Phantine. Nessa and Nour, sidelined for special ops by Gaunt. And Cuu.

Kolea didn't know what to think about that.

'We should maybe visit Cuu tonight, if we get the passes,' Lubba said as if somehow tuned to Kolea's thoughts. It was likely the subject was on every mind in the section.

'What do you mean?' Kolea said.

'Go see him. Wish him well. That'd be okay, wouldn't it, sarge?'

'Yeah, of course.'

Lubba, the squad's flamer operator, was a short, thick-set man covered in underhive tattoos. He leaned back against the fence. 'Well, we won't be seeing the poor gak again, will we?'

'What?'

'He'll be dead by this time tomorrow. Against the wall,' Jajjo said.

'Only if he's guilty–' Kolea began. 'I can't believe Cuu, even Cuu, would do a thing like that.'

'Doesn't matter though, does it?' said Lubba sitting up again. 'Old Gaunt put his balls on the block to get Caff released. He won't bother this time. Fact is, I reckon Cuu was the trade-off. Cuu in exchange for Caff.'

Kolea shook his head. 'Gaunt wouldn't do that–'

Several Verghastites laughed.

'He wouldn't!'

'Caff's Tanith, ain't he? Much more valuable.'

Kolea got up. 'It doesn't work like that, Lubba. We're all Ghosts.'

'Yeah, right.' Lubba sat back and closed his eyes.

There was a stillness for a moment, broken only by Skerral's distant yells. For the first time, Kolea felt the mood. The feeling that gnawed at the

Verghastites. The feeling they were second-class. He'd never sensed it before. He'd always got nothing but respect from Gaunt. But now...

'Come on!' he said, clapping his hands. 'Up and into the shower block! Go! Mess-call's in twenty minutes!'

There were moans and the men got despondently onto their feet. Kolea trailed them back towards the park hatch.

Ana Curth, dressed in old combat fatigues, was sitting on a rickety bench at the end of the path near the hatch. She was leaning back with her legs stretched out and crossed, reading a dog-eared old text.

'Good book?' Kolea asked, pausing by her.

She looked up. 'Gregorus of Okassis. The *Odes*. One of Dorden's recommendations. Either I'm very stupid or I'm just not getting it.'

'So,' Kolea said, turning to watch the men on the far side of the park doing star jumps. 'This is just a little down-time between shifts?'

'Yeah. I like the fresh air.' He looked round and saw the ironic smirk on her face.

'Actually. I was waiting for you. Obel said you'd be bringing your section back this way at the end of training.'

'Me?' Kolea said.

'You.'

'Why?'

'Because I felt like meddling where I wasn't wanted. Got a minute?'

He sat on the bench next to her.

'Remember what we talked about, back at Bhavnager? You confided in me.'

'I did. Who have you told?'

She slapped him playfully on the arm with her text. 'No one. But that's the point. You should.'

'Not this again.'

'Just answer me this, sergeant. Are you trying to get yourself killed?'

Kolea opened his mouth to reply and paused. He was taken aback. 'Of course I'm not. Unless you count enlistment in the Imperial Guard as a death wish.'

She shrugged. 'People are worried about you.'

'People?'

'Some people.'

'Which people?'

Curth smiled. He liked her smile. 'Come on, Gol,' she said. 'I'm not about to–'

'I let you into my confidence. Seems only fair you trust me as far.'

She put the text down and stretched her arms. 'Got me. Okay. Fair enough. One of the people would be Varl.'

'I ought to–'

'Not say anything to him,' she cut in, flippantly. 'Confidences, remember?'

'All right,' he growled.

'Varl... amongst others, I think... believes you're taking unnecessary risks. They think it's because you've lost your wife and kids, and that you're looking for a... what was it? A reuniting round.'

'Reunion round.'

'Uh-huh. That's it. That's what they think, anyway. But I know better, don't I?'

'So?' He picked up her text and began thumbing through the pages. Poems. Long, old poems like the kind he'd struggled through in Elementary Grade twenty-five years before.

'Well, are they right to be worried?'

'No.' He glanced at her quickly, and saw she was gazing at him intently. 'No. I'm not... not taking risks. I don't think I am. Not deliberately.'

'But?'

Kolea chewed his lip for a second. He looked down at the book with a little shake of the head. 'There was a moment. During the assault. I ran into the gunfire. I... I didn't care. Varl saw me. Even now, I can't imagine what I was thinking.'

'That you want to escape?'

He turned his head and met her eyes. There was no guile in them. Only care. The care that made her a great healer.

'What do you mean?'

'We all want escape. Escape from poverty, fear, death, pain. Escape from whatever we hate about life. And we all have our ways. The Ghosts who drink to drown the terrors of war. The ones who gamble. The ones who have a superstition for every thing they do.' As she was speaking, she slid a packet of lho-sticks out of her jacket pocket and lit one. 'Me, it's bad old poetry, a park bench in pretend sunlight, and these damn things.' She took a drag. She'd given up years before after her promotion to surgeon. The old habit had crept up on her again those last few months. 'And I like a glass of sacra now and then. Feth, I escape in all sorts of ways, don't I?'

He laughed, partly at her frank remark and partly at the way her Verghastite accent made the Tanith curse sound. She was one of the few from Vervunhive who had cheerfully borrowed that other world's oath.

'You, though,' she went on. 'Well, there's no escape, is there? Drink, narcotics... they must only make it worse. The hell of having your kids so near and yet so far away. For you, it must seem like there's only one escape. An escape from life itself.'

'You're a psychiatrist now, then?'

She blew a raspberry. 'There is another way, you know. Another escape.'

'I know.'

'Do you?'

'Yeah. I tell them. I tell Caff and Tona. I reveal myself to the kids. Don't think I haven't thought about it. Ana, it would hurt them all. Caffran and Criid... it would destroy them. It'd be like taking their children away. And

Dalin and Yoncy. Gak, the trauma. They've survived losing me. Finding me again might be too much.'

'I think they'd survive. All of them. I think they'd benefit in many ways. I think it would matter to them. More than you know.'

He flicked the pages of the text. 'Maybe.'

'Not to mention the good it will do you. Will you think about it?'

'What if I don't?'

'Oooh... you've no idea how persistent I can be. Or how many unnecessary medical checks I can order for you.'

'I'll make you a deal,' said Kolea. 'The assault on Ouranberg is close. Real close. Let me get through that. Then I'll... I'll come clean. If you think it's for the best.'

'I do. I really do.'

'But not before Ouranberg. Caffran and Criid will need their heads together for that. I'll not drop a bombshell like this just before a big show.'

Curth nodded and exhaled a plume of smoke. It shone blue in the artificial light as it billowed away. 'Fair enough.'

Kolea fidgeted with the book again, flipping the pages one last time before handing it back.

He stopped. The text had fallen open on the title page. A yellowing certificate had been pasted onto the endpaper. It was a scholam prize, awarding Mikal Dorden a merit in elementary comprehension.

'Dorden lent you this text?'

'Yes,' she said, leaning over. 'Oh. I hadn't noticed that. It must have been his son's.'

For the first few years of the regiment's life, Mikal and Tolin Dorden had been unique amongst the Ghosts. Father and son. Doc Dorden and his trooper boy. The only blood relationship to survive the fall of Tanith.

Mikal had died in the battle for Vervunhive.

Kolea gave her back the ragged old book.

'Gol?'

'Yeah?'

'Don't leave it too long. Don't leave it until it's too late.'

'I promise you I won't,' he said.

Seven

AT 08.00 IMPERIAL on the morning of the 222nd, the Ghosts assigned to Operation Larisel met in an office annexe off the training sub-hangar. They had exercised, showered and eaten a good breakfast brought in from the billet kitchens. There was a tension in the air, but it was a fine-tuned, taut feeling of readiness and an eagerness to get on and do.

The annexe had been cleared so as to accommodate a tactical desk, and folding chairs had been arranged in a circle around it.

'Take your seats,' Kersherin told them as they filed in.

When Captain Daur arrived, everyone was surprised to see him.

He walked in casually and took off his cap and jacket. 'Morning,' he said.

'Where's the colonel-commissar?' asked Mkoll.

'He's asked me to convey his apologies and take his place. Something came up.'

Daur walked over to the tac-desk and loaded a data-spool into the slot. The unit hummed and information scrolled across its glass screens. Daur typed in the password that would let him access the confidential files.

'What something?' Adare called out. Daur ignored him.

'Let's talk about Ouranberg,' he said, getting their attention. The Phantine troopers took their seats amongst the Ghosts.

Daur keyed a stud on the desk and a large hololithic image of the target city rose majestically into being above the optical emitters. A three-dimensional landscape, covering the table top.

'There it is,' he said.

They all craned forward.

'Stand up, if you want to. You need to get to know this place. Let's begin with basics. Two linked domes, Alpha and Beta, primary habitation. Built against and between them to the north is the main vapour mill complex. Here, you see? Adjoining that and Beta dome is Gamma, a smaller habitat sector. Minor habitat domes cluster around the north edges of the mill. The main aerodrome is here, in the cleavage between Gamma and Beta, if we want to think in anatomical terms.'

'Hey, let's not,' said Banda. Several men laughed.

Daur held up an apologetic hand. 'Fine. Here… you see? Here at the southern face, the main porta is–'

'What's a porta?' asked Larkin.

'Gateway, Larks.'

'Just so's I know,' Larkin said, making careful notes in his jotter.

'The main porta, anyway. A sixty metre square vacuum hatch called Ourangate. In front of it, extending out on an apron of rock for about a kilometre, give or take, is Pavia Fields, a kind of ornamental platform.'

What are those? Nessa signed.

'Standing stones. Monolithic war memorials,' said Daur, catching her gestures easily and answering at once. 'It's called the Avenue of the Polyandrons and it marks the formal approach to Ourangate. Linked to the Pavia Fields platform by a causeway is the Imperial Phantine Landing Station, the main dock point for drogues. Especially if they're carrying Imperial nobility. Extending on another causeway from the north-east of the city is the secondary vapour mill complex, built on a neighbouring peak. The mountain top Ouranberg is constructed on actually rises up through the city, hence this… Ouranpeak.'

Daur indicated the fang of rock that jutted out of the top of the city model, between the Beta and Gamma domes.

'What are those extensions to the west and north?' Mkvenner asked.

'Stacks,' Daur said. 'Linked by supported pipelines to the main mill. They use them to flare off waste gases.'

He looked round the room. 'Okay so far? Let's talk about drop zones. Any questions up to this point?'

'Yeah,' said Varl. 'What did you say Gaunt was doing again?'

'You've started?' Gaunt said.

'Yes we have,' Commissar Del Mar said wearily. 'Time is precious, so we moved the sessions up by half an hour.'

'I wasn't notified.'

'Gaunt, I understood you weren't bringing a challenge to this hearing.'

'I changed my mind,' said Gaunt. He stepped up onto the platform and walked to the empty row of seats on the defence side.

Cuu, hunched, shackled and defeated, stood where Caffran had been the morning before.

'Approach the bench,' said Del Mar. Gaunt walked over to him and lent down on the table.

'I just about tolerated your showboating with Caffran yesterday, Gaunt,' whispered Del Mar. 'I can't believe you've got the brass neck to turn up again today. This is the devil you put in the frame for the killing. It's a done thing. You said yourself he was the one.'

'I may have been wrong. A moment, please.'

Before Del Mar could protest, Gaunt walked back down the stage and faced Cuu.

'Did you do it?' he said simply.

'No, sir!' There was animal fear in Cuu's ugly, piercing eyes. 'I looted gold, enemy gold, for that I'll put my hand up. But I didn't do no killing. Sure as sure.'

Gaunt hesitated. Then he walked back to Del Mar, took a pack off his shoulder, and emptied the contents onto the desk in front of the commissar.

Ghost daggers, nine of them, each one wrapped in plastene.

'What is this?' asked Del Mar.

'Warknives. Straight silver, Tanith issue. Some are notched, as you can see. Any one of them might be the murder weapon.'

'And why should I believe that?'

'Because these were recovered from a Blood Pact cell operating in the undercity. They had acquired several sets of Tanith fatigues and these knives. They were using defaced coinage to bribe the locals. The evidence I sent you – the blade shard, the coin under the bath – it all points to Cuu there. Unless you take into account the notion that not everyone dressed as a Ghost that night was a Ghost.'

'You're truly pissing me off now, Gaunt,' said Del Mar. 'I won't stand for this.'

'I don't care. All I care about is my duty. There are reasonable grounds for the dismissal of charges against Trooper Cuu. As reasonable as the grounds you threw Caffran's case out on.'

'I'm warning you–'

'Don't even try. You know I'm right.'

Del Mar sat back, shaking his head. 'What about the old man? The witness?'

'I showed him a picture of Cuu and he didn't recognise him either.'

'I see. So the Ghost who was seen, the one who undoubtedly slew Onti Flyte...'

'...was very likely a Blood Pact trooper masquerading as a Ghost, yes.'

Del Mar sighed.

'Reasonable doubt,' said Gaunt.

'Damn you, Gaunt.'

'Sir, can we square this away so that I can get on with my real duties?' Gaunt said, sarcastically stressing the word 'real'.

'He admits looting?'

'Yes, sir.'

'Then he'll be flogged. Case dismissed.'

GAUNT DIDN'T STAY to see the sentence carried out. As he came down the steps of the Chamber of Justice, he met Hark hurrying in. The man looked tired, his eyes still puffy with sleep, and he was trying to smooth down his hair with his fingers.

Hark stopped in his tracks when he saw Gaunt.

'Sir?'

'It's done. Cuu has been cleared of the murder.'

Hark fell into step with him as they descended into the yard.

'I... I wish you had kept me informed, sir.'

'Informed, Viktor?'

'That you'd changed your mind about Cuu's guilt.'

Gaunt glanced at him. 'It was an eleventh hour decision. I thought you'd be pleased. Between the pair of you, you and ayatani Zweil have been on at me for days about being even-handed towards the Verghastites. And you were right. A popular Ghost gets into trouble, and I move heaven and earth to get him out of the mess. A less-popular Verghastite gets in trouble, and I cut him adrift. I dread to think what it would have done to Verghastite morale if I'd left Cuu to face the court alone this morning.'

'I am pleased, sir. For inevitable reasons, you do seem to have favoured the Tanith until now. Even if you didn't think that's what you were doing.'

'Captain Daur brought me up sharp, I'm glad to say.' He stopped walking and turned to Hark. 'You still seem... put out, Viktor.'

'Like I said, I wish you'd told me you had decided to go to bat for Cuu. I could have helped.'

'I managed fine.'

'Of course. But I could have done some leg work, organised evidence. That's what I'm here for.'

Gaunt raised a hand and the staff driver assigned to him started up the waiting car and drove it across the yard to collect him.

'I suppose you could have talked to witnesses. You probably would have preferred to do that yourself, rather than let me do it.'

'Sir?'

'I went to visit Mr Absolom, Hark. He'd seen the killer, after all. I had to make sure he didn't recognise Cuu. Mr Absolom's a fine old fellow. A service veteran, isn't he? He'd do anything for the Imperial Guard. Especially if a persuasive commissar came to see him and convinced him it was his duty.'

Hark's eyes darkened. 'You told me to guarantee Caffran's acquittal.'

'And a key witness would do that, wouldn't it? Absolom didn't recognise Cuu's picture, of course. But you knew that. He wouldn't recognise any picture. Because he didn't see the killer at all, did he, Viktor?'

Hark looked away. 'I suppose you'll want my resignation from the regiment?' he said bitterly.

'No. But I want you to learn from this. I will not break Imperial law. Better that Caffran had gone to execution innocent than lie to get him off. Commissars are often thought of as devious, Viktor. That reputation is justified. They are political animals who use all the tricks of politics to achieve their goals. That is not my way. And I will never sanction it in any man in my command. You could make an exemplary officer, Hark. My oh-so naive idea of an exemplary officer, anyway. Don't stoop to those methods again, or I will drum you out of this company and the Commissariate. Do we have an understanding?'

Hark nodded. Gaunt got into his car and was driven away out through the gate.

Hark watched him go. 'Naive. You said it.'

GAUNT STEPPED UP onto an empty ammo crate that Beltayn had lugged in. He raised his voice, and the sound of it silenced the men gathered round in the main billet.

'Men of Tanith, men of Verghast. Ghosts. The word has just been given. Weather permitting, we go for Ouranberg at dawn on the 226th. Make ready for the Emperor's work. That is all.'

As he got off the box and put his cap back on, Gaunt thought about the information he hadn't been at liberty to announce. By the time the invasion began, the squads of Operation Larisel would have been active in Ouranberg for over twenty-four hours.

God-Emperor willing.

THE DROP

OURANBERG, PHANTINE, 224.771, M41

'Never, ever, ever fething again.'

– Trooper Larkin, 2nd Team marksman,
Tanith First

JUST AFTER MIDNIGHT, in the first hour of the 224th, Scald-storms rose cyclonically in the cloud oceans north of Cirenholm. Jarring, superheated belts of fire, dozens of kilometres long, crackled up into the higher reaches of the sky, and the borealis flickered and roiled in queasy, phantom coils.

Air visibility and sensor ranges were cut to less than five kilometres. Plumes of rising ash blotted out the stars. The poisonous heart of Phantine raged against the night.

The storms had been predicted by the Navy's long-range auspex, and the twitching senses of the taskforce astropaths. This was what the tacticians had been waiting for.

The drogues *Zephyr* and *Trenchant* had reached their holding position several hours before midnight. Hugging a dense reef of altocumulus cloud forty kilometres across, they kept station in a shallow gulf of sky called the Leaward Races, almost in the dead centre of the great air desert known as the Western Continental Reaches.

On the flight deck of the *Zephyr*, Admiral Ornoff ordered the launch.

Ornoff had used the drogues judiciously to pursue his policy of nightly raids. By releasing the bomber shoals from carriers that varied their positions, he ensured that the defences of Ouranberg never knew from which direction to expect the next raid. Enemy hunter squadrons searched for the drogues by day, hoping to surprise them before they could unleash their armadas, but the Western Continental Reaches were vast, and Ornoff used the mammatocumulus of the regular Scald-storms as cover.

The night raid of the 224th would approach Ouranberg from the south-east, covering a distance to the target of about three hundred and forty kilometres. They would use the prevailing jet streams of the Reaches to maximise speed, hugging the ultra-violet void where the troposphere became the stratosphere.

Including the fighter escort of Imperial Navy Lightnings and Thunderbolts, the raiding force numbered some six hundred aircraft. Thirty matt-grey Marauders of the Phantine Air Corps took the role of the pathfinders, pressing ahead clear of the main formation to light up the target with illumination-mines and incendiary payloads. Six minutes behind them came a mass wave of over three hundred heavy bombers. Most of these were lumbering, six-engined Magogs, painted an unreflective black. The Magog was a prop-driven, atmospheric type that had been in service for centuries, but the wave also included two dozen Behemoths, the awesome and ancient giants of Phantine Bomber Command.

Following the first wave came a second pack of Marauders, from either Imperial Navy or Urdeshi regimental squadrons. The green mottle-camo of the former distinguished them from the silver-belly/beige-top two-tone of the latter. All seventy of them were laden with fuel-air explosive payloads.

The third wave numbered almost two hundred craft. More Magogs, as well as twenty Urdeshi Marauder Destroyers and thirty Phantine Shrikes. These destroyers, and the elderly hook-winged, single-engined Shrike jets, were specialist dive bombers that would finish the raid by carrying out pinpoint low-level runs into a target zone that, by then, should have been grievously punished.

Flying as part of the second wave were four void-blue Phantine Marauders that carried no bombs at all. Larisel 1, 2, 3 and 4.

KERSHERIN AND THE other Skyborne specialists checked the Ghosts over one by one, covering every detail down to boot laces and pocket studs with what would have seemed like obsessive fuss had the tension not been so high.

Each member of the Larisel teams wore a modified version of their standard Tanith uniform. In place of regulation underwear, they had been issued silk-lined, rubberised bodygloves that acted both as insulation against the extreme cold and a seal against the corrosive atmosphere. Over that went the black Tanith tunic, breeches and webbing, and over that a zip-up leather jump-smock that came down to the hips and was laced with chainmail. Light equipment that would normally have been carried in a kit bag or backpack was distributed into the uniform pockets of the tunic and the webbing pouches and the smock closed up tightly over the top. Gloves and boots were then pulled on, and gaiters buckled around the wrists and boot-tops to form a tight seal.

By then, the Ghosts were already sweating in the hot and abnormally heavy gear. They raised their arms as light belts-and-braces of outer webbing were fitted. These had pouches at the hips for additional kit items, and secure loops for lamp packs, flares, a rope-coil, a short-nose laspistol, a saw-edged cutting knife and the Tanith blade. Their camo-cloaks were tightly wound with a scrim-net around a pack of tube charges and grenades, and stuffed into a musette bag that was lashed horizontally from the front of the outer webbing across the groin. Medi-packs, bag-rations and power-cells for the lasrifles and pistols were loaded into the troopers' thigh pouches.

Not everyone was carrying a lasrifle. Apart from the four snipers with their long-las variants carried in covers with slings, Milo, Cocoer, Meryn and Varl had the U90 cannons. The solid ammunition took up a lot more space, so while the four of them carried spare cells in their thigh pouches for the other team members' guns, every member of the squad was strung with a bandolier of drum magazines. For the drop, the four U90's had slim, twenty-five round clips fitted and wrapped into place with adhesive tape. The higher capacity drum-mags they all carried in their bandoliers were too bulky to jump with. The cannons, like the lasrifles, had their muzzles plugged with wax stoppers to prevent them fouling on impact.

Camo paint was applied to their faces, and micro-beads fitted into their ears and tested. Then they pulled on their woollen hats and did up their smock collars ready for the helmets. Varl kissed the silver aquila that hung on a chain around his neck before dropping it down into his tunic and buckling up the neck of the over-jacket.

The helmets were black steel with integral visors. Inside, they had a leather liner-cap that buckled in place around the chin. A canvas frill around the bottom of the helmet tucked inside the smock collar and sealed with a zip. A pressurised air-bottle, which hooked to the chest webbing, would feed oxygen into the helmet cavity during the jump.

Finally, the jump-packs were lifted onto their backs, strapped on, and the power engaged for a final check. Main weapons were cinched tight across their chests. Safeties were double-checked. Kersherin offered up a brief but heartfelt prayer for them all.

They could see little, and hear even less, except the crackle of the vox. It was hard to walk under the weight, and they shuffled around, smacking hands with each other awkwardly for good luck.

Once the four Phantine Skyborne were suited – an operation that took a great deal less time – they were all escorted by ground crew across the

Trenchant's number five flight deck to the four Marauders and man-handled inside.

'Feth!' Milo heard Adare moan. 'I've had enough already.'

The Marauders they were using for the drop had been stripped for the job, with all bombs and weapons except the nose cannons removed. They normally required a crew of six including gunners, but for this raid only two flight crew, a pilot and a navigator, would take them up. The nose guns were slaved to the pilot's control, and the navigator would coordinate the drop with the Skyborne officer aboard. The flight crew was already in position in the cockpit above the cabin, completing final checks and blessings.

The squad members eased their overweight bulks down onto the bare cabin floor.

THE LAUNCH WENT smoothly. Ornoff took that to be a good sign. One Magog turned back almost at once, reporting bombs hung, and another aborted after about fifteen minutes, voxing in that it had suffered a critical instrument failure. The first landed safely on the *Zephyr's* runway deck. The other, presumably blind, missed the drogues completely and flew on east into the burning clouds. It was never seen again.

A raid launch with only two aborts. That was the best they'd managed since they'd begun bombing Ouranberg. On the bridge of the *Zephyr*, Ornoff felt a confidence rising within him. He summoned the drogue's chief ecclesiarch and ordered an impromptu service of deliverance.

THE PASSAGE WAS noisier, colder and more turbulent than anything the Ghosts had experienced riding the drops in over Cirenholm. They were much higher and travelling much faster. Not long after the violent take-off, with cabin temperature and pressure dropping away and skins of ice forming on the metal surfaces inside the cabin, they all began to appreciate the sweltering layers of clothing they were wearing.

There was a surprising amount to see, given that the cabin had limited ports and they were trussed up in helmets and visors. What had been the payload officer's pict-plate had been switched on in each of the Marauders, filling the darkness of each cabin with a chilly green glow, and displaying a detailed modar picture of the raid formation.

In Larisel 1, Varl eased forward, struggling with the weight on his body. He keyed his vox and gestured to the Phantine, Unterrio, who was tuning the pict-plate.

'That's the bomber waves?'

'Yeah,' answered Unterrio. Even using the vox, he had to raise his voice above the engine noise and the constant thunder of the wind. 'We're here in this belt.'

Varl looked closer, trying to focus through the visor's eye-plates. He realised each foggy band of modar returns was actually made up of hundreds of individual dots, each one accompanied by a graphic number.

'Every craft has an identifying transponder,' Unterrio explained. 'It helps us pick up bandits quicker. Time was, enemy cloud-hunters would slip in amongst the bomber shoals and bide their time, moving within the formation, choosing their kills. Now, if you don't display a code, you're fair game.'

'Gotcha,' said Varl. It made sense. He looked round at the cabin and saw that the other members of 1st Team – Banda, Vadim and Bonin – were listening in and looking with interest.

'Which ones are the other jump-craft?' voxed Vadim.

Unterrio raised a gloved paw and pointed to spots on the plate. 'That's Larisel 4, Sergeant Mkoll. That's Sergeant Adare's ship, Larisel 3. Here, just hidden by the graphic of that Navy Marauder... that's Larisel 2. Corporal Meryn's bird.'

It took a moment for Varl to make sense of the jumping, flickering display. It seemed that the four jump-craft were spread out thinly amongst the bomber wave.

The Marauder lurched, and the engines seemed to swoon and stutter.

'What was that?' Varl voxed, his voice sounding dry and hard over the link.

'Turbulence,' replied Unterrio.

In Larisel 3, Specialist Cardinale was conducting a similar explanation of the plate graphics for the benefit of Milo and Doyl. Nessa and Adare, perhaps resigned to being mercilessly insulated against the world, were playing blade, parchment, rock. Their giggles snickered over the vox-link as their heavy-gloved hands beat out the repetitive gestures of the game.

Larkin wished there was a window to see out of, but there wasn't. He sat on the bare floor of Larisel 2's cabin and gazed at the others. Kersherin was studying the aiming-plate display. Kuren and Meryn were chatting. Mkvenner looked like he was asleep.

'How long?' Larkin asked Kersherin.

'Forty minutes,' replied the Phantine.

Scout Sergeant Mkoll had not been designed to fly. But still he had not challenged Gaunt's decision to pick him for this operation. Mkoll didn't do things like that. And he knew that when the time came and he got onto the target, he would be the right man for the job.

But the flying. That was a fething nightmare. He'd never been higher than the top branches of a nalwood until Gaunt had taken the Tanith off-world. Space travel – which, like Colm Corbec, he reviled – at least didn't seem like flying.

This was much worse. The vibration, the elemental wrath beating at the craft. It was as if the air really didn't want you to forget you were eight kilometres up thanks only to its charitable physics.

And the waiting. That was the mind killer. Waiting for action. Waiting for the moment. It allowed fears to grow. It gave a man time to worry about the struggle ahead. Combat was hell, but at least it was against real enemies, people you could actually shoot. The enemies here were time and fear, imagination and turbulence... and cold.

Mkoll felt sick. He hated the waiting almost as much as he hated the weight they were forced to wear. He felt anchored to the metal deck. When the time came and the jump-call was given, he wasn't entirely convinced he would be able to get up.

He looked round Larisel 4's cabin. Babbist, the Phantine trooper, was fighting with the display plate. It kept rolling and flickering on him, showing nothing but green fuzz. Bad tubes, Mkoll decided. If Babbist didn't get it working, they would be going in blind.

Cocoer and Nour were sitting back as if sleep. Nour probably was. He switched off that way sometimes in the lag before combat. Twitchy and already running on adrenalin, Rilke the team sniper was stripping and reassembling the firing mechanism of his long-las, getting used to manipulating it with his heavy gloves. Mkoll wanted to grab him and tell him to stop, but he knew it was simply a coping strategy.

He keyed his vox and leant forward. 'Okay, Rilke?'

'Sure, yeah,' crackled the sniper, his hands repeating the process over and over again. 'Actually, I'm fething scared, sarge. I keep wanting to throw up, but I know I can't in this visor.'

'That would be horrible,' Mkoll agreed.

He heard Rilke laugh.

'I only do this to keep my mind off the nausea,' Rilke added, holding up the trigger plate briefly before speedily fitting it again. 'Feth, I feel sick. My stomach is doing flips. How do you cope, sarge?'

'I watch you,' said Mkoll.

THIRTY MINUTES FROM the target, an unidentified contact wavered on to the screens and ten of the fighter escorts broke south to hunt it out.

'Probably just a heavy scald-flare,' Unterrio told the Ghosts. 'We're fine.'

The Marauder lurched badly again, the fifth or sixth time it had done so during the flight. The others didn't seem to be noticing the jolts any more, but Bonin was convinced it wasn't turbulence. The acute wariness that Mkoll had trained into Bonin and all the Tanith scouts was ringing all sorts of alarms in his head.

He got up, slowly, heavily, and thumped forward to the short rungs that led up into the cockpit. Unterrio was hunched over the pict-plate with Varl and he looked up as Bonin shuffled past, unhappy that he was moving around but not about to stop him.

Bonin peered up at the flight crew. They seemed to be fighting with the controls.

'Problem?' he voxed.

'No,' said the pilot. 'None at all.'

Bonin thought he recognised the voice. 'You sure?'

'Yes!' the pilot snapped and looked back at him. There wasn't much to see of the face through the visor of the pressure mask, but Bonin recognised the eyes of Commander Jagdea.

'Hello,' he said.

'Scout Trooper Bonin,' she replied.

'I thought you were hurt?'

'The break was treated and fused and I'm all strapped up in a pressure sling. You can fly a Marauder one-handed anyway. Not like a Lightning.'

'Whatever. Just so long as you're okay. You volunteer for this?'

'They asked for volunteers, yes.'

'You must like us,' Bonin ventured. She didn't answer. 'The engines shouldn't be doing that, should they?'

She looked back at him again. 'No, all right? No, they shouldn't. We've got a misfire problem. But I'm not going to let it affect the mission. I'll get you there.'

'I'm sure you will,' said Bonin.

THE SHOAL'S LUCK lasted until they were almost in sight of Ouranberg. About ten kilometres out, the scald-storm suddenly collapsed and faded, sinking its fires into the lower stratum and leaving the air bare and empty.

The Ouranberg defences picked them up almost immediately. The fighters were on them about two minutes later.

The cloud-hunters went through the shoal on afterburner, crossing north/south. Two stricken Magogs, on fire, ploughed their way down on steep dives into the Scald. A Navy Marauder ceased to be in a blizzard of shrapnel and ignited gas.

As the enemy craft banked round for another pass, they met the Imperial fighter escort. Through the cabin's slit window, Milo could see streams of tracers and bright flashes flickering against the clouds.

A brilliant light suddenly shone back through the cockpit, shafting down into the cabin.

'What was that?' asked Adare.

'The pathfinders just lit up the target,' the pilot announced. 'Five minutes. Go to stand by.'

The Ghosts all struggled to their feet. Cardinale moved between them, tugging out the air hoses that had linked them to the ship's supply and cutting in their own air-bottles.

'You're running on internal now,' he voxed. They nodded their understanding.

Then he opened each jump pack back-plate in turn and threw the start-up rocker switches. Lift power, a blessed relief from the weight, kicked in. The outside roar was so great they couldn't even hear the turbines.

Cardinale unplugged and refitted his own air hose and then turned his back to Nessa so she could throw his pack switches. Doyl moved to the back hatch and put his hand on the release lever. They all watched the screen.

THE FIRST MAIN wave came over the vast bulk of Ouranberg, which was already lit up with flares and combustion bombs. Dragging slowly through the air, the Magogs began to spill bombs from their bellies. Air-cracking flashes slammed out from each hiss of fire.

Above and around the bomber shoal, the fighters danced with the enemy in a furious dog-fight guided mostly by modar. Already, the ground batteries had opened up in full force. Floral patterns of flak decorated the air. Rockets lashed upwards. Hydra batteries zippered the air with tracer rounds.

One of the Magogs blew apart, a single engine nacelle still spinning its prop as it dived downwards, on fire like a comet. Another was caught in the spotlights and hammered with flak until it fell apart. A Behemoth, hit in the wing-base by a rocket, dipped slowly towards the city, on fire, and struck the Beta dome edge, causing an explosion that sent flame out more than five hundred metres.

Another was hit as it was opening its bomb-bay. The explosion took out the craft either side of it.

ON A CUE FROM Babbist, Nour wrenched open the side hatch of Larisel 4. Typhoon-force wind galed in, rocking them all. Nour flinched back, seeing the Navy Marauder flying next to them in the formation suddenly ignite and veer towards them.

The stricken craft, bleeding flames from behind the cockpit, missed them by only a few metres and dropped away, its fire trail marking out a spiral as it accelerated to its doom.

All that Nour had seen in the split second before the Marauder had pitched away was the pilot and the fore-gunner, hammering at the perspex of their screens, trying to break out as fire sucked into the crew spaces they occupied.

'Ready for drop,' Mkoll cried.

Nour shook himself. He couldn't get the image of the burning, hammering pilot out of his head.

'Ready.'

Babbist ushered Cocoer and Rilke up to the hatch.

THE DZ'S FOR Larisel had been selected carefully. Larisel 1, Varl's mob, was to drop onto the main vapour mills, with Larisel 4, under Mkoll's command, dropping on the mill worker hab-domes to the north-west. Adare's unit, Larisel 3, was going after the secondary vapour mills, and Larisel 2, under Meryn's control, was jumping on Beta dome.

Flak whickered up at them from the city. The first wave of Magogs had hammered Beta dome. Patterns of throbbing fire pulsed below: pin-points or clusters. White-hot fires raged up into the night and secondary explosions rippled through the domes.

'Go! said Cardinale.

Milo leapt from the Marauder. He was instantly struck by a fierce sideways force, a hammerblow of slipstream that turned him over and over. He tumbled, stunned, and fell, gunning his pack. Nothing seemed to happen.

'Relax, relax into it...' Cardinale said over the link, barely audible over the raging wind.

Ouranberg was coming up very fast and very hard. Milo yanked at his thruster control. Training had been all well and good, but nothing could have prepared him for leaping into space in this kind of cross-wind. He was being swept clear of the DZ.

Milo saw Nessa and Adare dropping past him, spreadeagled, trimming their thrusters. He slid in behind them, the wind tearing at his mask.

The vast, dull-grey dome of the secondary mill rose up in front of him, a small city in its own right.

He coasted in.

LARKIN PASSED OUT as he left the hatch. It was partly fear, and partly the sledgehammer thump of the wind. He came round, felt his entire body vibrating and saw nothing but oily blackness.

'Larkin! Larkin!'

He realised he was falling on his back. He fought to right himself, over-cueing the jump-pack controls so he shot up like a cork. The wind was a thundering, buffeting howl in his ears. There was no sign of Mkvenner, Kersherin, Kuren or Meryn. The wounded, battered shape of the Beta dome was twinkling with hundreds of fires. He tried to make sense of it, tried to match what he saw to the carefully memorised picture of the cityscape and the DZ in his head.

Then he saw Meryn, passing him twenty metres to his left, looking stiff and awkward but at least in control. Squeezing his handgrip, he propelled himself after the sergeant.

LARISEL I WAS two minutes short of its DZ, juddering through flak, when the engines finally failed. Jagdea yelled at them to go, fighting to keep the nose of the leaden craft up as long as she could. They bailed: Vadim, Unterrio, Banda, Varl. Bonin hesitated, and clambered back to the cockpit ladder. The Marauder was beginning to vibrate wildly.

'Come on!' he cried. 'Move it! You've both got chutes! Come on!'

Jagdea pushed him back. There was a bright burst right outside the cockpit dome and flak sent ribbons of metal and glass spearing in at them. Bonin didn't have to look to see that the co-pilot was dead.

'Jagdea!' he bellowed, grabbing at her.

Stalling out, the Marauder rolled over onto its back and entered a terminal swan dive. Bonin was upside down, pressed into the roof, the harness of his jump-pack half-choking him.

Fighting the mounting G-force, Jagdea pulled a lever that fired the explosive bolts in the cockpit canopy's frame, and the damaged canopy ripped away entirely. She unbuckled her restraint harness and pulled at Bonin hard, yanking him up into the cockpit. The force of the wind did the rest, sucking them both up and out of the diving craft and scattering them away into the sky.

'ARE WE ON the target?' asked Mkoll.

'I don't know!' said Babbist.

'Are we on the target?'

'The damn aimer is off-line!' Babbist yelled, struggling to get the flickering, rolling image to freeze.

'We're going to overshoot if we're not careful,' said Nour.

'We go, we go now!' Mkoll decided.

'But–' Babbist began.

'We go *now!*'

Mkoll moved to the hatch. 'Come on! Line up and out!'

There was an odd bump, like something had flicked at his inner ear. Mkoll swayed and looked round. There was a smouldering hole in the deck of the cabin where a large calibre tracer round had punched through, killing Babbist on its way up to the roof. Nour had been knocked down, and Rilke and Cocoer were trying to lift him.

'Come on!' Mkoll cried. A shower of sparks blinded him. More tracer was riddling the cabin, ripping through the hull-skin. He heard Rilke scream and Nour yelling, 'It's going! It's going! It's going!'

VARL LANDED A damn sight harder than he might have wished, and lay for a moment on a section of reinforced roof plating, winded and bruised. Unterrio appeared over him, grabbing him by the hands and pulling him up.

'Feth,' said Varl.

They were on a wide manufactory roof structure adjoining the main vapour mill, high up above Ouranberg with only the mill chimneys and the crag of Ouranpeak rising above them. The sky was a bright fury, but the raid now seemed far away.

Banda had made it down on a roof section adjacent to theirs, and as they went down to join her, using the lift of the packs to bounce themselves along as if on springs, they heard Vadim calling urgently over the vox.

Unterrio spotted the young Verghastite up on the inspection walkway of a chimney flue. He was pointing up at the sky.

'There! There!' he said.

Varl looked. He wasn't sure what he was looking for, then he saw what Vadim's sharp eyes had already detected. A Marauder, about a kilometre and half away, turning south in a loop. It had to be Mkoll's bird, Larisel 4, making its pass on the mining habs.

Then he realised it was on fire.

'Feth, they had better–' he began. The Marauder exploded in mid-air. A big sphere of white light expanded in the sky and then was gone.

Mkoll, Rilke, Nour, Cocoer... just gone. Vital men, friends...

A whole team finished before they'd even begun.

LARISEL AND THUNDERHEAD

THE ASSAULT ON OURANBERG, PHANTINE, 224 to 226.771, M41

'Right through the specialist training, we'd all had this feeling of confidence, like the beloved Emperor was with us in all things. Then we were on the ground, and Mkoll and the others were dead, and we started to realise we didn't stand a chance.'

– Brin Milo, 3rd Team trooper, Tanith First

One

THEY HAD TO get off the roof-space fast. Thick streams of black smoke from petrochemical fires and incendiary bursts were washing back across them and across the roof structures of the Ouranberg's secondary vapour mill.

The smoke was pouring from the main city, carried by the powerful high-altitude winds and, if the Emperor was with them, it would have concealed them in the last stages of their jump.

But from the moment he was down, Doyl had been surveying the area. There were six defence towers in the immediate vicinity, all of them with decent views of the roof where they had landed, smoke or no smoke.

The five members of Larisel 3 hurried into the cover of a ventilator stack and got down. No firing had come their way; indeed, two of the towers were still spitting tracer streams at Imperial aircraft peeling off the target.

'Did they see us?' Milo voxed.

'We're alive, aren't we?' replied Sergeant Adare. 'I think their attention is on the sky above.'

'Check in,' voxed Specialist Cardinale. 'Any injuries? Any equipment losses?' There were none apparently. Adare made a special point of signing to Nessa to make sure she was okay.

'Did you hear what they said?' muttered Doyl. 'Sergeant Varl, on the vox, as we were coming in?'

Milo had. A brief, incomplete, dreadful message-burst. Mkoll's craft had gone up short of its drop point.

'I can't believe it–' he murmured.

'Me neither,' said Adare. 'God-Emperor rest their souls. But there's nothing we can do about it. Except go on with this and get some fething pay-back.'

Adare raised his gloved hand and exchanged palm-slaps with Doyl, Milo and Nessa. Cardinale hesitated and then smacked his own hand against Adare's proffered gauntlet. Milo knew Adare was trying to make sure the Phantine felt like part of the team.

In truth, Milo had returned Adare's palm-slap with little conviction himself. The loss of Mkoll was a profound shock. The scout sergeant had always seemed invulnerable, one of those Ghosts who would never fall. Milo even felt a little envious of Nessa. She couldn't read their lips because of the visors and no one had signed her the news. He'd been worried about how she might cope with the mission given her disability, but now it seemed she was lucky to be spared the bad news. At least for a while.

Doyl led them down the length of the ventilator stack and then across a narrow open space to the cover of some galvanised pipework. They moved sluggishly and heavily, even though the grav-units of their jump-packs were still on to ease the burden.

Cardinale helped Doyl out of his jump pack and the scout hurried on alone, looking for an entry point while the others got rid of their packs. Adare and Cardinale stowed the heavy units in a stack under the pipework, lashed them in place with rope and concealed them with a scrim net. Milo doubted there would be many foot patrols up here in the toxic atmosphere outside the dome, but the last thing they wanted was for the enemy to find traces of a troop landing.

They were still weighed down with kit, helmets and the armoured smocks, but now they felt a thousand times lighter. Nessa had taken her long-las out of its cover and assembled it, though with her visor in place, there was no point aligning the scope. Milo peeled the adhesive tape off his U90's twenty-five round clip and replaced it with a drum magazine marked with a red cross – the special armour-piercing load. Adare collected in and pocketed the plastic muzzle stoppers. Then he gently tried his vox-link. They'd picked up Varl's strangled message whilst still in the air. Now they were down, the hard structures of Ouranberg were blocking anything but short-range transmission. As Daur had predicted in his last briefing, there was going to be no contact between teams once the mission was underway. A full-gain vox-caster would have weighed one of them down unnecessarily. Besides, it wasn't impossible that the enemy was scanning for vox-calls on the known Imperial wavelengths.

Milo hunched down so that he had a good firing position, covering the space all the way from the pipework to what looked like a row of short exhaust flues on the edge of the roof section. Despite the bitter cold, he was hot, and he could feel cold sweat running down his spine. It was getting harder to breath. They were probably reaching the limit of their air-bottles.

Doyl reappeared. He had unshipped his camo-cloak and shrouded himself with it.

'Got a possible entry point. Thirty metres that way. Looks like a maintenance hatch and it's locked, but we should be able to force it.'

They ran forward, low, in single file, after his lead. The hatch was thick with rust and lay in the side of a raised hump in the roof, under the lea of an exposed roof spar. Milo and Cardinale stood look-out to either side with weapons ready as Adare and Doyl examined the hatch.

'I don't think it's pressurised,' said Adare.

'Me neither. We get through this and maybe down inside to a sealed door.'

'Cut it,' Adare said.

Doyl took out a compact cutting torch, said the prayer of ignition, lit its small energy blade and sliced into the lock. There were a few sparks and a slight glow, but Adare held his camo-cloak out to screen the work.

Once the teeth of the lock were cut, Doyl used his knife to force the corroded hatch out of its frame.

Adare led the way in, a lamp pack locked to his lasrifle's bayonet lug. The chamber appeared to be a circulation space around the head of an elevator assembly. Heavy machinery, caked in grease, jutted up out of the floor. Even with his helmet on, Milo could hear the wind moaning through rust holes in the metal roof-cover.

Doyl located a floor hatch in the far corner and they struggled down a short ladder into dark attic spaces that filled the cavity between the mill's outer roof and inner pressurised hull. It was now getting very hard to breathe.

The floor beneath them was a skin of clean metal ribbed with tension members. Unwilling to find out if the inner hull skin was load-bearing, they edged along the ribbing. After about fifty metres, they came across a break in the inner roof where rockcrete support piles of staggering proportions rose through to buttress the main roof.

One had metal rungs fused into the side, and they descended again, carefully, hand over hand, weapons slung on their backs.

Twenty metres down, the way was blocked. A huge moulded collar of industrial plastene sheathed the descending piles and sealed them against the downward sloping rim of roof-skin. Adare believed they would have to go back, but Milo spotted an almost invisible inspection plate in the metal skin. With Adare supporting his weight, Doyl leaned out from the rungs and pressed against the plate until it fell into the cavity behind. Doyl swung over and clambered through. A moment later, he voxed them to follow.

They were in a crawl space under the inner skin, and there was barely room to stand. Doyl replaced the plate, which had rubberised edging and formed a seal by being held in place by the internal pressure. Milo could feel the rush of air going out past him until Doyl got the plate back in position.

Gratefully, they unplugged their air-tubes and slid their visors up. The air was thin and cold and had a rough taste in it that stung their throats. But they were now inside the pressurised section of the mill.

'Did we trip an alarm?' Cardinale asked.

'I don't think so,' replied Doyl, checking the frame of the plate for signs of leads or breakers. 'The atmosphere processors might have lost a tiny amount of pressure while the plate was open, but I doubt it was enough for them to have noticed.'

'In case they did, and they're able to pinpoint the source, let's get moving anyway,' said Adare.

They hunched their way down the crawl space. It opened out dramatically, stretching out further than the eye could see, but didn't get any deeper. Doyl scouted around, and found a hatch in the floor some forty metres off. It was heavy-duty, Imperial design, and electronically locked.

The scout worked fast. He taped one of the six miniature circuit-breakers he carried in his tool-roll to the hatch frame, and secured its leads to either side of the lock. He waited until the little green rune on its casing lit up, indicating that the hatch's alarm circuit was now looping via the breaker, and then cut through the lock-tongue with his cutting torch. Though there was no immediate scream of klaxons, it was impossible to tell if the alarm had been bypassed, so they dropped through the hatch quickly and pulled it shut behind them.

The hatch had let them down into a maintenance corridor, old and dingy, and poorly lit. Centuries of condensation had rusted the walls, rotted the mat-boards and encouraged thick, lurid mould growths along the ceiling. The corridor ran north/south.

'South,' said Adare confidently, and they moved off. South, the direction of the main city structure of Ouranberg.

And the creature they had come to kill.

IT HAD TAKEN Bonin a full ninety seconds to gain control of his jump-pack, and that had felt like an eternity: tumbling, wheeling, spinning, with no sense of up or down. Somehow, Jagdea had shown the good sense to cling on to him, despite the violence of their drop.

By the time he had squeezed enough lift out of the grav-units to pull them both up, and begun to compensate for their drift with the turbines, they were well out to the east of Ouranberg.

'Hold on!' he voxed.

'My chute's intact! I'll drop!' she replied.

'Where to?' he asked. Below their dangling feet there was nothing but the frothing, fire-lit expanse of the Scald.

'It doesn't matter–'

'No! Just hold on!' His voice over the link sounded tinny and dull. The night winds beat and tugged at them.

Cautiously, Bonin nudged them towards the gloomy city, using little squirts of turbine power to buoy them along like a leaf on a racing stream. The crosswinds seemed to be with them, but every now and then, the gale suddenly gusted against them, and the pair were turned or blown back.

'Your grip still good?'

'Yes.' She had her hands and forearms locked up under his chest harness. He realised he had his right arm protectively clutched around her left shoulder, gripping the top of her inflator-chute's shoulder webbing.

'We're going to need more lift,' he said, depressing the red stud on the handgrip. The grey, eastern slopes of what had to be Gamma dome were looming in front of them like a mountain range.

They almost didn't clear Gamma dome. Bonin had to fight to stop the crosswinds smashing them into the outer hull, and the jump pack seemed to be struggling to find enough lift. Vortices of wind created by the dome's angular surface eddied them like chaff. And though, by the altimeter, they were climbing fast, the dome seemed to go on forever.

Gamma dome seemed to have been virtually untouched by the raid, though great flickers of orange and white lit the sky and the clouds behind it where Beta dome was ablaze.

As they hugged the curve of the dome up towards the summit, a different level of wind patterns took over and suddenly started to carry them up with increasing speed. The dome-hull flicked by underneath them, and Bonin had to pull hard to the left to avoid collision with a protruding mast.

Then they were over, passing the massive icy crag of Ouranpeak, and dropping towards the main vapour mill.

'Varl! Banda! Vadim! Respond!' Bonin voxed. Foolishly, he had imagined his biggest problem was going to be getting anywhere near the mill. Now, seeing the size of it, he realised that finding his team mates was going to be a much taller order.

He repeated his calls as often as he dared. They soared down past a scaffolding tower structure that suddenly lit up and roared with heavy anti-air fire.

They weren't the target. The tower was plugging away at a Shrike dive-bomber that had misjudged its run. But Bonin had been concentrating so hard on steering and guiding, he hadn't even thought about the defence points and towers Ouranberg bristled with.

It was a sudden, sobering thought. Perhaps it was that they presented such a tiny target, perhaps luck was with them, but it now seemed like a miracle that they hadn't been spotted, tracked and fired on by any of the gun emplacements on Gamma dome.

Luck, Bonin decided. He couldn't see it because of the high, covering cirrocumulus, but he was sure his lucky star was still up there somewhere.

However, it wouldn't be for long.

'Brace yourself, Jagdea,' he said

'What? Oh sh–'

They dipped onto a lattice-truss roof in the shadow of mill head, but the angle was bad, the deceleration a little premature, and the roof a good deal steeper than Bonin had judged.

They bounced once, denting the alloy siding hard, and rolled, flying apart. Jagdea bounced again, twice, cried out in pain as the impacts jarred her recently-knitted break, and slithered to the edge of the guttering.

Bonin tried to gun the turbine, but the first impact had buckled the control arm and he couldn't find it. He crashed over the gutter, slammed into the side of a storage tank, and blacked out.

'Nice landing,' he heard Jagdea say as he came round.

She was hunched over him, tugging loose the buckles of his harness.

'Anything broken?'

'I don't think so.'

He sat up. He had landed on a strip of roof between the tank and the raised section where they had first tried to set down. The strip was a tarnished sluice of metal matted with wet filth where the upper roof structures drained water away. Looking round he saw that if he had continued to roll or slide, he would have gone clean off a fifty metre drop into a derrick assembly.

Together, they scrambled up the strip and onto a slab roof behind the tanks. Bonin prepped his lasrifle and Jagdea took out a service issue Navy pistol. He tried the vox again, but there was still no signal from his team.

They hurried west, crossing a walkway over a storage vat full of oily water with a surface sheen like rainbows. Nearby, a cluster of bare metal flues breathed burning gases into the sky.

The vox crackled. Bonin thought it might be Varl and the others, and retuned to get a clearer signal. What he heard then was guttural and nothing like Low Gothic.

He pulled Jagdea into cover just as three Blood Pact troopers in full hostile environment armour appeared on their tail, running up to the far end of the walkway over the vat. Their bobbing crimson bowl-helms reflected brightly in the dark fluid.

One had already seen them, and squeezed off a burst from his lascarbine. The shots thumped into the ducting they were crouched behind.

Bonin took aim. He fired a snap shot that winged the first Blood Pact trooper and checked the advance of the others. They all started shooting, making the ducting ring with the rapid hits.

The trooper he had winged tried to sprint across the walkway as the others covered him. Bonin put a las-round through his shoulder and then another into his iron-masked face. The trooper fell off the walkway loose-limbed and splashed into the vat, throwing up a heavy surge in the viscous liquid.

Bonin grabbed the pilot by the hand and they ran back down the length of the roof towards a row of large heat-exchangers that sprouted from the galvanised panels like dove-cotes. Las-bolts licked through the air around them.

As soon as they were down behind one of the exchangers, Bonin fired again. Two more Blood Pact had appeared on an adjacent roof, firing down from a chain-fenced walkbridge. It wouldn't take long for the four Chaos soldiers to coordinate a crossfire.

Shots spanked into the metal housing of the exchanger. Bonin fired low and hit one of the troopers on the walkbridge in the chest. The man collapsed and hung where his webbing had caught on the chain rail.

Another flurry of rounds slammed into the exchanger, and the entire top casing, a dome of thin metal, was wrenched off. Jagdea fired her pistol, but her aim wasn't great.

A shot ripped past near to Bonin's shoulder. The second man on the walkbridge had moved up, and was close to having the drop on them. There was nowhere to run without risking the steady firing of the advancing pair on their level.

The Blood Pact trooper on the bridge suddenly lurched forward so hard his body snapped the chain rail and he tumbled into the void.

'What the feth...?' Bonin began.

The two on the roof glanced around for a second, puzzled, and in that time a single, fierce las-shot exploded the head of the nearest.

Bonin snatched up his las and fired a burst on auto at the remaining foe. The Blood Pact trooper ducked down again behind a stanchion and didn't reappear.

'Hold your fire, Bonin,' a voice said over the link.

Varl appeared from behind the stanchion, sheathing his warknife.

'We're clear. Banda?'

'Nothing from up here, sarge.'

'Vadim?'

'Clear.'

'Unterrio?'

'Clear also. No movement.'

Varl hurried across to Bonin and Jagdea.

'Gotta move. Come on. Thought we'd lost you.'

They ran after him, up a fire-stair onto an upper roof overlooking the walkbridge.

'How didn't you?' Bonin asked.

'We heard your calls, and followed the signal. The bastards have got men up on the roof. Not because of us, I don't think. They brought down a lot of planes in the raid, and they're checking for ditched air-crew.'

'You sure about that?'

'No,' said Varl.

Banda rose from cover on the upper roof as they clambered up. Bonin was sure her long-las had taken out two of the enemy. 'Nice shooting,' he said.

'S'what they give the shiny medals for,' she returned. She nodded at Jagdea. 'I see you brought a friend,' she remarked ironically.

'Jagdea got us here alive, Banda. Least I could do was return the favour.'

'Gak! Down boy! I was only saying.'

Vadim and Unterrio came up a side-ladder and joined them.

'Good,' said Varl. 'Maybe now we're all finally here, we can get on. Roofscape's crawling with bad guys. I suggest we get inside.'

'You found a way in?' asked Bonin.

Varl looked at him, his eyes staring sarcastically through his visor. 'No we haven't – a) because we were looking for your sorry arse, I don't recall why, and b) because isn't that your job, Mister Scout?'

'Point,' admitted Bonin.

'Can we do it soon?' said Banda. 'This air-bottle's choking me up.'

'Okay, follow Bonin's lead, fireteam cover!' Varl ordered.

Jagdea caught Varl by the sleeve. 'Sergeant. I know I'm... not meant to be here. I think it's best if I stay put and give myself up.'

'No!' said Bonin.

'Like Boney said, commander: no,' Varl agreed.

'I appreciate the loyalty, but I'm not infantry trained, and certainly not covert-skilled like you. I'm dead weight. You should ditch me now. I understood the importance of this mission when I volunteered. I don't want to compromise it.'

'You're coming with us. End of debate,' Varl said.

'I'll take my chances, sergeant–'

'No!' said Varl.

'Commander Jagdea has a point, sergeant,' said Unterrio. 'We will be quicker and safer without her. This operation is too vital to risk. And like me, the commander is a Phantine. We care about the liberation of this world more than we care about our own lives.'

'Listen to Unterrio, sergeant,' said Jagdea. 'You've just killed a search party up here. Leave me for the Blood Pact to find, and I'll tell them it was me. Just a downed pilot. All they're expecting. It'll cover your presence.'

Varl tightened the strap on his U90 thoughtfully. 'I said no, I meant no. For one thing, they'd know you didn't do it unless we leave you with a long-las and a warknife, which I'm not prepared to do, because it would make them ask even more questions. For another... I'm not taking you out of kindness. Have you any idea how savage their interrogations would be? You wouldn't last. None of us would. Your "downed pilot" story would collapse so fething quickly you'd be selling us and your planet and your family. No, commander. No. You're coming. For our sake, not yours.'

For Larisel 2, entry was easy. Huge sections of Beta dome were left punctured and shattered by the raid, and significant parts of it were still on fire. Gathering near the mast array at the dome's apex, the five-member team crossed onto the western side, and roped down to a collapsed roof section that was still issuing flame and smoke.

With Larkin covering them, Mkvenner and Meryn clambered down into the gash and secured the interior space. It was a habitat chamber, totally scorched through. Mkvenner picked his way across toasted carpet and found a door melted into its frame by the heat of the detonation that had blown out the room.

Sergeant Meryn kicked his way through smouldering plyboard and opened a side room that had also been gutted by the blast. A bomb had splintered straight through the floor here and gone off in the level beneath. There was a jagged hole in the flooring next to the atomised remains of a bed or a couch.

'Move down and form up,' Meryn voxed.

Kersherin, Larkin and Kuren dropped down through the roof, and Mkvenner led them through to Meryn. They looked down through the floor hole. Distant sirens were wailing, set off by the multiple breaches to the dome's pressurised shell.

'Nothing for the next two floors,' Mkvenner commented. The bomb had indeed demolished everything beneath them for two floors, partly through its impact and partly through its blast. Larkin glanced up and saw a standard dining fork impaled through a wall beam. The blast had turned even everyday objects into lethal shrapnel.

'Let's rope it,' Meryn decided. Mkvenner secured one end of his line-loop and lowered himself through the smouldering hole in the floor.

They swung down one level. Larkin tried to look away from the two blackened corpses that the detonation had crushed into the wall. The surviving shreds of the floor supported half a bureau, a litter of debris, the scattered pages of a book, and a miraculously unbroken vase.

Another level down and there was a floor again. The surface had been stripped off by extreme heat, and they balanced on the joists. One half of the room, a bed chamber, was eerily untouched. There was a tethwood chair, a shelf with drinking glasses and ornaments, and a good quality carpet that ended suddenly in a singed line where the floor had burned out. Discarded clothes hung over the chair. The only sign of damage in that half of the room was a slight blistering of the paint on the walls.

Mkvenner crossed to the door and opened it a slit. There was a corridor outside, plunged into emergency lighting.

'Let's go!' he voxed, and they followed him out into the hall in a fireteam spread.

Larkin was shaking. It was partly the trauma of the drop, partly combat tension, but mostly the shock of the news that Mkoll hadn't made it. He felt one of his migraine headaches pumping horror into his skull. He'd had the foresight to bring his tablets. Daur, Gaunt and Meryn had all insisted. But with his visor down and working off his air-bottle, he couldn't take one.

They'd got about ten metres down the hallway when a three man emergency crew appeared, dressed in flame retardant white overalls and rebreathers. They panicked at the sight of the troopers and turned to flee.

'Oh, feth. Take them.' Meryn's order was terse but necessary.

Kuren and Kersherin opened fire and cut down the trio. It didn't feel right, Kuren thought. It didn't feel right at all, but they had to preserve their secrecy. Another emergency worker appeared and started running towards the elevator at the end of the hall. He had abandoned a blast victim who lolled on a stretcher in the open doorway of a room.

Mkvenner fired and the worker slammed over against the wall, slid down, and lay for a moment drumming his feet against the deck before he died.

'Feth,' said Mkvenner with distaste.

'We have to blow this hall,' Meryn said. 'They find shot bodies, they'll know we're here as good as if we left these poor fethers to talk. Blow it, and it'll look like a delayed fuse bomb going off.'

Mkvenner nodded and pulled out a couple of tube charges from his musette. Larkin watched, still shaking. This ruthlessness was a side of Corporal Meryn he hadn't seen before. Meryn, one of the younger Ghosts, was an able and reliable soldier. His service record was excellent, but Gaunt had not yet advanced him. Rawne, however, had recently taken Meryn under his wing. Now, it seemed, he was aiming to prove himself, taking no chances that might vitiate successes for the mission. He was doing things the way his hard-arsed mentor Rawne would do them. It wasn't the Meryn Larkin knew. He didn't like it, even though he knew it was the smart way to go.

'Larkin! Come on! We're leaving!' said Meryn, and they hurried down into the stairwell next to the elevator as tube charge blasts blew the hall out of the side of the dome above them.

GAUNT TOOK THE data-slate from his adjutant Beltayn and looked it over. 'Is this confirmed?'

'The data came via Admiral Ornoff.'

As far as the admiral could report, two of the Larisel craft had been destroyed before they had reached the target. Larisel 2 and Larisel 3 had landed. Ornoff believed from pilot reports that some if not all of Larisel 1 had dropped before their Marauder had gone down.

That was something.

Larisel 4 had exploded outright well short of the city. No survivors. No chutes.

'Oh dear God-Emperor,' Gaunt sighed. 'Mkoll.'

Two

FIVE HUNDRED AIR-HORNS simultaneously rasped out a long, bleating note, and workers started to shuffle around Ouranberg's secondary vapour mill in their thousands. It was a shift change, but there would be no rest for the gangs coming off station. Grim tannoy announcements ordered them to collect meal pails from their designated canteens and then assemble at the main bascule. There they would be broken into work details and sent across the causeway to Ouranberg itself, to assist in the rebuild and recovery.

'Failure to report will result in reprisal punishment of all members of an individual's work gang,' the tannoy emphasised over and over. The voice, already distorted by the bass-heavy vox-repeater, had a thick, hard accent and spoke in a monotone as if reading the words without understanding them. 'Reprisal punishment will be immediate. No excuses. Report to the assembly yard of the main bascule in twenty minutes.'

The long, expressionless declaration repeated itself several times, the delays and echoes of the capacious turbine halls turning it into a tuneless canon of overlaps.

No one complained. No one dared. The workers trudged from their posts and filed silently into the wire-caged walks that led away from the mill, while others hobbled in the opposite direction down parallel cage-ways to take their places. The air was thick with dust, and smelled like it was rotting, a byproduct of the ozone and pollutants generated by the mill. Yellowish light glared from mesh-basket lamps, flickered by the turning rotors of the soot-heavy ceiling fans.

Blood Pact personnel, armed with pain-goads and synapse disrupters, walked above the cage-ways on grilled platforms. Some of them, stripped down to black leather bib-overalls and iron masks, restrained leashed packs of snarling cyber-mastiffs with sweat-slick, corded arms and shouted abuse at stragglers. These were brutes from Warlord Slaith's slaver force, a specialised unit of the Blood Pact which enforced the Chaos army's occupation. Their cruel, relentless methods ensured that the captured workforce maintained output and serviced the industries Slaith had conquered. On Gigar, the slavers had worked the captive locals, night and day, for eight weeks, setting their canines on twenty individuals every time one slackened or collapsed. At the end of eight weeks, the wells of Gigar had produced enough promethium to fuel sixty Blood Pact motorised regiments for a year. And the hate-dogs were fat.

The workers of Ouranberg had been reduced to an almost zombie-like state, deprived of sleep, of decent food, of enough fluids. Distinctions of sex and age had vanished. All were swaddled in overalls and rag bandages stiff with grey dust. Coarse canvas hoods or shawls, similarly grey, draped them like monks. They were hunched and submissive. Battered rebreathers and work gauntlets dangled beneath the edges of their shrouds. Raw, black-bandaged feet left limping trails of blood on the dusty floor.

Though Ornoff's persistent bombing campaign might have been hurting Slaith's forces, it was turning the lives of the slave workers from a living hell to something indescribably worse. Every waking hour had to be spent on repair and rebuild work.

Slaith knew an invasion was coming, and he intended to throw it back by making Ouranberg a fortress. It was believed that the slavers were lacing the workers' meagre rations with stimulants to force them into twenty-four hour activity. Already, many had died of convulsive fits, or gone berserk and thrown themselves at the Blood Pact guns.

The air-horns blared again. The tannoy repeated its monotone order. A work crew from the mill's ninth level channeled down the narrow cageway towards the stair flights that would take them to the assembly yard.

Just inside the mouth of the caged walk, a worker stumbled and fell against the chain-fence. A Blood Pact guard on the overhead platform jabbed down with his pain-goad, but the crumpled worker was out of reach. His fellow workers just hurried past him, not wanting to get involved. The slavers pushed their way into the cage, shoving aside the workers who were too slow-moving. The hate-dogs bayed.

'Don't,' hissed Adare, squeezing Milo's arm as they shuffled forward.

Screams echoed down the chamber. One of the Blood Pact started shooting into the crowd.

'Just keep going, for feth's sake,' Adare whispered.

Milo fought back the urge to throw off his filthy shawl and open fire with the U90 lashed tight under his right armpit. The screams were unbearable.

'We're dead if you even think about it,' Adare mumbled.

The members of Larisel 3 moved on with the trudging mob. All of them were shrouded with stolen rags, grey dust rubbed liberally into their hands and kit. Doyl had swathed their boots and lower legs with bandage wraps, and dirt had been rubbed in there too. They walked with shoulders bent.

More shots rang out behind them.

Milo choked back his rage. Peering out from under his hood, he saw a slaver standing just the other side of the chain fence, watching them all file past. Milo was close enough to smell the bastard's rancid body odour, and see the ritual scars on his misshapen hands, the eight-pointed brand of Chaos on his bare sternum. The slaver's iron grotesque seemed to be staring right at him.

Milo tensed his hand around the heavy cannon's trigger grip...

And then they were out, clanging down the metal stairs towards the assembly yard.

The secondary vapour mill was built into a volcanic plug, a sister peak to the main outcrop on which Ouranberg was constructed. It was linked to the main city by a two kilometre long cantilever causeway suspended between the two peaks. From the vast, dirt-filmed windows of the assembly yard, they could see out across the majestic causeway to the monumental, domed bulk of the city. Through cloud-haze, a thousand lights pulsed on masts and stacks and a million more glowed from ribbon windows and observation decks.

The yard was thronging with slave workers. Larisel 3 laced in amongst them. Milo stuck close to Nessa in case she missed a signal from Adare.

'Worship Slaith!' boomed the tannoy suddenly. 'Worship him for he is the overlord!' The Blood Pact cheered throatily, and the workers dutifully raised a suitable moan. 'Worship Slaith, and through your toil and blood, embrace the truth of *Khorne!*'

The very name made some workers wail and sob. Someone screamed. Whips cracked into the crowd. Milo felt his gorge rise and gooseflesh quiver across his hands and arms. That word. That foul, foul word, that name of darkness, an animal cry from the warp. It reeked with evil, far more than the simple combination of letters and sounds could convey. It was like a noise, pitched on a certain frequency, that triggered involuntary fear and revulsion.

Milo had seldom heard the True Names of Chaos spoken aloud. They were forbidden sounds, utterances that human mouths should not make.

He tried to forget it. He was terrified he would remember the name and speak it, or have it burn into his memory. Gaunt had once taught him there were four great names of darkness, that might arise alone, or in combination. Milo had made it a point of personal honour not to know any of them.

'Praise the warp! The warp is the one true way! The names of the warp are a billion and one, and each name is the lament of mankind! Worship the warp! Praise be the warp! Through the power of the warp, the Lord of Change will transmute the galaxy! The warp will engulf all things in a tide of blood!'

Milo sensed Nessa was shaking, and realised with an unexpected pang of fear that she was responding to the sounds even though she couldn't hear the words. He pushed her on through the crowd. He prayed to the God-Emperor of Mankind that the tannoy wouldn't utter that awful word again.

Cardinale had reached the gateway of the yard, where workers pressed in to approach the bascule. He tried to block out the sounds, his hand clamped so tight around his little silver aquila, the wingtips were puncturing his palm. He suddenly registered the pain, and flexed his hand.

Cardinale looked back, trying to find the other members of the team without raising his head. He spotted Adare, and Doyl. There was no sign of the boy or the female sniper.

The gate joined the causeway via the bascule, a massive ironwork drawbridge lowered on thick chains from the winch house overhanging the drop. As its great bulk dropped down with a shuddering crash, Blood Pact slavers started to whip the workers into line. They opened the gate's barred shutter.

An electro-lash caught the back of Cardinale's calf and he fell to one knee as his leg spasmed.

'Up! Up!' a nearby slaver roared, though his hoarse snarls were mainly directed at the workers who had been completely knocked down by the whip.

Cardinale felt a strong hand support his arm and he got to his feet. Doyl was right next to him.

'Your leg?' the scout whispered.

'It'll be fine. We have to get through this gate.'

'I know.' Doyl turned and saw Adare a few rows behind them.

'First fifty!' yelled a slaver, speaking, like the tannoy, in a language unfamiliar to him. 'First fifty to Beta dome!'

Whips cracked and they spilled through onto the bascule and the causeway beyond. The causeway was a rockcrete thoroughfare broad enough to take a cargo truck. It was roofed with pressurised, wire-reinforced glassite and lit by crude strip lamps buried in the walls.

'Are they with us?' Adare whispered.

'Yeah,' replied Doyl. 'Don't look round. Milo and Nessa are about twenty metres back. I saw them both.'

There was a hold-up. Slavers drove the work gangs against the causeway wall in single file to let a cargo transport speed through. Cardinale took the opportunity of the pause to stoop and rub his aching calf.

'Oh shit,' he said suddenly.

'What?'

Cardinale started to search his pockets and the folds of his clothing. The slender chain was still wrapped around his hand, but it was broken. The silver aquila was gone.

'Move! Move!' a slaver screamed now the transport had passed. The workers resumed their march over the causeway.

'It must have snapped off,' Cardinale said.

'Never mind that. It doesn't matter,' Adare said.

'What if they find it?' Cardinale said, rubbing at the wingtip punctures in his palm flesh.

'Shut up, all right? Let me worry about that.'

They were halfway across the causeway.

Okay? Milo signed surreptitiously to Nessa.

I'm fine. That was scary.

True.

They were coming up on the entry porta to Ouranberg, the cyclopean gate house that defended the causeway and the northern approaches. Blood Pact banners fluttered from the batteries.

Nearly there.

In the assembly yard, with the tannoy still screaming out its noxious sermon, one of the slavers yanked on his hate-dog's chain. It was worrying at the filthy flagstones.

It had found something.

The slaver hunched over and raked his scarred fingers through the greasy muck. Something silver glittered.

A tiny double-eagle. An aquila. An Imperial totem.

'Alarm!' he screamed, ejecting spittle from between his rotten teeth. 'Alarm! Alarm!'

SIRENS BEGAN TO whoop. The mass of slaves on the causeway looked round in panic as the strip lights in the wall started to flash amber. The porta into Ouranberg was so close.

'Keep going!' Adare said.

'What do we do?' Cardinale stammered.

'Keep going, like I said. We're nearly there! Keep going and lock and load!'

The trio elbowed their way through the milling workers, closing on the gateway.

Behind them, Blood Pact soldiers were surging out across the bascule onto the causeway, pushing aside mill workers, or simply gunning them down. There was a terrible howling. The hate-dogs had been unleashed.

* * *

'COME ON!' MILO urged Nessa, squeezing her arm.

She surprised him by pulling back.

'No!' she said aloud. She dragged him back against the causeway wall amongst the cowering workers, and pulled his hood down over his head.

Nessa had fought the Verghast hive war as a scratch company guerilla. She knew how to mingle in the ordinary, how to hide in plain sight. Though his gut instinct told him to run, Milo remembered that, and trusted her.

He bowed his head.

Blood Pact troopers and slavers rushed past them, kicking down anyone foolish enough to get in their way. The hate-dogs, trailing ropes of drool, bounded ahead of them, baying, making the air stink with their rancid pelts.

Two confused mill workers were gunned down right in front of Milo and Nessa by the Blood Pact. Their bodies lay crumpled in spreading lakes of blood, kicked and trampled by the Chaos troopers who rushed after.

INSIDE THE PORTA, alarms were also ringing. Enemy troops, their iron masks glaring, were corralling all the slaves who had crossed the causeway to one side of the entrance hall. They were shouting and gesturing with their weapons.

'Feth!' said Adare as they came through the gateway, setting foot on Ouranberg proper for the first time.

'Go with the flow,' Doyl urged. 'Get in line and don't draw attention to yourself.'

They could all hear the howling coming closer.

'The dogs! The damned dogs!' Cardinale whined. 'They've got my scent–'

'Forget it!' Doyl said as loudly as he dared.

'We have to go active,' Cardinale said, fear in his voice.

'You fething well won't until I say, Phantine!' Adare growled. 'Get over! Over to the side with the other workers!'

'But the dogs!'

The dogs were on them, bursting through the screaming workers in the gateway, surging in towards them.

'Holy Emperor!' Cardinale yelled. He pushed Adare aside.

'Oh feth! No! Don't! Don't!' Adare shouted. 'In the name of the Golden Throne, Cardinale–'

Cardinale threw back his cloak disguise and wheeled round, firing his lasrifle on full auto at the bounding hate-dogs.

He blew three of them apart, two in mid-air. The fourth, a two hundred pound cyber-mastiff, barrelled into him and smashed him to the floor. Its steel jaws tore into the left side of his face.

'Active!' Adare bellowed, all hope lost. 'Go active, Doyl! We've no fething choice!'

Sergeant Adare wrenched out his lasrifle and blasted the dog off Cardinale point-blank.

Doyl swept round and raked the nearby Blood Pact guards with his own rifle.

Cardinale was screaming. Blood was pouring out of his torn neck. Adare grabbed him, his hands becoming slick with the Phantine's gore.

'Go! Go!' Doyl yelled, shooting dead two more of the approaching dog-pack. A third hate-dog fled, howling, dragging a foreleg.

'Get him clear, sarge! Get him clear!' Doyl cried. He blasted his weapon in a wide arc that toppled two Blood Pact sentries out of an autocannon nest overlooking the porta's entrance hall.

The slaves were shrieking and running in panic. Adare dragged Cardinale to his feet and fired his lasrifle one-handed. Doyl started cutting a desperate path for them through the frenetic mob. If they could get clear and just find somewhere to hide...

Doyl recoiled as a las-round creased his forehead. Blood started to trickle into his eyes. Cursing, he pulled out a tube charge, ripped off the det-tape and hurled it to his left. The concussive blast hurled three Blood Pact infantrymen into the air and added to the wild confusion.

Firing indiscriminately at anything that looked like a Chaos trooper, Adare cut a swathe through the press towards the north-west exit of the entrance hall. He was virtually carrying Cardinale by then. Mill workers fled in terror before him.

'Doyl! This way! Out this way! Come on!' Adare shouted.

Doyl, half-blinded by his own blood, followed Adare's voice. He had to push and kick slaves out of his way. Several of them collided mindlessly with him.

'Adare!'

'Come on, Doyl!'

Autocannon fire chopped into the crowd, and felled a dozen workers. Doyl could smell fycelene and the metallic scent of blood. The cannon rattled again.

Wiping the back of his sleeve across his eyes, Doyl turned back, dropped to one knee, and aimed at the source of the heavy fire. Blood Pact troopers were shooting their way through the pandemonium of slaves. One had a support cannon on a bipod, and a slaver ran beside him, feeding belts of ammunition. The jagged muzzle flashes of the cannon illuminated the gun's brutal work like a strobe light. Each flare froze a snapshot of lurching figures, slaves falling, knocked off their feet, crashing into one another

Doyl managed to shoot the gunner through the throat before his wound blinded him again. Adare had reached the north-east exit, and stumbled into the doorway, spilling Cardinale over. He scrambled up and lobbed a grenade high over Doyl's head into the mob of enemy troopers.

'Come on!' Adare screamed at Doyl over the crump-whoosh of the grenade. 'We can still do this! First and Only! First and fething Only!'

Doyl ran towards Adare's cry.

Together, they broke out into a wide stone tunnel leading off from the entrance hall. Smoke from the main hall was blowing in and pooling under the arched roof. Slaves were staggering, stunned, everywhere.

'We're clear!' Adare said to Doyl. 'Help me with him!'

They each seized one of Cardinale's wrists and started to drag him. Doyl tried not to look at the Phantine's ruined face.

'Which way?' Adare asked.

'Left,' said Doyl.

They had only gone a few metres when a las-round caught Adare in the knee and knocked him over. Blood Pact squads were clattering into the tunnel from a side passage ahead of them.

'Feth!' Doyl despaired. He let go of Cardinale and fired from the hip and scored two hits. There were so many Blood Pact and so little cover they weren't hard to hit.

Neither am I, Doyl thought.

The enemy squads were firing as they charged. Hard rounds and las-bolts cracked and whined around the three Imperials. Doyl felt one pass through his cape and another kiss painfully across his thigh. Stone chips peppered his face from a ricochet off the tunnel wall.

Adare started shooting from a prone position, and the sergeant's efforts were suddenly bolstered by Cardinale. Soaked in his own blood, ignoring his wounds, the Phantine had struggled to his feet. He stood, swaying slightly, at Doyl's side, mowing down the cult warriors with haphazard bursts.

'Brace for det!' Doyl cried, and tossed another tube charge down the tunnel into the charge. The fireball collapsed part of the roof and buried the Blood Pact squads in masonry. A crimson bowl-helmet came spinning out of the blast and bounced off the tunnel wall.

'Cardinale! You hear me? You hear me? We can still make this!' Adare urged, trying to rise.

Cardinale nodded, unsteady on his feet.

'Back that way,' Adare ordered. 'Back down the tunnel!'

'Okay,' said Doyl. 'Okay, but we need to go to ground. We can't survive out in the open like this.'

'Agreed!' said Adare. He turned, his next words drowned by a buzzing roar.

Adare's chest exploded and he was slammed back against the wall with enough force to splinter bone. Hundreds of tiny, secondary impacts simultaneously peppered the stonework.

Doyl staggered backwards, trying to shield Cardinale. The Phantine had collapsed again. Doyl was sure Cardinale was dead. The scout could suddenly smell an odour of rancid milk mixed with mint.

The beast was moving so fast the Tanith scout could barely follow it. Using its dewclaws to grip the stones, it skittered along the tunnel roof, upside down. An armature frame of augmetic servo-limbs clamped around its torso automatically racked the xenos-pattern flechette blaster it had used to slay Adare. A crude leather bandolier dangled from its gleaming, mottled body. It gazed down its wattled snout at Doyl, doubled han lids flickering across its milky eyes protectively.

Doyl raked it with las-fire.

It barely flinched.

Doyl screamed and fired again. He emptied his size three clip into the beast until the power was gone.

It grabbed him by the throat with one of its powerful forelimbs and lifted him up. He gagged.

'The Emperor protects,' Doyl choked just before the loxatl pushed the muzzle of its flechette blaster into his eye and fired.

'MOVE THROUGH! MOVE through!' the slavers raged, making free use of their goads and lashes. Rounded up again, the slave details filed through into the entrance hall. The place was littered with debris and blood. Heretic troopers were dragging corpses away.

Are they...? Nessa signed.

Don't think about it, Milo replied. *It's down to us now.*

Following the crowd, heads down, the two survivors of Larisel 3 shuffled into the city.

VARL'S TEAM PROGRESSED steadily down through Ouranberg's main vapour mill complex, following back stairs and sub-corridors. Several times, they had to conceal themselves to avoid roaming patrols or hurrying work-gangs.

Bonin led the way. They'd ditched their extra jump kit, helmets and mail smocks, and the Ghosts had put on their stealth-cloaks. Varl had draped scrim-nets over Unterrio and Jagdea and smeared a little camo-paint on the pilot's face.

From all directions, the mill rang with the sounds of heavy labour. Drills chattered. Hoists whirred. Turbines rumbled and shook.

The tactical briefing had presumed Slaith to be secure somewhere in Alpha dome. Varl considered it a priority to obtain more specific information. Twice they stopped while Unterrio tried patching his data-slate into a city-system terminal, but it was futile. Slaith's forces had corrupted the Imperial database and flooded it with incompatible, unreadable sequences.

They crossed a series of storage halls, and skirted the edge of an air-wharf. Here, they had to wait in hiding for almost fifteen minutes while servitors loaded a cargo carrier. Only when the carrier lifted off the pad and flew off in the direction of the Alpha dome did the wharf clear, allowing them to continue. Banda paused to check a roster board hanging from one of the wharf's roof supports.

'Regular shipments to the Alpha dome,' she said. 'Every couple of hours.'

Varl nodded. He glanced at Jagdea. 'Could you handle one of those bulk carriers?'

'Yes,' she said.

They pressed on, but the way was blocked. Work-gangs under armed guard were clearing bomb damage from the next manufactory space. Bonin doubled them back, only to hear more escorted gangs tramping down the access tunnel in their direction.

'Feth!' Varl said. They were boxed in.

'Here! In here!' Bonin hissed. He'd forced the lock on a side door. They hurried through and he closed it behind them. They were in a small storeroom for machine parts. It stank of oil-based lubricant. Varl and Bonin flanked the door, weapons ready, listening to the feet marching past outside.

They could hear rough voices, and a series of vox-exchanges. Several individuals had stopped to converse just outside the door.

Vadim pushed to the back of the store. He quietly cleared some plyboard boxes from a grubby bench and hoisted himself up to reach a small fan-light window high in the wall. The window was crazed with dirt, and he had to use his pry-bar to move the latch.

Looks promising, he signed. Varl and the other Ghosts nodded. Jagdea and Unterrio, unfamiliar with gestures, frowned.

You first, I'll cover. Get those three through and Vadim after them, Varl's hands wrote in the air deftly. Bonin gave him a thumbs-up and went to the back of the room, taking Vadim's place on the bench. He squinted through the fanlight and felt cool air on his face. The little window looked out onto a circulation space between mill houses. He wedged the window open as wide as it would go with his warknife, and slithered through head first.

At the door, Varl watched Bonin's boots disappear. The voices outside were still arguing, but seemed to be moving away.

Bonin's face reappeared at the window and he reached an arm down. Banda got up, pushed her long-las through the gap and hauled herself after it. Vadim boosted her feet to help her on her way.

He turned and waved Jagdea up.

With Vadim pushing her feet, she was nimble enough, but the scrim-net Varl had insisted she wear snagged on the edge of the window frame.

She struggled, pinned. Vadim got up on the bench next to her and tried to unhook the netting. His efforts shook the old bench and wobbled the tall, spares-laden shelving next to it.

Varl kept glancing back. *Hurry the feth up!* he mouthed at Vadim. He was sure the harsh voices outside were getting closer again. He flexed his augmetic shoulder and adjusted his grip on the heavy U90.

Vadim drew his warknife and slit through the net, freeing Jagdea. She slithered out through the window, but the sudden motion of her release shook the bench again. Vadim swayed, and the shelf rocked.

A tin canister full of rivets dropped off the top shelf.

Varl saw it fall as if in slow motion. He closed his eyes, waiting for the inevitable.

There was no sound. He looked again. Unterrio had caught the canister a few centimetres from the rockcrete floor. The look of heart-stopped relief on the faces of Vadim and Unterrio almost made Varl burst out laughing.

Unterrio exited next. In the light of Jagdea's difficulties, he had the sense to take off his scrim-net and bundle it through the window ahead of him.

Vadim, crouching on the bench, looked back at Varl and beckoned him.

You go, Varl mouthed. He looked back at the door and then pressed his ear to it. The voices were right outside now. Right out fething side.

Bonin had broken the door lock to get them in, but Varl noticed a bolt, which he gingerly drew into place. He backed slowly from the door, keeping his gun aimed at it.

Vadim was through the window. He leaned back in to pull Varl up. Keeping his gun on the door, Varl sat on the bench and slowly drew his feet up. His left boot brushed the edge of the shelf.

Two litre-capacity flasks of lamp oil toppled and smashed on the storeroom floor.

Varl couldn't believe he'd been so stupid.

He could hear the voices, and saw the latch being waggled furiously.

'Come on!' Vadim hissed.

There was a hammering on the door now. Kicking. Shouting.

Then shots. The metal of the door around the latch deformed and burst under the impact of several las-rounds. The bolt still held.

Whoever was on the outside now opened fire directly at the door, punching six molten holes. Penetrating the door metal had robbed the las-rounds of most of their power, but they still had enough force to wind Varl and smash him off the bench.

'Varl!' Vadim shouted. Multiple holes now riddled the door and sparking las-shots rained into the storeroom.

'Feth!' said Varl. He was badly bruised on his shoulders and the backs of his legs from the hits. He got up, aimed his U90 at the door and opened fire, bracing against the recoil.

His weapon was loaded with a clip of standard .45 calibre rounds. Striking the metal door, they dented its surface wildly, but few penetrated. An answering storm of fire punished the door from the other side.

Varl popped the yellow-tagged drum out of his weapon, replaced it with a red, racked back the bolt, and blitzed the door with explosive armour piercing rounds. They went through the door like it was made of wet paper. The surrounding wall too. The explosive bullets blew bricks and metal shreds out into the corridor.

Varl turned, tossed the gun up to Vadim, and threw himself up through the fan-light.

An alarm was ringing. It was quickly answered by another. Larisel 1 dashed across the circulation space and towards a gulley that formed the waste-gutter for a small foundry.

'Not that way!' Bonin ordered, already spotting two guard towers on the far side of the foundry. 'Down here!' Another gulley, but it was piled with precast tiles for roofing repairs.

'Good one, Boney. There's no way through,' Banda said.

'Yes, there is,' Vadim announced and got up on the nearest pile of slabs without breaking stride. His sure-footed climbing skills exceeded theirs, but they followed, making it up to the top of a wall, and from there onto the pitched roof of a walkway cloister.

They hid under the tarpaulin covers of a barrel stack in the next work-yard.

'I think we had better lie low for a while,' Bonin said.

'Yeah,' panted Varl, 'and then I think we go back to that wharf.'

MERYN'S TEAM, LARISEL 2, was the first to see the face of Sagittar Slaith. Every street and plaza in Beta dome had its public address screens and pict-plates tuned to a mesmerisingly grim live feed of various Blood Pact preachers gibbering blasphemies and extolling the virtues of their daemonic faith. The broadcasts were constant and relentless, captured by a fuzzy, handheld viewer that regularly went out of focus trying to remain trained on the capering, lunging hierarchs. They were painted, pierced devils, ranting in a mix of their own warp-twisted language and bastardised Low Gothic. Some would preach for hours at a time, twitching and spasming as if they were thrashing through narcotic highs. Others would scream hysterically for a few short minutes before disappearing. The pict image would then jump and flicker as it cut to the next preacher.

The members of Larisel 2 tried to ignore the broadcasts, but they were pretty much inescapable. They echoed and rang around every street and access tunnel.

Of the team, Larkin was the most disturbed by the transmissions. On the way down through the bombed sections of the upper habs, they had ditched their jump kit and, freed of the visored helmet, Larkin had at last been able to take some of his powerful anticonvulsants. He felt better for a while, but the migraine itself merely subsided. It kept rumbling around the edges of his brain like a storm that refused to break.

Once they got into the primary sector levels, there was a pict-address plate on every other corner. Larisel 2 hugged back streets, sub-walkways and deserted yards, but there was no respite from the blaring voices and jerking pictures. Larkin felt his stress levels soaring, and the migraine began to boil up again.

The comprehensible, Low Gothic parts of the sermons were bad. The speech used, the concepts, the ideas, were all hard to take and often shocking. But the gabbled warp-words were much worse, as far as Larkin was concerned. His mind knotted as it imagined the meanings.

Worst of all, what really chilled Larkin, was the sight of Ouranberg citizens, ragged, often weeping, watching the broadcasts. They seemed to be under no duress. They simply stood at street corners, in squares and wide commercial parades, gazing at the screens, their minds gradually corroding under the poisonous bombardment of warp-lies.

Mkvenner steered them well. He had an unerring instinct for avoiding foot patrols, and swept them into cover each time a speeder went over. They stayed out of sight of crowds, and only once had to silence an individual who spotted them. A middle-aged man had simply walked out into a yard as they were sprinting across it. He had stared at them without saying a word and then just turned and wandered back into his hab.

Meryn had broken from the group and followed the man into the building. A few minutes later, he re-emerged and they moved on.

No one asked Meryn what he'd done. Everyone knew. Everyone knew it was absolutely paramount to maintain the mission's secrecy for as long as possible. It was a necessary evil. Just like shooting the rescue crews. A necessary evil.

Larkin didn't like it much at all. 'Necessary evil' seemed to him to be one of those too-clever phrases men used to excuse wrongs. And there was quite enough unnecessary evil in the fething galaxy without deliberately adding to it.

On balance, what he really didn't like was the fact that Meryn showed no emotion. He remained calm, unexpressive. Probably a quality Rawne, maybe even Gaunt, would admire as utterly professional devotion to duty. But Larkin thought that he might feel easier about stuff if Meryn showed just one ounce of regret or upset.

Just before dawn on the 224th, they stopped for a rest break, taking shelter on the first floor of an abandoned weaver's. Once the day cycle started, movement would be restricted, and they needed to get some bag-rations inside them and catch some sleep. The weaver's premises, which had been looted and then boarded up, overlooked a small municipal square full of burned-out vehicles and litters of debris. A public-address screen on the opposite side of the square boomed out the latest tirade of Slaith's preachers. Citizens stood around oil can fires gazing at the broadcast.

They ate, then Kuren took the first watch.

He woke them all after about two hours. It was still dark outside. The lamps that should have cut in automatically at the start of the day cycle had been shot out. Ouranberg seemed to be locked into a permanent twilight, which Mkvenner realised would help their progress immensely.

Kuren had woken them because of the broadcasts.

The preachers had shut up, and a good fifteen minutes had gone by with nothing on the screen but white noise.

Then Sagittar Slaith had appeared.

He was utterly terrifying.

They had been shown a few blurry longshots of a being believed to be Slaith during the pre-mission briefings, vague suggestions of someone tall and heavy-set, but nothing that could be called a likeness.

The face on the screen was entirely hairless: bald, shaven, lacking even eyebrows and lashes. His ears were grossly distended by the weight and number of the studs and rings that pierced them. They looked like a lizard's frill. Slaith's teeth were chrome triangles, like the tips of daggers. Three huge and old diagonal scars marked each cheek, ritual cuts made to seal his pact with Urlock Gaur. He wore a white fur cloak over a spiked suit of maroon power-armour. His eyes were pupil-less white slits.

His voice was the soft, muffled throb of a nightmare that had woken the sleeper in terror with no clear memory of why he was afraid.

He spoke to them. Directly to them. He used Low Gothic haltingly.

'Imperial soldiers. I know you are here. I know you are here in my city uninvited. Creeping like vermin in the shadows. I can smell you.'

'Feth!' stammered Larkin. Meryn shushed him.

'You will die,' Slaith continued. His eyes never blinked. 'You will die soon. You are beginning to die already. A hundred thousand agonies will carry you to your graves. Your death-screams will shake the Golden Throne and wake that rancid old puppet you claim to serve. I will cut your flesh and make you swear the Blood Pact. I will burn your hearts on the altar of Chaos. I will send your souls to the warp where my lord, the Blood God, mighty Korne, will remake you in his image. His alchemy will reforge your souls in the beauty of eternal darkness, where His Pain will be yours forever.'

At the mention of the forbidden name, Larkin felt his senses sway. He grew feverishly hot. He saw that the others had all gone pale. Kersherin was gulping hard, trying not to vomit.

'Give up your futile mission now, and I will grant you the mercy of a quick death. You have an hour.' Slaith glanced away, as if talking to someone off-camera, and then looked back. 'Slaves, dwellers in this place, hear me now. Search your habitats, your workplaces, your storehouses. Search your cellars and attics, your granaries and pantries. Find the uninvited Imperial vermin. It is your duty. Any amongst you I find to have aided them or sheltered them will suffer at my hands, and their kith and kin besides. Those that come forward to give up the Imperial vermin will be blessed in my eyes. Their rewards will be the greatest I can bestow. They will be honoured as my own blood kindred, for they will have shown true loyalty to my lord the Blood God.'

The screen view suddenly jolted and panned around, refocusing. The Ghosts caught a glimpse of a finely appointed chamber, backed by vast windows that looked out on a ruined statue. Then Slaith's fur-wrapped back filled the screen, the viewer following him across the chamber. He moved aside. The image blurred and refocused again.

The men of Larisel 2 caught their breaths.

Three bodies lay twisted on the floor under one of the windows. Two were unmistakably wearing Tanith uniform and unmistakably dead. Vast, ruinous wounds rendered them unrecognisable. Blood soaked the carpet under them. Sprawled across them was a mutilated man, naked except for Phantine-issue combat pants. He also looked dead, but he winced and writhed as Slaith slapped him with a steel-shod fist.

It was Cardinale. His face was a torn mask of blood. His wrists and ankles were bound with razor-wire.

'Sacred feth,' said Meryn.

'See how I know you are here, Imperial vermin. Your fellows are already discovered and broken. Your cause is lost.'

Slaith looked back at the screen. 'One hour,' he said and the picture went dead.

The screen fuzzed and rolled for a long while. They all jumped as another preacher suddenly appeared, howling out a stream of profanities.

Larkin's hands were shaking badly. His mouth was dry.

'They got Larisel 3,' Meryn said.

'Those bodies? Milo? Doyl?' Kuren asked quietly.

Mkvenner shrugged. 'Maybe. Maybe one of them was Adare.'

'So some of team 3 might have got clear?' Kuren pressed hopefully.

'Unless there wasn't enough left of the others to find,' said Mkvenner.

'I can't sleep now,' said Meryn. 'Not after that. Let's just get on. Let's find that bastard. Okay?'

Kersherin and Mkvenner nodded. 'Yeah,' Kuren agreed, his head bowed.

'Larkin? Okay with you?'

Larkin looked up at Meryn. 'Yes. Let's get on with it.'

THE STACKS OF Ouranberg's waste gas burners lay out to the north and west of the city, built up on slender crags of rock. Heavy pipelines carried by vast trestle frames of ironwork girders, some over four kilometres long, linked them to the main city structure. The burners themselves were fat, kiln-like brick chimneys twenty metres in diameter, capped with blackened-metal ignition frames.

It was mid-morning on the 224th. The sky was a blinding bowl of topaz altostratus and the morning pollution banks welling up from the Scald were dissolving into yellowish vapours as the headwind gathered force. Ominous clouds gathered in the western distances.

Ouranberg was three kilometres away at the end of a vast span of rusty girderwork. The city was still immense. Sunlight flared and glinted off its ribbons of windows. Thin black smoke, like smudged thumbprints, rose from the domes.

Out of breath from the last stint of climbing, he sat back on a thin ledge of rock about fifty metres from the top of the stack, one boot braced to stop the wind sweeping him off. The burner high above him hummed as the wind blew through the cavities of its burner brackets and every ten minutes or so there was a gigantic whoosh as gas ignited and blistered up into the sky. Cinders floated down like snowflakes.

His air bottle had long since been spent, and he was forced to use the helmet's rudimentary rebreather. That meant every lungful came in moist and warm, and it was impossible to breathe deeply. This was a climb that would have been hard even in clean air conditions. He'd sweated off about two kilos already. His head ached from oxygen starvation. His hands and knees and feet, despite gloves, reinforced leggings and boots, were bloody and raw.

He started to climb again, and managed about ten metres. That put him almost on a level with the bottom spars of the pipeline's scaffold. He lifted his visor quickly to suck water from his flask, and then lowered it. The temptation to inhale the cold air outside was almost overwhelming.

He clambered to the edge of the scaffolding. It had looked slender from a distance, but now he was up close, he appreciated the titanic scale of the I-beams and girder spars. Climbing it wouldn't be easy. The spars were far too wide apart. He would have to belly along the girders, hand over hand.

And reach Ouranberg sometime next century.

The alternative was to keep climbing and cross the bridge along the pipeline. That meant going vertically up the increasingly sheer rock stack for another forty metres or so.

He tested the tension on the rope that played out beneath him. There wasn't much give, so he spent ten minutes hoisting the kit up to his level. Climbing with full kit on would have been out of the question. He'd been forced to lash it together and drag it up after him every time he reached the limit of the rope. If only his jump-pack hadn't been crippled in the drop. He keyed his micro-bead and tried another call.

'Larisel, Larisel, do you read?'

Nothing.

'Larisel, Larisel, over.'

Still nothing. He knew he was well out of range but still he couldn't resist trying every now and then.

'Larisel, Larisel... this is Mkoll. Do you read? Do you read?'

Three

THEY WERE ON the countdown for the invasion now. O-Day. Operation Thunderhead. Just over a day away.

Gaunt and Rawne joined Lord General Van Voytz and the officers of the Urdeshi and the Phantine to review the mustered ranks of the Krassian Sixth. They were a newly founded regiment, out of the recently liberated agri-world Krassia in the Rimward Marginals. Two thousand men in copper-coloured battledress and grey shakos. Their commanding officer, Colonel Dalglesh, was a PDF veteran with beetle brows and a spectacular handlebar moustache.

'A fine bunch of men, colonel,' Gaunt told him at the end of the inspection.

'Thank you, sir,' Dalglesh said, appearing to be genuinely pleased. 'May I say, it is an honour to be serving with you.'

Gaunt raised an eyebrow.

'Truly, sir,' Dalglesh said. 'The reputation of the Tanith First is considerable. Krassia was settled thanks to the Martyr's crusade. Your work in her name on Hagia Shrineworld is regarded with great esteem amongst my people.'

'Thank you,' said Gaunt. 'It's always nice to be appreciated.'

'It's always novel to be appreciated,' Rawne murmured behind him.

Gaunt's micro-bead trilled.

'Excuse me, colonel... Gaunt, go ahead?'

'Colonel-commissar, it's Curth. You'd better get up to the infirmary.'

ANA CURTH SET down the vox-mic and hurried back down the corridor to the intensive ward. She pushed her way through the crowd of orderlies, nurses and walking wounded that had gathered in the doorway.

Dorden looked round at her. 'Did you reach him?'

'He's on his way now.'

Dorden turned back into the room. 'Did you find him like this?'

She shook her head. 'I found his bed empty. He'd pulled the drips out. We started to search for him and Lesp found him in here.'

Dorden took a step towards the cot where Corbec lay half curled in a sleep that the doctor doubted he would ever wake from.

Agun Soric, naked except for a sheet and the heavy wrap of bandages around his bulky torso, was sitting on a stool next to the colonel's cot, his head on Corbec's chest. His skin was dimpled with blood-blisters where the drips had been attached, and with the puckered white marks left by the adhesive tape that had held them in place.

Soric raised his head as Dorden approached, and slowly lifted the laspistol so that it was aimed at Dorden's belly.

'Not another step.'

'Hey now, Agun. Easy. Calm yourself.'

Soric's one good eye was bleary. He'd been unconscious for many days. Given the extent of his chest wound, Dorden wasn't sure how he was managing to remain alive divorced from the life support apparatus.

'Doc,' he murmured, as if he was recognising Dorden for the first time.

'It's me, Agun. What's with the weapon?'

Soric looked at the laspistol as if he was surprised to find himself holding it. Then some realisation crossed his face.

'Daemons,' he hissed.

'Daemons?'

'All around. All around in the air. I had a dream. They're coming to take Colm. Coming for him. I dreamt it. They're coming for him. In his bloodstream, chewing like rats. Nnh! Nnh! Nnh!' Soric made a graphic gnawing sound.

'And you're going to fight them, Agun? With the gun?'

'If I gakking well have to!' Soric said. He swung his head round awkwardly and focused on Corbec. 'He's not ready to die. It's not his time.'

Dorden hesitated. He remembered, with an unnerving clarity, Sergeant Varl saying the same thing.

'No, he's not ready, Agun,' Dorden agreed.

'I know. I dreamt it. But the daemon rats. They don't know. They're chewing at him.' Soric made the gnawing sound again, and then coughed.

'I'd shoot them if I could,' he added.

'Where the hell did he get a weapon?' murmured someone in the huddle of onlookers.

'Who's that?' demanded Soric loudly, looking up alertly and raising the gun. 'Daemons? More daemons? I dreamt about daemons!'

'No daemons, Agun! No daemons!' placated Dorden.

'Get them out of here,' he hissed at Curth.

'Move! Now!' Curth ordered, herding the bystanders out. She drew the screen behind them and looked back at Dorden.

'How is he still alive?' she whispered.

'Because I'm a tough old bastard, lovely Surgeon Curth,' Soric answered. 'Vervun Smeltery One, man and boy, ahh. Hardens you up, it does, smeltery work. She's a lovely girl, isn't she, doc? A lovely, lovely girl.'

'I've always thought so,' Dorden said calmly. 'Why don't you give me the laspistol, Agun? Maybe I can shoot these daemon rats?'

'Oh no!' Soric said. 'That wouldn't be fair on you, doc. You don't use guns. Always admired that in you. Life-saver. Not a life-taker.'

'Why don't I take it then, Agun?' Curth asked gently. 'Back in basic PDF training, I was top of my class at small arms. I bet I could nail those rats for you.'

Soric looked at her. With astonishing deftness, he spun the pistol in his paw so that the grip was suddenly pointing at her. 'Off you go then,' he said. 'Lovely, lovely girl,' he added sidelong to Dorden.

'Oh, I know,' said Dorden, breathing out.

Curth took the weapon gingerly and tossed it into a laundry bin.

'Let me look you over,' said Curth.

'No, I'm fine,' said the old Verghastite.

'I just want to check the rats aren't chewing at you too.'

'Hnnh. Okay.' He coughed again, and Dorden saw the spots of blood that speckled the cot sheets. Soric seemed to slump a little.

Curth went behind Soric and did a bimanual exam of his torso.

'Feth! He's respiring on both lungs! How is that possible?'

'Clearly?' asked Dorden, unconvinced.

'No... there's a fluid mass.' She took out her stethoscope and pressed the cup to Soric's back. 'But not much. This is amazing.'

'Absolutely,' Dorden whispered.

'Forget me, I'm fine,' said Soric, rousing suddenly and coughing again. 'The dream told me I would be fine. The dream made me fine. Said I had to be fine so's I could get up and keep the daemons away from Colm. They want his soul, doc. They're chewing in.'

'The dream told you that?'

Soric nodded. 'Did I tell you my great grandmother was a witch?'

Curth and Dorden both hesitated.

'A witch?' echoed Dorden.

'Had the second sight, most peculiar it was. Earned her keep in the out-habs for years, telling fortunes.'

'Like... a psyker?' Curth asked.

'Gak me, no!' Soric spluttered. 'Lovely, girl, but very foolish, eh, doc? My dear Ana, if my sainted old grandma had been a psyker, she'd have been gathered up by the Black Ships, wouldn't she? Gathered up by the Black Ships or shot as a heretic. No, no... she was a witch. She had a harmless knack of seeing the future. In dreams mostly. My old mam said I'd inherit the talent, being the seventh son of a seventh son, but I've not had so much as a twinge of it me whole life.'

'Until now,' he added.

'You dreamed Corbec had daemons chewing at him?' asked Curth.

'Clear as you like, that's what the dream said.'

'In his blood?'

'As you say.'

'And the dream said you'd come back to life so you could prevent that? Prevent the daemons carrying Colm off?'

'Yes, lady.'

Curth looked over at Dorden. 'Find Lesp. Have him do a toxicological spread test on Corbec.'

'You're kidding,' Dorden said.

'Just find Lesp, Tolin.'

'No need. I can do a tox-spread myself.'

'I had other dreams,' Soric said. His voice was distant now, as if he had exhausted himself.

'We need to get you back to bed, Agun,' Curth hushed. 'The dream will only heal you if you help it by resting.'

'Okay. Lovely, lovely girl, doc.'

Curth helped Soric to his feet as Dorden stripped sterile wraps off the instruments he was about to use on Corbec.

'Bad dreams,' Soric mumbled.

'I'm sure they were.'

'I saw Doyl. And Adare. They're dead. Breaks my heart. Both dead. And the cardinal is in terrible pain.'

'The cardinal?'

'Terrible pain. But tell Gaunt... Mkoll's not dead.'

Curth glanced at Dorden. She saw the look in his eyes. Torn between hope and dismissal.

'Come on, Agun,' she said.

'Lovely, lovely girl,' Soric mumbled. He sagged and collapsed.

'Lesp! Lesp!' Curth yelled.

By the time Gaunt reached the infirmary, Soric was strapped into a cot and back on life support.

'He said *what?*'

'He said daemons were after Corbec. And that he'd dreamed Doyl and Adare were dead, but Mkoll was alive. And he said something about the cardinal being in terrible pain.'

'The who?'

'The cardinal.'

Gaunt stood with Curth in the shadows of a service doorway down the hall from the intensive bay. Curth was trying to light a lho-stick, her hands unsteady.

'Give me that,' Gaunt snapped, and plucked the stick from her mouth. He walked over to a flamer pack that had been dumped amidst a clumsy pile of kit along the corridor wall by crash crews and lit the thing off a blue pilot flame from the nozzle.

He crossed back to Curth and handed her the lho-stick.

'Those things will kill you,' he said.

'Better them than the warp,' she replied, sucking hard.

'His actual words were "the cardinal"?'

'That's what I heard.'

'The Phantine specialist assigned to Adare's team was called Cardinale,' Gaunt told her.

'No crap,' she said simply.

Dorden approached down the hallway and joined them. Without comment, he took the lho-stick from Curth's hand, took a deep drag, regretted it in a fit of coughing, and handed it back to her.

'Corbec will live,' he said.

Gaunt smiled. 'And Soric?'

'Him too. I dread to think what it would take to bring Agun Soric down.'

'You don't look happy,' Gaunt noted.

Dorden shrugged. 'On Ana's advice I ran a tox-spread. Corbec was in a terminal decline thanks to a nosocomial infection.'

'A what?'

'In his injured state, he had picked up a secondary infection here in the infirmary.'

'Blood poisoning,' said Curth.

'Yes, Ana. Blood poisoning. If I hadn't shot him up with twenty cc's of morphomycin and an anticoagulant, he'd probably have been dead by nightfall.'

'Damn,' said Gaunt.

'Daemons in his blood stream, chewing like rats,' Curth said, mimicking Soric's gnawing sound.

'Don't start with that,' Dorden said.

'But you've got to admit–' Curth began.

'No, I haven't,' said Dorden.

THE GHOSTS IN the main billet were packing kits and stripping down weapons when Hark brought the punishment detail back in. Trooper Cuu was cuffed and hobbled, and scurried to keep up with the guards. His face was drawn and pale from too many nights in a cell, and it made his jagged scar all the more prominent.

'Stand to!' Hark cried, and the detail slammed to a halt.

'Keys!' demanded Hark.

The nearest trooper handed him a fob of geno-keys and the commissar unlocked Cuu's restraints.

Cuu stood blinking, rubbing his wrists.

'Do you understand the nature of your transgression and renounce it utterly before the eyes of the God-Emperor?'

'I do, sir.'

'Do you accept your guilt and understand it as a measure of the God-Emperor's forgiveness?'

'I do that, sir.'

'Do you promise to stay right out of my damned way, from now on?' Hark snarled, pushing his face into Cuu's.

'You can count on it.'

'Sir?'

'Sir. You can count on it, sir.'

Hark looked away. 'Prisoner is dismissed,' he said. The detail turned on their heels and marched out, Hark behind them.

Cuu crossed to his cot. He sat down and looked along the row at Bragg.

'What?' Bragg said, looking up from the half-oiled firing mechanism he was stripping down.

'You,' said Cuu.

'Me what?' Bragg asked, getting up.

'Let him be, Bragg,' said Fenix.

'He ain't worth it,' said Lubba.

'No, Cuu wants to say something,' said Bragg. 'Cuu, I'm glad Gaunt got you off. I'm glad it wasn't you. Made me sick to think someone in our regiment could do a thing like that.'

'You thought it was me, Bragg. You told them where to look.'

'Yeah,' said Bragg, turning away. 'Those coins... that was your fault.'

'And this is yours,' said Cuu, pulling up his tunic so they could see his narrow back and the bloody welts the lash had made thirty times across his torso.

Four

It was a long way down.

The late afternoon was bringing down a glowering weather pattern: low, dark nimbostratus swollen with rain and a stiff westerly wind. In sympathy, the Scald far below was seething up, churning with firestorms and electrochemical flares.

The driving acid rain was heavy enough to reduce Ouranberg to little more than a grey blur against the ominous sky. But it did little to reduce the scale of the yawning gulf beneath him.

Mkoll edged along the top of the pipeline. There was just enough room on the girders of the support cradle for him to put one foot exactly in front of the next, steadying himself with one hand against the side of the pipe itself. The rain was making everything slick: the metal under his feet, the pipe under his touch. There wasn't much in the way of anything to actually grasp onto except the occasional rivet. It was a matter of steady balance and total concentration.

For the first five hundred metres or so, he'd walked along the top of the great pipe, but then the weather had deteriorated and the rising wind had denied him that option. Walking along the edge of the cradle was much slower going.

He would have preferred not to look down, but it was essential. The girders were scabbed with rust and sticky lichens, and he had to place each step carefully. Below him was a sheer drop down into the toxic depths of Phantine. One slip, one patch of rust or moss, one rain-slick spar, and he would be falling without hope of survival. Mkoll was pretty sure that if he fell, he would collide with one of the span's cross members on the way, so at least he wouldn't know much about it.

He'd already had two close shaves. A sudden gust of updraft had nearly swept him off. And he'd accidentally trodden on one of the vile slug-like things that dwelt in this dismal place. Thermovores. Bonin and Milo had told him about them. The thing had squished and his boot had slid right away in the slime. Too close. Too, too close.

Mkoll figured he was about halfway across. The rain was getting heavier, sheeting down diagonally, and barks of thunder shook the air. It was almost twilight, and, apart from a few lights, the city was now utterly invisible.

The rain had brought the slugs out. Mkoll presumed they derived nutrients from the precipitation, or essential fluids, or maybe fed on micro-algae dissolved out of the metal by the rain's high acidity. Feth, he was no biologist! All he knew for sure was that the metalwork was covered with the disgusting things, ten times the number that had been there at the start of his crossing, before the rain. He tried not to touch them and certainly not to tread on them. The latter was difficult. He had to take long strides regularly to step over writhing piles of them. Twice, he had to use the stock of his lasrifle to sweep particularly large masses out of his way.

The skinwing presumably mistook him for a rival predator. Or perhaps it fancied bigger game. He saw it coming right at the last minute, a scrawny, attenuated rat-like thing with a ragged, two metre wingspan and a whip-thin tail four metres long. It flew into his visored face, trilling ultrasonic squeals frenziedly, and beating its wings at him. Mkoll stumbled, swung at it with a curse, and slipped off the girder.

He caught the girder edge with his left hand. The impact of arrest nearly dislocated his shoulder. Mkoll grunted in pain. His legs pinwheeled, trying to find something to tuck against. As his left fingertips began to slip off, he got his right hand on the girder too. His first grab came away with a handful of thermovores. He shook them off his fingers and got a better grip. His legs were still dangling and his forearms were on fire with the effort of gripping the spar and supporting his weight.

The skinwing came back, attacking him from behind, shrilling so loud his steel helmet vibrated.

'Get the feth off!' he yelled.

Teeth clenched, grunting, he got one elbow up on the girder, then the other, then one boot. Finally, he rolled himself up onto the beam and lay, shaking and choking for breath, face down in a mass of crushed slug-vermin.

He lay there for a long time, trying to slow his racing heart, feeling like he was going to die.

He finally moved again when the skinwing landed on his shoulder and started to gnaw at his neck-seal. He jerked round, caught it by the head and held on tight as it thrashed and fought. He kept his grip on it long enough to pull out his knife and kill it.

Mkoll dropped it off the edge and watched it tumble away, wings and long tail trailing, into the depths. Wretched fething thing had nearly killed him.

Just before it vanished into the clouds far below, an indistinct shape, much, much larger than the skinwing and sleekly black, emerged briefly from the Scald and took it gracefully in mid-air before vanishing again.

Mkoll had no idea what he had just glimpsed. But he became suddenly glad it had only been a skinwing that had decided he might make a meal.

He got up, unsteady and aching, wiped the slime off his tunic front, and resumed his arduous progress.

NESSA PLACED HER hand over Milo's mouth before she woke him. It seemed unfair to disturb him. He was profoundly sleeping, like a child, it seemed to her.

But it was getting on for 20.00 Imperial, and the dusk cycle was beginning. They had to get moving.

Milo woke and looked up at her. She smiled reassuringly and took her hand away, uncovering an answering smile.

He sat up and rubbed his face with his hands. 'You okay?' he whispered.

She didn't reply. He lowered his hands and repeated the whisper so she could see his lips.

'Yes,' she said. Then added, 'Too loud?'

She had difficulty gauging the volume of her own speech.

'That's fine,' he said.

Sneaking away from the slave gang they had mingled with to cross the causeway, they had spent the earlier part of the day progressing across the main mill areas and work yards, avoiding the eagerly searching patrols of the enemy. In the middle part of the afternoon, weary from effort and the sustained tension, they had broken into a derelict tenement hab on the outskirts of Alpha dome to steal a few hours' rest.

Neither of them had mentioned the terrible events of the causeway crossing. Milo hadn't known Doyl well, but he knew the Ghosts had lost a valuable and gifted scout. Adare's death affected him on a more direct, emotional level. Lhurn Adare; sharp, confident and strong, had been a well-liked Tanith and a personal friend. He had been one of Colonel Corbec's sacra-drinking cronies, a die-hard carouser who liked to see the dawn come up with the likes of Varl, Derin, Cown, Domor, Bragg and Brostin. Part of the inner circle, the heart and backbone of the Tanith First. Milo had seen plenty of action at Adare's side, right from the early days. He remembered the relentless practical jokes Adare had played on Baffels and Cluggan. He remembered getting fabulously legless with him the night Adare made sergeant. He remembered Adare's frequent, sound advice.

Now they were both gone. Adare and Doyl. Dead, Milo was sure. Like all the others. Baffels, on Hagia. Cluggan, long gone on Voltemand. Mkoll, in the skies over Ouranberg.

How much longer, Milo wondered, until all the last pieces of Tanith were worn away?

He got to his feet and stretched, trying to shake off the sadness so his mind could be sharp. The bare room was lit by a single chemical lamp that Nessa had dared to ignite because the windows were boarded with sheets of pulp-ply. Her long-las was laid out on her camo-cloak, disassembled. She was using a thimble sewn from vizzy-cloth to polish and oil the firing mechanism.

Milo took out some foil-sealed bag rations and wolfed them down, swigging water from his flask. He noticed his hands were grimed with dust, but didn't care.

He opened the tissue paper schematic of Ouranberg they had all been issued with and studied it again, plotting routes.

'Did you sleep?' he asked, touching her arm first so she knew to look at him.

'A little.'

'Enough?'

'I had a dream,' Nessa said as she worked on her sniping piece.

'A dream?' he asked.

'I dreamed Colonel Corbec and Sergeant Soric came to find us. They were alive.'

'They probably are,' Milo said. 'I mean, we don't know.'

'No, but they were close to dying when we left. It's one thing to lose someone in battle. It's another to leave them dying and then never know... never find out...'

'We'll find out. They'll be waiting for us when we get back. Soric will be full of jokes and terribly proud of you. Corbec will have a bottle of sacra open and be demanding I dig out my pipes for a tune or two.'

'Why will Soric be proud of me?' she asked.

'Because you will have put a hot-shot between Slaith's eyes.'

She laughed. 'It's good to know you have such confidence in me. And that you can see into the future, Brin.'

'It's a gift I have.'

She shook her head with a chuckle and started to slide her long-las together. Her hands worked with economical practice, clicking the components together. Milo doubted he could have reassembled a lasrifle in twice the time.

He watched her. She was commonly regarded as the most beautiful woman in the Ghosts, though the men had their favourites: Muril, Arilla, Banda, Solia, Ellan, Criid and, when they were drunk or in pain enough to actually dare admit it, Ana Curth. Criid and Banda were thought to be the most alluring, though it often impressed Milo that Criid was firmly considered out of bounds even in terms of conversational fantasy because of her tie to Caffran. Nessa wasn't sexy in the same way Banda or Solia were. It was partly her quietness, itself a scar of warfare. But it was mostly her fine-boned, stunning face, the perfect angles of her cheeks and nose and the deep blue of her eyes. Her streaming, glossy hair had seemed to be a key part of her appeal. That was gone now, and she was still utterly beautiful. Her hair was just beginning to grow in again, a fine down-like felt. The lack of hair emphasised her sculptural features.

Her eyes came up and caught his. 'What's so interesting?' she asked.

Milo shook his head.

He looked away, and saw a small slab of pulp-ply leaning against the wall. A knife tip had cut the words 'Nessa Bourah, 341.748 to 225.771 M41.' into it.

'What the feth is that?' he asked.

'Just a habit,' she replied.

'It's a fething grave marker!'

'Relax, Brin. We did it every day during the scratch fighting. I never got out of the habit.'

Milo shook his head, puzzled. 'You'll have to explain more than that,' he said.

She put down her long-las and faced him. 'We were going to die. Every day, fighting the guerilla war in the ruined out-habs of Vervunhive, we were going to die. The death rate was awful. So we got into the habit of carving our own grave markers in what little downtime there was. If we died, you see, there would be a marker ready. Easy. Simple. A quickly dug slit-trench, a scatter of earth over the body, a prayer... and a marker ready and waiting.'

'That's terrible.'

'That's... the way it was.' She paused and cleared her throat quietly. Then she continued, 'It became routine, and people started putting the next morning's date on the markers, as if daring fate to take them. It was a joke at first. A bad, dark joke. Then someone, I don't remember who, pointed out that, as a rule, the fighters who carved the next day's date as their death date survived.'

'Survived?'

'The sensible ones who left the death date blank tended to die. Those that gleefully etched in that the next day would be their last... lived. So they'd have to scrap the marker and make a new one because the date was wrong. After a week or two, it became a habit, a lucky charm. We all did it, daring the gods, or daemons or whatever rules the cosmic order, to make our grave markers useless.'

'And you still do it?'

She nodded. 'At times like this, I do.'

'I feel like I should make one,' he said.

'Only works for Verghastites, I'm afraid,' she said.

'Damn shame...' he grinned.

And froze.

He could hear a knocking, scraping sound from the floor below. Seeing his look, Nessa got up and loaded a cell magazine into her long-las.

Slowly, listening, Milo lifted his cannon.

More knocking, a crash.

Let's go, he signed.

They gathered up their kit rapidly, keeping an eye on the door. Nessa extinguished the lamp.

In the sudden, blue gloom, Milo gestured to the back door with his thumb, they moved slowly, silently towards it, weapons ready, camo-cloaks draped around them.

Milo gently pulled back the pulp-ply boarding the nearest window.

Three platoons of Blood Pact were assembling in the square outside.

Another search-patrol. Ever since Adare and Doyl had been discovered, the enemy had been scouring the mill district for other Imperial interlopers. The public address system had broadcast imploring appeals to 'find the vermin', alternating with demands that the 'Imperial scum' give themselves up.

Milo and Nessa backed to the rear door. They were expecting Blood Pact.

But it wasn't.

The hab-room door splintered in, exploded by some powerful shotgun blast, and the first loxatl scurried through.

In the half-light, Milo got a glimpse of a sinuous, grey body with a flat, snouted head and a short, muscular tail. It came in and went up the wall, dewclaws ripped into the plaster to gather purchase. An augmetic limb-frame strapped around its mottled belly tracked around the pepper-pot nose of an alien scattergun.

A second loxatl slithered in through the door and clawed its way rapidly up the other wall. Milo could smell spearmint mixed with sour milk.

Its bionic weapon-frame clicked around, sweeping the room. It aimed at Milo, shooting out a dull green aiming light that splashed on his cloak.

Nessa's long-las roared.

The second alien mercenary was ripped off the wall by the hot-shot and smashed, convulsing, into the doorframe.

The other one fired its weapon. A huge hole was chewed out of the pressed-fibre panelling beside Milo.

He opened fire, lurched back for a moment by the U90's almost unmanageable recoil.

The hi-ex AP rounds blew the lizard thing apart and hosed the wall with its unwholesome blood. Its smoking carcass fell off the wall and slammed onto the floor.

'Feth!' he heard Nessa scream. The creature she had shot was lurching up again, sweeping its flechette blaster towards Milo.

Milo emptied the rest of the drum mag into the second loxatl, pulping its head and chest.

He looked round at Nessa.

Come on! he signed. She nodded and pulled him towards the doorway the loxatl had come through. Trusting her, Milo realised she was right. The Blood Pact squads were storming up the rear of the hab, intending to pick off any fleeing stragglers the loxatl had missed.

No one was expecting anybody to exit from the front of the building.

Nessa and Milo, hand in hand, raced out of the hab tenement, and sprinted away towards the forbidding shells of residence blocks on the far side of the square.

In the hab behind them, Nessa's grave marker lay crushed under the bulk of a dead loxatl.

THEY'D HAD TO wait the best part of the day for a chance to sneak back to the air wharf, where it took them just ninety seconds to commandeer the carrier. Banda's long-shot took out the driver, and Bonin and Varl did the rest with warknives.

Jagdea ran forward across the air wharf and heaved the driver's corpse out of its seat.

'Do we leave them here?' Unterrio asked, nodding at the dead bodies.

'No, get them aboard,' said Vadim.

They hefted up the heretics' corpses and threw them on to the carrier's cargo bed.

It was a light hauler, with a roofed cabin section and a tarp-covered payload bay. Jagdea got behind the controls as the rest of Larisel 1 finished lugging the dead onto the vehicle's bay and climbed aboard.

'Commander?' Varl prompted.

'Just familiarising myself with the layout,' she said.

Expertly, Jagdea launched them, and they flew down a canyon of habs towards the porta of Alpha dome.

* * *

AT JUST ABOUT the same time, far to the north-west, Mkoll was scaling the granite outcrop where the pipeline finally joined Ouranberg. It was dark, freezing cold, and the wind was fearful, but he felt triumphant. He had made it all the way across.

Now all he had to do was get inside.

CONVOYS OF TRANSPORT vehicles loaded with munitions for Alpha dome's air defences had been rumbling down the access routes non-stop for over an hour. Larisel 2 had been forced into hiding until the activity died down. They waited, with nervy impatience, in the basement of a burned-out Ministorum chapel.

Kuren watched the door, armed with Meryn's U90. In the course of the day they'd seen plenty of the vile loxatl mercenaries accompanying the Blood Pact patrols.

'This remind you of anything?' Mkvenner said. He'd been searching through the broken litter that covered the basement floor, and now held up a cheap plaster figurine, one of a dozen he'd found in a box.

'It's a memento of Saint Phidolas, who led the first settlers to Phantine,' said Kersherin. 'Every church on the planet sells cheap souvenirs like it. For the pilgrims.'

'Yeah,' said Mkvenner, 'but what else?'

'I don't know...' said Kersherin.

Mkvenner casually smacked the figurine against a pillar, smashing off its head and upper body.

'How about now?'

They all looked at it, like it was a joke and they were ready for the punchline.

'Feth,' said Larkin suddenly. 'It was behind Slaith.'

'Right,' said Mkvenner.

'What?' Meryn snapped. 'Behind Slaith? What are you talking about?'

'When he was on the screen,' said Larkin, 'when he... he showed us Cardinale... there was a big window behind him and a ruined statue outside.'

'I don't remember any statue,' Kuren said.

'There was a statue,' said Mkvenner. 'Ruined. Right outside his windows.'

The scout turned the broken figurine over and examined a label on the bottom.

'An image of Saint Phidolas,' he read, 'copied from the great statue that may be seen in the Imperial concourse, Alpha dome, Ouranberg.'

'Well, well, well...' Meryn chuckled.

'I DON'T LIKE the look of this,' Jagdea said.

'Keep going,' Bonin told her. He was riding next to her in the hauler's cab.

They had got through the porta into Alpha dome with remarkable ease, and joined an access route that had seemed busy enough for them to blend in. Varl hoped they might get as far as the dome's core districts by midnight.

But the traffic was slowing, and armoured Blood Pact air-speeders with rotating orange lamps were forcing all vehicles down to road level so that they could be channelled through a check station.

'We need to get off this route,' said Jagdea. They were barely crawling, following the tail of a large munitions truck.

'They'll see us if we try and break away. Besides, the route has no obvious intersections.'

'Well, I don't think going through that checkpoint is going to be an especially healthy idea!' she hissed.

'Sarge?' Bonin called back through the mesh partition to Varl. 'Any stunningly good suggestions from you?'

Varl peered down the line of near stationary traffic ahead and behind them. The six-lane route itself was open, with little cover, and thirty storey tenements rose on either side. Not the place for a firefight.

He cursed himself. Using the hauler had been a smart idea, and it had saved them a lot of time. But Jagdea and Bonin had advised him to ditch it once they were inside Alpha dome. Varl had wanted to press on, to see how far they could get. He felt stupid now, like he'd let them down. Even though Gol Kolea was nowhere around, the Kolea-Varl devil-dare rivalry had landed them in this fix. Gol had been the hero at Cirenholm. Shutting down the power plant like that had effectively won the battle for them. He'd triumphed that round. When Operation Larisel came up, all Varl had been able to think of was that this might be his turn. His turn to be the hero. Devil-dare, Kolea! How d'you like that?

So he'd pushed them on, far further than they should ever have gone out in the open like this. He had pushed them so they would reach Slaith and be heroes. 'Stupid' didn't even begin to cover it.

'There's a road to the left, about seventy metres up,' Varl said through the mesh.

'I see it,' said Jagdea dubiously.

'We keep rolling forward like this, up to the checkpoint, and then break left fast and exit.'

'Just like that?'

'Commander, I have absolute faith in your ability to drive this thing like it was a Lightning on afterburner. We get down there, ditch this cart and go to ground.'

'That's your plan?' asked Unterrio.

'Yes, it fething is,' said Varl. 'We all clear?'

'What happens if they rumble us before we reach the turn?' asked Jagdea.

'Okay...' Varl said. 'We pull out of the queue anyway. Fly straight at the tenement.'

'What?'

'I've got hi-ex loaded. I'll make a hole. We'll get inside the building and then ditch and cover there. Okay? Clear?'

The traffic line crept forward. The air was thick with exhaust fumes and the sound of dozens of engines. An air-speeder droned by overhead, flying down the queue. Incomprehensible instructions boomed out of an amplifier at the checkpoint.

'Foot troops!' Bonin whispered sharply.

'Where?' asked Varl.

'Walking down the line towards us. On the median strip. There, by the crash barrier.'

'Oh feth.'

'They're checking papers,' Jagdea said. She tugged off her gloves, wiped her sweating hands dry on her jacket, and then gripped the wheel and the throttle lever again, tensed and ready.

'Wait for it. Wait for it,' Varl said. Banda, Vadim and Unterrio raised their weapons to their shoulders. Bonin put his laspistol on his lap.

'They may not come down this far,' Banda whispered hopefully.

The vehicles moved forward again, another few metres. A Blood Pact officer, standing on the route's central barrier, waved the three trucks immediately in front of them on with a torch stick.

Then he stepped out into their path and held up a hand.

'Shit!' said Jagdea.

Four more Blood Pact troopers and a slaver with a team of hate-dogs approached behind the officer. He walked towards the hauler.

'We're blown,' announced Bonin.

'I know!' said Varl. 'Wait to the last possible moment...'

The officer stepped up to the cab and peered in. They could smell his body odour and see his blood-shot eyes through the slits of his iron mask. He began to ask something in a language they didn't understand and then stopped as he saw Bonin and Jagdea and their Imperial combat gear.

'Go!' said Bonin, and shot the officer through the head with his pistol.

Jagdea threw the hauler out of the line, engaging the throttle so hard that Unterrio was thrown off his feet in the back. The air-truck screamed across the route towards the tenements as shouts, sirens and shots rang out after it. Heavy fire from an air-speeder stitched plumes of debris from the road surface as it tried to track them.

'Varl!' Jagdea screamed. The front of the tenement was approaching very fast.

Varl threw back the tarp and stood up so he could fire over the roof of the cab. He had to fight to stay upright. They were going to hit the wall in scant seconds.

He fired the U90 and created a rippling blister of overlapping explosions that blew the ground floor facade in.

They went through the hole.

Almost.

Varl had barely ducked in again when an overhang of brick caught the tarp of the speeding machine and ripped the entire cover frame off. That tipped the nose up and spun the back end out. The left rear engine mount sheared off against an exposed metal beam and a considerable portion of the hauler's underside shredded away.

The tenement's ground floor was one great, open space used for storage and presently empty, except for the metre square rockcrete pillars every thirty paces.

The stricken machine flew into the store-space almost sidelong. It hit the floor once with boneshaking force, bounced up under its own headlong momentum, and then impacted again, shrieking along the floor in an astonishing wake of sparks and fragmenting metal.

It hit the first pillar head-on with enough force to spin it off the ground and leave it crumpled and smoking, facing the way it had come.

Varl and Banda had both been thrown clear and lay unconscious on the ground nearby. Unterrio got to his feet and tried to get Vadim up. The young Verghastite had struck his head and was out cold.

'Come on! Come on!' Unterrio screamed.

Bonin came round. He was hanging out of the shattered cab section. It took him a moment to work out what was going on. He could hear Unterrio shouting.

Jagdea, saved by her harness belt, was alive but semi conscious. Bonin fought with her harness and began to drag her out.

Powerful searchlights lanced in through the street windows and the hole. Silhouetted against them, figures were surging in.

Unterrio leapt out of the carrier and opened fire with his lascarbine.

'Bonin! Get them clear! Get them clear!' he was shouting.

Bonin tried to work out how he could get four semi conscious people clear of anything. Banda was coming round, weeping with rage and pain, clutching a broken wrist.

Jagdea suddenly opened her eyes and looked up at Bonin with distant confusion. 'I keep crashing things,' she said weakly. 'I don't like it.'

'Jagdea!'

She began to pass out again, and murmured. 'I smell… milk. Bonin, I smell milk and mint…'

A flechette blaster roared and Unterrio's defiant stand came to a sudden, explosive end.

Something small and hard and metallic landed near to Bonin and came skittering to rest.

For a second, he thought it was a grenade, but then he realised it was a synapse mine.

'Run!' he howled, though he was pretty sure no one was in any state to obey.

The mine went off with a silent flash, like a falling star, that flared for a moment, bright and then went out.

And as he collapsed, paralysed, Bonin knew that his own lucky star had finally gone out too.

Five

IT WAS MIDNIGHT on the 225th. The massed forces of Operation Thunderhead were beginning to leave Cirenholm, streaming in convoy out into the night, heading for Ouranberg.

The vast bomber waves went out first with their interceptor escorts. It was a clear night, and up in the cockpits of the Magogs, it seemed to the aircrews like they were part of new constellations issuing from the city.

The drogues that would convey the main army forces began to depart, sliding up into the cold night air in the wake of the bombers, rotor blades chopping. Thunderbolt escorts cruised in beside them. The drogues *Zephyr*, *Aeolus* and *Trenchant*, heavy with Krassian and Urdeshi infantry regiments, headed out on a long path that would eventually turn them west to assault the main airwharfs and drome structure of Ouranberg.

The Ghosts were boarding the *Nimbus*, which, as part of a pack of six drogues, would convey the main assault force of Tanith, Phantine and Urdeshi to the southern face of Ouranberg.

O-Day. By dawn the next day, all hell would be unleashed.

Gaunt checked his despatch orders for a final time, signed them, and handed them to Beltayn, who hurried them off to Van Voytz. Rawne, Daur, Hark and the other senior officers waited for him outside the office. He rose, put on his cap, and led the Tanith commanders onto the main troop deck. No word had yet come from any Larisel group. He wondered how many of them might still be alive.

On the massive troop deck, thousands of battle-ready Ghosts were being conducted in prayer by ayatani Zweil.

Zweil saw the officers approach, and finished his reading from *The Gospel of Saint Sabbat*. He closed the old book and smoothed his robes.

'Let me say this, finally,' he projected, loud and effortless. 'To you all, so you know it and keep it in your minds through the danger that faces you. And let me say it now, before he does.' Zweil indicated Gaunt with a casual thumb and laughter rippled through the ranks. 'The Emperor protects. Know that, remember that, and he will.'

Zweil turned to Gaunt. 'All yours,' he said. He made the sign of the aquila and blessed Gaunt with a few words, and then went down the line of officers, repeating the same.

'It appears the venerable father has stolen my line,' Gaunt said, facing the Ghosts. There was more laughter. 'So let me tell you this. Colonel Corbec and Sergeant Soric are both out of danger.'

A considerable cheer went up. Gaunt raised a hand. 'They are expected to make good recoveries. So remember this. I'd like the first news they hear from their infirmary beds to be word that Ouranberg has fallen and that the Ghosts have acquitted themselves bravely. That sort of news will heal them faster than any drug Doc Dorden or Surgeon Curth can give them. What do you say?'

The cheers were deafening.

'Men of Tanith, men of Verghast–'

'And women!' Criid shouted.

Gaunt smiled. 'And women. I often ask you if you want to live forever. I won't tonight. I expect to see you all again this time tomorrow, raising the standard of the Tanith First above Ouranberg. Death is not an option. Fight hard and give the God-Emperor of Mankind the victory he asks of you all.'

Almost drowned out by the applause and the shouting, Gaunt turned to Hark.

'Viktor? Inform the admiral we're ready to cast off.'

THIS TIME, THE medics were going in with the troop assault. Curth's medi-pack was fully prepped, but she was struggling with the body armour Gaunt had issued.

'You've got the buckles misaligned,' said Kolea, coming into the drogue's hospital behind her.

'Really?' she said sourly, looking like a patient half-escaped from a strait jacket.

'Here, let me,' he said, stepping forward to fit her armour properly.

'Shouldn't you be on the troop decks?' she asked.

'Yes. But I had to see you first. I have a favour to ask.'

'Go on then.'

'How's that?' he said stepping back. She flexed her arms and patted the plated front of her armour vest. 'Excellent. Thank you. Now what's this favour?'

'You know I promised to tell Criid and Caffran about...'

'Yes.'

'That I'd do it after Ouranberg was done.'

'Yes.'

'And you know I'm not looking for that reunion round.'

'Yes, I do. Come on.'

'I don't think I'm going to be coming back from Ouranberg,' he said.

She gazed at his face. It was unreadable. 'What?'

'Listen to me, I'm not looking to find death, but I think it might be looking for me now. It's let me off too many times recently. I'm not saying

I'm going to do something foolhardy, but it's a feeling I have. Now I've made up my mind to tell Criid, I think death might be hoping to cheat me.'

'Feth, aren't you the fatalist?' She gripped him by the shoulders firmly and looked up into his eyes. 'You are not going to die, Gol. You are not going to let death take you.'

'I'll do my best. But I have this feeling. This feeling Gol Kolea's not going to come back from Ouranberg. You've been gakking good to me, Ana. I have this last favour to ask.'

He took a sealed letter out of his tunic pocket and handed it to her. 'If I don't come back, give this to Criid. It's all there. Everything.'

She looked at the letter. 'And if you do?'

'Burn it. I'll be able to tell her and Caffran what was in that letter myself.'

'Okay,' she said, and slid the letter into her fatigue's pocket.

'Thanks,' he said simply.

She rose up on tip-toe, put a hand behind his neck to pull him lower and kissed his cheek softly.

'Come back, Gol,' she said. 'Make me burn it.'

IN OURANBERG, DRUMS were beating. Long range auspex had detected the mass formations of air machines moving out from Cirenholm, and the Blood Pact was preparing for war. There was a sense of relief, that the hour had finally come. The preachers on the address-systems spouted their last blasphemies and then fell silent.

The address screens fizzled with white noise.

The invasion was coming.

ON ALPHA DOME'S Imperial concourse, a fifty acre rockcrete plaza in front of the central administratum palace, thousands of can-fires had been lit and the standard of the Blood Pact raised alongside the disturbing, semi-sentient fronds of algae the loxatl used as banners.

A rotund bronze cauldron, three metres across, had been set at the top of the palace steps, under the flags, below the desecrated statue of Saint Phidolas. Devotees of the warp-cult, Blood Pact troops and confused citizens were spilling into the concourse from all sides.

Blood Pact slavers led the prisoners out. There were fifty of them, all chained together, all beaten down and despairing. They were whipped to the base of the steps and ordered to sit.

Larisel 1 was amongst them. Bonin was chained up next to Jagdea, his head still swimming from the effects of the numbing synapse mine. She looked like she might pass out any minute.

Bonin could see Varl three rows away, and Vadim, both sullen and dazed. A little searching found Banda. The chains were chafing at her snapped wrist and she was ashen with pain.

Bonin and Jagdea were in the front row of the prisoners. At the head of their chain was Cardinale. Bonin barely recognised the Phantine specialist. Cardinale was very close to death.

The other prisoners were Imperial servants, captured aircrew or Ouranberg nobility.

Jagdea was staring at a man in the row opposite them. He was dressed in ragged Phantine flight-crew uniform, and his shoulder and neck were blotched with dried blood and signs of pollution burns.

'Viltry?' she said.

'Commander Jagdea?' he mumbled, looking up askance.

'God! I thought you were dead! What happened?'

'Lost my bird over the Southern Scald, thought I was windwaste… then one of Slaith's supply ships picked me up.'

'Golden Throne!' she said. 'It's good to see you!'

Viltry laughed darkly. 'Here? I don't think so.'

'We're not dead yet, Viltry,' Jagdea said. 'Someone once told me that death comes when it comes and only a fool would bring it early.'

'What kind of simple-minded crap is that?' Viltry said.

Jagdea looked across at Bonin and smiled. A weary smile, but not a defeated one. 'The best kind, I believe. All I'm saying is that it's only over when it's over.'

'Oh, for us, it's over,' Viltry said sourly. He gestured at the bronze cauldron.

'What is this about?' Bonin asked him.

'The invasion must be coming,' Viltry said. 'Slaith intends to symbolically renew his blood pact with Urlock Gaur so he can be strong when he meets the Imperial assault. We're the sacrifice. That cauldron… we're supposed to fill it. With our blood. Slaith will help, of course.'

'Feth…' murmured Bonin. 'I wondered why he hadn't killed us yet.' He looked at the huge bronze bowl. It was going to take an awful lot of blood to fill it.

Fifty prisoners, five litres each. That should do it.

THE CEREMONY BEGAN. Hundreds of Blood Pact warriors and dozens of loxatl flooded down the steps from the palace, passing the plinth of the shattered statue of Saint Phidolas, and stood aside as Sagittar Slaith descended.

They were beating their scarred fists against their weapons, and the clamour raised thundering applause from the gathered audience of thousands.

Slaith, magnificent in his armour and white fur, kissed the side of the bronze cauldron, and lifted the glinting, ritual adze.

Blood Pact troopers dragged Cardinale up the steps, pulling the chain of prisoners after him. Bonin and Jagdea found themselves yanked along closer to the foot of the steps.

Slaith raised the adze and bellowed arcane words. Cardinale was draped over the edge of the cauldron and held down by two slavers.

'BEFORE HE LOPS Cardinale, if you wouldn't mind,' Meryn hissed in Larkin's ear.

'Shut up and let me concentrate,' Larkin said. From the roof of the Ouranberg stock exchange, he had a perfect view over the Imperial concourse. There was zero wind, but the range was long. Larkin adjusted his sights, and wished he had been given the opportunity for a test round.

'Come on, Larks, you can do it,' Kuren said.

'I'd shut up, if I were you,' Larkin heard Mkvenner say. 'He's doing his thing.'

Below, Slaith declaimed something else and quickly raised the adze over Cardinale's exposed nape.

'Larks!' Meryn urged.

A hot-shot round sang out over the concourse and smashed into Slaith.

'Feth!' said Larkin. 'That wasn't me!'

Mkvenner looked up. Pandemonium had instantly overtaken the crowd below, and the Blood Pact were surging towards the eastern side of the concourse.

'It came from over there,' Mkvenner said, pointing to the Munitorium blocks that flanked the east edge of the square.

Larkin trained his long-las again, staring through the scope. He saw Slaith getting back to his feet beside the cauldron.

'Feth! He's got a personal shield!' Larkin said.

'Hit him anyway!' Meryn demanded.

Larkin fired, and Slaith was slammed over onto his back. At the same moment, a second hot-shot stabbed in from the Munitorium and clipped the edge of the cauldron. Then a third hit Slaith on the ground.

'Now we're in trouble,' Kersherin said.

Blood Pact and loxatl were tearing through the crowd towards the foot of the stock exchange.

Larkin fired again, hitting Slaith cleanly. But the warlord got up, assisted by his men. His personal shield had held.

'He's las-proof,' Larkin said.

'I suggest we get out of here,' said Meryn.

'No,' said Larkin, taking aim again. 'Wait...'

ON THE TOP floor of the Munitorium block, Nessa fell back from the window and looked at Milo.

'He's shielded! I hit him twice!'

'Okay, let's go. We did what we could.'

They ran to the exit door. Milo could hear boots thundering up the stairs towards them.

Mass panic had overtaken the square. People were fleeing everywhere. Bonin looked round at Jagdea and started to say something when he was lurched back by a powerful jerk on the chain. A pin-point las-round of extraordinary accuracy had severed the chain between them.

Bonin leapt to his feet and threw himself on the nearest Blood Pact guard, choking him with the dangling end of the slave-chain. As the red-clad warrior collapsed, Bonin grabbed his weapon.

It was a standard las. Good enough. Bonin gunned down three Blood Pact who ran towards him and then started firing at the enemy troops on the steps. Jagdea struggled forward and grabbed another of the fallen enemy weapons. She started to shoot away the chains confining the other prisoners.

'Death comes when it comes and only a fool would bring it early, eh?' Bonin yelled at her. 'What idiot told you that?'

'We get out of this mess alive, Bonin,' she shouted back, 'and I'll tell you!'

'And believe me,' she added, shooting a charging slaver through the head and shattering his iron visor. 'I intend to get out of this alive if it's the last thing I do.'

Bonin laughed aloud, and drove the fight towards the bewildered enemy.

Flanked by a bodyguard of three Blood Pact officers and two loxatl, Sagittar Slaith hurried back into the palace. He was cursing and swearing, bruised and shaken by the savage hits his personal shield had taken.

As he stormed back into his private apartment, the floor began to shake. It was nearly dawn and overhead the first waves of bombers had reached Ouranberg. Slaith turned slowly to his officers, smouldering with his infamous rage. The Blood Pact shook behind their iron grotesques, and even the xenos warriors closed their nictating han lids. Slaith opened his mouth, but it was not his fury that hit them.

A rain of shots from a lasrifle on full auto killed the Blood Pact officers instantly and exploded harmlessly off Slaith's screen and the reflective hides of the two loxatl.

There was a human standing in the rear doorway of the room. An Imperial soldier half-shrouded in a ragged camo-cape, his lasrifle aimed at them.

'Where the hell did you come from?' Slaith raged.

'Tanith,' said Mkoll, and fired again.

Slaith walked forward through the blasts unharmed, the flinching loxatl at his side, double-lids shut against the las-shots, armature cycling up their flechette cannons.

'A lasgun?' said Slaith. 'I'm shielded and the loxatl soak up las-fire. You're out of luck. You should have been better prepared.'

'Oh, this is just a distraction,' said Mkoll, gesturing with his lasrifle. 'The real surprise is under that table.'

The loxatl flechette guns spat their hails of lethal sub-munitions and exploded the doorway and the wall around it. Mkoll was already diving headlong out of sight.

Slaith stooped and peered under the table. What he saw was six tube charges wired together on a timer.

'No!' he screamed. 'Noooooo!'

THE DETONATION TOOK the roof off the state room. Slaith's personal shield managed to hold for 1.34 seconds before it was overwhelmed by the blast force.

Sagittar Slaith was still screaming with rage as he vaporised.

Six

PHANTINE, WITH ITS oceanic skies and tempestuous Scald, was a planet of storms, but the greatest storm that morning was the human one that engulfed Ouranberg.

In the pale, violet light of dawn, columns of dense black smoke and spiralling fireballs crowned the city, and the air streamed with las-fire, tracer shells and streaking rockets. Swarms of attack craft, like plagues of insects, buzzed over the domes through the crackling blossoms of flak. Raging infernos glowed dull red through ragged holes in the main domes.

Preceded by diving packs of Shrikes, the main force of drogues and troop barges assaulted the Imperial landing platform and the expanse of Pavia Fields behind it, setting down thousands of Imperial Guardsmen under withering fire from the fortifications of Ourangate and the Alpha dome emplacements. The gun turrets of the barges chattered and flashed as they hovered in, their gate-ramps crashing down to disgorge charging troops or the clanking Chimeras and Manticores of the Urdeshi Seventh Armoured.

The noise was total. A dreadful blur of sound out of which individual noises could hardly be distinguished. As the ramp of his own barge came down, Gaunt led his men out with urgent waves of his power sword. They were never going to hear his voice.

Urdeshi units took the landing platform after a brutal series of firefights and horrific hand to hand encounters. The Ghosts of Tanith, led to the west by Major Rawne and to the east by Captain Daur, pincered the Blood Pact ground forces defending the Avenue of the Polyandrons, and opened the way to Ourangate itself.

The drogue *Skyro*, supported by Marauder gunships, manoeuvred in over Beta dome and roped Phantine and Urdeshi troops down onto the main vapour mill. A brigade personally led by Major Fazalur took and held the main mill complex against bitter resistance until Gaunt broke through Ourangate and moved Tanith and Urdeshi elements to relieve him.

To the east, the secondary assault poured into the city's main drome. For about an hour, the fighting there was the most intense and furious of the whole battle. The Krassians were driven back twice until the resolve of the Blood Pact finally snapped. After that it was a rout.

The cost was high. Nearly two thousand Imperial Guardsmen were killed, the majority of them Krassian and Urdeshi. Forty aircraft were lost. The drogue *Aeolus*, heroically staying on station to ensure that the Krassian units could get enough troops down for their third and final push into the dome, was hammered by Ouranberg's western batteries and eventually listed, rudderless and on fire, towards Gamma dome where it foundered and exploded. The entire crew perished. The colossal explosion shot a vast doughnut of burning gas up into the air and scorched the west face of Gamma dome black.

But Imperial victory was pretty much guaranteed from the moment that word of Slaith's death began to spread through the enemy forces. The Blood Pact kept fighting, and in many ways became more savage. They were lost, and that made them suicidally vengeful.

Slaith's demise certainly did not rob them of their courage. But their coordination and discipline were gone. Without Slaith, they were like a brain-dead body, still twitching with involuntary responses.

Van Voytz had known all along that Ouranberg would be hard to capture, nigh on impossible, in fact, if he was to keep the vital vapour mills intact. As fighting raged through the hab-domes of the city, and report after report came in of losses and casualties, he consoled himself with the knowledge that it could have been a hundred times worse. His gamble with Operation Larisel had paid off. If Slaith had still been alive at the start of the assault, chances were the date 226.771 M41 would have been remembered as a tragic Imperial defeat.

It didn't feel like victory on the ground in the streets of Alpha dome. Fierce fighting continued until well into the evening. Whole hab-blocks were on fire, and in places the roadways had collapsed through into lower dome levels.

Gaunt led from the front, directly deploying his units into the heart of the dome. Squads under Bray, Burone, Theiss and Daur had secured a vital inner bascule and overrun a string of well-made Blood Pact emplacements. There were rumours that inside the domes the citizens of Ouranberg were rising up against their oppressors. Gaunt saw nothing of that, only hundreds of terrified civilians fleeing the main centres of fighting.

His primary concern was not the overall victory. Van Voytz could worry about that. As soon as he was within range, he made repeated efforts to contact the Larisel elements and was heartened to find that some of them at least were still alive. Beltayn relayed broken transmissions from Meryn's team, which had linked up with the survivors from Varl's Larisel 1 and were now besieged in the refectory of Ouranberg's Scholam Progenium near the Imperial concourse.

Gaunt swore to them he would break through and secure them. He pushed Rawne's elements to his left flank, supported by Urdeshi armour, and sent Haller, Maroy and Ewler's units to the right.

The right flank approach was hopeless. Maroy reported heavy resistance in the eastern market area. Rawne fared little better. His forces – the sections commanded by Kolea, Obel and Mkfin and a brigade of Urdeshi under young Shenko – ran foul of the loxatl and got caught up in a period of ugly street-fighting that lasted over two hours.

Gaunt himself managed to cut through eventually, leading the platoons of Domor, Skerral and Mkendrick along with forty-five Urdeshi pioneers and the units that had, until Cirenholm, been led by Corbec and Soric. These last two were temporarily commanded by Raglon and Arcuda, and Gaunt kept the inexperienced leaders close. He needn't have worried. Arcuda displayed a tactical gift that made Gaunt wish he'd advanced the man sooner, and Raglon was as confident and assured as he might have hoped. Raglon had come a long way from junior vox-carrier.

They broke through a half-defended line of buildings and saw off a loxatl counter-attack with their flamers. Dremmond and Lyse led the flamer repulse against the vile xenos mercenaries. They had a fantastic resistance to laser rounds, but fled moaning from the flames. With Nittori from his own platoon still injured, Gaunt had allowed Lyse to take his role. She was the first female flame-trooper in the regiment, another notable achievement for the Verghastites.

Just after 14.00 Imperial, Gaunt's force caught Blood Pact elements on the Imperial concourse from the side, put them to flight and relieved the besieged Ghosts in the scholam. Despite the fighting that continued to rattle outside as the Urdeshi stormed the main palace, Gaunt took the time to greet them all personally, and thank them for their bravery and determination.

Of the sixteen Ghosts and their four Urdeshi Specialists who had gone in as Operation Larisel, they appeared to be the only survivors. Banda, with a shattered wrist. Scout-trooper Bonin and Sergeant Varl, both wounded badly in the mayhem of fighting that had followed Slaith's death. Vadim, seriously concussed from the truck crash. Larkin, crying quietly with the pain of the migraine that had finally conquered him. Mkvenner, Kuren and Sergeant Meryn, all battered but miraculously intact. Specialist Kersherin, the only Skyborne who had survived. Commander Jagdea, who praised in particular Bonin's efforts to free and protect the captives during the running firefight, including a pilot named Viltry and Specialist Cardinale.

Cardinale, Gaunt learned, had perished from his terrible wounds during the siege.

Gaunt called up immediate medicae support for them and tried not to think about the ones who hadn't made it. Rilke, Cocoer, Nour, Doyl, Adare, Nessa, Mkoll... Milo.

Fifteen minutes later, Arcuda voxed Gaunt to say his men had found Milo and Nessa alive on the roof of the Ministry of Vapour Export. Gaunt closed his eyes. The Emperor protects.

Almost as an afterthought, he turned back to the survivors and asked, 'By the way... who made the shot in the end? Larkin?'

'None of us did,' said Meryn. 'Larkin hit the bastard several times, and so did Nessa I think. But he was shielded.'

'Then how the feth–?'

Gaunt's unfinished question was finally answered late that afternoon, when Urdeshi units searching the ruins of the palace found a lone Tanith scout unconscious in the rubble.

His tags said his name was Mkoll.

RAWNE'S FORCES WERE being hammered by the loxatl in the palatial habs west of the Alpha dome heartland. The aliens were using some kind of heavy fragmentation mortar, perhaps a larger-scale version of their signature flechette blasters. Obel had pressed his unit forward, and Bragg had managed to hose one loxatl position with cannonfire, but the deadly shells were still whooping down.

With Troopers Lubba and Jajjo, Gol Kolea had broken through the back wall of a ransacked kitchen into some kind of service tunnel that allowed them to advance right up to flank the main loxatl dug-outs. Emerging from the tunnel, hunched low, Kolea could hear the regular *punk-shiff!* of the loxatl mortars, and a human voice screaming for a medic.

The trio ran low across debris-littered rockcrete and scooted behind an exploded water main that was weeping frothy water into the road.

Caffran was lying on his back in a nearby shell-hole. His leg was lacerated with loxatl barb shrapnel.

'Don't be daft, sarge!' Lubba yelped, but Kolea was already running.

Flechette shot winnowed the air around him and he threw himself into the shell-hole.

'How's it going, Caff?' he asked.

'Kolea. Feth, it hurts. The fething alien freaks have got the end of the roadway locked up.'

Kolea looked at the wounds. 'Nasty, but the medicae are on the way. You'll live, Caffran.'

'I don't care about that!' Caffran said. 'I care about Tona!'

'What?'

'Rawne sent us all forward. I got caught here, she went on with Allo and Jenk. I think they were hit too. I can't reach her on the vox.'

'Oh gak,' Kolea said, peering out of the shell-hole. 'Stay here,' he said, as if Caffran was in any state to move.

'Sarge!'

'What?'

Caffran swallowed back his pain. 'Why... why did you come to me when I was arrested? You were acting so... so strange. When Tona came to visit me she gave me hell for getting into such a stupid fix. But I knew she was just frightened. You, though... it was like you were really afraid I'd actually done that stuff to that poor woman. What was that about?'

Kolea smiled at him. 'Caff, it must be the parent in me. I'll tell you when I get back.'

He jumped out of the shell-hole and started to run.

ALLO AND JENK were dead. Criid was sprawled beside their remains, wounded in the arm and side. Enemy fire wailed around them.

Kolea half-fell into her foxhole, banging his knee against a broken pipe.

'Hold tight, Tona,' he said. 'Caff's missing you.'

He scooped her up in his arms, ignoring her moans of pain and started to run back the way he had come.

'You're crazy!' she wailed as flechette shot exploded around them.

'Not the first time I've been accused of that,' he said, struggling. 'You and Varl ought to form a gakking club.'

He reached the edge of the shattered buildings and almost threw Criid into Jajjo's arms as he fell down.

He was smiling, and only when he fell did they see the bloody mess where the back of his skull had been.

'Sarge!' Lubba yelled, risking his own life to drag Kolea's body into cover from the crossfire. 'Sarge! Sergeant Kolea! Please! Don't be dead! Don't be dead!'

BRAGG LOOKED OVER at Caill. 'Last box?' he asked.

'We've got two more,' said his loader.

Bragg sighed. He looked out of the nearest hole in the wall and shook his head. Loxatl flechette fire was sweeping the street outside. 'Not going to be enough to get through that. I'll stay put and lay down some cover fire. You run back down the line and get us some more, eh?'

Caill nodded. 'I'll be two minutes,' he said. 'Don't leave without me.'

Caill hurried away. Bragg looked over at the other Ghosts in the shelled out basement: Tokar, Fenix, Cuu and Hwlan.

'Any bright ideas?' he said.

'You give me a good spread of protective fire with that land-hammer,' Hwlan said, 'and I reckon I can get a group into that block opposite.'

'You're on,' said Bragg and hefted the big support weapon into place. 'On three,' he said. 'One, two–'

The cannon exploded into life, strafing the street with a devastating rain of shots.

Hwlan, Fenix and Tokar surged out, running the gauntlet of fire.

The cannon clicked dry.

'Need another box?' Cuu asked.

'Yeah,' said Bragg. 'That would be–'

The corner of the ammo box cracked into the side of Bragg's head. He slumped to the side, and passed out for a second.

'What the feth?' he spluttered, coming round. 'Cuu? What the feth was that?' Bragg felt blood pouring out of his scalp. He was dizzy and sick.

Lijah Cuu was standing, staring at him.

'You sold me out,' he said.

'Oh feth, Cuu! This isn't the time to settle some stupid feud!'

'No? When would be a better time, Tanith? I don't know, sure as sure.'

Bragg tried to get up. 'You really have lost it, Cuu. Gaunt got you off. You just got lashes. You were lucky.'

'Lucky?'

'I mean… feth, I don't know what I mean. Feth, you're scum. Gaunt will have you shot for this and–'

'He ain't gonna know, is he?' said Cuu. 'Is he, you big dumbo?' In Cuu's right hand glittered thirty centimetres of silver Tanith warknife.

'Cuu? What the feth are you–'

Cuu plunged his straight silver into Bragg's heart.

Bragg's eyes widened. His lips gasped for a second, like a fish.

Cuu wrenched the dagger out and leaned forward so his mouth was right next to the dying Tanith's ear. 'Just so's you know… it *was* me. I did her. And it was beautiful. She fought, oh how she fought. Not like you, you big dumbo.'

Bragg suddenly lurched up and swung the autocannon around by the barrel like a club. If it had connected with the lean Verghastite it would surely have crippled him. But Cuu had jerked out of the way.

'Try again, Bragg,' he said, and stabbed the blade down again. And again. And again.

EPILOGUE: THE GUNS OF TANITH

PHANTINE,
227.771, M41

'I don't believe I had ever found a senior officer who appreciated the Ghosts' particular skills before. Now I have, I don't really think I'm any happier.'

– Ibram Gaunt, C-in-C, Tanith First

THE DROGUE HAD docked just a few minutes before, but already the children were running out and playing.

The Ghosts' entourage had reached Ouranberg as part of the mass reinforcement wave. Surly wharf masters oversaw the unloading of cargo freight, while men who would soon become jugglers, mimes, fire-eaters and knife-sharpeners haggled with them over the safe deposition of their worldly goods.

And the children were loose. Laughing, chanting, scampering around the docking bay. Yoncy tottered forward and half-threw a ball that Dalin went scampering after.

'Kids, huh?' said the woman behind Curth. The surgeon looked round.

'Kids,' said Aleksa scornfully. 'The battle's won, the dead are dead, and now the kids arrive to make us all soft and sad. Well, I'm not gakking sad. Life sucks. Get a bloody helmet.'

'Agreed,' said Curth, taking a lho-stick from her pack and offering the box to Aleksa. The blousy older woman with her boudoir finery took one and lit them both from a chased silver igniter.

'Dalin! Careful with your sister now, you hear me?' she shouted. She dropped her voice and added, 'You're the one he told, aren't you?'

'The one he told?'

'Kolea said to me the only other person who knew was the lady doctor. That's you, isn't it?'

'Yes,' Curth sighed.

After a while, Aleksa asked, 'How's Gol?'

'He's alive,' said Curth.

'But what?'

'His primary functions are intact. He's conscious. But the damage to his brain was considerable. He has total sociotypal memory loss. I mean total. He doesn't even know his own name. Or that he has kids. Nothing...'

Aleksa smiled. 'So that solves a lot, really.'

'No,' said Curth, taking out the sealed letter and staring at it. 'Gol Kolea came back... but he didn't come back. I... I don't know what to do.'

'Honey,' said Aleksa, pressing the letter back into Curth's coat, 'take my advice. Thank the Emperor and walk away.'

Curth folded up the letter and slowly wandered back up the docking ramp into the city.

VAN VOYTZ HAD been effusive in his praise. He was full of talk of commendations and decorations. He spoke about petitioning Macaroth to officially change the Tanith First's regimental designation to reflect its specialist stealth and infiltration strengths.

'The next time the guns of Tanith sound, I want it to be in support of my advances,' Van Voytz had declared, pouring large snifters of amasec for his assembled officers.

Gaunt hadn't really been listening. The arch-enemy had been deprived of Phantine. A significant heretic leader had been eliminated.

The Crusade force would now benefit from the planet's massive vapour mill output.

And he had kept alive as many men as possible in the pursuit of those goals.

It was a victory, and duty had been done. Gaunt just didn't share Van Voytz's desire to toast the living and the dead and talk about it all night. He walked alone through the Imperial concourse. Clearance teams were still searching the surrounding buildings for enemy survivors.

Gaunt supposed that the curse of mid-ranking officers like himself was that they were still close enough to the sharp end to feel the loss. The Gaunts and Rawnes and Fazalurs of this galaxy were the ones who got to cope with the bloody aftermath of victory. The lord generals got to celebrate each triumph because, to them, the dead were just names on data-slates. The chain of rank insulated them from the emotional consequence. It made a generally decent man like Van Voytz seem just as heartless as some of the callous bastards Gaunt had been forced to follow in his time.

At least the perceived rift between the Tanith and the Verghastite that Hark and Zweil had chided him about appeared to be easing. During the fight for Ouranberg, the regiment had seemed much more of a single, integrated whole.

Maybe sticking up for Cuu had sent the right message.

GAUNT RETURNED TO his section and had Beltayn transmit his respectful thanks to all Tanith and Verghastites alike via all section leaders, along with the order for the regiment to pull out. Urdeshi and Krassian reinforcements from Cirenholm were coming in to supervise the occupation.

The guns of Tanith could fall silent for a while, and rest.

'Order and signal of thanks sent, sir,' said Beltayn.

'That'll do,' said Ibram Gaunt.

STRAIGHT SILVER

FOR TANITH • FOR THE EMPEROR

For John Bergin and Gareth Branwyn
(for playing while I hammered)

*'T*HROUGHOUT THE *first six months of 772.M41, the seventeenth year of the Sabbat Worlds Campaign, the Imperial Crusade force under Warmaster Macaroth struggled to consolidate the wins it had achieved during the previous winter and turn them to its best advantage. Supremacy in the vital Cabal system now seemed possible, thanks to the lines of resource and supply – the so-called "victory veins" – opened up by the successful actions at Gigar, Aondrift Nova, Tanzina IV, Phantine and the mighty forge world Urdesh. But the infamous fortress world of Morlond still held out, and reports suggested that Urlock Gaur – who had, it seemed, become overlord of the arch-enemy forces since the death of Archon Nadzybar at Balhaut – was massing a renewed counter-attack in the Carcaradon Cluster. Furthermore, the Imperial Crusade was contesting hard along its coreward flank with Chaos hosts commanded by Anakwanar Sek, Shebol Red-hand and Enok Innokenti, three of Gaur's most capable warlords.*

'With typically instinctive flair, and against all the advice of his staff chiefs, Macaroth divided the Crusade force between his most trusted generals. Crusade Ninth Army, under Lord Militant Humel, was sent to Enothis to break the grip of Sek's vile host. The Eighth and Sixth Armies, commanded by General Kelso and Chapter Master Veegum of the Silver Guard, was directed to the Khan Group to prosecute Innokenti, while the Seventh, under Marshal Blackwood, struck out deep to coreward, towards Belshiir Binary and Alpha Madrigo. Lord General Bulledin, in command of the Second, was charged with holding and protecting the spinward supply lines through to Urdesh. Macaroth himself pressed on with the First, Third and Fourth to lead the renewed push for Morlond and, as the Warmaster put it, "grapple with Gaur in his own backyard".

'Many voices were raised in objection. The Navy commanders in particular believed that Macaroth had only survived his gamble at Cabal by the thinnest of luck, and now saw him repeating the risk on an even greater scale. Other generals expressed unhappiness at being passed over for army command. Van Voytz had hoped to get charge of the Fifth Army, but that was given to Luscheim and tasked with rearguarding Macaroth's push. Instead, Van Voytz was given a brigade-strength taskforce, nominally attached to the Fifth, and sent to Aexe Cardinal, an Imperial world that had held out throughout the Chaos domination of the Sabbat Worlds. There, he faced the unenviable labour of breaking a deadlocked land war that had been raging for forty years…'

— from *A History of the Later Imperial Crusades*

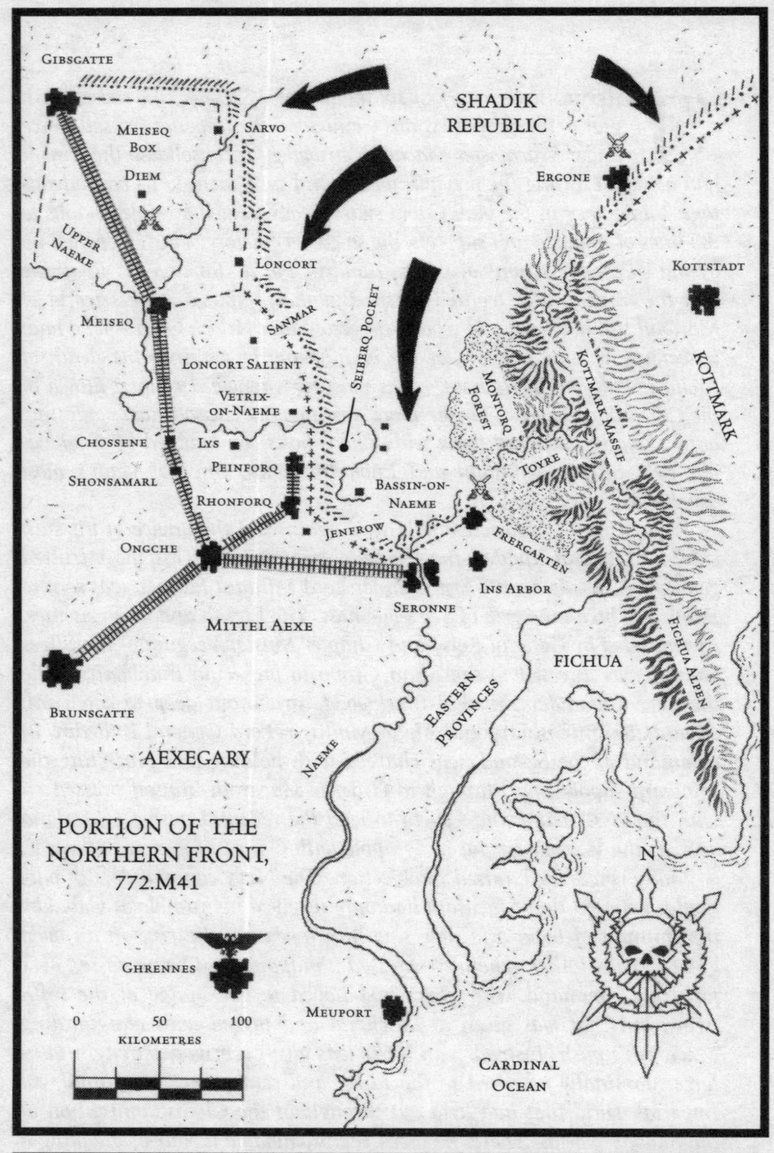
Gibsgatte
Shadik
Republic
Meiseq
Box
Sarvo
Diem
Ergone
Upper
Naeme
Loncort
Kottstadt
Meiseq
Sanmar
Seiberq Pocket
Loncort Salient
Montorq
Forest
Kottmark Massif
Kottmark
Vetrix-
on-Naeme
Chossene
Lys
Toyre
Peinforq
Shonsamarl
Bassin-on-
Naeme
Rhonforq
Jenfrow
Fregarten
Ongche
Ins Arbor
Seronne
Mittel Aexe
Fichua
Fichua Alpen
Eastern
Provinces
Brunsgatte
Naeme
Aexegary
Portion of the
Northern Front,
772.M41
N
Ghrennes
Meuport
0
50
100
kilometres
Cardinal
Ocean

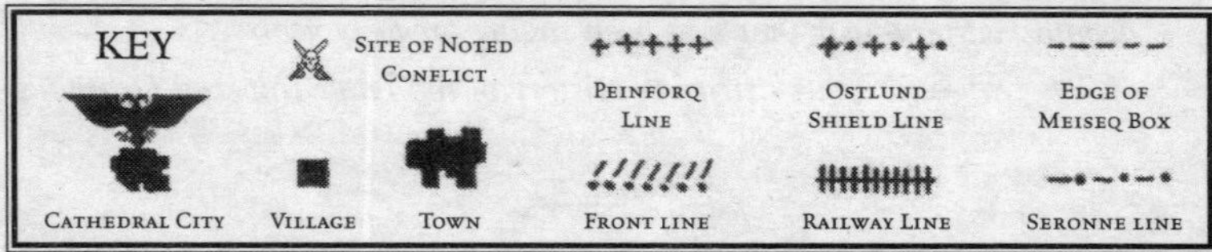
Key
Site of Noted
Conflict
Peinforq
Line
Ostlund
Shield Line
Edge of
Meiseq Box
Cathedral City
Village
Town
Front line
Railway Line
Seronne line

PROLOGUE

'There are three things an Aexegarian may be trusted to do well: make love, make war, and worship the Emperor. Of these, warmaking is our finest skill. We have been doing it for years. I think you'll find we have the hang of it.'

– Leonid Fep Krefuel, High Sezar of Aexegary

BRUNSGATTE TOWERED AROUND him like a badly-ordered dream. He was weary from the long train journey and, as he had moved westward, the weather had become increasingly poor and wet, so now the pin in his femur ached rheumatically. He had tried to distract himself by reviewing the despatches once again, but it was too dark in the back of the limousine. Instead, he sat back, hands clasped across his belly, and watched the city as it passed.

Dusk was closing, and the lamps along the strasseways were beginning to glow amber under their frosted-glass hoods. In twenty minutes, they would be little stars of pearl-white light. The rain was coming down. To the south, it made dark, blurry sheets under the clouds that frothed above the commercial district and the Brunsgatte docks.

The limousine, shiny black like a dress uniform shoe, was an old Ampara Furioso Vitesse, as solidly built as a Leman Russ. On either side of the silver leaping-behj ornament above the car's snarling chrome grille, a pennant fluttered. The blue and gold state flag to the left; the gold, white and magenta colours of the Aexe Alliance to the right. He could barely hear the eight litre engine, such was the thickness of the bodywork and the upholstery, but the stroking windshield wipers squealed every ten seconds like fingernails down a blackboard.

The car crossed Congressplatz, passed under the shadow of Sezar's Gate, where slopes of red wreaths were piled up, and ran the length of the Colonnade of Fishers to Trimercy.

Squeak, squeak, squeak, stroked the wipers.

They stopped at the lights at Trimercy, and the southerly flow of traffic passed before them. The outriders each put a boot down to steady their bikes. The limousine's climate control seemed to be circulating nothing but warm exhaust fumes. He leaned forward and fiddled with the dial, to no appreciable effect.

'What's wrong with the heater?' he snapped.

The driver lowered the lacquered communicating screen.

'What did you say, sire?'

'The heater.'

'It's on, sire.'

'Could it be off?'

'Of course, sire.' The driver made an adjustment to the dashboard controls. 'Better?'

It wasn't. He thumbed down the reardoor window and let in the cool rain-scents of the city. He could smell damp tarmac and wet rockcrete. He could hear motor engines and distant horns. At the roadside, by the junction, he could see a flower stand closing up for the night. The seller, swathed in a transparent slicker, was hand-folding the fractal blooms into their metal cups. The glittering mathematical petals crackled as deft, expert hands collapsed them.

Some were a particular red. He felt his pulse rate rise. Not now... not now...

He closed his eyes and swallowed hard, trying to retard his breathing the way his physician had taught him. But the Seiberq Pocket was only a heartbeat away. The lightning. The spraying mud. The dreadnoughts. The pools filling the shell craters. Red, red...

The lights changed and they pulled north, the outriders describing wide arcs as they roared away ahead, lamps flashing.

'Are you all right, sire?' the driver asked.

'Yes, I'm fine. Fine.' He closed the reardoor window to a thin slit.

Mons Sezari rose before them, dominating the skyline, dwarfing even the tallest of Brunsgatte's steeples and towers. They climbed the curling road and then pulled in under a glass awning behind the postern gate.

'Ready, sire?' asked the driver.

'Yes,' he said, and got out. A junior military aide held the limousine door for him.

In the days of the great sezars, generals had entered Brunsgatte from the Fortress Gate, carried in pomp on jewelled warcarts pulled by striding struthids.

Those times were long gone, but protocol demanded that he transferred from the car to a warcart for the final, formal approach.

A squadron of hussars had the warcart waiting. The struthids, some of the last of that dwindling species, were huge, proud beasts with massive, polished beaks and thick plumage, standing twenty hands high. He thought of the scabby, thin mounts the front-line cavalry were forced to make do with.

He stepped up onto the warcart's backplate, his attaché case tucked under his arm, and the hussar chief lashed the struthids forward. Their trimmed black claws drew sparks from the wet cobbles as they began to canter.

The fighting birds drew the warcart in under the entry arch of Mons Sezari and drew up at the west porch of the palace, a long aisle of electric lamps under a stained glass roof. Officers of the Bande Sezari were waiting in full dress uniform, struthid plumes in their shakos. They wore voluminous pantaloons of green silk, with gold chains linking the wide hips to their wrists, so that when they saluted, they seemed to spread wide green wings in his honour.

He dismounted, paid the driver his ritual scuto, and walked up the long blue carpet into the porch. The attaché case swung in his hand.

Sire Kido Fep Soten, the high sezar's chamberlain, was waiting for him under the glass portico. Soten parted the black velvet of his ermine-trimmed robes and made the aquila salute across his chest.

'My sire count, welcome. The sezar awaits you.'

He followed Soten down a long hallway decorated with heraldic motif wallpaper, through a chamber strung with stupendous chandeliers, and into the audience room. Halberdiers of the Bande Sezari opened the doors for them.

Soten bowed. 'My lord high sezar,' he proclaimed, 'Count Iaco Bousar Fep Golke, commander-in-chief of the Aexe Alliance forces, awaits your pleasure.'

The high sezar, Leonid Fep Krefuel, rose from his couch. He had been sitting near the fireplace, shielded from its direct heat by a fretwork screen. Through open doors on the far side of the room, the count could see a gathering of figures and hear the clink of glasses.

The sezar was clad in ceremonial gold battledress brocaded with silver wire and diamonds under a behj-skin mantle. He was a short, heavy-set man with a ruddy, colicky face, a wet, ample mouth and a thin, grey moustache.

'Count Golke, a pleasure as always,' he said.

'My high sezar, you do me an honour.'

'Welcome, welcome... take refreshment.'

A black metal-enhanced servitor whined up alongside them, carrying a tray of drinks. Golke took a small amasec and sipped it. He owned several estates, including a schloss in the eastern provinces, but still the sheer scale of the Mons Sezari architecture scared him. The ceilings were so high, the windows so sheer. Blue and gold silk banners, thirty metres long, hung down the walls, each one sporting the leaping-behj arms of Aexegary. Every month for four years he had come to the palace to deliver his war report, and still it humbled him.

'I could wait, lord, if you are with guests,' Golke said, gesturing to the figures in the adjacent room.

'No, no. We will join them directly. There are men I want you to meet.'

Golke wanted to ask who the men were, but he could tell the High Sezar of Aexegary was in one of his businesslike moods. He'd been the same when they'd met the week before the push on Jepel and Seiberq. He's preparing to give me instructions he knows I won't like, Golke thought. God help us, not another Seiberq.

Golke set down his drink. 'My report, lord?'

The sezar nodded. 'Let's have it,' he said, settling back onto his place on the couch.

Golke's fingers were shaking as he unbuckled the attaché case and slid the duplicate copies of the report out. Both were sleeved in blue covers and closed with gold ribbons. He passed one to his master, who took it and slit the ribbon with the behj-claw he wore on a signet ring.

Golke opened his own copy, stood before the high sezar and started to read.

'An account of the warfare between the forces of his glorious majesty the High Sezar of Aexegary and his allies, and the denounced oppressors of Shadik, in the period 181.772 and 212.772. Foremost, it must be seen that the concentration of artillery attacks along the Peinforq Line, and also in the Naeme Valley, has much harassed the progress of the enemy's infantry dispositions in that region. Observer estimates place a mortality figure of nine thousand on said enemy dispositions, with particular losses taken around Bassin-on-Naeme on the nights of 187-189. Munition expenditure in that period is given as forty-eight thousand nine hundred and eleven 0.12 medium explosive shells, nine thousand and forty-six 0.90 incendiary shells, two thousand three hundred and seventy-nine 0.50 heavy shells and–'

'Has the expenditure been costed?' asked the sezar.

'My lord, yes,' said Golke, skipping through the pages of his report. 'It is annotated in the fiscal appendix. Ahm... rounding up, two point two million scutos.'

'You say "harassed" the progress, count. Does that mean impeded? Halted? Denied?'

Golke cleared his throat. 'They suffered losses, as I said, and their advance was stalemated, though they retook the towns of Vilaq and Contae-Sanlur.'

'Move on.'

'My lord. Along the edge of the Meiseq Sector, I am pleased to report our line has held fast despite sequential attacks. On the afternoon of the 197th, a breakthrough was achieved by the Forty-First Brigade at Sarvo, and they managed to advance to hold the water mills at Selph.'

'How far is that?'

'Three... ah... three hundred and ten metres, lord.'

'Move on.'

'The north-western sector. At Gibsgatte, the Third Regiment of the Sezari Light held off a counter-push on the 199th. The regimental commander personally notes his gratitude to the high sezar for his foresight in disposing them to Gibsgatte so that they might achieve such glory.'

'Losses?'

'Twelve hundred and eighty-one, lord.'

The high sezar closed his copy of the report and put it down on the seat beside him.

'Should I continue, sire?' Golke asked.

'Will I hear anything new?' the high sezar asked. 'Will I hear anything apart from what is effectively a stalemate no matter how you dress it up? Will I hear anything apart from deadlock at the cost of thousands of men and millions of scutos?'

Golke lowered his report to his side. A loose page fell out and fluttered down onto the carpet.

'No, my lord.'

The sezar rose again. 'Forty years, count. Forty years of this. Forty years of waste and cost and stagnation. There are boy soldiers on the front these days whose grandfathers died in the first phases, when we stood against Shadik alone. Our allies are with us now, thank the Golden Throne, but...'

He looked into the fire for a moment. Golke thought how heavy the behj-skin mantle looked on his shoulders.

'Do you know what Soten told me the other morning?' the sezar asked quietly.

'No, sire.'

'He told me that since the Principality of Fichua added its strength to the Alliance back in... what was it? 764?'

'763, sire, with the Stromberg Pact.'

'Just so. Since 763, our Alliance armies have lost the equivalent of the entire population of Fichua nine times over.'

It was a stunning statistic. Golke blinked. He knew Fichua well, from vacations there in long-past days. The smallest country in Continental Aexe, to be sure, but still...

He felt his pulse rising again. Anger rose up in him like quicksilver in a thermometer that has been stuck in a furnace. He wanted to scream at the lord sezar.

It's because of you! You! You! You, and the staff chiefs who have gone before me, with your rules of war and your codes of battle! Damn you and your archaic strategies–

Instead, he bit his tongue and breathed deeply, the way his physician had taught him.

'The impasse is maddening, my lord,' he said. His voice sounded tiny and strained. 'But perhaps by the year's end, we might–'

The sezar turned to face him. 'Count Golke, please. I'm not blaming you for those forty years. I praise your efforts, the sterling work you have undertaken since you took over as commander-in-chief. I am not a stupid man, no matter what the popular press says–'

'Of course not, my lord!'

The sezar raised a hand. Firelight winked off the behj-claw ring. 'Let them blow off steam, I say. Let them rail in their editorials and goad me with their cartoons. I am beloved of the Aexegarian people.'

'You are high sezar, my lord.'

'And I will achieve my triumph, I have no doubt. I will break Shadik and drive its hosts out into the wilds.'

'I have no doubt, lord.'

'Neither have I. I never have doubted that, count. But as from tonight, I am assured of it.'

Golke glanced over at the room beyond where the visitors were talking and sipping drinks under the chandeliers.

'Why… tonight, my lord?'

'This day, Count Golke. It will be remembered in our history books. Our great-great-grandchildren will celebrate it.'

The sezar moved over to Golke and took him gently by the arm. 'It has not yet been publicly announced, count, nor will it be for some time. But you must be told. Five nights ago, Imperial starships arrived in orbit. The first of a liberation fleet.'

Golke swallowed and considered the words one by one. He felt a little giddy. The pin in his hip suddenly ached like a bastard.

'Imperial…?'

'The crusade has reached us, my dear friend. After all these years of fighting alone against Chaos in the dark. Warmaster Macaroth, praise be his name, has cut a swathe through the arch-enemy, putting them to flight. The Sabbat Worlds are his now, his for the taking. And, as is only right, he saw it as his first priority to despatch elite forces to relieve Aexe Cardinal. The first contingents are deploying as we speak. From next week, the war against Shadik will be bolstered by the Emperor's Imperial Guard. Our long struggle has not been in vain.'

'I am… overwhelmed, my lord.'

The sezar grinned. 'Take up your drink, Golke, and toast this redemption with me.'

Golke found his glass, and the sezar clinked his own against it.

'To victory, long pursued, rightfully ours.'

They threw their empty glasses into the grate.

'I have something for you, count,' said the sezar. 'Two things, actually.' He reached into his robes and produced a slim, oblong box covered in gold-flecked blue satin. The sezar opened it.

A Gold Aquila, pinned to a white silk ribbon, lay in the cushioned interior.

'My lord!'

'This is to acknowledge your devoted service to me, to the Alliance and to Aexegary. The Order of the Eagle. The greatest honour it is in my gift to bestow.'

The high sezar took the medal from the box and carefully fixed it to Golke's breast.

'You have done your country great service, Iaco Bousar Fep Golke, and you have acquitted yourself, in my name, with devotion, ability, obedience and humility. You have personally known the physical cost of war. I salute you.'

'High lord of all, it has been my duty and my duty only.'

The sezar clapped him gently on the arm. 'You've earned this, Golke. This – and my other gift.'

'Sir?'

'As of midnight tonight, you are honourably relieved of supreme command. Your toil is done.'

'Relieved of command...? My lord, why? Have I displeased you?'

The sezar laughed, loudly. It was forced, Golke could sense.

'Not one bit. But with the arrival of the Imperials, I am forced to make changes in the command structure. Radical changes. You understand, don't you, count? It's all tediously political.'

'My lord?'

'The Imperial general... Vonvoyze, I think he's called... he'll want authority, and space to cohere his forces. He and his senior staff need a liaison, someone who can help to acclimatize them and clasp them into our war effort efficiently. I trust you, Golke. I want you in that role.'

'Liaison?'

'Just so. Linking our forces with those of our liberators. You have the tact, I think. The objectivity. You are an educated man. And you deserve a rewarding job after the trials of supreme command.'

'I... I consider myself fortunate, my lord. So... who will take my place?'

'As commander-in-chief? I'm giving that to Lyntor-Sewq. He's all fired up and very much the coming man. He'll put a fire under our armies with that enthusiasm of his.'

Golke nodded, though it was just a mechanical gesture. 'This Imperial general... he will answer to Lyntor-Sewq?'

'Of course he will!' the sezar snorted. 'The Imperial Guard may have arrived at last to dig us out, but this is still *our* war. Aexegary will retain supreme command. Come...'

The high sezar put his hand on Count Golke's arm and steered him towards the cocktail party in the adjacent room.

'Come and meet these Imperial saviours we've been sent. Let them get the measure of you. You can congratulate Lyntor-Sewq while you're at it.'

'I can't wait, my lord.'

ONE
UP THE LINE TO THE NAEME

'It's all a matter of ratios.'

– Savil Fep Lyntor-Sewq, Supreme Commander,
Aexe Alliance Forces, on reviewing casualty lists

THE HULKING LIFT-CARRIERS had dispersed them onto lush green paddocks near a place they had been told was called Brunsgatte. They could see the city skyline in the distance, through leafy woodland and the low-rise roofs of outer boroughs. Some time that morning it had rained, but now the day was warm and clear and felt like spring.

Everything had come off in the paddocks: infantry, heavy support, munitions, supplies, even the disorderly, unofficial ranks of camp followers. Processions of big, dirty-sided trucks had begun to lurch onto the grass to gather them all up and transport them to the railhead. Two kilometres away, over the woodland, the drop-ships of the Krassian Sixth were visible in the air, gliding down onto their own assembly points.

Trooper Caffran of the Tanith First-and-Only wandered slowly away from the landing zone, where the grass was bent over by jetwash, and stood by a hedge, overlooking the belt of woods. He sort of liked this place already. There were trees. There was greenery.

Caffran, first name Dermon, was twenty-four standard years old. He was short but well-made, with a blue dragon tattooed on his temple. He had been born and bred on Tanith, a forest world that no longer existed. Caffran was an Imperial Guardsman – a highly effective one, according to his formal record.

He wore the standard issue kit of a Tanith soldier: cross-laced black boots, black fatigue trousers and blouse over standard issue vest and shorts, with webbing – which supported his field pouches and a plump musette bag – and lightweight, matt-grey cloth armour. A tight, black buckle-under helmet made of ceramite swung from his waist belt beside his warknife. On his collars he wore the skull and dagger crest of the Tanith First and around his shoulders was draped a camo cloak, the signature item of the Tanith regiment, the so-called 'Ghosts'.

A heavy pack was slung from his back. His standard pattern Mark III lasrifle, its stock and furniture made of nalwood, as were all Tanith-stamped lasguns, hung on a fylon sling over his shoulder.

Caffran could smell rain and beech-mast on the air, the wet odours of a woodland floor. Just for a second, the smell was unbearably evocative. His heart struggled to accommodate the feelings.

He glanced back to see if he was missed, but there already seemed some delay in loading the regiment onto the trucks. Engines idled and grumbled, and an occasional wheel spun in the muddy grass that the convoy was quickly chewing up. Local military had pegged out assembly points on the paddock with metal tent stakes and twine, but seeing the wait, few of the Tanith had stayed in their sections. Some sat on the grass. A few dropped their packs and started kicking a ball around. Stewards in long, tan greatcoats hurried about, shouting instructions, directing trucks and trying to gather guardsmen together as if they were escaped poultry.

At the end of the hedge, Caffran found a brick-paved path that ran away under an avenue of grey-barked trees. These paddocks were clearly a municipal park, he realised, turned into a makeshift landing zone.

There were benches facing the path, and he sat down on one in damp shade of the avenue trees. It was nice, he thought. Sure, the trees had none of the grandeur of Tanith trees, but still.

He wondered how Tona was doing. She was his girl, though she was a fellow trooper too. Tona had come in on a different carrier because they were in different squads now. Sergeant Criid. It still made him chuckle. Another first for the First-and-Only.

Between every other tree in the avenue, there was a large, smooth cube of white stone. Each had a faded oblong patch on the side facing the path. Caffran wondered what they were. Markers of some sort, maybe.

He heard someone coming up behind him and turned. It was Commissar Hark, the regiment's political officer. Caffran grabbed up his pack hurriedly and stood, but Hark waved him down with a relaxed hand. Sometimes Hark could be a bastard disciplinarian, but only when it mattered, and it clearly didn't matter now. He gave the bench a quick brush with his gloved hand and sat down next to Caffran, curtseying the tails of his stormcoat over his thighs so he could cross his legs.

'Some kind of general balls-up,' he said, indicating the dispersal area behind them with a sideways nod. 'I don't know. There's about twenty trucks packed with our people just sitting there, trying to leave the park. No wonder the war here's been going on for forty years. They can't even organise their way out of a field.'

Caffran smiled.

'Still,' said Hark, 'a chance to take the air. You had the right idea.'

'Thought I was about to get a reprimand,' said Caffran.

Hark glanced over at him and raised his eyebrows in a 'you never know' expression. Viktor Hark was a sturdy man, strong but fleshy from years of good living. His eyes were slightly hooded and his clean shaven cheeks slabby. He took off his commissariate cap and fiddled with the lining, revealing thick, cropped black hair on a skull that rose like the round tip of bullet from his broad neck.

'They've been at it forty years, sir?' Caffran asked.

'Oh, yes,' said Hark, gazing out through the trees at the rise and fall of lift-carriers at another dispersal field in the middle distance. 'Forty fething years. What do you think of that?'

'I'm afraid I don't know much about it at all, sir. I know this planet is called Aexe Cardinal, and that city over there is called Brunsgatte. Apart from that...'

'There'll be briefings, Caffran, don't worry. You're a guest of a nation called Aexegary, the chief amongst seven nation states that are at war with the Republic of Shadik. The brigade is here to bolster their forces and show Shadik how war really works.'

Caffran nodded. He didn't really care much, but it wasn't often he got to have a conversation with Hark.

'We're fighting a nation, then, sir?'

'No, we're fighting the same arch-enemy as ever. Chaos got its filthy claws into Shadik some time back, trying to use it as a foothold to conquer the entire planet.'

'I guess it's pretty impressive they've held them off so long,' Caffran ventured.

Hark shrugged. They were silent for a moment, then Hark said, 'How do you think that girl of yours will do?'

'Criid? I think she'll do fine, sir.'

'Bit of a gamble, giving a woman squad command, but Gaunt agrees it's worth it. Besides, we needed a Verghast to take the reins of Kolea's unit. You think she can take the pressure?'

'Easily. It's everyone else I'd worry about. Keeping up with her.'

Hark sniggered and put his cap back on. 'My appraisal precisely. Still, it's going to be interesting. Three new sergeants to test in the field.'

Criid wasn't the only trooper to have been promoted into dead men's boots after the tour on Phantine. A Verghast called Arcuda had been given charge of Indrimmo's platoon, and Raglon had been posted to lead Adare's. Best luck to all three, Caffran felt. Indrimmo had died at Cirenholm, and Adare had been killed during the penetration raid at Ouranberg. Kolea, one of the best loved Verghast troopers, wasn't dead, but a head wound during the final phase of fighting at Ouranberg had robbed him of memory and identity. He could still function, physically, but Gol Kolea wasn't living in Gol Kolea's body any more. He was a trooper now, serving under Criid as part of his old squad.

Tragic is what it was.

'I see the old heroes and worthies of Aexegary have gone back to fight the war,' Hark said.

'Sir?'

The commissar pointed at the white stone blocks under the trees. 'Those plinths. The statues have been removed. Even the placards. Recycled. Melted down for the war effort. Whoever used to stand on top of those is probably shrieking towards the Shadik lines right now as part of a shell case. Aexegary is on its last legs, Caffran. Drained to the limit. We got here just in time.'

'Sir.'

'I hope,' Hark added. 'Maybe they're already dead, just still twitching. Guess we'll find out.'

His tone was flippant, but his words made Caffran uneasy. No one wants to get into a fight that's already lost.

Whistles started to blow up on the field. They looked round and saw things were beginning to move. Stewards were urging Ghost troops onto the trucks.

'Up and at 'em,' Hark said, rising. He dusted his coat down as Caffran hoisted up his bergen.

'Do me a favour,' Hark said. 'Loop back down this path and check there are no stragglers. I'll hold your transport for you.'

'Yes, sir.'

As Hark walked back up the grass to the LZ, Caffran went the opposite way down the path, covering the trees and the line of the hedge. He found Derin and Costin leaning against a vacant plinth smoking lho-sticks.

'Look sharp,' Caffran said. 'We're moving at last.'

Both of them cursed.

'And Hark's on the prowl.'

Derin and Costin finished their smokes and gathered up their kit.

'Coming, Caff?' Derin asked.

'Be there in a sec,' he replied, and continued down the pathway, leaving them to wander back to the assembly areas.

It all seemed clear. Caffran was about to turn back himself when he spotted a lone figure right down at the edge of the adjoining paddock, lurking under a small stand of trees.

As he jogged closer, he could see who it was: Larkin.

The regiment's master sniper was so lost in his own thoughts, he didn't hear Caffran approach. He seemed to be listening to the rustle of the breeze through the branches above him. His kit and his bagged long-las were piled up on the grass beside him.

Caffran slowed his pace to a walk. Larkin had never been the most stable of the Tanith, but he'd become particularly withdrawn and distant since Bragg's death.

Everyone had been fond of Try Again Bragg. It was hard not to be. Genial and good-natured, almost gentle, he'd used his famous size and strength to great effect as a heavy weapons specialist... never mind his terrible aim, which had earned him the nickname. Bragg had fallen to enemy fire at Ouranberg and everyone missed him. He'd seemed to be one of the regiment's permanent features, immovable, like bedrock. His death had robbed them all of something. Confidence perhaps. Even the most gung-ho Ghosts had stopped believing they would live forever.

Bragg had been Larkin's closest friend. They'd been a double act, the wiry sniper and the giant gunner, like Clarco and Clop, the clowns in the Imperial mystery plays. Larkin had taken the big man's death hardest of all, probably, Caffran guessed, because Larkin hadn't been there. The sniper had been part of the penetration mission, sent in ahead of the main force, and by the time he had been picked up and returned to the Ghost's ranks, Bragg was already dead.

'Larks?' Caffran began.

The knife was there in a blink. Larkin's Tanith warknife, its straight silver blade thirty centimetres long. It appeared as fast as one of Varl's barrack room sleight-of-hand tricks. Caffran saw the blade, and the fear in Larkin's eyes.

'Feth!' he said, backing off, his hands raised. 'Steady!'

It seemed to take a moment for Larkin to recognise Caffran. He blinked, swallowed, then shook his head and put the knife away with a hand Caffran could see was shaking.

'Sorry, Caff,' Larkin said. 'You made me jump.'

'I did that,' agreed Caffran, raising his eyebrows. 'You okay?'

Larkin had turned aside and was gazing away into nothing again.

'Larks?'

'I'm fine. Just thinking.'

'About what?'

'Nothing. You... on your own?'

Caffran looked about. 'Yeah. Hark sent me to gather everyone up. We're rousting out.'

Larkin nodded. He seemed a little more composed. It was often hard to tell with Mad Hlaine Larkin. He picked up his bergen and rested his sniper weapon over his shoulder.

'You sure you're okay?' Caffran asked.

'Jumpy. Always get jumpy before a show. Got me an ill feeling about...'

'The Emperor protects,' said Caffran.

Larkin murmured something that Caffran didn't catch and hooked the little silver aquila he wore round his neck out so he could kiss it.

'Sometimes,' he said, 'I don't think the Emperor's even watching.'

AT THE PARK gates, the reason for the convoy's slow departure became evident. The Aexegarian people had come out to greet the liberators. They thronged around the gates, filling nearby streets, blocking the route with a mass of cheering bodies, despite the best efforts of the local arbites to control them. From the back of the troop trucks, the crowd was a sea of waving blue and gold flags, with the odd Imperial crest pennant mixed in. At least three brass bands were vying for attention. Hab-wives held babies up to the sides of the creeping transports, calling to the guardsmen to touch them and make them lucky. Local hierachs in full regalia had come out to bless the off-worlders, and the district mayor had arrived with a delegation of selectmen. Blue and gold bunting threaded the rockcrete lampposts, chirring in the breeze. The mayor's aides cornered the first Tanith officer to emerge from the park, and dragged him off to be presented to the mayor, who granted him the freedom of the city, strung garlands round his neck and generally shook his hand off on the assumption that he was in charge. He wasn't. He was Sergeant Varl of nine platoon who had just happened to get his men onto a truck first. Varl was quite enjoying the attention until he was asked to address the crowd.

It took over three hours to get the Tanith from their LZ to the railhead. The massive convoy finally shook free of the crowds and moved off through an industrial suburb of Brunsgatte where long straight avenues of identical red-brick habitat blocks alternated with guild halls, labourers' welfare clubs and shabby grey manufactories. It started to rain along the way, a shower at first and then heavier and heavier until the downpour hid the receding towers of the city and obscured the great palace overlooking it all.

In the rain, the railhead was a blur of steam. Troop trains, converted from livestock wagons, were lined up in siding areas, their maroon locomotives panting wet heat and hissing out vapours of sooty fumes. Tractors with fat bowser tanks watered the boilers, and mechanised chutes fed gleaming floods of coke straight into the tenders.

The air smelled of coal-tar. Whistles shrilled. The Tanith exited the trucks and huddled under dripping temporary awnings as the local militia moved amongst them, issuing embarkation numbers. Heavy equipment and vehicles were loaded aboard freight trains with wide conflat wagons. From under the awnings, the Tanith waved and exchanged cat-calls with the Krassian troops mustering on the far side of the tracks. The regiments had fought together at Ouranberg. Old friendships – and rivalries – were renewed.

Ditching the military staff car that had brought him from the LZ, Colonel-Commissar Ibram Gaunt strode in through the steam and the bustle. The liaison officer appointed to him, a Major Nyls Fep Buzzel, scurried to keep up. Buzzel was a short, plump man who kept his right hand stiffly in the pocket of his green overcoat, and Gaunt presumed him to be an invalid veteran. As Gaunt understood the circumstances on Aexe Cardinal, all able-bodied men not in reserved occupations were at the front. The fronts, he corrected himself. This was a global war, with theatres to the north and west of Aexegary, along the sovereign states of the southern oceans, and in the east.

Buzzel was pleasant enough. He wore an officer's cap with cockade made from some sort of plumage. The feather was wilting in the rain. He'd said something about serving with the Bande Sezari, a name he mentioned with pride as if to suggest it was something special, but Gaunt had never heard of it.

'When do I see data-slates? Tacticals? Charts of disposition?' Gaunt asked as he strode along.

'There will be time, sir!' Buzzel replied, side-stepping a munition cart.

Gaunt stopped and looked at the Aexegarian. 'I'm moving my troops to the front line, major. I'd like to have a feel for that area at least before they get there.'

'We will be breaking the transit to Rhonforq, the allied staff headquarters, sir. Briefing dossiers have been forwarded there.'

'Are these cattle trucks?' Gaunt asked, banging the side of the nearest wagon.

'Yes, but–' Buzzel began before realising Gaunt was already moving again.

'Sergeant Bray! Secure those tent rolls!' Gaunt called.

'Sir!'

'Obel? Ewler? Which train are you supposed to be on? Look at the dockets, for feth's sake!'

'Yes sir!'

'Varl? Nice speech. You're missing a few of your mob. I saw them down past the gangers' huts, smoking and dicing.'

'Right on it, sir!'

Buzzel watched the colonel-commissar curiously. Apparently, he was quite a war hero, so they said. Tall, imposing in his black leather stormcoat and commissariate cap, with a face like... like his name. Narrow, sculptural, noble. Buzzel reflected sourly that he didn't know what a war hero was meant to look like. Sixteen years of front-line service and he'd never met one.

He liked Gaunt's manner. Authoritative, brisk, disciplined, and he still seemed to know every man by name.

'Daur!'

A handsome young Tanith captain rushing past stopped to salute Gaunt.

'You making any sense of this?'

Captain Daur nodded, producing a data-slate. 'I borrowed this from one of the local marshals,' he said. 'Makes more sense than a lot of whistle blowing and shouting.'

'Let me look,' said Gaunt and reviewed the slate.

'Managing all right?' he asked as he read.

'Yes sir. Trying to find Grell's platoon. They should be aboard C Train already, but they've been lost in the mix.'

Gaunt turned and pointed. 'I saw them over there, behind the signal gantries, helping to load munition crates from a stalled tractor.'

'Thank you, sir,' Daur said as he took back the slate and hurried off.

'A car has been prepared for you in Train A,' Buzzel said, but Gaunt wasn't listening.

'Surgeon Curth? What's the problem?'

A woman had appeared. She was young and wore a borrowed rain-slicker over her red medicae overalls. A stern expression gave her appealing, heart-shaped face a hard edge.

'All the regimental medical supplies have gone walkabout, Gaunt,' she said. Buzzel was surprised to hear her use the colonel-commissar's surname without the respect of rank.

'Have you looked around?'

'We've all looked around. Dorden's hopping mad.'

Buzzel stepped forward. 'If I may, sir... the medical supplies would have been loaded onto Train E along with consumables. That's already on its way.'

'There's your answer, Ana,' said Gaunt. 'Aexegarian efficiency is a step ahead of you.'

The woman smiled and disappeared into the mêlée of hurrying bodies.

Gaunt moved on, jumping down off the rockcrete platform so he could walk down the side of a troop train along the gravelly sleeper bed. Tanith troops pressed themselves eagerly against the wagon window slits and dangled like apes out of the doorways, clapping their hands and chanting his name. 'Gaunt! Gaunt! Gaunt!'

Gaunt made a mock bow, doffed his cap to them and then stood again, clapping back at them. There were cheers.

'Soric! Mkoll! Haller! Domor! My thanks to your men for that warm support! Are you ready to move?'

A chorus of 'Ayes!'

'We're ready, sir!' called a thickset, older sergeant with one eye.

'Good for you, Soric. Tell your boys to get as comfortable as they can. It's a six-hour ride.'

'Aye, sir!'

'It's only four hours to Rhonforq, sir,' whispered Buzzel.

'I know. But if they steel themselves for six, four will seem like nothing. It's called psychology,' Gaunt whispered back.

He turned to face the train again. 'Sergeant Domor?'

'Sir!' replied a soldier with bulky augmetic optical implants.

'Where's Milo?'

'Here, sir!'

A lad appeared in the crowded wagon doorway, the youngest Tanith Buzzel had yet seen.

'Milo… pipe us on our way,' Gaunt said. The boy nodded and, after a few moments, a wailing, haunting note rose up above the frenetic activity. Buzzel recognised the tune: The old Imperial hymn 'Behold! the Triumph of Terra'.

THREE TRACKS AWAY, Colm Corbec, colonel and second officer of the Tanith regiment, heard the pipes as he slammed the wagon's side-door shut and dropped the latch.

Corbec was an oak of a man, bearded and hairy limbed, with a fighting temper and a playful good humour that made him beloved of the men.

'Ah, the pipes,' he sighed. 'Magnifying the glory of Terra to the heavens in bitter-sweet lament.'

'You talk a lot of old feth sometimes, chief,' said Muril, the sniper in Corbec's squad, and the other troopers laughed. Muril was a Verghastite, one of a host of men and women recruited from the city of Vervunhive to bolster the original Tanith strength. The divided loyalties and cultural differences of the two sides – Tanith and Verghast – had taken a long time to gel, but now they seemed to be pulling together as one fluid unit and for that Corbec was grateful. They'd fought well together, mixed well, complemented each other's strengths, but as far as Corbec was concerned, the real breakthrough had come when they'd started using each other's curse words. Once he'd heard Verghastites saying 'Feth!' and Tanith saying 'Gak!' he'd known they were home and dry.

Muril was one of his favourite troopers. Like many of the female Verghast volunteers, she'd excelled at marksmanship and had specialised as a sniper. Her bagged long-las lay beside her on the straw-littered floor of the wagon and the grey silk marksman's lanyard was displayed between the third button of her field jacket and the stud of the left-hand breast pocket. Muril was tall and lean, with long dark hair that she kept pinned back in a bun, and a slender, sharp-nosed face framing knowing dark eyes and a refreshing smile. Corbec had seen her injured during the fight for Cirenholm. In fact, he'd almost got himself killed dragging her to safety. Despite the fact the surgeon had been required to rebuild her pelvis, she had recovered a fething sight quicker than he had.

He was still shaky, still weak, though he put a brave face on it. Several people had commented on how much weight he had lost. I'm old, Corbec told himself. Recovery takes longer for a man of my distinguished years.

Old in so many ways, he reflected. Sehra Muril was as lovely as any girl he had courted back in his oat-sowing days in County Pryze, but he appreciated she was quite out of his league now. He knew several young troopers were competing for her attention. Muril paid Corbec attention all right, but he was rather afraid he knew that look. The look a girl would give her father.

Mkoll, the regiment's chief scout, had told Corbec that Muril had put in for scout training. If she was successful, Corbec would lose her, but he didn't begrudge it. Stealth scouts were the Tanith First's forte, and so far no Verghastite had made the grade. Mkoll was doing his best to bring some of them up to scratch, and if one of those was going to be Sehra Muril, Corbec was determined to be nothing but fething proud.

The train lurched and then began to roll. Corbec shot out a hand to steady himself against the wagon's side.

He pulled his dog-eared tarot pack from his blouse pocket and grinned. 'Okay, lads and lasses. Who's for a game of Strip Solon Naked?'

TRAIN E PULLED out, rattling as it hunted over the multiple points and gained speed.

Major Elim Rawne, third officer of the regiment under Gaunt and Corbec, sat back in the first troop wagon and accepted a lho-stick from his adjutant, Feygor.

'What do you reckon to this one, major?' Feygor asked.

Feygor was a vicious whip of a man, tall and thin, who had allied himself to Rawne right from the off. Some said they had a murky history that went back to their days on Tanith. They were alike. Rawne was handsome, in the way that weapons and snakes are handsome. Slim but well-built, Rawne had a fine profile and eyes that, as Corbec put it, could charm the drawers off a Sororitas nun. When this comment had filtered back to Rawne, his only remark had been, 'Oh. Do they wear drawers?'

Rawne hated Gaunt. It was that simple. He hated him for a number of things, but foremost he hated him for letting the Tanith homeworld die. But it was an old hatred, and it had become feeble with neglect. These days, he tolerated Gaunt. Even so, most of the troops thought Rawne was the nastiest piece of work the Tanith First could offer.

They were wrong.

Murtan Feygor had got his throat shot away during the fight for Vervunhive, and his every word came flat and monotone through a speech enhancer sewn into his larynx. Since then, he'd sounded permanently sarcastic, though several Ghosts, Varl and Corbec in particular, had opined that it was no great disability because he always had anyway. Fierce as a cornered plague-rat, he was snide and cunning and trusted no one except Rawne.

But he wasn't the nastiest piece of work the Tanith First could offer either.

Rawne exhaled a long bar of blue smoke as he thought about Feygor's question. 'Dug-in war, isn't it, Murt? Drawn out, old. It'll be trenches, you mark my words. Fething field fortifications. We'll spend our time either labouring with nine seventies like common navvies or ducking for cover in some other bastard's latrine.'

'I hear you,' said Feygor with disgust. 'Fething trenches. Fething n ine-seventies.'

A nine-seventy referred to the Imperial Guard's standard issue entrenching tool: a heavy, compact multi-purpose pick that could be stowed by detaching the helve from the head. Its official name was the 'Imperial Implement (General Field Fortification) Pattern 970'. Every Ghost wore one in a buttondown leather sheath on the back of his webbing.

'Trenches,' Rawne muttered blackly. 'It'll be just like Fortis Binary again.'

'Fortis fething Binary,' Feygor echoed.

'Where was that?' Banda whispered to Caffran. They were sitting a little way down the wagon with their backs to the door, close enough to overhear their platoon commander's remarks.

'Before your time,' Caffran told her. Jessi Banda was Verghast, another grade one sniper like Muril. Fortis Binary was a piece of hell the Tanith had endured several years before the fight at Vervunhive had brought the new recruits in.

'It was a forge world,' Caffran explained. 'We were trench-bound for a long time. It was... unpleasant.'

'What happened?' Banda asked.

'We survived,' growled Rawne, listening in.

It was a straight put-down, but Banda just raised her eyebrows and grinned, letting it wash over her. Major Rawne had never been able to disguise his contempt for the female troopers. He didn't believe they had any business being in the Tanith First. Banda had often wondered why. She'd have to ask him sometime.

'Any advice?' she asked.

The boldness of the question floored Rawne for a second, but that was the way of these fething women. He tried to come up with something good, but 'Keep your head down' was all he could manage.

'Fair enough,' she nodded, and settled back.

'You hear that?' Feygor asked suddenly.

'What?' asked Rawne.

'Raised voices. In the next wagon.'

Rawne glowered. 'Sort it out, will you?' he said.

'I WON'T TELL you again,' said Tona Criid.

'So don't,' replied Lijah Cuu, not even looking at her. Every member of Criid's platoon, crowded into the wagon space, had fallen silent and was watching the confrontation warily.

'You will service your kit and field strip your weapon, trooper.' Criid's voice was firm.

'It's a waste of time,' Cuu replied.

'You got something better to do?' she asked.

Cuu looked at her for the first time, fixing her with his cold green eyes. 'Plenty,' he said.

No one had dared mess with Tona Criid before her promotion. Thin and tough, with cropped bleached hair, Criid was a ganger from the slums of Vervunhive, an environment that had schooled her wits, reflexes and fighting smarts. Though young, she could more than look after herself, and was reckoned to be one of the hardest of the female troopers. Unlike Verghastites such as Banda and Muril, she hadn't specialised. She was a regular trooper with front-line experience.

Her promotion to sergeant, and the squad command that went with it, was never going to be an easy ride. Gaunt had done it on Hark's advice. Hark believed it would send the right message to all the troopers in the regiment... take the Verghastites seriously. Take the women seriously.

Certainly ten platoon needed a Verghastite officer now Kolea was incapacitated. He'd commanded almost automatic respect because of his record as a guerrilla company leader during the hive war. But his squad was tight, and everyone knew they wouldn't take kindly to any replacement, no matter how qualified. There were some tough customers in ten platoon, and none tougher than Lijah Cuu.

Cuu was a bad ploin and no mistake. A competent trooper, with abilities that could probably take him into either sniper or scout speciality, but he had a mean streak as deep and obvious as the scar that split his face from top to bottom. At Cirenholm, he'd been accused of the brutal rape-murder of a civilian and had come within sniffing distance of a firing squad before Gaunt had got him off. Innocent of that, perhaps, but guilty of so many other things. The plain fact was that he liked killing things. You got troopers like that in the Guard sometimes.

Gaunt had considered transferring Cuu out of ten platoon but knew that would undermine Criid's authority. The Ghosts would read that as him giving Criid an easy ride. He'd told her she'd have to deal with him.

Criid took Cuu's gaze without blinking. 'Let's review,' she said, slowly and clearly. 'You're a member of ten platoon. I'm the squad officer. I've just given Ten a direct order to make use of this transit time to service kit and weapons, and everyone else is happy to do that. Aren't you? Lubba?'

'Yes, ma'am,' grunted the gang-tattooed flamer bearer.

'Nessa?'

The squad's sniper, permanently deaf from shell-damage at the hive, signed back 'yes'.

'Jajjo? Hwlan? Any problems with my order?'

Jajjo, a mixed-race Verghastite with dark brown skin and darker eyes shrugged and smiled. Ten platoon's Tanith scout Hwlan nodded with a brisk 'Yes, m-sarge!'

'Only you seem to have a problem, Cuu.'

'Seems so. Sure as sure.' He smiled. It was the most unsettling smile in the Imperium. The most evil servants of Chaos would have killed to have a smile that lethal.

Tona Criid was not smiling. Deep inside, she was trembling. Her greatest fear was not death or torture or grievous injury. It was failure. Failure to live up to the opportunity Gaunt had given her. She would make this platoon her own. Or die trying. And die trying, seemed more likely the case.

'Do it now,' she said.

Cuu deliberately dropped his pack and weapon onto the floor and took out a lho-stick, which he lit with a tinder box. 'You know what I hate,' he said, blowing smoke at her. 'What I hate is the fact that you talk to me like I was one of your gakking kids.'

'Oh feth me!' Trooper Vril whispered to Hwlan. 'There's gonna be a fight now.'

'Sure as sure,' Hwlan whispered back sarcastically.

Unless you were going to make nice, you didn't mention Criid's kids. Yoncy and Dalin. They weren't hers biologically, just war-waifs she'd rescued from the killing grounds at Vervunhive and looked after ever since. She and her man Caffran were parents to them, and when they were off in action, the two kids were looked after by the regiment's camp followers. It was the Tanith First's one little happy-ending tale. Criid and Caffran, true love, kids saved from death... you couldn't make feth like that up.

'What did you say, trooper?' asked Criid.

'Here we go,' murmured Vril.

'Ah feth it,' whispered Hwlan. He slid the haft of his nine seventy out to use as a baton. If it came to fists, he'd get in on Criid's side. Cuu was a vicious worm. The scout saw that DaFelbe and Skeen both looked ready to jump in, and Nessa had got to her feet too.

But if it went off, Hwlan thought, would it help to get involved? Would Criid thank them? Probably not. She'd want to assert her command over Cuu alone, to make the point. Hwlan could feel Vril's hand on his arm, pulling him down. Vril clearly thought the same way too.

Cuu picked smoke-weed off his lip. 'I said I don't like it when you talk to me like I was one of your kids. Why? Did that upset you?'

'Not at all,' said Criid smoothly. 'But I notice you haven't shown respect to my rank since this conversation began. Would a "sergeant" or a "ma'am" really kill you?'

'Gakked if I'm gonna find out,' Cuu said, winking at the troopers around them.

'Don' you talk that way,' said a voice from the back of the wagon.

'What?' sneered Cuu.

'Don' talk that way. Don' be doin' that.' It was Kolea. He'd risen, slowly, and was staring at Cuu. There was a vague animosity in his eyes, but his face was blank. The headwound he'd taken at Ouranberg had made him very slow and direct. His mouth slurred words.

'Sit down, you dimwit,' said Cuu archly. 'Go hunt for your brain. I hear the loxatl have it in a little glass trophy box.'

Lubba, staunchly loyal to Kolea, threw himself at Cuu with a snarl, but Criid blocked him and kicked him down on his arse.

'Full marks for heart,' she told him. 'But I won't have brawling in this platoon.'

'Yes ma'am,' Lubba said.

'Why you bein' so bad?' Kolea asked Cuu. He shuffled forward, screwing up his eyes in confusion.

'It's all right, Gol. You sit down,' Criid said.

'Sit down, sarge?'

'Yeah, you go sit down and I'll deal with this.'

Kolea wavered. 'You sure, sarge? This... this man here was being bad.'

Criid knew that Kolea had been struggling to remember Cuu's name, and had failed. She also knew he only called her 'sarge' because he could see her pins.

'Sit down, Trooper Kolea.'

'Okay.'

Criid looked back at Cuu. 'Follow my order and service your kit.'

'Or what?'

Criid pushed a hand out towards Cuu's face, and he dodged back, but it was a ruse. The real sting was Criid's left leg, sweeping round at knee height.

Cuu crashed over onto the straw-covered floor, hard. Criid was on him in a heartbeat, one hand gripping his hair and yanking his head back, one knee in the small of his back.

'Or I exert my authority,' she said.

Cuu responded with a gender-related obscenity. In reply, the base of her hand against the back of his head, she smashed him nose-first into the decking. There was a crack that made them all wince, and it wasn't wood.

'You gakking bitch!' Cuu coughed as she yanked his head back again by the hair. Blood was running from his broken nose.

'You wanna go again, Trooper Cuu?'

'Gakking b–OW!'

Another headslam.

'Oooh, that's gonna smart!' Vril gasped.

'I can keep going until we get to where we're headed and then hand you off to Gaunt...' said Criid, digging her knee into his spine and making him cry out, '...or you can service your kit and your weapon and call me by rank. What do you say, Cuu? What do you gakking say?'

'I'll service my kit, sergeant!'

'…is the right answer. Get up.'

She got off him and he rolled over, his face dripping with blood.

'Off you go, Cuu.'

Cuu got up, and took his pack and lasgun off to the farthest corner of the wagon. The members of the platoon slow-handclapped and Criid performed a little bow.

'What don't you do?' she asked.

'Mess with you!' Lubba called out.

'Excellent. Carry on.'

'Everything okay in here?' Feygor called, pushing open the dividing shutter between the wagons.

'Just fine,' said Criid.

'What's wrong with Cuu?' Feygor asked.

'Nothing,' she said.

'Should he be bleeding like that?'

'Yes.'

Feygor shrugged. 'Rawne says keep it down.'

'We are.'

'Okay then,' said Feygor and left.

Criid walked down the rocking wagon and sat herself beside Kolea. 'That was nice what you did,' she said.

'What'd I do?' he asked, puzzled.

'Never mind,' she sighed.

Gaunt rode the A train. His carriage had once been a coach-class car, but its luxury days were long passed. Even so, he knew that the worn upholstery of the compartments was a fething sight sweeter than the transit arrangements of his Ghosts.

He sat in a compartment with Buzzel, Chief Medic Dorden, Hark and the regiment's chaplain, ayatani Zweil. Gaunt's adjutant, Corporal Beltayn, waited at the door.

Zweil and Hark were arguing about something, but Gaunt wasn't paying attention. He gazed out of the window, watching the vales and fields and woods and townships of Mittel Aexe flicker past.

Doc Dorden leaned over and tapped Gaunt's knee.

'Credit for them?'

Gaunt smiled at the grey-haired medicae. 'Not a lot of anything, to be honest. Just trying to focus.'

'An empty mind is like a pot for Chaos to piss in,' said Zweil. Buzzel looked shocked.

'Just kidding,' said the old priest, chortling into his long, wispy beard. He took out a clay pipe and began to stoke it with weed.

'This is a non-smoking area,' said Buzzel.

'I know that!' snapped Zweil testily, though he clearly didn't. He got up. 'I'm off to bless the poor bastards,' he announced, and stomped off down the connecting corridor.

'Your chaplain is an... unusual man,' said Buzzel.

'No kidding,' said Hark.

Gaunt returned his gaze to the landscape outside. Low, hilly country broken by stands of trees and small lakes. It would have been almost picturesque if not for the weather. Rain splashed along the windows of the speeding train.

'We're heading for Rhonforq, you say?' Dorden asked Buzzel.

'Yes, doctor.'

'Which is the gateway to the Naeme Valley?'

Buzzel nodded. 'The Naeme roughly demarcates the front line in the central sector.'

'It's dug-in?' Hark asked.

'Extensively,' said Buzzel, 'and has been for a long time.'

Hark scratched an earlobe. 'So the front's as stagnant as we've been told?'

'We make advances,' Buzzel said firmly.

'And so do they,' said Gaunt. 'As I understand it, there's a stretch of territory thirty kilometres wide and a thousand long that has remained disputed for forty years. That's one hell of a no-man's land.'

Buzzel shrugged. 'It's been a hard war.'

'An impasse,' said Hark. 'Which we're going to break. I take it you'll be using the Tanith to their strength as stealth infiltrators?'

Buzzel looked confused. 'I understood you were front-line troops. That's where you're being sent. The front line.'

Hark looked at Dorden and both men sighed. Gaunt beckoned Beltayn through the compartment window.

'Sir?'

'Can you patch me a link to the lord general?'

''Fraid not, sir. Something's awry. Vox is down.'

'When we get to Rhonforq, find Mkoll and tell him to move a recon team forward to the line. I want a detailed intelligence capture before we proceed.'

'Yes, sir!'

Gaunt looked at Buzzel. 'My Ghosts will fight to the last: harder, braver and stronger than any soldiers you have ever seen. But I will not see them wasted in the meatgrinder of a slow trench war. They have skills, and I'll have them use those skills.'

Buzzel smiled amiably. 'I'm sure the supreme commander understands that, sir,' he said.

The train slowed. Outside, Gaunt saw that the landscape had begun to change. The vegetation looked grey and sick, and acres of farmland had been rutted down to nothing but spongy brown waste. Stands of woodland had been felled leaving acres of dead stumps like badly planned cemeteries. They passed at least one team of timbermen denuding a hillside, their big, blacked-iron logging engine sheeting sparks and woodpulp up into the overcast sky. The roads were thick with drab motor transport and heavy carts drawn by oxen and hippines.

Towns and villages were scruffy and neglected, windows shuttered and boarded. Some had earthworks or pales raised around their eastern fringes, one in five had the steel mast of a shield generator rising from its midst. Apart from the masts and the motor vehicles, there was no other sign of metal in commonplace use.

They passed through one village where bells and horns were sounding. The westerly wind was bringing down not only rain but also a thin, yellowish smoke. Townsfolk in the street went about their business in canvas masks and rebreathers.

They clanked on through mercy stations – tent cities raised to cope with the exodus of injured, generated at the front. By Gaunt's estimation, they were still over a hundred kilometres from the real front. The war was so old, so chronic, it had spilled back this far.

He could smell it. War has its own smell. Not fyceline, not promethium, not water or mud or blood, not rank soil or ordure, not even the pungent decay of death itself. All of those scents were in the air.

War had a metallic tang. You could almost isolate it. A mineral smell quite subtracted from the diverse secondary odours it generated. A smell of steel and hate. Pure, repellent, universal.

Gaunt had smelled it on Balhaut, on Voltemand, on Caligula, Fortis Binary, Bucephalon, Monthax, Verghast, Hagia, Phantine and all the others. That diamond-tough scent of pure war, lurking behind the sweaty, more obvious perfumes that decorated human conflict.

This was going to be hard. Aexe Cardinal was going to cost them. It was in the air.

War. Waiting for them. Old and hard and cunning, like a wily, immortal beast, ready to pounce.

Ready to kill.

TWO
THE WOUNDED RIVER

'From Bassin to Seronne, the rural valley commends itself to the visitor, and in clement season there are many rewards to be had: the old parish churches, the cafes and inns, and the undemanding foot-paths and bridle ways of thetranquil riverbanks.'

– Fweber's Touring Guide
to Mittel Aexe, 720th edition

THE GROUND WAS peppered with ancient, rain-filled shell holes for as far as he could see. A pock-marked surface, like the cratered plain of some dead moon. The wet soil was greenish grey and the pools were dark emerald or black, though some were skinned with frothy white scum. Nothing seemed to stand taller than the height of a man's shoulder. A few poles and staves jutted from the mud, the occasional scourged remains of a tree, iron hoop-stakes and piquets and coils of barbed wire.

The sky was leaden and bulging with creased blotches of grey and yellow clouds. To the east, a dark haze of rain fuzzed the horizon into a filthy smudge.

Mkoll lowered his field scope and spat on the ground. The air was heavy with a dusty, chalky smell that got into the back of the throat. He could feel the grit abrading his teeth. It was the smell of dead land, of earth that had been disturbed and pulverised and thrown over so many times that it leaked its powdered essence into the air.

'Well, this is fething lovely,' muttered Bonin sarcastically. Mkoll glanced round at him and nodded. It was disturbing, this place. Tanith scouts had an unerring sense of direction, but the sheer featureless morass around them made it feel like they were nowhere at all. All of his men seemed uneasy: the usually cheerful Bonin, Caober from Gaunt's own platoon, Hwlan from ten, Baen from Varl's mob. Even Mkvenner, Corbec's lean, taciturn scout from two platoon, normally the model of composed calm, seemed unsettled.

Caober had a small map that Gaunt had given him. He held it up, flicking his index finger against the paper in frustration. 'Sitwale Wood,' he said at last.

'Sitwale *Wood*?' Hwlan echoed, stressing the second word.

Caober shrugged. 'The levelling glories of field artillery,' he said, 'beneath which all things are rendered equal.'

There was a track of sorts, rutted and mired. The scout party moved off behind Mkoll, following it north-east. About a kilometre further on, and the track made a crossroads marked by a temporary sign. '55th/9th rg' pointed one arm. '916th/88/ac' read another. 'R'forq ASHQ & 42nd rg' announced the arm that pointed the way they had come. The last one, pointing west, read 'Real Life'.

'Company!' Baen called. There were lights on the track behind them, and the sound of labouring engines. Mkoll waved his men off the track.

A jolting field truck, smeared in mud, rumbled past, turning east. Behind it came a staggering file of artillery tractors towing 0.12 feldkannone pieces. Aexe Alliance infantry in filthy green greatcoats walked beside the column. Their heads were covered with canvas bag-hoods with rough-cut slits for eyes and mouths. Most carried metal pry-bars or coils of wire matting to free up wheels when they bogged in. The hooded men reminded Bonin of the scarecrows used on the fruit farms back home in County Cuhulic. No one paid any attention to the Tanith team.

Twenty tractors, thirty, thirty-five, then twelve high-sided haycarts piled with shells that had been jacketed for protection in wicker sleeves. The carts were drawn by hippine teams, ten to a cart. These beasts were thin and wild-eyed, and stank of disease as they whinneyed and snorted along, every step a struggle.

After the slow carts came infantry, trudging under the weight of full field kit, their heads wrapped up in their dirty scarves. Mkoll watched an officer step out of file and stand by the signpost waving his troops around in the right direction.

After a few minutes, the officer turned and walked over to the Tanith. His greatcoat was stiff with mud and when he pulled the scarf away from his dirty face, Mkoll was shocked to see how young he was.

'Lost?' he began. Then he noticed Mkoll's rank pins and made a more formal salute.

'No,' said Mkoll, stepping up. 'Sergeant Mkoll, Tanith First.'

'You're from the Imperial expedition?'

'That's right.'

'Lieutenant Fevrierson, 30th battalion, Genswick Foot.' His accent was tight and clipped. Aexegarian. 'It's a pleasure to see you. Where is your main force?'

'Moving into reserve,' replied Mkoll. 'Our commander's sent us up to scope the leading edge.'

'Scope the...?'

'Assess the disposition of the forward line,' Mkoll glossed. The young man nodded. It was partly the accent, Mkoll thought. Mine's as unfamiliar to him as his is to me. That and the fact that they're still using old terms. He reminded himself that this war – this world – had been isolated for a good time.

'We're moving up to the 55th sector,' said Fevrierson. 'You're welcome to tag along.'

Mkoll nodded his thanks and made a brief hand signal that the lieutenant didn't catch. Immediately, the five men in his patrol were at his side. They fell in with the still plodding stream of Alliance infantry.

Fevrierson made light conversation as they walked. He was a little wary of the newcomers. Their kit was very clean and in good order, apart from the splashes they'd picked up on the day's hike. The fabric of their uniforms was of a type he didn't recognise. It looked comfortable and strong, possibly synthetic. They carried powerful-looking rifles that didn't seem to have any sort of ejection ports for spent cartridges. Could they be energy weapons? Fevrierson had never seen a lasgun close up, and they made him feel ashamed of his long, heavy bolt-action autorifle. The off-worlders also had tech items like power scopes and ear-bead comm-links. Individual trooper comm-links! They were truly from another place, like the characters in the demiscuto science-romance digests his brother used to buy from the newsvendor.

'This a rotation?' Mkoll asked.

'Yah. It used to be a week up and then two in reserve, but it's alternate on and off now.'

'You and your men have been in billets for a week?'

'Yah.' Mkoll bit back a comment about the filthy state of the locals, but Fevrierson had seen the look.

'There are no washing facilities at Jen-Frow. The billets are poor. No water for laundry.'

Mkoll nodded. 'I meant no disrespect.'

'Yah, of course,' said the Aexegarian earnestly.

'You'll soon be dirty, soon enough,' muttered one of his file. Men around sniggered.

'That's enough, Herxer!' Fevrierson growled.

'It's okay,' said Bonin. 'We do dirty good. We've been in dirty scraps before.'

'Where's your commanding officer?' Mkoll asked Fevrierson.

'I *am* the commanding officer,' he said.

A WHISTLE BLEW from the rear echelon, then a second, then another coming up the file.

Fevrierson took out his own and blew. 'Off the road! Off the road!'

Mkoll wondered if it was an attack, though there was no sign of anything and the chilly, wet landscape was otherwise virtually silent.

They heard hooves. Cavalry was moving up the road at a canter, and the infantry were standing off to let them through.

The Aexegarians cheered and waved their scarves and gensfilly bonnets as the riders went past. The cavaliers were dressed in blue and gold coats with bright green sashes and white, bell-top shakos. They sat upright and haughty, eyes front, saddle-sabres clattering at their hips. Their mounts were gigantic flightless birds with grey feathers and vast hooked beaks, powering along on massive, blue-fleshed limbs.

'Feth me!' said Hwlan.

The front riders held lances with fluttering bannerols, but the rest carried short-action rifles. None of them seemed to be holding any sort of reins or bridles.

'Hussars. Carbine-hussars,' said Fevrierson proudly. 'A fine sight.'

'What are those bird things?' asked Caober.

'Struthids,' said Fevrierson. He frowned. 'You've never seen a struthid before?'

'I've seen plenty,' said Caober. 'And now I've seen everything.'

'They don't have reins,' said Mkoll. 'Do they control with their feet?'

'They're psicavalry,' said Fevrierson. 'They need both hands to operate the carbines in a charge, so each man has a puppeteer, linking him to his steed.'

'An implant? Augmetic?'

'I don't know those words. A puppeteer's a little machine. They put them in the men's heads surgically. The struthid has one grafted in to match. It creates a brain link and lets the man drive the bird.'

Over sixty hussars galloped past and then the infantry returned to the road. Mkoll saw some of the Aexegarian troopers retrieving the odd feather from the mud and fixing them to their coat collars.

'Lucky charms,' Fevrierson said.

After another forty-five minutes, Mkoll realised the track was sloping down, though the landscape around remained spread out in its flat, pocked immensity. They were entering the rear portions of the trench network. The horizon had been clear earlier because everything vital had been sunk and dug in.

The workings were of immense size, some as wide as city streets and ten metres deep. Where they extended below the water table, duckboards had been laid down and teams of sappers were manning hand-pumped bilges. Strings of electrical lights ran down the carefully revetted walls and Mkoll could smell the ozone of shield generators. Armoured vehicles and trucks moved down the working line, and when one appeared, they had to stand to in lay-bys cut into the trench wall to allow them past. Troops hurried back and forth, some in greens, some in greys, a few in blues and golds or russets, all locals, all filthy. It was like entering a partially buried city. Some sections of trench were entirely roofed in with wired flakboard, with lighting hanging from the tunnel roofs.

'This is something,' said Baen to Mkoll. 'I expected trenches, but not like this.'

'They've had forty years to build it,' said Mkoll.

And they'd built it well. Massive, mainstreet-style reserve trenches, often shored up with rockcrete, off which ran barrack dugouts to the west and communication and support trenches to the east, towards the front. Running as they did from sap-heads and deep munition wells, the support trenches were shallower but zig-zagged, or were well provided with solid traverses to protect the vulnerable links and make them easier to defend compartmentally. To the east, about a kilometre away by Mkoll's estimation, lay the line of the fire trenches. To the west, rearwards, lay deeper pits accessed by communication trenches laid with narrow-gauge rails.

'The gun-pits,' Fevrierson said. Even the main artillery was dug in subsoil, Mkoll thought. The rails were for shell-carts. A few moments later they had to pause to allow barrows of massive wicker-wrapped shells to be heaved across the reserve trench and up the supply channels to the gun-pits. Fevrierson checked his watch. 'Readying for the night firing,' he said.

The Genswick Foot halted and stood easy in a firing trench as Fevrierson reported to the sector's staff blockhouse. He took Mkoll with him.

The blockhouse was a series of armoured rooms buried deep in the ground off the reserve mainway. It had folding shutters and gas curtains at the entrance.

Inside, it was warm and damp and busy. There was a chart room, and a vox-annex where a row of signallers chattered into bulky old-style field sets.

Sheafs of thick vox-line cables ran out along the entrance hall and away through loopholes. Inside the main entrance, sweating, ruddy-faced runners sat on a bench, waiting to be sent out again.

Mkoll waited at a reinforced door while Fevrierson signed in. From his vantage point, the Tanith could see a small command room filled with military aides grouped around a low map table. They were all in shabby but impressive number one uniforms: more blue and gold, more green, some yellow, some grey and some dark red.

Mkoll hadn't got the hang of the varied insignia or liveries yet. The men in grey tended to be quite dark skinned, and the few in red were pale and red or blond haired.

Fevrierson was reporting to a sallow-faced general whose green uniform seemed loose and ill-fitting. The man's face was drawn. He's lost weight since that kit was tailored for him, Mkoll thought.

The general talked to Fevrierson for a while; pointing to items on the map-table, and signed an order sheet. Then Fevrierson said something, and indicated Mkoll.

The general nodded and strode over to where the Tanith scout was waiting. Mkoll snapped a salute that the general gave back.

'We weren't expecting you for another two days,' said the general.

'We're not up in force, sir. My commanding officer ordered me forward in advance to assess the field.'

The general nodded and then surprised Mkoll by making the sign of the aquila across his chest and offering his hand.

'It's good to see you anyway and I thank the Throne you've come. I'm Hargunten, CoS, 55th region. Welcome to the Peinforq Line.'

'Sir. Mkoll, Tanith First.'

'What do you need, sergeant?'

'A look at the line and the chance to report back to Rhonforq,' said Mkoll. He produced the papers Gaunt had drawn up for him, countersigned by Buzzel.

General Hargunten looked them over. 'Wait here,' he said. 'The Genswick are moving forward to station 143, so you might as well go with them.'

He moved off to confer with other staff. As Mkoll waited he saw that one of the red-uniformed officers was looking him up and down. A colonel, by his pins. Mkoll didn't know the crossed-sabres and heraldic dragon of the man's insignia.

'Imperial?' he said after a while, his accent new to Mkoll. Thick, glottal, rich.

'Yes, sir.'

'Come to save us all.'

'Come to fight the arch-enemy, sir.'

The colonel snorted. His skin was very pale and slightly freckled and his side-shaved hair was red-gold.

'We can win this war,' he said.

'I have no doubt.'

'Without your help,' he finished.

'Not for me to say, sir.'

The colonel grunted and turned away. Fevrierson returned, with the general.

'Papers in order, sergeant,' Hargunten said, returning them to Mkoll. 'Go with the lieutenant here. See your way around. My compliments to your commander.'

Mkoll tucked the folded papers into his webbing pouch and saluted.

'See the front,' the colonel called out. 'See a war like you have never known.'

'I've known war, sir,' said Mkoll and, turning, strode out of the blockhouse.

'SCHLEIQ ME! I can't believe you did that!' Fevrierson exclaimed as they came out through the gas curtains into the damp evening air.

'Do what?'

'Smarted him like that!'

'Who was he?'

'Redjacq!'

'Who?'

Fevrierson blinked at Mkoll as if he was mad. 'Redjacq... Redjacq Ankre, of Kottmark?'

'Means nothing.'

'The Kottstadt Wyverns?'

'Really, I don't know. Kottmark is the neighbouring country, isn't it?'

'Yah... and the other senior partner in the Alliance. We'd be dead now if the Kottmarkers hadn't joined the war twenty years ago.'

'And this Redjacq... he's something special?'

'Their finest field commander. Leads the Wyverns. Furies, they are. We're lucky to have them in this sector.'

'I'm sure you are.'

IT WAS GETTING dark by then. Fevrierson got his infantry moving, and they went up through a series of zig-zagging communications trenches to the front-line position. There, things were more the way Mkoll had expected. No electrics, just the occasional promethium lamp or brazier. Dirty fire trenches dug in about three metres deep and heavily traversed with cross-spars and earth-filled gabions. A firestep made of stone lintels laid up against the base of the leading wall beneath the breastwork and iron loop holes. Despite the duckboards, the trenches were swilling with liquid mud and alive with vermin.

Wretched soldiers in blue coats stood down and began to retire in slow, weary lines as the Genswick Foot relieved them and took their places beneath the parapet.

The sky was clouding over and the light seemed to leak out of it. Thunder rumbled somewhere. The trenches stank. Mkoll turned to his men. 'Caober, Baen, Bonin... up that way. Mkvenner, Hwlan... back the other. Twenty minutes and back to me. See what you see.'

They moved away, but Mkoll caught Mkvenner's sleeve and held him back a moment. Unofficially, Mkvenner was Mkoll's number two in the scouts, totally dedicated and totally ruthless in a way that Mkoll, for all his reputation, could never hope to be. Some Tanith said Mkvenner had been trained in the old martial ways of cwlwhl, the fighting art of the Nalsheen, legendary warriors who had maintained law during Tanith's troubled feudal days. Mkoll always quashed those rumours, mainly because they were true and he knew how close Mkvenner guarded his background.

'Keep an eye on Hwlan,' Mkoll told him. 'Ten platoon is unsettled right now, with Criid taking over. Make sure he's together.'

Mkvenner nodded and made off. Mkoll watched the tall, lithe figure retreating down the busy trench.

Mkoll joined Fevrierson in the command dugout. It was little more than a shed built into the leading edge of the trench. There was a V-shaped binocular periscope on a tripod stand, and Mkoll took a lookout.

It was his first look at the battleground. In the twilight, it was a miserable place, though he was certain it would look even more miserable by day. Torn earth, incomprehensible wreckage, tall piquet fences of dangling wire. A kilometre away, the shattered land dipped a little and spread into a wide flood plain of poisoned water and stagnant pools interspersed with muddy islets and ridge-crests of shell-blown soil.

'A lot of water down there,' he said.

'That's the river.'

Mkoll looked again. 'It's no river…'

Fevrierson smiled at him. 'Oh yah! That's the beautiful Naeme, proud lifeflow of the borderlands!'

'But it's just pools and lakes and flooded flats…'

Mkoll's voice trailed off. He realised a river would look like that if it had been shelled for forty years. The banks, the environs, even the riverbed itself would have been ripped apart and pummelled into ruins. But the water still flowed. Where once it had been a proud, major river meandering through meadows and sleepy villages on its long journey to the sea, it was now cut loose, leaking out across the punished landscape like blood from a wound, its original form and structure lost to the war.

There was a soft 'pop' and the area below them was suddenly bathed in chilly white light. A few seconds more and other starshell flares burst, glowing, in the sky. Through the scope now, everything looked bleached and cold, hard shadows shivered as the flares slowly dropped.

'Corpse light,' said Fevrierson, putting on his steel helmet. 'Brace yourself,' he said.

'Why?'

'It's time for war.'

Distantly, a whistle blew. A bull-horn wound up and died again, its moan echoing across the front.

The gun-pits of the Peinforq Line woke up.

The sound and light split the darkness and eclipsed the tremulous glow of the starshells. The earth shook. In the deep pits and weapon-dens behind the line's spinal trenches, large calibre howitzers and mortars hurled munitions up into the gathering dusk. Elevated feldkannone and rocketshargen joined them.

Mkoll looked back at the Alliance lines and watched the thunderous light show. Two kilometres west of him and for twenty kilometres to north and south, the guns blazed and muzzle-fires strobed and danced. Massive, brilliant flashes flickered up and down the artillery line, some of them casting weird, momentary shadows from their pits. Mkoll heard the concussive screech of heavy shells lobbing overhead, the deeper, pneumatic twang of mortars, the huge crump of bombards. Rockets went up and over, squealing in the air and leaving trails of fire.

He'd never seen a bombardment on this scale before. Not even at Vervunhive.

Mkoll looked east, through the scope. A ragged strip of detonations and flame-storms was creeping across the ruined land on the far side of the wounded river. He could smell fyceline and iron in the wind, and then the stench of mud rendered into steam.

Fevrierson seemed content. He sat back and took a tin cup of caffeine from his subaltern.

'Want one?' he asked.

'No,' said Mkoll. The bombardment was shaking his marrow.

'They'll keep this up for a few hours, then they might signal us to advance.'

'Feth,' said Mkoll.

'You might as well have a cup,' said Fevrierson. 'We could be here for a w–'

There was a sudden roar and a shockwave of heat slammed across the front line from the west. Fevrierson stumbled to his feet. He stared back at the Aexe lines. A white hot cone of fire licked up from the direction of the allied artillery positions.

'Not a misfire, surely...' he began.

There was another colossal bang and a flash and this time it knocked them all over. Whistles were blowing.

'That's shellfire,' Mkoll said, getting up.

'But they've got nothing that–'

A third roar. Then a fourth. Then a dozen heavy impacts along the line to the north-west. Gargantuan fires blazed into the night.

'Schleiq!' Fevrierson cried. 'What the hell is that?'

'Something new?' Mkoll asked.

A runner almost fell into the dugout, dripping with perspiration. 'Order to repel!' he gasped.

'Repel?' Fevrierson said.

Mkoll grabbed the scope. Out in the no-man's land of the Naeme Valley, phantom shapes were advancing towards them.

'Get your men to stand ready,' he told the young lieutenant. 'We're being assaulted.'

MKOLL HURRIED OUT into the fire trench, unslinging his rifle. Men were shouting and running, knocking into each other. They'd panicked.

'Get them under control or we're dead,' the Tanith hissed at Fevrierson, who started blowing his whistle. Mkoll could hear the jangle of field phones and yelled exchanges begging for order confirmation.

He hadn't planned on this. He'd come for a little observation, not to get caught up in a storm assault.

He adjusted his micro-bead. 'Four! This is four! Sound off!'

'Thirty-two!' That was Bonin.

'Twenty-eight, four!' Caober.

'Thirteen. Moving up with sixty,' Mkvenner responded, accounting for Hwlan too.

'Forty-five, sir.' Baen.

'Four, got you. Close on me, at the dugout. Double time.'

'Thirty-two, I see contacts closing,' Bonin reported.

'Understood. Close on me. Permission granted to go active if you need to.'

More titanic impacts rocked the ground, and the sky to the west was underlit yellow with fire. The enemy's massive counter-bombardment had broken the discipline of the Allied barrage. Mkoll felt ultrasonic knocking and then smelled ozone as shields ignited along the Allied command line. In the semi-darkness, he could see the translucent white umbrellas of energy flickering over the main reserves. Still more enemy ordnance hammered down, splashing off the shields in great, deflected air blasts. In one place, a shield fizzled as it was struck and died out.

Mkoll was no artillery expert, but he knew the power and range of the enemy guns must be at least on a par with Imperial super-siege pieces. The front line, this 'Peinforq Line', had clearly been arranged to permit sustained artillery actions across ranges of five or six kilometres. The shells coming in had probably travelled more like fifteen or twenty. Fevrierson's astonished reaction alone was enough. He'd not seen anything like it. That wasn't a good sign.

Mkvenner and Hwlan rejoined Mkoll, as did Bonin a moment later. 'They're right on the parapet, less than thirty metres,' Bonin said.

'Why the feth aren't these idiots in place?' Hwlan said.

Fevrierson had got a few men onto the firestep and Mkoll heard the first dull bangs of trench mortars and the chatter of a machine cannon.

Almost immediately, as if in answer, the top of the trench's back wall started to take hits. Boards splintered and scads of earth flew out. Then one of the Genswick privates on the firestep flew backwards into the trench bottom as if he'd been clubbed in the face.

'Bayonets!' Fevrierson yelled. 'Stand by to repel!' The gathering mobs of Allied infantry slotted long, bill-tipped blades to their rifles.

'They've got to do more than repel,' Mkvenner said quietly. 'A few grenades or a well-timed push and the enemy'll be in the trench. They've got to go at them before they make the parapet...'

Mkoll looked round at Fevrierson. 'Well? While there's still time.'

'The order was to repel. Hold and repel...' Fevrierson's voice trailed off. His eyes were wide and wild in the gloom.

And then it was too late. Multiple explosions tore through the fire trench on the other side of the nearest traverse. Grenades. A second later, a stick bomb went over their heads, flung too hard. It landed on the top of the rear wall and covered them in dirt.

The infantry on the firestep started shooting. Their solid-ammo rifles made boxy, hollow bangs which overlapped with the clatter of the bolts as they were pulled back and forth. Enemy rounds whipped in low over the lip of the parapet. Two more men collapsed off the step, one spun right around by the impact.

'Hold to repel! Hold to repel!' Fevrierson was shouting.

Suddenly, a significant chunk of the facing parapet blew in, ripping panel-boards and brushwood revetting out of the wall and tossing men aside onto the duckboards. The first elements of the enemy wave scrambled down into the trench through the section their grenades had taken out. They wore khaki coats, brown corduroy breeches and slime-slick puttees, and dark green steel helmets over dirty woollen toques or chain-mail splinter masks. Most carried bulky autorifles with ugly saw-edged bayonets, but others had pistols and long-handled wire-cutters. Mkoll saw at least three who were wearing bulky grenadier waistcoats, the multiple canvas pockets stuffed with ball and stick bombs.

Spilling in through the breach, the trench raiders turned their guns and fired down the ditch line into the milling Genswick Foot. Other attackers breasted the parapet and started a rapid-fire enfilade into the heart of the section's defence.

There was a thick mob of Alliance men between Mkoll and the raiders, most of them trying to run or find cover. He could hear the whinnying smack of the enemy bullets thumping into the jostling bodies, punching through worsted and flannel, through canvas and leather, through flesh. Hit, some men convulsed but were held upright by the press. Others screamed because they were hit or because they were desperate not to be. One man was yanked up out of the mob by the force of an enfilading shot to the neck, his body cartwheeling over on top of the others. A ball bomb, round and black with a fizzing paper fuse, bounced off another man's shoulder and then blew the front of the command dugout into the air in a shower of planks.

There was general uproar from the Genswick troopers as they tried to flee from the breach and the crossfire. The bulk of them were penned in by their own confusion like animals in a slaughterhouse channel. Fevrierson and some of the men up on the firestep managed to return fire over the heads of the mob, and Mkoll counted at least two raiders go down. He thrust his way forward against the tide of panicking men.

'Feth this! Turn! Turn and fight! Come on!' he snapped.

Mkvenner and Hwlan got up onto the firestep and opened up sidelong down the trench. The sudden bursts of laser shots stunned the Genswick boys. Like they've never seen lasweapons before, Hwlan thought.

'Get down! Get down!' Mkoll yelled at the men in the trench and as they ducked and cowered, he and Bonin fired a storm of full auto-shots over their heads in support of the sideswiping fire of Mkvenner and Hwlan.

The raiders fell back under the hail of energy rounds. The front three or four were cut straight down, and fell onto the men behind them, tripping a few of them. Mkoll waded through the huddled Genswick soldiers in the trench base and opened up a field of fire on the raiders coming over the broken parapet, punishing their enfilade. He felt a rifle round thump into his chest armour, and others pass close by into the earthern wall, but he kept firing.

Fevrierson blew his whistle. 'Come on! Come on! The Imperials have got them on the turn!' Bolt-action rifles now began to volley at the intruding force. Bonin drew his lasrifle up to his shoulder and took a swift aim, snapping a single shot that dropped an enemy grenadier in the middle of the raider group. The ball bomb in his hand exploded and touched off the contents of his waistcoat. Channelled by the trench, the combined blast surged flame, shrapnel and broken pieces of duckboard in both directions.

'Go!' Mkoll yelled, storming forward with Bonin. The raided section had been effectively cleared by the blast. The air was full of soil dust, fine like flour, and it was settling across everything, making dark sticky patches where it mixed with spilled blood. The bodies of raiders, scorched black and twisted, lay across the firestep and the trench floor. One hung upside down from the parapet wire. Mkoll, Bonin and five of the Genswick Foot rushed the firestep at the broken section of the trench in time to intercept the next raiding party as it came over the parapet.

There was a savage flurry of point-blank shooting that knocked three of the raiders back out of the trench and one of the Genswickers off the step. Then it was hand-to-hand, brutal, blind. Mkoll used his rifle butt to deflect a bayonet that jabbed down at him, and then clubbed the attacker in the kneecap with it. One of the Genswick lads bayoneted an attacker through the belly and hoisted him up into the air like a labourer pitchforking a straw bale. Bonin, who'd had time to fix his silver Tanith warknife to his rifle's bayonet lug, killed one man outright and then slashed the thigh of another, cracking the man's head with his lasgun's butt as he fell. A pistol fired twice in Mkoll's ear and the Alliance private next to him screamed and fell, clutching his face. Mkoll fired his rifle and shot out the throat of the grenadier with the autopistol. The man slipped off the parapet where he had been standing, and ended up sitting, dead, on the firestep with his back to the trench wall.

Another few seconds of maniacal punching and clubbing, and the last of the raiders dropped back, denied.

Bonin and two Genswickers stood up at the parapet and started firing down into the dark to drive the raiders back out into the war-waste. Along the trench, Fevrierson and his men were now laying down a serious rifle fusillade from the step, the chatter of their solid round shots punctuated by the cracks of Mkvenner's and Hwlan's lasguns.

Mkoll crouched on the firestep and started to plunder the bombs from the dead grenadier's waistcoat. The balls had friction fuses that lit when a paper twist was yanked out. He fired them one by one, tossing them up and out over the parapet. The stick grenades had long wooden grips like brush handles with loops of linen dangling from pins in their bases. Mkoll realised you put your hand through the loops before swinging the grenades out. As each one sailed off, its pin was left hanging from his wrist on the loop. One of

Fevrierson's men, wounded in the arm, came up and helped him lob the bombs out into the night.

The Tanith sergeant switched round the moment he heard las-fire from his left. Caober and Baen, along with three Alliance soldiers, came around the next traverse, shooting into the space behind. 'Flank attack!' yelled one of the Alliance men. 'Raiders in the fire trench!'

'Hold this wall!' Mkoll yelled to Bonin, and jumped down off the firestep, running along the trench to support Caober and Baen. Mkvenner was running with him, along with a handful of Fevrierson's men.

The traverse shielded them all from the raiders in the next section, but also denied them aim. Baen hugged the end of the traverse and snapped off shots round the corner as often as he dared. A stick bomb came tumbling end over end across the traverse. Almost too fast to see, Mkvenner caught it in mid-air and slung it back. The blast curled smoke out round the end of the traverse.

'They'll be reeling! Rush them!' one of the Genswickers declared, and charged round the end of the defensive fortification with two of his comrades. All three were riddled with rifle shots and slammed back against the revetment wall. They hung there for a millisecond and then flopped onto their faces.

Mkoll glanced at Mkvenner.

'Topside, flank and down,' said the tall, grim scout.

Mkoll nodded. He waved Caober with them and pointed Baen to hold the corner of the traverse.

The three Ghosts threw out their camo-cloaks, and sheeted them over their shoulders, draping them expertly so that one hem-fold formed a hood over their heads.

Then they went up the back wall of the fire trench and over the top.

The surface behind the fire trench was packed earth and pools of mud. It was essentially dark, but the heavy barrage continued to strobe the entire line with fierce flashes. In the heat of the brutish trench fight, Mkoll had almost forgotten about the bombardment. It was still going on: the super-heavy long range shells plastering the command and supply trench areas of the entire Peinforq Line as far as he could see. Some shields still held, but only a half-hearted sporadic barrage answered the enemy thunder.

Mkoll, Caober and Mkvenner crawled forward, shrouded by their capes, hugging the mud. They'd sheathed their warknives and had slung their lasrifles over their shoulders under the capes so they wouldn't jar against stones or metal fragments on the ground. They slithered, feeling their way. Every time the light of a shell-blast lit the sky they froze.

Down in the trench to their right, they could hear Baen and the Genswick boys duelling patchily with the raiders, squeezing off shots around the traverse. Mkoll could hear the raiders shouting to each other in a language he didn't understand. But there was no mistaking the order 'Grenadze! Grenadze!'

They were just short of the rear lip now. Mkvenner undid a hoop of stiff but malleable wire from around his waist, straightened it, and pushed it out ahead of him until the tip just poked over the back edge of the fire trench. The wire had a strand of fibre optic cable wrapped around it. The tip was a tiny optical cell and at Mkvenner's end was a little pin-plug that he attached to his scope. Gently, he moved the wire around and studied the poor resolution images the cell was sending back down the cable to his scope's eyepiece.

He raised his hand just high enough for Mkoll and Caober to see. Five fingers, then three. Eight raiders. He moved his hand laterally, indicating four at the traverse corner, two below them and two more to the left.

Mkoll nodded, and reached back to slide a tube-charge from his webbing pouch. All three of them took off their lasrifles and laid them on the mud. This was going to be too tight, too constrained for rifle work. They drew out their pistols and warknives. Mkoll and Caober had standard pattern laspistols and Mkvenner had a .38 calibre auto with a twelve shot clip that he'd acquired on Nacedon. Caober and Mkvenner armed their pistols and lay face down with hand guns in their right hands and warknives in their left. Mkoll lay his laspistol on the mud beside his right hand and clamped his warknife between his teeth. Then he ripped the det-tape off the tube-charge and hurled it down into the corner of the traverse.

The blast threw the shredded form of one of the raiders right up out of the fire trench. His burning corpse bounced over the parapet and rolled into no-man's land.

By then, the three Ghosts had thrown off their cloaks and leapt down into the trench.

Mkoll landed awkwardly but squarely enough to coil into a firing crouch. He aimed right, and put las-rounds through the backs of two raiders stumbling blindly out of the blast smoke.

Mkvenner came down like a feline between the two raiders directly under their position. He headshot one point-blank, and as the man spasmed away, spun round and broke the neck of the other with a powerful sideways kick.

Caober's leap brought him down hard on top of the other two and all three collapsed in a writhing scrum on the floor of the trench. Fighting to rise, one of the raiders stood on Caober's ankle and wrenched it badly. The Tanith yowled and shot him through the pelvis. The raider went over again, screaming and hammering with his arms like a broken toy. The other raider rolled clear and slashed at Caober with his bayonet. Straight-armed, Caober blocked the spearing blade with his warknife and shot at the man, but missed. The raider drove on and Caober lost his pistol in his frantic effort to dodge.

The laspistol lay close by on the duckboards, but Caober didn't waste time trying for it. He grabbed the barrel of the raider's rifle with his now free hand and tugged it past him, stabbing the bayonet into the trench wall under his armpit and dragging the enemy's throat onto his extended knife blade. Blood squirted across Caober's chest. In his earbead, he heard Mkvenner say, 'drop,' and he did so, falling even as the corpse fell.

Five more raiders were hurtling down the trench onto them. Mkvenner ignored the rifle rounds whizzing past him and strode towards them, firing his pistol. The first and second raiders lurched backwards as if they'd been pole-axed. The third slumped on his face. The fourth was struggling with a jammed bolt when Mkvenner's shot snapped his head round and blew out his cheek. The fifth got off a shot that knocked Mkvenner sideways, blood gouting from his head.

'Ven!' Caober screamed, and threw himself at the raider, slamming him down hard. Caober pinned the soldier with his right forearm and expertly rotated his warknife in his left hand, switching the blade from tip up to tip down. Once it was down, Caober thumped the blade repeatedly into the raider's chest.

Mkoll had finished off the raiders half-killed by the tube-charge and came running back down the fire trench with Baen and the Genswick troopers on his heels. Still more raiders, including a grenadier, were behind the second five.

Mkoll's pistol toppled one, and then Baen was firing on full auto with his lasgun. The Alliance troopers beside him supported with fire from their rifles.

Mkoll moved forward over the crumpled bodies. 'You two! Ahead and secure the trench!' he ordered and a pair of infantry men ran ahead. 'You others, up on the firestep!' The rest clambered up onto the step and began shooting into the night.

'Trench secure!' one of the Genswickers shouted back. He'd linked up with members of his own platoon pushing out from behind the next traverse.

'Onto the step, then!' Mkoll urged. 'See them off!'

Caober struggled up and ran to where Baen was kneeling over Mkvenner. There was an appalling spill of blood.

'Sacred Feth!' Caober stammered. 'Ven!'

'Oh, shut up,' growled Mkvenner tersely. He had a nub of cloth jammed to his ear and when he took it away, blood squirted from his ear. 'It took my ear lobe off. That's all.'

'Feth!' Caober gasped with such relief Baen and Mkvenner both started to laugh.

THERE WERE NO more raids against station 143 that night, though Fevrierson's men stood to on the firestep at alert drill. Word filtered back that stations 129, 131, 146 and 147 had been intruded with serious losses, though by midnight only 146 was still the scene of fighting as Alliance troops doggedly drove the raiders out. Unconfirmed reports said that an entire section had been overrun between stations 287 and

311, and from the noise of combat washing down the line, Mkoll could believe it.

The enemy barrage ended, abruptly, at midnight, leaving just a dismal fog of ash vapour and fyceline smoke drifting down over the allied lines. At 01.00, the Alliance gun-dens commenced a counter-bombardment that mercilessly whipped the Shadik front-line positions across the Naeme until dawn.

At 02.15, with the punitive artillery searing the sky behind them, Mkoll assembled his team and bade farewell to Fevrierson. The young lieutenant saluted and shook Mkoll's hand, and many of his weary company clapped and cheered.

'You're going back?' Fevrierson asked.

'Should have been back long since. We've a reconnoitre to report.'

'Thanks,' said Fevrierson. 'Thank you. Emperor bless you.'

'These are good men,' said Mkoll, nodding to the mud-spattered infantry all around them. 'Keep them tight and you'll keep them alive.'

'I hope I never see you again.' said Fevrierson. 'I'd never wish this shit-hole on anybody, especially not for a second time.'

Mkoll nodded. Bonin grinned.

'What will you tell this commander of yours?' Fevrierson asked.

'The truth,' said Mkoll. 'The front's everything he was afraid it would be.'

THREE
A.S. HQ RHONFORQ

'...and to the general disposition of auxiliary support elements, officers of said elements are to answer to (i) the primary commander of their given area/sector, and (ii) the ranking Alliance officer in their specific line subdivision.'

– Aexe Alliance *General Order Book*, 772th edition,
section 45f, paragraph iv, 'Command Protocol'

FROM RHONFORQ, YOU could see the massive smoke spume rising from the Peinforq Line ten kilometres away to the east. During the night, the old chafstone buildings of the town had vibrated to the distant symphony of the guns.

Dawn was at 04.37 Imperial. The sun rose, dull and veiled, over the woods towards Ongche, and mist fumed over the strand meadows and market gardens west of the town. The Tanith First had slept for about five hours in poor billets on the southern edge of the town, but most of their motor pool staff and armourers had been up all night. They'd laid off from the trains at 21.00 the previous evening, along with two companies of Krassians and a motorised battalion of Seqgewehr coming up from Seronne.

Gaunt rose at 05.00, stiff and sour. All night, despatch riders and material transports had rattled by down the street under his window. He'd been billeted in a pension off the town square. Daur and Rawne occupied rooms there too, along with five of the Krassian officers and a number of Aexe Alliance staffers. Corbec had elected to billet with the Ghosts.

Gaunt's room was small and spare, with low, sloped ceilings and a window that wouldn't close properly. Beltayn knocked and brought him a canister of caffeine and a bowl of lukewarm water.

'Mkoll back yet?' Gaunt asked, attempting to shave using the tepid water. Beltayn was laying out Gaunt's service uniform on the bed.

'On his way, sir.'

'Delayed?'

'Something was awry.'

'For instance?'

'You heard the shelling, sir. The whole place is buzzing with it. New super-siege guns. The line took a pasting last night.'

'I thought as much,' said Gaunt . 'I wo–oow!'

Beltayn looked up. 'Sir?'

'Nicked myself,' said Gaunt, raising his chin to study the razor wound on his throat in the mirror. 'This water's almost cold, Beltayn.'

'That water's as warm as it gets unless it decides to be caffeine,' Beltayn said. He brushed the crown of Gaunt's cap and set it on the bed. Then he came over to Gaunt and peered at his cut. 'You've had worse,' he said.

Gaunt smiled. 'Thank you for that.'

'What you want is a needle,' said Beltayn.

'A needle?'

'Old family trick. A needle. Excellent when it comes to shaving nicks.'

'How does it work?'

'When you cut yourself with the razor, you take the needle and poke it into your gums.'

'That works?'

Beltayn winked. 'Sure as feth blots out the pain of the nick.'

DRESSED, AND WITH a tab of Beltayn's cigarette paper stuck to his shaving wound, Gaunt took his caffeine outside. The day was clear and promisingly warm, though the stink of fyceline was everywhere. He stopped on the pension's terrace to chat with a Krassian major and two officers from the Seqgewehr, and saw Rawne and Feygor demolishing a fried breakfast in the small dining room.

A column of tanks clanked past through the square. Gaunt finished his drink, put the empty cup on one of the terrace tables, and walked across the road to the Chapel St Avigns where the Allied staff headquarters was sited.

Rhonforq was one of the Octal Burgs – eight high church municipalities that sustained the authority of the See of Ghrennes through Mittel Aexe. Its church and cloister had been built in 502, ten years after the first colony footing at Samonparliane, and before the war its chief activities had been wool-carding, button manufacture and cheese making. Visitors were invited to throw a coin into the fountain of Beati Hagia or, if they were sound of limb, take in the hike to the Sheffurd Hills to view the birthplace of Governor-General Daner Fep Kvelsteen, whose autograph and seal were included in the famous four at the bottom of the Great Aexe Declaration of Sovereignty.

Gaunt knew that much from a dog-eared, obsolete touring guide he'd discovered under his bed the night before.

Allied staff headquarters was thronging with activity. In the inner cloister, a rank of despatch riders waited on humming motorcycles. Sheafs of telegraph and vox-cable trunked out of windows and noodled up into the dish arrays anchored to the rooves. A shield mast attached to a portable generator dominated the quadrangle, the grass beneath it brown and dead from radiation.

Gaunt hurried up the front steps of the main chapel, accepting the salutes of passing Alliance officers.

'Where's Van Voytz?' he asked an adjutant at the desk.

'You mean General Van Voytz?' the adjutant replied testily without looking up.

'If we're going to be formal, you say "Lord General Van Voytz, colonel-commissar", sir,' Gaunt growled, snapping his fingers so that the adjutant would look up. He did and gulped.

'Beg pardon, sir. The lord general has gone ahead to Meiseq, but he's expected back tomorrow night.'

'I want to vox him.'

'Vox-lines have been cut by last night's barrage, sir.'

Put another way, something's awry, Gaunt thought.

'What about Lyntor-Sewq?'

'The supreme commander has been called away, sir.'

'Feth it!' snarled Gaunt. 'I need to be briefed. I need to see charts! I need–'

'One moment, sir. I'll ring through.'

The adjutant hurriedly lifted the receiver of his field telephone and cranked the handle. 'Colonel-Commissar Gaunt, for briefing,' he said and paused.

'Wait one moment, sir,' he told Gaunt, replacing the handset.

'Colonel-Commissar!' the voice echoed around the hall. Gaunt looked round to see a tall, pale, ginger haired officer in a dark red uniform advancing towards him across the paved hallway.

Gaunt saluted him.

'Gaunt, Tanith First-and-Only.'

'Redjacq Ankre, Kottstadt Wyverns. I'm acting authority for the Alliance in Lyntor-Sewq's absence. Follow me.'

Gaunt fell into step with the taller man, and they walked down towards the doors of the main situations room. There was something about Ankre, something in his bearing and manner, that made Gaunt bristle. But he ignored the feeling. He'd been Guard long enough to know that you often didn't like the men you had to count as allies. Stifling personal opinion usually helped get the job done.

'I met some of your men last night,' Ankre said, apropos of nothing.

'Indeed?'

'A scout party.'

'Ah yes, I sent them ahead.'

'You didn't trust our intelligence reports?'

Gaunt stopped and made eye contact with the big red-head. 'I'm sure they're fine. I haven't actually seen one,' he said venomously. Ankre paused, not sure how best to deal with the criticism. Before he had time to make his mind up, Gaunt smoothed past the remark by saying, 'So, you were at the front last night?'

'Yes, I was,' the colonel replied stiffly.

'It seemed like you took a bruising. New heavy siege weapons, I hear.'

'I didn't think you'd read a briefing,' Ankre said, enjoying the slyness of his retort.

'I have eyes and ears. So... new enemy tactics, then? New weapons?'

'Yes,' said Ankre. A sentry in green Alliance fatigues saluted and held the door for them.

The nave of the old chapel had been converted for military use. The windows were taped and blacked, though Gaunt could make out the lead ridges of the old stained glass. Flakboard baffles lined the room, banked with sandbags, and the air was dry and warm and smelled of electricity. Glow-globes floated beneath the rafters, illuminating a central area busy with technicians, aides and officers. Portable codifiers and high-gain vox-casters had been uncrated and set up on trestles. There was a constant murmur of voices, a chatter of machines, the occasional whistle of tuning vox-channels, background static. A pair of hooded acolytes from the Adeptus Mechanicus were blessing the servitors that were being installed at the new Imperial vox-units.

The situations room was a confidential area. Inside the door, Gaunt had to give his name and serial code to a clerk and was issued with a small green pin-badge. High Command wanted a thorough record of everyone who came and went.

Ankre led Gaunt across to a chart table, which Gaunt studied keenly. It was a complete mess of over-mapped gibberish. Ankre gave him a blurred, low-detail map showing only a small field section. It had been printed on flimsy paper.

'Your regiment is to move up to the 55th sector along communication line 2319 at dusk tonight and take position along the front to secure stations 287 to 295. Your chain of command is to Major Neillands at station 280 and then to General Hargunten at Area/Sector. Here are the day's challenge codes and vox frequencies.' Ankre handed Gaunt a data-slate. 'Familiarise yourself with them and then erase the slate.'

'My chain of command runs through a major?' asked Gaunt.

'Is there a problem?'

'This Neillands will relay orders from area/sector?'

'Of course, in the event that you can't receive them yourself... if, say, vox is down.'

'What if Neillands can't receive orders from area/sector... if, say, his vox is down? I answer to him?'

Ankre shrugged as if he still couldn't see what the problem was. 'Yes, as I have said–'

'I heard what you said, colonel. I just don't believe it. You are saying that, in certain circumstances, most likely the kind of circumstances when it really matters, I am supposed to answer to a junior officer? I am expected to put my command... my regiment... into his hands?'

Ankre frowned. 'Get me the *General Order Book*,' he told an aide. The man returned in a few seconds bearing a fat, red-sleeved folder stamped with the Alliance crest and the words 'Most Secret – Destroy in Case of Jeopardy'. Ankre leafed through it. Gaunt could see that most of the pages were typewritten inserts, pasted or stapled in. 'The supreme commander has this arranged in black and white,' he said, unamused. 'His tactical staff working party drew it up once we'd been advised of your approach. Here... chain of command as I said.'

'Let me see that,' said Gaunt. Ankre seemed reluctant to let the book go, but handed it over after a pause. Gaunt read down the badly typed order docket. 'This says nothing about our position. No specifics. It simply says that we are to answer to the primary officer of whatever sector we are sent to–'

'That's General Hargunten.'

'And secondarily to the senior Alliance officer in our line area.'

'Exactly what I said. The senior Alliance officer in your line area is Major Neillands of the Feinster Highlanders.'

Gaunt shook his head. 'I don't think so. I think rather that Major Neillands should answer to me. In the event that we lose contact with area/sector, that would be the best protocol.'

'Well, that's unfortunate,' said Ankre. 'The word you seem to be ignoring is "Alliance". You are to answer to the Alliance chain of command. The supreme commander is merely following the will of the high sezar. He has made it clear that the Aexe Alliance forces are to remain in control of this war. If that means you have to swallow your pride and answer to a major, then deal with it. You have come here to fight for the Alliance.'

'I have come here to fight for the Emperor,' Gaunt hissed. 'We stand together against Shadik. We of the Guard are now part of the Alliance.'

'Not technically,' said Ankre, taking the folder out of Gaunt's hands and thumbing to another page. 'Here. It is quite specific. The Imperial expedition is termed "auxiliary support".'

He closed the folder and smiled as if to suggest he had won the short debate. Gaunt knew there was absolutely no point arguing with him. He'd met men like Ankre before. He'd go over his head.

Gaunt turned to the chart and found, with some difficulty, the station points Ankre had mentioned.

'This is the front line?'

'Yes.'

'My men are light infantry, specialising in covert action. It's a waste to put them there.'

'We do not have the luxury of being choosy. Stations 287 through to 311 were overrun last night by the enemy, the largest breach in the Peinforq Line. The enemy has been driven out, but reinforcement is essential in that area. Vital. A brigade of Krassians will move forward to fill stations 296 to 311, to the north of you.'

'I repeat my objection.'

'Are you afraid your men will be unable to hold a trench line?'

Gaunt took off his cap and his gloves and set them down on the edge of the chart table. This action gave him a few seconds to breathe deeply and still his rage.

'I am afraid of nothing except the stupidity of a blinkered high command system,' he replied.

Ankre stepped back a pace and lowered his head slightly, aggressively. 'The supreme commander selected the Tanith for this position entirely on the basis of the good account your scout party made of itself last night. The whole of 55th sector is talking about it this morning. A handful of men, but they turned the tide at station 143. That's the kind of expertise the commander wants at the line, especially at a stretch that is weak and vulnerable.'

'Even if we are merely auxiliary support?'

Ankre handed the folder back to the waiting aide. 'I think we're done here, colonel-commissar,' he said.

'I want a copy of the field charts,' said Gaunt.

'Why?' asked Ankre, now clearly beginning to lose his patience.

Gaunt held up the flimsy field map. 'Because this shows only my immediate position.'

'Your point?'

'How can I effect optimal command if I only get to see the specific vicinity? How can I appreciate the battle as a whole?'

'You don't need to. You have a specific duty. That is what you must perform. That is all you should be interested in.'

Gaunt slid the map and the data-slate into his coat and put his gloves and cap back on. 'I can't believe that in this day and age you're still fighting wars like this,' he said. 'Have you never read Macharius? Solon? Slaydo?'

'None of those fine warriors are here on Aexe,' said Ankre.

'More's the pity,' snapped Gaunt. He strode away, then turned and glared back at Ankre. 'I'll mobilise my troops. But I will not move them up the line until I have met with an Alliance commander – any Alliance commander – who can verify these orders more satisfactorily than you. Make that happen, colonel. Make that happen fast.'

Ankre's look was murderous. 'This is tantamount to insubordination. I could have you–'

'Word of advice,' said Gaunt, cutting in sharply. 'You do not ever want to mess with me. Bite your tongue, find me someone more useful than yourself, and never threaten me again. Are we clear?'

Ankre said nothing. The whole situations room had fallen silent. Gaunt turned his back on them all and marched out.

'Do me a favour,' sighed Dorden. 'Hold the feth still, eh?'

Trooper Caober shrugged. 'It's sore as a scalded shoggy, doc,' he moaned.

'You're a big boy. Shut up. Do you see Ven making a fuss? You do not. He's bleeding like a stuck hog, but do we hear a whimper? We do not at all. So shut up.'

Caober sighed and gritted his teeth. He was sitting up on a wooden table in the Ghosts' temporary medicae station, a derelict woollen mill on the southern fringe of Rhonforq. The mill was big and old, built from flinty, black stone, and straddled a gushing stream that the wool-workers had once used for washing excess lanolin from the fleeces. There was a damp, fatty smell, and every surface was sticky with grease. The orderlies had offered to scrub it down with bristle-brushes, but Dorden didn't suppose they would be there long enough for it to be worth the elbow. Midday sunlight, hard and yellow, stabbed down through ventilator panels in the high, tiled roof, and lit the hall with a sickly light. Most of the mill equipment had been shifted out long since. Tiny shreds of wool fibre still clung to nicks in beams and rough brick edges.

Mkoll's team had arrived back in Rhonforq at 11.30 that morning, and Mkoll, Caober and Mkvenner had reported immediately to the medicae station. Dorden was tending to Caober's wrenched ankle while Lesp dressed Mkvenner's ear-wound. Mkoll had said his own injuries could wait. An adjoining mill hall had been occupied by the Krassian medics, and many voices echoed through from the Krassian troops lining up for inoculator shots.

'How did this happen again?' asked Dorden, examining the scout's bared foot and ankle. The flesh was puffy and lilac with bruising.

'It – ow! – it got stood on. There was a fight.'

'So Mkoll says. A good one?'

'So-so. You know.'

Dorden glanced up at Caober. 'No, I don't. Tell me about it. Allow me to live the war vicariously through your bravado while I stay back here soaking bandages.'

'There was a fight. Ow! A fight. In the trench. Enemies came in, so we fought them. I – ow! – got my ankle stood on.' Caober faltered and his voice tailed off. He was a fine scout, but his story-telling ability left everything to be desired.

Dorden continued to wind bandages tightly around Caober's ankle. 'Somebody fill me in. Ven?'

Mkvenner looked up, his ear packed with gauze. 'Pardon?'

Dorden laughed, and so did everyone else – Lesp, washing his hands in a tin bowl, Chayker and Foskin sorting surgical tools. Even Mkoll, sitting on a chair in the corner.

'What's funny? I can't hear,' growled Mkvenner. The laughter stopped. No one wanted Mkvenner to think they were taking the piss out of him. Mkvenner was one of those Ghosts you respected, every second of the day.

'When the barrage started, they tested the line with trench raiders,' Mkoll said as he got up. Dorden could tell at a glance he was holding himself stiffly as he moved. 'It got very messy. The locals weren't at all prepared.'

Dorden tied off the bandage and called over to Foskin. 'Get Caober's boot back on, loose, and find him a crutch. Stay off it for a few days and you'll be good to go.' He wiped his hands and moved over to Mkoll. 'Let's take a look,' he said.

Mkoll started to take off his webbing and jacket, but it clearly hurt him to lift his arms, so Dorden helped him strip down to the waist. The bruise across the pale flesh of his chest was ugly and black.

'Feth! You been playing smack-stick again?' asked Dorden.

'Rifle round. Took it last night. Didn't notice it at the time. Adrenalin, I suppose. Been hurting like a fether since dawn, though.'

Dorden tutted and sprayed Mkoll's wound with counter-septic. By his side, Foskin clucked in amazement. He'd been folding Mkoll's clothes and kit. He held up a mangled large calibre round. 'Your chest armour stopped this,' he said. 'It was buried in your breast-guard. You want me to throw it away?'

Mkoll took it and put in his trouser pocket. He had his own battlefield superstitions.

'I see the war's started without me,' said a voice from behind them. Gaunt had entered the mill. 'Carry on,' he added, before they all started throwing salutes. He peered at Mkoll's hefty bruise. 'First blood to them, I take it?'

'We gave a good account,' said Mkoll.

'So I hear. I met your fan club. A Colonel Ankre.'

'Who?' murmured Mkoll. 'Oh, him. The red-head. I didn't think he'd taken to us much.'

'You're the heroes of the line, my friend,' said Gaunt sarcastically. 'The locals are so impressed, they've given us a whole front trench to hold.'

'Feth,' Mkoll said.

'You told them–' Dorden began.

'Oh, I told them all right. I don't think they were listening.' Gaunt sighed. He handed the flimsy map to Mkoll. 'This is what we're taking on, if they have their way.'

Mkoll looked over the slip. 'Bad place. Took the worst of it last night. The very worst. The river comes in close here, you see? The parapet is low and waterlogged. Ideal for storming. I wasn't sure they'd even got it clear.'

'Tell me what you saw up front,' Gaunt said, sitting down as Dorden dressed Mkoll's nasty wound.

'The Alliance soldiers we saw were tired and over-stretched. Ill too, most of them. Low sanitation, low hygiene. What's worse, they have precious little discipline. They fight well enough when they're ordered up and controlled, but there's no sign of initiative.'

'They panicked when the raid started,' said Caober.

'To be fair,' said Mkvenner, 'they panicked when the shelling started. They'd never seen that before, not like that. I think they were fairly fit as front-line infantry, but when those new super-guns opened up, they were milling and broken and scared. And the enemy raiders punched right in through them.'

Gaunt nodded. 'The enemy?'

'Good, tight, professional. Solid ammo weapons, some body armour. The grenadiers are their strength. Simple explosives, but effective, and in large numbers.'

Gaunt listened to his chief scout and then said, 'So... what does Lord General Mkoll think?'

It was a private joke. Gaunt trusted Mkoll's tactical mind absolutely, and often voiced this hypothetical question. If Mkoll was supreme commander here, what would he do?

'This fight'll go on till doomsday,' said Mkoll, once he'd considered things. 'It's been going on forty years. A deadlock. You might think that Guard reinforcements like us might overtip the balance in favour of the Alliance, but then so might these new super-guns, in favour of the enemy. What I'm saying is it'll take something new, something lateral, to break this. Can't say what with only this fething map to go by.'

'I'm working on that,' Gaunt assured him.

Mkoll shrugged, and then winced and wished he hadn't. 'I don't know. Something new. Something different or unexpected. Something from a new angle. We'd better find out what. Before they do.'

'I know something,' said Mkvenner quietly. 'These new super-guns they've got. They might have been developing them for years, but don't you think it's funny they first use them a day or two after we arrive? They must've seen our ships coming in. They must know the Guard is here and that the Alliance has off-world reinforcements at last. They're afraid the Alliance has got the edge. They want the edge back.'

'I'll give 'em the edge back,' Caober chuckled, testing the sharpness of his straight silver warknife.

'Hold that thought,' Gaunt told him with a smile. He looked at Mkoll. 'Write me up a full report. Everything and anything.'

'Will do, sir.'

Gaunt was about to say something else when angry voices broke into the mill hall. Ana Curth burst in. 'Dorden, where the feth are– Oh! My apologies, sir.'

Gaunt stood. 'As you were, Surgeon Curth. I believe you were about to cuss again.'

'Fething right,' she said. 'I can't find our fething supplies and the supplies should be there and the Krassians are blaming–'

'Whoa, whoa!' said Dorden. 'From the top and remember to breathe this time.'

Ana Curth took a deep breath. She'd been a well-respected and well-paid civilian medic on Verghast before the Zoican War and, to the amazement of Dorden and Gaunt, had elected to join the Tanith regiment at the Act of Consolation. No one had ever found out why she'd cast aside a comfortable, rewarding lifestyle in favour of the thankless miseries of an Imperial Guard medicae posting. Gaunt believed it was because she had a sense of duty that probably put them all to shame.

They were fething lucky to have her.

'Our supplies are missing,' she said. 'All of them. Everything we shipped in from the Munitorium vessels. I looked for them at embarkation and was told they had been trained ahead. But they're not here.'

'No, no,' said Chayker. 'I saw them. Piled up in the lean-to behind the mill.'

'Oh, there are plenty of gakking crates there, Chayks,' said Curth. 'And they're all marked with the Tanith and Krassian symbols. But they've got nothing in them except dirty cotton wool and straw. The Krassian medics are trying to give their men field shots, and there's nothing to use, and they're claiming we pinched them all–'

'All right, all right...' Gaunt said. 'What have we got?'

'About thirty cases of one-shot mire-fever doses and about the same in anti-toxin pills,' said Lesp. 'Everything we brought up the line ourselves, sir.'

'Give them to the Krassians.'

'Gaunt!' Curth started.

'Do it. I won't have bad feeling with good allies like the Krassians. I'll find our supplies, and the Krassians' supplies too. We'll make do until then.'

'Ever the diplomat, eh, Ibram?' smiled Dorden.

'They once invited me to join the Imperial diplomatic officium,' said Gaunt. 'I told them to feth off.'

* * *

THERE WAS LAUGHTER ringing from the old wool mill. His driver had told him this was the place set aside for the Imperial Guard medicae units. Laughter seemed a strange sound to hear. He walked in from the car, entering a large hall where eight men and a woman stood around, hooting and chuckling. It seemed like the officer had just told a really good joke. Four of the men and the woman were medics. The others, apart from the officer in his stern cap, were black-tunicked troopers, all of them injured.

He cleared his throat and the laughter stopped. They all looked round.

'I believe you were asking for me,' he said. 'I am Count Iaco Bousar Fep Golke.'

COUNT GOLKE WAS a quiet, silver-haired Aexegarian dressed in a dark green uniform that showed no decoration apart from the insignia of Aexegary on the collar and shoulder boards, and the golden aquila medal pinned at his throat. He walked with a slight limp, and Gaunt could see that his neatly trimmed silver beard had been grown, in part, to disguise old burns on his cheek and throat. He introduced himself as chief of staff/liaison.

They walked together across the yard outside the mill.

'We've met already,' Gaunt said. 'In passing. I was one of the Imperial officers presented to you that night at the high sezar's palace.'

'I thought so,' replied Golke. 'I confess that night I was rather distant. Forgive me if I was distracted. The surprise news of the Imperial arrival, my unexpected decoration...' He patted the gold eagle medal. Gaunt knew Golke wasn't mentioning the fact that he had just been stripped of rank too. That night had marked the end of Golke's four year tenure as supreme commander of the Aexe Alliance forces. A blow to his pride, Gaunt imagined. Another little puffed up aristo general, who'd made his rank by dint of noble blood rather than command merit, now drummed out of office to make way for the newcomers. Gaunt expected bitterness and resentment. He was surprised when he detected none. Golke seemed to be nothing except tired and disenchanted.

'My new role,' said Golke, leaning against a gatepost to ease his leg, 'as I understand it at least, is to facilitate communication between the Alliance and the Imperial expedition. It's all rather formless and vague, so I have to thank you.'

'How so?'

'Giving me something decent to do, colonel-commissar. Something other than the futile round of cocktail welcome parties and handshaking. You've quite rattled Redjacq Ankre.'

'If I may speak freely?'

Golke made an ushering sweep with his hand.

'Colonel Ankre displayed to me a real ignorance of modern warfare methods. He is blinkered, clinging to outmoded and discredited principles and strategies. Indeed, this whole war–' Gaunt stopped.

'Go on, colonel-commissar.'

'I should not, sir. I barely know you and I don't feel it is my place to deliver a critique of your nation's war-making.'

Golke smiled. It was quite a winning smile, even if one corner of his mouth, fused by scar tissue, refused to bend. 'Colonel-Commissar Gaunt, I was twenty-nine years old when this bloody war began. I served as a front-line infantry officer for twelve years, then joined the Office of Strategy for another fifteen, then some time in the east, then five years as area general in sector 59, then four as supreme commander. Never in that time was I one hundred per cent happy about the way Aexegary prosecuted this war. I criticised, objected, used my rank to try to make changes I thought would be beneficial. It was like pushing water uphill. So let's make a deal. Speak freely and speak your mind. If I am offended, we'll agree to disagree.'

Gaunt nodded. 'Then I'd say this war would have been over thirty years ago if the Alliance had for one moment overhauled their martial philosophies. You're fighting this like a pre-firearm campaign, like something from the days of antiquity. The use of infantry and cavalry, the dependence on cannon, the expenditure of manpower. And, forgive me, the reliance on the nobility for command personnel.'

Golke chuckled ruefully.

'There is a concept that we in the Guard hold true. Total war. The prosecution of an enemy that takes no account of national boundaries or political structure. War with a single, unswerving objective, to defeat the foe. War that never stays still but is constantly looking for new opportunities. True to such a concept, the Imperial Guard has triumphed over the enemies of the Emperor in all theatres. We advance, both physically and mentally. You have stagnated, intellectually, as truly and deeply as your front line.'

'You don't pull punches, do you, Gaunt?'

'Not when I'm invited to throw one for free. Look, sir, I know Aexegary has a long and illustrious history of military success, but you're still fighting wars the way your ancestors did. Shadik is not a bellicose neighbour state to be bested on the field and then invited over for diplomatic reparations. It is a cancer, a spreading evil of Chaos that will not, ever, play by the old rules. It will grind you down, invade you and consume you.'

'I know that.'

'Then you seem to be alone. Ankre doesn't know it. Not at all.'

'Ankre is old school. He's a Kottmarker. They're anxious to prove their worth in the Alliance. What am I saying? We're all old school.' Golke looked over at the roofscape of Rhonforq, squinting as if the afternoon light hurt his eyes. 'Enlighten me, then.'

'In the first place, the Tanith are stealth experts. They'll fight like bastards in a front line, but that'd be wasting them. They need to be used, not as cannon fodder, but as the incisive weapons they are.'

'That makes sense.'

'Second... dispersal of information. I know that it's vital to guard dispositional data from enemy eyes, but this is plainly ridiculous.'

Gaunt pulled out the scrappy map Ankre had given him. 'I think I speak for every Imperial officer when I say that we need an overall perspective. How can I press any advantages I might make if I have no clear idea of the bigger picture?'

'Ankre told me you were after general charts. The idea appalled him. Our way of warmaking revolves around individual commanders performing their appointed tasks and leaving the concerns of general strategy to the staff chiefs.'

'That's like fighting blindfold, or at least fighting with just a narrow view through a little slit.'

Golke put his hand in his jacket pocket and produced a data-slate. 'Copy everything on this,' he said. 'These are the full charts you wanted. But be circumspect. Ankre and the Alliance generals would have me shot if they thought I'd given these to you.'

'I'll be careful.'

'Give me time, and I'll get the idea accepted by the GSC. If we can prove the advantage, it'll make it easier for them to swallow. Your commander, Van Voytz, is working on them too. I don't believe he's terribly happy with the situation either.'

'I didn't expect he would be,' smiled Gaunt.

'Now do me a favour. Advance your regiment to the appointed stations. Show willing. I'll go back to the supreme commander and petition him to act on your advice. A day or two, perhaps three. Then we might see results.'

Gaunt nodded, and shook the count's hand. 'You have the chance to win this war, sir,' he said. 'Don't let the Alliance waste it.'

FOUR
287–311

'Sergeant Tona Criid? Sergeant Tona Criid? I like the sound of that. No other gak-face will, though.'

– Tona Criid, sergeant

IT WAS THE Ghosts' third day on the line. They'd got used to the routines: the patrol circuits, the wire-expeditions, the bilge-pumping, the observations, the manhandling of latrine buckets out up the communication trench, the man-handling of food buckets back down from the cookhouse ('I swear they get those fething buckets mixed up most times,' Rawne was heard to say). They'd even got used to what Corbec called the 'trench walk' – stooped, head down, so nothing projected above the parapet.

The tension remained. Since the night of Mkoll's advance party, there'd been no bombardment. On day two, the enemy had assaulted the line twenty-five kilometres north at station 317, but otherwise it had been quiet.

One-third of the regiment had advanced to the line, leaving the other two-thirds in reserve at Rhonforq. At the end of the first week, they were to rotate, and begin a pattern that meant no trooper stayed on the line for more than a week, and every trooper got two weeks' rest in reserve in every three. Gaunt, of course, hoped the Tanith wouldn't be staying at the front for anything like that long.

At the line, the Ghosts were caked in mud after the first few hours, and crawling with lice after the first day. They slept, as best they could, curled up under the lip of the parapet, or in hand-scooped dugouts.

Criid had become so muddy she'd decided not to fight it any more. She'd plastered mud across her face and matted it into her hair.

'What the feth are you doing, sarge?' Skeen had asked.

'Camouflage,' she said.

Fifteen minutes later, all but two of her platoon had followed suit and daubed themselves with mud. Kolea hadn't, because he hadn't understood what was going on.

Cuu hadn't, because, well, he was Cuu.

Still, Criid congratulated herself, I seem to have most of the platoon pulling together. Maybe I can do this.

Ten platoon occupied station 290, with eleven platoon, Obel's, to their north, and sixteen platoon, Maroy's, to their south.

Each station represented about a kilometre of fire trench, broken in twenty metre intervals by traverses. They had a dugout bunker with a field telephone and vox, but the Ghosts' personal vox-links had made that obsolete most of the time.

Three times a day, Criid did her tour, accompanied by Hwlan and DaFelbe. She checked trench integrity, she checked that food was getting through, she checked the obs stations. She individually inspected each trooper's kit, ammo supply, and feet for trench foot.

The third day was dismal. Rain blew in from the west, angled in such a manner that the trench sides offered absolutely no shelter. The rain also tasted of something, something faintly metallic, faintly chemical. Someone said that blister gas had been used the day before up north in the Meiseq Box, and some troopers put on their breather hoods or tied cloth over their mouths. The sky was low and oppressive, churning with fast-moving cloud that was almost black. It sapped the colour from the day. Faces became pale, eye sockets shadowed.

Some of the trench's previous incumbents – the Seventy-seventh Lunsgatte Rifle Brigade – had stayed behind. A detachment of thirty had been remaindered to man the trench mortars in the pocket dugouts spaced behind the main fire trench. Their fire-officer, a sergeant called Hartwig, joined Criid when she toured the mortar dens. He was tall and humourless, huddled in a mud-flecked grey oilskin, toque and a green kepi with a metal badge that showed some sort of bear-like animal. His men didn't mix much with the Tanith. They seemed content to live in the cramped hollows of the dens. Criid got the impression Hartwig and his men didn't think much of a unit that included women, let alone one that was led by one.

The mortars were squat, blue-metal machines called feldwerfers, and used compressed gas to fire the three kilo shells pneumatically. The crews kept the weapons spotlessly clean, they were forever polishing and oiling them. In contrast, the men themselves were filthy and their uniforms piecemeal. Most wore toques or loose hoods, with sleeveless leather jackets or fleeces, and many had flat sheets of armour tied or strung across their chests. Dirt caked their hands and faces black.

Interspersed with the mortars were Favell-pattern spring guns, a heavy little catapult engine that looked to Criid like some kind of pipe organ. It took two men to operate the double windlass and crank back the long throwing arm to the cock-stop. When the trigger lanyard was pulled, the cluster of massive springs in the main body of the weapon slammed the arm up and lobbed grenades or ball bombs out over the fire trench and into the battlefield.

Hartwig assured Criid that the Favell could send a grenade over two hundred and fifty metres. The trick was to set the grenade's fuse so that it didn't detonate high in its arc. They needed to blow on the ground, or near it, but if the grenadiers left the fuse too long, there was a risk that the enemy would have time to gather them up and toss them back. One member of each spring gun team had a clay pipe on the go at all times, an ignition source ready and waiting to start fuses that was a lot less fiddly than matches or gun-string.

The Seventy-seventh Lunsgatte weren't the only prior inhabitants who had stayed in the fire trench. Shrunken, eroded body parts protruded from the trench floor and sometimes the wall, usually where the rain had exposed them. During a heavy period of action three years before, Criid learned, the troops at these stations had been obliged to bury their dead in the trench itself. Water damage was slowly raising them back into the daylight.

During her midday tour on the third day, Criid found Lubba and Vril trying to shore up a section of revetment that was falling in thanks to the rain. Part of the parapet overhang had become a gutter for the rainwater, which was now gushing into the trench in a thick stream. The task was made all the more unpleasant because where the timber had come away, ancient cadavers had been exposed, curled and almost mummified.

'Gak,' she said, viewing the scene.

'We need more planks,' said Lubba. 'Even if we get these back in place, they're rotten through.'

Criid looked at Hartwig. 'Planking? Flakboard?'

He laughed at her. 'You're joking.'

'Any suggestions, then?' she said. She was quickly becoming tired with Hartwig's dreary resignation.

'There's sometimes some brushwood at station 282. They bring it forward along the supply trench there when its available.'

'Brushwood?'

'Anything will do,' said Vril.

Criid turned to Hwlan. 'Go on down to 282 and see if you can get your hands on some.'

'Yes, sarge.'

'What about damming that stream?' DaFelbe suggested, pointing at the liquid mud gushing down over the lip.

'We'd have to get up over the parapet. So I'd rather be wet than dead,' said Vril.

'After dark, then?' Criid ventured.

'Sure, sarge. Once it's dark.'

There was a wet, loose gurgle and another section of the revet slumped into the trench where Lubba was trying to force it back in. Greasy mud slithered out, shedding another vile body with it. The corpse was staring, its jaws open in a scream, but its eyes and mouth were full of mud.

'Oh gak... Hwlan!' Criid called after the scout. He stopped and looked back.

'See if you can find Zweil too.'

Hwlan nodded.

They moved on a little way. Criid checked the next two or three troopers at the firestep: Vulli, Jajjo, Kenfeld, Subeno. Kenfeld's boots were leaking and he needed foot-powder.

Then they reached Cuu, or at least Cuu's position. The firestep was empty.

'Mkhef!' Criid called to the next man along. 'Where's Cuu?'

'Latrine, sarge!' the trooper called back.

They waited, and Cuu reappeared. As soon as he saw Criid, he unslung his rifle and held it out for inspection, wordlessly. There was no expression in his eyes. His face still bore the bruise marks where she'd dented it.

'You left your post, Cuu.'

'Had to.'

'You wait until change-over.'

He shook his head. 'Couldn't wait. My belly's a mess. Gakking food round here. An emergency, sure as sure.'

'How long have you been sick?'

'A day.' He did look pale and unwell, now she came to look.

'You keeping anything in?'

'Going right through me,' he said with unnecessary relish.

'Signal a man up to cover,' she told DaFelbe, then she looked back at Cuu. 'Report to Dorden. Get him to fix you up with salts or a shot. Then right back here, you understand me? I want you back before 13.00, no excuses.'

'Okay,' said Cuu, picking up his kit. 'Back by one, sure as sure.'

Criid watched Cuu walk away until he was out of sight round the next traverse.

'He's trouble, that one,' said DaFelbe.

'Sure as sure,' she replied.

In the next fire bay, Criid found Pozetine, Mosark and Nessa Bourah huddled in scrapes hulled out under the dripping parapet. They were playing dice, but she could tell their hearts weren't in it. She ran a quick inspection, though the three were able troopers who didn't need much steering, and asked if there were any problems.

'Only the waiting,' said Pozetine. He was a short, square-set Vervunhiver with a boxer's splayed nose, ex-Vervun Primary, and a hell of a shot. A shoe-in for sniper specialisation in fact, had it not been for his grievous lack of patience. He worried, he fidgeted. A sniper he was not.

'Waiting's always the killer,' said Criid.

Pozetine nodded. 'S'why I hate digging in, sarge,' he said. His fingers were working the dice, making them move in and out between his knuckles. An edgy and all too practiced tick.

'Bide your time,' said Criid.

'What I keep telling him,' signed Nessa, a model of calm.

It was easy to say. No soldier liked the waiting hours. They had a habit of magnifying fears and gnawing at nerves. But they got to Pozetine worse than most.

'Do something,' Criid suggested. 'I could find you a job. Latrines–'

'Gak that,' growled Pozetine. Mosark laughed.

'Then take a turn on lookout.'

'I offered, but he's happy and set.' The 'he' Pozetine referred to was Kolea, down at the end of the bay. He was motionless, peering through a stereoscope rigged to peak out over the parapet.

Criid walked along the duckboards to him. 'Kolea?'

He didn't move. She put a hand gently on his arm and he looked up. She could tell it took a moment for him to work out who she was.

'You okay? You've been watching a long time.'

'Don' mind it. I can watch.'

He could at that. If Pozetine was the most impatient man in the platoon – gak, the entire regiment – then Kolea had become the most focused and tranquil.

She knew for a fact that he'd been manning the scope for at least two hours, slowly playing it back and forth through a one-eighty arc. He didn't get bored, he didn't get tired. She'd have pulled any other man off the duty ages before for fear that fatigue would make him sloppy. Not Kolea.

Criid didn't know precisely what the loxatl munition had done to Kolea's brain. Surgeon Curth had tried to explain it to her, but the technical terms had been beyond Criid. Something to do with memory and personality. All of it, ruined. Gol Kolea, the scratch company hero, wise, smart, strong... lost, and only this physical shell of him left with them. His dependability had survived, and expressed itself in an extraordinary attention span.

Or at least, Criid told herself, an ability not to get bored with the most mundane tasks. Kolea could watch the line vigilantly for hours. Pick up a conversation five minutes after it had lapsed and he wouldn't know what you were talking about.

Criid had admitted it to no one, but Kolea was the biggest problem in her command. Gaunt assumed it would be Cuu, but she knew she could handle that gak-pellet. No, it was Kolea. Ten was Kolea's platoon, for a start. He'd forged the unit. It was his still. If he'd died, that would have been a different ball game, but he was still here, a constant reminder of his mental absence, of the void where his inspired leadership had been.

Worse still, he'd only ended up this way because of her. She'd been wounded during the fight for Ouranberg. Kolea had carried her to safety and taken his headwound as a consequence. She'd never found out why, really. Varl had said that it was simply Kolea's way. He'd never leave a trooper down and in danger. Maybe so. But it felt like something else. Like Kolea had needed to save her for some reason, something more than simple loyalty.

Caffran reckoned it was because of the kids. Kolea had sometimes referred to the two orphans Criid had rescued from Vervunhive as a 'little piece of good', and Caffran believed Kolea had taken an almost patriarchal interest in looking after Criid and Caffran, the kids' ersatz parents.

Whatever. She'd never know. She'd never be able to ask Kolea, because Kolea couldn't even remember Ouranberg, let alone the motives that had once driven his life.

'You get tired, you sing out,' she said.

'Don' worry, sarge.'

'You see anything, you sing too.'

His big fingers reached into the neck of his field coat and held out the tin whistle. He beamed. 'Got my blower.'

'Good,' she said. 'Carry on, Trooper Kolea.'

She got up, but his next words stopped her in her tracks.

'The kids.'

'What?'

'What?' he echoed.

'What did you say, Gol? Just then?'

'Um…' he thought about it. 'The kids. They gonna be okay? They all right?'

'They're fine,' she said. Her heart was banging in her ribcage. It was almost like the old Gol Kolea was in arm's reach.

'They're young,' he said.

'Yes, they are.'

'But I guess they'll manage. If you say they're all right.'

'They will.'

He nodded. 'So young. S'pose war is all they've known. But so young, most of them. Boys. Not even shaving yet. Acting like soldiers.'

The Aexe Alliance troopers. That's what he was talking about. Everyone in the regiment had been shocked to see how terribly young most of the local soldiery was. 'Kids' Lubba had said.

Dear God-Emperor. Not her kids at all. She'd seen a spark, just for a second, but it had been false. 'Carry on,' she said.

* * *

'You okay there, sarge?' asked DaFelbe.
'Yeah. Grit in my eyes,' said Tona Criid.

The canteen barrow had passed along the fire trench north of station 290 about fifteen minutes before, dishing out pieces of dry rye-bread and a watery gruel made of fish stock and tough root vegetables to the men of eleven platoon. Now Trooper Gutes was coming along through the rain with the wash bin, collecting up the troopers' mess tins to take them up the supply trench and rinse them at the standpipe tap at rear/290.

It was a rota task, and Gutes had drawn for the day. He didn't grumble, but it was a scummy job. By the time he'd collected all the mess tins, the wash bin would be slopping and full. Piet Gutes was one of the older Tanith troopers, drawn and tired. It wasn't physical fatigue he suffered from. It was the wearying attrition of Guard life. The hopeless struggle to get through each day, knowing there was no happy ending waiting for them. No homeworld. No family embrace to return to.

The day Tanith had died, Gutes's daughter Finra had been twenty-one, and her daughter Foona just four months old. It had been a wrench leaving them, but the Emperor called, and the Emperor was the Emperor.

Piet Gutes woke up some nights, sit-up-straight awake, with the last fire-flash of Tanith fading in his mind's eye. That final, shuddering cough of flame and light that signalled the death of the world that'd raised him. It had been just a little thing, a wink in the night. He'd witnessed it from the obs ports of the troop ship. Just a tiny, silent flash.

How could that have been Tanith dying, he often wondered. The mantle splitting. The oceans evaporating. The continents sliding into each other and disintegrating. The great nalwood forests licking into cinders in a wall of white heat. The core, cut loose, erupting and boiling out into the vacuum. Piet Gutes supposed that anything, even the most important and profound event in his life or anyone's life, would seem like nothing more than a tiny, silent flash if you saw it from far enough away.

He wondered about it, sometimes, washing grease off mess tins, sorting power clips, sewing buttons back onto his tunic. The galaxy was big and everything in it was small, and he was small too. The Emperor's dead! Really? Yeah... that tiny flash just then. Did you see it? The Imperium's fallen! Sacred feth, you kidding? No... just that little flash. You must've noticed.

Far away. That's where he'd like to be. 'Far away up in the mountains', like the old song. It was all he wanted these days. To be so far away that everything looked small and insignificant.

'Tins! Tins!' he called, plodding down the fire bay with both hands on the yoke of the big metal pail. Garond tipped his in, then Fenix and Tokar.

'Thank you kindly,' Gutes said to each, his voice so rich with sarcasm it made them laugh.

He struggled into the gun-nest, where Caill and Melyr were hunched down beside their support weapon. Caill tossed his tin in, half-finished, but Melyr was still chasing the last drips of gravy with a scrap of Caill's left over bread.

'Feth, you like that stuff?'

'Good eating, if you've a hunger,' said Melyr.

Gutes liked Melyr. Heavy-set, solid, an ace with a fat cannon or a rocket tube. But he hated seeing him there. Bragg had been eleven's cannon man. Hark had switched Melyr in from twenty-seven when Bragg was killed. It was almost unseemly. Caill, the best ammo humper in the regiment, in Gutes's opinion, had just about been wedded to Bragg. Now here he was running boxes and feeding belts for someone else.

Times change. Needs must. Get far enough away and none of it looks big enough to be important anyway.

Melyr finished up, smacked his lips appreciatively, and plonked his mess tin into Gutes's wash bin.

'My compliments to the chef,' he said.

'Melyr, man, you're a fething lunatic,' said Gutes.

'You wanna worry,' said Caill. 'I have to sit beside this feth-head.'

'Sit further back and it won't seem to matter so much,' Gutes suggested.

'What?'

Gutes shook his head. He was glad Caill was settling in with his new partner. That's what really counted. He knew Caill was still down on himself. He'd left Bragg to run for fresh ammo, and by the time he'd got back, Bragg was done. Three loxatl flechette rounds at close range, that's what Gutes had heard. Like he'd eaten a tube-charge. So much mess they'd been hard pushed to find enough to bury, and Bragg had been a big guy.

Feth happens, Gutes thought.

He stumbled on, under a reinforced arch, into the next fire bay, wishing he had a hand free to brush away the biter-flies that buzzed around his face. Loglas had told him about a trooper up the line who'd let those things settle and then woke up with his brain eaten out by hatching larvae.

Piet Gutes didn't fancy that. He did however wonder how someone with his brain eaten out by larvae had managed to wake up at all. An inconsistency in the story. Maybe Loglas had been pulling his leg.

'Everything all right, Piet?' called Sergeant Obel, coming the other way down the trench with his runner.

'Fine, sir.'

'You got mine already,' said Obel.

'I did so,' said Gutes. Every Ghost's mess tin was etched with his surname and pin code. The fun part of this job was getting the right tin back to the right body.

Fun part. Yeah, right. There was nothing about the collection, cleaning and redistribution of mess tins that could be considered fun.

'Carry on, Gutes,' Obel said.

Gutes stopped at the end of the bay and put his bucket down. Greasy slops rocked out over the lip.

'Hey, Larks?'

Mad Larkin slowly turned back from the loophole where his long-las was resting. He smiled slightly when he saw Gutes. They'd been good buddies since the Founding Fields. It was nice to see him smile. Larkin seemed edgier than ever these days. He and Bragg had been particularly close.

'Got your tin?' Gutes asked.

Larkin looked around and eventually produced his mess tin from a shelf in the revet side. It was full of gruel, the hunk of bread disintegrating into it.

'Ah, Larks, you gotta eat.'

'Not hungry, Piet.'

'You gotta eat, but.'

Larkin shrugged.

Gutes picked up the tin. 'You sure you don't want this?'

'Yeah. No appetite.'

'Okay, then.' Gutes left his slop bucket next to Larkin's firestep and went back down the trench. Melyr accepted the bonus rations with delight. 'You gotta wash that up yourself and get it back to Larks,' Gutes told him.

He went back to his wash bin.

'What you doing, Larks?' he asked.

Larkin had been working a screwdriver into the setting of his rifle scope.

'Calibrating,' he said.

Every sniper calibrated their scopes. It was a given. An adjustment to the milled ring on the back-sight, a moment to let the sighting scanner read your retina and set up the hairs, but Larkin played around more. He tweaked off the inspection cover and overrode the reader, calibrating his weapon to nuances of windspeed and shot-drop that were too subtle for the scope to set automatically. Gutes had heard him say sometimes that he saw the truth through his scope. The view through the scope was the one reality Larkin trusted.

'You wanna be careful no tech-priest catches you doing that,' Gutes admonished. 'They'd have you burned at the stake.'

'So don't tell 'em,' said Larkin.

'I won't,' said Gutes. Larkin was the best shot in the regiment, and Gutes wasn't about to tell him his job, even if tinkering with military tech was strictly forbidden. That was the province of the tech-priests, who guarded their secrets jealously. If Larkin had to be a heretic to shoot so well, that was fine with Gutes.

Gutes pulled up his sloshing bin and trotted on, picking up the last of the mess tins and then heading west up the supply trench.

* * *

'HEY, LARKS.'

Larkin looked up from his scope, thinking Piet Gutes had come back for some reason.

It wasn't Piet Gutes.

'How you doing?' said Lijah Cuu.

'What the feth?' Larkin cowered back into the corner of the firebay, his hand trying to find the hilt of his knife. 'What the feth are you doing here?'

'Oh, now, that's not nice.' Cuu crouched on the firestep, elbows resting on his knees. 'Just dropped by to say hello to a friend. And you're acting all unfriendly.'

'No,' mumbled Larkin.

'Yes, you are, sure as sure.'

'What do you want?'

Cuu straightened out his lean legs and sat down on the step with his back to the parapet.

'Like I said, just saying hello.'

'You shouldn't be here,' said Larkin.

'Who's gonna know, tell me that? I'm meant to be seeing the doc. Who's gonna miss me? Who's gonna worry about two buddies chatting together?'

'I'm not your buddy,' Larkin said bravely. His hand had found the knife now. He kept it behind his back.

Cuu thought about that. 'Maybe not. Maybe not.'

He leaned forward, pushing his scar-split face right up into Larkin's. 'Buddies ain't the right word, is it, Tanith? We got a score, you and me. You sold me out, sold me out to the commissars, back on Phantine. You and that big dumbo.'

'Don't call him that!'

'Big dumbo? Why the gak shouldn't I call that big dumbo a big dumbo? He was a big dumbo, sure as sure.'

'Shut up!'

'Hey, I'm just being nice and saying hello.' Cuu's voice dropped to a raw whisper. 'We got a score, Tanith. You know it, I know it. It's gonna get settled. Thanks to you, I got flog-scars on my back. I think about you, most nights. You and that holier-than-thou big dumbo. Sooner or later, you're gonna pay.'

Larkin pulled back even further. He knew he had no hope of getting his long-las free from the loop-hole. He wanted to shout out, but there was no one around.

'What do you mean, pay?'

'Sooner or later, sure as sure. War's a messy thing, Tanith. Confused and all shit like that. Middle of combat, all crap flying this way and that. Who's gonna notice if I get my payback? You'd just be another body in the count.'

'You wouldn't dare!'

'Oh, wouldn't I now? You'll get yours, just like big dumbo got his.'

Hlaine Larkin was petrified. Ever since Phantine, he'd been guarding his back, waiting for this moment. And now Lijah fething Cuu had just come up on him when he least expected it. But those last few words bit clean through his terror.

'What do you mean, he got his? What the feth does that mean?'

'Terrible shame. Big dumbo buying the farm like that.'

'No… no, that's not what you meant. Not at all! Feth… feth, you bastard… you killed him!'

'As if,' smiled Cuu.

'You bastard! I'll take this to Gaunt–'

Cuu snapped out a hand and closed it tightly around Larkin's throat. His eyes went dark, like a cloud had passed across the sun.

'Oh no you won't, you little gak. Who'd believe you, eh? Where's your gakking proof? This is just between you and me. You and me. Our little score. And it'll get settled, sure as sure. You'll know why. And I'll know why, and everyone else can take a gakking jump. You'll pay for the flog-scars I got. You'll pay with scars of your own.'

Larkin yanked out his knife. Straight silver, thirty centimetres. Tanith First-and-Only warblade. In simple desperation, he lunged at Cuu.

Cuu was ready. He blocked Larkin's wrist with his left fist, turning the knife aside, and tightened his choke hold. Larkin writhed away, but he was penned in and trapped, like an animal, like prey.

Cuu cuffed him around the temple and, as he swayed, dazed, threw him off the firestep. Larkin landed shoulders first on the duckboards, feeling them squelch underneath him.

His fingers groped for his warknife.

It was in Lijah Cuu's hand.

Cuu stood over him, raised Larkin's knife to his mouth and slowly licked the blade. The tiniest drop of blood welled up and fell onto Larkin's forehead.

'You're fething crazy!' Larkin gasped.

'Sure,' said Cuu, 'as sure. We've come this far. Let's do it.'

He flew at Larkin, blade extended. Larkin remembered the combat moves Corbec had told him, and rolled, kicking Cuu's legs away. Cuu crashed over, ripping the blade sideways and tearing a strip out of Larkin's trousers. Larkin squealed and kicked out again. But Cuu moved like a snake, wrapping himself over and under Larkin's jerking limbs.

The blade was at Larkin's throat. He felt its edge bite into his skin.

'What the feth is this?'

Loglas was coming down the trench bay towards them, his hands balled into fists. 'Cuu? What the feth are you doing?'

Fighting the pressure at his neck, Larkin screamed. Oddly, his scream sounded like a whistle.

A whistle. Two more blew. Then another.

Loglas halted and looked up. The shell hit the back wall of the firebay and went off, kicking mud and slime and pieces of flakboard fifty metres into the air. A twenty-pounder at the very least.

Larkin saw it, saw the actual shell. The flint-grey casing, the barbed fins, like it was a pict playing in slow motion. He saw the huge flash. He saw one of the fins, a broken chunk of metal twenty centimetres by ten, whizzing out from the impact, turning in the air like a kid's throw-toy.

Loglas was reeling back from the concussive force of the blast when the flying fin hit him in the face. In slow motion, Larkin saw the way it made Loglas frown, then grimace, then twist his features into an expression no human face could make while it was alive.

Loglas's face caved in nose first, and his forehead tore away from his scalp like a yanked curtain. His head convulsed with the whiplash, his neck shattering as it bowed back. His face vanished, sucked into the hole that was being driven into the front of his head, and then the whirling fin came out the back, strewing skull shards and bloody matter ahead of it.

'Nooo!' Larkin howled. Then he went deaf as the blast roar hammered him.

COLM CORBEC HAD emerged from his dugout at station 295 approximately sixty seconds before the first shell landed. He paused on the firestep, frowning, cupping his hands to shield his eyes from the rain.

'Chief?' asked Rerval, his vox-officer. 'Something up?'

Corbec had smelled ammonil wadding on the wind. Batteries loading up for barrage. Rerval watched with horrid fascination as Corbec slowly raised his whistle and blew.

Rerval grabbed up the vox-horn and started to yell. 'Incoming barrage!'

He repeated the cry three times before there was an ominous click which announced that the e-mag pulse of the enemy guns had killed the vox-signal.

Then the shells started to land.

THEY FELL IN the rain. They fell like rain. They scattered in and out of the leading fire trench of the Peinforq Line's 55th sector from station 251 right up to 315 and over into 56th sector as far as 349.

Ten shells a second, heavy gauge from the deep super-siege batteries, and smaller howitzer rounds from the Shadik front. In a space of two minutes, the air was full of mud fog and the atomised steam of debris over a stretch of fifteen kilometres. The ground was quaking.

Between 293 and 294, Rawne and Domor got their troopers into cover. Amongst three platoon, Wheln and Leclan took shrapnel hits, Torez lost an arm and Famoss was decapitated. Five metres of fire trench and a traverse simply vanished in a blizzard of spraying earth.

* * *

Sergeant Agun Soric slept through the first thirty seconds of the onslaught. The roar and vibration didn't wake him. It took Trooper Vivvo, shaking him and yelling in his face.

Soric blinked open his single eye and looked up at Vivvo's pale face in the halflight of station 292's dugout.

'What?' he asked, tersely. But there was a background clamour of thunder and voices, and the little camp table was jarring.

'Gak!' Soric snorted, and scrambled up. How could he have slept through this?

Over the constant howl of shells, he could hear debris spattering off the dugout wall. Someone was screaming for a medic.

Short, stocky, grizzled, possessed of a mighty laugh and a temper corrosive as acid, Soric had been a smeltery boss back on Verghast. In the war there, he'd become a troop leader ad hoc, a resistance fighter. His exploits had left him with scartissue in place of one eye, a limp, and the eternal respect of Vervunhivers. Ibram Gaunt hadn't thought twice about making Soric a senior platoon leader.

His ability to sleep was a throwback to the old days, when he'd been able to catch a nap despite the tumult of the smeltery line. Now the knack seemed like a liability.

He bundled Vivvo outside, pressing a hand down on the younger man's shoulders to keep him low. The air was full of billowing, opaque fog that made them both choke and gasp violently. They couldn't see anything except the swirling vapour and fuzzy, bright flashes. The parapet at 292 was particularly low and waterlogged; a wide lake formed against its outside lip. The shells falling into it had raised the dense steam and coiling vapour.

'Gak! Back inside, son!' Soric coughed, and shoved Vivvo back into the dugout. He stood alone for a moment, though how alone he couldn't tell. There could be men just a few metres away, Soric thought, and I can't see them. He tried to shout out, but his mouth filled with mud droplets and he started choking again. Besides, the continuous noise of detonations totally drowned him out.

Soric staggered back into the dugout. Vivvo was on his hands and knees, his arms wrapped protectively over his head, retching up muddy liquid.

'We're going to die, boss!' he hacked.

'Did we die on Verghast?'

'N-no...'

'Then I'm sure as gak not going to die on this arse-wipe world.' Soric sat down on the canvas stool. Something jabbed into his hip and he discovered a message shell in the pocket of his breeches. He couldn't remember putting a message shell in his pocket.

He unscrewed the brass cap and shook out a small fold of blue tissue paper. A sheet from a Guard issue despatch pack. Every sergeant had one, though they were seldom needed because of the vox-link. They were for emergencies, and Soric was sure he hadn't used his pack since they'd arrived. But when he looked around, he saw it lying on the dugout's shelf, the paper seal torn off and the top sheet missing.

Soric unfolded the sheet. The brief message was hand written in pencil. 'Bombardment for sixteen minutes, then foot assault from the north-east, under cover of the drain outfall.'

He read it again. His fingers shook a little. There was no mistake about it.

It was his handwriting.

A WHOOPING SHELL struck the third traverse along from station 289, and threw clods of earth and pieces of wood and brick out along the fire trench. Gaunt threw himself flat, dragging Beltayn down with him. The troopers around them were hurled over by the concussion.

As debris and rain spattered down over them, Gaunt got up. He'd lost his cap. A man was wailing pitifully nearby.

'Beltayn?'

His adjutant rose slowly.

'You all right?'

'Feth,' Beltayn grumbled, fiddling with his left hand. His thumb was dislocated. 'Something's awry here...'

Beltayn's voice faded off as he saw the corpse of Trooper Sheric on the duckboards at his feet. The blast had mutilated the side of Sheric's head and jammed a broken plank through his upper torso. It made Beltayn's dislocated thumb suddenly seem quite insignificant.

Nearby, two other men from fifteen platoon were trying to field dress Trooper Kell's torn belly. It was Kell doing the wailing: a feeble, sick-animal sound. Yellowish loops of intestine were spilling from the bright red gashes in his black tunic.

Sergeant Theiss, the normally cheerful commander of fifteen platoon, ran up with one of his corpsmen. He said something to Gaunt that was inaudible over the shell fall. Gaunt waved him off and pointed to Kell.

Gaunt had been at station 289, reviewing muster, when the bombardment started. He cursed the sense of displacement. His own platoon, one, was at station 291, with Caober in charge. There was no way he'd be able to rejoin them in this.

He got up onto the firestep and viewed back down the line through the scope Beltayn handed up to him.

'Throne of Terra...' he murmured.

The valley was an inferno for as far as he could see. Banks of smoke, as vast and dense as thunderheads, hung over the fire trenches, obscuring the view. Shell blasts stippled through the smoke, catastrophic and murderous. An immense fire burned down in the vicinity of 256. At 260, it looked as if an entire section had been gutted. The barrage was creeping back into the supply and communication trenches. Shields had come on over the rearline and command sections, but they weren't the day's targets. Today, the Shadik guns were striking at the infantry lines. And that could mean only one thing.

It was the prelude to an offensive.

A WHISTLE BLEW. It was Kolea at his spotter scope.

'They're coming!' he cried.

Criid tumbled out of the scrape she'd been sheltering in. Steam and fyceline fumes clogged the trenchway. Station 290 had taken some hits in her post, but nothing like the punishment she'd seen fall on Maroy's section.

She blew her own whistle. 'Fix blades! Stand ready to repel!' She dearly wanted to check on Maroy's mob, but there was no time for that. Around her, the troops of nine platoon got up onto the firestep, warknives locked into the lugs of their lasrifles.

The shells were still falling. It seemed to her impossible that the enemy would advance into this.

But she trusted Gol Kolea. He'd never lied before and he wouldn't lie now.

Crouched on the rain-slick paving slabs of the step, she peered out through a loophole. Through the churning vapour, she saw figures, running forward at a halting pace, weapons swinging. Mkoll had briefed the First. Don't let them get close enough to deploy grenades. Hand bombs are their way into the line.

But a spring gun or a pneumatic mortar could throw a lot further than a man.

'Hartwig! Target the slopes, now!'

'Yes, ma'am!'

In the face of the bombardment, their little answering barrage seemed feeble as it began. Spring guns cracked and mortars drummed. There was a satisfying ripple of light munitions from beyond the parapet.

'Keep it up!' she yelled. She risked another look and saw the advancing line of Shadik troopers, just blurs in the fog. Many staggered or were thrown up as ball bombs and mortar rounds fell amongst them.

She glanced down the line. Nine platoon was crouched, ready. She saw Vril spit and shake out his neck. She saw Jajjo drying the grip of his las on his cloak. She saw Nessa, still as a statue at her long-las. Nessa's hair was still boyishly short from the pre-mission buzz-cut she'd had on Phantine, and from some angles she could be mistaken for one of the younger men. One trooper – Criid thought it was Subeno – was vomiting with nerves, but still holding his place.

'Straight silver!' Criid bellowed. 'Step up and fire at will!' Her first battlefield order to the troops.

As one, nine platoon rose and rested their lasrifles on the parapet. They started shooting, dropping the nearest Shadik assaulters as support blasts from Hartwig's gun-dens lofted up over them.

Criid tried to find a target, but it was like aiming into murky water such was the density of the smoke boiling back off no-man's land. A raider in a chain-veil helmet suddenly loomed, winding up to hurl a stick bomb, and she squeezed the trigger. By her side, DaFelbe saw him too, and they killed the raider simultaneously. The stick grenade bounced away and blew up.

Now there were more, and they were running for the line. Some moved in groups, carrying makeshift storm-shields made of overlapped flak-board. Criid slammed off five shots at one shield, but it didn't slow down. It was just six metres from the parapet when a spray of fluid fire washed across it and turned it into a squealing mass of flames and thrashing human torches.

Lubba fired again, hosing the immediate vicinity with his flamer. Criid could distinctly hear his tanks knocking and spluttering despite the fury of the shells. Tracer shots began stitching across the muddy slope from the platoon's support weapon. Figures danced and jerked. Some hung in the wire.

Hand bombs started to bounce in at them. Criid had to duck fast as one went off right under the parapet. DaFelbe toppled off the step, clutching his right cheek where a hunk of shrapnel had punched into his jaw.

'Medic!' Criid yelled. She started firing again. They were so damn close now, and despite everything, there were so damn many.

BRIN MILO, THE youngest Ghost of all, was right beside his platoon sergeant when the raiders came leaping in. One went right over Milo's head and fell down as he landed awkwardly on the duckboards. Sergeant Domor turned and shot him dead where he lay.

They'd been swarmed. Sheer numbers had flung themselves at 293 and 294 and made it over the parapet. Now three and twelve platoon faced the very worst that trench warfare had to offer. Hand-to-hand in the narrow trench gully.

The raiders wore khaki and brown, and most had gas-hoods and heavy helmets clamped over their heads. They carried old-pattern autorifles, pistols and curved hangers.

The world became very, very small. Just a tight space between earthen walls, deafened by shells, full of jostling bodies. Milo slashed and jabbed with his bayonet, staggering back a step as blood gouted over him, and then fired point-blank at a khaki figure clawing at him.

For a while – longer than most of the Ghosts had been comfortable about, to be truthful – Milo had been the only civilian to escape the fall of Tanith. Gaunt had rescued him, though sometimes Milo liked to explain it had been the other way around. Because of that, he'd been seen by all as one part mascot, one part lucky charm... and his skill with the Tanith pipes had come in handy.

Milo had made trooper as soon as he was old enough. According to Corbec, Varl, Larkin, Bragg – God-Emperor rest him – Milo had received more combat experience by the time he sewed on his first cap badge than many Guardsmen did in five years.

That was how it went when you were one of Gaunt's chosen. At his own request, Milo had been placed in Domor's platoon. He knew a spot in one, Gaunt's own, was likely, but he wanted to distance himself a little from his 'saviour'. And from the notion that he was Gaunt's lucky mascot.

Brin Milo was no mascot. He was twenty-one years old standard, tall and strong, and he'd take no feth from anyone now. Despite his age, the Ghosts – especially the Tanith – took him quite seriously. Though Milo only suspected it, both Gaunt and Corbec considered him squad leader material.

Brin Milo had something to prove. It would be his destiny to have something to prove until the day he died.

BARELY TWENTY METRES north of Milo, Rawne's platoon was fending off an assault too. The trench was packed with wrestling, stinking, sweaty bodies. Rawne couldn't see more than a few metres in any direction. He fired his laspistol, and slashed out with his warknife.

Feygor, soaked in blood, appeared alongside him, and together they smashed a little way into the khaki bodies bottled in the trench. They were treading over the wounded and the dead of both sides alike. Melwid was with them, and, briefly, Caffran and Leyr.

'Crush them against the traverse!' Rawne shouted. 'Where's Neskon? Where the feth is Neskon?'

The squad's flame trooper was nowhere to be seen. Nothing was anywhere to be seen, except the churning, stabbing figures of the enemy.

Then a pistol banged, its noise muffled by the close-packed bodies. Rawne saw Melwid fall, clutching his belly. He felt a dull ache in his own midriff. Feygor yelled something and impaled the owner of the pistol on his bayonet.

Rawne fell over. He didn't mean to, but his legs had gone numb. He slumped sideways and hit his head on the revetment. Sounds had become dull and distant.

What a fething stupid way to fight a war, Rawne thought.

'A fething stupid what?' said a voice behind him.

He struggled over and looked up. He dearly wished his legs would work. Jessi Banda, the platoon sniper, was curled into a scrape in the trench wall behind him.

'What?' said Rawne.

'A fething stupid what did you say?' she asked, her voice hoarse.

'Way to fight a war,' he replied. 'Did I say that out loud then?'

'More kinda screamed it,' she said.

Someone stood on his legs and he yelped. Banda reached down and dragged him up into her scrape, holding him tightly so he wouldn't slip back into the base of the trench.

'You'll be okay,' Banda said.

'Of course!' Rawne snapped. He paused. 'Why?'

She didn't reply. He looked down and saw the blood soaking his lower tunic and his breeches. He saw how limp and lifeless his legs were.

'Oh feth!' he barked. That wasn't right. Not right at all.

He turned his head, angry now, and looked at Banda. 'Why the feth aren't you fighting, woman? I thought you females were meant to be tough!'

'Oh, I'd love to,' she said. A shell went off overhead, and Rawne flinched into her. When he did, it made her cough. She aspirated blood out over her chin.

'Not today though, I think,' she said.

'Feth! Where are you hit?'

'Worry about yourself, not me,' she answered.

'Banda! Trooper Banda! Where are you hit?'

She didn't reply. She'd passed out. Rawne found the broken chunk of Shadik bayonet still sticking out of her rib cage.

Banda was so limp, she nearly toppled into the fire trench. Rawne clawed onto her and held her in place, helpless himself, trying to stop the both of them getting trampled in the vicious, endless welter of close combat seething along the trench.

'Medic! Medic!' he cried. No one was listening.

Her head nodded down. Rawne tried to support her.

'You'll be okay,' he told her. 'I fething order you to be okay...'

HEAD LOW, COLM Corbec scurried down the zig-zag defence trench that joined his dugout to the main front facing of 295. The fury of the long range Shadik artillery was still smashing up the day, but it seemed eerily still in his part of the line. There was nobody coming at them.

He came up along the step, patting Surch, Orrin, Irvinn and Cown reassuringly on their shoulders as he came by. Each one was crouched at the parapet with his gun slotted into a loophole or bracket.

Corbec dropped in beside Muril. She was training her long-las back and forth, her eye pressed to the rubber gusset of her scope.

'Care to guess where the feth the enemy is today?' he asked.

She chuckled. That dirty laugh he liked so much.

'They don't seem to be interested in us, chief.'

'You making anything?' he wondered.

Muril shook her head. 'I thought I saw a wire-cutting party out there at the fifty-metre mark a few minutes ago. But it wasn't. Just bodies on the wire, stirred by the blasts. Nothing else.'

'May I?' he asked. She slid her long-las out of the loop and passed it to him. He set it to his shoulder and rose slowly to the top of the parapet.

'Chief!' she hissed.

He knew he was taking a risk, but this total lack of activity was driving him spare. Corbec peered into the scope, adjusting the setting ring, waiting a second as the optic scanner read his retina and automatically recalibrated for his eyesight.

There was nothing out front but mud, wire tangles, twisted piquets, craters and streams of white and grey smoke driven almost horizontal by the crosswind.

He looked to his right. Just five hundred metres south, at 294 and 293, he could see a hellish trenchfight tearing through the positions occupied by Rawne and Domor. Swarms of khaki-clad troopers were pushing up from the mire and assaulting the main line. To his left, again no more than half a kilometre away, the defences held by their Krassian allies were swamped with raiders. Corbec could hear the frantic crackle of small-arms and the bang of grenades.

He dropped back down. 'This is fething... peculiar,' he said, passing the sniper weapon back to Muril with a grateful nod. 'Why the feth aren't they coming at us?'

'They know the great Colonel Corbec is here and they don't want to risk it?' Muril suggested.

'You're a sweet girl, and obviously correct, but there has to be more than that.'

Muril deftly calibrated her gunsight back to her own requirements and sat back on the step, straightening her right leg and flexing it. Maintaining the firing crouch clearly caused her discomfort in her freshly rebuilt pelvis.

'Maybe put yourself in their place?' she said.

'Like what?'

'If you were ordered to take this line, what would you do?'

'I'd attack under the barrage,' he said simply.

'And go for the weakest point,' said Cown from his place behind Muril.

'Well, feth... yes!' Corbec said.

He jumped off the step and planted a kiss on Muril's dirty brow. 'Thank you for your suggestion!' he declared. She was nonplussed. Then he put a smacker on Cown's forehead too. 'And thank you for your insight!'

'What, chief?'

'Imagine! You're going for a line. Frontal assault. But before you get there, the units either side of you break through into their areas. Why lose men pressing home at an unbroken line? Any field commander worth his water would divert towards one of the holes already kicked in. You can bet the bastards intended for us are in support at 294 or 296 right now. Text book. Secure and hold and then hit us from the sides, along the trench. Vox-man!'

Rerval ran up. 'Sir?'

'We got links again yet?'

'No sir.'

'Okay... here's what we do. Every second man, stand down from the step. Those still on station, hold and stay vigilant. Irvinn, you've got fire command here on the step. First sign of action, set up will-fire response and blow your fething whistle.'

'Yes, chief.'

'The rest split into two groups. Where's Bewl?'

'Chief?'

'Take half. Move south. Support Domor's mob. Hold the trench lengthways.'

Bewl nodded, and moved off to communicate the instruction to the troops along the south end of the line section.

'The rest with me,' Corbec said.

THE REST WERE Rerval, Cown, Mkvenner, Sillo, Veddekin and Ponore. Detowine, two platoon's new flamer man made the cut too, but Corbec sent him back to the step. If an assault did come late, he'd need the flamer on the line, along with Surch and Loell's .30 support.

Corbec double-timed the six men up along the trench, moving north. Every Ghost still on the firestep wished them the God-Emperor's grace as they went by.

The attack had been going on for seventeen minutes according to Corbec's timepiece. The smoke and steam kicked up by the immense barrage had now become so chronic, someone, presumably in the support lines, had started to fire off starshells to light the field. The flares served no good purpose except to turn everything into a white haze.

Corbec's team ran on, pausing and flinching every few metres as yet another shell went in over them, shook the ground, and anointed them with a rain of loose earth. By the time they reached the armoured traverse that marked the edge of station 295, Corbec realised he was out of breath.

'You okay, chief?' Mkvenner asked him quietly, so the others couldn't hear.

'My bones are too fething old, son, and they've seen too much war.' Corbec paused a moment and coughed. He'd always led from the front, and that had cost him. He'd lost the little finger of his left hand at Voltis City. That had been the start of it. The start of the tally. Menazoid had hurt him hard. Hagia worse. On Phantine, he'd been lucky to come out alive. Deep wounds to the body and leg, taken during the Cirenholm feth-for-all, followed up with a nosocomial dose of blood-poisoning.

It was a wonder he wasn't made up of augmetic prosthetics.

It was a wonder his luck had lasted this long.

A VERGHASTITE TROOPER named Androby occupied the last slot before the traverse.

'Lot of noise, these last few minutes,' he reported. 'Not much to see.' He'd been using a battered artillery scope borrowed from the mortar teams to keep a watch round the blind end of the traverse.

'Hold here, and stand ready to relay an alarm shout back down the line,' Corbec told him.

They moved around the traverse. For the second time in a week, Mkvenner was advancing around a defence-divide into what could well be an enemy-stormed trench. Corbec knew that. He'd heard Mkoll's debrief about the fight at station 143.

Mkvenner didn't show any nerves at all. He was quiet, expressionless, his camo-cape draped over him. He led the way with his lasrifle up against his shoulder so that everywhere he looked, his gun pointed. He was so silent, Corbec couldn't tell he was there unless he could see him.

Corbec followed him, laspistol in one hand and a grenade in the other. The pin was already out and Corbec was holding the spoon tightly in place with his big, hairy fist.

Behind Corbec were Sillo and Cown. Both had rifles with warknives fixed. Sillo had been a dye-cutter on Verghast, and he was quick and dependable. Cown, good old Cown, was one of the Tanith die-hards, who'd been at the front of just about everything since the awful day they'd first shipped out. He was still getting used to the augmetic bicep and collarbone he'd won at Cirenholm.

To their rear came Ponore and Veddekin, both Verghastites. Ponore was a young, lank prematurely bald fellow who complained incessantly, and Corbec didn't like him much. Veddekin was taller, buck-toothed and younger. Both of them knew how to use a lasgun, and both had seen action, most particularly on Phantine. Corbec wondered if either of them had killed yet. He didn't know, and it was too late to ask.

Rerval brought up the back. He'd left his vox-set with Androby, and carried an extra bag of field dressings. Corbec knew Rerval was a solid fighter. It was easy to forget the war-skills of the vox-troopers. Corbec hoped Raglon would change that conception now he'd been promoted from vox ops to platoon leader. Besides his rifle, Rerval carried a Pharos-pattern flare pistol so they could signal back if things started to cook.

The trench seemed empty. The light was bad and the air was misty with ordnance fumes. Corbec could smell wet soil, promethium, the raw stink of the untreated timber used for the duckboards.

This section of fire trench ran for ten metres, curving slightly north-west, and ended in another solid traverse. There was an opening in the back wall four metres in that went through to a gun-den. Mkvenner checked it, and reported it was empty. A pneumo-mortar and shells, but no gunners.

'This is gakking w–' Ponore began.

Mkvenner put a finger to his lips and the Verghastite shut up.

They crocodiled along, squad members hugging alternate walls.

Here was a discarded lasrifle. Here, the broken haft of an entrenching tool. Items of personal kit were visible in the scrapes. Musette bags, picts of loved ones, igniters and smokes, respirator masks, vacuum-packed ration bricks, bed rolls, balled-up woollen vests.

Like they'd left in a hurry, Corbec thought.

They reached the second traverse. Mkvenner held up a hand. He pointed to the flakboarded back wall of the trench. There was a clotted splatter of blood, matted with strands of hair.

Mkvenner made a signal, one hand over the other, and dropped onto his belly. Corbec stepped aside and let Cown through. Cown and Mkvenner edged round the end of the sturdy earthwork divide, Mkvenner on his front, Cown crouched over him so that two lasguns, stacked, would greet whatever was round there.

'Ahead,' Cown whispered.

Corbec led the others around.

The next fire-bay was empty too, of the living at least.

Fresh corpses virtually filled the trench bottom. Slaughtered Krassian troopers, dead Shadik raiders, all twisted and wrapped under and over each other in an orgiastic celebration of feral murder. Smoke plumes drifted out from some las-punctures where uniform fabric had started to burn. Fountains of blood had splashed up the wall and step in some places. In others, grenades had rendered bodies down into abattoir chunks, and scorched the earth walls black with soot. Where they stepped, the duckboards sank and bright pools of blood welled up through the slats.

The smell was truly nauseating. Blood, cordite, offal, sweat, fyceline, faeces.

All the Ghosts had seen war before, to a greater or lesser extent, but this sight stung them. So many bodies, packed in so tight, into such a little space.

'Gak...' said Ponore.

'Shut up,' Corbec told him. He tried to walk forward, but there was nowhere except bodies to step on. Corpses groaned and sighed, burped and farted as he put his weight on them, squeezing lungs and guts. He was trying to make his way to the mouth of the communications trench that opened into this strand of fire trench halfway along.

It was hard balancing on the dead. Corbec reached his hands out to brace himself against the sides of the trenchway. He spat a disgusted curse as his weight caused a little geyser of blood to squirt from a Krassian's chest wound.

Veddekin suddenly swivelled, and the movement startled Corbec. Veddekin's lasrifle banged and a bright bolt of energy whickered across the width of the trench and punched through the face of a Shadik raider who had just appeared at the parapet.

The raider jerked with whiplash and then toppled head first onto the firestep before falling over, back and feet first, into the bottom of the defence. Corbec had jumped so much at the shot he'd lost his footing and fallen over amongst the heaped dead.

'Sharp eyes,' Mkvenner growled in approval to Veddekin. The scout leapt onto the step, and swung his weapon up, shooting dead the next two Shadik who loomed up at the parapet.

The Ghosts rushed the step then, joining Mkvenner and firing down into the smoke-thickened reaches of no-man's land at the assault party that was trying to get in.

'Gak! There's too many of them!' Ponore yelled.

'Aim. Fire. Repeat,' Mkvenner urged.

Corbec looked up at the backs of his boys on the step and struggled to rise out of the warm layers of bodies. He got his left hand on a timber support and–

He froze. The grenade spoon tumbled from his clawing hand.

He'd dropped the fething bomb.

He looked down, looked down into twisted limbs and staring faces and spools of steaming guts. It was down there somewhere.

If he cried out a warning, he knew his squad would break and the assaulters would be all over them. If he didn't, he and most likely two or three of his team would be killed.

'Sacred feth!' Corbec howled, lunging his hand down into the sticky mess of burst viscera, exposed bone and burnt fabric beneath him. He groped for the grenade. Of all the stupid fething ways of dying. How long had the fuse been set to? Ten seconds? Fifteen?

How long had he been scrabbling for it?

His fingers closed on the bomb. It felt red-hot, toxic, and he wanted to let it go.

But he daren't. He yanked it up and threw it. Threw it as hard as his big, tired, old arm could manage. Threw it up and out, hoping it would fly all the way to the Republic of Shadik and never come back. Threw it as desperately as he'd thrown the sewn-leather batter-balls that had come his way across the rec-field at Pryze County Ground when he'd been just eleven and detesting his forced participation in the County Scholam Tournament.

He'd hated batter-ball. He'd never been able to catch. Never been able to field. He'd been doomed, as a kid, to be the last boy picked for teams.

'Feth!' he screamed, and threw. Threw hard. The best throw of his life.

The hurtling bomb went off in the air, three metres up, as it spun into no-man's land. Shrapnel from the airburst caught five of the raiders at the heart of the attacking platoon.

They broke and fell back, shots from Mkvenner, Cown, Veddekin and Rerval punishing them further. Veddekin hit one in the back as he ran away and ignited the poor bastard's ammo web. The retreating figure caught fire in a flash and carried on running, burning, jolting erratically over shell holes and mud-ridges until he dropped out of sight.

'Are we clear?' Corbec asked, on his feet again. His voice was hoarse with stress. He prayed to every pantheon imaginable that no one had noticed how fething close he'd come to screwing up. Especially Mkvenner. Corbec was meant to be top dog. Mkvenner would never have screwed up like that, not in a million years. And Mkvenner would most certainly have picked Corbec last for his ball team. Old and tired and slow, Colm Corbec, old and tired and slow.

'We're clear,' said Cown.

'Should we stay here?' asked Rerval.

'They won't come back any time soon if they think the line's secure,' said Mkvenner, wisely.

Corbec beckoned them after him and advanced up the jink-cut communications trench. He led the way now, his officer's pistol holstered and his rifle pulled off his back. He'd fixed his bayonet.

There were more bodies up the communications cut, Krassians most of them, distinguished by their copper-coloured coats and grey helmets. Rerval recognised a face or two from Ouranberg. Poor fething bastards. They'd fought to hold every miserable centimetre of this arbitrary hole in the ground. The way some of them had died beggared belief. The suffering, the indignity...

They were four zags down when Corbec stopped them. Small-arms fire was whizzing back and forth along the next angled stretch.

'Way I see it,' Corbec told them quietly, 'the enemy got in and overran the line, killing the Krassys or driving them back up the communications. Probably lost a lot themselves on the way. So we're coming in behind them. Let's make it count.'

The Ghosts nodded and checked weapons.

'Three abreast,' Corbec instructed. 'Me, Ven and Veddey. There's no more room than that. Sillo, Cown, get some tube bombs ready and lob them over the divide as we go. Lob them far – you hear me, you fethers?'

They did.

'And get in behind us,' Corbec said to Ponore and Rerval. 'If we go down, fill our spots. Cown, Sillo, you too, after them. Let's show them how it's done.'

On Corbec's signal, they came round the zag-end and onto the backs of a pack of Shadik raiders clustered in at the next turn. Some of the enemy troopers began to turn as the first las-rounds sliced into them.

'First-and-Only!' Corbec yelled, firing on full auto, smacking las-shots into khaki backs.

Veddekin fell back, his weapon jammed.

Rerval pushed past him, and maintained the tight line. Tube-charges wobbled through the air above them, hurled by Sillo and Cown from behind the trench turn. The blasts filled the narrow defile.

'Straight silver!' Corbec shouted, and, without further warning, charged the enemy. He'd charged because he'd spotted that their angle wasn't secure. Not by a long way. A secondary trench, probably a munitions track, intersected with their stretch from the right on a dog-leg. If there were more Shadik up there...

There were.

Corbec crunched his bayonet into the ribs of one of the Shadik, then kicked the man off the blade as he turned to shoot another raider behind the first. Somehow the first Shadik managed to wrench Corbec's blade off his gun as he went down. As a third came in, swinging a trench club with an iron head, Corbec speared him with his lasrifle anyway. For all he bemoaned his age and diminishing strength, Corbec was still one of the biggest, strongest men in the First. Bayonet or no bayonet, you didn't get up again if Colm Corbec put his weight behind the steel muzzle of a lasgun and rammed it into your sternum.

Now Corbec had an angle into the secondary trench. It was narrow and well-boarded, and sloped away from him downhill in a slight incline. He dropped to his knees and fired down it. His shots hit two of the enemy bunched up fifteen metres away, then a third. A fourth returned fire with a compact sub-autogun, a little bull-nosed slugger with a hooked magazine obviously designed with trench-war in mind.

The burst of small-calibre bullets ripped into the support palings of the trench gabion behind Corbec, showering out splinters. Corbec fired twice, unruffled, and knocked the shooter off his feet and sideways into the revetment. The man slithered down and rolled over.

There were other figures deeper in the secondary trench, veiled by the shadows and the smoke. Corbec fired on them a couple more times, and then ducked back into cover as a ball bomb landed near the mouth of the secondary and threw mud and broken duckboards into the air.

Corbec took stock. He, Mkvenner and Rerval were on one side of the secondary's opening, the rest still back at the start of the zag. Cown tried to dart across to them, but jerked back when rifle rounds and what seemed to be buckshot came stinging up the munitions track.

Corbec looked up the zag. His squad had cleared out the raiders right up to the next turn, about ten metres away.

'Check ahead,' he told Mkvenner. 'I'm hoping there's Krassians round that bend. Don't let 'em shoot you.'

Mkvenner nodded and grinned. He got to the end and peered round. Serious las-fire made him dip back at once.

'Guard! We're Guard!' he hollered. More las-shots. The Krassians, a new outfit with comparatively little battlefield experience, had taken a pounding in the last forty-five minutes. They were spooked and angry and shooting at anything.

Rerval joined Mkvenner.

'They're not taking the chance we're not Shadik,' Mkvenner said.

'We better get their attention,' Rerval said. He pulled out his flare pistol, broke it open, and began sorting through his satchel of smoke and colour pellets. 'What's today's recognition colour?' he asked.

'Blue,' said Mkvenner. He knew full well Rerval knew that. Rerval was vox-ops, up there with Beltayn and Rafflan as one of the best signals specialists in the regiment. The question had been Rerval's way of stress management. A coping strategy. A chance to find out what Mkvenner thought of the idea without actually asking it.

'Blue. Right,' said Rerval. He slid a colour-coded cartridge into the flare pistol, snapped it shut, cocked it, and said, 'Look away.'

They both averted their eyes. Rerval fired the signal gun round the corner of the zag so that the flare embedded itself in the muddy wall beyond. It began to burn with phosphorescent white light, tinged blue by the smoke it was spilling out. The light was fierce and harsh. It threw off long, inky shadows and made everything look cold.

The las-fire stopped.

'Guard! We're Guard here!' Mkvenner tried again. 'You Krassian up there?'

A pause. An answering shout.

'Krassian?' Mkvenner called again.

'Aye! What's the day code?'

'Alpha blue pentacost!' Rerval called.

'Blue eleven salutant!' came the correct answer.

'I'm coming out,' called Mkvenner. 'Hold fire!'

He walked slowly into a trench still lit by the brilliant glare of the fizzling signal round. Blue smoke wafted around him. It was a theatrical entrance, and Rerval was rather proud of it.

Krassian troopers came down the trench to meet them. Their weapons were still raised, and they all looked edgy and scared. Young, a lot of them. Faces white against the copper worsted of their coats.

'Where the hell did you come from?' asked the officer in charge.

'The nalwoods west of Attica,' replied Mkvenner with typical inscrutability. The officer looked puzzled.

'We're Tanith First-and-Only,' said Rerval. 'We pushed in from the south.'

'Tanith?' echoed the officer. Two or three of his younger men had tears in their eyes. Relief, Mkvenner presumed.

'They hit us bad, so bad,' said the officer. 'Are they gone? Did you get them?'

'Not yet,' said Mkvenner.

Fifteen metres back around the zag, Corbec was negotiating the clearance of the secondary trench. Along with Cown, Veddekin and Ponore, he'd been squirting off shots down the length of it on a regular basis, but the response was firm. The worst part of it was that at least one of the raiders had a shotgun, probably a sawn-off, an ideal weapon for trench fights. Ducking in and risking a bullet was one thing, and Murten Feygor would probably give you odds on it. But a shotgun blanketed the space.

Sillo had found that out. Ponore had dragged him back from the junction and dressed his wound, but Corbec knew a scatter-shot hit like that was gangrene waiting to happen, even if the enemy hadn't treated their lead with bacterials as he'd known to be the tactics amongst the arch-enemy.

Sillo had been hit in the left thigh with such force it had shredded his trouser-leg off, broken his belt, and gouged the flesh so deeply Corbec had seen yellow fat and bone. Sillo had screamed, passed out, then woken again screaming. He shut up when Ponore stuck him in the buttock with a one-shot disposable full of morphosia.

'Might be another way round,' Veddekin suggested, his back to the wall by the junction.

'Might be. Who knows?' Corbec grumbled. 'If we had a fething map...'

He did have a fething map. All XOs had been given one when they checked in at 55th sector HQ on their way up the line. The map was deficient in three particulars. First, it showed only the immediate locale of the XO's posting, which meant Corbec's finished at station 295. Second, it showed no minor detail of supply trenches, communication lines, munition tracks or ops centres, because Aexe Alliance Command feared that a map showing such detail would be too sensitive to risk it being captured. So even if Corbec had possessed a map of 296 and northwards, it wouldn't have shown him this track anyway.

Third, perhaps most importantly, it looked like it had been made by a hallucinating, ink-dipped cockroach that had been allowed to run across a piece of used latrine paper.

'We could go over the top,' Cown said, thinking aloud. 'That's what the scouts did at 143 the other night.'

Well, they were fething scouts, the best of our best, half a century younger than me and tough enough to crack nalnuts in their armpits, Corbec wanted to say. But he bit it back. Cown was only trying to help.

'I'd wager they're expecting that, pal,' Corbec said. He picked up a Shadik helmet, hung it on the nose of his las and hefted it up above the revet.

He only had to wiggle it for a second before a rifle round cracked it and sent it spinning away into the air.

Cown smiled at Corbec feebly, and shrugged.

Ponore was looking around. 'Holy gak!' he began. 'We're lucky we didn't go up like bonfires when we started fire-fighting down this!'

More complaints. Corbec wasn't really interested in what Ponore had to say any more. He'd march over and slap him quiet if it wasn't for fact he'd have to get in line of shot to do it.

Ponore wouldn't shut up. He'd crossed to the other side of the zag and yanked up a tarpaulin. As was the case with many supply trenches, funk-holes had been dug out of the sides to make space for storage and then veiled with canvas curtains. Ponore was revealing stacked bags of dressings, tins of vegetable soup, muslin bags of candles, and three or four drums of lamp oil.

'If a shot had hit this,' Ponore moaned, 'whoomff! That'd been us.'

Corbec suddenly grinned. 'Ponore?'

'Yes sir, chief?'

'I could kiss you.'

'He does that,' Cown warned earnestly.

'Get those drums out. Careful, mind.'

Veddekin and Ponore manhandled the first one up to the junction.

Corbec peered around the corner again. He saw what he'd seen the first time he'd looked down the munitions track. Back then, he'd been too busy killing Shadik to pay attention.

The secondary trench sloped away from them. Not much, barely, in fact. But enough. That's why the duckboarding was good. Water drained away down this side trench.

'What now?' asked Veddekin.

'We need a tube or something,' Corbec improvised. 'Cown? There must be a syphon or a funnel or something in there.'

Cown searched the funk hole store, cursing every time the curtain fell back, blocking him in darkness. Ponore went over and held the tarp back for him. Cown emerged with a tin jug.

'What about this?'

'Toss it over.'

Cown threw the jug across the junction and Corbec caught it by the handle. Four or five shots whined up the secondary at the movement.

Corbec recovered his warknife from the ribs of the raider who'd somehow managed to rip it off. He mumbled an apology to the knife for what he was about to do.

It took him about a minute of chopping and levering to bend out the base of the jug and cut it lengthways. He ended up bracing it against a trench post and ripping the curled-away half off by hand.

He'd made a little trough. Not the best trough in the world, but a little trough all the same, with a spout end and everything. His machinesmith father would have been proud.

He flipped it back to Cown. More shots.

'Dig it into the earth there,' he instructed. 'No, at the corner so the spout hangs over the edge. That's it. Keep the back end in cover. That's the lad. Dig it in if you have to. Make it stable.'

Cown raked the earth away with the head of his nine seventy and made the trough stable.

'Fine and lovely,' approved Corbec. 'Now start pouring the oil down it.'

Ponore unplugged the first drum and then tipped it over with Veddekin's help. Clear, sweet-smelling lamp oil glugged out, swirling down the makeshift trough. It began to run down the secondary, gurgling under the duckboards.

'And the rest,' urged Corbec, as Cown and Ponore rolled the first drum away, empty, and Veddekin tipped the second. Corbec realised he was fidgeting from foot to foot. He so wanted to be on the other side of the junction, mucking in with the work, but he could only stand and issue instructions.

A sudden thought hit him. An epiphany. That's what it was called. He'd heard Captain Daur talk about epiphanies. Daur was an educated lad. He understood these fine, subtle things.

A moment of unexpected clarity. That's what Corbec believed it to mean. A sudden revelatory instant of comprehension.

He should never have become an officer. Never. Not even a sergeant, let alone XO of the Tanith regiment. Sure, he had the presence and the charisma, so he was told. He was a personality, and the men rallied round him. That was what Gaunt had seen in him, first time they'd met. Must've been. And Corbec was happy to serve.

But there it was. Gaunt had made him colonel. He'd not asked for it. He'd not chased for it. He wasn't a career man, like Daur or, Emperor protect them all, Rawne. He had no ambition.

What was it they all said about him? That compliment? He led from the front. Just so. He was never happier than when he was at the very workface of fighting, confronting the practicals.

He was the big, strong son of a machinesmith from County Pryze. He should have been a trooper, a dog-grunt, fething well mucking in. Mucking in over there, in fact. Not standing this side of the junction, yakking out orders.

Corbec thought about that for a moment, watching the oil swirl away down the secondary.

'Third drum going in now!' Cown hissed. 'Is this going to work?'

'Let's find out,' Corbec grinned. He looked up-zag to the turn where Mkvenner and Rerval were talking with a bunch of bewildered-looking Krassians.

'Rerval! Over here, son!'

The vox trooper hurried down to Corbec.

'Gimme your flare gun. What burns best?'

'Sir?' Rerval said, handing over the fat-nosed signal gun. Corbec cracked it open.

'Your flares, Rerval. Which one burns best?'

Rerval searched in his bag. 'Red, I guess, chief. It's got the biggest powder charge. But we're only supposed to thump one of them out in predicaments. It's the emergency signal.'

'Give me one. If this works, I'm sure as fething certain our Shadik friends yonder will consider this a predicament, and no mistake.'

Rerval shrugged and handed Corbec a red-tabbed cartridge.

Corbec slotted it into the gun and closed the spring-loaded mechanism.

'Clear?' he asked Cown.

The Ghosts on the other side had rolled the last drum away. Cown nodded.

'Duck and cover,' Corbec told them. 'Fire in the hole!'

He pointed the flare pistol down the secondary and squeezed the trigger.

Nothing happened.

'What the feth is wrong with this piece of crap?' he snarled, bringing his hand back in.

'There's a safety lock,' said Rerval, fussing and trying to be helpful. 'Just there. No, the lever there by your thumb. Uh huh.'

'Well, I knew that,' said Corbec and fired the flare down the munitions track.

Superheated, glowing like a laser torpedo, it ricocheted off the right-hand wall, tumbled left, bounced off a timber post and went spinning away towards the cowering Shadik raiders, kicking off streams of bright red smoke.

Corbec pulled Rerval back against the side wall of the zag.

There was a distant yell. A crump of ignition. Then forty metres of the secondary trench went off like a flamer's kiss. Fire leapt up into the sky, clearing the tops of the walls. Thick, intense, sweet-smelling like the wick-burn of the little lamps they'd given them.

Then there was another smell. A terrible smell. Cooking fat and meat.

'Good job,' Corbec told his boys, wincing into the bright flame light. 'Good fething job.'

THE FOOT ASSAULT on 292 came at precisely sixteen minutes after the start of the bombardment. It came from the north-east, the Shadik using the big, rusting tube of the drain outfall as cover.

Just like the note had said.

Not a single raider made it closer to the parapet than fifteen metres. Agun Soric had clustered his rifles around the outfall, and they blazed at the advancing khaki.

Trooper Kazel reckoned they slaughtered at least fifty, maybe sixty even. It was hard to tell. Five platoon had certainly blown them back to wherever they'd come from.

Soric missed Doyl. Doyl had been his platoon's scout. He'd died on the special mission at Ouranberg. Doyl would have been counting. Doyl would have known.

Soric stood on the step and closed his good eye. He'd always refused a patch or an implant for the eye he'd lost at Vervunhive. He wore the rouched scar with some defiance. It made him look as if he was perpetually winking.

He closed his eye and waited. He saw they'd killed at least seventy-six raiders, a multi-platoon force. Kazel had been underestimating.

Sometimes, Soric saw better with his good eye closed. It was just one of those things. He didn't think much of it. His eye was dead, and so he reckoned it saw things only the dead could see. It had a vantage his good eye didn't.

That had been particularly the case since Cirenholm. He'd been badly wounded there. Recovering, he'd had such strange dreams.

Soric knew he should've kept quiet about them, but secrecy wasn't his way. He'd talked about the dreams, and now Gaunt and Dorden and that sweet girl Ana Curth regarded him with mistrust. He should never have told them about his great-grandmother.

Grandam had possessed the sight. Some called her a witch. So what? It wasn't like she was a psyker, for gak's sake! Grandam had just been able to… to see stuff others didn't. Now Agun could, being the seventh son of a seventh son, as Grandam had always assured him.

It hadn't always been that way. Not until Cirenholm. Passage so close under death's black wing and out the other side, that marked a man. That woke him up. That opened his senses.

Opened his eyes.

The handwritten note though, that was another thing altogether. Soric felt his heart skip as he thought about that.

How had he known that? How had he written it to himself?

'Stand down,' he told his men, and the word was passed along. There'd be no more Shadik at 292 today.

Soric realised he knew that for a fact. Why was that?

He felt scared, really scared suddenly. He limped back to his dugout, ignoring the calls and questions of his men.

'Vivvo?'

'Boss?'

'Get them settled,' he said and dropped the gas curtain after himself.

In the dim lamp-light, he sat down at the little raw-wood table. The brass message shell was sitting there, on end, casting a little blunt shadow. There was no sign of the scrap of blue paper.

Soric breathed slowly, clutching the edge of the table tightly with his gnarled hands. A drink. That might help.

He got up, and waddled his stiff leg over to the shelf. Scope, ammo clips, candles... 'spare water bottle'.

Gaunt had said he'd have men shot for drinking on duty. Except in special cases.

This was a special case.

Soric unstoppered the flask with hands that were quaking more than he'd have liked them to. He took a slug of sacra. Good old Bragg had supplied him with the stuff. Soric had developed a taste for the Tanith liquor. Who'd get him sacra now Bragg was gone?

The blue-paper despatch pad lay on the shelf beside the flask. Soric thought about picking it up, then took another swig instead. The grain alcohol burned in his belly. He felt better. He looked at the pad again.

The first two sheets were missing.

Soric glanced over at the table. The brass message shell sat there, ominous.

'Go away!' he said.

'Uh, I did knock,' said the shell.

But it wasn't the shell. It was Commissar Hark.

The commissar peered in at Soric, holding the gas curtain back.

'Sergeant?'

'Oh, oh! Come in.'

Hark entered.

Soric felt hugely exposed. He tried to keep his mouth clamped shut so he wouldn't exude the smell of liquor. Gaunt might have forgiven him. Hark was a different matter. Hark was a commissar, unqualified, unalloyed.

'Everything all right?' Hark asked. He seemed suspicious.

'Fine, fine,' said Soric, breathing through his nose.

Hark looked at him. 'You could relax, sergeant.'

Mouth clamped shut, Soric grinned and shrugged.

Hark sat down on the stool, removing his cap. 'Good work today, sergeant. Excellent, in fact. How did you guess the Shadik's approach route?'

Soric shrugged again.

'Lucky, huh?' Hark nodded. 'Shrewd is a better word. You're very shrewd. You know your stuff, Agun. Can I call you Agun? It doesn't offend your sense of rank?'

'Not at all, sir,' Soric muttered, trying not breathe as he spoke.

'The bombardment's stopped,' Hark said. Soric realised he hadn't noticed.

'We've held them off for the most part,' Hark added. 'Tough stuff around 293 and 294, and also with Criid, Obel and Theiss. And Maroy's dead.'

'Shit, no!' said Soric, despite himself.

'Yeah, it's too bad. Good soldier. But his section took seventy per cent losses. Shells caught them hard. Lasko, Fewtin, Bisroya, Mkdil. All gone. Not you, though, eh?'

'Sir.'

Hark gestured expansively. 'I don't have the full picture yet, but I'm pretty sure your platoon gave the best today, unit for unit. A hell of a job, Agun. Good work. Smart to pick up on their route of attack. I'm impressed.'

'Thank you, sir.'

'I'll be commending your unit to Gaunt. Any one you want to pick out?'

'Uh… Vivvo and Kazel.'

Hark nodded. 'I tell you what you could do now.'

'Sir?'

'I don't know about you, Agun, but I'm shaking fit to drop. Man like you must have some hard stuff hereabouts.'

'Oh,' said Soric. He rattled round on the shelf. 'Forgive my inhospitality, commissar.'

He poured sacra into two of the least chipped shot glasses cluttering his shelf and handed one to Hark.

'Excellent. Knew I could count on a trusty Vervunhiver like you.'

Hark knocked back the shot. Soric sipped his own. He refilled Hark's glass and breathed more naturally.

Hark finished the second shot. 'Takes a while, but that Tanith stuff is good, isn't it?'

'Becoming a favourite, sir,' said Soric.

'You'll have to tell me how you did it, some time,' said Hark.

'Did what, sir?'

'Outguessed the Shadik. Good work, though. Excellent. The regiment is proud of you.'

Hark got up.

'I have to get down the line now. Rawne's been hit. His section is a mess.'

'Hit bad?'

'I'm going to find out. Again, good work, Agun. My compliments to your boys.'

Hark pulled back the gas curtain to leave.

'Thanks for the drink,' he added, and disappeared.

Soric sat down hard as soon as the commissar had gone. He played with his shot glass, and then finished the dregs.

Vivvo stuck his head through the curtain.

'Boss? Do you w–'

'Go away,' said Soric.

'Yes, boss.'

Alone, Soric picked up the message shell and unscrewed the top. He had to thump the base of the canister twice to get the fold of blue paper out.

The message was written in his own handwriting, just like before. It said: 'Don't drink. Commissar Hark is coming.'

FIVE
SILVER, RED AND BLACK

'Waiting is crap. It's crap for a hungry man in a canteen line, it's shit for a groom at his wedding supper, and it's double triple quadrilateral crap for a soldier boy like yours truly.'

– Colm Corbec, colonel

IT HAD BEEN a bad day at the front. The Tanith First reserves at Rhonforq could tell that just from the false dusk caused by the wall of black smoke rising in the distance. They waited for news, hoping for good, steeled for bad.

Gaunt had left Captain Ban Daur in command of the First's reserve section, a full two-thirds of the regiment's strength, and Daur fretted miserably throughout the afternoon. Every ten, twenty minutes he wandered outside and watched the flickering lights and puffing smogs of the distant battle. At first, the thump of the shells had been like the thunder of a distant storm; muffled, remote, lagging behind the flashes. Then the sound had become continuous, without break or breath or pause. A constant rumble, as if the earth was slowly faulting and tearing.

Sometimes, the ground shook, even this far away.

Once in a while, there came a blast roar so loud and plangent that it rose out of the rumble. Daur couldn't work out if these noises came from shells that had landed closer to his position, or bigger shells landing with the rest. They'd been told the enemy had brought up some big-reach, huge calibre weapons. All the men were talking about 'super-siege' guns.

Daur tried to occupy himself, but the rumble was too distracting. At around 14.00, he went to eat at one of the pensions, and got a curious look from the matronly owner when he ordered scrambled eggs. Only when it arrived did he remember that he'd already taken lunch – scrambled eggs – just an hour before.

He thought of visiting Zweil. The unit's chaplain was refreshing company sometimes, and good at distracting a man's mind with provocative conversation. But he was told that Zweil had gone to the front that morning with Gaunt, as if he'd known he'd be needed today.

Daur toured the billets instead. The Ghosts had occupied the stableblocks and barns of a pair of farmsteads in the south of the town, their overspill camped out in a sea of tents pitched in the paddocks behind. The paddocks adjoined an old tannery occupied by a company of Krassians, and a little vee of derelict shops and outbuildings at the junction of the two southern roads, which was the billet of a local brigade, the Twelth Ostlund 'Shielders'.

Daur wandered into the muddy yard of one of the stableblocks. Burone, Bray and Ewler had taken the long, left-hand barn for their platoons. The men mostly lurked around, dejected in the light rain, like prisoners of war in a blockhouse pen. Daur saw the coals of burning lho-sticks in the shadows of the high-loft hatches. Under the slope of a lean-to roof, Pollo from seven platoon was trying to teach card tricks to a crowd of onlookers. Pollo had been bodyguard for a noble house back on Verghast, and his nerves were augmented by extravagantly expensive neural enhancers, so his fingers split and spread the cards faster than the eye could follow. It was a little piece of magic to watch, and the men around him were captivated. Daur watched for a little while, until Pollo had exhausted his repertoire of tricks and produced three cups and a shell case instead. The audience groaned.

'Who wants a try?' Pollo asked, his hands circling the up-turned cups in a blur. He caught Daur's eye and winked. 'You, sir?'

Daur smiled. 'You see my rank pins, Trooper Pollo? I get those for being smart. No thanks.'

Pollo grinned. 'Your loss.'

'I don't think so,' said Daur and wandered on. At the back end of the yard, Haller's men were kicking a ball around with some of the Krassians. It was a lively, muddy game. Noa Vadim was running circles around the Krassians, his squad mates urging him on. Daur was sure they were really shouting and whooping to shut out the distant growl of the battle.

Daur heard low-level gunfire coming from one of the stable pens and went to investigate. He found Trooper Merrt practising his aim against old bottles ranged on the cross-beams of the end wall.

Merrt looked up as Daur appeared. 'Sorry, sir.' he said. 'Just gn... gn... practising. I've set it to gn... gn... low-charge.' He looked a little shamefaced, though it was hard to tell. Merrt's jaw and one side of his face were crude metal implants, poorly disguised by a flesh-coloured mask. Daur knew why he was practising. Merrt practised every chance he got. A Tanith, he'd been one of the regiment's original snipers, with a hit rate lower than Larkin's or Rilke's but still impressive. Then, on Monthax, he'd taken a horrific head wound and his aim had gone to hell. Gaunt had kept him as sniper for a time – too generous a time, according to Hark – but Merrt's lack of success on Phantine had finally obliged Gaunt, reluctantly, to reassign him back to a standard trooper role.

Daur knew Merrt hated his loss of status even more than he hated the loss of his face. Merrt practised and practised, striving to regain his prowess and win back his marksman's lanyard.

'How's it going?' Daur asked.

Merrt shrugged. 'I'd like to be working with a gn... gn... long-las, but they took it off me and gn... gn... gave it to some girl,' he said bleakly, indicating the standard-pattern lasrifle he was holding. His speech was distorted by the rebuilt portions of his head. Merrt seemed to gnaw the words out. He stammered a lot, thanks to that ugly replacement jaw.

'Some of those girls are good shots,' said Daur smoothly. He knew too well a lot of the Tanith resented the Verghastite volunteers, particularly the females, and especially the females like Banda, Muril and Nessa who excelled at shooting.

Daur wouldn't hear them bad-mouthed. They were the Verghastites' one claim to excellence in the regiment.

Merrt stammered particularly badly, realising he'd spoken out of turn to the senior Verghastite officer. 'I didn't mean anything gn... gn... by that, sir.'

'I know,' said Daur. There was no real anti-Verghast or misogynistic rancour in Merrt. He was just a damaged man struggling with his own failure.

'Gn... gn... sorry.'

Daur nodded. 'You carry on,' he said.

Daur felt wretched as he walked away from the stall. There had been plenty of scorch marks on the end wall, but precious few broken bottles.

Daur crossed the end of the back paddock, passing the time with a few soldiers there. Then he followed a quaggy path up onto a bank that ran down through what had once been an orchard, before the men in the billets had felled most of it for firewood. Arcuda and Raglon were sheltering from the rain by a low wall, their capes pulled up around them.

Daur knew they were both nervous. Both had been promoted, along with Criid, to platoon command just prior to Aexe. Both were anticipating their first taste of field command.

But both had reason to be proud, in Daur's book. Arcuda, a Verghastite with a long, thin doleful face, had proved himself in the ranks and won his pins. Raglon had made his way to squad command through distinguished service in company signals. It was odd not to see Raglon with his vox-set. Daur was pleased to find them together; Verghastite and Tanith, on equal footing, counting on each other.

They greeted him and he squatted down beside them.

'Action at the front,' Daur said.

'We noticed,' said Raglon.

'Chances are, we may move forward early,' Daur added.

Arcuda nodded. 'I want to get up there, sir,' he said. 'I just want to get in it. Sort of... get it over with. Did you feel that way on your first command?'

Daur smiled. 'My first command was a sentry detail at Hass West, Vervunhive. Very pedestrian,' he said. 'I was nineteen. I didn't see action for four years. Not until... the War.'

Someone sniggered. Daur looked up and saw Sergeant Meryn leaning over the wall and listening in.

'Something funny, Meryn?'

Meryn shook his head. 'No, captain. I'm just always amused the way you Verghasts refer to Vervunhive as "The War", capital emphasis and all. It was a big do, certainly, and hard as fething bastardy for everyone involved. But it wasn't "The War". The War's what we're fighting now. We were fighting it before Verghast and we'll be fighting it still in years to come.'

Daur got up and faced Meryn. The man was young, one of the youngest Tanith-born officers, several years junior to Daur. He was trim, compact, good-looking, and had recently taken to cultivating a moustache that made him look sinister in Daur's opinion. Meryn had charm, and a fine record, and his brevet-ranking to sergeant as part of Operation Larisel on Phantine had become a permanent thing. His pins were as new as Arcuda's and Raglon's.

'I know there's war and there's war, sergeant,' Daur said. 'You'll have to excuse a Verghast his memories.' Daur deliberately used the word Meryn had used. 'Verghast' not 'Verghastite'. All the Tanith did that. To them, it was a contraction. To Verghastites, it was insulting slang. 'We know we're fighting The War now. But you'll forgive us if we tend to focus on the fight that saw our home-hive ransacked.'

Meryn shrugged. 'And Tanith died. We all have our memories. We all have our wars.'

Daur frowned and looked away, the drizzle splashing off his face. He didn't like Meryn much. He'd been an obvious choice for platoon command, some said an overdue choice, but he'd become unpleasantly hard-edged and cocky. Sometimes, he reminded Daur of Caffran. Both Tanith were of a similar age, a similar build even. But where Caffran was young and eager and good-natured, Meryn was young and ruthless and arrogant.

Colm Corbec had a private theory about that. The theory was called Major Rawne. According to Corbec, Meryn had been 'a fine, honest lad' for some time until he'd made corporal and, thanks to the vagaries of regimental structure, fallen under Rawne's wing. Rawne was Meryn's mentor now, and Meryn was learning well. The fresh-faced attitude had vanished, and been replaced by a bitter, hostile air. The stain of Rawne's corrosive influence, Daur believed. Rawne was grooming Meryn. Unofficially, the rumour was that Meryn had ordered, or performed, some excessively brutal actions during Operation Larisel. Certainly Larkin and Mkvenner were tight-lipped about him. Meryn had been zealous to achieve his Larisel mission targets and prove himself for promotion.

Too zealous, maybe.

'So, any word from the line yet?' Meryn asked. Daur wished Meryn would go away so he could spend some time bolstering Arcuda and Raglon without an audience.

'No,' said Daur. 'Not yet.'

'If there are casualties, you can figure we'll be moving up before tonight,' Meryn said.

'If there are casualties...' Daur admitted.

Meryn made a sarcastic gesture at the smoke rising from the front. 'There'll be casualties,' he said.

'You'd wish that, would you?' snapped Daur.

'Not for a moment,' said Meryn, his face turning stony. 'But I'm a realist. That's bad feth up there. "The War", you know? Someone's going to get hurt.'

Daur wanted to tell Meryn to go away, but Raglon and Arcuda had got to their feet, shaking the water off their capes.

'We're going to check on our units, sir,' said Raglon.

'Get them ready, if and when,' Arcuda added.

'Good idea,' said Daur.

The two novice sergeants walked away down the bank towards the village and the tower of the Chapel St Avigns. As soon as they were out of earshot, Daur turned on Meryn.

'Do you understand the concept of morale, Meryn?'

Meryn shrugged.

'Those two are on the verge of their first field command. They're scared. They need building up, not knocking down.'

'It's a crime to be realistic now, is it, captain?' Meryn asked, insolently. 'This is my first action as sergeant too, if you'll recall.'

'You've had command, Meryn. At Ouranberg. You did all right there. Too well, maybe.'

'What does that mean?'

'Whatever you like,' said Daur, walking away. He uttered a silent prayer of thanks that within a week or so, Meryn would be Rawne's responsibility again.

* * *

THERE WAS A lot of noise coming from the end sheds of the tannery. Daur pushed his way into a barn space that stank of sweat and bodies. The place was full of Ghosts and Krassians and a good number of the red-tunicked Ostlunders.

The Ostlunders were from Kottmark, the country that bordered Aexegary to the east. They were a fair-skinned, hardy breed, generally much taller than the Imperials.

Daur peered through the crowd, trying to establish the source of the commotion.

'Varl,' he sighed to himself. 'Why am I surprised?'

Sergeant Varl, head of nine platoon, had found himself a new game to bet on. Varl, a likeable, handsome rogue, had come up through the ranks and earned his sergeant pins with sweat and blood. His own, for a start. On Fortis Binary, he'd taken an upper torso wound that had resulted in serious augmetic work to his shoulder, collarbone and upper arm. Not long after that, Gaunt had made him sergeant. He'd done it to prove there was no pecking order in the Tanith. Varl was one of the boys, common as grox muck, but he had attitude and charisma in bucket loads, and that made him an ideal leader of men.

You couldn't help but like Varl. All the men did. He was a joker, a prankster, a troublemaker. He also proved that a dog-grunt could have the mettle to lead.

Gaunt had hoped he'd bring a common touch to the command echelon of the First. Varl had brought it in spades.

Daur knew that Varl had made sergeant long before the more upstanding and clean-cut Meryn. Maybe that was why Meryn was such an insufferable feth-head.

Ceglan Varl was playing ringmaster here. His men had made a pit from straw bales, and they appeared to be orchestrating fights between chickens.

Daur moved his way to the front of the press. No, not chickens...

'Struthids! Lovely young struthids, fit to fight and tough as hell!' Varl was declaiming from the wooden loading dock above the pit. He lofted one of the birds by the scruff of its neck, expertly avoiding its clacking blade of a beak and its windmilling, clawed feet. Expertly, that was the word. Daur chuckled. They'd only been on this world five minutes, and Varl was suddenly an expert handler of the local wildlife.

'Look at this jolly fellow! Look at him, eh?' Varl bantered. 'We call him the Major, because he's nasty as all feth!'

The Ghosts in the crowd laughed at this.

'Look at his foot-claws! Look here!' Varl grabbed one of the bird's pistoning feet and splayed the vicious claws for the crowd to admire. 'Three centimetres long, sharp as straight silver! What more do you want?'

A Krassian shouted something.

'Beak? Beak?' Varl replied, looking over and swinging the squirming struthid round. 'I'll give you beak! Mr Brostin, if you'd be so kind?'

Brostin, the heavy-set flame-trooper from Varl's platoon, strode out into the straw-strewn ring and held out a spent brass case from a .30. The bird lunged and cracked the case in two with its scissoring beak.

The crowd roared. Brostin retrieved the broken parts and threw them into the press. Men huddled and fought for them.

'He's tough, all right! Yes, sir! The Major is a tough old bird! We all saw what he did to the Captain just now, didn't we?'

More shouting.

'The Captain?' called Daur.

Varl saw Daur and balked. 'Ah... hello there, sir! How are you? The Captain I refer to... rest his poor soul... was named after another captain who in no way was meant to resemble you... uh...'

'I'm sure. How much on the Major?'

Varl's smile returned. 'Perhaps you'd care to place your wager with one of my friendly assistants, sir?' Daur saw Baen, Mkfeyd, Ifvan and Rafflan moving through the crowd, collecting cash and quoting odds.

'What's he up against, this Major?' Daur shouted.

'Three rounds, no holding, first bleeds, first pays...' said Varl, '...against Mighty Ibram here!'

There was a throaty bellow of approval. Trooper Etron appeared on the other side of the stage, clutching a white-plumed struthid juvenile with a silvery beak. He was having trouble holding on to it. Feather fibres drifted in the warm air.

'No, thanks,' smiled Daur. 'My money's on Mighty Ibram every time.'

'This is fixed! You fix this!' some of the Kottmarkers were yelling.

'Calm yourselves, friends,' said Varl.

'We have our own fighter!' called the tallest of the Ostlund Shielders.

Varl addressed the crowd. 'A new contender, gents and gents, trained by our worthy Kottland allies here... what's the bird's name?'

The clique of Kottmakers had brought a snapping, scarred struthid fledgling forward. 'Redjacq!' their leader hollered.

'Redjacq indeed! He's a fine looking beak-brain, and no mistake!' Varl yelled. 'Place your bets, folks... next round is the Major, Tanith-reared and hard as feth, facing off against Redjacq, trained and maintained by our delightful Kottmark allies there! Ante up! Who's for the Major?'

'Ten!' shouted a Verghastite.

'Twenty on Redjacq!' howled a Krassian.

'My warknife says the Major guts him.'

Daur peered through the crowd to identify the source of the voice. It was Mkoll. The chief scout was standing, arms folded, in the middle of the frenzy.

'We spit on your knife!' cried one of the Kottmarkers.

'I… uh… wouldn't do that if I were you,' said Daur, but the Kottmarkers weren't listening.

'Gentlemen! All bets now stand!' Varl said, taking a nod from Baen. 'Round one! Release your fighters!'

The juvenile struthids exploded into the ring from either side to a cacophony of jeers and taunts. Feathers fluttered up from them. Redjacq sliced and chopped at the Major and more plumage flew. Then the Major lunged in and broke Redjacq's neck with a clean bite of its formidable beak.

The tannery's roof tiles rattled with the uproar that followed. Tanith – and some Krassians – were shouting and dancing. Wagers were paid out, back and forth: local currency, Imperial coin, trophies, badges, mementos…

Up on the loading dock, Varl did a strutting chicken walk, back and forth, his head bobbing in and out, his elbows beating chicken wings.

Caught up in the middle of it all, Daur laughed. For a moment, he almost managed to forget how bad things were.

A firm hand gripped his arm. It was Mkoll.

'Stay sharp, sir,' the chief scout said softly. He nodded towards the door. 'Over there.'

Daur looked. Varl's lackey Ifvan was trying to get a group of Kottmarkers to pay out. Daur couldn't hear the exchange, but he could read the body language. More Kottmarkers were closing in through the oblivious, dancing Tanith.

'Back me up,' Daur said.

'I will,' said Mkoll.

Daur pushed through the dancing men. Nine or ten Kottmarkers were gathered around Ifvan now, and others looked like they were bang out of sportsmanship.

One of the Ostlund troops started shoving Ifvan in the chest. They were all a lot taller than him. They were all a lot taller than Daur.

Daur cleared his throat and prepared to intervene. At that moment, the Kottmarker behind Ifvan suddenly produced a trench club. It was a thick cylinder of hardwood with a metal boss, the size of a stick grenade.

Daur lunged forward. The club came down–

–and stopped. There was a solid, meaty thunk that shut the room up suddenly.

The Kottmarker had dropped the club. His sleeve was pinned to the doorpost by a Tanith warknife. There was a terrible, pregnant silence.

Daur glanced back at Mkoll, but the scout chief simply shrugged in bemusement.

'I hate a bad loser,' said Varl, from the stage ten metres away. He was staring at the Kottmarkers surrounding Ifvan. 'This is an entertainment. Sport. It isn't war. We come in here in the spirit of friendly competition and leave the killing at the door. You're pissed off. Well, tough. In the spirit of this place, I say take your money. We don't want it. Your bets are wiped. Take your money and get out.'

Some of the Kottmarkers took a step towards the stage.

'Or,' said Varl, sharply, 'I start chucking a few more warknives. Someone give me some straight silver.'

Daur blinked. An extraordinary thing happened. There was a ripple of thuds, and a semi-circle of Tanith blades appeared around Varl's feet, tips buried in the wood, thrown without hesitation and with complete accuracy from the crowd.

Varl bent down and plucked out one of the still vibrating blades.

He tossed it up in the air without even looking at it, and caught it again by the grip.

'Well?'

The Kottmarkers fled. So did some of the Krassians. The owner of the club left part of his sleeve pinned to the doorpost.

The men of the First began to cheer and clap. Varl did a little bow and then balanced the knife on his nose, tip down.

'That's enough!' Daur raised his voice. 'Let's clear out and get ready for kit inspection!'

The Ghosts filed out, chattering and laughing. One by one, the knives were retrieved from the stage planks. Brostin recovered Varl's blade from the doorpost and tossed it back to the sergeant. Varl returned Brostin's. The knives passed in mid-air. Neither man was looking as he deftly caught his weapon.

The shed was almost empty. Mkoll lingered. Daur climbed up onto the loading dock next to Varl.

'I'm impressed,' said Daur. 'You kept control.'

'You don't start something like this if you can't police it,' Varl said. 'First rule of showmanship.'

'Still, it was magnanimous of you to let them go without paying.'

Varl smiled. 'All part of the show. Besides, Ifvan and Baen picked their pockets on the way out.'

'Captain?'

Daur looked down into the body of the shed. Mkoll stood in the doorway.

'Signal's come through,' Mkoll said. 'They're moving the wounded back up the line.'

THE FIRST WOUNDED had begun to filter back during the late afternoon, and by the time the bombardment ended and the assault had subsided, they were streaming into the field stations. Some came walking, others carried by stretcher bearers or supported by their comrades, some were borne on barrows or on shellcarts.

Dorden, the First's chief medic, had moved his team up to a triage station just after lunch. The station, designated 4077, was just four kilometres to the rear of the front line. They endured the later stages of the bombardment while they prepped the area. The ground shook. Tent canvas flapped. Surgical tools rattled on their trays.

'There's no mains water supply,' reported Mtane, one of the regiment's three qualified medics.

'None at all?' asked Curth, laying out clean blades on a cloth-covered tray.

Mtane shook his head. 'There's a bowser. About half-full. The Alliance orderlies can't promise it's clean.'

'Lesp!' Dorden called. The lean orderly ran up. 'Set up some stoves and start boiling water. Wait!' Lesp paused as he prepared to dash off again. Dorden handed him a small paper packet. 'Sterilising tablets. Do your best.'

Curth broke open a box of anti-bacterial gel packed in fat metal tubes and passed them around. 'Use them sparingly,' she admonished. 'It's the only carton we've got.'

The triage station was a collection of dirty, long-frame tents pitched to the west of a dead woodland. The access ramps into the first dugouts of the 55th sector workings began just fifty metres east of them. They were terribly exposed, the first above-ground features this side of the Peinforq Line. The wood – Hambley Wood, apparently – was proof of their vulnerability. It was a sea of soft mud and old craters, stubbled with the burnt stumps of thousands of trees. The whole area smelled of wet-rot and mulch.

The First's medicae team shared the station with a Krassian detail and a gang of Alliance corpsmen. When Curth went outside the Ghosts' tent for a final lho-stick before the real work began, she was surprised and disgusted at the filthy state of the locals. Their scrubs and – worse – their hands, were soiled. Many were ill. Some were intoxicated, probably from drinking neat rubbing alcohol.

Foskin, the most junior orderly, joined her for a smoke.

'How many are they going to kill by transmitting infection?' she asked.

'Let's just make sure all the Ghosts come to us,' he said.

It was nothing like that simple. The bodies and the walking wounded that began to pass back to the triage station were so drenched in mud it was impossible to distinguish rank or regiment or even gender.

Curth spent five minutes sewing up a thigh wound before she realised it was Flame-Trooper Lubba she was treating.

One of Kolea's old mob, from nine platoon.

She rinsed his face and smiled when the tattoos were revealed. 'How's Gol?' she asked.

'He's okay, ma'am. Came through it, last I saw.'

'And how's Tona shaping up?'

'The sarge? She was fine.'

Curth was pleased. They were calling Tona Criid 'the sarge' already. Ana Curth was the only person in the First who knew the secret. Kolea had known, but it had been lost along with his identity. There was a madam called Aleksa who knew too, but Curth hadn't seen her since Phantine. The two children Criid and Caffran had 'adopted', two kids who now waited with the camp followers at Rhonforq, were, in truth, Kolea's. He'd presumed them lost. When he'd found out they were alive after all, it was too late. Orphans, they'd bonded with Criid. It was too late to wreck their world again.

That's what Kolea had believed anyway, before injury had robbed them of his character.

Curth felt it was her responsibility to watch over them all.

The anonymous wounded plodded in, through the late afternoon. Dorden found cases of shrapnel wounding, concussive damage and several chronic examples of harm done by gas, both caustic and lachrymatory. He extracted a five centimetre piece of hand-bomb casing from DaFelbe's jaw, twenty-two nails from the foot and leg of Trooper Charel, and a broken length of bayonet from the ribcage of Jessi Banda.

She came round on the table as he was cleaning the wound prior to excising the foreign body.

'Rawne!' she gasped. 'Rawne!'

'Easy there,' he scolded. He looked at Lesp. 'Any morphosia?'

Lesp shook his head.

'How's Major Rawne?' Banda called out, convulsing.

'Easy,' said Dorden. 'You'll be okay.'

'Rawne...' she murmured.

'Was he hurt?' Dorden asked.

Banda had passed out.

'No breath sounds on the left,' Lesp reported. 'We're losing her.'

'Her lung's collapsed,' said Dorden matter-of-factly, and set to work.

Some of the most terribly wounded came from sixteen platoon, though there weren't many of them. One of the Krassians told Curth that sixteen had been virtually wiped out by shellfire.

Trooper Kuren, who'd made it through the horrors of Operation Larisel on Phantine unscathed, had lost part of his leg. 'They're all dead,' he told Curth. 'Maroy's dead.'

She shivered. 'Dead?'

'Almost all of us. The fething shells, like murder...'

She looked across the station. Mtane was trying to pull together a Krassian's gaping chest. Foskin and Chayker were holding down a man who was going into a grand mal seizure and vomiting blood. Dorden was fighting to save Banda's life.

'Sergeant Maroy's dead,' said Curth.

Dorden nodded sadly. 'Rawne may be too,' he said.

Around 17.00 hours, the tide of wounded ebbed. Dorden's triage station alone had dealt with nearly five hundred bodies.

The light was bad, choked by the shell-smoke. Drizzle pattered in. The ground inside and outside of the tents was awash with blood, and pieces of discarded uniform and equipment were scattered everywhere.

Light wounded had been sent along the road to Rhonforq and the other reserve stations. The really sick and injured were being ferried by cart and stretcher to the main field hospitals. Dorden made sure that all the seriously wounded Ghosts were labelled so they would be conveyed to his mill infirmary at Rhonforq.

Curth and Dorden exited their triage tent during the lull, complaining to each other about their parlous lack of supplies. Curth smoked another lho-stick, which Dorden shared briefly, though it made him cough. She was afraid she was teaching him bad habits.

'Hey,' she said, nudging him. 'Over there.' Across the churned mud of the station, Alliance orderlies were conveying medical supplies to their tents on sack-barrows.

Curth ran over, tossing her stick-butt into the mud. 'Hey!'

Dorden tried to stop her. 'No, Ana! Don't!'

It was too late. Curth had reached the sack-barrows. She grabbed a box off the nearest and ripped open the lid, the Alliance orderlies objecting angrily.

'Imperial supplies! This stuff is stamped for use by the First-and-Only! You bastards! You stole this!'

'Be off!' growled an Aexegarian.

'I will not! Our supplies went missing, and we've been fighting to survive without them! You had them diverted, didn't you? You fething well stole our med supplies!'

'Ana! Please! It's not worth it!' Dorden cried as he came over. He'd seen this kind of despair-induced corruption too many times before. The Alliance was running painfully short of essential supplies. A big shipment of fresh medical goods must have seemed too choice a treasure to ignore. He'd get some more, he'd get some more shipped in from the Munitorium vessels. It wasn't worth confronting these miserable, desperate wretches.

'Hell, no!' Curth exclaimed, and tried to gather up some of the cartons.

A thuggish Alliance trooper with a dirty bandage around his head struck out at her, and knocked her over into the mud. The cartons went flying.

'No, oh no... no you don't!' Dorden yelled and leapt at the Alliance orderlies, pulling them back off the fallen Curth, who was hunched in a foetal position in the mud to protect herself from their toecaps.

They turned on him. One punched him in the mouth, another kicked him in the hip. Dorden yelped, and then threw a jab that laid one of the Aexegarians out. Then they really started to pound on him. Curth got up and threw herself back into the fray, clawing and punching and kicking.

A bolt-round went off, very loud in the close air.

The brawling figures broke away from Curth and Dorden at the sound. Ibram Gaunt walked across the muck, white smoke escaping through the vents of his bolt pistol's flash retarder. He was splashed from head to toe in mud and blood, and powder burns marked his cheeks.

'I am Imperial Commissar Gaunt,' he said. 'I am known to be a fair man, until I am pushed. You've just pushed me.'

Gaunt lowered his weapon and shot two of the Aexegarians dead where they stood. The rest fled. For good measure, Gaunt sighted and shot down one of the escapees too. Guardsmen, medics and Aexe personnel all around the field station stood and gawped in shock.

Gaunt helped Dorden and Curth to their feet.

'No one does that to my medicae core,' he said.

Curth looked at him in frank fear. She'd never seen him like this.

'I'm a commissar,' he said to her. 'I don't think you realise what a commissar is, Ana. Get used to it.'

Gaunt looked away. 'You men!' he shouted at a group of stunned onlookers. 'Gather up these supplies and distribute them evenly between the Guard and Alliance medical teams at this station. Surgeon Curth here will supervise.'

She nodded.

'Dorden?' Gaunt turned to the old medicae. He had a swollen eye and his lip was split.

'All right?'

'I'll survive,' said Dorden. Gaunt could tell he was more angry than hurt. Angry that the fight had started at all, angry that he'd been stupid enough to get involved. And more than anything else, angry at the way Gaunt had just demonstrated the bleak side of Imperial Guard discipline. Dorden had vowed never to kill. He'd broken that vow once, on Menazoid Epsilon, in order to save Gaunt's life. Now he saw Gaunt take life wantonly, in the name of iron discipline.

'Doctor?' Gaunt said.

'Sir?'

'See to Rawne, please.'

GAUNT'S ARRIVAL HAD marked a fresh influx of casualties, the majority of them Krassians and Alliance, but also a good number from at least seven

Ghost platoons, including those of Rawne, Domor, Theiss and Obel. The injuries in Theiss's and Obels's units were mainly from shells. Some of these wounds, like Trooper Kell's, were devastating. Others were insidious.

Trooper Tokar would be the first Tanith man to have to learn as a necessity the sign language used by previously blast-deafened Verghastites.

In Domor's platoon, and in Rawne's, the injuries were from close-quarters fighting. Milo, unharmed himself apart from a few bruises, carried in Trooper Nehn, who'd had his skull cracked by a trench club. Trooper Osket had lost an eye, and then had suffered the misfortune of grabbing a bayonet thrust at him. The blade had chopped in between his middle and third finger, right down through the palm to the base of the thumb. Corporal Chiria, one of the Verghastite girls in Domor's outfit, had massive lacerations that would scar her plain but cheerful face forever.

Rawne was unconscious. Feygor and Leclan carried him in on an improvised stretcher made of duckboards.

'What do you know?' asked Dorden briskly as he started to cut away the major's tunic and undershirt.

'Solid round to the gut,' said Leclan, three platoon's corpsman. 'Close range.'

'How long ago?'

'Two, maybe two and a half hours. It was mayhem in the trench. Bloody mayhem. I found him in a funkhole. Banda was holding on to him, but he'd passed out long before that.'

'Banda was brought in earlier,' said Dorden, washing the filth from Rawne's stomach.

'I sent her up,' said Leclan. 'In the first wave. I didn't want to move Rawne. I called for a surgeon to come to him at the front, but the vox was down and the runners I sent never came back.'

'Feth!' Dorden said, examining the gunshot. 'He's lost a lot of blood. A feth of a lot.' He leaned over and grabbed Rawne's dog-tags, calling out the blood type printed on them to a waiting orderly.

'Is Banda all right?' Leclan asked.

Dorden stopped his relentless work, and looked at Leclan. The man was frightened and worried. Corpsmen like Leclan were standard troopers trained to administer only the most basic first aid. They weren't medics. They were just there to do the fundamentals until medics came. 'Jessi Banda's going to live. It was touch and go. But she'll be fine.'

Leclan sagged visibly with relief.

'You did all right,' Dorden said, returning to his work.

'He's not going to die, is he?' Feygor asked. The involuntary sarcasm injected into his voice by his augmetic throat made Dorden snort.

'We'll see.'

* * *

'How's the thumb?'

Beltayn looked up and saw Gaunt. He scrambled up from the ammo hopper he'd been sitting on and showed the colonel-commissar his bandaged hand.

'Hurt a bit when they reset it, but it's fine. Doc Mtane says no heavy lifting, and absolutely no complicated vox work. In fact, he recommends a vacation somewhere where there's no gunfire.'

'Nice try,' said Gaunt.

They were alone at the edge of the triage station, by the side of the trackway where long grass bushed out from broken fence posts. The sun had begun to come out, its light turned sooty by the vapour of war.

A train of stretcher bearers went past, heading west.

Gaunt sat down on the grass bank, and Beltayn resumed his seat on the old hopper.

'You have the casualty lists?' Gaunt asked.

Beltayn produced a data-slate.

Rawne had once joked, bleakly, that the Tanith spared Gaunt that one grim responsibility of commanding officers everywhere, the letter home. In truth, few Guard COs bothered to inform next of kin, though a handful of regiments were famous for the scrupulous way they did it. Gaunt had no one to write to, even if he'd felt the inclination. Tanith was gone, and most of the Verghastites who'd joined the Ghosts had done so because they were leaving no one behind.

Gaunt remembered the old days, when Oktar had charged him with composing the LIA notices for the families of the Hyrkan dead. After Balhaut, it had taken him the best part of a week.

Gaunt studied the data-slate.

'Sixteen platoon pretty much doesn't exist any more,' said Beltayn. 'I suppose we fold the survivors into squads that need making up.'

Gaunt nodded. From the list, he realised that the Ghosts' strength had dropped to less than one hundred platoons for the first time since Verghast. He felt his anger returning. War consumed manpower. That was one of the first things they drummed into you at the commissariate.

But this war… this war consumed manpower like a glutton. It fed on death, even though it was bloated and full.

'Can you get me a link to Van Voytz?' Gaunt asked.

'I can try,' said Beltayn.

As his adjutant began to set up his vox-caster, Gaunt got to his feet, and wandered a little way down the track. Columns of Aexe Alliance foot soldiers were moving towards him from the reserves, weary and dirty. More bodies for the war machine.

Gaunt saw a lone figure trudging his way, overtaking the toiling infantry ranks.

'Captain Daur?'

'Sir,' Daur saluted. He was out of breath. He'd been jogging all the way from Rhonforq.

'The reserves are in safe hands, I trust?'

'Mkoll, sir,' Daur panted.

'And you're here?'

'It looked bad. The vox was down. I wanted to... to know.'

'It was bad. Over a hundred casualties. Thirty-six dead that I know of, including Maroy. Rawne may not make it, either.'

Daur looked away, gazing across the neglected fields and the withered woodlands.

'It's going to chew us all up, isn't it, sir?' he said.

'Not if I have anything to say about it,' Gaunt replied. 'Be advised, Ban... with Rawne out, you have third ranking as of now.'

'Understood.'

'I want you to bring up five platoons early to replace two, three, eleven, twelve and sixteen. You call it. We'd best forget the standing rota. Any platoon that sees hard action gets rotated for fresh from now on.'

Daur nodded. 'You want me at the front now?'

'I understand Colm saw some feth today too. I'll drop him back in favour of you.'

'He's all right?'

'Far as I know. But I want to go easier on him. He's had a rough time these past eighteen months. He's still not... not his old self.'

'That's fine, sir,' Daur said.

'Colm will take the reserve, and you and I will lead at the front.'

'Yes sir.' Daur registered a certain pride. For the first time it would be Gaunt and a Verghastite in command at the sharp end. It felt like a coming of age. But his feelings were mixed. Rawne wounded, Corbec pulled back... would the Ghosts still be Ghosts without them?

When he first signed up, at the Act of Consolation, Daur had imagined a time when he'd be Gaunt's XO. He'd all but willed death on Rawne and Corbec so that he could bring the Verghast strength to the fore.

Now it was happening, and he felt nothing but keen loss.

'Sir?' Beltayn called out. Gaunt strode over to his adjutant, who was listening intently to the phones of his vox-set.

'No luck with the general, sir,' Beltayn explained, 'but I've spoken to his aide. You're invited to dinner with the staff chiefs at Meiseq tomorrow night. Sixteen hundred hours. Dress uniform.'

LARKIN WANDERED DOWN the fire trench between stations 290 and 291, his long-las hanging from one hand and his Tanith blade hanging from the other. Troopers got out of his way. Mad Larkin was mad again.

'Larks?' Corbec called out, approaching him. 'How you doing?'

Corbec had been shipping Sillo off to a triage station when word had reached him that Larkin was on the prowl. 'He looks like he's gone right over!' Trooper Bewl had said excitedly.

Larkin blinked and slowly recognised Corbec. He glanced down at the weapons he was carrying as if he'd only just become aware of them, and carefully set them down on the firestep. Then he sat down next to them.

Corbec shooed the gawking troopers around him back to their duties and went down to Larkin's side.

'Bad day, Larks?'

'Horrible.'

'It's been tough all round. Anything you want to talk about?'

'Yes.' Larkin paused. He opened his mouth to speak the name 'Lijah Cuu', but stopped himself. So badly, he wanted to tell Corbec about Cuu. Cuu the maniac. Cuu the psycho. Cuu, who would have killed him but for the sudden shelling.

Cuu, who had killed Bragg.

But now it seemed pointless. Loglas, the only witness, was very dead. If Larkin brought a charge, it would be Cuu's word against his. And Cuu had proved to be bulletproof up till now.

Larkin knew Colm would take him seriously. But he also knew that Colm was hidebound by the rules.

As soon as the shells started to fall, Cuu had fled, leaving Larkin alone. Larkin had been so terrified, arms up over his head, eyes closed, it had taken him a moment to realise Cuu had actually gone and only Larkin's fear of Cuu was left behind.

No, there was no point, Larkin decided. The only way to be free from his fear was to face it. Corbec couldn't help him. Gaunt couldn't. The system couldn't.

Lijah Cuu had to die. It was that simple. Cuu wanted the score settled, didn't he? So it would be settled. Fething straight, sure as sure, one way or another.

'Larks?' Corbec said. 'What did you want to tell me about? You look like you're all upset.'

'I am,' said Hlaine Larkin. 'Loglas died,' he confessed.

That was true, but it was also a lie. That wasn't why Larkin was most upset.

But it was all Corbec needed to know.

SIX
ONE HAND GIVES, ONE HAND TAKES

'I say, if they want to skulk, let them. I'd be interested to see great skulkers at work.'

– Colonel Ankre

THAT NIGHT, AND the morning that followed, it was mercifully quiet in 55th sector. It was as if the tide of war had drawn out from that part of the line, slack, low.

It was flood tide elsewhere. Further south down the Naeme Valley, the 47th and 46th sectors were brutalised by twelve straight hours of heavy bombardment. A considerable stretch of the so-called Seronne Line, which ran east from the end of the Peinforq Sectors right across country to the Kottmark Massif, came under shellfire, and then armoured assault. The worst clashes were just south of the Vostl Delta.

To the north, there were intermittent light attacks and raids all through the night at Loncort and the Salient. Unconfirmed reports were circulating that sectors north of Gibsgatte had endured the biggest offensive of the year, and that battle still raged there.

The morning was damp and fog-bound. With Beltayn his only companion, Gaunt travelled north for Meiseq. Beltayn said little. He could tell Gaunt was in a foul temper, and didn't want to provoke anything.

A staff car conveyed them as far as Ongche, where they boarded a despatch train bound for the north. The train was half-empty, and rattled along through misty farmland and rain-swept heath.

Prior to departure, just after dawn, Gaunt had made a final inspection of the First's positions. Daur's relief squads were at the front by then, though Corbec was to remain as line XO until Gaunt's return.

At the end of his tour, Gaunt had made a call at the military hospital in Rhonforq, spending time with the injured and looking in on the critical cases. Rawne had survived the night, though he'd required secondary surgery in the small hours to staunch internal bleeding.

Dorden was so fatigued by then he seemed almost asleep on his feet, and the bruises he'd taken in the beating were starting to nag at him. Gaunt had been intending to ask the chief medic to accompany him to Meiseq, but one look at Dorden stifled the idea. Dorden was needed at Rhonforq, if only to get some rest.

Gaunt knew that Dorden was still angry with him about the discipline killings. He had a right to be, in Gaunt's opinion. Gaunt had been in a dazed rage the afternoon before, weary with the pointless losses he'd witnessed at station 289. He'd just snapped.

As an Imperial commissar, Gaunt was unusual, quite apart from the fact that he held command rank. Commissars were universally feared. They were the Guard's instruments of discipline and control, the lash that kept the soldiery in line and drove them forward. They were there to drum the tenets of the Imperial creed into the minds of the enlisted men, and then give them stark, regular reminders of that truth. Summary execution, even for minor violations, was acceptable stock-in-trade for a commissar. The great Yarrick himself had once said that it was a commissar's job to be a figure of greater fear and threat to an Imperial Guardsman than any enemy.

That was not Gaunt's way. Experience had shown him that morale was better served by encouragement and trust than by an unpredictable temper and a pistol. He'd had a good example in the form of his mentor, the late Delane Oktar. Oktar's philosophy of morale had been based on trust and tolerance too. There had been times when a firm hand had been called for, a few more when action had worked better than words.

But Gaunt prided himself on his fairness, and knew that he was able to count men like Dorden as friends because of it. At the field hospital, he'd acted just like a typical commissar. Dorden hadn't said anything, but Gaunt had seen the disappointment in his eyes.

As the train rattled north, he turned the incident over in his mind. There was no point setting the blame on fatigue. Fatigue implied weakness, and a commissar could never be weak. He realised it was more a matter of futility. He'd come into the Aexe war with reservations, and each step of the way to the front had confirmed his fears. War was not senseless of itself. Faced with the immortal obscenity of Chaos, humankind had a true cause to rally around and fight for. There was a greater good, a purpose, even here on Aexe.

It was the manner of this war that was senseless. The dismissive contempt with which the Alliance threw men and materiel at the enemy. The antique thinking that believed brute strength was the main determining factor behind victory. It made Gaunt angry to see this, angrier still to have the First caught up in it. The afternoon before, he'd been smothered by the futility, and it had worked its ministry on him.

Outside, the world went by. One world, just one of thousands, hundreds of thousands, that combined to form the greatest achievement in human history. The Imperium of Mankind. Many believed that the Imperium was so vast in scale, so huge in scope, that the actions of one man could not affect it. That wasn't true. If everyone thought that way, the Imperium would simply collapse in upon itself overnight. Each and every human soul determined their part of Imperial culture. That was the only thing the Emperor asked of a man. Be true to yourself, and all those myriad tiny contributions would combine to build a culture that could endure until the stars went out.

Beltayn was asleep, his head nodding onto his chest, his bandaged hand cradled in the other. Beyond the window pane, broken woodland flickered by, cut by hillsides dark with rain. A stream flashed like a drawn sword. Meadows lay invisible beneath cloaks of white mist. Uplands broke through fog like the tips of grey reefs. A lone, lightning-scarred tree stood vigil on a bare hill. A village slumbered, derelict. Clouds as thick as ruffled taffeta chased each other across the sky.

GAUNT WOKE FROM a recurring dream about Balhaut, and realised the train had stopped. The rain drummed down and gloomy woodlands surrounded the carriage windows. He checked his timepiece: an hour past noon. They should be in Chossene by now.

He got up and walked down the empty carriage to the door. Opening the window, he smelt the damp undergrowth and soil of the wood, and heard birdcalls and the batter of rain on the leaves. Other passengers were peering out. Down at the locomotive, engineers had dismounted.

Gaunt opened the door and jumped down onto the overgrown track side.

The locomotive had broken down, one of the engineers told him. Repairs were beyond them. They were going to have to wait until a relief tender could come out from Chossene.

'How long will that be?' Gaunt asked.

'Three or four hours, sir.'

GAUNT SHOOK BELTAYN to wake him up.

'Come on,' he said. 'We've some walking to do.'

'What's wrong, sir?' asked Beltayn sleepily.

Gaunt smiled. 'Something's awry.'

THE MISTS WERE beginning to clear as they trudged up through the woods, heading west on a little-used path. Pale sunlight shone down through the branches of the wood. The rain had stopped, but still rainwater fell, dripping down from the canopy. The air smelled of wet, and the scent of some wildflower.

The engineer had given them directions. A village, Veniq, lay half an hour's walk to the west. Someone there could provide the Imperial officer with transport, the engineer supposed. In his opinion, it was better to stay with the train. Help was coming. Eventually.

Beltayn had been in favour of waiting too. 'We might walk for hours. Or get lost. Or–'

'If we wait for the relief tender, we'll miss my appointment for sure. Meiseq's still a good way away. We walk.'

The track was muddy and it was slow going. Beltayn insisted on carrying Gaunt's overnight pack but, with his own kit and his damaged hand, he was over-encumbered and kept stopping to put something down and resettle his load.

The cool air was bracing. Gaunt realised he was raising a sweat, and took off his stormcoat, flopping it over his left shoulder. Behind them, back down through the woods, they heard a train whistle. If that was the relief tender, then they really had made a bad choice and wasted a lot of effort.

'You want to go back, sir?' asked Beltayn when he heard the whistle note.

Gaunt shook his head. This brisk walk through the empty calm of the wood was like a balm. His lungs were full of cool, smoke-free air and his nostrils full of flower scent. It was amazingly strong now. He didn't know what it was. Little bright-blue flowers with odd-shaped petals covered the ground between the trees, showing over the wet moss and ivy. He wondered if it was them.

He turned to Beltayn and took his overnight bag from him. Then he took Beltayn's pack too.

'That's not necessary,' said Beltayn.

'Ah, let me carry them a while,' said Gaunt.

THE TRACK WOUND through the wood, but there was no sign of farmland or the village. They crossed a rushing brook by way of an ancient stone bridge, black with mould. Bird calls and the burr of insects floated eerily through the trees. In one dense thicket, the beythorne was strung with spider webs that glinted with beads of rainwater like quartz.

'What did the engineer mean about brigands?' Beltayn asked, pausing to get a stone out of his boot.

'Deserters, I believe,' said Gaunt. 'Over the years, bands of them have run to ground out here in the wooded country. They live by pilfering from farms, poaching…'

'Brigandry?' Beltayn added. 'Being, as it seems, brigands.'

Gaunt shrugged.

'Well, maybe this was a bad id–' Beltayn began, but shut up as Gaunt raised a hand.

Across the next clearing, a stand of white birch with gleaming bark, a deer had emerged from the smoke of mist. It stood for a moment, regarding them with its head cocked. Then it turned and darted away.

A heartbeat later, and they saw others, distantly, chasing soundlessly through the woods.

Like ghosts.

A FULL HOUR after they had begun their hike, they emerged from the edge of the wood at a point where the land became planted fields. Swaying heads of young, green wheat covered the slopes down the waist of a hill towards a fresh line of woodland in the valley.

It was a decent vantage point, but there was no sign of any village.

'I'm hungry,' said Beltayn.

Gaunt looked at him.

'Just saying,' he said.

Gaunt put the bags down and mopped his brow. The walk had reinvigorated him, but he was beginning to agree with Beltayn. This had been a bad idea.

He checked the position of the sun, and read his timepiece. He wished he'd brought his compass, or his locator, or even his auspex, but there had seemed no need that morning. His bag contained nothing but his shaving kit, his number one uniform, and his copy of *The Spheres of Longing.*

He wanted to ask Beltayn which way he favoured, but to do so would be to admit he was lost. He decided they should follow the track down the edge of the field where it curved into the bottom of the valley. Perhaps there'd be a road down there.

They'd gone about a hundred paces, when he stopped again. 'You see that?' he asked.

Beltayn squinted. Down in the valley, hidden in the woodland there, was a building. Grey chafstone, the roof made of slate. Some sort of tower poked up through the canopy.

'You've got sharp eyes, sir,' said Beltayn. 'I'd never have seen that in a thousand years.'

'Come on,' said Gaunt.

IT WAS A chapel, old and rundown, buried in the green twilight of the wood. Trailing ivy and fleece-flower clung to its walls. Bright green lichens gnawed the chafstone. They walked around the partially-collapsed wall, in through the old gate, and up the path to the door. The scent was back, that flower scent. It was so strong, it made Gaunt feel like sneezing. He could see no flowers.

Gaunt pushed open the door and walked into the cold gloom of the chapel. The interior was plain, but well-kept. At the end of the rows of hardwood pews, a taper burned at the Imperial altar. Both men made the sign of the aquila, and Gaunt walked down the aisle towards the graven image of the Emperor. In the stained glass of the lancet windows, he saw the image of Saint Sabbat amongst the worthies.

'Well,' murmured a voice from the darkness. 'There you are at last.'

SHE WAS VERY old, and blind. A strip of black silk was wound around her head across her eyes. Her silver hair had been plaited tightly against the back of her skull. Age had hunched her, but stood erect she would have towered over Gaunt.

There was no mistaking her red and black robes.

'Sister,' Gaunt said, and bowed.

'Welcome here. There is no need for obeisance.'

Gaunt looked up. How had she known he was bowing? For a scant second, he wondered if she was some gifted seer, but then he caught himself. Stupid. Her senses were sharp, and attuned to her blindness. She'd simply noted the direction of his voice. 'I am Colonel-Commissar Ibram Gaunt,' he said.

She nodded, as if she didn't especially care. Or, Gaunt thought, as if she already knew. 'Welcome to the Chapel of the Holy Light Abundant, Veniq.'

'We're near the village then?'

'Well, the name is a little misleading. Veniq is about four kilometres south of here.'

Beltayn groaned quietly.

'Your boy is disheartened to hear that,' she said.

'My boy? My adjutant?'

'I hear two of you. Am I mistaken?'

'No. We're trying to reach Veniq, to find transport. Our train... well, it doesn't matter. I need to be in Meiseq tonight.'

She sat down on one of the pews, feeling her way with one hand, leaning on her staff with the other. 'That's a long way,' she said.

'I know,' said Gaunt. 'Can you perhaps set us on the right road?'

'You're on the right road already, Ibram, but you won't reach your destination for a while.'

'Meiseq?'

'Oh, you'll be there tonight. I meant...'

'What?'

She settled herself against the stiff back of the pew. 'My name is Elinor Zaker, once of the Adepta Sororitas Militant, the order of Our Martyred Lady. Now warden and keeper of this chapel.'

'I am honoured to meet you, sister. What... what did you mean about my destination?'

She turned her head towards him. It was the fluid neck-swivel of a human who had been habituated to helmet-display target sensors. For a moment, Gaunt felt like she was aiming at him.

'I should speak less. There are things that mustn't be said, not yet. You'll have to excuse me. I get so few visitors, I feel the urge to gabble.'

'What things mustn't be said?' Gaunt started to say, but Beltayn spoke over him.

'How long have you been here, lady?' he asked.

'Years and years,' she said. 'So many, now. I tend the place, as well as I am able. Does it look trim and clean?'

'Yes,' said Gaunt, glancing around.

She smiled a little. 'I can't tell. I do my best. Some things I see clearly, but not my environment. He doesn't sound very young.'

Gaunt realised this last comment had been made about Beltayn. 'My adjutant? He's... what, thirty-two?'

'Thirty-one last birthday, sir,' said Beltayn from the far end of the aisle.

'Well, he's no boy, then.'

'No,' said Gaunt.

'I understood it would be a boy. No disrespect, Ibram. You're important too. But the boy, he's the crux.'

'You seem to be speaking in riddles, sister.'

'I know. It must be very distressing. There are so many things I can't say. It would ruin everything if I did. And it's really too important, so that mustn't happen. Was there a boy? Very young? The youngest of all?'

'My previous adjutant was a boy,' said Gaunt, suddenly very unsettled. 'His name was Milo. He's a trooper now.'

'Ah,' she said, nodding. 'It gets it wrong sometimes.'

'What does?' asked Gaunt.

'The tarot.'

'How can you read cards when you can't see?' Beltayn asked warily.

She turned her head towards the sound of his voice. Another careful aim. Beltayn stepped back slightly as if he had been target-acquired. 'I don't,' she said. 'It reads me.'

With her head turned, Gaunt could see the long, pink line of the scar that ran over the top of her skull, seaming her white hair like a plough-furrow through corn, down to the left side base of her neck. He sighed inwardly. He'd almost been taken in by her talk. He'd been on the verge of believing they had stumbled upon – or been fatefully drawn to – a prophetic being. But now everything, even her peculiarly apt references to Milo, took on another meaning.

She was mad. Brain-damaged in some long-ago action. Rambling, talking at shadows, deprived of contact by her lonely vigil.

Gaunt needed to get on. 'Look, sister... we are heading for Meiseq. I believe lives depend on us getting there. Is there any way you can help us?'

'Not really. Not in the grand scheme of things. You're going to have to help yourselves. You and the boy, I mean. As far as Meiseq goes... I wouldn't want to go there. Ugly place. An affront to the eyes. But you can borrow my car, if you like.'

'Your car?'

'No use to me any more. It's garaged in one of the barns across the lane. You might have to clear undergrowth from the doors, but the car runs. I turn it over every day. The keys are on the doorpost hook.'

Gaunt nodded to Beltayn, and the adjutant hurried out of the chapel.

'Has he gone?' she asked.

'Gone to find the car,' Gaunt said.

'Sit with me,' she whispered.

Gaunt sat beside her on the pew. Rambling though she was, Sister Zaker was doing him a favour, so he could at least humour her for a minute or two.

He could smell the flower-scent again. Where had he smelled that before?

'It will be hard,' she confided.

'What will?'

'Herodor,' she replied.

'Herodor?' The only Herodor Gaunt knew of was a tactically insignificant colony world some distance to coreward. He shrugged.

'I've been allowed to pass on a few things,' she said. 'There is harm throughout. But the greatest harm, ultimately, is within. Within your body.'

'My body?' Gaunt echoed. He didn't really want to get drawn into this. But she deserved civility.

'Figuratively, Ibram. Your body, as DeMarchese describes the body. Have you read DeMarchese?'

'No, sister.' Gaunt wasn't even sure who DeMarchese was.

'Well, do so. The harm is in two parts. Two dangers, one truly evil, one misunderstood. The latter holds the key. It's important you remember that, because you commissars are terribly trigger happy. I think that's it. Oh, there is something else. Let your sharpest eye show you the truth. That's it. Your sharpest eye. Well, that about does it. I hope I've made myself clear.'

'I–' Gaunt began.

'I have to sweep the floor now,' she said.

She paused and turned her head towards him. 'I really shouldn't say this. I'm stepping way beyond my role... but when you see her, commend me to her. Please. I miss her.'

From outside, the cough and snarl of a motor engine racing into life broke the stillness.

'Of course,' said Gaunt. He gently took her hand and kissed it.

'The Emperor protect you, sister.'

'He'll have his hands full protecting you, Ibram,' she replied. 'You, and that boy.'

Gaunt retreated down the aisle. 'We'll return the car.'

'Ah, keep it,' she said with a dismissive wave of her hand.

OUTSIDE, IN THE damp trackway, Beltayn sat behind the wheel of a massive old limousine. Its night-blue body was chipped with rust and lichen caked its running boards. Weeds had sprouted from the grille and fender. Beltayn had turned on the headlamps, which burned like the eyes of a nocturnal predator.

Gaunt walked up to the car and ran his hand along the grey hide of the retractable roof.

'This come down?' he called.

Beltayn fiddled with the dashboard controls. With a creak, the hood retracted on concertinaing iron hoops so that the car was open-topped.

Gaunt got into the back. Beltayn looked back at him and raised his bandaged hand in a rather pathetic gesture.

'I... uh... don't think I can handle the transmission, sir,' he said.

Gaunt shook his head, amused. 'Change places,' he said.

THEY ROARED AWAY down the woodland lane, leaving the chapel behind. Sunlight dappled and flickered all over them.

'So...' shouted Beltayn from the back over the roar of the eight cylinder engine, '...how strange was that?'

'Forget it!' yelled Gaunt into the slipstream, changing down as he took the massive, elderly automobile around a hard bend. 'She was just hankering for company.'

'But she knew about Brin–'

'No, she didn't. A few enigmatic remarks. That's all. Hive-market preachers use that kind of routine all the time. It works on the gullible.'

'Okay. So she was trying to fool us?'

'Nothing so calculating. She was just... not altogether there.'

A DROVE ROAD brought them through Veniq, and then on across open arable tracts to Shonsamarl where they joined the Northern Highway. Southbound, the highway was thick with munition trains and troop carriers. Northbound, they caught the end of a convoy of Guard Thunderers and light armour moving up to Gibsgatte. They played leapfrog up the line of heavy tanks as well as the passing traffic would allow, until the convoy turned off at Chossene, and then they raced on over the Naeme viaduct and into the cornfield flats of Loncort County.

Fitful light rain and patchy sun followed them through the afternoon along metalled roads that lay like ribbons over the salty-green fields. They saw slow formations of Alliance triplanes buzzing east towards the front, and once or twice the glint of Imperial air support banging in supersonically, taking a new kind of war to this lingering, old-fashioned theatre.

Shortly before 18.00, Gaunt saw the skyline of Meiseq rising over the fields.

MEISEQ WAS A new town built on old roots. It had been almost entirely razed in the early years of the Aexe War, when the initial Shadik advance had sliced mercilessly right across country to the Upper Naeme. Five years of counter-fighting, focused especially on the Battle of Diem, had eventually ousted the enemy from a portion of territory marked in the north-west corner by the city of Gibsgatte and in the south-east by Loncort. This, the so-called 'Meiseq Box', was now perhaps the most sturdy of the Alliance's line defences, forming as it did the middle section of the Northern Front. To the south, from Loncort, ran the Peinforq Line that held the Naeme Valley. To the north ran the hotly contested sectors beyond Gibsgatte. The Alliance considered the Box so sound it had turned the areas around Diem into a Memorial Park for the fallen. An eternal flame burned at the site of Diem's cathedral, and the oceans of grass around it were lined with row upon row of white, obcordate grave markers.

Meiseq had been rebuilt. Its buildings were made from pressure treated wood-pulp, coated with an emulsion of rock cement. It perched on an escarpment above a bend in the Upper Naeme, encircled by pales of timber and flakboard. At its centre rose the wooden cathedral of San Jeval.

It was getting dark by the time they drove up through the fortress gate in the south face of the walls and entered the town. The cathedral bells were ringing, and lamplighters were igniting the caged chemical torches that lined the streets.

Meiseq reminded Gaunt of a frontier city. Its prefabricated bulk smelled new and entirely at odds with the old, stone-built population centres he'd experienced so far on Aexe. It was strategically important, and wanted visitors to know that, but it seemed little more than a camp, an earthwork. The air smelled of roofing pitch and sweating wood. He remembered moving in to occupy Rakerville, years ago, with the Hyrkans. That had smelled the same. An outpost. A brief statement of Imperial activity. A gesture made without confidence at a frontier.

They parked near to the cathedral in a yard surrounded by trees. The trees were old and withered, but the Aexegarians who had remade Meiseq had remade the trees too, grafting new boughs onto the old trunks shattered by war. Late blossom and fresh green growth formed a roof over the gnarled, grey trunks.

Gaunt and Beltayn walked down the neighbouring streets, through the light crowds, and found the military hall, a grim, twin-towered edifice with a walled precinct of its own.

It was nearly 20.00 hours.

* * *

WASHED AND CHANGED, Gaunt left Beltayn in the officio suite appointed to him, and went down to dinner. His guides were two subalterns of the Bande Sezari, dignified in their plumed head-dresses and green silks. Night had fallen, and the narrow passages of the military hall were caves of fluttering rushlights.

The dinner had just begun in a terrace room overlooking the river to the west. The last scraps of day-fade smudged the sky outside, and drum-fires flickered along the low river bend.

There were nineteen officers present, and all stood briefly as Gaunt took his place at the empty twentieth place. He sat, and the mumble of conversation resumed. The long table was dressed in white cloth, and lit by four large candelabra. Gaunt's place setting twinkled with nine separate pieces of cutlery. A steward brought him an oval white bowl and filled it with chilled, blush-red soup.

'Imperial?' asked the man to his right, a short thin-faced Aexegarian who had clearly drunk too much already.

'Yes, sir,' said Gaunt, careful to acknowledge the man's rank boards. A general.

The man stuck out his hand. 'Siquem Fep Ortern, C-in-C. 60th sector.'

'Gaunt, Tanith First.'

'Ah,' said the drunk. 'You're the one they've been talking about.'

Gaunt looked down the table. He saw Golke nearby, and Lord General Van Voytz at the head of the table. He didn't recognise any other faces, except for Van Voytz's chief tactician, Biota. Like Ortern, all the others were senior Alliance officers, either Aexegarians or Kottmarkers. Gaunt began to feel like he'd walked into a lion's den. He'd assumed Van Voytz had summoned him to attend a private dinner where he could voice his disquiet at Alliance tactics in the company of chosen staff chiefs. He hadn't expected this, a full, high brass banquet. Though Van Voytz, imposing in his dark green dress uniform, dominated the head of the table, the presiding influence seemed to come from the man to Van Voytz's left, a bullish Kottmark general with a disturbingly bland, pale face, half-moon clerk's spectacles and white-blond hair.

Gaunt said little, and ate quietly, catching the conversation strands as they cut back and forth along the table. There were a lot of thinly veiled, disrespectful remarks about Imperial soldiery, which Gaunt felt were entirely for his benefit. The Alliance staff were goading him, seeing what they could get away with, seeing what would make him comment.

Three courses came and went, including the main course of braised game, and were followed by a sticky, over-sweet pudding called sonso that the Alliance officers greeted with much approval. It was a local speciality. Ortern, and some of the others nearby, extolled its virtues. To Gaunt, it was almost unbearably sugared. He left a good deal of it.

The stewards cleared the tables, brushed off the cloth, and served sweet black caffeine and amasec in large, green-glass balloons. The locals, who had all dined with their pressed white napkins tucked into the buttons of their dress frocks like bibs, now tossed the loose ends over their left shoulders, apparently a custom that showed they were finished. Gaunt folded his own loosely and left it on his setting.

A tiny servitor drone circled the table, clipping and lighting cigars. One of the Kottmarkers pushed his chair back and started to smoke a long-stemmed flute-pipe with a water bowl. Ortern offered Gaunt a fat, loose-rolled cigar, which he declined.

Ortern chuckled. 'Your customs, sir, are rather alien. On Aexe Cardinal, a gentleman never leaves his sonso unfinished. And he never declines the offer of another man's smokes, for when can he be sure he'll sample such delights again?'

'I mean no offence,' said Gaunt. 'Is it protocol to accept a cigar and save it for a later time?'

'Of course.'

Gaunt nodded, and took one of the proffered cigars. He knew Corbec would appreciate it.

The conversation now opened up more freely across the table.

'Ibram,' Van Voytz greeted Gaunt from the table-head with a toast of his amasec, 'you joined us late.'

'My apologies, lord. I encountered transit problems on my way from Rhonforq.'

'I was afraid you wouldn't make it,' said the bespectacled Kottmark general. 'I was looking forward to meeting you.'

'Sir,' Gaunt acknowledged.

'Ibram, this is Vice General Carn Martane, commander in chief of the Kottmark Forces West, and deputy supreme commander of the Alliance.'

Lyntor-Sewq's right hand man, then.

Martane smiled blandly at Gaunt and sipped his amasec delicately. 'I have been intrigued by certain reports,' he began.

'Come now, Martane!' Van Voytz cut in, good humouredly. 'This is a social event. We can leave the war room talk for the morning.'

'But of course, lord general,' said Martane deftly, sitting back in his seat. 'The war consumes our every waking moment in ways I forget must seem strange to visitors.'

Van Voytz's face darkened. It was a tremendous but subtle slight. Martane was deferring to Van Voytz, but doing so in such a way that suggested the Imperials took the Aexe struggle far less seriously than the locals.

'Actually, my lord,' said Gaunt brightly, 'I'd be interested to hear the vice general's comments.'

The conversation stilled. It was a duel, no more or less, verbal but still vicious. Imperials versus Alliance. Martane's remark had been cutting and poised, allowing Van Voytz two options: pass over it and take the put-down, or trigger a more obvious clash by marking it.

Either way, Van Voytz would lose grace. Now Gaunt had stepped up and deflected the slur as deftly as Martane had made it.

Martane chose his words carefully. 'Colonel Ankre, that worthy son of Kottmark, has suggested to me in despatches that you have been... less than impressed with our military organisations.'

'Colonel Ankre and I enjoyed a robust exchange of views, sir,' said Gaunt. 'I imagine that is what you are referring to. I admit I'm surprised he took them so to heart he needed to bother you with them.'

Gaunt saw Van Voytz disguise a smile. There was a word that usually followed a remark like Gaunt's latest. The word was 'touché'.

'I was not bothered by them, colonel-commissar. I was glad Redjacq took the time to instruct me. I would hate to think that our new Imperial allies are fighting against us. Administratively, I mean.'

Martane was a skilled political operator. There was another comment that seemed light and warm yet had sharp steel running through it.

'Why would you think that?' Gaunt asked, parrying directly.

'Ankre said you took issue with the workings of chain of command and field etiquette. That you remonstrated with him over a lack of intelligence.' Martane was more direct now. He clearly felt he had Gaunt on the back foot and was about to force him into damning himself.

Gaunt saw Golke across the table. The man was impassive. Gaunt recalled clearly how direct and brutal he'd been with Golke at Rhonforq, Ankre too. He could tell Golke was willing him not to be similarly forthright now.

As if I'd be that stupid, Gaunt thought to himself. 'I did, sir,' he said.

'You admit it?' Martane caught the eyes of some of his fellow officers slyly. Gaunt saw Van Voytz ever so slightly shake his head.

'The Imperial Expedition has come here to be your comrade in arms, vice general. To be, as it were, part of your determined Alliance against the Shadik Republic. Surely it is right we enmesh ourselves properly into the Alliance forces? Elements of field etiquette and intelligence were particular to this war, and I needed clarification. I've fought many battles, sir, but I can't pretend to understand the nuances of this one yet. My question came, vice general, simply from a desire to best serve the high sezar and the free people of Aexe.'

Martane's pale cheeks flushed briefly as red as the first course soup. Behind a guard of honesty, Gaunt had just outstepped him. Martane fumbled. 'Ankre also suggested you believed your men too good for front-line combat,' he began, but it was the blunt move both Gaunt and Van Voytz had been waiting for. Unable to force Gaunt to condemn himself with his own words, Martane had stumbled and voiced an actual insult.

'For shame, vice general,' growled Van Voytz.

'I am affronted, sir,' Gaunt said.

'Come now, Martane,' Golke said, speaking for the first time. 'That is hardly the courtesy we of Aexe extend to voluntary allies.'

Voices rumbled round the table. Many of the officers were embarrassed by their commander's comment.

Gaunt smiled to himself. As with war, so with decorum, Aexe was so old-fashioned. He remembered some of the staff dinners when Imperial commanders had hurled abuse at each other across the table and then sat laughing over the port. There was no such frankness here. There was simply a culture of martial formality that stifled any hope of victory.

'My apologies, colonel-commissar,' Martane said. He made his excuses, and left the table.

'Nicely done, Ibram,' said Van Voytz. 'I see the old political skills of the commissar haven't left you.'

Gaunt had retired with Van Voytz, Golke and Biota to a small library room. Servitors adjusted the lamps, refreshed drinks and then left them alone.

'Did you summon me here to make a fool of Martane, sir?' Gaunt asked.

'Maybe,' smiled Van Voytz, as if the idea was delicious.

'Vice General Martane needs no help making a fool of himself,' Golke said.

'I was hoping I would come away with more than that satisfaction tonight,' Gaunt said.

'Just so,' said Van Voytz. 'I've studied your despatches, and listened to the comments our friend Count Golke here has passed along... unofficially, of course. You could have caused trouble with Ankre, Ibram. He speaks as he finds, and he speaks ill of you.'

'Quite obviously. But I won't stand by and see Guard units hammered for no reason.'

Van Voytz sat down in a large padded armchair by the fireplace, and took a book at random off the nearest shelf. 'This is a difficult theatre, Ibram. One that requires tact. If we had supreme command here, I'd gladly take the Alliance and shake it by the scruff until it worked properly. Worked like a modern army. God-Emperor, a full Guard army employed here purposefully could turn Shadik back in a month.' He looked up at Gaunt. 'But we don't have that luxury. Albeit nominally, the Alliance leaders – Lyntor-Sewq, who I'll confess I cannot stand, and the high sezar himself – have battlefield command. My Lord Warmaster Macaroth himself made it clear we were here to support the Alliance, not take command from them. Our hands are tied.'

'Then men will die, sir,' said Gaunt.

'They will. We are obliged to fight this war at the Alliance's pace, to the Alliance's rules, and following the Alliance's traditions. Aexegary and its allies are desperate to retain control of the fight. No offence, count.'

Golke shrugged. 'I'm with you on that, lord general. I tried to change things for years. Tried to modernise tactics and strategy. The simple fact is that Aexegary has a long and illustrious martial history. They will not admit, not ever, that they are capable of losing a war. Aexegary never has, you see. And especially against an old foe like the Shadik.'

'The Alliance won't admit they are fighting a modern foe,' said Biota quietly. 'They will not accept that the Shadik Republic has changed, been corrupted, that it is no longer the neighbouring power Aexegary has bested in five wars.'

'And the Alliance members don't see it either?' asked Gaunt.

'No,' said Golke. 'Kottmark especially. They see their entry into the war as an opportunity to prove their worth on the world stage.'

'Pride,' said Gaunt. 'That's what we're fighting. Not Shadik. Not the archenemy. We're fighting the pride of the Alliance.'

'I think so,' said Van Voytz.

'Undoubtedly,' said Biota.

'Then I am ashamed of my country,' Golke said sadly. 'When the high sezar told me the Guard was coming to assist us, my heart leapt. Until I saw the look in his eyes.'

'What look?' asked Van Voytz.

'The look that told me he saw you Imperials as brand new toys... toys that he would use in just the same way as the old ones. I had hoped that the Alliance might learn things from the Guard... new ways of fighting... things like fluid field orders and unit-level decision making...'

'You've been reading your Slaydo,' said Gaunt with a smile.

Golke nodded. 'I have. I think I'm the only man on Aexe Cardinal who has. To no avail. The Alliance is still living in the glory days of the great sezars. They will not change.'

'A dutiful father,' said Biota softly, 'is distressed to find his son mourning the death of the family pet, a feline. The boy complains that he looked after it, groomed it, fed it, and yet it passed away despite his care. Anxious to please, the father purchases a new pet for his son, a hound. He is horrified when he catches his son pushing the hound off the balcony of the family house to its death. The son is distressed once more. "That pet wouldn't fly either," he tells his father.'

Biota looked around at them. 'We are the hound,' he said.

DAWN FOG FROM the Upper Naeme shrouded Meiseq the next morning when Gaunt rose. He had made sure Beltayn woke him early for the return trip to Rhonforq. While he was shaving in the cold, new light, a messenger arrived and asked him to attend Lord General Van Voytz.

Van Voytz was taking breakfast in his staff apartments, along with Biota and a small group of aides. At Van Voytz's instruction, a steward brought caffeine and fried fish and egg mash for Gaunt, so he could eat with them.

'You're starting back to Rhonforq today, Ibram?' Van Voytz said, eating heartily. He was dressed in an embroidered cape and a linen field suit of dark red.

'I've been away too long as it is, sir. And you?'

'North. Lyntor-Sewq awaits me at Gibsgatte to address the Northern generals. It's a mess up there. We're deploying our Urdeshi units there tomorrow. I've good news for you, however.'

'Sir?'

Van Voytz dabbed his mouth with his napkin and munched, taking a sip of fruit juice. 'Well, it was good news until five-thirty this morning. Then it simply became interesting.'

'Go on.'

'Our friend Count Golke has been working his influence on the Alliance GSC planners for the last few days, and after last night's dinner it paid off. The First is to be reassigned, in keeping with their scouting abilities. Right over to the west, an area called... what is it, Biota?'

'The Montorq Forest, sir.'

'That's it. Orders will follow. But you've got your way. The Tanith will be used to its strength at last. Don't let me down.'

'I won't, sir.'

'Me or Golke. It was the devil's effort to convince them.'

'What's the interesting part, sir?' Gaunt asked.

Van Voytz paused, chewing, and emptied his mouth. Then he picked up his glass. 'Come with me, Ibram.'

Van Voytz led Gaunt out onto a verandah overlooking the river. The landscape below them was barred with chalky mist.

'There's a rider,' Van Voytz said. 'Golke talked your mob up, emphasising how terrific they were as stealth scouts so the GSC would agree to reassign them. Trouble is, he may have talked them up too well. They've taken the idea to heart. Suddenly, they like the idea of scouts. They see uses of their own.'

'Right, and what does that mean?'

'It's a give and take thing, Ibram. Fifty per cent of your force gets to scout the Montorq Woods. In return for that, the other half gets deployed into the Pocket.'

'The Pocket?'

'The Seiberq Pocket. Front line. Their job is to penetrate the Shadik defences and locate... and maybe disable... these new super-siege guns. They reckon if you're so good at recon...'

'Feth!' said Gaunt. 'There's a word for a deal like that.'

'I know. "Ironic", I think it is. I'm pretty sure Martane and Ankre had something to do with it. Give and take. You get to play to your strengths in the west... provided you show the same skills at the blunt end. I'm sorry, Ibram.'

'Sorry? I play the odds, my lord. All of my men on the front or half of them.'

'Good lad. One hand gives, one hand takes, as Solon used to say.'

Overnight bag in hand and his mind full of troubles, Gaunt walked out of the military hall into the Meiseq sunlight. It was 08.30. Imperial personnel threaded between the Alliance sentries as they loaded Van Voytz's transports.

Gaunt looked around for Beltayn and the car. He found only Beltayn.

'What's up? Where's the car?'

'It's really weird, sir. Something's awry. I think the car's been stolen.'

'Stolen?'

'It's not where we parked it.'

Gaunt put his bag down. 'Give me the keys, then. I'll find it.'

Beltayn grimaced. 'That's the other weird part, sir. I can't find the keys either.'

'Feth! What'll I tell her?'

'The old woman?'

'Yes, the old wo–'

Gaunt sighed. 'Don't bother, let's not waste any more time. Scare us up some transport... or at least get us tickets on the next southbound train.'

Beltayn nodded and hurried away.

'A problem, colonel-commissar?'

Gaunt turned and found Biota behind him.

'Nothing much, nothing I can't deal with.'

Biota did up the neck clasps of his red, tactical division body-glove and nodded.

'That story last night. About the feline and the hound. Very pertinent. Very sharp,' said Gaunt.

'I can't presume credit,' Biota said, off-hand. 'One of DeMarchese's fables.'

Biota walked away towards the waiting vehicles.

'Tactician Biota! A moment!'

'Gaunt?'

'DeMarchese? You said DeMarchese. Who is that?'

Biota paused. 'A minor philosopher. Very minor. You know the name?'

'I've heard it.'

'DeMarchese served as an advisor to Kiodrus, who in turn stood at the right hand of the beati during the First Crusade. His contribution is rather eclipsed by Faltornus, who was the real architect of Saint Sabbat's strategy, but still his homely fables have some merit. Gaunt? What is it?'

'Nothing,' said Gaunt. 'Nothing.' He looked up at the pale sun and then said, 'Elinor Zaker. Does that name mean anything to you?'

'Elinor Zaker?'

'Of the Adepta Sororitas Militant, the order of Our Martyred Lady?'

Biota shook his head.

'All right. Never mind. Good luck at Gibsgatte. May the Emperor protect.'

Gaunt walked off to find Beltayn. He had seldom felt so uneasy. He had finally identified the pervasive flower-scent from the previous day.

Islumbine. The sacred flower of Hagia.

SEVEN
POACHING

'And this, my friends, is what they call sweet.'

– Murtan Feygor

THE FOREST BECKONED.

They could smell it. From Ins Arbor, coming off the transports, they could see it. Rolled like green fur around the uplands east of them. Big. Silent. Inscrutable.

It wasn't as if the Tanith hadn't seen forest since the Founding. There'd been plenty. The thick rainwoods north of Bhavnager, the tropical groves of Monthax, the Voltemand Mirewoods. But there was something about this forest, something temperate, old and cool, that reminded them all achingly of the lost nalwoods.

Ins Arbor was a shabby dump of a town, ill-supplied and stinking in the summer heat. There were no proper billets, virtually no water, and the worst rations they'd yet experienced.

But morale had improved overnight.

THE FOREST BECKONED.

Corbec could see the renewed spirit in the faces of the men around the camp. He sat back on the fender of a half-track, and made a last few adjustments to squad lists he was drawing up. Each ten-man detail needed a good mix of scouts and fireteam, and Hark had requested Corbec spread the scout-trainees evenly.

Corbec sucked on the big cigar smouldering between his teeth. A gift from Gaunt. He'd been going to save it for a special occasion, but the smoke was doing a fine job of screening out the odour of the Ins Arbor latrines.

Gaunt's real gift had been this mission. Half of the First taken out of the Naeme meatgrinder and given something useful to do. That was what had lifted morale, despite the grim facilities of the staging town. Anything was better than the line, and the prospect of forest work was better than anything. Tanith were smiling. Verghastites, who had no special affinity with woodland, were smiling too, simply lifted by the mood and the last minute reprieve from trench postings.

He called Varl over and sent him to round up the troops for the first details.

THE FOREST BECKONED.

Brostin kept going on about it. Thuggish, brutal, tattooed, one of the most barbarian of all the enlisted Tanith, he would not shut up about the wonder of it all.

'Smell that!' he said. He paused, cocking his head, wistful. 'Not the leaves. The smell of wet earth beneath trees. Hmmmmm.'

'All I smell is your gakking p-tanks, Tanith,' Cuu said mildly.

'You've got no soul, Cuu. No soul at all.'

'So they say, sure as sure.'

'Here's an idea,' said Feygor, his voice a quiet hiss through his throatbox. 'Why don't the two of you shut up?'

Brostin shrugged and smiled, and picked up his sloshing fuel tanks again. Cuu melted away into the bracken.

Feygor raised his right hand and swept the fingers round twice in a paddling motion. The members of nineteen detail fanned forward through the underbrush.

It was late afternoon. The sun was a yellow dapple to the west behind the leaf cover. The glades of the forest were misty hollows pillared by black trunks. Wild birds called aloud through the wood spaces, and the air smelled of damp bark, wood-poppy and beythorn.

Nineteen detail had been out now for three hours, having left the company command at Ins Arbor with the other details after Corbec's briefing. On the hike up through the villages, the details had separated, one by one, each striking off towards their own designated patrol. Nineteen had been ordered to sweep the Bascuol Valley as far as the pass road down to Frergarten. Two, maybe three days, out and back. They'd made decent time, moving in country. A gentle stroll into the woods.

'I thought Brostin was born and raised in the slums of Tanith Magna,' whispered Caffran.

Gutes shrugged. 'Me too. I guess even the city-boys amongst us get sentimental once in a while.'

Caffran nodded. He didn't begrudge Brostin's enthusiasm. These were dark pine woods, the nearest thing to Tanith they'd experienced since the loss. The spark of recognition he himself had felt at the landing zones was magnified here. Forest. Trees. Aexe Cardinal felt enough like home to please him.

The Verghastites in the detail were less settled. Muril and Jajjo, children of the hive, were jumping at shadows, moving their weapons to cover every last mysterious creak and crack the forest made.

'Cool it down,' Caffran whispered to Muril as she snapped round, her lasrifle aimed.

'Easy for you to say, tree-boy,' she said. 'This is spooky.'

Feygor raised his hand to signal a stop and turned back to face his scout-team.

'Feth!' he said, 'I've heard quieter beer-dances! Could we act professionally? Could we?'

They nodded.

'And tell me... ' Feygor added, 'isn't this better than slogging it at the front?'

'Yes, Mister Feygor,' they all agreed.

'Good. Excellent. Now come on.'

Feygor turned and walked smack into Mkvenner.

'Feth me backwards! Ven! Damn!'

Mkvenner looked at Feygor dourly. He had no love for Rawne's adjutant. A speck of feth, if you pressed him for an opinion, and few dared.

'Way's clear,' Mkvenner said. 'Through to the big oak at the dip. Want me to spread forward?'

'Yeah, why don't you do that?' Feygor said, recovering his composure. 'And take one of the fething wannabes. That's the idea of this, isn't it?'

'So I'm told,' said Mkvenner. He glanced back at the spread out members of the detail. 'Trooper Jajjo! Front to me!'

Jajjo tumbled forward to join the lean, scary Tanith scout. Jajjo was one of the few Verghasts to show potential as a scout.

'Ahead and low, fan south. Calls are standard,' Mkvenner said to the eager Jajjo. 'Go!'

Mkvenner and Jajjo forked away ahead of the detail. Feygor kept his eyes on them. He could still see Jajjo's creeping, hunched shape after two minutes. Mkvenner had vanished almost immediately.

Rerval made a vox-check to make sure they were still in range. He looked up and saw Muril with a grim expression on her face.

'What's up, Verghast?' he said.

'Nothing. Nothing...' she answered. Rerval shrugged. He knew what was bothering her. Muril and Jajjo had both signed up for scout training, and this tour in the woods was meant to be their proving ground. So far, only Jajjo had benefited from Mkvenner's expertise and tutoring.

It's a female thing, Rerval thought. Just like Rawne, though I'd never have expected that kind of prejudice from Ven.

'Let's pick it up!' Feygor called back down the line. 'Moving on!'

They advanced, spread out, through the dim forest space: Feygor, Gutes, Brostin, Muril, Caffran, Cuu.

Cuu paused to look back at the tenth and final member of the detail. 'You with us?'

'Sure,' said Hlaine Larkin. 'Sure as sure.'

FEYGOR WAS PRETTY pleased with himself. He'd made the cut into what had become known as the 'lucky half' of the First, and now here he was with command of a foot patrol. Minimal effort, a little walk-and-look job, and open ended. And if they found somewhere nice, maybe an old farm or something, then a two-day patrol might turn itself into three or four days of R and R.

He'd have preferred to pick his own detail. Nineteen was a mixed bag, but Brostin, Rerval and Gutes were okay, Cuu had his moments, and Caff was all right in his way. Larks was a nut, but what else was new? He could shoot. Maybe he'd bag them something for supper. Feygor acknowledged to himself that he had no idea what sort of wildlife lived out here, but he was pretty sure there would be something with a mouth at one end, an arse at the other, and decent eating in between.

The Verghasts he could do without. Jajjo was a stiff, and in Feygor's opinion, no Verghast was ever going to cut it as a scout. It wasn't in the genes. The girl was better. Decorative. Maybe he'd get really lucky and bag another kind of game out here in the wild woods.

The real pain was Ven. Sure, Feygor respected the scout, everyone did. But everyone was afraid of Mkvenner too. He was straight as a die. Feygor knew he'd have to plan very carefully if they were going to have any fun without Ven getting in the way.

Of course, there was meant to be a job to do, too. The Montorq Forest covered upwards of three thousand square kilometres and ran down from the Toyre, bearding the western flanks of the Kottmark Massif, a wall of mountains that split the eastern provinces of Aexegary from Kottmark. Most of the Montorq terrain was steep, thick woodland slopes, pretty much impassible unless you were on foot or had time to scout out a decent track.

The Shadik Republic lay to the north. The nominal border was about eighty kilometres away, beyond the headwaters of the Toyre. During the long years of the war, Shadik had pressed Aexegary and Kottmark along all viable routes, gradually establishing the pattern of the front line. Seen on a tactical map, the forest uplands were the one break in that line. West of them lay the Seronne Line, the Naeme Sectors and Meiseq, tight as a drum. North and east, the so-called Ostlund Shield Line that blocked the

Shadik thrusts into Kottmark. Shadik had never touched Montorq. It had been spared the war because of geography. Just a few hours' walking in the skirts of the forest showed how hard the going would be. Only a fool would try and push an army through the forest. Feygor had heard the Republican commanders called a lot of things, but fool wasn't one of them.

However, times change. The Alliance had become concerned with the idea that Shadik was about to change tactics in an attempt to throw the deadlock. Instead of directly assaulting Frergarten, the Alliance's great eastern bastion, they might push elite infantry with light support down through the Montorq, and encircle Frergarten, achieving by stealth where three previous assaults had failed. They could take Frergarten, Ins Arbor, snap the Seronne Line and be marching into the Eastern Provinces in under six weeks.

It was unlikely, but it was possible. The Ghosts' orders were to assess enemy disposition and communication routes in the Montorq area. To bring early warning, if necessary. And, Corbec had suggested during the briefing, work out the feasibility of the Alliance pulling the trick in reverse. By the autumn, maybe an Alliance force would be heading through the forest, marching north…

Feygor didn't care. He didn't actually care who won, who lost. He wouldn't give a feth if the Shadik President came along and took a dump in the high sezar's ear. Just as long as Feygor was left alone. He was tired. It had been a long fething road from Tanith, and they'd been through plenty.

Rawne always said that Gaunt led them like he had something to prove. Well, they'd fething well proved it enough, hadn't they? It was some other bastard's turn. Maybe when they were done with this feth-hole, the First would get rotated back to regimental reserve for a few months. Six, maybe. A year. Feygor had seen other companies get the call back out. The fething Vitrians, for instance. They'd gone back into crusade reserve about eighteen months earlier and as far as Feygor knew they were still there, sitting with their fething glass boots up on a table, smoking someone else's lhos, playing at garrison. The Bluebloods too, those bastards had been pulled to the rear after Vervunhive.

There was no fething justice.

Feygor reached the next crest, a slope of loose rocks and ferns that bounded a deep dell where a thin stream splashed down its course under the dark trees. The trees, mountain ash, link-alder and some kind of spruce, creaked and moved their heads gently. A slight rise in the wind. Westerly. The scent of rain.

On one of the rocks lay a leaf, fresh, curled into a loop with the stalk stabbed through the blade of the leaf. Feygor picked it up. One of Ven's waymarkers. All the scouts left marks like this to show the squad behind them they'd cleared and passed ahead. You wouldn't notice them unless you knew to look. Ven and Jajjo would be half a kilometre ahead of them by now.

As the detail made their way up the fern trail behind him, Feygor pushed on, clambering up the tumble of rocks on the crest into a break in the trees where the sunlight could fall on him. The sky was tinged yellow, what he could see of it. Clouds chased, gathering. Rain definitely. Maybe even a summer storm.

Feygor knew the signs. Like Brostin – and like his mentor Rawne – Feygor was a city boy. But even if you grew up in a place like Tanith Attica, you were never far from forest. Feygor had got to know woodcraft and how to read the weather as a teenager, making the early morning runs out of Attica's mercantile district into the Attican woods. You'd needed the skills in his trade. Skills to find a particular clearing at a particular time, skills to get home the long way round without getting lost. Skills to avoid the arbites and the excise men. The movers and shakers in Attica's black market didn't go much on excuses like 'I got lost' or 'There was a sudden downpour and I ran late'.

Feygor sat down and waited as the members of the detail came up over the crest. Cuu, then Caff, then Gutes and Rerval. Brostin came back in the line, so that the betraying smell of his flamer's fuel tanks would be minimised. Muril next, quiet as a feline. Feygor watched her move by, his gaze lingering once she'd gone past and afforded him a rear view.

Larkin was right in the tail. According to Brostin, Larkin had specifically requested this detail, which seemed odd to Feygor. Everyone knew that Larkin and Cuu were not exactly best buddies. Larks usually did his level best to find occupation as far away from Lijah Cuu as possible. Indeed, Cuu had seemed puzzled by Larkin's inclusion. Puzzled. Almost annoyed.

But Larkin seemed strangely relaxed. That was good, in Murtan Feygor's book. The last kind of crap he needed out here was Larks in one of his manic phases. He'd keep an eye on the sniper. He'd asked Piet Gutes to do the same.

Feygor got up and slithered back down the crest to join Larkin as he made the top.

'Gonna be looking for shelter soon,' Feygor said. 'Wind's up. Would be good to eat. Fancy your eye?'

Larkin shrugged. 'Why not?'

'Don't go far.' Feygor looked back down the trail. 'Muril!'

She turned and made her way back to them.

'Larks is on dinner duty. Buddy him up. Don't get lost.'

'Okay,' she said. The order clearly pleased her. Half an hour poaching with Larkin wasn't scout training with Ven, but it was better than nothing. Feygor knew she was itching to show her ability. Anything to get in her good books.

'I saw some spoor down on the path,' Larkin said. 'Let's try that way.'

The pair of them began to descend the slope the way they'd come.

Feygor moved ahead, catching up with the rest of the detail. Brostin had stopped to take a swig from his billy. Right at the front, coming up the next rise in the shadow of the trees, Cuu had paused too. He was staring back down the dell at the departing figure of Larkin.

LARKIN KNELT AND checked the spoor. It was fresh. Some small animal, probably a grazer. He sat on a rock for a moment, exchanging his hot-shot ammunition clip for a low-volt pack.

'What's that?' Muril asked.

'You hunted before?'

She shook her head.

'A hot-shot'll mince anything smaller than a deer. We wanna eat. We don't wanna paint the scenery with liquid animal.'

She smiled. She sat down and put her lasrifle on the earth beside her. Larkin had got used to seeing her with a long-las. It seemed odd for her to be carrying a standard Mark III carbine.

'Miss it?' he asked.

'Sort of,' she admitted. 'But I want to be a scout. I really want to make that grade. And that means packing in my beloved long-las for a standard Mark III. Besides, I get the hat as compensation.'

She was referring to the soft, black wool cap she was wearing. Standard kit order for troopers was the ceramite helmet for line duties, and a choice of black beret or forage cap otherwise. Unless you were a scout, or a trainee scout like Muril. Then you got to wear the wool cap for all duties. It didn't obstruct movement or vision like a helmet, and there was no danger of it clinking against your weapon during a crawl. The caps were the mark of the First's elite, one of those subtle but crucial uniform differences that lent prestige. If she made scout, she'd get to wear the matt-black speciality badge on the brim. No Verghast had done that. No woman, either.

Larkin smiled. Whatever standard kit order said about headwear, the First was extraordinarily lax about it. Many went bare-headed. Berets were common under fire. He'd once heard Corbec tell Hark that more Ghosts had used their hard-bowls as buckets than had worn them in combat. Here was this girl keen to win the right to wear a hat she'd probably never use anyway.

Except, of course, on parade. That's where it would matter. That's where Sehra Muril in a scout cap would be a fething big deal.

'What's funny?' she asked.

'Nothing,' he said.

He got up and practised sighting his long-las into the trees.

'You don't think I'll make it?' she said.

He shrugged. 'You made marksman. I know this. If any of you hivers ever make scout, it'll be one of you girls.'

'Mkvenner doesn't seem keen on the idea,' she muttered. 'When the colonel told me he'd put me in this detail to shadow Ven, I got really excited. I mean, Ven's the real deal. Him or Mkoll. The very best. I thought this was it. The big step forward. But he only seems interested in Jajjo.'

'Jajjo's okay.'

'Sure. But Jajjo's getting all the attention. Who did Ven call up just now? Me? I don't think so. Did I do something wrong? Or am I fooling myself? Or does Ven have a thing?'

'A thing?'

'About girls.'

Larkin lowered his weapon and squinted over at her. 'We all have a thing about girls.'

Muril laughed. 'But really…'

Larkin raised his weapon again. Distantly, through the trees, he could see the members of nineteen detail skirting up the next slope under a bank of spruce.

'It ever occur to you,' he said softly, 'that Ven's taking time with Jajjo because Jajjo's the one who needs the work?'

'Gak!' she said. A broad smile spread across her slender face. 'That's a way of looking at it that hadn't occurred to me.'

'You gotta see all the angles…' Larkin said. His voice had dropped to a hush. He let the las float in his hands, the aim fluid. He coasted the muzzle around. He wasn't blinking. Through the sight, he saw the distant figures, crossing in and out of the leaf-cover. He waited for the scope to lock. The read-out lit up in his eye. Target-fix. Four hundred and seventy two metres. The back of Feygor's head. Coast. Target-fix. Four seventy-nine and half. Brostin's promethium tanks. Coast.

Four eighty-one. Target-fix. Lijah Cuu. Side of the skull. Adjusted for cross-wind. Tracking.

'What are you doing?' Muril asked.

Larkin had stopped breathing. The long-las felt weightless. The target-fix rune was flashing steady now. His right index finger slowly tightened on the trigger. Lijah Cuu stopped and turned to speak to Gutes. The horizontal of Larkin's cross hairs made a bar across Cuu's eyes. The vertical almost followed the line of the trademark scar. Right there. Right now. Kill-shot.

Larkin lowered the gun, breathed out and snapped the safety.

'Just getting my eye in,' he said.

HEQTA JAJJO COULDN'T get the gakking leaf to bend. Every time he looped it, it sprang back, and when he'd finally got the stalk pushed through the leaf, it tore.

'Problem?' said a voice.

Jajjo looked up. Mkvenner was standing over him.

'Gak, you made me jump.'

'That's a good thing because I'm a scout. And it's a bad thing because that's what you want to be too.'

'Sorry.'

'Don't be sorry. Be better. What's the problem?'

'You told me to leave a sign here. I can't get it to make the shape.'

Ven hunkered down and plucked a fresh leaf from a nearby clump of beythorn. 'You're trying too hard. It's just a twist. It has to look casual.'

Mkvenner made a perfect loop and set it on a crop of white stone.

Jajjo sighed.

'You'll get it,' said Mkvenner, almost encouragingly.

'You think we're wasting our time, don't you?' said Jajjo.

'Why?'

'Because we're not fit. Not fit for scouting.' Jajjo didn't have to qualify the 'we're'. They both knew he meant 'Verghastites'.

'If that's what you think, then the only thing I'm wasting is my effort. Take the point.'

'Only if–'

'Take the point, Jajjo. Show me you can work terrain.'

Jajjo picked up his Mark III, and advanced, head low. They'd reached a long, curved valley of pine wood with a steeply tilted rake that was thick with last year's needles. The wind was up now, and the trees swayed and shushed over him.

The air was cold. The sunlight had died off and plunged the forest floor into twilight. Jajjo tried to make as little sound as possible. His foot cracked a piece of dead bark, and he looked back guiltily towards the place where he'd left Mkvenner.

The scout had gone. How the gak did he do that?

Jajjo worked the cover all the way down to a thick copse of link-alder. Halfway down, he knocked his rifle-stock against a sapling. Then he realised he hadn't draped himself with his camo-cape properly. Gak on a flakboard, was there anything else he could get wrong?

The sound of the wind in the trees was mesmeric now. Like a sea, Jajjo thought. His family had come from Imjahive originally, down in the archipelago, one of Verghast's tropical cities. He knew what the sea sounded like. He'd missed it when his family had moved to Vervunhive, the year he turned six.

Jajjo stole past the copse, and crossed a spread of swishing ferns. The first spots of rain started to come down, smacking hard impacts into the leaves of the ground cover. Jajjo tried to stick to the shadows. Through the stand of pines ahead, there seemed to be something, he couldn't tell what. He switched cover, making short runs between trees, the way he'd been taught in scout preparation. Now the sounds he made were being masked by the gathering rainstorm and wind. He kept his Mark III tucked up under his right armpit, barrel down, so it wouldn't catch on anything.

The rain got heavier. The drops beat down like a non-stop drum roll on the leaves. The temperature immediately rose by a few degrees, lifting skeins of mist from the ground and choking his nose with a damp, mulchy reek.

Jajjo reached the pine stand, and slid through the trees. What the hell was that up there? There was definitely some sort of clearing. A break in the trees. He could tell that simply from the light.

He got down in the ferns and crawled for the last twenty metres to the edge of the clearing, pushing his weapon in front of him. He raised his head, and saw, through the rain, what lay beyond.

'Gak!' he stammered. He turned to rise and work back, but Mkvenner was crouched right behind him.

'Good work,' said Mkvenner quietly. 'Look what you found...'

IT WASN'T ON any of the maps. Mainly because it was old, and the maps were new. Ven and Jajjo back-tracked to meet the detail, and led them forward.

It was a house. A big house. A retreat. Rerval described it as a manse, and the name stuck. Derelict and overgrown, it occupied a cleared stretch of hillside within the forest, facing west. Lime-washed grey stone, black slate. Two storeys and maybe an attic. Blind windows looked out across an unkempt garden from the front. There was a weed-choked path leading to the front porch, and the signs of an old wall and gate in the overgrown hedges. Gutes and Caffran circled round the rear and found a single-storey wing extending from the back, and a clutch of outbuildings clogged against the back garden wall around a paved yard. Beyond that, a wild garden and lawn stretched up hill to the edge of the pine woods. There was an old wall at the top of the lawn, against which sat several more dilapidated outhouses.

The rain was torrential now.

'Let's check it,' Feygor said.

They split. Feygor, Gutes, Cuu and Brostin to the front door; Caffran, Rerval, Jajjo and Mkvenner to the back.

'Armed,' Feygor said on the front steps. The dripping Ghosts with him nodded. Gutes and Cuu dropped in either side of the big, old doors. Paint was flaking off the panels. Feygor peeked in through ground floor windows, but saw nothing except dust and shadows.

'Going in,' he said over his micro-bead.

'Read you,' crackled Caffran.

Feygor nodded. Brostin stepped up and put his shoulder into the doors. It took two shoves, but the wood splintered and the doors swung open.

Gutes and Cuu, lasrifles aimed, screwed in behind him.

The hallway was dark and the air was stale. Mildew. Old carpets. Damp. They edged into the gloom, making out a staircase and several doors off the hall on the ground floor. Water dripped from the ceiling and the stairwell. Feygor crept inside, his rifle at a hunting tilt.

He snapped his fingers and he, Gutes and Cuu turned on lamp-packs. They slung them from the bayonet lugs of their weapons and played them around the hall. The spots of light revealed a lacquered sideboard with cobweb-strung candle stands, a massive gilt-edged mirror that threw their inquisitive lights back at them. A coatstand, hung with a single, lonely raincoat. An embroidered rug. Dried flowers in a dedemican vase. A console table with a brass letter rack.

Cuu tried the wall switch. The big chandelier remained dark. 'No power,' he said.

'Yeah,' Feygor smiled, 'but it's a roof.'

The rain pelted down. Thunder rolled. Feygor worked his way over to the left hand door off the hall.

Brostin hand-cranked the feeder reservoir of his flamer's broom, and clicked the lighter flint. There was a wet cough, and then a hiss as the flamer came to life. Brostin had it turned right down, so that just a cone of blue-heat sizzled around the nozzle. The hiss of the burner filled the air. They could all smell promethium.

Brostin edged his way over to Feygor, using the barely-lit flamer like a lamp. 'After you,' he said.

Feygor opened the inner door and pushed it wide, keeping his back to the doorpost. Brostin went in, revving the flamer up into little, quick flares of hot yellow flame.

'Dining room,' he said. Feygor prowled in, sliding his lamp beam off the walls. Old oil paintings, grim faces. Vases and porcelain. A long, dark-varnished table lined by twenty chairs. A single plate at one setting, decorated with a pair of fruit stones, and a small paring knife.

Feygor went back out into the hall. Gutes and Cuu had opened the room on the other side. Some kind of sitting room, with armchairs and sofas covered in dust sheets. A big fireplace with a basket of logs. More cobwebs.

Feygor moved through the space to another door at the end. He pushed it open, aiming his lamp and gun through the slit. A small room, lined with empty shelves. Dust. A library? A study? He edged inside, covered by Gutes. There was a desk and a captain's chair on brass castors. Racks and hooks on the walls that had once held something. He swung his beam right.

Framed by his light-beam, the monster loomed out of the darkness, its lips pulled back from its huge teeth, its clawed paws raised to strike.

'Holy feth!' squeaked Feygor and shot it.

He hit it in the belly and there was a loud burst of fur and dust. Gutes, startled by the sudden shot, rolled round through the doorway and blasted off a burst himself.

'Stop! Stop!' Feygor shouted over Gute's fire. The monster continued to snarl at them. The micro-bead link went wild.

'Who's shooting?' That was Caffran.

'Confirm contact! Confirm contact!' Jajjo.

'Feygor? Sign back.' Ven.

Feygor was laughing, his giggles rolling flat and dry from his voice box. 'Relax. No contact.'

Gutes was sniggering with relief too.

'What the feth?' said Brostin, shouldering in through the door and raising his flamer. He gunned the torch and the flare lit up the room. The huge beast in the corner was starkly lit, poised on its plinth, paws raised to strike. Sawdust dribbled from its shot-open gut, and the flames reflected in its glass eyes.

'Feth!' said Brostin. 'Are you trigger-happy or what?'

'I thought it was a real fething thing!' Feygor protested and chortled. 'Took me by surprise.'

'Well,' said Brostin, 'you pair sure killed it.'

Feygor walked over to the stuffed trophy. It was quite a beast. Raised on its hind legs, three metres tall, covered in black fur and sporting teeth the length of his fingers.

'What the feth is it?' asked Piet Gutes.

'Some kind of ursa,' said Feygor, truculently punching it in the chest. It was hollow.

'It's a behj,' said Cuu, from the doorway. 'Big deal here on Aexe. The totem animal, the king predator. I heard the sezar wears a pelt, and the locals barter the claws as lucky charms.'

'How the feth d'you know that, Lijah?' asked Brostin.

Cuu smiled. 'I made a cred or two playing the trench markets. It always helps to have local knowledge. A struthid feather is lucky, but a behj-claw–'

'Always got your eye on the main chance, eh, Cuu?' admired Feygor.

'Sure as sure,' said Lijah Cuu.

CAFFRAN HAD LED his team into the back kitchen.

'Odd,' Mkvenner said.

'What is?'

'Everything's clean and put away... except that cup and dish by the sink.'

'Someone left in a hurry,' said Rerval. 'This whole region is supposed to have been evacuated.'

'Then why do I smell garlic?' Ven asked.

Aiming his lamp beam into the shadows, Caffran edged through the scullery and an empty, damp-smelling washroom. Jajjo followed him.

Jajjo found a door off the kitchen that came free with a kick. It was a walk-in pantry, the shelves lined with fruit pickles and jars of preserved vegetables. Four haunches of salted meat hung from the beam hooks.

'Gak me, my mouth is watering,' said Jajjo. They'd been on lousy rations since landfall.

The vox chimed.

'Come see what I've found, boys,' said Feygor.

CAFFRAN'S TEAM FOUND Feygor's in the cellar of the house. A short run of stone steps let down into it via a door in the hall. Labelled by vintage, the wine racks were arranged in five rows of shelves.

Feygor took a bottle off one of the racks, cracked its neck off against the cellar wall, and splashed a large measure into his upturned mouth.

'Gutes, Cuu,' he said, belching and licking his lips. 'Go light the fire. Stoke it up, mind. We've found our billet.'

'We should secure it,' said Mkvenner.

'Okay, so secure it,' Feygor snapped. They could all hear the wind and rain beating down outside. 'Do what you want.'

Mkvenner glared at Feygor for a moment. Then he turned to Jajjo. 'Come on.'

The pair of them left the cellar.

Feygor took another knock from the bottle and glanced over at Caffran. 'It ain't sacra,' he said, 'but I think I'm gonna like it here.'

EIGHT
THE POCKET

'The worst day of my life. The worst part of the line.
I wouldn't wish it on any bastard. I don't ever want
to go back there.'

– Count Golke, on the Seiberq Pocket

IN SILENCE, THEY waited until the guns had stopped. Then they went out. Up over scaling ladders, up over the parapet. Into the blackness and the mud. Into little, individual worlds of suffocating gas-hoods.

It was just before 03.30 in the morning, and day seemed a whole lifetime away.

'Keep it tight,' Criid grunted into her micro-bead, the sound of her own breathing resonating inside her canvas gas-mask. Her platoon was straggled out. Somewhere to their left was five platoon, Soric's band. Somewhere to her right was seventeen, Raglon's. Somewhere around her was her own gakking platoon, not that she could see them. The damn hoods: blindfolds, gags, earmuffs all rolled into one.

There was a kind of light. It twinkled through the imperfect plastic lenses of her hood. Amber, dull. Just enough to pick out the landscape of no-man's land. Smoggy vapour fumed from the craters. It hid the wires. Pools of chemical water in deep shell holes gave off a leery phosphorescent glow.

This was a game. Not a fun one. Nobody had been looking forward to it. Not since they'd been transferred to 58th sector.

Criid missed having DaFelbe with her. Word was he was recovering from the face wound. She'd had to move Mkhef up as her adjutant, and she didn't get on with the lanky Tanith as well.

The ground was wet and sticky. It was like striding through caramel. All she could hear was the muffled pant of her own lungs inside the hood.

'Wire!' said a muffled voice. She turned her head. It was Mkhef, waiting while Kenfeld and Vulli came up with the cutters.

Criid crouched down. All around her, anonymous, hooded ghosts were slipping in, just shadows in the bad light. Everyone was cloaked up, shrouded in their camouflage capes.

'Breached!' Kenfeld reported, his voice sounding like it came from a box. He stood up, pulling the broken strands of wire aside with his gloved hands.

'Move up, with me,' Criid whispered.

Barely fifty metres to Criid's left, Soric guided his platoon ahead. Despite the proximity, he couldn't see any of Criid's bunch, or Obel's, which was allegedly running to his left flank.

Agun Soric was sweating inside his hood. He hated hood work. He was blind and stifled, his already reduced vision cut down to a pathetic scrap.

The mud was hell. Wet-soft and deep. It sucked at boots, pulled feet down at every stride, like the earth was hungry. Soric had to pause to cover Trooper Hefron, who hadn't secured his boots well enough and had therefore lost one to the grab of the ground.

'Get your gakking boot back on!' Soric barked, panting in the humid darkness of his hood.

'I'm sorry, sarge, I'm sorry...' Hefron was repeating.

'Shut up and get it tied!' Soric stood back, trying to let his lungs fill. All he could taste was damp, hot air. Perspiration was running into his one good eye. He couldn't wipe it.

'Gak!'

Hefron got back up and Soric sent him on his way with a cuff to the back of the head. He'd gone a pace or two himself when he tripped on something hard buried in the muck and went down.

Liquid mud drowned his hood's visor. He couldn't see. He could taste filthy water pouring in through the gauze filter.

Hands grabbed him and pulled him up.

'Sarge? You okay?'

It was Vivvo, his voice crackling over the link.

'Yeah.'

'You hit?'

'No. I fell.'

'Gak, I thought you were hit.'

'Wipe me gakking eye slits, for god's sake,' Soric said.

There was a squeak and vision returned. Vivvo was scooping the mud from Soric's hood-lenses with his fingers.

'You hurt?' he asked.

'No. Yes, bruised my leg. Fell on something.' It was even harder to breathe now. Soric had never felt so stifled. The infernal hood…

'Give me a moment, Vivvo. Step on. Get the platoon focused before they run too far ahead.'

Soric trudged forward, feeling his leg for the bruise. Something had smacked into it hard when he fell.

There was something in his pocket. Blindly, he took it out and held it up. It was the brass message shell.

Soric's heart began to race even harder. He was sure he'd left that fething thing in his dugout.

Fumbling with muddy, gloved fists, he unscrewed the cap. There was the folded sheet of blue tissue paper he'd been expecting.

It was hard to read through the smeared hood visor.

It said. 'Air's clean. No need for hoods. Warn ten about mill house.'

Something else was written underneath that he couldn't make out.

Soric tore open the buckles and pulled off his hood. He took big lungfuls of the cold exterior air, air thick with the taste of fuel and mud and water.

But not gas.

He pulled off his gloves and wiped his good eye, shoving the sweat back into his hair.

'Signals! Signals!' he called.

Mohr, his vox-man, came stumbling over the mud-plain towards him and started visibly when he saw Soric bareheaded.

'Feth, sarge! Orders was hoods!'

'Air's clean,' Soric told him. 'Vox it out. Air's clean and you have my word on that.'

Mohr knelt down in a shell hole and adjusted his set, removing his gas-hood as he did so. His young face was flushed and beaded.

'Give me the mic,' said Soric. 'This is twenty, twenty to all. The air is clean, repeat, clean. Ditch the hoods.'

Soric sat down, still holding the vox-horn to his mouth. He twisted the paper scrap until the feeble light caught it so he could read.

'Twenty, ninety-one.'

'Ninety-one, twenty. You certain about the hoods?'

'Certain. Trust me, Tona.'

'Read that, twenty.'

'Twenty, ninety-one. I think you're coming up on some kind of mill house. A building.'

'Ninety-one, twenty. Not on the maps.'

'There's nothing on the maps, Tona. Just watch it, okay. You see a structure, be wary.'

'You got inside information, Soric?'

'Just be careful.'

'Ninety-one, twenty. Careful. Confirmed.'

Soric clicked off the mic and sat back for a moment, gazing up. The sky was dark, fumed with a haze of yellow. There were no stars. He wished there could be stars.

'Finished, sir?' asked Mohr. He was getting anxious. The platoon was leaving them behind.

'Not quite,' said Soric, looking down at the piece of paper clenched in his dirty fist. That line under the first. His wet fingers had blurred the ink. It was just a smudge. He peered at it. What the gak did it say? He ought to know. He'd gakking written it.

Or something with handwriting just like his had, anyway.

Something, Soric knew, even if it scared the living gak out of him, he had to trust.

Something something don't let something... what was that? It looked like 'Raglon'. Was it? Shit, what had this said? The first part had been a warning to Tona. Was Raglon going to get into a mess too? God-Emperor, what did it say?

'Next time write it in gakking pencil!' he said.

'Sarge?' Mohr asked nervously.

I said that out loud, thought Soric. He lifted the vox-mic. 'Twenty, two-oh-three?'

'Two-oh-three, twenty.' Raglon's voice came back swiftly, as prompt on the link as any ex-vox man.

'Twenty, two-oh-three... uh, just watch yourself, okay?'

'Say again, Soric?'

'I said watch yourself. Don't know why, don't know what. Just... be extra careful, okay?'

'Understood. Two-oh-three out.'

Soric tossed the mic back to Mohr. 'Let's go,' he said, and levered his squat frame up. The mud and darkness closed in on all sides. There was no sign of Vivvo or the rest of five platoon.

Soric grabbed Mohr by the arm and started to trudge forward.

THERE WAS NO landscape out here to read in any proper sense. Just burst earth and wreckage. For all Criid knew, they could be heading back to their own lines. But somehow Hwlan saw the way.

The Tanith scout had the lead, nudging the extended line of ten platoon across the wasteland. At least they had the relief of losing the hoods. How'd Soric known it was clear? A message from the atmos-sniffers at the line, Criid presumed.

The darkness seemed solid, vicing them in. The odour of death and soiled water was almost suffocating. Criid ducked into a shallow crater with Nessa and Vril, and they found themselves swimming alongside bloated, swollen corpses. Mkhef splashed in with them a moment later and recoiled in disgust.

'Feth!'

'Shut up, for gak's sake!' Criid whispered. 'We must be getting close to the Shadik lines.'

Nessa crawled up the forward edge of the crater and scoped with her long-las.

'Wire, about twenty metres up. No movement.'

'Feth this,' murmured Mkhef, trying to shoo away a gas-distended corpse that kept bobbing towards him.

The link chimed. Criid heard Hwlan's voice.

'Got some sort of structure, sarge. Nine points west. Looks like... I dunno...'

'Stay put,' said Criid into her micro-bead.

She hand-signalled over to Nessa, Vril and Mkhef. 'With me.'

The four of them scrambled up out of the wet slick of the crater and ran west over the pock-marked mud, ducking under an old stretch of rusted wire. They came in behind the jagged, partial boarding of a stretch of fence where Hwlan was hiding in a scrape.

The building beyond was backlit by a yellowish fog rising off the enemy lines. It was a ruin, a shell, one wall gone, the remains of a chimney stack rising like a tombstone. The structure lay in a hollow, swimming with creek water, festooned with wire. It looked like some kind of... mill. Some kind of water mill.

Criid had an unpleasant nagging feeling left over from Soric's last transmission.

She glanced up again at the ruin, a blankness against the yellowy dark. Caffran had a great rep for building assaults. What would he do?

The thought stopped her. Caff. Criid felt a terrible ache. Where was he? What was he doing, right now? Was he even alive?

How fething stupid was this, scampering through darkness and mud with a gun in your hand, when some things really mattered?

Caff...

'You okay, sarge?' Mkhef whispered.

'Yeah, why?'

'You looked kind of funny–'

'I'm fine,' she said. She was. She was fine. She was Sergeant Tona Criid, Tanith First-and-fething-Only, the only fem who'd ever made that grade. She wasn't going to gak it up now. It didn't matter what she felt about Caff, or Yoncy or Dalin.

She'd chosen to be a soldier, and worked to get the pins. Love was just an anchor she didn't need.

Not right now.

'Kenfeld?' she said quietly into her bead.

'Sarge?' the vox link crackled.

'Report?'

'I'm east of you, round the front with Mosark, Pozetine and Lubba.'

'See anything?'

'Just a ruin.'

'Okay, send Lubba forward with Pozetine. Cover space. But wait for my word. We're going to stealth assault from this side.'

'Read you, sarge.'

'Stealth assault,' Criid repeated to her companions, removing her blade from her bayonet lug and slinging her rifle over her shoulder. The others did the same.

'Why the caution, sarge?' Vril asked.

'I've got a hunch,' she said. 'This could be nasty, but I want it quiet.'

The four of them advanced over the black mud towards the shattered ruin. It was bigger than Criid had first thought. Tall. Thick walls, what was left of them. She snuggled in behind a fallen section of roof, and waved Hwlan through. Vril followed him. Criid dropped in behind them, Mkhef at her heels. Nessa hung back, scope raised.

Inside the mill, it was like a cave. Water dripped in through the open roof, and through the punctured second floor above. The ground was a mess of fractured rockcrete and tumbled girders.

Criid moved forward almost blind through the mess of debris. She climbed up over a slumped girder, tossing her knife into her left hand to brace herself with her right. To her west, Hwlan crawled forward under a slumped beam, and then folded himself through a blast hole in what remained of one of the interior walls.

She waited, then heard two, quick taps click through her micro-bead. It was a standard First non-verbal signal made by gently flicking the mic of your intercom. Two taps... clear.

She edged forward again, trying to fit herself through a narrow gap between rockcrete slabs, but her cape kept getting hung up on some of the twisted reinforcement bars jutting from one of the slabs. She had to back off, and go round.

A single tap. Not clear. She froze.

Two taps. She resumed her crawl, moving through a stagnant pool on her hands and knees and then making her way slowly up a mound of rubble that climbed out of the water, trying hard not to dislodge any loose chunks.

Hwlan was waiting for her at the top in what remained of an old doorway. There was a nondescript dark lump lying in the shadows near his feet. Criid realised it was the corpse of a Shadik sentry.

They waited until Vril and Mkhef caught up with them, and then went through the doorway into the next portion of the ruined mill. It was very dark here too, but down at the far end, there was a flickering light, like shadows cast by flames. Then they saw movement. Larger shadows moving against the meagre firelight.

There was a Shadik forward observation post in the far end of the mill. Three, maybe four men in hoods and long, grey coats moved about the end room. They had a fire, for warmth, in an oil can, its light shielded from the outside. Hwlan caught at Criid's arm and directed her attention upwards. Through missing floorboards, they could see another Shadik up in the remains of the second floor, crouching at a tripod-mounted spotter scope and gazing out over the wasteland to the west.

They'd never get near him without him noticing them.

Criid signalled the other three to move up, ready to take the Shadik on the ground floor level with their blades. She unslid her rifle, and took careful aim on the dim figure overhead. She'd have to risk one shot. But it had to be a good one.

She waited for Hwlan's signal. She had a good angle. One shot was worth the risk.

HALF A KILOMETRE south of the mill, Sergeant Raglon's platoon had reached the water-logged remains of an old field trench. There was no sure way of telling which side had constructed it, and certainly no way of knowing why it had been dug east-west. Once upon a time, its orientation had made some kind of tactical sense.

Raglon was sweating hard, more nervous than he dared admit. He'd seen plenty of combat before, and had brevet-led a unit on Phantine, but this was his first formal command in an active operation.

Raglon was a serious, thoughtful man, determined, just like Criid and Arcuda, the other neophyte sergeants, to prove to Gaunt and Hark that they'd made a good choice of promotions. He envied Criid the fact that she'd had a chance to blood her platoon in combat at the line. Then again, he envied Arcuda, who was still waiting in reserve back at the fire trench. Gaunt had made no bones about the hazards of these scouting raids into the waste. And Raglon had learned from the Alliance soldiery he'd met that the Seiberq Pocket had a particularly bad reputation as one of the hardest contested regions of the Peinforq Line.

He signalled his men down into the abandoned trench. At the very least, it offered his platoon a means of pushing east out of sight.

The trench was littered with dead. Old dead. The unidentifiable remains of men who had fallen out here perhaps years before, their bodies never recovered. Brown bones stippled the mud like broken twigs.

Seventeen moved single file, heads down, occasionally having to crawl on their bellies to pass sections where the trench walls had caved and filled the ditch.

Raglon had ordered Lukas, his vox-operator, to rig his set for headphones only, so that the caster wouldn't suddenly blare into life and give them away. It was a smart move, the sort of thing that another novice team leader might have overlooked. But Raglon had come from signals and knew about these things.

Where Raglon lacked experience, it was in character judgement. Since taking command of seventeen, his primary efforts had been to establish authority. Seventeen had been Lhurn Adare's platoon, and Raglon was all too aware of the fact he had nothing of the mourned sergeant's charisma. He'd just never be popular the way Adare had been.

So he'd decided the best way to run seventeen was to let them function the way they had under Adare. He didn't want to mess around with habits and established routines. If seventeen had evolved field practices they were happy with, who liked to buddy who in fire-teams for instance, he didn't see the point in changing things. He thought arbitrary changes would make the platoon resent him, and that was true, up to a point. But some habits stemmed from sloppiness.

When they reached the dead trench, the men formed a file automatically, as they saw fit, and Raglon didn't question it. So it was that they advanced now with Suth, the scout, in the lead, and Costin right behind him. Raglon fell into place about four men back.

It was his first command error.

Suth was a good scout. Costin, his buddy, was a drunk.

Adare had known that Costin drank too much. He'd tried to keep a lid on it. Costin was a nice guy, despite his carousing, and a decent trooper if kept away from the sacra. In a situation like this, Costin would inevitably want to get in beside his friend Suth. Adare would have stopped him, pushed him back down the file, just to be safe.

When Costin moved up eagerly with Suth, Raglon hadn't thought to object. Everyone knew Costin liked the drink. Raglon didn't realise how much Costin had been knocking back since Adare's death.

The abandoned trench had actually been constructed by the Alliance during an early phase of fighting, before the full bulk of the Peinforq Line had been built. The Shadik, to whose lines it was now closest, had never filled it in, because it afforded them excellent cover for raid-teams and wire-cutting parties. Indeed, they had extended its eastern end into the verges of their own fire trench system.

As Raglon's platoon advanced along it, a raiding squad was coming the other way.

Suth stopped, and signalled back down the line for a halt. He'd heard something, and wanted to check it.

'I'm coming with,' hissed Costin.

Suth shook his head. He could smell the liquor on Costin's breath. *Stay put,* he mouthed. Costin was making too much damn noise.

'Fine!' said Costin, and sat down, glancing back at Azayda, the next man in line with a 'what can you do?' shrug.

Angry, Suth took hold of Costin by the jaw and gave him a sharp slap on the cheek. *Be quiet!* he mouthed, urgently.

Glowering, Costin sat back.

Suth turned, and began to edge forward along the watery swill of the trench pit, then levered himself out of the trench on his belly and started to crawl.

Costin stared after Suth for a moment, his pride wounded. He wiped his hand across his mouth, and then spat the slime he'd inadvertently deposited there. It tasted foul.

He leaned up to see how far Suth had got, but the scout was out of sight.

Costin sniffed, and then took a flask bottle out of his fatigue pocket. He took a swig, but it was virtually empty and he tasted only fumes. So he tipped it back. Tipped it right back to get at the dregs.

The glass bottle flashed as the background light caught it.

Costin wailed as a rifle round exploded his hand and the bottle it was holding. A second later, and another shot tore open his tunic across the right shoulder.

Costin began to whimper as he fell into the bottom of the trench.

Azayda leapt forward, desperate to quieten Costin, and a third round burst the Verghastite's head like a ripe fruit.

Back down the line, Raglon heard the cries and the sudden shots, and cursed aloud. He tried to push forward, but his men were being driven back by furious sniper fire and quick bursts of semi-automatic shooting. Zemel dropped, killed outright. Tyne took a hit in the knee and another through the arm. Lukas lurched over with a yell as a shot smashed his vox-caster.

Suth was down, alone, out in the open. He could see the glitter of shots cutting up the trench towards his platoon. He could see the shapes of the raiders as they hurried forward.

He felt the worst possible feeling a Tanith scout can ever feel: that he had led his comrades into danger.

He didn't hesitate. He got up, and ran the trench from the side, his lasgun blazing, assaulting the stormers from the flank.

He made several kills before their massed firepower cut him down.

TO THE NORTH, Soric's platoon froze and dropped as they heard the gunfire start up. Agun Soric heard solid fire, and then las-rounds.

'Gak,' he said, 'Some poor bastard's engaged.'

And though he hated to admit it, he knew for certain who that poor bastard was.

Raglon.

THE ABRUPT GUNFIRE just a half kilometre south startled Criid and made her lower her aim for an instant. She'd been about to take the gakking shot.

She saw the spotter on the second floor of the mill get up and hurry over to the other side of the building, stepping expertly over gaps in the planks. She heard voices in the rear room of the obs post.

Do I wait or do I go for it, she asked herself?

She took aim again.

'Bets are off,' she said into her link and fired.

Her shot punched through a floorboard from below and severed the right shin of the spotter. He screamed out, fell, and came crashing through the rotten planks, bouncing off a jut of girder-post on his way down.

Vril, Mkhef and Hwlan ploughed in, killing the others below with quick, merciless shots.

Criid ran in to join them, ordering the rest of her group to hold position. The sounds of a serious firefight was rolling in from the south. Vril and Hwlan stood cover as Criid and Mkhef searched the obs post area. Cooking pots, boxes of ammo for a .45 cannon set up in a broken window, cans of processed meat, a field telephone. A strange, ugly statuette made of painted clay that Criid smashed against the wall the moment she saw it.

'Check around!' she said.

'Here!' Mkhef called.

At the back end of the chamber, corrugated metal sheets roofed in the entrance to a tunnel. They peered in. It was dark, but well shored up with flakboard.

Chances were it ran directly back to the Shadik lines.

'What do we do?' asked Vril.

Criid ignored him. She was looking at the field telephone. The light on top of it was blinking.

Feth.

'We can't stay here. They'll either close this tunnel when they don't get an answer or they'll start coming through in force.'

Away across the no-man's land they could hear cannons and mortars opening up from the Shadik front.

She looked back at the tunnel mouth. Such a great chance to reach into the enemy lines. But not tonight.

'Fall back!' she ordered, her micro-bead set on the platoon channel. She was last out of the mill. Pausing as she left, she tossed a tube-charge into the mouth of the communications tunnel, closing it off in a flurry of mud and earth spoil. If they couldn't use it, neither would the Shadik.

DAYLIGHT CAME EARLY over the Peinforq Line, dirty and hazy. It had begun to rain again, and an early bombardment was thumping to the north.

Gaunt waited in his dugout station, toying with an almost empty cup of caffeine.

The gas curtain was pushed back and Daur came in.

'What's the story?' Gaunt asked him curtly.

'Five, ten and eleven came back in. Ten just a few minutes ago.'

'Losses?'

Daur shook his head. 'They didn't make much contact, they just dropped back when things got lively.'

'Anything useful?'

'Criid did well. Her gang reconnoitred some old mill structure that isn't on the maps. Obs post. They picked off the troopers manning it. It had a dugout run back to the enemy line. Criid sealed it.'

'How?'

'Tube-charge. She's annoyed. I think she'd have taken a team down it to see what was what if things hadn't woken up.'

'She did the right thing.'

Daur nodded.

'Seventeen?' asked Gaunt.

'Nothing yet. No sign. Zero on the vox. Soric and Criid both confirm the commotion came from Raglon's area.'

Gaunt put the porcelain cup down on the table carefully because he was aware he'd been about to throw it. He'd sent four platoons out on this first night to play the Alliance's new game, and he'd only got three back. Raglon. He'd been Gaunt's vox-officer for several years. He'd been so proud to get his pins and his command.

'What do we do, sir?' asked Daur.

'We do it by the book,' Gaunt replied. 'Stand everyone down. Tomorrow night, four more platoons, four new areas. Haller, Bray, Domor, Arcuda. Get them ready. Tell them–'

'What, sir?'

'Tomorrow night, I'm going with them.'

Daur paused. 'As your XO, sir, I have to recommend you don't.'

'Noted.'

'Just for the record, you understand, sir.'

'I do. Thank you for observing your duty, Ban.'

'I'd like to go too, sir.'

Gaunt managed a thin smile. 'You know I can't allow that. Not both of us.'

'Then let me go in your place.'

'Not this time, Ban. I won a decent operation for half the Ghosts. I'm damn well going to stand by the ones who got the lousy half of the deal. Maybe you go the night after. Deal?'

'Deal, sir.'

DAUR HAD BEEN gone for some minutes when the gas curtain was pulled back again. It was Zweil.

'I hear we're missing some people,' said the old Hagian cleric, setting down without being invited.

'Raglon's platoon.'

'I want to go out tonight. If there's a chance we find them, I'd like to be there.'

'We won't even be covering that area again, father. There's no point.'

Zweil frowned. 'You won't even go back to look?'

'We are obliged to try other areas, father. Not the zones where the Shadik are expecting us. Standard field policy.'

'Whose?'

'Mine.'

'Hmmmm,' said Zweil. He sat down facing Gaunt. 'Tough job you've got here.'

'It's always a tough job.'

'Yes, but sending your platoons out into that... wasteland... hoping you'll find a gap in their lines. Why would that be again?'

'You know damn well, Zweil. Don't pretend Daur hasn't told you.'

Zweil grinned. Gaunt had always liked that grin, from the moment he'd first met the old priest on Hagia. It was confident, wise.

'Very well, Ibram. Pretend I'm Daur. Confide in me your plans.'

'I don't think so. You haven't got the clearance.'

'I could have the clearance, if you allowed it.'

'No, Zweil.'

The old man held out his hand, knuckles bunched, palm down. 'Play you for it. Knuckles.'

'Oh, for goodness' sake...'

'Unless you're afraid an old priest'll beat you?'

Gaunt turned round smartly and put his bent knuckles against Zweil's. 'Never taunt a Guard officer,' he said.

Zweil nodded. In a flash, he'd cracked Gaunt's knuckles with a blow from the right.

'Ow!' cried Gaunt. 'I didn't think we'd started!'

'Now you do. Best of three?'

Gaunt paused, then rapped down, missing as Zweil's hand pulled away.

In reply, Zweil snapped his hand round in a feint, and then smacked Gaunt's knuckles again from the right.

'Best of five?' asked Zweil, grinning.

'No. Enough.'

'So you'll grant me clearance?'

'No.'

Zweil sighed and sat back. 'Got you twice.'

'Yes, yes–'

'Both from the same angle.'

'What?'

'The same angle.'

'Do you have a point?'

Zweil nodded. 'I caught you because you didn't think I'd try the same thing twice. What if the Shadik think the same way?'

'Very clever. Now get out.'

Zweil got to his feet. 'Promise me something. I think that's the least you can do seeing as how I won.'

'Go on.'

'If you decide to go out into the same zones again tonight, take me with you.'

Gaunt hesitated. 'Yes, father.'

'Bless you,' said Zweil.

GAUNT HAD CALLED Criid to his dugout. He wanted to know more about this mill she'd found. But when the knock came, it wasn't Criid. It was Count Golke.

He was wearing battledress.

'Going somewhere?' Gaunt asked.

'When you head out again tonight, I'll be with you.'

'Why would you do that, sir? You're liaison. Front-line work is behind you.'

'I know the Pocket, Gaunt. I served here. I got you into this mess, though it wasn't my intention. I think I can help you.'

'Really?'

Golke nodded.

'So... what about the mill.'

'I'm guessing it's the old Santrebar watermill. I didn't know any of it was still standing.'

'Well,' said Gaunt. 'You've given it a name. But I don't think–'

'I was a soldier, Gaunt, before I was anything else. Before I got drawn into the political nonsense running this war. I think I've outlived my usefulness as a staff officer. Let me be a soldier again.'

There was a knock.

Criid entered. 'Reporting as ordered, sir,' she said.

'Sit down, sergeant, and tell me and the count about this mill...'

[illegible] thought the Shadow [illegible]?

[illegible]

[illegible] to the [illegible] Phantasm [illegible]

[illegible] nothing [illegible]

[illegible] through the [illegible]

[illegible]

[illegible] Guard.

[illegible] found that [illegible]

[illegible]

[illegible]

Where [illegible] about [illegible]

[illegible]

[illegible] can help you.

[illegible]

[illegible]

[illegible] was [illegible]

[illegible] before [illegible]

[illegible] Prince [illegible] said.

[illegible] tell [illegible] about [illegible]

[illegible]

[illegible] were [illegible]

It [illegible]

[illegible]

NINE
THE MANSE

'Haunted? Well, there are ghosts here, that's for certain.'

– Trooper Brostin

THE STORM THAT had begun the previous evening showed no sign of easing up. Rain drummed the roof of the manse and pattered against the windows all night. Past midnight, peals of thunder and brilliant flashes of lightning had made it seem like they were still back at the line, enduring shelling.

By dawn, the electrical tumult had stopped, but the rain had got harder. It was as if the vast, black thunderheads were too heavy to clear the peaks of the Massif and had hooked there, deluging the forest like dirigibles trying to shed ballast.

From the streaming porch windows of the manse, Caffran could see out onto the gloomy garden at the front. Already overgrown by the time they'd pitched up the night before, it was now littered with torn leaves and broken boughs brought down in the night. Swirling rivers of rainwater gushed from the higher slopes of the rear gardens, via a hedged ditch on the east side of the manse, to the gate. A lower part of the lawn was actually underwater.

He went back down the hall to the kitchen. It was early still. From the drawing room, he could hear loud, bellicose snoring. No point disturbing those sleepers, he decided. Various pots and pans from the kitchen shelves stood on the floor of the hall and up some of the stairs, pinging and beating as they caught steady drips coming in from above. Caffran nudged one around with his foot, so it was more completely under a particularly busy trickle.

Mkvenner, Jajjo and Muril were in the kitchen. Ven was sitting at the table, studying the map and chewing on a C-bar ration. Muril was occupying the window bench, sipping a can of caffeine. Jajjo greeted Caffran and offered him a cup from the pot on the stove. He was munching on some leftovers from the previous night's meal.

Muril and Larkin had caught up with them about an hour after they'd entered the manse. Soaked through, they were carrying a knife-trimmed branch from which hung a plump buck. Nineteen detail had eaten well. Some of them had drunk well too.

'What's the plan?' Caffran asked, sitting down opposite Mkvenner.

'Don't ask me,' Mkvenner replied tersely, without looking up.

Caffran held up his hands in a gesture of surrender. 'Only asking,' he said.

Mkvenner sighed and sat back. 'Sorry, Caff. Didn't mean to snap.' He folded up his map, got up, and pulled his camo cape around him. 'I'll be outside, checking the perimeter.'

He stepped out into the torrential downpour and closed the door after him. The old latch fell with a clack.

'Feth!' said Caffran. 'What bit him on the arse?'

'He seems pretty normal to me,' muttered Muril. Her tone was as dreary as the daylight.

'Come on, that's grim, even by Ven's standards,' said Caffran.

'I think he's pretty gakked off with Feygor's attitude,' Jajjo said. 'He wanted to get an early start, move on into the woods, but they're all still sleeping it off. And... no one stood watch last night.'

'I did,' said Caffran.

Jajjo nodded. 'Yeah, all three of us did. But Brostin and Cuu were meant to do the small hours, and they didn't bother. They were too busy being unconscious.'

'Feth...' Caffran said. The idea alarmed him. He couldn't remember the last time he'd spent a night in the field without someone on perimeter. Anyone could have snuck up in the dark. The whole fething Shadik Republic could have snuck up in the dark.

'I'm gonna go wake Feygor up,' Caffran announced.

'Is that really a good idea?' asked Muril.

'No, maybe not.' Caffran reconsidered, sitting back down. 'The amount he was putting away last night, it's not going to be pretty this morning.'

'Him and Brostin and Gutes and Cuu,' said Jajjo, the level of his disapproval obvious. 'Like they were off duty.'

Caffran smiled. He liked Jajjo, but the man could be a real stuff-shirt sometimes. Though only Feygor and his drinking buddies had got wasted the night before, everyone had enjoyed the luxury of a glass or two, even Ven. But not Jajjo. Come to think of it, Caffran had never seen Jajjo drink.

'You got to cut them some slack,' Caffran told the Verghastite. 'I know we're on a tour here, but this is easy-hive compared to the line we were in. They're gonna blow off steam a little, given these opportunities.'

Jajjo sniffed. 'Whatever.'

They heard voices in the 'hall, and Larkin and Rerval entered the kitchen. Neither one of them had disgraced themselves the night before either, though Rerval had become a little tipsy. Larkin had disappeared early.

'Could be the weather,' Larkin was saying.

'It doesn't feel right,' replied Rerval. 'I'm not getting a signal at all.'

'What's the problem?' asked Caffran.

'Vox is down,' said Larkin, helping himself to caffeine.

'Vox isn't down,' Rerval insisted. 'There's something up with the caster set.'

'You sure?' said Muril. 'Could be the weather.'

'Don't you start,' Rerval said, shaking his head. 'I'm gonna have to strip it down. Once I've got some brew inside me.'

'Heavy head?' Jajjo asked, without sympathy.

'No,' replied Rerval. The intended rebuke had annoyed him. 'I slept badly. Kept waking up. This place is full of the strangest noises.'

'Yeah, I know what you mean,' said Caffran. 'How'd you sleep, Larks?'

'Like a baby,' said Larkin quietly. Caffran wondered where. The heavy drinkers had spent the night in the drawing room by the fire. The rest of them had occupied bedrooms on the first floor: Jajjo and Mkvenner in one, Rerval, Muril and Caffran in another.

'Well, I'm going to do something useful,' Jajjo announced. 'Cleaning up, maybe.'

'You're kidding!' said Muril.

'We left a mess in that dining room last night. This is somebody's house.'

'Somebody who left years ago,' said Rerval. 'This whole sector has been evacuated. Corbec told us so.'

'I still think it's polite. We're not looters. Well, I'm not anyway. Someday maybe, someone will come home here again.'

They were all looking at him.

'Oh, all right. If we stay here another day, we're going to need clean plates ourselves.'

Caffran sighed. 'I'll help,' he said.

The pair of them left the kitchen and walked back down the hall towards the dining room. The hall was dark, and they easily saw the little flash that briefly lit the windows. A short delay, and thunder growled distantly.

'Feth,' said Caffran. 'Is it ever going to let up?'

Jajjo paused in the doorway of the dining room. He was staring at something.

'What's up?' asked Caffran.

'That raincoat. It was on the coatstand last night when we came in.'

'Yeah, and it's still there.'

'Right. But now it's wet.'

A little puddle had collected on the tiles under the wooden stand.

Caffran glanced round and saw the look on Jajjo's face.

'Don't start. Someone used it last night, that's all.'

'Who?'

Caffran shrugged. 'I don't know! Someone very drunk, maybe? There are several candidates.'

Jajjo smiled, reassured. They went into the dining room and stopped dead.

The table was clean and wiped. The chairs set back in place. All the crockery was gone.

'What the feth–?' Caffran began.

'I thought we were supposed to be the ghosts,' Jajjo muttered.

'I said don't start–' Caffran snapped. His words were cut off by a sudden yelling from the drawing room.

And by a blast of las-fire.

'YOU FETHERS! You fethers!' Feygor was howling. Naked except for his undershorts, he was sitting up on his crumpled bedroll, his rifle in his hands. Caffran and Jajjo rushed in, blades drawn. A second later, Rerval, Larkin and Muril burst in from the kitchen.

The stuffed behj was lying on its back in front of Feygor, its head shot off. Sawdust drifted down in the air. On their own bedrolls around the room, Brostin, Gutes and Cuu were blinking awake.

'What the feth's going on?' asked Caffran.

'Those fethers!' Feygor squawked. 'I woke up and that fething thing was standing over me! Ha ha... very fething funny, you bastards! Who put it there?'

'You killed it for sure this time,' said Cuu and slumped back onto his mat.

'Who put it there?' demanded Feygor again.

Gutes shook his head.

'Bastards!' cried Feygor and kicked out at the stuffed beast.

'Did anyone put it there?' asked Caffran. There was a chorus of 'no' and 'not me'. He glanced at Jajjo before the dark-skinned trooper could speak. 'Don't even think about it,' he warned.

'I think this place is haunted,' Jajjo said anyway.

'Feth off!'

'You dumb gak!'

'I said don't go there,' Caffran admonished.

'Well, who washed up then, eh?' asked Jajjo.

There was a pause.

'I did,' said Gutes. Rerval and Caffran groaned.

'Feth you! Old habits die hard.' Gutes got to his feet and wandered off to find the can.

'Good old wash-bin Gutes,' smiled Larkin.

'I heard that, you fether,' Gutes's voice trailed back from the hall.

'And the stuffed animal?' snapped Caffran. 'Brostin? Had to be someone with a bit of muscle to move that thing.'

Brostin turned over in his bedroll, and put his hands behind his head. The pose emphasised the huge girth of his arms and pecs. He stared at Caffran. 'You accusing me, Caff?'

'Seems like your style, yeah.'

'Yeah, well... it was. Funny as feth, eh?' He closed his eyes and rolled over again.

'Bastard!' Feygor snarled, and threw a boot at him.

Caffran turned and ushered Larkin, Rerval, Muril and Jajjo out. 'Leave them to it,' he said.

Gutes was in the kitchen, drinking the last of the brewed caffeine.

'Thanks for putting the stuff away, though,' he said.

'What?' asked Caffran.

'The plates and stuff. I washed it all up, but I didn't know where it went, so I left it by the sink.'

He looked at their faces. 'What? What?'

BY NOON, EVERYBODY was up. Brostin, Feygor and Cuu were still in their underwear, grim and hungover. The rest of nineteen were kitted up, filling time.

Muril had found a regicide set from somewhere, and was playing a game with Larkin.

Rerval came into the kitchen. 'Which of you fethers took it?' he asked.

'Took what?' Feygor asked.

'The caster's down because someone took out the main transmission circuit. I don't carry a spare for that. Who's got it?'

There was a general shrugging and shaking of heads.

'Come on–'

'We're not tech-heads, Rerval. We don't feth around with tech-kit,' said Brostin. 'Do I look like an adept of the Mechanicus?'

'Someone did it. Clean job too. Mister Feygor?'

'Why are you looking at me, trooper?'

'Maybe you thought we'd get to stay here an extra night or two and enjoy the facilities if we unexpectedly lost contact.'

Feygor set down his mug. 'You know what, Rerval? I wish I'd thought of that. I really do. It's neat, it's sneaky. It serves my purpose. But I was planning on staying here a while anyway, vox-link or no vox-link. I didn't feth with your beloved caster.'

He leaned forward, staring Rerval in the face. 'Don't ever fething accuse me of crap again, you little bastard.'

Rerval blinked and looked away suddenly.

'Sorry,' he said.

'Sorry what?' snapped Feygor. Everyone looked on, stony-faced. Caffran didn't like what he was seeing. Feygor was a bully, with a mean-streak as wide as the Kottmark Massif.

'Sorry, "Mister Feygor".'

'Better,' said Feygor, leaning back.

'Sure as sure,' murmured Cuu from the rear of the room.

Feygor yawned. 'Anyone want to tell me about this circuit? While we're on the topic? Like I said, it suits me fine, the vox being down, but I'd like to know who sabotaged it. Anyone?'

No one spoke.

'Okay–' said Feygor with a wicked smile. 'If our culprit would like to fit it back into the little whining bastard's caster-set in... oh, three days? That'd be fine and I won't mention it to Corbec. Understood?'

The troopers shifted awkwardly. Thunder was still grumbling around the forest and the rain was lashing down. Feygor looked over at Brostin. 'Go and get some wine,' he said.

Brostin got up and shambled out.

'Are we not moving today?' asked Caffran.

'Do I look like I'm moving, Caff? Do I?'

'No, Mister Feygor.'

'Then I'm probably not moving.'

'We should–' Jajjo began.

'And not a word from you, Verghast. Okay?' Feygor rocked his chair onto its back legs. 'Look,' he said, slightly more softly. 'Have you seen this weather? It isn't letting up. The way I call it, we stay put until it breaks. We'd be mad to try and push on in this. No offence, Larks.'

'None taken,' said Larkin.

'Anybody else got a problem with that? Anybody else got a problem with me being in charge? Because I seem to remember that's the way Colonel Corbec wanted it.'

The back door opened, and Mkvenner came in, water streaming off the folds of his cape. He looked around at the silent assembly of figures.

'I take it we're not going anywhere,' he said darkly.

'Any contacts?' Feygor asked him.

Mkvenner shook his head. 'Nothing. Perimeter's secure. The area's quiet. Though someone or something's disturbed one of the outhouses. Like someone's been sleeping out there.'

'Recently?' Feygor asked.

'Couldn't tell,' Mkvenner said.

'We won't worry about it, then.'

'Your call,' said Mkvenner.

'Why, yes it is,' said Feygor.

Mkvenner paused. 'Mission requirements call for us to scope this valley,' he said.

'And we will,' said Feygor.

'When?'

'When I'm ready,' Feygor said, looking round at Mkvenner. 'You ought to relax, Ven.'

'There're many things I ought to do, Mister Feygor. But I won't.'

Feth, thought Caffran. This could turn really ugly.

'Tell you what, Ven,' said Feygor. 'You want to scope so badly, you go ahead. You'll move faster without us. Head out, get the lie of the land, and swing back. By then, the weather may have cleared.'

'Is that an order?'

'Yeah, why not? Run a deep patrol, check things out, come back here. Once the storm's gone, we'll move out and finish the sweep with you. Think of us as base camp. As HQ. We'll hold things here.'

Mkvenner had an icy look in his eyes. 'Should we check that with Ins Arbor base?' he asked.

'Ah, sadly, vox is down,' Feygor said, with a contented smile.

Mkvenner looked around the kitchen. 'Okay. I'll be gone a day, tops.'

'The Emperor protects,' said Feygor.

Brostin came back in, his arms full of wine bottles. 'These do?' he asked.

'They most certainly will,' said Feygor.

Mkvenner took one last contemptuous look at Brostin, Feygor and the bottles, and left.

'VEN! VEN!' CAFFRAN called out as he ran through the rain, up the back plot of the manse, after the retreating scout.

Mkvenner stopped and waited for him. Thunder clashed above them.

'This isn't right,' said Caffran.

'Yeah, but it's what's happening.'

'Feygor's out of line.'

Mkvenner nodded. 'He is. But he's got command of this detail. What are you going to do? Mutiny?'

'Corbec would understand.'

'Yes, he would. But if you or I get into a clash with Feygor, it could get nasty long before Corbec arrives to intervene. It's crap, but it's better just left.'

Caffran shrugged. 'We could just go with you.'

'We?'

'Me, Muril, Rerval... probably Larks. Jajjo definitely. Maybe even Gutes.'

Thunder rolled again.

'I'll take Jajjo. Send him on up.'

'That's it?'

Mkvenner fixed Caffran with a fierce stare. 'Think about it this way. I'd be happy to sit out a few days in that place, getting plastered and telling old stories. But there's a job to do. There's a chance... just a chance... that there's enemy activity in this forest. And while that chance exists, I'm going to look for it.'

'Yeah and–'

Ven held up a finger to silence Caffran. 'In an ideal galaxy, we'd all go. The way we were meant to. But thanks to Murtan Feygor, this isn't an ideal galaxy. So we improvise. That's what we're good at, after all. If I find something out there, Emperor protect me, I'd like to have a patrol fire-team at my back. Failing that, I'd like to know there's a secure, well-defended strongpoint position not too far away at my heels. Stay here, Caff. Right here. Get Muril, Rerval, Larkin – maybe even Gutes, like you said – and lock this place up ready. Just in case.'

'Okay. If that's what you want.'

'It's what I want. Not what I'd wish for, but it'll do. As far as I'm concerned, you're in charge here now. Hold the manse and wait for me. Feygor can get his when we get back. I'll see to it personally. For now, let's just worry about getting the job done and not fething up.'

Caffran nodded.

Mkvenner took his hand and gripped it tight. 'I'm relying on you.'

'Signal when you can.'

'Not a lot of range on these micro-beads. No more than a league or two in these woods.'

'Do it anyway. If it's bad news... make the signal "comeuppance".'

Mkvenner smiled. Caffran hadn't seen him do that very often.

'Okay. Send Jajjo up. I'll see you in a day and a night.'

Caffran stood and watched Mkvenner stride away through the rain until he had vanished into the edge of the wood.

Thunder boomed.

'WHERE'S JAJJO?' ASKED Muril, wandering into the kitchen. The storm had worsened and the light was bad. From the drawing room, they could hear sounds of laughter and drunken antics.

'He's gone with Ven,' said Caffran.

Muril sat down on the window bench. 'Oh, that's just typical!' she said venomously.

'Calm down,' said Rerval.

'Bite me, Tanith! This whole tour's turning into crap,' she complained.

There was a particularly loud roar from the drawing room. A crash. Laughter.

'What are they doing?' asked Caffran.

'Using that stuffed thing as a battering ram,' said Rerval. 'I think the game is to see how long one of them can stay on its back with the others running it around the room.'

'Children,' Muril said, acidly.

'Listen,' said Caffran. 'I spoke to Ven. He thinks there's no point going up against Feygor. But he wants us to hold this place, in case.'

'In case of what?' asked Rerval.

'In case he and Jajjo find something out there. Okay? Where's Larkin?'

Rerval shrugged.

'Muril, you seen Larks recently?'

'No,' she said, preoccupied. 'Why the gak does Jajjo get to scout? Why the gak does that happen?'

'Just forget it,' said Caffran. 'We have to focus. We'll take watches. Two hours on. You handle the first one, Muril?'

'Sure,' she said.

'Rerval. Sweep the perimeter and then start building cover for us. Anything you can find.'

Rerval nodded. 'What'll you be doing, Caff?'

'I'm going to find Larks,' he said.

NIGHT FELL. THE rainstorm continued to hammer the forest and drench the manse. In one of the outbuildings, an old greenhouse at the edge of the rear yard, facing north, Muril cowered and shivered, watching the tree-line. It was just a dark expanse of trunks half-screened by the sheeting rain.

Rerval brought her a cup of hot caffeine and a plate of sliced salt beef.

'Been busy?' she asked him.

'There's not a lot to use, but I managed to raise a barricade across the yard at the back of the kitchen. And I boarded up some of the ground floor windows at the back.

'Where's Caffran?'

'Doing the rounds,' he said.

CAFFRAN WAS ACTUALLY emptying pots. No one had bothered to tip out the pots and pans that had been standing under the drips, and now some of them were overflowing. He opened the front door and slung each one empty into the downpour.

Light bled into the hallway from the drawing room, along with raucous noise and the smell of a decent fire. Caffran could hear Brostin telling a coarse story, and Cuu and Gutes exploding into laughter. A bottle broke. There was another, stranger sound that Caffran realised was Feygor laughing too, choking the noise in and out of his augmetic throat.

Caffran shuddered.

He closed the front door. He hadn't been able to find Larkin anywhere. He looked at the coatstand. The raincoat had gone.

The drawing room door burst open and Gutes tumbled out. Light and heat and laughter spilled out around him.

'More wine!' he exclaimed.

'Haven't you had enough?' Caffran asked.

'Don't be so fething uptight, Caff!' Gutes replied. 'Why don't you join us. We're having a fine time.'

'So I heard.'

'Makes a change from the fething war!' Gutes slurred.

'The war's still going on,' smiled Caffran.

Gutes looked sad. He pulled the door shut, cutting out the sounds of merrymaking. He leaned against the hall wall and slid down until he was sitting.

'I know. I know. It never lets up, does it? War. There's only war. It's the only future we've got. Dark? Yes! Grim? Oh, yes, sir! There's only ever war!'

'Don't worry about it, Piet,' Caffran reassured.

'I don't, Caff, I don't,' Gutes mumbled. 'I'm just so tired, you know? Just so very fething tired of it all. I'm worn out. I've had enough.'

Caffran crouched down beside the intoxicated trooper.

'Get off to bed, Piet. Things'll seem better in the morning.'

Gutes struggled up to his feet. Caffran had to help him.

'Things seem better now, Caff! They really do. I gotta get more bottles.' He lurched away towards the cellar door.

Caffran thought about trying to stop him, but decided not to. Gutes was too far gone.

He heard a creak on the stairs above him, and quickly brought round his lasrifle, switching on the lamp pack under the barrel.

Halfway down the stairs, a little old woman flinched at the sudden, fierce beam of light. She was wearing a raincoat, and it was dripping wet.

Caffran's light illuminated Larkin beside her. He was smiling as he steadied the old woman's arm.

'Hey, Caff,' he said. 'Look who I found…'

TEN
SANTREBAR MILL

'Blood for land: the commerce of war.'

– Satacus, 'Of the Great Sezars'

The Republic subjected sectors 57 and 58 of the Peinforq Line to a sustained gas attack during the morning. The wind, a brisk westerly, favoured their enterprise, and carried the gas swiftly into the Alliance fire trenches: so swiftly, in fact, Alliance respirator drill was found wanting. Men died in dreadful numbers. Three hundred and forty-eight in one five-kilometre stretch alone. Hundreds more were brought out of the reeking amber mist, frothing and blistering, screaming and crying.

A fitful barrage responded to the gas attack. Less modest artillery quaked the earth for over an hour to the north, in 59th sector.

The gas took a long time to dissipate, and the Shadik had undoubtedly been planning on that. At a few minutes before 15.00, a considerable portion of the 57th sector fire trench was assaulted by a brigade of raiders who had advanced under cover of the chemical fog. For a period of about twenty-five minutes, savage, blind fighting occurred at the 57th, and there seemed a genuine danger that the line would be penetrated. The timely arrival of a detachment of the Bande Sezari, as well as a company of elite Kottsmark chemtroops, tipped the scales. Then the wind turned, and the poison smog began to drift east off the Peinforq defences. The Shadik raiders beat their retreat.

By then, this possible opportunity had been anticipated, and Alliance Staff Command 57th/58th opted to press. Cavalry and light foot elements were pushed through to overtake the raiders then continue on for a counter-attack. They were supplemented by armour.

Alliance armour was in the main ponderous, primitive, rhomboidal tanks with heavy roof or sponson guns. These sluggish giants rumbled their way out into the Pocket. They were menacing, but had not achieved much success in anything but psychological terms since their first employment twelve years earlier. However, on this day, five Imperial Guard Thunderers, spared from the action at Gibsgatte, led them out. By evening, they had made a memorable dent in the Shadik lines. It was the first demonstration of modern armour superiority witnessed on Aexe Cardinal.

At the time of the first toxin shelling, the First was laid up in a secondary line, awaiting the evening advance to the fire trench. They had decent warning time on their side, but their respirator drill was excellent anyway. They sat tight, until word started to come in of the raid on the 57th sector. Daur went to see Gaunt immediately.

'We can reinforce,' he suggested. 'We're close enough to do some good.'

Gaunt refused the idea. He'd worked hard to secure a legitimate role in the Alliance for both arms of the First, and he wasn't about to upset that stability with a show of unilateral bravado. However much he wanted to.

'Stand three platoons to,' he conceded to Daur finally. 'If command requests us, we'll move at once.'

They waited, tense, for an hour or so. When the wind turned and the counter-assault pushed through, Gaunt and Golke moved down to an observation post on the hem of the secondary line.

Borrowing Gaunt's magnoculars, Golke watched the steady advance of the tanks, his gaze lingering over the heavy-set, trundling shapes of the Guard armour pieces. The Thunderers were painted mustard drab, and moved forward with their siege-dozers lowered, ripping through piquet lines and thorny barricades of wire. Sprays of liquid mud kicked up from their churning treads.

Golke was seriously impressed. He spoke for a while about armour clashes he'd witnessed, though he was so preoccupied with what he was seeing there was no real thread to his talk. Gaunt understood that Golke had received his injuries during one of these clashes, but he didn't want to press the count for details. Golke mentioned 'dreadnoughts', yet the word did not seem to mean the same thing for him as it did for Gaunt. To an Aexegarian, 'dreadnought' was a catch-all word for any armoured war machine.

Whistles were blowing all along the trench system to sound all-clear. The gas had washed out of the line. Gaunt took off his respirator and wiped his sweat-damp face. The afternoon light was good and clear, grey and bright, except for the roiling yellow fume of the departing gas that blanketed no-man's land.

'Nightfall's at 19.40,' Golke remarked. He produced a data-slate. 'I have a schedule for tonight's barrages. When do you want to move out?'

It was a legitimate question. Provided he informed Allied GSC, the timing of the Ghosts' next raid was down to him.

Gaunt looked at the Aexegarian. 'Now,' he said.

THE MAIN FIELD infirmary of 58th sector was a large system of bunkers situated amidst the reserve and tiring trenches at the back of the line, west of the main gun-pits and artillery dens. Set well underground, beneath a roof of rockcrete and flak-sacks, it was said to have its own shield umbrella too, but Dorden didn't believe that.

However, the facilities were decent. Curth had made strenuous efforts, since they'd moved north, to secure fresh supplies from the Munitorium fleet, and Mkoll had taken his own platoon back to escort the supplies and make sure they arrived unmolested. Many of the First, Dorden included, had been surprised that Mkoll had not been part of the regiment's eastward deployment to the Montorq.

'Scouts are needed here too,' Mkoll had told Dorden when the subject came up. 'I'm not about to head for the forest and expect the lads I leave here to do something I wouldn't do myself.'

There was an implication in the master-scout's remark, Dorden felt. Whatever happened out in the Montorq, good or bad, only bad was going to happen here. The Pocket was going to see action, no matter what. Mkoll's selfless sense of duty wasn't going to let him shirk.

When the First had been moved up to the 58th sector, Dorden had packed up his field hospital at Rhonforq and brought it with him, wounded and all, so he could maintain personal care for them and be on hand for the new fighting. That afternoon, gas-attack victims poured into the infirmary's triage hall. None of them were Ghosts, but Dorden and his medicae staff didn't hesitate. They sprang up to support the Alliance surgeons, bathing eyes, treating burns, washing poisons out of cloth and bubbling flesh. The respiratory damage was the worst. There was little they could do for the victims with fluid-filled, drowning lungs except try to stabilise them.

Dorden worked urgently. He dearly missed Foskin and Doctor Mtane, who had both gone west with the Montorq mission. He wanted to trust the ministrations of the Alliance surgeons, many of whom were devoted, good men, but their medical practices seemed so terribly outmoded. He took careful note of the treatment deficiencies he saw, and hoped there would be an opportunity for him to advise the sector's chief of medicine on better, less barbarous techniques. At least three troopers he saved that afternoon were dying as a direct result of treatment rather than gas.

A terrible stench of chemical burns and corrupted blood filled the infirmary. Frothy, discoloured waste matter wept in lakes across the stone floor. Corpsmen turned on the roof vents and hosed with disinfectant, but it didn't do much good.

'Feth!' muttered Rawne. 'The smell is going to choke me to death!'

'Will it make you stop talking?' asked Banda. He looked across the aisle at her cot with a withering stare, but she just grinned. She was pale, and a cut above her right eye was black with stitches. Her mending lungs were having a hard time coping with the wretched air. Still, she found the breath to taunt him.

Rawne got up off his cot, and sat carefully. The ward hall was full of Ghosts, as well as a few Krassians, casualties from that first trench fight at the 55th sector. Many, like Rawne, were healing well, but it would be a long time before they could be pronounced fit for active duty. Rawne wondered how many more Ghosts would come through these halls before the present occupants made their way out.

The days since he had been wounded had passed at a dishearteningly slow crawl. Rawne felt detached and very much out of the loop, even though he'd been brought regular reports. He wanted to get up and out, but not because he was such a dutiful soldier he needed to get back to play his part.

He was distressed at the prospect of what feth-heads like Daur might be doing in his absence.

'What are you doing?' asked Banda.

He didn't reply. He grabbed hold of the back of a wooden chair and slowly dragged himself to his feet. The pain in his stomach, which had been a dormant ache for the last thirty hours, started to throb again.

'What are you doing?' Banda repeated. 'Doc Dorden'll have your guts.'

'Feels like he already has,' Rawne snapped.

He took a deep breath, and let go of the chair back.

God-Emperor, it was hard. It felt like his legs had atrophied. It felt like someone had upturned a live brazier in his belly. It felt like someone was stabbing a bayonet into his spine.

'What are you doing?' Banda repeated for the third time. Then added, 'Major?'

That did it. Rawne hadn't been addressed by rank for what seemed like an age. Especially by Jessi Banda. If he but admitted it, that had been the best part of this enforced stay in the ward. Jammed together by the proximity of their beds, the comatose nature of their immediate neighbours, and their shared suffering at station 293, they had provided conversational company for one another. It wasn't a friendship, exactly. Rawne certainly wouldn't acknowledge anything like that, but they'd talked, and played boredom-defeating word games, and joked occasionally. After the first few hours of them being cooped up together involuntarily, she had stopped calling him major and he'd stopped calling her trooper. They had formed a cordial, sparring companionship as a reaction to their situation.

'I'm going for a breath of fresh air,' Rawne said, panting.

'Oh, what? And leave me here? And I thought we were mates.'

It was too much effort to shoot her another withering stare. It was almost too much effort to remain standing. 'Just...' he said. 'Just...'

'What?' Banda asked.

He sighed. 'Can you get up?'

'Can I gak.'

'Oh, for feth's sake...' Slowly, very slowly, he plodded round the end of his cot and grabbed hold of a wheelchair that had been folded up against the foot of the next bunk. It took him a moment to force the spring-shot seat back into place, and he almost fell doing it.

'Careful!' she said.

'Like you care...'

He got the chair stable and shuffled it across to her bedside, leaning hard on the handles.

'Come on,' he said.

She looked up at him. 'Gakking well help, then.'

Setting the chair's brake, he got her by the wrists, and levered her forward to the edge of the cot. He could hear the wheeze in her lungs.

'Maybe we shouldn't–'

'You started this, Rawne,' she said.

'On three. You'll have to help me. One, two...'

She almost missed the seat completely. As it was, she had to wriggle around once she'd got her breath back. Rawne leaned over, doubled up, dizzy from the pain in his gut.

'Okay?' she said.

'Oh, sure...'

He grabbed the handles of the chair, kicked off the brake after a couple of feeble tries, and trundled her up the aisle towards the exit. Pushing really hurt his fethed-up gut.

But at least now he had something to lean on.

BANDA WAS CHUCKLING to herself. Despite the real and growing pain in his stomach, Rawne realised he was smiling too. There was a genuine sense of escape. A comradely feel of fellow prisoners sticking together and making a break for freedom.

And there was an agreeable sensation of flaunting the system that Rawne hadn't felt since he'd been coining it as part of Tanith Attica's black market.

The two invalids edged up the infirmary's exit ramp and out into the firing trench. It was their first sight of daylight in a while. He wheeled Banda along the duckboards as far as a waystation, pausing every few metres to rest, and then got an arm around her and manhandled her up into a vacant obs post. By then, they were both exhausted, and they flopped down onto the sandbags, leaning their backs to the parapet face.

Yet they were both sniggering too.

The pain in Rawne's belly flared for a while, but slowly it subsided now he was no longer exerting himself. They both took deep breaths, enjoying the fresh air. It wasn't fresh, exactly. There was a reek of mud, general sweat, wet sacking, fyceline, promethium, fungus, sour food, latrines. But it was light years better than the gas-corrupted waste-stink that permeated the infirmary.

'We ought to do this more often,' she quipped, clearly in pain but relishing the escape.

'Now I know what Corbec meant,' he replied.

'What?'

Rawne looked at her. 'He's had a tough run, this last while. Wounded, bedridden. He told me the thing he missed worst, what hurt him worst, was missing stuff. The physical pain of injuries didn't matter so much. It was losing his place in things.'

She nodded.

'I didn't appreciate what he meant, really. I thought getting wounded was a vacation. And that you'd be too taken up with your injury to worry about anything else. But he was right. It feels like I've been buried and left for dead and the galaxy has moved on without me.'

There was a long pause. A detachment of Fichuan Infantry tramped past along the reserve trench below them. Somewhere, muffled, a field-vox jangled.

'Why did you order me not to die?' she asked.

'What?'

'In the trench. I heard you. I couldn't answer, but I heard you. You ordered me not to die.'

He thought about it. 'Because I didn't want the bother of finding a new platoon sniper,' he said.

The trace of a smile crossed her lips and she nodded sagely. 'That's what I thought,' she said.

Rawne got up and looked down over the sandbag wall into the reserve trench. Troops were coming and going. A dirty, black ATV grumbled past, laden with shells for the feldkannones and hessian-bagged rockets for the shargen-launchers.

'Something's up,' he commented.

'What?'

'Beltayn just came running up and went into the infirmary.'

'Ah,' Banda said, knowingly. 'You mean something's awry…'

* * *

'I'm a little occupied, Adjutant Beltayn,' Dorden remarked as he made yet another attempt to rinse the eyes of a screaming, thrashing Aexe trooper.

'I can see that, doctor,' Beltayn said.

'So it'll have to wait.'

'With respect, doctor, the colonel-commissar said you'd say that. He said to tell you that the infiltration unit is moving out in fifteen minutes and–'

'And?'

'And you should move your fething arse. His words.'

'Really?' said Dorden. 'I thought he wasn't mobilising until tonight?'

Beltayn said something that was drowned out by a particularly curdled shriek from the man on the gurney.

'I said... change of plan, doctor. We've got daylight cover. The gas, you see? And a whole bundle of distractions. There's a counter-push going on. Tanks and everything.'

'I just can't leave this, Beltayn,' Dorden said. He'd promised Gaunt he'd move out with the next patrol in the hope they'd find some of Raglon's platoon, but he hadn't counted on a triage hall full of chem-burned men.

'Go, Tolin. I can handle it,' said Curth, appearing from nowhere, her apron stained with bile and foam.

'You sure, Ana?'

'Yes. Just go.' She started to apply herself to the thrashing victim.

'Hold him!' she snarled at the stretcher bearers standing nearby. They jumped to help.

Dorden yanked off his smeared gloves and scrub-top and tossed them into a soil-bin. He took a fresh apron from the laundered rack, and started to fill his medicae kit from the supply shelves.

'We haven't got much time,' Beltayn urged.

'Then be a good man and get my jacket and camo-cape from the side office. They're on the peg.'

Dorden buttoned up his kit and slung it over his shoulder. 'Attention!' he yelled above the tumult of the ward. 'Be advised that Surgeon Curth is now in operational control here. No excuses, no exceptions. Go through her.'

Beltayn returned, and helped Dorden into his black, First-issue field jacket.

'Good luck!' called Curth.

'Keep it,' he replied. 'You'll need it more.'

Pulling his cape around his shoulders, Dorden hurried up the entrance ramp of the infirmary behind Beltayn.

'You say he's decided to go in daylight?' he asked.

'Yes, doctor. I heard him telling Count Golke that stealth works even when it's not quiet. He wants to make use of the noise and gas and confusion to get back to where the teams were last night.'

'I see. We have to go back. I've left my respirator behind.'

Beltayn turned and winked. 'I brought that too,' he said.

'You think of everything,' Dorden mocked.

'That's my job,' said Beltayn, without a hint of irony.

They ran out into the reserve trench and hurried along north towards the first communications spur running east. Dorden suddenly stopped and looked back. Beltayn skidded to a halt.

'What the feth are you doing up there?' Dorden yelled at a nearby obs tower.

'Feeling better already!' Rawne shouted back, giving a little wave. 'Good hunting, doctor!'

'Just... just take your medicine!' Dorden yelled at Rawne in frustration, then followed Beltayn up the trench.

RAWNE SAT BACK down and produced a hip-flask from his pocket. He unscrewed the cap and offered it to Banda.

'What is it?' she asked.

'Sacra. The best. The very last of Bragg's legendary brew.'

'Don't know if I should,' she said.

'You heard our venerable medic,' Rawne said. 'Take your medicine.'

Laughing as hard as their painful wounds permitted, they drank to one another's health.

THE INFILTRATORS WENT over the top and into the dead lands of the Pocket at a minute before five in the afternoon. Four platoons – Criid's, Domor's, Mkoll's and Arcuda's – along with a command team of Gaunt, Dorden, Zweil, Beltayn, Count Golke and four elite troopers from the Bande Sezari.

Respirator masks clamped on, they extended into the soupy veil of the drifting gas, which wrapped the landscape with a tobacco-yellow stain. Visibility was down to twenty metres, though the overall light was good. A bland glow of daylight bathed them through the toxin clouds, white and flat.

Scout Hwlan, from Criid's platoon, took point, along with Mkoll himself and 'Lucky' Bonin from Domor's mob. Hwlan had found the mill the night before, and they were trusting his instincts to lead them in.

To Hwlan, an experienced scout with many years as a tracker in the nalwoods of Tanith in his past, it was a strange experience. Many said the Tanith could never get lost, and claimed they had the most unerring sense of direction. The constantly shifting trees of Tanith had bred that into them.

That was the theory, anyway.

The chemical attack had changed the ground, baking the mud so dry it had begun to crack. Underneath it was wet and soft, and the feet of the troopers cracked the surface as they advanced, spilling up mud as fluid and yellow as custard.

Vague landmarks from the previous night – a broken tree, a fence of wire, a dead tank – had solidified and become permanent, but they'd also been changed by the action of gas. The Pocket had become a dead space of embalmed features, desiccated, fused, chemically transmuted.

The point men reached a wire barricade that collapsed into rust as they touched it. The liquid chemicals accreted in some crater holes were burning.

And there were so many corpses. Dorden was shocked. Fresh corpses, hooked in wire or lying on the ground, so florid they looked like they were still alive. Others, older, hunched and flattened into the postures of submission only dead men can afford. Others, older still, cadaverous and dry, opening their bones to the sky.

It was also grimly silent. There was no wind, and the gas clouds stifled all noise. A bright, dry desert of war, lethal to the touch and the merest breath.

Gaunt placed Milo and Nehn from Domor's platoon with Zweil. The old ayatani was a newcomer to gas gear and was clearly uncomfortable with the mask and the thick gloves. He'd cinched up the skirts of his long coat so that they wouldn't drag in the mire, revealing an incongruous, borrowed pair of heavy Aexegarian army boots. Gaunt could hear a mumbling over the vox. Zweil was quietly reciting a prayer of protection. Gaunt signalled Milo to show the priest how to turn off his micro-bead.

'I appreciate your blessings, father,' he said, 'but perhaps for now you could keep them to yourself inside your hood. We need the link quiet.'

The riven landscape curled up over a long ridge where the mud was covered in a mosaic of bones, human and hippine. They saw the occasional rusting scrap of a respirator valve, a saddle buckle, the bent barrel of a carbine. On the far side of the ridge, the ground shelved away into a wide basin where a brackish crescent of water shone in the flat light. Old piquets marched in a line down the slope and disappeared into the pool. Along the eastern shore of the water, the mud was crinkled into strange patches that reminded Gaunt of rose blooms. Shards of ashy glass clung to the folds of each patch. He realised they were the impact marks of gas bottles from a previous attack. The mud had baked and puckered with the intensity of the leaking toxins.

An Alliance trooper stood on the far side of the pool, headless. His rotting body was held up by the metal stake he'd fallen against.

The trio of scouts led them round the side of the basin, and out over its lowest lip. They entered a flat area covered in shell craters some large enough to swallow a man, others just pock-marks the size of a fist. The craters overlapped each other, small inside large, large intersecting with larger. The pattern was so dense and seemed so deliberate, it was surreal. To their north, on a bank of mud, lay the burnt-black carcass of a Shadik tank.

Mkoll indicated they should turn south a little, but Golke consulted his chart and advised against it. A row of crossed timbers suggested to him the edge of a mined area. Old munitions, but it was stupid to risk it, and they weren't set for sweeping work. In order to move light, landmine experts like Domor had left their sweeper sets at the line.

They moved north-east instead, following a mangled ridge, plodding through murky strands of water and oil. To their left was a series of waterlogged pits absolutely choked with bodies, as if the dead had all decided to congregate in one place. Zweil realised he was glad of his mask.

Since they'd set out, they'd been able to hear the roaring of the counter-assault pushing ahead of them, a little to the south. Now they heard a deeper, more booming noise. Boxed in by the gas-clouded air, they could see nothing, but Gaunt was sure it was the Shadik super-siege weapons opening up at the Peinforq Line in response to the push.

'Any way we can fix a source at all?' Gaunt asked Mkoll without much hope. Mkoll gestured at the hood he was wearing.

'Not really,' he replied. He thought about it and listened to the thumps. 'Best guess is that way,' he pointed. 'But it's vague.'

Gaunt turned to Hwlan. 'How far to this mill?'

'Another half kilometre. We're approaching from a slightly different angle to last night. There's a creek, with a fence nearby, and then the mill itself in a wide hollow.'

'It's more like three-quarters of a kilometre,' said Golke over the link, wiping specks of mud off his chart's plastic cover. 'And slightly more to the south.'

Gaunt looked back at Hwlan. Through the lens-plates of his bulky hood, he could see Hwlan shake his head slightly.

'With respect, sir,' Gaunt told Golke, 'I have to trust my scout.'

Golke didn't seem abashed. He was quickly coming to admire the First's field skills.

They moved on. In less than fifteen minutes, they were drawing in on the south-eastern side of the ruined mill, just a vague shape in the fog of gas.

Hwlan had been spot on.

It looked quiet, empty. Perhaps the Shadik had been unable to resecure it since the previous night. No sense taking chances, though.

The Ghosts advanced, low. Gaunt spread Criid's platoon in a semicircle to his right, and Mkoll's and Domor's wider to the left, with Arcuda's in place to the rear, ready to support.

The troop got to within fifty metres of the shattered mill.

'Hold,' Gaunt signalled. Down, hidden under their capes, the Ghosts lined up their weapons, studying the ruin for movement. Gaunt gestured to Mkoll.

The master scout began to slide forward under his cape. To Golke, he seemed to all but vanish. Bonin and Hwlan quickly followed Mkoll, along with Oflyn, the scout from Arcuda's platoon.

After ten seconds, Mkoll voxed. 'Clear. We're at the outside wall. Two big rockcrete beams fallen in a V-shape. See them?'

Gaunt acknowledged. Golke tried to see the beams. Even when he found them, he couldn't see the Tanith.

'Move up the assault squad,' Mkoll linked.

The squad came up, and Gaunt advanced with them. Six men: Domor, Luhan, Vril and Harjeon, with Dremmond and Lubba and their flamers. Gaunt left fire command with Criid.

They reached Mkoll's position. The scouts were ready to go in. Dremmond and Lubba prepped their flames.

'On three–' said Gaunt.

'Wait!' Bonin voxed. 'Movement. Up, to the left. The rafters over the far window.'

Before Gaunt had time to take a look, a shot zipped out of the mill and went over their heads, followed by another that smacked off a tie-beam Luhan was using for cover.

'Wait!' Gaunt yelled, just before his men started to return fire and hose the south face of the mill.

The shots had been las-rounds.

Gaunt adjusted the setting of his micro-bead. 'One, who's up there?'

A pause. Faint static on the link.

'One,' Gaunt repeated. 'Identify.'

'Two-oh-three, one,' came the response.

It was Raglon.

ELEVEN
THE DUTIFUL

'Cuu's a fething maniac, Larks…'

– Trooper Bragg (deceased), on Phantine

SHE WOULDN'T TALK. She wouldn't even take off her raincoat. She allowed Larkin and Caffran to lead her into the gloomy kitchen and sit her at one of the chairs by the table.

She flinched as Rerval suddenly came in from outside. He looked at the old woman in confusion.

'She was hiding upstairs,' Larkin told him. 'I was… patrolling and I heard a noise and I found her. She's our ghost.'

Caffran poured a hot drink from the stove and set it on the table beside her.

'Drink up,' he said. 'You look hungry. And cold.'

She looked up at Caffran slowly, her old eyes not blinking. There was something far away in her gaze that suggested she didn't really see him.

'Drink up, ma'am,' said Caffran again, encouragingly. She didn't. Her gaze returned to the glow of the stove plate.

'What do you mean she's our ghost?' Rerval asked Larkin.

'Moving things, you know. Putting the plates away. She's been here all the time, hiding from us.'

'How do you know?'

Larkin shrugged.

'Hey, do you think she took the circuit out of my vox?' Rerval said suddenly. 'Did you mess with my vox-caster, mother?' he asked.

The sudden voice made her flinch again.

Larkin took Rerval by the arm and tugged him back. 'Have a heart, lad. She's scared witless. I promised her we wouldn't hurt her.'

'Of course we won't hurt her,' said Caffran. 'We won't, ma'am.'

'Besides,' Larkin added, 'I don't see an old girl like this having the knack to disable a piece of Guard kit. Smash it, maybe. Lift the primary transmission circuit? I don't think so.'

'Who the feth is she?' Rerval whispered. 'Apart from being our ghost, I mean. Do you think she just came here to shelter?'

'Doesn't feel like that to me,' said Larkin. 'The way she cares about the place. Tidies stuff away, hangs up her coat. I think this house is hers. Her home.'

'But this whole area was evacuated years ago,' said Rerval. 'That's what the colonel told us. Why would she still be here?'

'Sometimes people don't want to leave,' said Larkin. 'Old, set in her ways, tied by memories to this place. Maybe she chose not to.'

'Then she could have been here for ages. Years.'

'Waiting for the invaders to come. Hoping they wouldn't,' Larkin murmured.

Caffran looked at the frail old woman. She was still immobile, placid. Her hair was silver, almost white, pinned back tightly with small metal clips. Her clothes were clean, but old and faded, and her little leather buckle-on shoes were worn. He could see the sole was coming away from one of them. The only reaction she made, every once in a while, was to wince and look round at any loud noise emanating from the drawing room. The crash of a glass breaking. A thump. Brostin's booming laugh.

We're invaders, he thought, invaders in her home.

'Why's her coat wet?' he asked suddenly.

'What?'

'If she's been hiding from us here, why's she been going outside? In the rain? And if she's been hiding, why hang her coat up where we can see it?'

Larkin frowned. 'I don't know. Maybe we should check around outside again when it gets light. The outhouse Ven mentioned. He said he thought someone had been sleeping out there.'

'Someone else?' asked Caffran.

'Maybe.'

'Should we tell Feygor about her?' Rerval asked.

'Feth, no! Not tonight. Not the state he's in. Do you want to scare her even more?'

Rerval considered Caffran's words. 'No,' he said. 'There must be some clue as to who she is. I'll nose around.'

'Okay,' said Caffran. 'Stay with her, Larks. I'll go tell Muril about her and advise her to keep her eyes peeled for any other houseguests.'

* * *

Rerval and Caffran had both been gone for ten minutes, and Larkin had simply sat there in the kitchen with the old woman, listening to the rain and the spit of the stove. The wind was getting up again, and the thunder was rumbling closer.

Cuu was suddenly just standing there in the kitchen doorway. The old woman started, and Larkin looked up sharply.

'Hey, Tanith. Who's your girlfriend?' Cuu said. His eyes were hooded and he swayed slightly.

'Go back to your drinking, Cuu,' said Larkin softly.

'We got hungry. I came for some food. Where'd you get this old witch from?'

'She was hiding,' said Larkin.

'Hiding? In the house? Gak. What's she got to say for herself?'

'Nothing. Just go away.'

Cuu drunkenly flapped a hand at Larkin, his attention on the old woman. He leaned down, putting his leering face close to hers. She pulled away, avoiding eye contact.

'Stop it,' said Larkin.

'Who are you, witch? Eh? Speak up, I can't gakking hear you? Where the gak were you hiding? Eh?'

She drew back as far as the chair would allow.

'Back off, Cuu,' Larkin warned.

'Shut up, Tanith. Come on, you old witch! Who are you?' Cuu reached out and grabbed her roughly by one thin shoulder. She let out a little gasp of fear. 'Who the hell are you?'

Larkin leaned forward and grasped Cuu tightly by the wrist. He yanked Cuu's arm back, tearing his grip from the old woman's shoulder, and slowly rose to his feet, pushing the drunken Verghastite backwards.

'Get the hell off,' snapped Cuu, his attention switching entirely to Larkin. He fell back unsteadily, drink slowing his reactions, but quickly locked and pushed back. Larkin wasn't giving.

'Get your hand off me, Tanith,' Cuu growled.

'If you leave her alone.'

'Oooh, that's it. You've done it now, sure as sure.'

Intoxication made him telegraph the punch. Larkin dodged it easily, and pushed Cuu right back across the kitchen. He fell heavily against the dresser and several plates and pots fell off with a crash.

'You piece of shit,' Cuu said, reaching instinctively for his blade. But his kit was lying back in the drawing room. In the instant it took him to realise the dagger he was groping for wasn't there, Larkin had thrown a left hook that twisted Cuu's head round and dropped him to the floor. Cuu lay there, moaned, and spat bloody saliva onto the red-glazed tiles.

Larkin paused. He could do it now. He'd even have a cover story. He could fething well–

But the old woman was staring at him. Her hands were up over her head, protectively, though she was still sitting in the chair. He could see the glint of her eyes staring out between her gnarled fingers.

'Feth, it's okay!' said Larkin. 'He won't hurt you. I swear he won't!' He crossed to her and bent down, trying to calm her.

'Please, it's okay. It's really okay. I–'

He blacked out. There was a dull thump, like a muffled peal of thunder, and he blacked out.

He came to, sprawled face down across the table. The back of his head hurt really badly. His vision swam.

He tried to rise, but lost his balance and fell off the side of the table onto the floor.

The fall saved him. Cuu brought the iron skillet pan down for a second blow and hit the table where Larkin had just been crumpled. The pan exploded the cup and sprayed porcelain shards and tepid caffeine across the polished wood.

Larkin tried to crawl backwards away from Cuu, but the Verghastite came for him, swinging the pan again. It caught Larkin on the shoulder. He kicked out at Cuu's legs.

Cuu reached down and grabbed Larkin by the throat. With a snarl that flecked spittle out between his clenched teeth, Cuu hauled Larkin up and threw him against the side counter. He pinned Larkin with the flat of his forearm, and hit him with the pan again. Larkin squealed as he felt a rib go. Another savage blow and pain flared through his left elbow. But for that raised arm, the heavy pan would have mashed his face.

'You Tanith gak! You little shit! You stupid bastard!' Cuu rained down slurs and blows alike in a berserk fury.

Suddenly, Cuu shrieked and collapsed off Larkin, dropping the pan with a clang. The metal frame stock of a Mark III lasrifle had just smashed up between his legs from behind.

Cuu hit the floor, convulsing and choking, tears washing down his screwed up face. He fell in a foetal position, clutched at his groin and threw up.

Dripping with storm water, Muril turned her lasrifle round so that the muzzle was pointing at Cuu's temple.

'Any more from you, Cuu, any more, and I use this end on you instead.'

'What the feth's going on?' demanded Caffran pulling down his cape hood as he came in through the kitchen door behind Muril. The old woman made a sudden dash for the open door, but Caffran intercepted her gently and sat her back down. She didn't protest.

Muril helped Larkin up. He was shaking. One cheek was swelling and turning blue, and blood streamed from his nose. The back of his head had left more blood on the countertop.

Muril dragged out a chair and helped Larkin sit down.

'Cuu... Cuu was gonna hurt her–' he stammered.

Muril looked round at Caffran. 'Little bastard nearly beat Larkin to death. If we hadn't come back...'

Caffran looked down at Cuu, who was still curled up and weeping out jagged groans. Every few breaths, he retched again and added to the expanding pool of liquid vomit around his head.

'Feth,' Caffran murmured. He was reaching down to grab hold of Cuu when Feygor and Brostin stormed in. They were both very drunk, more obviously drunk than Cuu had been. Feygor was having trouble walking. They reeled to a halt and blinked repeatedly, trying to take in the scene before them and understand it.

'Where's the fething food, Lijah?' Feygor said.

'You want some food?' asked Caffran. 'I'll bring you some. Go back to the drawing room and I'll bring you some.'

His head swaying back and forth like his neck was rubber, Feygor frowned and made several vague pointing gestures around the room.

'What the feth?' he barked, his augmetic voice box coarse and indistinct as it tried to cope with his inebriated sounds. He looked at the old woman and tried to focus his eyes. 'Who the feth is this?'

'It's likely we're all guests of hers here, so show some respect,' Caffran said. 'She's old and she's scared.'

Feygor snorted. 'What's with Larks? And why's Cuu down?'

'Cuu was making trouble for the old lady,' Muril said. 'Larks tried to stop him and he went wild with a skillet.'

'We had to subdue him,' Caffran added, hoping to take a little heat off Muril if necessary.

'Cuu was hurting the old lady?' slurred Brostin. The idea seemed to offend him.

'He's drunk,' said Muril.

'No excuse,' said Brostin with great certainty.

'Who the feth is she?' Feygor wanted to know. He took a step forward, approaching her. Caffran stepped in and carefully steadied Feygor.

'She's the owner of the house,' he said. He didn't know that for sure, but it had a certain weight Feygor's addled brain might take in.

'Where'd she come from?'

'She was here all the time. Hiding.'

'Fething spy!' Feygor said, clapping his hands. The old woman jumped.

'No, sir.'

'I fething say so. Sneaking and hiding.'

'She was scared of us. Does she look like a Shadik agent?'

'Fethed if I know!' Feygor said. He stood straight and waggled a finger. 'Lock her up somewhere. Lock her up. I'll question her in the morning.'

'We can't lock her up,' Muril began.

'Lock her the feth up!' Feygor spluttered. 'Who's in charge here, bitch?'

Good question, Caffran thought.

Brostin tugged at Feygor's arm. 'You can't lock her up, Murt. Wouldn't be right. Not an old lady.'

''Kay, what then?'

'I'll look after her. I'll stay with her,' said Caffran. 'You can talk to her tomorrow.'

'All right,' Feygor said, satisfied. He wheeled around, unsteadily, and wandered into the pantry. They could hear the smash of breaking jars as he foraged for food.

Brostin stood for a moment, and then followed Feygor out.

'Feth,' murmured Caffran. He looked over at Muril, who shook her head. Caffran bent down and hauled Cuu towards the door. He threw the coughing Verghastite out into the rain.

'Sober up, you little swine!' he snarled after him. Cuu lay in the yard, whining like a canine in the beating rain.

When Caffran came back into the kitchen, he saw that the old lady was carefully picking up the objects that had fallen during the fight. Pans went back onto the dresser. Shards of china were picked up one by one.

'She just started doing that,' Muril said, dabbing disinfectant pads from her field kit to the back of Larkin's head.

Caffran watched. The old lady threw the broken cups into the kitchen waste, and then swept up the bits she couldn't pick up with a dustpan and brush. She took the skillet Cuu had used to beat Larkin and hung it back on its hook over the stove. Then she shuffled into the wash house and re-emerged with a mop.

Caffran stepped forward and took it from her. She gave it up without resistance. 'Let me do that,' he said, and started to clean Cuu's spew off the tiles.

He wouldn't watch her do that.

IT WAS WELL past midnight. The electrical storm had returned with a show of force even greater than the previous night. Rerval gave up his search of the upstairs. There was no sign of anything personal apart from the old furniture and bedclothes. Wardrobes were mostly empty except for a few dry pomanders rolling about their floors. Just about every upstairs room was damp, some saturated, from the leaking roof. Trickles of water streamed down. The air stank of mildew and rotting linen.

He played his flashlight around the halls and the walls of the rooms. There were few pictures, but in places his light revealed the pale oblongs where pictures had once hung. There was an ormolu clock on the mantle of one bedroom. It had stopped at half past four. The gilt decoration showed two soldiers in plumed hats, standing either side of the face and supporting it with their hands.

He found a linen closet where the old, piled sheets were generally dry. There were a few items of kit and some hot-shot clips stacked in the corners. This was evidently where Larkin had chosen to make his lair.

Rerval left it alone.

He saw the attic hatch, and got a chair. Pushing up through the hatch, he shone his light around. The attic was swimming. Many tiles had gone. His beam picked out black, mouldering rafters, streams of rainwater and stacks of rotting junk. He decided not to waste his time.

He wandered back to the stairs. How had she lived here for so long? Alone? Had the isolation snapped her mind? Was that why she wouldn't speak?

He went down the stairs, avoiding the plinking pots and water catchers. Lightning flashed.

Lamp light was shining from the half-open drawing room door, and he could hear voices and the clink of glasses.

A paler light was coming from under the dining room door.

Rerval switched off his flashlight and drew his laspistol. He put his hand on the door knob and carefully opened the door.

A single candle was guttering in the middle of the long dining table, its twisting flame reflecting off the dark, varnished top.

Piet Gutes sat on his own halfway down, his head in his hands. There was a half-finished bottle of red wine next to him, and some pieces of paper spread out on the tabletop.

'Gutes?'

Gutes looked up. He was drunk, but that didn't completely explain the redness of his eyes.

'You all right, Piet?'

Gutes shrugged. 'Doesn't matter where you go,' he said, 'it always finds you.'

'What does?'

'The war. You think you're so far away it can't touch you, but it finds you anyway.'

Rerval sat down beside him. 'War's our life, you know that. First-and-Only.'

Gutes smiled bitterly. 'I'm tired,' he said.

'Get some sleep. We–'

'No, not like that. Tired. Tired of it all. When we got sent out here–'

'Aexe Cardinal?'

'No, Rerval. The woods. This mission. When we got sent out here, I was thankful. We might get a few days, leave the war behind. Get out from its embrace. And when Ven and Jajjo found this place… feth, it seemed like a little paradise. A little paradise, just for a day or two. I'm not greedy.'

'Sure.'

Gutes drummed his fingers on the table top and then took a swig of the wine. He offered the bottle to Rerval, and Rerval knocked back a sip himself.

'Everything's okay from far away,' Gutes said. 'I mean, when you get back far enough, nothing matters.'

'I suppose,' said Rerval, handing the bottle back to Gutes.

'I was far away when Finra died. And little Foona too.'

'Finra? Your wife?'

'No,' Gutes chuckled. 'My daughter. My wife died eighteen... no, nineteen years back. I raised Finra on my own, you know? Did a good job, I think. She was a beautiful girl. And Foona. A little darling, my first grandchild.'

Rerval hesitated. He didn't know what to say. It was ironic, he thought. I'm signals, a vox-officer. Communication is my speciality. But I have no idea what to say to this man.

'I wish I had pictures of them,' Gutes said. 'There was no time, when I signed up. It was last minute. We agreed she'd send some on via the Munitorium. She promised me a care package. Letters.'

'They didn't suffer, Piet,' Rerval said.

'No, I know that. Just a little flash and Tanith was dead. Bang, goodnight. Like I said, nothing matters if you're far enough away. You know that song? "Far away, up in the mountains"? Brin Milo plays it sometimes.'

'I know it.'

The candle flame fluttered and almost went out. Then it flared again, as wax dribbled from the lip. Thunder slammed above the percussion of rain outside.

'I always thought,' Gutes said, 'that she'd be the one getting the letter. My daughter, I mean. The one that comes in the vellum envelope. The one that says blah blah blah regret to inform you that your father, etc.'

'That letter,' Rerval nodded, taking another sip from the bottle.

'Turns out, it was the other way round. Except I didn't get any letter. Just saw a little flash from far away.'

'You should get some sleep,' Rerval said.

'I know. I know, Rerval.'

'Come on then.'

'Far away. That's what this place is. So I thought. A chance to be far away at last, just for a few days. But it doesn't matter where you go. It always finds you.'

He fumbled with the old papers in front of him and pushed them over towards Rerval. A letter sheet, brown with age, and its envelope. The letter was embossed with the crest of the Aexe Alliance.

Rerval read it.

'Feth, where did you find this?'

'In the rack, in the hall. It was there when we came in. I didn't pay it much heed before.'

The letterhead date told Rerval it had been sent nearly seventeen years before. It began: 'Dear Madam Pridny, on behalf of the General Staff Command of the Aexe Alliance, I regret to inform you that your son, Masim Pridny, corporal, was reported missing during action at Loncort earlier this week...'

* * *

'RAIN'S STOPPED,' MURIL said. A pre-dawn glow was spreading in through the kitchen windows.

The old woman was asleep, curled up on the bench seat. Larkin was sitting hunched at the table, nursing a glass of sacra. The bruises on his face were almost black, and Muril was worried about the wound on the back of his head.

Everyone else was long since asleep, except Caffran and Rerval, who were standing guard.

Muril got up and used a cloth to open the stove plate. She tossed some more logs in, and raked them around with the poker.

'You okay?' she asked.

'Yeah,' said Larkin. He was still studying the letter Rerval had shown them. 'Poor old girl, waiting all this time... seventeen years... waiting for her son...'

'You suppose that's why she didn't leave this place?'

'Yeah, I suppose. Waiting at home for a son who's never actually coming back.'

'Poor woman,' Muril said, looking over at the sleeping figure. She sat down opposite Larkin.

'Tell me about Cuu.'

'Cuu?'

'Lijah gakking Cuu. He nearly killed you, Larks. That wasn't about some old lady, was it?'

'He was drunk. He was hurting her.'

'Still... there's more to it than that, isn't there.'

Larkin shrugged. The gesture was painful. Muril wished they had Dorden around, or Curth, or even a corpsman, to check Larkin's ribs and elbow.

And his head.

'Don't know what you mean,' he said.

'What I mean,' she said, 'is that you and Cuu have a thing. Everyone knows it. Don't know when and why it started, but you have a thing.'

'A thing?'

'A feud.'

'Maybe.'

'For gak's sake, Larks! I could help you!'

'Help me? No, Muril, you don't want to help me. No one would want to get dragged into what I'm doing.'

'What are you doing? I mean, why the gak did you volunteer for this detail when you knew Cuu was part of it?'

Larkin smiled. He sipped his drink. Muril could see the blood blossoming in the clear liquor as he lowered the glass from his mouth.

'I mean... the two of you have a famous feud that everyone knows about. He treats you like crap. And here you are, signing up to join a squad that you know he's in too. You usually do your best to stay away from him, but now it's like you wanted to be close, you wanted to… oh gak!'

'Now you're getting it,' Larkin smiled.

Muril blanched. 'What the gak are you planning?'

'Nothing you need to know about. Forget it.'

'I will not, Hlaine! What is this about?'

'Payback,' he said.

'Payback? For what?'

'Doesn't matter. I should go relieve Caff.' He knocked back the drink and stood up.

'With your head? Are you sure?'

He sat back down, blinking, and felt the back of his skull with cautious fingers.

'Maybe not.'

'So tell me about payback.'

'You wouldn't understand.'

'Try me.'

Larkin smiled. 'You're a good girl, Muril.'

'So they say. Don't change the subject. Payback.'

'What can I tell you? What if I said I want to get even for the way Cuu has persecuted me since the day we first met? Would that be okay? He's made my life a misery, leant on me, beaten me down. Would that be enough?'

She shrugged. 'Probably. Cuu's a bastard. A predator. He bullies anyone he can. Caff hates him, you know? After that thing on Phantine. I know Gaunt got Cuu off, but Caff believes Cuu killed that woman. And Caff nearly went to the wall for it.'

'I got Caff off,' Larkin said. 'Me and Try. We got Caff's case dismissed and got Cuu sent up in his place. Bragg ratted on him. Then Gaunt got Cuu off on a technicality. Got him the lash rather than a firing squad. That's why he hates me. He blames me for the lashes. Me and Try.'

'So his hate is focused on you now Bragg is gone?'

'Kind of,' Larkin said, with a smile Muril didn't like the look of.

'So that's why you want–'

Larkin raised a finger. 'I never said that. What if I want payback on Cuu because I'm crazy? Everyone knows I'm crazy. Mad Larkin, you know the form.'

'Yeah, but–'

'I'm not right in the head. Everyone knows that. Maybe I want Cuu because I'm insane.'

'You're not insane.'

'Thanks, but the jury is still out. I don't care. Maybe I am crazy. Look out, Lijah Cuu.'

'What's the real reason?' she asked.

Larkin hesitated. He wanted to tell her, but he knew how the others treated him. Mad Larkin. Untrustworthy. Crazy. His head hurt.

'He killed Bragg,' he said simply.

'He what?'

'I can't prove it. Not even slightly. But from what he's said to me, he killed Bragg. For ratting on him. And now he wants me too. So I thought I'd cut to the chase and get in first.'

She stared at him. 'Really?'

'I believe it. I don't expect you to. In fact, I've probably just proved to you that I'm crazy after all.'

'No,' she said. She leaned forward towards him.

'Larks... tell Gaunt about it. Gaunt or Corbec or Daur. They'll help you. Don't do something you'll regret.'

'Like killing Cuu before he kills me? Too late. And it doesn't matter what Gaunt and Corbec and Daur believe. With what little I've got, their hands would be tied. Don't you think I've thought of that? It goes as it goes.'

He got up unsteadily and hefted his long-las. 'Thanks for smacking Cuu off me,' he said, 'but do me a favour. Forget this whole conversation. It'll be better that way.'

STARK DAWN LIGHT spread across the back lawns of the manse. Mist wisped up from the wet grass.

He caught the movement out of the corner of his eye. Not much, just a flicker of something. The vaguest flicker.

Caffran left his sentry post in the greenhouse and ran up the main back lawn. Daybreak birdsong rang around him. He reached one of the most distant sheds, and yanked open the door.

'Out! Now!' he barked, his lasrifle aimed inside.

The Aexegarian trooper was young and matted with filth. He had a dirty twist of beard. He came out into the open, blinking, his hands over his head.

'Don't hurt her,' he said. 'It wasn't her fault.'

'Shut up and get your hands on the wall!' Caffran snapped.

The trooper turned and spread against the side of the shed.

Caffran reached forward to pat him down. He kept his lasrifle at the man's back.

His vox crackled suddenly.

He backed off and adjusted his micro-bead's setting.

'Say again? Say again?' he called.

The vox buzzed again, and he heard a single word.

'Comeuppance.'

TWELVE
ANYWHERE BUT HERE

'So I'm a plucky soldier boy,
My country I hold dear,
Find me somewhere to fight for, sir,
Anywhere but here.'

– refrain of popular Aexegarian song

NINE MEN DEAD. Six injured. Three more sick with gas-related injuries caused by tears in their kit. Seventeen platoon was a mess. And Raglon knew it. Gaunt could tell the novice sergeant was badly shaken and terribly ashamed of himself. His first field office, and he'd ended up with less then fifty per cent of his platoon alive or able-bodied.

Gaunt's infiltration force moved up to occupy the ghastly ruins of the Santrebar Mill, and as the four platoons took station at windows and likely firepoints, Dorden co-opted half a dozen of them to help him deal with Raglon's wounded.

Two were close to death. Sicre and Mkwyl; there was no hope for them. Dorden called for Zweil.

It was getting on for 19.00 hours, and the day was beginning to fade. The dull bluster of the counter-push still rolled across the wasteland towards them from the south, and the deep booming of the super-siege guns continued. Everything was still closed in and swaddled by the yellow gas vapour.

Just after the hour, it began to rain. The light changed, a soft blush across the low yellow sky. It reminded Golke of the way a brush wash could alter a watercolour. Painting had been his hobby, years before. He stood, looking out from one of the mill's low windows, almost admiring the view. It was stark and unlovely, but there was a quality to it. The dark, rusty ground, the off-white sky slowly saturating with blue-grey.

Weighed down with his battlefield mail, heavy coat and respirator, he felt distanced. This was the land he was fighting for, the land he had spent his adult life fighting for. As far as his eyes could see, there was nothing but the scarring of warfare. This wasn't the site of a battle, this was landscape transformed by the brute sorcery of relentless fighting. Stripped, burned, poisoned, malformed, killed.

He wondered why, then, he admired its eerie beauty. Surely it wasn't just the amateur painter in him making a trite aesthetic response. This was the Pocket, he told himself. The Seiberq Pocket. That murderous slab of country that had robbed him of his friends, his men and his health.

He'd emerged from this place a wreck, so dismayed by its horrors that he'd been receiving counselling from his physician ever since. The memories still lacerated his mind.

He tried to picture it living again. Ten, fifty years in the future, a hundred... whatever it might take. He tried to imagine the war over, and peace slowly restoring the rule of nature. Trees. Fields. Life of any kind.

Golke could imagine it, but the vision was not convincing. This, the ravaged vista before him, was the only truth.

He knew why it was important to him. The Pocket had haunted him for years, lurking in his nightmares and daydreams. And now he'd come back to face it. That's really why he had volunteered to assist Gaunt's mission. This was aversion therapy. He'd come back to face his daemons and deny them, exorcise them, banish them. He'd come back to recover something lost by his younger self. The Pocket was a hell-hole, an unfeasibly ugly ruin. But already he could see some beauty in it.

He'd taken the first step. He'd looked upon the landscape of his nightmares and hadn't frozen in terror.

He could do this. He could break the Pocket just like it had once broken him.

Two months earlier, his aides had dragged him out for a night at the musical hall in Ongche. A popular touring show was in town, and they'd insisted he'd enjoy it. The gaudily-painted theatre had been packed with rowdy soldiers on furlough, but Golke had enjoyed the performance from one of the balcony-boxes. It had all been amusing enough, though the common troopers loved it as if it was the best thing ever. A conjuror, an acrobat troupe, a virtuoso viol player, a clown act with trained canines, singers, bandsmen, a rather feeble soprano. A famous comedian in a too-small hat who strutted the stage and made off-colour remarks about Shadik sexuality and hygiene to furious approval.

Then had come the girl, the little girl from Fichua, the top of the bill. This, his senior aide told him excitedly, was what the boys were all waiting for.

She didn't seem much, just a child in a hoop skirt and bodice. But her voice…

She sang three songs. They were funny and saucy and patriotic. The last was a ditty Golke had heard the men singing from time to time. An ironic piece about doing your bit in which the soldier assured his superiors he was willing to fight, but expressed the wish to do so somewhere safe. The chorus went something like 'I want to find a place to fight, anywhere but here.'

The crowd had gone mad. The little Fichuan girl had repeated the song as an encore. Flowers had been tossed onto the stage.

It had stayed with him. Golke had found himself humming it. 'Anywhere but here, your lordships, anywhere but here.' Three curtain calls and goodnight.

It was in his head now. The refrain went round and round.

Anywhere but here.

He understood why the men, sentimental fools the lot of them, like all soldiers off-duty, loved it so. It was catchy and bright and funny. It voiced their secret desires. It let them laugh away their dearest and most hidden wishes.

The tune died away in his head. Staring out at the misery of the Pocket, it simply faded away. Golke could see through its reassuring lie.

This was where he wanted to be. This was where he needed to be.

Not anywhere but here.

Right here. And right now.

THE RAIN FELL harder, sizzling on the poisoned ground, gushing through the crippled drainage of the mill. It was so intense that within fifteen minutes the air had cleared and the sky had become greyer and bigger.

Dorden used his atmosphere sniffer and declared that the gas-level had dropped under advised limits.

Gratefully, the troopers began to unbuckle their hoods.

The open air was cold and damp, and retained the metallic scent of the gas, muddled with rot and soaked earth. Some of the men were so relieved to be out of their hoods, they started laughing and chatting. Gaunt got Beltayn to circuit the mill and relay orders for them to hold it down.

Zweil, his head bared again, said a blessing to the sky, and then went back to Sicre and Mkwyl. Both were dead, and he'd said last rites over both of them already. Now he repeated the duty. 'So they can hear me,' he told Dorden.

It was getting darker. Apart from drifting streams of artillery smoke, they could see for several kilometres. The sky was turning black, and the lights of the lines, both friend and foe, were visible. Over in the east, the false dawn of a flare barrage lit the landscape white. From the south came the flashes and glows of the counter-push. Beyond the eastern horizon, the great blinks of light from the super-siege guns backlit the land.

Overhead, in the dark, muddy blue, Gaunt could see stars, for the first time since he'd set foot on Aexe Cardinal. They were twinkling and blurred by the thinning smoke in the upper atmosphere, but he could make them out. Every now and then, a red or orange line scored the sky as rockets flew over. Part of the Peinforq Line – Sector 56, Gaunt guessed – began to strobe as it started off the night's barrage. They could hear the whine and squeal of shells in flight. Fires began to burn along the reciprocal edge of the Shadik lines.

Mortars pounded from somewhere. Feldkannone crumped.

Another night on the Front began.

'WHAT HAPPENED?' GAUNT asked. He led Raglon to a quieter corner of the mill ruin and sat him down. Raglon was strung out and shaking.

'I'm sorry, sir,' he said.

'What for?'

'For fething up so badly.'

'Skip it, sergeant. What happened last night?'

'We got pounced on. We were following a dead trench and we ran smack into enemy raiders. The fight didn't last long. But it was furious. Back and forth, almost single file. We gave a decent account, I think. They fell back and we moved north, dragging the wounded with us, hoping to join up with ten. We'd heard Criid had taken the mill.'

'And?'

Raglon sighed. 'I don't know how much we missed them by, but they'd already fallen back. The enemy had begun to shell. So we stayed put. It seemed like the right choice. I thought I could feasibly hold the mill, even cut to half strength.'

'Any contact in the night?'

'None, sir.'

Gaunt nodded. 'Did you leave any men behind, Raglon?'

'No, sir!'

'Then I think you did all right. You should stop beating yourself up.'

Raglon looked at Gaunt. 'I thought you'd take my pins right away, sir.'

'For what, Rags?'

'For fething up. For losing so many men.'

'One of my earliest actions, Rags. One of my first real command actions, you understand, I led a ten-man unit of Hyrkans into a forest ward on Folion. We had been told it had been cleared. It had not. I lost seven men. Seventy per cent losses. I hated myself for it, but I retained my rank. Oktar knew I'd just got myself into a bad place. It happens. It happens to all Guards, sooner or later. When you're in a position of authority, it seems to matter all the more. You did all right. You were just unlucky.'

Raglon nodded, but he still seemed unsettled. 'I just hate the responsibility–'

'Of the deaths?'

'And the mistake...'

Gaunt paused. 'Raglon, this is your first real test of command. Not the fight, not the actions afterwards. Truth is the test. If it all went off the way you say it did, fine. If you're covering for someone, then it's not. If you want to be an officer in my regiment, then you have to deal in the truth, right from the start. So... is there anything else you want to tell me?'

'I was in command, sir.'

'Yes, you were. So who fethed up?'

'I did. I was in command.'

'Sergeant, the mark of a good squad leader is that he or she recognises weaknesses and brings them to the attention of his commanding officer. Take it on the chin by all means. Feth knows, you'll have to live with the pain. But if there's a loose link, tell me now.'

Raglon sighed. 'I think we'd have run into the raiders anyway, although I'm told Scout Suth had advance warning. I had allowed myself to be spaced too far back in the file. As I understand it, Trooper Costin blew our cover.'

'How?'

'He was drinking on duty, sir. He gave away our position by failing to observe proper stealth discipline.'

Gaunt nodded and got to his feet.

'For the God-Emperor's sake, sir!' Raglon moaned. 'Don't!'

'Sergeant Adare, may the Emperor rest him, advised me of Costin's unguarded drinking last year. Adare should have come down on it. I should have come down on it. At the very least, I should have warned you about it when you took over seventeen. This is my fault, primarily, and then Adare's, long before it's yours. First and foremost, it's Costin's.'

'Sir...'

'Speak?'

'I only got half my platoon out of that trench. Please don't reduce the number of survivors.'

Gaunt put a hand on Raglon's shoulder. 'See to your duty and regret nothing. I'll see to mine. You'll make a first class platoon leader, Raglon.'

Gaunt walked through the mill. Mkoll hurried up to him.

'Sir?'

'In a moment, Mkoll.'

Gaunt reached the dingy alcove of rockcrete where Costin was lying. Dorden was changing the dressings of the trooper's shattered hand.

The doctor looked up, and recognised the grim set of Gaunt's face.

'No,' he said, rising. 'No. No way, Gaunt. Not now. He's half bled to death and I've spent the last twenty minutes saving his hand.'

'I'm sorry,' said Gaunt.

'Fething no! No, I said! I will not stand by and let you do this! Where the feth is your humanity? I respected you, Gaunt! I'd have followed you to the ends of the worlds, because you weren't like the others! That shit at the triage station... that I understood! I hated you for it, but I forgave you! But not this.'

'He confessed to you, then?'

'It all came out,' Dorden looked down at Costin. 'He told me about it. He's traumatised. Remorseful. Suicidal, probably.'

'Suicide is no option. His laxity caused the death of several Ghosts.'

'So what? You'll shoot him for it?'

'Yes,' said Ibram Gaunt.

Dorden stood in front of Costin. 'Through me, then. Go on, you bastard. Do it.'

Gaunt slid his bolt pistol from its holster. 'Stand aside, Doctor.'

'I will not. I fething well will not.'

'Stand aside, doctor, or I will have you stood aside.'

Dorden leaned in, standing on tip-toe so his eyes were level with Gaunt's. 'Shoot me,' he snarled. 'Go on. I'm defying your orders. If Costin deserves the bullet for breaking your orders, so do I. So, shoot me. Or have everyone know you as an inconstent leader... one rule for one, another for another.'

Gaunt didn't blink. He slowly raised the bolt pistol until the muzzle was pressing at Dorden's adam's apple.

'You're forcing an issue that shouldn't be forced, doctor. You are the backbone of the First, depended on by everyone. You are loved by the men. I consider myself lucky to count you as a friend. But if you choose to take a stand on this, I will shoot you. It is my duty. My duty to the Guard, to the Warmaster and to the God-Emperor of Mankind. I cannot make exceptions. Not Costin. Not you. Please, doctor... stand aside.'

'I will not.'

Gaunt raised the bolter a little so that Dorden was forced to tilt his head back.

'Please, doctor. Stand aside.'

'I will not.'

'We are mirrors, Tolin, you and me. Mirrors of war. I break them. You put them back together. For every gramme of your soul that wishes war would end, mine matches it tenfold. But until the killing ends, I won't back down from my duty. Don't make the next round I fire be the one that kills Tolin Dorden.'

'You really would shoot me,' Dorden marvelled softly, 'wouldn't you?'

'Yes.'

'Holy feth... then that just makes me want to stand here all the more.'

Gaunt's finger tightened on the trigger.

Tighter.

Tighter.

He turned away and lowered the weapon, clicking on the safety.

'Tolin,' he said quietly. 'You've just undermined me in front of my men. You've just weakened my authority. I'm glad to the bottom of my heart that I couldn't shoot you, because of our friendship. But I hope you're ready to cope with the consequences.'

'There won't be any consequences, Ibram,' Dorden said.

'Oh yes, there will,' said Gaunt. 'Oh, most certainly there will.'

MKOLL STOOD NEARBY, alarmed by the confrontation. For a minute, he'd thought Gaunt was going to ask him to step in and bundle Dorden away.

He should have known better. Gaunt would never involve another man in a personal fight.

But it was bad. There wasn't a trooper in the First who'd take a gun to Doc Dorden. The idea was criminal. Time would tell what Gaunt's loss of face would lead to.

The stand-off had shown Gaunt was human. Ironically, that wasn't necessarily a good thing. Even more ironically, most of the First probably knew it already.

GAUNT STOOD ALONE for a few minutes. Around the mill, troopers whispered to each other. The Colonel-Commissar suddenly turned and walked back towards Costin. A hush fell. Dorden looked up from treating another man and saw where Gaunt was heading. He rose, but Milo stopped him.

'Don't,' whispered Milo. 'Not all over again.'

'But–'

'Milo's right,' said Mkoll, stepping closer to the pair. 'Don't.'

Gaunt crouched down by Costin and took off his cap. He smoothed out the brim.

Costin lay against the pock-marked wall, fear overlaying the pain in his face.

'This is a regiment to be proud of, Costin,' Gaunt said finally.

'Yes, sir.'

'We stick up for one another. Look out for one another. That's the way we've always done it. It's the way I like it.'

'Yes, sir.'

'The doctor is my friend. We don't see eye to eye on some things, but that's the mark of friendship, isn't it? I think you deserve to be executed. Right here and now, because of your neglect. The doctor believes otherwise. I'm not about to shoot him. It turns out, in fact, I couldn't even if I thought it was the correct thing to do. So that puts me in a hard place. I have to be fair. Even-handed. If I don't shoot him for breaking orders, I can't very well shoot you for the same, can I? So you should consider yourself lucky.'

'I do, sir.'

'You should also know I hold you in the deepest contempt for what you did. I can never trust you. Your comrades can never trust you. Many, in fact, may hate you for this. You better watch your back.'

'Yes, sir.'

Gaunt put his cap back on. 'Consider this your first and only chance. Clean up your act. From this moment onwards. Become the model of the perfect trooper. Prove Dorden right. If I see you take another drink, *ever*, or if I learn from others that you have, on duty or off, I will come down on you with the fury of a righteous god. It's all up to you.'

'Sir?'

'What?'

'I'm... I'm sorry. Truly sorry.'

Gaunt got to his feet. 'Words, Costin. Just words. Actions speak louder. Don't tell me you're sorry. *Be* sorry.'

GOOD ADVICE, GAUNT mused to himself as he rejoined Mkoll. Deeds not words. Time was getting on and they were in danger of losing the lead they'd gained earlier. Either they moved on the Shadik lines now, or packed it in.

Gaunt called Golke, Beltayn and the platoon leaders to join them.

'I estimate from the light flashes the target guns are about seven kilometres away, sir,' Mkoll said. 'North-east. It could be more, given their range, but their firing lights are brighter than the last time I saw them so they've like as not moved up.'

'They're heavy. Rail-mounted. Do the Shadik have tracks in that area, count?'

Golke shrugged. 'There was a rail line up the east side of the Naeme Valley, years ago, but these days? No one from the Alliance has seen past the Shadik front in decades. Even our aerial obs is limited. Of course, they may well have purpose-built something.'

'So how do we get there?' Gaunt said, inviting opinions.

'It's straight across no-man's-land,' said Domor. 'About a kilometre and a half from here. There's some decent cover apart from the last few hundred metres. We'd have to go slow, the Ghost way.'

'What about this dugout, Criid?' Gaunt asked.

She walked them to the back of the mill and showed them the pile of blast-collapsed rubble that marked the tunnel mouth. 'I've every reason to think this runs right back to their lines,' she said. 'A covered arterial route for getting obs patrols back and forth from the mill. I'd have checked it if there'd been time last night, but there wasn't, so I sealed it.'

'Something Raglon and his boys are grateful for, no doubt. You used a single tube?'

'Yes sir.'

'So, if we clear this opening, the rest of the run should be sound?'

'They'll have it guarded,' Golke said. 'They may well even be trying to clear it now.'

Mkoll shook his head. 'I can't hear anything. No sounds of picks or shovels. I think they've just assumed we hold the mill now. Either that, or they haven't had time to detail sappers in.'

'If we go that way, we can be on them a lot quicker,' Gaunt mused. 'It's going to get nasty at the far end, whichever way we go. I think I'd rather come up through a guarded tunnel and take my chances. The alternative, as Domor said, is a run at the lines, and that could get messy.'

'We'd still have to clear it,' said Golke.

Gaunt smiled. 'An opportunity for the Verghastite element of the First to shine. Arcuda... round up every man you can find who used to be a miner or an ore worker. We need six or seven. Any more and they'll be getting in each other's way. Move Dremmond and Lubba in to cover them. We'll flame the hole the moment anything moves.'

Arcuda nodded and hurried off.

Gaunt looked at the rest of them. 'Once we go, we'll have to work to fluid plans. This is going to be hit and run. Opportunistic. We're going to need everyone ready to improvise. Best case, we find these weapons and throw a rod in their spokes. Worst case, we simply find them and relay their precise location back to the Alliance. Everyone clear on that? Minimum result is locate. Any questions?'

'What about the wounded?' asked Mkoll. There were seven men from seventeen unfit to move.

'They stay here. Zweil stays with them, along with a backstop team. I'll select it. Anything else?'

'One thing that might be useful, sir,' said Beltayn. 'I've been monitoring vox traffic. About five minutes ago, the Alliance distributed the signal "rogue behj".'

'By which they mean?'

'There's another assault due,' said Golke. 'The counter-push must have produced results in the 57th. GSC must have decided to capitalise on that, and send out a second wave. What was the qualifying code, Beltayn?'

'Eleven one decimal two, sir.'

Golke nodded, impressed. 'They're coming on force. Right across 57th and 58th. We can expect a serious bombardment to start with, and then skirmishers followed by main assault. This part of the front is going to be lively tonight.'

'Works in our favour,' said Gaunt. 'Confusion, line assault. We couldn't want for better distractions. And being underground during the bombardment can't hurt either.'

'Unless a stray shell brings the roof down,' muttered Criid.

Her pessimism made Gaunt laugh.

'Let's get set,' he told them. 'The clock's running. I want to be coming up on the Shadik lines during or after the first assault. Then we play it as it comes.'

Arcuda had rounded up six Verghastites with mine experience: Trillo, Ezlan, Gunsfeld, Subeno, Pozetine and, of course, Kolea. Stripped down, they got to work with their nine-seventies and their bare hands. Other troops were brought in to form chains and clear the rubble the Verghastites were digging out. Lubba and Dremmond, their flamers ready, stood by to hose the opening if anything stirred.

Gaunt stood and watched the work for a while. He was fascinated by Gol Kolea. Criid had had to explain to Kolea what was needed, because his mind lacked even the most basic memories of his long years as a miner in Number Seventeen Deep Working, Vervunhive. But his body had not forgotten the skills. He set to work, relentless, inexhaustible, clearing the rubble and dirt with expert efficiency. He wasn't just a powerful man mucking in, he knew what he was doing. He was able to advise on clearance and support measures. He set up the work chain so it moved effectively.

Except he didn't know what he was doing. It was all automatic. The physical memory of mining practices informed his limbs. His eyes were vacant.

Gaunt considered that of all the men the First had lost, Kolea was the one to be most dearly mourned. A superb soldier. A fine leader. If it hadn't been for Ouranberg, Kolea might have made serious rank in the Ghosts.

Most of all, Gaunt missed Kolea's quiet, insightful character.

When men died, you simply mourned their absence. The lack of them. You missed their presence. He could think of many like that: Baffels, Adare, Doyl, Cluggan, Maroy, Cocoer, Rilke, Lerod, Hasker, Baru, Blane, Bragg...

God-Emperor! That was just scratching the surface.

But with Kolea it was worse. He was still there, in body, in voice. A constant reminder of the warrior they'd lost.

Gaunt walked back from the tunnel mouth and found Milo.

'Got a duty for you,' he said.

'Ready and willing, sir,' said Milo.

'I want you to hold this mill. Zweil's staying, and the wounded need looking after. I also want a team here in case we come back in a hurry. You and four men. You've the command, so you pick.'

Milo looked crestfallen. He was clearly disappointed not to be advancing with the main mission.

'Isn't there someone better suited for the job, sir?' he asked.

'Like?'

'Arcuda? Raglon? They've both got rank. And they're–'

'They're what, Milo?'

Inexperienced, Milo wanted to say. 'Good choices,' he said, uncertainly.

Gaunt sighed and nodded. Milo had turned out to be a first class soldier, with a real promise of leadership qualities, despite his age. Either of the suggestions – Arcuda, green and nervous, and Raglon, shaken and tired – would make more sense. Indeed, Gaunt knew he'd rather have Milo in his fire-team than either of the sergeants.

There was another reason for his choice, one that had been nagging at him for days. He wanted to tell Milo about the old Sororitas woman in the forgotten woodland chapel, but every time he turned it over in his mind, it sounded stupid. He didn't really even believe it himself.

She'd said Milo was important. Not here, important elsewhere. Then again, she'd been barking mad.

If, he acknowledged to himself, she'd even been there at all. That whole incident had taken on a very dreamlike quality in his head.

But Ibram Gaunt had been alive long enough to know that the galaxy moved in ways far stranger than he could ever divine. His whole life had been bisected and intercut with mysterious truths and consequences. Coincidences. Destinies. Truths that didn't seem to be truths until years afterwards.

He could not risk it. He could not risk Milo.

'I want you to do it,' he said. 'I trust you. Think of it as a test.'

'A test, sir?'

'Maroy's dead, Milo. Sixteen platoon needs a new sergeant. I'm considering you for that. Get on with your duty, and I'll consider you more seriously. Pick your four.'

Milo shrugged. He was quite taken aback by the prospect of a promotion and a command. At Vervunhive, it had been a toss up between Milo and Baffels, and Gaunt had given the command to Baffels on the basis of age and experience. Milo was so very young. But war had aged him since then. So had experience. Gaunt knew that if he offered the rank to Milo now, it wouldn't be turned down. He wasn't a boy any more. Vervunhive, Hagia, Phantine and Aexe Cardinal had turned him into a soldier.

'So?' said Gaunt. 'Your four?'

'I'll need a sniper, Nessa.' That made sense. Milo and Nessa had formed a good bond during the Ouranberg raid. 'A flamer to cover the tunnel. Dremmond. Beyond that... I dunno. Mosark? Mkillian?'

'You've got them. Do me proud. If we're not back by dawn, retreat towards the line if you can. Identifier from me is "piper", challenge is "boy". Failing that, one long tap and two short ones. Make sure it's not us before you get Dremmond to roast the tunnel.'

Milo nodded.

'Watch Zweil. He can be a handful. Consider yourself in receipt of the brevet rank of sergeant.'

'Thank you, sir.'

Gaunt smiled and saluted Milo. Milo returned the gesture.

'You've come a long way from Tanith Magna, Brin. Be proud of yourself.'

'I am, sir.'

THE HOLE WAS a dark, sinister space.

'Clear?' hissed Gaunt.

Two micro-bead taps from Mkoll said yes.

'Advance,' Gaunt said.

The infiltration team filed quickly into the dugout run. Mkoll and Domor had the lead, followed by Lubba and Hwlan. Gaunt was right behind them with Bonin.

INITIALLY, THE EARTH-DUG tunnel dropped away rather sharply. The floor was a congealed mass of soil-waste. But after about ten metres, it levelled out and its nature changed. Rather than earth-cut walls, the tunnel was made of mouldering stone, old, but well-laid. It reminded Gaunt of a storm-drain or a sewer.

It was far too elaborate and significant to have been built to cover Republican troops out to the forward observation point at the mill. This was ancient. Gaunt realised it was most likely some part of the mill's old water-system, a drain or possibly a feeder sluice. The Shadik had unearthed it and put it to use.

It was quite narrow and low, and the wet, slime-covered stones were treacherous, especially in the near-pitch darkness. They dared not use lamp packs for fear of advertising their approach. That was why he'd put Sergeant Domor in the lead. 'Shoggy' Domor had been blinded on Menazoid Epsilon, and his eyes had been replaced with bulky augmetic optics, which made him resemble a certain bug-eyed amphibean and thus earned him his nickname. Domor adjusted his optics to night-vision mode.

After a further twenty metres, the tunnel dropped again, this time suddenly, and they had to wade through knee-deep water. There was greater damage to the stone work – evidently this part of the tunnel had subsided or dropped badly.

Gaunt looked back down the file. His eyes had adjusted to the gloom, as much as they were going to, anyway. He could see grey-black shapes moving against the darkness, and hear the occasional splash or clink of rock. It was hard effort, and the men were trying to keep their breathing quiet. It was also hot and airless, and everyone was sweating freely.

About three hundred metres along, Mkoll called a stop. A secondary tunnel opened up to the left, also stone-built, and water gurgled out of it. They waited while the master scout checked it. A minute. Two. Three.

Then a double-tap on the micro-bead link.

Gaunt risked vocals, keeping his voice low. 'One, four?'

'Four, one,' Mkoll responded, barely audible. 'A side chute. Dead-end. It's collapsed.'

They moved on. In the space of the next two hundred metres, three more side chutes opened. The party waited as Mkoll checked each one scrupulously.

A few minutes more, and Gaunt felt cool air moving past his face. He could smell water. In another step or two, he could hear it. A torrent, fast moving.

The tunnel opened out. Gaunt couldn't see enough, but he could feel the space in front of him.

'Some kind of vault,' Domor reported over the link. There was a sudden scrabbling noise and a low curse.

'Report!' Gaunt said.

'Lubba nearly slipped over. Sir, I think we're going to have to risk lamps.'

'How clear is the way ahead?'

'No sign of contact. Wait.'

They heard soft boot-steps on stone, a wooden creak, and then it fell silent for a few seconds.

'Domor?'

'It's clear. I think we should use lamps. Someone's gonna fall, otherwise.'

'Your call, Domor, you're in the best position to decide.'

'Do it, sir.'

'Two lamps only. Hwlan. Bonin.'

The scouts switched on their packs. The pools of light they cast seemed alarmingly bright. They illuminated the chamber, and Gaunt realised at once that Domor had been correct.

The tunnel they had been following came out halfway up the stone walls of a deep cistern area. It dropped away below them. Narrow, rail-less stone steps led down from the tunnel to a stone buttress where lengths of duckboards had been placed as a bridge across the gap over onto a matching buttress. From there, another flight of steps led up to the resumption of the tunnel. Domor was on the far side, crouched at the top of the opposite steps, watching the way ahead.

There was nothing to hold on to, and every surface was dripping with slime. Without the light, a good many of them would have lost their footing on either set of steps, and the narrow duckboard bridge would have been impossible to negotiate.

Far below them, water thundered through the bottom of the stone vault.

Holding his lamp, Hwlan went across the bridge. He stood at the foot of the opposite steps to light the way. Bonin waited with his own lamp at the bottom of the near flight.

Gaunt and Mkoll went across with Lubba. Gaunt turned back and signalled the troop to follow, single file. He wanted Bonin and Hwlan free to move up at the front. He instructed every third man to stop and take over the job of holding the lamps. The last man through would collect in the lamps and turn them off.

THEY'D BEEN UNDERGROUND for about fifty minutes, and had advanced what Mkoll reckoned was about two-thirds of a kilometre, when the barrage began.

It sounded like a distant hammering at first, then rose in volume and tempo until they could actually feel the earth around them vibrating. Gaunt calculated there was between eight and twelve metres of solid earth above their heads, but still everything jarred. Spoil and water squirted and dribbled out of the roof, shaken loose or forced out through ground distortions. Every once in a while, a whole stone block popped out of the wall and fell on the floor.

Agitation rose. Gaunt could feel it. It wasn't hard to imagine what would happen if a heavy shell scored a direct hit above them. Crushed, suffocated, buried alive. The tunnel could cave or collapse. They'd already seen it had done that further back.

Even the most confident Ghosts wanted to be out of this potential grave. They wanted to be taking their chances in the open. It didn't matter that they were probably at less risk from the shelling and the shrapnel down in the drain.

Indeed, Gaunt felt his own pulse rate rising steeply. Claustrophobia had never been a private fear of his, but down here, like this…

The earth shook with an especially violent jar. Someone back in the line moaned in fear.

'Quiet!' Gaunt hissed.

Then he realised how stupid the comment had been. If it was loud down here, it would be deafening above ground. The shelling would cover their noise. They could advance now at double time, not worrying about stealth.

He issued the order and they started to move, almost fleeing down the line of the tunnel. The deluge of explosives continued to roar above them.

'Hold it!' Mkoll cried.

They skidded up. 'What is it?' Gaunt asked.

'You hear that?'

Gaunt couldn't hear anything above the shell blasts and the panting of the men. 'What?'

'A scratching noise. A rattling…'

'Sacred feth!' Domor suddenly cried out. He could see further than any of them. He could see what was coming.

'Vermin!' he said in horror. 'A swarm of vermin, coming this way! Oh God-Emperor!'

'Sir?' urged Lubba, slightly frantic. He had his flamer ready.

'No,' said Gaunt. The shelling might be covering their advance, but sustained flamer-bursts would be an insane risk to take. 'Stand your ground!' Gaunt said. 'They're fleeing the shelling. Just grin and bear it. That's an order.'

The rats hit them.

A river of squealing, matted bodies, surging in a tide back along the tunnel, filling the floor space to shin-depth, some scampering along the walls. Gaunt felt them collide with his legs, rocking him back, and then pouring around and under him. Men cried out. The noise and stench of the living river was atrocious. The writhing pressure of the rats' bodies was even worse.

Frantic, seeking cover in the deeper drains, the rats clawed and bit as they swept past. Gaunt had to steady his hands against the tunnel wall to prevent himself being knocked over. He felt sharp needle-bites on his shins and calves.

There was a scream, and frantic activity behind him. Harjeon had been carried over, and had virtually disappeared into the streaming mass of black bodies.

Criid and Livara struggled and swore, trying to get him up again.

We're probably all dead, Gaunt thought to himself. All of us infected with the multitude of filthy plagues and infections these vile things carry. Golden Throne! Of all the things that I imagined might end my service to the Imperium, it was never rats.

As suddenly as it had begun, the vermin tide stopped. A last few squeaking things scuttled by in the gloom. Gaunt heard men stamping at them.

'Report!' he said.

There were general moans and comments of loathing. Not a single member of the mission had avoided bites or tears. Harjeon was covered in them, and started shaking and vomiting in loathing.

'They got on my face... in my mouth–' he wailed.

'Shut him up, Criid.'

'Yes, sir.'

'Let's move.'

THE SOUNDS OF the shelling grew louder, but not because they were closer. There was a faint, cold light ahead, and the noise of the barrage was being carried back along to them from the tunnel mouth.

Just a hundred metres to go.

Gaunt ordered Mkoll, Bonin and Hwlan forward.

'Ready order,' he said to the rest. 'Straight silver. Let's keep the surprise on our side as long as possible.'

Two taps.

'Forward,' he said.

UP AHEAD, THE three scouts emerged into the open air. It was cold and foggy from the shelling, and the shock-flashes of blasts backlit the misted air. The sound of the barrage was deafening: whooping shell-falls, some high-pitched, some low and basso, others still oddly melodic and expressive. Most detonations were huge and so loud they shook the diaphragm. Others made hotter, flatter sounds. Some made no sound at all, just a flash and a quake of the ground. After every single one there was a surging, pattering hush, like breakers on a shingle beach, as soil and shrapnel rained down.

Finding their way by the strobing flicker of the impacts, Mkoll, Bonin and Hwlan scurried out of the tunnel mouth, heads down. There was a sandbagged revetment and a guard point at the Shadik end of the tunnel, but it was unmanned. The guards had fled for cover.

The scouts found themselves in a deep bay off the main fire trench. They fanned out to the exit, and then ducked back as three Shadik troopers ran past, boots clumping the duckboards. These disappeared, and then two more came by, carrying a screaming man on a stretcher. They too vanished into the glowing smoke.

Mkoll signalled the other two up with him. They emerged into the fire trench proper. It was deeper and better laid than the Alliance trenches, with a wider firestep and a back-slanted parapet of rockcrete blocks. The trench, as far as they could see, which was to the next traverse, was empty.

'Move up,' Mkoll said.

A moment later, five Shadik troopers, running hell for leather, appeared round the traverse to their left. They didn't seem to register the Tanith until the last moment.

The scouts didn't give them a chance to react. Mkoll brought down the first one, sliding his silver knife through gas-mask and windpipe. Hwlan skewered another in the sternum and then propelled himself and the corpse into a third.

Bonin crashed his rifle-butt into the belly of the enemy soldier nearest him, and sent him tumbling away, winded, then put his weight into a stinging sidekick that snapped the fifth trooper's neck and dropped him abruptly onto the duckboards. Bonin leapt over him, and quickly killed the winded man with his bare hands.

Hwlan tried to make a clean kill of the last trooper, but the fether was struggling hard. The Tanith man got his lasrifle braced across the man's neck and wrenched it around, twisting the helmeted skull down hard against the trench floor.

Five men dealt with in just a few seconds.

They were dragging the bodies into cover behind the camo-nets of a funk hole as Gaunt led the first of the main party into the fire trench.

'Which way?' Gaunt asked.

Mkoll pointed left.

'Lead off with Hwlan,' Gaunt told him. He turned to Bonin. 'Set here with Oflyn, and take up the rear of the file. Stay in close contact.'

'Sir,' nodded Bonin.

The party moved off quickly behind Mkoll and Hwlan. Two scouts at the head and two at the rear was the best insurance Gaunt could muster.

Beyond the second traverse they came to, a Shadik fire-team was trying to set up a pair of autocannons at the parapet. Nine men, all told.

Mkoll and Hwlan came at them from behind, knives out. Gaunt followed them, drawing his power sword, along with Criid, Ezlan and LaSalle. Brutal killing followed. One of the Shadik got a shot off, but Gaunt hoped its sound would be drowned by the barrage. He decapitated a man with his sword, and then impaled another. Nothing stopped his ancient blade, not mail-armour, not battle-plate, not leather and certainly not flesh.

Criid finished off the last man, and looked up at Gaunt.

The shelling had just suddenly ceased.

That meant the ground attack was coming. And it also meant that the Shadik would be streaming back out of their bunkers and shelters to man the step and repel.

THIRTEEN
CORPSE LIGHT

'Sometimes, y'know, I really miss my slum.
Times like this, for instance.'

– Flame-Trooper Lubba

FIFTEEN REGIMENTS OF Alliance troops assaulted the line in the wake of the barrage. A wave attack, welling up from the smoke-skeined darkness of no-man's-land. The twenty-kilometre stretch of line had been lit up for half an hour by the salvos of the bombardment. After a moment's eerie silence, it lit up again. Small-arms. Machine guns. Grenades. Flamers. From the air, the wide band of massive light bursts reduced to a thinner, fizzling line of fire.

It was the most significant attack mounted on the Shadik line in eighteen months. An offensive, the officers of the GSC were calling it back in the safety of the rear-line bunkers. Lyntor-Sewq and Martane had been prepping for it since Lyntor-Sewq's promotion to supreme commander. Lyntor-Sewq had dearly wanted to make his mark early, and prove to the high sezar how lax his predecessor, Count Golke, had been in his accomplishments. It was all part of a greater strategy that incorporated the northern push through Gibsgatte, where the supreme commander had invested the bulk of his Imperial Guard armour. The idea was to sucker punch Shadik by a northern thrust and then take him hard in the belly at the Pocket and Bassin-on-Naeme. Lyntor-Sewq's overall scheme was to divert the enemy's strengths to the north and retake the river valley, establishing a new front he called the Frergarten Line before winter set in. If successful, the Peinforq Line would become obsolete for the first time in twenty-six years.

Over winter, the new line could be reinforced using Alliance troops, and be ready by spring not only to hold against the inevitable counter-push, but also to launch an invasion of the Southern Republic, in concerted effort with the Kottmark armies on the Ostlund Line.

It was an over-ambitious scheme, typical of a new commander trying to be emphatic and break the deadlock apparently imposed by his predecessor. If Golke had been privy to the planning meetings, he'd have been able to tell Lyntor-Sewq frankly that the same thing had been tried before, three times, in point of fact. The 'Oust-and-Out' strategy was an old one, and it had never worked.

If Ibram Gaunt had been privy to the planning meetings, his comments would have been earthier still. Lyntor-Sewq was playing the war like a game of regicide. The first thing a commander learns that's of any use at all is that army groups do not behave like playing pieces. They don't obey set rules, they don't have preset 'moves'. Often a strong group signally fails to do what was expected of it. Often, too, a 'weak' piece can win the game by being used cleverly.

Unfortunately, neither officer was present at the meetings. By the time it was getting too late to advise Lyntor-Sewq differently, both Gaunt and Golke, the latter by choice, were at the sharp end of things.

Van Voytz was at the meetings, most of them anyway. His counselling efforts were completely eclipsed by the determination of the new supreme commander. When, months later, Van Voytz finally withdrew from Aexe Cardinal, he would come to regard his time there as the most frustrating and impotent of his career.

Most GSC staffers believed that this particular night had been chosen to launch the offensive because of the opening the counter-strike at 57th had provided. Its success had jibed in a timely way with the frontal press at Gibsgatte. This was only partially true.

Though Gaunt never learned the truth, the offensive had been launched because of Redjacq Ankre. Discovering, from logged notes, that the First was infiltrating that night, he'd persuaded Martane to put the call in. Ankre was a proud man. His pride would eventually cost him his life, many years later. He hated the idea that the Tanith could have found an opening, and he used that hate to fuel his persuasive powers. If the stealthers of the First could break the Shadik line, then so could the Alliance ground forces. Ankre was actually afraid that the off-worlders of the Guard might actually achieve something that the Alliance had failed to do. He could not stomach the idea.

He personified the emotion-led failing of the Alliance top brass, a failing that had prolonged this war by decades. As with all efforts of such scale, his failing went unnoticed in the general scheme of things.

Almost three thousand Alliance troops fell casualty on the line assault that night. No figure, not even an estimation, was made for the Shadik forces. At one stretch of the line, one hundred and seventy-eight men of the Genswick Foot, including Lieutenant Fevrierson, became encumbered in lines of wire and were slaughtered by machine guns. At another section, no more than fifty metres long, three hundred Fichuan infantrymen died in the storm charge. The trench filled up, level with the surrounding terrain, packed with bodies so deeply the Shadik were forced to fall back and hold a reserve trench. Trench mortars killed sixty men of the Meuport Fifth as they came towards the parapet and were illuminated by starshells sent up by a nearby Brunsgatte unit who had become disoriented. The surviving men of the Meuport Fifth later took the fire trench, held it for an hour, lost it again and then retook it before dawn. The action entered their regimental legend.

At the northern tip of the assault, a detachment of struthid cavalry overran the held position under cover of autocannons, and stormed the main reserve trench. Then a counter-strike of gas shells and nail grenades broke their sturdy advance and left them dead and dying. Hussars, individually untouched, lay twitching and screaming in the foggy dark, sharing through the mind-links the death-throes of their wounded mounts. Alliance troopers advancing through the area started to mercy kill the birds, and then found themselves, in tearful desperation, mercy killing the hussars too.

They could not bear the screams.

The Kottstadt Wyverns, under Major Benedice, assaulted, took and held a kilometre stretch of fire trench, and then storm-fought their way back down the communication alleys to secure a line of gun-pits. South of them, a brigade of Mittel Aexe dragoons, the Seventh Ghrennes or 'Steeplers', did likewise, and then tried to spike the guns and destroy their munitions. Ninety-three men were incinerated when a high explosive dump was enthusiastically flamed, blowing a hole in the earth two hundred metres in diameter. The rest of them, along with a fair number of Wyverns, subsequently died in the clouds of toxic gas that spewed from storage pits ruptured by the main blast.

All the while, set far back, the Shadik super-siege guns continued to bombard. Their immense shells broke shield umbrellas on the Peinforq Line, and obliterated an ammunition dump, a command bunker, nineteen artillery stations – including five heavy howitzer mounts – a sector infirmary and a reserve trench full of young, conscripted Fichuans who thought they'd managed to skip the war for a night.

Some of the massive shells even struck Peinforq itself. The Manorial House was destroyed, and the abattoir, along with the burial chapel, two cafés, and a street of billet-housing full of Krassian troopers.

Despite the monumental losses, the Alliance offensive didn't lose momentum that night, or the day after. Lyntor-Sewq, determined to press for the victory he saw beckoning, deployed greater and greater numbers into the push until it ran out of steam on the fourth day and he conceded defeat.

But for Gaunt's mission, that was in the unknowable future. By midnight on that first night of offensive, they were a kilometre inside the Shadik lines, following a supply trench.

All hell was breaking loose behind them at the Shadik front, lighting up the sky and filling the valley with smoke fumes.

But they were pushing forward, silent, relentless, into the depths of the enemy fortifications.

CORPSE LIGHT BROKE above them, white and pale. More flares. The roar of the battle was distant and muffled. They'd just slaughtered twelve Shadik infantrymen in their fifth skirmish of the night. The First had suffered no losses so far, but Gaunt wondered how much longer they would be able to work with blades alone.

The sound of the siege guns was deafening now, even though they were still several kilometres away. The ground vibrated, not from impacts but from firing.

'I'd say there were six guns at least,' Mkoll told Gaunt. 'I've been counting the flashes and the rhythm.

'Seven,' said Bonin. 'Definitely seven.'

'If Bonin says seven, seven it is,' said Mkoll. 'He's got an ear for these things.'

'How far?' asked Gaunt.

'Well, it's not like we can't find them,' said Mkoll, pointing to the superheated flashes of discharge lighting up the north-eastern sky.

'Yes,' said Gaunt, 'But there's no sense of scale. How far?'

'Two, maybe three kilometres.'

Gaunt sighed and looked around. The supply trench system they were in was dark and quiet. Everything had been pushed towards the front.

Once in a while, Shadik personnel appeared, and were knifed to silence by the Ghosts.

But Gaunt knew they'd been lucky. All it would take was for them to meet an advancing brigade head on.

Then it would come down to firepower. Firepower and numbers.

If only they had a decent fix on the guns. Something concrete to take back with them. He'd told them all that locate was the minimum requirement of the mission.

Two or three kilometres to the north-east wasn't precise enough.

Round the next traverse of the supply trench, they found themselves in a deep ammunition corridor laid with track. It was twice the width of the infantry burrows, and ran north-east, dead straight.

The feeder roads for the big guns. Wide enough to take the girth of the shells on munition trains.

They were closing on it.

'Fan out and follow,' Gaunt ordered, and dropped his team into the bottom of the wide, man-made gulley.

A rifle cracked, twice. Trooper Sekko convulsed and fell.

Gaunt looked back and saw Shadik elements emerging from the gloom, weapons blazing. The Ghosts returned fire, lasguns cracking. Lubba spat fire down the wide space of the ammunition corridor.

The game was up. They'd been rumbled.

FOURTEEN
THE FIRST STAND

'This one's for Try.'

– Hlaine Larkin

'WHAT DOES IT mean?' Feygor asked, angry.

'It means trouble,' said Caffran.

'What sort of trouble?' Feygor snapped.

'I don't know! I agreed the word with Ven before he left. If he found trouble, that was the signal: "Comeuppance". I don't even know if it was him who sent it or Jajjo.'

'Anything else? Anything more?' Feygor asked. Rerval looked up from the micro-bead set he'd been playing with. 'Nothing. Not enough gain. Now, if my main set was working–'

'Feth take your main set,' Feygor replied. He sat down at the kitchen table and drummed his fingers in agitation. 'Define trouble,' he said, looking at Caffran.

'Ven wasn't specific. It could mean they've run into enemy scouts, a patrol… maybe brigands… maybe Jajjo's fallen and broken a leg… or it could be there's an entire army group moving this way.'

'Next time you agree on a code word, you fether, make sure you know what it means!'

Caffran looked Feygor in the eyes. 'At least I bothered to check with him before he left. You just let him walk out of here.'

'Shut your damn mouth,' Feygor growled. He looked round at the others. They were all watching the exchange. 'Pack your kits. We're leaving.'

'What?' cried Caffran.

'You heard me! We've no idea what's coming. There's eight of us here. What good are we going to do holding a place like this?'

Brostin and Cuu began to head for the door.

'I'm not going,' said Caffran. They stopped in their tracks.

'I gave you a fething order,' said Feygor, slowly rising to his feet.

'And you can stick it. Mkvenner asked me to secure this place until he got back. So that's what I'm doing. A strongpoint. We've been building cover around the back area.'

'Who's we?' asked Gutes.

'Me, Muril, Rerval and Larks. You lot can split if you want. I'm not going to let Ven and Jajjo down. If they sent the signal, they meant it. And given the range on the beads, they can't be more than a few kilometres away. So... go if you want to.'

'I gave you an order,' Feygor repeated, malevolently.

'Any notion that you're actually in charge vanished when you decided to take a holiday here. You've hardly been following orders since we arrived, so don't give me that. We're staying, at least until Ven gets here or we hear more from him.'

Feygor's glare moved across their faces. 'You all feel this way?'

'Yes,' said Rerval.

'I'm staying,' said Muril.

Larkin just nodded.

'I'm staying too,' said Gutes suddenly. He looked at the old woman huddled in the corner. 'I don't think she's going anywhere, not if she's stayed here this long. I ain't leaving her for the wolves.'

'Feth it!' said Feygor. He looked at Brostin and Cuu.

'I'm with you, Murt, sure as sure,' said Cuu. 'Just say the word.'

Brostin shrugged. He looked uncomfortable.

Feygor scratched his neck. The idea of running clearly appealed to him but he was considering the consequences. If trouble was that close, they'd stand a better chance of survival here as a group than alone and moving through the forest.

'Okay,' said Feygor, 'okay, we stay. For now. Prepare for contact. Caffran, get everyone deployed.'

The Ghosts began to ready themselves, Brostin and Cuu hurrying out of the kitchen to gather kit. Feygor turned and faced the Aexe trooper Caffran had found.

'Of course, we haven't even started with you,' he said. 'Get talking.'

The dishevelled young man refused to make eye contact. Feygor hit him and knocked him onto the floor. He was about to hit him again when Caffran grabbed his arm.

'He's a deserter. That much is obvious, isn't it? He ran into these woods and he's been hiding here, probably because it was out of the way and the old lady fed him.'

'Why?'

'Gak it, Feygor,' said Muril, 'how dense do you have to be? She must think it's her son, come home again after all this time.'

'This sounding like the truth to you?' Feygor asked the young man, who was picking himself up.

'Don't hurt her. Please,' he whispered.

'And don't hit him again in front of her,' Caffran advised. 'If she does think he's her son, you might find yourself with a bread knife stuck in your back.'

'What's your name?' Muril asked the young man.

'Private First Class Rufo Peterik, Sixteenth Brunsgatters.'

'How long ago did you... run?' Caffran asked gently.

'Six months,' said Peterik.

'You been here ever since?'

'Couple of months living rough, then here.'

'Did you disable my vox-caster?' Rerval asked from across the kitchen. It was a blunt but obvious question. It was just the sort of thing a desperate deserter might have done.

'No, sir,' said Peterik straight away. 'I did not.'

'We haven't got time for this,' said Feygor. 'Lock him up or tie him to a chair. Or something.'

There was no point objecting. None of them could predict what the youth might do, though Caffran had a hunch they didn't have to worry about him. Caffran tied him to a chair anyway.

'Piet, Larks... sweep the ground,' said Feygor. His manner was calmer now. Having made the decision to stay, he was eager to reimpose his leadership.

Both Larkin and Gutes looked at Caffran first and only left the kitchen when he nodded.

OUTSIDE, THE MIST had grown heavier, gauzing out the rising sun. There was no wind, but the air had a tang of rain. They still hadn't quite shaken off that storm.

Larkin and Gutes hurried up the back lawn, following the line of the garden wall, their boots and trouser legs becoming soaked with dew from the wet undergrowth.

It was terribly still, terribly quiet. Birds called intermittently from the woodlands beyond. They reached the tumbledown, overgrown sheds at the edge of the property and crouched down, watching the trees. The softly billowing mists created brief shapes occasionally that made them tense up, but it was just mist.

'You took the circuit, didn't you?' Gutes said at length.

'What?' Larkin's tone was short. His skull felt like it was splitting from the blow Cuu had given it, and he could taste one of his migraines creeping in.

'The circuit from Rerval's vox. You took it, didn't you? I've seen the way you mess with tech-kit. You're the only person apart from Rerval who's got the skills.'

'Piet, considering how dumb you like to play, you're a smart man.'

Gutes grinned. He scanned the woods again.

'Why'd you do it, Larks?' he said after a pause.

'I...' Larkin hesitated. 'I wanted to make sure we were left alone for a while.'

'Oh,' said Gutes.

Then, 'I think maybe we need that vox again now. I think maybe we've been alone long enough.'

'Yeah,' said Larkin.

'You'll give it back?'

'Yeah.'

'I won't say nothing, Larks.'

'Thanks, Piet.'

AN HOUR PASSED, slow and taut. It began to rain, lightly at first and then with greater force. Despite the rain, the mist refused to budge. The light ebbed as it became overcast, and the early morning seemed like wet twilight.

There was no signal on the beads. Caffran began to wonder if he'd imagined it.

All fully kitted and prepped, the members of the detail took station to cover the back of the manse. Caffran was set up in the greenhouse, one of the western most outhouses running off the back yard, with a good angle across the rear lawn, and a decent view left into the patch of kitchen garden behind the pantry. He and Rerval had strengthened the defences in the greenhouse with packing crates, earth-filled sacking and part of an old iron bedstead they'd found on a bonfire heap. They'd carefully knocked out the last of the glass panels.

East of him, across the mouth of the yard area, Cuu was crouching in place at the end of a long barricade Muril and Larkin had built from fence timbers and corrugated iron sheets. They'd had to dismantle several of the lean-tos to cannibalize for material.

Rerval was positioned further along the same barricade, hunched in the corner it made with the stone wall of the old coal bunker.

Brostin was sitting on a chair just inside the half-open kitchen door, his flamer broom across his lap, his tanks beside him. He checked the power cells of the two laspistols – his and Feygor's – that he carried as small-arms. Feygor, his rifle primed, was a few metres away at the main kitchen window. A thick wall separated him from Gutes, who was in the dining room, dug-in at the rear window overlooking the coal house and the hedges of the side ditch. Larkin was on station on the first floor above them all, using a bedroom window as his fire point.

Muril, insisting she was the closest thing they had to a scout, was up at the top of the rear lawn in the derelict sheds at the end of the garden wall. She knelt, perfectly still, watching the trees.

About twenty minutes earlier, as they'd run final checks before taking up station, Rerval had found the missing transmission circuit on the kitchen table. Assuming that it was Feygor, or one of Feygor's cronies, who'd left it there for him to find, Rerval made little fuss. They were all in this together now and there was no point racking up the tension any more.

He'd fitted it back into the caster and, after consulting with Feygor, sent a message back to Ins Arbor. Position, situation, the prospect of enemy contact.

Ironically, there had been no reply, apart from a few strangulated whines of static. Rerval didn't know if it was atmospherics or some slip-up he'd made repairing the vox. There was no time to strip it out and start again. He prayed company command had heard him. He prayed there'd be help coming. Failing help, he hoped that a warning had got through.

IN THE DAMP, mouldering back bedroom, Larkin settled himself on the pungent mattress he'd pulled up to lie on, and rested his long-las on the paint-flaked sill. He shook out his neck, tried to ignore the pain clawing into his brain from the top of the spine and across the back of his head, and scoped up.

His swollen face ached as he pushed it against the eye-piece. His cracked rib stung and he had to alter his stance.

He had a good sweep of the entire back lawn. He panned the rifle around, taking distance readings off the various features: the end sheds, the sundial at the centre of the lawn, the coal bunker, Caff's greenhouse.

Down below him, in the yard, he saw Cuu crouching at the barricade with his back to him.

Larkin turned the rifle down and took aim on Cuu. No more than fifteen metres. Clear. An easy shot. Target-fix. Larkin's fingers twitched on the trigger.

Not yet. But maybe soon. If there was shooting, if there was a fight, he'd take Cuu and damn the consequences. He'd take Cuu Cuu's way: in battle, when no one would know. What was it that little bastard had said? War's a messy thing, Tanith. Confused and all shit like that. Middle of combat, all crap flying this way and that. Who's gonna notice if I get my payback? You'd just be another body in the count.

Good advice, Lijah Cuu. Good advice.

* * *

RAINWATER DRIPPED FROM the shed roof and hit Muril's cheek with a plick. She wiped it away, and then realised it wasn't the drip that had made the noise.

Her micro-bead had tapped.

'Who goes there?' she said into the mic.

Silence.

She waited. Something moved in the trees, but it seemed likely it was just a bird.

She was about to ask if any of the Ghosts at the house had signalled when a figure tore out of the trees, running towards her position, leaping fallen logs and ripping through undergrowth. Her rifle came up and she had a clear shot.

She froze.

It was Jajjo. Filthy, covered in mud, his uniform ripped, Jajjo was running almost blindly towards her.

'Jajjo!' She called. He skidded to a halt, looking around.

'The wall, man, the wall! Get in here!'

He started forward again and vaulted the low stone wall, then came crawling round on his hands and knees into her shed.

'M-Muril?'

'Gak! Look at you. What happened?'

'En-enemy p-patrol,' Jajjo stammered, so exhausted and out of breath he could barely speak.

'I've got Jajjo here,' Muril voxed to the manse. 'Stand by.'

She dragged Jajjo over against the shed wall. He was in a bad way, thin, pale and dehydrated.

'Report!' she hissed.

'W-where's Ven?' he asked.

She shrugged. 'Haven't seen him.'

'He should be here already! He was ahead of me!'

'Slow down! Slow down! Tell me about your contact. What did you find out there?'

'Shit, Muril,' he said, and clambered over the window slit. He peered out.

'Twenty, maybe thirty of them. They're right behind me. Didn't you get my call?'

'Just the signal. Comeuppance.'

'Gak, I knew the link was bad! I–'

He shut up and ducked down.

'They're here!' he hissed.

She wasn't about to cower with him. She got up to the shed's window and looked out.

Figures, three or four of them, were approaching through the mist and the trees. Big men, in battledress.

Carrying lasrifles.

She recognized their blood-red tunics and their leering iron face masks at once.

Not Shadik. Not Shadik at all.

Blood Pact.

As if they had smelled her sudden fear, three of the Chaos infantry swung round and opened fire on the outhouses. Laser rounds chopped into the roof tiles and shattered old brick and chafstone. Support fire – three or four more lasrifles and then what felt like an autocannon – whickered out of the trees.

Muril yelped and covered Jajjo's head with her arms as las-rounds punched in through the woodwork of the window and tore apart the leading edge of the roof.

'Contact!' she yelled into her bead. 'Contact!

'GOLDEN THRONE!' SAID Feygor, peering out of the window. 'That's las-fire! Eight, maybe nine shooters.'

Brostin was on his feet. He took a glance round at Peterik, who was shielding the old woman in the corner of the pantry.

'Shadik don't have las weapons,' he said, in gruff confusion. 'Murt? How come they have las weapons?'

'I don't know!' snapped Feygor. 'Muril! Muril! Report!'

The bead-link crackled. '–od Pact! I say again, contact is Blood Pact!'

'Oh, sacred feth!' Feygor said.

CAFFRAN HEARD THE signal too and his blood ran cold. They'd met the Blood Pact before, on Phantine. The Pact was the devoted vanguard of the arch-enemy. Not cultists, not rebels. Drilled and trained infantry, highly motivated, highly skilled and well equipped. If they were here, fighting for the Republic... well, that meant a forty year old war had just changed as radically as it had done when the Guard arrived in support of the Alliance. This had ceased to be a global matter. Now it was well and truly part of the Crusade.

From his position, all he could see was the back of the outhouse and the sprays of tile and stone smashing off it under the heavy fire. He yearned for a target.

'Keep it close! Wait until they commit!' Feygor urged over the link. The hell with that! Muril and Jajjo were dead meat if no one took up the fight. Feygor clearly didn't want to give away the fact that a unit was dug-in here. Not until he had to.

A slightly different noise now rose from the beleaguered outhouse. The whine-crack, higher-pitched, of first one Imperial lasrifle, then another. Muril and Jajjo were returning fire.

That was play, as far as Caffran was concerned.

'Larkin!' he voxed. 'You got a target?'

'Yes, Caff. At least two.'

'I've got an angle on one too,' reported Gutes.

'I think it's time for us to go to work,' Caffran said.

'Hold fire!' Feygor snarled over the link. 'They don't know we're here yet! Hold fire!'

'Feth that,' said Larkin and took his first shot.

The overcharged sniper-round zapped off up the length of the garden and blew out the head of one Blood Pact trooper in a sideways spray of blood, tissue and metal. His almost headless body toppled over into the ferns. The others started running for cover. From the dining room, Gutes took one out with hits to the hip and the side of the neck.

'Holy Feth!' Feygor was screaming. 'I didn't give the fire order! Who's firing? Who the feth is firing?'

'I am,' said Larkin and did it again. Target-fix. Seventy-three metres.

Another head shot. The Blood Pact trooper flew off his feet, his legs kicking slackly up into the air as he cartwheeled.

'I think we're in this now,' said Rerval and started to clip las-shots up over the lawn.

'Sure as sure,' agreed Cuu, opening fire alongside him.

'Holy Feth! Won't any of you take a fething order?' Feygor shouted over the vox, almost apoplectic.

In the perimeter outhouse, Muril and Jajjo were blasting away and rejoiced as first one Pacter dropped, then two more thanks to fire from the house. Muril recognised and admired the work of a long-las.

She tracked another one into the trees as he sought cover, and sprayed the area on full auto, kicking up a fuss of torn leaves and stalks.

Jajjo was firing on single shot. His gun followed a Blood Pact trooper who was dashing back into the misty shadows of the pines. Jajjo squeezed the trigger.

The dazzling round hit the figure in the spine and tumbled him over.

Autocannon fire continued to strafe the sheds where Jajjo and Muril hid. After a couple more fierce bursts, the side wall came down in a tumble of dislodged chafstone, and the two Ghosts had to crawl out from under the slumped roof and move in a rapid crouch back along the garden wall.

'Can't someone tag that fething cannon?' Muril barked.

'Negative, can't see it,' Caffran voxed, his opinion swiftly agreed with by Gutes.

'Larks? You see it?' Muril called.

'Too deep in the woods,' Larkin replied. 'Can't even see a snout flash.'

'Gak that!' said Muril. She and Jajjo were pinned down behind the narrow stone wall, and cannon fire was gradually creeping their way. They needed a break, enough time to run back down the lawn to the main house.

It didn't look like they were going to get it.

'Hold tight and wait for my word,' said Larkin over the link. 'Wait for it...'

He couldn't see the cannon crew, even from his raised vantage, and he couldn't see any muzzle flash. But he watched the dipping line of the cannon's tracer rounds as they tore out of the woodland. The high calibre shots punished the garden wall and made sappy steam out of the undergrowth. Another few seconds and it would be punching through the wall where Muril and Jajjo were sheltering.

Larkin rolled his aim back, following the line of tracers until it vanished at its mysterious source. He made an educated adjustment to his aim, and fired into the woods.

The cannon fire stopped abruptly.

'Go! Muril! Go!' he cried, as he reloaded and fired another shot exactly where he'd placed the first.

Muril and Jajjo fled down the garden towards the barricade. A few loose las-rounds from rifles chased them, chewing up the turf.

The cannon started up again, but it was lacking confidence now, as if someone else had taken over. Its shots bombarded the back wall of the garden or shot clear over it, smacking into the rear face of the house. A window smashed.

By then, Muril and Jajjo had reached the barricade and had hurled themselves over it.

The cannon continued to spray.

'First thing you learn,' Larkin said to himself, 'is move if someone knows where you are.'

He fired another shot, aiming exactly at the point he'd placed the last two. For the second time in thirty seconds, the cannon fell suddenly silent.

'Nice bit of shooting that, Larks,' voxed Gutes.

Now Caffran felt exposed. With Muril and Jajjo dropping back, he now occupied point position in the defence.

He kept scanning the end of the garden, the wall, the chokes of undergrowth leading into the trees.

He didn't have to wait long.

At least two dozen Blood Pact troopers came out of the tree-line and assaulted the rear wall, sheeting fire at the manse. All of the Ghosts, even Larkin, had to drop down to avoid the ferocity. The attackers were now using the rear garden wall and the ruined sheds abandoned by Muril and Jajjo as cover.

Caffran was the first to begin return fire. He lanced shots along the back of the wall that hit at least one attacker and caused several more to duck. This interruption in firing gave Cuu and Larkin an opening. Cuu sprayed the back of the outhouses with fire, and Larkin fired another hot-shot that took a Blood Pact trooper in the chest.

To the east, from the dining room window, Gutes took up the slack, firing his trademark way: slow, methodical, jaggedly. Two Blood Pact troopers tried to flank by sprinting down the side wall of the property, following the hedges into the ditch. Gutes got them both. Then a third that he didn't kill outright. Then a fourth who emerged, trying to drag the injured man back into cover.

As an afterthought, Gutes picked off the wounded bastard too.

A flurry of fire was hitting down at the manse and the barricade from the central portion of the rear wall. Cuu and Rerval replied, supplemented by Jajjo and Muril, who were now up the barricade with them. Feygor added his own support from the kitchen window, and Brostin suddenly broke from the kitchen doorway and ran up the yard to the side of Caffran's station, leaving his flamer behind. The big thug wriggled in beside Caffran and started to fire his pistols, one in each meaty hand.

'What I wouldn't give for a tread-fether right now,' Brostin grumbled.

'I hear that!' said Caffran.

A shot spat across them from the left. Blood Pacters moving west to flank them from the other side. Brostin rolled to his feet and slid out of Caffran's greenhouse, swung round behind it and came up over the low wall to meet the three Pacters rushing them across the kitchen garden. His laspistols chattered as he raked them back and forth. He killed two and winged a third.

Down at the barricade, Cuu deselected rapid fire and switched his Mark III to single shot. He hunted the garden wall, waiting for Blood Pacters to pop up for a shot. Every time they did, he shot them in the face. Three in a row. Four. The fifth one was smacked over by one of Larkin's shots before Cuu could fire.

Ducking round the kitchen doorway for cover, Feygor dared the yard and ran for the barricade as a welter of shots rained down, exploding plaster, brick, gutters, tiles.

He ducked in beside Muril.

'Get up with Larkin!' he said. 'I know you don't have a long-las any more, but you'll do more good up there.'

She nodded and ran back for the kitchen door.

Feygor got up and started firing. He looked over at Jajjo.

'Where's Ven?'

Jajjo shook his head.

Beside Jajjo, Rerval fired and scored a killshot. He distinctly saw the Blood Pact trooper fall.

He turned to grin triumphantly at Feygor and a las-round hit the side of his head.

Jajjo ducked down to help him, but Rerval was getting up without assistance. 'I'm okay,' he said, but it didn't sound like that. From the corner of his mouth back to his jaw-line, his cheek was flopped open and blood was streaming out down his neck. Rerval fired one more shot, then reached up and felt the rip in his face.

'Feth–' he slurred and fell over.

Jajjo dragged him back into the kitchen. The amount of blood pouring out of Rerval's torn face was extraordinary. 'Help me!' Jajjo shouted to the old woman and the young boy he saw cowering in the corner. He had no idea who they were.

Las-fire smacked and punched through the kitchen window and covered the tiles with glass shards. Several more shots exploded fibres from the kitchen door. Jajjo tried to hold Rerval's face together.

The old woman ran across the kitchen, her head down, and took over. She pinched the wound tight and started to wrap it with her shawl.

'Let me free! Let me free, for god's sake! I can help!' bellowed the young man. Jajjo realised the youth was tied to his chair.

Jajjo got up, went across to the boy, and cut his bonds with his dagger. 'I don't know why you're tied up,' he said, 'but don't gak with me.'

The young man – Jajjo realised how dirty and unshaven he was – darted across to the field dressing kit Gutes had left on the bench seat. He recovered it and ran over to join the old woman cradling Rerval. An astonishingly wide pool of blood had spread out under her.

'Do you know what you're doing?' Jajjo asked.

'I was a corpsman. I know field aid,' replied the boy.

'Don't let him bleed out,' said Jajjo, and ran out into the fight again.

LAS-FIRE FLICKERED UP and down the lawn, fierce and heavy. Caffran thought he'd scored another hit but it was hard to tell. There were at least a dozen shooters up there.

Muril arrived on the first floor, and tried to find the window with the best sweep.

She could hear the hot-shot whine of Larkin's weapon from nearby.

Larkin reloaded again and took aim. He'd switched bedrooms three times since the fight had begun so his shots didn't come from the same place each time. In the far end bedroom, he knelt and sighted.

A steel helmet over a grotesque iron mask.

Bang!

The Blood Pact trooper fell. Larkin reloaded.

He hunted for targets. The back of his skull hurt worse than ever, and he could taste blood. Every now and then, his vision faltered. The blizzard of las-fire coming down at them was almost overwhelming. Middle of combat, all crap flying this way and that...

Larkin stroked his long-las and tilted the aim down. Lijah Cuu was below him in the yard, firing away up hill.

The scope's crosshairs made a luminous frame around the back of Cuu's head.

Larkin paused. He breathed carefully. His head was really aching now, that terrible stabbing migraine that had haunted him all his life.

He blinked away sweat. He would fething do this.

Cuu, right in his sights. Lijah Cuu. His nemesis. The embodiment of his fear. The man who had killed Try Again Bragg.

One shot.

Pop.

Easy.

Larkin's finger tightened on the trigger.

Target-fix. Cuu. Nine point seven metres.

Larkin whined aloud, a pitiful sound. He wanted to do it, yet he couldn't. He was a sniper, a marksman, a killer. But not a murderer. He couldn't shoot one of their own in the back, even if it was Lijah fething Cuu.

He wanted to. He had to. It was the only way. It was why he'd come.

But...

Cuu would have done it without hesitation, Larkin thought. That thought and that thought alone convinced him to take his finger off the trigger.

'Larks! What the gak are you doing?'

Larkin looked up from his carefully laid gun. Muril stood behind him, appalled.

'Don't do it,' she said. 'Please. I know you want to. I know he deserves it. But don't...'

'Sehra,' he said quietly. 'I can't anyway.'

'That's good,' she said. 'Really, Larks. Don't descend to that animal's level.'

'Oh, feth,' sighed Larkin. His head was truly spinning now. His vision was closing in with flashes and lumps of colour. She was right. He was so fething glad he hadn't stained his soul the way Cuu had stained his. There was honour. There was morality. There was sleeping at night without waking up screaming. Bragg would understand. Wherever he was, Bragg would understand.

Larkin turned and took a last look out of his scope. Cuu was looking right back at them.

Lijah Cuu saw the aimed rifle.

And smiled.

BROSTIN AND CAFFRAN finally drove the last of the Pacters back from the left hand flank of the house. Feygor and Gutes smacked shots against the rear wall, and Feygor hit another body.

Then the Blood Pact fell silent.

The Ghosts waited. No contact. No sound. The rain got heavier and washed the traces of Rerval's blood out of the yard.

'Stand down,' said Feygor, at last.

'They'll be back,' said Caffran.

'LIE DOWN,' MURIL advised him.

'My head really hurts.'

'Cuu smacked you a good one with that skillet, Larks. I've been worried.'

Larkin lay back on the dirty mattress in the upstairs room. 'It's not that. I get headaches. Really bad ones. I've always had them.'

'Whatever,' said Muril. 'I think it's that headwound. Cuu really hurt you. I don't want to worry you, Hlaine, but it needs to be looked at. I wish for gak's sake Curth or Dorden was here.'

Larkin had already passed out on the mattress. Watery blood wept into the padding behind his head.

'Gak,' said Muril. 'You really need a doc fast...'

She froze. Down below, she could hear Feygor and the others repairing defences and reloading for the next wave.

She'd heard a sound from the front of the house.

She took up her lasgun and went out onto the landing. Another tiny sound, a movement at the porch.

She went down the staircase slowly, gun raised.

At the foot of the stairs, she wheeled round, and found herself aiming at Cuu. He winked at her.

'Careful, girl.'

'What are you doing here?'

'I heard something out the front,' he said.

She covered him with her weapon. 'Check it out,' she said.

'Why the hostility?' he asked.

'You know why, you bastard. Now... check it out.'

Cuu went down to the front door, Muril watching him every centimetre of the way. He drew his blade.

Cuu threw open the door.

The dagger flew from his hand as a tall figure took him in a choke hold.

'Do you realise how easy it was to get round the front of this place?' asked Mkvenner.

FIFTEEN
THE MONSTERS

'In the long run, a man with a brain is more dangerous than a man with brawn.'

– Warmaster Slaydo,
from *A Treatise on the Nature of Warfare*

FIREBREATHING, LIKE THE giant creatures of old myth, the monsters lay before them.

When the monsters roared, the ground shook and the air came past, hot and acrid, in a pressurised shockwave. The light flashes were painful and immense, like grounded stars being switched on and off in the night. The sound shook teeth and bone and marrow.

The battle in the ammunition corridor had taken seven minutes to conclude in the Ghosts' favour. Squaring off against a Shadik battalion of slightly greater size, Gaunt's infiltration group had lost five men – four Ghosts and one of Golke's Bande Sezari troopers. But their superior weaponry and, in Gaunt's opinion, far superior battlecraft had left nearly thirty Shadik troopers dead. Broken, the rest had fallen back.

Undoubtedly, the Shadik commanders knew they had intruders now. Despite the open invitation to the siege guns' location offered by the corridor, Gaunt and Mkoll had pulled the mission team off east into a muddy, trackless wasteland beyond.

The area was lightless and cold, rambling with old lines of wire and jumbles of wreckage. Weeds and thorny scrub grew in clumps and thickets, sprouting around the split rockcrete of old pill boxes and between the axles of rusted trucks. This was an old battlefield, years old, that the war had passed over and left behind. Now it was just dead ground in the hinterland of the Republican line.

The Ghosts advanced silently through the dark terrain, heading north, towards the titanic blasts of the guns. They kept the ammunition corridor just in sight to their left, and moved parallel to its course.

There would be troops out searching for them. Gaunt was sure of that. Even with the huge offensive going on, drawing on Shadik manpower, the enemy commanders would not allow a suspected infiltration so close to their super-guns to go unchecked.

On three occasions, the Ghosts dropped down into cover when the scouts alerted them to Shadik patrols in the corridor. Gaunt didn't need another stand-up fight at this stage. Better to hide and wait and move on once the jeopardy had passed.

The night sky was amber, tinged by the vast doughnut of smoke drifting out from the guns. On occasions, they glimpsed the moon, an orange semi-circle dancing in and out of the bars of cloudy exhaust.

Nearly three hours after they had first emerged from the mill tunnel, they came up to a ridge that overlooked the guns.

The monsters.

It was physically hard to observe them directly. For the last forty minutes the Imperials had been trudging through a wasteland made spectral by the almighty flashes going off beyond the black horizon. They had almost become acclimatised to the noise and the light and the trembling soil.

But looking on the guns was virtually impossible. The flashes seared eye-sight, leaving idiot repeats glowing on the back of the eyelids. The shockwaves came like slaps. The discharge blasts felt like they were exploding eardrums. Beltayn reported that the pulse shock had killed all vox-links.

Lying on his side on the earth near the top of the ridge, with the men spread out below him, Gaunt pondered his next move. He felt frustration gnawing at him. They'd got so close, against all expectations except his own, and now they couldn't go the last distance.

It was like one of the myths he'd read as a child in the scholam progenium. Monsters so ghastly that the very breath or sight of them blinded men and turned them to stone.

He adjusted his data-slate and took a compass bearing. At least now he had accomplished something. The precise location of the siege guns was known to them. Without other options to hand, their imperative now was to get that information back to GSC. And that meant physically, with the vox dead.

Gaunt turned to Mkoll and the sergeants and used Verghast scratch-company sign language to communicate his intention to pull back and break out. Halfway through, a chillingly eerie thing happened. Darkness and silence fell.

It wasn't complete silence. The distant, frenzied commotion of the offen-sive was now audible, and it wasn't true darkness either because of the ambient background firelight.

But the guns had stopped firing.

Gaunt crawled back to the top of the ridge. What he had only vaguely glimpsed before was now laid out below him. The monster guns, each one set on a huge rail cart, their massive barrels, the size of manufactory chimneys, elevated to the sky. There were seven of them, just like Bonin had insisted. Smoke lay thick like ground fog around them, blurring their shapes and distorting the bare white glow of the chemical lanterns strung up around the area. Gaunt saw figures moving around, gun-crew dwarfed by the huge railway cannons. Electric hoists and flatbed loading carts, which had been occupied serving shells into the automatic arming mechanisms, were now busy clearing unused shells and propellant-mix cartridges clear of the firing site. Some laden carts were being attached to a greasy shunting engine that began puffing them away down the ammunition corridor.

'Why d'you think they've stopped?' whispered Golke.

'They've been firing all night,' Gaunt replied. 'I imagine there comes a point when the barrels get so hot, you have to let them cool. God-Emperor! Now we've found them, what do we do?'

Golke shrugged. Even dormant, the massive guns and their rivetted steel cars looked invincible. Oil and condensation dripped from their huge shock-absorber pylons and clung in glittering droplets to the taut wires of the warping winches. The shells alone were taller than a man.

The Ghosts had proved their bravery, tenacity and ability to Golke without doubt, but what could they, with lasrifles or even tube-charges, do against such juggernauts?

'I don't think there's much chance of us spiking them,' Mkoll said to Gaunt, as if reading Golke's thoughts. 'I reckon I could feth up a field gun or a howitzer fairly permanently, but I wouldn't know where to begin with one of these. Let alone seven.'

'What about the munitions?' Domor suggested.

Gaunt thought about it. None of them were demolitions experts. Domor's landmine skills were as close as that got. Although a big explosion was the basic result he was looking for, he didn't want to go fiddling around with the shells or the cartridges.

They didn't even know what mixes and forces the Shadik were using, or what type of explosives or propellants. They might get a big explosion all right, but one that incinerated them and left the guns standing. Besides, the Shadik were shipping the spare munitions away even as they watched. They knew the risks.

'I think we have to cut our losses,' said Gaunt. 'Getting these co-ordinates back to the GSC is going to be a job in itself, and I think we're going to have to settle for being content with that.'

'If we can't screw with the guns themselves,' said Dorden suddenly, 'why don't we screw up their use?'

'What, doctor?'

'Their mobility. They're too big for us to deal with, so we use their size against them. You fancy moving one of those without rails?'

Gaunt chuckled to himself. Obvious, elegant, simple. The Republic had constructed a major system of wide-gauge tracks along their front line, connected with service lines, sidings and ammunition corridors, so that the siege guns could be shunted from one firing position to the next. At locations like the one they overlooked, the double line fanned out into reinforced spurs so that the guns could sit alongside each other. But that main double line was their only way of moving.

'What are we carrying in the way of tube-charges?' Gaunt asked Mkoll.

'Enough to blow the main line here and on the far side for a good distance.'

'They'll repair them,' said Golke.

'Of course, but how long will that take, sir?' asked Gaunt. 'A day? Two days? Besides, struggling back with this location setting will be a pointless effort if by the time we've got an airstrike or an armour push lined up the guns have been moved again. I don't think we've got a choice, realistically. We have to blow the line. If we take out the ammo corridor too, they won't even be able to fire the guns let alone shift them until the repairs are done.'

Golke nodded. 'How do we do this?' he asked.

THEY BROKE INTO four groups roughly along platoon lines. Mkoll's unit would move up, skirting the firing site, and wire the track sections north of the guns. Gaunt allowed him ten minutes' head start to get into position. Domor's squad went east, to rig the ammunition corridor's line. Arcuda's dropped back west and right of the ridge to set their charges along the southern stretch. Gaunt stayed with Criid's platoon and the elements of Raglon's on the ridge, ready to provide fire support if things woke up.

Ideally, the blasts should happen pretty much simultaneously. Co-ordination was hard without the vox. Gaunt had them synchronise their timepieces. The deadline was at 04.00 hours. Charges should be laid by then. At 04.00, each team leader would fire a red starshell to signal readiness, then Gaunt would fire a white shell to order detonation. If any reds hadn't fired by that time, then Gaunt would wait two minutes. After that, it was white flare anyway and pull out. They agreed a rendezvous back in the deadlands.

'Remember,' Gaunt told them, 'if it comes to a choice between sticking to the deadline and blowing the tracks, blow the tracks. We can always improvise if we have to. The Emperor protects, so serve him well.'

IT WAS TWO minutes to four. The sounds of battle were still rolling in from the front line. The cover team left on the ridge waited nervously. They felt vulnerable and alone now there were so few of them.

Beltayn snapped a white signal pellet into his flare pistol and handed it to Gaunt. 'Safety's off, sir,' he said.

'Problem!' Criid hissed urgently. Gaunt looked where she was pointing. A detachment of Shadik troopers was filing out into the siege gun firing area from a trench head to their west. Gaunt counted at least sixty men. Clad in long coats and helmets, their weapons ready and lowered in their hands, they were searching between the gun cars and the loading hoists.

Looking for us, Gaunt thought. Looking for the infiltrators.

'Ready your weapons,' he called down the line. 'Wait for my word.'

Some of the Shadik had lanterns. Two had teams of snarling canines.

Gaunt tucked the flare pistol into his pocket and took out his boltgun. Full clip. He drew his power sword and laid it on the earth beside him.

Down the line, the Ghosts in Criid and Raglon's squads fitted new clips to their Mark III's and fixed their blades to the barrels, each trooper stabbing the warknife into the ridge soil first to dull its shine.

Golke and the Bande Sezari soldiers got their solid-round weapons ready.

One more minute.

Be on time, all of you, Gaunt willed. Be on time.

Alarm whistles suddenly blew. The enemy detachment abruptly began running, moving in a flood to the east. Gaunt saw muzzle flashes and heard the crack of rifles.

They were heading into the ammunition corridor. Domor's team had been spotted.

'On them!' Gaunt yelled. 'First-and-Only!' The cover team broke from the ridge and came down the slope, guns blazing. The Shadik unit faltered, suddenly under fire from their left. The Ghosts ripped into them.

Gaunt was right in the middle of it. His boltgun howled and blew an enemy infantryman apart. His majestic blade, the power sword of Heironymo Sondar, gifted to him in gratitude by the people of Vervunhive, flickered with blue lightning. Beside him, Beltayn was firing from the shoulder as he ran, thumping bright las-bolts into the greatcoated enemy.

Beyond Beltayn, Criid was urging her Ghosts on, deploying them in tight groups even in the mêlée of an impromptu charge.

I made a good choice in Tona, Gaunt thought.

A second later, a Shadik battletrooper was in his face, lunging with a serrated bayonet. Gaunt deflected with the sword, shearing off the front half of the man's gun and an arm with it. A bolt-round settled the man right behind him.

Lubba's flamer roared and lit up the night. Gaunt saw two Shadik lurching away, burning from head to toe. Hwlan, Vulli and Kolea laid in side by side. Kolea seemed to have forgotten how a lasrifle worked. He was scything into the enemy with his bayonet fixed, reaping them down like corn stalks, hacking like a miner at an ore-face.

It was a blur of frantic, face-to-face killing. Golke blasted with his revolver until it was empty, and then grabbed up a Shadik submachine-gun that had fallen on the gravel of the track bed.

One of the Bande Sezari men beside him convulsed as rifle rounds tore through him. Golke swung round and cracked away with the compact weapon, knocking three of the enemy troopers off their feet.

'More of them!' Raglon yelled above the din of combat. Gaunt could see another company of Shadik troopers streaming out of the eastern trench-head to reinforce the first. Grenades blared and flashed in the night.

Domor's squad had been pinned down and then driven off by the first fusillades. They had taken cover around a parked munitions truck about two hundred metres down the corridor.

'Sir!' Beltayn yelled. Gaunt looked up and saw two red starshells fading away. In the frenzy of it all, he'd almost missed the signals from Mkoll and Arcuda.

Two out of three. Good enough. It would have to do.

'Break off and retreat!' he bellowed, and fired the white flare.

As soon as the corpse light of the white signal bloomed above them, a hot yellow burst exploded to the north, and then another, seconds later, to the west.

The cover team, firing behind them as they went, battled up the ridge and back into the darkness of the wasteland. They left the sidings and track beds littered with Shadik dead.

GAUNT CHECKED HIS bearings by the luminous dial of his compass. They were right on the rendezvous point. 'Head count!' he ordered to Beltayn.

Behind them, yellow light flickered the night. The main line was severed both north and south of the gun sidings.

Two minutes passed, and Arcuda's team emerged out of the gloom. Then Domor's squad struggled in, breathlessly.

'I'm sorry, sir,' Domor panted. 'We were almost set when they hit us. I tried to go back and finish the job, but they had the area bracketed.'

'Don't worry, Domor. You did your best. We hit the main transit line, that's the important thing. Those guns aren't going anywhere.'

'But they'll still be able to fire with the corridor open to supply them.' Domor looked forlorn with disappointment.

Gaunt gripped him by the shoulders. 'You did all right, Shoggy. Really. You did your best, that's all I ever ask for. We sit tight here now until Mkoll's mob rejoins us and then we have fun and games getting out of here. All right?'

Domor nodded.

Beltayn reappeared. 'We left a few dead behind us, sir, but everyone's accounted for. Except–'

'Except?'

'Count Golke, sir.'

SHADIK TROOPERS WERE milling around the firing site, and spreading out down the lines, surveying the damage with lanterns. Two huge craters marred the tracks, one on each side of the siege gun emplacement. More troopers, muffled in their heavy, drab coats and trench armour, shambled south down the corridor line, picking over the bodies. One called for an officer as he found the half-laid tube-charges between the sleepers.

Count Golke crouched behind the bogies of the munition cart, barely twenty metres from the nearest enemy soldier. He watched as they grouped around and cut apart the wires connecting the tube-bombs, pulling them off the tracks. The officer waved a hand and barked orders, sending a squad of about ten down to check the cart.

The troopers approached, rifles ready, the lamplight glinting off their helmets and bayonets.

Golke limped round the back end of the cart. It was actually a linked line of three, laden with propellant cartridges, waiting for the next shunting engine to move in and pull it down to the armoured magazines.

Golke climbed up onto the middle cart. It was hard work with his hip. He winced and grunted.

The bullet wound in his chest made it harder still.

He got onto the top, and sat down between the canister hoppers. He smiled. He'd come back into the Pocket, faced his demons, and come through it. Now he was going to his victory too. It was due him.

What he'd failed to achieve as a commander, he would do as a trooper.

The enemy soldiers were around the carts now. He could hear their voices. One called out. He'd found the trail of Golke's blood.

Golke heard more voices, and boots clunking on rungs of the cart's metal side ladder.

Those Shadik voices. The voices of the enemy.

Golke wished the whole war could have been as simple as this.

He coughed, and blood welled out of his mouth and down his chin. A Shadik called out, he'd heard the cough. Golke caught the sound of bolt-actions cranking.

He lifted up the tube-charge. It was the only one he'd been able to tear free from the tangle Domor's team had wired to the tracks. There'd been no time for more.

He wasn't sure how it worked, but there was a paper tab on the top that looked like an igniter strip.

He felt footsteps on the body of the truck. A Shadik trooper appeared around the side of the right hand hopper and called out as he saw Golke lying there.

The trooper raised his rifle.

'For the Emperor,' Golke said, and tore the det-tape away.

THE TUBE FIRED. Canisters around ruptured. Propellant cartridges ignited. The blast lit up the valley for a moment. One hundred metres of ammunition corridor and the land around it vanished in a geyser of flame.

SIXTEEN
COMEUPPANCE

'I hate last stands. You never get an opportunity to practise for them.'

– Piet Gutes

THE SKY WAS full of stars. They were pink, and vaguely oblong. On the horizon, sheaves of white fireworks danced and burst, like the firecrackers of a victory parade. The air was pulsing with a strange humming sound, like a moaning human voice swimming in and out of hearing. A dark shadow suddenly eclipsed the stars. A big shadow that filled the sky.

'Wake up,' said a voice.

He obeyed, moving. The strange sky, with its ghastly, wrong stars, drained away. He smelled cold air and heard the patter of heavy rain close by.

'Larks,' said Bragg, 'it's time to wake up.'

'Try?'

Try Again Bragg smiled his big, genial smile. 'Time to wake up,' he said.

Larkin blinked and sat up quickly. The movement made him dizzy and he felt nausea rise through him. The hind part of his brain felt like someone was repeatedly clubbing it with a nine-seventy, spike first. At the edges of his vision, obscure lights danced and fire crackers burst.

He was on the dirty mattress in a damp bedroom of the Manse. Rain sheeted down outside, accompanied by lightning. It was late afternoon.

Bragg wasn't there any more.

'See you later,' said Larkin.

* * *

APART FROM THE rainstorm, things had been quiet since they'd driven the assault back first thing. They'd repaired the defences, and added a few more at Mkvenner's suggestion.

The scout explained how he and Jajjo had run across the Blood Pact unit late the previous night. A fair-sized patrol force, which Mkvenner was certain was just the spearhead of a larger advance. Shadik had been reinforced from off-world by the elite infantry of the arch-enemy, and the first action of that elite had been to pave the way for an invasion through the Montorq Forest.

Ironic, Caffran thought, that both Chaos and Imperial elements had brought the same advice to the warring nations of Aexe Cardinal.

Rerval was stable, thanks to the deserter's field aid, though weak from loss of blood. They put him in the drawing room out of the way, and Caffran asked Peterik to look after him. No one complained that Peterik wasn't tied up any more. The old woman sat with them and banked up the drawing room fire.

With Rerval out of commission, Mkvenner operated the vox-caster, and sent a more detailed repeat of the original message. Again, there was no reply. There was still no way of telling if anyone had heard either warning.

'We're done here now, anyway,' announced Feygor. 'I mean, now Ven and Jajjo are back. We know the situation. So we can get out of here now. Just get up and go.'

'And how far would we get?' asked Mkvenner. 'With an old lady and a man who can't walk?'

Feygor shrugged. 'Then we fething well leave them! I know, tough. I don't like it. But aren't we obliged to carry a warning back now? I mean, the vox is probably down. We'd be failing in our duty if we didn't get off our arses and try to get word back to company command.'

Mkvenner frowned. He didn't want to get into his thoughts on the subject of Murtan Feygor and failure of duty.

'He's right,' he said instead, surprising them all, including Feygor. 'Up to a point, anyway. We have to assume the vox is dead. We have to get a warning through to Ins Arbor, or this could turn into a first class feth-up. But even without the old lady and Rerval, even moving as fast as we can, I don't think we'd outrun them. They're swift, they're good and they're right on us.'

'So?' asked Cuu.

'So, we maintain the defence of this place. For as long as we can. We keep the Blood Pact busy right here.'

'Because?'

'Because we'll be buying time for someone to get word back. Someone fast might have a chance if the enemy push was delayed here.'

Caffran, Muril and Jajjo looked solemn. Feygor shook his head. Gutes sat down, tutting. Brostin growled an unhappy curse.

Cuu asked the obvious question. 'Who goes?'

'Who's fast?' Mkvenner replied.

'You,' said Feygor.

'I'll be staying here,' said Mkvenner. He'd suggested the plan. He wouldn't leave the hard part to them.

'Then Muril or Jajjo,' said Feygor. 'Maybe Cuu. He's light on his toes.'

'Who's going to decide?' asked Caffran.

'I am,' said Mkvenner, and no one argued. 'Jajjo. You're up. Take the bare minimum so you move light. Don't stop for anything.'

The young Vervunhiver nodded. He was swallowing hard. The weight of responsibility scared him. So did Mkvenner's trust. Worst of all was the idea he was leaving them behind. They were going to die to buy him time.

'Come on,' said Mkvenner. 'Get going. There's no time to waste.'

They all said their goodbyes to Jajjo in turn. Caffran and Gutes helped him pare down his kit and wished him well. Feygor tried to say something and then just nodded, lost for words. Brostin slapped him on the back and told him not to feth up. Muril filled a pair of water canteens for Jajjo to take with him. 'Good luck,' she said.

'I wish he'd picked you,' Jajjo told her.

'Me too,' she smiled, 'but not for the reason you think.'

'You can do it, Jaj,' Cuu said, winking at the cadet scout. 'Sure as sure, you can.'

Jajjo left by the front door, into the rain and the bad light.

He turned back once, to look at Mkvenner. 'Sir, I–'

'Go,' said Mkvenner.

And Jajjo was gone.

MKVENNER SHUT AND bolted the front door. Feygor was already deploying the remaining members of the detail to fire positions. He sent Muril to the first floor, to check what shape Larkin was in and take up a sniping position. 'Use Larkin's long-las if he's out of it,' Feygor instructed.

In the hallway, she passed Mkvenner heading back from the front door.

'Sir,' she said.

'Trooper?'

'I know things have gone... bad,' she began. 'But for the record... for what that's worth... I wish you'd taken me more seriously during this patrol.'

'You don't think I've taken you seriously?'

'I want to be a scout, sir. All the way along, you've given the opportunities to Jajjo, brought him along. Even now, even this. He gets trusted with the break out run.'

'You know why I chose him over you?'

'No sir.'

'You're a better shot, Muril. We need you here. When we... if we get back, I'll be making a recommendation to Mkoll. Scout advancement.'

'For Jajjo?'

'For both of you. I've been impressed with your work from the moment you signed up. Jajjo needed a bit of extra coaching to make the grade.'

She opened her mouth, then closed it again. She wasn't quite sure what to say.

Then the opportunity was gone anyway. They both started as they heard a flurry of explosions from the back of the house.

NINETEEN DETAIL HAD set half their tube-charges in the undergrowth and outbuildings along the back of the rear plot. Brostin had found some bales of fence twine in the cellar and they'd rigged tripwires.

The first intruders into the garden, moving clumsily in the heavy rain, found the wires with their boots. A whole cluster of charges had gone off along the ragged rear wall and demolished it completely. Two more had been triggered at the top of the ditch on the east side of the garden. The Blood Pact troopers, so far invisible in the downpour, began shooting at the house. The defenders at the manse fired back a few discouraging blasts. After a minute or so there was another flash and boom from the left side of the property line as another set of charges was tripped.

The firing stopped. The Blood Pact had fallen back again.

MURIL WENT TO fetch Larkin's long-las, but found it in his hands. He was crouched by one of the bedroom windows, scanning the rain outside.

'You all right?' she asked.

'Yeah,' he said. He didn't look it. He looked dreadful. His thin face was almost white except for the livid bruising, and his eyes were dark hollows.

'I feel better,' he said. 'Really. I feel better for not... taking that shot.'

'Good,' she said. 'We'll get Cuu, Larks. We'll get out of this and get him. I saw him try to kill you, remember? We'll talk to Corbec. Tell him everything.'

'Okay,' said Larkin.

'I mean... Cuu, Feygor, Brostin... Gutes too, I guess. They're going to be up on charges for what they did here. Feygor as good as deserted for a few days. I can't believe Ven won't make a full report. And we'll make a full report of our own about Cuu.'

'Good,' he said.

'So... you fit to do some hunting?'

'I'm fit,' he nodded, settling his long-las.

'I'll be down the landing in the end bedroom.'

'Okay.'

She disappeared. He turned back to his scope. For a moment, he couldn't see the garden or the fringe of woods at all. Just oblong pink stars and firecrackers.

He blinked, then blinked again, until his vision cleared.

HALF AN HOUR later, the Blood Pact returned. In the makeshift pillbox of the greenhouse, Caffran thought he saw movement in the rain, and craned his head up over the edge of the old bedstead and the sacking.

He heard a noise. A hollow puff followed by a whine. Then another. Then yet another.

He knew that sound.

'Incoming!' he yelled.

The first mortar shell blew a hole in the middle of the lawn and threw clods of torn earth into the air. Another made a fireball halfway down the garden's east wall and stone chips rattled down with the rain. A third hit the roofless coal bunker.

The shells kept coming, pounding the rear lawn with fierce explosions. Then autocannons opened up in the tree-line, stitching the back of the house.

Mkvenner was down at the barricade with Cuu. Any moment now, and a mortar round would flatten the greenhouse and Caffran with it.

'Fall back! Caff, fall back!' he shouted. The heavy structure of the house itself at least offered some protection.

Caffran was curled up protectively, trying to keep an eye out. A shell went off right outside, shaking the greenhouse and spraying him with dirt.

'Caffran!'

'Wait!' he shouted back.

Under cover of the furious mortar and cannon fire, the troopers began their assault. Caffran glimpsed red-clad figures pouring in through the rubble at the back of the lawn, some crawling along the side ditches or below what was left of the back wall. Now small-arms fire came their way too.

He waited as long as he dared, until enemy shapes had almost reached the sundial half-way down the lawn.

He yanked the twine in his hand. The cord was tied off to the det-tapes of their remaining tubes, buried in the lawn itself. They went off in rapid series, hurling two or three bodies into the air.

Satisfied, Caffran leapt up, and scrambled out through the back of the greenhouse into the yard. Las-rounds flew past him. A mortar bomb exploded in the kitchen garden off to his left, and then another hit the greenhouse squarely.

The blast threw him onto his face. Mkvenner dashed across to him and dragged him back towards the kitchen doorway where Brostin was covering them. Cuu had already run inside out of the deluge.

Mkvenner got Caffran into the kitchen as two more mortar shells hit the barricade and the remains of the coal bunker. Stone fragments peppered the back wall of the manse. Everyone firing from a window ducked. A further shell hit the west side of the wall and brought the roof down into the pantry with a terrible crash.

'Okay?' Mkvenner snapped at Caffran. Caffran was dazed, and his shoulders and the backs of his legs were covered in shrapnel cuts.

'Fine!' he gasped, and got up to join Brostin at the door.

'Get that flamer up!' Mkvenner said. 'They'll be in range soon!'

The house shook as another mortar struck it. Broken tiles avalanched down into the yard. There were Blood Pact troopers all over the rear lawn now, coming in low on the far side of the barricade and the shredded greenhouse. Thick smoke and the flash of explosions fogged most of the view. The Ghosts fired at every target they could make out. From the first floor, Muril and Larkin were making the best of the kills.

'Somebody else get upstairs!' Feygor bellowed, blasting from the main kitchen window. Cuu leapt up and ran.

'The right! They're getting round from the fething right!' Gutes yelled over the link from the dining room. Mkvenner moved to the kitchen door and peered out east. Over the burning vestiges of the coal bunker, he could see Gutes's las-fire hammering at the hedge-veiled ditch running up the side of the manse.

'Keep that up, Gutes!' he snarled. 'Keep them ducking! I'll come around the front and set up a crossfire!'

'Read that!' Gutes sang back.

Mkvenner ran back along the hall from the kitchen, and unbolted the front door. The house vibrated with the rattle of gunfire and the batter of the mortars. The pots and pans on the stairs were quivering and spilling their contents as the whole manse shook. He felt a particularly loud bang that sounded like a mortar had taken the roof in. Mkvenner realised it was simply the thunder splitting right overhead.

He got the door open and edged out into the rain, weapon up, moving round the eastern side of the building. The roar of battle floated round from the rear.

The Blood Pact was already tearing through the ditch hedge into the front lawn area. One spotted Mkvenner, but the scout shot him dead before he could raise either weapon or cry. He fired again. Two more toppled backwards into the hedge, arms flailing.

Three more opened fire, and Mkvenner was forced to dodge back into the cover of the porch. Las-rounds whirred off the stone porch posts. From cover, he managed to hit two of the attackers and then made a dash for the hedge, hoping to cut off the ditch with an enfilade.

A grenade tumbled through the rain. Mkvenner threw himself out of the way, but still the blast lifted him and slammed him into the long, wet grass of the lawn.

He came round again moments later to see an iron mask leering at him, and a blade striking at his throat.

Mkvenner rolled and kicked his legs round, smashing the Blood Pact trooper over. Another one lunged at the Tanith with his bayonet, but Mkvenner grabbed the barrel, wrenched it out of the enemy's hands, and killed him with a savage blow using the stock. A las-round cracked at him from point-blank range, but Mkvenner had crouched low, and came up, scything the bayonet of the captured weapon through the belly of the third attacker. Without looking, he planted a kick backwards, breaking the neck of the first man, who was now trying to get up from the grass.

But there were more of them, so many more. Almost a dozen, rushing him, some firing. He sidestepped another bayonet, and a las-round ripped through his right thigh. Fuelled with pain, he rammed the blade of his borrowed rifle through the neck of the closest invader.

Full auto las-fire tore across the lawn, making trails of steam in the downpour. Three Blood Pacters fell immediately, then a fourth. Mkvenner opened fire with his lasrifle and took out two more before turning and sprinting for the porch.

In the porch doorway, Peterik stood, blasting furiously with Rerval's lasgun. Full auto.

The remaining Blood Pact exposed on the lawn either died or fled.

Mkvenner tumbled in beside him.

'Thank you,' he said.

'You need to get that leg wound treated,' said Peterik.

'I'll do it later, if there's a later,' said Mkvenner. 'Right now, we have to hold the front of the house. You up to that?'

Peterik nodded. 'Yes, sir. I am.'

At the rear, a series of mortar rounds had struck the yard and blown paving slabs through the kitchen wall. Another two shells had slammed into the pantry, already a ruin. Caffran and Feygor were down behind the cast-iron bulk of the stove, firing through the shattered hole that had once been the main window. The kitchen door had been blown off its hinges, but Brostin was in the doorway, revving his flamer.

A trio of Blood Pact troops leapt the barricade and charged the kitchen. Brostin hosed them and they torched in their tracks, the grenades they carried blowing out and showering the fractured yard with metal chips, pieces of gristle and burning scraps of fabric. Brostin nursed the flamer, and sent a second flare right over the barricade, sizzling in the rain. They could hear screams. An enemy trooper, burning across his back and legs, ran hopelessly towards the greenhouse and fell when Feygor shot him.

Brostin had an infamous affinity with fire. Now the enemy was in range, he started bursting sprays of liquid flame up over the barricade and the wall of the kitchen garden, sliding it round angles that las-rounds couldn't touch. He washed the jumbled wood of the felled green house with a blanket of warm, orange fire, blistering the old paint and cooking the wood, and then ignited the toasted kindling with a spear of blue, super-hot fire. Another enemy voice rose up in a scream. A blizzard of touched-off grenades added to the raging fire.

The mortar rounds still thumped in. Caffran flinched as he heard one go through the roof. Cannon fire raked the back wall, splitting exposed brickwork and stone. The manse's original lime wash render had long since been shot away.

Feygor looked across at Caffran as they ducked another salvo.

'This what you wanted to stay here for?' he asked, sarcastically. Feygor always sounded sarcastic, but this was the real thing.

'No,' said Caffran. He pointed to the Tanith regimental badge on his jacket. 'I wanted to stay for this.'

Brostin's flamer spluttered and whooshed again. The stink of burning promethium filled the kitchen.

'They're rushing us!' Brostin yelled. 'They're rushing us!'

It was over, Larkin knew. The manse was falling apart under the mortar rounds, and the back of the house was under assault from a battalion-strength enemy unit. The Blood Pact was in the side ditch too, he could hear that, and round the front.

He made what shots he could, knocking down scarlet shapes on the lawn and behind the barricade. But one thing was for sure. There were more enemy troopers outside than he had hot-shots left in his satchel.

He wondered if they'd bought enough time. He wondered where Jajjo was. He wondered if anyone would ever know what a thing they'd done there this day. That handful of them, against an army.

His vision was going again. The lights were dancing. He blinked hard and shook his head, trying to clear his eyes. Shaking his head made it feel like he was sloshing his brains around.

He wondered if the pain would overcome him before the Blood Pact reached him. Which would be quicker? Which would hurt less?

He took another shot, but missed. He fired again, and missed a second time. His eyes were so foggy and the pain so almighty. Pink, oblong stars. Firecrackers. Firecrackers...

A hand grabbed him by the back of the neck and slammed his face into the window sill. Larkin squealed in pain and passed out briefly.

Lijah Cuu held him by the back of his head, fingers pressing like iron tongs into the damaged region of the sniper's skull.

Larkin writhed, tears of pain rushing down his ashen cheeks.

'What...? What...?' he mumbled.

'We're dead now, Tanith, sure as sure. They're in at the doors and windows. We're finished. Except I'm not finished. I'm not going anywhere, even all the way to hell, without settling my business.'

'Feth!' screamed Larkin, trying to struggle free. Cuu's hands twisted at the fracture in the back of his skull and he gagged and howled. Blood spurted from Larkin's nostrils. 'You crazy bastard!' he spluttered. 'This isn't–'

'What? What, you little Tanith gak-face? The right time? That's funny, sure as sure. You have to pay, and if this isn't the time, there'll never be another.'

Cuu wrenched at Larkin's head again, and the sniper threw up. Cuu shoved him off onto the mattress.

Larkin tried to move, but the oblong pink stars filled his vision, merged into one huge firecracker that blasted through his mind.

He went into spasms. His back arched and his eyes rolled back until they were just bloodshot whites. Blood spattered as he bit his tongue. As the seizure smashed through his stringy body and limbs, he made an unearthly groan.

Cuu stepped back for a second in disgust. He drew his blade. Tanith straight silver, thirty centimetres long.

'You animal,' he growled, avoiding Larkin's thrashing limbs. 'Looks like I'll be doing you a favour, you freak.'

He raised the knife.

'Get off him, you bastard!' Muril spat. She stood in the doorway of the bedroom, her lasrifle aimed at Cuu's scar-split face.

She edged towards him. 'You shit. You little shit.'

Cuu rose, grinned his grin. 'I was just trying to help him, girly. Look at him. He's spazzing out. Let's help him before he bites through his gakking tongue.'

'Leave him alone! I saw you, Cuu. I saw what you were doing.'

'I wasn't doing nothing.'

'You were going to kill him. Like you killed Bragg. And God-Emperor knows who else. You piece of shit.'

'So what are you going to do, eh? Eh, girly? You gonna shoot me?'

'I might.'

'We're all dead anyway. Listen to the crap out there. They must be into the kitchen by now. Go ahead, shoot. It won't matter.'

'It'll matter to me, Cuu. I'll die happy.'

There was a stunning flash and a noise that sounded like thunder but wasn't. The bedroom wall exploded in, strewing bricks and plaster across the room. Another mortar shell came in through the attic overhead and blew out the landing behind them.

Muril tried to get up in the choking dust and smoke. There was no sign of her weapon in the debris, so she drew her warknife. Covered in shreds of plaster and curls of wallpaper, Larkin was still alive, and still convulsing and groaning on the mattress by the window.

Muril stumbled towards him, searching for Cuu's body in the rubble.

He was behind her, his blade in his hand.

With a cry, she swept round, as fast as any Tanith scout had ever moved, before or since.

Straight silver punched through flesh and bone and didn't stop until it had impaled the beating heart.

PART OF THE roof collapsed. Piet Gutes ducked as falling rafters tore through the ceiling of the dining room, crushing the long, polished table. The vases and precious porcelain tumbled off the shelves and smashed. The oil paintings had caught fire.

Gutes got up, spitting out dust. The ceiling was open right to the sky and rain drizzled down. He took a look up through the smashed window hole he had been defending. A red-painted light tank was rolling down the back lawn from the trees, enemy troops surging around it. It raked up the overgrown grass and knocked over the sundial. When it fired again, Gutes felt the manse shake. One of the pictures fell off the wall.

For the first time, he wondered who they were. Those solemn faces, dark with age, looking out from the frames. Staring at him from so far away.

The pictures burned, despite the rain.

Gutes saw movement at the window and fired. An iron mask lurched back. Shots came in, ripping into the floor. Gutes backed down the dining room, rainwater pattering off him, avoiding the smashed furniture and firing at the gap. Multiple points of gunfire tore through in reply.

A single dining chair had survived the collapse of the rafters. Gutes sat down on it and continued to fire at the window until his cell ran dry.

Half a dozen Blood Pact troopers scrambled in through the window, aiming their weapons at the lone figure sitting on a chair at the end of the room.

They started to shoot.

Gutes wondered if the old woman would make it. He hoped so, though he doubted it.

But it didn't matter any more.

Nothing matters if you're far enough away. That's what Piet Gutes had always told himself.

And now, at last, he was as far away as he could possibly be.

SEVENTEEN
FIRST AND LAST

'There can be honour in life, and honour in courage,
and honour in action, but the most certain honour of all,
to man's regret, is the honour in death.'

– Iaco Bousar Fep Golke, from his diaries

SMOKE WEPT OUT of the forest like blood from a wound. The storm had passed, heading out at last across the peaks of the Massif, but the air was still damp and the sky still black.

The sound of warfare continued to drift back through the pine stands of the Montorq. Small-arms, vehicle-mounted cannon, grenades.

Colm Corbec jumped down from the eight-wheeler APC he'd been riding in and called out to the unit groups ahead.

'Are we clear?' he yelled.

'Clear!' Varl shouted back.

'Go get me a sit-rep!' Corbec hollered.

'Sir,' said Jajjo, rising from his seat in the APC. 'I'd like to–'

'I know you would, son,' said Corbec. 'But I think maybe you should stay here for now.'

'I–'

'That's an order, lad.'

Corbec wandered up through the trees towards the smoking shell of the old, lonely house. 'The manse', Jajjo had called it.

To his left, light tanks and clanking sentinels of the Krassian Armoured ploughed up the valley through the trees, lending fire support to the First fire-teams Corbec had sent in ahead of him. A fairly serious firefight was occurring in the woods behind the house.

Commissar Hark trudged back to meet him. He was swinging a helmet in his hand.

'Trooper Jajjo was right,' Hark said, showing Corbec the helmet's iron mask. 'Blood Pact.'

'I never doubted Jajjo's word for a moment,' said Corbec quietly. 'The vox messages were plain enough.'

Hark nodded. 'Just so, Corbec. I'm just glad we mustered up and got here in time.'

'Did we, but?' Corbec said wearily.

'We've driven the Blood Pact force right back into the woods. Major Vikkers of the Krassian armour says they're in retreat, falling back up the valley to the high pass. Looks like the Krassian tanks scored a good few kills against enemy armour pieces and–'

'We've won, for today. I know that, Hark. I meant... did we get here in time for our own?' Corbec fell silent, looking at the smoking ruin of the manse.

'Nine platoon's checking it now. We–'

'Round up the rearguard and send them through,' Corbec told him abruptly. 'I'm going to see for myself.'

VARL WAS WAITING for him at the battered porch of the manse. Enemy dead littered the lawn. An old woman – Corbec had no idea who the feth she was – was kneeling on the gravel path and weeping over the body of a young Alliance soldier. On the steps of the porch, a Krassian corpsman was treating a Tanith trooper for multiple injuries. He was shouting out for a medic as he worked. The Tanith man was so covered in blood he was unrecognisable at first. A bad leg wound, a gut shot, a scalp wound, something messy through the left shoulder.

Corbec ignored Varl and knelt down beside the man. Only then did he realise it was Mkvenner.

'Feth, Ven! It was only meant to be a patrol!'

'That's all it was,' said Mkvenner, weakly blinking blood out of his eyes.

'You'll be okay,' Corbec said. 'Make him okay, feth it!' he said, looking up at the frantic corpsman.

'You got our signal then?' Mkvenner whispered.

'If you're going to waste talk, don't state the fething obvious. We got it, Ven, we came. We kicked their arses back into the woods. You did a fine job, you and the rest.'

'Commendations,' Mkvenner sighed.

'Just shut up now,' said Corbec.

Mkvenner shook his head. 'I may not get another chance to say this, Colm. I commend them all. All of them. They were true to the last. First and last. If

Jajjo made it, then he deserves scout rank. Muril too, no question. Make sure she knows I commended her. And I want a special mention put in to Alliance GSC. Will you do that for me, sir?'

'Of course I will.'

'Private First Class Rufo Peterik, Sixteenth Brunsgatters. For valour. Can you remember that name, Colm?'

'I will, but I won't have to, Ven. 'Cause you're fething well not going to die.'

Krassian medicae ran up the front lawn to assist the corpsman. Corbec rose and turned to Varl.

'Tell me. How bad?'

'Piet Gutes is dead in that room there. Looks like he gave a good account of himself. Rerval's alive. Took a hit to the face in an earlier phase of action. Docs are with him now.'

'That's something,' Corbec sighed. He'd missed his vox man these last few days.

'Brostin, Feygor and Caffran made it too, though Brostin and Caff are hurt bad. Somehow Feygor came out without a scratch.'

'Luck of the devil,' Corbec said. 'What about the rest?'

'Larkin's touch and go. Doc Mtane's with him. Head wound. The doc doesn't know if he'll make it. Says we have to get Larks back to Ins Arbor for surgery.'

'Feth,' said Corbec.

'I–' Varl began.

'What?'

'I found Muril upstairs with Larks. The bastards had bayonetted her.'

Corbec closed his eyes. He felt a pain worse than any injury he'd ever received. 'I want to go see her,' he said.

'Chief–' Varl tried to stop him. 'You don't want to see that.'

'I need to, Varl. I need to.' Corbec pushed past the sergeant and walked up the steps into the house.

In the doorway, he paused and glanced back at Varl.

'What about Cuu?'

'Oh, he made it,' Varl said.

THERE WAS A lot of commotion around the house. Not the same sort of commotion that had all but demolished it, but still. Troop carriers were gliding up. Krassian tanks were churning up over the lawns and into the woods.

There was a gak of a fight going on up there in the trees.

Not his problem any more.

Lijah Cuu sat on an old bench at the side of the front lawn and watched it all.

He licked the blood from the straight silver of his warknife and slid it away into its scabbard.

EIGHTEEN
ENDING IN THE MIDDLE

'When I speak of a body in this way, I mean the body as a figure for an armed force. To the leader, that force becomes his body. He must care for it and drive it and feed it and see to its well-being and its ills. It thuswise becomes his limbs, and organs of life and sense, the body militant. Thus the scale magnifies. All commanders and their men are bodies in war, fighting and falling in the way of things as sole men fight and fall and shew their woundings.'

– DeMarchese, *On The Use of Armies*

A WEEK LATER, in the dismal streets of Gibsgatte, more rain fell.

Colonel-Commissar Ibram Gaunt, still limping slightly from the rifle-round that had scraped him during the six-hour break-out from the Shadik lines, came up the steps of the Sezaria, a gold-domed building that dominated the skyline of the dirty northern city.

Bande Sezari sentries at the door checked his papers and then bowed to admit him, the struthid plumes in their caps touching the floor.

Gaunt nodded to them with genuine respect. He knew who the Bande Sezari were now. He'd seen several of them fight to the last.

An Alliance adjutant escorted him up three flights and along a splendid corridor of gilt-framed paintings. The adjutant knocked at a set of painted doors and announced him.

'Colonel-Commissar Gaunt, sir.'

Gaunt stepped in, the doors closing behind him, and saluted.

Supreme Commander Lyntor-Sewq rose, and came round his desk to greet Gaunt.

'Good to see you, Gaunt.'

'Sir.'

Lyntor-Sewq was a thin, bald man with a plucked moustache and limpid eyes. 'How are you, sir?' he asked.

'Well enough.'

'Leg troubling you?'

'Not so much, thank you for asking.'

'Rough ride you must have had, getting out from the enemy lines that night.'

'Indeed, sir. It took us a day and a half, all told, laying low, moving when it was clear.'

'Your stealthing arts. Why, they're the talk of the General Staff! You ran into trouble, though?'

'Yes, sir. Twice. The last time when we were almost clear. I lost a few good soldiers there.'

'A terrible shame, Gaunt. Drink?'

'I'll take a small amasec, sir.'

Lyntor-Sewq poured two drinks into priceless crystal glasses. He handed one to Gaunt.

'Here's to your efforts, sir,' said the supreme commander.

'And my dead,' returned Gaunt.

'Quite so.

They sipped.

Lyntor-Sewq led him over to a chart table on which the full expanse of the Aexe Cardinal war was laid out.

'Many doubted you, Gaunt. You and the Imperials. Of course, we were grateful for your intervention. But still... I won't ever mention your name to Redjacq Ankre.'

'If I never see him again, sir, I will not be forlorn.'

Lyntor-Sewq chuckled. 'We got the guns. The siege-guns. I'm sure you've been told. They were stuck right where you'd stranded them. A flight of marauder aircraft destroyed them the following night. Those marauders. Fine vessels. I'd dearly like a few to bolster the Alliance Air Corps.'

'I'm sure General Van Voytz will oblige. Actually, I expected to see him here today.'

Lyntor-Sewq smiled. 'He's gone south. To Frergarten. We're pushing up through the Montorq now, you know. And that's where I must thank you again. Your scout units, stemming the tide, calling a warning. Alerting us to the presence of the arch-enemy elite on Aexegarian soil. My plans have changed, of course. Radically. But I'm focusing on the new initiative, and I think we may have turned a corner. The war will be over by Candlemas.'

Gaunt finished his drink. 'I hope so, sir,' he said. 'Either that, or this war will last forever.'

Lyntor-Sewq looked down into his glass grimly. 'It takes as long as it takes,' he said.

Gaunt nodded. He'd been reviewing battle reports for the last week. They'd killed the super-guns and fronted the invasion through the Montorq and even so both actions seemed like tiny pieces of a whole.

Sarvo had been lost. The Meiseq Box punctured. The lower Naeme Valley overrun. The Ostlund Shield broken in two places. For every victory, a loss. For every metre taken, a death. The war simply ground on, like a furnace fed by manpower.

'I presume you'll be deploying my units to new locations?'

'Actually, no.' The supreme commander handed Gaunt a data-slate. 'New orders. From the Warmaster, relayed by the Astropathicus. Your regiment is being retasked. Navy transports are moving in system to collect you.'

Gaunt looked at the slate.

He felt a peculiar sense of shock. He'd never been pulled out of a warzone before the fighting was done. In his opinion, there was still a year or more of bloodshed to go on Aexe Cardinal before the Imperium could claim victory. Macaroth was pulling the Tanith First out. It was like ending in the middle of things. According to the slate, elements of the Second Crusade Army were moving in to replace them and finish the job.

And his heart skipped when he saw the destination the Ghosts were heading to.

'The Emperor protect you, where you're going,' Lyntor-Sewq said.

'Thank you, sir.'

'I only asked you here today to give you this.'

He reached into his desk and produced a slim, oblong box covered in gold-flecked blue satin. Lyntor-Sewq opened it.

A Gold Aquila, pinned to a white silk ribbon, lay in the cushioned interior.

'This is to acknowledge your devoted service to Aexe Cardinal. The Order of the Eagle. The greatest honour it is in the high sezar's gift to bestow.'

Gaunt had seen one before, pinned proudly to Iaco Fep Golke's coat. He dearly wanted to take the medal and stuff it into Lyntor-Sewq's throat until he choked. Or at least refuse it. But he knew the trouble that would follow if he did either.

He allowed the supreme commander to pin it on him, and saluted. He'd wear it now, and never again.

As Gaunt strode out through the echoing hallway of the Sezaria, an officer of the Bande Sezari raced up to him with a package wrapped in brown paper.

'Sir,' he said. 'Tactician Biota said to expect you and give this to you with his compliments.'

Gaunt took the package with a vague nod.

Beltayn was waiting outside, sitting behind the wheel of a huge black staff car. His thumb was better. He could do gears now.

Gaunt got in the back.

'Sir?'

'Take us back to Rhonforq, Beltayn,' Gaunt said.

The motor car roared off from the long steps and turned into Gibsgatte's cross-town traffic, heading south.

In the back of the car, Gaunt stripped the brown paper off the parcel. Inside was an old edition of a book. He checked the spine: DeMarchese, '*On The Use of Armies*'.

Gaunt smiled, despite the deep misgivings aching through his heart.

There was a handwritten note from Biota tucked inside the cover.

'Colonel-commissar,' it began, 'I hope you find this instructive. I salvaged it from the lord general's library and I'm sure he won't miss it. As to the question you asked me...'

At Gaunt's urging, they drove through the woodlands around Shonsamarl on their way back to Rhonforq. The sunlight played through the trees, dappling the car as it switched back and forth down the narrow, meandering lanes.

Beltayn pulled the car to a halt.

'We're lost, aren't we?' Gaunt said.

'No, sir,' said Beltayn. 'I'm Tanith. I don't get lost.'

'You got lost on the way through here.'

Beltayn shrugged. 'All I know is, sir, this is the place. Don't ask me why it's not here anymore.'

Gaunt got out of the car. The woodland looked familiar, very familiar. He was sure Beltayn was right.

There just wasn't a chapel there any more. There was no trace of the Chapel of the Holy Light Abundant, Veniq. Nothing, except the lingering perfume of a particular flower.

Beltayn stepped over to join him. 'Where did it go, sir?' he asked.

Gaunt handed Beltayn Biota's note so he could read it.

'As to the question you asked me, I have researched the Imperial records and found a mention of an Adeptus Sororitas warrior named Elinor Zaker. She was a key member of Saint Sabbat's retinue during the original crusade, and died on Herodor six thousand years ago.'

Beltayn shivered. 'Something's awry, sir,' he said.

'I think so,' said Ibram Gaunt.

All along the 58th sector of the Peinforq Line, the word was spreading. The Ghosts were being pulled out. Enervated, Daur went down the line, distributing marshalling orders to the platoons. They were to pull back the following night to the cathedral city of Ghrennes and await Navy collection.

The orders didn't say where they were heading, but all the troops were excited. It sounded significant. And most of them were just desperate to get out of the trench horror of Aexe.

Daur was torn. He wanted to see the First out of the murderous front line, but he was going to miss the XO role. Ana Curth had told him that Rawne was almost fit. In a day or two, the major would return to duty.

Daur conveyed the orders dutifully, getting the regiment to prep for off-lift.

He got Haller's platoon roused up, then Obel's.

Then he walked down the zagging trench to Soric's command post.

Daur looked in through the gas curtain. 'Chief? Get your men ready,' he said. 'We're shipping out tomorrow night.'

Soric was seated at the table in his gloomy dugout. He held a twist of blue paper in his fingers.

'Right you are, captain,' he said. 'I know.'

Daur shrugged and left.

Soric looked down at the paper in his hands. 'Ghosts leaving. Tomorrow night,' it read.

Soric balled it up and threw it aside.

Vivvo suddenly peered in through the curtain. 'Word is we're moving on, chief. Any idea where to?'

'No,' snapped Soric.

'Okay,' said Vivvo warily, backing out and leaving him alone.

Soric sat back. The gleaming brass message shell sat on the camp table in front of him. He waited, hoping, wishing. Then he reached forward and grabbed the shell.

Agun Soric unscrewed the cap and shook out the spill of blue paper.

He unfolded it and read what was written there, written in his own hand.

One word.

'Herodor.'

SABBAT MARTYR

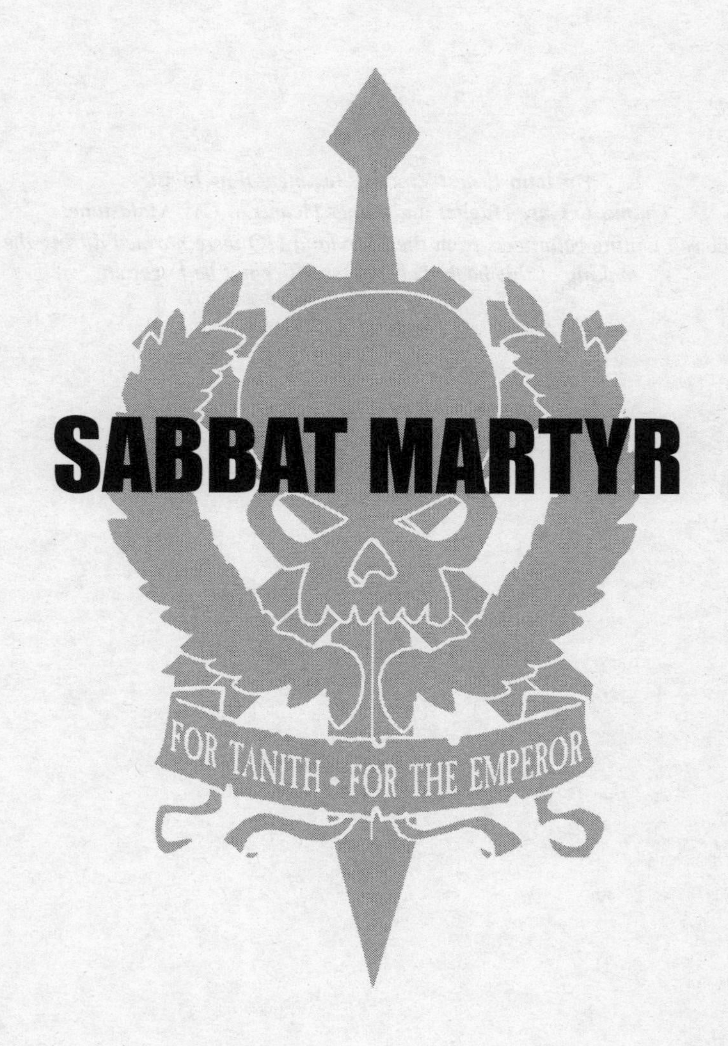

For John Ernest Vincent, regimental archivist.
Thanks to Gary Hughes and James Hewitt at GW Maidstone.
Eleven willing volunteers from the Maryland HQ were harmed during the making of this book. Let their sacrifice not be forgotten.

'BY 773.M41, the eighteenth year of the Sabbat Worlds Campaign, the Imperial crusade force under Warmaster Macaroth had yet failed to take the notorious fortress world Morlond. As long as Morlond stood, the thrust of the crusade was stalled, and Macaroth could not drive his forces onwards into a decisive war with the core military strengths of the archenemy overlord ("Archon"), Urlock Gaur, in the Carcaradon Cluster. More than ever, the crusade host seemed disastrously overstretched and increasingly vulnerable to flank attack. Already, Chaos hosts commanded by two of Gaur's most ruthless lieutenant warlords, Anakwanar Sek and Enok Innokenti, had enjoyed considerable success by counter-striking along the coreward portion of the Imperial thrust. If such successes continued, the crusade force risked being split in two, and the greater part of it, along with the Warmaster himself, becoming cut off, surrounded and annihilated.

'Macaroth was all too aware of the danger, and all too aware of the imponderable nature of the problem. He could not remain overstretched for fear of flank attack, but neither could he spare any forces from the Morlond front, as a weakening there would leave his vanguard vulnerable to Gaur. Either option seemed cursed with failure. Macaroth simply had to decide which one to risk. Famously, he showed one of his generals two identical cups of wine and asked him to pick one. "One is elixir, one is poison," he said. "How can I tell them apart?" the general asked. "By taking one up and tasting it," replied the Warmaster.

'Macaroth eventually decided to remain as he was, risking overstretch, and fight on to take Morlond with one last effort. In the third quarter of 773, Enok Innokenti began his murderous, catastrophic flank attack in the Khan Group.

'It was a time of disaster, looming failure.

'And miracles...'

— from *A History of the Later Imperial Crusades*

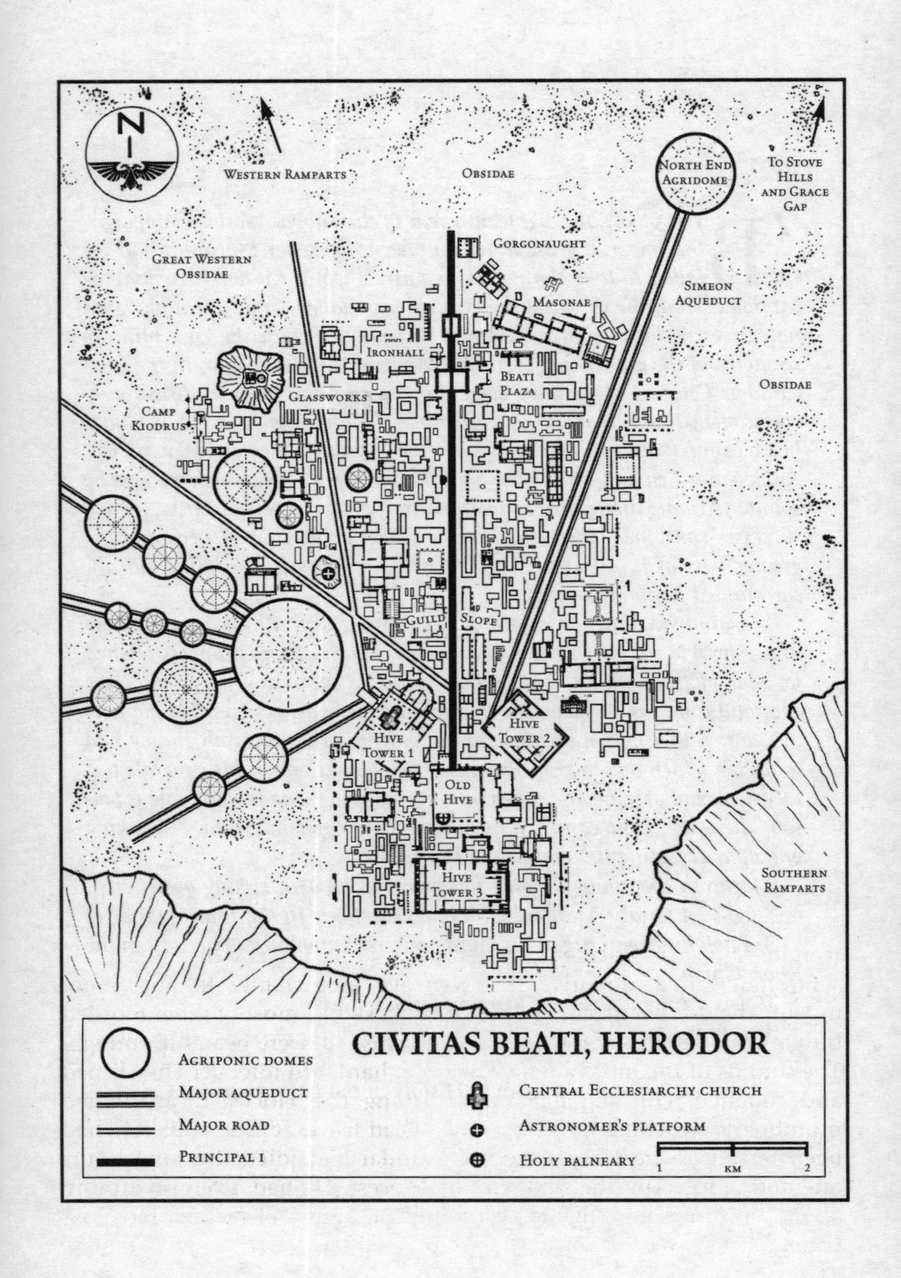

Western Ramparts
Obsidae
North End Agridome
To Stove Hills and Grace Gap
Great Western Obsidae
Gorgonaught
Simeon Aqueduct
Masonae
Ironhall
Beati Plaza
Obsidae
Camp Kiodrus
Glassworks
Guild
Slope
Hive Tower 1
Hive Tower 2
Old Hive
Hive Tower 3
Southern Ramparts
CIVITAS BEATI, HERODOR
Agriponic domes
Major aqueduct
Major road
Principal I
Central Ecclesiarchy church
Astronomer's platform
Holy balneary
1
km
2

PROLOGUE

THE INTELLIGENCE, SUCH as it was, had been in their possession for a week. Yet two or three times a day, and more often during the watches of the night, He would review it, as if somehow He expected it to change.

Etrodai wasn't sure what that meant. He wasn't sure if it meant He was excited by the news, or disquieted. That troubled Etrodai enormously, for he prided himself on knowing His whims and moods like no other. Etrodai had been His life-ward for ninety-two years, had won that vaunted position by besting the previous holder of the office in a legal murder-fight. No one knew Him better than Etrodai.

Except now, Etrodai was no wiser than the rest.

All along the tarnished pillars and dusty alcoves of the Process, the cobwebs fluttered and the bones began to chatter. It meant He was restless again. Before the onyx door had even opened, Etrodai was on his feet, his changeling blade skinned and raised in front of his face.

Etrodai waited, attentive, apprehensive. The chatter became more urgent. The dry, beetle-clicks of the human skulls, most of them mottled brown with decay as if they had been varnished, were bearable enough. The sounds of the more alien skulls were harder to tolerate. They lisped and coughed, clucking like birds, ticking like clocks, disarticulated mouthparts twitching in the dust like dead leaves. Once, while He had been resting to heal a psi wound, Etrodai had idled the long hours attempting to count the skulls in the Process. He had given up around about ten thousand. They kept interrupting him and making him lose count.

A soft rumble, and the onyx door, tall as five men and as broad, slid back into the wet marrow of its hatch seal. Warm air exhaled through the gap. The bones fell silent.

He emerged from His inviolable chamber. The null field popped like surface tension around Him.

'Magister,' said Etrodai, keeping the blade raised but averting his gaze respectfully. 'What is your will?'

'I have made psyk-audience with the Archon, and now know his mind on this. He says that if the news is true, I must act according to my heart.' His voice was brittle, yet musical, like the notes of a bale-pipe or a sonoret, and always made Etrodai feel ashamed of his own ugly, mechanically-formed speech. 'And my heart tells me we must make this our first duty above all other concerns. Now, the instruments?'

'They're assembled, Magister. On the hinterdeck. All of those it was safe to assemble, that is.'

'I'll speak with them and charge them,' He said, then hesitated. 'But first… I will review this great truth one last time.'

Etrodai was not surprised. He turned and led the way down the Process, hearing each and every skull grate in its alcove as it turned to watch Him pass.

The Process, tomb-dark and lit only by ancient, crazed glow-spheres, was a kilometre long. At the far end, goat-headed slave-carls turned the iron keys and swung the towering brass doors open. The slave-carls looked at the walls and sobbed, terrified lest they should catch the slightest glimpse of Him.

Seven times thirteen men of the Retinue waited in the anteroom, under the gilt-arched ceiling and the flaking murals of the Five Atrocities. Their heavy boots slammed to attention in one perfect motion and they shouldered arms. Their flanged body-armour was blue-black like Etrodai's, and their heads were concealed under broad-tailed helmets and visors with bulbous, insectoid goggles.

With Etrodai leading, his sword pointing at the roof and skinned for so long now that beads of blood were welling up along its thorny edge, the Retinue fell in around them and marched in escort, right arms bent and locked around each shouldered weapon, left arms snapping free like pendulums at their sides. Two men ran ahead to open each set of doors in turn.

Access to the data crypt was sealed by a void shield that shimmered in the air like oil on water. It disengaged at His merest touch. Any other man would have lost his arm to the elbow if he had made contact. The Retinue waited outside as Etrodai stepped into the crypt with Him.

The data crypt was cold and dim, and ribbed with a porous tissue like calcified sinew. In the panels between the ribbing, the walls were etched with words from a pre-Imperial language. A foggy, hazy light billowed around their feet.

The secrets kept here whispered about them, hissing like steam or fat on a skillet. Their murmur was not as loud as the chatter of the countless skulls in the Process, but it was more insistent and far more repellent. Vile whispers settled around Etrodai, penetrating his armour, his skull and crawling into his brain, telling him things that he, even he, had no desire to know.

The intelligence had been placed on a pedestal near the centre of the crypt. It had been teased from the fused synapses of an expended seer gestalt and kept in its latent thought-form to preserve its accuracy. This glowing engram was a ribbon of light circling in a figure-of-eight path around a doughy lump of vat-farmed cerebral tissue, on which it had been anchored onto to give it focus.

Etrodai stood back as He stepped to the pedestal and ungloved His hands. The chrome gauntlets hung from the wrist straps of His vambraces as His long, quadruple-jointed fingers slid into the light and began to knead the tissue with lascivious strokes. The winding ribbon of light faltered and broke, and then the luminous strands of information began to flow up His outstretched arms, across His wide shoulders and into the base of His brain.

He sighed and His head rolled back. Light shone out of His mouth and illuminated a tiny spot on the crypt roof.

Etrodai waited...

The long fingers withdrew, and the engram streamed back into its orbit around the lump of tissue. He replaced His gloves.

'There's no mistake,' He said. 'I have examined this every way I know, testing for invention and falsehood. This is not a lie. This is a manifest truth from the sentiences of the immaterium.'

The notion chilled Etrodai and He seemed to notice the look on the lifeward's face.

'Don't be troubled. While it might appear that this is a great blow to us, I believe this is rather our perfect moment of triumph, and the feeble godlings of human order have given it to us themselves.'

'Then my heart rejoices, Magister,' said Etrodai.

A respectful silence awaited them on the hinterdeck. The only sound was the gusty hiss of the air scrubbers and the sub-threshold harmonic thrum of the massive warp engines twenty decks above. The hinterdeck was a subsidiary landing platform, reserved for the Magister's personal use. It jutted out like a shelf high above the long, gothic vault, fifteen hectares square, that formed the primary flight deck for the colossal flagship's fighter screen. The squadrons had been ramped out to secure storage during the voyage. The echoing space below was empty now except for rows of energy bowsers, electric munition trains, and the launch cradles hanging like open crab claws from the high roof. Yellow lights winked in series along the runways scribed into the battered floor.

There were eight beings assembled there in the middle of the empty metal platform. He had specifically requested nine for, according to Him, nine was a significant number. The ninth, too dangerous for direct intercourse, was suspended in a null field outside the hull, in the mouth of the main bay, connected by tele-audience relay to the proceedings on the high platform.

Etrodai ordered the Retinue to wait by the entry hatch, and then stood beside Him as He presented Himself to the assembled figures. Etrodai's skinned blade was so hungry by then that blood was dripping off his knuckles and his arms ached with it. But Etrodai would not reskin his blade until it was all done.

'I've a task for you,' He said. 'A task of significance. I charge you nine with it.'

They murmured. The triplets slithered and coiled their clammy grey hides around each other. The other trio bowed their heads. The two loners remained stiff and unmoving. An obscene rasp of digital filth crackled via the vox relay from the thing in the null field outside.

'A martyr. A martyr once, a martyr always. Our enemies think they have us, so we'll abuse them of that idea. We'll take this, their latest burst of vitality, and make it their last. One amongst you will perform this deed. I don't care who. You will break their renewed hopes and cast them into the dust. This trust I put in you.'

They murmured again, a vow of promise.

'Look at me,' He said.

They had all been standing with their backs to Him, fearful of gazing directly upon His form. Now, one by one and hesitantly, they turned. The triplets hissed at the sight of Him and regurgitated venom-soaked lumps of their last meal, which had been digesting in their throat sacks. The other trio turned, but only their leader, the tall one with the green silk robes and intricate body art, blanched to look on Him. The tattooed leader was as tall and thickly muscled as Etrodai, but his two companions were little base-formed things with the morbidly blind eyes of psykers. The two loners turned too. The figure in the crimson armour of the Blood Pact dropped to his knees and uttered a stifled prayer. The other, the cadaverously pale xenosbreed in glossy black, just stared.

'Good,' He sighed. He turned around and stared out of the main deck's mouth at the feral thing trapped in the force-sphere. 'And you, Karess? Are you ready?'

From the null field outside, a brutal curse rasped over the vox-link. It was as ingenious as it was anatomically horrific.

He smiled. That was the one thing Etrodai could not stand. His Magister's smile was the most terrible thing in creation. He shuddered and felt as though he were about to retch.

'Two rotations from now,' said Enok Innokenti, Magister and Warlord, 'the word will be given and my host will fall upon this cluster and quench the fires of its suns with blood. The crusade of the Imperium of Mankind will break and beg for a quick death.'

He paused. He was still smiling. 'Under cover of that great attack, the real work will begin.'

ONE
THE BRINK OF MIDNIGHT

'How many times have we stood here, you and I,
surveying the field before battle? How many times have we won?
How many times must we lose to have lost all those
victories and promises of victory? Once, old friend.
Once. Once. Once.'

— Warmaster Slaydo,
to an aide, before Balhaut

'BAD DAY COMING!' the man cried aloud. 'Bad day coming! Bad day in the morning!'

He had clambered up onto an almsman's wagon, ignoring attempts to pull him down, and was now shouting, arms outstretched and fingers clawing, at both the sky and the gathering crowd.

'Bad day is coming down upon us all! On you! And you, sir! And you, madam! Nine more wounds! Nine times nine!'

Some in the crowd were booing him. Others made the sign of the aquila or the beati mark to ward off any evil luck he was bringing on with his words. Others, Anton Alphant noticed wryly, were listening quite intently.

There was nothing new in the man's rantings. He, and others like him throughout the camps, had been causing scenes like this regularly in recent days. It wasn't good for morale, and it certainly wasn't endearing the pilgrim mass to the city authorities.

Almsmen, their rank denoted by the blue ribbons that fluttered from their long dust-cloaks, were trying to coax the man down off the wagon. His feet had already knocked over several sacks of the corn-wafers and hardtack they had brought to distribute through the camp. An ayatani from one of the farworld congregations had elbowed his way through the crowd and was holding up a prayer-paddle as he shouted benedictions at the man. Two junior Ecclesiarchy adepts were clutching pewter cups and using their silver aspergillums to shake water at the improvising preacher. Holy water, Alphant was sure, that they had purchased at great expense from the stoups of the Holy Balneary.

Alphant closed his fingers around the ampulla of holy water in his own coat pocket. He'd come an awfully long way to get it, and it had cost him the last of his coins. He wasn't about to waste it so generously.

'Maybe we should stop him,' Karel said.

'We?' smiled Alphant. 'You mean me.'

'Everyone listens to you.'

'He's entitled to his opinion. Every last soul here came because it mattered to them more than anything else. You can't deny his passion.'

'He's scaring people,' said Karel, and a fair few of the other infardi grouped around the clock shrine with them agreed. 'Things could get ugly.'

They were right. Several penitents in the crowd had become so agitated by the man's preaching they had begun to scourge themselves. The row had even captured the attention of some of the nearest stylites. They turned round on their pillar tops to watch, and some shouted out over the heads of the crowd. Other pilgrim troupes had wheeled or carried their clock shrines up close to the wagon, pointing them at him as if the symbolism might deter him.

It seemed to make him worse.

'The brink of midnight, and then the bad day dawns! Fire from the heavens and the precious blood spilled!'

'Can't you make him stop, Alphant?' Valmont asked.

'I'm no priest,' said Alphant. How many times had he said that? Just an agri-worker from Khan II who had made the pilgrimage here when he'd heard the news because it seemed like the right thing to do. Along the way – and it had been a hard journey – he'd somehow become the nominal leader of those he'd travelled with. They looked to him for opinion and direction, more than ever since they'd reached the cold, austere reality of the camps. He'd never asked for the responsibility.

Then, of course, she'd never asked for hers.

Alphant had no idea where that sudden, sobering notion had sprung from. But it was enough to make him change his mind, hand his bowl and breviary to Karel, and walk towards the ruckus around the wagon.

He'd gone no more than three steps when someone in the angry crowd hurled a lump of quartz at the gibbering man. It missed, but others followed. One cracked against his forehead and he toppled back off the wagon top.

'Damn!' said Alphant.

The crowd went mad. Fighting broke out, and more missiles flew – rocks, ampullas, bless-bottles. The alms wagon overturned with a crash and people started shrieking.

Alphant put his head down and shouldered into the surging mob. The hapless preacher would be torn apart in this, and the last thing the camp needed was a death. Alphant was still a strong man, and he found he remembered some of the old moves, enough to tackle and dissuade the most boisterous rioters in his path anyway. Nothing too vicious, just a little deflection and the occasional squeeze of a nerve point.

He got round the upturned wagon, and paused to prevent three screaming infardi from throttling one of the almsmen. Then he looked for the preacher who had started it all.

And saw an amazing thing.

The preacher was sitting on the rough ground, both hands clamped to his forehead. Blood was pouring out through his fingers, staining his robes and making dark patches in the dust. He was in no state to protect himself.

But no one was touching him. A girl, a young girl no more than eighteen, was standing over him. Her face, thin and pale, was confident, the look in her green eyes soft. She had one hand extended, palm out, to ward off the riot. Every time a part of it spilled towards her, she moved her hand in that direction and the people drew back. That simply, that quietly, she was maintaining a tiny circle of calm around the preacher, keeping at bay a crowd lusting for his blood.

He moved towards her. She looked at him, but did not turn her palm towards him, as if recognising his peaceful intentions.

'Do you need help?' Alphant asked.

'This man does,' she said. Her voice was tiny, but he heard her clearly over the uproar. He bent down at her side, and examined the preacher's injury. It was deep and dirty. He tore a strip off his shirt, and wetted it with water from his ampulla without even thinking of the cost. Wasn't it said to cure all wounds?

'Bad day coming,' the man murmured as Alphant wiped the blood away.

'Enough of that,' Alphant said. 'It's already here as far as you're concerned.' He wondered how long the frail girl could hold the commotion at bay. He wondered how she was doing it.

'What's your name?' he asked, looking up at her.

'Sabbatine,' she said. He laughed at that. Saint names and their diminutives were common enough in this part of the Imperium, and there was, as might be expected, a disproportionately high number of Sabbats, Sabbatas, Sabbatines, Sabbeens, Battendos and the like in the camps. But for her, it seemed terribly appropriate.

'I think he's right,' she said.

'What?'

'I think something bad is about to happen.'

There was a quality to the way she said this that was more alarming than the entirety of the preacher's manic declamation.

'You mean like another attack? The raiders again?'

'Yes. Get to safety.'

Alphant didn't question her any further. He got his hands under the preacher's arms and hoisted him up. When he'd got the lolling man upright he realised that the girl had disappeared.

And the nature of the uproar around him had changed. It wasn't a riot any more. It was a panic. People were fleeing, screaming, falling over one another in their anxiety to leave. Something was burning. Smoke filled the low sky above the Ironhall camp.

'Bad day...' the blood-streaked man gurgled.

'Yeah,' said Alphant. He'd just heard a sound that he hadn't heard in twenty years, not since he'd handed back his standard issue mark IV, put his cap pins and badge away in a dresser drawer, and used his Guard-muster pay-out as deposit on a nice little parcel of cropland in the agri-collective west of the primary hive of Khan II.

The snap-crack of a lasrifle.

THE TAC LOGIS situation reports were urgently identifying a heretic raid in progress in the pilgrim encampment just west of the Ironhall Pylon, and true enough there was a furious plume of smoke rising from that quarter, a plume ominously undercut by the blink of weapons fire.

But as Udol rode a lurching carrier down the Guild Slope, through the deafening uproar of the panicked suburb, he caught sight of fat brown vapour clouds wallowing up heavily from the obsidae east of the Simeon Aqueduct.

'Is that the aqueduct?' he shouted.

'Fixing it now, major!' answered his signals officer, dropping back inside the carrier's rusty top hatch to man the tactical station.

'It is the aqueduct, sir!' the signalman called back a moment later.

'What?'

'The aqueduct, and the obsidae on the other side of it!'

Their helmet mics were turned up full, but it was still nigh on impossible to hear one another over the din. The engines of the APCs were revving, and the vast crowds packing the street were wailing and shouting. Gorgonaught, the great prayer horn at the northern end of Principal I, was booming at the white sky from its ancient tower. Udol was sure he could also hear the slap of distant detonations and the sizzling kiss of impacts against the outer fan of shield cover. It was coming down again, fourth day in a row.

Udol slithered down inside the hull and cranked his bare-metal rocker seat around so he could look over the signalman's shoulder at the screen.

'What does tac logis have?'

'Nothing on that, major. They're directing us forward to the Ironhall zone. Captain Lamm has engaged. Heretic raid coming in from the wastes. He–'

'They're in at the east door too,' Udol muttered. He adjusted his vox set's channel. 'Pento? Udol here. Take the front six with you and go look after Lamm's interests. Seven and eight? Move off with me.'

Objections and several requests for clarification crackled back, but Udol ignored them. He tapped his driver on the arm and pointed.

The carrier obediently veered east, parting the rushing crowds with blares from its warning sirens. Two other units from the convoy turned with it. They got off the Guild Slope and rumbled down a gravel linkway deeply shadowed by the tall buildings on either side. At the end of the linkway, the buildings framed an oblong of sky stained with clots of smoke.

They emerged onto Principal VI, flanked by low-rise habs, and crossed the wide boulevard until they were facing the towering lime-brick arches of the Simeon Aqueduct. Beyond that massive arched structure lay the open reaches of a glass field. Like so many vacant spaces at the city edges, the area had become a pilgrim shanty over the last two months, a sea of rough canvas tents, survival blisters and hastily raised clock shrines. Another makeshift expansion of the city's limits to accommodate the massive influx of believers.

Filthy brown smoke billowed across the whole campsite and washed out between the arches of the aqueduct. Dirty pilgrims were pouring out with it, struggling with children and belongings.

'Some damn infardi's knocked over a campstove in his jubilation,' said the signalman. 'It happened the other week over at Camp Kiodrus. Whole row of tents went up and–'

'I don't think that's what it is, Inkerz,' Udol snapped. 'Driver! Get us in through there!'

The driver dropped the gears down to the lowest ratio and began to roll the carrier through the nearest arch span onto the obsidae. Almost at once they were crushing tent structures and lean-tos under their heavy, solid wheels. Frantic pilgrims, flowing around the vehicle as they fled the area, hammered their fists on the armoured sides and implored them to stop.

'No go, major,' said the driver, hauling on the brake. 'Not unless you want to, you know, crush them.'

'Everybody out!' Udol ordered. 'Rove-team spread! Get on with it!'

The side hatches on all three troop carriers rattled open and the troops dismounted, fifteen from each. They lunged their way forward against the tide of the crowd, carrying their weapons upright. Udol paused long enough for Inkerz to strap the compact accelerant tank to his back and connect the hose, then he took off, pushing to the head of his men. He raised his armour-sleeved left arm, squeezed the stirrup built into the palm of the glove, and scorched off a little rippling halo of flame into the air so they could pick him out in the crush. Once he had their attention, he dispersed them left and right through the forest of tents and personal detritus.

Fifty paces into the shanty, the place was almost deserted. The smoke was thicker. Udol was appalled but unsurprised at the wretched conditions the pilgrims had been living in. Junk, rubbish and human waste covered the narrow tracks that wound between the pathetic tents. It was hard to see more than a few metres in any direction. Quite apart from the smoke and the shelters, there were clock shrines everywhere. No two were identical, but they all followed the same essential pattern: a timepiece of some sort – domestic clock, electric timer, digital chronometer, hand-sprung horolog – set in a home-made wooden box, the taller and more gaudily painted the better, it seemed. He looked at one nearby. As tall as a man, with reclaimed tin shutters open at the top to reveal the clock face, it was set on a wooden handcart and anchored in place with industrial rivets. The thing had been painted gold and silver and, in places, green, and skirts of plastic sheeting had been wrapped around the towering body. Inside that upright box, a stationary pendulum hung down, festooned with dried flowers, crystals, keepsakes, coins and a hundred other votive offerings. At the top, inside the shutters, the old clock face and the hands had been sprayed green and then the dial and the tips of the hands picked out again in gold. The hands were set at a heartbeat before midnight.

Major Udol knew precisely the significance of that.

He went around the shrine, waving the troopers behind him close. The pilgrim shelters ahead of them were burning freely. Dirty yellow flames licked away shelter cloth and canvas and leapt up into the morning air, swirling into dense, dark smoke. Udol saw a clock shrine in the heart of the fire succumb and topple.

The trooper beside him suddenly jumped back, as if in surprise. Then he did it again and fell on his back.

Shot through the torso, twice. Udol didn't even have to look.

He barked a hasty warning into his vox. The men around him scattered into cover. Two-thirds of them made it. The bastards had been waiting.

Udol crouched down behind the relative shelter of an overturned flatbed as energy bolts spat and whistled overhead. One of his men nearby got in behind the frame of a plastic tent and then rolled over onto his side as a las-round came through the fabric skin and into the back of his head. Another man, caught in the open, was knocked over by a laser bolt that broke both his legs. He fell hard, and started crawling until another shot hit him in the face.

Udol felt his heart race. He glimpsed movement on the pathway next to the fire, drew his laspistol, and fired a few bright bars of energy down the narrow track. The troopers around him began to open up with their carbines.

'Inkerz!' Udol voxed. 'Get tac logis. Tell them there's another hot raid coming in right down here under the aqueduct!'

'Acknowledged, sir.'

It was hot, all right, and getting hotter. Udol counted forty-plus hostiles out there, in amongst the abandoned tents. He glimpsed drab red body armour and dust-cloaks. They matched the description of the hostiles that had been hitting and running all around the city skirts for the last four days. Heretic zealots, drawn to the city as surely as the pilgrims, as anxious to deny the truth occurring here as the pilgrims were to celebrate it. Marshal Biagi had told Udol personally that the hostiles were most probably militant cultists from a world in the local group. They'd made their way to the planet under cover of the mass pilgrim influx to stage terror attacks on the city.

The bastards could fight. Fight disciplined, and that was what made them really scary. Udol had tangled with warp scum many times before – had the scars to prove it – and Imperial military rigour had triumphed over zealot fanaticism every time.

Maybe it was the Imperium's turn to play the fanatic, Udol considered. According to every clock in sight, the hour was on them. They certainly had something to be fanatical about at last.

A sudden wind picked up, and began to drive the smoke cover hard north. A great part of the hostiles' position in amongst the tents was abruptly unveiled. Udol coordinated his shooters and began systematic counter-fire. His troop pounded rapid fire into the shamble of tents and bivouacs, and then pushed forward through the shanty, keeping their heads low.

A weapon cracked close to Udol, and the man to his left tumbled over onto the remains of a survival blister. Udol swung round and fired his sidearm, hitting the hostile square in the snarling iron visor he was wearing. Before the bastard's body had even folded up under him, another two came charging out of cover, firing wildly. Udol dropped to one knee, raised his left arm straight and clenched the stirrup grip. A long spear of incandescent flame leapt from the torch-vent behind the knuckles of his glove and broke around their torsos. Both staggered, ablaze, screaming. The flames cooked off the powercells in the nearest one's webbing and blew him apart, shredding his arms and torso right off his collapsing legs in a searing flash. The explosion felled his companion, who lay writhing and burning on the ground. Udol walked over to him and executed him with a single shot from his laspistol.

'Farenx. Beresi. Get forward on the double,' Udol told the men behind him. They were close to the edge of the shanty spread, and the hostiles were falling back fast. Just heretics, Udol thought. Maniac cultists testing the faith and resolve of the city with their cowardly terror-tactics. Exactly what the Regiment Civitas Beati had been formed to fight.

But when he reached the hem of the shanty, he realised he was wrong. It was more than that, far more. The open vista of the obsidae lay before him: a flat, cold waste of grey pumice and dust flecked by litters of black volcanic glass. It stretched away north for three kilometres towards Grace Gorge and the murky crags of the Stove Hills.

Three vehicles were approaching, striding in towards the shelter camp. Stalk-tanks. Behind them, at their plodding heels, came a fanned out line of over two hundred hostiles on foot, draped in dull red dust-capes. Since when did cult heretics have armour? Since when did they assault like a military force?

'Oh crap!' Udol heard himself say. 'Fall back! Fall back!'

The stalk-tanks came on, scuttling like arachnids. Each had six piston-geared legs that supported the low-slung body casings. Udol could see the drivers in the underslung bubbles beneath the tails. On each raised head section, dual mini-turrets rotated and began to fire.

The blistering shots came in constant, rippling waves as the barrels of the double pulse lasers in each mini-turret pumped, recoiled and fired again with brutal, mechanised rhythm. Udol saw Beresi cut in two, and three other troopers lifted off the ground by the overpressure of impact blasts. Detonations threw pumice and obsidian chips into the air. Twinkling scratches of light flickered along the advancing row of blood-red troopers as they began to fire their weapons too. Udol fell into cover. He heard men he'd known since childhood screaming their last words into their moulded rebreather masks.

He did the only thing he could think of. He prayed to the Saint.

FIFTEEN KILOMETRES SOUTH, at the crest levels of the inner city, the immortal choir was tuning up. Rampshel, the choir-master, was limping to and fro, waving his baton, and calling for the second vocids to 'pitch yourselves, for Terra's sake!' The children in the front rank, some no more than six years old standard, were fidgeting with their formal ruffs and vestments, and gazing into the distance. The fumes of incense burners filled the cool air, and the temple slaves were setting out the last of the golden reliquary boxes under direction of the High Ecclesiarch and his black-robed provosts.

'Almost there, first officiary,' assured Rampshel as he shuffled past, leaning on his silver-knobbed cane. 'Absolutely nearly almost there.'

'Very good, choir master. Carry on,' said Bruno Leger, elected first officiary of Beati City. He was a small man, with a cleanly shaved scalp and a neatly clipped goatee. He settled his mantle of office around his shoulders with a fastidious gesture, and double-checked that his amulet was hanging squarely on his chest. By his side, Marshal Biagi folded his huge arms and sighed.

'We're good, I think,' muttered the first officiary. 'Are we good?'

'We're good, sir,' replied Biagi.

'Are we? Fine. Excellent. I mean, is this… you know… sufficient?'

'It's fine, first officiary,' said Biagi. He smoothed his regimental sash. 'If the bloody choir can hit a note, we'll be laughing.'

'Are they off-key? Are they? Off-key?' First Officiary Leger craned his head and cupped a hand around his ear. 'They're off, aren't they? I'll have a word…'

'Sir, please,' said Ayatani Kilosh, extending a gnarled hand out of the folds of his long, blue silk robes and placing it reassuringly on Leger's arm. 'Everything is quite perfect.'

'Is it? Is it perfect? Good. Excellent. Why are those little boys wandering off? Shouldn't they be in the front rank of the choir?'

'Rampshel will see to it, sir,' said Biagi.

'Will he? I hope so. I want everything to be perfect. These are heroes we're welcoming today. Veterans. Their reputation precedes them.'

'Certainly it does, sir,' said Ayatani Kilosh.

A shadow flickered past overhead, momentarily blotting out the skylights of the ceremonial docking terrace. They all felt the thump of touch down.

'Well, they're here,' said Leger.

Rampshel raised his arms and the choir began to sing. He was conducting them strenuously when the first set of the terrace's inner hatches cycled open and steam hissed in.

First Officiary Leger wasn't quite sure what to expect, except something heroic. The choir, lungs bursting and antiphonals held open in front of them, voiced the Great Supplication of the Beati. They were bloody well almost in tune too.

Two figures sauntered down out of the steam. They came side by side. A louche male with a handsome face and the eyes of a joker, and a slender female with cropped bleached hair and an attitude. Both were dressed in matt-black fatigues and body armour; both had lasrifles slung casually over their shoulders. The man had an augmetic shoulder, and winked the moment he saw Leger. The woman was wearing a fur-trimmed bomber jacket, and carried her lasrifle yoked horizontally so that her right arm could hang near the trigger grip and her left folded casually over the top like it was a speeder's door.

They stalked down into the docking terrace, ignoring the efforts of the choir.

Leger stepped forward. 'On behalf of the people of–'

The man with the augmetic implant turned, smiled, and put a finger to his lips. Behind him, the female completed her sight check of the area and raised a hand to her headset.

'Site's clean,' Biagi heard her say. 'Come on out.'

A silhouette appeared in the hatchway, back lit at first by the vapour. An imposing figure in a long coat and a peaked cap. First Officiary Leger breathed in expectantly.

The figure walked into the light. He was a tall, lean man in the field dress of a commissar, but his epaulettes showed the rank of colonel. His face was as hard as a knife. He came down the ramp to face the trio of dignitaries, knelt before the first officiary and took his cap off.

'Ibram Gaunt, Tanith First, reporting as ordered,' he said.

So this was the famous Gaunt, thought Biagi. He wasn't especially impressed. Gaunt and his men, so the briefing files had said, were front-line grunts. They certainly had that mad dog smell about them. Not house-trained. Biagi had serious doubts they were suitable for the task they had been chosen to perform.

Gaunt rose.

'Welcome, welcome, colonel-commissar,' said Leger, taking Gaunt daintily by the shoulders and kissing him on the cheeks. He had to stand on tiptoe to do this. Gaunt seemed to tolerate the custom the way a guard dog tolerates the occasional brisk rub between the ears. Leger began to make a fuller and longer speech of welcome in High Gothic.

'You arrive cautious of your own safety,' Biagi cut in, nodding at the pair of troopers who had preceded Gaunt out of his lander. Gaunt narrowed his eyes and looked at Biagi questioningly.

'Marshal Timon Biagi, commanding the PDF and civic regiments.'

Gaunt saluted. 'My sergeants here insisted,' he said, indicating the waiting pair. 'During our descent, we were informed that a raid was underway.'

'In the city fringes, not here,' Biagi replied. 'My forces have it contained. We have a minor ongoing problem with heretic dissidents. There was no threat to your safety.'

'We prefer to check that sort of thing for ourselves,' said the female sergeant, addressing Biagi directly.

'Criid,' Gaunt scolded softly.

'My apologies,' she said. 'We prefer to check that sort of thing for ourselves, sir.'

Biagi grinned. Seemed this famous pack leader couldn't even keep his dogs in line. He looked the female – Criid, was it? – up and down and said, with a mocking tone, 'A woman?'

She fixed Biagi with an unblinking stare and then repeated his head-to-toe appraisal. 'A man?' she said. The male sergeant with the augmetic limb sniggered.

'Zip it, Varl,' said Gaunt. He faced Biagi. 'Let's not get off on the wrong foot, marshal,' he said. 'I won't reprimand my people for being dutiful.'

'What about for speaking out of turn?' Biagi said.

'Of course, the moment I hear one of them do so.'

'Well, it's quite wonderful to have you here!' the first officiary said with a rush of false enthusiasm, clearly desperate to brush over the awkwardness. 'Isn't it? Quite wonderful?'

'I'm here because I was ordered to be here by the Warmaster himself,' Gaunt said. 'It remains to be seen what else is wonderful about it.'

'May I say, colonel-commissar,' said Kilosh, speaking for the first time, 'that remark disturbs me.' Though tall, he was a very old man, yet his gaze had more strength and confidence in it than that of either the marshal or the first officiary. 'It might easily have been mistaken for heresy.'

Gaunt stiffened and said carefully 'No such offence was intended. I was not referring to the wonder that has taken place here, rather I meant the grave consequences that might be set off by such a thing.'

Kilosh nodded, as if appeased. 'We have met before,' he began.

'I remember, Ayatani Kilosh,' said Gaunt making him a small, formal bow. 'Three years ago, sidereal. In the Doctrinopolis of Hagia. A brief meeting, but it would be rude of me not to recall it. Your king, Infareem Infardus, was dead, and I was the bearer of that ill news.'

'That was a dark moment in the history of Hagia,' Kilosh agreed, rather flattered by Gaunt's precise recollection. 'And a bleak time for my holy order. But times have changed. The miracle has happened. The galaxy is a brighter place now, and you deserve thanks for your part in that.'

'My part?'

'The efforts of your regiment. You protected the Shrinehold and drove away the enemy. That's why you're here.'

'You requested it?'

'No, colonel-commissar,' Kilosh smiled. '*She* did.'

Gaunt hesitated, and stroked his fingers down one side of his lean chin thoughtfully. 'I look forward to talking with you more on this subject, ayatani-father,' he said. 'First, I would like the permission of the first officiary... and the honourable marshal... to dispose my men.'

Leger nodded eagerly, and made another little bow. Gaunt turned away and walked back towards the docking hatches.

'What do you make of him?' Kilosh whispered.

'Not enough to care about,' said Biagi.

'He seems like a decent fellow,' said Leger brightly. 'Doesn't he? Decent sort?'

'Oh, I think he is,' said Kilosh. 'Almost too decent. And that's where we might have a problem. It almost seems to me he doesn't believe.'

'Then he must be made to believe,' said Biagi. He paused as he saw a thick set man in the uniform of a line commissar emerge from one of the hatches. 'Excuse me,' he said, and walked away.

TANITH PERSONNEL POURED out onto the assembly floor. As he strode down the metal deckway, Biagi could see hatch after hatch opening along the ornamental terrace. Men and, in places, women, clad in the same dirty black and draped with camo-capes, were exiting the fleet of drop craft, lugging munition boxes, stow crates and kitbags. They had a smell to them. The smell of dirt and fyceline and jellied promethium that no amount of bathing could scrub out. The shadows of other landing ships flickered across the terrace skylights, and there was the thump and clank of landing clamps engaging. Steam vented through the floor grates.

The newcomers gave Biagi a courteous wide berth. He was a senior officer, and also an imposing figure. Shaven-headed, with dark olive skin and amber eyes, he wore the ceremonial battledress of the city regiment: gleaming brown leather embossed with gold-wire detailing. His left arm and chest were covered with polished, segmented armour plating and, on his back, under the fold of the scarlet sash, his accelerant tank was locked in place.

Biagi stopped as he came on three troopers hefting a pallet of promethium tanks out of a landing hatch.

'You. What is this?'

'Sir?' said the nearest, a bear-like oaf with a shaggy moustache.

'What are your names?' asked Biagi.

'Trooper Brostin, sir,' said the bear. He gestured to his fellows. 'This here's Lubba and Dremmond.' The other two men saluted quickly. Lubba was a short, heavy brute covered in the most barbaric tattoos. Dremmond was younger and more plainly made, his hair short and dark.

'You're flame troopers?'

'Sir, yes sir,' said Brostin. 'Emperor's own. He puts the fire in us and we put his fire into his enemies.'

'Well, you can put those tanks and those burner pumps back on the lander, trooper.'

'Sir?'

'City bye-laws. Only the officer class of the Regiment Civitas Beati is permitted flamers in battle.'

'Begging your pardon, your sir-ship... why?' asked Lubba.

'On this world, water is power, and the enemy of water – flame – is a privilege exercised only by the high-born warrior class. Do you require more of an explanation?'

'No, sir, we don't,' said Brostin.

Biagi moved on. 'Commissar Hark?'

The commissar turned, and quickly saluted.

'Biagi, Marshal Civitas Beati. Welcome to Herodor,' Biagi said, returning the salute and shaking Hark by the hand. 'I was asked to look out for you.'

'Really?'

'The general would like a word in private.'

'I thought he might,' said Viktor Hark.

GINGERLY LOWERING HIS aged frame, Ayatani Zweil prostrated himself and kissed the metal deck, murmuring prayers that he had known most of his days but which only now seemed to have meaning.

There were Ghosts all around him, off-loading from the landers. Many knelt down around him, producing their own green silk faith ribbons and kissing them the way he had taught them. They were faithful, these boys and girls, these soldiers. It was a glorious thing to see. He unwound his own beaded green ribbon from around his wizened knuckles and began to recite the litany.

Gaunt appeared beside him and gently raised him to his feet.

'I must finish–' Zweil began.

'I know. But you're in the middle of a landing deck and liable to be crushed underfoot if you stay there.'

Zweil huffed but allowed Gaunt to lead him out of the way as Obel and Garond manhandled a crate of rockets out onto the docking terrace with an anti-grav hoist.

'Are you all right?' Gaunt asked.

The imhava ayatani stared up at Gaunt with ferociously beady eyes. 'Of course I am! How could I not be?'

'You are over-tired, ayatani-father. The long voyage has drained you.'

Zweil snorted. If Gaunt had suggested such a thing back on Aexe, he might well have agreed. Back there, he'd tried to ignore the signs, but there had been no denying that his great age was catching up with him. He had honestly begun to wonder how much longer fate was going to give him.

Then, the news had come. And new vitality had filled his arthritic joints and dimming mind.

Zweil looked at Gaunt and regretted his sharpness. 'Ignore me. I'm old and wishful and I've spent the last few months on a Navy packet ship dreaming of what awaits us here. I expected...'

'What?'

Zweil shook his head.

'A smell of sweet, uncorrupted flesh permeating the entire planet? A scent of islumbine?'

Zweil chuckled. 'Yes, probably. All this long voyage from Aexe Cardinal, I've been wondering what to expect.'

'Me too,' said Gaunt.

'Ibram... I almost can't believe it's true.'

'Nor I, father.'

There was something in Gaunt's voice that made Zweil pause. He glanced at his friend the colonel-commissar and saw from the look on his face that Gaunt had let something slip in the tone of his reply.

Zweil stared at him and frowned. 'What's the matter?'

'Nothing. Skip it.'

'I will not. Gaunt? If I didn't know better, I'd take you to be a doubter. What aren't you telling me?'

'Nothing, like I said.'

'On Aexe, she spoke to you–'

Gaunt's voice dropped to a whisper. 'Please, ayatani-father. That must remain between us. It's a very private thing. All I meant was…'

'What?'

'Has anything ever seemed too good to be true to you?'

Zweil grinned. 'Of course. There was a rather limber girl on Frenghold, but that matter is even more privy than your incident on Aexe Cardinal. I understand doubts, Ibram. The Beati herself warned us against false idols in her epistles. But the divinations cannot lie. Every Ecclesiarchy church in the subsector has been sent signs and prophesies. And you… you have more reason to trust than any living being on this world.'

Gaunt breathed deeply. 'I trust in the ministry of the Saint, and the inscrutable workings of the God-Emperor. It's men I don't trust.'

Zweil was disconcerted, but he managed a smile and patted Gaunt on the arm. 'Forget the frailties of men, Ibram. On Herodor, there is emphatic wonder.'

'Good. If you see Ana… never mind, there she is.'

Gaunt left the old priest and edged through the press of disembarking Ghosts.

'Ana?'

Surgeon Ana Curth looked up from a shipment of sterilised theatre tools she had been itemising. She rose, tucking her data-slate under her arm and smoothing her short, bob-cut hair away from her heart-shaped face.

'Colonel-commissar?'

'The matter we spoke of during the voyage…'

She sighed. 'You know what? I was humouring you, Ibram. All those weeks stuck with you on a transport. It was easier to nod along than speak my mind. Well, we're here now, and I'm speaking my mind. You should be talking to Dorden about this.'

Gaunt winced. 'The chief medic and I aren't getting along at the moment.'

'Well, that's because you're both stubborn fools and I for one–'

'Shut up, Curth.'

'Shutting up, sir.'

'I want you to do this for me. Please. Privately. Quietly.'

'It's a matter of faith–'

'You may question me on anything, surgeon, except faith.'

She shrugged. 'Okay. You win. I'll get my kit, even though… even though, mind… I don't like it.'

She moved away, and then turned and called back: 'You understand I'm only doing this because you're so amazing in bed.'

The Ghosts around them came to a sudden halt. Several dropped their kitbags. Curth scowled at them all. 'A joke. It's a joke. Oh for feth's sake, you people…'

She disappeared into the press. Gaunt looked at the staring troopers around him. 'As you were,' he began and then sighed and made a dismissive gesture.

'Sir?'

It was Beltayn, Gaunt's adjutant. Gaunt didn't like the look on his face.

'Out with it.'

'Sir?'

Gaunt tipped his head down and looked at Beltayn. 'Something's awry. I can tell.'

Beltayn grimaced toothily and nodded. 'We're... we're missing a couple of landers.'

'A couple?'

'Three or so.'

'Three or so?'

'Well. Four actually.'

'Which ones?'

'Two, three, four and five.'

'Corbec, Rawne, Mkoll and Soric. I know I'm going to regret asking this, Beltayn, but do you have any idea why that might be?'

'They diverted during descent, sir.'

'Diverted? On whose authority? Let me guess... Corbec?'

'Yes sir.'

'And they are now where?'

'As I understand it, sir, they were alerted to the action at the city perimeter and Colonel Corbec – as it were – decided they should...'

'Should?'

'Muck in, sir.'

'Oh feth,' said Gaunt.

Major Udol rolled. Fire from the stalk-tanks was smashing up the terrain all around him. The high-pitched *whoop-whoop* of their pumping guns was all he could hear. He was bleeding from a scalp wound. The scorched remains of one of his men was hanging from a semi-collapsed tentframe in front of him.

A shadow passed overhead, and he saw from the dust the wind had changed again. It was blowing a gale suddenly. Grit pattered against him. What the hell was *that*?

Udol looked up and froze. Thrusters flaring and sunlight glinting off its hull, a drop-ship was coming in right on top of them. A second was dropped down not five hundred metres away, and there were two more besides, falling like giant beetles out of the sky.

They were standard pattern Imperial Guard landers. Bug-nosed, bulk-made delivery ships. The Imperial Guard. He'd been praying to the Saint for deliverance. What kind of answer was this?

Udol felt the ground shake as the first drop-ship zeroed, bouncing hard on its hydraulic landing struts. Men leapt out of the drop-ship's opening hatches. Men in black fatigues and body armour. Men wrapped in camouflage capes. Guardsmen. They were spreading out into the barrens of the obsidae, laying down a fire pattern against the advancing hostiles, facing them down, and the damn stalk-tanks too. The dust-filled air was thick with rapid las-fire.

Udol got to his feet in time to see the closest stalk-tank re-aim and fire on the first drop-ship as it dusted off again. The impact slewed the nose round hard and made the engines wail with protest, but it lifted clear, right over his head, gear still down and hatches still wide open.

There was a puff of smoke from the newcomers' hasty file and a rocket spat at the first stalk-tank. Another followed it. A fireball bloomed around the tank's forebody, and it came to a standstill, its leg frame rocking back and forth. It hesitated, took another step, and another rocket smacked it in the snout. A blast-flash lit the glass field for a moment, and when it was gone, so had the stalk-tank, and hot fragments of Chaos-fashioned engineering were raining down out of the smoke.

Udol tried to raise his men on the vox, but an alien signal washed through the channel. He only caught snatches of it. Something like '...fething waiting for?' followed by '...live forever!'

He ran forward, rousing his men. The Guard had the phalanx of raiders on the turn. Another fireball briefly lit the sky, bright like a rising sun. A second stalk-tank had gone up.

The air was full of ashy debris. Through it, the soldiers in black poured forward, guns crackling, only half-visible in the haze.

They were like ghosts, Udol thought.

WHOEVER THEY WERE, they seemed insufferably pleased with themselves. As Udol approached, the black-clad troopers were whooping congratulatory exchanges as they jogged back to recover the heavy packs and bergens they'd ditched in haste as they'd come out of the landers. The hostiles, those few that had survived, had fled away into the dusty distance of the obsidae. The third and last stalk-tank was a burning mass on the glass field. Corpses in red uniforms littered the ground.

Udol tried to identify an officer amongst the Guardsmen. These men seemed to have no disclosing marks except a dagger-thrust skull pin and the aquila of the Imperial Guard. Their faces were hidden by crude, bulk-issue rebreather masks.

'Are your boys okay?' asked a deep voice from behind him.

Udol turned. The man addressing him was big and broad, the unruly tufts of a thick black beard emerging around the edges of his mask. His accent was strange.

'What did you say?' Udol asked.

'Your boys. I was asking after them. You were in a bit of a spot there.'

'We–' Udol began. He didn't quite know what to say. 'You came in on drop-ships,' was all he could come up with.

The big stranger jerked a thumb at the sky. 'We've been stacked orbital for the last sixteen hours, then we got the word to go to landers, for which everyone gave thanks. So, we're on the way down and the word comes up there's an attack and we gotta abort the drop. Feth that, I say, 'sides it was too late for going back, if you know what I mean. We spied the LZ from way up, then we spied the feth-storm–'

'The what?'

'The shooty-shooty. Friends in trouble, says I, so we wriggle out of the pattern and fall in where, as it might be, we could be most advantageous.'

'You… you dropped into the firefight rather than the LZ?' asked Udol.

'Yes, we did. I see it as an economy of effort, myself. If we were going to drop anyways, we might as well drop for a purpose. And so we did. Fething good thing too. By the way, who are you?'

Udol gazed at the gloved hand held out to him. 'Major Erik Udol, Third Company, Regiment Civitas Beati.'

'Clearly pleased and all that, Udol. Pardon me but this old wardog's still riding the combat high. Got my boys here boisterous too. Too many months in a belly hold, too little killing. This is Herodor, eh? Heard so fething much about it.'

'Do you know…' Udol began. 'Do you know how counter-regs it is to drop troop landers into the path of an assault?'

The big stranger paused, as if thinking about this. 'Fairly sure the answer to that is "yes". Do you know how effective it is to drop-assault an ongoing ground attack? Or would you rather not live forever?'

'I–'

'See for yourself,' the stranger said, extending a big arm in a wide gesture. 'Observe the debris, the pleasant lack of incoming fire, and the arses of many enemies fleeing for safety. Was there something else, major?'

'Who *are* you?'

'Colonel Corbec, Tanith First-and-Only.'

'Oh,' said Udol, understanding at last. 'The Tanith. You're the ones. The ones she's been waiting for.'

CORBEC'S IMPROMPTU RELIEF force, four platoons strong, assembled itself into vaguely ordered groups at the edge of the fight zone. Word was the officer in charge of the local force had voxed tactical logistical command to request transports to take them into the city proper.

Major Rawne of the Tanith Ghosts, ranking third officer beneath Gaunt and commander of third platoon, wandered away from the makeshift assembly point and stood alone, slowly turning in a circle to take in the scene. This was his first look at Herodor, a world that had taken them months of monotonous travel to reach. A world, so he understood, that contained a great miracle.

It was not a pretty place, and didn't look at all miraculous, but it had a sort of cold beauty, Rawne conceded. The sky was a flat, bright white, with the merest smudges of grey-blue along the horizon, particularly in the north, where dirty crusts of rock pushed up into the air. The ground around them – an obsidae, the locals called it – was a bare field of blue dust, littered with black volcanic glass. The thin air was cold, and abrasively dry. Rawne had been told most of Herodor was an arctic desert: a dry, sub-zero waste of dust fields, glass crags and crumbling escarpments. It reminded him, unpleasantly, of death, of the cold, desiccated, brittle truth contained in all tombs. The Ghosts had yet to go to a world that did not cost them life and blood. What price was Herodor going to demand? Whose last sight would be these forlorn wastes?

Any of us, he thought. *All of us. Death is never choosy, never selective.* On Aexe Cardinal, he'd come to within touching distance of death himself. He sensed that cold grasp was still on him, reluctant to let him go again.

Or maybe that was just the chill wind gusting in across the obsidae.

Rawne's slow circle of contemplation brought him up at last looking south at the city itself. The Civitas Beati, the city of the saint, a minor shrine, just another of the many places and many worlds touched by Sabbat thousands of years earlier and made holy. It was a sprawling place, the main population centre on Herodor. Three slab-like hive towers of white ashlar stood like bodyguards around a higher, older, darker central steeple, encircled by sloping skirts of lower level habs, manufactories, transitways and brick viaducts. To the west lay the tinted domes of the many agriponic farms that fed the city, farms that were themselves kept alive by the hot mineral springs on which the city had been founded. That's what made it a special place, Rawne thought pragmatically. It wasn't who might have been here or what they might have done. This city was here only by the grace of the thermal water that gushed up through the cold crust of the world in this one place.

Rawne heard someone shout his name. The shout was muffled by a rebreather mask. He turned and saw Mkoll, the regiment's chief scout, jogging over to him.

'Mkoll?'

'Transport's here, sir.'

There was an aqueduct at the edge of the obsidae, and a string of battered carriers was rolling out from under the arches.

'Let's get everybody moving,' Rawne told the chief scout.

By the time the two of them rejoined the main group, the Ghosts were boarding the waiting transports. Mkoll checked his own platoon had their equipment stowed. He looked over and saw Sergeant Soric of five platoon, who seemed to be taking his time getting settled with his men. Mkoll ran across to him. The last of five were finding their places in the carrier's rear payload bay. Soric, the old rogue, was studying a piece of paper.

'Everything all right?' Mkoll asked him.

Soric looked up, as if Mkoll had made him jump. He balled up the piece of paper, a scrap of blue tissue, and tossed it away. 'Everything's fine!' he told Mkoll, and then reached up to the tailgate so the nearest men could help haul his bulk up into the truck.

Mkoll thumped twice on the rear bodywork and the carrier started away in a splutter of exhaust and over-revved engine. He turned back towards his own transport.

The ball of blue paper blew across his path, carried by the wasteland wind across the flinty shards of the glass field. Mkoll stooped and caught it. It was torn from a despatch pack, one of the flimsy blank forms for written messages if the vox was down. Soric's vox was fine, wasn't it?

Mkoll unfolded the paper. A single line was handwritten there: *Trouble before you even reach the ground.*

What in the name of Terra, Mkoll wondered, did that mean?

TWO
THE GIRL FROM THE HILLS

'That which was will be.
That which dieth will live. That which falleth will rise up.
This, I say to you, is the nature of things,
if you but once believe.'

— Saint Sabbat, Epistles

He stood on one of the highest decks of the inner hive and looked down over the sprawl of Beati City, across the ceramite and white-ashlar slopes of the hive towers, the mosaic of brick-tile rooftops lower down, crosscut by the lines of boulevards and viaducts, the mouldering stone of the old districts, the stained metal sides of the processors and agriponic domes, the maze of alleys and slums, the warrens of low-rise habs.

Not a secure town. Not secure or securable. There were no curtain walls or encircling fortifications, except the natural bowl of rocky headlands around the valley site. There was a shield system, generated by pylon stations around the city limits which, along with main sequence masts on the roofs of the hive towers, could raise a coherent energy field like a carnival marquee above the city. But the shield system had been designed to ward off dust storms and glass blizzards, not munitions.

And that was what was coming. Full-scale war, drawn inexorably towards Herodor as surely as the pilgrim flocks had been drawn. The Civitas Beati would not survive. It hadn't been constructed for war, and he didn't know how he would begin to defend it. He thought of Vervunhive – great, solid Vervunhive – and how hard that had been to hold on to. Vervunhive had been designed by military planners with principles of defence uppermost in their minds. Its Main Spine and curtain walls had formed a solid fortress within which the entire hive population could shelter during times of attack and siege. Beati City, in contrast, had simply grown, spilling low-rent, low-rise habs out further and further from its more modest and overcrowded hive towers.

God-Emperor, but this was going to be fething bloody.

Gaunt turned from the tinted observation window and scribbled some more notes down on the data-slate he'd kept at his side since arriving, every last idea he had to make the city as proof against assault as possible. Stronger shield generators, for a start. Mobile artillery batteries, and some real armour. Reinforcements, naturally. The damnably wide boulevards would have to be blocked, and the aqua system managed. Food and power and munitions had to be stockpiled. According to the last Navy report, the Munitorum fleet was two days out, and a three regiment force, including armour, was inbound from Khan. Herodor needed battlefleet cover too, and he'd put in a request, through channels, for assistance from the Adeptus Mechanicus, though no answer had yet come.

He heard the door to the wood-panelled deck open and presumed it was Beltayn, returning at long last with caffeine and a snack. It wasn't.

'Nice of you to decide to join me,' Gaunt said. Corbec grinned and nodded. He was munching on a cut of bread filled with salt-meat, and carried a hot cup of caffeine in his other hand. Rawne, coming in behind him, carried two more cups and handed one to Gaunt.

'We intercepted Beltayn on the way in,' Rawne said.

'There was supposed to be food too,' said Gaunt. Corbec stopped chewing immediately and looked down at the cut in his hand guiltily. 'Sorry,' he said.

Gaunt shook his head dismissively. 'Take seats. You've had a busy day, as I understand it.'

'Couldn't just leave 'em to fry out there. It was a pretty major assault, worst they've had, so I'm told,' said Corbec. Both he and Rawne had dust adhering to their uniforms, and Corbec's face still displayed the ruddy pressure marks where his rebreather mask had cut into his skin.

'Armour?'

'Three stalk-tanks. Light stuff, but even so. Caff and Feygor messed them up good with a brace of tread-fethers. More particularly, we got a positive ID.'

He reached into his musette bag and pulled out a snarling iron visor. There was a las-hole in the middle of the mask's forehead.

'Feth,' said Gaunt.

'The Blood Pact are here. In big numbers.'

Gaunt gestured to the iron visor Corbec was holding. 'It could just be–'

'I'd know the fethers anywhere,' said Rawne.

Gaunt nodded. 'The local military seems to think the raids are down to some heretic-dissident cells. They've been hitting the city for the last four days.' He took the mask from Corbec's hand. 'They have no idea, have they?'

'About time they did,' said Corbec.

Gaunt put the mask down. 'I think we're dealing with an advanced unit ordered to keep us busy until the main force arrives.'

'And you think that main force is inbound?'

Gaunt laughed darkly at Rawne's question. 'Find me someone in this sector who doesn't know what's happening here! If you were the enemy–'

'If?' smiled Rawne.

'If you were the enemy,' Gaunt continued, passing over the jibe, 'wouldn't you consider this world a primary target?'

Rawne looked at Corbec, who simply shrugged. 'So... any sign of this impending doom?'

Gaunt shook his head again. 'Fleet has nothing. Too many pilgrim ships confusing the picture.'

'Forget what might be. What about an operational base for the ones already here?' asked Rawne.

'Orbital surveys found what might be some landers in a deep glass desert a thousand kilometres west of here, but there were no life readings. The active hostiles here on Herodor are well hidden. Probably in the range of volcanic uplands called the Stove Hills, but that's just conjecture.'

'I say we–' Rawne started.

'We haven't got the manpower, Rawne. It'd take us weeks to find them, even with our skills. This is a big, bleak world with a lot of corners and holes to hide in.'

'But not an important world,' said Rawne darkly.

'No, major,' agreed Gaunt. 'Not an important world at all.'

'Then why–' Rawne began, and stopped dead when he saw the look in Gaunt's eyes.

'Have you... seen her?' Rawne said instead.

'Not yet.'

'You said the pilgrim ships were confusing things,' Corbec said. 'There are plenty of pilgrims here already. Hundreds of thousands. Orbital space is thick with them.'

'More ships arriving all the time,' Gaunt said. 'Some have come from beyond the subsector.'

'Probably should stop them,' Corbec ventured. 'I mean, we have to get this place locked tight. Can't just have anyone wandering in, even if they are harmless happy-clappies. Remember on Hagia, the way they came in with the pilgrim traffic?'

'I remember, Colm. I just don't know how we stop it. Some of these ships are old, barely serviceable and woefully unsupplied. If we try to form a picket and turn them away, we'll be consigning Imperial citizens to their deaths. Tac logis here tells me that ninety per cent of the pilgrim ships would not survive the return voyage. In most cases, they've spent their last savings on a one-way trip here. A trip to salvation.'

Corbec set down his empty cup and brushed crumbs off his tunic. 'The poor, sorry bastards,' he said bitterly.

Gaunt shrugged. 'The whole cluster and beyond knows what's happening here on Herodor, so you can bet the enemy does too. I can't begin to imagine why the information was released publicly.'

'Because she insisted,' said a voice behind him. Rawne had left the door open and no one had heard the newcomer walk in. They leapt to their feet and saluted.

'At ease,' said Lord General Lugo.

'I was told to report to you at 1700, sir,' said Gaunt.

'I know. I finished up earlier than expected and thought I'd move things along. Welcome to Herodor, Gaunt.'

'Thank you, lord general.'

Lugo glanced at Corbec and Rawne. 'Perhaps a moment alone...?' he suggested.

'Of course.' Gaunt turned to the others and waved them out. 'Dismissed, you two. Get the regiment settled.'

Corbec and Rawne hastened from the room and closed the door behind them.

'Feth,' whispered Corbec as soon as he was outside. 'I had hoped we'd never see that bastard again.'

'Not as much as Gaunt had, I'll be bound,' said Rawne.

'I SUGGEST, IF I may, man to man,' said Lugo, 'that we put all previous unpleasantness behind us.' Lugo was a tall, bony individual with thin, greasy skin that clung like parchment to the curves of his shaved skull. He wore a stark white dress uniform, the chest covered in medals.

'That might be advantageous, sir,' said Gaunt.

'Things were said on Hagia, Gaunt. Deeds were done. You redeemed your reputation and abilities in my eyes with that little excursion to the Shrinehold. So... say no more about it, that's my motto.'

Gaunt nodded. He found it difficult to answer. Lord General Lugo was, in his opinion, one of the most inept and self-aggrandising officers in the Crusade's upper command echelon, a political animal rather than a military leader. In 770, he had negotiated for himself command of the liberation of the shrineworld Hagia, believing it to be a simple task that would win him much glory and bolster his political ambitions. When the liberation effort went disastrously wrong, he had blamed Gaunt and tried to make the Tanith First's commander carry the can. In doing so, he nearly lost the entire shrineworld to Chaos, a calamity only averted by the Tanith during the peculiar happenings at the Shrinehold itself. After Hagia, his slate clean, Gaunt had been transferred with his forces to the Phantine theatre. Lugo, though not actually disgraced, had remained on Hagia as Imperial Governor, his ambitions in tatters.

Sadly, that meant he had been in exactly the right place to benefit from the extraordinary events that then took place there. His star was now in the ascendant again. He was, by default, in control of what might prove to be the most influential part of the entire Imperial interest in the Sabbat Worlds. Rumours were already spreading that Lugo could be looking to replace Macaroth as Warmaster if the current stagnation continued. He was very much the coming man.

Gaunt could almost smell that confidence and ambition on the lord general. It was actually the smell of hair tonic and cologne, but to Gaunt such pampering scents were the same thing. Lugo had his sights on power. Real power. It gave him an appetite so great you could almost hear his stomach growling.

And it was absolutely obvious that the last thing Lugo wanted in his path was Ibram Gaunt, who had shamed him so on Hagia.

'Why is there a smile on your face, Gaunt?'

Gaunt shrugged. 'No reason, my lord. Just pleased that things can be square between us.' No reason indeed. Gaunt was smiling because, for the first time since he'd received his orders on Aexe Cardinal, he was pleased to be on Herodor.

As he understood it, he was only here because she had requested it. Lugo would never have sent for Gaunt. Whoever – whatever – she was, she had clout. She was in charge here, really in charge, and Lugo was forced to obey her will. Lugo and his tacticians were taking her seriously. Either that, or Lugo's capacity for intrigue was so great Gaunt couldn't even begin to see its devious mechanisms.

'You say she insisted that word of her return be broadcast?' Gaunt asked.

Lugo nodded. He had stalked over to the window and was staring out at the city as the first shrouds of evening began to fall across the scene. 'She would not have it kept secret, no matter how strenuously my advisors objected. She cannot... as I understand it... see why her return should be kept from common knowledge. She calls herself an instrument, Gaunt. An instrument of the Golden Throne. She embodies a power and a purpose for the good of Mankind. Kept secret, she has no power or purpose at all. It makes a certain sense.'

'It makes her vulnerable. It makes this world and this... forgive my candor... feeble city vulnerable.'

Lugo watched the city lights as they came on in the covering darkness. A wind from the wastes had picked up and pattered glass flecks against the thick window pane. 'It does. It does indeed.'

'Then why here, sir? Why this backwater? Surely her power and purpose could be put to better use at the vanguard of the crusade. With the Warmaster on Morlond, for example?'

Lugo turned from the window. He was smiling now. 'It pleases me no end to hear you speak this way, Gaunt. It agrees entirely with my thinking. She should not be here. We must persuade her to… relocate.'

'Of course,' said Gaunt, 'though this all presumes she is what she says she is.'

Lugo's expression suddenly darkened. 'You don't believe?'

'I–' Gaunt began.

Lugo took a step forward. 'If you don't believe, I can scarcely see the point of you being here.'

'I remain to be convinced, lord general.'

'You what? You're talking like a damned heretic, Gaunt.'

'No, sir. I–'

'Saint Sabbat has been reincarnated. She is made flesh so that she might lead us to victory here in the worlds that bear her name. This is a moment undreamt of in human history! A moment of sacred wonder! And you *remain to be convinced?*'

Gaunt opened his mouth and then closed it again. He met the lord general's hard stare.

'I think it's high time you met her,' said Lugo. 'Either that, or it's high time I had you burned at the stake.'

On a cold, forlorn night just like the one presently bearing down on the Civitas Beati, but six thousand years earlier, the Saint had left her mark on Herodor. The Civitas Beati hadn't been called that then. It was but a single colony tower, the basis of what would one day become Old Hive, the central hive steeple, and back then it was called Habitat Alpha (colonial). The Saint, at the head of her flotsam cavalcade of an army, a host made up of colonial regiments, armed pilgrim retinues, a commandery of the Sisters Militant later to form the Order of Our Martyred Lady, and an echelon of the now extinct Astartes Chapter the Brazen Skulls, had bested and driven off a Chaos force at Grace Gorge, and she had come to Habitat Alpha to cleanse her wounds. She and her chosen bathed in the thermal springs and made them blessed for all time. The next morning, the Saint's host arose, refreshed, and annihilated the renewed thrust of the Chaos force in the Battle of the Shard Valley where, it was said, she alone disposed of eighteen hundred enemy warriors, including their Archon, Marak Vore.

It was all in the annals, and the storybooks. Gaunt had known them since childhood. Under Slaydo, he had committed them to memory.

The Balneary Shrine where Sabbat had washed her wounds lay in the lowest depths of Old Hive. It was constructed from black basalt and lit only by electro-candles and biolumin globes. Attendants and shrine priests hurried out as Lugo, with his chief staffers and life company troopers, approached down the long stone corridor. The air was hot and damp, and smelled of sulphur and iron.

They reached the doorway. 'We will wait here,' Lugo said. 'All of us,' he added, looking pointedly at Surgeon Curth, whom Gaunt had summoned to join him before following the lord general into the depths of the hive tower. Curth caught Gaunt's eye and he nodded.

'Stay here. I'll call if I want you.'

Gaunt stepped through the heavy doors, and they closed behind him. It was dim and quiet, and the close air was clogged with steam rising from the deep-cut bathing pools. A narrow staircase of a hundred steps cut from gleaming white limestone led down from the doorway, thousands of electrocandles lining the edges of the flight. The candlelight reflected off the slowly lapping water below. To the east lay the Chapel of the Emperor, to the west the votive chapel of the Saint. Gaunt went down the pale, polished steps, and took off his cap. He was sweating already. He walked to the side of the main bath, and stared down at his chopped reflection in the rust-stained water. The water rose from an aquifer deep beneath the city, broiled and heated by the volcanic vents in the crust. It was said to heal all wounds. Along the edge of the bath, Gaunt could see hundreds of brass spoons, cups and ladles that were used by the faithful to drink or baptise or cleanse themselves. Deep in the pool, shimmering, he saw millions of coins and blades, badges, medals and other offerings.

He knelt down at the poolside, plucked off a glove, and ran his bare fingers through the warm water.

There was a splash on the far side of the bathing pool, and ripples circled across towards him. He looked up in time to see a pale figure rising from the water, its back to him. It was a woman, clad in a simple white shift. She came up the bath's side steps, dripping, the wet linen sticking to her body, and he averted his gaze. Two shrine adepts emerged from the steam and draped her in a long, grey robe. She pulled it close, and brought the hood up over her head.

Then she turned, facing Gaunt across the water of the sacred balneary.

'Ibram.'

He looked up. 'You know my name?'

'Of course.' Her voice was soft and breathy. He longed to see her face. A sweet scent reached his nostrils as if the departing adepts had thrown incense on the lamp flames. Islumbine, that was it. The smell of islumbine, sacred flower of the Saint.

'I'm glad you're here,' she said.

'I came because I was told to come,' Gaunt said. 'I was ordered.'

She folded her arms, facing him across the steaming pool.

'You can stand up, if you like. You don't have to bow.'

He rose, slowly.

'I requested you. I requested the Tanith Ghosts. It pleases me that Gaunt's Ghosts are here with me on Herodor.'

The voice was so sweet. So penetrating. It was almost as if he already knew it.

'Why us?' Gaunt asked.

'Because of what you did on Hagia. You and your men put up their lives to vouchsafe my remains against the archenemy. You defended the Shrinehold to the last. It is only right I ask for you here, now, to protect me as you did before. I want the Ghosts to be my inner circle. My honour guard.'

'We will not shrink from that task,' Gaunt said. He took a few steps and began to move around the side of the pool. 'I had a... well, I don't know what it was. I had a vision on Aexe Cardinal that this would come to pass. A woman six millennia dead told me to find you here.'

'Really?' she said, as if thinking for a moment. 'That is good. That is as I intended it to be.'

'Did you?'

'Of course.'

He took another step closer. 'You intended that? That vision of the sororitas? You created that chapel in the woods out of nothing?'

'Of course, Ibram.'

'I believed that. It was real. Beltayn and I, we were totally convinced by it. We felt... touched by a strangeness beyond our power to explain.' He took a step closer. She began to back away slightly.

'Not like now,' he added.

'Ibram, you alarm me. What is this agitation in you? Why do you approach me?'

'Because I want to see your face.'

'No.'

'Why not?'

'Because–'

'I want to see your face because I know your voice!'

He lunged at her and grabbed her. She thrust out a hand and pushed his face aside, but he shook it off and yanked back her hood.

'I know your voice,' he said again, as she fought to break free.

'Sanian.'

Sanian pulled away from him and dragged her robe tight. She stared at him with eyes he couldn't fathom.

'You don't believe.'

Gaunt took a step back and shook his head, laughing out loud. 'I wanted to. Oh, believe me, I wanted to. Five months in a transit ship, waiting to see the truth? I've longed for this moment since Slaydo first explained the mysteries of Sabbat to me. I expected all sorts of things... truth, lies, fantasies. But not *you*, Sanian.'

She glared at him. Her black hair fell in wet ringlets around her beautiful face. It had grown long since he'd last seen her, a far cry from the shaved scalp and braid she'd worn as an esholi student. 'Understand this, Ibram. I'm not Sanian.'

'You are. I know you. You were the esholi who guided my men to the Shrinehold. Milo still talks about you.'

The look in her eyes changed suddenly and unnerved him. 'Oh, Ibram. Of course I am Sanian. My flesh is, at least. I needed a vessel, and she was the right one. She was a sweet girl and she gave her flesh to me. I look like Sanian. I sound like her. But I am not her. I am Sabbat. The girl from the hills of Hagia, reborn into this fragile body.'

'No...'

'Answer me this, Ibram. How else might I come back? How else might I find flesh to clothe me?'

He shook his head. 'This is a trick. Lugo is using you. You're not my Saint.'

GAUNT STRODE OUT into the corridor outside the balneary and Lugo's party stood back to let him pass.

'Well?' asked Lugo.

Gaunt stared at Lugo for a moment. 'It doesn't matter what I believe, does it?'

'Why?'

'Because as far as the Imperium is concerned, as far as hundreds of thousands of pilgrims are concerned... and as far as the archenemy is concerned... we have a reincarnated saint here on Herodor. And that's all that matters.'

Lugo grinned. 'At last, Gaunt, you're grasping the idea.'

GAUNT MARCHED AWAY from the balneary and the lord general's retinue, and headed down the long, stone colonnade that led to the nearest elevator bank. The attendants from the balneary, the hierarchs and adepts who had withdrawn from the place at Lugo's approach, were waiting quietly in the colonnade, silent robed figures in the gloom. He pushed through their huddled groups, knowing they were all watching him.

'Gaunt! Gaunt!' Curth called as she ran after him. He didn't break stride. When she finally caught up with him, he was waiting outside the iron cage door of the elevator for a lift car to arrive.

'You want to tell me what's going on?' she snapped.

He looked at her, his eyes in shadow. 'Ever have a secret, Curth? One that will hurt as many by telling it as it will by keeping it?'

'Yes,' she said honestly, the thought of Gol Kolea flashing through her mind.

He seemed surprised at her reply, as if he'd been expecting her to say no. 'How did you decide?'

'I didn't. It was decided for me.'

'That's what I'm afraid will happen here.' The mechanically wound elevator car clanked and moaned to a halt, and he wrenched open the collapsible cage door. Curth had to leap in after him to stop him closing the cage in her face. For a moment, she thought he was going to pull the cage open again and order her out. Instead, he walked to the wall panel and pulled on the brass lever. The elevator began to rise, gears whirring in the blackness of the shaft.

'Did you see her?' she asked, watching the lights of passing floors slide down his face.

'I saw her.'

'And it's put you in this mood?'

He let out a slow, dangerous breath and looked like he might punch something.

'You asked me to help you, Gaunt. You said you needed proof to put your mind at rest.' She patted the equipment satchel slung over her shoulder. 'I brought the bio-scanner. Did you not need proof after all?'

'Apparently not,' he said.

'It's not her, is it?' Curth asked. Gaunt said nothing. With a sigh, she leaned over and pulled the brass lever down to suspend motion. The elevator clanked to a halt between floors. Somewhere, a buzzer rang. An amber light began to flash on the control panel.

'Talk to me,' she said.

'Let it alone, please, surgeon.'

Curth shook her head. 'I've watched you, Ibram. All the way from Aexe Cardinal, ever since the news broke. Part of you wants it to be her, part of you is afraid it won't be. Know what I thought? I thought the moment you saw her, you'd be sure. Just like that. No need for me to do a gene procedure to get the answer for you. I knew you'd know. And you do.'

'I do.'

'It's not her.'

'It's not.'

'Throne!' she gasped, then recovered her train of thought. 'So what is this? Disappointment? Anger? You came here needing proof one way or the other, and you've got it. That at least should satisfy you.'

'Do you remember Sanian?'

She shrugged. 'No, I... oh, wait. Hagian girl, a student... esholi, that's what they were called, wasn't it? She went along with Corbec's mob.'

'That's her.' He stared at her.

Her eyes widened. 'You are fething kidding me, Gaunt! Her? She's the Saint?'

'Far as I can tell, Sanian believes she is the reincarnation of Sabbat. She's quite lucid, and convincing, I would imagine, to someone who didn't know her already. She needs psychiatric treatment in an Imperial asylum. But her potential value has been recognised. Her value as propaganda.'

'By Lugo?'

'You can see how delighted he is his career's back on track. He doesn't care if she's real or not. All he cares about is the fact that she's convincing. The crusade needs a miracle right now... and he's the one who's going to be remembered forever as the man who made that miracle happen.'

She reached out tentatively and chaffed his shoulder reassuringly. 'So, tell the truth. As a servant of the God-Emperor, you've always been honest to a fault.'

'It's not that simple. She is strategically valuable, there's no getting away from that. As an icon, a rallying point, she could win this war for us. Her presence could bolster our morale and destroy the enemy's resolve. If she continues to play the part, and we all go along with it and say we believe, we could liberate the entire cluster. But I don't think I can lie about something like this. Not to Zweil... not to Corbec and Dorden and Daur and the others who were touched by the Saint on Hagia. They believed in a truth there, a truth that I felt too. I can't ask them to believe this lie instead.'

'Let them make their own minds up,' she said.

'AH, THERE YOU are,' said Corbec, looking up from the data-slate he had been fiddling with. 'You'll be pleased to know we're settling in. Billets are fine. I've got a list of their locations here, if you want.'

Gaunt ignored the slate Corbec held out to him.

'Or maybe you don't. Anyway, we're getting the lie of the land. Rawne and Mkoll are out there right now, deploying platoons around the city perimeter. We got about nineteen in the field, setting up waystations in cooperation with the local militia. It won't be much, but by dawn we should have a basic defence established around the north and east flanks of the city. The locals add about twelve thousand to the numbers, along with medium armour, and the lord general's landing force has about a thousand more, plus light armour and some special weapons units.'

'Where's Milo?'

'Milo?' Corbec furrowed his brow and scrolled down the disposition lists on his slate. 'Right now, I'd say he was out with his platoon at the Glassworks. That's... ah... up in the north-west sector.'

Gaunt nodded. 'Get on the vox and get him back here.'

'Well, they're due for return rotation to the billets at ten tomorrow and–'

'Now please, colonel.'

'Right. Yes, sir.'

Gaunt walked past him into the wide, vaulted chamber on the eightieth level of the third hive tower where the Tanith First had set up their operations post. The wide room, with shuttered windows on two sides, was busy with regiment personnel, working with members of the Regiment

Civitas Beati and tech-adepts from the regular Herodian PDF to set up main-caster vox stations, tactical superimpositionals and relay nodes. Power cables and data-flexes snaked across the floor. Technicians were wiring up the portable comm-desks and holo-chart tables.

'Is he all right?' Corbec asked Curth, who had followed Gaunt into the room.

'Not really,' she said.

Gaunt turned and looked back at Corbec. 'What's through here?' he asked, gesturing to a side arch into another room.

Corbec hastened over to join him. 'Just an annexe. Daur thought it might do as a briefing room. The Munitorum's bringing chairs up, and a few tables. Beltayn's organised some food too. Down the hall on the left, plenty of grub for–'

Gaunt cut him off. 'Two minutes. I want you, Dorden, Zweil and Daur in the annexe for a privy briefing. Hark too, if he's around.'

Corbec shrugged and nodded. 'As you ask, sir.'

THEY TOOK THEIR seats. Corbec; the old ayatani priest Zweil; Captain Ban Daur, the Verghastite third officer; Dorden, the chief medic and Viktor Hark, the regiment's commissar. Curth slipped in and sat at the back. Before he sat down, Daur configured and activated the portable confidence screen that would generate electroference patterns to keep the meeting private.

'What I've got to say doesn't leave this room,' said Gaunt.

The men nodded. Curth, at the back, folded her arms and hunched her shoulders.

'I've met the Saint,' said Gaunt.

'Praise be!' Zweil murmured.

Hark had a sick look on his face that indicated he knew what must be coming next.

'She isn't real.'

There was a long silence. Corbec stared blankly at the wall opposite him. Daur groaned and put his head in his hands, fingers wrapped with a green silk faith ribbon. Dorden closed his eyes and folded one hand around the other. Zweil blinked.

'She... I'm sorry, what?' Zweil said.

'She is a fake. An invention. A subterfuge.'

'Oh, feth...' sighed Corbec.

'Seriously?' Daur asked. His eyes were welling up.

'More particularly,' Gaunt said, 'she is known to us. To you, Colm, and you Dorden, and Daur too. As far as I can tell, she truly believes she is Sabbat incarnate. But when I met her, face to face, I realised it was the poor girl we'd met on Hagia: Sanian.'

'Sanian?' Corbec started.

'No, no... this... no, this isn't right,' Zweil said, agitated. 'The Saint has come back, the Beati. This is what we were told. She is here...'

'She isn't. It's... a scam,' said Gaunt.

'Absolutely not!' Zweil cried, and got up.

'Father... father, please. I understand this is hard for you to hear.'

'It is her! It has to be!' Zweil had become so upset that Dorden and Curth had both risen to their feet. 'This is the Saint returned, not some esholi child with her head all messed up!'

'I believe,' said Hark, slowly pulling on his black leather gloves, 'that Zweil ought to know. He is an ayatani of the Beati Cult, after all.'

Gaunt shot a dangerous look in Hark's direction. 'She isn't real,' he repeated.

'She was on Hagia,' said Dorden, his arm around Zweil's shoulders. He was staring at Gaunt. 'She spoke to me.'

'I know she did, Tolin,' said Gaunt.

'She spoke to me too,' said Daur.

'And me, boss,' said Corbec.

'I know, Colm. I fully believe that on Hagia you and Ban and Tolin... and others too... had a communication from the Saint that drove you to do what you did. All I'm saying is... this isn't the Saint. Not here. Not now.'

'But–' Daur began.

'Has she spoken to you since?' Gaunt asked.

The men were silent.

'Heretic! She spoke to you,' Zweil cried suddenly.

'What?'

'You... and Beltayn. On Aexe Cardinal. Through her servant.'

Gaunt closed his eyes, trying to master the anger that boiled inside him. 'Ayatani Zweil... I told you that in strictest confidence. It was meant to remain between just us. An act of confession, sacrosanct. I trusted you would keep it to yourself.'

'Well, this is too important!' snapped Zweil. The bone-thin old priest swayed, and for a moment Gaunt was afraid he was about to keel over. 'Devil take my vows, you're lying about this and I won't have it!'

'What's he talking about, Gaunt?' asked Dorden.

'He's speaking out of turn, doctor,' said Gaunt.

'He knows!' Zweil cried.

'I think you should tell us, sir,' said Corbec.

'This is hardly the time or–'

'Tell them!' Zweil screamed. 'Tell them what you told me! Tell them what made me believe!'

Gaunt looked from one face to the next slowly. He realised that, right then, he didn't have a friend in the room.

'All right. On Aexe, I took a trip from the frontline to Meiseq to meet with Van Voytz. Beltayn was with me. Our train was delayed and we went on foot for a while, and we found this chapel in the woods. There was an old woman there. She seemed to know us, and she warned me about Herodor, long before the orders came through. Later, Beltayn and I tried to find the chapel again. We... couldn't, and I can't explain that.'

'Tell them the rest,' said Zweil.

'It's not pertinent,' Gaunt said.

'It is! It speaks volumes! The woman they met identified herself, and later they discovered she had died here on Herodor six thousand years ago!'

'That's enough,' snarled Gaunt.

'Yes, it is,' said Zweil. 'It's enough. Enough proof by anyone's standards. The Saint told you to come here and serve her! How dare you deny her now!'

Gaunt took off his cap and sat down. Everyone was staring at him.

'I don't know what happened in the woods on Aexe. It has been with me ever since. I'm sorry I never told any of you about it. But it doesn't change the facts. The Saint here is not the Saint. She is a pretender.'

'And for the record,' Gaunt added, looking at Zweil, 'I'm appalled by your lack of confidence, father.'

'Oh, get over it!' Zweil spat. He shook Dorden's arm off him. 'Tell me this, Ibram Gaunt... if this Saint is such an obvious fake, why did she request you here? You, the one man who could expose her?'

Gaunt shrugged. 'I don't know the answer to that.'

'And if Lugo is really calling the shots,' added Corbec, 'why would he let that happen?'

'I don't know,' said Gaunt.

'I know this,' said Hark, rising to his feet. 'It doesn't matter if she's the Saint or not. As far as millions, maybe billions, of Imperial citizens are concerned, she is Sabbat reborn. Truth or lie, we have to uphold that, or Imperial morale will collapse overnight.'

'I was getting to that part, Hark,' said Gaunt. 'We have a duty here, whether we like it or not...'

'To lie?' asked Dorden coldly.

'Even that,' said Gaunt.

Zweil let out a low moan and shuffled towards the door. He paused there and looked back at Gaunt. 'Why here?' he asked. 'If it's a lie, why the hell here?'

Gaunt couldn't answer him. Zweil paced out of the room, and Curth and Dorden followed him in concern.

'Dismissed,' said Gaunt. Corbec and Daur both left, uneasily.

Gaunt looked at Hark. 'I see your old master has been working on you.'

Hark shook his head. 'Lugo? He's not my–'

'Shut up, Viktor. Lugo placed you with the Tanith on Hagia. You were meant to be my replacement. He–'

'No, Ibram. I was meant to be your judge and executioner. That was what Lugo wanted of me. I'd like to think that I have proved myself to you and the Ghosts since then. Yes, Lugo spoke to me when we arrived. I won't lie. He asked me to work on you. He thought you could persuade Sabbat to relocate to Morlond. That would really do his cause no end of good.'

'I see. And?'

Hark smiled. 'I told him you'd make your own mind up.'

Gaunt nodded.

'Zweil will calm down,' said Hark. 'It's in his nature to blow hot and cold. What interests me is how right he was.'

'What do you mean, Viktor?

'If this Saint Sabbat is a fake… why us… and why here?'

THREE
UNHOLY NIGHT

'Everyone has a choice. Me, I choose to not make a choice. What? What? Why is that funny?'

— Hlaine Larkin, Ghost

IF HE'D LEARNED anything about Herodor so far, it was that the nights were fething cold. The city shield was lit, and for that they might be somewhat thankful, but the wasteland wind, with a cutting edge like a chainsword, slid in under the canopy of energy and bit them to the bone.

If Larkin had understood his sergeant's pre-brief right, the area the carriers had dropped them off in was called the Glassworks, a ramshackle, two thousand hectare arrangement of dingy workshops, storebarns and manufactories in the north-west of the city. It seemed a long, long way from anywhere nice. The main bulk of the Civitas, well-lit and cosy-looking, was a good distance behind them. Here, the light of drum-fires and phospha lamps combined with the gauzy glow of the shield overhead to produce a blue, submarine halflight.

Above, in the night sky, stars twinkled that were not stars. Those indistinct pinpricks of light were the hundreds – possibly thousands – of pilgrim ships that had swarmed to Herodor.

Larkin's platoon, number eleven, had been sent to the Glassworks with ten and twelve to secure that section of perimeter. Easy job, to say it. In practice, it was hard to even find the perimeter in the first place. The whole area had been overrun by pilgrims, and their tent towns had grown like forest fungus between the empty buildings – inside some of them, in fact – and out into the edges of the wasteland itself, beyond the limits of the crackling shield. There was no definable edge to the city at all.

Weapons slung, uneasy, the Ghosts moved through the twilight world of the camp. The pilgrim contingent was huddled around feeble fires, cooking late meals or forming prayer circles. Infardi worshippers in green silk were performing rituals around their clock shrines, or moving through the camp passing out pamphlets. Many were tonsured or had their napes shaved, others hugged placards or emblems of the Saint. The most extreme had pierced themselves with the stigmata of the nine wounds, or inscribed holy tracts on their skin. Some had whips or sticks to scourge themselves with. Every single one displayed his or her pilgrim badge proudly, and every one looked pinched and painfully cold.

'Keep it tight, Larks,' Sergeant Obel called. Larkin hurried to catch up. Just for the hell of it, he shouldered his long-las and panned the scope around. Through the enhanced and magnifying viewfinder, he spot-picked locations in the fuzzy cold of the obsidae beyond the camp. For one brief second, he thought he glimpsed movement in the distance. Just wind blowing the dust up. That's all, he told himself. Not the enemy.

As far as Hlaine Larkin – the regiment's finest marksman – was concerned, the enemy wasn't really out there anywhere. He was already inside the city, inside with them.

And his name was Lijah Cuu.

JUST FIVE HUNDRED metres from where Larkin was standing, in another part of the straggled-out camp, Trooper Cuu raised his standard pattern lasrifle to fire.

'Not another step, gak-head,' he hissed. 'Or I'll ventilate your torso, sure as sure.'

'Put that up,' Sergeant Criid snapped, pushing past Cuu and jerking his gun-muzzle skywards with an off-hand gesture. 'Sir? Mister? I need you to identify yourself.'

Anton Alphant turned and looked at her. He raised his arms so she could see his hands were empty.

'I don't mean any trouble, trooper,' he said.

'Sergeant,' she corrected, and moved forward to face him as her platoon – the tenth – closed in behind her.

'My apologies, sergeant. It's been a few years.'

'Since what?' she asked. Alphant liked her already. Sharp to the point of brittle, fast-eyed, confident. A looker too, if you liked hard, thin girls. A little beyond an old man like himself, of course.

'I was Guard. Years back. Sorry, that's not important, is it?'

Criid shrugged. 'We've been told to secure this area, sir. It's okay if the pilgrims keep to their camp areas, but we can't have them moving around after dark.'

'Because of the raiders?' he said.

She nodded. 'You are a pilgrim, I suppose? You've got papers?'

Alphant affirmed with another quick nod, and then gently opened his robe so she could see what his hands were doing at all times. He pulled out his sheaf of certificates.

DaFelbe, Criid's number two, a tall, thin, earnest young man, hurried forward and examined Alphant's papers with a handheld verity-reader.

'Anton Alphant,' DaFelbe called back. 'Registered infardi pilgrim. Place of origin, Khan II, place of birth–'

'Enough,' said Criid. She took the papers and walked over to face Alphant. 'Says here you were assigned camp space in the Ironhall district. You've roamed a little too far.

'I... I was looking for someone,' said Alphant.

'Who?'

'It's not important now. I got sidetracked, I'm afraid. I was just going to see if the doors on that manufactory were open. There are a lot young children in this part of the camp and I was hoping to get them into shelter.'

'Why? Are you some kind of elected leader?'

'No, not at all. It's just... the nights are cold.'

'Aren't they just?' said Criid. 'Hwlan?'

The tenth platoon scout hurried up.

Criid nodded to the empty building nearby. 'Get that place open, please. Some kids here who could do with shelter tonight.'

'On it,' Hwlan said.

'Nessa... watch his back,' Criid added, signing to the platoon sniper. Nessa Bourah scooped up her long-las and hurried after the scout.

There was movement behind them, but it was just Sergeant 'Shoggy' Domor and twelfth platoon closing up.

'See much?' asked Domor.

Criid chuckled at the unintended irony of his question. 'You tell me.' His bulbous, augmetic eyes were clicking and whirring as they scanned the horizon.

'Not enough to spit on, Tona,' he said.

'Be thankful for that,' she said.

Back down the file of Ghosts, Brin Milo chaffed his cold hands and looked into the distance.

'What the feth are those people doing?' he asked.

'Them there?' Nehn replied. 'Keeping their fething balance, I'd say.'

Throughout the fire-lit sprawl of the pilgrim camp, as ubiquitous as the bizarre clock shrines, thin towers rose up into space. Wood, mostly, some steel, some stone on wheeled trolleys. On top of each one stood a pilgrim, poised vulnerably on the summit of his or her thin pillar.

'Stylites,' said Corporal Chiria, as if she knew. She was a heavy-made Verghastite, her plain face badly scarred by the last campaign they had gone through. 'Stylites, you know? They stand on top of plinths and pillars, Milo.'

'Uh... why?'

'Well,' considered Chiria, 'I don't exactly know.'

'Brings them closer to the Saint,' said a voice from behind them. 'Proves their faith.'

'Really, Gol?' asked Milo.

Gol Kolea set his lasrifle down and thought hard. It was painful to watch. Gol Kolea had once been leader of tenth platoon, with a fine war record behind him. Some said he was senior officer material. But on Phantine, two years before, the spraying fragments of a loxatl flechette round had ripped into his head and torn away his wits and his personality. It was a crying shame, a real tragedy. Kolea seldom said more than a few words. His last comment was a downright magnum opus.

'How do you know that, Gol?' asked Milo.

'Dunno,' said Kolea. He scratched at the side of his head. 'Just is a thing.'

'Oh, you know the sergeant,' said Cuu, sauntering up. He was the only man who still referred to Kolea by his former rank. 'Talks a lot of gak, don't you, gak-head? Eh? Eh? Sure as sure.'

'One day, Lijah,' said Chiria, venomously, 'someone's gonna plant a las-round straight between your eyes.'

'Uh huh. Who'd that be? You?' giggled Cuu. 'You haven't got the balls, Chiria. Sure as sure.'

Milo turned to face Cuu and stared into his deep set, scar-cut face. 'You don't stop mocking Kolea and I'll do it myself, you understand?' Milo said.

Cuu grinned. 'Whoo, careful, mascot. You'll bust a seam!'

Milo dropped his lasrifle and balled his fists.

'Enough! That's enough!' said Bonin, the twelfth platoon scout. He put himself in between Milo and Cuu. 'Milo... signals is asking after you.'

'Me?'

'Yes, you. Cuu. Go and be busy elsewhere.'

Cuu sniggered and wandered off.

'NOT EXACTLY HOMELY,' Hwlan sniffed, looking around. The manufactory interior was dark and empty, and smelled of woodrot, motor oil and ozone. Nessa moved past him, scoping around with her long-las. DaFelbe advanced with her, shining his lamp pack into the darker corners. There were holes in the roof over their heads, and through them, they could see the shifting luminescence of the city shield.

'It's out of the wind, that's the important thing,' said Alphant. 'A few drum fires in here and it'll be almost cosy.'

'I guess,' said Hwlan.

'All right if I bring some of the families in?' Alphant asked Criid.

She nodded. 'As many as there's room for.'

In less than fifteen minutes, the place was teeming. The pilgrims dragged belongings with them on barrows and litters, and some manhandled clock shrines in through the doorway. Fires were laid. The pilgrims were singing a slow, pastoral hymn as they settled themselves. Alphant moved amongst them, helping them get comfortable. Criid watched him for a while. The man might not claim to be a leader, but he had a natural, reassuring air of command that the pilgrims all responded to. He was, however, clearly preoccupied, and kept looking at the door as newcomers entered. Who was he hoping to find in the Ironhall camp?

Criid was helping an elderly man find a corner to sit in. The old man had a handcart loaded with crudely painted plaster busts of the Saint, undoubtedly copied cheaply and in bulk using a fabric replicator, which he sold to the faithful to keep himself in soup money. Once Criid got him bedded down on his ragged mattress roll in a corner of the manufactory, he pressed one into Criid's hand.

'No, that's all right.'

'Please.'

'Honestly, I have no money.'

'No, no,' the old man shook his head. 'Not for money. It is my thanks for your kindness.'

'Oh,' Criid looked at the plaster effigy. It was hideous. The paint had been applied so badly and so clumsily that Saint Sabbat looked like a pre-teen clangirl wannabe from Vervunhive who had just that morning discovered cosmetics and applied them enthusiastically.

'Thank you,' Criid said, tucking the plaster bust into her jacket pocket. It was a non-uniform garment, a fur-trimmed Shadik army field jacket that she'd appropriated on Aexe Cardinal. She'd slit the insignia off. So far, no one had brought her up for wearing it, and she was glad of the warmth.

'May the Saint bless you,' the old man said.

'Thanks for that too,' she added, but her attention wasn't really on him. She could hear raised voices coming from the factory entrance.

In the doorway, DaFelbe and Lubba were having an altercation with a tall man dressed in the ornate demi-armour of the local military.

'...just have to get them out of here, then,' she heard the man say as she walked up.

'Problem?' she asked.

The local turned to look at her. He was clad in brown synth-leather and his torso and left arm were cased with segmented steel. Behind him were over a dozen Herodian city troopers with bullnose carbines.

'Are you in charge?' he asked.

'Sergeant Criid, Tanith First,' she answered smoothly. With a flick of her head, she signalled DaFelbe and Lubba to back off. Lubba seemed curiously naked without his trademark flamer pack. Gakking city ordinances.

'Captain Lamm, Civitas Beati. This is an unauthorised use of civil property. Get these lowlifes out of here.'

'No,' said Criid.

The captain bristled. 'No?' he said.

'These *people*,' Criid emphasized the word, 'needed shelter. This building was not in use. Derelict in fact. This isn't unauthorised because I authorised it.'

'Use of property is a matter for the city council to decide. Did you break the lock?'

'Not personally, but I take responsibility. Let's be nice about this, Captain Lamm. There's no need for unpleasantness. We're on the same side.'

From the look on Lamm's face, he didn't quite agree. His men shuffled, edgy.

'Get these vagrants out of this building,' Lamm said, slowly and deliberately.

Criid had one of the choicest and most vulgar replies of her life ready to throw back at him, but a sound from beyond the factory interrupted her.

It was the sound of gunfire. The first shots of the night.

And it was swiftly followed by the sound of screaming.

'FIND A POSITION!' Obel yelled. 'Find a position and hold it!' The Ghosts in eleven platoon had started moving the moment they heard the first shots, but they were met by a surge of panicking pilgrims rushing out of the camp area. Two or three guardsmen were knocked off their feet by the moving crush.

The initial bursts of enemy fire had appeared only as flashes of light in the distance behind the press of bodies, but now actual laser bolts were visible, bright and hard, searing over the heads of the crowd. Hot red or hotter white, the lines of shots walked and bent like tracer rounds through the gloom. A series of them struck the warehouse wall behind Obel's location and blew out thick chunks of plaster and brick. Two loose rounds hit a stylite in the middle distance and knocked him, flailing, off his pillar. Other shots arced down mercilessly into the terrified masses.

'Oh feth!' Obel cursed, down in cover behind a handcart with his vox-officer. The vox-man was shouting to be heard as he relayed the situation in.

'Estimates?' Obel yelled.

'I can't see a bloody thing, sarge!' Brehenden barked back, trying to push through the disorder.

Larkin had managed to reach a doorway on the other side of the thoroughfare. He narrowed his eyes and watched the light show for a few seconds.

'At least a dozen shooters. Light or standard las,' he called out once he'd assessed the pattern. 'But they've got something heavier. A grunt cannon or even some kind of plasma cooker.'

That was what was doing the real harm. Potent firepower, auto-cycle, indiscriminate. Dozens of pilgrims were already dead. The heavy had so much kick, it brought down another of the hapless stylites by chopping clean through the pillar he was standing on. Larkin observed with astonishment that the other pillar-dwellers didn't try to flee or climb down. They simply sank to their knees on the precarious perches and started to pray.

'Can you knock it out?' Obel yelled.

Larkin studied the play of las-bolts in the air, watching for the fat, dull red ones. About two hundred metres north and east.

'I can try,' he said, without enthusiasm.

Obel waved Jajjo and Unkin forward to partner Larkin. Jajjo, dark-skinned and handsome, was eleven's new scout and the first Vervunhiver to achieve promotion to that elite speciality. Larkin knew Mkoll had high hopes of Jajjo's abilities.

'Call it, Larks,' Jajjo said. Ordinarily, the scout would take point, but this was now the sniper's play.

'Left, down there,' Larkin said. The trio pushed across the flow of the screaming crowd and hurried down a short flight of flagstone steps onto an arched walkway that ran along the back of a factory blockhouse. Several dozen pilgrims had elected to hide along here, and cowered into the walls as the three guardsmen ran past.

The walkway reached a corner where it split, continuing on over a stone footbridge into the side of a fabrication mill or descending to the lower service street by a wooden staircase. Pilgrims flooded along the street below. Larkin stood at the top of the steps for a moment and cocked his head. The gunfire sounds had altered slightly, relative to his location.

'Down,' he said and the three of them thumped down the wooden steps and began following the street by hugging the wall as civilians ran past the other way.

They reached a cross street. The flow of pilgrims had ebbed. Bodies sprawled all around on the rutted roadway. A clock shrine lay overturned at the junction.

Larkin darted out and got in cover behind the clock shrine. Immediately, the street lit up; light las-fire, hissing like quenched steel, and the heavy, diaphragm-vibrating belch of the cannon. Peppered, the carcass of the clock shrine shook and pieces of wood and plastic splintered off into the air. Shots chopped into the street paving too, or thudded dully into the draped and hunched corpses.

Larkin kept his head down. The fusillade he'd stirred up was so intense there wasn't a chance of Jajjo or Unkin making it across to join him. They were still pinned around the corner.

Several cannon rounds came right through the twisted clock that sheltered him and missed his head by a short margin. Larkin rolled and pulled his long-las up to his shoulder. Prone, he had a very limited field of view under the shrine's cart base, but it was enough for him to slide his long-las through and clear the sights.

The street beyond resolved in the cold, green shimmer of his night scope. He had to tweak the visual gain down because the las-flashes swooping his way were testing the limits of the radiance contrast.

Better. A hot spot. Very hot. A superheated muzzle, something big. He looked again, identifying three shadows working a heavy cannon on a tripod behind a parked motor truck forty metres away. More hot spots, smaller, cooler. Men with lasrifles. One in a doorway, another behind a row of fuel drums, another low against a side wall. All of them pumping fire at him.

He reached back and opened his musette bag, pulling a handful of powerclips out and selecting a standard low volt cell. He did it all by touch, reading the difference between the upright and diagonal crosses of tape he'd marked the sides with. He'd have preferred to go with a hot-shot for maximum power, but there were too many targets. A hot-shot was a one-use cell and he didn't have the time to keep changing between hits.

Larkin popped the hot-shot clip out of the long-las and replaced it with a low volt. He made sure he had a green 'armed' tell-tale showing on the backsight, and then snuggled in. Feth, but they weren't letting up. Another minute, no more, and the clock shrine would start falling apart and he might as well be naked in the middle of the street with a target painted on his face and a feather up his arse.

The cannon was the obvious initial target, but the noise it was whooping out would cover him as he picked off the others first. He set on the shooter in the doorway, waited for him to blaze away again to pick him out of the shadows properly, and then fired. The enemy probably didn't even see his muzzle flash in the confusion.

The one by the side wall now. *That's it, keep shooting. Show me right where you are…*

The long-las kicked. The figure by the wall flopped over.

The shooter by the drums suddenly realised that his cronies were down. He started to run back towards the cannon. That was when Larkin put his third shot through the man's spine.

The cannon started to crank up and fire right at him instead of hosing the street. No time for chances. Larkin ejected the low volt and slammed a hot-shot home. Each blast of the cannon had many times more power than the long-las, even with a hot-shot in the pipe, and it was cycling them out at a rate of five a second. The clock part of the toppled shrine disintegrated and a wheel went spinning off the cart, dismembered and shedding spokes.

'Yeah, yeah,' said Larkin and fired.

The hot-shot made a growling howl and the stock banged back against the permanent bruise on Larkin's right shoulder. It hurt. It always did. He liked the pain because he always associated it with a kill-shot.

The gunner's head vaporised and he pitched forward over the cannon. Sudden silence. Larkin could see the gunner's two teammates scrambling to pull him aside as the Tanith sniper locked another hot-shot in place.

Power-cell pack, one metre left of the tripod stand, feed cable attached...

Shoulder smack.

The cell pack exploded with the force of several grenades and tossed the whole cannon, tripod and all, into the air, along with all three figures, lifting balletically in a bright bloom of fire.

The tripod carriage bounced twice, making hard, metal clangs. The bodies didn't bounce.

'Clear!' Larkin yelled, reloading and getting up. Jajjo and Unkin swept out of cover and started running past him, snapping off semi-auto bursts to wash the street. Larkin ran after them, keeping close to the wall.

'Feth me, Larks!' said Unkin, surveying the sniper's handiwork as he got into a covering position at the next corner, near to where the destruction of the cannon had made a burning crater in the roadway. 'You don't mess about!'

'Pat him on the back later,' said Jajjo. He was crouching beside the truck and had begun firing down the left hand street.

More assaulters were moving up towards them. Lots of them. And Jajjo recognised their blood-red uniforms at once.

BLOOD PACT. So it was true, Tona Criid thought to herself. Up to a point, at least. The 'heretic dissidents' raiding Beati City were actually trained, drilled and seasoned infantry from the archenemy's elite field corps. What Corbec's briefing had omitted was the scale. This wasn't a skirmish raid. This was a full-on assault.

The enemy was pouring out of the wasteland into the Glassworks sector in force, heavily serviced by infantry support weapons and portable shields. By her own estimate, fifty or more pilgrims had been slaughtered in the opening phase, caught between the ruthless shock-fire of the attackers and the virtually helpless Imperials. Now the pilgrims had mostly fled into cover nearby, or en masse up into the inner city, and the battle had opened up, a ferocious street-fight running up through the obsidae, the camps and into the manufactories in the zone. Criid's platoon, supported by Domor's, held a three block area, with Obel's unit not far away to their west. She was reinforced fifteen minutes into the fight by three more platoons transitting in from the east, and by the column of local warriors voxed up by Captain Lamm.

It was ugly, as ugly as anything she'd ever known, and that was saying something. It felt a little like the street war she'd been caught up in back at Vervunhive, but there the enemy had been the well-equipped but drone-like Zoicans. The Blood Pact were a different thing altogether. They knew how to fight the streets. They were as skilled as the Ghosts and more disciplined than any Chaos force she'd ever encountered. It also compared unfavorably with the trench war on Aexe Cardinal that they'd only recently left behind. At the time, she'd believed that to be the benchmark of bad in terms of combat. Trapped – like rats and with rats – in narrow, filthy dugouts, sometimes fighting hand to hand.

But this was a gakking nightmare. The Glassworks was too open, too meandering. Every corner and twist of walkway, every sub-alley and back run, was a death trap. In a trench, you at least knew the enemy was in front of you.

Laughing, she burst off a spray of las-shots and slammed a Blood Pacter backwards through an archway. Two more appeared, and she felled them both as well.

'What the feth is funny?' Lubba shouted at her, blasting with his newly issued lasrifle. It seemed too small for his meaty, tattooed hands. She knew he dearly missed his flamer. Gak, but how useful would a flamer have been right then?

'I caught myself longing for trenches,' she said, re-celling her weapon. 'Struck me as laugh-your-brains-out funny.'

'Left! Left!' Subeno was yelling suddenly. A torrent of las-fire whickered down a side street and Criid and Lubba had to dive to find cover. Domor ran past her, with Nehn, Bonin and Milo. They closed down the fresh angle of attack with a heavy sheet of rapid fire. Several more Ghosts, led by Chiria and Ezlan, pushed through the gap and drove the fight back down the street. One of the Ghosts lurched and dropped. Criid couldn't see who it was. But she could see for sure they were dead.

Lamm's men had the cross street down from them locked up. Every few seconds, Criid could hear the hiss-burp of his sanctioned flamer. Behind them, in the next street block, Herodian PDF were engaged in a running battle with the enemy inside a row of iron-framed tithe barns.

'How's our back looking?' she called to Lubba. He was covered in plaster dust and looked like he'd been rolled in flour.

'Like I have the remotest fething idea,' he replied.

She got up and ran back down the narrow street, picking her way between the bodies of slaughtered pilgrims. DaFelbe, with nine troops in a good location, had the back end of the street sealed, but was coming under increasingly heavy fire. She saw Posetine and Vulli dragging Mkhef back out of the firing line. He'd been shot through the neck and chest. She doubted he'd see sunrise.

Rounding the corner, she ran right into Captain Daur leading his platoon up through the smoke.

'Report!' he yelled over the shooting.

Criid made a vague gesture around her. 'They're fething well all over us!' she began. 'Get back!'

'Cover!' he yelled, and his platoon broke towards the doorways and shattered windows of the barn opposite.

Criid moved the other way into a rubble strewn alley and straight into three Blood Pact troopers coming the other way.

Criid yelped and dropped. A las-round burned across her scalp.

It knocked the sense out of her. She lay face down in the rubble, unable to move, to see...

Something came down off the roof behind the Blood Pacters. A single Ghost, laspistol in one hand, straight silver in the other. In less than two seconds, all three enemy troopers were dead, two shot point-blank, the other slit open.

Breathing hard, Lijah Cuu lowered his hands. He was dripping with blood. He walked over to Criid and crouched down beside her. Figures ran past the end of the alley. Shots whined.

He holstered his pistol, and twitched the combat knife over so it was point-down from his bloody fist. Then he rested the tip of it against the nape of her neck. A drop of dark blood welled up around the razor-sharp point.

With his other hand, he stroked her hair, matted with blood, and then dragged a dirty finger down the slope of her exposed cheek.

'Sure as sure,' he muttered hoarsely. He raised the blade to slam it down.

A big hand closed around his rising wrist and held it dead. Cuu gasped in pain and glanced up.

'Don' you hurt nobody,' Kolea said.

'Get off me!' Cuu said.

'Don' you hurt nobody, Lijah-Cuu,' Kolea repeated, rising. Cuu was forced to come up with him, his wrist viced in Kolea's monumentally strong grasp.

'I was trying to help her! She needs help! Look at her!' Cuu squealed. 'Her gas-hood is twisted around her throat! Look! Look, gak it! I was gonna cut it off!'

'You go 'way,' Kolea said. 'Go 'way now.'

He released Cuu's wrist. Cuu backed off, staring at Kolea. Kolea returned the gaze, placid.

'You help her then,' Cuu said, 'you stupid gak-head.' He raised the war knife slightly, then wiped the blood off it on his trouser leg and sheathed it.

'Go 'way!' Kolea said. Cuu vanished into the shadows.

Kolea bent down and rolled Criid over, stripping off her constricting gas-hood. Then he gathered her up in his arms and started to walk.

Out on the street, Lubba saw him coming and felt his heart freeze. He'd been there, on Phantine two years before, and seen this exact thing. Kolea carrying the injured Criid to safety. Seconds later, Kolea had been hit and the man they all knew and loved had disappeared.

Lubba leapt up before it could happen again and pulled Kolea into cover. 'Medic!' he shouted. 'Medic here now!'

TWO STREETS AWAY, mortar rounds were falling on the sheds and factory spaces. Seething sheets of flame rushed out of doorways and windows, spraying glass into the air and shaking the earth. A roof caved in. Two long assembly shops were ablaze.

Milo cowered in the cover of a half-fallen wall. His ears rang with over-pressure. Blood from a shrapnel wound dribbled down his cheek. Bonin lay beside him, trying to tug a sliver of glass out of his palm.

'Well, this is fething nice, isn't it,' he said over the roar of detonations.

'Indeed,' Milo answered. He was rattled and dazed by the explosions but, beyond that, he had the oddest feeling. Like...

Like on Hagia.

He never had found out what signals had wanted him for.

'Wise up!' Bonin suddenly hissed, and rolled over, bringing his lasrifle up. He cracked off a couple of rounds and Milo joined his efforts. Red-clad figures had just emerged from the bombed-out buildings ahead of them.

They fired with care and precision. Bonin, a hugely able scout, had been trained in warfare by Mkoll, and knew how to shoot and how to wait to shoot. Milo had learned his battle-craft from a variety of sources... Colonel Corbec, Gaunt himself and, most especially, Hlaine Larkin. Milo picked his targets with a huntsman's expertise.

Between them, they shot down nine Blood Pact attackers as they emerged from the ruins and tried to push down the street.

They huddled in the rubble for a few minutes, and when the mortars started up again, they slid back in the direction of the main force.

'Help me!' someone was shouting. Flames were licking up around the buildings nearby and spitting sparks up at the fluttering shield.

Milo broke into a run, Bonin alongside him. They saw a man up ahead, a well-built man in late middle age wearing the robes of an infardi pilgrim. He was trying to drag an elderly man out of a burning manufactory.

'There are more inside!' Alphant yelled at the two Ghosts as they reached him. 'By the Saint, the place is on fire!'

The abandoned barn Criid had opened for Alphant's faithful just a short while before was now riven with flames. Many of those inside were too old or infirm to save themselves. Or they were children, helplessly lost and terrified.

Milo and Bonin went back in with Alphant and shooed the screaming children out. Rafters came down in scuds of flame. Bonin and Alphant grabbed an old woman in a litter seat and struggled out with her, patting out the flames which had caught on her dress.

Milo grabbed up two small children and scrambled them through into the night air.

Outside, they were met by a rain of las-fire and hard rounds. The Blood Pact had caught up with them. The old woman Bonin and Alphant had carried to safety died in her chair. Milo couldn't bear to look at the other casualties.

He and Bonin dragged their lasrifles off their shoulders and began returning fire, using the masonry of a disintegrated store front as a barricade.

'Give me something! Anything!' Alphant yelled from cover in a doorway, children huddled around him.

'You know what to do with it?' Milo shouted back.

'I was Guard! I know!'

Milo fetched out his laspistol and threw it to Alphant. Then he chucked over some spare clips from his musette bag. The three of them began to fire down the street.

Ducking in and out and shooting, Alphant suddenly saw the girl, Sabbatine. He'd been looking for her all night... ever since their encounter in the Ironhall camp, in fact. There was something about the girl, something remarkable, something that had driven him to seek her out.

She came out of a lathe shop down the street, rushing a group of child pilgrims from a block where flames were leaping up. They ran in line, holding hands. She looked like a scholam teacher on an outing.

'Get back! Get back!' Alphant shouted out to her.

She turned, saw him, and began hurrying the children towards the cover position where Alphant and the two Ghosts lay.

'For feth's sake!' Milo exclaimed, seeing them come. Las-fire whipped around the heads of the little, urgent procession. How was it missing? How were they not dead?

Bonin and Milo rose up a little, and fired to give them cover, then began dragging the wailing children down behind the barricade as they reached them.

'Come on!' Alphant yelled at the girl. She seemed to be making no effort to duck or keep low. He risked his own skin and ran out of cover to grab her and the last of the children. A shot grazed his thigh. Somehow, the tiny girl kept him upright until they tumbled back into shelter.

'I was looking for you,' he said.

Sabbatine smiled. 'I know.'

Milo crawled over to them, urging the sobbing children to stay low, trying to make it sound like a game.

'That was a very brave thing you did,' he said to the girl. She looked over at him and Milo was lost for words. He'd never seen her before in his life, but he knew her. As if he'd always known her.

Milo shook himself to clear the distraction from his mind. 'We have to get these children out of here,' he said. 'Bonin?'

'No go!' Bonin yelled from nearby, in amongst the cowering kids and other pilgrims himself. 'The fire's choked off the back end of the street. We can't get through that way.'

Milo slithered forward and dared a look out down the street ahead. Spark-filled coils of smoke washed across the trashed, shot-up accessway. He saw men moving up through it, men with rifles and chilling iron masks. Every few seconds, one or more raised his weapon and fired in their direction. Far too many for just the three of them to repel.

Then even that became academic. The advancing Blood Pact infantry were drawing aside into the edges of the ruined street. Something was approaching from behind them.

'Oh feth...' groaned Milo as the assault tank, painted crimson and defiled with abhorrent symbols, rolled into view.

'THIS IS NOT an appropriate time for an audience,' said the Civitas Beati staff officer. 'The city is under attack.'

'Really? Make a list of more appropriate occasions then, feth you!' Zweil snarled. The soldier, in his heavy battledress and polished armour segments, towered over the aged ayatani, and in the candlelight of the atrium it was impossible to read the expression on his hard-set face. Behind him, the massive bronze doors of the city's chief Ecclesiarchy cathedral, situated near the summit of hive tower one, were engraved with images of Kiodrus holding up the bowl for the Saint to cleanse her wounds. The doors were shut resolutely.

'Father, please,' the staff officer began.

'I've come a long way to see her,' Zweil told him.

'So have very many people.'

Zweil waggled his bony hands in frustration. 'Do you know who I am?'

'You are Imhava Ayatani Zweil, and only an old rogue like you would see fit to make a ruckus like this.'

The voice came from behind him. Zweil glanced round and found himself facing another old man in priestly robes.

'Kilosh,' he said, bowing. Kilosh returned the gesture. 'You're a long way from home for a tempelum ayatani, brother,' said Zweil.

'The circumstances of our devotion change, brother.' Kilosh smiled. 'It's surprisingly good to see you again, you cantankerous old troublemaker.'

'And you, though you seem as starchy and straight-laced as ever. I need to see her, brother.'

'That much is evident to everyone in shouting distance. I might see what I can arrange, except…'

'Except what?' Zweil scowled.

'There is enough trouble for us all tonight. I'll not have you causing more.'

Zweil drew Kilosh to one side and lowered his voice. 'I know what you think. Not only do I have a less than pristine reputation, I've been consorting with these Tanith heathens for longer than might have done me good.'

'Brother, I do not regard Gaunt and his men as heathens.'

Zweil paused. 'Neither do I, as it goes. But you're afraid I'll go in there and denounce her to her face. Disbelieve as Gaunt disbelieves.'

'His lack of faith indeed pains me, brother.'

'Not half so much as it does me. He is a good man, and honest, and I've hitched myself to his regiment this last while because he seemed a true devotee of the Saint. I do not know what has occurred to break his faith, but it saddens me.'

Kilosh nodded. 'So you haven't come as his emissary, to unmask the false idol?'

'Rather the reverse. Brother, I need to seek audience so I can go back and affirm the truth to him. Make him see. Make him believe.'

'You entertain no doubts of your own?'

Zweil shook his head. 'There have been signs, portents, omens, enough to mass an exodus of pilgrims, enough to turn this part of the Imperium on its head. The divination of a dozen temples of a dozen worlds has foretold, emphatically, that the Saint is reborn and come here to Herodor. The evidence is unequivocal. I believe she is here. I believe full stop. I will do everything in my power to make Gaunt believe too. For without his faith, we are doomed.'

Kilosh studied Zweil's face for a long moment, then beckoned him to follow.

The Civitas Beati regimentals drew back the bronze doors, and the two old priests hobbled into the vast chancel of the great church. The marble walls and pillars were laced with gilt, and obsidian mosaics had been chased into the stone facings. Clock shrines had been clustered inside the entrance, along with glacial heaps of islumbine garlands. A massive, sculptural eagle wrought from black iron, thirty metres from wingtip to wingtip, was suspended from the domed roof. The deep rows of pews, arranged in a semi-circle fan, were made of a dark, varnished wood and, at the high altar, great candlesticks worked from gleaming chelon shell fluttered with yellow flame. The altar itself was a large, rectangular basin of stone, filled with holy water from the balneary. The water was smooth and unrippled, like a brown mirror.

Zweil knelt and made devotion for a moment facing the altar. Then Kilosh helped him back to his feet and led him through to the inner chapel. Esholi handmaids, robed in violet albs and white bicorn headdresses, waited outside the gilded screen of the iconostasis. Kilosh opened the old screen door and the pair descended the few, worn steps into the tiny crypt.

It was dark, save for phospha lamps and a shaft of faint exterior light, swirling with the glow of the city shield, that fell through a narrow slit high up the wall above the simple shrine altar. A woman was kneeling there, in prayer, the window light dipping onto her.

She heard them and rose, turning. She wore long, blue robes and a white stole, and her glossy black hair was tied up away from her face. Kilosh bowed at once. Zweil stared at her, unable to express himself. He felt his heart pound as if it was about to rupture, as if he had come this far and this long only for his ancient body to fail him now.

'Ayatani Zweil,' said the Saint, her voice like silk. Islumbine. He could smell islumbine strongly on the air.

He gasped and fell to his knees. Words would not come.

'I–'

'Shhhh, loyal father,' she said, and reached out a hand. He took it between his own.

Something thrilled through his skin, like an electric charge. Like needles. He broke the grip sharply and looked up at her, confused.

'Sanian...' he said.

Her smile had not faded. 'You know the vessel I am in, Ayatani Zweil. You recognise it, but–'

'No!' he said, struggling to his feet. He was blinking hard, as if trying not to cry. 'Oh, God-Emperor, he was right. You're Sanian...'

She backed from him. Kilosh rose, grunting with effort. 'Damn you, Zweil!' he hissed. 'You said you would not do this! You tricked me!'

'No, no...' Zweil said, still staring at her. 'With all my heart, Kilosh, I meant what I said back there. But now I see the truth. It is not the truth I wanted to see, but it is the truth nevertheless.'

Kilosh angrily pulled at Zweil's sleeve to drag him back. The imhava ayatani pushed him away. 'The Saint is here. I feel her in every stone and every breath of air. But this is not her!'

THE TANK FIRED again, burying a shell in the facade of the burning manufactory behind them. Rock and glass was hurled into the air. The children and the pilgrims were screaming.

'Tube-charge!' Bonin yelled.

'You'll never get close enough!' Milo bawled back, shielding his head from the fluttering debris. He scrambled over to Bonin and pushed the tube-charges from his satchel into Bonin's hands. 'Not unless it's distracted! On three!'

Another shell howled over their heads. The tank was just twenty metres off now. Its hardpoint stubber started chattering, raking the rubble barricade.

The two Ghosts started to run in opposite directions, heads down. Bonin hurtled down the left side of the roadway, tight to the wall, trying to strap the tube-charges together as he ran. Milo crossed to the right side, went on hands and knees until he reached a doorway, and then flopped round. Through the smoke, he could see Alphant and the other adult pilgrims trying to squeeze the children into what little cover remained.

'Ready?' Bonin's voice crackled over the micro-bead.

'Go!' Milo said. He swung up out of hiding and let rip with his lasrifle on full auto. The shots pinged and flashed against the bruised metal hull of the war machine. It lurched to a stop and then the stubber came round to aim at him.

He barely got down in time. The hefty, solid-slug weapon blew the wall and doorway over his curled up body into fragments. It wasn't enough. He hadn't distracted it for anything like long enough for Bonin to get close.

Milo started to crawl again as more flurries of shrieking stub rounds went over him. If only he could–

He heard Alphant shouting and looked up.

The girl was running from cover. Running into the middle of the war-wounded street, right out in front of the tank.

'Feth, no!' Milo yelled, and started to dash after her.

She was right in front of the tank, both hands raised like an arbites officer controlling road traffic. The tank stopped as if puzzled. The main turret turned, lowering the massive cannon, like a cyclops eye-stalk, to stare at her.

Bonin came out of the smoke alongside the tank and hurled the tube-charges. They bounced along the hind-part of the hull, and came to rest under the lip of the turret's aft cowling.

Milo dived headlong and brought the girl down hard, smashing her aside just as the main tank weapon fired.

And the tube-charges detonated.

At that moment, on a sliproad leading down between manufactory sites into the Ironhall sector, Captain Daur fell down so hard and so suddenly the troopers around him thought he'd been hit.

'Captain!' Brennan yelled, running to him. A few sparkling las-shots from the raiders down the slope drifted past like fireflies. Trooper Solia was yelling for a medic.

'I'm allright,' Daur said. His teeth were chattering, like he was cold. 'I mean, I'm not hit.'

'Why did you fall down, captain?' Solia asked, fierce concern on her dust-smudged face.

'I just had... the most awful feeling,' Daur said, and then laughed at how stupid it sounded.

There was nothing stupid about the expression on his face.

* * *

In the back of the transport, in the rancid, recycled air, Curth stepped back from the Herodian trooper she'd been trying to sew back together and shook her head with a sigh. Many more injured, most of them infardi, were gathered around the entry ramp of the heavy vehicle. Every now and then, it vibrated as the ground shook from nearby shell-falls.

Curth heard a clatter and looked round. Chief Medic Dorden, working at a gurney beside her, had just knocked an entire tray of surgical instruments over.

'Dorden?'

He swayed. His face, behind his plastic mask, was grey and unhealthy.

'Dorden!' Curth cried, hurrying to him.

'Ana? What just happened?'

'What do you mean?'

'Didn't you see that flash? It was so bright...'

'No... nothing more than the barrage we're already getting.'

'So bright...' he whispered.

The Tanith reinforcements leapt out of their transports the moment the column of trucks pulled up. They'd reached a crossroads on Principal I, facing north on the Guild Slope, where the southern boundary of the Ironhall and Glassworks sectors began. One by one, light tanks and self-propelled guns of the Regiment Civitas Beati powered past, moving up to the front line, along with Salamanders and light cannon-platforms from Lugo's landing force.

Gaunt checked his bolt-pistol clip and walked the length of one of the stationary troop carriers to where Corbec was briefing squad leaders.

'I know these babies have nice, thick armour,' Corbec was saying, slapping the hull of the carrier, 'but they're also big fat targets. We've got close-engage street fights up ahead, and you'll be more use – and safer – on foot. Get ready to disperse by squad.'

He glanced round at Gaunt. 'Anything you want to add, sir?'

Gaunt was about to answer when Corbec suddenly put a hand to his head and swayed.

'Colonel?'

'Oh my God-Emperor...' said Corbec, looking up into Gaunt's eyes. 'Did you not just feel that? *Did you not just feel that?*'

'Ayatani Zweil! Ayatani Zweil, withdraw yourself now!' Kilosh was shouting.

'Don't you understand, Kilosh? Can't you unbend enough to see it?' Zweil pointed across the chapel at the Saint, who watched him with reproachful silence.

'I will summon the temple guards and have you ejected if you do not cease and depart now!' Kilosh stormed.

Zweil, his head pulsing, was about to reply when he felt a smoky, rusty tang in his mouth.

He looked at Kilosh and coughed. Blood spattered into his raised hand.

'Zweil? What's the matter with you?'

Oh my dear lord Emperor, Zweil thought. *This is it. I'm having a stroke and–*

And that was all he thought. Soundlessly, he pitched forward and cracked his head on the flagstones.

'Zweil?' Kilosh said, more mystified than anything else. He stooped beside his elderly colleague, felt for a pulse and started to call for help. There was a shriek from behind him.

He turned to see that the Saint had fallen to her knees. In the light of the phospha lamps, he saw a frightened, horrified look on her face. Her shaking hands were dabbing at the blood streaming from her nose.

'Help me!' Kilosh screamed. 'Help me here!'

THERE WAS NOTHING left of the tank apart from a heap of blackened metal shreds. Dense blue smoke filled the narrow street, making it hard to breathe, Bonin was coughing and choking as he ran back. His ears were still ringing.

'Milo! Milo!'

The boy was face down in a ditch, covered in ash and pebbles. Bonin reached him about the same time as Alphant did. Milo came to as they rolled him over. He was miraculously alive and intact.

But the girl, nearby, curled up by a broken kerb, was not. The blast of the tank round, which had dug the ground up beneath both of them and hurled them into the air, had landed her hard. Her neck was broken and she was dead.

Alphant cried out in despair.

Milo hadn't seen any of this, but at the sound of the cry, his guts tightened.

He got up and knew, long before he actually saw her body, that something awful had just happened. Something huge, something dark, something more than all the waste and death and slaughter around them.

Something unholy.

FOUR
MAGNIFICAT

'I know what I saw then. And I know what I see now.'

— Zweil, ayatani

FROM THE STREETS of the Guild Slope in mid-city, a nimbus of russet-pink and yellow could be seen suffusing the darkness over the north-west skirts of the metropolitan area. Individual sparks of light flickered in that blanket glow like grounded lightning. Dull booms and roars, pent in by the acoustic lid formed by the city shield, rolled back to their ears, and smoke, similarly trapped by the shield, collected into a wispy roof like low cloud. According to the now frenetic reports of Civitas tac logis, over a thousand hostiles, with supporting armour, were assaulting the city.

And the city was falling. Partly under the fury of the attack, and partly beneath the weight of an inexplicable sense of defeat and loss that had settled over the population during the hours of the night.

Viktor Hark could not account for it, but he could feel it. An ache, a feeling of disillusion, a sapping misery. Perhaps it was the unexpected speed and ferocity of the chaos onslaught. Perhaps it was a general realisation of how fragile the Imperial position really was.

Even in his worst-case contemplations of disaster, Gaunt had never expected things to go so badly wrong so rapidly. Hark knew that as a certainty. He'd spent considerable time with Gaunt, risk-assessing the woeful defensive opportunities afforded by the Civitas Beati, the far from adequate numerical strengths at their disposal, the complete lack of preparation time. It was a bleak picture, and Gaunt had made no secret of his fear that once the archenemy's main force arrived, the fight for Herodor would be as good as done.

But that main force had still to reach Herodor, and yet the city already seemed close to collapsing in one night.

Tac logis was still referring to the invaders as 'heretic dissidents'. Hark sighed when he heard this and tugged the micro-bead from his ear. He didn't want to listen any more.

The streets were clogged, by people and by lamentation. That was it. This was not the sound of terror and alarm rising from the crowds. This was the sound of woe.

Hark was riding in a heavy-fendered troop transporter near the front of a reinforcement column. There were twelve transporters, all identical grey, long-bodied Munitorum vehicles, and they were only making any headway through the crowds at all because of the three Chimera heavies from the lord general's life company that were leading them through. The sight of tracked armour made the distressed crowds part sharply.

Colonel Kaldenbach, Lugo's field commander, had command of the column, and the Tanith and Herodian PDF squads in the troop carriers answered to him. Hark knew Kaldenbach fairly well from his time on the lord general's staff, an uncompromising but gifted officer who had crowned a good career in the Ardelean Colonials with elevation to Lugo's personal life company.

The column turned west off Principal II, under the broad aqueducts that serviced the agriponic district, and rolled into the wide plaza of Astronomer's Circle in the shadow of the great volcanic plug on which sat the Astronomer's Platform, that bastion of Herodian science and learning. It was up there, in the ancient observatories that had been operating permanently for over two thousand years, that Cazalon had devised and written his treatise on non-baryonic matter and Hazmun Zeng, three centuries later, had doggedly completed his Theory of Gravitation in the face of fierce Inquisitorial displeasure. Hark had been told that it was possible to visit Zeng's workshop study, which had been preserved, by order of the first officiary, exactly as the great man had left it. The idea appealed to Hark immensely. To climb the steps rough-hewn in the side of the rock plug up into that quiet little island of observatories, macroscope towers, sidereal calculators and libraries high above the murmur of the city and spend a few quiet moments in the dusty room where Zeng had made such a staggering contribution to Imperial science, filling notebooks with mirror-script to fool the watching eyes of the Inquisition.

But war, as ever, anchored Hark to the ground. In twenty years, he had travelled to and served on over forty worlds, many of them rich with cultural treasures and sites of significance. He had never enjoyed the indulgence of visiting any of them. There was always fighting to be done, or battle orders to review and, when that was over, a troop-ship waiting to convey him to the next theatre.

The column drew up in the Circle and the units disembarked. Kaldenbach, sturdy in his long green coat and cap, marched the line of assembly, issuing orders. There were fifty troopers from Lugo's life company in the support force, all of them clad in heavy green fatigues and camo-helms. A major called Pento from the Regiment Civitas Beati was in charge of the Herodian portion, two platoons of Civitas Beati elite and five of regular Herodian PDF. Sergeant Varl drew up the Ghost element of five platoons: his own, Haller's, Arcuda's, Raglon's and Ewler's.

Putting his commissar's cap on brim first – 'Gaunt-style', the Ghosts called it – Hark felt somewhat surplus to requirements. Kaldenbach even had his own commissars, an inseparable pair of identical twins called Keetle. They were thin, bony redheads with fair skin and thyroid eyes, dressed in black, patent leather stormcoats that creaked as they strode along, singing out incendiary and fortifying mottoes in stereo. Bad form, in Hark's book. The assembling soldiers were clearly spooked. They were on the doorstep of a savage urban fight zone and about to go in head first, and around them lay a city that seemed to have already given up.

'Soldiers of the Imperium!' yelled Keetle One.

'You see that up there?' bawled his brother, pointing up at the Astronomer's Platform.

'The seat of Herodian learning! From there, astronomers maintain a permanent study of the enfolding majesty of the heavens, comprehending their secrets and discerning their truths!'

'But even their vigilance,' yelled Keetle Two, 'is but a brief glance compared to the eternal vigilance of the holy God-Emperor!'

'Praise be the God-Emperor!'

'Praise be the God-Emperor, who watches over us all, at all times, and in all things!'

'His eyes are on you all now,' declared Keetle One. 'They do not stray, they judge and consider your every action!'

'So do not disappoint him! Do not fail in this great hour of warfare!'

They rattled on for a good while like this. Hark could kindle a rousing speech like the best of them when necessary, but this seemed like overkill. Just as Gaunt sometimes allowed himself to play genial soft fiddle to Hark's brimstone, so now Hark felt it was his time to be more sympathetic.

He started with Sergeants Arcuda and Raglon. Both were newly lifted to squad command. They were still finding their feet, and on Aexe Cardinal, Raglon's first taste of combat leadership had been cursed by massive bad luck and heavy losses.

They tensed as he walked up, so he smiled, and that seemed so unusual to them they both sniggered.

'Ready to go?'

'Sir,' they both affirmed. He looked at their platoons, drawn up in triple lines, sparing a particular moment to study Trooper Costin in Raglon's outfit. It had been Costin's drunken errors that had proved so expensive to Raglon's unit on Aexe. Gaunt should have shot him by rights, and would have done too, but for the passionate intervention of Dorden. Dorden had put his neck on the line to spare Costin, and had undermined Gaunt's authority in the process. The once-warm friendship between the colonel-commissar and his chief medic had been seriously strained ever since. Hark had his eye on Costin, but the man seemed to have cleaned up his act in a real effort to redeem himself.

'Let me tell you something,' Hark said quietly to Raglon and Arcuda. 'I know what's in your heads right now. Fear. Fear of pain and death, fear of failure. The weight of your new responsibilities. That sick feeling you'll feth up and let the side down. And those two are not helping your nerves with their pompous yakking.'

He thumbed sidelong at the Keetles, who were now leading the reluctant Herodians in a declaration of the Imperial creed. Raglon and Arcuda both laughed nervously.

'Forget about them,' Hark said. 'Think about this. The men out there, our friends and comrades, our fellow Ghosts, down there in the battle zone, up to their necks in the worst kind of feth. Think about them and think about this... it's you they most want to see. Not just reinforcements, Ghosts. The fething best field troops it's ever been my honour to know. There is nothing they are hoping for more than the sight of these five platoons storming in, guns blazing and hearts afire, to ease their heavy burden. To them, you'll be a dream come true. Think about what it'll mean to them, and I promise you, all your worries will seem insignificant by comparison.'

They both nodded, firm and resolved. Hark clapped them both on the shoulders. 'You'll be fine, sergeants. Spread the word amongst your men, get them set.'

Hark walked on to Haller, a Verghast vet, and Ewler, a grizzled old Tanith career soldier. They needed no soft soap, and his chat with them was a more workmanlike discussion of tactics and deployment. He answered their queries, complimented them on their squad turn-out, and told them a joke about an Ecclesiarchy convent and a curiously shaped fruit that made them laugh so loud it drew disapproving stares from the Keetles.

Finally, he strolled towards Varl. To the Ghosts, Varl was the soldier's soldier, smart-mouthed, cock-sure, roguish but utterly cool under fire. He'd slogged up through the ranks from common dog-grunt to get squad command, earning it on sheer merit, and was loved by all. He'd lost a shoulder on Fortis Binary, and had a hefty augmetic inbuild to replace it. If there was a hot centre to any fight, Varl would most likely be in it. If there was a scam or practical joke in the barracks, Varl would be in the thick of that too. The joke about the nuns and the fruit was one of his. Hark had overheard it just thirty minutes earlier, during Varl's platoon warm-up.

'Ready?' Hark asked.

'I was born ready, sir,' Varl replied, then paused. 'That's a lie. I was born horny. I got ready during my early teens.'

Hark laughed, but he could tell from Varl's manner something was bothering him. 'What's up, Ceg?'

Varl looked uncomfortable. He tapped a finger to the micro-bead plug in his left ear. 'I've been tuned to the local channel, the tac logis, monitoring the chatter,' he said quietly. 'It sounds like shit in a nalnut is going on down there. And the mood on the street tonight is like we've already lost.'

'Yes, I feel it. I won't lie, I think this is going to be bad.'

'It's not just that, sir,' said Varl. 'Report came in, five minutes back. Said the Tanith second officer was down.'

'Down?'

'Dead or hit real bad, they weren't sure. And then no confirmation.'

'Do they mean Corbec or Rawne?'

Varl shrugged. 'Could be either, both are in there. Then again, before the first wave of reinforcement went in, Captain Daur was the second officer on the ground.'

Corbec, Rawne or Daur dead. Any of those things would be a critical blow to the Tanith morale.

'You've not said anything to the men?' Hark asked.

'I'm not stupid,' Varl replied acidly, and Hark knew he'd deserved the rebuke.

'Of course not.'

'I just wish we could move. Get on in there and find out,' Varl said. He looked over at Kaldenbach who, with the ubiquitous Keetles, was now addressing the lord general's life company troopers. 'I mean, we're here. All this fannying around, what are we waiting for?'

'We're waiting,' said Hark, 'for Lugo to vox us the word to advance.' He thought for a moment. 'Come with me,' he said.

They walked over to the colonel's side. 'What is it, Hark?' Kaldenbach asked.

'Shall we advance, colonel? We are deposed and ready, and the night isn't getting any younger.'

'We await word to go,' said Kaldenbach, a pale, handsome man in his fifties with clean-cut features and wiry grey hair. Given that, from the sounds of it, tac logis was having difficulty differentiating its arse from its elbow, that word could be a long time coming in Hark's opinion.

'Well, sir,' said Hark gently, 'my troopers are famous for their scout specialisation. We should be going in already, preparing the way for your force.'

Kaldenbach frowned. 'I wasn't aware they were *your* troopers, Hark. Last time I checked, you were commissar, not... a ranking colonel as well.' This, an unwelcome reference to Gaunt's unusual and unpopular dual status, was a thinly veiled dig.

'My troopers are famous for their scout specialisation, sir,' said Varl quickly, beautifully timing his interjection, 'and last time I checked, I was ranking Tanith officer. I'm sure Commissar Hark will agree.'

Hark smiled and nodded.

Kaldenbach looked coldly at Varl, and the Keetles whispered darkly to each other.

'Anxious to die, sergeant?' Kaldenbach asked.

'Anxious to serve the God-Emperor... and you, sir.'

'Very well,' Kaldenbach snapped. 'Move in. We will stand to until word is given. Pave the way for us, if you're so damn good at it. And stay in constant vox-contact.'

Varl saluted and hurried away with Hark beside him. 'Ghosts of Tanith!' he shouted. 'Let's get wriggling! Game's on!'

The Ghost units massed forward to join him.

'Nicely done, Ceg,' Hark whispered.

'You set him up, sir. I was just there to finish him off.'

The Ghost force surged forward across the paved Circle, dressing their camo-cloaks, and melted into the narrow streets beyond.

Pento, the Herodian officer, watched them disappear. The last thing he or any of his men wanted to do was rush prematurely into combat.

Not, it seemed, like the off-worlders in black.

THE SCRIVENER'S OFFICE ruptured and collapsed, all eight storeys of it. Dust and fire flushed out from the avalanche of masonry, and the men of five platoon ran for cover.

Squat, robust, one-eyed and nothing like as mobile as his younger troopers, Agun Soric threw himself flat and the dust flow rushed over him like a breaker. The air was full of smouldering paper scraps, millions of pages of notation physically liberated by the explosion.

'Chief! Chief!' Vivvo's voice rang through the billowing smoke. Soric pulled himself up.

'Hold your gakking water, Vivvo. I'm not so much as half dead yet.' Even so, Soric didn't object as Vivvo steadied him.

'We have got to find that gakking tank,' Soric said.

'Round up! Round up!' Vivvo yelled, and the scattered elements of five platoon came out of cover. The street was a mess. White rubble covered the cobbles and most of the buildings on the west side of the road were ablaze. Soric hobbled forward, sending hand signals to fan his beleaguered troopers out. Then he sat his wide rump down on a slab of alabaster, took off his mask and spat.

Kazel, Mallor and Venar suddenly switched round, rifles aimed, as they picked up movement south of them.

'Twenty, seventeen! Hold your fire!'

'Safeties, boys!' Soric urged, as Sergeant Meryn's platoon ran up to join them out of the drifting smoke.

Meryn was a young, slickly handsome Tanith with more front than the entire fething crusade. It was said Rawne was grooming him, and that, Soric believed, explained why the previously amiable Meryn had become such a hardboiled bastard of late. He was openly ambitious in all the wrong ways, and there were dirty rumours that during the insurgency mission on Phantine, he'd exposed a cruel, almost psychotic side to his character. It was said he'd murdered civilians. Soric didn't know about that, and didn't want to, and there was no arguing with the pretty boy's combat record. But of all the squads he could have meshed with, Meryn's was about last on the list, save Rawne's platoon, of course.

And then there was the matter of that ridiculously sinister moustache Meryn had been cultivating.

'Taking a breather, chief?' Meryn suggested as he approached the seated Soric.

Soric didn't rise to the bait. 'Just waiting for you to win the gakking war single-handed, lad,' he said, replacing his rebreather. 'There's a tank somewhere in the streets yonder. It's making a gakking mess.'

Meryn turned and yelled: 'Guheen?'

Trooper Guheen hurried up, a compact missile tube slung over one shoulder. Coreas came with him lugging the satchel of long-snouted rockets.

'Treads to feth,' Meryn told him. He turned to Soric. 'So where's this tank?'

Soric rose to his feet. He was a head shorter than Meryn and as ugly as Meryn was handsome. 'If I knew that,' he said, 'I'd have fethed the bastard myself.'

'Sure you would,' said Meryn, dubiously. He waved his platoon forward into the maze of side alleys behind the ruin of the scrivener's. 'Keep low!' he shouted. 'Find this armour for me!'

Meryn's platoon, fourteen, was tight and well-drilled, Soric had to give the pretty bastard that much.

He was about to yell at Vivvo to drag five platoon to order and show Meryn's lot how it should be done when a scrap of paper landed at his feet. It was just one from the blizzard that had been blown up and out of the office collapse. Drifts of them, many burning, were settling over the ruins. But where all the others were white, Munitorum grade sheets, this was blue and lightweight.

He looked down at it, sighed deeply, then scooped it up.

On it, written in his own handwriting, were the words: *Guheen's going to get himself pulped if he goes that way. The tank is behind the cabinet maker's shop.*

Just like that. Bold as gak.

Soric shivered, tossed the scrap aside and yelled at the top of his voice: 'Guheen! Hit the bricks!'

Guheen and Coreas both heard him, halted and looked back.

'Get down, you gakkers!' Soric bellowed, running forward. He slammed into Hefron from his own squad, and wrenched the tread fether out of his bemused hands.

'What the feth is–' Meryn yelled.

Guheen and Coreas dropped flat about a half-second before a tank shell slammed through the side wall of the laundry they were passing. The wall blew out and showered bricks in all directions. The shell, shrieking and leaving an eddying vapour-trail in the still settling white dust, went over their heads and hit the corner of a shuttered café. The blast deafened them all and collapsed the café frontage in a welter of flame and flying stone chips.

Everyone was down, dazed and bewildered.

Except Soric. Panting, he ran through the rubble until he had a clear view down the side of what had to be the cabinet maker's shop. There was the tank, a hefty mid-sized model painted crimson and daubed with markings that flopped Soric's stomach. A flayed human hide was stapled across the front of its hull. Its fat turret was traversing. Soric could hear the clank of the chain drive.

With his trick leg there would be no kneeling down to soften the recoil... or hide. He stood his ground as the heavy-gauge barrel tracked round towards him and sat the missile tube he had wrenched from Hefron's grip onto his broad shoulder.

'Hello, gakkers,' he hissed and squeezed the trigger-spoon. The rocket banged away, kicking smoke out of the tube's back end with such fury it threw Soric over. The missile flamed across the rubble and hit the tank just under the edge of the waist plating. There was a loud explosion, and pieces of shrapnel zinged through the air, hot and hard as las-rounds.

When Soric looked up, the tank was gutted with fire.

He got to his feet and turned to his men, arms raised and brandishing the launcher. 'Who's the chief? Who's the gakking chief?'

They cheered him vigorously.

Meryn crossed to him, pausing to check on Guheen and Coreas, who were temporarily deaf but otherwise unhurt.

'How the feth did you know?' he asked Soric.

'Lucky guess,' Soric replied.

The vox clicked, and another Ghost platoon closed in on them out of the dust. It was two platoon, Corbec's mob, or at least what was left of it. Mkvenner was in charge, with Rerval at his side.

The tall, lean scout had still not properly recovered from the serious wounding he had taken on Aexe Cardinal. Mkvenner's long face was gripped by swallowed pain.

'Ven!' cried Soric. 'Where are the rest of your boys?'

Mkvenner shrugged. 'We came under fire. Tank fire. Three or four units. Got out all I could. I think–'

'What?'

'I think Corbec might have bought it. We can't find him anywhere.'

Soric looked away, blinking hard. 'Gak, that's... that's not good.' He looked at Rerval. The young signals officer was trying hard not to cry.

'You tried the channels?' Soric asked.

Rerval nodded.

'Try 'em again,' Soric said.

Two closed up with five and fourteen. Vivvo hurried over to Soric and handed him a brass shell.

'What's this?'

'Found it in the rubble, sir,' Vivvo said.

Soric took it. He didn't even have to check now. It was his message shell. Like a bad penny...

He unscrewed the cap and knocked out the fold of flimsy blue paper inside.

It read: *Colm's alive, but he's pinned down by cannon fire. Ven will be dead in two days unless you get him help. Two stalk-tanks south of you, well hidden. Be wary... a lot more Blood Pact are about to hit.*

Soric breathed out hard. 'Corbec's alive,' he told Mkvenner.

'How the feth do you know that?'

'Call it a hunch. Let's fan west. Rockets to the front. There are a couple of stalk-tanks out there, hulls down, if I know anything. But we can do this.'

Mkvenner nodded and wiped blood away from the corner of his mouth with his cuff. Why in the name of the God-Emperor hadn't he sat back and let himself heal? What sort of internal damage was he doing to his body?

'Get to a field hospital, Ven,' Soric said.

'I'm fine.'

Soric faced him, brows furrowed. Tall and lean and deadly, Mkvenner was about the most frightening man in the Ghosts, and that was before you knew anything about him. No one ever chose to confront him. Life wasn't worth that much hurt. But Soric persisted.

'That's an order, Mkvenner. Find Dorden or Curth and find them now,' said Soric.

Mkvenner stared at the thick-set, older man and finally nodded. 'Sure,' he said, and shambled away through the enclosing smoke.

'Move it up! You heard me!' Soric yelled. 'Two platoon, you answer to me now!'

'Jumped up runt,' Meryn said, watching Soric rally the troops around him. They loved him, the fools.

'Sir?' said Fargher, approaching Meryn. He held out a crumpled ball of flimsy blue paper.

'What's this?' Meryn demanded.

'Chief Soric was looking at it before... before he took out the tank, sir. I thought you'd like to see it.'

Meryn unballed the paper and read it: *Guheen's going to get himself pulped if he goes that way. The tank is behind the cabinet maker's shop.*

'What is this... warpcraft?' he whispered.

'Sir?' asked Fargher.

'Never mind, Fargher,' Meryn said as he folded the paper carefully and tucked it into his jacket pocket. 'Just thinking out loud...'

For the fourth time in twenty minutes, third platoon attempted to get around the same street corner without dying. They were bunched up in a little access terrace behind an oil and gas separation plant in the Ironhall district. The terrace joined the main street at right angles, and something down that thoroughfare had them pinned with heavy fire.

With the bulk of his unit huddled low in the terrace way behind him, Rawne cautiously approached the junction with his platoon scout, Leyr, and Troopers Caffran and Feygor. If they stayed put much longer, they'd be swamped by the advancing enemy ground troops, and the terrace was no place for a firefight.

Most of the Tanith scouts had their own signature trick for looking round blind corners. Leyr's was a sweet little pocket periscope, a precision brass instrument that he'd picked up on Aexe Cardinal. 'I got it from an Aexegarian colonel,' Leyr told anyone who asked, 'who stood when he should have ducked. He had no use for it any more. Likewise, he had no use for his spectacles, his moustache comb or his hat.' The periscope was powerful but small enough to slip into the chart-pocket of his fatigues. He slid the business end round the fractured brick corner and took a squint. Fifty metres down the rubble-strewn main street, a stalk-tank sat in the centre of the roadway, its weapon pods pointing in their direction.

'You were right,' Leyr whispered. 'Scuttle-armour.'

Rawne curled his lip in annoyance. 'Any AT rockets left?' he asked, already knowing the likely answer.

'No, sir,' said Caffran. 'We're out. The tread fethers are dry.'

'Suggestions?'

'How far down is it?' Feygor asked Leyr.

'Forty, maybe fifty,' Leyr replied, looking again. Too far for even the strongest of them to throw a tube-charge. 'We better think of something quick,' he added. 'There are troops moving up.'

'I don't think we've got much choice,' Rawne said. 'We'll have to pull back, maybe reform a position a few streets that way.'

The men nodded. No one liked giving ground, but no one liked dying needlessly either.

Feygor relayed the orders with a series of quick, clear gestures, and the platoon began pulling back down the terrace.

The terrace led along to an iron walkway over a chemical drain trench, and then down into a wide, paved concourse from the centre of which rose the aluminium tubes and flanges of an atmosphere processor. Units like it, fed by ducts from the main hive structures, were dotted throughout the outer city, pumping air to maintain the thin, local atmosphere of the Civitas.

The platoon came to a sudden halt. Rawne hurried up to the front, keeping low. Banda, the platoon's sniper, had brought them to a standstill. She was huddled in beside a low wall, long-las raised. Rawne, a spectacularly unreconstructed Imperial male, had been dead against the admission of women troopers from the outset, and Banda – oozing self-confidence and physical appeal – had long been a particular thorn in his side. But in the trench hell of Aexe they had been wounded together, and had helped each other through, and in the process had reached an understanding. Rawne relied on Banda's good counsel now as much as he did that of Feygor or Caffran. Some even rumoured that Rawne and Banda were lovers, but no one dared ask either of them to confirm it.

'Movement,' she reported.

'Identity?'

'Can't tell.'

Rawne hand-signalled 'ready to engage' back down the file. 'Head shot as soon as you see a head,' he told the girl.

She took aim, and waited until something bobbed into sight in her scope. At the last moment, she relaxed her finger from the trigger.

'Friendlies,' she said.

A ramshackle squad of Civitas Beati guards was moving warily into the concourse. Rawne got on the vox and hailed them. Their leader was Udol, the major he had met during their unorthodox arrival on Herodor just the day before.

'No going that way,' Udol said, gesturing in the direction he and his men had approached from. 'They're pasting the area with mortars mounted on tractor units.' Rawne had already heard the distant, persistent *whoop-crump* echoing in their direction.

'It's as bad behind us,' he said simply. 'Blood Pact ground troops advancing, with at least one stalk-tank. They've got the up-street locked.'

'Blood Pact?' Udol asked. 'We weren't told anything about Blood Pact. Tac logis says its heretic raiders.'

'With respect,' Rawne replied, clearly expressing none at all, 'your tac logis is voxing out of its arse. It's Blood Pact all right. Trained, tight, well-supported and systematic. Their handiwork identifies them. Besides, I've met them before.'

'What do we do?' Udol asked, hoping the tremble in his voice wasn't too obvious.

'Do?' sneered Rawne. 'I don't think we've a great many options.'

The words were scarcely out of his mouth when their meagre options fizzled away dramatically. The peeling energy rounds of a stalk-tank's cannons splashed across the concourse area, blasting sections of paving up into the air. Several more punched through the metal duct-work of the processor and it began emitting an eerie, wounded moan as air escaped from the holes.

The troops – Tanith and Civitas alike – scattered for cover. Several troopers fell, cut down.

The options had been reduced to two.

Fight, or die.

A KILOMETRE-LONG stretch of the wide Principal I, from the tower of the prayer horn Gorgonaught back through Hazgul Square towards Beati Plaza, was then the scene of a major armour battle. Twenty-nine vehicles of the archenemy's main force were driving south, countered by twelve Civitas Beati light tanks, and six Vanquishers from Lugo's life company.

The broad, and once majestic, boulevard was littered with burning wrecks and dimpled with shell-craters. Most of the Chaos armour was stalk-tanks or light standards, but they had at least one super-heavy, a crimson monster that annihilated all before it.

Gaunt's platoon held position in the ground floor of a glassblower's fabricatory on the west side of Hazgul Square. They had exhausted their anti-tank munitions long since, and could do precious little about the armour. They concentrated their efforts on the enemy ground troops instead. But it wouldn't be long before their continued harassment of the infantry drew the attention of a Chaos battle tank.

Keeping low to avoid the occasional stray shot that whined in through the holes in the brickwork, Gaunt moved along his platoon's position, distributing encouraging remarks and quiet comments. In a fight-zone like this, he would have normally gone up a gear or two, maybe resorting to one of his favourite quotations or an ad hoc speech to rally the mood.

But this mood was flatter than any he'd known. Had he become so transparent that his men instantly saw in him the looming prospect of failure? Now he knew the painful truth about the 'Saint', Gaunt could hardly swallow the rage and disappointment he felt. Without that one spark of light and hope, the fight here on Herodor seemed no better than suicide.

Strangely, it was as if the whole city sensed that too. As if its heart had been torn out, as if it felt as lost and despairing as he did himself. Gaunt couldn't forget the look on Colm Corbec's face just before they'd deployed an hour before. 'Did you not just feel that? *Did you not just feel that?*'

Corbec hadn't been able to explain it, but Gaunt had seen other troopers in the vicinity similarly upset for no apparent reason at the very same moment. And the vox traffic had been abruptly flooded with anguished calls of dismay. That had been the moment the mood had truly crashed.

Corbec had pulled himself together, and they'd pressed into the zone. The last time Gaunt had seen his number two, Corbec was shaken and uneasy, leading his platoon off down a smoke-hazed side-street.

Everything shook as two tank rounds hit home nearby. The fabricatory rocked and dust spattered down from the ceiling. Gaunt checked the box-mag of his bolt pistol, and clambered across the rubble to where troopers Lyse and Derin were guarding a doorway. They were both pinking the occasional shot out of the broken entrance with their lasrifles.

'How are you holding?' Gaunt whispered, crouching behind them.

Lyse raised a dusty hand and indicated some features of the fire-lit battlefield outside for her commander's benefit. 'They've got foot units moving up behind that wall there, and behind the dead truck,' she said. 'We can't get a clear shot.'

'But you'd have 'em finished by now with your torch, right?' he asked. Lyse nodded. On Phantine, she'd become the first female trooper to become squad flamer, and was proud of that role. A tough, broad-shouldered Verghastite in her late thirties, Lyse preferred to wear her black vest top to show off arms that were as well muscled as any male's. Like all the Tanith flame-troopers, she missed her speciality weapon, and so did Gaunt. A few spurts of an Imperial standard man-portable flamer Mk.VIII would have cooked the Blood Pact now edging up to their position in the blindside of the building.

Beside them, Derin started firing more urgently. A few figures in red-brown battledress had emerged from behind the burning vehicle wreck outside and were attempting to rush the side wall. Lyse began shooting too, and Gaunt scrunched forward on his knees and added his own firepower to the repulse. Lasrifle shots and bolt rounds rattled out from the doorway. One of the figures simply fell over and vanished in the rubble. Another jerked back dramatically in mid-stride. The rest ran back for cover.

'Right,' said Gaunt, about to move on. 'Keep sharp and do that every time they try something.'

'It's like she's abandoned us, sir,' said Derin suddenly. Gaunt stopped. For a second, he assumed Derin was talking about Lyse, which made no sense. Then he looked into Derin's face and realised that wasn't what he'd meant at all.

'The Saint, sir. It feels like we've come all this way for her and now she's abandoned us.'

Gaunt remembered that Derin had been one of the misfit band Corbec had led on his private mission back on Hagia. Derin had not shown the same signs of beatific inspiration at the time as the likes of Corbec and Daur and Dorden – he'd simply joined Corbec's endeavour out of loyalty to the old man – but the experience had clearly affected him.

'She hasn't,' Gaunt said simply. 'She's here with us. She always is.'

'H-have you met her?' Derin asked.

'Yes, soldier, I have,' Gaunt said, trying not to say anything that was an outright lie.

'It doesn't feel like she's here. Not any more. It did when we first got here. It was like there was something in the air. But it's gone now. Just gone.'

'The Beati Sabbat is right here still, Derin. She will not abandon the defenders of her shrine. And never forget… the Emperor protects.'

Derin was comforted slightly, but the troubled look didn't completely leave his face.

Gaunt was called to the rear of the hab, where his platoon scout Caober had just slipped back inside from a run down through the shelled street to their left.

'We're gonna have to start moving, sir,' he said. 'Three or four of the enemy tanks have turned west, and they're coming round the back. We're gonna get pinned if we stay in here.'

'Where do you suggest?' Gaunt asked.

Caober shrugged. 'I linked up with Sergeant Mkoll's platoon and Captain Daur's, sir. They've both already been forced back across the intersection into those habs there.'

'Retreat, in other words?'

'Sir, back is the only operative direction. There's no forward any more.'

Gaunt nodded. 'Any sign of Corbec?'

'No, sir.'

'Let's peel out, odds then evens, through those blast holes in the back. Caober, find us a hab to take position in and show the Ghosts the way as they come through. Beltayn?'

His adjutant hurried over.

'Odds and evens, out that way. Caober has point. Spread the word and let's make it snappy.'

Beltayn turned to distribute instructions when the hab was struck squarely by a shell that blew a section of wall in on them and killed two members of first platoon. A shrieking *whoop*, a blitzing, gritty fire-burst and then everyone still alive was picking themselves up in the choking smoke.

Gaunt could hear heavy assault fire from outside. Over the micro-bead he heard Derin.

'They're coming in! They're charging us! They're coming in!'

Gaunt knew there'd be no retreating now. He drew his power sword and ignited it. 'Ghosts of Tanith!' he shouted. 'In the name of the God-Emperor of Mankind... give them hell!'

'WHAT ARE YOU doing here, chief?' asked Domor in surprise. Corbec, his fatigues and pack layered with grey dust, had just scrambled into the manufactory basement where Domor's platoon was guarding the wounded. Above ground, the district was ablaze for the most part, and artillery was pounding it. There was no hope of carrying injured troopers out.

'I got lost,' Corbec said. 'In all the confusion. It's hairier than me out there. Any of my lads show up here?'

Domor shook his head. 'We've got people from ten, eleven and thirteen here, but no sign of anyone from your unit.'

'Vox?'

'You're joking, in this?' The ground above them shook with the heavy shelling. Even short-range micro-beads were only barely making it. Corbec saw Criid lying on a pile of sacking nearby. Kolea and Lubba were with her.

'How is she?'

'Okay,' said Domor. 'Head wound. Nothing too bad. Others are worse.'

Corbec could see that for himself. It was ugly and going to get a lot uglier before daylight. There were civilians down here too. In one corner, Corbec saw several adults trying to comfort a group of terrified children. Everyone was black with ash-soot. He wandered over. The adults with the kids were all civvies, pilgrims by the look of them. Bonin was standing nearby, leaning his tired body against a wall and sipping from his water bottle.

'Taking a personal interest?' Corbec asked him.

'Me and Milo had to fight like bastards to get those kids out. We were all penned in a few streets away. It was close.'

'Armour?'

Bonin nodded. 'You might want to have a word with Milo,' he said softly.

'Milo? Why?'

Bonin just shrugged and said nothing.

Corbec found Milo in the furthest, darkest corner of the basement space. He was hunched over, bruised and exhausted. A small shape lay under a dirty sack beside him.

'Brinny boy?'

Milo looked up. The grief on his face took Corbec's breath away.

'You look like I feel,' he tried to joke, but Milo was too burdened by emotion to even respond.

Corbec sat down next to him.

'What happened?'

'There was a girl,' he said. He spoke so quietly, Corbec had to lean forward to hear him above the bombardment.

'A girl?'

'Yes…' Milo looked at the crumpled form under the sack. Corbec put the rest together.

'It's always hard, that. Take your eye, did she? You'll just have to–'

'You don't understand, sir. She was… I don't know. There was something about her. Something amazing.'

'Well, y–'

'I thought she was the Saint.'

Corbec paused. 'What?'

'I knew the Saint was with us. I could feel it. Like on Hagia, you know?'

Corbec nodded. He knew the feeling. It had got into his soul on Hagia and never really left.

'I knew she was with us, really with us. Not just on this planet like we've been told, but right there on the street, in the middle of everything.'

'She watches over us,' Corbec murmured.

'She was there. I saw this girl and I just knew.'

'And?'

'She died. She saved the children and then she died. It wasn't meant to happen. I can feel it wasn't. It wasn't meant to happen like that. What will we do without her?'

Corbec didn't reply. He lifted the corner of the sacking. The girl was very peaceful and very dead. Just a young girl, another victim of the endless war. He laid the sacking back.

'It wasn't meant to happen,' Milo repeated.

'None of this was,' Corbec growled.

From outside came the rattle of small-arms close by. Domor, Bonin and the other able-bodied troops in the basement shelter grabbed up their weapons and headed for the exit.

'Come on,' said Corbec, getting up and checking his rifle's power cell. 'Come on, Milo. It's a long way from over yet.'

THE FIRST BLOOD Pact warrior who made it into the shattered hab was a massive brute, even bigger than the late, lamented Trooper Bragg. He came through a gap in the east wall that Trooper Loff had, until a moment before, been defending.

The heretic warrior was clad in heavy fatigue battledress coloured a dark, patchy russet, with steel-plated boots and iron armour strapped around his thighs, shoulders and belly. His face, under the red bowl-helmet, was visored by a black metal mask, an iron grotesque shaped into a snarling, hook-nosed, feral face. His hands, thick with the scar tissue of the heinous Pact ritual, clutched a laser pistol and a wickedly curved bill-hook.

Loff lay dead on his face in the gap where a blow from the bill-hook had dropped him. The Blood Pact warrior howled out an obscene war-cry and ploughed into the hab, firing wildly. There were others behind him.

Gaunt met him head on. His scything, energised blade, the power sword of Heironymo Sondar, glowed like a sliver of ice as it deflected two of the storm-warrior's laser bolts up into the blackened roof. Then he brought it sidelong and the murderous bill-hook – along with several scarred fingers – spun into the air in a puff of blood. Borne forward by his own momentum, Gaunt slammed the blunt nose of his bolt pistol up against the howling grotesque and fired. The brute, his head demolished, crashed backwards. Gaunt began firing over his collapsing corpse into the weight of enemy troopers scrambling through the gap at his heels.

Beltayn and Neith jumped forward beside him, shooting point blank with their lasrifles and thrusting with the Tanith warknives they had fitted as bayonets. 'Straight silver! Straight silver!' Beltayn was yelling.

It wasn't the only breach. The hab reverberated with the clash of hand-to-hand combat as Blood Pact storm-squads burst in through window lights, doorways and shell holes, driving first platoon backwards into the ruins. It was a killing frenzy, the malevolent, red-hot heart of pure war. The smoke-filled chamber, murky and firelit like daemon hell, was thick with screams, blows, spraying shots and thrashing figures. They were enveloped in chaos.

Gaunt's bolt pistol was spent. There were spare mags in his belt-pouches, but absolutely no chance of reloading in the turmoil. He let it go and wrenched out his Tanith warknife, plunging into the nearest enemy trooper with both blades. Blood soaked his jacket and his cloak so much the cloth slapped heavily around him. He realised he was screaming wordless sounds of rage at the swarming enemy.

They stank. They brought their abattoir reek with them: foul breath, sour sweat, dried blood and the noxious aroma of the oils and paints with which they anointed their bodies.

The sword of Sondar split a black-iron visor in two. Blood sizzled off the charged blade. Gaunt's warknife hacked into a throat. Something knocked his cap off. A Blood Pact trooper crashed sideways into him and staggered him, but the wretch was already dead. Then a laser round clipped the top of Gaunt's left shoulder and knocked him to his knees. He put the power sword through the armoured thighs in front of him, and was flattened as the severed bodyweight toppled forward onto him.

Beltayn had lost his lasgun. He snatched up a fallen bill-hook and slammed it with both hands into the nearest enemy sternum, then leapt forward and grabbed Gaunt by the shoulders, trying to drag him to his feet. Vanette and Starck charged in to support him, firing full auto into the scrum of Blood Pact all around.

'Back! Get back!' Beltayn yelled in Gaunt's face. The colonel-commissar didn't even seem to recognise him. He was dripping with gore. 'We have to get back!' Beltayn repeated, his throat raw from the smoke. Gaunt shoved him out of the way and butchered another Blood Pacter who was surging at them. The power sword cut him in two and cracked stone chips out of the pillar beside him.

An explosion knocked them all off their feet. Masonry rubble rained down from the roof and the end wall of the hab fell like a stack of child's play-bricks. Cold air washed in, thick with the smell of fyceline, and contorted the dense smoke around them into weird eddies and gusting coils.

Sword still clamped in one blood-smeared hand, Gaunt grabbed Beltayn by the arm and dragged him towards the caved section of wall. Vanette and Starck followed them, backing their way, emptying the last of their power cells from the hip as they went. There was no sign of any other member of first, just dark red figures scrambling through the smoke at their heels.

The four men fell out down the mound of rubble into the open. Las-shots sizzled out of the hab building after them.

They were in the wide concourse of Hazgul Square itself. The whole area was on fire. Buildings, reduced to hollow shells by the firestorm, spurting flames and sparks from their blind windows. Three tanks – one Imperial light and two enemy models – were burning where they had died. Bodies littered the ground, half-covered by the ash falling like snow from the boiling smoke. The heat was so fierce it felt like a summer noon on Caligula.

There was no way of telling where anything or anyone was. It was as if they had washed up in the middle of the apocalypse.

Gaunt recovered his wits enough for his hands to start to tremble. His heart was banging like an autoloader. Limping from a wound he couldn't remember receiving, he hurried the other three across the twenty metres of open square to the nearest cover. It was a burned-out RCB troop carrier. They cowered down, scanning the nightmare around them.

'One! This is one!' Gaunt cried, and then realised the lack of response was because his micro-bead was no longer in his ear. Its snapped flex dangled from his collar clip.

He looked at the other three. All of them were covered in dirt and blood and multiple minor wounds. Vanette's jacket was shredded and blood streamed down his right forearm from a wound at his elbow. Starck had his head in his hands, shaking with nervous energy and adrenaline. Both still had their lasrifles. Beltayn's grazed, cut hands were empty. He sat with his back against the troop carrier wreck, staring out at the firestorms with the blank look of a man who had reached his limits.

'Vox?' Gaunt said, shaking him.

'Sir?'

'Vox?'

Beltayn shook his head. A las-round had blown the vox-caster off his back during the melee in the hab.

Melee, Beltayn thought. How inadequately did that stupid fething word describe what they'd just come from.

'Micro-bead, then? Beltayn? Beltayn!'

The signalman snapped out of it. He fumbled to his ear and started to call into his intercom.

Gaunt heard the clanking even before Starck called him. Two hundred metres north of them, across the shattered square, an Imperial light tank was reversing hard, smashing debris and ruined vehicles out of its way. As Gaunt watched, an AP shell hit the pavement beside it, showering it with dirt and stone, and then another blew its turret in half. It veered wildly, trailing thick smoke, and came to a halt. Gaunt saw the driver struggle clear. The man started to run, then fell as small-arms fire cut him down.

Two Blood Pact battle tanks, with a stalk-tank clattering up on their left flank, advanced into the square. The tanks rocked as they fired, sending shells screaming over Gaunt and his comrades and into the buildings on the south face of the plaza. Loose formations of Blood Pact fire-teams were hurrying forward with the armour. Whilst Gaunt and his platoon had been caught up in the hell of the fabricatory fight, the battle outside had been lost. The enemy had broken the Imperial resistance, crushed the armour, and was storming down Principal I.

Las-fire began to hit the bodywork of the troop carrier. It was coming sidelong, from the ruined hab. The Blood Pact unit that had driven first platoon from its position – and most likely slaughtered them all – was now spilling out of the hab over the shelled wall the way Gaunt and his men had come. They were shooting across the open ground towards the huddled Imperials.

The four of them scrambled around into cover at the rear of the carrier, but even that offered precious little protection from the crossfire. To their right, the main advance and the rolling armour; to their left, the flank push of the infantry.

Vanette and Starck returned fire with their lasrifles, concentrating on the enemy unit advancing from the hab. Gaunt wished he had something more than his sword left. Beltayn gave up with the micro-bead and took out his service pistol, squeezing off shots around the end of the truck. The wrecked vehicle shuddered as incoming fire struck it, denting the metal and spalling off the scorched paintwork.

'Starck! Vanette! A pistol, either of you!'

Starck had lost his – lost the entire holster, in fact – but Vanette unshipped his laspistol and slid it across the rockcrete to Gaunt. Gaunt sheathed his sword and ducked down by the buckled rear wheel, taking shots at the main advance. By the counter display on the pistol's butt, he had about thirty shots left before the cell expired.

Thirty shots. That was the measure of life left to him.

'Munitions?' he shouted over the crackle of enemy fire.

'One cell left!' replied Vanette.

'Half a cell!' reported Starck.

'Two clips!' Beltayn stammered.

'Make them count,' said Gaunt.

The fire they were receiving was getting heavier. Both infantry fronts were targetting the troop carrier, and the stalk-tank had begun to spit cyclic pulses at them. The wreck rattled and shook, and actually moved more than once under the impacts. Bodywork casing fragmented off into the air. Beltayn howled out as a piece of shrapnel tore into his arm. Vanette's cheek was scorched by spall bursting from a hull-strike. Any moment now, Gaunt knew, a tank round or a rocket grenade would finish them off.

Ten shots left.

'Sabbat Martyr,' Gaunt began to murmur, 'in the name of the hallowed Emperor of Terra, deliverer of the Imperium of Man, I commend my soul and my dying deeds, and the souls of these three brave soldiers, into your hands that you–'

Fire sheeted across the square from the south, cones of flame, white hot and hungry, spraying like water from pressure hoses, it gushed across the archenemy troops emerging from the hab and turned those that didn't break and flee into jerking, stumbling torches.

'Something...' Beltayn gasped. 'Something's...'

Not awry. Not by any stretch of the imagination.

Four Chimeras, displaying the insignia of the lord general's life company, stormed into the square, crashing through burning buildings with their toothed dozer blades. They were moving fast, their hulls rocking back on their treads as they accelerated out of the rubble. In their top turrets, troopers manned the autocannons, blazing tracer fire into the air. Behind the fast, armoured carriers, lumbering tanks emerged. Civitas Beati armour, PDF lights and two life company Vanquishers. They began firing as soon as they had visual target on the enemy vanguard. Flooding in around the vehicle charge were troopers, many carrying company banners, flags and aquila standards on long poles. Leading the ground troops with a standard clenched in one hand, Gaunt could see Marshal Biagi. He was striding forward at the head of a dozen officers of the Regiment Civitas. They were razing the ground before them with their flamer packs.

The four Ghosts crawled under the wreck for safety as shells and heavy cannon fire whipped over their heads in both directions. The noise and concussion were physically painful. From where he lay, Gaunt could see Biagi directing the ground forces forward. Someone, Lugo himself most probably, had mobilised all the reserves into this counter-push. The damn fool! If this failed, there would be nothing, absolutely nothing, left to defend the inner hives with.

Gaunt knew Lugo was hardly the most gifted tactician ever to emerge from officer candidate scholam, but this was an act of madness even by his dismal standards. Already this night they had been surprised at the sheer scale of the advance force the archenemy had managed to land on Herodor. Who was to say that another force of equal size wasn't now waiting to strike at the southern agriponic zone, or another poised in the Eastern Obsidae? What would Lugo do then, if his entire military strength was committed here?

It was madness. It was...

...it *was* madness, but not the kind Gaunt supposed.

He blinked.

Something odd was happening. Every sound was dulling, everything in sight beginning to shimmer. Shards of glass on the floor under his bloodied hands twinkled like diamonds. The scabby metal of the tailgate above his head looked like mother of pearl. Tank shells slid overhead in perfect clarity, leaving slow billows in their wake, the smoke turning and spiralling into perfect double-helix trails.

Everything seemed

to slow

down.

Feth!

For a moment, Ibram Gaunt thought he'd been shot. He felt no pain, no impact, but he'd heard invalided veterans describe the way really bad wounds happened without you knowing it, turning the world into a slow motion wonderland as your failing senses registered the simple, profound splendour in everything.

There was a light in his eyes. A golden light. A life company Salamander, squat and heavy on its tracks, rolled up into his view, coming to a halt just a few metres from where he lay under the wrecked carrier. A figure stood upright in its open-topped cabin.

She was beautiful.

She wore a suit of intricately-worked golden battle armour so fine and form-fitting that it had been clearly fashioned for her by master metallurgists. Pieces of polished chelon shell had been set into the bodice and wide pauldrons. Imperial eagles formed the couters at the elbows and the poleyns at the knees, and the same symbol was also etched in repeated ribbons down the thigh plates and along the vambraces. Her left hand was covered with a gilded glove that had silver eagle claws extending from the fingertips. Her right hand was bare. Beneath the dazzling golden plate, she wore a suit of tightly-wound black mail, each link formed in the shape of an islumbine bloom. A white skirt, long and flowing and fixed with purity seals and prayer streamers, billowed from her waist. The heavy golden gorget rose up high to her chin, but her head was uncovered. She'd cut her hair short, sheared it off crudely in fact, so it fell in a glossy black bowl over her pale head. Her eyes were green, as green as an infardi's silk, as green as the rainwoods of Hagia.

The Beati looked down at Gaunt. A halo of light surrounded her, so fierce and bright it made her seem almost translucent. Nine cyber-skull drones hovered around her in the radiant glow, forming a circle behind her head, their eyes lit, their miniature weapon pods armed. She was terrible to behold.

She smiled.

'I've been waiting for this, Ibram. Haven't you?'

'Yes,' was all he could say. He realised he was weeping, but he didn't care.

She raised her arms wide. A green cloak unfurled from her back and became wings. A perfect aquila form spread out around her, five metres on either side, not silk but shimmering green light. Behind her head, the double-heads of the Imperial eagle clacked and hissed, encircled by the skull drones.

Gaunt got to his feet. He was so intent on her he knocked his head against the rear fender of the carrier, but his eyes didn't waver from the vision before him.

He drew his sword and held it out to her, grip first.

'You'll need that, Ibram,' she admonished quietly, and drew her own blade. It was slender, silver and well over a metre long. Islumbine garlands were looped around the hilt and jewelled pendants dangled from the pommel. She activated it and the blade thrummed into life.

'Let us educate the archenemy of mankind,' she said.

'What lesson do we teach?' Gaunt asked.

'The Emperor protects,' she said.

She raised the sword and pointed it at the enemy. The unseen driver slammed the Salamander forward but she didn't even stir. On either side, Imperial warriors surged forward towards the recoiling foe. Flamers hissed, cannons barked, lasguns cracked and the heavy tank guns roared. The Imperial banners fluttered.

Sword in hand, Gaunt ran after her.

FIVE
TRIUMPHS AND MIRACLES

'Where there is an enemy, rage!
Where there is a victory, rejoice!'

— Saint Sabbat, Epistles

THERE WERE CROWDS everywhere.

It was barely daybreak, but the streets were packed. Teeming masses of chanting pilgrims, celebrating soldiers and rejoicing citizens clogged the transitways and boulevards of the Civitas Beati, united in a raucous and unstinting expression of triumph. The wounded city had woken up to find it was, miraculously, still alive.

Wide slicks of black smoke stained the early daylight, wiping deep smudges across the flat, cold whiteness of the sky. Outlying northern sectors of the city were still-burning ruins littered with wrecked war machines and the uncounted bodies of the dead.

An early estimate suggested hundreds of military personnel and citizens had perished. The pilgrim community had suffered the most. Thousands had not made it through the gruelling night.

But the body count and the serious destruction inflicted on the Civitas seemed to bother no one in the crowd. They were as abnormally excited now as they had been inexplicably deflated in the small hours of the night. Easy to explain perhaps, for humans are simple things: they were alive, they had won, and they were rejoicing in that fact.

The greatest concentration of people was mobbing in around Beati Plaza, hundreds of thousands of exhilarated human beings, all of them chanting and whooping and dancing and cheering. Banners were flapping in the dawn air, white petals swirling like confetti from the garlands the people wore. Soldiers, their grinning teeth white against the caked dirt on their faces, were hugged and kissed, and lifted up on shoulders. Drums pounded. The ancient prayer horns of the city boomed. Fabricatory sirens wailed.

People had got up on roofs and balconies, or waved eagerly from upper floor windows. Streamers and fireworks flashed in the sky. On several street corners approaching the plaza, infardi preachers had climbed up onto the carts of their clock shrines and were leading prayers and hymn singing. Ecclesiarchy processions, led by choirs, carried reliquaries from the hive shrines through the streets. Ministorum workers scattered petals and flower heads harvested at random from the agriponic farms.

By the time Gaunt reached the heaviest crowds in the plaza area, he had garlands of islumbine and irridox around his neck, and had been kissed and hugged more times than he could count. His clothes were ragged and torn and he was covered in cuts and bruises. He still carried the aquila standard that he'd picked up from a fallen RCB trooper in the thick of the fighting before daybreak.

He felt strange, dazed, dislocated. The noise of the jubilation around him seemed louder and more oppressive than the bitter warfare of the night. Everything felt like a dream, but that was just his fatigue, he was sure.

On the cold, flinty plain of the Great Western Obsidae, as dawn came up, he had helped undertake the extinction of the enemy forces. There had been no quarter, and that was all right, for the Blood Pact were devoted and sworn servants of the archenemy of mankind.

But they had slaughtered them. All of them.

The glass fields beyond the city's north-western perimeter were scattered with corpses and with the smouldering hulls of fighting vehicles. Faced with the Beati, and with the renewed vigour she had inspired in the warriors of the Imperium, the Blood Pact had snapped and run. Biagi and Kaldenbach, the acknowledged victors of the fight, had led the pursuit and annihilated the enemy in the obsidae. Now the winds of the ice-desert, gusting in over the Western Ramparts, would shrivel the Blood Pact bodies, and the ground frost freeze-dry their flesh, and they would remain as fragile mummies amidst the litter of their ruined armour, a testimony to the brutal zeal of an Imperial army inspired by faith.

Gaunt reached the plaza. The crowds were packed fifty deep, but they parted to let him through. Pilgrims and citizens reached out to touch him or to clap him on the shoulders. He was limping and using the banner for support.

She was at the centre of the plaza, standing on top of a Chimera, raising her hands to the exulting crowds.

'Sir! Sir!' Gaunt glanced around and was almost knocked over by Raglon's enthusiastic hug of a greeting.

'We feared you were dead, sir!' Raglon cried.

'I'm not, Rags.'

'I see that, sir. God-Emperor, it's good to see you! What a day this is! What a moment!'

Gaunt smiled a tired smile. Raglon's excitement was contagious. Too seldom had he seen his men filled with the simple joy of victory.

'How's your platoon, Rags?'

'In fine shape, sir.'

'You came through it all right?'

Raglon nodded eagerly. 'We came through. No losses. But we gave them hell. I'll be filing a report... recommendations...'

'I look forward to it.'

Raglon turned and looked towards the centre of the plaza. 'I can't believe this, sir,' he said. 'I mean... she's here. Really here.'

'Yes, she is, Rags,' he said. 'She really is. Enjoy this moment. They don't come often in our walk of life.'

Gaunt looked at the Saint as Raglon pulled away, laughing. She seemed to be staring directly at him.

'I'M HAPPY AND all, but I wish she'd stop doing that.'

'Doing what?' asked Feygor, raising his voice to be heard over the din.

'Looking at me like that,' replied Rawne. Third platoon were in the crowd on the far side of the plaza from Gaunt. 'She won't stop looking at me.'

'It's me she's looking at,' Feygor said. 'Not you. Why would she look at you?'

'Well, I don't know...' Rawne said, rolling his eyes.

'I do,' said Banda. 'The major's sex on legs, real catnip for us womenfolk.'

Feygor laughed. Rawne looked at Banda with disdain.

'But I hate to disappoint you,' Banda continued. 'Her holiness the Beati is actually looking at me.'

'IT IS A good day,' said Gol Kolea quietly.

'Yes, Gol, it is,' Criid replied. She patted him on the arm. Around them, the crowd was going mad with chants. The Beati was a distant figure at the heart of the packed square.

'A good day,' Kolea repeated. 'She looks at me and sees me and sees I'm happy that it's a good day.'

'Who does, Gol?'

'The sainty-woman.'

'Uh huh.'

'Hey, sarge.' Criid looked round and saw Jajjo shouldering his way through the press. 'Found him,' he said, with a grin.

Caffran appeared behind Jajjo and grabbed Criid in a tight embrace.

'Thought I'd lost you!' he breathed, kissing her cheek and neck. He raised a hand and gently touched the bandage around her head.

'You're hurt.'

'Nothing that won't mend. Kolea got me to a medic.'

'I din't think I'd ever see you again, Tona,' Caffran said.

'It'll take more'n a few Blood Pact to keep me from you,' she replied and met his mouth with hers.

'Yeah, yeah... not in front of the troops,' said Lijah Cuu as he wandered past.

'SEE HER?'

'Of course I do.'

'Then be thankful,' said Colm Corbec, 'your little nightmare was just that... a little nightmare. There she is. Alive and well and... saintly.'

Milo nodded. 'Yes, I suppose so. She's amazing. She seems to be looking right at me.'

'At you? At me, more like. Right at me.'

Milo smiled. 'Believe what you want, colonel.'

'I believe I will.'

'That she's looking at you?' scoffed Mkoll dryly. 'I think she's certainly looking at me.'

The vast crowd around them suddenly sent up a booming cheer and the Ghosts in their midst joined in.

'Me, definitely,' murmured Mkoll.

LARKIN STARED. IT was like he had her in his crosshairs and she had him the same. If it had been a kill-sight, it would have been tough. Ninety metres, with a crosswind and hundreds of cheering bodies between him and her. But he'd have made it. Larkin was sure.

And even more sure that she'd have made it too. The way she looked at him. Like a marksman.

HARK PUSHED THROUGH the crowd. He almost fell over Daur, who was sobbing his heart out, and then bumped into Meryn, who was just staring.

'Meryn?'

'She's real.'

'I think that's the idea, sergeant.'

Beside them, Sergeant Varl had climbed up on a clock shrine cart and started to dance, putting on a beret plumed with struthid feathers and pulling it down comically over his ears.

Hark laughed despite himself.

* * *

'CHIEF?' VIVVO HANDED Soric the brass message shell.

'Thank you,' Soric said, and nodded Vivvo away. The crowd around them was going crazy. The cheering was so loud it was making him twitchy.

Soric undid the shell's cap and used his fingers as tweezers to fish the note out.

It said: *It's you she's looking at. She knows.*

Soric dropped the paper scrap and pushed the message shell into his pocket.

A moment later and Vivvo re-emerged from the bustling crowd.

He held out a message shell.

'This yours, chief?' he asked.

Soric patted his pant pockets. They were empty.

'Must be,' he said.

Vivvo handed him the shell and turned away. He glanced back over his shoulder. Soric knew Vivvo was catching on.

Soric opened the shell. This one said: *Tell Gaunt. Nine are coming. Nine are coming.*

The handwriting was hasty. Really rushed and badly formed, like he'd been writing in a hurry.

Despite the celebration around him, Soric felt his heart sink.

THE LITTLE GLADE was quiet. It was a spring morning, early, the first rays of sunlight gleaming through the leaves. A vague mist covered the path to the chapel door.

Each step he took sounded too loud in the cool silence. There were no birds singing. That seemed odd. His boots crunched on the stone pavers.

His pulse was racing. There was nothing to be afraid of, but he was afraid anyway. Why was that? He wanted to be here. He wanted to go inside, but his heart was thumping.

He reached the door. Dew glittered on the iron handle. He reached out to take hold of it, but the door began to open of its own accord. It began to open and behind it he saw–

GAUNT WOKE WITH a start. He had to fight to catch his breath. The room around him was dark and over-warm. He had no idea what time it was.

He got up off the bed and started to walk towards the windows to open the shutters. Only then did he feel the terrible aches of his tired body. Every step was painful.

He opened a shutter, and white light shafted into the small chamber. Outside it was late afternoon, and the sweep of the city-scape below showed that the celebration was still going on. He could see banners, the occasional spark of a firework, and crowds still streaming along the narrow streets.

He fiddled with the climate control vents built into the window sill, but no amount of jiggling eased the oppressive heat. He wished he could open the chamber window, but it was a hermetically sealed unit. This level of hive tower three was too high above the city shield and the Civitas's atmosphere envelope.

Gaunt tried to remember the dream he'd been having. It had been so vivid, but it had melted away the moment he woke. Aexe Cardinal. He had been back on Aexe Cardinal, at the chapel. More than that, he couldn't say.

He caught sight of his own reflection in the heavy dressing mirror in the corner of the room. He was dressed only in his under shorts, and his lean, muscled flesh looked unnaturally pale and white. The dark furrows of old scars looked like relief features on the surface of a chalky moon, especially the long, ugly rip across his belly that Dercius had left him with so many years before.

The newer wounds, the ones Herodor had given him, were more livid. So many abrasions and scratches he didn't care to count, scabbing black with blood. Bruises too, dark black and sickly yellow. The most serious were the las-burn across the top of his left shoulder and the gash in his right calf. Lesp had cleaned him up pretty well, dressed the worst, and sutured a few of the deepest cuts.

He limped out of the bedchamber into the outer room. His personal effects had been set out on the dresser and his spare uniform was laid out over the back of the chair.

'Beltayn?' he called out. There was no sign of his adjutant.

He was dressing when the door opened and Rerval came in.

'Sorry, sir. I should have knocked. Thought you were asleep.'

'As you were.'

Rerval, Corbec's signalman and adjutant, entered and closed the door. He was carrying a musette bag.

'Where's Beltayn?' Gaunt asked.

'He was bushed, sir. Corbec ordered him to billets and asked me to cover. I hope that's all right.'

Gaunt nodded, buttoning up his dress jacket.

'How long have I been asleep?'

'About four hours, sir. Everything's calming down a bit. Captain Daur's running things in operations.'

'Have we got any numbers yet?'

'Not for me to say, sir. Lugo's throwing a banquet tonight, which you're expected to attend.'

'Do you mean Lord General Lugo, Rerval?'

Rerval blushed. His cheeks went red apart from the white puckering of the long scar he'd taken across the face on Aexe. 'I do, sir.'

'I don't honestly care what you call him... except a bad habit might get you into trouble.'

'I'll remember that, sir.'

Gaunt finished buttoning his jacket and started to look around for his cap. Rerval reached into the musette bag he was carrying.

'Looking for this, sir?'

The cap was a little dusty and the worse for wear, though Rerval had done his best to clean it up.

'Colonel Corbec sent a scout back to the hab to find it, sir. No sign of your bolt pistol though, I'm afraid, so I requisitioned you this for the time being.' Rerval produced a brand new laspistol in a black leather holster.

'Thank you, Rerval,' said Gaunt, strapping it on. He buckled on his sheathed sword and warknife too and then put on his cap. Then he paused. 'I... I must have lost my cape somewhere along the way,' he said ruefully. He felt ashamed to admit it.

Rerval took off his own camo-cape. 'Take mine, sir. Please, it'd be an honour. I'll get myself another.'

Gaunt took the trademark Tanith garment and nodded his thanks. Rerval's gift was astonishingly generous, given how fiercely the Tanith protected their knives and capes.

'How do I look?' Gaunt asked.

'Like a conqueror of worlds, sir.'

'Very kind. How do I look really?'

'Tired, sir.'

THE OPERATIONS CENTRE was quiet. Only half the console positions were manned, and in most cases it was Munitorum clerics who were on duty. Daur was sitting in the side annexe, working his way through a stack of data-slates.

He started to get up when he saw Gaunt enter, but Gaunt waved him back into his seat.

'Long night, Ban. How're you holding up?'

Daur smiled reassuringly. 'I came through pretty much intact. Feel like a million credits now. You?'

'Weary, but a victory is a victory. Puts fire into even the most exhausted bones.'

'Not just that, though. Not just victory. I mean... after everything you said to us in here yesterday. You were wrong, weren't you?'

Gaunt sat down beside him. 'About the Beati?'

Daur nodded. 'I saw her. We all did. In the fight, and afterwards, down at the triumph. That was no fraud.'

Gaunt sighed. 'No. No, I can't think it could have been. The moment I saw her I was sure... as sure as I had been yesterday she wasn't real.'

'You must have been mistaken yesterday, sir,' Daur said.

'Do me a favour, Ban? Keep an open mind. The girl I met yesterday was not the Martyr. I know that in my heart as well as I know anything. For all her passion and conviction and self-belief, she was not the real thing. The woman who appeared last night... well, she was everything the other had not been. I don't know what happened... but something very strange took place as the battle was raging.'

'Thank the God-Emperor for that!'

'Indeed, the Emperor protects. But keep an open mind.'

'Because what can change one way might change back?'

'Quite so. Now why don't you bring me up to speed on the situation?'

Daur handed Gaunt a data-slate imprinted with the general operations report. 'I've rotated every Ghost who saw action last night off active to rest and resupply. Marshal Biagi wanted some bodies to add to his perimeter patrols, but Lord General Lugo seems to think we've got nothing to worry about now, so he went easy. Everyone's in billets, either standing ready or sleeping. Except those in the infirmary.'

'How many?'

'Thirty-nine. Eleven serious, including Mkhef, Sapes and Bewl. And Mkvenner.'

'Not again, not after Aexe.'

'Indeed no. He still hasn't recovered from the pasting he took on Aexe. Soric encountered him in the field last night and saw he was ailing, so he sent him back to the field hospital. Dorden reckons Ven's been pushing himself too hard and started bleeding internally from some of the old injuries. In a bad way, apparently.'

'How bad?'

Daur shrugged. 'I'm not the chief medic.'

'Is Ven going to die?'

'Probably.'

'Feth,' Gaunt took off his cap and set it on the desk beside him. 'I'll go and see him.'

'Make it fast. The Lord General's summoned all the senior staff to a banquet tonight.'

'I thought it was customary to *invite* officers to a banquet, not summon them.'

'I don't believe this is optional, sir.'

Gaunt shook his head. He didn't feel much like hobnobbing with Lugo's officer cadre. He looked across at Daur. 'I might as well get the rest of the bad news over with now. How many fates?'

'Thirty-two,' said Daur. He passed another data-slate to Gaunt. 'That's pending, of course. We've still got about twenty unaccounted for.'

The Tanith dead were listed by squad. The first six were from Gaunt's own platoon, number one. Reading each name gave him a twinge of pain, but he was relieved. The storm-fight in the hab had been so vile, so brutal, he'd been expecting to see many more names there. He knew Beltayn, Vanette and Starck had made it because they'd come out with him. It turned out that Caober, Wersun, Myska, Derin, Neith, Lyse, Bool, Mkan and another eight had made it out alive too.

'Mkoll says it was Caober, Derin and Lyse who led them out safe. A real fighting retreat, well ordered despite the vicious hand-to-hand. They got them far enough back for Mkoll's platoon to cover them. He's recommending honours for the three of them. I spoke to Derin myself. It sounds like it was hell in there.'

'It was hell everywhere, wasn't it?'

Daur sighed. 'I think so. But I get the feeling your stand in the hab there was the worst bout of close-quarters.'

'It shouldn't have happened. If we'd had flamers, they'd never have got within spitting distance of staging a storm.'

'You know the rules here, sir.'

'Know 'em, loathe 'em, gonna fight to change 'em. I won't get us caught like that again. When the next wave comes, we're going to be ready, and that means flamers to the front.'

Daur picked up his caffeine and sipped it, grimacing when he realised it had gone cold. 'Next wave? You think we're honestly going to get more?'

'I have no doubt, Ban,' said Gaunt, getting to his feet. 'We had a tough few hours there, and I'd not want to relive them, but we'd be fools to think that was anything except an unexpectedly heavy advance. The main force is coming. And they'll be loaded for behj.'

'There may also be a bright side, Gaunt.'

They looked up as Viktor Hark entered the annexe. He paused to sign off some slates a Munitorum scribe was holding for him, exchanged a few words with the robed, implanted functionary, and then strode in to join them.

'Are you rested, sir?' Hark asked, sweeping up his coattail and seating himself facing them.

'Well enough, thank you, Viktor. See much action?'

'In the closing stages. Enough to keep my hand in. Not enough to merit honours. Many did though; I have a list.'

'I look forward to reading it.'

'The lord general has a list too,' said Hark. 'You're on it.'

'Me?' said Gaunt.

'Both of you. Kaldenbach and Biagi are being given the credit for winning the fight, but Lugo wants to cite you and all the other senior officers – Tanith and Civitas alike – who were out in the thick of the first phase. But for your actions, the lord general says, there would have been no fight left to win. He's called the banquet to issue the citation pins.'

Gaunt was about to retort, but he saw how pleased and excited Daur looked and bit it back instead. He had no wish to be decorated by Lugo, but men like Daur, Rawne and Corbec deserved the recognition. It was about fething time.

'What did you mean when you said there was a bright side?' he asked.

'Astropathic signals from the reinforcement fleet, just received. I took the liberty of signing them off and passing them on to Lugo. Our replenishment will be here tomorrow at dawn, warp permitting. Nine Munitorum packets laden with munitions and medical supplies, three regiments of Khan Heavy Ground, and an Ardelean tank company out of San Velabo. Word is there's a Fleet Mechanicus pioneer ship inbound too, carrying a batch of mid-range plasma reactors to beef up the city shield. Plus five warships and a fighter carrier from the Segmentum battlefleet. Two days from now, Herodor's going to be a much tougher nut to crack.'

'Bright side indeed. What about enemy movements?'

Hark shrugged. 'Nothing. The balloon went up on Khan VI last night, according to transmits. Their far-listening stations thought they'd locked up an incoming warfleet heading our way. Turned out to be a flotilla of pilgrim ships from the Hagia system.'

Gaunt picked up his cap and put it on. 'Consider me a great deal happier than I was five minutes ago. I'll be in the infirmary if anyone needs me.'

'The function starts at 20.00, sir,' Hark reminded him.

'I won't be late.'

Gaunt left Daur and Hark talking and limped out through the quiet operations centre. At the door, he met Sergeant Meryn on his way in. Meryn saluted sharply.

'Problem, Meryn?'

'I was looking for Commissar Hark, actually, sir.'

'Nothing I can help you with?'

'I wouldn't want to trouble you, sir,' said Meryn.

THE PRIMARY TANITH billet was in a scholam on the thirtieth level of hive tower three. The double-bunked dorms had been cleaned out to accommodate the off-world troopers. The shutters were closed and the phospha lamps turned down, and smoke from lho-sticks filled the dim air.

Soric limped down the aisle between the bunks in dorm five, exchanging quiet greetings with those men that weren't asleep. Many were just unconscious, sprawled out on their cots, still wearing their battledress and the dirt and dried blood of the night before.

Soric himself was tired, but he was edgy too and he couldn't sleep. His lost eye ached like a bastard.

'You all right there, chief?' Corbec called to him. Soric stopped and stomped over to Corbec's cot.

'Fine, Colm. Fine and dandy. You know me.'

'Indeed I do,' said Corbec. He'd been stretched back in his undershirt on his cot, but now he sat up and pulled out a hip flask.

He offered it to Soric, who took it and sat down on the edge of the bunk.

'Good stuff,' he said, smacking his lips and handing it back. 'Surely that's not the sacra?'

That's what the Ghosts had begun to call it: *the* sacra. Several of the men, and many of the sutlers and traders accompanying the regiment, had become very handy at distilling the Tanith's beloved liquor. But none of them had quite the same knack as the lamented Bragg. His stuff had always been the best. A few flasks of it were rumoured to remain. And that stuff, like some mythical relic, was called *the* sacra.

'Indeed not,' smiled Corbec. 'But I commend your palate. Not many Verghasts can tell the difference.'

Soric shrugged. 'We're getting the taste for it. I've heard rumours that Trooper Lillo is close to perfecting the first Verghast distilled brand. He's calling it Gak Me Number One.'

Corbec chuckled. 'I know. With respect to Lillo – and let me confide in you that he's had me, Domor and Varl in for intensive taste tests – Gak Me Number One will get you blind pissed and clean brushes. It is not, however, sacra. This little job, which has, I'm sure you will agree, a fine nose, an agreeable undertaste, and a soft hint of ploins, vanilla and antifreeze, is the product of dear old Brostin who, let's face it, knows how to boil things. It's about the best there is in these dreary, post-Bragg days.'

Soric took another swig. 'He's got a bright future in illegal intoxication head of him, that Brostin.'

'So... what's got you wandering around at this hour?'

'Can't sleep.'

'Me neither. Got the itch.'

'The itch?' Soric blinked his one good eye at Corbec.

'Not something I picked up from one of Aleksa's girls, I assure you. The combat itch. Seems like I've been out of it for too long. Too, too long. Oh, I saw some shooty-shooty on Aexe, but it wasn't after much. I feel like I need to get back in the game.'

Soric nodded. On Phantine, both he and Corbec had been badly wounded. It had been the latest in a long series of injuries the colonel had suffered. He'd almost died on his medi-bed, but for Soric.

Because that had been where it had started.

Injured, Soric had suffered some kind of transformation. He couldn't say what exactly, and he'd kept it quiet. But it was like something inside him had woken up. Something he knew he had to keep secret from his friends and comrades. There had been twitches of craft in his family line, though never enough of anything to cause trouble. He'd believed the trait had passed him by, until the wounding on Phantine.

There, he'd known – simply known – that Corbec had been dying of a nosocomial infection. His warning had saved Corbec's life. And that had just been the start. Since then, the messages had been coming more and more frequently.

Gak, but he wanted them to stop.

Still, he knew what Corbec meant. Corbec wasn't a young man any more – neither of them were – and one injury too many would spell the end of their careers. Neither of them wanted that. But still...

'Don't push it,' he said.

'What do you mean?'

'You want to prove you're young still, young and fit. But don't push it. The shooty-shooty isn't known for its mercy.'

Corbec smiled at him. 'I'm first officer of the finest regiment in the Imperium, Agun... and it's a place I want to be for a long time. Don't worry about me. Me, I'm gonna live forever.'

'Make sure you do,' Soric said and got to his feet. 'Milo around?'

'Down yonder,' Corbec said with a flip of his thumb.

Soric shuffled his squat bulk down the aisle. He saw Larkin fast asleep on a lower bunk, his long-las wrapped in his arms like a favourite girl.

Soric stopped dead and slowly looked around. Something... something nagged him. Something he didn't even have to open his damn message shell to know.

Two bunk rows away, he saw Lijah Cuu. Cuu was flat on his belly on a top bunk, appearing to all around him to be asleep. But Soric could see Cuu's feline eyes were open, open and staring at Larkin.

He shuddered. Cuu was a piece of work. If he had it in for Larks, Soric pitied the poor bastard sniper. Maybe he should tell someone about–

He stopped himself. Cuu was looking at him now, returning the stare. Soric looked away and walked on. What would he tell anyone anyway? That he'd got a feeling? A bad feeling? A hand-written note from himself saying Cuu was a mad feth who needed to be watched at all times?

'What's up, chief?' Soric had come to a halt next to Milo's bunk. The youngest Ghost had spread his Tanith pipes out on his bedroll and was cleaning the chanters with a wire brush.

'Hello, Brinny. Got a moment?'

'Sure.'

Milo moved the chanter pipes so that Soric could sit down. The old Verghastite pulled a scrap of blue paper from his pocket.

'I need your help. It's a delicate matter. Can you promise me you'll be discreet?'

'Of course,' whispered Milo, sitting up, wondering what the hell Soric was going to tell him. Instead of speaking, Soric handed the scrap of paper to him.

'What's this?'

'Read it.'

Milo did. Hand-written on the sheet was the line: *Ask Milo. Trust Milo. He'll know.*

'What does that mean?' Milo asked.

Soric shrugged.

'Well, who wrote it?'

'I did.'

'When?'

'I have absolutely no idea,' said Soric.

GAUNT HATED COMBAT hospitals. They reminded him too much of the consequences of his profession.

The Civitas Beati had assigned a public health clinic on the tenth floor of hive tower three as the Tanith infirmary. It was a spartan hall of metal tiles and plastic screens. As he limped through the entranceway, he was assailed by the reek of antiseptic, which was so sharp and strong it almost but not quite masked the underlying aroma of blood and human waste.

A hand bell was ringing. Infardi volunteers and local medicae staff moved between the beds in the dim light, and in one corner an Ecclesiarchy provost was delivering the last rites. Candles flickered under their glass hoods. Someone was crying out with pain. Through a partly-drawn screen, Gaunt saw Curth and Lesp fighting with a thrashing body. Blood was pooling on the floor under the gurney.

He took off his cap and limped further into the chamber. Looking left and right, he finally located Mkvenner, lying in a cot at the far western end under the windows. Night was falling outside, and Mkvenner's bed was bathed in bars of cold, blue light. Gaunt saw Kolea sitting by Ven's side in silent vigil. Though his mind was ruined, Kolea seemed to know things, sense things. Gaunt was glad that Mkvenner wasn't alone at this time.

He started to walk towards Ven's bed when Dorden appeared from a side room.

'Ibram,' he said, as if surprised to see Gaunt.

'Doctor. I came to check on the wounded. Ven in particular.'

Dorden nodded. There was tension between them. Both of them hated how awkward things had become. 'Look, if you've got a moment,' Dorden said. 'I'd like you to look in on Zweil.'

'Zweil? He was wounded?'

Dorden shook his head. 'He collapsed from a stroke in the cathedral last night.'

'Feth, why wasn't I told?'

'I didn't know you hadn't been.'

'What's the prognosis?'

'He's stable. It's hard to say at this early stage.'

'Any idea what caused it?'

Dorden looked at him. 'Stress. Upset. I'm sure you remember that the ayatani was fairly worked up last night.'

'Are you blaming me?'

'No, of course not!' Dorden snapped. 'Not everything is about you, Gaunt.'

Trying not to rise to this, Gaunt walked past Dorden and into the side room. Zweil lay on his cot, as white as the sheets wrapped around him.

'Ayatani father,' Gaunt whispered, sitting down beside the bed.

'Oh, it's you,' said Zweil. The words came out slurred. The left half of his face seemed reluctant to move.

'How are you?'

'The feth you care!'

'I care a great deal. Stop it with the hostility, Zweil. You'll only make things worse.'

Zweil closed his eyes, as if in regret. 'You were right,' he hissed. 'I went to see her. I met her. She's just a lie, a fething lie. Just that silly girl Sanian. You were right.'

'I wasn't,' said Gaunt.

Zweil turned his head slowly and looked at Gaunt.

'What?' he gasped.

'Last night she was a lie. Today, she isn't.'

'Don't torture him, Gaunt,' said Dorden from the shadows of the doorway behind him.

Gaunt looked round at Dorden sharply. 'Have you not seen what's been happening today, doctor?'

Dorden shrugged. 'I've been busy. I understand we won.'

'The Saint is here,' Gaunt said. 'She led us to that victory. I don't understand it at all, but it's true.'

Dorden stepped into the room and into the light cast by the electro candles around the old priest's bed. 'Is this another of your games?'

'You know me. I don't play games.'

'I thought I knew you, Ibram. Aexe Cardinal proved me wrong. But... I guess you wouldn't.'

'Doctor, you went through hell on Hagia because you believed. I only said what I said last night to protect your faith. Last night there was no Saint Sabbat on Herodor, at least not one I had seen. This morning, there is.'

'I want to see her,' Zweil said suddenly.

'He's too sick to–' Dorden began.

'I want to see her!'

'He wants to see her, and I think he should,' said Gaunt. 'You too, Tolin.'

Dorden shrugged. 'I don't know...'

'Get a wheelchair. And get some orderlies to lift Zweil.' Gaunt checked his pocket watch. It was a quarter after seven and he wasn't even changed. 'Do it!' he insisted. He turned back and squeezed Zweil's hand. 'I'll take you to see her. Let me check on Ven first.'

Zweil nodded.

Gaunt limped out into the main infirmary hall and started down to Mkvenner's bed. Then he stopped.

Mkvenner and Kolea were gone.

THE HOLY BALNEARY was empty. There was no sound except the gentle slap of the water in the main pool. The dim air was wreathed with steam and the tangy smell of iron.

By the light of the fluttering candles that lined the long, limestone staircase, Kolea helped Mkvenner plod his way down. Biolumin globes shone on the steam below, their light picked out on the ripples of the sacred pool.

Mkvenner coughed violently, and his hand was wet with blood as he took it from his mouth. Kolea held on to him tightly to stop him falling.

'Take me back, Gol,' Mkvenner said, his voice husky with rattling fluid.

Kolea shook his head. 'Make you better. This will, it will. It will make you all better. It heals all the wounds. That's what they said. You'll see.'

'I'm tired. Too tired. I can't...'

'Don' you stop now, Ven. Don' you stop. Hold me tight and I'll get you there. You won' fall.'

'Gol, please. Let me die in my bed. Let me–'

He started coughing again. The wracks hit him so hard that he bent over and blood spattered on the gleaming limestone stairs. Mkvenner sank to his knees.

'This is madness,' Mkvenner gasped.

Kolea shook his head. 'She'll fix you better,' he said. He reached into the pocket of his jacket and produced a truly awful plaster effigy of the Saint, a pilgrim nick-nack. Kolea displayed it with huge pride. 'Found this. Lucky charm. Lucky lucky. Was Tona's. In her pocket.'

'Criid?'

Kolea nodded and smiled encouragingly. 'Found her hurt. Found it on her. Lucky lucky. It kept her safe. Real safe. Keep you safe too. Make you better.'

'Just take me back, Gol.'

'Saint make you better. Water make you better. You'll see.'

Kolea put the effigy back into his coat. Mkvenner started coughing again. More blood came up and Mkvenner's wracks became so violent, he passed out.

Kolea bent over and picked the big Tanith up. Grunting with effort, his legs shaking, he continued on down the steps, carrying Mkvenner in his arms.

He reached the bottom, and crossed the pool side towards the deep steps that ran down into the fuming water.

'Make you all better,' he repeated, over and over. Mkvenner didn't answer. His head hung limply.

Carrying the dying scout, Kolea descended into the water, up to his shins, his knees, his thighs, his waist. The buoyancy of the water collected Mkvenner's limp form up and floated him. Kolea pushed out, the water up to his throat, keeping Mkvenner on the surface.

Blood stained out in a wide fan around them.

'Be better! Be better now!' Kolea cried out.

He looked up suddenly. On the far side of the pool, a figure had appeared, indistinct in the smoking steam.

'Make him better!' Kolea demanded, trying to keep Mkvenner's limp body above the water level.

'Make him better!'

'WHAT NOW? You want me to walk?' Zweil leaned forward in the bathchair Lesp was pushing and stared at the candlelit flight of white steps below them. They could smell the sulphurous water.

Zweil made an effort to turn his head to look up at Gaunt. 'Do you expect me to get up and walk down that?' he snarled.

'No,' said Gaunt. 'Lesp? Help me.'

Between them, the Tanith commander and the slender orderly gathered Zweil up in a chair-lift between them and started to edge down the stairs. It was hard. Gaunt realised how unreliable his wounded leg was. If he fell now…

Behind them, Dorden shook his head wearily and pushed the empty bathchair to one side. Then he began to follow the others down the steps into the humid chamber of the Holy Balneary.

'Could you stop fidgeting?' Lesp grunted.

'I'm not!' Zweil complained.

'I think you are. This isn't easy,' said Gaunt. Sweat was beading on his forehead from the effort, and Lesp was panting. Moisture coated every smooth limestone stair, and every step they took was a disaster waiting to happen.

'What… what the feth is happening down there?' Dorden said suddenly from behind them.

Gaunt nearly fell. They were halfway down the white staircase. 'Put him down! Lesp, put him down!'

They eased Zweil's paralysed body onto a step and let go. Lesp had to crouch and hold on to Zweil to stop him slithering away down the stairs. Gaunt rose and looked at what Dorden was pointing at. Below them, in the pool, three figures were standing in the water.

'Wait here,' Gaunt said. Dorden bent down beside Lesp and helped to keep Zweil stable. The three of them watched Gaunt stagger his way down to the pool.

Gaunt limped from the foot of the staircase to the edge of the balneary pool. The three bodies in the water were now submerged, one of them pressing hands down on the backs of the others' heads to dunk them.

Or drown them. Or baptise them.

Gaunt couldn't tell. He thumped down the bath steps into the water himself.

The figures surfaced in a rush of bubbles and spray. Kolea. Mkvenner.

And her.

'What the hell is this?' Gaunt cried.

The Beati, clad only in a white shift, smiled at him, wiping away the water that dripped down her face from the fringes of her bowl-cut hair.

'The water heals, Ibram,' she said.

Just the sight of her stilled his fears. He stopped where he was, the warm water rocking against his legs.

Mkvenner turned and splashed his way towards him.

'Ven?'

Mkvenner got up on the steps and sat down, soaked through. He started to laugh.

'Ven? Are you all right?'

Mkvenner was laughing heartily, as if at some enormous cosmic joke. A man in his condition surely shouldn't be able to laugh so violently. Unless...

'I told you,' said Kolea, splashing up to the foot of the steps and clambering up beside Mkvenner. 'Didn't I tell you? Heals everything. That's the thing about this place, it–'

Kolea paused, and looked around, blinking in the wet air. His gaze finally found Gaunt's face.

'I–' he said. 'Sir, I think I may have missed something. How did I get here?'

SIX
PERTURBATION

'Bad day coming!'

— Unidentified preacher, Herodor

'SAY THAT... AGAIN, if you please.'

Lord General Lugo exuded power and authority in his white, high-collared dress uniform, but his tone didn't match his appearance at all. He sounded positively nervous.

'I said, lord, that I apologise for attending this function late, but I was delayed by an extraordinary event in the Holy Balneary. Before my eyes, the Beati performed a sacred miracle. Two, in fact. Sacred miracles of healing.'

Gaunt paused and allowed the silence to last. The room, a high-tier ballroom in Old Hive that Lugo's staff had requisitioned for the banquet, was full of formally attired officers – Herodian PDF, life company, Regiment Civitas and Tanith – who were all staring at Gaunt and the lord general. They'd been standing around, sipping preprandial amasecs and chatting, when Gaunt entered, and they'd heard every word.

'A miracle? What miracle?' Lugo asked, edgily. Biagi and Kaldenbach were nearby, and Gaunt could see Rawne, Mkoll, Daur and Hark in amongst the gathering. Behind the huddle of officers, servitors and household staff putting the finishing touches to the long table ceased their activity, as if realising something was in the air.

'Two of my troopers went to the Holy Balneary tonight. One, Mkvenner by name, was at death's door. He was wounded on Aexe, and had never made a full recovery. The other, Sergeant Kolea, had been left a mental cripple during action on Phantine. It was a chronic condition that no amount of surgery could fix. As I understand it, Kolea had taken Mkvenner down the balneary. It was an act of comradeship. I think Kolea's simple mind had seized on what he had been told about the holy waters and so he believed he was doing the right thing.'

Lugo's eyes narrowed as he listened.

'When I arrived,' Gaunt went on, 'they were in the main pool, and the Saint was present. She was with them, in the water, almost as if she was...'

'...baptising them?' murmured Biagi.

'Just so, marshal,' said Gaunt. 'When it was done, both men were healed. Completely healed.'

'You must be mistaken, sir,' said Kaldenbach.

Gaunt shook his head. 'I admit, truth and falsehood seem to keep switching places with each other here on Herodor, but I know what I saw.'

'Were you alone in witnessing this, Gaunt?' Lugo asked.

'No, sir. It was also witnessed by my chief medic, an orderly named Lesp, and by Ayatani Zweil.'

Lugo and Biagi exchanged quick glances. Gaunt could see the disguised unease on both their faces.

'When did this happen?' asked Lugo.

'An hour ago, sir.'

'And only now do you come here and tell me?'

Gaunt paused. 'Ayatani Zweil made me conversant with the etiquette concerning such events. I made haste to summon the senior ayatani, the provosts of the Ecclesiarchy, and the first officiary, so that the miracles could be corroborated and documented, and entered into the holy record.'

'You informed church and state before you informed me?'

Gaunt nodded. 'I wasn't aware miracles were a military matter, lord. Ayatani Zweil told me that being a site of proven miracles would greatly increase Herodor's significance as a sacred place. This made it a matter for the Imperial Church. All Imperial subjects are legally obliged to inform the Ecclesiarchy of wonders and portents. And of course, it adds provenance to the authenticity of the Beati herself.'

'She needs no provenance!' Lugo snapped.

'Sir, I don't understand,' said Gaunt. 'The Saint is reborn here on Herodor and she has proved her divinity by performing genuine miracles. That surely is a cause for universal rejoicing. Why do you seem angry?'

Lugo stiffened and looked around, suddenly aware of the image he was projecting. He forced a smile. 'You misunderstand me, my dear colonel-commissar. I am just... astonished. Miracles, as you say, are beyond our understanding, beyond the remit of normal life, and I confess I am alarmed by anything that does not fit into the pragmatic, physical world of soldiering. I'm sure my brothers here will agree?'

There was a general murmur of assent from around the room.

Lugo looked at Gaunt. 'I'm not ashamed to admit that the notion of miracles terrifies me, Gaunt. The unseen universe exerting its power over our material lives. That sort of... magic is so often the stock in trade of our archenemy. So, please forgive my tone just then. Of course it is a cause for joyful thanks.'

It was an excellent recovery, Gaunt had to give him that much.

'I will go to the first officiary at once, and consult with him about how we should proceed.'

The assembly saluted as Lugo strode out, Biagi at his side. Then the chatter renewed, urgent.

'Is this true?' Hark asked softly, as he reached Gaunt's side.

Gaunt nodded.

'But Kolea was...'

'Permanently crippled, I know. Dorden doesn't know what happened. It's quite scared him.'

'And Lugo too.'

'That's different,' Gaunt said. 'I think Lugo's scared because he was in control of his game here until five minutes ago and now he most definitely isn't.'

THE SCARS WERE still there: old, pink, smooth, knotted across the back of the head from the base of the neck up to the crown. The hair had never properly grown back through the crumpled tissue, and Kolea had kept his head shaved.

'Let me see it once more,' he said. Ana Curth paused and then lifted the hand mirror again. Kolea craned his eyes sideways to study the marks on the back of his skull.

'A real mess.'

'Yes, it was,' she said. She put the mirror down because her hands were trembling and she didn't want to drop it. 'Just a few more tests,' she said, hoping she sounded breezy.

'Haven't you done enough?' he asked. She met his eyes and swallowed. There was a light there, a human spark back in them that hadn't been around since that day on Phantine two years earlier. It was like he'd risen from the dead, and though she was overjoyed to have him back, it terrified her. It was beyond her professional expertise to explain it.

'Why don't you sit down?' he suggested. 'You look like you've seen a ghost.'

She laughed, stupidly delighted by the awful joke, and sat on a wooden stool facing the bedside where he was perched. The infirmary was quiet, though those patients still awake had heard what was going on and were whispering from cot to cot. From nearby came the soft whir of a medicae resonancer as Dorden ran the machine over

Mkvenner's torso for the umpteenth time. Dorden glanced up from his work, saw Curth looking at him, and shrugged. They were both spooked. They'd seen plenty in their days with the regiment, but nothing like this.

'How much do you remember, Gol?' she asked.

He frowned, his lips pursed, for a brief second resembling the brain-damaged Gol Kolea, struggling to remember someone's name or what he was supposed to be doing.

'With any clarity, I remember a street in Ouranberg, in the habs of the Alpha Dome. Criid was down. Hurt. Enemy fire. Those damn loxatl freaks. I remember the impacts of their flechette blasters. That distinctive sound... the hiss, the rattle of the shrapnel barbs. I went to get Tona. She was with Allo and Jenk, and they were dead. She'd caught shrap in the arm and the side. It looked bad. I picked her up and started to run. I...'

'What?'

'I don't remember anything after that. It's just a blur from there. You know how when you're swimming and you dive down, and sounds from above you become all muffled and hollow? It feels like my memories since then are like that. Vague, out of focus. When my head came back up out of the water in that pool all the sounds flooded back and I remembered who I was.'

'It's been two years.'

'Two years?' he gasped. 'Tell me.'

'Tell you what?'

'Tell me where I've been. Tell me what happened.'

She breathed out and looked at the floor. 'It was a loxatl round. It hit you in the back of the head and... and there was nothing we could do. You nearly died. You have to understand, Gol...'

'I understand you did your best.'

'No, I mean... this isn't normal. You'd lost a considerable percentage of brain tissue. Your personality was destroyed. You could barely answer to your own name. You were just a shadow. An empty body.'

'And now I'm not.'

She stared at him. 'Gol, I've scanned your skull with the infra-ometer and the mag resonator. There's no change. Your brain is still as damaged as before. There's been no real reconstruction, just basic tissue healing. There is absolutely no way you should be... cogent again like this.'

Kolea reached up and ran his fingers over the mess of scar-tissue.

'You said it was a miracle.'

'It is. In the strictest, most literal sense of the word. You and Ven both.'

'That scares you.'

'Yes, it does.' He blinked at this and looked away. Curth jumped to her feet.

'Oh, Gol! no! Don't misunderstand me! I'm only scared of the unknown. Dorden's the same... God-Emperor, everyone is!'

She reached out and hugged him tightly, pecking a quick kiss on his cheek before pulling away again.

'But we're fething glad to have you back.'

He smiled. The old smile. The one she'd once been rather keen on.

'Tell me the rest,' he said. 'Where is this place again?'

'Herodor,' she said.

'And before that we were where?'

'On Aexe Cardinal. Trench war.'

He nodded slowly. 'I have a vague, muffled recollection of mud and water. And bombardment. Huge bombardment. Who's been leading the squad?'

'Criid,' Curth said and laughed when he opened his mouth in surprise. 'First female sergeant. Things have moved along a bit in two years. Jajjo made scout.'

'Our first Verghast scout? Oh Holy Terra...' Kolea murmured, genuinely moved and proud. 'About gakking time.'

'Muril almost made the grade too. She was in the program, and Ven says he would have recommended her to the specialty.' Curth's face darkened. 'But she died on Aexe.'

'Who else?' he asked quietly. 'Get it over with. Who else have we lost while I was in the dark?'

'So... CAN I go?' asked Mkvenner.

Dorden was packing up the instruments and glanced over at him. 'You seem astonishingly unmoved by this, Ven,' he said. He was trying to disconnect the power lead from the base of the resonator paddle, but his mind was everywhere and he couldn't remember how the lead-lock worked. He had to put the device down quickly so Mkvenner wouldn't notice his distraction.

Mkvenner shrugged. 'You say I'm fit?'

'Rudely healthy. There's no trace of any internal bleeding. There's not even a residue of blood pooled in your abdomen.'

Mkvenner started to pull on his black vest. 'So I can go?'

'Do you know what just happened?'

'Yes,' said Mkvenner.

'Well, I fething don't! Explain it to me.'

Mkvenner shrugged again. 'It is my honour to serve the Imperium of Man, and in so doing the God-Emperor who protects us all. Tonight, in his infinite wisdom, he spared me, and he did so through the instrument of his chosen one. I'm not going to argue with that. I'm not going to be scared by that, either.'

'Yes, but–'

'There are no "buts", Dorden. We fight the archenemy because we believe in the Holy Truths. Terrible things happen, unnatural things, warp-magic things, and we accept them because we believe. Now a good thing happens and you think we should question it?'

Dorden frowned. 'No, put like that.'

Mkvenner looked up. There were sounds coming from outside. Voices.

'Stay here,' Dorden said, and walked towards the infirmary exit.

A crowd was gathering in the torch-lit hall outside the hospital facility. Dorden saw huddles of ayatani and esholi, groups of ecclesiarchs and adepts, even a few infardi. Most of them had prayer beads, pilgrim badges, ampullas of holy water or placard boards with pictures of the Saint pasted onto them. Some were incanting, or swinging incense burners. Many carried votive candles.

'What is this?' he asked.

'We want to see the Miraculous,' said one ecclesiarch.

'That's not possible. This is a hospital, and there are sick men here who need rest.'

'The Saint has touched men here!' an ayatani declared. 'We must have audience with these men and test them for faith and truth.'

'Go away,' said Dorden.

Ayatani Kilosh moved towards him through the gathering crowd.

'Show me the men,' he said to the old doctor.

'Can't this wait?'

Kilosh shook his head. 'Corroboration must be had and witnessed, and testimony recorded so that these miracles may be written into the holy record.'

'Why?'

'Why? Doctor, if a plague breaks out do you not try to contain it, identify it and document it for the good of the Imperium?'

Dorden blinked. 'Of course.'

'Well, a wonder has happened here that has profound significance for the Church of Man. We must investigate it and document it so we can understand fully what it means. The God-Emperor has spoken to us, and we need to find out what it is He has said.'

Dorden sighed. 'Just you then, Ayatani Kilosh. You and your scribes. I will not have the other patients discomforted.'

THE AIR WAS heavy with the hot smell of baking bread. Down the promenade from the scholam where the Tanith were billeted there was an arcade of merchant shops – a weaver, a milliner, a measure-arbitrator, a meat-packer and a bakery. It was nearly dawn, and a civic light-keeper, a long-bodied servitor, was clunking down the arcade, adjusting the wall-mounted phospha lamps to the day setting. The bakery was the only business up at that hour. The ovens were running in the back of the store, and the lamps were lit in the windows. In less than an hour, the hive's morning function pattern would begin, and the area would be busy with workers walking from their habs to the main-hive elevator banks to get to work. The bakery, which did a busy trade every morning in breakfast rolls and sugar-loaves, was preparing for the morning rush.

This early, it was still eerily empty. The antique speaker horns along the promenade were playing the same soft music they had been broadcasting throughout the night cycle, and the public address screens were scrolling random, soothing texts from the Imperial creed.

It reminded Soric of Vervunhive. He felt sadly nostalgic. He'd always loved this time, the early calm at the start of a day in the hive, the brief hiatus between night shift and day shift. He remembered rising at this time, walking to work, purchasing caffeine and a sosal from the food-house on his hab-block, seeing the open gates of the smeltery as he approached.

He'd knocked on the door of the bakery and got the bleary assistant to sell him some soft dough-twists, still warm from the ovens. Not sosals, but still… Now he and Milo sat under the gantries of the upper walkway, munching the food. A pair of arbites wandered past, but they didn't spare them a second glance. Two off-duty soldiers, heading home after a night in the taverns.

'So… you think you're a psyker?'

Soric's mouth turned into a firm, upside-down U. 'That's not what I said, Brin.'

'But you're worried about these… these happenings?'

'Of course I am! Worried… terrified.'

Milo ate the last of his dough-twist and wiped his mouth on his sleeve.

'You know what happens, chief.'

'I know. I know, gak it.'

'Seriously, I don't know why you're talking to me.'

'Because–'

'Because this said so?' Milo produced the crumpled blue paper from his pocket.

'I don't want to die, Milo,' Soric said.

'No one said anything about d–'

Soric shook his head. 'A bullet in the head. That's what I'll get. They don't even have to prove anything. If anyone thinks, or even thinks they think, that I'm touched by the warp, I'll be executed. No hesitation.'

'Gaunt wouldn't–'

'Wouldn't he? It's his job. It's the duty of every one of us. If I found out one of my boys was touched, I'd do them myself. No question. I'm not an idiot. You don't take chances with gak like that.'

Milo thought for a moment. 'By rights, then, I should shoot you. Or report you at least. Why have you trusted me?'

'I heard things.'

'Heard what?'

'Things. Things about you. I thought you might be sympathetic. I thought you might know what to do.'

'Why?'

'Because you're still here. Gaunt never shot you.'

Milo widened his eyes. 'Chief, I'd be lying if I said you don't scare me. The feth you've told me tonight... I should be running away and screaming for you to be gunned down.'

'But you're not.'

'No. I was interrogated. By an inquisitor. Did you know that?'

Soric blanched. 'No!'

'Back on Monthax. It was before your time. Before Verghast. Right from the Founding, I was regarded as a bit of a lucky charm. You know the story.'

'Corbec told me a little. You were the only civilian to get off the world alive.'

'Right.'

'Because of Gaunt.'

'Right. He saved my life. I was the only non-com to make it off Tanith. And the youngest. All the men looked at me like I was special. Like I was a little piece of Tanith, saved and preserved.'

'But you were special, weren't you?'

Milo sniggered. 'Oh, yes. A kid, surrounded by grown-up soldiers that I so desperately wanted to impress. Corbec, Cluggan, Rawne – I guess. Gaunt himself, certainly. I loved the fact they paid attention to me, took me seriously. I think I milked it a bit.'

'Milked it?' Soric sat back.

'I had a knack of knowing things. Well, that's what they all thought. I was the mascot, the lucky charm. If I had a funny feeling, they all took notice of it. Believe me, chief, it was child's play.'

'You faked it? Gak!'

Milo shook his head. 'No, no... nothing like that. I did get a feeling every now and then. A sense of premonition. But look at it this way. I was a kid, following men round into war zones. Shit was likely to happen at any moment. Bombardments. Raids. Sneak attacks. I mean, probability law alone means I got it right a lot of the time. I was scared and jumpy. When I jumped, the men listened. When I jumped and they listened and something happened... well, bingo. As far as they were concerned, I was a lucky charm who had a sixth sense for danger. You know troopers, chief. They're a superstitious lot.'

'Gak me,' said Soric, deflated. 'So it was all a turn. Little Brinny-boy doing his thing so the troops would love him.'

'Not quite,' said Milo. 'Are you going to finish that?' he asked, nodding at the half-eaten twist in Soric's hand.

Soric shook his head and passed it to Milo.

'There were times,' Milo said, through a mouthful, 'there were times when it seemed real. I know Gaunt was worried. He didn't know what to do. If I did have a touch about me, he knew he'd have no choice but to execute me. But he didn't dare.'

'Because?'

'Come on, chief! I was the kid, the lucky mascot, the last living civilian from Tanith. What the feth would it have done to the Ghosts' morale if he'd shot me?'

'I see your point...'

'Anyway, this inquisitor got wind of it. Varl had been playing on my rep to stage a few "entertainments" on the troop transport and some of the other regiments got nervous. I was reported. Next thing I know, I was in front of this inquisitor.'

'I've never had the pleasure. Was he a bastard? I've heard they are.'

'He was a she. Lilith. But yes, she was a bastard. Put me through the wringer. Gaunt was there. Tried his best to keep me out of the crap.'

'And?'

'And... she did her job, Agun. She got to the truth and uncovered it. She found out I was a fake and exposed me. And that's why I'm still alive.'

Soric breathed heavily and rubbed his dry hands together. 'You were a fake...'

'Not deliberately. I had been starting to believe myself. But she got the truth out. And I realised I'd been playing with fire. If that's all this is, chief, stop now.'

'It isn't,' said Soric. He reached into the thigh pocket of his fatigue pants and fished out a crumpled packet of lho-sticks.

'I thought you'd given those up.'

'So did I,' Soric said, lighting one. 'They help with the headaches. I get this pain across my skull, and in my dead eye.' He reached up with his left hand and splayed the fingers across his scarred head. 'It hurts, a lot.'

'You should tell Gaunt,' said Milo.

'About my headaches?'

'About everything. Tell him. If I know anything about Gaunt it's that he's no bastard. He'll protect you. He'll do what is necessary to keep you safe without breaking Imperial law.'

'The black ships...' Soric murmured.

'Maybe. I don't know. All I know is, I'm not touched. Never was. I'm not in any way special. But I know how hard it can get if they suspect you. So tell Gaunt. Maybe that's why the message told you to speak to me. Sound advice.'

Soric exhaled a plume of fragrant smoke. 'I need to do something. The messages are getting...'

'What?'

'More urgent. I've had a warning. I don't know what it means, but it's gonna be bad. I have to tell someone... Gaunt, who knows? But if I tell, that's the end for me. Goodbye, Agun, nice to have known you. I don't know, Brinny. Should I be looking after myself or looking to the greater good?'

Milo got up, dusting crumbs from his lap. 'I think you know the answer to that, chief.'

Milo walked away down the promenade.

Soric sat for a moment in silence. 'All right, already!' he hissed, reaching into his leg pouch. The brass shell had been wriggling like a rat.

He unscrewed it and routinely tipped out the note.

Nine are coming. Stop gakking around and be a man. Milo can be trusted, but he's lying. He IS special. Don't tell him. Don't scare him. The clock's reached midnight.

'I PRESUME YOU have a pass, trooper?'

Milo stopped in his tracks in the scholam entrance.

'Sir?'

Hark stepped out of the shadows. 'An exeunt pass, permitting you to stray from quarters.'

'I haven't, sir.'

Hark nodded. 'Who were you with?'

'No one, sir. I was just taking a walk.'

'With Sergeant Soric. I saw you.'

'It's nothing, sir.'

Hark raised a gloved hand and beckoned Milo over to him with one crooked finger.

'I will judge what is something and what is nothing. I have my eye on Soric.'

'Why, sir?'

Hark's eyes were hooded. 'Reports. I don't intend to divulge my sources to a common trooper.'

'Of course not, sir.'

'You lead a charmed life, Brin Milo. The Tanith dote on you. Gaunt dotes on you. All I care about is the well being of this regiment. Its health... spiritual, physical... mental. I believe that you, like any of the Ghosts, would tell me if there was something – wrong – going on. It would be your duty.'

'It would, sir.'

'Tell me about Soric.'

'The chief is upset, sir.'

'Upset?'

'He is suffering from headaches.'

'And?'

Milo shook his head. 'And nothing. Headaches.'

Milo stiffened as Hark produced a scrumpled piece of blue paper from his storm-coat pocket and opened it out, holding it so that Milo could see.

It read: *Guheen's going to get himself pulped if he goes that way. The tank is behind the cabinet maker's shop.*

'I have no idea what that means, sir,' said Milo.

'Soric is warp-touched, isn't he?'

'Not that I know, sir.'

'If I find out he is, and that you've been covering for him, I'll have your neck as well as his. Clear, trooper?'

'Crystal, sir.'

'Get to your billet!' snapped Hark.

Milo hurried away and Hark turned and stared up at the massive window lights that ran along the promenade bay. Up in the deep blue, stars were shining.

SOME OF THE stars were ships.

On the wide bridge of the frigate *Navarre*, Executive Officer Kreff leaned forward in his padded seat and said, 'Authorise.'

The bridge crew nodded, touching console switches. There was a low hum as the gravitic assemblies in the massive ship's underbelly cycled and flat-banded mag waves to compensate for the ship's orbital drift.

A proximity horn started to wail.

Kreff tutted and got up, sauntering over to the main pilot well where the helm servitors sat in recessed floor sockets. The demi-human crew sat hunched forward, their plug-crusted skulls looping hoses behind them like braids.

'Station keeping,' he ordered.

'Maximal one oh one,' the nearest servitor croaked from its augmetic voice-box.

With a press of his hand on the imprint reader, Kreff cancelled the siren. Orbital space above Herodor was thick with ships, most of them informally registered pilgrim tubs. Every few minutes, as the elegant frigate reclined in orbit, tracking sensors would fire off, warning of another near miss. It had become routine.

Kreff walked into the actuality sphere in the centre of the bridge space, and looked around at the speckle of glowing ship-phantoms that appeared in 3D in the light-impressed sphere around him. Tactical readouts glowed beside the various images, blinking as the images slowly tracked. There was a mass conveyance called the *Troubadour*, part of a newly arrived pilgrim caravan, that kept wandering into the *Navarre's* collision cone.

The vox beeped. It was the captain.

'Alarms woke me, Kreff.'

'Nothing to worry about, captain. Just routine.'

Captain Wysmark signed off.

'Bloody hulk is wandering again...' Kreff said.

'*Troubadour* is signaling, sir,' said one of the deck officers. 'They have a fire on board. Major fire, in the hold space. Requesting urgent assist.'

'Check it.'

'*Navarre* is reading massive heat build in the hold section. They're burning alive.'

Kreff nodded. 'Fire suppression teams to standby. Board teams to ready. Move us in, helm, and tell the*Troubadour* to stand by for immediate docking. Let's hustle.'

'Should I have the troops stand by, sir?' asked Colonel Zebbs, the ship's senior armsman, standing to attention behind Kreff.

'It's a bloody pilgrim ship, not a hostile,' said Kreff.

ENSIGN VALDEEMER TOOK the data-slate from the waiting deck servitor, reviewed it quickly, and then began to stride purposefully across the steel deck of the *Omnia Vincit* towards the fleet captain's pulpit. To his left, where the edge of the bridge deck dropped away, the dozens of helm servitors, tech-priests and astropath navigators were arranged in descending tiers, like the upper circle of a great theatre. It took a massive crew to control a battleship the size of the *Omnia Vincit,* a massive bridge crew alone. The bridge space was vast and vaulted like a gigantic basilica, its high domed roof painted with beautiful frescos of the actes sanctorum.

Valdeemer was just a small part of that crew, and a recent part too. He'd joined the ship just eighteen months before, but already he was a junior deck officer. He knew he had a bright future. One day, it would be him sitting up there in that magnificent throne, bio-linked to the ship's systems, commanding the power of a god in the Emperor's name.

To get there, he had to shine. To excel. To do his job in exemplary fashion and be seen to be doing it too. He could have voxed the report for the fleet captain's attention, but it was important, and suited personal delivery. Besides, it brought him to the fleet captain's attention.

He hurried up the alabaster steps of the pulpit, pausing briefly at the top as the Navy armsmen guards scanned him and then stood aside.

Fleet Captain Esquine terrified every member of the great ship's crew. Even Valdeemer, for all his confidence, was cowed by him. It was hard to tell where the fleet captain's gilded throne ended and his own body began. He was encased in golden armour, intricately wrought and etched, and his armour engaged directly with the throne so he formed a solid, engraved structure. His hands and arms were fused into the arms of the seat, and the back of his head, in its skullcap of gold, was locked against the throne's high back.

Esquine's hands were set palm-down on the arms of the throne, and only his gold-jacketed fingers moved, dancing like a pianist's. At their bidding, multi-jointed servo arms raised and lowered in front of the fleet captain's eyes, presenting pict-plates, larger actuality screens, and data-slates. The fleet captain held them up, sometimes four or more at a time, overlaying, comparing, transferring data from one to another with a blink, interlocking and compressing information into tight holographic spheres that floated around the throne.

Esquine's face was long-browed and noble. His blade of a nose had a slight hook to it, and his pale eyes were lashed with nearly invisible white hairs. The gold tracery of circuitry was woven into his ears, his cheekbones and the skin of his forehead from the edges of the skullcap, giving his flesh a jaundiced tinge. His mouth was invisible behind the grille of a vox-caster that rose from his gilded chest plate like a breathing mask.

Valdeemer smoothed the crisp front of his uniform jacket, shook out his braided cuffs, adjusted the sit of his emerald sash, and stood to attention.

'You have a report for me, ensign?' Esquine asked. His voice was soft and fluid, each word sounding like a rounded stone dropped into a deep pool.

'Sir,' Valdeemer nodded, and held out the data-slate. Esquine's fingers flickered, and a servo arm extended out from the throne's side and took the slate, swinging it back before the fleet captain's eyes.

'From the astropathicae,' Valdeemer went on. 'They have detected an advance perturbation in the Empyrean, warp modulus eleven two nine nine seven, at a point–'

'Nine AU out from Herodor. I can read, ensign. A standard Imperial arrival vector.'

'I thought I should bring it to you at once, sir.'

Locked in place, Esquine's head could not turn, but his pallid eyes glanced sidelong at Valdeemer for a moment.

'Of course.' Esquine's gaze returned to the slate, and a servo-arm moved in to offer up another for comparison. 'The reinforcement fleet is approaching. That worm Lugo will be pleased, no doubt. Let us prepare. Ensign, step onto the throne plate.'

Valdeemer blinked and looked down. He was standing on the outer decking of the command pulpit. The throne itself was set on a raised disc of polished plasteel in the centre. He quickly stepped up onto the edge of this inner platform.

There was a slight vibration. The disc began to move, sliding backwards. The adamantine bulkhead wall behind the throne parted with a hiss of disengaging magnetic locks, and the entire throne platform – and Valdeemer along with it – retracted through the opening space.

As the shadow of the bulkhead passed over him, Valdeemer felt the retracting throne-platform begin to rotate too. It turned them through one hundred and eighty degrees until Esquine's throne was now facing into the secret, armoured chamber behind his pulpit. The strategium.

The bulkhead shutters closed, sealing them in. Valdeemer felt a rush of excitement. This was the first time he had been invited into the inner sanctum of command.

The dim, heavily buttressed chamber was ovoid. Tech-priests and senior deck officers stood or sat at console stations built into the walls between the buttress stanchions, and seven more perched at high podium consoles facing inwards around the actuality sphere that flickered and glowed in the centre of the room. There was a constant background murmur of vox chatter, cursor chimes and machine language.

Commander Velosade was in charge here. He snapped to attention as the throne rotated in and called out, 'Captain on the strategium.' Everyone made formal salute.

'At ease and continue,' said Esquine. 'Display the warp perturbation, if you will.'

Velosade cracked his fingers, and a dimple of mauve light appeared in the lower hemisphere of the actuality globe.

'Reduce scale and give me tactical,' said Esquine.

The actuality sphere flickered, dissolved and reformed, slightly wider and sparer in detail. Valdeemer recognised immediately they were looking at a 3D verisim of the entire inner system. There, the bright fuzz of the local star, there Herodor, and the other four inner planets, the bright band of the asteroid belt. The mauve dimple lay outside this inner group, as far from Herodor as Herodor was from its star.

'Overlay tactical!' Velosade ordered.

A geometric grid graphic flowed into the sphere, graphing its dimensions, and the disposition of Esquine's vessels – along with the myriad pilgrim and merchant ships – appeared as slowly drifting, numbered light-points.

'Astropathicae report parameters verified. Perturbation reads at warp modulus eleven two nine nine seven, nine AU out. Tracking cogents. Concordance estimated at ninety-three minutes. Awaiting confirmation.'

Velosade turned and looked at the fleet captain. 'Orders, sir?'

'Remain as they were, commander. Warmaster Macaroth has charged us to exercise extreme caution. Move a frigate up in front of the modulus point, fighter screens up. They can greet arriving friends... or deny arriving enemies. The remainder of the fleet stays as vanguard.'

A flutter of Esquine's fingers made cursor points appear on the glowing sphere. Valdeemer knew the commander was using the word 'fleet' ironically. An officer of Esquine's rank – and a ship like the *Omnia Vincit* – could normally expect to have a considerable attendant fleet in support. However, Esquine's battleship, with only two frigates in attendance, had been sent to carry Lord General Lugo to Herodor by the Warmaster as a mark of special respect, and the recently arrived Tanith had brought only one frigate and one heavy cruiser as escort vessels. Three frigates, a cruiser, a ship of the line, and fleet tender vessels – not too shabby as far as a flotilla detail went, but badly under strength in terms of fleet engagements.

'Inform the surface,' Esquine continued, 'and alert the civilian traffic that there is a manoeuvre, code magenta, and that we expect their cooperation and their careful station-keeping for its duration.'

Velosade nodded, and started growling orders. All the strategium crew began working, many of them suddenly speaking loudly and urgently into their vox-links.

'Your choice of frigate, sir?' called Velosade.

'The *Navarre*,' replied Esquine without hesitation.

'The *Navarre* is occupied, sir,' Veldeemer said suddenly and winced at the sharp look the commander gave him for speaking out of turn.

'Let him talk, Velosade,' said the fleet captain. 'Occupied how, ensign?'

'A mercantile mass conveyance in difficulties, sir. The *Navarre* signaled it was moving to assist.'

'Let them carry on,' said the fleet captain. 'Charge the *Berengaria* instead.'

'Sir,' affirmed Velosade.

'Well appreciated, ensign,' said the fleet captain softly to Valdeemer. 'A slight diversion I hadn't accounted. You read sphere tactics well.'

'I like to stay on top of things, sir.'

'Keep it up,' said Esquine.

Valdeemer felt a flush of pride run through him.

ITS VAST ENGINES cycling up to one tenth power, the frigate *Berengaria* moved away from Herodor, prowling forward into the interplanetary gulf. Though only classified as a light cruiser, it was massive by any standards of measure: a long, fortified, angular vessel, its barbed hull dull green. Frigates of the *Berengaria's* pattern were fast and well-armed, the blade-edge of any serious Navy group.

'We have broken orbit and are advancing to the advised modulus,' Captain Sodak said quietly, standing in the actuality sphere of the *Berengaria's* bridge.

'Signal sent and noted by fleet command, sir,' an ensign replied.

'Flight decks?'

'Fighter screen reports ready aye.'

'So noted. Cycle up the launch ramps.'

'Aye, captain.'

Sodak looked at the warp dimple in the depths of the impressed-light sphere in front of him. It was getting larger and darker.

'Order is launch.'

'Order is launch, aye!'

TINY SPECKS OF light darted from the flanks of the *Berengaria*. The specks raced ahead of the massive warship, catching the backscattered light of the distant sun as they fanned out into a cloud like dust-flies at twilight.

They were Lightning-pattern fighters, swift and deadly one-man craft, spat out of the frigate's launch decks by mag-catapult. In wide formation, they spread out before their mighty parent craft.

Squadron Leader Shumlen, a thrice-decorated ace and flight commander of the *Berengaria's* fighter wing, dropped his heads-up scope into place and gunned his Lightning forward into the apex point of the fighter screen. Despite the physical rush of launch and the metabolic rush of the prospect of combat, Shumlen's vitals-reader showed that his cardiac rate was astonishingly level and calm.

'Keep it spread,' he said unhurriedly over his vox-comm.

'Concordance in forty-two minutes and counting,' vox-link from the frigate reported.

THE NAVARRE SHIVERED as its docking clamps secured the mass conveyance *Troubadour*. On the frigate's bridge, alert sirens rang and hazard lights flashed.

Kreff cancelled them with a wave of his wand. He took the vox-horn from a waiting servitor.

'Open the hatches. Boarding parties to ready. Transfer the wounded out. Medicae, stand by to receive injured.'

'Sir?'

'What is it?' Kreff snapped impatiently.

'That heat source sir, on the *Troubadour*...' The aide looked confused. 'It's gone.'

'Gone?'

'Faded, sir. I guess they could have got the fire under control...'

Kreff looked at Zebbs.

'Go!' he said, and the soldier was running to the bridge exit.

'Shall I alert the captain?' asked the aide.

'No!' Kreff halted. 'Yes, yes. Wake him.'

A DETAIL OF Navy armsmen was waiting for Zebbs in the prep-chamber of the mid-starboard air-gate. The colonel was pulling on his armour-jacket as he entered. The detail stood to attention, bulky in their emerald green armour suits, their combat shotcannons held ready, their faces hidden behind tinted visors.

'Safeties, but let's go careful!' he said, taking his own shotgun from his number two.

He racked the grip of his powerful weapon and stepped to the gate.

'Open up mid-two!' he shouted.

The hatch ground open. There was no one on the other side. No sirens, no alarms, no smell of fire or scenes of panic.

Zebbs stepped through. His armsmen hurried in after him, spreading out.

The hallway was dark, and it smelled of stale air as if the scrubbers were malfunctioning. Zebbs wasn't surprised. This was an old ship, poorly maintained. It was a wonder it had ever made a warp-transition.

'Floor's wet, sir,' popped one of his men over the inert vox.

'Coolant leak,' said another, his voice punctuated by the crackle of the link.

'You think?' said Zebbs, looking down. The deck was awash, about two centimetres deep in dark liquid. It looked for all the world like–

There was a little splash as something landed in the liquid and rolled towards them. It ended up between Zebbs and his point man. They both looked down at it.

It was a grenade.

'Shit,' was all Zebbs had time to say.

'ZEBBS? ZEBBS? COLONEL, report!' Kreff yelled into the vox horn. He'd just heard a loud and suddenly cut-off roar over the channel that had wiped signals out. Now there was only a dull murmur of static.

'Clean it up!' Kreff shouted at his aides. 'I want Zebbs on the link now!'

They rushed to obey. A second later, from a different vox source, they tuned in the sounds of shouting. Confused, demented shouting. And the smack of gunfire.

Kreff lowered the vox-horn in dismay.

'Sever the dock-clamps! Break us off!'

'Clamps are locked out, sir!'

'What? What?'

'Docking clamps one through nine are locked out, sir,' said his aide.

'Holy Throne, no!'

'Is there a problem, Kreff?'

Kreff turned to see Captain Wysmark striding towards him across the bridge.

'We've... we've been boarded, sir,' he said.

Wysmark, tall and saturnine in his green dress uniform, seemed unflustered. He took the vox-horn from Kreff's trembling hands and spoke into it.

'Armsmen to all active airgates. On the double. Repel boarders. Repeat, repel boarders.'

SPACE BUCKLED. SPACE shimmered, and tore. Out of the splitting dark fabric, the inscrutable light of warp space flashed and seared.

Out of the breach, ships thundered into view.

They came fast at first, as if flung out of the Chaotic reality, and then slid down to a more dignified drift. Imperial ships. Three Munitorum conveyances, then a Navy frigate, then four more heavy transporters.

'Open formation,' Shumlen ordered. 'They're friendlies. Repeat, they are friendlies.'

The fighter screen broke around him, spreading wide and zipping like tiny silver reef fish along the lengths of the ponderous new arrivals. The vox-channels were suddenly busy with hailing signals.

'Request permission to return to carrier decks,' Shumlen voxed.

'THE FRIGATE *Glory of Cadia* sends greetings and compliments,' Sodak's ensign reported.

'Respond as per form, ensign.'

'The perturbation is not dissipating, captain,' called a tech-priest.

Sodak would have been surprised if it had. According to the watch briefing, they were expecting something in the order of sixteen ships, and the actuality sphere showed only eight newcomer vessels. A fleet disposition emerging from warp space often came through in several waves.

'Instruct the *Glory of Cadia* to escort its charges into Herodor high anchor. Inform fleet command that we will remain on station to await the next wave.'

'Yes sir.'

'Fighter screen, captain?' asked the flight controller from his raised, glasteel-bubbled console station.

'Keep them aloft,' replied Sodak. He was a cautious man. Without that caution, he'd never have lived long enough to become a warship's commander.

A CREW-SERVITOR, short and broad with circuitry glinting across its black metalwork, turned from its station and handed Valdeemer a data-slate. The ensign immediately hurried it across to the fleet captain's throne. Esquine was watching the fleet arrivals at the concordance point.

'Distress report, sir,' said Valdeemer anxiously. 'The *Navarre*.'

'Show me,' said Esquine softly.

'They are under internal attack,' said Valdeemer, handing the slate to one of the fleet captain's grasping servo limbs. 'Captain Wysmark reports intruder hostiles attempting to board from the merchant ship.'

'Signal Wysmark. Ask him if he requires assistance.'

HARD ROUNDS WHINED down the companionway and rattled off the metal partitioning, causing the armsmen in Sublieutenant Epsin's team to duck for cover. Something was wrong with the deck lights. Only the frosty green auxilary lighting panels were illuminated and, from the smell of the air, the circulators were out or dying too.

There was a buzzing noise too, very faint, that came and went. Cabling fritzing out, Epsin thought.

Another volley of shots. Epsin saw the deformed slugs bounce onto the deck plating and roll. They looked like the crushed butts of lho-sticks.

It was sweep-fire. Random auto-bursts fired around corners and down blind halls to clear a path.

'Hold fire,' Epsin whispered. 'Let 'em think the way's clean...'

Hunched down along the companionway behind bulkhead stanchions, his men shifted uneasily, their shotcannons raised ready.

The enemy appeared. Three... then four, five... man-shadows hefting short-pattern autoguns, hurrying down the hallway ahead.

'Repel,' Epsin whispered.

His cannon boomed, barking out a bright white flash in the dim green light. Other shotcannons around him did the same. The shadows ahead collapsed, hurled back violently by the heavy firepower. Acrid smoke filled the air and, without the circulators in operation, stayed there.

'Forward!' Epsin ordered. The armsmen party hurried ahead, hugging the metal walls of the companionway. Almost immediately, more hostiles appeared around the junction turn ahead, rattling auto-fire in their direction. Epsin's pointman let out a cry and slumped sideways against the wall. The man behind him recoiled, bent double and collapsed on his face.

'Bastards!' Epsin yelled. 'For the Emperor! For the *Navarre*!' The shotcannon bucked in his hands as he blasted with it. His team had almost fought its way to the intersection leading down to the nearest airgate.

It was just then, above the roaring gunfire, Epsin heard the buzzing again.

'THE FLEET CAPTAIN enquires if we require assistance, sir,' said Kreff.

Captain Wysmark looked up from the situations monitor at his exec. 'What do you think, Kreff?'

'I think we're in for a hell of a dirty fight along the airgates, sir. But I hardly think the fleet captain wants to lose another fifth of his flotilla to a boarding action when we're at magenta stand-by awaiting arrivals. We can manage. The *Navarre's* armsmen are the best in the fleet.'

Wysmark smiled slightly. 'My reading exactly. Signal the *Omnia Vincit* so. We'll have this contained in another fifteen minutes.'

Kreff turned smartly and instructed the signals officer. He turned back to his captain's side.

'What was that?' Wysmark asked.

'Sir?'

'That buzzing. Did you not hear it, Kreff?'

'No sir.'

Wysmark shook his head and returned his attention to the monitor. 'This is the price we pay for wet-nursing the pilgrim craft.'

'Sir?'

'A mass of unregistered, unregulated traffic, filling orbit, packed with citizens it's our duty to protect. The odds were high there'd be infiltrators and heretics amongst them. We're obliged to help a ship in distress, even if it turns out to be a trap. All part of the job, Kreff.'

'I was wondering, sir...'

'What?'

'Why now, sir? If there are heretics aboard the *Troubadour*, then they've been here in orbit for three days. Why choose this moment to act?'

'I was thinking that myself. Coincidence that we're at magenta standby and thus stretched?'

'There's no such think as coincidence, captain.'

Wysmark nodded. 'Get me a verisim link to the fleet captain.'

'INCOMING VERISIM!' VELOSADE called. 'Captain Wysmark of the *Navarre*.'

'Display,' said Esquine.

A half-size holoform image of Wysmark appeared like a pale red phantom in front of the fleet captain's throne, projected up from the holo-emitters in the strategium's decking.

'Wysmark?'

'I wanted to advise extreme caution, fleet captain,' Wysmark's voice crackled over the vox-relay. 'The boarding action we are enduring would seem pointless unless it is part of a larger scheme.'

'The enemies of mankind are not famed for their tactical brilliance,' said Esquine.

There was a slight time-lag delay before Wysmark's image nodded and smiled at the fleet captain's remark. 'Agreed, sir. But I fear this is a strategy to take the *Navarre* out of useful disposition.'

'I see.'

'I simply wished to advise caution.'

'So noted. Thank you, Wysmark.'

The holoform faded. Esquine fixed Velosade with his hard, pale eyes. 'Wysmark is a sound commander not given to over reaction. Arm the main batteries, captain.'

EPSIN PLUNGED THROUGH the thick smoke pluming down the air-gate's entry deck. The walls were marred with shot damage, and several bodies lay on the deck. Rough, dirty men in drab red armour, their faces covered in black iron masks.

More than simple heretics, Epsin thought.

He waved his men up. Along the side hallway that led to the other gate entries, he heard sporadic gunfire.

And the buzzing again, that damn buzzing. Like an insect in a jar.

Epsin saw a figure in front of him, through the smoke. A tall figure...

No, three figures. One tall man, cloaked in pilgrim green and hooded, clutching two smaller figures to his sides with thick, powerful arms that were laced with tattoos. The smaller figures were dressed in rags, shivering and clinging to the man in green like frightened children. They turned their faces towards him, and Epsin gasped as he beheld their twisted, runtish, eyeless visages.

In unison, they opened their mouths, and the buzzing grew much louder, as if the lid had come off the jar and freed the insect. Epsin coughed and staggered, shaking his head frantically to get rid of the buzz.

He knew what this was. He tried to adjust his headset to send a warning to the captain.

The armsman beside him, a stalwart ship-trooper who had been in Epsin's team for nine years, turned slowly. His mouth was slack, and blood ran copiously from his nose and tear-ducts.

He brought his shotcannon up and blew Epsin's head off.

'CONCORDANCE NOW IN two minutes,' the vox-link rasped.

'Thank you, *Berengaria*,' responded Shumlen, tilting slightly in the tight embrace of his grav-seat as he brought the Lightning round in a tight turn. 'Flight leader to screen elements, form on me for a second pass. More traffic inbound.'

The pilots of the squadron chattered back in confirmation and the Lightning flight, like a flock of racing birds, turned as one and made course towards the calculated real-space entry point about seven hundred and fifty kilometres ahead.

There was nothing to see. The starfield at this speed was a striated blur, and the warp perturbation that preceded a re-entry was visible only on instruments.

Shumlen checked his scope, and saw the swirling dimple of colour on the low-res screen swell and flutter. 'Arm weapons,' he said.

His pulse was barely idling.

FOR THE SECOND time in less than an hour, space tore open. The reality fissure leapt and crackled like a luminous cephalopod, lashing tendrils of warp energy into real space that twisted out, fizzled and faded. Non-baryonic light flared brilliantly through the tear, backlighting the arriving ships. Monumental silhouettes, they were shot forward into real space.

They did not slow down. They were moving at cruise speed. Attack speed.

Shumlen blinked. The arriving ships were just dots against the glare-spot ahead of his squadron, but his pattern recognition systems began to hoot and warble.

'Hostiles, hostiles, hostiles,' he said, matter-of-factly. 'We have hostile vessels in system and advancing. Flight leader to screen elements... accelerate to attack velocity.'

'HOSTILES REPORTED!' THE ensign sang out, a tremor in his voice.

'Battle stations,' said Sodak. The sirens began to wail. 'Shields up. Arm batteries. Power to main lances.'

'Shields aye!'

'Fighters are engaging,' said the flight controller.

Sodak gazed at the flickering images on the actuality sphere. 'Increase magnification. Get me a clearer picture.' At the current resolution, the holographic display was overlaying tag cursors and disposition icons. Code numbers were jumping and blinking.

'Tenfold mag aye!' said the ensign.

The tactical image enlarged rapidly. It looked like three enemy ships, possibly four, but the overlay icon of the fighter screen was making it hard to read the details.

'Take out the fighter icon,' snapped Sodak, and an aide cancelled the overlay image of the *Berengaria's* attack squadron.

Four ships. One of them very large. And they were moving. Point seven five light at least, cutting straight towards Herodor.

'Enginarium,' said Sodak. 'Flank speed, please. Reactor output to ninety per cent. Last ready call for weapons.'

'Weapons aye. All green.'

'Firing solutions, all batteries and lances. Target the big one.'

'Aye sir.'

'HOSTILES, SIR,' SAID Velosade. 'Four marks. We believe three cruisers and a capital ship.'

'Hold position.'

'*Berengaria* is engaging.'

'Hold position,' Esquine repeated.

'Signal from the *Glory of Cadia*, sir,' Valdeemer called out. 'Requesting permission to come about in support of the *Berengaria*.'

'Denied. I want them here, in line with us. Get that order confirmed.'

'Yes, fleet captain.'

'Status?' Esquine asked.

'*Solstice* is standing by. *Laudate Divinitus* is standing by. They both report battle readiness.'

'The *Navarre*?'

'Still locked in the boarding fight, sir.'

Esquine fell silent. Around him, above the machine-code chatter of the strategium, he could hear the ship's priesthood chanting their blessings to secure victory in combat. The Imperial creed was being broadcast over the intercom system.

'Battle stations,' said Esquine softly. Bright red lamps began to cycle and flash and a moaning alarm siren started to sound. Esquine felt a shiver run through him as the neuro-plugs linking him to the ship's systems delivered the multiple responses of an Imperial battleship rising to full combat mode. Esquine's heart pounded as the reactors came to full power, his fingers twitched as the weapon batteries made ready to fire, his flesh tingled as the shields rose. He closed his eyes and experienced a rushing sense of expanded vision as power was diverted from non-essential systems to boost the main sensor cone.

He looked, and saw the enemy bearing down.

* * *

THE VOID WAS incandescent with rippling fireballs and traceries of light. Shumlen gunned in under the rake of the enemy's forward anti-ship batteries and headed under the belly of the main vessel.

It was huge, easily the size of the *Omnia Vincit*, a Chaos battleship, its black hull so covered with turret clusters and shield pods it looked diseased and blistered. Three Chaos cruisers ran with it, fearsomely lithe warships with serrated hulls. Two were decked in red and gold, the third black with its ribbed superstructure painted white.

The *Berengaria's* fighter screen had met the ships head on, so as to minimise the angles of fire available to the enemy gunners, but even so Shumlen had already lost about thirty ships to the massive anti-fighter barrage. Every pilot knew the drill. Once they were on the enemy, it was individual action. There was no hope of formation tactics in a fight zone this confused.

Shumlen hugged the enemy hull as close as he dared. He loosed one underwing missile, but was already well past by the time it detonated and he was unable to tell what surface damage he might have inflicted.

A Lightning tumbled past in front of him, causing him to veer as his collision warning system blared briefly. The Lightning was coming apart, shredding as it fell like a comet towards the hulking surface of the battleship's hull.

Pulse lasers chased Shumlen, stitching the darkness with phosphorescent bolts. He banked hard left, saw a raised missile turret ahead, and fired his second missile. The blast dazzled him and his whole ship shook violently as he flew out of the blastwash.

A Lightning slid close to him, almost in formation, and then exploded as pulse fire from the hull found it. Another two shot over the top of him and began strafing runs along the underhull. Shumlen lost sight of them in the vivid firestorm.

Shumlen half-heard a transmission on the vox.

'Repeat, repeat,' he said. His pulse was just beginning to lift.

'Bats, bats, bats!' one of his wingmen repeated.

The enemy had got its fighter screen launched.

FLICKERING WITH TWINKLING flashes of light from the small-ship fight racing around their hulls, the Chaos vessels bore on.

'Archive sweep results, captain,' said Persson, Sodak's tactical officer.

Sodak looked over the data. Two of the enemy cruisers were positively identified: the *Cicatrice*, with its white-ribbed superstructure, and the *Revenant*, its red hull laced with gold. The third cruiser was either the *Harm's Way* or the *Suture*. The identity of the main battleship was vague, for such giants were much more seldom seen, but Persson's pattern recognition program suggested the monster was the *Incarnadine*, an ancient, infamous craft.

'Master of ordnance? Have we firing solutions?'

'Solutions and range, captain,' replied Adept Yarden.

'Fire!' snarled Sodak.

The deck rocked beneath him slightly. Streaks of light from the lances and main batteries spat into the darkness.

'Main batteries have fired. Lances have fired. Torpedoes are running.'

On the augur-scope, blips of light crackled around the dark bulk of the approaching *Incarnadine*.

'Damage?'

'Their shields have held, captain,' said the master of ordnance.

'Second cycle, fire!'

Berengaria trembled again.

'Third cycle, fire!'

'Torpedoes have reached target, captain.'

'Damage... give me something, Yarden!'

The master of ordnance glanced over at the captain from his position at the fire control station.

'I'm sorry, sir. Nothing.'

'The *Revenant* is breaking formation, captain!'

Sodak turned his attention to the actuality sphere. One of the enemy cruisers was accelerating away from the battle group and advancing ahead of it.

'Engaging us?' asked an ensign.

'No,' said Sodak. 'They're going for the convoy.' The *Revenant's* course was vectoring it in after the slow moving Munitorum ships that had come out of the warp.

'Maintain course. All forward batteries and lances to sustain firing cycles at the primary target. Torpedoes too, if you please. As the *Revenant* passes us and presents, I want sustained fire on it from the flank batteries.'

'Aye, captain,' replied Yarden, swiftly moving to task his gunnery officers and their servitor crews.

The *Revenant,* swooping in like an interstellar predator, seemed to fine-tune its path as it passed the *Berengaria* as if to taunt Sodak. Its main weapons blasting forward, the *Berengaria* lit up its port side with fierce fire from its flank batteries. The *Revenant* made a desultory return of fire from its own side armaments as it thundered past.

'We hit them sir. Minor hull damage. Not enough to slow them.'

'Us?'

'Shields held.'

'Signal the fleet captain and verify his instructions. Does he want us to maintain assault?'

The bridge suddenly lurched hard, and damage klaxons beeped wildly.

'The *Incarnadine* has begun firing on us, sir. Minor shield damage.'

The ensign had barely finished when the ship shook again. Several crew-men were thrown off their feet, and the wail of the klaxons got louder.

Sodak could see from the main console that they'd been hit hard on the upper hull. Moderate damage, hull punctures, interdeck fires...

'Auxiliary power to the shields!' he cried.

The *Berengaria* yawed as it was struck again. And again.

AT THE HIGH anchor point above Herodor, the *Glory of Cadia* rumbled in well ahead of the reinforcement convoy it had been escorting. As per Esquine's firm orders, it came about in a wide arc and took up station in battle formation with the massive *Omnia Vincit* and its smaller sisters the *Solstice* and the heavy cruiser *Laudate Divinitus*. Behind and below them, the mass of pilgrim ships formed a wide scatter of small, vulnerable targets, huddled close to the upper atmospheric reaches of the cold planet. Despite Esquine's command edicts, some of this motley host had begun to break orbit and flee, a few directly out into interplanetary space, chasing off towards Herodor's star and the further reaches of the system. Others were moving to geo-sync orbits behind Herodor, hoping to keep the planet between them and the terrifying attackers.

At a twitch of Esquine's fingers, an aft lance battery on the mighty *Omnia Vincit* fired, and crippled the merchantman *Somnambulist* as it attempted to break anchor.

That was all the time and firepower the fleet captain intended to waste. 'Signal the civilian fleet again, Velosade. We will punish any further infringement of the edict in a similar fashion. I will not have non-military vessels confusing the issue with unauthorised movement. Tell them any such action will force us to suspect they harbour heretic agents and that we will fire on them accordingly.'

'Sir!'

'The *Berengaria's* in trouble, sir,' whispered Valdeemer.

'I see that plainly, ensign. We will hold position. If we move to assist them, we will lose our formation initiative. Sodak knows when to fight and when to break and run.'

Valdeemer frowned. He knew Sodak's orders had been an unequivocal instruction to engage. There had been no discretionary option for flight.

'Should I inform him of such, sir?' asked Valdeemer.

'No,' said the fleet captain.

HE HAD FIRE on nine decks, a reactor crippled and shields close to failure. There was no longer enough power for the lances.

'Torpedoes!' Sodak ordered.

'Torpedoes aye!' cried Yarden.

'Cancel some of these damn alarms,' Sodak added. The air was ringing with overlapping klaxons. He could smell acrid smoke. Smoke gathering in the circulator system, too thick and dense to be expunged by the air scrubbers.

The massive enemy warship was right on them now, so close Sodak could actually see it as a dot through the glasteel windows of the bridge.

'Keep us true! Keep us face on!' he shouted at the helm officers. The frigate's strongest hull armour was concentrated around the prow. He didn't want to expose the flanks. Moreover, he wanted to maintain as small a target as possible.

'Aye, sir!'

'We're yawing, helm!'

'Attitude control is damaged, captain. We're trying to compensate...'

The *Incarnadine* fired on them again. Sodak didn't have time to even register the salvo on the augur scope.

The *Berengaria* pitched wildly. Parts of the upper hull splintered away in a spray of micro-fragments. Power failed for a few seconds on the bridge as an explosion tore across the forward helm position, incinerating three helm officers, five servitors and Tactical Officer Persson.

Yarden was still at his post, blood gushing from a shrapnel wound in his chest. Blood bubbled at his lips as he tried to call out a situation report, his dripping hands fumbling with the fire control console.

Sodak knew the situation, even though Yarden couldn't report, even though the actuality sphere had failed and the augur-scopes were dead. They were mortally wounded and helm-less, drifting now under the momentum of impact to present their starboard side to the archenemy monsters.

'Signal the *Omnia Vincit*,' Sodak cried. 'Signal begins... The Emperor protects–'

A salvo of torpedoes from the *Harm's Way* hit the *Berengaria* amidships, followed a scant moment later by a lance strike from the *Incarnadine*. The *Berengaria* seemed to blink and twitch for a second as plasma fire coiled and rippled like lava along its broken flank.

And then it vaporised in a shockwave of expanding white light.

IN THE OMNIA VINCIT's strategium, Valdeemer almost didn't notice the death flare of the *Berengaria*. He was staring at the actuality sphere with horrid fascination as the enemy frigate the *Revenant* powered in after the desperate relief convoy. The indicator icons of two mass transports flickered and died. The others tried to break and evade, but the archenemy killer was directly astern.

'Commence formation advance,' Esquine called. 'Battle engagement pattern. Signal Wysmark and tell him to stop wasting time. We need the *Navarre* now.'

In a wide, firm line, the four Imperial warships prowled forward from high anchor, shields raised, to meet and deny the enemy assault.

SEVEN
PLANET FALL

'Nine are coming.'

— Message written in Soric's hand

Gaunt had arrived half asleep at the hastily called meeting just before dawn. After the night's curious events, he'd tried to nap for a few hours, only to be woken by Beltayn in the middle of the afternoon.

'The lord general wants to see you, sir,' Beltayn said.

Lugo and his house staff had occupied a mansion on the ninety-seventh level of Old Hive. It was a place of faded grandeur. The walls and high ceilings were cased in shiny black ebonite inlaid with matt detailing in arthrocite, and the floor was paved with pink, earth-fired tiles throughout. On every fourth wall panel in the entry hall, an electrolamp was set in a brass wall sconce, and long webs of glinting steel-lace hung as drapes at each arched doorway.

It wasn't made clear to Gaunt whose palace-home this was, or where they had gone to make way for Lugo.

To be honest, he wasn't thinking much of that. He was bleary headed as the postern sentries let him in and showed him the way down two long hallways and up a flight of brick steps to the room where Lugo was waiting.

Gaunt had been expecting some kind of formal staff summit, and was surprised to find Lugo alone except for Kaldenbach.

The room was cold – the whole mansion was cold – as if the ancient heating pipes and hypercausts of the crumbling Old Hive were weak and inefficient at this high level. Lugo sat in a suspensor chair, dressed in a thick houserobe over his uniform shirt and breeches. His jacket and cap lay on a tall wooden dressing stand beside him.

He was sipping caffeine from a porcelain cup. A portable thermal heater was standing on the floor, warming his booted feet.

The room had tall, lancet windows of touched, coloured glass in two walls, and a set of ornate glass doors in the third that appeared, through the veil of a steel-lace drape, to give access out onto some kind of balcony or roof terrace. Kaldenbach stood beside these doors, arms folded, looking either stubborn or threatening. Gaunt wasn't quite sure what the man was shooting for. Threatening, he guessed.

'Sir.'

'Come in, Gaunt. A hot drink?'

'Thank you, no, sir.'

Kaldenbach, who had started to move at Lugo's offer, continued anyway even when it was refused, and helped himself to a cup from a silver vacuum-jug that stood on a dresser against the wall.

'I apologise for the early call,' Lugo said, almost cordially. 'I wish to speak with you about the Beati.'

'About the Beati...'

'About what we should do.'

'In what respect, sir?'

Lugo cleared his throat delicately and took another sip. 'I have so far made myself and my resources available to the Beati. To, shall I say, the whim of the Beati. Her sanctified mind perceives the cosmos in a way ours do not, so I trust her judgment, even if it might seem... wayward.'

Gaunt smiled slightly.

'At her urgings, we decamped here to this... place of insignificance. I suggested that her person might be of greater use alongside the Warmaster at the front, but no. She was very polite, as you might expect, but she refused the idea. Herodor was what she insisted on, and to Herodor I escorted her.'

'We have spoken of this before, sir,' said Gaunt. 'You hoped to enlist my aid in convincing her to change her mind. Indeed, you applied pressure on my commissar to get me to do just that.'

Lugo shrugged as if this was trifling. 'We are past such shadow play now, Gaunt. The Beati must go to Morlond. She must quit this place and go directly to Morlond. I'm not asking for your help. I'm ordering that you give it.'

'I see,' said Gaunt.

'Come, come,' said Lugo, smiling. 'We're all friends here, Ibram. Tell me your thoughts.'

'You want to know what I think?' Gaunt asked.

'The lord general was quite clear,' said Kaldenbach sharply.

Gaunt glanced at him, and Kaldenbach looked down. 'Very well,' said Gaunt. 'I think you knew the truth all along. From the moment on Hagia when Sanian first became known to you. You were completely aware that she was a fake... a troubled, delusional girl who believed she was the incarnation of Sabbat and played the part reasonably well. You saw the currency in this, and backed her claim, for the good of Imperial morale... and to advance your own interests.'

'You insult the lord general with such slander–' Kaldenbach started. Lugo held up a hand smartly.

'Allow Gaunt to talk or leave the room, colonel.'

'I'm sorry if I'm too honest, sir,' said Gaunt. 'You did say the time for shadow play was over.'

Lugo nodded, and gestured for Gaunt to continue.

'You saw the best way to control her was to let her have her way for a while. Let her make decisions, grow into the role with confidence. A pilgrimage here... well, that sounds like the sort of inexplicable but lofty thing a reincarnated saint would do. To cleanse herself before the coming war. You'd indulge her for a few months, working on her all the while, and then make the journey to the front seem like her own idea. You'd join the Warmaster, no doubt inspiring his forces to a conclusive victory, and your eminence would be assured. What were you hoping for? A sector governorship? Host command? Higher than that?'

Lugo retained his smile, but there was a glaze of bitter ice in it. Gaunt knew he had hit the mark.

'And everything was going so well... apart from a few unpredicted inconveniences like the fact she requested the Tanith as bodyguards. That must have rankled, having me arrive and get in the way. But nothing you couldn't handle. Your plan was still intact. Until last night.'

'Last night?' echoed Lugo.

'Last night, lord general. When your little pawn did something you weren't expecting. When Sanian – and don't ask me to explain this, for it defies rational explanation – when Sanian became the real thing after all. She is the Beati, she is truly everything she believed herself to be, everything you pretended she was. A miraculous being in the strictest sense of the term. And that changed things. You have no idea what to do. You can't manipulate her any more. She is suddenly beyond your powers of reason and control, beyond your basic understanding. You're afraid. You're out of your depth. And your plan is coming apart at the seams.'

Lugo sucked his teeth thoughtfully, then got to his feet, shed his houserobe and started to put on his dress jacket. Kaldenbach started forward like a valet to hold the garment for him.

'A gripping piece of speculation, Ibram,' said the lord general, 'and quite convincing in its own way. Thank you for being so open.'

He turned to Gaunt, buttoning up the jacket's frogging. 'Utterly specious, of course. I have known the Saint to be genuine from the very start, and have supported her in that light. Nothing has changed. She has always been a miraculous figure to me. I bless the God-Emperor of mankind for placing me in this role of trust.'

'Just so,' said Kaldenbach.

'Just so indeed,' said Gaunt with a light shrug. 'As I said before, it doesn't matter what I think anyway. The important thing is that you realise I agree with you. Fake or real, the Beati should be with the Warmaster on Morlond. For the good of the Imperium, the Sabbat Worlds, the entire Crusade. I'm not going to fight you over that. I'll do everything I can to help persuade her. I don't, of course, know if I have any influence over her at all. But I will try.'

Lugo put on his cap, looked Gaunt in the eyes, and then stretched out his hand. Gaunt, surprised, shook it.

'Thank you, Ibram,' Lugo said. 'I knew you were a team player.'

'One last thing you should know, sir,' Gaunt added as their hands parted.

'What?'

'I am pretty sure this event we are part of, this incarnation, this manifestation... I'm pretty sure it is more significant than we realise. Space and time and... fate, if you will... are all coming together, and synchronising. Even before Sanian truly manifested as the Beati last night, the ripples of that happening were spreading through this sector and beyond. Signs, portents, auguries. You've heard them all, and put them down to hysteria amongst the faithful, I'm sure. But they are more than that. Every psyker in the sector – ours and theirs – must have felt as much. The cosmos is turning for a purpose, lord general, and this is one of those rare occasions when we can hear its machinery whirring and see its handiwork.'

'You speak like a prophet, Gaunt!'

'No prophet me... but still. I knew about Herodor long before I was summoned here. I was told to expect the Saint. My troopers have told me numberless stories from the pilgrim camps of men and women who share that supernatural inkling. Not the fanatics, not the stylites and the flagellants and the mystics who jump at any rumour. You'd be amazed how many normal, regular people there are out there. People who have thrown their lives and homes away to make the journey here because they simply, indelibly knew something.'

'Are you trying to scare me, Gaunt?' Lugo said with a falsely hearty chuckle.

'No, sir. But a healthy sense of fear would not be amiss. We stand in a time of wonder, sir. There is no telling what it might bring, but it will be momentous.'

Gaunt heard voices and footsteps in the hallway outside the room, but ignored them. 'Let us hope,' he said directly, 'that we are witnessing the end of the Crusade. Victory in the Sabbat Worlds, the archenemy put to fire and flight. With the Beati at Morlond–'

'I will not go to Morlond,' said a voice from behind him.

Gaunt turned. Sabbat stood in the doorway of the chamber, one hand raised to hold back the steel-lace drapes. She was wearing simple, grey combat fatigues and heavy black troop boots. Her skin was deathly pale and her eyes showed signs of upset and reproach.

'Beati,' said Gaunt, bowing his head. Lugo and Kaldenbach did likewise.

'I will not go to Morlond,' she repeated, stepping into the room and letting the steel-lace fall back into place. Through its patterned folds, Gaunt could see the household troopers hovering outside, too scared to come in after her.

'There is work to be accomplished here,' she said. 'Vital work. That is my purpose. Morlond can wait, or be tamed without me.'

'Lady, we–' Gaunt began.

Sabbat placed a hand gently on his arm and he fell silent, unable to speak.

'Herodor is the key, Ibram. The warp has shown this. I will not leave until this work is done.'

'How…' Lugo began. 'How can we serve you, lady?'

'I was looking for Ibram. It's time. They're coming, and I am afraid. I was looking for my protector. My honour guard.'

'The Tanith?' Gaunt whispered.

'You and the Tanith. I need you now.'

'What do you mean, "it's time"?' Gaunt asked.

She took him by the hand and led him over to the glass doors, which she opened with a press of her fingers. They went through, out onto the roof terrace. Lugo and Kaldenbach followed.

The terrace was a semi-circle of rockcrete jutting like a shelf from the steep roof levels of the Old Hive spire. A glasteel dome shielded them from the arctic atmosphere. The great sprawl of the Civitas Beati spread out below them, far below, a brown maze of angular shadows. The massive shape of the second hive tower rose up nearby, almost to their level, a slabby silhouette against the just rising sun.

Around the edge of the terrace were terracotta planters. The roses and sambluscus planted in them had withered and died into gnarled twigs, untended, but they reminded Gaunt of Lord Chass's roof garden in the upper Spine of Vervunhive.

Gaunt felt a twinge of fear and melancholy. But for a metal flower from that garden, he would have died on Verghast.

There were no flowers here.

Sabbat pointed up at the sky. It was thin blue, creased by bars of lustrous yellow and furrows of cloud in the east. The last stars were still visible.

'They are coming,' she said again. 'They are here. That's why I will not go to Morlond. I can't go anywhere now.'

Gaunt stared up at the part of the sky her slender fingers had indicated.

'What do you–'

A flash. For a moment. A little spark high up among the stars. Then another. Like impossible lightning, up in space.

'What does she mean?' Lugo hissed to Gaunt, shivering in the unheated air of the high garden.

'Ship to ship fire. The fleet has engaged. A planetary assault has begun.'

'Surely not,' said Kaldenbach. 'We would have heard…'

'It's only just started,' said Gaunt. 'Circulate orders, sir. Prepare for ground assault.'

'Oh, premature!' Kaldenbach scoffed. 'Fleet Captain Esquine has our interests protected. Four ships of the line… the *Omnia Vincit* alone could–'

Gaunt ignored him. 'Lady?'

'They're here, Ibram. Now I need you. You will protect me, won't you? You and your Ghosts? You will protect me until the work is done here?'

'You have my word, lady.'

A junior officer in the uniform of Lugo's life company hurried onto the terrace behind them, clutching a data-slate.

'Lord general! A signal from the fleet captain, sir. He's engaged with an incoming hostile battle group, sir and–'

Lugo took the slate from him abruptly. 'I know already. Dismissed.' As the junior backed off, bemused, Lugo read the slate data and handed it to Kaldenbach.

'Four archenemy ships. Potent, but Esquine should be able to hold them.'

'He won't.' Her voice was soft, almost a whisper.

Gaunt looked straight at Lugo. 'Prepare for ground assault,' he repeated firmly.

Lugo held his gaze for several seconds. Gaunt could almost see his mind working through possibilities, necessities and maybes. Lugo closed his eyes and sighed deeply.

'Do as he says,' he told the life company colonel.

'Lord General, I–'

'Now!' barked Lugo, and Kaldenbach turned and ran.

Now that was interesting.

Shumlen's vitals-reader had just shown his pulse rate spike the highest it had been in seventeen years. One for the log-book, he thought.

He'd just pulled a turn so tight the G-force had all but crushed him and blinded him for about fifteen seconds. He blinked hard to get his squeezed eyeballs to refocus.

Where the hell was that bat?

He hit the thrusters and spun his bird down into a wide evade. Blitz fire and enemy cannonades fluttered brightly in the darkness outside his canopy. He saw a Lightning far to his left, two bats on its back. Twenty-seven? Was that Liebholtz?

Las-fire chattered and pinked, studding the blackness, brilliant, then gone. The Lightning dogged, banked and came around, but the bats were still on him.

'Twenty-seven, twenty-seven, rake-turn to port,' Shumlen said over his vox as he soared down through the AF fire. A bat he hadn't even seen, wings hooked, chin-cannon flashing, went by and over him, away. Damage alerts beeped from his instrumentation and he cancelled them out.

His heads-up display swam and shifted, crosshairs drifting as he turned again.

'They're all over me! All over me!' Liebholtz's voice squealed over the link.

'Turn one-eight-one and come around hard,' Shumlen said.

His thumb trembled over the fire-stud in the top of his stick.

He was head on. He kicked the burners to full, crossing the Lightning coming the other way. The nearest bat, right on its tail, slammed into his display and the finders locked it up. The crosshairs went bright and hard and started to flash. The lock-tone sounded, a rising shrill.

He depressed his thumb and fell into a roll. He felt the shudder of his cannon pumping, the rhythmic grind of the autoloaders.

The bat flamed out in a bright fireball. Winnowing pieces of debris clattered off his hull and canopy.

Liebholtz wasn't clear yet. He was trying to climb out of the horizontal vector.

Typical air-boy, Shumlen thought. Liebholtz was a great pilot, truly gifted, but he'd come out of planetary airforce, like so many pilots. He still thought in terms of up and down, right and left.

No such things. Any true void-fighter knew that. And Shumlen was a true void-fighter. Oh yeah, this close to a planet or super-massive ships there was a marginal grav-element to allow for, but that was just part of the game. To void-fight, you had to think in three dimensions at once.

Shumlen flipped his bird up and over. Liebholtz was trying to cut up, but the bat was sticking with him.

Shumlen's heads-up hunted, washing left and right.

He saw the bat. A Locust-pattern interceptor, painted in tiger stripes. Long nosed, twin-boomed, spiky. Its chin-gun was already spelling out Liebholtz's doom.

Liebholtz's inarticulate last words spluttered out of the vox. His bird was consumed in a bright yellow flare.

Shumlen had the bat. The killer. It jinked back and forth, but he kept it in field. God-Emperor, but this jockey was good.

Shumlen tried a shot and missed.

He snatched his thumb off to conserve ammo. Thirty-seven per cent munitions left. One missile. Twenty-two per cent fuel remaining.

The Locust rolled back and over, coming down facing the other way and spiralling.

Neat... but not neat enough. Shumlen powered past him, and began to dive down towards the vast hull landscape of the archenemy battleship as it slid by, taunting the gun batteries.

They didn't let him down. Neither did the bat.

The batteries started pounding the moment Shumlen went over them, but he was too fast for them to make a kill.

They were still pounding when the bat chased after him, hungry for Shumlen's bird.

The bat went up in a messy spray of burning gases and hull debris.

Shumlen switched back up, got a lock almost immediately, and killed another bat on the turn with a drumming salvo from his cannon.

A cannon shell from somewhere punched through his port wing and he turned hard again, right into the backwash of an AF blitz.

Shumlen slunk away, circling in a deep, open turn. The bat zipped past him and he locked it tight. His cannon shuddered.

It blew out like a flower, the fuselage peeling away into silver shreds. He saw the pilot vaporise as he tried to eject.

A dismal toll rang from his instruments. He looked at his ammo counter and saw the worst.

Count zero. And the fuel load wasn't much better.

He flipped back. One missile left. Time to make it count.

Sweeping in and out of the bursting patterns of AF, he powered towards the bow of the archenemy battleship. The forward launch decks, open like mouths in the front snout of the beast. A missile there...

Bats passed in front of him, chasing Lightnings. More AF, incandescent. Then a bat with a bird on its tail, spraying rounds.

The bow of the super-massive craft dropped away under him, and Shumlen turned tightly, thrusters burning away the last dregs of his fuel as he came in for the final run of his career.

'SIGNAL FROM THE *Omnia Vincit*, sir!' Kreff yelled. Captain Wysmark didn't seem to hear him. The captain was standing by the master console, adjusting settings.

'Sir?'

That buzzing. Kreff could hear it. What the hell was it? It made his ears ache.

'Sir!'

Wysmark glanced up at him. 'Kreff?'

'*Omnia Vincit* is ordering us to join formation. The fleet captain says we should seal internals and blow the *Troubadour* off us.'

'Does he, indeed?'

Wysmark's hands danced over the master console.

'Sir?' said Kreff, alarmed. 'We should issue an emergency brace warning and clear the gates before we–'

There was an almighty thump. It shook the bridge of the *Navarre* so hard that Kreff was thrown over. Wysmark remained on his feet.

In a blizzard cloud of fragments, the *Navarre* had blown locks and torn away from the *Troubadour*. In the process, it had opened three of its skin-level decks to hard vacuum, but Wysmark had sealed the internal hatches and prevented a total breach.

Even so, ninety-six armsmen, who had spent the last half hour fighting for the very life of the *Navarre,* were locked out and voided to their deaths by the drastic manoeuvre.

The *Troubadour* slumped away from the frigate, spilling material and debris. It dropped away towards the glinting shoals of pilgrim ships in the high atmosphere.

As its engines ignited, the *Navarre* came nose up, and turned away from the bright planet below it.

Wysmark co-opted fire control to his console, and tasked the *Navarre's* batteries. When the actuality sphere gave him solution, he fired.

The *Navarre* blew the tumbling *Troubadour* into a billion glittering fragments.

'Sir! We need to get into the fleet formation!' Kreff stammered, getting up. He was astonished at the captain's brutality. Crewmen had just died, unnecessarily. Wysmark ignored him, but the *Navarre* was coming around nevertheless.

Kreff joined his captain at the master console, reading the display. Enginarium to full motive, shields up, weapons to power...

And a red light Kreff didn't recognise.

Kreff flinched back as he realised it was a drop of blood on the console, underlit by an enginarium rune.

Another drip fell next to it.

Blood was running out of the captain's left tear duct.

The buzzing was back, so loud, so very loud–

'Captain?

'Firing solution, please, exec.'

'Firing solution?' Kreff recoiled in dismay. The *Solstice,* the *Navarre's* sister ship, was rolling into view ahead, side on as it faced the incoming enemy.

'Now, if you please, Kreff!'

'Sir, it's one of ours!'

The knuckles crushed his nose and made him bite through his lip. Crying out in pain and spitting blood, Kreff fell sideways.

'Captain!'

Buzzing, buzzing, buzzing…

The *Navarre* lurched as its main lances fired. The beams, on full load, cut through the *Solstice's* flank plating and opened its inner decks to space. All two thousand metres of it crumpled like metal foil and tore apart. A moment later, its reactors went up. Where the *Solstice* had been, only a white hot blast radius remained.

The expanding shockwave hit the *Navarre* bow-on. The ship bucked and threw like an unbroken steed. Kreff hit the deck for a third time.

Prone, he looked up at Wysmark. He had been with the captain for ten years, ten years of loyalty and love. Blood was dribbling from Wysmark's nose and eyes, and his expression was oddly slack.

He was no longer the officer Kreff had followed into the mouth of death and back too many times to count.

Kreff fumbled with his uniform's holster and pulled out his service pistol.

Wysmark, without looking, had already produced the compact auto-mag anchored under the master console. He pointed it down at Kreff and fired, his attention on the main screen all the while.

The first shot smashed Kreff's pelvis. The second broke three ribs and ruptured a lung. The third pulped Kreff's right ear and spanked off the deck plating.

Gasping in pain, sobbing in ragged breaths, Kreff lay on his back in a widening pool of his own blood. He raised his service pistol in a shaking hand and shot Wysmark in the side of the head.

Wymark swayed. The impact of the round rocked him. The left side of his skull burst outwards, and bloody tissue dripped onto his braided collar.

He fell over to his left, hard.

'Help me! Help me!' Kreff gasped. Ensigns and servitors ran over to him, picking him up.

'*Navarre* to *Omnia Vincit*! *Navarre* to *Omnia Vincit*!' Kreff yelled into the vox.

'THE SOLSTICE... IS gone…' Valdeemer stammered.

'Gone? How?' Esquine demanded.

'The *Navarre*… it fired on her. Direct, sustained hit to midships.'

'Heretics have taken the *Navarre*. Emperor protect us!'

'What are your orders, sir?' Velosade asked.

'Cleanse my ship,' said Esquine. There were furious tears in his inlaid eyes.

'Firing solutions! The *Navarre*!' Velosade bellowed.

THE SIDE BATTERIES of the *Omnia Vincit* lit up and stayed lit. The *Navarre's* shields soaked up the merciless bombardment for several seconds, swirling and coruscating like molten glass. Then they began to buckle and fail. The *Navarre* heeled over, its hull shredding and burning. Its gravitic assemblies shut down and it started to fall, stern-first, into the gravity well of the planet. A vast internal explosion disintegrated it before it hit the atmosphere.

On the *Navarre's* bridge, Executive Officer Kreff was still trying to raise the *Omnia Vincit* on the fleet channel as he died.

The debris from the *Navarre* rained down towards the surface of Herodor, becoming meteors in the upper atmosphere.

One of those meteors was a standard pattern escape pod. It rocked and tumbled violently, rattling and vibrating as it plunged.

The two runt psykers were wailing in terror, flinching at every lurch. The big man in green silk robes murmured soothing words of reassurance and comfort to them as if they were his children, his massive tattooed arms holding them tight.

'Almost there,' said Pater Sin. 'Almost there...'

'You ready for this?' Mkvenner asked lightly.

Gol Kolea straightened the front of his fatigue jacket and nodded. Side by side, they walked in through the entrance of the Tanith billet.

The dawn call had sounded some minutes before, and the troops were rousing. Water pots were clattering onto stove rings, and men were dressing.

It was exactly the same as every morning in the Guard, simple routine. Only the place – a scholam by the look of it, Kolea thought – was different.

It made him smile.

'Morning, Gol,' said Obel, wandering past. Kolea nodded. No one gave him a second look. News hadn't reached here yet.

He wandered down the rows of bunks, looking around, hungry for the sight of familiar faces. There was a little ache in the back of his heart that some faces wouldn't be there. Muril... Piet Gutes... Try Again Bragg...

'This one's yours,' said Mkvenner.

Kolea stopped, and sat down on an unmade bunk. His pack was there.

He looked up at Mkvenner. The lean Tanith gazed down at him and shook his head. 'A night I won't forget. A favour I intend to repay.'

'No need, Ven.'

'You saved my life,' said Mkvenner. 'You're going to have to make it up to me.'

Kolea smiled.

'I'll see you later, Kolea,' said Mkvenner, and moved off through the dorm.

Kolea sat for a moment as the bustle went on around him. Then he took off his jacket and undervest and opened his pack to find a fresh shirt. The weight of the plaster effigy in his jacket pocket made him remember it was there. He took it out, looked at it for a moment, and stuffed it down inside his pack for safety.

He found a folded vest and shook it out to put it on.

'Know how to dress yourself, do you, gak-head?'

Kolea looked up. Cuu had been walking by, dressed in his under-shorts, fresh from the shower block. He had a towel over his shoulder. The painfully white, unhealthy skin of his scrawny, corded torso was covered in crude tattoos. He sneered at Kolea.

'Want me to help, gak-head? Want me to help you dress, you pathetic gak-head?' Cuu's voice was low but sharp. 'Want me to wipe your arse for you too? Sure as sure you do.'

He laughed.

'You must have got away with murder while I was absent,' said Kolea softly.

'Huh?'

'You always were a little shit, Cuu, but bullying a brain-damaged vet? Where the gak is your sense of regimental honour, you insidious pus-ball?'

Cuu's eyes and mouth opened very wide. He took a step back. The area immediately around them had fallen very quiet.

Kolea rose to his feet. He towered over the trooper, and his naked torso and arms were massive, especially next to Cuu's bony frame.

'You... you...' Cuu stammered.

'Yeah, me. I'm back. Now run away before I break your rodent neck.'

Cuu ran.

'Sarge?' Lubba said, getting up off his bunk. He was staring at Gol, blinking fast. 'Sarge?'

'Morning, Lubba. So, how's it going?' Kolea said lightly, sitting back down.

Whispers were spreading, voices talking fast.

'Gol?' Corbec said, appearing from the row end and walking towards him. Mkvenner was with him.

'Hello, sir.'

Corbec shook his shaggy head. 'Gaunt told me about what went on, but I was keeping it to myself until... until... feth! What happened?'

'Well, it's a funny thing...' Kolea began. The rest of his sentence was lost beneath the crushing pressure of Corbec's bearhug.

'I GET THE impression his return has been popular,' said Dorden. Zweil made a chuckling sound and nodded. The doctor pushed Zweil's chair down the aisles between the rows of vacated bunks towards the mobbing, clamouring concentration of troopers in the centre of the billet chamber. Kolea was at the heart of it, laughing and chatting, answering the barrage of excited questions as best he could.

Everyone was there, morning drill forgotten. Somebody had ordered in boxes of hot loaves from a nearby bakery, and sutlers had arrived with wheeled barrows laden with heated caffeine urns.

No, not everyone, Dorden noted. Away through the rows of bunks, he saw Lijah Cuu, getting dressed. Every now and then Cuu looked up as laughter rose from the throng.

'So tell it again...' Varl called. 'You did what?'

Kolea shrugged. 'I don't really remember. I was worried about Ven, and someone had said the baths healed all wounds.'

'That's what they say,' Lubba nodded, solemnly.

'And she healed you?' asked Soric.

'I guess so. Actually, I think she healed Ven. I was just in the way.'

The Ghosts laughed.

'Do you hear me complaining?' asked Mkvenner.

'Will she heal me?' Varl asked, tapping his augmetic shoulder.

'Not a chance, Ceg. She only cures the deserving.'

More gales of laughter.

'What about me?' asked Domor.

'You're as bad as Varl, Shoggy,' said Kolea. 'And besides, you wouldn't be without that enhanced vision now, would you?'

Domor shrugged. 'The Emperor protects,' he admitted.

'What about me?' cried Larkin from the back.

'I dunno, Larks. What's wrong with you?'

'Where do we start?' blurted Bonin. The crowd broke up in guffaws again.

'Will she cure me?' Chiria asked quietly.

Kolea looked down at her scarred face. She'd never been pretty, but he knew the scars on her face were the worst thing that had ever happened to her. He sighed.

'Who knows? I'll ask her.'

Chiria smiled. Nessa put her arm around her.

'I guess you'll be wanting your platoon back, Gol,' Criid said.

Kolea shook his head. 'I see you've been doing a fine job, sergeant. It'll be an honour to serve.'

There were cheers and whoops of affirmation. Criid blushed, and Caffran looked at her with a proud smile.

'I need to thank you, though,' Kolea said as the noise died down.

'Me?' asked Criid. 'Should be the other way around. You've saved me twice now, and the first time got you... hurt.'

'Maybe. But the second time got me cured.'

'What?'

'I don't remember much about it, as you will no doubt appreciate, but when I picked you up in that street, you had this... this effigy thing in your pocket. A plaster bust. Fething awful thing, it was.'

Criid nodded. 'An old guy gave it to me. A pilgrim. It was out in the Glassworks. He was trying to thank me for looking after him.'

'I found it. It reminded me... reminded my thick head, as was. Made me think about the Saint and how she cured people. I think that's what made me take Ven to the balneary.'

'You kept going on about the fething thing,' Mkvenner confirmed.

'It's yours anyway,' said Kolea, looking at Criid. 'I was just looking after it.'

She shrugged. 'I don't want it. Gakking eyesore. Just glad it had a use.'

'I would like to see it, if I may,' Zweil slurred. The mob parted politely to admit the doctor and the old man he was pushing in the chair. Zweil sat at a strange angle, half his face curiously limp.

'Of course, father,' said Kolea.

'I normally wouldn't bother over such trinkets,' Zweil said, carefully enunciating every word, 'but my brethren demand that every last detail surrounding a palpable miracle be scrutinised. It is the holy order of things.'

'It's in my pack,' Kolea said. He looked round at the troopers.

'I'll get it, sarge,' said Criid. She disengaged herself from Caffran's firm embrace and pushed away through the crowd.

'So, what did it feel like?' called Feygor through his throaty, monotone vox-box. 'Did it hurt?'

'What?'

'The miracle, you feth.'

'Yes,' said Zweil, nodding. 'What did it feel like, Gol?'

'I was wondering that myself,' added Dorden.

'Well...' Kolea began.

BEHIND HER, THEY were laughing and shouting out. Criid moved down through the rows of empty cots. She could feel the smile on her face. It wouldn't go. Kolea was back. *Kolea was back!* This had to be about the best day of her life, ever. Right up there along with the day she made sergeant and the day Caff told her he loved her.

She'd missed Kolea so much she hadn't realised, and she knew all too well she owed him everything. She'd have been dead on the streets of Ouranberg but for him.

She found Kolea's bunk and was digging through his pack. Everything was so neat and precise, everything folded and pressed. Kolea would gakking hate her for the mess she was making.

There was no sign of the effigy. She up-ended the pack and spilled its contents out onto the mattress. Clothes, ammo packs, a shaving kit, a boot-blacker, a pack of cards, a clutch of hololithic prints stuffed into a yellowing envelope.

And the effigy. Ugly gakking thing. The garish paint job was worse than she remembered.

She put it to one side, and began to repack Kolea's kitbag. The photo-prints fell out of the old envelope as she picked it up.

She looked at them.

A man. A woman. A young boy. A baby. Group shots, individuals. A father holding his newborn. A mother and her kids.

The man was Gol Kolea. Younger, true. Cleaner. One of him dressed as an ore-face worker.

She stopped dead.

Though they were years younger, she recognised the faces of the children. Dalin and Yoncy. And the mother. She'd only known the mother for a few brief minutes. In carriage station C4/a, Vervunhive. Criid had tried to help her with her toddler and her baby-cart. Then the shells had started to fall.

Gak! She'd seen this woman die, this woman in the pictures. The mother of the children Criid now counted as hers.

What the hell were the pictures doing in Gol Kolea's p–

'No,' she said. 'Holy Emperor, no!'

She got up and fell over, pulling the open pack down off the bunk. Kolea's stuff fell out onto the floor. She started to scrabble around, collecting them up and pushing them back into the bag.

An alarm started to sound, so loud, it made her jump.

'SORRY TO BREAK things up, ladies,' Rawne cried, sounding anything but sorry. He pushed his way through the throng of Ghosts around Kolea. Klaxons were bleating.

'Time for work. The archenemy is orbital and inbound, and we're expecting mass ground assault in the next hour. Get dressed, get kitted, get ready and get moving. If you're of a faithful disposition, ask the God-Emperor for his blessing. If you're a layman, put your head between your legs and kiss your fething ass goodbye. This is it. The real thing.'

The crowd of Ghosts broke up immediately, troopers running to their bunks, struggling into clothes, prepping weapons.

'Bad as that?' Corbec asked, coming up alongside Rawne.

'Worse than you can possibly imagine,' replied the major.

ON THEY CAME. The *Incarnadine*, the *Cicatrice*, the *Harm's Way*. Running side by side like hunting dogs, angling in at twenty degrees to the plane of the ecliptic. And the *Revenant*? Where was that?

Flanking in from sunward, obliterating pilgrim ships. It had already incinerated all the transports in the relief convoy.

Esquine tensed. This was still manageable. This was still a tactical possibility. He had three ships. The *Omnia Vincit* was a vastly powerful flagship. The *Laudate Divinitus* was also capable. The frigate *Glory of Cadia* ought to be up to the mark.

Their commanders appeared before him on the deck of the strategium, red-shot holoforms.

Captain Cask of the *Glory*.

Captain Massinga of the *Laudate*.

'The Emperor who gives us life also trials us now,' said Esquine.

Both holoforms nodded.

'The odds are not impossible, though they are against us. Massinga, the *Revenant* is yours. Take it to hell with all hands.'

'I will, fleet captain.'

'Cask, with me. We take this fight to the heart.'

'The Emperor protects,' crackled Cask's holoform over the vox.

'Attack speed!' Esquine commanded.

'Attack speed!' Velosade relayed across the strategium.

Valdeemer leaned back against a bulkhead. His heart was thumping.

THE GIGANTIC CAPITAL ship *Omnia Vincit*, flanked by its much smaller sister the frigate *Glory of Cadia*, powered away from the chilly light of Herodor towards the trio of archenemy warships.

Beside them for a while, the heavy cruiser *Laudate Divinitus* turned away to port, and lit up its thrusters as it burned down towards the *Revenant*.

The *Revenant* was picking off pilgrim ships, exploding them like paper targets on a circus showman's stall. Some started to run. That just gave the *Revenant* moving solutions. Its guns raked through the translucent skein of the upper atmosphere. Ships exploded and burned.

A flurry of torpedoes from the closing heavy cruiser unsettled the *Revenant's* shields, and it swung up to meet the Imperial warship.

The heavy cruiser was a third again as big as the gold-laced enemy ship. Its fighter screen puffed out from it like a cloud of dust, and was met immediately by the rival's own screen. As the massive vessels closed, spitting beams of light and sprays of plasma, the tiny fighters billowed around each other, cloud into cloud, dust particles whirling away to infinity.

The *Laudate Divinitus* fired a full volley of lances and torpedoes. The *Revenant* gunned away, shields flaring flat white. It fired its own cannonade broadside as it fled across the *Laudate's* bows.

The Imperial heavy cruiser shook. One of its shields ruptured. It fired back.

The *Revenant* brought its hind part in tight, turning in a forty-five degree angle on its prow. It came up facing the *Laudate*, facing the failed shield.

It fired its main lances.

The *Laudate Divinitus* didn't explode. It came apart in a series of coughing, jerking seizures. The final shudder kicked off the enginarium, and sent out a shockwave that destroyed nine pilgrim ships at anchor.

The *Revenant* dipped low into the thin reaches of the upper atmosphere, and began to disgorge drop-pods and landing craft.

Hundreds of them.

THE GLORY OF CADIA hit the *Cicatrice* so hard and with such sustain it began to burn. Esquine was savouring the victory when he saw the enemy ship turn.

The *Cicatrice,* immolating, spent the last of its reactor power pushing itself forward. It rammed the *Glory* amidships and the two vessels locked together, burning like a small star in close orbit space.

The *Harm's Way* and the massive *Incarnadine* were pummeling the *Omnia Vincit* with their batteries. Esquine felt the pain from the shields.

'Target the main ship, Velosade,' he gasped.

SHUMLEN HIT THRUST and came in at the open and lit port of the *Incarnadine's* starboard launch deck. He felt himself pressed back in the grav seat as the thrusters kicked in. His heads-up locked in at the hangar bay mouth.

One missile left.

Something flew out at him.

A bat, yes. But really like a bat. A dark, hooked shape. Small, fast, not a Locust-pattern ship, he was certain. Something xenos. Very xenos.

He banked, hunting. The bat zipped around and was behind him. Shumlen tried to turn, tried to get an angle so he could loose his last missile. The bat wouldn't let him be.

Shumlen turned hard again, and again. He couldn't lose it.

He turned for one last time and the stall siren howled.

Fuel out. He was drifting.

The bat zipped past him and then turned back, sliding up and coasting up alongside him.

Shumlen looked at it. His pattern recognition systems bleeped out confirmation.

A Raven.

A dark eldar Raven attack ship.

It hovered beside him for a second, and then flitted away.

There was no power left in his Lightning. Shumlen looked round, dead in space. The vast superstructure of the *Incarnadine* ploughed towards him.

And met him like a cliff face. His tiny craft burst and flared for a second as it was run down against the massive prow of the battleship. The *Incarnadine* didn't even feel it.

The Raven, circling nearby, dipped its barbed wings once to acknowledge the fall of a fine pilot, and then turned and burned towards the pallid glow of Herodor.

The control console of the sleek Raven reflected yellow light up across the features of Skarwael. He was grinning, a rictus of bared fangs and tight white flesh.

The bloody game was on.

EVERY ALARM AND klaxon in the Civitas Beati was blaring. Even the great prayer horns at the city quarter-points were wailing terrible rising notes. Storm shields began to close on all the windows, decks and apertures in the hive towers, and through the inner precinct of the Civitas. Segmented plating slid up to protect the glass domes of the agriponic farms.

There was uproar on the streets. Citizens fled en masse to the sub-level bunkers, to the storm cellars, to the lower levels of the hive towers. Technically, there were appointed shelters for all, but the protocols were old and hadn't been used for generations. Citizens ignored them, or had never known them, and fled hysterically to the nearest shelter.

The highways and principals of the mid-city and skirt districts were choked with road traffic. A lot of it had already been mobile at dawn, and it was swelled by private vehicles heading across town towards imagined places of safety. The traffic jammed up the routes, solid and nose-to-tail in places, and transports were quickly abandoned. In some outer streets, the roads were deserted but for rows of immobile vehicles, some with the engines still running, most with doors and hatches open.

THE MAIN BARRACKS of the Regiment Civitas Beati was an imposing keep that overlooked Principal I in the high town area, between the gigantic stacks of hive towers one and two. In the main yard inside the walls, the regiment was assembling and breaking up into troop elements. Columns of APCs and light armour units were grumbling up the ramps from the garages under the keep, directed by marshals to embarkation points where in theory they would pick up their assigned squads. There was no time for briefing. Instructions would be delivered en route via tac logis. All anyone knew was that they were following GAR3 – Ground Assault Response 3 – one of Biagi's pre-formed emergency strategies.

Timon Biagi himself stood in the open top of an armoured command vehicle, listening to the tac logis flow in his earpiece, watching the disposition. Troopers, some still buckling up armour, poured out of the keep and into the yard, filing past the armourers' platforms to collect munitions and combat supplies. Biagi was the two hundred and fifth marshal of the Civitas. From this hour forward it would be his name, and his name alone, that historians would think of when considering the Regiment Civitas. For he would be the marshal that stood alongside Sabbat at her Returning. Would they think of him like they thought of Kiodrus, he wondered? A second Kiodrus. He liked the feel of that idea.

Biagi looked up at the sky. It was unseasonably clear, and the violet dawn was turning into a cool white haze. In a corner of the sky, the future was making itself visible. Flashes and strobes of light, a thicket of twinkling stripes just visible in the growing glare, identified the monumental war now underway in orbital space. A war between gods, Biagi thought.

From down here where he stood, it looked like firecrackers.

THE GHOST AND life company elements moved out of the hive towers in rows of troop trucks and transporters, heading out into the skirt fan of the city. Life company tanks and tracked armour led the way, smashing rows of stationary, abandoned vehicles out of their path where they blocked thoroughfares and junctions.

Gaunt rode in a Salamander with Corbec and Hark. Hydra gun platforms travelled alongside them for a few streets, and then turned off to left and right to occupy good firing positions in open squares and plazas in the hilly inner reaches of the Civitas.

'This is Lugo's plan?' Hark asked.

Gaunt shook his head. 'He'll take the credit, but it's actually Kaldenbach's.'

'I thought it was too smart for that feth-wipe,' said Corbec, and then glanced at Hark's disapproving look.

'Did I say that out loud?' he smiled.

The plan was to assemble the main troop strengths in the city's geographical centre, towards the bottom of the Guild Slope, and wait. Even combined, the Tanith, life company, Regiment Civitas and Herodian PDF had nothing like enough numbers to cordon the entire perimeter of the sprawling city. First Officiary Leger had even seconded the city arbites and the local civic militia forces to bolster the military presence, and still that left them lacking in numerical resources.

The Imperial forces would loiter in the city centre, from which point any part of the city extent was as near as any other, and wait to see what direction the ground assault came from. Then they would respond fast, using transports, and channel their efforts in that particular area.

It was impossible to tell where the first wave of assault would come from. Gaunt had been through too many assaults from orbit – as assaulter and assaulted both – to think otherwise. There were so many variables.

From the data, Gaunt had seen, there were at least four archenemy warships up above them. Unopposed, their combined firepower could raze the Civitas down to the bedrock: streets, habs, hive-towers, even the armoured shelters underground. If the enemy decided not to bother with the complexity and effort of a ground assault, and simply went for the kill, this war would be over before it started.

There was one saving grace Gaunt was counting on–

'Sir!' Gaunt looked round as Corbec called out. The big Tanith was pointing up at the northern sky.

High up, streaks of orange fire were slashing across the pale sky. A few dozen at first, and then more. Hundreds more. Like a shower of meteorites, they rained down from high orbit overhead, diving north, leaving long, perfectly straight, perfectly parallel trails of flame and vapour in the sky behind them.

They weren't meteorites.

Gaunt saw distant flashes light up the northern horizon as the first hit. A second later, a distant sound like continuous thunder rolled in from the Great Western Obsidae.

drop-pods. For a half-second, Gaunt felt relieved. The archenemy was going for ground assault after all. Then he reconsidered. Death was not going to be swift and total. It was going to be slow and painful and hard.

But at least, if that was the case, he and his men had a chance to make it mutual.

'ENSIGN! ENSIGN!'

There was a voice in Valdeemer's dream, calling his name, and it wouldn't go away.

He blinked and found himself lying on his back in the strategium of the *Omnia Vincit*.

'Ensign Valdeemer! Are you alive?'

Valdeemer sat up and looked around. The air was full of smoke and flashing alarm lights and the baleful screech of klaxons and damage alarms.

'Ensign!'

He got up. The deck shook hard, and he steadied himself against a console. The crew servitor at the console was still working furiously, augmetic hands rippling over the display. The mechanical was totally oblivious to the chaos around them.

Valdeemer shook his head, trying to lose the swollen muzziness. Blood spattered on the deck. He raised his hand and felt a deep gash across his forehead.

They'd been hit.

He'd been at Esquine's side when the torpedo had struck them under the bridge tower. He remembered the numbing concussion, bodies flying. Yes, that's right. He'd been thrown to the deck.

How long had he been out?

'Ensign!'

He lurched forward towards Fleet Captain Esquine's throne.

'Sir?'

'I need you to man the main station. Can you do that?' Esquine looked like he was in pain, struggling, but there wasn't a mark on him.

'Sir? That's the commander's post.'

'Do it!'

Valdeemer turned and hurried through the smoke towards the main station. The deck was littered with smouldering debris and fallen panelling. He had to step over several bodies. Crewmen, deck aides, servitors, ripped apart by blast force or killed by flying debris.

One of them was Velosade. A piece of deck plating the size of a dinner plate had almost, but not quite, decapitated him.

Swallowing hard, Valdeemer got to the station and reviewed the board. Three shield failures. Two hull breaches. Fires on decks seven through eighteen and also in carrier bay four. Lances were out. Structural integrity was down to forty-seven per cent.

'Help me, Valdeemer,' Esquine whispered, his fingers flexing.

Valdeemer tried to assemble a plan in his mind. His fingers flew across the console, activating and deactivating runes as they lit up, calling up displays – enginarium, structural, shielding, deck-to-deck – and then cancelling them. He routed power away from the huge firestorm on deck eight. He bypassed two cogitator nodes damaged on deck eleven and brought lance number three back on line. He sealed the deck hatches that had not closed automatically and shut off the oxygen supply fuelling the lower deck fires. He shut down reactor two, which was red-lining and clearly damaged, and kicked in auxiliary power from the redundant reactor in the *Omnia Vincit's* belly.

Why hadn't Esquine already done these things? They were obvious, standard. The great capital ship was bleeding and burning to death, and Esquine hadn't even begun to apply emergency procedures.

'Report?'

'Damage is contained. I've got a lance back on line. We're painfully weak, but I'd like to divert all power from the engines to the shields.'

'Do it, Valdeemer!'

'I... I need the command override, sir. I'm not rank authorised!'

'The code is Vesta 1123!'

Valdeemer's bloody hands shook as they entered the code. He diverted power, ignoring the protesting howls of the tech-priests.

'Fighter screen?' Esquine urged.

'All but gone. Their small ships are all over us.'

'Where is the enemy?' Esquine asked.

Valdeemer looked round at the fleet captain. 'The *Incarnadine* is flanking us to port, sir, and returning full and sustained broadsides. Shields at thirty-five per cent. The *Harm's Way* is off the starboard bow, training main lances. Sir... can't you see this?'

'No,' said Esquine, his voice barely audible above the alarms and vox chatter.

The torpedo strike had vaporised the fleet captain's mind-impulse link, severing his connection to the massive ship. He was blind and deaf and lacking in all telepresent or hardwired connection to the *Omnia Vincit*, except for the waves of pain that washed through the ship into him as it took damage.

'Oh Holy Terra...' breathed Valdeemer, realising this. That meant he was in command. He, a junior ensign, was actually in control of the Imperial battleship *Omnia Vincit*.

How many times had he dreamed of command? How many hours had he spent longing for such a role?

Not like this. Gods of Terra, not at *all* like this...

'Orders, fleet captain?' he shouted over the din.

Esquine's answer was just a whisper. 'Kill them all... and if you can't do that, make the price of our lives a dear one.'

THE INCARNADINE USED its attitude thrusters to push in closer to the stricken *Omnia Vincit*. Its port batteries maintained their savage bombardment. The *Incarnadine's* constant scan-sweeps of the *Omnia Vincit* showed that it was dead in the water, its combined reactor power channelled from engines to shields. Massively protected, it was still a sitting target.

The *Harm's Way*, sitting off to bow-starboard of the Imperial warship, began to concentrate its lance blasts at the weak points of shielding, at the hasty overlap that barely covered the torpedo wound which had blown the fifth dorsal shield away and crippled the fleet captain.

The *Omnia Vincit* shook as the *Harm's Way* got a good, solid hit in. A huge section of upper hull splintered and peeled away.

The *Omnia Vincit* fired its reactivated lance and struck the *Harm's Way's* shields so hard it was forced to back off. The Imperial gunnery crews, sweating and half dead, cheered.

The combined fighter fleets of the *Incarnadine* and the *Harm's Way*, which had already obliterated the *Omnia Vincit's* fighter screen, concentrated their efforts around carrier bay three on the starboard side. The last of the Lightnings were atomised by the waves of Locusts – 'bats', as the Imperial Navy slang called them – gunning in, cannons flashing.

Three Locusts managed to enter the deck mouth. One was destroyed by AF turret emplacements inside the deckway. The second was also hit by AF fire, but managed to fire all six of its missiles into the belly of the carrier hold before it went up.

The third, accelerating to hypersonic, made it in down the main launch deck, strafing as it went, and banked right into the munitions loading bay. There, just before it catastrophically ran out of flying space, it dumped its payload into the sub-deck autoloader shafts that lifted munitions up to the carrier deck from the armoured heart of the *Omnia Vincit*.

The chain reaction blew the side off the noble Imperial ship in a vast flurry of underdeck explosions and fragmenting hull plates. Gored, its guts exposed, the *Omnia Vincit* yawed. In the strategium, Valdeemer desperately converted three per cent of shield power back to the engines and pushed the battleship out from between the vicing archenemy ships.

The *Omnia Vincit* slid forward out of the *Incarnadine's* fire-field. A three per cent drop on shield power wasn't much, but the *Harm's Way*, waiting at the bow like a jackal on a kill, didn't hesitate. It cycled up full load power from its main reactors and fired its lances at the overlay weakness.

Valdeemer turned from his post to look at Esquine. The fleet captain was shaking with rage and sorrow, impotent and agonised.

'I'm sorry, sir,' said Valdeemer, 'but I'm afraid–'

He was incinerated before he could speak another word. Esquine was incinerated too, his golden throne melting around his combusting body. Blaze-fire swept through the strategium and out across the bridge, burning crewmen where they stood and vaporising control stations. The deep, glasteel ports fronting the bridge shattered and blew outwards under the superheated overpressure. The remaining shields failed.

The *Incarnadine* flurried off one final broadside to put the *Omnia Vincit* out of its death throes. Blown open, twisted, ruptured, its hull crackling with diffusing electric discharges, the *Omnia Vincit* rolled over.

The archenemy ships, satisfied, depowered their weapon systems, cancelled shields, and coasted away into high anchor station.

The burned-out ruin of the *Omnia Vincit* remained in orbit around Herodor for nine hundred and three years, until slowly decaying, unadjusted orbit rates finally sank it down through the gravity well into the atmosphere, where it burned up. The parts of it that survived atmosphere-kiss and heat-shear filled the skies of the southern continent like shooting stars, and hailed down onto the Lesser Southern Dry Sea, creating impact scars and craters that later became radioactive lakes in that distant wilderness.

But that, of course, took place a long time after every person in this account was many centuries dead.

THE MIGHTY INCARNADINE and the frigate *Harm's Way* drew in tight alongside the *Revenant*, and began to disgorge the drop-pods and landers of the assault force. What had been hundreds became thousands. Troop pods banged down like tracer bullets. Drop-ships swam away from the carrier decks and began to bank down towards the surface. Heavy landers uncoupled and entered descent mode.

At the rear end of the *Incarnadine's* belly, an armoured iris valve slunked open and a small object fired out. Tiny, it had its own integral void shield, and shot like a missile down through the Herodian atmosphere. It left a smoking contrail behind it.

Its solitary occupant had set the trajectory. Now he rode, numb, down towards the planet surface. He had no other awareness except the hunger for blood.

Her blood.

The tumult and concussion of the steep, fast fall was nothing to him.

He dropped like a rocket just beyond the Glassworks quarter of the Civitas. His impact cratered the obsidae for five hundred metres in all directions and kicked out a shockwave flash so hard and bright the Imperials thought for a moment that the archenemy had decided to fire from orbit after all.

He had been very precise about his landing site. The force of his landing drove him down through the planet's crust and into the deep-seated darkness of the aquifer itself.

His pod splintered through sediment, rolled and came to rest, steaming.

He fired the explosive bolts and got out slowly. He was in a subterranean cavern, steaming with thermal waters.

He got to his feet and shambled forward. His every step shook the ground. His feet were massive, hydraulic limbs. His augmetic sensors began to chase and hunt, reflecting off the glossy limestone walls of the cave.

He set off, hunting his quarry.

His name was Karess.

OUT ON THE Great Western Obsidae, the drop-pods were raining in. A thick wave of dust was kicking out from their impacts. Drop-ships were circling down too, landing claws extended as they settled in.

The lander's hatch dropped open and fifty Blood Pact troopers hurled themselves out into the cold waste. Ahead, through the dust walls, they could see the rising terraces and towers of the Civitas Beati.

Following the troopers out, the Marksman looked at the city. His brethren were fanning off in a wide formation.

The Marksman took off his pack and set it on the dusty ground. He pulled out the sections of his long-las and fitted it together. He kept the scope in his pocket, away from the dust. He was dressed in the dull red uniform of the Blood Pact, and had the iron visor and palm-scars to prove his association.

His name was Saul. He was, by any standards of measure, the finest sniper currently attached to the Blood Pact coterie.

Resting the long-las across his shoulder, he began to jog towards the city.

THE TROOP LANDER settled down in a halo of dust but, unlike its companions, it did not lift off again. It sat there on the obsidae, its turbofan engines dying.

They'd got bored. It had only been a twenty minute ride down from the *Incarnadine's* carrier bays to the surface, but they'd got bored and hungry.

The co-pilot had been a fine plaything for a few minutes, but he had ultimately disappointed: heart failure through terror before they'd got to the kill. The pilot himself had been better sport. They'd pinned him and forced him to execute a safe landing, peeling off his scalp with their talons all the while.

The moment they had set down safely, they had cracked his bared skull and fed on his brains.

Now there was work to be done. That meant they had to go to the human mass living-structure in the distance. The idea was distasteful, but Chto, who had brood command, reminded the other two about the rewards on offer. Their memories were short. Once they were reminded, they got excited.

The triplets slipped away from the dormant lander, their wet grey bodies sliding together as they coursed through the obsidae on their bellies.

Their flechette cannons were loaded and armed.

HE SETTLED HIS Raven in to land on an outcrop of the Stove Hills. The Civitas looked far away.

Skarwael popped his canopy and climbed out of his tiny craft. Between him and the city, assault landers and drop-pods were falling like torrential rain.

If he didn't get started, it would all be over. And he didn't want that.

Hellfire take the sniper, and the Pater with his runt-psykers, and the loxatl filth, and the death-machine too.

This was his kill. His kill. The martyr would be his, and he would wear her screams like precious stones.

He was a mandrake, after all. Nothing in creation understood the art of secret murder better than him.

EIGHT
GAR 3

'If you are the last man standing,
you're not fighting hard enough.'

— attr. Kaldenbach's commissars

MKOLL CRIED 'DOWN!' His voice, seldom heard so forcefully, echoed over the vox link and everyone, even Gaunt and Rawne, obeyed.

Casting a brief, blurred shadow and visible only for a second, something hook-winged swept low across the hab-block streets. A moment later, blasts tore through the buildings to their left.

The Locust had come in against the wind, its jet-whine inaudible until the last minute. Gaunt had no idea how Mkoll had spotted it.

'The city-shield must be down already,' Rawne muttered, getting up. Ash and brick dust from the blasts were drifting across them.

'Not necessarily,' Gaunt replied. 'It's only a climate shield. A surface bomber like that, with its forward screens maxed up...'

As if demonstrating the colonel-commissar's point, two more Locusts, in fore and aft formation, whooshed east-west across the city limits about half a kilometre ahead of them. The one-man assault craft, black bodies glinting in the sun, were travelling at rooftop height. They banked up and away into the sunlight, one rolling. In their wake, fireballs rippled and flared along the surface. The Ghosts could hear the popping, banging reports.

There were other sounds too. The constant *thump* and *slam* of artillery and armour guns from all along the city's northern skirt. Occasionally, when the wind was in the right direction, they could hear the fierce crackle of small-arms exchanges.

Lugo and his staff strategae had taken over the Civitas tac logis, and were overseeing, literally, the Imperial efforts from the high levels of the hive towers. From there, they were able to despatch remarkably accurate and current assessments of the archenemy invasion. All of it was bad news.

Four strike columns had assembled in the Great Western and Northern Obsidaes within fifty minutes of set down, mobilising fast and spearing into the northern city limits. One was driving into the Glassworks from the north-west, two directly south into Ironhall, and the fourth from the north-east into the Masonae district. Most of this seemed to be light assault armour from landers and storm-troop brigades from the first wave of drop-pods. In total, close to three hundred vehicle elements and eight thousand men, well supported by air cover and the artillery sections setting up in the obsidaes.

That, under any circumstances, would have been bad enough. Imperial numbers in the Civitas Beati hovered just under the seventeen thousand mark, provided militia and arbites units were figured in. But the Imperials had only something in the order of one hundred and eighty armoured machines, of which seventy were unarmed carriers. No air cover. No artillery apart from some light Regiment Civitas field pieces.

This lop-sided equation became a joke when the rest of the picture was factored in. Out in the drop zone, behind the initial, fast mobilising enemy spearhead, a vast force was assembling. It was taking its time, ferrying armour and squads down in wave after wave of drop-ships and heavy lander-transports. It would let the spearhead forces take the brunt and crack the city open. Then it would move in to consolidate. Out on the obsidaes, tac logis calculated, over half a million men and a hundred thousand fighting machines waited to mount the second wave. And the count was rising with every incoming wave.

Well commanded, and with a feth-load of luck on their side, Gaunt estimated, the Imperial resistance would last five, maybe six days before annihilation. With Lugo in the chair, they probably had about two. It was death either way. The only variable was time.

Supported by sections of the Regiment Civitas Beati, the Ghosts advanced through the Masonae district, over which Gaunt had defence command. Kaldenbach was leading the Ironhall resistance, and a Herodian PDF colonel called Vibreson headed the Glassworks line. Biagi, and a life company officer, Major Landfreed, held most of the remaining four thousand troop strengths in the middle city, ready for short-notice deployment. Five hundred men of the Regiment Civitas garrisoned the hive quarter, mainly, Gaunt believed, to buy enough time in the final, inevitable phase of the invasion for Lugo to flee via shuttle from the crest level platforms. Flee to where, only the God-Emperor knew.

The Ghosts and their allies moved up through the narrow streets east of Beati Plaza. This district was largely untouched by war, apart from the strafing damage of the enemy air cover. The thoroughfares were ominously empty. The citizenry had fled. Homes and commercial properties stood empty and lifeless, and discarded possessions littered the roads.

As they prowled forward, bounding cover by squad from block corner to block corner, Gaunt considered they had, despite everything, a kind of luck on their side. Unopposed as they now were, the archenemy warships far above them could have ended the war quickly with aerial bombardment. Instead, the enemy had opted for the gross effort and huge cost of a ground assault. He knew what that meant.

They wanted the Beati.

Poorly protected and underdefended as it was, the Civitas Beati was still large, and taking it a street at a time would be a bloody, painfully expensive task for any army. The archenemy was only undertaking it because of the prize. Indeed, the archenemy had only come to Herodor, only bothered with the place at all, because of that prize. The enemy commander wanted the Saint. A body, at least... but a prisoner, that would be the greatest trophy. So an annihilating orbital bombardment was out of the question. No tangible proof of the Beati's presence would be left.

This was all about Sabbat. Everything they did, everything the enemy did. It was all about Sabbat.

Tac logis crackled in Gaunt's ear. Kaldenbach's forces had engaged.

Gaunt was about to relay this to his officers when Mkoll voxed again.

'Contact!'

INITIALLY UNOPPOSED, THE invaders rolled into the northern edges of the Masonae district. To the west of them, smoke and low-level flashes above the roofs showed where their associated columns were lancing through the Ironhall.

Phalanxes of Blood Pact led the way, backed by files of stalk-armour, STeG 4 lights and AT70 Reaver-pattern tanks. Their way was unhindered. Two AT70s peeled off to destroy the prayer horn Gorgonaught in a hail of close range fire, and a trio of stalk-tanks assisted Blood Pact sappers in blowing and cutting the ancient arches of the Simeon Aqueduct. Water, the city's precious life-blood, poured from the shattered aqueduct and flooded several low-lying street blocks. Locust dive bombing had already ruined the North End Agridome. Burning crop produce was billowing yellow-grey smoke into the sky through the ruptured dome seals.

Without seeing a trace of the vaunted Imperial forces, the archenemy crossed Brigat Street into Actes Hill, and began to spread out into the Masonae.

The troopers, moving ahead of the armour, were singing. The song made Mkoll's stomach heave.

'We'll have to put a stop to that at least,' he murmured. He took aim. 'Ease!' he warned.

Mkoll squeezed the tube's trigger spoon and an AT rocket roared down the street, neatly killing the third STeG 4 in the approaching file.

The AT70 behind it started to rev, and spattered fire from its coaxial cannon, but it was pretty much blinded by the black smoke ripping out of the dead STeG.

The two STeGs in front of the kill spurred forward on their heavy, solid wheels, their compact turrets traversing as they hunted for the source of the ambush. The Blood Pact stopped singing and raced for cover positions.

They didn't get very far. Surch and Loell were set up on the west side of the street, Melyr and Caill on the east. The two .50 cannons had a tight, interlocking field of fire, and preyed on the scattering ground troops mercilessly. Red-armoured bodies tumbled, sprawled, flew backwards, flew apart.

The two STeGs up front wheeled round, now firing, raking the lines of the street and blowing out windows and plaster facades. In another few seconds they would lock on to one of the .50 positions.

But they didn't have anything like a few seconds.

Caffran's tread fether bucked and banged, and a smoking rocket slammed down from his upper storey position, blowing one of the STeGs in half.

'Ease,' Mkoll said again, reloaded by Harjeon. He hit the remaining STeG's munitions locker. The shockwave brought the front of a nearby house down.

The AT70 lurched forward, grinding up and over the blazing wreckage of the first kill. As it came over, it fired its main gun. The roar was loud and impressive, but the shot was premature and whined away into the empty end of the street.

Caffran put his second rocket through the big, red tank's port tracks and crippled it. It slewed around, broken wheel bearings shrieking raw on the rockcrete.

Ghosts slipped from cover and leapt up onto its superstructure: Bonin, Domor and Dremmond. Bonin nailed the top hatch with a tube-charge, and left the rest to Dremmond. Gleefully reunited with his flamer, Dremmond pushed the hose muzzle down into the smoking hatch-hole and gutted the tank with combusting promethium.

Bonin dropped down, grabbing the dead 70's pintle mount – a twin-linked bolter – and swung back to face down the street. He started to fire at the Blood Pact infantry squads pressing up to meet the ambush.

'Duck or dance, choice is yours,' he chuckled grimly as the heavy weapon mount shuddered in his hands.

'That's enough! Off and out!' Mkoll called over the link.

Bonin, Domor and Dremmond quit the top of the tank and disappeared into the alleys off the street. At the same moment, the .50 teams dismantled their support weapons and hastened out of their positions.

Pushing forward rather more tentatively now, the Blood Pact advance reached the dead AT70. There was no sign of enemy resistance.

But there was a pack of three tube-charges strapped to the AT70's shell magazine, courtesy of Shoggy Domor.

THREE STREETS AWAY, the lead stalk-tank was hit simultaneously by two tread fether rounds. Wrapped in a brilliant fireball, it spun around, some of its legs thrashing out slackly like a carousel's arms. One leg severed entirely, and flew off, crashing through the front of a habitat unit.

Unfazed, the two stalk-tanks behind it scuttled forward over the burning debris, weapons pods tracking and firing, and each one was greeted by a rocket that blew its main hull to pieces. One collapsed, the other remained on its feet, limb segments dead and locked out, central body ablaze.

'That's the way to do it,' Colm Corbec grinned, lowering his empty rocket tube. He was up on the low roof of a hab building, behind the parapet. Varl's platoon was dashing forward, along the line of the wall beneath him, in single file, firing into the bewildered Blood Pact troopers who suddenly found themselves without armour support.

Brostin's flamer gushed. Corbec could hear the enemy screaming.

'NOW!' ORDERED MERYN, stone-faced.

Guheen pulled the trip wire and the tube-charges fourteen platoon had laid across the roadway ignited in geysers of fire and rockcrete. The AT70 almost flipped, its tracks blown away. It came down hard on its nose, the long snout of its main gun biting into the roadway before it came up.

It made the mistake of trying to fire. Either its barrel was deformed by the impact or clogged. Whichever, the hi-ex shell choked, and blew back so hard the rear portion of the turret vented out like a burst paper bag.

Blood Pact infantry flooded up around the burning beast and began firing. One, an officer, had a missile tube on his shoulder, and he dropped to one knee, aiming it at the store front where Meryn and Guheen were down in cover.

He never got to fire it. At least, not alive. A hot-shot round from Nessa Bourah, up on a nearby roof, tore out his throat. He fell sideways and his dead hand spasmed on the spoon.

The rocket winnowed away across the ground, spewing sparks and white flames. One Blood Pact trooper actually managed to leap up over it. He then died, along with the other dozen around him, when the rocket met the kerb and detonated.

* * *

The archenemy forces penetrating the Masonae suddenly realised they were in for a fight after all. They pushed on, resolved now.

In Latinate Road, a slender, picturesque street of tailors' shops and leatherworkers' habs, Daur, Raglon and Ewler brought their platoons in tight to meet the Blood Pact storm-thrust. A ferocious small-arms battle began.

Nearby, Arcuda's platoon – twenty-three – met a flanking push from another five Blood Pact fire-teams. Criid pulled her platoon back from Meryn's position and joined with Curral's, Haller's and Rask's at the junction of Toborio Street and Mason Yard, where a vicious, mid-range infantry duel was developing.

Grell and Theiss scurried their platoons in across the Lanxlyn Road and Principal III, smoking two STeGs and a stalk-tank before meeting the infantry rush head on.

In Skye Alley, Soric's platoon was pinned down by a pair of stalk-tanks that wouldn't go away. They cowered under the deluge of laser fire, stone chips and debris fluttering around them.

'Gak!' Soric coughed. 'Gak this!'

'Support fire! Support fire needed now!' Commissar Hark, crouching nearby, snarled into his vox. 'Support to grid two-six, five-nine! Respond!'

'Ask it for help, chief,' Vivvo yelled over the gunfire. 'For gak's sake!'

'Ask what?' Soric replied, ducking down.

'The thing in your pocket!' Vivvo bawled.

'The what?'

'The thing, chief! The thing that knows!'

'What thing?' asked Hark, looking round at them.

'The kid's just being funny,' Soric said.

'Trooper Vivvo?'

'I... I was just being funny, commissar, sir...' stammered Vivvo, realising the implications of his words. He was loyal to Soric above all things.

Another salvo rained in.

Soric scurried away head down. Once he was behind a door frame, and out of Hark's sight, he scooped the twitching message shell out of his pocket and opened it.

Kazel has the angle, but he can't see it. Tell him to go for the window. He'll know.

What about the rest, Agun? She's going to die and her blood will be on your hands.

'Shut up!' Soric yelled aloud, tearing the paper into scraps. He got on the micro-bead link.

'Kazel? Go for the window. Go for the window.'

'Chief?'

'Go for the gakking window, Kazel!'

Up in a fourth storey room, Kazel turned and fired his tread fether out of the window. It was a hasty, automatic response to Soric's command. The back-blast, contained in the room, almost killed him.

The rocket spat out of the window, deflected sideways off a lamp-bracket and dropped down, entering one of the stalk-tanks through the roof hatch.

As it died, it went into death throes, destroying its companion with insensible, random weapon-pod bursts.

'Shit…' said Kazel, looking down out of the window, his ears still ringing. 'Did I do that?'

As his Ghosts engaged, Gaunt conceeded he had to hand it to Biagi. Biagi had drawn up GAR 3 – Ground Assault Response 3 – and it was on the money. Rather than wasting time attempting to hold badly provisioned outer streets, Biagi's plan had identified and described the various junctions and street-meets where ambush and defence would work most effectively. It was pragmatic in that it gave ground to an invading enemy until good advantage could be had in defence, but it was thorough. Biagi had analysed every street – not by slate-chart but by eye, by methodical observation – and worked out the strengths and weaknesses. He had read the city well. The Ghosts' initial successes were as much down to Biagi's tactical intelligence as they were the Tanith battle skills.

Gaunt carried GAR 3 on him in a data-slate file, encrypted in case the device fell into enemy hands. Each time he read it, adjusting the fluid disposition of his force, he admired Biagi's work. He regretted the fact that the next time he and the marshal met up, it would no doubt be to clash. It was inevitable. Biagi had yet to find out that Gaunt had deployed flamers.

Even with GAR 3, it was down to the wire. The battle for the Masonae district had become focused on Latinate Road and Mason Yard, with minor skirmishes along Principal III and the atmosphere processor in Tesk Hill Square.

Gaunt waved Beltayn over and got on the vox, moving Daur's platoon and three PDF sections right up Principal III to a sub-access lane that let out into the east side of Mason Yard. Within fifteen minutes, Daur's force had the enemy's Mason Yard action in flank assault.

Gaunt's own trick to complement GAR 3, based on years of experience, was to keep his forces tightly engaged with the leading edge of the enemy advance. The invasive force was like an arm reaching blindly around an obstacle. Every time it came forward, the Ghosts grabbed it by the fingers and severed it at the wrist. By staying close to that leading edge, they discouraged air-cover attacks. The Locust pilots, even on low passes, even with the aid of smoke canisters and ident transponders, could not differentiate between friend or foe in the narrow, clustered streets.

Just before noon, stymied across a nine-block front, the invaders pulled back sharply and tried to redirect along Principal III itself. They led off this new phase with an armour charge – nine AT70s and four stalk-tanks, advancing at cruise speed behind a pair of AT83 Brigand-pattern giants. Corbec and Domor had their platoons in cover in a side-street off the Principal highway, and heard the revving turbines and clattering tracks before anyone else.

'Treads! Treads! On the highway!' Corbec voxed urgently. The Ghosts had to stay low. As they spurred on, the enemy AFVs were raking the sides of the wide boulevard with their pintle-mounts and coaxial cannons. Gaunt had pretty much anticipated this push. Domor's squad had already laced the Principal with tube-charges, the detonation of which took out one AT70 and slowed the entire charge right down as the AT83s lowered their dozer blades and began to clear the way.

Slowed down was good enough for Gaunt. His next signal brought three life company Vanquishers out of hiding in the warehouses beside Mason Yard. The *Wild One*, the *Demands With Menaces* and the *Access Denied*, all Gryphonne IV-pattern Leman Russ battle tanks with the trademark long guns.

Hurling specialist AT shells, the three Imperial tanks got down to business, their first three or four salvoes turning the Blood Pact's well-ordered chase advance into a bloody riot. The *Wild One* crippled one of the big AT83s with its first shot and killed it with its second. The AT83 Brigands, larger than their more primitive cousins the 70s, were, on paper, the Urdeshi forge world's equivalent of the Leman Russ. They had auspex guidance, weapon stabilisers and torsion bar suspension. They were the Blood Pact's best battle machines, not counting the very few ancient super-heavies they had inherited from defeated Guard units.

But there was just something about the Leman Russ. Its pedigree and reputation was second to none. When a Vanquisher or Conqueror appeared, the very sight of it filled Imperial hearts with pride and enemy hearts with fear. This, Corbec thought as he watched the engagement from a sheltered doorway, seemed to be the case now. Apparently numbed at the sight of three Vanquishers powering up in formation, the remaining 83 began to reverse hard. So hard, it ran into and over a stalk-tank, splintering its comparatively fragile frame.

An AT70 blew out under fire from the *Demands With Menaces*, and two more were rendered into scrap by the *Wild One*. One of the stalk-tanks strutted forward past the burning carcass of the first Brigand, its metal hooves chipping at the rockcrete roadway, and trained its weapon pods on the *Access Denied*. Twin double-pulse lasers flickered and chattered, and blast flashes blossomed across the Vanquisher's upper hull and turret. The *Access Denied*, seemingly oblivious, rolled forward, trailing smoke from burning ablative plates and scorched paintwork, and fired a single shell that disintegrated the stalk-tank's body segment so completely the port and starboard limb structures collapsed outwards, bisected.

An AT70 lobbed a shell at the *Wild One* that tore away its sponson and part of its track skirt. Another hit the *Demands With Menaces* on the turret, destroying its vox-mast, pintle mount and laser range-finder, and killing the assistant gunner with explosive spalling.

Wounded but not down, the *Demands With Menaces* plunged forward, laying its guns at the Reaver responsible. Corbec saw the top-hatch pop and the commander emerge, oblivious to the danger, to verify aim with a handscope now his range-finder was junked.

He knew his job. The *Demands* rolled to a halt and jolted hard as it fired, jerking plumes of accumulated white dust off its surfaces and hull grooves like sifted flour. The sound of the hypervelocity AT shell was just a crisp, flat clap in the augmented air. The AT70 made a much fuller and more satisfying sound as it exploded.

'Sir!' Corbec looked away from the show the life company tankers were putting on, and glanced at Domor.

'What's up, Shoggy?'

Domor pointed, looking across the street into the shadowed alleys that came up through a hab compound onto the highway. Corbec glimpsed movement behind the roadway's rockcrete revetment.

Enemy infantry. Fanning forward under the cover of the tank duel.

No, more than that. There were two or maybe three fire-teams over there, lugging tube launchers and long-stemmed rocket grenade bulbs.

They were going for the Vanquishers while they were occupied.

'Smart eyes, Shoggy,' Corbec called, stating the fething obvious. 'Five men... with me now!' he added, not caring who responded but knowing at least five would. Milo, Nehn, Bonin, Chiria and Guthrie were the first up, scrambling after him, heads down.

Corbec followed the enemy's example, and moved back down the side of the Principal behind the high revetment. He came to a break about fifteen metres south of the *Wild One's* rumbling hindquarters, and dropped down, adjusting his micro-bead.

'Shoggy, this is two, come back to me.'

'Two, clear.'

'Gonna rush across, mate. On a count of five–'

'Across the highway, chief?'

'Don't interrupt a man in the grip of a suicidal urge, Shogs. The count will be five. Draw up your unit and the rest of mine and hose that far side. Don't worry about hitting anything, just keep 'em ducking.'

'Understood is not quite the right word, but okay.'

'Good. Five, four, three, two–'

The rapidly assembled guns of twelve and two platoons started to rip and crackle, firing across the wide, sunlit roadway in front of the Imperial tanks.

The las-rounds, and the solid slugs from the .50 teams, mottled the rockcrete revetment furiously until it looked like waxy cheese or the surface of a particularly unlucky moon.

Corbec started to run. The others went with him, Milo and Bonin overtaking him. They came up hard, backs to the outer side of the revetment, and waited. Corbec checked his rifle's load and then shot them all a wink.

'You want to live forever?' he asked.

They all nodded. Milo laughed.

'Then follow me.'

They were up in a second and round the revetment through the nearby gap, into the cool shadows of the highway's far-side walkway.

The nearest Blood Pact fire-team was crouching down, locking an RPG into their tube. They looked up in surprise.

That was about all they had time for. The six Imperial lasguns killed them all so fast they didn't even have time to rise. Bodies fell, crouched or squatting.

Ten metres behind them, the second ambush team had time to react. Lasfire chopped in the Ghosts' direction and Guthrie fell over with a moaning curse.

Milo and Chiria led the firefight, firing on auto. Milo shot the tube-gunner in the neck, and his ammo-man in the hand, shoulder and face. Chiria whooped as she aced the Pacter who had hit Guthrie, and wasted the man beside him.

The other two started to run for cover. Nehn crisped off a shot that hit one in the back of the head and dropped him flat on his face. Bonin got the other.

Corbec had knelt down beside Guthrie.

'You still with me, lad?'

'Yes... yes... feth, it hurts!'

A las-round had gone through Guthrie's left thigh. It had cauterised itself, but he'd lost a good chunk of meat and it was so clean-through you could see daylight from the other side.

Corbec took out his field dressings and started to patch Guthrie's leg, smacking a one-shot needle-vial of morphia into the flesh above his hip first.

'Colonel!' Corbec heard Milo cry out.

He started to turn. A las-round. In flight, at full velocity, passing so close beside his face that he felt its stinging heat. He smelt the sheath of ozone fuming off it.

If he hadn't turned his head at the sound of Milo's warning, it would have hit him squarely between ear and eye. The round exploded harmlessly against the roadwall.

'Feth me...' Corbec gasped.

There was a third Blood Pact fire-team, and it had gone into cover when the first two were attacked.

They had the very positive advantage of decent cover. There were six of them, counting by the muzzle flashes from the shadowed doorways and arches down the walkway. Las-shots smashed into the ground and wall around the pinned Imperials. Chiria threw Nehn flat and most probably saved his life. Bonin started to fire back from the hip. Milo grabbed Guthrie and began to haul him towards the nearest cover... ten metres back down the walkway.

Corbec knew they would all be dead in seconds.

He grabbed the fallen Blood Pact rocket tube off the deck, swung it end over end like a baton to get it across his shoulder pointing the right way and yelled, 'Ease!'

Automatically, Nehn, Chiria, Bonin, Milo and even Guthrie, cried the same word aloud. The drilled answer-response meant their mouths would be open when the rocket fired, and therefore their eardrums wouldn't burst under the savagely unequal pressure.

The bulbous rocket flared down the walkway, passing over Bonin so close it scorched the fabric of his jacket's back. It entered the narrow angle of a doorway ten metres beyond and detonated. The flash was blinding, and the concussion wave brutal. Fragments of stone and pieces of enemy trooper flushed out in the firewash and pelted the inside face of the roadwall.

One surviving Blood Pact trooper, caught by the edges of the blast, stumbled out into the walkway, tearing off his helmet and iron visor, screaming. Bonin had been knocked flat by the concussion, but Milo got up fast and aimed his lasgun.

He saw the naked face of the tormented, wounded Blood Pact soldier. Hairless, pale, ear lobes and brows distended by the multiple piercings, the face brutally scarred from top to bottom with thick folds of rouched tissue. The blast had not done that. The Blood Pact's heinous initiation rituals had made those fearful, lifetime marks.

'Feth!' Milo gasped, and fired. The red-armoured figure buckled and fell. His screaming ceased.

'Colonel?' Chiria called anxiously, getting to her feet and pulling Nehn up after her.

Corbec was on his face on the walkway. His makeshift ploy with the launcher had ignored one crucial detail. The revetment had been right behind him when he fired and the huge exhaust kick of the tube had had nowhere to vent. The force had thrown Corbec forward five metres like a hammer blow. He'd made an even bigger balls-up of using a tread fether than Kazel had done a few hours before.

'Colm? Colm!' Bonin cried, running to him.

Bruised and battered, Corbec rolled over on to his back, giggling.

'Teach me to be fething spontaneous,' he sniggered.

There was a loud explosion from the other side of the revetment wall. Dragging Corbec to his feet and leaving Nehn to finish Guthrie's dressing, Milo, Bonin and Chiria hurried to the nearest gap.

The Vanquisher *Wild One* was dead. It was hard to tell what had done the work. The remaining Reavers and the AT83 were throttling back down the Principal, the stalk-tanks clattering away behind them.

Emboldened by the sight of a Leman Russ burning, the Brigand stirred forward again, and hammered a shot at the *Access Denied* that crushed its front bracings and fore-hull plating. By now, the roadway was punctured in dozens of places by deep shell craters.

'Feth all that,' Corbec declared, still woozy. 'Load me up, somebody.' He had picked up the Blood Pact rocket launcher again.

'Come on, now I know how the fething thing works...'

Chiria ran to the fallen satchel of shell spares and came back with one. With some discussion, the four of them figured out how to slot it into place, lock it in, prime it and arm the launcher.

This time, Corbec checked there was plenty of venting room behind him. 'Stand well back,' he told them. 'I've heard that's the smart move with these things.'

Bonin, Milo and Chiria backed right off, laughing despite the tension of the moment.

Corbec got down on one knee and rested the weight of the snout-heavy launcher on his right shoulder. The scope was an open sight, just a wire cross inside a metal bracket. He settled the centre of the sight against the junction between turret and hull on the AT83, then lowered this estimate by a few centimetres. Recent experience had taught him Blood Pact launchers pulled up like a fething bastard when fired.

'Ease!'

The RPG shot across the highway and hit the 83 in the side turret plates. The tank shook, but came no closer to death. It rapidly traversed its main gun towards Corbec's position.

'Not good...' Corbec admitted, starting to run.

But the distraction had given the *Demands* a good shot at the 83's throat. It fired, main-load AT, and took the big tread's turret off with the precision of a ceremonial guillotine.

The *Access* and the *Demands* stood their ground now on the ruined highway, whipping shells at the rapidly retreating Reavers and stalk-tanks. A pall of fuel-oil burn smoke and fyceline discharge hung over the area.

'One, this is two,' Corbec voxed.

'Two, you're clear.'

'The assault here is over, boss. We've turned them back and–'

Corbec broke off.

'Repeat, two. Repeat, two. Transmission interrupted.'

'Ibram? Corbec. I'm still here. Forget what I just said. The bastards just got serious.'

The reversing enemy tanks, now two hundred metres back down Principal III, were pulling over to the edges of the highway to allow something to pass. It came up monstrously fast, too fast, it seemed, for something so huge.

Access Denied and *Demands With Menaces* started to retreat rapidly, slamming into full reverse. A huge shell impact ripped the *Demands* apart catastrophically, spraying armour parts into the air on the hard tide of an expanding fireball.

Coming down the highway towards them was a Baneblade super-heavy war tank. All three hundred and sixteen tonnes of it were painted bright crimson, even the drive wheels and tracks, and foul symbols were inscribed along the massive hull.

Corbec dropped the empty launcher tube with a clatter. It had no purpose any more. This was an entirely different scale of feth.

'Oh my bollocks,' Corbec gasped.

JUST OFF LATINATE Street, Soric dropped to his knees, panting. He cursed himself for being too old for this gak, but it didn't take away the thumping of his heart and the lactic acid burning in his leg muscles.

They'd had to run. His platoon and Criid's and Raglon's and Meryn's. The lingering infantry fight had suddenly turned on its head, just when they thought they were gaining ground.

A couple of Reavers, and at least three N20 halftracks with flamer mounts in their pulpits, had come steaming into the street fight, driving the Imperials back. A squad of Herodian PDF had tried to counter strike, and had been cooked and boiled for their efforts.

Running had turned into the only viable option.

Soric had tried hailing Gaunt and tac logis to call up armour cover, but the blurting sheet-fire bursts of the enemy 'tracks seemed to be interfering with the signal.

He crawled into a doorway, sucking air. Men ran past. Vivvo stumbled up and collapsed next to him.

'All right, son?' Soric asked.

'I'm sorry, chief,' Vivvo replied.

'Sorry? Sorry for what?'

'For speaking about the... the thing. In front of the commissar like that.'

'Don't you worry, son. I can look after myself.'

'I should have thought, chief. I should have realised the commissar was there.'

Soric shrugged. 'Vivvo... can I ask you a question?'

'O-of course, chief!'

'How long have you known?'

'Known what, chief?' Vivvo asked honestly.

'About me. And the messages I get.'

Vivvo frowned. 'I've suspected it since Aexe, tell the truth. But I've known since we got here.'

'Known what?'

'That the message shell keeps coming back to you with stuff in it.'

'Stuff?'

'Data. Info. The gakking truth, chief.'

Soric nodded. 'You told anyone?'

'No! Well, yeah. Kazel, Venar. Maybe Hefron.'

'They all sound?'

'I think so. They wouldn't go shooting their mouths off about–'

'About what, son?'

'About you, sir. You and what you've got.'

Men from Meryn's platoon thundered past where they were hiding. Behind them, a hundred metres down the street, heavy flamers hissed.

'And what have I got, son?' Soric asked.

He was expecting all sorts of answers. The hidden eye. The oracle. The touch of the warp. The sixth sense. The psyk.

'The lucky charm,' Vivvo said. The honest simplicity of it almost brought a tear to Soric's eye. Milo had told him they'd called him that too. That was the truth of things. In this dark galaxy, superstitious soldiers didn't set up a hue and cry for the execution of their touched ones. They regarded them as lucky charms, touchstones, fate-wards against the entirely luck-free doom that awaited all of Imperial culture.

'You're not afraid of me, then?' Soric asked.

'Afraid of you? Why the gak would I be afraid of you?'

'Because of what's in me. Because of... of the warp. A commissar, an inquisitor... they'd have me for buttons because of what I can do.'

Vivvo blinked away dust and stared into Soric's lined features. 'Everything you do, everything that shell tells you... it's luck speaking to us, giving us the edge. Like with Kazel back there. I believe... really, sir... that it's the Emperor himself, speaking through you and looking out for us all. So long as you give us the good stuff, chief, I'll never question where it comes from.'

'They'll be on to me sooner or later, son. Best case, the black ships, worst... a bolt-round in the head. People like me, lucky charms or not... we're liabilities.'

'They come for you, they'll have to go through me first.'

Soric reached out a hand and grabbed Vivvo's tight. 'No. Promise me you won't get in the way when it comes. Promise me that.'

'I swear.'

'You don't want that kind of trouble,' Soric assured him. He let go of Vivvo's hand. Almost at once, Vivvo grabbed Soric's dust-caked fist.

'Promise *me* then, chief,' he said. 'Everything the shell tells you... share it. Act on it. If I ever find out you've been holding stuff back... I dunno. I can't threaten you, but you must know what I mean. All the while the things it tells you are fit for general consumption, then be our lucky charm. If it tells you shit you don't share... well, that's where we start running to the commissar.'

Soric swallowed. He nodded. 'Fair point. Beyond fair, son.'

'We better move, chief.' The sucking, rushing breath of the flamers was closer now. They could both hear the clanking of the N20 tracks.

'Go!' Soric said, and Vivvo ran off down the street.

Soric tugged the message shell from his pocket and opened it.

What about it, Agun? Vivvo's right... and very forgiving too. You want to see him shot? Him and Kazel and Hefron and everyone else who knows? Shot for harbouring a piece of warp-filth? You're not telling everything. You're betraying them. Be a man. Tell Gaunt. Tell Gaunt about the nine.

'Nine? What nine are you talking about?' Soric raised the empty shell-case and yelled the words into its hollow body.

'Nine what?'

But the N20 was too close now. Soric ran.

'MORE ARMOUR! I said we need more armour!' Gaunt yelled into the vox-horn, but nothing except static-chopped distortion caterwauled back.

'What's wrong with this thing?' he barked at Beltayn. The signals officer was trying to tune the dial of his voxcaster.

'Something's awry, sir,' he said, too busy concentrating on his job to form a proper reply.

'What?'

'Jamming, most like. Heavy-grade electroference.'

Gaunt had feared as much. The invaders were adding to their advantages by muzzling the Imperial comms and chain of command. They were probably fething up their own vox-links too, but no doubt the Blood Pact was relying on psykers to coordinate their forces.

'Pack that up and round up the platoon here,' Gaunt told Beltayn, and then ran off down the dusty street. The air was full of the sounds of combat from the thoroughfares all around. 'Rawne!' he yelled. 'Rawne!'

Rawne's platoon was holding the end of the narrow street where it joined Tesk Hill Square. The small-arms exchange was fierce. Gaunt saw Feygor in cover behind a garbage drum, snapping off shots. He came up behind him, head low.

'Feygor!'

Feygor glanced round. 'Little busy, sir.'

'Where's Rawne?'

Feygor shrugged. 'Micro-bead's down.'

'All vox is down. Where's Rawne?'

'Last I saw, up in that hab block. Third floor.'

Gaunt nodded and sprinted across the debris-littered road to the side door of the hab. A decent kick or two had taken it off its hinges. He went inside.

The unlit stairwell within led up to all nine of the hab's levels. There was a scrappy notice panel screwed to the wall facing the door that listed the names of the occupant families next to their hab module numbers.

Gaunt ran up the stairs two at a time, drawing his laspistol. Fething thing seemed lightweight and inconsequential next to the solid memory of his lost bolt pistol.

He didn't bother with the first two floors, and went into the third level through the spring-latched entry.

'Rawne?'

A long hallway stretched out before him, scattered with scraps of paper and discarded clothes. On either side, numbered doors identified the separate hab modules. Some were open, and despite the fact the phospha lamps were dead in their brackets, the hall was filled with thin daylight from the open rooms.

'Rawne?'

Nothing but the rattle and slam of fighting down below.

He stepped into one open module. It was a mess. Furniture was overturned, and shelves cleared. Tape had been put in an X over the main window in the vain hope that it would protect the glass from blast damage. Whoever lived here had left in a hurry. Gaunt hoped they were tucked up safely in a Civitas shelter now.

He crossed to the window, keeping out of sight, and took a look. Gunfire was being exchanged savagely across the open space of Tesk Hill Square below. There were shell holes in the paving, and a five storey building on the far side of the square was on fire. The massive atmosphere processor in the centre of the open space was dented and buckled by countless stray shots. Several bodies lay out in the open. Most, Gaunt noted with satisfaction, were clad in dirty red.

From his vantage point, Gaunt could see a good way west across the northern sectors of the Civitas. Huge banks of firesmoke were puffing up from the Ironhall sector. Last he'd heard, before the vox went to feth, was that Kaldenbach's line of defence was taking the worst of it. He hoped to Terra that Kaldenbach was following GAR 3 too. Kaldenbach, so cocksure and confident of his own abilities, had strategic ideas of his own. It would be just like him to ignore Biagi's fine prep-work and choreograph his own fight.

If he did, they'd all pay.

Further off, in the smoggy distance, he saw that enemy landers were still dipping in over the obsidaes. The downpour of drop-pods had all but ceased, but the landers still came on, ferrying men and munitions down, retreating empty, refuelling and repeating the process.

Gaunt had, for obvious reasons, a basic faith in the Guard being the backbone of the Imperium's fighting power. He had a healthy respect for the Astartes, for the Titan Legions, for the armoured regiments and the Navy, but the basic fething infantry was, in his book, the four square basis of victory. That's the way he'd been taught, after all, by his father, by Oktar, by Slaydo... even by Dercius. But right then, like never before, he longed for a squadron of Furies, or Lightnings, or anything air-mobile with a good rate of climb and armour-penetrator ammunition. Those landers were so vulnerable. One well led squadron could exterminate a huge chunk of the enemy strength in transit before it had even made surface-touch. It would be like a gamebird shoot.

He left the module and tried the next few. 'Rawne?' he called as he went.

Most of the hab flats were like the first one he'd entered – abandoned and untidy. He tried one where the door was locked, and came into a module that was completely empty except for a console table placed oddly in the middle of the floor. There was a book on it. The walls of the room were stripped bare, and there was no carpet or matting, just bare boards. Even the single phospha overhead was missing its shade.

He paused for a moment. It was very odd. There was a door – closed – off to the left. Why was this room so empty?

He took a step forward, and then heard the distinctive crack of a hot-shot load from nearby.

He hustled out into the hallway again, and went down five more doors into another scruffy module.

As he came through the doorway, Banda swung round from the window and aimed her long-las at him. The target light from her scope glowed on his solar plexus.

'Sir!' she said, putting up her weapon.

'Sorry to spook you, Banda. Where's Rawne?'

'Right here,' said Rawne, behind him.

Gaunt turned.

'Looking for me?'

'What are you doing up here?'

'Link's down, so I was trying to get a better picture of what was going on by eyeball. Bastards have us locked. I was looking for an opening.'

Gaunt nodded. 'There's bad feth going down at Principal III.'

'Corbec?'

'Something about a super-heavy tank. I think that's where the emphasis is switching. This...' Gaunt gestured towards the window and the fighting immediately outside. 'This is just a holding pattern.'

Rawne shrugged. 'Tell that to my Ghosts.'

'Look, I'm taking my squad, and Haller's and Raglon's, and we're going to head east to see if we can help Corbec. That means you're in charge of this area. Okay?'

'Of course.'

'You've got GAR 3?'

Rawne patted the data-slate in his jacket pocket.

'Use it, Elim. We've got no vox to communicate with, but we can hold this together if we're all singing from the same sheet. Here and Latinate are the hold points. Failing that, back to Armonsfahl Boulevard.'

'Latinate may already be gone. A runner came through from Soric. Hard push by flamer 'tracks.'

'Armonsfahl then. Send your own runner and get Soric back into the game. Get him to group the platoons with him and–'

Gaunt stopped.

'You know how to run a defence, don't you?'

Rawne shrugged slightly.

'I'm wasting my breath, aren't I?'

Rawne nodded.

'The Emperor protects,' Gaunt said, giving Rawne a quick salute and hurrying out and away down the hall.

'Gaunt?'

He paused at the sound of Rawne's voice, and turned. Rawne stood in the module's doorway, looking back at him.

'Yeah?'

'Good luck hunting that super-heavy. Give it feth. Give 'em all feth.'

Gaunt nodded, and hit the stairs.

THE SPRING DOOR banged shut after him. Rawne wandered back into the module. At the window, Banda was lining up her long-las

'What's–'

'Shhh,' she said. 'I'm working. Second floor window. Blood Pact officer with a rocket launcher. Thinks that noooo-body can see him...'

Her voice was just a soft hiss. Her breathing dropped to a very low rate. The long-las bucked hard as it fired.

'Got him?' Rawne asked.

She turned and smiled sardonically at him. 'What do you think?'

He leaned forward and kissed her mouth. It was a brief but hungry kiss.

'You know what I think,' he said, moving back. 'Kill something else for me.'

'Like what? I could run to a side window and get a decent angle on Gaunt as he ponces off.'

Rawne smiled, and shook his head. 'Thanks, but no. Either the archenemy gets him or I do. No favours.'

She shrugged, and slapped in a new clip.

'I appreciate the thought though,' Rawne added.

'Ah, I couldn't anyway. Gaunt's all right. I like him.'

She saw the look in his eyes and added sweetly, 'Not like I like you, naturally.'

'Naturally.'

'So,' Banda said, lining up and scoping for a new shot. 'You're in charge now. What's the plan?'

'We keep killing them until they're all dead... or we are. Or was that a trick question?'

* * *

'Everyone set?' Gaunt asked. There was a general assent. 'Let's move,' he told them.

With his own platoon, and Haller's and Raglon's, Gaunt set off away from Tesk Hill, into the middle streets of the Masonae District. The scouts moved ahead – Caober, Mkeller and Preed. Preed was Suth's replacement in seventeen. An older Tanith, he'd steadfastly remained a regular trooper until Mkoll had urged him to specialise. In his previous life as a game-keeper, he'd developed great woodcraft, but he'd not joined the scout fraternity because of a lack of confidence. He thought himself too old. Gaunt hoped Preed was not finding his true calling too late.

Half a kilometre east of Tesk Hill, they ran into trouble. A serious wedge of Blood Pact infantry was biting down around Hisson Street, trying to break through to Principal III. The platoons commanded by Skerral, Folore, Mkendrick and Burone – respectively nineteen, twenty-six, eighteen and seven – were packing a splendid but tight resistance to that attack. But the neighbourhood streets were no go.

'Suggestions?' Gaunt asked.

'We go through those buildings there,' Caober said firmly. Haller nodded. Caober consulted his data-slate chart. 'Cut through them and we should come out on Fancible Street, clear of this mess.'

The buildings were a manufactory and a hab block. They had been bolted tight and secure by their departing owners. Mkeller las-knifed the padlock on the manufactory's outer door.

'What?' Haller asked Gaunt.

'Let's go careful. If this is the way through, then you can bet the enemy will have thought of it too.'

'Coming the other way, you reckon?' asked the tall Verghast.

'I think so,' said Gaunt.

The interior of the manufactory was cold and dark. Generally, the air in the Masonae District had become increasingly stale, so much so that many of the Ghosts were wearing their rebreathers. Too many atmosphere processors knocked out of action, Gaunt thought.

The machine shops and assembly sheds were quiet. As they moved along, they checked every side door and storeroom, just in case.

They exited the manufactory and crossed via a covered walkway into the worker habitat. The procedure resumed. A careful checking of rooms to cover their backs as they crossed the hab's lower halls.

'This one's locked,' Caober said.

Gaunt approached, the Ghosts behind him down in cover, weapons raised. He turned the door handle.

'No, it's not.'

Caober furrowed his brow in surprise.

Gaunt threw the door open and they looked in, guns aimed. Another hab module, standard, except…

...this one was entirely bare. No carpet or rugs, no shade on the overhead lamp, walls stripped. A door to one side, closed. A console table drawn up in the centre of the floor, with a book on it.

'Clear!' said Caober. 'Move forward...'

'Wait!' Gaunt hissed. He had a terribly uneasy feeling. He walked into the bare room, and smelt its musty cool. What was going on? Some kind of coincidence?

He walked to the small table oddly set in the centre of the room, and reached out to the book lying there. It was old. So very old, it was falling apart and dissolving into dust.

He opened the cover and read the title page.

It was a first edition of *On The Use of Armies* by Marchese.

Gaunt had his own copy of this obscure work. Tactician Biota had given it to him just before he'd left Aexe Cardinal.

What the hell...? What gross coincidence was this? Gaunt felt a rising sense of panic and fear. Warp magic was around him. He looked at the closed side door. What was beyond that? What?

He stepped towards it, and turned the handle. The door opened gently. Gaunt smelled fresh, clean air. There were plants in the doorway. Climbers and shrubs. This side room was obviously some kind of indoor herbarium, an agri-room for–

'Hostiles!' Caober yelled from the doorway, and started to fire.

Gaunt slammed the door shut and ran to join him.

A Blood Pact platoon was coming to meet them down the hab hallway, using doorways for cover and firing their lasrifles and solid-slug weapons.

It took ten minutes of brutal fighting to kill them.

By the time the fight was over, Gaunt was at the east exit of the hab. He thought for a second about going back to that strange, bare room, but it didn't seem to matter so much any more. His blood was up. He'd just impaled a Blood Pact officer on his power sword. And by the time the three platoon group was out and into Fancible Street, he'd forgotten entirely about the old book and the bare room.

GOL KOLEA DROPPED down out of the hab window onto the slip-road beneath and ran forty metres, fast, towards the rear wall of the dingy storebarn facing him. Every black, glass-less window along the road staring down on him seemed to hold the threat of hidden shooters, but no fire came his way. He was breathing hard by the time he crunched against the gritty wall and slid down, but he could still hear the clattering rattle of a belt-fed weapon nearby.

DaFelbe was trying to raise him on the vox, demanding to know his position. The link was very bad, very chopped. Kolea could only just make DaFelbe out. Kolea flicked the mic of his comm-link twice in quick succession, the non-verbal acknowledgement, the *can't talk now*.

He crawled to the end of the store-barn's retaining wall and then quickly swung up over the low barrier, firing from the chest. Two Blood Pact troopers, their backs to him at the next wall line, toppled over, taken completely by surprise.

He ducked back down. More belt-fed rattling. Some shouting now. A couple of shots whined over him.

Chancing it, he took a dash towards the looming doorway of the barn and threw himself into cover. Renewed shouts, in a harsh language that made him cringe.

He worked his way down the inside wall in the gloom, up onto a loading dock, and across to a shell hole in the wall. The fractured puncture gave him a view out into the freight yard behind the barn. From there, he could see the two-man team with the belt-fed cannon, nestled behind a stack of pre-fab rockcrete sheets. He could see them, but the firing angle was lousy.

He needed to be higher...

A metal ladder, secured to the wall on brackets, led up from the loading dock to a first floor stowage platform. Slinging his lasgun over his shoulder, he went up the ladder.

He was just climbing off onto the stowage decking when he realised he wasn't alone. He threw himself forward as the figure came for him out of the dark, and they tumbled over together, grunting and thrashing. His opponent was quick, and Kolea got a warning glimpse of a bared blade. A flash of steel in the dimness. Gak to that. Kolea put all his upper body strength into a hooking punch and slammed the figure away onto its back.

He darted forward to finish the business scratch-company style, with his bare hands, and pulled up.

It was Cuu.

Cuu was writhing on the deck, cursing and clutching his bloody mouth.

'You!' Cuu hissed.

Kolea shrugged. 'Didn't you recognise me?'

Cuu shook his head. 'Thought you were one of them...'

That, disturbingly, didn't ring true to Kolea at all. Cuu had been up on the platform before Kolea, so his eyes would have had longer to adjust to the gloom. Surely, he should have been able to tell...

Unless he'd chosen not to. A quick slash with a warknife, and who'd have known better?

Kolea shook himself. Lijah Cuu was a scumbag, but he wasn't that much of a scumbag...

'Get up,' said Kolea. As Cuu rose, oathing and hawking bloody phlegm, Kolea crossed to the ventilator window in the wall, levered open the metal louvres, and looked out. Down below, at a steeper but better angle, he saw the gun-nest. He slid the barrel of his lasrifle through the louvres and took aim, even though he was going to fire on auto.

His shots rained down over the gun-position. The gunner himself flopped back dead at once. His loader turned, twitched as he was winged, and walloped over onto his back.

'The cannon's dead. Way's clear,' Kolea voxed to DaFelbe, hoping that the essence of his message would get through the fierce interference.

He turned to Cuu. 'Come on,' he said.

The platoon was moving up through the freight yard when they got down.

'Did I do that?' Criid asked Cuu as she brushed past him, glancing at his bloodied nose and mouth.

'No, sarge.'

She shrugged. 'Must be losing my touch.' Criid clicked her fingers and pointed, and Hwlan took the point men forward.

'Nice work,' Criid told Kolea with a smile. He nodded. He was still getting used to the odd looks his old friends and comrades were giving him, but there was something particular about Criid's manner. She'd been fine at first, but now there was a wary reserve. What was that about?

'Criid okay?' he asked Lubba.

Lubba was adjusting the feeder pipe of his flamer's P-tanks. 'Sure. Why?'

'Keeps looking at me.'

'Probably thinks your gonna get your rank back off her.'

Kolea shook his head. 'I told her...'

'She's gonna worry. That's all it is.'

'Flamer here!' Criid's order echoed down the concourse. They hurried to join her.

It was a false alarm. Varl's platoon was coming in from the next street over. Baen, Varl's scout, had picked up an enemy grouping at the nearby crossroads.

'About thirty of them,' Baen reported. 'And they seem to have a stalk-tank... but it's not active.'

'Not active?' Criid asked.

Baen hunched his shoulders in a 'what can I tell you?' gesture. 'Looks like they're guarding it.'

'We set up a holding fire here to keep 'em busy,' Varl proposed, 'then we could sneak a fire-team round the side. Through there–' he pointed.

'I'll take it,' said Kolea. Criid looked at him. Again, that strange tension.

'Fine by me,' Varl grinned. He'd missed his old sparring partner Kolea. 'So long as you don't feth it up.'

'Okay,' Criid said, reluctantly. 'Nessa, Hwlan, Baen... with Kolea.'

The four of them ran off to the left into the twilight of a narrow, tall sidestreet as the combined platoons laid in. Kolea could hear the crackle of las-arms and the hiss of flamers.

The scouts led the way, followed by Nessa with her long-las. Kolea brought up the back. There were worse places to be in the galaxy than directly behind Nessa Bourah when she ran, he considered.

A sort of realisation hit him. He felt – at a gentle, normal, human level – desire. Appreciation of a sexy female's well-made backside. Gak, but it had been a long, long time since he'd registered anything like that.

Since he'd registered anything like anything.

It really did feel like this was the first day of his life and he was seeing everything new. Like he'd woken up from a deep, numb slumber. How had he described it to Curth? Like surfacing from deep water.

I'm alive again, he thought. Thanks be the Beati.

Baen and Hwlan led them off the street, through the cluttered, ransacked ground floor classrooms of a hab-district scholam, and up onto the first floor of a Munitorum laundry. The air was stale and damp from the water stagnating in the big steel wash-presses. Vermin gnawed and scurried in the mounds of wet overalls. Soap crystals littered the floorboards and lint clogged the grilles of the overhead ducts.

They reached a row of windows that a shell fall had blown in. The stalk-tank was below them, crouching against the side wall of a suburban chapel. Baen had been right – the enemy troopers down there were holding the street as if defending the machine.

Nessa took a look through her scope.

Something's not right, she signed.

'May I?' Kolea asked. Nessa handed him her long-las.

He spotted down, letting the auto-settings of the scope adjust to his eyeball.

The stalk-tank wasn't standard. It was lacking weapon pods and fore-turrets. Instead, its underslung body compartments were fat and distended, like a swollen belly. Within the gross, glassteel bubble, Kolea could see a human figure in front of the driver. The figure was leaning back, twitching and spasming. Hundreds of plug-wires snaked from its body into the guts of the tank's body assembly.

'Psyker,' he said, handing the long-las back to Nessa.

'Psyk-weapon?' Hwlan asked.

'No,' said Kolea. 'I reckon it's that... and things like it... that are fething up our comm-links.'

Do the honours, Baen signed to Nessa.

She took aim, her breathing slowing. She fired.

The hot-shot round ruptured the belly-bubble and blew the psyker's head and shoulders into meat shrapnel. The stalk-tank itself shuddered and then started to burn. A non-verbal scream shrilled into the air and made them all recoil and gasp.

Kolea, Baen and Hwlan got back up to the window and began firing down on the rapidly breaking Blood Pact units. Criid and Varl took advantage of the confusion and pressed in.

In under five minutes, they had the street cleared.

* * *

THE CRIMSON BANEBLADE was a horrifying thing, terror made into physical form. Corbec doubted the fething Archon himself, Urlock wassissname, would have more presence in person.

The sound it made was enough. Not a growl, not a rumble, not a roar. A profoundly deep, almost infrasonic howl that vibrated the diaphragm and harrowed the soul. Someone – Daur maybe, or Ana Curth – had once told Corbec that infrasound noise, down around the 18Hz level, triggered a primaeval fear-response in humans. It was as old as caves and darkness and the first fire. The infrasonic rumble in the snarls of Old Terra hunter-felids made humans freeze with terror. It was a base response, inherited from the primates.

When it fired its main gun, or its hull-mounted Demolisher cannon, it was worse. The ground quaked. Shells seared away into the mid-city and fireballs bloomed up over the roofline. There was nothing he could do against that. Nothing any lone human could do.

'Come on! Come on!' Milo was dragging at his sleeve desperately. His assault team was ready to flee into the eastern streets. The Baneblade crunched over the mangled wreck of the *Demands With Menaces*.

'Okay!' Corbec started, and struggled to his feet.

'What the gak is that?' Chiria asked.

Corbec turned to look.

A figure was striding out onto the highway in front of the super-heavy tank. She was clad in golden armour and a sword glittered in her hand.

NINE
THE JOURNEY INTO NIGHT

'Stand with me, for as long as you are able.
A day, a week, a year, a minute. Whatever you can give,
however long you can stand, I welcome that.'

— Sabbat, epistles

IT WAS HER.

'Oh, feth me! The Beati!' Corbec whispered.

Milo stared. He had not yet got over the shock of the pilgrim girl's death. He could see her still, in his mind's eye, running out in front of the tank, waving her arms to distract it. This seemed too much like history repeating itself.

'Brin!' Corbec yelled, but Milo was already running out of cover.

'You'll be the death of me, boy!' Corbec added, as he shook off Chiria's hands and went after him.

Milo ran out onto the highway. The Beati didn't seem to see him. God-Emperor, but she looked so beautiful in her gilded, engraved armour.

He cried out. A second later, Corbec crashed into him and brought him down with a flying tackle. They both bruised hard on the road surface.

The Baneblade's coaxial sub-weapons swung to target the golden figure ahead of it and blazed away, but the Saint was no longer there. The vacant stretch of roadway ripped up in a messy blitz.

With a single leap, she had come up onto the fore-hull of the huge vehicle, behind the squat Demolisher mount and beside the main weapon. Her sword scythed in her hand.

The massive main barrel severed, the cut length of it crashing onto the hull before rolling off onto the ground. The sliced edges of the barrel stump crackled with discharging blue energy.

'Dear God-Emperor…' Corbec stammered in disbelief.

The Beati swung her sword up, grabbed the hilt with both hands and plunged it down, blade-first, between her well-planted feet, deep into the body of the tank's main hull.

It slewed to a stop. She had pin-pointed and executed the driver.

The top-hatch popped and a crew commander scrambled up, grabbing the yokes of the pintle-mounted bolter. She leapt again, somersaulting, and landed on her feet on the turret-top behind his hatch. Her purring blade cut through neck and pintle mount alike.

'Corbec… Corbec, did you see…?' Milo gasped, watching.

'The Emperor surely protects, lad,' muttered Corbec.

The Beati unclasped a golden tube-charge from her belt, thumbed off the spring and dropped it down into the open hatch. Then she dived headlong off the top of the tank.

Milo and Corbec started running for cover.

The Baneblade did not explode, but fire gusted through its heart, and blew off several hatches. One crewman staggered out, burning, and fell onto the highway.

Sword hanging low from her right hand, the Beati walked towards them, gleaming in her armour, backlit by the burning tank.

Milo and Corbec turned to face her.

'Well met, brothers,' she said.

They both found themselves smiling.

'That was astonishing, Holiness,' Milo said.

'Holiness?' she admonished. 'Is that how you greet a friend? I am Sabbat. Call me that if you must call me anything.'

Corbec glanced at Milo. He was amazed. The boy really didn't see it. This was Sanian, a girl Milo had spent years dreaming about. But he didn't recognise her, face to face.

But, when he came to think of it, Corbec realised he wouldn't have recognised her either. He only knew it was Sanian because Gaunt had told him so. This woman, this creature, was nothing like the esholi he'd met on Hagia. Sanian had been quiet, modest, restrained. This female blazed with confidence, power and drive.

And, while Sanian had been a treat for the eyes, the woman before them was beautiful. So beautiful it hurt. She was luminous. Beyond sex, beyond desire. A divine incarnation of beauty.

And she'd just killed a super-heavy tank outright in single combat.

Corbec suddenly felt awkward and pathetic.

'Nothing like the feats of valour you've performed in your time, Colm,' she said to him, as if reading his thoughts.

'You're too kind,' he mumbled.

Milo started to say something and then brought his lasrifle up rapidly, aiming – so it appeared – right at her head.

He fired, and the shot went over her left shoulder. The Baneblade crewman, bolt pistol raised, was half-out of the dead tank's side hatch, his weapon levelled at the Beati's back. Milo's shot hit him in the throat and he fell down on his face, the gun clattering to the deck.

The Beati flinched and looked round. When she turned back to look at Milo, she was smiling broadly.

'You see?' she said. 'You see? Without you, I am nothing. The Emperor, blessed be His divine grace, has given me strength and speed and power beyond the scope of man. But I can't fight the enemy alone. Alone, I will be overwhelmed. To live, and to be victorious, I rely on you... on you, Milo, and you Colm, on the brave men and women of the Imperial Guard, on all my fellow warriors... a fact that Milo has just demonstrated very clearly.'

'We only serve, Beati,' mumbled Corbec.

'We all only serve, Colm,' she assured him, placing her hand on his forehead. A raging headache he had not even begun to acknowledge, the after-effects of the Baneblade's awful infrasound, faded and vanished. He felt good. Feth! He felt twenty-one again!

'All of us, together, on the journey into night. I may be something... something... I don't know what. A figurehead, at least. A rallying point. A leader. But I am nothing without you. A leader is nothing if she has no one to lead.'

She looked at them both.

'Do you understand? I feel like I'm rambling...'

'N-no!' Corbec assured her.

'We understand,' said Milo.

'This is not about me,' she said. 'This is about all of us. Imperial souls, banding together to see off the dark.'

'We understand,' Milo repeated. She turned to look at him and smiled again.

'I knew you would, Milo. It is set, as a fact, in the warp. You will stay with me now. Now, until this is done. You will protect me. Gaunt has promised as much.'

'I will, lady,' Milo said.

'You're not scared, are you?' she asked.

He shook his head.

'I would be,' she told him.

GAUNT AND HIS force arrived on Principal III a few minutes later. Gaunt stared in amazement at the ruined super-heavy.

'What happened?' he asked.

'The Beati happened,' Corbec said.

'Where is she now?'

'Advancing. Domor's platoon went with her. Milo too.'

'Milo?'

'Looked to me like he'd been seconded. As her personal sidekick.'

Gaunt frowned. 'You look tired,' he said to Corbec.

'Been a long day, sir.'

And it would be longer, and without end. The Imperials had barely held back the archenemy's first wave, and the second was coming hard on its heels. There would be no break in this fight. The enemy would assault the Civitas until it fell.

'I've called for reinforcements,' Gaunt told his colonel. 'I want set units to drop back and refresh. Make yours one of them.'

'We're fine, sir,' Corbec protested.

'I know. But retire anyway. Soric's falling back, Haller, Burone, Ewler, Scafond, Folore, Meryn. Join them, please. Get your wounds patched. It'll make a difference tomorrow if I can pull platoons like yours fresh out of the hat.'

'If there is a tomorrow,' Corbec sighed.

'There will be,' said Gaunt emphatically. 'Now round up your platoon and retire.'

Corbec's platoon meandered back through empty streets towards the inner guard stations, sandbagged emplacements manned by Regiment Civitas and PDF along the Guild Slope.

They could all hear the fighting raging on at the city limits.

'Medic station,' said a PDF officer, pointing. Dorden and Curth had set up shop in a vacant livestock hall. Corbec sent his injured in that direction, but he was distracted.

He'd heard something. A sound from his past, nostalgic, eddying out of a hab across from the hall.

He walked over, and ducked into the hab. That noise! The shriek of a woodsaw. That dusty smell, that memory...

There was a stack of seasoned timber just inside the low door. Pale stuff with a fine bloom. Corbec ran his fingers along the grain. He'd forgotten how much the smell and feel of wood had been part of his life. A part of every Tanith's life.

'Help you, trooper?'

Corbec turned and peered into the dark interior of the building. An old man with sawdust flakes in his wiry hair was feeding planks into a table saw beneath the light of a single phospha lamp.

'Just... didn't expect to find a place like this here,' Corbec shrugged. The old man frowned as if he didn't know what to say to that, and hefted up another board in his gloved hands. The saw whined.

'Colm Corbec,' Corbec nodded to the old man, holding out his hand. The man finished his cut, then set the wood aside, and removed a glove to shake Corbec's hand.

'Guffrey Wyze. Sure I can't help you?'

Corbec scratched his head, looking around. 'I used to work in a place like this. My father ran a machine shop back home, but he did a lot of timber cutting too. It was timber country.'

Wyze nodded. 'Where was that?'

'Tanith.'

Wyze thought for a moment then said a single word that shocked Corbec. 'Nalwood.'

'You know it?'

'Of course,' said the old man. He hit the rubber-sleeved switch on the side of the table saw and powered it down so they could talk without raising their voices.

'You know it?' Corbec repeated.

'You see many forests here on Herodor? Plantations? Sustainable woodstocks? We import from all over. People like wood. It's reassuring. And it's versatile too. Furniture, frames, panels, whatever.'

He wiggled a finger at Corbec, beckoning him towards a side door between laden shelves of tools, pots and junk. Beyond was the wood store. A great mass of timber was seasoning there, in floor-to-ceiling open shelves, divided by aisle gangways. The air smelled of resin and heartwood.

'All imported,' said Wyze. 'Most of it's coloci and sap-maple and white toft from Khan, cheap stuff. Everyday. But I sometimes get shipments of choicer grades. There, that's half-cut supple pine from Estima. You ever see better?'

'It's nice,' agreed Corbec, stroking the velvet surface of the exposed pile top.

'And this is mature shiln from Brunce. I've got some genuine Helican spruce somewhere.'

Wyze walked down the nearest aisle and bent down to a low shelf. He tore some pulp-paper freight wrapping away from a small consignment of dark wood. It was dusty. It hadn't been touched in a while.

'Here you go. Thought I had some left. Only use it for special jobs.'

Corbec bent down beside him and knew immediately what he was looking at. He swallowed hard.

'Nalwood.'

'That's right. Beautiful stuff. Costs too.'

'I know it,' Corbec said. Quality timber had been Tanith's one major export. He'd worked the mills himself, years back, rough cutting wood for off-world shipment.

'Can't remember what I paid. Must be a while back now, but when I saw what the merchant had, I didn't argue about the price. This stuff is worth the outlay.'

Corbec reached down. The shipment's paper wrapper had the vestiges of a merchant's excise ticket pasted to it. He read off the fading shipping date. It was fifteen years old.

'I've been thinking about ordering some more,' Wyze said.

Corbec sighed. 'You can't get it any more,' he said. 'The supply's run out.'

'Well, that's a shame,' said the old man.

'Indeed it is.' Corbec could scarcely credit what he was seeing. He – and every other man of Tanith – had assumed that every last part of their world was dead, except for them and the stuff they'd taken off world with them. But here was a piece of Tanith that had survived, spared from the fires. How many other small relics remained, in woodshops and carpenter's stores across the sector?

And how fething right it seemed for it to have found its way here with them. Gaunt believed that fate had bound them to Herodor, that some great, invisible process of coincidence and cosmic synchronicity had tied them to this place and time. And here was the proof of it.

'I was wondering...' Corbec began.

'What?'

'I was wondering what you were doing here. I mean, with the invasion going on. The streets are cleaned out and everyone's pulled back to the hives. Why are you still at work?'

'Reserved occupation,' said Wyze. 'All part of the war effort.'

'Reserved? What's the work, then?'

'Making coffins,' said Wyze. 'We're going to need a lot of them.'

NIGHT WAS FALLING. The fierce fighting in the northern sectors of the Civitas did not abate. It lit the darkness with its flashes and beams. Deeper into the city heart, thousands of yellow fires flickered and glowed, the legacy of the shelling and the constant airstrikes. Every few minutes, Locusts loomed out of the closing darkness and streaked over the Civitas at low level, dropping payloads or firing cannons.

Beyond, in the obsidaes, the invasion force continued to land. The belly lamps of landers, frost white, burning in the air like flares. Rigs of phospha lamps had been built around makeshift drop points and, under their glare, as the cold night wind rose in the desert, armour columns assembled under marshals, and infantry brigades formed up. The glass fields were bright with circles of brilliance. Locust formations criss-crossed the area at speed. Massive transports came in, raising walls of dust, and shook the soil with their land fall. Iris valve belly hatches yawned open along their fat flanks and they gave birth to litters of stalk-tanks. Others landed, ramp mouths open like basking crocodilians, and lines of tracked armour, APCs, self-propelled guns and gref-carriers spewed from them onto the dusty plain.

Overhead, the low, baleful stars of the watching enemy warships shone.

SAUL, THE MARKSMAN, entered the city through the Glassworks sector. He spent most of the first day shadowing the frontline forces as they ploughed into the Civitas, street by street. Saul had no aversion to fighting, but assault scrapping was not his business here on Herodor, so he preferred not to get his hands dirty. He left the slog to the death-brigades and the armour. He spoke to no one, for he was preparing his mind for the task the Magister had set him, but he kept his helmet link open and listened throughout the day to the comm-traffic of his own forces.

Occasionally, he retuned to the enemy channel. It was meant to be encrypted, but their tech-mages had broken the Imperial cryptography in the first few hours of the assault. Saul spoke Low Gothic fluently. He found it useful to understand the chatter of the weak souls he preyed on. When, in the middle part of the day, his forces had launched their jamming weapons, he'd been frustrated to lose the Imperial signal.

It was back on again now. This pleased him, even though it meant the enemy must have taken out at least a few of the specialist psyker vehicles.

By nightfall, he had reached the junction of Principal VI and Brazen Street. He knew this from his chart-slate. The tech mages in the first wave had almost literally ripped detailed street plans and schematics from the Civitas's tac logis data banks, which were protected by laughably crude protection programs. The information flowed from the tech-mages on the surface back to the warships, where it was collated and transmitted back down to any one with the appropriate field gear. That meant officers, squad leaders, tank chiefs and Saul. A constantly updating, constantly refining picture of the city was made available to him on his hand-held.

The Imperials had fought well on that first day, to give them their credit. They'd held onto the Masonae and Ironhall districts, though it had cost them. By morning, Saul was certain, it would be a different picture.

In the Glassworks, the Imperials had been broken three times during the course of daylight, falling back on each occasion and redoubling their resistance. Monitoring the comm lines, Saul had learned that the Glassworks was defended in the main by local PDF and Regiment Civitas soldiers. Their area commander was a colonel called Vibreson.

This Vibreson was doing well in a bad situation. Nightfall had his forces stalling the Blood Pact push along Brazen Street and the Glass Road hab estates. The death-brigade units Saul had been shadowing all day were now dug in and stationary.

That didn't suit Saul at all. He needed to get on, deeper into the city, where his goal awaited him. He realised the time had come to make an opening for himself.

The Marksman sat down on a kerb beside a torched hab, just a few hundred metres from the fierce front of the fight, and took out his chart. He scrolled the specific map reference onto the little screen and studied it as he listened to the enemy's channel.

Blood Pact units moved up past him, and he ignored them. The night was coming down, and that was his hour, a time to capitalise on shadows and move forward. Night could get him within rifle-range of the target, and then he could simply wait, still and silent like just another corpse, until the moment came.

Saul switched channels and listened for a while to his own side's chatter. Officers, using the name of the Magister as a threat and a promise, were screaming for more armour to push up into the Brazen Street defences and crack them. Saul smiled. That was no good. The Imperials were too well established. Their line would hold for a good time yet.

It would hold against force, that was. Against physical attack.

But Saul had murderous experience of war. Their line would not hold against fear and confusion. Not for a moment. Fear and confusion would do in a minute what it would take a full motor division a day to accomplish.

He flicked back to the Imperial channel. He listened for the word 'Drumroll'. The Imperials – those poor fools – so loved their code names. They thought they were so clever. They never mentioned Vibreson in person, but that was what 'Drumroll' meant. Drumroll was needed at Casten Street. Drumroll was moving with twelve platoon up to Ravenor Crossing. Would Drumroll approve the repositioning of PDF eleven to the Sespre Aqueduct?

Idiots. It was like a child's game, trying to hide the truth from adults. That was always the Imperial failing. They regarded the armies of the warp as scum, so they also assumed they were stupid.

Where was Drumroll now?

'Drumroll, this is Sentry. Respond.'

'Sentry, go. Situation?'

'Taking heavy fire now, major fire. Junction of Brazen and Filipi. Request support.'

'Hang tight, Sentry. Switching rolling one and rolling two to your position in five. Got a shit-storm here on VI. Chapel of Kiodrus under heavy, sustained.'

'Read that, Drumroll. Can you deal?'

'Stand by.'

Saul looked at his slate. He took off his right glove and traced the line of Principal VI with a scar-disfigured middle finger. He kept his right index finger curled protectively against his palm. It was the only part of his hands that was not ritual-scarred. It was his trigger finger, after all.

The Chapel of Kiodrus. There it was. A temple raised to the memory of some half-arsed commander who had stood with the Saint in the early times. Apparently, that made him a big deal.

Saul got to his feet and tucked his slate in his thigh pouch. He put his glove back on and picked up his long-las.

It took him twenty minutes to skirt round the back of the habs, avoiding his own forces as much as the enemy, before he came out onto Principal VI.

He could see the chapel, a tall, dignified place raised from ashlar. Its facade was dented with shell holes. Las crossfire whipped across the roadway in front of it. Smoke hazed the early night air.

Saul crossed to a hab on the other side of the wide avenue, keeping low, and knocked the entry door off its hinges with a single kick. The building was dirty and stale. The stench of decomposing food wafted from the shared larders on each block level.

The Marksman went up five flights and broke into a hab apartment. A glance told him the window view wasn't quite right, so he went back out and up another floor.

Better.

He slid the window up and braced it with a leg he snapped off a chair. Then he lined up.

Saul fired up his scope. It whirred and blinked, then the image resolved. In green and black, light-boosted, high res. He panned around. The front of the chapel. The side. The alley beside it. The barricades. Now he got winks of brilliant light. Las-fire. The muzzle flash of several cannons. He adjusted the scope's glare setting.

He saw figures. Imperials. Dark blobs. PDF and Regiment Civitas, manning the defences, invisible from the street behind the solid defences, but oh so vulnerable from this lofty viewpoint.

Where are you, Drumroll?

'Drumroll, this is Sentry. Respond, urgent!'

'I hear you, Sentry. Little busy just now.'

'They're pushing hard, Drumroll.'

'Dammit, I said wait!'

Saul panned around again. Figures. An ammo runner scrambling up to the barricade with pannier boxes. A medic, bent over a sprawled body. Three riflemen in cover, firing. A vox-officer on one knee, offering up a speaker horn.

Offering up a speaker horn to a man whose very body language told of frustrated anger.

'Hello, Drumroll,' Saul said softly in Low Gothic, sniggering to himself at the odd sound of it.

He'd taken off his right glove so his hand was bare, and settled it around the grip. His one perfect finger hooked gently against the trigger.

With his gloved left hand he pulled a kill-clip from his belt pouch and snapped it into the long-las's belly.

The weapon pinged and a little red light lit up.

Charged to power.

'In the name of the Beati, Drumroll! We're getting pasted here!'

'Shut up, Sentry! Keep it together. Rolling is inbound to you. Keep it together and no one will get killed.'

Not a promise you're really in any position to make, Saul thought.

He didn't slow his breathing for the shot. He didn't have to. His lungs had been replaced thirty years before by augmetic air-exchangers which did the work with no moving parts and therefore no body motion. He simply shut them off and went rigid, a flesh statue.

The long-las cracked.

Saul pulled the weapon in and sat back against the wall.

'Say again?'

'Down! He's down!'

'Say again, Drumroll!'

'He's dead! Vibreson's dead!'

So much for your silly code names, Saul thought.

FEAR AND CONFUSION. More devastating than a full motor division. The PDF around the chapel panicked when their beloved leader went down. In under fifteen minutes, that panic turned into a fatal flaw.

Rushed by death-brigades, the line broke. It broke at six other places along the Principal at roughly the same time. Headless, the Imperial defenders went into a mindless spiral and were slaughtered.

By midnight, the invaders had smashed their way into the Civitas as far as Loman Street, just a few blocks short of Astronomer's Circle, deep in the western sectors of the city. Saul followed the tide, walking in its bloody wake through burning streets piled with PDF dead.

Just after midnight, alone and on foot, he pushed past the front-line of his own forces and slipped away into the dark streets of the mid-city and the Guild Slope. The rapidly retreating, badly organised Imperial defences were easy to avoid.

The target awaited him.

THE WAR GRUMBLED far above him like someone else's nightmare. Leg-mounts splashing through warm water, Karess advanced. Where the limestone chambers became too tight and encumbering, he used his cutting beams to burn them smooth and open. The reek of cooked stone and ash filled the air.

Karess couldn't smell it. He couldn't feel the heat. He felt nothing but the machine-induced pain of his being. He strode forward, metre by metre, into the belly of the Civitas.

'THE WEST HAS fallen,' said the life company aide.

Kaldenbach turned to face him, a harrowed look on his face.

'Fallen?'

'Broken, sir. Gone. Vibreson's dead. They're pouring in through the Glassworks now.'

The room, a small sub-chamber in the basement of an Ironhall manufactory, fell silent. The phospha lamps flickered. Vox officers looked up from the portable rigs and apparatus they'd set up in the makeshift command space.

Kaldenbach had been holding the Ironhall for nearly eighteen hours, and was excessively proud of that achievement. The Guard forces under Gaunt in the east had done well too, but Kaldenbach felt their efforts had been nothing compared to those of himself and his men. Two spearheads of the archenemy had struck at the Ironhall, and he'd fended them off.

If the Glassworks had gone, then his entire left flank was open suddenly.

Kaldenbach waved Captain Lamm over to the hololithic tactical display. 'We're down to the wire here, mister. I need you to mount a counterguard. Here, here and here. Use Principal II as a line defence.'

'Gladly. What can you give me?'

'Nine units. Your own carriers. I'll signal the marshal and get him to send reinforcements up.'

'He needs to do more than that, sir,' said Captain Lamm. 'He needs to extend his forces along the Guild Slope, or we might as well give up now.'

Kaldenbach nodded. 'Get out there, Lamm,' he ordered. 'Vox officer... to me!'

THE NIGHT AIR was bitter and dry. Lamm moved his units forward through the emptied city streets towards the swell of fire light that marked the archenemy advance. They had all switched to rebreathers. Too many processors had been choked and destroyed in the invasion.

Fanning out, his overstretched forces reached Principal II and some of them engaged. Lamm broke into a hab unit and went up to the top floor with a vox man and three of his officers to get a good overview.

Lamm knelt at the sill of an upper floor window and swung his field glasses over the burning, dying Civitas below. Fires and explosions showed up as points of white light so bright they baffled the instrument's filters. 'There,' said Lamm. 'There on the walkway. Bring a unit in there now.'

The vox-man didn't reply.

Lamm looked round, blinking to adjust his sight to the gloomy room. There was no sign of Forbes, his vox-man. Or of his three fellow officers.

Lamm rose, bemused.

'What...?' he began.

He heard something stir in the apartment's adjoining bathroom.

'This is out of order, you idiots!' he barked, drawing his pistol all the same. 'Where the hell are you? Forbes? This is no time for a joke!'

'Respond!'

The crackly voice made Lamm jump. It came from the voxcaster. It was leaning against the wall, straps dangling. There was no sign of the vox-man who had been carrying it.

There was another noise from the bathroom. Lamm raised his pistol and fired at the door. The las-round punched a hole in the fibre-board.

Light shone through it. With the snout of his pistol, he pushed the bathroom door open.

The overhead light was on, shade-less, bright, harsh.

Lamm found Forbes and his three officers. They were in the moulded plastic bathtub.

They had been stripped of their clothes and their skins and of all semblance of articulation. The tub was full to the brim with a thick, gleaming bouillabaisse of blood and meat and bones and organs. Blood trickled down the side onto the tiled floor.

Lamm gasped in disbelief then fell to his knees and vomited.

He heard a swish behind him, in the dark. It was the swish of a cloak. A cloak of wet, human skin.

Lamm rolled and fired, blasting shot after shot against the far wall of the room.

He stopped firing and rose, gun clenched in a shaking hand. His own breath rasped in his ears. He swung the gun round, left and right. Had he killed it? Had he?

Lamm's chest suddenly felt warm. He blinked and raised his hand. His chest was awash with thick, hot blood.

His hand went up to his throat and two of his fingers unexpectedly went in through a slit in the flesh that hadn't been there ten seconds before. His fingertips nudged his exposed larynx, neck tendons and oesophagus. His throat had been cut. He felt no real pain, just enormous surprise.

Skarwael finished his artistry. His boline, double-bladed, each edge mono-molecular sharp, punched into Lamm's teetering, choking form. He revealed the length of the spine while the man was still standing upright, and cut down through his kidneys and lumbar muscles.

Blood squirted out under pressure. Skarwael opened his mouth and stuck out his long, grey tongue as it spattered over him.

Lamm fell over onto his face.

Skarwael smeared the blood on his cheeks up and around his deep eye sockets. It made them seem even blacker and deeper against his stretched, white flesh.

He sighed. He would not be so patient and merciful with the Beati.

PATER SIN HUSHED his eyeless charges and cuddled them to his sides. They were walking down the middle of Principal I in the dark, fires around them, and the runt psykers were skittish. They were right in the middle of the wide highway.

Figures emerged from cover ahead of them. Imperial men. Their lasguns were raised. They shouted challenges, certain no enemy would approach so brazenly and out in the open. A shell-shocked pilgrim and his children, in desperate need of help, wandering blind... that's who they were...

Sin leant down and whispered into the ears of his runts and they trembled. They opened their wet, slit mouths wide. A deep buzzing filled the air.

The Imperial troopers came to a halt and turned to look at one another dimly. Then they opened fire. Within five seconds they were all dead, comrade killed by comrade.

The little malformed creatures closed their mouths and Sin used the hem of his silk robes to dab the spittle away from the corners of their mouths. Then he took them by the hands, one on each side, and led them on past the scattered bodies. The psykers stumbled, reluctant, like very young children. One began to open and close its mouth in a soft, agitated manner. The other had his free arm up and crooked, and was waving his hand back and forth next to his ear.

'We're almost there,' Sin crooned over and over to his runts. 'Almost there...'

VIKTOR HARK CREPT forward through the firelit rubble of the Masonae. His plasma pistol was drawn.

'Mkendrick?' he voxed impatiently. 'Mkendrick? Where the feth are you?'

There was no response from eighteen platoon. They had been holding the cross street at Armonsfahl Boulevard West, but they hadn't answered standard vox in fifteen minutes.

Hark didn't need this delay. His mind was on Soric. He wasn't sure how to break it to Gaunt, but his duty was clear. Soric had to die. He was a liability. A psyk-stain. He was a danger. Meryn had been right. Even Soric's own men, people like Vivvo, couldn't hide him any longer.

Hark felt sad about it. Soric was a good man and the Verghastite Ghosts loved him. But that didn't hide the truth that Soric was too lethal to live. Far, far too lethal. He needed a round in the head before it came to anything worse.

That was a commissar's job. In simple terms. In black and white. That was the duty. And Hark was nothing if not a slave to duty.

Hark tripped and fell flat on his face. His pistol bounced away into the street shadows. He cursed his stupid self and looked back at what he'd fallen over.

Hark froze.

He'd tripped over Mkendrick. The Tanith was dead, exploded, ripped apart. In the street around, Hark slowly resolved the other bodies in the darkness. Lentrim, Mkauley, Dill, Commo... all the men and women of eighteen platoon. All dead.

'Oh Holy Terra...' Hark mumbled and reached for his micro-bead. Then he froze again. Above the smell of soot and blood, he could suddenly detect a stink like crushed mint, and rancid milk.

He glanced up and saw them.

Sliding their clammy grey hides against one another, the triplets slithered down the street. Though three, they moved sinuously as one. Their weapon frames clacked as they reloaded.

Hark reached for his fallen plasma pistol, but it was too far away. Rolling, he wrenched out his back-up, a snub-nose Hostec Livery hard-slug revolver.

He fired it. The cut-nose round smacked into the greasy flank of one of the loxatl, and it began to hiss and whistle like a kettle on a burner ring.

Its two brethren fired their flechette cannons.

Hark rocked, as if caught in the slipstream of some large, fast-moving vehicle that had passed close by. But he did not fall, nor did he feel any pain. He looked round slowly. Three metres away from him, he saw his left arm, cleanly severed, lying in a widening pool of arterial blood. He couldn't see out of his left eye either.

With an angry, helpless cry, Hark slumped over onto his back and began the swift and involuntary job of bleeding to death.

TEN
THE SECOND DAY

'Our high and mighty Lord General Lugo
says "victory or death!"
What gives him the idea we're being offered a choice?'

— Rawne

A FEW MINUTES before sunrise on the second day, from his command post high in the hives, Lugo sent out the order to withdraw.

With the north-western suburbs of the Civitas wide open, the Ironhall district came under increasing pressure during the second half of the night, and Kaldenbach had finally, reluctantly, signalled that his forces could no longer hold onto it.

When the order reached Gaunt, he cursed even though he saw the sense of it. If Kaldenbach fell back, the Masonae would be left alone, a salient vulnerable to the pincer of the archenemy forces flowing in around it.

The northern Civitas sectors had to be given up.

Fortunately, Kaldenbach was a sound leader and a man of method. He did not simply throw his overstretched forces into flight. He knew the vital importance of a measured retreat, knew that ground must be given only for tactical consolidation. He coordinated with Gaunt so that the entire line could be withdrawn as cleanly as possible, supplying mutual cover and support.

It was a tough and bloody process, and it took five hours. On more than a dozen occasions, it nearly failed. Twice, PDF armour on the Glassworks flank retreated too fast, without provisioning cover for the infantry sections north of it, and created gaps that Kaldenbach managed to plug through the narrowest of luck. Then a charge of enemy AFVs against Kaldenbach's own command section almost managed a coup de grâce which was only held off by an improvised counter-strike by men of the Regiment Civitas. Gaunt's withdrawing sections were harried by airstrikes, three of which damaged the line badly and led to precarious moments of redeployment as invader units tried to capitalise on the weaknesses. Then Daur's units were sent east along Farkindle Street to take the pressure off a brace of platoons trying to withdraw under fire, but found their route impossibly blocked by a street-wide firestorm. Raglon's platoon, already backed into a certain measure of safety, extemporised courageously, and pushed forward again, in time to provide the cover Daur had been prevented from supplying.

Any one of these near-disasters might have cut a hole in the retreating Guard line, and that would have quickly ensured a miserable doom for every soldier in the withdrawing forces.

In the hour before noon, under a pale sky leaden with the smoke of the burning outer city, the last of Gaunt's and Kaldenbach's forces reached the defences of the Guild Slope and were absorbed into the second line. To their north, at their heels, the monstrous regiments of the archenemy surged down through the abandoned suburbs to begin the concentrated assault of the Guild Slope.

The second phase of the battle for the Civitas Beati had begun.

SHELLS AND OTHER ranged munitions were now falling on the inner city, and striking the hive towers too. The explosions dotting the vast faces of the soaring hives seemed like match-sparks on the slopes of mountains, but the damage was progressive. Heavier artillery was advanced from the obsidaes to positions inside the captured north up-city. The enemy's airpower also began to concentrate its attacks on the hive superstructures. Anti-fighter batteries on the roofs and upper levels of all four hive towers, most of them hastily erected during the previous days, set up brusque resistance. From the Guild Slope, the display was intense, even if smoke cover frequently obscured it: the attack craft, zipping and circling like flies through air striped and fretted with tracer and laser fire and the blossom of detonations.

Other sounds rolled in across the Civitas too: ghastly sounds. Filthy proclamations of warp-texts were flooding the vox channels, or being broadcast from the speakers of advancing armour at high volume.

The fallen prayer horn, Gorgonaught, was set back on its shot-up tower and directed at the hives. Through it, obscenity was blasted, often the amplified screams of Imperial troops, citizens or pilgrims captured during the first phase. The aural assault chilled and unsettled the already rattled and weary defenders. Life company commissars – the Keetle twins especially – were kept busy chastening, by execution, those soldiers whose mettle broke under the psychological torment.

For it became hard to think. It became hard to want to be alive. By the early afternoon, though the effects of the noise bombardment had yet to fully penetrate the interior of the hive towers, all those in the open Guild Slope and mid-city, including the bulk of the defenders, were sweating and sick. Nerves were frayed, stomachs acid and swilling. Even so, they had to fight on. The death-brigades assaulted the Guild Slope from north-east and north-west. At the barricades, defence lines and strong points, Imperial troopers fought and died with tears in their eyes, driven to anguish by the sputtering, hissing sounds of evil incarnate.

SORIC HAD STOPPED reading the message shell notes that came to him. The writing had become increasingly spidery and frantic, and where it was legible, it was simply abuse. He was a *weak fool*. He was a *coward*. He was *gakking scum*. The author, whatever it was, whatever part of him it might be, had become incoherent and desperate.

He rested his platoon for fifteen minutes between artillery barrages, and sat on his own in a doorway, hunched up, hands twitching, smoking a lho-stick. There was a taste of bile in his mouth that would not go away, and his eye kept watering. He kept looking for Hark. Hark knew.

Soric had been a brave man all his life. For all the sickness and fear he felt, now more than ever he knew Milo had been right. Soric just had to be brave enough now to do it the right way.

If it wasn't already too late.

'MOHR!' SORIC SHOUTED as he got up and squashed the stub underfoot. His unit's vox-officer ran up smartly.

'Find Gaunt for me, if you please.'

Mohr nodded, set his caster down, and started to speak into the horn as he adjusted the tuning dials.

'Heading for the field station on Tarif Street, chief.'

Soric checked his chart. Tarif Street was close.

'He's been summoned to see Commissar Hark, chief,' Mohr added.

Soric's face darkened. Too late, too late, too late...

'Vivvo!' he yelled.

'Chief?'

'You have platoon command here for the duration, lad. Listen to orders and make a good job of it.'

'Chief? Where are you going? Chief?'

But Soric was already thumping away down the street.

FILMY GREY SMOKE from tank shelling wafted down the narrow roadway in the Guild Slope. Ornate guild-owned warehouses stood on either side of the cobbled lane, and to the south, up the gentle incline, the colossal masses of the hive towers rose above the rooftops.

There was little, Varl considered, that distinguished this particular street from the one immediately north of it, or the one directly south. They were all part of the mid-city maze, all shell-pummelled and smoke-choked.

This street, however, marked the second line, the defensive ring around the mid-city to which all Imperial forces had withdrawn. More particularly, this street was the assigned part of the second line that was his platoon's duty to hold. A block away to the west was a company of PDF riflemen. A block to the east, Varl had it on good authority – well, tac logis at least – was a quartet of life company tanks. He hadn't seen them, but he trusted they were there.

Since noon, it had been quiet in his immediate neighbourhood, apart from the echoing torment of the archenemy's broadcasts and a single push-assault from a Blood Pact death-brigade that his men had discouraged with their excellently positioned enfilade.

Varl took a squint down the street where the men of number nine platoon were all in cover, waiting. He saw Baen, his platoon's scout, hurrying back to him from a foray down to the crossroads.

Pater Sin and his two charges were walking in step behind Baen.

Varl slid a lho-stick out of his jacket pocket and held it out to Brostin, in cover beside him. Brostin obligingly singed the tip of his sergeant's smoke with the hot-blue pilot light of his flamer.

Drawing deep and exhaling, Varl nodded to Baen as he drew close. The Pater and the psykers were virtually at Baen's heels.

'Anything?' Varl asked.

Baen shook his head. 'Not a fething sign. I checked the crossroads and just over. They're shelling Katz Street for all they're worth, poor PDF bastards. But nothing. Except–'

'Except what?'

Baen shrugged. Sin placed his massive hands firmly on the shoulders of his two runts and walked them forward. All three passed between Varl and Baen.

'Got this funny feeling we're being watched,' said Baen.

Varl smiled. 'It's nothing. Just edge. We all feel it.'

Sin paused, and kept his psykers huddled close to him as he stepped back and gazed into Varl's face. He recognised the man's uniform. Tanith. These men were Ghosts. The ones who had robbed him of his victory on Hagia. He'd come so close there, and had only escaped with his life thanks to a warning from his guide psykers. Very few of his breed had escaped Hagia alive.

Resentment and vengeance simmered inside him. Sin's lips curled back from his implanted steel fangs. These were the wretches who had denied him. This one, a sergeant by his markings, slovenly, casual, disfigured by an augmetic shoulder. A worthless little bastard who–

For a moment, Sin almost let the psyk-cloak drop so they could see him. He could kill them all, slaughter them, turning their own guns on them.

But patience and devotion to his sworn duty kept him true. He'd overtaxed his children already, and he wanted them strong and refreshed for the work ahead. They were tired, and that made them harder to control. One of them persisted in waving his hand. Masking was easier than goading, otherwise he'd have turned this street into a charnel place to make passage.

Besides, his revenge on the Tanith would be total when his work was complete. These men would all be dead soon. Better still, they would die stripped of all hope and faith.

He led his children away, up the climbing street. They crossed three more blocks, ignored by the Imperial defenders, and then turned directly south. Sin put his hands flat on the tops of his psykers' heads. They both winced and murmured.

Sin felt his way. He was close enough now.

He hurried the pair of them off the roadway into a covered market. The produce shops were all closed up and shuttered, and wooden screens had been partially raised to protect the glass roof.

He led the runts down the tiled walkway of one of the marketplace's aisles, and then crouched them down behind a buttonmaker's cart.

Sin soothed them with his low, sweet moaning, and lulled them into a calm, trance state by repeated use of their ritual command words.

They both became motionless. Even the waving stopped.

'Reach out,' he whispered. 'Find the instrument...'

His tattooed skin flushed and prickled as he felt their nightmarish minds seethe and boil. The low buzzing began. Slowly, a street at a time, they reached out, hunting.

Hunting for the flawed. The dangerous. The suitable.

There was one. No, too strong.

There! Another, weaker... but, no. Injured.

Another... and it recoiled, too fragile to be imprinted.

'More, more...' he soothed.

There...

Rawne blinked. He put his hand to his mouth, coughed, and when he brought the hand away again, the palm was wet with aspirated blood.

'You all right?' Banda asked.

Rawne didn't answer her. He started to walk away towards the exit that led out from the hab into the street.

'Major?' Banda called, more urgently.

'Major Rawne?' Caffran said, getting up out of cover at a broken window to hurry after his platoon leader.

'As you were, trooper,' Rawne said sharply, and coughed again.

Outside, tank rounds from the latest wave of Blood Pact assault whizzed and thumped into the nearby manufactories. Small-arms fire rattled and cracked up the open street.

Leyr, three platoon's scout, was watching the door, head down, and looked in dismay as Rawne started to walk past him.

'Sir!'

'Get out of my way,' said Rawne.

'Sir!' Leyr cried, more insistently. 'You'll be dead in five seconds if you stick your head out of that d–'

He reached out a hand to grab Rawne's arm. Rawne lashed around, blood dripping from his nose. His fist caught Leyr around the side of the head and smacked the scout to the ground.

Feygor lunged, leaping over the sprawled Leyr and crashing into Rawne. He brought the major down hard in the doorway, nudging the wooden door open. Enemy fire, fierce and unabating, smashed into the door and its surround, filling the air with wood chips and dust.

Rawne had landed on his back. Prone, he lashed out a kick with both legs that propelled Feygor, doubled up, right across the room, and also flipped Rawne back onto his feet. Caffran came in fast from the side, throwing a punch that Rawne blocked with a raised forearm. Caffran rallied with another smash, and Rawne turned that away with a hard, open palm, sidestepping Caffran's third blow, and elbowed the trooper in the throat.

Caffran fell down on all fours, gasping. Leyr was up again by then, swinging a hook at the side of Rawne's head. Rawne grabbed the scout's wrist and twisted so hard it almost broke. Leyr cried out in pain, and fell to his knees. Feygor clubbed Rawne across the shoulders and neck with both fists locked together.

Rawne staggered, blood flying from his nose. He swung out with a side kick that threw Feygor back against the wall, and then turned and staggered towards the door.

Banda brought him down.

She rolled Rawne over under her, and pressed her straight silver to his neck. Desperate, she glared down into his face.

'Elim! Elim! What the gak are you trying to do?'

He looked up at her, and then went limp, his unfocused eyes refocusing.

'Feth...' he stammered.

She climbed off him, keeping her warknife raised, point towards him. Rawne got up as Caffran, Feygor and Leyr closed in again.

Rawne blinked at them all.

'Caff? Jessi? Murt? What the feth was I just doing...?'

NO! TOO STRONG. Too willful. Too beloved by other souls that anchored him and dragged him back.

The twins were upset. They started to howl and whimper, and the buzzing leaked out of their open mouths.

'Sssshhh!' Sin cooed at them. 'There'll be another. Find him. Find the instrument. Reach out.'

Calming, they sent out their minds again.

There was one... no, too agitated.

Another... useless, about to be killed by the Blood Pact.

'Find one, find one... find the one who will serve and mark him out. Imprint him. Brand him with the purpose. Make him the instrument...'

The twin minds stopped with a sudden jolt. For a moment, Sin thought he'd have to start again, but then he realised they had stopped because they had found exactly what they were looking for.

Without doubt.

Pater Sin smiled. Through his empathic rapport with the runts, he could taste the chosen instrument's mind. It was delicious. *Perfect.*

'Brand that one!' he hissed, and the imprinting began.

BRIN MILO BLINKED. His head hurt and he was beyond any fatigue he had ever known.

'You need to sleep,' she said.

Milo looked up. He wasn't sure if it had been an instruction or an assessment. He couldn't tell with her.

'I'm tired,' he said.

Sabbat smiled. 'We're all tired, Milo. But it won't be much longer now. Fate has made its decision. It's coming.'

He wondered if she meant the overwhelming assault that was falling on their position at the second line, but she seemed to be gazing at the sky for some reason.

Milo was caked in dust and cut in a dozen places from shrapnel. Most of Domor's platoon, moving with them, were the same. The Beati was unmarked and unblemished. If anything, her pale skin and golden armour seemed brighter and cleaner than ever.

'How will this end?' he asked.

'The way fate wishes it,' she replied.

'You seem to trust in fate,' he said. 'I thought you'd trust in the God-Emperor.'

'If there is any law, any justice to this cosmos, Milo, they're the same thing. I have found my way, and the way is set.'

Rocket grenades slammed into the buildings west of them, and in their wake came a ripple of mortar rounds. Milo heard Domor yelling for his platoon to fall back. Milo got up and led the Beati after them.

All around the vaunted second line, the Imperials were withdrawing now. Before nightfall, it would be street fighting right back through the Guild Slope towards the hives. They were losing.

Fighting hard, fighting well, but losing anyway.

Milo and Sabbat got into cover, hearing the clank of advancing enemy tanks and the crunch of broken walls driven over under churning treads.

'I knew someone once who said that,' Milo said.

'Said what?' she asked, wiping dust from her sword blade.

'That she was looking for her way. That she had found her way.'

'Had she?'

'I don't know. She said that she thought her way was in war… but I didn't believe her.'

Sabbat frowned. 'Why? Wasn't she telling the truth?'

Milo laughed and shook his head. 'Nothing like that. I just don't know if she realised what war means.'

'What was her name?'

'Sanian. Her name was Sanian. I knew her for a while on Hagia. We were protecting y–'

'I know what you were doing on Hagia, Milo.'

Milo shrugged. 'I think I was in love with her. She was very strong. Very beautiful. I would have stayed with her if I could.'

'What stopped you?' asked the Beati. She turned and waved Domor's .50 crew up to a spot where they could crossfire the advancing death-brigade push.

'Duty?' Milo suggested.

'Duty is its own reward,' she said.

'So they say,' he replied.

'Who am I?' she asked, leaning close to him.

'You are Sabbat. You are the Beati,' he answered.

She nodded. 'He'll soon be coming.'

'Who?'

'The reason I'm here and not elsewhere. The reason we're all here.'

'I don't understand.'

'You will,' she said. Another RPG fell close to them and blew in a wall ten paces from where they were concealed. Milo gasped.

'Are you hurt?' she asked.

'My head. I have the worst headache.'

The Beati nodded. She crawled back under the firing line and called to Domor.

'Shoggy!' She was delighted by the way his smile lit up when he heard her use his nickname.

'Pull them back to Saenz Crossing. Get them dug in. Armour support is coming.'

'How do you know that, Holiness?' Domor called back. 'The vox is down!'

'Trust me,' she said. 'Do it. I won't be long.'

Somehow oblivious to – or invulnerable to – the shells and crossfire drumming around them, she led Milo through the devastated streets to a small Civitas chapel whose roof had been taken off by the recent efforts of the archenemy. The chapel had been dedicated to Faltornus.

The cracked rafters smouldered, and the floor was littered with chafstone tiles and broken pews. She beckoned him forward across the debris until they were standing in front of the aquila altarblock. Milo's head throbbed and rolled. He could hear how close to the bloody front of the fight they were. Why had she brought him here? She was so vital, so valuable. She was taking such a risk. This was crazy…

With gentle hands, she turned his dirty face towards the altar and pressed the middle three fingers of her right hand against his brow.

In a second, a single wonderful second of glass-cold clarity, his headache cleared and he saw everything.

Everything.

'You know it all now. Will you stand with me?'

'I would have done anyway.'

'I know. But I mean it. Gaunt does not understand. Will you stand with me, even in the face of his displeasure? I know you love him like a father.'

'This is too important, Sabbat. I will. And Gaunt will understand.'

Sabbat nodded. A golden glow seemed to back-light her eyes. 'Let us–'

'I think we should make observance first,' Milo said. 'I mean, this undertaking is so dangerous, we should offer a prayer to the God-Emperor… to fate… while we still have a chance.'

'You're right. You're here to remind me such things are right,' she said. They settled to their knees before the altar.

SAUL SUCKED IN his breath. The tagger points of his scope now blinked on empty space. Just a second before, he'd had a near-perfect shot. The broken lancet window looking into the Chapel of Faltornus, five hundred metres, negligible cross-wind… no adjustment he couldn't make.

For a while, she'd been screened by the boy, the young Guard trooper, who'd kept getting in the line of sight. Saul was confident one of his custom rounds would penetrate the boy's body and waste the Beati too, but he didn't want to risk it. Neither did he want the impurity. He wanted a clean head-shot. The Beati. In his sights. As the Magister would have wanted it. One shot.

But the bloody boy would not get out of the way. Not until the last minute, when he had disappeared suddenly below the level of the broken sill. Kneeling, presumably.

For one brief moment, the Beati was exposed, a clear shot through the broken lancet.

Then she too dropped from view beside the boy. What were they doing? Praying, he supposed. As if that would do any good now.

Saul slid his long-las back from the gap. The hab he was in was almost a kilometre long, bridging over six Guild Slope streets, and there were windows all along it. He could easily slip down to another firing position and get her on the way back up.

Saul started to gather his kit up and paused. He suddenly felt that rush only a sniper ever feels. He ducked.

Six hundred plus metres west, Hlaine Larkin raised his aim and sighed. He could have sworn he'd seen something at that hab window. A shooter lining up. Gone now.

Sliding quietly to one side, he touched his micro-bead.

'See him?'

A pause. 'No.'

'Keep her looking,' Larkin said. 'He's there. I swear.'

Saul snuggled up against a window five arches down and took the scope off his gun. He peered out, using the device free, like a telescope. There was the chapel. Still no movement.

He waited. How long does a prayer last?

He couldn't shake off that feeling, that six sense *rush*.

Just to be safe, he dropped back to the next window.

He scoped again. This time, a movement. The briefest suggestion of heads.

He fitted his scope back onto his long-las and rolled over to the window's far corner, lining up.

The prayer finished, Milo and Sabbat rose back into view. He saw her nod to him and say something. Saul had his shot. Clean... no, the boy was in the way *again*. If he leant out further...

There he was! Larkin tensed and then slumped back. He saw movement in the hab window, but a chimney stack was blocking direct shot from his position.

'Have you got it? Tell me you've got it!' he snarled into his vox-link.

Saul's unscarred finger began to squeeze the trigger. There was a crack-whine, a distant echo, and for one glorious moment, Saul thought he'd fired.

But the counter on his lasgun still read full.

Exploded by a hot-shot round, Saul's head came away entirely. His corpse, smoking at the neck, fell back into the hab. The long-las clattered from his hands, unfired.

'She got him, Larks!' Jajjo voxed gleefully.

Kneeling beside him, in the shelter of the dorm window, Nessa Bourah raised her smoking long-las and grinned.

The recirculated air in the Tarif Street triage was clammy, and stank of chemicals. A stream of trucks, driven by civilian volunteers, nosed into the yard, shifting the mobile wounded back to the infirmaries in the hives.

Gaunt pushed his way in through the crowds of casualties. Screams and moans and frantic voices came at him from all sides.

'Where's Dorden?' Gaunt yelled.

Foskin, his smock spattered with blood, glanced up from a thrashing life company trooper on a stretcher and pointed down the hall.

'Doctor?'

Dorden appeared through a makeshift screen made from a plastic sheet nailed to a door frame. He too was soiled in blood, and his face was sunk with fatigue.

'In here,' he said.

Several orderlies were lifting Hark onto a trolley for evacuation to the hives. Gaunt could barely see the commissar under the plastic hood of the medicae respirator and the sterile packing wadded to his left side. Thick IV drips and other tubes snaked out of his body, hooked up to fluid packs hanging from a wire stand at the head of the gurney, and to a resuscitrex unit and a haemopump stowed underneath.

'Feth...' said Gaunt. He glanced at Dorden.

'Massive trauma to the left body. Lost his arm, his left eye, his ear, and a lot of bone mass and tissue. Grell's boys found him, got him back here. He'd almost bled out.'

'Will he make it?'

The floor shook.

'Will any of us?' Dorden asked darkly.

'You know what I mean!'

Dorden sighed. 'He's strong. Determined. He might. We're shipping him back for intensive. Ibram...'

'What?'

'When Grell found him, Hark was surrounded by the corpses of Mkendrick and his entire platoon.'

'All... all dead?'

'Yes. Grell said it was like a butcher's shop. Something really did a number on them.'

'The Blood Pact are–'

Dorden shook his head, and picked up a little stainless steel surgical dish. He held it out. Several objects lay in it, matted with blood. Gaunt reached in to take one, curious.

'Don't,' Dorden said. 'Unless you want to slice off your finger tips.'

'Are they what I think they are?'

Dorden nodded. 'Blade slivers from a loxatl flechette round. I dug them out of Hark's shoulder.'

'God-Emperor, they're throwing everything at us.'

'It's the only report I've had of loxatl injuries, but I thought you should know.'

'Thanks,' Gaunt said. 'I need to get back out there.'

'One more I want you to see,' said Dorden.

The ward room was reserved for the most seriously injured, including those that Dorden didn't dare move. The doctor led Gaunt over to a corner bunk where a Tanith trooper lay on vital support. It was Costin, the drunk whose carelessness had damaged Raglon's platoon so badly on Aexe.

'You heard what Raglon's platoon did this afternoon?' Dorden asked.

Gaunt nodded. He was proud of them. They'd improvised a cover action when Daur had been cut off, and in doing so had saved more than seventy men.

'Raglon brought Costin in. Gut-shot in the fight. Probably won't last the day. But Raglon wanted him cared for particularly. The cover action was Costin's work. Raglon told me this himself. Raglon got pinned down, so Costin took point and led the platoon in. Set up some fierce cover. Got all those men out. Raglon wants to recommend him for valour.'

Gaunt looked at Dorden. Weariness had robbed the medic of his usual subtlety.

'So if I'd had my way and executed Costin on Aexe, all these lives would have been forfeit. You're saying I should thank you for–'

'Don't be an arse, Gaunt!' Dorden snarled, turning away. 'I was just telling you how it was.'

'You're right,' said Gaunt. Dorden stopped. 'I'm a commissar, and you're a medic. There are always going to be times when our first duties clash... clash in the worst ways. Hard discipline and selfless care do not overlap comfortably. I suppose it's a problem two friends on either side of that divide have to live with.'

'I suppose it is.

'But now, here... I'm sorry. You were right.'

Dorden looked away, awkwardly. 'Okay, then. Haven't you got a war to win or something?'

GAUNT PUSHED HIS way back out through the screen and found himself facing Soric in the hallway.

'Chief? What are you doing here?'

Soric's face was set firmly. 'I'm sorry, sir. I hope you will believe me when I say I meant no harm. I was always loyal, despite what he might tell you.'

'Who? What is this?

'Just do me one thing, sir. Hear me out and then make it quick.'

'Make what quick, Agun?'

'My execution, sir.'

'Soric? What the feth are you talking about?'

'I know Hark's told you everything, sir. I blame myself for not coming forward earlier.'

The plastic screen behind Gaunt wrenched back, and three orderlies emerged, wheeling Hark's gurney to the boarding ramp.

Soric's eyes widened as he saw the body roll past.

'I'm here because Hark's been hit bad, Soric. He's not been in a position to say anything to me. So… why don't you?'

Soric straightened up, pulling his ramshackle bulk to attention. 'Colonel-Commissar, sir. It is my duty and my shame to admit to you here that I… I have the touch of the warp in me. It's been in me since Phantine, and I have pretended for too long. The curse of the psyker corrupts my mind. I have been receiving messages, sir. Guidance, advice, warnings. All of them have been true. I am so sorry, sir.'

'Is this a joke, Soric?'

'No, sir. I wish it was.'

Gaunt was stunned. 'You realise I can take no chances, Sergeant? I have no choice. If there is any truth in this… if you are warp-touched, I must–'

'I know it, sir.'

'What are you going to do, Gaunt? Shoot him?' Dorden stood behind Gaunt. He'd overheard the whole exchange.

'I don't believe even selfless medics take chances with the warp, doctor.'

'This isn't some enemy warp-scum, Ibram,' Dorden said. 'It's fething Agun Soric!'

'Don't fight my corner, doc,' Soric said. 'Please, it's not right. You know yourself what's in me. Back on Phantine, with Corbec. I know it spooked you.'

Both Gaunt and Dorden remembered the incident well. It had indeed rattled them.

'It's been getting worse since then. A lot worse.' Soric seemed to be getting agitated, as if there was something alive in his pocket that was nagging at him.

'Standard practice says I should shoot you right here,' said Gaunt. 'But it's you, Agun, and I've never heard of a warp-freak turning himself in. Duty troopers?'

Three sentries from the Herodian PDF hurried over. 'Take this man's weapons, and his rank pins, and bind his limbs. Escort him to the hives and lock him down in the securest cell they have. If he tries anything, shoot him. And when you get to the hive, summon the local Guild Astropathicae to examine him.'

'Yes sir.'

'Sir, please. Before they take me. I have to warn you.'

'Agun, go. Before I change my mind.'

'Sir, please!' The troopers grabbed Soric, and pinned him hard. 'Please! For the good of us all! It told me nine are coming! Nine are coming! They will kill her and the blood will be on my hands! Please, sir! In the name of all that's holy! Please listen to me!'

Dragged by the troopers, shouting, Soric disappeared down the busy triage station hallway.

'Should you have listened?' Dorden asked.

Gaunt shook his head. 'Either he's snapped under pressure, in which case, I lament his passing, because he was a damn good soldier. Or... he's warp-touched like he says he is. I favour the former explanation. Whichever, he has nothing to say that I should trust. The rantings of a lunatic, or the perverse lies of the warp.'

'Because the warp never reveals truth to mankind?'

'Not to the untrained and the unsanctioned, doctor. No, it doesn't.'

'PSYKER TRICKS,' SAID Corbec. 'Sounds like it to me.'

'Fething psykers,' Feygor agreed.

'Felt like it had hold of my mind. I wasn't me any more. I...' Rawne's voice trailed off.

'What?' asked Corbec.

'If I hadn't shaken it off, Colm. Feth. I was going to kill her.'

'Who, Banda?'

'Feth, no! Her. The Beati.'

Feygor swore colourfully. It sounded, as always, curiously funny coming out of his flat-pitched augmetic voice box.

'Something got in your head and made you decide to kill the Saint?' Caffran asked.

Rawne shrugged. He couldn't tell them the truth. How would they ever trust him again?

Something had got into his head, all right. Something so soft and strong and seductive, he'd forgotten everything. Every loyalty, every friendship, every oath he'd ever sworn, even his startling intense affection for Jessi Banda.

All of it, forgotten. The only thing that had remained had been his ruthless streak of hate. His killer instinct. The part of his character that made others eternally wary of him, the part of his character that made sure Ibram Gaunt never quite turned his back.

The very, very worst part of him. It had swelled and grown and taken over his mind, body and soul completely. For that brief moment, he would have happily killed anything and anyone.

Then it had gone again, rushing out like a fast ebbing tide.

One terrible thought remained. If it had done that to him, what might it do to others? If it had cast him aside, where had it gone now?

MILO BLINKED AGAIN, his mind unsteady. He was so damn tired. The effects of the Beati's touch were fading, and the headache was returning. Voices seemed to be calling, as from a dream, as from the edge of sleep.

'You okay there, Brin?' Dremmond asked.

'Yeah, sure,' Milo said.

Twelve platoon was retreating carefully down a low alley in the Guild Slope, falling back towards the hives. The second line hadn't broken so much as compressed. Shells sang overhead from the massed enemy batteries down in the suburbs.

The sun was setting. Already, it was out of sight behind the rooftops. By nightfall, they would be into the hives, sealing the hatches, making those massive towers the site of their last stand.

Domor suddenly held up a hand, and the troopers in his company dropped into cover positions.

All, except the Beati. Gleaming bright, she walked down the alley to the head of the position, in open view.

'Get down!' Milo hissed.

'Get down, ma'am!' Domor added, urgently.

A death-brigade stormed the street. They came running, howling, charging, weapons blasting. Stone flecks exploded off the alley's side walls as they advanced.

Milo sighted up and fired. His shot brought down the closest of the iron-masked Blood Pact. The men around him began to fire too.

Sabbat stood her ground, her power sword whirling, ricocheting las-rounds off in all directions. She gutted the first two Blood Pacters who reached her, and decapitated the next one.

'Into them! Into them! Straight silver!' Domor yelled, and the platoon rose and charged, surging up around the defiant Beati, meeting the enemy head on.

Milo ran forward, his head pounding. He lanced his rifle-mounted warknife into the face of the nearest Blood Pact trooper, twisting it to pull it free.

He saw her. She looked so vulnerable. Just one shot. One last shot, and she'd be finished.

He threw himself against the enemy tide.

THE LAST DREGS of fading daylight filtered slantwise through the partially shuttered glass hoarding of the covered market, and gleamed off Pater Sin's steel teeth as he mouthed soothing words to his twins. They had done their work. They were linked to the instrument, and with each passing moment, they were imprinting the task deeper and deeper into its mind.

The twins were the most potent psykers in the sector. They were alpha level. Between them, their combined minds packed more power than all the astropaths and psykers on Herodor, Imperial and foe alike.

His children. The children of Sin.

KARESS WAS SUBMERGED now, ten metres deep in chalybeate spring water that pushed at him, heavy with current. Beads of escaped gas twinkled along the seams of his adamite casing and around the perforated cowls of his heavy weapons. His auditory tracts rippled with the *swoosh* of aquatic pressure.

The rock base of the aquifer was soft, and Karess's massive hooves churned up silt and eyeless mote-creatures, bacterium and thermal scum.

Machine-pain thrummed through his superstructure. He checked his positioning systems.

True south, true south. There, he would rise and kill.

TLFEH WAS DEAD. The human's bullet had lodged deep inside it and killed it. Chto, who had brood command, ordered Reghh to let Tlfeh drop. The cold, rank body slipped to the ground. Chto and Reghh stood up on their heels and howled at the sky in mourning. There was no sound audible to human ears, just a deep, sickening throb that shook the air.

Wet and gleaming, the two remaining loxatl wound round each other and slithered away down the next street.

Their harness cannons were armed. Woe betide anything that met them now.

'ORDERS, SIR!' THE signals officer yelled. Major Landfreed ran over to him, ducking down below the parapet. Shrapnel fluttered through the air from the nearby bombardment.

Orders were for the life company elements under Landfreed to fall back to Old Hive.

Landfreed relayed the orders to his men. Since noon, he had lost sixty troopers to the Blood Pact death-brigades. He was determined that those who remained would stay alive. His men started to move out: two squads, tight order.

A hi-ex shell landed just the other side of the ruined wall and the blast shook the ground. Tiles rattled down from the remains of the rafters. Landfreed threw himself down hard.

When he got up again, he was surrounded by smoke. He couldn't see any of his men.

Blinking, his eyes watering, he peered around, and found himself face to face with a black-robed figure that appeared out of nowhere.

Landfreed froze. Terror locked up his limbs and his reflexes. He gazed up into a face materialising just twenty centimetres from his.

It was bald and white, and utterly hairless. Deep folds criss-crossed the skin, and made furrows around the smiling mouth and the dark eyes. A dried, brown residue soiled the eye-sockets. It was the face of death, the bogey man that Landfreed had been taught to fear.

The haunter of the dark.

Skarwael slowly slid the tip of his boline up Landfreed's tunic front, effortlessly slicing off every button in turn. The silver fastenings cascaded to the floor, bouncing and clattering.

Skarwael's boline stopped when it reached Landfreed's bare throat.

Skarwael smiled. The smile made furrows deepen. Predatory teeth, whiter than the pallid flesh that cased them, were distressingly revealed.

Landfreed tried to find a scream.

'Sir? Sir? Major Landfreed?' Some of his men – Sanchez, Grohowski, Landis, Boles – came blundering forward through the acrid shell-smoke looking for him, and drew to a halt, astonished by what they saw.

Landis yelled out, bringing his lasrifle up. He didn't know precisely what the cadaverous thing in black was, but his gut told him enough.

Skarwael wheeled, his leathery black robes swishing out and twisting vortices in the dust-thick air. Landis's shots rippled the dust patterns but struck nothing solid.

Like a shadow, thrown suddenly elsewhere by a switching light-source, Skarwael reappeared on the other side of them. A glinting splinter pistol came up from under his cloak of raw human hides, gripped by long, pale fingers. Energy-charged filaments of toxic crystal spat from the barrel, and Grohowski doubled over, explosively gutted. Landis fired again, and missed again.

'Move! Move!' Landfreed yelled, finding his voice at last. And his laspistol.

He opened fire on the monstrous shadow, but it had vanished. With a baffled gurgle, Landis fell on his back, shot apart by his commander's blasts.

Boles and Sanchez fired together, hosing the ruined brick wall in front of them with auto-fire. They had the shadow in their sights, but it moved like a black flicker up the wall, around their raking shots, and into the air. It turned for a moment in mid-flight, the ghastly black cape flowing out behind it like wings, then fell on Sanchez. The life company trooper struggled and yelled and came apart as the near invisible shadow mauled him and then threw him aside.

Backing away, Boles looked at Landfreed.

'Run,' Landfreed said simply.

Boles ran. Behind him, Landfreed turned to face the monster, raising his arm to shoot.

But there was no pistol. No hand. Just a cleanly severed wrist-stump.

Skarwael materialised in front of Landfreed and impaled him on his boline.

Boles threw himself forward through the smoke and rubble. He could hear his commander dying back there. In the back of his terrified mind, he wondered one thing. What could make a death scream last so long?

'What's awry?' Gaunt asked Beltayn, pre-empting his signals officer's usual remark.

'How about... everything?' Beltayn replied.

First platoon was dug down in Digre Street, a commercial block off Principal I in the Guild Slope, when Gaunt rejoined them from the triage station. The pull back from the second line was a mess compared with the one the Imperials had staged from the northern suburbs at first light. They hadn't held the second line for anything like as long as Gaunt had hoped. The arch-enemy was ploughing deep furrows up through the dense Guild Slope and was already threatening the agridomes to the west. The defenders were meant to be withdrawing to the hive towers for the last stand, a tactical move overseen by Biagi and Lugo. Landfreed had gone off line and his forces were in rout. Kaldenbach's retreat was fundamentally impaired too – it seemed from the vox-log that he'd somehow lost several of his key subordinates, including Lamm from the Regiment Civitas. Even the Ghosts were in disarray. Gaunt tried and failed to coordinate with Corbec and Rawne. Their actions had been delayed by incidents that the vox-log gave no details of.

The last contact from the Beati had been a report of a hellish firefight in the low Slope region.

On Digre Street, it was getting bloody. First, fourth and twentieth platoons were heads down under heavy bombardment. The archenemy had drawn up a serious wedge of self-propelled guns into the skirts of the Guild Slope below their position, and now they were pasting the area.

Bright green-yellow geysers of fire erupted from the buildings around them, showering roof tiles and slabs into the air, and cascading rivulets of fire down off the intact rooftops. The air smelled of burned brick dust, so earthy and intense, it made the nostrils close.

Gaunt knew they were right on the edge now. They had a very narrow hope of getting the withdrawal to work. If they fumbled it – and fate wasn't with them – they wouldn't even live long enough to stage a last stand at the hives. If the enemy kept this pressure up, the Imperial defence on Herodor would be annihilated before it even reached the hives.

Gaunt ran across a burning street with Beltayn, and joined with Mkoll and Ewler in the shelter of a half-tumbled wall.

'We need to get out now. Back to the hives.'

Mkoll nodded. 'It'll be tight.'

'Wish I could get Corbec or Rawne on the vox.'

'Too much interference,' said Mkoll. 'The shelling alone is scrambling basic signals.'

'If I put up a line here, can you start leading the men out south?' Gaunt asked.

Ewler nodded. Mkoll shrugged. 'We have to look for snipers.'

'This deep in?'

Mkoll looked at his commander darkly. 'I got a report earlier. Larks and Nessa aced a sniper right up in the Guild Slopes. He'd almost drawn the Beati. They got him before he could take the shot.'

Mkoll showed Gaunt the location on the chart.

'Feth,' murmured Gaunt. 'Really, that far in?'

'Yes,' said Mkoll. 'I think they've got specialists deep into us now. Far, far deeper than their main front. And they're gunning for one thing.'

'Her,' said Gaunt.

Mkoll nodded.

Gaunt looked over at Beltayn. 'Bel... raise the Beati. Raise her or anyone with her. Tell her to fall back to the hives. My orders. She's what they're after.'

Beltayn flipped the dust-cover up off his caster-set. 'Do my best, sir,' he said.

'I just got Domor,' he said, a moment later. 'He says the Beati's with him. He'll urge her to withdraw.'

'Tell him to do more than urge, Bel. If she dies, it's all over.'

Beltayn nodded and turned back to his work.

Shells hammered down around them again. They all ducked.

'Right,' said Gaunt. 'Let's try and find a way out of this rat-trap. Ewler? Take the south side there. Mkoll, with me. You too, Bel.'

They ran from cover, dodging the sprays of debris and flame. Unsteady with his heavy vox-pack, Beltayn stumbled. Mkoll dragged him to his feet and pushed him into cover in a hab doorway beside Gaunt.

Gaunt's power sword took the lock off and they went inside, into a dark, drafty hallway where the air-rush of the shells outside ebbed and sucked like a giant respirator, fluttering paper scraps and dust back and forth.

It was pitch black. Mkoll kicked open a door and revealed an untidy hab module. Beltayn opened another, a blank room. Mkoll hurried on, and revealed another cluttered apartment with his boot.

'Mkoll!'

Mkoll backtracked and rejoined Gaunt and Beltayn at the door of the empty room Beltayn had opened.

There was nothing to see, an entirely bare hab module. No carpet or rugs, no shade on the overhead lamp, walls stripped. A door to one side, closed. A console table drawn up in the centre of the floor, with a book on it.

'What's the matter?' Mkoll said.

'Cover me,' Gaunt said, walking in. He had drawn his laspistol and sheathed his sword. Mkoll glanced at Beltayn, and Beltayn shrugged.

Gaunt walked to the small table oddly set in the centre of the room, and reached out to the book lying there. It was old. So very old it was falling apart and dissolving into dust.

He opened the cover and read the title page, knowing, with a sick feeling, what he would find there. It was another first edition of *On The Use of Armies* by Marchese.

He reached out towards it and the cover fell open, as if flipped by a strong wind. The pages fluttered and turned.

Gaunt stared down at the open book, and began to read:

When I speak of a body in this way, I mean the body as a figure for an armed force. To the leader, that force becomes his body…

He took a step back. He had been mindful of the things that had been shown to him, yet now they seemed to repeat with unsubtle reinforcement. Had he missed so much? Was he not being careful?

The closed door nearby rattled in its frame, as if shaken by a strong wind.

'Time's short, sir,' Mkoll cried out to him from the doorway.

Gaunt beckoned the two of them in to join him.

'What is this?' Beltayn asked.

'Sir?' said Mkoll.

'Do me this one service, my friends. Come with me and prove I'm not insane.'

Gaunt opened the door.

ELEVEN
THE CHAPEL AT NOWHERE

'Two dangers, one truly evil, one misunderstood.'

— Elinor Zaker, of the Herodian Commandery

IT WAS A chapel, old and rundown, buried in the green twilight of the wood. Trailing ivy and fleece-flower clung to its walls. Bright green lichens gnawed the chafstone. Bemused, afraid, Mkoll and Beltayn followed Gaunt around the partially collapsed wall, in through the old gate, and up the path to the door. The scent was back, that flower scent. It was so strong it made Gaunt feel like sneezing. It was islumbine.

Gaunt pushed open the door and stepped into the cold gloom of the chapel. The interior was plain, but well-kept. At the end of the rows of hardwood pews, a taper burned at the Imperial altar. Gaunt walked down the aisle towards the graven image of the Emperor. In the stained glass of the lancet windows, he saw the image of Saint Sabbat amongst the worthies. Mkoll and Beltayn hung back.

'How could this be here?' Mkoll asked.

Beltayn didn't answer. He knew what this was and the thought of it made him too terrified to speak.

'Well,' murmured a voice from the darkness. 'There you are at last.'

SHE WAS AS she had been the last time: very old, and blind. A strip of black silk was wound around her head across her eyes. Her silver hair had been plaited tightly against the back of her skull. Age had hunched her, but standing erect she would have towered over Gaunt.

There was no mistaking her red and black robes.

'Sister Elinor,' Gaunt said. 'We meet again.'

'We do, Ibram.'

'This seems like the Chapel of the Holy Light Abundant, Veniq,' he said.

'It is.'

'Which I thought was on Aexe Cardinal, a great distance from here.'

'It was once,' said Elinor Zaker. 'It hasn't been for a long time, not even when you last visited it. It exists only as a memory now, a memory where I can dwell.'

Beltayn groaned quietly. Mkoll blinked fast.

'Someone is disheartened to hear that,' she said, cocking her head. 'You are not alone?'

'There are three of us this time. Myself, Beltayn and my chief scout.'

She sat down on one of the pews, feeling her way with one hand, leaning on her staff with the other. 'So... this is Herodor already?' she said. 'Has it really drawn so late?'

'Yes,' said Gaunt. 'And dangers press. Can you guide us?'

She settled herself against the stiff back of the pew. 'The divine powers allow me only to advise. But things have become more perilous since I last spoke to you. Forces and elements that the tarot did not foresee have entered the mechanism. To counterbalance this, I have been permitted to speak to you again.'

'You've been trying to make contact. I apologise for ignoring the signs. I've been busy.' He paused. 'Permitted by who?'

She turned her head towards him. It was the fluid neck-swivel of a human who had been habituated to helmet-display target sensors. Just like at their first meeting, Gaunt felt as if she was aiming at him.

'The divine powers. Their name may not be uttered for it is too bright.'

'So, speak, sister,' Gaunt said. 'The hour is on us. The Beati is with me, but she may yet die by the hand of the archenemy. No more riddles.'

Elinor Zaker started. 'She's with you?'

'Yes,' said Gaunt.

She smiled a little. 'Oh my God-Emperor, at last...'

'There is so little time...' Gaunt urged.

'The mechanism is delicate–'

'Shut up!' Gaunt snarled. The force of his voice made Beltayn jump. Mkoll stared in fascination through narrowed eyes. He had seen – and, more importantly, accepted – visions before.

'I've had enough of the vagueness and the enigmatic crap!' Gaunt snapped. 'Tell me! Just tell me! If you can help me win, help me win! If not, why the feth did you ever draw me into this nonsense in the first place?'

She didn't reply.

'Sister?'

She folded her hands in her lap. 'You drew yourself in when you served the Beati on Hagia. You drew yourself in when you spared Brin Milo from the flames of Tanith. You drew yourself in when you listened to Warmaster Slaydo retell the struggles of the Age of Sabbat and swore your blood oath to finish his work. You drew yourself in long before you were even born, before your ancestors were born, for you and your Ghosts are a small part of a manifest destiny so great in dimension that from here, even at this high point of it, we cannot see the beginning or the end.'

Gaunt swallowed. 'I see,' he stammered.

She nodded to him. 'I know you don't. This is all you need to understand to play your part. Milo, first. He is vital. Vital to what will come hereafter. But understand there will be no hereafter if you fail here.'

'Here? On Herodor?'

'On Herodor,' she echoed. "There is harm throughout, more than was originally anticipated. But still, the greatest harm is within. Within your body.'

'You use the word as DeMarchese used it. Body, meaning an armed force. My Ghosts?'

'Indeed. You've been studying since we last met.'

'Yes, sister,' said Gaunt.

'Well, then. For the last time. The harm is in two parts. Two dangers: one truly evil, one misunderstood. The latter holds the key. It's important you remember that, because you commissars are terribly trigger happy. That key is more important to you now than ever before. Lastly, let your sharpest eye show you the truth. That's it. There will be nine.'

'What did you say–?' Gaunt began.

Reality popped like a soap bubble.

Gaunt was beside Mkoll and Beltayn in a very empty, very ruined hab module.

'What in the name of feth just happened?' Mkoll asked.

Beltayn was quivering with fear and confusion.

'Nine...' Gaunt murmured. 'Bel. Get on the vox. Find out where Soric is.'

In darkness, the spread of carnage through the Civitas was more visible. Whole sections of the outer skirts and slopes were ablaze, and fires clustered and spread around the north faces of hive towers one and two as well. Gaunt wasn't entirely sure when the city shield had failed, but it was long gone now, and winds from the north blew in across the Civitas basin and fanned the firestorms.

Imperial troop units and support crews fled south up the streets of the high Guild Slope, some on foot, some in roaring carriers and trucks. The second line had entirely broken.

Pressing hard at a trot, Gaunt's three platoon force got as far as the atmosphere processor in Fenzy Yard, and there managed to hop a ride on a quartet of PDF troop carriers that raced them up the last third of the Guild Slope to the keep in the high town district that served as main barracks for the Regiment Civitas.

The keep was largely intact. It had been hit by some long-range shelling, but its main structure, overlooking Principal I, had survived. Inside the assembly yard, hundreds of Herodian troopers were massing, loading spare ordnance into waiting transports.

Gaunt jumped down from his ride and looked around as Mkoll and Ewler did a head count. The night air was pungent with exhaust fumes, and ringing with the urgent shouts of men from all around. Gaunt looked up. The high town district was the base area of the hives, and their immense forms rose up above him, giddyingly tall and reassuringly massive. They weren't towers, they were vertical cities, and they were of cyclopean construction. Gaunt took a deep breath. He had forgotten how massive they were. They might hold, for a while at least.

'Gaunt!' He turned at the sound of his name and saw Biagi pushing through the crowds towards him. The marshal had clearly seen his own share of the combat. A hasty field dressing was taped across a wound to his hip.

Gaunt saluted. 'We look to the hives now, I suppose?' he said.

'Old Hive,' said Biagi. 'The lord general and the Civitas officiaries have withdrawn there. We will compose our defence around them.'

'Isn't Old Hive the most vulnerable?' Gaunt asked. 'It's ancient, and far less robust than the other towers.'

'Old Hive is the seat of Herodian culture,' Biagi said. 'It is our heart. The Holy Balneary is there, and the oldest shrines. If we concentrate anywhere, it must be there.'

The implication was grim. The other towers would be left unprotected. Their citizens would perish. It must have been a hard decision for Biagi to make.

Gaunt caught himself. No, the decision was easy. It was precisely the same one that he had made during the fall of Tanith. The whole could not be saved, and any attempt to do so would be doomed. The only course of action was to concentrate all combat efforts to save one part of it.

Biagi stared out at the rippling fireglow lighting the northern sky.

'To think I forbade your use of flamers, Gaunt. Look how my city burns.'

'Be thankful, sir, that I ignored your orders. But for my flamers, your city would have been burning far more, far sooner.'

Gaunt looked at Biagi. 'I sent a signal on my way up. Concerning a trooper of mine. Sergeant Soric?'

'Indeed. I've had him escorted down from the hives as you asked. What's so important about him?'

'Come with me and we may find out.'

Escorted by Beltayn, and Biagi's own signals officer Sires, Gaunt and the marshal strode into the Regiment Civitas keep. Emergency lighting was on, and the corridors were flushed with a dull green glow. Men hurried past them in teams, carrying boxes of supplies or pushing munitions on carts. The old fortress was being stripped bare of anything that might prove useful.

'Anything from Kaldenbach?' Gaunt asked.

'Brief signals. He's caught in a pocket to the west, but he has some armour left.'

'And the Beati herself?'

'We're having difficulty pinpointing her right now. I have implored her to retreat.'

'So have I. It's imperative. You understand this war is entirely symbolic?'

'The thought had crossed my mind,' said Biagi.

'Don't let it cross. Keep it centred. She's what this is all about. Herodor has no strategic importance. By coming here, she made this world a target. This invasion has one purpose. To find her and kill her. She's the lure. If we recognise that and use it, we might be in with a chance.'

'Does she recognise it?' Biagi said.

Gaunt glanced at him. 'I'm rather afraid that's why she came here in the first place, marshal.'

'I see,' said Biagi.

They came to a halt outside a security hatch, triple locked. Two PDF sentries stood aside for them, and beat a hasty retreat when Biagi dismissed them. The marshal fitted his authority key into the socket and the hatch whirred open. The chamber beyond was starkly lit by white phospha lamps. It was the keep's brig.

A group of armed Ghosts waited for them inside: Meryn and his unit, serving as guard detail.

'Sir!' said Meryn sharply.

'We can handle this, sergeant. Head for the evac transports. I'll see you in Old Hive.'

Meryn nodded. He looked angry. 'You should have shot him, sir,' he said.

'I beg your pardon, Meryn?'

'He's scum. Filth. I knew it. I told Commissar Hark. The bastard should have been executed long since.'

'That's your opinion, is it, Meryn?'

'Sir, every moment he lives, he brings shame on our regiment! I don't know why you didn't do your job as commissar and shoot the bastard thr–'

Gaunt's blow caught Meryn unawares and surprised everyone around them. Meryn sprawled on his back, clutching at his bloody mouth.

'Agun Soric has served the Ghosts with distinction, Meryn. He volunteered himself for detention, and he may yet prove to be something quite different from the bogey man you fear. As far as the bringing shame thing goes, you're doing fine all by yourself.'

Gaunt looked up at the men of Meryn's platoon. 'I am a commissar. It's my business to judge. But unlike the Keetles of this bloody cosmos, I will not be hasty in that judgment. Soric lives or dies by my word alone. Understood?'

There was a nervous growl of voices. Gaunt glanced down at Meryn. 'Get out of my sight, and pray I've forgotten your insolence the next time we meet.'

Fargher and Guheen dragged their sergeant to his feet, and fourteenth platoon left the chamber.

'I thought Meryn was one of your best?' Biagi said.

'He is, in a sound, unimaginative way.'

'What did he mean, then? About this Soric?'

'I need you to be patient, Biagi. Soric came to me earlier and confessed. He's a psyker.'

'HE'S IN HERE,' said Dorden, showing the four soldiers to the door of the fifth cell. The Tanith doctor had taken it upon himself to escort Soric personally. A robed astropath and two bullish men in long grey leather coats stood by the cell door. The grey men, clutching power-goads, were officer-handlers from the life company's sanctioned psyker cadre. Wire-grilled augmetic damper units were sutured into their ears and eyesockets.

'I heard what you said. To Meryn, just then,' said Dorden.

'Did you? I trust I'm starting to live up to your high standards, doctor?'

Dorden smiled sarcastically. 'One thing I don't get,' he said. 'Earlier, you told me you believed the warp never revealed truth to mankind, especially not to the untrained and the unsanctioned.'

'I changed my mind,' said Gaunt. 'I'm not trained or sanctioned but, as Zweil has freely pointed out, powers divine or otherwise have chosen to speak to me. Just this afternoon, in a little chapel, I–'

'What?'

'Never mind. This it?'

Dorden opened the cell hatch.

Soric was lying on the perforated metal cot, bathed in the hard light of the overhead phosphas. He had been badly beaten. Dorden had done his best to patch him up.

'Feth! What happened?'

'Meryn's platoon happened. They gave him hell on the transit down.'

'Bastards. Ignorant bastards…'

'What the hell is this?' Biagi muttered, bending down to collect up some of the hundreds of crumpled scraps of blue paper that littered the cell floor. Gaunt looked over his shoulder. The papers in the marshal's hands were covered in hasty, incomprehensible scrawl.

'I'd say that was torn from a standard Guard issue message pad,' Beltayn said.

'Did you give him paper? Writing tools?' Biagi asked the handlers.

'No sir,' one of them grunted, his voice a slabby monotone processed through an augmetic voicebox. 'We took all personal items from the prisoner. But they keep returning to him.'

'What the hell does that mean?' Biagi asked.

The handler crossed to Soric and searched him. Soric moaned at the touch. The handler produced a brass shell case from Soric's thigh pocket.

'I cannot count the number of times we've taken this off him. Every few seconds, it disappears from our evidence bag and reappears in his pocket.' The handler opened the message shell and shook out another fold of blue paper. 'And every time, there's another note in it.'

'Have you seen this before?' Gaunt asked.

'No, sir,' said the handler.

Gaunt knelt down beside Soric. 'Agun? Chief? You hear me?'

Soric's single eye opened, squeezed to a slit by the swollen flesh of his puffy face. The eye was bloodshot.

'Colonel-commissar, sir,' he sighed.

'There's not much time, chief. Tell me about the nine.'

'So tired... hurts so much...'

'Chief! You were desperate to tell me before! Tell me now!'

Soric nodded slowly, and, with Dorden's help, got himself up to a half-sitting position.

'Nine are coming,' he said.

'Nine?'

'Nine,' he repeated, swallowing pain. 'I'm so sorry, sir. I never meant to risk yo–'

'Save it for later, Agun. Tell me about the nine.'

'Nine. The shell told me there would be nine. Because nine is the sacred number of the Beati...'

'The nine holy wounds,' said Biagi solemnly.

'The nine holy wounds,' Soric nodded. 'I saw her. She was looking at me. Right at me. She knew...'

'Chief! Chief! Come on, stay with me!'

Soric had faded and slumped. Gaunt looked over at Dorden. 'Can't you do something?'

'That will help us? Of course. That will help him? No. Besides, if he's what you're afraid he is, a stimm-shot might not be a good idea.'

'I think we might have to take that chance,' said Gaunt. 'Agreed?'

Biagi nodded. The handlers charged their goads. The sharp stink of ozone filled the little cell.

Dorden thumped the one-dose derma-ject into Soric's arm and wiped the puncture with a swab loaded with rubbing alcohol. Soric trembled, shivered and convulsed.

Then he snapped awake, staring at Gaunt with his one good eye.

'Sir?'

'Tell me about the nine, chief.'

'Nine. That's what it said. It wouldn't shut up about it.' Soric raised his hand, and Gaunt saw it was holding the brass message shell. How the feth had it got back into his hand?

'Ever since Phantine, when I was hurt on Phantine, the thing has been there. Not speaking to me, you understand. Writing to me. All very civilised. I would open the shell and ooops! There's another message. Split left, split right, head down the wall there... all that shit. Combat shit. Just a word to the wise. I never worried about it. God-Emperor, I know I should have! I should have told you about it long ago!'

'Why didn't you worry about it?' asked Gaunt.

'Because it was in my handwriting. I like a drink or two, you know that, sir. I wondered... had I written it and forgotten...?'

'All these messages?'

'No. No! But at the start of it, a little. Then, when I realised it was more than that, I was too scared.'

'Of what?'

'Of men like you,' Soric said, pointing at Gaunt. 'Of men like them,' he added sourly, gesturing to the handlers.

'Milo told me what I should do,' said Soric. Gaunt glanced at Beltayn. 'He told me to be a man and fess up.'

'What... what is the shell telling you now, chief?'

'The shell always knows. It knew about Herodor long before we were marked up and shipped out. It knew. It just knows. Nine. Nine are coming.'

'Nine what?'

'Nine killers.'

'Coming to kill the Beati?'

Soric nodded.

'There is a vast army on Herodor trying to kill the Beati,' said Biagi.

'But the nine are special. They have been charged by the Magister. They are deep inside us. The shell says so. Deeper inside us than we dare realise.'

'What are they?' Gaunt asked.

'Wait,' said Soric. He put the message shell back into his pocket and then drew it out again. When he opened it, there was a flimsy sheet of blue paper folded up inside.

He flattened the sheet out to read it, and held it up close to his deformed eye.

'Nine. A marksman. Three psykers. Three reptiles. A phantom. A death-machine.'

OUTSIDE THE SIMPLE cell, Gaunt leaned heavily against the wall and wiped the rank sweat from his brow.

'Did you feel it in there?'

Biagi nodded.

'Like a swamp suddenly, so hot, so damp...'

'He's a psyker. He should burn.'

'Not while he's useful. Forget the invasion force, the archenemy has deployed specialist assassins into the Civitas. We have to find them fast.'

'But–'

'Think, Biagi! I told you this war was symbolic! All that matters, all that your world is worth, is the life or death of the Beati. We have to find these killers and kill them before they win this outright.'

Biagi shrugged. 'What do we know? He told us so little. A marksman…?'

'Dead already, I think,' said Gaunt. 'One down. The reptiles…'

'We know there are loxatl active,' said Dorden. Gaunt nodded.

'He mentioned a phantom,' said Biagi. 'I interviewed a life company trooper called Boles just thirty minutes ago. He told me how Landfreed and a whole fire-team were taken down by a ghost that came out of nowhere.'

'Ghost?' Dorden echoed.

Biagi smiled. 'Forgive me. A spectre. Boles is an experienced veteran. He was sure it was of the piratical devil-breed.'

Gaunt shuddered. Not since his days as a cadet, many years before Balhaut, had he been forced to deal with those vicious killers, the so-called dark eldar.

'What about the three psykers? And this… what did he call it? This death-machine?'

'We'll find them,' said Gaunt.

'How?' Biagi laughed.

'We'll find the Beati. They're all looking for her.'

'WHAT DID THE prophecy mean, sir?' Beltayn asked as he walked with Gaunt out through the exit hatches of the keep.

'Sister Elinor said there were two dangers: one truly evil, one misunderstood. I believe that misunderstood one is Soric. Remember, she told me to be wary, because commissars are trigger happy? That seems to fit. He's the key and I could have had him executed before I found that out.'

'What about the other?'

'Well, that's what we're looking for.'

'And what did she say at the end… "Let your sharpest eye show you the truth"?'

Gaunt nodded. 'Raise all sections still in the field. Tell them the Beati is at risk and they should locate her and safeguard her. And get me Mkoll on the link. He's my sharpest eye.'

Gaunt paused. 'And get me Larkin too.'

'HOLINESS! YOUR HOLINESS!' Domor ran across the yard to where the Beati stood. Milo was with her. She seemed to be staring at the sky.

Domor had to shout to make himself heard over the bombardment rippling through the nearby streets.

'Another vox-signal! From Marshal Biagi this time. He repeats Colonel-commissar Gaunt's instructions. We must make our way to Old Hive. It's imperative! Holiness?'

'I think she understands,' said Milo. The ground shook as a tank round demolished a commercial property not seventy metres away. 'We can't stay out here much longer anyway.'

Sabbat shivered, as if the night air was cold. In truth, it was sweltering hot from the raging firestorms.

'What is it?' Milo asked.

'He's coming. The endgame is on us.'

'Who is she talking about?' Domor asked Milo.

Milo shook his head. 'We have to go to Old Hive now, Sabbat,' Milo said. 'They're waiting for us. They need us.'

The Beati turned and looked at him with a half-smile. Sometimes, like now with the flame-light starkly side-lighting her features, she had a terrible, terrifying aspect.

'Soon,' she assured. 'One last venture. We must get to the agridomes.'

OUT ON THE bare wastes of the Great Western Obsidae, the night was a hard, dry sub-zero, cut by merciless winds from the outer zones. Phospha lamps glowed and swung in the wind, coldly illuminating the row upon row of empty landers and transport ships. Their mouth hatches were open, pointing south.

There, distantly, the Civitas lay, submerged in the murk and flash of war. The orange glow of the firestorms lit the low sky.

Thrusters whining and cycling hard a single lander, more massively armoured than the rest, came in low, sheeting up dust waves more fiercely than the desert winds. Its Locust escort turned and banked away. Burners flared blue. Hydraulic landing claws extended, and the battle transport settled like a giant mosquito.

The ramps opened. Light shone out. Crews of slave-carls spewed from the hatches, followed by a formal marching block of Retinue in full armour. The Retinue, five hundred strong, divided with parade ground precision, swung their weapons to shoulder in a perfectly synchronised movement, and formed two lines of honour guard.

Etrodai, his changeling blade skinned and hungry, strode down the ramp and He followed.

He was dressed for war in gleaming beetle-black armour. His face was masked by His antlered helmet. The Retinue murmured their moan of respect.

Enok Innokenti, Magister, Warlord, chosen disciple of the Archon, set foot on the dusty soil of Herodor. He raised His arms in salutation.

The Retinue screamed His name.

TWELVE
IN THE NAME OF SABBAT

'As the Emperor protects, so must we.'

— Ibram Gaunt

SOME OF THE men in Corbec's platoon were getting vocal with their complaints, and Corbec could half understand why.

'When the feth do we get to fall back?' said Bewl.

'For feth's sake, why are we still out here?' said Cown.

'We have a job to do, boys,' Corbec assured them. Instructions had been simple. Find the Beati and get her back to Old Hive. And watch out in particular for the really bad things. Of which there were nine, apparently.

They weren't fighting any more. They were sneaking. Cloaked up, stealthy, using every shred of Tanith woodcraft to edge through the splintered ruins of Guild Slope. They dodged advancing Blood Pact units, and hid while crimson tanks grumbled past, lamps blazing. There was the odd firefight or three, when circumstances demanded, but then it was strictly hit and run.

They were working the shadows and staying alive.

Corbec was glad to have Mkvenner back with him. He'd lost count of the Blood Pact throats Ven had sliced that night as he led them at point. There was no getting away from the fact that they were all going to die here on Herodor, one way or another. That was the way the odds were stacked, and not even Varl or Feygor would have given better. But by feth, they were going to make a good account of themselves.

His camo-cloak pulled up around him like a hood, Corbec scuttled forward at a signal from Ven, passing Orrin, Cown, Cole and Irvinn in cover. He reached the street turn and used the shadows cast by a burning community hall to blend into the scenery. He raised a hand, made a signal of his own. Veddekin, Ponore, Sillo, Androby and Brown sprinted up on his heels and vanished into the shot-up print shop to his left. Then Surch and Loell moved up smartly, lugging the .50 and its panniers of ammo.

Corbec scurried over to fresh cover. He was quiet for a big man. Rerval and Roskil covered him, and then slipped in behind him.

The three of them were running, in file, down to the end of the block. A tank, or something similar, had flattened the building there and left nothing but ragged rockcrete sections, sprouting the broken strands of their internal metal reinforcement.

Mkvenner reappeared, jogging back to them, light on his feet.

'Some kind of covered market to the left there. The road to the right is blocked. We could carry on down the hill if we follow that side street.'

'Can we go through the market?' Corbec asked.

'I haven't scoped it.'

'Let's try.' Corbec rose, and flashed a finger signal back. Then he and Ven were running forward again, with Brown, Cole, Sillo and Roskil behind them.

The covered market had once had a glass roof, but the shockwaves from the shelling had brought it down. Some wooden screens remained. The produce shops and trader barrows inside were all locked up and shuttered.

'Doesn't look promising,' Ven said.

Corbec nodded, and turned to go back. Then he stopped. He had smelt something. It was faint, very faint, almost masked by the rich stink of smoke and burning fuel.

Something like cinnamon. He knew that smell, vividly. That particular reek. From Hagia, the Doctrinopolis... what was it now? Four years ago?

He'd never forget it. It was in his nightmares still. A moment in his life no amount of good nights' sleep could wear away. Him and the poor boy Yael. Prisoners of the Infardi. And that thing, that monster in human form. The one who'd butchered Yael just to hear him scream.

It couldn't be! That bastard was long dead...

Corbec breathed in again: cinnamon, sweat, decay. Faint, but lingering.

'Cover me,' he said to Ven, and ignored the askance look the scout gave him.

Corbec advanced into the market, lasrifle low and ready. He took care with every step. The floor was covered in chips of broken glass from the roof. On the edge of his nerves and as fine as any Tanith scout, Corbec made no sound.

He prowled in, checking from side to side. Twice, he jumped at shadows and almost discharged his weapon. The smell grew stronger.

Corbec saw movement. Low down, under a trader's barrow. He circled, switching his lasrifle to a single-handed grip as he fished out a lamp-pack.

He edged round the cart, and saw there were two kids hiding between the wheels. Little, hunched up kids. One of them was waving his hand beside his head, as if he was trying to fan the close air. Corbec came around further, and clicked on the pack. He lit the kids up with a hard-light beam and they didn't flinch. He saw their faces.

'Oh feth!' he growled.

Something hit him from behind, a heavy, powerful mass that reeked of sweat and cinnamon. Corbec lurched forward and crashed into the cart, overturning it.

The weight was on him. He felt a knifing pain in his left shoulder.

Corbec yowled and smacked back with his elbow. The weight reduced, and he rolled, groping for his rifle. He blundered into the kids... though from his brief glimpse of them he knew they were not kids... and felt them grab at him.

'Colonel? Sir?' Corbec could hear Ven shouting. He heard men running forward over the glass litter. A lasrifle fired.

Mkvenner came charging in, with Brown and Cole beside him. Roskil and Sillo were close behind. Cole had already fired, shredding the shutters of a produce shop behind the shuffling twins. The twins seized each other and switched their sightless heads around in unison, looking at Cole. The concussive psi-wave hit him and broke every bone in his body. His limp, flopping form flew backwards into the air like a weighted sack, up and out through the market's roof, snapping a support truss with a sickening crunch.

Corbec leapt up, and switched around. He saw a flash of green silk and a glint of exposed fangs.

'Sin!' he screamed, and slammed out a fist that met Pater Sin in the face. The huge Infardi crumpled and crashed away, smashing over another two carts. Buttons and beads spilled across the floor.

'Pater Sin!' Corbec yelled again, and dived at the rolling bulk. The twins heard his cry and switched their heads towards him. The psi-shock caught him a glancing blow and tumbled him head over heels into the shutters of a shop on the far side of the aisle. He broke several slats, and fell onto the ground.

Mkvenner leapt onto Sin as he tried to get up. They grappled furiously, and the scout brought him down again. Sin slammed out a tattooed arm and smacked Mkvenner sideways.

The twins opened their mouths and the buzzing sound gushed out. Brown and Roskil skidded to a halt, and swayed, blood gushing from their nostrils and ears. Roskil raised his lasrifle and shot Brown between the eyes. Then he swung round drunkenly and aimed at Sillo, who was backing away in terror.

There was a blurt of las-fire on auto. Mkvenner was up on one knee, blasting. The twins slammed back against the wall together, and slid down, leaving sticky swipes of blood behind them. Roskil, brain-fried, collapsed as they died.

Howling, Pater Sin threw himself at Corbec. His lethal implants gnashed and bit at the Ghost's neck. Corbec fended Sin off with his left arm, groping with his right to find something to use against the maniac. Something. Anything.

He got his fingers around something metallic and hard. He hoped to feth it was his warknife. He pulled it and stabbed it into the side of Sin's skull. It didn't penetrate, but the blow cracked Sin back for a second.

It wasn't Corbec's straight silver at all. It was a tube-charge.

Corbec swore and flinched as Sin came in again. His massive body pinned Corbec, and his augmetic fangs opened to rip his enemy's throat out.

Corbec jammed the tube into the yawning mouth as Sin bit down. His razor teeth clamped solidly into the tube's metal casing. Sin tried to pull away. Corbec got his legs up under Sin's torso and kicked out, throwing the heretic backwards off him.

A torn strand of det tape remained between Corbec's fingers.

'That's for Yael, feth-face!' Corbec yelled as he threw himself flat.

The tube-charge anchored in Pater Sin's teeth detonated.

Spattered in Sin's vaporised remains, Corbec rose. He hurried over to Mkvenner, who'd been thrown flat by the blast.

'Got the bastard,' Corbec said.

Caffran suddenly realised what he was looking at. He'd taken point down a side street, and was hunched in cover as the Ghosts moved up behind him. The view ahead was dark and empty, heavily shadowed by the bulk of an aqueduct that ran overhead and down the slope into the lower city where the night was firelit orange.

Caffran was looking for movement at street level, but he was distracted by a motion up in the shadows of the aqueduct. Roosting birds, he thought, and then remembered that he'd not seen any bird life on Herodor.

He stared up. A pale shape seemed to be moving along the outside of the aqueduct, insubstantial as smoke.

'Stand by,' he voxed. 'There's something–'

And he realised what he was seeing. Two loxatl, sleek and fluid as fish in water, racing along the sheer brickwork, about to cross right over their position.

'Hostiles! Eleven o'clock!' he yelled and opened fire up into the shadows of the arch. The gunfire rolled in the echoing space and his shots, bright and furious, lit up the bricks beside creatures. One immediately disappeared up over the top of the aqueduct, and the other one came down the support pier at a stupendous rate, its long body undulating and glinting. About three metres from the street, it propelled itself over onto the facing wall of the hab opposite, its dewclaws allowing it to skitter up the vertical surface.

Caffran ran forward, firing again. Feygor, Leyr and Dunik were up beside him, but they hadn't seen what he had seen.

'Caff?'

'Loxatl! Feth, up there!'

Caffran shot at the front of the hab, though in truth he couldn't see the thing clearly any more. Dunik and Feygor blasted with him, blindly following his lead. The Ghosts had a particular revulsion for the loxatl kind.

The thing reappeared, lower than Caffran was estimating. Little augmetic servo-limbs in its weapons harness clacked its blaster round and it fired.

The first two flechette rounds hit the wall behind Feygor making deep holes haloed by hundreds of lesser micro-impacts. The third atomised Dunik's head and shoulders in a bloody vapour.

Caffran and Feygor threw themselves flat. Leyr, cut along the hand and arm by stray barbs, yelped and stumbled.

They dragged him into cover. 'Down! Stay the feth down!' Caffran yelled, seeing Rawne and a half dozen other Ghosts rushing up the street to assist them. The loxatl's cannon repeated its distinctive rattling cough and hailed splinters along the street wall at head height. Someone screamed.

Rawne was on his hands and knees behind an abandoned ground car and glanced up in horror at the huge, ragged holes the xenos weapon was punching in the wall above him. Each impact was actually a thousand razor barbs hitting simultaneously.

'Where the feth is it?' he yelled.

Caffran couldn't see. 'Facing us, about two floors up,' he voxed. 'There's another one gone over the top of the aqueduct. For feth's sake, someone cover that angle!'

Fifty metres back, Kolea and Criid heard his signal and glanced at each other. The whining cough of loxatl cannons had a particular resonance for them both. Ouranberg. Criid in trouble. Kolea effectively giving up his life to save her.

As if reading her thoughts, Kolea said, 'Not this time.'

They doubled back under the aqueduct, hunting for the second creature. On the far side, visibility was better. The street was well lit by the amber glow of the firestorms. Guns raised, twitchy, they fanned forward, trying to hug cover. Criid and Kolea first... Jajjo... Skeen, Pozetine... Kenfeld.

Jajjo saw firelight reflecting off inhuman eyes clouded by protective han lids. He dived forward as flechette rounds shattered the cobbles around him. Several barbs sliced into his calves and shins, but he managed to land and roll, and came up firing.

Jajjo's las-fire peppered the wall where the thing had been, but sharp dewclaws and chillingly nimble reflexes had propelled the thing ten metres up the front facade of the tenement and along under the edge of the roof.

Criid saw it go, and fired at it, Kenfeld joining in.

'Gak, it's so fething fast!' she wailed.

'I think–' Kenfeld began and then suddenly wasn't beside her any more. She flinched. Her face was sticky and wet. It was Kenfeld's blood. His mangled body had been thrown five metres backwards, as hard and fast as if a speeding truck had run into it.

Criid ducked into cover and started to recell her weapon with shaking hands. She heard las-shots, the answering cough of the blaster, and then footsteps running. Gol Kolea threw himself down beside her.

'Where is it?' she asked.

'Up to the left, but moving. You okay?'

She nodded. Her earpiece was ringing with calls and alerts from the rest of the squad, trying to move up but pinned down by the mercilessly switching fire.

Kolea made ready to run out again, but she grabbed his arm and pulled him back.

'No heroics now,' she said. 'We've only just got you back.'

'That an order?'

'Yes, and–'

'And what?'

'I want you alive when we're done. We need to talk about... about your children.'

He looked at her strangely. 'My kids died in the hive-war, Tona. My wife too. The only children we need to worry about these days are yours.'

'But–'

'Yours,' he said emphatically. 'The Emperor protects, and when he's busy, Tona Criid performs miracles for him. It's enough to know they're alive and loved. More than I could ever have hoped for.'

He embraced her, and held her tight for a second. Then he scooped up his weapon and ran. The cannon coughed and roared.

ON THE OTHER side of the aqueduct, Rawne was running too. Three more of his platoon were messily dead now, but the loxatl had stopped shooting for a moment. He figured it had gone up over the roof of the hab.

He ran right across the street and came up against the front wall of the tenement, pressing his back to it, edging along. The street was quiet. Thin wisps of smoke drifted down it. Across the road, he could see Ghosts creeping forward behind cover.

Rawne's nostrils were suddenly assailed by a rancid stink of milk. Milk and mint.

His shoulders pressed to the wall, he tilted his head back and looked straight up. The loxatl gazed down at him. It was directly above him, about three metres up the wall, head down, snuffling its wattled snout. Its augmetic harness clicked and aimed the cannon's barrel into his eyes.

'Well, shit,' said Rawne.

From across the street, Banda's hot-shot hit it in the base of the tail and blew it off the wall. It crashed down beside Rawne in a shower of shattered bricks, thrashing its sinuous body in agony. Fluid leaked out of its lipless mouth. Rawne pressed the muzzle of his lasrifle into the exposed folds of its throat and fired.

'Nice decoy work, baby,' Banda said, sauntering out of cover with her long-las over her shoulder.

'Ha fething ha,' said Rawne.

CHTO BROOD LEADER was dead. Reghh had heard his subsonic pain-wails. Anger-hunger swamped his mind, and his gleaming skin began to pulse with grief-codes. Iridescent patterns flashed along his snaking body. He scuttled down a wall, across a stretch of pavement, and then up a side wall into the next alley. These mammals were not the target. They were delaying him and making him waste shots.

Loxatl senses were dull tools. Out of water, their vision, hearing and smell were poor. Taste and vibration were their primary skills. Reghh could feel the mammal soldiers running up along the street he'd just left, looking for him. He could feel their footsteps, their mouth noises, their heartbeats and their lung-puffs. He could taste their fear-sweat and skin-scents.

He started to scurry back down the length of the wall, moving south, when pain slammed into his torso. White-cold, brutal pain. He staggered, double-lids blinking.

The mammal wrenched his rifle back and tugged the long, silver bayonet out. How had Reghh not tasted him or known he was there?

Reghh coiled round. The ground was awash with the life-fluid draining out of him. He dimly saw the mammal.

The mammal had no taste. No taste at all. As if he was somehow new-born: pure and as yet unsoured by the rank flavours accumulated in their filthy skins during their lives.

How could that be? The mammal was full grown.

Reghh tried to turn around enough to bring his harness weapon to bear. The pain in his belly was too great. The mammal-with-no-taste lunged again.

Gol Kolea rammed the bayonet into the thing's twitching body twice more to make sure it was dead. Loxatl blood dripped off the straight silver clamped to his rifle's barrel. Dark spirals of colour flashed up and down the animal's gleaming hide and then it went a dull white.

Breathing hard, Kolea tapped his micro-bead. 'Sarge?' he said. 'I got it.'

THE STRANGEST THING. In all his years of kill-hunts, he'd never had this feeling before. He was being hunted.

Skarwael shifted silently through the abandoned avenues of the Guild Slope, invisible to all. The Imperial city towers rose before him, but the neighbourhood was quiet and dead. The humans had fled, leaving ruin in their wake. Rumbling, like a sinister threat, the invading host was twenty minutes behind him.

Skarwael had preyed a few times on his approach to the hives, not because he had to but because he was thirsty for pain. Herodor was smashed. In less than a day, the hives would burn and the Magister would have his victory.

The task remained. She was elusive, this martyr. That made the hunt all the sweeter.

And this strange feeling. It made the whole enterprise rewarding. Skarwael had accepted the task on the basis of the price the Magister was offering – a fortune in territory and inner transition metals, and a tolerance treaty between his kabal and the Archon Gaur. But this thrill now was reward enough. The hunter was hunted.

He'd not felt like this since his bitter years as a novitiate, when Lord Kaah had hunted them all in the miserable vaults of the murderdromes to hone their skills.

What could it be out there? Certainly no human. No human could ever hope to best the stealth and guile of a mandrake.

Skarwael melted into shadow, and doubled back. Like a phantom, he flowed through the shadows of a burned-out hab and came out onto the street. Darkness swam about him, unnaturally extending his flesh-cloak, bonding him to the night.

Where are you, he wondered?

The street was empty. Patchy fires burned in several buildings. The stiff corpses of Imperial soldiers decorated the ground. A wounded man, a PDF private, ran past him up the street, terrified, hoping to reach the towers before the gate hatches locked. The human didn't even see Skarwael, even though he was standing in the middle of the thoroughfare. The oblivious human passed so close by Skarwael could have reached out with his boline and cut his throat.

Still that feeling.

Skarwael turned, became brick, became glass, became stone, shifting his visual form against the backdrop behind him. His unseen adversary was close by. He could feel it. His pallid skin prickled. Behind him? No! To the left...

He passed through shadow and firelight, bending light and sound around himself as he moved. His chameleon powers segued him into walls and doorways, like a spectre from the afterlife.

There! Skarwael turned and flowed back through the night. At last his peerless skills as a stalker had paid off. There was his adversary, huddled down behind a railing, trying to hide.

You were good, Skarwael conceded. *A pleasure to hunt, a pleasure to test my skill against. But you are no match for a mandrake. Don't move. I will honour you with a slow, delicious death.*

Skarwael lunged with his sacred knife. The boline stabbed between the railings and speared through lifeless cloth.

Surprised, Skarwael dragged the cloth through the bars and sniffed it. A cloak, an empty cloak, made of some camouflage material. He turned and saw the rifle aimed at him.

'You're good,' said Mkoll grudgingly.

The single las-round hit the mandrake between the eyes.

THIRTEEN
THE LAST HOURS

'Nine is still one.'

— Message written in Soric's hand

CLOSURE REQUIRED THE gene-print of the first officiary. Leger was frightened, and had to be talked through the procedure, but Biagi was patient.

'Are they all in? Are they?' Leger mumbled.

Cannon teams guarded the slopes of the hive gate below. Gaunt had already checked in Criid's platoon, Rawne's and Obel's. 'Wait,' he said.

Rolling gunfire was hitting Old Hive's base level precincts. Waves of arch-enemy units, most of them motorised, stormed in towards the towers at ground level, and the air assault had redoubled.

It was close to dawn.

A string of shot-up carriers rumbled in under the gate, and thundered down the slip road into Old Hive's vast entry halls. As soon as they stopped, they popped their hatches. Domor's platoon scrambled out. The Beati and Milo were with them.

'Sabbat,' said Gaunt, bowing. 'We were fearful for your life.'

'I'm sorry for that, Ibram. But I'm here now. Your Ghosts have kept me safe.'

'Gaunt?' Biagi yelled from the walkway above. 'Now?'

Gaunt paused and consulted his data-slate. They were all inside Old Hive now, all the surviving Regiment Civitas, the PDF and life company. All that could be expected anyway.

On his own list, the Tanith list, one unit was missing. Sergeant Skerral's, number nineteen, last seen in a firefight with the death brigades on Nesh-ion Street.

'Sir?' Corbec gazed at Gaunt. 'I think we have to draw the line now.'

Gaunt nodded.

'Seal the gates!' Biagi yelled. Leger placed his hand on the gene-reader plate and declared his authority. The massive blast shutters of the Old Hive gates clanged into place.

NINETEENTH PLATOON WERE about five hundred metres from Old Hive's north entrance when they saw the gates close.

Skerral stopped in his tracks, and pulled the men up. Half his unit were dead. He ejected a cell from his lasrifle and slammed in a new one.

'Come on,' he said, turning back to face down the slope at the waves of assault sweeping in. 'Let's see how many we can kill.'

The remnants of nineteenth lasted seventeen minutes from the time the gates closed. They accounted for one hundred and eighty-nine enemy casualties. No one witnessed their heroism.

OLD HIVE, AS massive as it was, throbbed under the attack hailing at it from outside. Many upper levels were on fire. The massed forces of the Magister slammed against the outer walls again and again.

Word came through that hive tower two had been taken. Innokenti himself was there, receiving civilian sacrifices.

The main gates of Old Hive fell at mid morning. The death brigades flowed in, fighting street by street and compartment by compartment to overrun the tower.

GAUNT WALKED DOWN the staircase into the Holy Balneary in the base of Old Hive. The thousands of electrocandles flickered and twinkled. Most of the notables were already assembled below at the poolside. Lugo, Biagi, Leger, Kilosh and the ayatanis, Kaldenbach, the chief astropaths, the senior ecclesiarchs.

The service had been the Beati's idea. A final blessing for her loyal forces before the end came.

Gaunt felt resigned to it all. They were just hours from death now. Ferocious hive fighting tore through the outer levels of the tower. Parts of the external superstructure were beginning to collapse under intense bombardment.

Even so, he'd allowed just a bare minimum of Ghosts to attend. Fighting the enemy took priority over any sacred blessing. The only Ghosts who he had permitted to accompany him marched in a double file down the steps behind him. The Tanith flame troopers. They carried their tanks and hoses proudly. Biagi had personally requested their attendance. He wanted to honour them, and recognise the vital role they'd played, despite the ancient Civitas laws.

Gaunt ushered them onto the poolside, and they formed up in neat ranks. Some of the city officiaries and life company officers regarded the dirty flame-troopers with disdain.

'Ignore them,' Gaunt said.

The Beati, encased in her golden armour, stood thigh deep in the pool, proclaiming the devotional of Kiodrus. Milo waited nearby, with the temple adepts, at the top of the bath steps. Sabbat's voice echoed through the warm, damp air. She praised the forces that had drawn about her on Herodor, and mentioned the officers and unit commanders by name. Seventy per cent of the names she spoke were the names of dead men.

Gaunt, standing to attention with his troopers, started to blank out her words. The air was warm, and he was filled with a sense of mortality. This was all just fine talk. Battle awaited them, above in the hive, and it would be their last. Gaunt found his attention drifting to a pulse of bubbles that rippled the water at the far end of the balneary pool from Sabbat. Some kind of vent.

More bubbles. Bigger, more violent. 'Beati–' Gaunt began, breaking rank to step forward.

Karess erupted from the balneary pool.

His hull was rank and filthy from his passage through the deep places under the Civitas. His weapon limbs swung up and started to fire. A heavy bolter cannon and a plasma gun.

Horrified panic seized the congregation in the Holy Balneary. Priests and soldiers scattered in all directions, some slipping on the wet stone. No one quite believed a Chaos dreadnought could suddenly reveal itself like this.

Karess strode forward through the swirling water of the pool, weapon-limbs firing, broadcasting obscenities. Basalt chips spattered out of the pool side. Bolter rounds slaughtered five temple adepts and three life company officers. Kilosh was incinerated by a plasma beam. Kaldenbach fell over, blood pouring from a gut-wound.

Karess advanced onto the pool steps, emerging more fully from the water. He traversed his hull to target the left side of the bathhouse. His heavy bolter slammed and roared and the side wall was plastered with blood and exploded tissue. First Officiary Leger and the civitas master astropath both ceased to exist in that salvo. Sabbat stumbled up the pool steps and Milo started to drag her towards the cover of one of the balneary's massive stone columns.

Biagi ran to help him, firing his service pistol into the pool. A bolt round hit him in the chest and threw his ruptured corpse back across the chamber, knocking several people over as they tried to flee.

One of them was Lord General Lugo.

Shrieking, Lugo tore himself clear of the fallen bodies and rose. The killing machine was now nearly at the top of the pool steps, setting its first massive claw-foot on the poolside proper. Milo had got the Beati behind a pillar and just about everybody else still alive in the room was in cover. Karess's sensor augmetics dialled and clicked as it swung its bulk around, hunting for targets.

Hunting for *the* target.

It saw Lugo, eyes wild in terror as he staggered backwards. Karess emitted another stream of strangled obscenity and aimed his bolter.

It didn't fire. A blow had rocked it. Spitting filth, it swung its massive iron torso round to locate the source and felt another strike at its flank.

Gaunt drew back the power blade of Heironymo Sondar and struck again. The war machine was monumental and vastly powerful, but it was slow and cumbersome. It fired, but Gaunt was behind it, splashing through the shallow water at the top of the steps. He lashed out with the sword again and split a deep gash right through Karess's rear hull casing.

Karess uttered an electronic squeal, and rocked around with a grinding clank of gears. The edge of his plasma cannon smashed into Gaunt and hurled him back into the pool.

The dreadnought turned back, screaming blasphemies, and located the pillar where the Beati was sheltering.

Clutching his terrible belly wound, Kaldenbach struggled to his knees. He was only a few metres from the killer. Gasping with pain, he pulled a stick grenade and rolled it across the flagstones. It came to rest between Karess's massive foot-claws.

The blast blew the upper part of the pool steps into fragments. It barely damaged Karess, but it pitched him off his feet. The brute machine crashed backwards into the pool, sheeting water up into the air.

Ghosts ran forward from cover to drag Gaunt up onto the pool's edge. Coughing, Gaunt gazed back at the seething frenzy of water where the infuriated Karess was attempting to right himself.

'Brostin! Lubba!' Gaunt spluttered. 'Boil the bastard!'

Five Tanith flame-troops ran to the edge of the pool and hosed the water with liquid fire. In the enclosed stone chamber, the heat was immense. Steam gouted up. They continued to hose... Brostin, Lubba, Dremmond, Lyse, Neskon... churning the water into a scalding, bubbling froth.

Karess's armoured hull was proof against just about anything, but Gaunt's sword had sliced a hole in it. Boiling water squirted in, into his casing, broiling the living vestige inside. Karess sank, his hull lights dimmed, and went out.

Brostin and his brethren ceased fire and raised their burner-guns. The air was sweltering hot and thick with steam and smoke. Blood coated almost every surface of the ancient chamber.

At terrible cost, the last of the nine had been stopped.

* * *

In his cell, much further up in Old Hive, Agun Soric felt a sudden rush of relief. He lay back on his cot, his heart pounding.

Then he felt something twitch in the pocket of his jacket.

'There were times,' Sabbat said quietly, 'when I did not think we would get this far.'

He didn't know what to say. She seemed to be speaking as if there was some chance of victory remaining. 'Lugo has a ship,' he said. 'I doubt very much if it will survive an escape run, but he wants you aboard it.'

'Do you?'

Gaunt shook his head. 'I think there are few chances of you surviving this war, my Saint, and Lugo's ship is not one of them. Mkoll has suggested an escape on foot through the rear of the city basin, into the Southern Ramparts. It would be hard, but you and a small force might remain alive out there, hidden.'

'While you keep Innokenti busy with a final stand here?'

'No one else is going to do it. Biagi's dead, Kaldenbach as good as. Lugo's too far gone with fear.'

Gaunt and the Beati sat alone in a debate chamber of the Herodian Officiate, on the ninth level of Old Hive. Despite the monolithic build of the city tower around them, they could feel the vibration of warfare tearing through the lowest districts.

'Ibram?' she smiled. 'Did you suppose I had no purpose to play here?'

'If you have a purpose, Sabbat, it is beyond my grasp. I have never understood why you chose to come to Herodor. You're too valuable – to us and to the archenemy. You could have swept our forces to victory on Morlond. Here, you've trapped yourself, for no gain at all. The only ones you've served by coming here are the forces of Chaos. Your death will boost their morale for years to come.'

'You understand risk, Ibram. Tell me, is it better to risk a little for an easy victory, or everything for a great one?'

Gaunt laughed sadly. 'I can't see the p–'

'If I had gone to Morlond, Ibram, I would indeed have assured a fast victory there. But the Crusade would have been lost. Macaroth has overstretched himself. Innokenti's flank attack now bites deep into the Khan Group. The Warmaster and I would have achieved victory on Morlond, only to see the forces behind us destroyed by counter-attack. We would have been cut off, and exterminated.'

'So you go to the Khan Group instead? Without any significant forces?'

'How important is Herodor, Ibram?'

'Compared to the major Khan worlds, and the main population centres? It's worth is zero.'

'So why is the Magister himself… and such a large portion of his host… bothering with it?'

Gaunt shrugged. 'Because you're here.'

She nodded. 'Innokenti could have won the war outright for Chaos with one merciless thrust up through the Khan flank. We did not have the forces available to stop him. But it occurred to me we could distract him entirely and make him waste vital time on a pointless invasion of a worthless world.'

'You... you used yourself as bait?'

'You said yourself, I'm too valuable. To us and the archenemy. Innokenti could not ignore me.' She reached into her cloak and produced a data-slate. 'This was received via the astropaths a few minutes before we sealed the hive gates. I intended to announce it at the ceremony in the balneary, but we were interrupted.'

Gaunt took the slate and read it. The text had been deciphered from a very high level encryption. In a final, bloody push, Macaroth's forces had taken Morlond. Urlock Gaur was in frantic retreat. It would take time, but Imperial divisions could now be spared to bolster the defences of the Khan Group against Innokenti's attack.

An attack that, despite every advantage, had stalled at Herodor.

'By the Golden Throne...!' Gaunt sighed, astonished.

'We may yet die here, Ibram. But we will have died in the name of victory.'

'Thanks be to the Emperor,' he said.

She rose to her feet. 'And if I am to perish here, I would like to make it count for as much as possible. Milo?'

Milo had been waiting in the chamber's anteroom. He hurried in and bowed to her before saluting Gaunt.

'The time has come,' she said. 'My message?'

'I took it to tac logis command. They have it loaded into the Civitas public address system. Just say the word.'

'Now, Milo.'

He adjusted his micro-bead and sent a quick voice command.

THE PICT MESSAGE was brief. She had recorded it straight to camera, speaking quickly and clearly. Every operational public address screen, comm monitor and view plate in the Civitas broadcast it, and the vocal strand boomed out of all the vox horns and speakers still wired into the city systems. It lasted about fifty seconds. Tac logis set it to a looping repeat. For hours, it could be seen and heard throughout the Civitas Beati, by friend and foe alike.

The broadcast told of the great victory at Morlond. It defiantly declared that Innokenti's murderous gamble had failed. It dared him to flee before the wrath of the God-Emperor overtook him for the brutalities he had heaped upon Herodor. The final words were as follows:

'All living souls of men still in this city, all people of the Civitas left alive, know this. With overwhelming forces, the monster Innokenti has crushed us physically, but he cannot crush our spirit. Our sacrifice has ensured great victory. Do not die in fear and hiding. Make the price of your lives dear. The Emperor of Mankind has room for all in his Imperial army.'

THEY CAME FROM the agridomes at first. The archenemy's ground assault had ignored the western agri-sectors in its efforts to concentrate on the main hives. Blood Pact field observers on the invader's western flank suddenly saw figures pouring from the agridomes in their thousands.

Children of the Beati. The pilgrim mass.

Despite the losses they had suffered in the short but ferocious war so far, they still numbered in their hundreds of thousands. The giant agridomes had offered them shelter when the city started to fall. They were men and women who had come to Herodor without really knowing why, except that the Beati had called them.

And now she called them again, directly, through the broadcast.

Some had captured enemy weapons, or PDF ordnance, some had horticultural implements or broken pipes or staves of wood. Some had nothing but their own bare hands.

Thousands of them died, miserably outclassed by the weapons and equipment of the enemy host. But they did not falter for a moment.

An hour after they first appeared to unleash their holy rage into the Magister's legions, similar tides began to flow from hive tower one and hive tower three, and from public shelters and basements through the Guild Slope and the low town.

The Civitas Beati, crushed almost to death by Enok Innokenti, turned like a mortally wounded animal in a trap and bit out at the hunter.

AGUN SORIC HAMMERED his fists against the door of his cell. His hands were bloody and swollen from his efforts, and left smears of blood on the steel.

'Please!' he yelled. 'Please! You have to let me out! I need to warn her! I need to warn her!'

No one answered. At this late hour, with the city falling, there was in truth no one left on duty in the detention block to hear him anyway.

He screamed and hammered again, tears coursing down his craggy face.

The open shell case, and its fold of blue paper, lay on the cot behind him.

FOURTEEN
SABBAT MARTYR

'Know him for what he truly is. A killer.'

— Message written in Soric's hand

FOR THE FIRST hour or so of the fight, Anton Alphant had used a pistol looted from an enemy corpse, but then they'd found a PDF carrier abandoned at the side of one of the approach streets to hive tower one, and they'd recovered half a dozen lasrifles from it.

It had a wire stock instead of the pressed metal one he'd been used to in his Guard days, but apart from that it was shockingly familiar.

Night, wild with firestorms and a monumental roar of war, had engulfed the Civitas, and Alphant found himself caught up in the bloodiest fighting he had ever known, his former days of soldiering included. He did his best to try and make sense of the street combat, and to guide the pilgrim forces with him through.

There was no formal structure to the pilgrim army. It was essentially a gigantic mob. But the Beati had come to them in the agridomes, drawing men like Alphant out of the crowd, and telling the pilgrims to look to them for leadership. Most already did. Sabbat had unerringly picked on those people who had some military background, or on men or women who had already become the natural leaders of pilgrim bands.

They had no plan as such... except to throw themselves against the enemy. Alphant tried to rally his part of the zealot tide towards Old Hive, where the Beati was said to be under siege.

Her life was all that mattered.

* * *

Etrodai had never known Him so deranged by rage. The Magister's fury was so great that Etrodai even feared for his own life. Howling, a blinding sphere of crackling corposant around Him, Enok Innokenti drove the Retinue and three of the Blood Pact's veteran death-brigades into the bowels of Old Hive, through hallways and gallery levels shattered by fighting and littered with the bodies of the slain.

Hatchway by hatchway, hall by hall, they ground into the failing defences of the tower city. At the forefront, Etrodai swept his changeling blade through PDF troopers, Imperial Guardsmen and frantic civilian fighters.

Over a hundred thousand Blood Pact soldiers, along with armoured vehicles, were now inside Old Hive, spreading like wildfire through the lower levels. Hundreds of thousands more massed outside in the ruins of the high town as the city burned behind them.

There were reports of counter attacks to the flank, but Etrodai was sure they couldn't be right. There were no other Imperial forces here on Herodor to stage such attacks.

The saint's defiant broadcast had driven the Magister to His pitch of rage. He wanted her. He would kill her Himself.

Her life was all that mattered.

Just before midnight, a death brigade managed to mine two central power generators in the sub-ground levels of Old Hive, mainly in an effort to shut off the continued broadcasts of the saint's message, which so maddened their master. The blast tore out two hive levels, and caused a great internal collapse that killed thousands. Power was cut on eighteen city levels above. Where the slaughter raged in the lower levels, the halls and hive thoroughfares became like infernal caves, lit only by flames and the flash of weapons fire. Fires burned out of control with the suppression systems cut, and smoke collected in the uncirculating airspaces.

Innokenti and his vanguard swept through it all, lit by the glittering fires of his psyker malice and by the lethal ribbons of energy that were his blood-rage made manifest. The invaders surged in behind them.

In the cell block high above, darkness fell. Soric, hoarse and exhausted, waited for the secondary systems to kick in, but none did.

He wedged his hands against the cell door and started to pull at it. If the power had comprehensively failed, then the mag-locks would have failed too.

The door refused to budge. He tried again, snorting with effort, and at last the steel plate began to slide back in its groove. Soric pulled until he could get his bloodied fingers into the gap and grab more purchase.

He slid the cell door open and staggered out. The cell dock was dark. Stumbling and groping, he made his way out and down into an assembly yard. The main gates of the detention unit were open. Outside, the hive thoroughfare was pitch black and abandoned. He felt a rumbling from below, distant. The air was stale and smelled of smoke. Through the big riser vents in the thoroughfare he could hear noises echoing upwards through the vast structure of the hive.

Sounds of carnage and destruction, sounds of death.

Soric limped down the empty hallway in search of a stairwell.

THE MAGISTER'S ARRIVAL on the Great Concourse, a vast public space on the ninth level of Old Hive, was announced by the stalk-tanks that came blasting up the three great ashlar staircases that ascended from the transit terminals and ornamental gardens below. Such was the scale of the staircases, the war machines were able to climb five or six abreast, with Retinue and Blood Pact troopers rushing on foot in their wake, firing up at the Imperials dug in around the ornate basalt rails of the concourse level. The vast space was three hive levels deep, and the massive glass pendant lights that hung from the arched roof had been dark since the power failure. Great windows thirty metres high overlooked the staircases and lit the concourse with the glow of the burning city outside.

Major Udol, now ranking commander of the planetary forces, had assembled the last of his armour on the concourse, and their guns met the stalk-tanks as they came up from the steps. Shell blasts tore across the pavements, hurling stone slabs and men into the air. Pulse-lasers spat their pumping streams through the hellish gloom, ripping open the fronts of the buildings lining the concourse and shattering the huge obsidian sculptures that hung down from the roof. Glass images of the aquila and other Imperial crests crashed down in avalanches of glass shards, exploding into fragments like falling ice.

The Magister's forces surged up onto the concourse.

Gaunt had drawn up half the Tanith regiment and the last of the life company behind the armour for this stand. All remaining forces were occupied on other levels, meeting other invasions, but this, Gaunt knew, was the key.

She had told him so. She had felt the wrath of Innokenti approaching.

Udol's armour rolled back slowly across the pavements, crunching over the vast heaps of broken glass, firing as it went. They took heavy losses, but not a single stalk-tank made it more than twenty metres from the head of the steps. Udol's gentle retreat was designed to lure a good portion of enemy infantry up onto the concourse, where there was no cover.

'In the Emperor's name... now!' Gaunt signalled, and his infantry strength emerged from around the sides of the huge public space, firing as it came. The first fifty seconds were a blistering massacre. The concourse lit up as bright as day with the las-weapon discharge. Hundreds of Blood Pact and Retinue troopers were cut down or blown apart. Then the archenemy rallied, and the firefight began in earnest. Still the Imperials punished them.

'Hold the line! Hold cover!' Gaunt ordered. His men had the full advantage of the buildings on either side of the pavements, and the still advancing enemy had nothing but open space.

Gaunt saw a ripple of light at the top of the steps. Unearthly, malevolent light, crackling like lightning. In horror, he realised that the Beati and the life company had broken cover formation and were charging onto the concourse towards it. The Beati herself was lit up in a halo of green fire.

Alone, despite that great power suffusing her, she would die.

'Ghosts of Tanith!' he yelled, raising his sword. 'Charge!'

Only on Balhaut, in that hell of war, had Gaunt known pitched fighting on such a great scale. Like seas clashing, the waves of soldiers tore into one another, stabbing and firing. Flamers roared. The force of the clash made the ancient concourse shake. Gaunt ran with his men, laspistol blasting in his left hand, power sword scything in his right. Within seconds, he had been hit twice, glancing shots to his body, and a half dozen tears had ripped through his clothes. The sword of Heironymo Sondar bit through Blood Pact veterans who lunged at him with fixed bayonets, and hacked open the dark blue armour of the Magister's elite troopers, savage brutes with bulbous insectoid goggles.

He tried to find the Saint. His face was wet with blood and his breath was rancid in his throat. The din around him was so immense he was deafened. Every second, every part of a second, he was striking and moving, dodging, stabbing, caught up at the heart of a combat melee so feral it seemed to be an echo from the barbaric wars of the past.

He saw Rawne and Caffran for a moment, blasting into the enemy as they ran forward. Feygor, kneeling over a fallen Ghost and firing on auto. Varl, Criid, Obel, Domor, Meryn, their men around them as they charged into the enemy mass. He saw Daur shoot a Blood Pact officer through the head. He saw Brostin spraying flamer-fire into a collapsing pack of Retinue troops. He saw straight silver and blood and courage.

He saw men he'd known for almost seven years fight and die.

The men and women of Verghast, true Ghosts all, stalwart and brave.

The men of Tanith, staunchest warriors he'd ever known, who so surely deserved to live forever.

Gaunt knew war was fickle, and seldom let a warrior choose his place of death. But this, this was enough. As good, as worthy, as honorable, as any he could have chosen.

The flare of unholy radiance was close to him, and he hacked through closing ranks of Retinue soldiers to reach it. His pistol had gone. Only the charged blade of his sword remained. A las-round creased his cheek but he ignored the burning pain and took the head off a member of the Retinue, leaping forward into the lightning.

Surrounded by the heaped dead, Innokenti stood before him. The Magister, more vile and wretched than anything Gaunt could have imagined, was locked sword to sword with the Beati.

Every blow they exchanged, every strike, crashed like thunder. Sparks flew. Shockwaves from the meeting blades threw men around them – friend and foe alike – off their feet. Hideous corposant writhed and seared around the Magister. Cold green fire, in the form of a great eagle with its wings unfurled, lit up the Saint.

Gaunt charged forward, his boots slipping on the blood-wet stone.

A daemon sprang at him, blocking his path. The beast was huge. It was cased in the blue-black armour of the Retinue, but its head was bare, the pink flesh grievously marked with ritual scars. Its mouth and nose were hidden behind an augmetic grille and its eyes were glowing yellow slits. It wielded a ghastly sword of serrated bone which grew out of its right fist. The flesh of that fist had peeled back, exposing grey finger bones that were fused into the long blade. It swung at Gaunt.

Blood saved him. His boot slipped and he fell. The bone-blade whistled over his head and Gaunt rolled before it could slice back. He jumped to his feet and parried the daemon's sword as it came at him, and then drove hard with a thrust that the beast turned aside.

They circled amid the whirling carnage, trading blows with all their strength. Gaunt could no longer see the Beati. Only a greenish light in the air suggested she was still alive. Desperately, Gaunt lunged, but the daemon hooked the strike away, countering with a thrust that juddered Gaunt's power sword down.

His guard was open. The bone-blade came at his throat.

A las-round smacked into the side of the daemon's neck, and a second ripped open its shoulder guard. It stumbled away from Gaunt, turning.

Brin Milo charged forward, power-cell spent, and rammed his straight silver up to the hilt in the daemon's chest.

Eaten by the beast's acid blood, the blade snapped off. Milo staggered back. With a wordless scream, Gaunt swung around and put his power blade clean through the thing's neck.

Etrodai, life-ward of the Magister, fell dead, his changeling blade crumbling to dust.

Gaunt and Milo turned and ran towards the Beati. Living fire was sizzling around her, and pouring like burning oil out across the pavements of the concourse.

The fire was pouring from the disembowelled corpse of Enok Innokenti.

'Holy Terra...' Gaunt stammered.

Sabbat rose, the sightless, gaping head of the Magister dangling from her raised fist.

'In the name of the Emperor!' she yelled. The luminous aquila around her flared to three times its size, snapping and beating at the high roof.

The sound of her voice was so clear, so loud, it blew out the great windows of the concourse in a vast blizzard of glass.

To a man, every archenemy warrior on Herodor shrieked.

WHERE HE HAD been hard-pressed just a minute before, Corbec now found himself facing an empty hallway. Weary and nervous, he edged his forces forward, clearing through to the western gate of the hive.

Something had most definitely happened. The enemy forces had been all over them and now they were in flight.

'Rerval? What's the story, son?'

Rerval shook his head. A huge and devastating rush of psyk-noise had just burned out all the comm channels and fused every vox-set in the hive area.

'Could be a trick,' said Mkvenner.

Corbec nodded. 'Hold it here. The fethers don't give up that easily. We've got a breathing space at least.'

Mkvenner nodded. He rounded up the Ghosts and PDF in the immediate area and put them to work building barricades with the debris in the hall.

Haller ran up as the work began.

'Something's going on,' he told Corbec. 'Got no vox, but word of mouth says the enemy is falling back all over.'

Corbec scratched his head. 'Damned if I know what this is about.'

'Colm?'

Corbec looked round. Mkoll was approaching now. Some of his squad came up behind, battered and bleeding like the rest of them, escorting a figure.

It was Soric.

'He... he demands to talk to you,' said Mkoll.

'Agun's never had to ask for my ear in his life, Mkoll. He won't start now either.'

Corbec walked over to Soric. The old Verghastite was shaking and exhausted.

'You have to warn Gaunt.'

'Warn him?'

'It's not over.'

'I'll not argue with you, Agun. Something fishy's going on but I d–'

'No, Colm!' Soric pulled a brass message shell out of his pocket and opened it. 'The nine. The nine are not finished. The psykers–'

Corbec smiled. 'I killed the psykers, Agun. Pater Sin and his two freaks. I sent them to hell.'

Soric swallowed. 'I know you did. It told me.'

'What did?'

'Doesn't matter. Colm, they'd already imprinted their task. That's what they were for. Not to kill the Beati like the others, but to choose and direct a killer who would do it for them. Someone close to her. And he's still out there.'

Corbec's eyes widened. 'Feth… What? Who?'

'It showed me everything, Colm. It showed me what he was,' he said, holding out the ragged sheet of blue paper for Corbec to see.

Milo put his arm around the Beati's shoulders and led her across the concourse. She was shaking with exhaustion, and deep slashes from Innokenti's blade were bleeding freely.

'Medic! Medic here!' he called.

The enemy had gone, in rapid retreat, their morale broken as much by the death of their overlord as by the victory of the Beati. Even now, the fleeing enemy forces were engaging with the pilgrim army in the high town as they tried to break off.

It was not over. Indeed, the fight for Herodor was a long way from done. But for now, the looming defeat was postponed.

The ruined concourse, adrift with smoke and crackling fires, was littered with the dead of both sides. Men picked their way through the rubble, looking for the wounded, for fallen comrades. Where they found the enemy alive, they were merciless.

Dorden led a gaggle of medic teams out into the battlefield.

'Here!' Milo called, and Dorden came running over.

Gaunt and other officers stood warily by as Dorden treated the Beati's wounds. 'Can we get vox?' he asked Beltayn.

'It's all out, sir. The death scream of the enemy leader fried every circuit.'

Gaunt turned to the men around him. 'We've done a great thing this day. We've pulled back from a brink I was sure we would topple over. We have struck a great blow at the archenemy of mankind. Gather your units, see to the wounded, and spread this word, by mouth, to all you meet. The Beati is triumphant. Innokenti is dead. Make sure everyone knows it. Make sure every last damn citizen in the hives knows it.'

The officers nodded and spread out.

'I need to get her to an infirmary where there's power,' Dorden said. 'And I'll need a stretcher…'

'I can walk,' said Sabbat, rising.

'Then we'll walk with you,' said Gaunt. 'Honour guard, here!'

Milo stepped up, as well as Daur and Derin. Nessa also took a step forward. Gaunt nodded.

Larkin, sat wearily against a wall nearby, got to his feet.

'Me too, sir,' he said.

Gaunt looked at him. 'Any special reason, Larks?'

Larkin gestured at the Ghosts around the Beati. 'They were the honour guard. On Hagia. The ones she called.'

Gaunt looked and realised the old sniper was right. Dorden, Daur, Nessa, Milo and Derin had all been part of Corbec's inspired mission on the Shrineworld. Apart from Corbec himself, the only ones missing were the ones no longer alive. Greer, Vamberfeld and Bragg.

'Try would've wanted me to fill in for him,' Larkin said. 'It mattered to him. She mattered. I... I can see why now.'

'Carry on,' said Gaunt.

USING LAMP PACKS to light their way, and moving slowly, the escort left the Great Concourse and headed down the connective hallways towards the main stairwell. They walked through abandoned hive streets littered by warfare and looting. Terrified and stunned civilians huddled in the ruins and watched them pass by, bowing at the sight of the Saint.

Edgy, Gaunt walked with them, desperate for the vox to come back so he could get a picture of the situation. He'd have to trust Rawne and Udol to get things solid without him.

They were clearing another hallway, close to the access shafts, when Gaunt saw a flash of torchlight and heard a voice calling his name.

Panting hard, Corbec ran up, followed by Soric.

'What's he doing here?' Gaunt asked.

'His duty,' said Corbec. 'There's a killer out there still. One of the nine.'

'What?'

'The psyker's imprinted someone,' Corbec said. 'Someone suitable.' He held out the rag of blue paper to Gaunt.

'Get her in cover!' Gaunt yelled and raised his lamp to read the scrap as Dorden and the honour guard hurried the Beati towards shelter. Nessa and Larkin immediately raised their long-lases and started to scan for trouble through their scopes.

'No...' Gaunt said, reading the name on the paper. He swung round. 'Milo! Get h–'

A las-shot seared out of the darkness around them and hit the wall centimetres from the Beati's head.

Everyone dropped. Another two shots zapped at them. One hit Derin in the shoulder and threw him off his feet.

'I can't see him!' Larkin moaned, training his weapon.

Two more shots whined in. Nessa tried a return, and banged a hot-shot into the darkness. The killer's reply, a semi-auto flurry, hit Daur in the hip and slammed Dorden over against the wall.

'He's all over us!' Corbec yelled, down in cover beside Gaunt. 'Did you see Soric's note? Did you read what he did?'

Fury boiled through Ibram Gaunt. Soric's talent had not only identified the killer imprinted by Sin's psykers, it had exposed him for all he was. Soric had seen into the hateful mind of a stone killer and revealed all his crimes.

Lijah Cuu. Murderer. Rapist. Killer of Bragg. Killer of Sehra Muril.

Corbec held out his laspistol to Gaunt.

'On three?' he suggested.

Gaunt looked back at the beleaguered escort. Daur and Derin were both writhing in pain. Dorden was lying on the ground and looked like he was dead. Nessa was pumping his chest frantically. Milo and Larkin, weapons raised, were shielding the Beati with their bodies.

'Get ready to move her!' Gaunt yelled.

He and Corbec leapt up and charged, firing into the dark. The laspistol cracked in Gaunt's hand, spitting bars of light into the shadows. Corbec was beside him, spraying auto-fire from his lasrifle.

A flurry of shots burned back at them.

Gaunt leapt over a scatter of fallen wall stones and darted along the far wall. He fired into the shadows. 'Cuu! Cuu, you bastard! I will have you!'

A las-round hit Gaunt in the back and threw him hard onto his face. He felt the hot rush of blood leaking out of him. He tried to turn.

'You first, sure as sure, then the bitch Beati,' Cuu said, kneeling on Gaunt's back and making him yell with pain. 'I'll kill you all.'

The straight silver came down to Gaunt's throat.

The hot-shot was so loud the noise of it rolled up and back down the hallway. Gaunt felt Cuu's deadweight slam down across him. He struggled out from under Cuu's body. Larkin bent down and dragged him up.

Gaunt swayed. The wound in his back was agonising. He gazed down at Cuu's ruined corpse.

'Never did like him,' Larkin said.

'He killed Bragg.'

'I know, sir,' Larkin said.

'Good shot. In the dark like that.'

'I just fething wish I could have got a bead on him sooner,' said Larkin. His voice was low, as if strained by massive emotion.

'What do you mean?' Gaunt asked. He stirred up and looked back down the hall. Pain flared through his back, but what he saw hurt him so much more.

Twenty metres back down the hall, face down in a pool of blood, Colm Corbec lay dead.

EPILOGUE

The battle for Herodor lasted another six weeks. The vast invasion force fell back after Innokenti's death, harried and harassed by the militant pilgrim army. Two days later, renewed and using its strengths to the full, it re-assaulted the Civitas. Thousands of pilgrims perished in the resistance. The Beati, limping from her wounds, led the counter push with the remnants of the Imperial strength – Ghosts, Regiment Civitas, PDF and the pilgrim host – and kept the massive force at bay for a week.

Then the reinforcement fleet arrived, sent by the Warmaster. The initial fleet engagement lit up the night sky. A far greater and more bloody combat than is recorded in this account then took place. Over a period of weeks, the Magister's forces were driven out of the Civitas, and extinguished in a final pitched land battle in the Stove Hills.

The Tanith Ghosts played no part in that.

Nor did they play a part in the overall victory. Freed from their obligations at Morlond and the front, large segments of the Crusade force were loosed to defend the Khan flank. The details of those actions is recorded in other works. It is sufficient to point out that had the Magister's warhost not been so detained with the business of Herodor, the entire Khan Group would most likely have fallen, and the Crusade efforts been lost.

The Beati's efforts had been emphatic. She had forced the flank attack to be stillborn, and furthermore she had killed one of Gaur's most senior lieutenants. The message sent to the enemy was devastating. As the Archon's forces tumbled back into the edge systems of the

Sabbat Worlds, Macaroth prepared for the final, triumphant era of the Crusade.

As history records, it would not be easy. But for the while, the advantage was entirely his.

GAUNT TURNED HIS face away from the stinging dust as the lander came in. It settled on the roofpad of Old Hive, and the thrusters died.

He turned to face the Beati and knelt. She lifted him up again with both hands.

'Not to me,' she said. 'I should kneel to you.'

'Do you know where they're sending you?' Gaunt asked.

'The front line. Carcaradon. To Macaroth's side... as Lugo kept advising.'

Gaunt smiled. 'You knew better.'

'Now, he's right. I will not forget the service of the Ghosts, Ibram.'

'Just do me a favour and look after him.'

She smiled and nodded. 'His destiny awaits us, Ibram Gaunt. It is more than you could possibly imagine.'

She kissed Gaunt's forehead and walked away towards the open ramp of the lander. Gaunt looked at Milo. He seemed happy and terrified, all at once. He ran over to Gaunt as if to hug him and then, at the last minute, stopped and threw a hard salute.

Gaunt returned the salute. Then he drew his warknife and handed it to Milo.

'You lost yours. Take mine with you now.'

Milo looked at the straight silver in his hands for a moment and then ran to join Sabbat. The lander's ramp closed, and it lifted away into the colourless sky on a roar of jets.

'Goodbye, Brin,' Gaunt said, certain he would never see the boy again.

THE SHUTTLE FROM the black ship was waiting. Ominous men in long dark robes paced about the platform. He could smell the ozone stink of power-goads. His hands shook in their cuffs.

A black-robed figure strode down the landing ramp, glanced at a data-slate offered by a servitor, and walked towards him.

'Name?'

'Agun S–'

A power-goad lashed him into silence.

'His name is Agun Soric,' said the man standing beside him.

'Evaluation?'

'Psyker, level beta.'

The black robed figure nodded. 'Sign the release, please.'

Viktor Hark took hold of the data-slate with his newly implanted augmetic limb and studied it. He put his signature on the plate with the stylus and handed the slate back to the inquisitor.

'Where are you taking him?' Hark asked.

'Where he belongs. It's no concern of yours,' said the robed inquisitor. 'Advance him!' he yelled, and the handlers goaded the shackled Soric up the ramp.

Hark could hear Soric sobbing. He turned away, shutting it out.

A brass message shell sat on the deck grille at his feet. Hark leaned down and picked it up in his augmetic hand. He opened it and knocked out the paper.

Two words were written on the blue scrap.

Help me

Hark turned back and watched as the shuttle lifted off and swung up and away into the sky.

THE SAW WAS shrilling. The lovely whine of good wood splitting. The air was thick with aromatic dust.

Colm Corbec walked into the little woodshop off Guild Slope and watched for a while as the old man – what was his name again... Wyze? – worked the wood. Business had been brisk. Feth, yes! Coffins for the departed. God-Emperor, that was supply and demand!

Corbec stepped into the pungent, dry air of the woodshop, and ran his hand down a length of mature timber. Not nalwood, but good.

This Wyze. He was all on his own, without any assistance. Not the way Corbec's father would have run it. He needed a hand.

Corbec rolled up his sleeves. He knew this work. He liked it. He'd stay awhile and help out.

'NO OTHER WOOD will do. You understand?'

'Yes, Mister Gaunt,' said Guffrey Wyze.

'That's Colonel-commissar–' Gaunt began and then shook his head. 'Nalwood. All of it.'

'It's your money, sir. Friend of yours, was it?'

'Friend. Brother. Ghost,' said Gaunt.

Wyze smiled. 'Plenty of them hereabouts.'

ABOUT THE AUTHOR

Dan Abnett lives and works in Maidstone, Kent, in England. Well known for his comic work, he has written everything from the *Mr Men* to the *X-Men*. His work for the Black Library includes the popular strips *Titan* and *Darkblade*, the best-selling *Gaunt's Ghosts* novels, the Inquisitor Eisenhorn and Ravenor trilogies, and the acclaimed Horus Heresy novel, *Horus Rising*.